Max Hermann Ohnefalsch-Richter

Kypros, the Bible, and Homer [electronic resource] : oriental

civilization, art and religion in ancient times

Max Hermann Ohnefalsch-Richter

Kypros, the Bible, and Homer [electronic resource] : oriental civilization, art and religion in ancient times

ISBN/EAN: 9783741171901

Manufactured in Europe, USA, Canada, Australia, Japa

Cover: Foto ©Andreas Hilbeck / pixelio.de

Manufactured and distributed by brebook publishing software
(www.brebook.com)

Max Hermann Ohnefalsch-Richter

Kypros, the Bible, and Homer [electronic resource] : oriental civilization, art and religion in ancient times

Kypros.
Marion-Arsinoë 1886.

Karac. C. Watkins.

A class of attic vases specially destined to Cyprus and unknown until now. The author was the first to excavate and recognize this ware which is described at the end of this book.

Eine bisher unbekannte, für Cypern bestimmte attische Vasengattung ein welcher würde Jahrhunderts, vom Autor zuerst gefunden, zuerkennt und am Ende dieses Werkes beschrieben.

KYPROS

THE BIBLE AND HOMER.

ORIENTAL CIVILIZATION, ART AND RELIGION IN ANCIENT TIMES.

ELUCIDATED BY THE AUTHOR'S OWN RESEARCHES AND EXCAVATIONS DURING TWELVE YEARS'

WORK IN CYPRUS

BY

MAX OHNEFALSCH-RICHTER, PH. D.

WITH A LETTER TO THE AUTHOR FROM THE RIGHT HON. W. E. GLADSTONE.

TEXT.

LONDON.

ASHER & Co., 13, BEDFORD STREET, COVENT GARDEN.

1893.

DEDICATED TO

HIS HIGHNESS

BERNHARD,

HEREDITARY PRINCE OF SAXE-MEININGEN-HILDBURGHAUSEN.

PATRON AND FRIEND OF THE STUDY OF ANTIQUITIES

BY

MAX OHNEFALSCH-RICHTER.

10, Downing Street,
Whitehall.

Feb. 3. 1893

Dear Sir

A thorough examination of your work,
which would have been my first concern
for compliance with your desire, has unfortunately been out of my power, in
consequence of the heavy demands upon

my time together with some other causes.

Aided, however, by the references which you kindly supplied, I have made myself sufficiently acquainted with it to be deeply impressed with its importance as a substantial contribution to the great work of unifying and integrating the archaic knowledge which has recently been obtained in so many branches, and so many quarters.

Cyprus was I apprehend a great advanced post of Phœnician navigation, commerce and civilisation, and it may prove to have been the richest storehouse of illustrative remains supplied by the race, which played so momentous a part in human development.

Your views of the Associate Cephaloidibi, so far as I have been able to examine them, appear to me to be in close correspondence with the evidence supplied by the text of Homer. And it may be worthy of note, with reference to the Gorgoneion, that while the Shield of Agamemnon associates it with Cyprus, the only other mention (if I remember right) of the Gorgon in Homer is in the Underworld of the Eleventh Odyssey which is as I conceive altogether exotic, that is to say Phœnician, in its character.

I could wish that this letter were more worthy

of its occasion but you will I am sure excuse its insufficiency on account of the circumstances under which it is written. I have the honour to remain

dear Sir

Yours very faithful & obedient,

W E Gladstone

I take the liberty of inclosing a recent paper of my own, somewhat slight in its texture, which has certain points of relations with your work.

PREFACE.

The island of Cyprus affords perhaps the most striking instance in the whole history of the world, of a country where century after century the streams of diverse civilizations converging from different sources met and mingled at full flood. The highways of commerce now pass the island by, but in the early days of the world it was at once the centre of civilized impulse, the link between either shore of the Mediterranean and the remoter East and West, and as such the cynosure of many an ancient people.

The beginnings of civilization in Cyprus can be traced back to the same pre-historic period of which we find evidence on the banks of the Nile, Euphrates and Tigris, in Syria and in Asia Minor, and seem to point to a Thraco-Phrygian origin. The remains are neither Semitic nor continental in character, but Indo-Germanic and proper to an island or coast population. The first Greek colonization of the island must have taken place centuries before the period of the Homeric poems. There were Phoenician colonies on the island at a very early period, how early it is impossible exactly to determine until a larger number of older tombs in Phoenicia proper have been opened. The Greek colonists in early times employed a peculiar syllabic written character and adhered to it till about the 4th century B. C. How they came by this written character is a question to which a solution will be offered in the present work. The oldest extant Phoenician inscriptions, themselves the earliest examples of letters properly so called, come from Cyprus. This point too I have, with the kind help of other scholars, demonstrated for the first time. These inscriptions occur on bronze vessels dedicated to the Baal of Lebanon by a Cyprian in the time of the biblical Kings Solomon and Hiram, and deposited on the altar to that divinity which stood on a sacred High Place in Cyprus. In Cyprus, then, we are standing in the very midst of ancient Canaanitish civilization as depicted in the old Testament. On the other hand the worship of Aphrodite, the myth of King Kinyras and the accounts of the armour of the Achaian heroes, of Agamemnon's coat of mail and of Achilles' shield, bring us back again to Cyprus, but from an entirely different cycle of ideas. My excavations and researches during twelve years of unremitting toil in Cyprus brought me on the one hand to the Greeks and Homer, and on the other to the Semites and the Bible. The results of my labours are embodied in the present book

Kypros, the Bible and Homer.

The early civilization of Troy has found so far its only analogy in Cyprus. The influence of Cyprus and Mycknae on each other was mutual and contemporaneous. Influences of every kind passed to and fro between Cyprus and Egypt (especially Naukratis) and between Cyprus and

Phoenicia (especially Byblos). We find analogies both in religious practices and in the history of civilization reaching far and wide into Syria, the newly discovered country of Samal, Empire of the Hittites and among the nations of Asia Minor, Carians, Lycians and Lydians. The Greek islands, large and small, early interchanged with Cyprus not only all manner of utensils, vessels, weapons, ornaments and garments but also many a custom both sacred and secular. Similar links were formed early between Cyprus and the mainland of Greece. The only extensive parallels to the remains found in the earliest strata at Olympia are furnished by our Cyprian discoveries. From time to time the inhabitants of the "Copper Island" carried on a brisk trade with Cyrene and Carthage, with Etruria, Malta, Sicily and Sardinia. The exports consisted not only in copper ore, but in axes, bronze or iron, in copper shields and cups and in silver vessels. Even in Hungary, as far away as Hallstadt, in Central and Northern Europe we can track the influence of Cyprus in weapons made there or carried there by commerce. Very probably the sword was invented in Kypros. The kyanos of Cyprus, a subsidiary product of copper smelting, in the rough or worked up, competed early with that of Egypt. To utilize the waste product side by side with the smelting of copper and the forging of arms a subordinate industry sprang up — glass manufacture — the existence of which in Cyprus I was the first to prove. Cyprian masters also play an important part in the development and perfecting of the metal industry in general, of the glyptic and ceramic arts, of wood and iron carving as well as in terra-cotta work, sculpture and bronze casting, although they never reached the high level of perfection attained by the Greek artists.

The campaigns of mercenary soldiers, immigration, wars, payment of tribute, foundation of colonies by foreigners in Cyprus and by Cyprians in foreign lands favoured an exchange of commodities. The gods, with their ritual and images, brought art in their train. From Cyprus the little golden images of Astarte passed to Mykenae, and the stone ones to Naukratis. Images of Tammuz found their way from Cyprus to Malta, Carthage and Etruria. From Cyprus Aphrodite and Adonis started on their triumphal progress through the ancient world.

But in many respects the island received more than it gave. In particular the two great centres of Oriental antiquity, Mesopotamia and Egypt, exercised a most decisive influence on Cyprian civilization.

A clear picture of this cannot be presented by words alone. Therefore it has been my special care to give as full a collection of illustrations as possible, the most important part of which consists in a large number of antiquities hitherto unpublished. In order to make the work of comparison easier and more thorough, I have been obliged to repeat some already published in other works, chiefly in Perrot's "Histoire de l'Art". I hope that the defective arrangement, necessarily inherent in the book, will be pardoned for the sake of the new and important facts that I have been able to bring forward. Reference is facilitated by the Index and the description of the plates.

As a solid basis to the whole I have made a list (in great part based on my own discoveries) of all Cyprian sanctuaries, and have amply illustrated it with maps, plans and restorations.

Starting from the fact that the holy tree — e. g. the biblical Tree of Life and Tree of Knowledge — holds a very important position in the worship of ancient Oriental peoples, I have devoted a large part of my work to tree and grove worship in Cyprus, Mesopotamia, Egypt, Syria and Judaea, adding thereto the worship of post and pillar, — Ashera and Masseba — so well known from the Bible.

The exceptional abundance of votive offerings of all kinds will be dealt with in the sections devoted to the different divinities to whom the offerings are dedicated. Under this head come Cyprian examples of curious ornaments, rings for ears, nose, fingers, or feet, breast-plates and girdles, which in many cases serve to explain passages in the Bible and Homer.

Besides the sanctuaries the most important sites of excavation are the Cypriote tombs. These also are illustrated by a number of plans, sections, views, architectural details and pictures of the various articles buried with the dead.

Among the works of art we may specially notice the Greek statues and vases, some of which were imported and some made on the island. Of these many are published here for the first time.

A perfectly new feature is presented by the class of black-figured vases of the sixth century B. C. manufactured in Athens specially for Cyprus.

I attach special importance to the accurate plans of a Cyprian citadel in the Heroic Age, of which the previous publication was so inadequate.

The publication of the work in its present full and elaborate form is entirely and solely due to the exceeding kindness of my Uncle Geheime Ober-Regierungsrath Professor Dr. Julius Kühn. He has not only become responsible for the whole expenses of the work, which are considerable but has afforded me the opportunity of finishing my task here in Berlin, the principal centre of German science, where I enjoy the double advantage of reference to a large Museum and of the aid of scholars, who are specialists in their own departments. I am glad to take this opportunity of publicly expressing my sentiments of filial gratitude to Dr. Julius Kühn.

I am indebted in the very highest degree to Dr. Chr. Belger, one of the editors of the Berliner Philologische Wochenschrift, who followed with unflagging interest the course of my work, checked many mistakes, and called my attention to several points which otherwise might have escaped my notice; my thanks are also due to Herren DD. O Jessen and H. Schmidt.

In the preparation of the English edition I have had the assistance of many English scholars, both ladies and gentlemen. The chief part of the work was undertaken with great devotion by the well-known archaeologist W. R. Paton M. A. (Aberdeen). A further portion was translated by Miss E. Sellers (London), who is equally well known to the world of learning and justly so. The translation of the conclusion and of the greater part of the explanation of the Plates has been completed by Miss K. A. Raleigh (London), with great kindness, energy and industry. Mr. C. H. Jeafferson (Liverpool) also translated a few sheets. In Berlin the well-known Professor H. Nettleship of Oxford had the kindness to revise a great part of the proof-sheets. To them, my English associates, I offer my best thanks.

From the Central-Gewerbeverein für Rheinland and Westfalen and the head of the same, Herr Director Frauberger I received an important contribution, in the form of good photographs of the Cyprian gold ornaments belonging to the Museum at Düsseldorf. These photographs were made specially for me free of cost, and Herr Director Frauberger added an admirable description which has been printed in the Appendix. I must also express my gratitude for illustrations and descriptions received from the Albertinum at Dresden, from the Director of the same, Herr Professor Dr. Treu and his assistant Herr Dr. P. Herrmann, from the Historical Art Collection of the Imperial House of Vienna, and the Keeper of the same, Herr Dr. R. von Schneider, from Herr A. Brockhaus in Leipzig, from Herr Professor Dr. Th. Schreiber in Leipzig, from the Grand Ducal Museum at Karlsruhe and the Director of the same Herr Hofrath Dr. Wagner, and from the University Museum in Bonn and the Director of the same Herr Professor Dr. Löschcke. Messrs. C. Watkins, C. Christian and J. W. Williamson afforded me hearty co-operation in Cyprus and through their intervention I was able to illustrate the rich discoveries of Marion-Arsinoë in a full and satisfactory manner. The Kaiserliches Deutsches Archäologisches Institut and the First Secretary of the same in Athens, Herr Dr. W. Dörpfeld, placed at my disposal for this work some hitherto unpublished photographic views.

M. Pottier of the Louvre in Paris and Mr. Cecil Smith of the British Museum in London have given me valuable aid. Herr Generalconsul E. Landau lent me some of my own original water colour drawings which were in his possession and which I used in the preparation of the coloured plates. His brother too, Baron Dr. W. von Landau, supported me with advice and practical help.

It is to Herr Geheimrath Professor Dr. E. Curtius and Herr Professor Dr. A. Furtwängler that I owe the possibility of publishing on so complete a scale the antiquities in the Cyprian collection of the Antiquarium of the Royal Museum at Berlin. I also enjoyed the valuable co-operation of Herr Professor Dr. Erman, Director of the Syrian and Egyptian section of the Royal Berlin Museum, and of his assistant Herr Dr. Steindorff. To these gentlemen, as well as to Herr Professor Dr. Schrader, Herren DD. Abel, Schäfer and C. F. Lehmann I am indebted for important information on the Syrian and Egyptian antiquities which I have incorporated in my treatise. The books necessary for my studies were freely lent me from the Royal Library at Berlin.

Most of the drawings are by Herr Lübcke and are admirably executed. The remainder of the drawings are the work of Herr Siegert and Herr Couvé. All the phototypes, among them nine coloured ones, were prepared with the utmost care in the workshop of Herr A. Frisch. The zinc etchings, which occur partly in the text and partly among the plates, come from the photochemigraphic workshop of Herren Dr. Diesterweg & Co., Fischer and Dr. Bröckelmann, A. Frisch, E. Galliard and P. Meurer. I have been industriously collecting materials in Cyprus since 1879, consisting not only of notices of finds and descriptions of excavations, but of plans, photographs, drawings and water colours. Most of them are made by myself. Without these it would have been impossible to publish the work at all.

I cannot refrain from mentioning in addition the names of some to whom my gratitude is due for aid given me and interest used on my behalf whereby I was able to go to Cyprus and pursue my archaeological studies there. An English lady, who wishes to remain unnamed, provided the means for my journey to Cyprus in 1878. His Excellency Herr Baron von Keudell, at that time German Ambassador in Rome, who knew me personally, used his influence with the Reichskanzleramt to obtain for me diplomatic introductions for Cyprus. When I arrived in the island Mr. C. D. Cobham, the English Royal Commissioner of Larnaka (known by his bibliography on Cyprus) and Mr. D. Pierides (known by his works on epigraphy and numismatics) began to take an interest in my proceedings. They recommended me to Sir Charles Newton, who was at that time Keeper of the Greek and Roman Antiquities in the British Museum, and towards the end of the year 1879 he entrusted me with the conduct of the first excavations.

The French scholar Sal. Reinach, in his Chroniques d'Orient, which first appeared in the Révue Archéologique, and were then collected in a volume, assigned a considerable space to my investigations. My work has been discussed in England especially in the Contemporary Review and the Academy by the Oxford scholar A. H. Sayce, and in America in the American Journal of Archaeology. In Germany my discoveries and studies were made the property ot a wider circle by means of the Berliner Philologische Wochenschrift edited by Chr. Belger and O. Seyffert. Among German scholars who have up to the present time published the materials afforded them by my new discoveries, I may mention the names of the professors DD. Herr A. Furtwängler, Herr F. Dümmler, Herr W. Helbig, and also Herr DD. P. Herrmann and Herr Julius Naue. The powerful influence which Herr Dr. H. Schliemann exercised on my studies will be best understood by a perusal of my work. The death of this distinguished man was a peculiar loss to me. On the very day on which the sad news was published I received a letter from Herr Dr. W. Dörpfeld, which gave me to understand, that I was to consider myself engaged to take part in Schliemann's excavation projected for the spring of 1891. His unexpected death destroyed one of my most cherished dreams.

Besides the gentlemen whom I have already named as affording me aid in Cyprus I must express my warm gratitude to their Excellencies Sir Robert Biddulph and Sir Henry Bulwer for the ready and substantial encouragement which they always gave to my studies. Many other persons still living in Cyprus, Englishmen as well as Greeks, have shown me kindness and sympathy. These are named in my Dissertation, the appearance of which is due to a suggestion of Herr Hofrath Professor Dr. Overbeck in Leipzig.

Shortly before publication the value of this work was greatly enhanced by a letter from Mr. W. E. Gladstone, which I have reproduced in facsimile. I felt much pleasure in being honoured with a letter from a man of so high a position, especially as the House of Commons had just begun its sittings.

Once more let me repeat my heart-felt thanks to all those who have helped me in my labours.

BERLIN, February, 1893.

Max Ohnefalsch-Richter.

CHAPTER 1.

Ancient Places of Worship in Cyprus.

I describe, at the outset, the six most important Places of Worship which I excavated, because they will occupy a large share of our attention in the present work, and because they give the key to the proper comprehension of Cyprian sacred precincts in general. In their descriptions of the Olympian apparatus of worship as revealed by the excavations, Curtius*) and Furtwängler**) could only cite Cyprian parallels. The material for comparison at the disposal of these scholars, when they wrote, will appear as but a tiny and not always reliable fragment of the History of Cyprian Worships, when compared with the numerous and, in some instances, quite complete pictures of religious observance in ancient Cyprus which I here lay before the reader for what, to all intents and purposes, I may call the first time. Such of my discoveries as have been already made public by myself and others are only a very small fraction of a whole the remainder of which I have purposely withheld; and as regards discoveries since made by others, my long experience as a practical excavator should make me better able to turn them to good account than the discoverers themselves.

I begin with No. 1, the temenos of Artemis Kybele at Achna in the East of the Island.***)

If we draw a straight line from Larnaka, the best known port on the south-east coast of the island, to the ancient Salamis, situated on the east coast north of Famagusta, Achna, a small modern village, will be found about half way between the two. It lies on the edges of a well-watered and fertile depression in the otherwise unfertile or sterile plain. To the S. and SE., in the direction of the village Xylotimbo, there is nothing but bare rock; to the N. and NE., in the direction of Akhyritou, the rock has a scanty covering of ferruginous soil. In the fertile and winding valley of Achna, at a spot where it is tolerable narrow, about 50 metres from the last houses and not far from the road, the peasants, in the spring of 1882, came by accident upon the Artemis-Temenos.

---

*) Die Altäre von Olympia. Berlin 1882. (Extract from the Abhandlungen der Königl. Akademie der Wissenschaften. Berlin 1881.)

**) Die Bronzefunde von Olympia. Berlin 1880. (Extract from the Abhandlungen der Königl. Akad. der Wissensch. Berlin 1879.)

***) In order to enable the reader to find the places easily in the Map (Pl. I), I have there inserted *in red*, at the spots to which they refer, the numbers of the present list. I have also *underlined in red* all the places in the island in which I have made excavations. I have not added an itinerary, as this would have involved connecting by lines most of the villages in the island. Nor did I think it was any use to insert all the spots at which I saw ancient remains or tombs opened by others. I will discuss these in works more specially dealing with Topography.

2*

They were digging for the government, at intervals along the valley, a number of square holes, such as it is usual to make for the extermination of the locusts. *) On Plate IV I give a plan of the temenos as far as it could be determined; the northern portion, lying towards the village, was destroyed many years ago, when an orchard was laid out there. We owe the preservation of a portion of the temenos to the fact that the land has only been occasionally turned by the Cyprian plough, a primitive implement which happily scratches only to the depth of a few centimetres. Nevertheless, at some date in the course of two thousand years,**) violent hands must have been laid on the great mass of the votive offerings which once stood here. We can reckon from the existing fragments of the great terracotta statues that they stood at least 12 feet (3,5 m.) high. It was only to be expected that these huge statues protruding from the ground, and standing "sub divo" should fall a prey to the destroyer. The greatest depth at which the virgin soil was reached was 4 feet. All the bases and feet of statues entered on the plan were found in situ at a higher level (some at no more than 1½ feet below the present surface), resting on the ancient trodden surface. — In digging down at the spot PHT (Pl. IV) the peasants came upon rough terracotta statues (like those on Pl. XI. 1—3 and 8, and Pl. XII, 1—4) packed as close as sardines in a box. (I found similar piles of statues in the excavations of September and October 1882). They were found in such quantities that the children in the village were using them as play-things. Some of the best were sold to a barber at Larnaka, and it was thus that I was led to the discovery of the site. †)

I have found no dedications giving the name of Artemis-Kybele, but the finds testify to her worship here.

Only one inscription was discovered, complete with the exception of two letters, but incomprehensible. It runs in one line round the lower edge of a censer or lustral vessel shaped like a column or altar and about 9 cm. high (reproduced in "The Owl" 1889, p. 76—77 and Pl. IX 26). It is as follows:

ΤΟΚΡΕΤΕΝΕΟΣΝΙΚΟΔΗΜΟΣΟ Θ ΡΟΟΣΙΕΡΟΝ

The name Nicodemos recurs in the Apollo-Temenos at Voni (No. 3). The last word ἱερόν taken together with the circumstances of the discovery, tells us that we are on holy ground, on ground consecrated to some god. Perhaps the penultimate word is to be restored ἥρωος "of the hero"; the other words cannot be understood. It would seem that an illiterate mason had copied the inscription imperfectly.

Site 2, Voni: We here find ourselves in a far more fertile region, watered by one of the most abundant springs in the island. This spring rises at the north end of the village of Kythræa, and a number of villages on, and at the foot of, the southern slope of the northern range owe their existence entirely to it. One of these villages is Voni. The scene of our excavations, near the

---

*) Cp. in the "Nation" (Berlin 1891) page 710 of my Essay "Cypern unter englischer Verwaltung."

**) The temenos has been disused since the fourth century B.C., as the finds clearly show.

***) Part of the breast of a female colossus is exhibited with the other finds of Achna in the British Museum.

†) S. Reinach, Chron. d'Or. p. 187 [5,354—5]. I shall often have to quote this work, which gives the best information about Cyprus and my discoveries; the numbers in brackets refer to the year and pages of the Revue Archéologique, i. e. in this case 1885, p. 354—5.

westernmost houses of the village, is, as the crow flies, about 8¹/₄ miles (13.6 km) to the N.E. of Nicosia, the capital of the island.

On Pl. V, 1, I reproduce the plan of the walls of the Apollo-temenos as far as they can be determined. Pl. V, 2 gives a vivid picture of the excavation and its surroundings. In the background we see the graceful outline of the northern chain, and, beneath it, the olive wood which skirts the village. Propped against the walls of the mud-built house, the last of the village, stand a row of life-size or colossal lime-stone statues, just dug up. In the foreground are my tents and cases, and the excavation in progress. Two of the numerous channels of the system of irrigation fed by the Kythraea spring meet just at the S. W. corner of our Apollo-sanctuary, and the united stream runs across the picture into, and then through, the village. On the near side of the watercourse we see two of my workmen engaged in hoisting on to a cart one of the life-size beardless limestone statues, while, in the immediate foreground, another bearded Græco-Phœnician statue is lying ready for removal. The heads of these statues were, as a fact, found separately, but in the picture I have attached them to their bodies in order to make the whole more graphic.

The drums of columns united and surmounted by a rude doric basis, visible to the left, chanced to have been so disposed at the time the photograph for this picture was taken, and were not found at the spot they occupy in the picture.

Ten drums of columns were found nearly in a row in the wall running from North to South: it is evident that this wall had a stoa adjacent to it on the East.

The architecture and finds will be dealt with in subsequent sections. The view is taken from S. S. E. To the north, between the olive wood and the mountain range, on the southern spurs of the latter, lies the ancient town of Chytroi, a little east of the modern Kythræa. The picturesque region there is now called Ayios Dimitrianos after an old church now completely ruined and overgrown.*)

Our picture of Voni shows once again with what a fine appreciation of natural beauty the ancients chose the sites for their settlements and for the houses of their gods.

Productive excavations had been going on at this place for more than ten years, and the inhabitants continued to dig in secret even after the English occupation, until at length the Government intervened and confiscated the antiquities. When I had formed a committee for the foundation of a Cyprus Museum, I turned my eyes to the site at Voni, and, on the 21ˢᵗ of May 1883, commenced the excavations at the cost of the Museum. I reproduce here the inscriptions found on this spot and published by me in the Athenischen Mittheilungen **), adding a few further remarks.

1. Rectangular basis; length 4 feet (= 1,22 m); depth 2 feet 7 inches (= 78 cm); height 1 foot 1 inch (= 33 cm). On the upper surface three quadrangular depressions. The stone evidently supported a group of three small statues:

ΚΑΡΥΣΟΝΥΣΑΓΟΡΟΥ   Κᾶρυς ᾿Ονυσαγόρου
ΑΠΟΛΛΩΝΙΕΥΧΗΝ   ᾿Απόλλωνι εὐχήν.

---

*) See the Map (Pl. I Nos. 23 and 24) and Nos. 23 and 24 of my list below.
**) Chron. d'Or. p. 186—187 [5, 354] and Mittheilungen des Kaiserlichen Deutschen Archäologischen Instituts zu Athen. 1884, p. 127—139 and Pl. IV and V.

2. Similar basis; length $2^1/_2$ ft. (= 66 cm); depth 1 ft. 10 in. (= 52 cm); height 12—13 in. (= 30,4—33 cm).

I   CIΔΩPOC
KAPYOCAΠOΛ
ΛΩNIEYXHN

σίδωρος
Κάρυος Ἀπόλ-
λωνι εὐχήν.

The dedicants οι Nos. 1 and 2 seem to be father and son.

3. Rectangular block of stone; length 3 ft. (= 91 cm); depth 2 ft. 2 in. (= 66 cm); lenght 10 in. (= 25 cm). The inscription is on one of the narrow sides.

NIKOΔHMOΣYIOIKAPYOΣAΠOΛΛΩNI
ΣIA   [EY]XHN

- - - Νικόδημος υἱοὶ Κάρυος Ἀπόλλωνι
- - - σια   [εὐ]χήν.

The inscription is incomplete on the left; the remainder was probably engraved on another block which has not been found. In line 1 one or more brothers of Nikodemos were mentioned.

4. Scratched on the dress of a badly preserved, headless statue (rather over life-size), near the knee, KAPYC, i. e. the word Κάρυς in the nominative. This is the fourth instance of the occurrence at Voni of this hitherto unknown proper name.

5. and 6. Quadrangular basis; length 2 ft. 8 in. (= 80 cm); depth 1 ft. 8 in. (= 51 cm); height 10 in. (= 25 cm). The two inscriptions are engraved on the front at the same level; each inscription has corresponding to it a quadrangular depression on the upper surface, meant to receive a statue.

5.

AΠOΛΛΩNIEYXHNIOAPXOΣ
YΠEPMHNHKPATOYΣTOY
YIOYENTY𝑥XHI

Ἀπόλλωνι εὐχὴν Ζόαρχος
ὑπὲρ Μηνηκράτους τοῦ
υἱοῦ ἐν τύχῃ.

6.

AΠOΛΛΩNIEYXHNTIMOKPATHΣ
YΠEPONAΣIOPOYTOYIOY
EITYXHI

Ἀπόλλωνι εὐχὴν Τιμοκράτης
ὑπὲρ Ὀνασιόρου το(ῦ) υἱοῦ
ἐ[ν] τύχῃ.

In No. 5 l. 3, the stone was already damaged when the inscription was engraved. The names Ζόαρχος and Μηνηκράτης are new.

7. Fragments of a rude stone vase standing on a low foot; it may have served to certain holy-water. It was built into the Altar (A on the plan, Pl. V) the inscribed side being concealed. The fragmentary inscription is on the outer side of the body of the vase.

AΠOΛΛШNOCIEPE

Ἀπόλλωνος ἱερέ[ως].

8. Quadrangular basis; length 10 in. (= 25 cm); depth 6 in. (= 15 cm); height 4 in. (= about 10 cm); damaged.

AIAΘHTYXHI
KPATEIAAΓOPIAAI
TEMIΔIEYX

Ἀ[γ]αθῇ(ι) Τύχῃ
Κράτεια Ἀγορία Ἀ[ρ]-
τέμιδι εὐχ[ήν].

This stone was built into the southern wall of the square altar-enclosure (at the spot marked Ar. Jn. on Pl. V.) and, in this case also the inscription was concealed.

9. The inscription, well preserved with the exception of one or two indistinct letters, is tolerably well engraved on a triangular, wedge-shaped, blackish stone (Diorite?), quite unhewn and formed thus by nature; height (in its longest axis) about 5 in (= 12,5 cm). I describe this stone and the circumstances under which it was found in greater detail in the Chapter relating to Stone-worship.

ΛΓΓΟΡΓΙΑΙΟΙΘΙΑCΟC	ΛΓ *Γορπιαῖοι θίασος*
ΤΗCΑΠΟCΚΕΥΗC	*κῆς ἀποσκευῆς*
ΕΟΥCΕΝΤΟΙΕΡΕΟΝ	*ἔθυσεν τὸ ἱερέον.*
ΛΔΤΟΙΕΡΕΟΝΟΘΙΑ	ΛΔ *τὸ ἱερέον ὁ θία-*
5 CΟCΤωΝΗΔΥΛΛΙωΝ	*σος τῶν ἡδυλλίων.*
ΛΕΟΘΙΑCΟCΤω	ΛΕ *ὁ θίασος τῶ[ν]*
ΚΙCΑωΝΤΟΙΕΡΕΟΝ	*Κιτάων τὸ ἱερέον.*

Γορπιαῖος (Banquet-month) is the name of a Cyprian month falling in August and September.

10. Female torso; the head and the legs from the knees downwards are missing; height 3 ft 5 in (= 1,04 m); draped in an inner and outer garment both clinging to the limbs; the outer garment leaves the right shoulder free; the treatment of the draperies in Egyptian; the arms hang down at the sides; the right hands holds a holy-w.ater sprinkler. A little below the missing left hand a small nearly square tablet width $3^1{}_4$ in = 8.3 cm., height $3^1/_2$ in = 9,2 cm.) is carved on the thigh; we may suppose it to have been carried in the left hand by means of a handle or cord. On this tablet is engraved the inscription in Cyprian syllabary; beyond one or two perhaps doubtful characters, it is in excellent preservation.

R. Meister[*] reads the inscription as follow:

Γιλ(λ)ίκα ἀμὲ | κὰτ ἔστασε | ὁ Στασιχ | ρέτεος.

The name *Γιλλίκας* or *Γιλλίκα*, which occurs also in other Cyprian inscriptions, is Phoenician. The sanctuary was therefore consecrated in the first place to Apollo. In his retinue, but quite subordinate to him, appears his sister Artemis. I will return to this question when I discuss the statues.

No. 3. Taking leave of Voni, we will now turn our steps inland towards the central district of the island, the kingdom of Idalion and its capital of the same name. Idalion will be found a little to the S.W. of a direct line drawn from Larnaka (Kition) to Nicosia (Ledrai), and about half way between the two.

Plate II shows the position of the ancient town Idalion and of the modern more northerly village of Dali, which, for Cyprus, is a flourishing place and lies in the midst of well watered gardens. No. 36 here marks the position of our site 3.

Plate III exhibits on a larger scale the ancient Idalion.

The interesting temenos lies to the N. of the old town, on the river of Dali (in which that excellent traveller and archaeologist L. Ross[**]) rightly recognised the ancient Satrachos), and close to one of the last houses of the more compact north-westerly portion of the village. Further to the N., N.W., and W., the irrigated gardens and fields on both sides of the stream are dotted with

---

[*] Die griechischen Dialekte. Band 2. Göttingen 1889; p. 169. Cp. now Hoffmann, Die griechischen Dialekte. p. 46.

[**] Reisen nach Kos, Halikarnassos, Rhodos und der Insel Cypern. Halle 1852. p. 102.

houses and farms. The land in which our temenos was found is itself part of this garden-land, called by the peasants περβόλια, i. e. gardens.

Plate XVI gives a view of part of the excavations and the neighbourhood of the river bed, taken from the S. E. The land is owned by two people: the northern strip, behind the fig tree in the middle, belongs to Philippi Michaili, the somewhat higher ground on the south to Giorgi Pieri. At point hy on Pl. VII the virgin soil was reached at the maximum depth of 5 feet (or 1½ m.) In á later chapter it will be shewn that the greater height of the rubbish-layer in Georgi Pieri's land contributes to demonstrate the existence of a roofed building.

Plate VII gives a carefully made plan of the whole temenos, after it had been laid bare. I convinced myself, by digging trenches or sinking shafts all round, that there was no hope of finding anything else in the way of antiquities, walls, or traces of sacrifice. The site was accidentally discovered in the spring of 1883 by labourers who were digging a ditch round the garden-land. The peasants at once begun [to rummage, but, in my then capacity of Superintendent of Excavations to the Cyprus Museum, I succeeded in having the ringleader brought to justice.*) At the same time, I confiscated the things which had been [found and brought them to the Museum. When I went to Europe in 1884, I-proposed the site to various Museums and Scientific Institutes in Berlin, Paris, and London, but with no result.**) On my return, I persuaded Mr. C. Watkins, then manager of the Ottoman Bank in Larnaka, to supply the funds for the excavation, and set to work in February 1885. Following sections of this work will contain a more detailed account of the rich results of this excavation. By the old Turkish law relating to antiquities, which still holds good in Cyprus, one third of the finds belongs to the government, one third to the proprietor, and one third to the excavator. Mr. Watkins, by my advice, bought up, at a small cost, the rights of the proprietor and those of the government, and had therefore only to give up a few duplicates to the Island Museum. After I had vainly attempted to dispose of the great mass of the finds in London, I secured for them a home in the Museum of Berlin.

No inscriptions were discovered; but the numerous finds point clearly to the temenos having been consecrated to Astarte-Aphrodite.

On Pl. XIII are illustrations of four heads (two terracotta and two stone) from life-size statues found here.***)

No. 4. We will now quit Idalion and, journeying due west, reach, at a distance of 10 miles in a direct line, the region of the ancient Tamassos. This district, so populous in early times owing to its copper-mines and the fertility of the soil, is now occupied by the villages of Pera, Politiko, Episkopio, Kambia, Kappedhes and Analyonda. The ancient town of the 6th and 7th centuries B. C. lay between Pera and Politiko. In my work on Tamassos I will publish a large scale map of the district, indicating the ancient settlements, necropoleis, holy places &c.

I examined the ground here practically, with pick and shovel, for the first time in 1885, on my own account; and, having convinced myself of the importance of this almost virgin site, I begged

---

*) See my article in the Repertorium für Kunstwissenschaft 1886: "Das Museum und die Ausgrabungen auf Cypern seit 1878", I.

**) S. Reinach. Chron. d'Or p. 190 [5², 356—7].

***) Reinach, Chron. d'Or. p. 189—197 [5, 356—62]; he there gives illustrations of five statues.

first Col. F. Warren, then Chief Secretary, and afterwards Mr. Watkins to apply to the Government for permission to excavate at, and near, Tamassos. I begun by working for Col. Warren and found the large, richly ornamented, vase of which an illustration will be given below.*)

While engaged in excavating for Col. Warren, I heard that a shepherd, tending his flocks, had lighted on a pile of ancient statues in a valley called Frangissa, between the villages of Pera, Kambia and Analygonda (at no great distance from the last). The credit opened for me by Col. Warren was almost exhausted, and his instructions were that I was to find for him only good Greek things and good Greek glass. At the close of Col. Warren's excavations, I had engaged to go to Amathus for Mr. Watkins. The shepherd's chance discovery and my own examination of the place induced me to write to Mr. Watkins asking him to take out his permit for Tamassos instead of Amathus; but he happened to be then absent at Beirût in Syria, and my letter was delayed. On my communicating to Col. Warren my project of excavating Frangissa for Mr. Watkins and the high expectations I entertained with regard to the site, he begged me to proceed at once to dig there for himself, his own permit for Tamassos not having expired, and Mr. Watkins having none. I was still awaiting a reply from Mr. Watkins, for whom I was anxious to reserve the site; it was now the middle of October; the rains were imminent; the place in question was on the banks of a torrent, far away from all roads, and the soil was stiff. Col. Warren was Chief-Secretary to the Government and Hon. Keeper of the Museum. I was at once his private agent, and Superintendent of Excavations for both the Government and the Museum. My choice lay between excavating the site at once for Col. Warren and letting the work stand over until April or May 1886. I was too well aware that, unless the excavations were taken in hand at once, by next spring little or nothing would be left to find. I knew that the peasants, having once got wind of the place, would ransack it, smash most things, and sell to the first dealer or amateur such objects as to their eyes seemed valuable. My preliminary investigation had told me that unique results were to be expected. I had observed that, owing partly to a landslip, and partly to the action of the torrent when swollen by the winter rains, the statues, many of them still in situ, were covered by a deposit which attained a depth of almost two metres, and, under the circumstances, it was possible that colossal statues still erect might be found. It was clear, from the nature and circumstances of the finds made on the spot discovered by the shepherd, that we had just struck one end of the space containing votive offerings; here, it seemed, stood the altar with its layer of ashes crowded with such objects and reaching to a much greater depth. I further saw, from the quantity of the finds, and their modelling and colouring, that the temenos must have been founded at least as early as the sixth century B.C. Here was, obviously, an important place of worship, where one could count upon finding interesting Phoenician and Greek inscriptions, and good votive bronzes.

Under these circumstances, I decided to excavate the place for Col. Warren, rather than let it be for ever lost to Science.**) I contemplated offering to Mr. Watkins, in compensation, a temenos-site at Amathus which I had rented at my own risk, as well as other important ground (the right

---

*) S. Reinach, Chron. d'Or. p. 293—300 [7, 76—82]. I hear quite recently from Dümmler that the vase is now in the British Museum.

**) As was, to a very great extent, the case with regard to the temenos at Limniti (infr. No. 52), where the English found that most things had been destroyed, broken, or abstracted, by the peasants.

to excavate in which I had also secured in my own name and at my own expense) at Poli tis Chrysokhu, where I felt sure of finding tombs of good Greek period containing objects of value. I therefore wrote to Col. Warren telling him that I would, although I was a little averse to it, excavate Frangissa for him, and prophesying the discovery of most interesting Phoenician and Cyprian inscriptions. At that date no inscribed fragments had been found. I begun the work on the 17th of October 1885, carried it out as rapidly as possible owing to the lateness of the season, and finished on the 2nd of November. The finds exceeded even the high expectations I had formed.

The plan of the temenos is given on Pl. VI. My work on Tamassos will contain a series of good illustrations of the highly interesting sculptures, and a second publication by J. Euting and W. Deecke of the two bilingual Phoenician and Cyprian inscriptions.*)

I had at once set to work to make a road across the torrent-bed, through a vineyard and up a hill to the nearest highway, and had just completed the transport from Frangissa to Nicosia of the numerous statues, some of them colossal, when, two days afterwards, the rains began. The excavation, and especially the transport of these heavy objects, would have been now impossible, as the carts, oxen, and camels would have sunk into the ground.

During these 18 days, occupied as I was besides in building the road, I had to draw up a detailed description of the finds. I was at the same time obliged to watch the work from daylight to dark, and to go over, assisted by a trained workman, the very numerous fragments, in order to pick out pieces which could be connected and discard what was of no worth. Many bits had to be cleaned and put together on the spot, as it would have been scarcely possible at a later date to discover their points of connection, and without cleaning and treatment with acids, valuable painted fragments might well have escaped the most practised eye. I had to be content with making an exact general plan, and inserting the most important finds; in this task I was, on the last Sunday, personally assisted by Col. Warren himself. Every stone of any significance, and all the bases of statues entered in the plan, are drawn to scale, and this holds good for all my other plans: most accurate measurements were everywhere taken.

Unfortunately, want of time and money did not allow me in October to carry the excavation further north, where probing trenches and shafts had convinced me that walls existed of considerable thickness, and of a better construction than the wall, already excavated, enclosing the space in which the votive offerings stood.

It was still more regrettable that, although I had my photographic apparatus with me, I had no money to obtain from Nicosia silver and collodion, my stock of which was exhausted (I at that time used the wet process). All that I had saved from my salary had gone towards working up in scientific form the results of my excavations, a task for which neither the Museum nor individuals would pay me; I had even contracted debts in the cause of science. My urgent representations to Col. Warren that he should give me the means of making photographs had no result: he was only concerned for antiquities which could be easily transported, and would find a ready sale. Consequently he would not, owing to the expense, allow me to pull down the peribolos-wall of the temenos, but ordered me to proceed at once to level the ground, as we were bound to do by the terms of

---

*) The Tamassos finds in general will only be sufficiently discussed here to give completeness to the present picture of the ancient worships. A monograph on Tamassos will appear next year.

our contract with the proprietor Gianni Krasopoulos of Pera. Although I received these instructions on the spot from Col. Warren on November 1st, I, nevertheless, proceeded on the following day to carefully demolish the walls. We have already seen at Voni, how two inscriptions were there built into the wall, with the inscribed face turned inwards, and I looked for something similar at Frangissa. In pulling down the walls in defiance of Col. Warren's orders, the great bilingual inscription was found on the South side at the point Jn., built in with the inscribed side concealed: the smaller bilinguis had been previously discovered inside the enclosure at the point Jn². Such are the facts; and it is clear that Col. Warren had little share in the discovery of the temenos of Apollo-Resef.*) In addition to the two bilingues, I found the fragment of a dedication to Apollo in ordinary Greek characters. The inscription is cut in one line round the edge of a large stone "benitier." This was found inside the enclosure, about the middle, a little to the N. of the terracotta colossus.

But, as I have said, the larger of the two altar-shaped marble cubes, with the longer and more perfect inscription, would have been lost to the world, had I followed Col. Warren's instructions. I have felt much hurt by his having represented himself as the discoverer of the inscription and the temenos, making not the slightest mention of myself.**)

The temenos at Frangissa is the only one yet known in Cyprus, where life-size and colossal statues with their heads on have been found erect in situ. To mention a few examples. —

In the small enclosure at the south end a life-size archaic stone statue was found in situ on the stone NA (Pl. VI). Almost in the centre of the main enclosure, on the stone slab C, stood the largest of the archaic terracotta colossi; the upper portion of this statue had, however, owing to cracks, been a little jammed into the middle part in a vertical direction. The head was on the body, but as there were other cracks in the neck, I was obliged to take the whole out piece-meal. Numbers of other statues of various sizes were lying in rows where they had fallen when the landslip did its work of destruction.

Unhappily these splendid discoveries — discoveries the like of which had never been made, and will never perhaps be made again, in Cyprus — were the means of causing a very regrettable lawsuit in the Insular Court at Nicosia between Col. Warren and Mr. Watkins, in which I was the principal witness. Mr. Watkins was the only person in Cyprus who had supplied the means for excavating on a somewhat generous scale and had allowed me freedom to do or leave undone what I thought fit. The best proof of this lies in the model excavation at Dali (No. 3).

The action Watkins v. Warren was also the means of preventing me from drawing up in Nicosia a detailed description of the finds. By an order of the Court the antiquities were removed

---

*) Reinach, Chron. d'Or, p. 300—302 [7, 81—4]: Sitzungsberichte der K. Preuss. Akad. der Wiss, 1887, p. 116—123, "Zwei bilingue Inschriften aus Tamassos. Von Jul. Euting and W. Deecke." My plan (our Pl. VI) is there reproduced on a smaller scale.

**) The Cyprus Museum. "A bilingual inscription (Phoenician and Kypriote). Recently discovered near the ancient town of Tamassos, Cyprus, during excavations carried out by Colonel Falk. Warren R A." Proceedings of the Society of Biblical Archaeology for. December 1886 and January 1887. "Phoenician and Cypriote Inscriptions. By professor W. Wright, P. Le Page Renouf and P. Berger." A correction of mine is printed in the following number (February 1887).

Cp. also Mémoire sur deux nouvelles inscriptions Phéniciennes de l'île de Chypre par M. Philippe Berger. (Paris 1887). p. 1: "Vers la fin de november 1886, M. Renan eut connaissance par une lettre de M. Max Ohnefalsch-Richter, de la découverte de deux nouvelles inscriptions bilingues, phéniciennes et cypriotes qui avaient été trouvées à Tamasus, près de l'autel à bruler, dans le temenos d'Apollon."

from my house. As in spite of my protest, no trained workman (not even one of those who had taken part in the excavations) was present on the occasion of their removal, the connection of many pieces was lost, and it was afterwards found impossible to fit the largest terracotta head on to its body. Such is, in brief, the.true and.melancholy story of the excavations.

The neighbourhood of Frangissa is one of the most picturesque in the island. It lies on one of the northern spurs of Mt. Machairas. The gentle upper slopes are broken by terraces of rock, furrowed and pierced by deep chasms, and at the foot a sheer precipice descends into the great plain. I will give some views of the neighbourhood in my work on Tamassos.

With Nos. 5 and 6, two places of worship which I excavated in 1889 for the Berlin Museum, I will not deal here at any length, as they, like No. 4, will be dealt with in the special work.

No. 5. By this I designate a sanctuary of the Mother of the Gods, certified as such by epigraphical evidence. I discovered it just inside the northern city-wall of Tamassos, to the N. of the village of Politiko, and to the S. of Pera and the river Pidias (the Pedaios of the ancients), which passes between the two villages. This, the chief stream of the island, has a general northerly course, and the ancient town of Tamassos lies on its left bank nearer Politiko than the temenos. I found the remains of walls which had belonged either to a house or to a primitive sanctuary. Of these I made a plan and section. At present, I will only say that the votive offerings, chiefly statues, were lying in a deep shaft-like cutting on the western side of the temenos. The above-mentioned fragment of a dedication, also found in this cutting, is on the upper edge of a fictile vessel, which had evidently been used for lustral purposes.

No. 6 is another temenos discovered, like the last, at Tamassos in 1889. It lies about a thousand metres further north, close to the left bank, and partly in the present bed, of the river. By the help of the villagers, I was successful in finding the spot, where, a few years before Ludwig Ross's visit,*) a life-size (probably archaic) statue was found, chopped up by the peasants, and sold for old bronze. The head is said to have been preserved and to have found its way to England, but its present abode, if it exists, is unknown. I certified by an excavation, begun on a large scale, that here, at flood-mark on the left bank of the stream, a large temenos consecrated to Apollo existed in ancient times. It contained gigantic stone statues. I found one of these, headless and damaged, but measuring 3,57 by 1,30 metres, as well as fragments of bronze statues over life-size, and two bronze statuettes. The largest of the latter is rather more than 26 cm. in height, and is now one of the treasures of the Berlin Museum. It is of archaic Cyprian workmanship: in the modelling of the face one can already trace the expression of an archaic Greek art that is just beginning to evolve itself independently.

The excavations here begun on the 3ʳᵈ of October 1889. Unfortunately the rainy season arrived much earlier than usual, and ushered itself in by a deluge which put an abrupt end to our work. Although I was not yet able to fix the precise limits of the votive area, enough antiquities had been found in the stratum excavated to make a resumption of the works desirable.

Inscriptions of great value and important bronzes were, doubtless, still underground; but as yet, no inscription had come to light. I had 100 men working for me,·but the excavations had only continued for 16 days.

---

*) Inselreisen IV (Cypern), p. 161.

The scenery of the valley in which the temenos lies is of a character to charm the beholder. The fertile fields and luxuriant olive-woods form a rich contrast to the steep and barren mountain-slopes above.

I have here, as a first instalment of the documents at my disposal, given some account of six sites, at all of which I made important discoveries. Five of these had been scarcely touched before; at Voni alone had extensive depredations gone on. In addition to these six sites, I was enabled to examine closely no less than forty-six others, and to dig in most of them. Of others I had word; Hogarth's Devia Cypria*) added six to my list; the Excavations of the Cyprus Exploration Fund at Salamis an additional five.**) The list comprises in all 72 examples, and in the text I shall have to speak of some further sites not contained therein. This material is so extensive, that it enables us, on many points, to reach sure conclusions, claiming to possess permanent value.

No. 7. Kition. Temenos of Artemis Paralia, as shown by inscriptions***); near Larnaka, on the eastern edge of the salt lake; repeatedly examined by me in 1879. I dug there, and found that the site had been terribly ransacked.

No. 8. Kition. Hillock with temenos, which a series of inscriptions show to have been consecrated to Ešmûn-Melqart. It is situated in the salt lake, on a tongue of land which projects for a considerable distance from its western bank. I examined it in 1879. It is easily recognisable in Colonna Ceccaldi's (very incomplete) plan of Larnaka and environs†), and has been also correctly described and distinguished from the foregoing by Isaac H. Hall.††) It is, therefore, surprising that L. Heuzey mixes up the two sites, and converts them into a "monte testaccio" containing vast quantities of worthless ex-votos.†††)

No. 9. Kition. Sanctuary of Astarte on the Acropolis or harbour-fortress, between Old Larnaka and the modern Skala. My assignment of the temenos to Astarte, resting on no epigraphical evidence§), was subsequently confirmed by two Phoenician inscriptions. I watched the removal of the hill, made photographs and measurements of the works which were being demolished, and drew for the Government a still unpublished plan. I also published in the Graphic §§) sketches of the architectural and other finds.

No. 10. Achna. In addition to the temenos described above (No. 1), a second primitive sanctuary, yielding somewhat similar finds, came to light further east, on a gentle slope in the river valley. I made some further excavations there and found, inter alia, a most interesting very old terracotta statuette of Artemis-Kybele, now in the British Museum.

---

*) London 1889. P. 66, 71 and 83.

**) Journ. of Hell. Stud. XII (1891), p. 59—198.

***) Cesnola-Stern, p. 56. L. P. di Cesnola confuses Demeter with Artemis. See Al. P. di Cesnola, Salaminia. p. 95.

†) Monuments antiques de Chvpre de Syrie et d'Egypte. (Paris 1882), p. 17—19. Corpus Inscriptionum Semiticarum. Nos. 23—28.

††) On the Phoenician inscriptions of the Cesnola Collection in New-York. (Proceedings of the American Oriental Society, October 1883. CLXVI.)

†††) I have not the reference to Heuzey's work. I read of it in an American periodical.

§) Ausland 1879, p. 970 sq. Corpus Inscriptionum Semiticarum, p. 92—99 and Nos. 86. A and B. Reinach. Chron. d'Or, p. 176 [5², 346—7.]

§§) London 1880.

No. 11. Also near Achna, but more in the direction of Avgoru, on the rocky plain above the ravine. The same class of finds as at Nos. 1 and 10, pointing to Artemis. I examined the site in 1882. Not distant is Vrisudi, the property of Mr. M. Westorf.

No. 12. Between Achna and Xylotimbo, on ferruginous soil. The finds show that Apollo was here worshipped in conjunction with Artemis. I dug here also in 1882.

No. 13. Close to the village of Xylotimbo, by the threshing-floor: examined at the same date as the last: Artemis-finds like those of Nos. 1, 10 and 11.

No. 14. At a place called Pharangas, between Achna and Akhyritou, and N. E. of the former. Here Alexander di Cesnola's workman discovered an Artemis-Kybele temenos, equalling our No. 1 on the extent and value of its finds, which now form one of the attractions of the Cyprian collection in the British Museum.*) Alex. di Cesnola seems throughout his book "Salaminia," to have ticketed the Pharangas finds as Salamis finds. Figs. 196 (p. 191), 198 (p. 193), 201 (p. 195), 206 (p. 202), 213 and 214 (p. 224) are obviously all from Pharangas, for I found at Achna (No. 1) the same types, exactly corresponding as regards style, technique, material, colouring, and dimensions. My own researches with the spade on the site converted my suspicion into certainty, and enough yet remains there to enable others to judge of our respective accuracy. **) I will deal with this question at greater length when I come to speak of the statues.

No. 15 is a site Ormidhia, on the coast to the South of Achna and Xylotymbo. I found, in digging here in 1882, a terracotta statuette of a man with a little ox under his arm, together with a few other votive figures. The name of the god is uncertain.

No. 16. At Cap Greco, the ancient Pedalion, on the level "col" at the foot of the summit, are the remains of a large temenos, and many stone figures, some larger than life. Mr. Dörpfeld and I discovered the place in 1890.***)

No. 17. South of the great tumulus in the plain of Salamis. I dug here in 1879 and 1880. Aphrodite with the tympanon, evidently an Aphrodite-Kybele, was worshipped here. The site has suffered much.†

No. 18. Near Arsos, east of Tremithousha, west-south-west of Salamis. The ancient word ὅλσος "holy grove" has survived in the name of the modern village.††) To the N.E. of the village are the remains of a temenos dedicated to a male divinity. I investigated the spot in 1883. A small bronze votive ox, and a small bronze group of a man leading an ox to sacrifice (now in the Louvre had been found here by the peasants. I discovered, among other things, fragments of figures representing Geryon, who often in Cyprus appears us a companion of Apollo.†††)

---

*) No. 1 supra.

**) The terracottas figured and described by Cesnola in Salaminia, come, however, as he says (p. 222 "from Salamis and other Cyprian sites," so the figures here mentioned have not a false attribution, in as much as they have none.

***) The colossal head of Aphrodite-Kybele, now in the Berlin Museum (Cesnola-Stern, pl. XXXIX, 1 and p. 159) probably comes from here. I have said something of this holy hill of Aphrodite in the Berl. Philol. Wochenschr., 1891, p. 962—963.

†) Chron. d'Or., p. 181 [5², 349—50.]

††) There is another village of the same name, high up in the mountains in the western part of he island.

†††) Cesnola-Stern, pl. XXXIV, 1.

No. 19. Near Marathovouno, north of Arsos, north-west of Salamis, nearly due east of Nicosia. Some peasants commenced digging here in 1890. I proceeded to the spot and examined the site. A male divinity, probably Apollo, and numerous helmeted figures came to light.

No. 20. Near Goshi,*) about nine miles from Larnaka in a north-westerly direction, on the Nicosia road. I took both Dümmler and Furtwängler up to see this wonderful "place of worship" situated on a steep hill-side in the midst of beautiful mountain scenery. In the days of Turkish rule valuable finds were made here and sold to the Consuls in Larnaka. The grove was consecrated primarily to Apollo. The ground falls so rapidly that we can scarcely suppose there was a building, unless an artificial terrace had been formed.

The work of destruction and depredation that has gone on here is indescribable. The ground on every side is thickly strewn with the remains of smashed statues (some of great size), stone bases, and quantities of small terracotta fragments. The chief divinity was evidently the martial Apollo. Here, just as in the sanctuary of this god at Frangissa near Tamassos, numerous terracottas representing chariots in combat had been dedicated. Here too, as at Frangissa, and in the older of the two Apollo groves at Athienu, whence L. di Cesnola obtained his most important statues, by the side of Apollo stands first Herakles-Melqart. I discovered a fragment of the upper portion of the head of a stone statue somewhat larger than life, which shows the same design and the same tendency of style as Cesnola's Herakles-Melqart statue (Cesnola-Stern, pl. XXIII). Next in rank to Apollo and Herakles we find at Goshi the seated Baal-Hammon-Zeus. Such was also the case at Frangissa.

No. 21. A temenos, of which little now remains, on an eminence between Nicosia and the nearest village to the South, Ayios Omologitades. The site is now occupied by the English church. A Greek church, dedicated to I know not whom of their saints, is said to have formerly stood on the spot, and until a few years ago, the ground was still looked upon as consecrated, and on certain occasions candles were lit, and service performed. In digging the foundations for the Protestant church, the workmen came upon stone statues and ancient votive offerings, as well as large Hellenistic draped statues of good treatment, portions of an older chariot combat executed in stone, and fragments of columns.**)

No. 22. To the W. of the ancient Chytroi (now Ayios Dimitrianos), between it and the modern Kythraea, is a temenos, shown by more than one inscription to have been dedicated to (Aphrodite) Paphia. It is situated on a considerable hill commanding a splendid view. Although already, in Cesnola's time the ground had been thoroughly ransacked, I succeeded in digging up some very important terracotta fragments, among them a life-size head, and the upper two thirds of a large statuette: they are now in the Cyprus Museum.***) Both represent Aphrodite: the statuette is nude, and wears a nose-ring. These statues (as far as the style, my notes of other similar discoveries, and my general knowledge permit me to judge) date, in part at least, from as early as the end of the 7th, or beginning of the 6th, century B. C.

L. P. di Cesnola had obtained from this site eleven Cyprian inscriptions, all of them dedi-

---

*) Kosci in Reinach, Chron. d'Or, p. 175 [5² 345—6].
**) Described by me in the "Repertorium für Kunstwissenschaft IX, 1886, p. 206.
***) Reinach, Chron. d'Or, p. 187 [5, 534 - 5].

cations to the goddess of Paphos, the Paphia, as Aphrodite is here, in most cases, briefly styled; one other is published by Deecke, Hall, and Meister;*) A. di Cesnola contributes two more.**) I found two others (now in the Cyprus Museum). In 14 out of the 16 she is called "Paphia" or "Paphian Goddess"; one gives the full name "Paphian Aphrodite"; ***) in another all that remains of her name is A.

No. 24. At the S. W. corner of the upper portion of the town of Chytroi, and within the walls, I made in 1883 some excavations for the Cyprus Museum in an Aphrodite-temenos, which had been much ransacked at an earlier date. Here groups of woman dancing round a sacred tree are of frequent occurrence. The objects discovered — they are now exhibited in the Museum at Nicosia — prove that, by the side of Astarte-Aphrodite, Tammuz-Adonis was especially venerated here.

Nos. 25 and 26. Two primitives sanctuaries or holy groves of Apollo, near Athiænou, at a place called Hag. Photios. The two sites excavated are several hundred metres apart,†) and between them is a hill. The older and more wealthy temenos lies to the S. W., near the ruined church of Hag. Photios visible to the N. The later temenos, with work of a more Greek character and of the 4th and later centuries, lies eastward of the church and at a somewhat greater distance from the village of Athiænou. I took Messr. Dümmler, Furtwängler, Oberhummer and Dörpfeld to see this place. There are enough fragments lying about to make both sites recognizable, but excavation would reveal much more. When I first visited the site, and also on the occasion when I visited it with Dümmler, I was accompanied by the late Andreas Vondiziano, the supervisor — I may say the conductor — of Cesnola's excavations, and Georgi Sotiri of Athiænou, one of those who was present when the colossal head was found. Dümmler questioned these people in Greek. The later eastern temenos, lying, as I have said, to the east of the hill, formed a tetragon 18 metres by 9, and was surrounded by a peribolos-wall of quarried stones and boulders about 3 feet in height. Nearly in the middle of the western side of this rough enclosing wall, and facing the slope, we observed an opening resembling a gate; according to Vondiziano a few rude stone steps lead from this gate down into the votive area. There were also entrances on the North and on the East. It is probable — I should say certain — that similar rude walls once enclosed the other more important western temenos lying to the S. W. of the hill and nearer to the ruined church. The peasants had here been at work ere Cesnola came, and the excavations made at Cesnola's expense consisted only of burrowing holes in the find-stratum after the fashion of moles. The later eastern site has been since levelled and for

---

*) I follow the excellent guidance of the American scholar, J. H. Hall, who tentatively corrects the earlier editors in the Journal of the American Oriental Society XI, 1885, p. 210—214, Nos. 1—14, "Inscriptions from Kythraea." There are eleven Cyprian dedicatory inscriptions in the Metropolitan Museum of Art at New York; a twelfth (Deecke No. 13) comes also from Kythraea-Chytroi, but is not in New York.

**) Salaminia, p. 84—86, figs. 78 and 79. The inscriptions are there stated to have been found at Cerina (Kerynia?), but there is no doubt that they came from our site at Chytroi.

***) Nos. 1 and 2 first published by Pieridis in the "Cyprus Museum" 1883; republished, with improved readings, by Meister. Die griechischen Dialekte, II, p. 168.

†) "According to Ceccaldi 200 metres, according to Cesnola 200 yards." So Holwerda: Die alten Kyprier in Kunst und Cultus, p. 1. — The first to recognise in the two sites Τιμίνη of Apollo was R. Neubauer in his essay: Die angebliche Aphroditetempel zu Golgoi und die daselbst gefundenen Inschriften in kyprischer Schrift, (Comm. philol. in honorem Theod. Mommsen, Berlin 1887, p. 673—693) For dove-priests and dove-sacrifices, which testify neither for nor against Apollo, see below.

long cultivated, but this is not the case with the western site — the site which has given us the priest with the pigeon, the colossal head, the Herakles*) &c. One can still see the row of enormous mole-hills here, just like those which testify to the excavations at the temenos of Artemis-Paralia by the salt lake near Larnaka (our No. 7).

No. 27. I mention next in order a holy grove which I have not yet personally examined. It is in the neighbourhood of Pyla, and Mr. Lang obtained some valuable finds from it. The inscriptions tell us that it was dedicated to Apollo Magirios: Apollo is the chief figure of a group of divinities comprising Herakles, Pan (ithyphallic) and Artemis. There were found here numerous terracotta statuettes of single dancing priestesses, and stone groups of priestesses dancing in a circle round the sacred cypress tree.**)

Nos. 28—38. From Idalion in addition to No. 3, I can cite no fewer than eleven other examples of holy groves or simple altars.—

No. 28. Grove or altar of the Idalian Anat-Athene, attested by inscriptions; situated on the hill now called Ambilleri—the westernmost of the two Akropolis summits and the chief Akropolis of Idalion. See on Pl. III the points marked 2 and 3, and Ambilleri on Pl. II. Here, affixed to some portion of the temenos or perhaps simply to a tree, was the perforated bronze tablet with the long Cyprian inscription, now in the Cabinet des médailles in Paris and known to scholars as the Luynes tablet. Close at hand, certainly inside the sacred precinct of Athene (perhaps within the walls of a roughly built chamber) were stored votive offerings of price—a number of silver paterae, and bronze weapons: such of these as survive are also in Paris. Inscribed on one of the bronze objects, which may be either the handle of a sceptre, a club, or part of a carriage, is a dedication in Cyprian syllabary to the Athene of Idalion.***) A portion of a cuirass found in the same place bears a short Phoenician inscription:†) it belonged to a cuirass similar to one found by me in 1889 in excavating for the Berlin Museum which the circumstances of its discovery show to belong to the sixth century B. C. The great inscription (of such value for the list of the Phoenician kings of Kition and Idalion), found in 1887 by myself and Mr. Evstathios Konstantinides (a Greek gentleman educated in Germany), is a dedication to the goddess Anat, who is evidently to be identified with the Greek Athene.††) This inscription was built into the wall of a small Greek church (9 church on Pl. III), constructed on the former city wall of the lower town of Idalion. We may assume with some approach to certainty that this block of marble belongs to the temenos of Athene on the Akropolis, and was brought down to be used in building the church. The inscription, which is Phoenician, tells us that an object of beaten copper was dedicated to Anat, but the word statue is avoided, and while, in almost all other cases, τεμένη and the precincts of altars are crowded with terracotta, stone, and bronze figures, their frequency being in most places still attested by the numerous fragments lying on the surface of the abandoned excavation sites, here, on the spot where the bronze tablets with Cyprian inscrip-

---

*) Cesnola-Stern, Pls. XXI, 1, XXII, XXIII and XXIV.

**) G. Colonna Ceccaldi, Monuments antiques de Chypre, de Syrie et d'Égypte (Paris 1882), p. 21. Hogarth, Devia Cypria, p 26

***) For further details see my notice in The Owl p. 46—47, and Perrot & Chipiez III, p. 772, 779, 866—869

†) Perrot & Chipiez III, Fig. 348. (p. 494)—the bronze object with Cyprian inscription   Fig 633 (p. 867)—the bronze piece of a cuirass with Phoenician inscription.

††) See below, No. 61 Bilinguis Anat-Athene at Larnaka tou Lapithou.

4

tions were found, statuary fragments are wholly absent. Below we shall meet with an aniconic spring-
and tree-worship at Lithrodonda (No. 42). We may well assume, in the present case also, the
existence of a fortified summit, consecrated to Anat-Athene, where no votive statues were erected,
but beasts were sacrificed, and paterae, arms, and inscribed tablets of metal were dedicated.*) There
was never here, at any time, any kind of image-worship.

We cannot help recalling the sanctuary of Athene Telchinia at Teumessos in Boeotia,
where, as Pausanias expressly tells us,**) there was no image. "We might conjecture" adds Pausanias "as regards the name, that Cyprian Telchines had emigrated to Boeotia and there founded
the temple of their Athene. The absence of all idolatry is also characteristic of the oldest find-
stratum at Olympia, as Furtwängler in his „Bronzefunden von Olympia" (p. 32) first pointed out.
He there cites Cyprus as a parallel and refers both to Cesnola's finds and to the sanctuary excavated by Lang (No. 37 in the present list). I will recur to this subject below.

Nos. 29 and 30. The western Akropolis-hill at Idalion was, as we have seen, consecrated to
Anat-Athene***); that on the east was consecrated to Astarte-Aphrodite.†) This great grove of
Aphrodite, held in such high esteem by the ancients, is not to be sought, as Holwerda and others
before him, suppose, in the depression between the two Akropolis-hills, for the temenos there excavated by Lang is shown by numerous inscriptions to belong to Rešef-Apollo.††) There is no room
here for the extensive grove described by ancient writers, which was rather a hill-forest, a hill holy
to Aphrodite, like that on Cape Pedalion. I have (in 1887) shown that it is to be sought on the
smaller and more easterly of the two Akropolis-hills, at the spot marked 8 Temenos on Pl. III. An
examination of the walls and the nature of the finds made at point *n*, demonstrated that the great
grove of Aphrodite lay originally quite outside the city wall. At a date not earlier than the sixth
century B. C., and perhaps later, a portion of the great grove was marked off from the rest as a
smaller temenos, and comprised within the city walls by an extension of the fortified area made with
this purpose.

The finds showed, that already previous to the fortification of the holy precinct, buildings
with an interesting disposition of columns had stood in the grove. Earlier discoveries made in the
sanctuary and grove, and a group of Aphrodite κουροτρόφος with two children, (one in swaddling
clothes) leave no room for doubt that this goddess was worshipped here,

I designate by No. 30 the sanctuary of Rešef-Mikal-Apollo-Amyklos, excavated by
Mr. Lang, to which reference has just been made. It seems to have stood by one of the principal
gates of the lower town, on the main road, which ran in a notherly direction exactly in the track o

---

*) We are reminded of the consecration of the tabernacles in the Old Testament.

**) IX, 19, 1. Καὶ Ἀθηνᾶς ἐν Τευμησῷ Τελχινίας ἐστὶν ἱερόν, ἄγαλμα οὐκ ἔχον· ἐς δὲ τὴν ἐπίκλησιν
αὐτῆς ἔστιν εἰκάζειν ὡς τῶν ἐν Κύπρῳ ποτὲ οἰκησάντων Τελχίνων ἀφικομένη μοῖρα ἐς Βοιωτοὺς ἱερὸν
ἱδρύσατο Ἀθηνᾶς Τελχινίας.

***) Pl. III, Nos. 1—3.

†) Pl. III, 6, The Owl 1888, p. 55—56.

††) Pl. III, No. 8. B. H. Lang, Narrative of Excavations in a Temple at Dali (Idalium) in Cyprus
with observations on the various Antiquities found therein by R. S. Poole Esq. (Transactions of the Royal
Society of Literature. Second series Vol. XI. Part. I. p. 30.) G. Colonna Ceccaldi, Monuments antiques de
Chypre, de Syrie et d'Égypte. (Paris 1882). p. 29—31 and Pl. I. A. E. J. Holwerda. Die alten Kyprier in
Kunst und Cultus. Leiden 1886.

the modern road coming from the villages Alambra and Lymbia and passing between the two summits on its way to Dali. This road and the position of the shrine are shown on Pl. II and Pl. III, 6.

Two plans of this temenos have been published, one by Lang, the other by Ceccaldi (see the references on the preceding page). I have with the permission of the publishers (Messrs. John Murray and Didier & Cie.), reproduced both these plans on Pl. VIII, 1 and 2. Lang's plan was edited by himself; Ceccaldi's, after his death, by the publishers of his work.*)

Lang (p. 35) calls his a "rough ground plan." I can personally attest the care and conscientiousness which both these writers have exhibited in their works dealing with Cyprus, as I have been enabled in many cases to revise their statements on the spot. I therefore thought it necessary to take both these plans into account in the section of this work dealing with the Cyprian temenos (with roofed buildings). Ceccaldi's plan gives one the impression of having been carefully sketched on the spot after accurate measurements: it is more elaborate than Lang's. Although the two plans do not exactly correspond throughout, yet certain details, e. g. a small tetragonal building (Lang's L, Ceccaldi's R), are of precisely the same dimensions in both, and both exhibit, in the main, the same distribution of walls, steps, stone vessels, and bases of columns, and the same find-spots of inscriptions and coins. I only became acquainted with these two works at a date when I had already made and entered with the greatest care the measurements of my own plans (Plates IV—VII), and drawn up the annexed report of discoveries, so that Messrs. Lang and Ceccaldi's results and my own mutually check each other. It will be seen that we all give (with a few variants) the same general scheme of constructions intended to serve purposes of worship. It is all the more to be regretted that M. Perrot, in his and M. Chipiez' admirable Histoire de l'art dans l'antiquité seems to be ignorant of both these plans.**) Lang's description will always rank as one of the most valuable records of Cyprian excavation that we possess.

No. 31. A little to the west of this large sanctuary of Aphrodite, at the spot marked 7 on Pl. III, within the oldest city wall, there is another small house, shrine, or temenos also consecrated to Aphrodite.***) I found it in 1883 during the course of excavations carried out for Sir Charles Newton.

No. 32. On the northern slope of the principal Akropolis-hill Ambilleri, below the Anat-

---

*) P. 30 of the "Monuments": L'on a reproduit, planche I, le plan de ces fouilles tel qu'on l'a retrouvé dans les papiers de l'auteur.

**) III, p. 278, M. Lang découvrit à Dali un temple, dont il a négligé de relever le plan; il n'a même pas donné la moindre indication sur l'état du terrain où il a retrouvé un butin si précieux et sur les dispositions architecturales dont il a dû y relever la trace.

***) The name Ambelleri is, in Ceccaldi's work (p. 295—296) and in Cesnola-Stern erroneously given to both Akropoleis: this name belongs to the western hill, the eastern being known as I Mouti tou Arvili. The two Ceccaldis' description of the scenery is otherwise excellent, and their descriptions show that they correctly distinguished the two shrines on the eastern hill, our No. 31 (on Pl. II) on the lower eminence and the great Aphrodite temenos, our No. 29 (8 on Pl. III), on the higher. The Ceccaldis also mention that the life-size statue, illustrated on their Pl. XVIII 1 and purchased by the Louvre, comes from this last place. I learnt that the colossal statue of which the lower part is missing (Ceccaldi Pl. XVIII, 2, and Perrot III, p. 542, Fig. 368) comes also from No. 29. At our No. 31, where the Ceccaldis still saw a cistern and thought they recognised a flight of steps leading down the hill side, I found remains of lime-stone statues, in various sizes and styles, all of them female figures and evidently belonging to an Aphrodite-temenos: among them a head of Aphrodite, rather more than half as large as life, of fine, developed Greek style.

4*

Athene temenos and the theatre, Aphrodite had yet another small place of worship, temenos, or primitive shrine (Pl. III, 4). The famous sanctuary of the Idalian Aphrodite had been wrongly sought on this spot also.*) The situation, the extent, and the relative productiveness of this place all speak to the contrary, while our point 8 is well qualified in all these respects.

No. 33. In the course of other excavations for Sir C. Newton (1883), I found, on the next hill to the west of the Ambilleri Akropolis, a temenos of Aphrodite κουροτρόφος (Pl. II, 15). Although the place had been ransacked, I was able to fix the position of the altar of sacrifice and the limits of the votive area, and found sufficient iconic fragments to determine the character of the worship. By the side of Astarte-Aphrodite with maternal attributes, Tammuz-Adonis was especially venerated here.

No. 34. If we now turn our steps eastward, we find, outside the eastern city wall and to the north of the great hill grove of Aphrodite on the Mouti tou Arvili, a temenos of a male divinity situated at the foot of the slope. (17 on Plates II and III).

No. 35. South-east of the great Aphrodite-grove, (Aloupofournos 8 on Plates II and III) and on the same ridge at a greater height, another hill god, evidently Apollo, was worshipped. Besides the fragments of numerous statues, the remains of a cistern used for lustral purposes are visible.

If we now descend into the plain, we re-find, to the north of the ancient Idalion, on the banks of the stream just where the last houses of the modern Dali stand, our No. 3, the Aphrodite temenos excavated in 1885 (Pl. VII).

No. 36. Close to the last, to the east (37 on Plate II), I was able to demonstrate the existence in ancient times of a sacred tree on which terracotta masks of men and animals were hung. The tree decayed, the antifixes survived, and were found lying in a heap. They have holes both in the sides and at the top, so that they could be either strung round the tree or hung up separately. I communicated this discovery to Mr. Helbig.***)

No. 37. To the south of this site (Nos. 36 and 37 will be found on Pl. II near 41) an ancient well or pit was found, full of portions of statues, the bones of animals, ashes, and charcoal. Since excavating the house-sanctuary of the Mother of the Gods at Tamassos (No. 5), where the statues were lying in a consecrated pit, I think that here and at No. 29 (41 on Pl. II) something similar was the case.†)

No. 38. Outside the village of Dali, on the east, near the point marked 21 on Pl. II, where four large underground tombs, built of stone, were found, stood another small temenos belonging to an unknown goddess. In 1887 some shepherds found here a few female stone heads, which came into my hands. I also visited the spot.

No. 39. About a mile (= 1,60 km.) to the north of Dali, at point 31 on Pl. II, stood a temenos consecrated to an animal divinity. All the figures I found there represent beasts single and in groups e. g. birds, cows suckling calves &c.

No. 40. Rather more than a mile and a half (= 2,40 km.) to the north-east of Dali, just

---

*) Ross, Reisen nach Kos &c., und der Insel Cypern, p. 99.

***) Das Homerische Epos (2nd edition), p. 417, Note.

†) Similar trenches or pits, with or without a casing of masonry) are not infrequent in Cyprus, and I will speak of them below. We may compare the dispositions of Greek heroa, as described in Roscher's Lexikon, col. 2497, on the evidence of the latest finds.

before we reach the village of Potamia, are the remains of an ancient shrine where Rešef-Apollo and Melqart-Herakles were worshipped. The spot is marked 28 on Pl. II.

No. 41. A sanctuary lying north-west of the village of Nisou, about 6 miles (= 9,60 km.) west-north-west of Dali. Votive groups in terracotta representing chariot combats, similar to those found by Lang at Idalion (No. 30), and by myself at Goshi (No. 20) and Frangissa (No. 4), are frequent here.

No. 42. Near Lythrodonda, a village lying about six miles (= 9,60 km.) south-east of Tamassos and distant about nine miles (= 14,40 km.) from Idalion. We are here in the oldest copper-mining district. East and west of Lythrodonda the slag-heaps left by the ancient workings are visible from a long way off. In a mountain valley to the south I found (1883) the traces of an imageless worship. The offerings, consisting solely of lamps and coins, were deposited on the banks of the stream, at a spot where a spring rises at the foot of a precipitous rock. The possibility of a necropolis is excluded. W. Helbig mentions this place in his Homerische Epos.[*]) The lamps and coins belong to the times of the later Ptolemies and the early Roman emperors.

No. 43. Near Amathus, just outside the north-east end of the town, I found, in 1885, a precinct sacred to several divinities, male and female. It has still to be excavated. I have rented the land.

No. 44. In the southern outskirts of the lower town of Amathus is the shrine in which the colossus of Melqart-Herakles-Bes-Typhon[**]) now at Constantinople was worshipped.

No. 45. A holy place on the highest summit of the Akropolis of Amathus, where two gigantic stone vessels were used for ritual purposes. One of these is still lying broken on the spot, parts of it remaining in situ; the other is in the Louvre.

No. 46. Near the village of Pasoulla, on a hill about 6½ miles (= 10,40 km.) north of Limassol, and 7 miles (11,20 km.) north-west of Amathus, is a temenos sacred to Zeus Labranios. This is one of the few important sites which I have not personally examined, but besides the brief mention in Cesnola-Stern, we have Cesnola's detailed description, published by Mr. Hall in the Journal of the American Oriental Society, Proceedings at New Haven 1883, "A temple of Zeus."

No. 47. A hill now known as Mouti Sinoas was the scene of a highly interesting altar-worship of Baal Libanon, practised already, as the Phoenician inscriptions from the site show, early in the 10th century B. C. This hill is in the mountainous district between the villages of Kellaki and Sanidha, not far from the village of Sinoas, and seven miles (= 11,20 km.) in a straight line north of Amathus. Here again we are in the region of the old copper mines,[***]) and Lythrodonda (No. 42) is only eleven miles (= 17,60 km.) away.

No. 48 and 49 are two places of worship at Hyle, both evidently consecrated to Apollo Hylates. The reader will find this place one mile (= 1,60 km.) west of the ancient city of Kurion at the south-west corner of the island. On the Paphos road, in the little ravine mentioned by Ross[†])

---

[*]) P. 240, Note 2.
[**]) Perrot and Chipiez, Fig. 386. The Christian church has converted Typhon into Ayios Typhonos or Tykhonos. This is the name of a small village near Amathus.
[***]) Corp. Inscr. Semit., p. 22—26. See also my article "Cypern, die Bibel und Homer" in Ausland, No. 26 and 28 (1891).
[†]) Reisen nach Kos &c., p. 176.

there came to light in Cesnola's time the remains of a temenos (No. 48) with numerous statues, which belong to an older and deeper deposit than that of No. 49, a larger precinct situated about five minutes ' walk to the north-west.*) I accompanied Mr. Oberhummer (1887), and Mr. Dörpfeld **) (1890) on their visits to the spot. In the older temenos three fragments of Cyprian texts were found. ***)

No. 50. There is another temenos of Apollo Hylates at a place called Drymou in the west of the island about nine miles (= 14,40 km.) south of Poli tis Khrysokhou (Marion-Arsinoe), and about twelve miles (=19,20 km.) north of New-Paphos. Two dedications in Cyprian syllabary found here style the god simply Hylates, without Apollo†). It would seem to have been the custom in Cyprus thus to designate the different forms of the same divinity, the simple epithet in time acquiring substantival force.

No. 51. An altar consecrated to Aphrodite on Cape Boumo. ††) This promontory will be found on the map between Morphou Bay and Khrysokhou Bay on the north coast, in the extreme west of the island. There are two villages called Boumo, one on the mountains at some distance from the sea, the other, smaller and of more recent growth, on the shore close to the road leading from Karavostasi (Soloi) to Poli tis Khrysokhou (Marion-Arsinoe). The houses of the village by the sea belong to the people of the upper village, who come down to the coast for a certain portion of the year to cultivate their fields. Since the English occupation, a growing sense of security from the inroads of pirates has tempted many of them to abandon their mountain fastness for good and all, and take up their abode at the sea-side. The name Boumo is nothing else than the Greek βωμός "altar." It is most interesting to find that, while the altar of a church is called here (and throughout the Greek east) ἡ ἅγια τράπεζα "the holy table," the Cypriots call a deposit of ashes and charcoal containing ancient remains, a βωμός. I have paid frequent visits to the place, and in 1890 made a practical examination of it in company with Mr. Dörpfeld.

No. 52. A temenos at Limniti, probably belonging to Apollo (perhaps not exclusively). Having heard that the peasants were ransacking this site, I took steps to make the Government intervene, and induced Mr. Watkins to rent the ground with a view to excavation. Unfortunately, I found that nearly everything of value had been abstracted. I was, however, able to secure the best things for the Berlin Museum. When the Cyprus Exploration Fund came and really excavated the place, there was little left to find.†††)

No. 53. A temenos of Aphrodite near the villages of Katydhata-Linou, in the valley of Solia, about five miles (= 8 km.) south-east of Karavostasi (Soloi). I made some researches here in 1882.

---

*) Cesnola-Stern, p. 281—283.

**) Dörpfeld photographed some of the fragments which were lying about. Prints can be obtained from the Kais. Deutschen Archaeologischen Institut in Athen, (Nos. 2 and 3 of the Cyprian collection. See Jahrbuch des Instituts VI (1891), p. 89 of the Anzeiger).

***) Published by Deecke in Collitz' Sammlung der griechischen Dialekt-Inschriften I, page 23 and pages 42—44.

†) Published ibid., p. 19, No. 28 and 29. Compare Paphia for Aphrodite Paphia.

††) On Kitchener's map and the more recent map of Sakellarios the name is written Pomos or Πωμός. The native pronunciation is Boumos.

†††) Reinach, Chroniques d'Orient, p. 421—422 [80, 80--82] Journal of Hellenic Studies, IX (1890), p. 83—99.

Groups of figures dancing round male or female flute-players were among the votive offerings. I also found fragments of a silver patera with flowers in relief, and of a bronze patera with a battle of Greeks and Amazons in relief.*)

Nos. 54—57 comprise a series of sites in the vincinity of Old Paphos and New Paphos.

No. 54. By this I designate the great temenos of Astarte-Aphrodite at Paphos excavated by the Cyprus Exploration Fund in 1888,**) which, it seems, even in Roman times, included a temple differing widely from what we understand by a Greek or Roman temple. It would appear that if the excavation had been continued further to the west, where there seem to be traces of adjoining buildings, the real temple might have been found.

I here feel myself compelled to reprint word for word from the Journal of Hellenic Studies IX (1888), p. 158 a note of Hogarth's.***) The facts are as follows. The Imperial German Archaeological Institute had as a result of my repeated representations resolved upon initiating excavations in Cyprus, Sir Henry Bulwer having expressed himself as favourably disposed to the project. Mr. Dörpfeld's original plan was to excavate the temple at Paphos with me; but when the English entered on the field, the Imperial German Institute at once recognised with proper tact that in Cyprus, which had been under British rule since 1878, the English should have precedence, and that no untimely spirit of rivalry should be allowed to mar our gratitude to the insular Government for allowing us, as foreigners, to excavate at all. When, at the end of 1887, the English archaeologists reached Cyprus in force, they did not, as I know from Mr. Sayce and others, at first contemplate Old Paphos. When Hogarth says they had been "informed through a very indirect channel" as to the intentions of the Imperial German Archaeological Institute, he can only mean myself, and indeed I still possess the letter which he addressed to me on this matter from Old Paphos. How, under the circumstances, he can speak of "an excessively vague and untrustworthy rumour" is to me incomprehensible.

No. 55. The Astarte-Aphrodite of Paphos has been notorious from all time. I was able in 1890, with the assistance of Messrs. Dörpfeld and Meister†) to show that Apollo also was worshipped here. The remarkable inscription containing proof of this (now in the Berlin Museum) was found by us in a wall of loose stones separating the courtyard of one Turkish house from that of another. A few of the (Cyprian) characters were visible, and Mr. Dörpfeld's practised eye at once lighted on them. The English excavators would have done well to examine more closely the modern walls adjacent to their excavations.

No. 56. Apollo again appears at New Paphos and here as Hylates. I should, perhaps, have mentioned the well-known rock-caves or rock-tombs there, with their votive inscriptions to this

---

*) Reinach, Chroniques d'Orient, p. 185 [5², 352—3].

**) Journal of Hellenic Studies IX, p. 149—271.

***) We had been informed through a very indirect channel that the Royal Archaeological Institute of Berlin had formed a definite plan for excavation at Kuklia in the coming autumn. Had we discovered this to be the case we should of course have yielded in their favour and selected another site, but, as we could hear of no sort of preparation having been made, and the rumour being excessively vague and untrustworthv, we perservered with our original intention. As a matter of fact the subject of Cyprus had been discussed at Berlin together with other likely fields of operation, but indefinitely postponed for want of opportunity and funds.

†) Berliner Philologische Wochenschrift, 1890, col. 618.

woodland god*) after Nos. 48—50, but I have classed them here with the other sanctuaries of Apollo which follow.

No. 57. In spite of the elaborate arguments of Hogarth, who sees in the monoliths on the Paphian shore nothing but oil-presses, and denies any religious significance to the site, I venture to conjecture that this was a place of worship. I think that this is also the view of Mr. Dörpfeld, whom, in 1890, I accompanied to the spot. I give on Pl. XVIII a new view of the monoliths and their surroundings from a photograph. When I come to speak of stone- and pillar-worship, I will support my conjecture by proof. The distance in a straight line from the hill of Old Paphos to the monoliths is about a mile and a half (= 2 km.)

No. 58. Twelve miles (= 19,20 km.) nearly due north of Old Paphos, **) the village of Amaryeti will be found on the map. Here in Cesnola's time, successful, but irregular, excavations were repeatedly made: it is even not impossible that two dedications to the god or hero Opaon Melanthios, stated by him to have been found at Old Paphos, really came from Amaryeti, where Hogarth excavated in 1888 a temenos of Apollo Melanthios and Opaon Melanthios.***) But Cesnola has not been clearly convicted of error. The existence of a far older Apollo-worship at Paphos in the immediate vicinity of the temple of Aphrodite is now attested by the inscription I found there, (see above). It is impossible to say whether Apollo were there worshipped in a distinct temenos or sanctuary, or whether a separate altar, with or without an enclosing fence ($\varphi\varrho\acute{\alpha}\gamma\mu\alpha$), were consecrated to Apollo inside the great temenos: either alternativ ewould suit the facts of early religious usage, as established by the German excavations at Olympia,†) and (as I will comprehensively show in the present work) holding good also, with certain local variations, for Cyprus. If Apollo were worshipped at Paphos, it may very well have been under the style and titlo of Melanthios or Opaon-Melanthios. Apollo Hylates, as we have seen, was worshipped at New Paphos and Drymou, both of which are in the kingdom of Paphos, but his original home is Hyle, in the kingdom of Kurion. Similarly, the Paphia (No. 23) was worshipped in the distant kingdom of Chytroi and its capital of the same name; and as regards this very Opaon Melanthios, we know that his cult was not confined to one spot, for S. Reinach has recently pointed out that two dedications to him come from Kition. G. Colonna Ceccaldi, who first published these two inscriptions, inferred the existence of a sanctuary of Opaon on the spot where they were found — near the salt-lake of Larnaka. ††) I cite this heroon of Apollo-Opaon-Melanthios at Kition under No. 72 at the end of the present list Unfortunately, I have not yet been able to obtain any accurate information about the spot and the circumstances of the discovery.

No. 59. Another Apollo, whose name $Mv\varrho\iota\acute{\alpha}\tau\eta\varsigma$ connects him with the myrtle, is placed by Hogarth at Episkopi, between Marathounta and Amaryeti, 6½ miles (= 10,40 km.) in a straight line north-west of Old Paphos and 4½ miles (=7,20 km.) from Amaryeti. This small village must not be confounded with the larger Episkopi further to the South near Kurion. Hogarth saw

---

*) Here he has his full name Apollo Hylates. Cp. Griechische Dialekt-Inschriften I, p. 20, 31, 32.
**) Hogarth has 12 engl. miles and wrongly northwest.
***) Cesnola-Stern, p. 368, Nos. 3 and 4.
†) Compare especially Curtius, Die Altäre von Olympia.
††) Revue Archéologique 1874, XXVII, p. 87. Monuments de Chypre, de Syrie et d'Égypte: p. 193 and 194, Nos. 2 and 3.

numerous ancient remains here, and is perhaps right in supposing that the small altar with the dedication to Apollo Myrtates now in the church at Marathounta, where no ancient remains are visible,
was brought from Episkopi.*) In any case, epigraphical evidence shows that in the region of
Paphos Apollo occupied, by the side of Aphrodite, a conspicuous position.

No. 60. Quitting this region and going up into the mountains, we find ourselves, at a height
of 3000 (= 941 mt.) feet, in the neighbourhood of the monastery of Khrysoroyatissa. The monastery
is to the north-east of Ktima, the principal place of the Paphos district, at a distance of 18 miles
(= 28,8 km.) as the crow flies. One mile (= 1,60 km.) west of Khrysoroyatissa is another small
monastery called Ayia Moni, a dependency not of Khrysoroyatissa, but of Kykkou the largest and
wealthiest foundation in the island. Built into the church of Ayia Moni are two dedecations to Hera
in Cyprian characters **) Hogarth rightly infers that this is the site of an ancient shrine of Hera.
He cites the dedication from Old Paphos, in which the names of Aphrodite, Zeus Polieus, and
Hera occur in this order, and the inscription from Amathus (C. I. G. 2643) which makes mention of
plantations near the Heraion.***)

No. 61 at Larnaka tou Lapithou, on the south slope of the northern range. This hamlet is
distinguished from the town of Larnaka by the addition tou Lapithou, Lapithos being the name of the
nearest large village (distant about 2 miles = 3,20 km.) In my remarks on altar-worship in a following
chapter will recur to the bilingual (Phoenician and Greek) dedication of an altar to Anat-Athene,
cut on a rock here.

No. 62. Passing still further eastward, we betake ourselves to Trikomo, 8 miles (= 12,80 km.)
north of Salamis. In T. Colonna Ceccaldi's time two large stone statues, evidently belonging to
a temenos, were found in the neighbourhood and acquired by him.†) This is perhaps the site near
Trikomo called Monarga mentioned by Hogarth and entered in his map of the Karpas.††) Men
repairing a road found here some rude statuettes. These rude statuettes and the great erect figures
the workmanship of which Ceccaldi praises so highly may have belonged to the same temenos.

Nos. 63—67 comprise five places of worship at Salamis · wholly or partially excavated by
the Cyprus Exploration Fund.†††)

No. 63. The site of the granite colums (Munro-Tubbs' A) must, although the editors do not
seem to think so, have been originally a holy place. The terracottas found at a great depth and
other circumstances point to this. The site was not laid bare.

No. 64 is the "Sand site, B," in Munro-Tubbs' report, a great temenos evidently belonging
to Zeus, at the north-east corner of the old town, near the spot where the forester's house now

---

*) Devia Cypria p. 24—28.
  Ἀπόλλωνι
  Μυρτάτη
  Ξά(νϑ)[ος
  ὑπὲρ Ὀνασᾶ
  Βοίσκου.
**) Compare Hogarth, Devia Cypria p. 34 and 35.
***) Compare Engel, Kypros I, p. 115, II, p 661.
  †) Mon. de Chypre &c., p. 299—300.
  ††) Devia Cypria, p. 65.
  †††· Journ. of Hell. Stud., 1891, XII, p. 59—198.

stands. It was, unfortunately, only partially excavated by the English explorers. They mention that at the south-east end of the precinct a fragmentary dedication to Zeus was found built into a later wall.*) As I have often found, in the comparatively recent peribolos-walls of "temene," inscriptions and statuary fragments of a much earlier date,**) I infer with certainty that this place was consecrated to Zeus, and the quantities of ἀγάλματα found here, as well as other circumstances, confirm this view. The editiors themselves believe that, in this case, they have hit upon a sanctuary and suppose that the actual temple may be still concealed further to the east.

I myself discovered this site in 1881—82, when I held the post of Superintendent of Works for Replanting in the Forest Department, and the discovery was not entirely accidental, as Messrs. Munro and Tubbs state. ***) In the year 1882 it was arranged that I should commence excavations at this spot for Sir Charles Newton then Keeper in the British Museum, as soon as I had retired from the Forest-Department and was again at leisure to work for him. I had been sent in 1881 to the mouth of the Pidias to select the best sites for plantation on the state lands. The Government had at that time conceived the notion of improving the climate of Famagusta by drying the marshes and planting the river banks. I chose two pieces of land, one to the north and north-west of the ancient Salamis, and the other close to the Pidias, south and south-east of Salamis. During the course of the winter, while these plantation-works were yet in progress, it struck my former chief Mr. Madon and Sir Robert Biddulph the High-Commissioner, that the two plantations I had designed might be connected by a belt running right across the ruins of Old Salamis. The idea was a good one from the forester's point of view, but scarcely commended itself to the archaeologist. Protests on my part were useless, and on pain of instant dismissal, I had to commence the work necessary for uniting the two plantations. I managed to obtain instructions to the effect that if in cutting holes for planting or sowing, in probing for water or in extracting building material from the ruins, I met with antiquities, I was to make a report and suspend the works at the place indicated. I selected, especially in digging for water, where it was necessary to go to some depth, places at which I thought I had a good chance of finding ancient remains, and discovered by this method the site of the temenos of Zeus. I at once wrote and telegraphed; but although Sir C. Newton expressed his desire that I should, after my approaching retirement from the Forestry Department, make some trial of the spot, I was obliged to sow over the site and mark off the space in seed by a rope barrier, which, in my own subsequent excavation of April 1883, I was forbidden to overstep. By 1890 the seedling trees had almost perished, and the Cyprus Exploration Fund was permitted to dig within the barrier. On page 59 of their report Messrs. Munro & Tubbs write as follows: "Among the most important of Herr Richter's many services to Cypriote archaelogy may be reckoned the accidental discovery of two small marble capitals under the sand near the Forest guard house, which occurred while he was employed in the Forest Department and subsequently gave us a clue to one of our sites."

By this they mean this site of the Zeus temenos. On pages 62 and 66 of the same report

---

*) Ibid, p. 119: the inscription is given there on p. 194.

**) Cp. No. 2 (Voni), No. 4 (Frangissa).

***) Journ. of Hell. Stud., XII, p. 59. I have already spoken of this site and the circumstances under which I discovered it in an article entitled "Das Museum und die Ausgrabungen auf Cypern seit 1878," published in the Repertorium für Kunstwissenschaft, 1886.

it is no longer I myself but my workmen who are credited with the discovery and in addition to the two marble capitals only one basis of a column and two limestone statues are mentioned.

My discovery of all. these things was made on the 11th of February 1882, and next day using the chambre claire I made sketches of the two statues and one of the capitals. These sketches are still by me and will probably be published shortly.

I have said enough to show that I have some cause for complaint.

I have again and again called attention to the importance of making excavations at Salamil.

Among the numerous objects found here by the English excavators are a marble statue of Sarapis with Cerberus, and a female draped statue akin, in motive and treatment, to small stone figures found by me at Akhna (No. 1).

No. 65. The Agora (C) on the western side of the town, only partially excavated. Messrs. Munro & Tubbs believe that the remains found at the south end are those of a Roman temple, and that the ruins of an older shrine must exist beneath.*) This may be so; it is at all events clear from the inscriptions and statues discovered that Zeus Olympios had a shrine here.

No. 66. The Daemonostasium and Cistern (D);**) east of the agora, at the southern end of the old town. The English explorers believe that the remains of a neighbouring temple had been collected here. The objects found and the circumstances of their discovery indicate clearly that the site itself was once the scene of some worship. Among the numerous finds are many which show the closest correspondence to those of the Artemis groves at, and near, Akhna, and the Artemis grove by the salt lake at Kition. Others point to Apollo. I should suppose that Artemis and Apollo were here worshipped under holy trees. Many ox-head masks, 2—3 inches in height, with holes for suspension, were found. At Dali (No. 36) I found, together with a quantity of human masks, one such ox-head mask of about the same dimensions.

No. 67. Toumpa (G.): on an eminence in a little Delta formed by two arms of the Pidias (the Pediaios of the ancients). This site produced interesting finds in great numbers, of a character which enabled Munro to point out that the principal divinity worshipped here was a bearded male god (Apollo?); only I do not think we should follow him in supposing a simple altar worship without any enclosure. There must have been an enclosure formed by peribolos-walls or by a φράγμα. The piece of rough walling, 4 feet in lengh, 3 ft., 5 in. in breadth, and 1 foot 8 in. in height, which was found running in a north-easterly direction is evidently part of the fence of the holy enclosure. The black stratum consisting of the vestiges of sacrifice—charcoal and fragments of bones—was reached at a depth of 5 ft., 6 in., but the actual altar of sacrifice was not found, (the same was the case at Amaryeti and Limniti).

The finds, described in the Hellenic Journal pages 146 f, are very extensive, but the excavators were not successful in discovering many large objects in good preservation. Here, as at Frangissa, terracotta and limestone figures in great number, ranging from colossi fifteen feet high, to lilliputian statuettes, had once stood. Munro quite rightly points out the correspondence as regards period, style, motives, and dimensions between the unhappily very fragmentary discoveries of Toumpa and the magnificient series of objects from Frangissa (No. 4.) At Toumpa also the statues were

---

*) Journ. of Hell. Stud. XII (1891), p. 77.

**) Ibid., p. 91 and p. 137.

***) Ibid., p. 98 and p 163.

painted: indeed, to judge from plates IX and X of the Hellenic Journal (1891), painted statuettes and fragments of painted colossi were found here of an excellence unparalleled elsewhere. The only objects which can at all be compared with the painted male figurines on plate IX are the painted female figurines from Akhna (No. 1) which are reproduced in colours on one of the Plates of the present work. The fragments of painted masculine terracotta colossi (pl. X of the Journal) show, for the first time, figures, animals, and winged monsters painted on smooth surfaces of drapery. I can supply an interesting parallel to them in the fragments of feminine terracotta colossal from the Dali sanctuary (No. 3), now in the Berlin Museum. In this case, the figures of men and animals are first moulded on the draperies, diadems &c., the effect being afterwards heightened by colouring. Some coloured illustrations of these marvellous specimens will also be given in the present work.

The richly decorated Frangissa statues, the colouring of which is in many instances remarkably vivid and distinct, will be published in my forthcoming work on Tamassos. In subsequent sections I shall have more to say on the subject of the Toumpa finds.

No. 68 takes us into the Karpas, the eastern tongue of Cyprus. On the south-east coast of this peninsula, near the village of Gastria,[°]) Hogarth has perhaps rightly fixed the site of the ancient Knidos. The place where the inscription mentioning Knidos was found is known as Vallia. At a distance hence of about 150 yards (= 137 mt.), and close to the sea, Hogarth and Guillemard found an ancient oblong peribolos constructed of more or less carefully hewn limestone blocks— evidently a temenos-enclosure. The long axis lies almost due east and west and measures 37 feet; (=11,47 m.) the short axis, lying north and south, measures 21 feet 5 inches, (= 6.41 m.) The single stones are 1 foot (= 30.4 cm.) in breadth, and rise to the height of 2 ft. (= 61 cm.) above the present surface: the thickness of the whole varies, according to the number of stones, from 2 to 6 ft. (0,61 to 1,82 m.) The north-west corner is formed by a large erect block rising 6 ft. 9 in. (= 2,05 m.) above the surface and measuring 2 ft. 10 in. by 2 ft. 10 in. (= 86 cm.) This pillar-shaped stone is slightly pointed at the top. It is not pierced, like the Paphos monoliths, but on one side a small incision, according to Hogarth quite accidental, has been made. Hogarth recognises on the worn surface of this block the traces of what we call rustica work, which he is perhaps right in stating to be a not unfrequent characteristic of Phoenician masonry. He takes the block to be a sacred menhir, and calls attention to the fact that the single menhirs standing in English stone-circles are nearly always at the north-east corner.

Hogarth mentions three other monoliths as existing in the same neighbourhood, on the eastern edge of the level expansion of the valley of Vallia, about an hour's ride from Akrotiri. They stand above the doors of tombs at a place called Kamarais or Tria Litharia. The tombs have long oblique approaches or "dromoi"; the monoliths over the doors are about a man's height, 2½ feet (= 91 cm.) in breadth, and 1 ft. (= 30 cm.) in thickness; they are bluntly pointed at the top: two have fallen down, the third remains erect in situ.

Between these tombs and the stone enclosure, at a place called Pallura, in the middle of thick brushwood, Hogarth found fragments of Cyprian stone statues "of the ordinary old type" (what type?), evidently again the relics of an ancient holy grove in which image worship was practised.

---

*) Devia Cypria, p 65.
**) Ibid., p. 70—71.

No. 69. Continuing eastward along the Karpas we reach a place called Peristephani, about half an hour north-west of the village of Leonarisso. Here again Hogarth found numerous remains of a temenos; he describes four objects thus:

1. Fragment of a nude female colossal statue which must have been about 9 feet. (= 2,73 m.) high.

2. A female head larger then life, which may have belonged to the statue.

3. Fragments of a bearded colossus.

4. Fragments of a female life-size draped statue with the right hand resting on the breast: style and attitude recall the more archaic examples of Dali.

No. 70. We have now reached the extreme north-east point of Cyprus, Cape Dinareton and the adjacent islets called Kleides in antiquity. The cape is now called Cap Andrea from the monastery of St Andreas, with its cave, rock-church, and spring, situated about $2^1/_2$ miles (= 4 km.) to the south. Hogarth has rightly placed on the cape the temple of Aphrodite Akraia mentioned by Strabo, who tells us that women were forbidden to enter it..[*]) I saw the ruins in 1879, but did not observe the statuary fragments discovered by Hogarth. A headless female statue exhibited the same rude style as the Peristephani figures: a draped arm was of later date.

No. 71. We retrace our steps to the flourishingn garde village of Rizokarpaso. It lies in a fertile upland plain, which commands a view of the sea in both sides. On the east an abrupt path leads down to the shore, following the windings of a deep ravine. As we descend we are suddenly confronted by an abrupt and lofty hill, which, with its almost flat summit, has all the appearance of a natural fortress. The hill is called by the Cypriots To Rani, and here stood the ancient mountain-fortress and city of Urania, which played so important a part in the history of the island at the end of the 4th century B.C. Demetrios Poliorketes, in 306 B.C., undertook an expedition against Cyprus and Salamis the capital of Menelaos. Dr. P. Schröder[**]) describes the campaign. Demetrios, coming from Cilicia, landed at Karpasia. Before marching on Salamis, he had to capture the fortress of Urania. Schröder has rightly identified the site.[***]) At the north-east end of the hill, a natural grotto has been so cut as to form a hypaethral subterranean, sanctuary. The only access is from below, and by no means easy: one must climb along the precipice and between huge fallen masses of rock, and creep in through a square hole at the north-west corner. A chamber (5 metres long, 3,90 m. broad and 2 m. high) is hewn in the rock. Exactly in the centre a long rectangular shaft, rather more than 1 metre square, admits the light from above. At the four corners of this square opening rudely-built pillars support the rock which forms the roof of the chamber. The walls and the pillars show traces of a former stucco covering.

On the plateau at the summit of the hill of Urania, I observed many ruins and some cisterns cut in the rock. The last time I visited the place was in May 1890; it had entirely escaped Hogarth.

With No. 72 closes our list of the more important sites supplying material for our subject. I return here to Larnaka (Kition), to make good the omission of certain other sites of worship there, which will concern us later on.

---

[*]) Devia Cypria, p. 83.

[**]) In an article in the Globus XXXIV (1878) p. 153—154, entitled "Meine zweite Reise auf Cypern im Frühjahr 1873."

[***]) See my review of Hogarth's Devia Cypria in the Berl. Phil. Woch., 1891, col. 1000.

The first is an altar of the same Opaon Melanthios, Apollo Melanthios or Apollo Opaon whom we found at Amaryeti (No. 58). Ceccaldi in his Monuments *) published two dedications to this Opaon Melanthios found near the salt lake at Larnaka, and inferred the existence here of a sacellum of this god. Nothing more is known of the discovery.

We must, further, either assume the existence of another sanctuary belonging to Ešmun-Adonis, or suppose that a triad, consisting of Ešmun, Melqart, and Adonis, was worshipped on the hill by the salt lake consecrated to Ešmun-Melqart. (No. 8 of our list.) In the latter case the Ešmun-Adonis inscriptions and the Ešmun-Melqart inscriptions come from one and the same site.

*) P. 192 and 194, Nos. 3 and 4. Cp. S. Reinach, Revue des Études Grecques II p. 225—233.

CHAPTER 2.

Tree Worship and the Transition to anthropomorphic Image Worship.

I. The holy Tree on Cyprian antiquities.

1. In the Pre-Graeco-Phoenician Copper-Bronze Period.

Fig. 1

In this early period, reaching back to two or even three thousand years before the Christian era, the holy tree is only found engraved on seal-cylinders or worked in relief on hand-made vases.

Fig. 2

a) The oldest forms show always a realistic representation of a tree or branch, probably intended for one of the native conifers. With it occur indigenous animals only (or the heads of such) and rudely executed human figures; lions and wild beasts, as well as fabulous creatures compounded of man and beast or of different beasts, are absent; there are no cuneiform incriptions.

Fig. 3.

Fig. 1. Impression of a stone cylinder dug up at Ayia Paraskevi near Nicosia; no further information as to discovery obtainable: Konstantinides Collection, Nicosia. In the middle a man praying with uplifted arms; on his right the sacred tree; on his left an ox-head and an object which is a compromise between a star and the tailed disc of the sun.

Fig. 2. Impression of a stone cylinder from the same spot: formerly in my possession. Before a tree (evidently meant to represent either the pinus aricio or the cypress) stands a man (perhaps a sacrificant), holding in his left hand an ox-head, in his right hand a tailed sun disc (?) or rudely indicated axe (?); above the latter a disc with knob in the centre.

Fig. 3. Hand-made, polished vase of red clay with ornaments in relief; excavated in an earth-tomb at Ayia Paraskevi by myself in the presence of Mr. Dümmler: on the body of the vase, at equal distances from each other, a snake, a stag, and a tree. I reproduce only the reliefs of the vase.

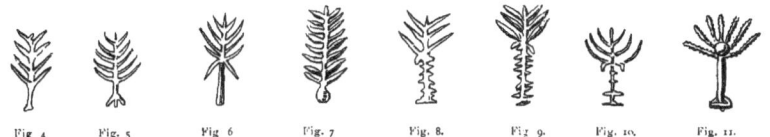

Fig 4   Fig. 5   Fig 6   Fig. 7   Fig. 8.   Fiz 9.   Fig. 10,   Fig. 11.

Figs. 4—11 show eight further examples from Cyprian seal-cylinders of the realistically treated sacred tree: I take these from the works of Louis and Alexander Palma di Cesnola.*)

b) First traces of Mesopotamian influence. Side by side with cylinders imported from Babylon and Assyria we find local imitations. Lions, all kinds of fabulous and winged monsters demons with human bodies and the heads of beasts, griffins, sphinxes &c., begin to appear. The tree loses its realistic form, and is pecularity schematized; it appears now as a kind of combination of altar, tree, flower, plant, and candelabrum, now as an aniconic ἄγαλμα of peculiar form, a post with fillets tied round it &c.

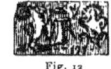

Fig. 12

Fig. 12. From the same place as figs. 1 and 2. Stone cylinder. A man stands between a rampant lion and a schematized sacred tree, which seems to burn at the top. A sun-disc, and a three-lobed object occupy the rest of the field.

Fig. 13.

Fig. 13. From the same place: A stone cylinder (perhaps more Hittite in character): now in the Oriental Department of the Berlin Museum. A winged sphinx and griffin sit opposite each other in heraldic attitude; they are coupled by straps: behind and between them a conventional tree, sacrificial flame, or burning candelabrum with several arms. Beneath the bellies of the monsters are spirals; beneath the griffins' wings three pellets.

Fig. 14.   Fig. 15.   Fig. 16.   Fig. 17.   Fig 18.   Fig. 19.   Fig 20.   Fig. 21.

Figs. 14—21 lay before the reader further variants of this sacred object, which, so it seems, developed itself from the Assyrian holy tree with its peculiar stylization. These cuts, like Figs. 4—11 above, are borrowed from the plates in, A. P. di Cesnola's Salaminia **) containing engravings of

*) Fig. 4: A. P. Cesnola's Salaminia, Pl. XIII, No. 20.
   Fig. 5: Ibid., No. 21.
   Fig. 6: Ibid., No. 17.
   Fig. 7: Cesnola-Stern's Cypern, Pl. LXXVI, No. 14.
   Fig. 8: A. di Cesnola's Salaminia, Pl. XIII, No. 18.
   Fig. 9: Cesnola-Stern's Cypern, Pl. LXXVI, No. 15.
   Fig. 10: A. di Cesnola's Salaminia, Pl. XII, No. 16.
   Fig. 11: Cesnola-Sterns Cypern, Pl. LXXVI, No. 13.
**) Fig. 14: Pl. XII, 1. Fig. 15: Pl. XIV, 43. Fig. 16: Pl. XII, 5. Fig. 17: Pl. XII, 8. Fig. 18: Pl. XII, 7.
Fig. 19: Pl. XII, 6. Fig. 20: Pl. XII, 2. Fig. 21: Pl. XII, 3.

Cyprian cylinders. Mr. Sayce there*) would see in this remarkably formed object of worship, peculiar as it is to Cyprus, the emblem or image of the Paphian goddess, and M. Menant in his " Recherches sur la Glyptique Orientale " **) seems to adopt this interpretation.

When I come to speak of the idol of the Paphian goddess, I shall have more to say with regard to the views of these two scholars.

Fig. 22.　　Fig. 24.　　Fig. 26.　　Fig. 27.　　Fig. 28.

Fig. 23.　　Fig. 25.

c) Figs. 22—28 show us impressions of seven further Cyprian cylinder seals. Numbers of these cylinders with representations of trees cannot be classed under types a and b; they exhibit all kinds of divergencies in subject, style, and technique.

Fig. 22. Also from Ayia Paraskevi: in the Kostantinidis collection, Nicosia. Two very rude human figures sitting, crouching, or standing among four or five trees; it looks as if they were clutching the trees with their hands: the work is highly primitive and scratchy: the branches of the realistically treated trees (approximating to type a) are directed downwards.

Fig. 23. Two figures standing, inclined to the right, among all kinds of signs and symbols: they seem to reach out their hands to grasp some of these objects. On the left we see first a kind of aniconic ἄγαλμα, or an object of worship not unlike the decorative Cyprian tree of our type b (according to Sayce and Menant the idol of the Paphian Aphrodite). It is formed by the symmetrical grouping of various distinct symbols; beneath are the disc of the sun and the crescent of the moon; above these a sun-disc with a tail and four horns, between two pellets and charged with another pellet; this is again surmounted by an ox-head with a disc and crescent on each side and another crescent resting on its horns. The first figure is in the act of grasping this ἄγαλμα with its right hand and holds up in its left hand a tree of the realistic form a. Beneath this tree and between the

---

*) Salaminia, p. 121.

**) (Paris 1886), II, p. 250. As Dümmler has pointed out in the Athen. Mittheilungen X (1886) p. 242, Menant has often been led into error as to the date and character of Cyprian cylinders by placing too much reliance on the unsubstantial data of the brothers di Cesnola. Dümmler and I established by enquiry and excavating on the spot that Louis di Cesnola never found a " temple treasure of Kurion." The cylinders of the pre-Graeco-Phoenician Bronze Period figured on plates LXXV—LXXVII of Cesnola-Stern's Cypern do not belong to those strata of the Graeco-Phoenician Iron Period which yielded the very remarkable antiquities obtained by Cesnola from Kurion, but come principally from the necropolis of Ayia Paraskevi near Nicosia, one specimen (Cesnola-Stern, Pl. LXXV, 3) probably from Maroni-Zaroukas (See our Pl. I). From the same necropolis or from other kindred necropoleis of the pre-Graeco-Phoenician Bronze Period come the interesting cylinders figured in Alexander di Cesnola's Salaminia. No cylinders occur in Salamis, for there, as at Kurion, the Copper-Bronze Period is unrepresented.

two figures is a couched quadruped. The interstices are occupied by four single pellets, and four pairs of pellets united by bars and resembling dumb-bells.

In Fig. 24 (from the same spot as the last) we have a speaking example of another sub-species of cylinders of Cyprian fabric, where the Cyprian imitation is almost as obvious as the Assyrian model. The holy tree is of our type a. A human figure stands between the tree and a large long-horned quadruped represented us crouching; it is meant for a wild goat, antelope, or moufflon. The way in which the animal's head is turned back is characteristic of the whole group;*) the creature turns its back to the man, but twists round its head and looks at him. He seems to be feeding or caressing it with his left hand, while with his right hand he touches the tree. These crouching or erect quadrupeds looking over their shoulders are absent from the cylinders of our type a, but occasionally occur on those of type b, and are proper to the genuine Assyrian cylinders of Mesopo-tamia itself.

Fig. 25 (same provenance) is an example of a small group of cylinders of a totally divergent technique, and exhibiting quite other motives. The quadruped is engraved in outline only, the lines standing out like ribs on the impression. It is half walking, half sitting, and carries its tail erect; it is about to advance towards an upright tree or branch; above it a similar branch is placed hori-zontally: both trees or branches are of the realistic type a.

Fig. 26 (from the same place) ...nts yet another peculiar class of Cyprian cylinders, on which we often meet with an act of sacrifice in the presence of the holy tree. Between the female figure seated on a chair (either a goddess or the idol of a goddess or her priestess) and the erect male figure (a god, priest, or sacrificant) we see floating in the air the holy tree in the form of our type b (according to Sayce and Menant the idol of the Paphia). The man holds in his left hand an object resembling a single-bladed axe and in his right hand what seems to be a double axe. Behind the female figure's chair a wild goat or moufflon stands erect; his body is turned towards her but he twists his head backwards and downwards just like the animal with similar horns and other characteristics on the cylinder No. 24. Three pellets occupy the space between his hind legs and the chair.

Fig. 27 (same provenance) supplies an example of a very remarkable class of Cyprian engraved cylinder; strikingly analogous is the specimen figured in A. P. di Cesnola's Salaminia, p. 120, fig. 114 and described there by Mr. Sayce. In both cases we have evidently to deal with a Cyprian imitation of a Babylonian cylinder: the god Merodach is engaged in combat with the demon-birds. But on our cylinder we have the horned ram's head introduced as a symbol, and the action is supposed to take place in front of the holy tree (here realistically treated.)

Fig. 28 is a very rare and remarkable example; very few of its class have met my eyes. It represents the latter end of the Cyprian manufacture of cylinders. I am particularly sorry, in this case, that I did not find the specimen myself. I bought it from a dealer in Nicosia; but I should have no hesitation in saying that it comes, like the proceeding ones, from Ayia Paraskevi. Here a human being and a beast are adoring the holy tree which stands between them. The seated human figure appears to be nude and feminine; it lifts up its left hand in the attitude of prayer; the beast

---

*) Cp. e. g. A. P. di Cesnola, Salaminia, Pl. XIV, 40.

(a wild goat or moufflon) is arrested in its career by the sacred object and bows down before it: beneath it is a three-pronged implement. The execution and the rendering of the forms are quite different from anything we have seen; this is especially noticeable in the general character and the "coiffure" of the human head, the most striking parallel to which is the series of heads on the well-known bronze patera of Idalion (below fig. 49). We are also reminded of the human heads on early Cyprian vases e.g. our plate XIX. The beast, with those curious lines like saddle-girths encircling its middle, reminds us of the beasts on our Tamassos vase (figs. 37 and 38). I parted with this interesting specimen to Col. Warren.

The oldest tree-worship, far older than these monumental evidences, eludes the methods of proof, but in its beginnings it was, doubtless, part of an aniconic fetish-worship. Soon, those objects which claimed attention or veneration, such as trees, snakes, stags &c., came to be reproduced in pictures, and we now find the tree appearing on Cyprian vases and cylinders (type a). This old, realistically treated tree would seem to belong to the primitive inhabitants of Cyprus before the advent of any Mesopotamian influences. It is, however, true that on Mesopotamian cylinders, and especially on archaic Babylonian cylinders, representations of trees do sometimes occur which bear a very strong resemblance to those on our Cyprian cylinders. Of these Babylonian realistic trees I will speak in a subsequent section. The idols which occur in the same stratum with the vases decorated with designs of trees in relief (fig. 3) are always of tabular form and draped.

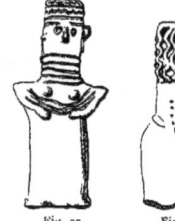

Fig. 29.   Fig. 30.

Fig. 29 represents a terracotta idol of this type, found by me at Phoenijais in 1883 and now in the British Museum.

Fig. 30. Back view of the upper portion of a tabular idol from Ayia Paraskevi; thus figured in order to show that it is clothed. Such is the type of idol which occurs with cylinders and vases bearing trees of our type a.

A rude terracotta, discovered by me in an early earth-tomb at Ayia Paraskevi, and first published by Dümmler in the Mitth. des Arch. Inst. von Athen, vol. XI, p. 209 and Beilage III fig. 1, represents a tetrapod on which two pairs of divinities (male and female) are seated. These figures also are to be regarded as draped idols of tabular form, although in this case the small dimensions combined with the potter's lack of skill have caused them to appear thicker in proportion to their width than was intended. The little wooden idols must have been of very similar form, sometimes indeed not flat åt all but cylindrical I will recur to them when I come to speak of the post idols.

Figs 31 and 32 introduce us to the two chief idol-types which appear with trees of types b, but never earlier. The ornaments on fig. 32 are all incised: on fig. 31 the διάζωμα alone is incised, the necklaces consisting of alternate black and red painted rings. I found among the objects discovered by von Luschan and Koldewey at Senjerli in North Syria, (the ancient Samal) very instructive parallels to the Cyprian idols like fig. 32 with the enormous pierced ears and double pairs of earrings. The Berlin Museum possesses several examples of this Cyprus-Senjerli type, as well as some very fine replicas and variants of the Cyprian tabular type (figs. 29 and 30).

6*

Fig. 31 (No. 8103 in the Antiquarium of the Royal Berlin Museum) was found in a rock-tomb at Ayia Paraskevi in company with a number of Mykenaean vases among which was the fine crater painted with oxen here figured (fig. 33). This idol measures 22 cm. (= 8³/₄ in.) in height.

The other idol, fig. 32 (No. 109 in the Antiquarium) was obtained at an earlier date and nothing is known as to the circumstances of its discovery. Its height is 20 cm. (= 8 in.)

Fig. 31

Fig. 32.

34,5 cm. high.
Fig. 33

In the third volume of Perrot's Histoire de l'Art, a terracotta like our fig. 31 is reproduced on p. 211 fig. 150; and figs. 374 and 375 (p. 552 and p. 553) of the same volume are replicas of our fig. 32. The first has the cavity of the navel indicated; the third has a round disc immediately under the breasts. I have already said that these idols closely resemble the terracotta idols of Senjerli, and their resemblance to Schliemann's lead idols from Hissarlik (Ilios, p. 330, fig. 226) is scarcely less striking.

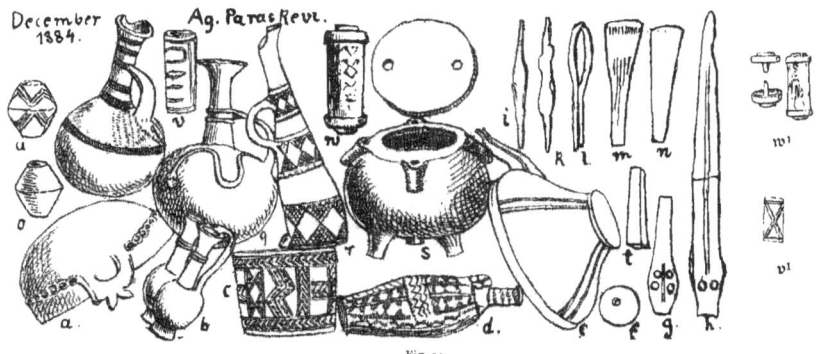

Fig. 34.

In the same stratum with the Cyprian cylinders of type b real Babylonian and Assyrian cylinders occur. Fig. 34 contains sketches of twenty-four different objects which I found together in a rock tomb at Ayia Paraskevi (excavated in December 1884): fig. 36 gives a plan and section of the tomb.

Fig. 34 w shows in actual size a real Babylonian cylinder with cuneiform inscription in its original gold setting, which is made to be taken off and on; the impression of this cylinder is reproduced

Fig. 35.

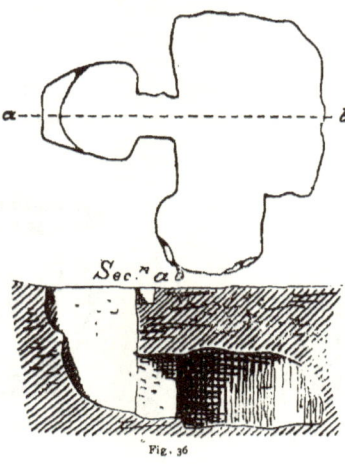

Sec.ⁿ a b

Fig. 36

in fig. 36 (it was first published by Carl Bezold in the Zeitschrift für Keilschriftforschung, Leipzig 1885, II page 191.

Fig. 34 v shows us a Cyprian cylinder from the same tomb.*)

*) a. Semi-circular bowl (diameter 0,136 m. = 5³/₈ in, height 0,071 m. = 2¹³/₁₆ in.) of uncoloured clay A chain-pattern in relief runs round the rim.

b. A vase composed of two united bottles (height 0,109 m. = 4³/₈ in.) with coating of dull-black clay: on the neck a raised ring-ornament.

c. Cup of fine porcelain-like yellowish clay (height 0,071 m. = 2¹³/₁₆ in): incised ornaments without white filling: two holes opposite each other near the rim.

r. Bottle of the same technique: a loop attached to the foot: height 0,205 m. (= 8¹/₁₈ in.)

f. Bowl of the same technique as b: diameter 0,138 m. (= 5¹/₈ in.), height 0,095 m. (= 3³/₄ in.)

q. Technique the same as b: two snakes in relief on the body of the vase: height 0,166 m. (=6⁵/₈ in.)

s. Remarkable three-legged vessel (height 0,13 m. = 5³/₁₆ in.) with coating of dull-black clay, four long tubular holes just below the edge: the lid, not coloured black and pierced with two holes, was found in its place on the vase. Cp. Schliemann, Ilios p. 251, fig. 44.

d. Small bottle (height circa 0.085 m. = 3¹/₈ in.) The ornaments are smudgily painted on the unprepared surface in a colour passing from blackish-brown to bluish-black. Another vase of the same technique is 0,107 m. (= 4¹/₄ in.) high. All the vases are hand-made.

u. Spinning whorl of terracotta: incised ornaments: height 0,017 m. (= ³/₈ in.)

o. Stone whorl: height 0,015 m. (= ⁵/₈ in.)

t. Four-cornered whetstone of slate: length 0,049 m. (= circ. 2 in.)

f. Bead (the boring 0,01 m. long) of a baked whitish substance resembling porcelain.

g, h, i, k, l, m, n. Seven objects of bronze containing a very small percentage of tin, all forms peculiar to the Cyprian Bronze Period. g. h. daggers, i. k. awls, l. m. pincers, n. chisel. The length of i is 0,08 m. (= ⁵/₁₆ in.) and the dimensions of the others accordingly.

v and v¹. Cylinder made of a white compound, drawn from two sides and in two sizes; v actual size, v¹ reduced. It had been coloured deep-red, perhaps in imitation of stàined ivory.

w and w¹. The cylinder with cuneiform inscription and its gold mounting. w actual size; w¹ (right) reduced and without the mounting; w¹ (left) the two separate parts of the gold mounting (the spike of one of the caps should be longer). This gold mounting, intended to be put off on, was found in its place, and by its help we can explain as cylinder-mounts certain small golden objects from Hissarlik, which Schliemann thought were earrings (Ilios p. 514, figs. 705—708.)

2. Tree worship in the Graeco-Phoenician Iron Period down to Roman times.

In this long period, embracing more than a thousand years, we meet with frequent evidences of tree worship on Cyprian monuments.

As the earlist know Phoenician inscriptions from Cyprus, the dedications from the altar of

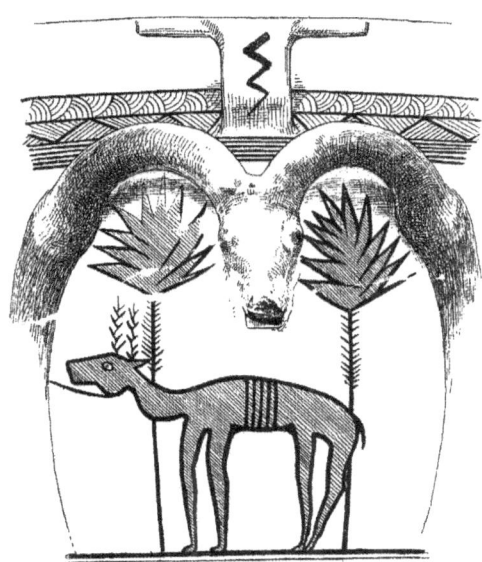

Fig. 37.

Baal Libanon, must be placed in the time of King Hiram the contemporary of David and Salomon*), we may carry the beginnings of the Graeco-Phoenician Iron Period certainly as far back as the first half of the tenth century B. C. and presumptively a few centuries further.

Fig. 37. A portion of the great crater excavated by me in a tomb at Tamassos in 1885. The two double handles on the shoulder of the vase, of which one is visible here, are formed by large coloured cow's or calve's heads. Underneath this handle two realistically formed trees with a stag in front of them are painted in black and red. Whether the trees are meant to represent palms or conifers is an open question.**) On the opposite side of the vase the two trees recur in the same place with, in this case, a bird flying upwards between them. (See fig. 75 below). The style and technique of this vase show it to belong to the period of transition from bronze to iron; it is a Cyprian development of that later Mykenaean ware of which the most remarkable specimen is the well-known Mykenae crater.***) In fig. 38 I give once more a picture of the entire vase; the foot, as restored by the artist is, however, too slender, and should have been drawnto resemble that of the Mykenae crater. The vase was found with the foot broken away, and had doubtless been deposited in this imperfect condition in the tomb of the original owner, who had valued it highly during his lifetime. The first detailed description of the vase was given by S. Reinach, who published at the same time the whole cycle of paintings which decorate its shoulder and body.†) The present sketches are rather better than Reinach's and (what is most important)

---

*) See above, Ch. I, No. 47.
**) Cp. S. Reinach, Chroniques d'Orient, p. 294—300. [7, 76—7 and 81—2].
***) Furtwängler und Löschke, Mykenische Vasen. Plates XLII, XLIII, and XLIV, 75.
†) See Reinach, Chroniques d'Orient, p. 294—300 and again p. 360—362 [7² 89—90].

show the two bands immediately underneath the neck with their geometrical patterns. The lower band is
formed of two interlocking rows of
triangles filled in with parallel lines;
the upper band is formed of segments
of circles similarly filled in, a form of
ornament very characteristic of Myke-
naen vase painting. That the vase is
a product of Cyprian art is evinced
by the clay and the technique,
especially by the manner in which the
colours, dull-black and blood-red, are
applied on the rough surface of the
clay. The red on vases of this class
has been put on quite superficially,
probably at a time when they had
been already half-baked, and, in this
particular case, the black also was
much inclined to peel off. As Sandwith rightly observes in his admirable
paper on Cyprian pottery read before
the Society of Antiquaries in 1871*),
this red colour is very apt to be

Fig. 38.

washed off by water. I will on another occasion deal at length with the whole series of pictures on
this unique vase; at present we are concerned with the trees and the question whether they are
holy trees or not or have any sacral significance. If we compare the manner in which these trees
are here introduced with the dispositions of the trees on the following vase (fig. 39), on the bronze
patera from Idalion, and on the Cyprian silver paterae, various possibilities present themselves. In
some cases the action seems to be taking place in a holy grove, under holy trees to which divine
honours are being paid; elsewhere it would seem that the trees only indicate the hunting forest in
which the wild beasts dwell.

Fig. 39. Portion of a barrel-shaped vase painted in black and red**), found near Kition.
Four conventional holy trees stand at equal distances from each other; round the trees stags and
birds are grouped. That these are unquestionably holy trees to which divine honours are paid, as to
actual simulacra, will be at once evident when I have demonstrated by a comparison with other
monuments that the object here which we call a tree is nothing less than the old fantastic tree-idol or
aniconic ἄγαλμα already developing into the anthropomorphic ἄγαλμα.

---

*) Printed in the Archaeologia XLV (1887) p. 127—142: see especially p. 133.
**) Published by me in the Journal of Hellenic Studies V (1884), p. 102—104. "On a Phoenician vase
found in Cyprus."

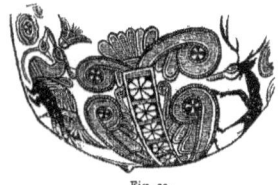

Fig. 39.

There is in the Berlin Museum (Antiquarium No. 228) another vase from Kition,*) on which two quadrupeds (goats?) are represented in heraldic attitude with the holy tree between them. On Plate XIX I give a photographical reproduction of the vase after my own photograph of the original; on Plate LXI a reduced drawing in colours of the picture on it. On Plate XIX 2 we see a good phototype of another vase in the Berlin Museum (No. a 72 and 255 in the Catalogue of the Cyprian Collection: height 36,5 cm. = 13³/₈ in.). It is the same vase of which an imperfect illustration is given

*) Faultily reproduced in Cesnola-Stern Pl. IV, 1 = Perrot III, fig. 518. Reinach has narrated at length in his Chroniques d'Orient (p. 360—362) the misfortunes which befel the Tamassos vase; but I may be permitted to recur to the subject and give a more complete version of the real facts. I extracted the vase myself, in company with Abraami, one of my best hands, with the knife, from a deep earth-tomb. The vase was lying in the tomb complete with the exception of the missing foot, and so placed that the representation of the lion hunt first met our eyes. We saw that the vase showed a number of breaks and cracks and could only be taken out piece-meal. The pieces were sent up with the greatest care in baskets and carried by myself and Loiso, another workman highly experienced in cleaning and joining, (I have spoken of him in the introduction to my Dissertation "Ancient Places of Worship in Kypros" p V.) to a tent spread near the scene of the excavation and there laid on tables. The valuable parts of the vase were on the spot carefully wrapped in cotton-wool and paper and packed is baskets. I was then putting up at the monastery of Ayios Heraklides (at no great distance to the E. of the spot where the vase was found: see the map Pl. I). Partly in the tent and partly at the monastery, Loiso and I undertook the cleaning and putting together of the pieces: the vase was finally mended and photographed in the monastery. I had already made independently in the course of many years' experience the same discovery as Sandwith, viz. that certain colours on this pottery are most evanescent and disappear when rubbed with water; but I knew that if extreme care is exercised as to the strength of the solution, and rubbing entirely avoided, a treatment with dilute acid is not injurious. Some parts of this vase were so incrusted with a coating of hard lime-like earth, that only bits of the painting were visible here and there, and we accordingly set to work to free the surface entirely from this deposit by treatment with weak acid. This once accomplished, we proceeded to put the vase finally together and secure it by cement; I used in this process a cement, long employed at Stuttgart with good results, composed of joiner's glue, pounded chalk and terracotta, linseed-oil, turpentine-oil and water in certain proportions. The interstices where the pieces did not exactly fit and the few holes where bits were missing were filled in with cement, and in order that the whole should not be disfigured by these few white lines and patches, I painted the cement with water-colour the same shade as the ground of the vase, but in a way which made it easy to detect the restaurations at first sight, and entirely without re-touching the paintings. The mending was as successful as it could well have been under the circumstances, and I then made photographs of the vase which unfortunately did not turn out very well, as I had a stock of very inferior chemicals and was obliged to work with old half-spoilt collodion. But in spite of this the photographs were good enough to serve as a basis for the illustration given by Reinach in the Revue Archéologique, and for that in the present work. I had a good double case made for the transport of the vase from the monastery to Nicosia and from thence to Europe; it reached my house at Nicosia carefully packed in the beginning of November 1885, and I then put the last touches to the mending and made it additionally secure. Col. Warren, to whom the vase belonged, now asked me to give the whole a lining of plaster, a request which I ought not to have complied with; but as I was not sufficiently awake to the danger of such an operation, I acted acording to his instructions with the result that the vase, as a necessary consequence of the application of the plaster coating, fell to pieces and had to be put together again. While I and Loiso were occupied in mending it for the second time, a law-suit commenced between Col. Warren and Mr. Watkins, the Director of the Ottoman Bank, with regard to the right of ownership in a certain site of excavation, and in this suit I was involved as principal witness. Col. Warren lost his temper and in spite of my refusal and protestations, had the vase in its half-restored condition forcibly removed from my house by the officers of the law. As he subsequently declared at a séance of the Museum Council on the 13th of April 1887, the vase was afterwards restored in England. It was exhibited in 1886 at the Colonial and Indian Exhibition, and

in Cesnola-Stern, Pl. LXXXV, 1 = Perrot-Chipiez III, p. 710, fig. 522. On Plate XX I give in the correct tones a reduced grisaille tracing of part of the painting, the obverse with the human figure. A man in a long robe holds up a flower in his left hand, and carries in his right hand a bird hanging down. In front of this figure the holy tree or plant is seen somewhat realistically treated; behind him it appears in its more conventionalised Assyrian form. The neck of the vase terminates in a female head hollow and open at the top. High up on the shoulder of the vase two knobs indicate the nipples. The chain which passes round the neck and the circular locket or amulet hanging from it are not in relief, but are painted on in black and white. This necklace and locket do not appear on the earlier illustrations, and are also invisible on our photo-type and tracing; I therefore give the adjoining sketch of the upper part of the vase (Fig. 40) on which I show this detail.

Fig. 40

On Plate XIX, 3 will be found a reproduction in phototype of another vase at Berlin (No. 71 in the Cyprian section of the Antiquarium: height 32,3 cm = 12³/₄ in.)*). A slightly reduced tracing of the important part of the paintings on it is given on Plate XXI. They are executed in black and brown on the rough uncoloured ground of the shoulder We see at the first glance that an act of worship before the sacred tree is here represented. The principal picture begins to the left of the tubular spout. In the centre stands the great mystic tree surmounted by a tress-ornament; at its foot two birds are fluttering upwards and picking at its arabesques. Two priests in long cloaks with large capes stand before it and each touches with one extended hand the summit of the tree, while his other hand hangs behind him and grasps a long-handled pitcher. Between the men and the birds small trees or plants are growing; that on the right resembles a cypress, that on the left the flower of an umbelliferous plant. The space under-neath the spout of the vase is filled by the same tress-pattern which surmounts the tree, between horizontal lines, a zig-zag line, and a denticulated border; a little cypress-tree to the left of the handle, behind and to the right of the first man, and a long branch to the right of the handle and left of the peacock are introduced from the same dread of a vacuum. The man on the right pushes up against the top of the holy tree with his right shoulder: he on the left stands at a more respectful distance and the space between him and the tree is occupied by a little branch. This, the principal picture of the vase, representing the adoration of the holy tree by two men and two birds, is in itself

---

*) sent in 1887 to Paris, as the authorities at the Louvre were anxious to purchase it. An employé of the Louvre discovered that parts of the antique work had been painted over and requested permission to wash the vase with water, a permission which Col. Warren granted. The employé at the Louvre, possessing as little experience as Col. Warren himself of Cyprian pottery and the variety of its techniques washed off, together with the evidently insignificant modern restorations, the greater part of the genuine antique painting. The vase with the miserable remains of what were once deeply interesting and hitherto unparalleled Cyprian paintings, is now in the British Museum. If my advice had only been asked at the right time and followed when given, these remarkable paintings would have been saved; as things stand, Reinach's and my own illustrations and my photographs are the only documents testifying to what we once possessed and have now almost entirely lost by improper measures.

*) In Cesnola-Stern Pl. LXXXVI, 2 a faulty illustration is given.

7

complete: beside it we see a second and smaller picture of a gigantic bird perched on another holy tree which has here more the form of a palmette or capital. Two flower-buds grow from its trunk on the right, and the bird, which looks to the right, seems disposed to peck at the stalk of one of them. A second flowering branch with pendant leaves fills the space between this second scene and the left end of the first scene: a small flower fills the space on the left of the holy tree beneath and behind the bird's tail. This bird is evidently meant for a peacock; and on the vases figured on Pl. XXII, I and Pl. XXIII. 1 and 2 the roughly sketched birds walking in single file have a greater resemblance to peacocks than to any other feathered creatures. The peacock, as we know, was among the rare and costly things which king Solomon had collected at his court for purposes of entertainment or effect*); and as our vase belongs to the period between 1000 and 700 B.C., it may be contemporary with Solomon. On the other hand the way in which this fabulous-looking bird is sitting on the fabulous tree would seem to indicate that it is meant to represent the phoenix, which is also known to the Bible, and appears on Egyptian monuments in the form of a heron or some other water-fowl.

Plate XIX, 4 is a phototype of another Cyprian vase accidentally discovered, while I was in Cyprus, by a peasant near the village of Athiaenou. This valuable specimen is still in Nicosia in the

Fig. 41.

collection of my friend Mr. Evstathios Konstantinides. I originally communicated it to M. Reinach who published it in his Chroniques d'Orient**), and I subsequently published it more completely myself in the Jahrbuch des kaiserlich deutschen Archäeologischen Instituts 1886.***) The coloured plate is a reduction from my own water-colour tracing. The height of the vase is 0,296 m. = (11¾ in.) The paintings are executed in black and two shades of red on the unprepared yellowish surface of the day. We see a man standing in front of two gigantic flowers and holding in his left hand a third smaller flower, which he seems to be smelling; the flowers are perhaps those of the lotus. In his right hand he holds by a string a bird which is attempting to fly over his head. The subject is evidently the same as that of the vase just discussed (Pl. XIX, 2 and XX), but in a different stylistic dress. In both cases two flowers, bushes, or trees; in both cases a man with a flower in his left hand, a bird in his right. Here the bird is flying up, there it is hanging down.

Figure 41†) shows a third variant of the same substantially identical motive. Here we

---

*) 1st Kings X. 22. Compare the section on the peacock in V. Hehn's Kulturpflanzen und Hausthiere (Berlin 1883) p. 286—294.

**) Cp. Chroniques d'Orient p. 194 [5², 359—60].

***) "Cyprische Vase aus Athiaenou" p. 79 82 and Pl 8. Perrot and Chipiez have republished the vase in the IVth volume of their Histoire de l'Art, p. 564, fig 286 in illustration of the Hittite shoes (τζαϱούχια) with toes pointing upwards. In my publication in the Jahrbuch I should have laid stress on the evident Hittite influence and the peaked shoes; but my friend Dümmler, who supervised the publication of my article ,See p. 79 of the Jahrbuch) considered that the objective originals for the paintings of this vase were to be sought in Egypt and referred the peaked shoes to the pointed feet on Egyptian paintings. I will recur to this question in another connection

†) After Perrot III, p. 709, fig. 521.

have a human figure, walking to the left and looking over its shoulder, between a huge, fantastically formed tree and a gigantic bird. Between man and bird is a large flower; beneath the bird's beak a bud.

On Cyprian vases of this Graeco-Phoenician stratum, which extends from circa 1000 to the middle ot the 6th century B. C., the juxtaposition of birds and tholy trees or flowers is very frequent. The annexed cut (figs. 42 and 43) are reproduced from A. P. di Cesnola's Salaminia, Plate XIX Nós. 30 and 31. On fig. 42 a bird seems to be pecking at the holy tree with its beak; on fig. 43 three birds in single file are flying towards the tree.

Fig 42.   Fig. 43.

I was able in 1886 by means of my extensive excavations at Poli tis Khrysokhou (Marion-Arsinoe: see the Map, Pl. I) to demonstrate the very general existence in the Greek colonies in Cyprus of a custom frequently referred to in the Homeric poems, and I have discussed the subject in some detail in P. Hermann's Winckelmannsprogramm "Das Gräberfeld von Marion auf Cypern".*) It is the custom of pouring water from a ewer over guests' hands before, and probably after, meals and receiving the water in a bowl.**) I found most frequent traces of this custom at Marion-Arsinoe (Poli tis Khrysokhou) in the West of the island and at Kurion in the South (the modern Episkopi);***) but the whole Paphos district,†) comprising, besides Marion-Arsinoe, the towns of Palae-Paphos and Nea-Paphos††) supplied numerous illustrations of it. I will deal with this custom (which still holds in Cyprus) and the ewers and basins which attest it in the chapter treating of the cultus of the Dead. In the present place I will speak of certain ewers from Marion-Arsinoe (found in the course of excavations conducted for Messrs. Watkins, Christian and Williamson) only in so far as they throw light on tree worship and the decorative use of the tree. The shoulders of these ewers are often painted with water-fowls and trees along with plants, flowers, rosettes, palmettes &c. Sometimes the birds stand in heraldic attitude on either side of the plastically ornamented spout, sometimes we have a number of birds (often swans and geese) marching in single file. At times the holy birds seem to be represented as adoring a holy tree which may be either realistically formed, or of the unnatural and conventional type; elsewhere the birds are walking about underneath the trees or between them. In very many cases the same vase shows two distinct species of tree, clearly differentiated by the painter. It often looks as if the holy birds were reared and preserved in the holy grove of a divinity who was worshipped under the semblance of a natural or artificial tree. The same phenomenon has met us on some of the vases described and figured above, e. g. Pl. XIX. fig. 3 and Pl. XXI.

Fig. 44 is a reproduction of an illustration in the Winckelmannsprogramm (fig. 29) for which my own water-colour drawing of the original was used. On Plate XXIII, 1 I give for the first time

---

*) (Berlin 1888: G. Reimer) pages 46—62.
**) E g. Od. α 136.
***) Cp. the Map, Pl. I.
†) Cp. Kitchener's Map of Cyprus (Stanford 1885.)
††) See Pl. I.

good reproductions in phototype of my drawings. In the upper left-hand corner we see a sketch of the ewer (its height is 14 inches = 35,56 cm.) showing its condition and preservation. Beneath are the paintings on the shoulder reduced from the original water-colour tracing, those on the left of the spout above, those on the right beneath. The spout is here, as in many other cases, formed by the seated figure of a slave girl holding a pitcher, the busy ἀμφίπολος, who pours a fine jet of water over the hands of the guests. Fig. 46 shows a well-preserved specimen of this class of ewer — the πρόχοις, as we meet with it in Homer's discriptions. On our vase (fig. 44, Pl. XXIII, 1) five black aquatic birds, walking one behind the other, are painted on a surface artificially coloured a deep brownish-red, while a sixth bird is proceeding in the opposite direction. A broad band composed of black and white lines (produced on the wheel) represents the ground on which the birds are standing and from which rise the trees, plants, flowers, stars, and rosettes painted in transparent black with touches of surface-white.

Fig. 45 (fig. 30 in Herrmann's Programm) is a somewhat careless reproduction of my own water-colour sketch of one of the fragments of a similar prochus which could not be entirely restored. The vase was so much broken, that I did not attempt to put the pieces together on the spot, in 1886; but the most important portions—the paintings on the shoulder, and the spout with the adjacent part

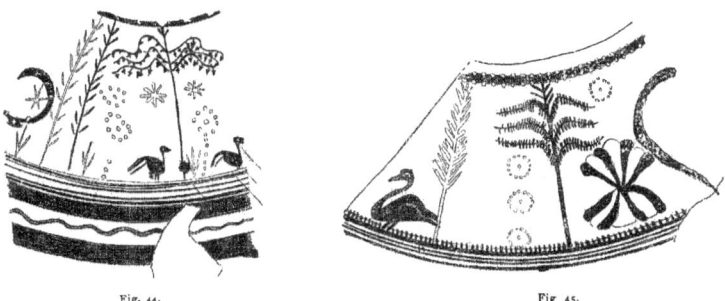

Fig. 44.   Fig 45.

of the neck—were preserved in such good condition that I thought they merited reproduction here on Plate XXII, 2. The spout is again formed by a seated figure of an amphipolos pouring water from a jug, modelled in archaic Graeco-Cyprian style. The height of the figure is $5\frac{1}{2}$ in. (= 14 cm.) the height of the painted strip from the feet of the swans and trees to the top of the highest tree, 3,8 inches (= 9,8 cm.) The groups on each side of the spout are here heraldically treated. On either side stands a black swan, and behind the swan on either side are three trees of identical forms and identically grouped. We see first a white tree resembling a palm-leaf; next stands a black tree also realistically formed and perhaps meant to represent an entire palm-tree; then follows a conventional tree—or, since exception might well be taken to the use of the word "tree" here, we may call it a palmette—composed of alternate white and black petals. Six rosettes composed of white dots, and a black horn-ornament studded with two rows of white beads and springing from the root of the vase-handle complete the main decoration of the shoulder on both sides of the spout. My own illustrations, carefully drawn from the original, give the best idea of the ornamental borders which frame the picture above and below, and the details of the colouring on the female figure are admirably rendered on Pl. XXII, 2, with the sole exception that the lights on the hair where the black passes into dark blue should be of a deeper shade. The figure, like the body of the vase, is painted red, white, and black. The head has been made in a mould and, in all probability, subsequently retouched with a modelling stick: the body and extremities have been kneaded and joined to the head in the rudest possible way by the potter himself, who evidently was neither gifted with much talent nor possessed the technical cleverness we expect from a sculptor or coroplast.*)

On Plates XXI, I and XXII, 2 I give illustrations of two other ewers from the same excavation and their decorations. In both cases six aquatic birds are doing the goose-step under trees. The technique of these vases and the colours employed on them are the same as those of the other vases on the same plates just described. The illustrations are in every way so excellent that any description would be superfluous. The ewer figured on Pl. XXI, 1 measures 13⁷/₈ inches (= 35,28 cm.) in height; the height of that on Plate XXII, 2 is 13¹/₈ in. (= 33,33 cm.) Fig. 46 shows us a well-preserved ewer from the same excavation, acquired for the Berlin Museum at the auction held in Paris in 1886, and now exhibited in the Cyprian section of the Antiquarium along with other objects from the same site (Poli tís Khrysokhou, Marion-Arsinoe).**) While the older Cyprian vases with birds, flowers, and holy trees (such as figs. 42 and 43***) above or Cesnola-Stern Plates LXXXIX, 1, 3, 4, 6, XCII, 1, XCIII, 2) disappear from the tombs in the middle, or at the beginning, of the 6th century B.C., we continue to find representations of these subjects on ewers in the Greek colonies, such as Marion-Arsinoe, up to the end of this century or even later. The accurate journal kept during the excavations of 1886 at Poli, chronicling, as it does, the contents of each

Fig. 46.

tomb, combined with the experience I had gained from twelve years observant work on other sites, made it possible for me, as time went on, to classify the finds by centuries, in some cases even by

---

*) Cp. Herrmann's Winckelmannsprogramm, p. 54 and especially my remark on page 95 ibid. On these ewers with seated or erect female statuettes as spouts we meet with all kinds of peculiar adaptations, not unexampled in other classes of monuments, e. g. the terracotta groups of dancers. The potter, for example, uses the mould of a throned figure with both hands resting on her knees. He sticks his figure on to the ewer above the little jug which forms the spout, but as neither of the two arms of the statuette are available to hold the jug, he is obliged to attach a third arm to it. In other cases it is an erect figure holding a flower which he presses into his service for the purpose of grasping the little jug.

**) Herrmann's Programm, p. 53, fig. 36.

***) A. P. di Cesnola, Salaminia, Pl. XIX, 30 and 21.

decades. Besides several Cypriots possessing natural ability there were three Englishman Messrs. Christian,*) J. W. Williamson and E. Foot to whom I had imparted my methods; and their cooperation was of great value to me in these excavations. Mr. Foot especially, who was acting as the Government overseer of the excavations, when I had once initiated him into the correct methods of observing and recording the results of observation with pen and pencil, showed the greatest conscientiousness in all his work.**) The ewer, fig. 46, must, from the circumstances of its discovery and from its stylistic peculiarities, be placed in the 5th century B. C.***) The picture is executed on the shoulder in one colour with touches of surface-white. The birds are marching round the vase in file under trees of two varieties, a foliage-tree resembling the fig-tree and another tree which may be a palm.

On Pl. XXIV, 1—10 the paintings on the shoulders of ten other ewers are reproduced in phototype. Pl. XXIV 3 is here repeated as fig. 47. These illustrations are all taken from my own grisaille drawings of the originals. Pl. XXIV, 10 shows a vase with black horizontal bands, the paintings between these bands being executed in surface-white alone. At the top we see two narrow strips occupied by processions of somewhat long-legged water-fowl—storks, cranes, or herons. The principal field below these, or that portion of it which remains, shows us a huge holy tree of the conventional type, formed entirely of dotted rosettes strung together. Right and left of the trunk are two large birds (of one only a part remains). Another bird is standing in the air to the left of the tree-top.

The other vase-paintings figured on the plate exhibit only trees, plants, branches, rosettes, palmettes, stars, zigzag or wavy lines. Men and beasts are absent.

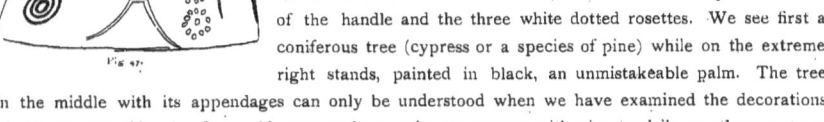

Fig. 47.

Fig. 47 (= Pl. XXIV, 3) seems to represent the holy tree between three concentric circles on the one side and four dotted rosettes on the other.

The paintings on Pl. XXIV, 8a and 8b are very peculiar. 8a shows three trees on the left, close to the black-painted horns of the handle and the three white dotted rosettes. We see first a coniferous tree (cypress or a species of pine) while on the extreme right stands, painted in black, an unmistakeable palm. The tree in the middle with its appendages can only be understood when we have examined the decorations of the reverse side 8b. It would seem to be a palm or cypress with vine-tendrils or other creepers hanging from it. On 8b we see one of the black horns studded with white beads which are common on these vases: through it grows a cypress, from which depend long vine-tendrils.

The annexed cut shows an interesting fragment of another of these ewers from Marion.†) We see on the shoulder of the vase a tree or shrub with trifoliate flowers. The stem, the branches, and the flowers-petals are white, the centres of the flowers black.

In many cases the trees had doubtless no exclusively sacral significance. Sometimes indeed

----

*) Mr Christian, a brother of Mr. C. Christian, the Manager of the Ottoman Bank and still a young man, unhappily died during the excavation at Poli of an insidious fever of a kind hitherto unknown in Cyprus, and so fatal that he was dead in less than twenty-four hours after the first attack, the district doctor arriving only when all was over.

**) Mr. Foot is also a very expert draughtsman, so that his assistance proved very useful to me in preparing illustrations and especially in making tracings from Greek vases.

***) Herrmann's Programm, p. 53—55.

†) Ibid., p. 54, fig. 37.

we can only look upon them as decorations pure and simple; elsewhere they seem to serve in the main a decorative purpose while retaining their sacral character. But granting to the full the frequent employment of the tree as an ornamental motive and all that this implies, we have nevertheless in the monuments already presented to the reader and others which I will now lay before him a material quite adequate to prove the extensive practice of Tree-worship in Kypros during a certain period, and the important place occupied by the symbols and scenes of this worship in the repertory of contemporary art. We have seen that the long period during which the Cyprian potter continues to employ these motives corresponds with the period during which the greater part of the Old Testament from Deborah's song (Judg. 5, 12th century B. C. to the post-exilic works of Ezra and Nehemiah (444 B. C.), was composed; and all the great names of Greek poetic literature from Homer to Euripides fall likewise within its limits. In the following sections we will briefly trace the analogies to Tree-worship and the decorative use of the tree in Kypros which meet us in the contemporary literatures of Judaea and Greece and in the traditions of other lands.

Fig. 18.

Let us, in the first place, turn to the products of Cyprian work in metal, and look for representations of the holy tree.

Here the Cyprian metal paterae concern us most. All the known examples, with one single exception, are of silver.*) This exception is the famous and much discussed Dali patera of bronze or copper, discovered in an early Graeco-Phoenician earth-tomb not far from the western limit of the lower town of Idalion. On Plate III will be found a plan of the ancient city of Idalion made with all possible care and conscientiousness by myself and the British Government-Surveyor Mr. E. Carletti (a gentleman of Italian birth). I took especial pains to ascertain the exact places at which the more important of the earlier finds had been made.**) No. 12 marks the spot where the Dali bronze bowl was found.

In fig. 49 I once more reproduce this celebrated patera, round which a whole literature has grown***) and deservedly, for it is up to now quite unique. On it are represented a sacrifice and a

---

*) I myself unearthed at Tamassos in 1889, during excavations undertaken on behalf of the Berlin Museum, a silver patera decorated with a horse in relief. It fell to the share of the Cyprus Museum in Nicosia, the law as to excavations still valid in Cyprus allowing one third of the results to the Insular Government, one third to the proprietor of the site, and one third to the excavators.

**) See the Explanation of the Plates and pages 6—7 and 16—20 above. Cp. too The Owl (Nicosia) 1888, p. 43.

***) I will speak in another place of the significance of the reliefs on this patera—the oldest known specimen of such work from Cyprus—for the history of Art Religion, and Civilization. Many of the paterae

round dance to the accompaniment of music. The scene is a holy grove, under the trees of which we are meant to understand that the religious dance is executed;*) the sacrifice being performed before the altars and seated idol of the goddess. There is, however, no holy tree which is itself an object of adoration.

It is otherwise on the silver patera from Amathus, which, like the last, has been very

frequently illustrated, discussed, and cited in the literature of archaeology**) While the exterior zone is here ornamented with the representation of a military campagn, the subjects of the pictures in the two interior zones are religious. On the outer and more extensive of these latter we see a tree of the conventional type dependent on Assysian models, to the right and left of which stand two priests in the symmetrical attitude ot armorial supporters, performing

Fig. 49.

some function connected with a sacrifice.***) Their near arms (respectively right and left) hang down behind them, and each hand grasps the Nile-cross; with their other arms elevated and directed

and shields with decorations in relief from the Zeus cave in Crete (See Halbherr and Orsi, Antichíta dell' Antro di Zeus Ideo in Creta" in the Museo Italiano di Antichita Classica vol. II.) offer very remarkable resemblances to it. The Dali bowl is discribed or figured or both by Ceccaldi in the Revue Archéologique N. S XXIV (1872 II), p. 304 ff. and Pl. 14; Cesnola-Stern pages 74 and 404 and Pl. IX; Ceccaldi, Monuments de Chypre, de Syrie, et d'Égypte (Paris 1882), p. 92 ff. and Pl. VII; Furtwängler, Die Bronzefunde von Olympia, p 55; Helbig, Das homerische Epos (2nd ed.) p. 34, fig. 4. I may say that the details as to its discovery given by Helbig after Cesnola-Stern p. 74 are certainly, in part at least, incorrect. See also Holwerda, Die alten Kyprier in Kunst und Cultus (Leiden 1885), p. 31—36 and Pl. VII, 20; Perrot et Chipiez III, p. 673, fig. 482. Our figure 49 is borrowed from Perrot & Chipiez.

*) These objects between the figures have been thought to be not trees but columns. This is a question the discussion of which I must reserve for the sections of this work dealing with pillar worship and ring dances.

**) Cesnola-Stern, Pl. LI; Perrot & Chipiez III, p. 775, fig 547 (our fig. 50 is taken from hence); Ceccaldi, Monuments, Pl. VIII; Helbig, Das homerische Epos, Pl. I.

***) I will not attempt to analyse here those portions of the design which are dominated by Egyptian influence.

towards the tree, they are in the act of either attaching flowers to it or pulling flowers from it.   On the exterior zone we see the besiegers felling with double-bladed axes the grove of palms and fig-trees outside the walls of the fortress.   The graceful realism of these trees, in which we can detect the feeling and the handiwork of an artist, is in striking and intentional contrast with the stiff and conventional treatment of the holy tree in the second zone.

The sacred precinct of Anat-Athene, on the western Akropolis of Idalion*) contained no

Fig. 50.

votive agalmata, but arms and armour were suspended in it.   Among the objects found on this spot are a double-bladed axe,**) portions of a suit of armour,***) a sceptre,†) battle-club, or part of the pole of a chariot, and fragments of a shield††)—all of bronze.   A bronze tablet, inscribed on both sides with Kyprian characters, had also been suspended in the sacred area, most probably on a holy tree.†††)   The two Kyprian inscriptions on the bronze sceptre (?)§) and the bronze tablet§§) both mention the Idalian or Edalian Athene (Athana).   The first is symply a dedication to her; the second is a contract between the community of the Idalians (Edalians) and the physician Onasilos: at the

---

*) See No. 26 (p. 15 supra) and Plate III, 2. Cp. also The Owl (Nicosia) 1888, p. 46.
**) Figured ͻ Perrot & Chipiez III, p. 867, fig. 634.
***) Ibid., fig. 633, (with Phoenician inscription) wrongly described by Perrot as a géniastère de casque.
†) Ibid., p. 494, fig. 348 (with Kyprian inscription.)
††) Ibid., p. 869, fig. 636.
†††) See above, p 15, No. 28.
§) Meister, Die griechischen Dialekte II, p. 156, No. 62.
§§) Ibid., p 150—156, No. 60.

end we read: "And the King and the city deposited this tablet, with these words inscribed thereon, beside the goddess Athana who is in Edalion, with oaths not to break this covenant for all time." I have above (p. 15) pointed out that a Phoenician dedication to the goddess Anat*) inscribed on marble, discovered as recently as 1887 in the plain (at point 9 on Plate III) comes evidently from this holy grove. In the same place I called attention to the aniconic Tree- or Grove-worship once practised at this spot, and I cited as a parallel the aniconic cultus of Athene in Boeotia which Pausanias expressly

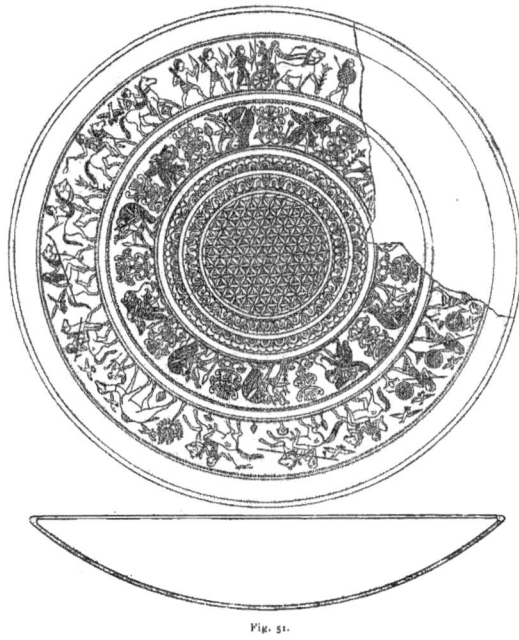

Fig. 51.

connects with the Kyprian Telchines. I also mentioned there the fact that in this same holy precinct of Anat-Athene a considerable number of silver paterae had been deposited, and I now give (fig. 51**) an illustration of one of these. The spot where this discovery was made and the plateau on which the grove of Anat-Athene stood have been described by me at greater length in "The Owl"***) the English journal (started and conducted in Cyprus by myself and an English gentleman) in which the plans, Plates II and III of the present work, were originally published. The silver paterae, the bronze inscribed tablet, and the bronze weapons were found at points 2 and 3: at point 1 was found a heap of heavy iron swords of the Homeric type known to us from Mykenae and from my own excavations for the Berlin Museu .i at Tamassos, which produced a

large number of unmistakeable specimens of this class. The spot (point 1) where the swords were discovered was pointed out to me by the peasants, and I soon found a sufficient number of fragments left behind by the excavators to remove all doubt as to my informants' correctness. Perrot gives

---

*) P. Berger "Une nouvelle inscription Royale d'Idalie," p. 15—22 of the "Mémoire sur deux nouvelles inscriptions Phéniciennes de l'île de Chypre" (Extrait des Comptes rendus de l'Académie des inscriptions et belles lettres pour Avril 1887); Jul. Euting, "Epigraphische Miscellen" in the Sitzungsberichte der Berliner Akademie der Wissenschaften, 1887, p. 420—422; Dr. Pierides in the Academy of April 23rd 1887; p. 293, and May 7th 1889, p. 329.

**) After Perrot III, p. 779, fig. 548.

***) 1888, p. 45 ff.

in his Histoire de l'art*) a description of the place and circumstances of the find which is only in part correct. By the "narrow plain on which the remains of several tumuli were to be seen"**) he means the narrow plateau on the hill with the still visible traces of the excavation. (See Nos. 1—3 on our plate III, and Plate LX A and D***). Certain portions of his account of the objects discovered can hardly be correct. I do not believe that, as Perrot reports, copper or bronze axes shaped like simple stone chisels†) can have occured in this stratum of the Graeco-Phoenician Iron Period even though the stage of this Period here represented be an early one, not reaching later than the fifth century B. C.; for this particular form is associated exclusively with the Pre-Graeco-Phoenician Copper-Bronze Period.

I have felt myself called upon to make a place here for the above corrections of the received account of these finds, their locality and circumstances. Although in the present section it is simply my aim to exhibit the different forms under which the holy tree makes its appearance on Cyprian antiquities, the treatment of tree-worship and grove-worship in Cyprus and of their relations to the Bible and Homer being reserved for subsequent sections, I may be allowed to mention here a very obvious and happy comparison of Cyprian usage with the sacred writings, derived, as it is, from the very circumstances connected with this particular find which I have just been laying before the reader. Perrot (p. 771, note 1) narrates, after L. P. di Cesnola, the true and very melancholy story of the discovery of the twelve silver pateræ. They were found in one pile, each laid on the top of the other, "just like a dozen dinner-plates" as several of the older inhabitants of Dali who were present at their unearthing described it to me.††) Ten were melted up, and two (now in the Louvre) saved.†††) These 12 silver-gilt pateræ deposited in the grove of Anaṭ-Athene on the western Akropolis of Idalion remind us of the 12 sets of votive offerings presented on 12 successive days by the princes of the 12 tribes of Israel at the consecration of the Tabernacle and its altar. (See Numbers chap. 7.) Each prince brought, among other offerings, a massive silver charger, a silver bowl, and a flat golden patera (spoon in the A. V.) We have then here a speaking testimony to a Semitic rite as actually practised by the Hebrews. The further our knowledge reaches, the more clearly do we perceive how true in all particulars are the pictures of worship which the Bible gives us. Here at Idalion and there at Jerusalem we find the same imageless worship at an altar. In both cases we have the deposition of precious vessels of gold or silver; in both cases we have the number twelve.

The patera of which an illustration is here given (fig. 51) is one of the pair, now in the

---

*) III. p. 866—869.

**) 'Près de Dali, dans une plaine étroite, où se voyaient les restes de plusieurs tumulus'. In Colonna-Ceccaldi's Monuments (see above p. 15—17) the spots where the bronze and iron weapons, the bronze inscribed tablet, and the silver bowls were found are correctly given, if we allow for his having misnamed the eastern Akropolis hill. See above, p. 17 note 3.

***) Pl. LX shows the reader four views of Idalion (cp. Plates II and III). Compare also the Description of the Plates below.

†) Described and figured by Perrot III, p. 888, fig. 635.

††) Perrot mentions twelve, and my informants gave the same number. Ceccaldi (Monuments, p. 295) puts the number at fourteen. As Ceccaldi is wrong in his statement as to the number saved (he says that only one was saved, whereas there were two) I consider that more dence is to be placed in the number as told to myself and Cesnola by the peasants. I suppose that they told Ceccaldi that twelve were found, and that he added to this number the two still existing specimens, instead of reckoning them in.

†††) Perrot III, p. 771, Fig. 546, and p. 779, fig. 548.

Louvre, which were saved about 40 years ago by the French Consul Tastu. Its diameter is 0,195 m. (= 7⅝ in.) Here the two outer zones alone are decorated with figure subjects; the centre is occupied by a medallion of a pattern borrowed from textile work, encircled by two rings of continuous lotus and lotus-bud pattern. On the larger exterior zone we see the departure to the wars or the triumphant return of a king; he himself leads the procession mounted on a chariot and surrounded by his foot-guards; next come the cavalry, and in the middle of it the commissariat represented by a loaded camel. The royal chariot is followed by three light-armed archers and preceded by squires carrying short spears. Just that bit of the patera is broken away which contained the van and rear of the procession and the division between the two; but the procession seems to have been closed by a troop of heavy-armed soldiers carrying round shields and long spears, of whom three are still visible. As on many other silver bowls, e. g. those from Praeneste (Perrot III. p. 759, fig. 543) and Caere (ibid. p. 769, fig. 544, and p. 780, fig. 549), birds, the omens or heralds of victory, are flying over the heads of the army, which is doubtless either setting out on, or returning from, a successful expedition. The trees, plants and flowers of different sizes which are introduced between the figures serve the double purpose of indicating the country through which the troops are marching and of satisfying the taste of the period, which could ill dispense with these favourite accessories. The subjects of the narrower second zone are taken from the domain of religion or mythology. We see ten holy trees, and an eleventh evidently stood on the portion which has been broken away. These artificial trees are of massive proportions, and are schematically represented in the manner of our type b (fig. 14—21): by the side of eight out of the ten rises a small tree more realistically sketched and doubt-less intended for a natural tree.*) In some cases it would appear to be meant for a cypress, in others for a lotus tree. Between each pair of the large mystic trees (or tree-like aniconic agalmata) we see one those single combats between man and beast which belong to the mythological repertory of the sixth century B. C. Two different scenes alternate with each other — in one instance the same scene occurs, with slight variations, twice in succession. We see in the one case a four winged demon clothed in a long robe fighting with a lion, in the other a winged griffin in a peculiarly distorted pose is attacked by a hero who wears only a short loin-cloth.

On Plate XXIV̌ an illustration is given of the silver girdle which I unearthed at Poli tis Khrysokhou (Marion-Arsinoe) in 1884, and placed at the disposal of my friend F. Dümmler for the purpose of publication. I would refer the reader to his admirable article in the Jahrbuch des Instituts.**) There will be found there the plan and section (made from my measurements and draw-ings) of the tomb in which this rare, in fact unique, specimen was found. Dümmler has also repro-duced my sketches (made to scale with the help of the chambre claire) of the principal types of pottery and one of the archaic lamps found in the same tomb with the girdle. Resting his argument on the character of the other objects found in the tomb, the general circumstances of the dis-covery***) and a comprehensive comparative review, Dümmler has dated this curious product of

---

*) It appears to me that in this case we should suppose that in front of the cultus-image, in the form of a mystic tree or pole hung with bands, there is erected a natural tree resembling our May-trees. I will recur to this question in speaking of the Ashera.

**) Band II (1887), pages 85—94 and Plate 8.

***) Dümmler describes on page 87 of the Jahrbuch, from the report with which I had furnished him, all the other finds made in the tomb, and figures the most important gold objects on Plate 8, figs. 3 and 5.

Cyprian local silversmith's work in the middle of the sixth century B. C. at latest—a result perfectly in accord with my own series of observations made before and since. The oblong plaques united by hinge-fastenings of which the actual girdle is composed are ornamented, like the inner zone of the Idalion silver patera (fig. 51), with two alternating designs. It is probable that there were originally eight such plaques in the girdle, four with the pair of griffins and four with the figure holding wild beasts. The griffins sit symmetrically like watch dogs with their backs turned to each other; they are separated only by a small lanceolate tree, evidently a little cypress. Still smaller dwarf trees of the same shape are growing in front of the griffins at the extreme edge of the field. These little cypresses, now larger now smaller, occur sporadically on the outer zone of the Idalion bowl, (fig. 51) and are more lavishly scattered about the Kurion bowl (fig. 52). The demonic personage, subduer of beasts, on the second design is here wingless; he grasps by their hind legs two pairs of beasts also wingless. The upper pair, two lions, are (in heraldic phraseology) passant, regardant; the lower pair, two wild goats, rest their fore-paws on the ground, and like the lions, look back over their shoulders at their captor. He himself is marching towards the spectator's left, but his head and trunk face us. Two flowers spring from the ground and fill the space under the heads of the wild goats. Dümmler attaches great importance to these stalked palmettes springing from the ground, since this motive, as he says, is peculiar to a strictly limited class of artistic works which are among the earliest Greek importations into Italy. As a palmette-tendril of exactly the same style and form as that here is found e. g. on Cyprian stone capitals*) and decidedly belongs to the repertory of Cyprian art in the period about 600 B. C. and earlier (see Dümmler, p. 92 and the shield from Amathus, Cesnola-Stern, Pl. LII) we must concede that in these Cyprian products the first essays of Greek art may be detected—essays too showing a considerable degree of independence. Or should we say that the palmette tendrils are not Greek at all? In any case the specific form which meets us on the silver girdle of Marion and the stone capital of Idalion seems to be a Graeco-Phoenician variant or modification, peculiar to Cyprus, of an oriental type, into the origin of which we cannot here pause to enquire. Of its relation to Tree-worship and Tree-ornament there can, however, be little doubt. The griffin designs are framed in a double border following the oblong outline of the plaque and composed of an exterior meander pattern**) and an interior pattern of alternating flowers and buds of the lotus, a decoration already quite familiar to us.***) The larger fields containing the subduer of beasts are enclosed in a simpler frame composed only of linked palmettes and tree-ornaments, a pattern also familiar enough to us as occuring on numerous works of Cyprian art.†) From these

---

　　* In "The Owl" (Nicosia) 1888, on page 60 of my essay: "New discoveries at the most celebrated temenos of Aphrodite" and Plate V, 3 ibid., I give an illustration of such a capital showing precisely similar palmette-tendrils springing from the ground. I will reproduce this illustration in a later portion of the present work and shall then have something more to say on the subject of these tendrils.

　　**) The meander pattern is rare in Cyprus, but occurs e. g. on the border of the dress of a winged sphinx supporting a censer. A description and illustration will be given below.

　　***) E. g. on the Idalion silver bowl (fig. 51); on the stone sarcophagus from Amathus (Cesnola-Stern, Plates LIV and LV = Perrot III, figs. 415—418); on vases like those figured by Perrot III, p. 699, fig. 501 and A. P. di Cesnola, Salaminia, p. 253, fig. 238.

　　†) E. g. on the Amathus sarcophagus (Cesnola-Stern Plates LIV and LV). This ornament appears in many modifications. Holy trees, flowers, palmettes, capitals, the ends of cuirass-plates, and other articles of adornment or decorations are formed either by simplifying or by further elaborating it. The palm with its crown of foliage seems to have given the original suggestion. In speaking of the palm I will recur to this question.

eight silver plaques of uniform size forming the actual girdle, there hang by means of twisted chains attached to rings a number of hollow bells of the same metal, about twenty to each plaque. Evidently we have here an imitation in silver repoussé work of an embroidered or brocaded girdle from which tassels hung by cords. The two narrower plaques of the same height, which were next to the clasp of the girdle, are decorated with figures of winged sphinxes symmetrically seated on either side of a holy tree. We have already seen the same motive of two sphinxes almost identically rendered on the silver bowl from Kurion (fig. 52), and it recurs on the stone relief illustrated on Plate XXVI. The holy tree between the griffins on our silver girdle corresponds to that with which we meet on the Amathus bowl (fig. 50), the Idalion bowl (fig. 51), the Kurion bowl (fig. 52), and the Kurion gem fig. 53. The sphinx designs on the girdle are framed in a simple tress.*) The portions of the girdle which form the clasp are gilded, and are divided by mouldings into a number of compartments of different sizes, fifteen in all. Seven of these compartments are ornamented with parallel lines in relief, running horizontally; the four compartments at the corner are occupied by delicately finished rosettes, while the four others contain designs of animals. The two spaces on the right and left are each occupied by a pair of lions placed in reverse positions, and standing, like the sphinxes, not on the horizontal but on the vertical plane. The two on the left are couched ready to spring; the two on the right are standing and look back over their shoulders. The two remaining spaces, the upper and lower, contain antelopes feeding between cypress trees and recalling in all points the browsing animals on the Kurion patera (fig. 52).

Dümmler in his article cites other Cyprian parallels of the existence of which I had informed him, viz. objects found by myself at Kurion in 1883 which belong to the same artistic repertory, and show the same types of decoration as this girdle. Since then (in 1889), while digging at Tamassos for the Berlin Museum, I unearthed in a tomb there dating also from the sixth century B. C. the remains of a similar silver girdle: unhappily it was only possible to rescue a few tiny fragments. The plaques of this Tamassos silver girdle were thinly plated with gold leaf, while its little silver bells were ungilded, but were attached to the girdle by delicate chains of pale gold (electron). On the single plaque which is tolerably well preserved we see in repoussé a column with volutes and palmette-capital between two cypresses. To all appearance the vocabulary of design at the disposal of the artist is here the same as in the case of the Marion-Arsinoe girdle.

There are thus, as I have shown, three different centres of civilization, Marion-Arsinoe, Kurion and Tamassos, which have given to us these silver (in parts silver-gilt) girdles, with in all three cases similar designs in relief similarly disposed and with fringes of little bells hanging from chainlets and tinkling when set in motion. We have therefore to deal with a wide-spread custom. We see a similar tasselled girdle round the waist of the heavy-armed warrior on the Tamassos vase. In more advanced sections of this work I shall have occasion to point, in another connection, to the occurrence in other lands of parallels to these Cyprian girdles and more especially to that of Poli tis Khrysokhou illustrated on Plate XXV.

At present I will content myself with mentioning that, as Dümmler**) and Helbig***) have

---

*) This tress occurs on the bronze patera of Idalion (fig. 49), and the silver paterae of Amathus (fig. 50 and Kurion (fig. 52). See also the vases on Plates XX, XXI &c.

**) Jahrbuch des Instituts, II, p. 92.

***) Homerisches Epos, p. 209. Helbig gives a cut (fig. 61) of a portion of my girdle, but refers only

not failed to observe, of all existing monuments these Cyprian girdles best serve to bring before our eyes a certain form of the Homeric girdle. The girdle which Hera puts on has a hundred tassels.*) Below, when we come to speak of Cyprian costume, we shall be able to show how vividly

Cyprian monuments illustrate certain articles of apparel and ornament described partly in the Old Testament and partly in the Homeric Poems. My main purpose here has been to indicate how representations of the worship of holy trees, and that tree-ornamentation which, while it originated in the significance of the tree as an object of worship, subsequently let fall all religious associations, had an influence on the details of ancient Cyprian every-day costume, no less profound and tenacious than that which they exercised on vase manufacture, and relief work in clay, stone, and metal.

We now return to the silver bowls, and in fig. 52 I give an illustration of one of the most interesting examples (Cesnola-Stern,

Fig. 52.

Plate LXVI 1). This patera measures 0,20 m. (= 8 inches) in diameter and is now in New York: our illustration is reproduced from Ceccaldi's Monuments pl. X. Here religious subjects prevail, occupying, as they do, the whole of the outer zone and the central medallion. The inner zone contains hunting and pastoral scenes; but even here too a religious figure, the couched sphinx, is intruded. In this inner zone a forest of cypress trees serves to indicate at once the haunts of the wild animals, the feeding-ground of the other animals, and the holy grove in which the sphinx is lying surrounded by cartouches. One of the scenes alone—that where the hunter faces a wild beast (lion or bear), and thrusts his spear into its jaws, while a bowman aims at it from behind— is being enacted not under the cypresses, but among undergrowth of an unrecognizable variety. The outer zone, composed on a larger scale, has more interest for us here. We see five holy mystical trees, graceful variants, already betraying a Greek sense of style, of that Cyprian type with which we are now familiar. In three cases two animals are heraldically placed to the right and left of the tree. Starting from the upper

---

to Dümmler, while in reality the discovery of the girdle and the illustrations of it are mine. True, he mentions me in his preface among his collaborators, I having furnished him with numerous observations gained from excavation.

*) Iliad Ξ 181. ζώσατο δὲ ζώνην ἑκατὸν θυσάνοις ἀραρυῖαν.

left-hand part of the illustration and proceeding towards the left, we see first two winged griffins, placing their fore-paws on the lower branches of the tree, as if they intended to climb it, and picking at the upper branches with their beaks. Then follows, under tall, realistica lly formed cypresses, the scene of the battle between a lion and an ox or bear. This is succeeded by another conventional holy tree between two rampant antelopes or moufflons*), whose pose is precisely similar to that of the two griffins. Another scene of tree-adoration immediately follows, and it is the most graceful of the five. The mystic tree is here treated with a stylistic excellence which shows that the Greek sense of beauty had already dawned**). From its roots, from its trunk, and from its top spring blossoms; the delicately drawn winged sphinxes rest their fore-paws on the root- and trunk-flowers of the tree, grasping them with their claws; then reaching up and throwing back their heads, they kiss the blossoms which spring from its topmost branches. The gracefulness of this heraldic design of animals adoring a tree is only equalled by the reliefs on certain columns and capitals of which L. Palma di Cesnola has published admirable illustrations***) (reproduced on a smaller scale on our Plate XXVI). The group of the mystic tree and sphinxes is succeeded by two further mystic trees resembling the two first, their composition being more elaborate only in that they have blossoms issuing from their stems, in addition to those issuing from the roots which are common to all five trees. These two last trees are not flanked by heraldic animals, but between them stands a two-winged female figure, copied from an Egyptian design,†) almost certainly a goddess,††) holding flowers in both hands and with two cartouches behind her. The remainder of the zone is occupied by further religious scenes, sacrifices, and battles with monsters. I will only remark that the group of the man clothed only in short drawers engaged in combat with a winged griffin in a distorted pose, here introduced next to the fifth holy tree, is, as we have already seen, repeated six times, with no essential variations, on the Idalion silver patera fig. 51. At the other or left end of the religious scenes, just behind the group of winged griffins and holy tree, we again see a man, here partly mailed, engaged in combat with a winged griffin, but this griffin is in the erect pose which is usual in the case of lions. The combat between a four-winged demon and a lion which we saw repeated four times on the silver bowl from Dali (fig. 51) reappears here on a larger scale as the central medallion of the patera, two birds, omens of victory, being introduced to fill the vacant spaces. On the inner zone of reliefs (in addition to the sphinx and the lion- or bear-hunt

---

*) The moufflon still frequents the hill-forests of Cyprus, and is increasing in numbers owing to the operation of an English game-law specially enforced in its favour.

**) Cp. G. Perrot II (Chaldée et Assyrie), p. 321, fig. 138. Layard, Monuments, 1st series, Pl. 43.

***) A descriptive Atlas of the Cesnola Collection of Cypriot Antiquities in the Metropolitan Museum of Art, New York. By Louis P. di Cesnola LLD, Director of the Museum. In three volumes with introduction by Professor Ernst Curtius of the Berlin Museum. Berlin. A. Asher & Co. 1885). The Introduction by E. Curtius promised on the Title Page was never written.

†) Cp. G. Perrot, Histoire de l'Art, I p. 800, fig. 531 and III, p. 787.

††) Here as on the Amathus bowl (p. 47 fig. 50) the goddess is Isis, who like Hathor, was worshipped in Kypros, and united with the Kyprian Astarte-Aphrodite, herself originally none other than the Babylonian Nana-Istar, to form the single great Kyprian goddess. In the sections of this work dealing with feminine divinities I recur to this subject. Cp. also Roschers' Mythol. Lexikon II, cols. 379 and 380, (Isis auf Kypros) and I col. 1868. (Hathor auf Kypros.) In 1885 I demonstrated the existence at Kition of a temple dedicate to this chief goddess of Kypros, Astarte-Aphrodite, where the Hathor-Isis element is particularly prominent, and the Louvre and Berlin Museums each possess a capital from this sanctuary with the representation of Hathor. An illustration of the capital in the Louvre is given by Reinach in his Chroniques d'Orient (Paris 1891) p. 178 (Revue Archéologique 1885 2, 347).

already described) we observe a lion in a position which shows that he is intent upon surprising a herd of cattle. The herd is represented by a browsing horse, a cow suckling her calf, two oxen marching the one behind the other, and two others butting at each other. The large cypress-trees mentioned above are not the only trees on the outer zone. Little baby cypresses are to be seen sprouting up beside the mystic tree with the griffins and the mailed man and griffin. The principal design on this outer zone, round which the holy trees with their guardian monsters, and the single combats, are grouped, does not nearly concern us here, and I have therefore left it hitherto undescribed. The manner is quite Egyptian. A king is striking a group of prisoners with his uplifted club-sceptre;*) in front of him stands the hawk-headed god and blesses the victory; behind him is a soldier carrying a corpse.

On Plate XXVI 1—3 I give a reduced phototypical reproduction, from L. P. di Cesnola's above-cited Atlas, of an admirably preserved stele (1) and two fragments of similar stelae or capitals (2 and 3). The stele No. 1, 4 feet, 6$^1/_8$ inches (= 1,45 m.) in height, said, like the two fragments, to come from Athiaenou, has been already figured and described in the third volume of Perrot's History of Art***) but these fragments (No. 2 measures 2 feet, 1$^3/_4$ inches = 65,5 cm. in height, No. 3 2 feet, 6 inches = 76,2 cm.) were, as far as I am aware, first made known by the admirable illustrations of them in the Atlas. The fragmentary condition of Nos. 2 and 3 does not admit of our deciding whether they form parts of stelae of the same form as No. 1 or of capitals like those illustrated by Perrot†) and myself.††) But in view of the facts that on these fragments groups of winged sphinxes before the holy tree occupy the large central space, exactly as on the stele No. 1, and that such winged sphinxes frequently occur in Cyprian Art either surmounting sepulcral stelae or as independent sepulcral figures, while their occurrence on capitals is hitherto unattested, it may be regarded as highly probable that the fragments should be restored as stelae of the type of No. 1. In all three cases the two sphinxes occupy similar symmetrical positions to the right and left of the holy tree. No. 3 conveys an impression of higher antiquity than the others. The sphinxes here are swarming up the tree like men or monkeys. All the details, when compared with those of Nos 1 and 2, have a rough appearance and exhibit a lack of fluidity and executive skill.†††) In the triangle from which both the two volutes of ionic style curving outwards and downwards and the six palm-leaves curving upwards and inwards spring, we see the disc of the sun and the crescent of the moon surmounted by a pendent lotus-flower. The admirably preserved specimen No. 1 is executed with much greater care and in a more advanced archaic-Greek style. The triangle in the middle is occupied by a large lotus flower alone. Here the holy tree, especially in its upper portions, has much more of the palmette character. The sphinxes are worked in a freeer archaic-Greek style and their pose, drawing, and modelling are distinctly superior. They still, it is true, stand on their hind legs, but their position as a whole—the manner in which they climb up the tree and bring their breasts nearly into contact with each other- is more natural and graceful than that of those on No. 3. No. 2

---

*) Cp. Perrot I, p. 127, fig. 85 and III figs. 36, 543, and 546.
**) Plate XCIX 671 c, 672, and 673.
***) P. 217, fig. 152.
†) Vol. III. p. 116, fig. 52
††) The Owl, 1888, pages 60 and 61 and Plate V, 1—3
†††) I will speak in another place of the importance of these specimens for the history of Art.

bespeaks further progress. We cannot tell in this case how the central triangle was ornamented, as this portion of the relief is broken away. The decorative group, here of much larger dimensions, is enclosed on each side by only two inward-curving leaves from whose short terminal spirals delicate lotus flowers depend. The holy tree issues from a column resembling the ionic, which in its turn springs from a large lotus-bud. The tree itself is formed by four superimposed palmettes, and from its foot, as well as from the summit of the column-capital, long spirals grow: on either side two large long-stalked lotus-flowers, describing bold and elegant curves, shoot out from the con-junction of the first and second palmettes. On these flower-stalks stand the winged sphinxes in armorial attitude, each resting one fore-paw on the second palmette of the tree. On all three specimens, 1—3, the extremities of the great wings of the sphinxes curve forwards in a fashion which has been hitherto often spoken of as a peculiarity of early Greek style; but the curve of the wing-points is here on No. 3 more pronounced than on Nos. 1 and 2, the closest parallel being the wings of the horses on the Melos vase published by Conze.*) The hair of the sphinxes falls in graceful locks on their necks and shoulders: their heads are surmounted by mural crowns. The style in which their bodies, heads, and hair are modelled points to a date when the archaic period was drawing to a close, and the purer ionic forms of the capital of the column are also an indication that Greek Art has now reached a somewhat more advanced stage of development. We cannot shut our eyes to the relation-ship in style, forms, and motives between our stone reliefs No. 1 and 2 and the silver "repoussé" designs of sphinxes on the Kurion bowl (fig. 52) and the girdle of Marion (Plate XXV), but the severer conventionalism of these products of the silversmith's art vindicates for them a date of a few decades earlier than that of the stelae. Knowing as we do the exact surroundings among which the Marion girdle (Plate XXV) was found, we shall not be far wrong if we date the stone relief Pl. XXVI 3 and the Kurion patera somewhere in the early years of the 6th century or at the extreme end of the preceding 7th century; while the remaining relief Pl. XXVI 2 would belong to the very end of the 6th, or the beginning of the 5th century.

I reproduce here (fig. 53) from Cesnola-Stern, Pl. LXXIX 1 a, a cut of an intaglio on a Cyprian scarab**) which gives material for instructive comparisons. We meet here with the same

Fig. 53.

design that we have already seen on the intermediate zone of the Amathus silver bowl underneath the fortress. The position and costume of the two men and the form of the tree which they are adoring are the same in both instances. On the vase (Plate XXI) the same motive is employed, there but the group is modified in accordance with the specifically Kyprian, Early Graeco-Phoenician style of the work. The men's heads are uncovered, and they have long flowing hair, but their dress and pose are still the same, and the tree retains its form. The gem (fig. 53) gives us a welcome cue to the reason for the presence of a segment of a tress above the tree-top on the vase. The vase-painter found the winged sun-disc which we see on the gem either too difficult a subject, or unsympathetic, or incomprehensible, and there-fore substituted for it the piece of tress, a pattern which came as readily to his hand as to those of

---

*) Conze, Melische Thongefässe (Leipzig 1872) Pl. IV. Of the sphinxes more anon.
**) Cp. also p. 336 of King's Essay "Die Ringe und Gemmen des Schatzes von Curium" in Cesnola-Stern. As is well known, the tress belongs to the repertory of Assyrian Art.

the goldsmiths and silversmiths of whose familiarity with this tress-pattern I have already spoken in discussing the Marion silver girdle.

Fig. 54 shows another variation of this motive. The Egyptian tendencies are here strongly marked, but the style is withal local Kyprian. The design is cut on a chalcedony  scarab. Two hawk-headed deities in the same position as the men on the preceding gem, the vase, and the silver bowl, are adoring a remarkable aniconic agalma which here takes the place of the tree and is (like the tree in fig. 53) surmounted by the sun-disc. Here it would indeed seem that, as King has already observed*), the cone of the Paphian goddess forms the base of the agalma. From the sides of the summit of this cone two snakes emerge, and between them on its actual summit rests a ball from which issues a composite object the significance of

Fig. 54.

which is by no means clear: it would seem to be either a palmette, or several snakes fantastically grouped. It is evident that we have here a curious Kyprian version of the tree-adoration, highly modified by Egyptian influence.**)

The next cut, fig. 55,***) shows the engraving on a large scarab. The holy tree is here adored by two bearded sphinxes, who each raise one of their fore paws. A crescent rests on the top of the vertical tree-stem.†)

Lastly I give (fig. 56) in the size of the original the incised designs on a steatite weight.††) On the four sides, which are slightly broader at the foot than at the top, we see respectively (1) a

Fig. 55.

Fig. 56.

seated human figure holding a tree or branch, (2) a maned quadruped, perhaps a horse, stepping to the right; above its back in the air is branch, (3) a man engaged in adoring a tree or branch, (4) another quadruped in motion with a branch above it. The under surface of the weight is also decorated with a similar branch and animal.†††) I have no doubt at all that we have both in this case

---

*) Cp. King's description p. 339 in Cesnola-Stern. Our figure 54 is a reproduction of Plate LXXX, 10 there. Kings calls attention to a similar gem with Phoenician inscription, Gesenius No. LXX.

**) More will be said on this subject below in the sections dealing with the transformation of the tree post, and aniconic agalma into the anthropomorphic idol.

***) Cesnola-Stern, Plate LXXX, 13.

†) King (Cesnola-Stern, p. 340) again points out the occurrence of a similar type with Phoenician inscription in Gesenius (Mon. Phoen. No. LXXter.)

††) A. P. di Cesnola, Salaminia, p. 134, fig. 137.

†††) The manufacture of these and other similar Kyprian weights (I cite some other examples below) seems from the circumstances of their discovery, as far as these are known with certainty, to extend over a space of time which commencing in the Bronze Period about the middle of the second millennium B. C. finishes in the Iron Period about six or seven hundred years B. C. Various manners in the manufacture and ornamentation of these weights, as well as certain formal divergencies, can be discriminated, but their consideration must be reserved for future enquiry.

9*

and the others to do with scenes of tree-worship. In a subsequent section I will lay before the reader terracotta idols of tree form, which I myself dug up in more than one holy precinct, and further testimony to the existence of such idols in Kypros reaches us through literary sources. Our numerous illustrations alone have, I think, sufficiently shown that the adoration of holy trees played during different periods a great part in the religious observances of the Kyprians, although it is indisputable that the sanctity and ritual significance of the tree cannot in many cases be isolated from its profane utilization as a decorative element, and must in some cases be distinctly postponed to the latter. In this section I have, in selecting the material on which my conclusions rest, purposely set aside Hellenistic and Roman times. In fact of the many examples I have cited the most recent reach no further than the 5th century B. C. The vases, e. g. fig. 48, are among the latest.

II. Kyprian Tree Worship and Tree Ornament compared with those of other Eastern Countries.

In this section the representations of trees sacred or profane and the use of arboreal ornament in the arts of other oriental countries will concern us, and we will show how this group of forms and ideas, as revealed to us in the designs employed on all classes of artistic handwork, again teaches us to what an extent the foreign and native elements in Kyprian Art, Civilization and Religion mingle, interpenetrate, and amalgamate. We open the series with:

1. Hissarlik and Kypros.

Heinrich Schliemann, whose loss we are still deploring, found, as all know, at Hissarlik that Troy the fortunes of which are the theme of those glorious products of single or united genius,

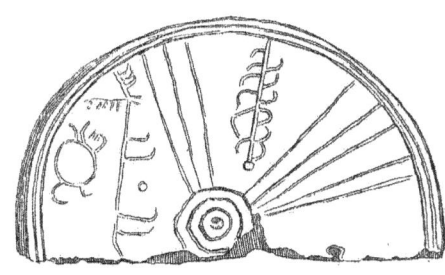

the Homeric poems. The Iliad pictures to us the conflicts in remote antiquity of Hellenic and non-Hellenic tribes on the soil of Asia Minor. Homer clothes this primitive and legendary Greek world in the dress of his own time. Up to the present day it is only in Cyprus that modern research has been able to discover strata of civilization showing a close relation with the oldest and immediately succeeding strata of Hissarlik. It has been reserved for myself to point out in full the extent

Fig. 57.

and intimacy of these relations.*) Tree-ornament and tree-worship play no small part here.

I give, in fig. 57, a cut of the vase-cover found in the third town of Hissarlik and represented

---

*) Cp. F. Dümmler: "Aelteste Nekropolen auf Cypern," in the Mittheilungen des Instituts zu Athen XI, p. 212.

by Schliemann in fig. 484 of his Ilios (p. 461). Beside it I place (fig. 58, a, b, c, d, e, f, g, h) pictures of Kyprian hand-made vases of red clay with reliefs. Fig. 58c is the entire vase the reliefs on the body of which alone, tree, stag, and snake, are reproduced above in fig. 3. It is here drawn from a point of view which shows the tree only. As we see, other snakes in relief curl round the neck and handle of the vase. On the vase-cover from Troy are engraved a tree, a stag, and a beast which may be either a cuttle-fish or a tortoise. The technique and style, the subjects and the arrangement of the

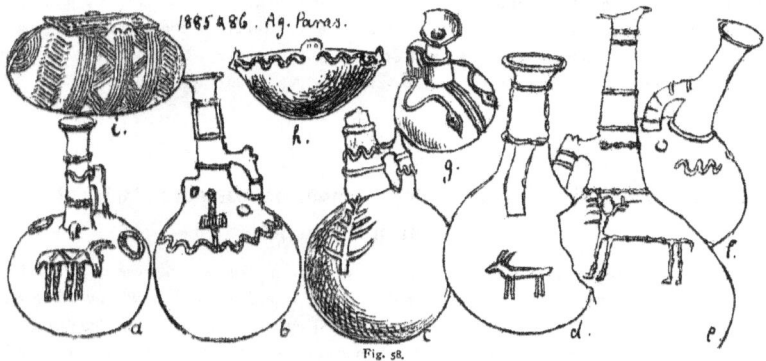

Fig. 58.

incised designs on the Trojan vase show just the same peculiarities as the designs in relief on these Cyprian vases of the Copper-Bronze Period, unearthed (in 1885) by myself, in Dümmler's presence, at Ayia Paraskevi near Nicosia.

Fig. 59 shows in the dimensions of the original the impression of a Cyprian seal-cylinder of

Fig. 59.

Fig. 60.

Fig. 61.

stone. A man stands in front of a large tree, probably to be regarded as holy. He holds in his left hand a branch, in his right hand a cresset, pole, cross or other utensil of worship. The rest of the space is occupied by the figures of four beasts. In regard to the Cyprian vases with reliefs, of which figs. 3, 18 and 58 exhibit specimens, Dümmler in his above-cited paper: "Die ältesten Ne-kropole auf Cypern"*) says that, while no exact parallels to them have hitherto been met with, yet a striking analogy to the linear style of the figure-designs is supplied by Trojan spinning whorls with engraved ornaments, and by a certain definite class of local-Cyprian cylinders. In the same paper**) he discusses the various groups of cylinders occurring in Cyprus, some manufactured in

*) Mittheilungen des Instituts zu Athen XI, p. 229.
**) Ibid, p. 242.

the island, others imported from abroad in ancient times. The conclusions he there reaches quite coincide with those at which I had myself arrived.*) As the first discoverer of these remarkable relief-vases of early date, so often exhibiting designs of trees, I had been led to devote considerable study to the subject of their relation to the cylinders and the classification of the latter. We must distinguished the Kyprian cylinders with rude and realistic designs not traceable to any definite originals (fig. 1 and 2) from the Babylonio-Assyrian (fig. 12) and Hittite

 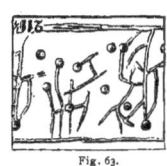 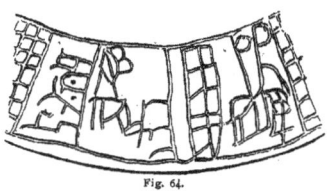

Fig. 62.   Fig. 63.   Fig. 64.

cylinders (fig. 5) on the one hand, and from the Kyprian cylinders copied from, or affected by, Babylonio-Assyrian originals (fig. 4) on the other. After Dümmler had quitted Cyprus, there were found in the necropolis of Ayia Paraskevi four cylinders and a clay spinning whorl with linear designs of figures which show still more striking analogies to the incised figures on Trojan cylinders, whorls, and vases and to those on a whet-stone from Troy. I therefor, for the sake of completeness, insert in this place the illustrations of these specimens, figs. 60—64. Only on one of the cylinders, No. 63, has a rude attempt been made to represent a human figure before a tree.

In Figs. 65—67 I reproduce from Schliemann's Ilios pictures of the incised designs on two vases (Nos. 1532 and 1533) and on a whet-stone (No. 1534). I think that the exhibition of such

Fig. 65. (Ilios 1532).

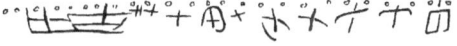

Fig. 66 (Ilios 1533).   Fig. 67 (Ilios 1524).

parallels is of permanent value, even though it be too early to come to a decision as to the ethnological position to be assigned to the peoples and civilizations in question.

Mykenae and Kypros.

Leaving Hissarlik-Troy we turn our steps to Mykenae itself. Here we are considerable nearer to the period in which the Homeric Poems were composed.

---

*) Furtwängler in his article "Gryps" in Roscher's Mythologisches Lexikon, col. 1753 also adopts my classification of Kyprian cylinders.

Fig. 68 represents one of the two identical pictures which decorate a vase found in Cyprus and already figured in more than one other work.*) It is a two-handled amphora, turned on the wheel, the very remarkable decorations being painted in glaze-colour, and belongs to the

Fig. 68.

Mykenaean class of vases. Most probably it was found in the same nekropolis at Ayia Paraskevi, from which comes the amphora with the procession of oxen illustrated above (fig. 10). We see to the right two men mounted on a biga; in front of the chariot are two other figures standing in what seems to be an attitude of adoration on either side of a tree to which we may confidently assign a holy character.

Figs. 69 and 70 show us, in the size of the originals, impressions of two stone cylinder-seals unearthed by the peasants in the necropolis of the Pre-Graeco-Phoenician Copper-Bronze Period

Fig. 69.

Fig. 70.

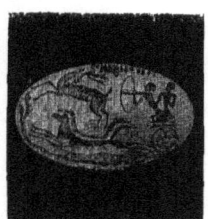

Fig. 71.

above the village of Kythraea and close to the great fountain of Kephalovrisi. On No. 69 stands a man in a long dress. He holds up his right hand as if taking an oath or offering a prayer; with his left hand he grasp the trunk of the holy tree. A couched quadruped, a bucranium, and a bird fill up the rest of the space. The identity in point of style of No. 70 is evident at the first glance;

*) Comp. Catalogue Barre, Pl. IV. Perrot IV, p. 715, No. 526. Furtwängler und Löschke, Mykenische Vasen, p. 28, fig. 16. Dümmler, Athen. Mittheilungen XI, p. 235.

I have accurately indicted in the drawings the similarity of the engraving and the outlines. The man, who in this case stands on a chariot drawn by a single horse, wears the same costume as the

Fig. 71.

man on No. 69; he looks in the same direction, his head is similarly formed, and his right hand is uplifted in the same manner. The chariot-driver is here himself the huntsman, or, perhaps, the presence of the missing huntsman is indicated by the bow and arrows. A stag, a small quadruped, and two birds represent his quarry.

No. 72 is an illustration of one of the gold rings*) discovered by Schliemann at Mykenae. The archer, standing on the chariot and bending forward, is in the act of releasing the arrow aimed at the stag, which here, owing to want of space, is placed above the two horses. The charioteer looks on. Either the more life-like scene on the Mykenaean gold ring is a free imitation of a corresponding variant of our Cyprian stone cylinder, or both one and the other go back to the same original.

Fig. 73 (after Menant**). We have here the impression of a chalcedony cylinder from the

Fig 73.

collection of the Duc de Luynes, which again reveals to us the same design that we have seen on the two preceding examples, the Cyprian cylinder (fig. 70) and the Mykenaean gold ring (fig. 72). The resemblances to the gold ring are especially striking and numerous. The forms, positions, and movements of the horse and of the large animal which is being pursued by the huntsman are in both cases strikingly similar; the manner in which this animal twists its neck round being especially noteworthy.

Fig. 71 exhibits on a larger scale one of the scenes from the series which decorate the vase excavated by me at Tamassos in 1885; two illustrations of

---

*) Schliemann, Mykenae, No. 334.
**) Recherches sur la Glytique Orientale (Paris 1886) II, p. 82, fig. 87. Hence our fig. 73. Lajard in his large book of plates "Mithra" engraves several variants of the same motive.

it, one showing the complete vase, have been given above (fig. 37 and 38). We see a lion-hunt among trees. The charioteer whips the horse up, while the archer, who here wears a sword in his belt and is also provided with a lance, gazes with a helpless and terrified air at the lion which is just in the act of charging. A fellow-sportsman on foot, approaching the lion from behind, is just about to catch it by the left ear with his right hand and to deal it a blow with the double hammer which he holds in his left hand. This man wears a small circular shield suspended on his left side.

Two trees (see the illustration in fig. 36) under each handle of the vase mark the limits of the picture. In Fig. 37 we made the acquaintance of the stag which stands under the trees on the left; in fig. 75 we see the two trees on the right surmounted by the double-handle of the vase. In this case a bird on the wing

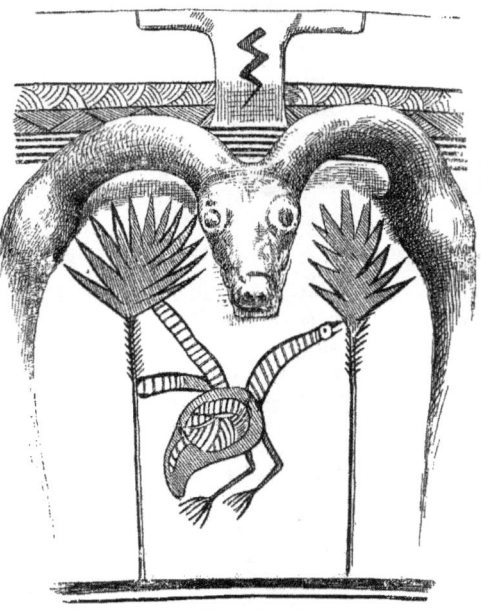

Fig. 74.

Fig. 75.

takes the place of the stag. It is drawn and characterized in the same manner as the bird of victory which is flying above the chariot.

The vase (cp. pages 37 and 38 above) is closely related to Schliemann's well-known vase with the procession of warriors. (fig. 74.) Here as in the case of the Tamassos vase, the double handles are formed by horned calves heads. Aquatic birds, remarkably similar in style to the Kyprian birds and heraldically grouped, are introduced in the vacant space beneath the handles. Even the concentric circles recall the form of the Kyprian concentric cirles. In the costumes, the form and outline of the figures, in the technique of the paintings, the choice of colours &c. the two craters show numerous points of contact. The band of contiguous groups of parallel curved lines, placed

---

*) Furtwängler und Löschke, Myk. Vasen (Berlin 1886) Pl. XLIII.

10

alternately bend-wise and bar-wise, which runs round the shoulder of the Tamassos vase is quite Mykenaean. See, for example, Furtwängler and Löschke, Mykenische Vasen, Pl. XXXVII. 380, Pl. XXXVIII, 393 and many others.

In Figs, 76 and 82 I give illustrations of a two-handled cup and the decorations on a funnel-shaped vase both found at Haliki in Attica.*) Beside these I place the series af designs from Cyprian cylinders (14—21) figured and discussed above, and I append (figs. 78—83) pictures of six further Cyprian objects. Fig. 78a and b and fig. 79a and b show the two engraved sides of two cubical, pierced steatite beads, or possibly small weights.**) Fig. 80 gives in the size of the original the impression of a steatite seal-cylinder.***) Three human figures in long robes join hands and seem to execute a ring-dance. The lower interstices between the figures are filled by two stars composed of dots, and a sun-disc with crescent; the upper interstices by two ox-heads surmounted by pellets, and a holy tree or blossoming bush. Fig. 81a and b is an illustration of a cylinder taken from A. P. di Cesnola's Salaminia p. 124, fig. 117. As Mr. Sayce in his description of it says, a man is represented standing between two holy trees. We again observe here the ox-head which plays the same prominent part on this group of Cyprian cylinders as on Mykenaean monuments. The design of this cylinder is exceedingly similar to that of the one published above as No. 69;†) the tree resembles those on the Mykenaean vases (figs. 82 and 83). Fig. 77 shows us a two-handled amphora, already illustrated on a smaller scale in Cesnola-Stern (Pl. XLII. 3).††) We observe behind the car a standing figure, obviously female,†††) and between her and the handle three flowering shrubs or trees. The vases figs. 76 and 82 (Haliki, Attica) and 77 (Ayia Paraskevi, Cyprus) belong to the bright-glazed Mykenaean class The painted representations of trees and bushes on this Mykenaean ware bear a quite surprising resemblance to the engraved designs on Cyprian stone cylinders and stone cubes. The engraved objects of stone and the painted vases come from the same find-stratum,′ as is amply evinced by the numerous discoveries of Mykenaean vases in the necropolis of Ayia Paraskevi. We observe the same, or a very similar, tree, prone or erect, on a Mykenaean vase from Ialysos,§) four trees of much the same type and two birds on a Mykenaean vase from Crete,§§) similar trees on Mykenaean vases from Haliki,§§§) Boeotia°) &c.

Fig. 83: Fragment of a Mykenaean vase from Charvati.°°) Two swans face each other with a tree, resembling a palmette, between them. Furtwängler and Löschke cite the cor-

---

*) Furtwängler and Löschke, Myk. Vasen (Berlin 1886) Pl. XVIII, 122 and Pl. XIX 134a.
**) From A. P di Cesnola's Salaminia p. 145, fig. 138 and Pl. XV. No. 61.
***) Ibid., Pl. XII, No. 9.
†) Cp. M. de Clerq et S. Menant, Antiquités Assyriennes (Paris 1888) Plate IV, figs. 30, 32 and 39.
††) Reproduced from Furtwängler and Löschke, Mykenische Vasen p. 29, fig. 17. Also in Perrot, Hist. de l'Art III, p. 714, fig. 525.
†††) She stands as if engaged in prayer with uplifted arms, an attitude of frequent occurrence both on Cyprian cylinder-seals from tombs and in Cyprian terracotta figures from sites of worship. The prayer seems to be addressed to the holy plants on the left. We should compare the adoration of the holy tree on the Mykenaean amphora from Cyprus, fig. 68 above.
§) Furtwängler and Löschke, Myk. Vasen Pl. IX, 53.
§§) Ibid. Pl. XIII, 81.
§§§) Ibid., Pl. XVIII, 124.
°) Ibid., Pl. XX, 142. P. Orsi has recently (1892) excavated at Paterno in Sicily a Mykenaean vase bearing a quite remarkable resemblance to our fig. 76.
°°) Ibid., p. 67, fig. 36.

Fig. 14.   Fig. 15.   Fig. 16.   Fig. 17.   Fig 18.   Fig. 19.   Fig. 20.   Fig. 21.

Fig. 76.

Fig. 77.

Fig. 14—21. 78—81. Antiquities from Kypros — Fig. 76, 77, 80 and 83. Mykenaean Vases from Haliki, Kypros and Charvati

a. Fig. 78 b.   a. Fig 79 b   Fig. 80.

Fig. 81.

Fig. 82.

Fig. 83.

10

responding groups on a Dipylon vase from Cyprus (Cesnola Stern Plate LXVIII) and an intaglio (Perrot and Chipiez III p. 641). Fig. 84 (a Cyprian vase with unpolished surface, here reproduced from Cesnola-Stern Pl. LXVIII), may also be compared. Beside it I place the paintings on a Mykenaean vase with unpolished surface (figs. 85—88).*) Let the character, style, and outlines of the Mykenaean be compared with those of the Cyprian birds on figs. 84, 37, 42 and 43 (the two last repeated here to facilitate comparison). Scarcely a half-year goes by without rendering its contribution towards the correct dating and resolution into definitely marked sub-sections of the Mykenaean Period of Art.**) Research into the origin and destribution of the Mykenaean civilization is still in a stage where the truest service we can render it is to gather new material: every new excavation by Flinders Petrie in Egypt or by Tsountas at Mykenae has taught us something fresh. But there is not a little still to be gained by reviewing and ordering the materials already made public. Cyprus, of a surety, contributes in no poor measure to the elucidation of Homer: the Cyprian silver paterae supply the best known analogy to the shield of Achilles as regards both the arrangement in concentric zones and the wealth and variety of the subjects represented. The author of that description must have had similar works of art before his eyes. Fresh collocations and comparisons, in themselves apparently insignificant, may yet create links which will take their place in the great chain of evidence. We will go on our way gathering and storing, conscious that our labour is not in vain: a great mosaic is formed of countless little bits not one of which must be missing.

3. Representations of trees, holy and profane, in Egypt and Cyprus.

The Bible and Homer have from all time pointed to Egypt as the repository of many of their secrets; but it is only during the last few decades—I might even say during the last ten years—that practical excavations, no longer directed to purposes of robbery but to the accurate observation of facts, have compelled her to utter them; with the result that to-day not only does much which formerly we could only perceive through the veil of traditionary lore stand revealed and, in many cases, confirmed to the letter before our eyes, but on many points our knowledge of things Egyptian is fuller than that of those who wrote the books of the Old Testament and the Homeric Poems. It is astonishing to see how few things there are of which Egypt is not the ultimate parent, be they motives employed in Art-handiwork and Art, or religious notions and representations. The early civilizations of Mesopotamia have of course also succeeded in making fashionable much that is peculiar to them, and nowhere is their influence more marked than in the province of Tree-worship. It is certainly true that the monuments from the cities on the Euphrates and Tigris testify to a much more developed Tree-worship, than those from the banks of the Nile. But even here

---

*) The form too of this Mykenaean vase is representative of a type peculiar at once to the early pottery of Mykenae and to a certain stratum in Cyprus. The distinction, a very vital one, is that in Cyprus aquatic birds never occur on hand-made vases of this paunched shape, while at Mykenae the reverse is the case.

**) Cp. W. M. F. Petrie: "The Egyptian bases of Greek History." in the Journal of Hellenic Studies Vol. XI (1890), p. 271—277 and Plate XV: Notes on the Antiquities of Mykenae. Ibid. vol. XII (1891) p. 199. (Petrie's conclusions are subjected to close criticism by Cecil Torr in the Classical Review 1892, p. 127): Steindorff's adress "Aegypten und die Mykenische Kultur" delivered at the Winckelmannsfeste 1891 and reported in the Berl. Phil. Wochenschrift 1892, Nos. 11 and 12.

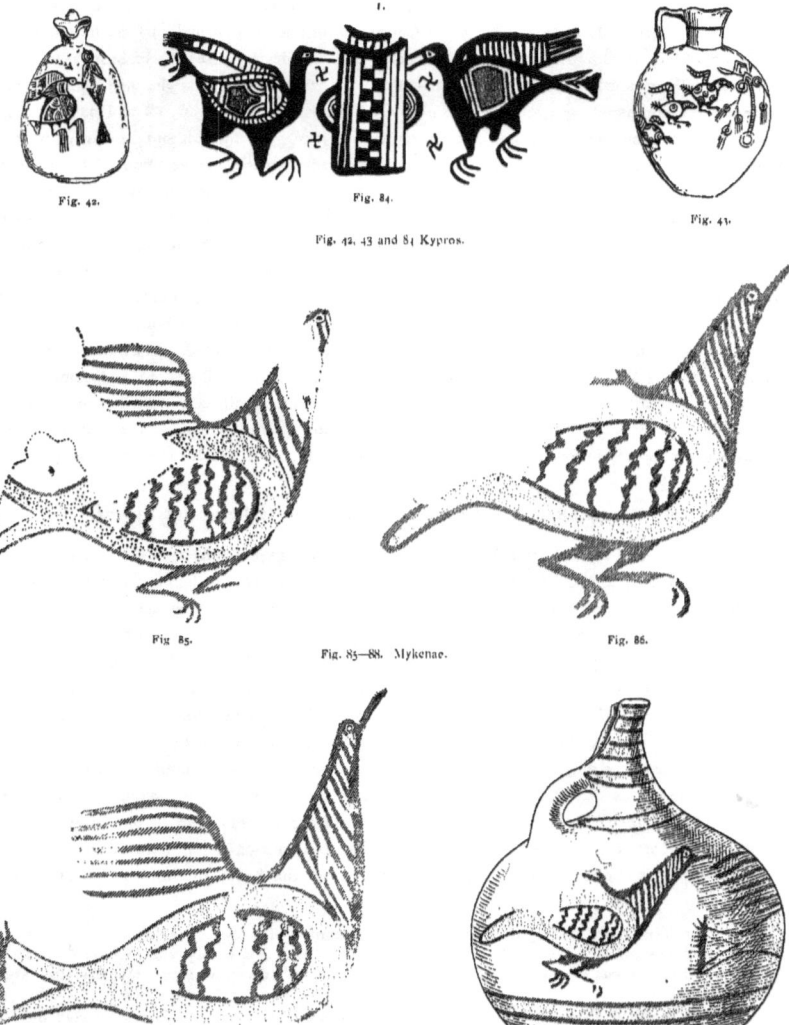

Fig. 42.

Fig. 84.

Fig. 43.

Fig. 42, 43 and 84 Kypros.

Fig. 85.

Fig. 86.

Fig. 85—88. Mykenae.

Fig. 87.

Fig. 88.

Egyptian mouments now contribute much more than they appeared to do some years ago, and not a year passes but supplies new material. We are indeed now in a position to say that very numerous elements and details of the decorative tree as a whole or of its parts which were supposed and still are supposed to be old-Assyrian or old-Babylonian creations, in reality came originally from Egypt, travelling to the Euphrates and Tigris just as they travelled to the Orontes, to Asia Minor, to the Greek islands and Greece itself—yes and even to more distant lands, to Italy, to the Italian islands, Sardinia and Sicily, and to Carthage. In many cases Egyptian creations may have been propagated through Mesopotamia; in others they were carried afield by the peoples of Syria and Asia Minor. More often, as the Egyptian hieroglyphic inscriptions told us long ago, their purveyors are the people of the "Great Green", the coast and island populations of the Lēvant; and not at all the least but perhaps, indeed, the most prominent part in this carrying trade must have been played throughout by the Kyprians. When we talk of Phoenicians, we must often understand there by Kyprian Phoenicians. That this was so is attested by the ancient remains and inscriptions and inevitable resulted from the island's geographical position and its wealth in timber and copper.

On the other hand it would seem that, with the beginning of the New Empire, certain representations of holy trees and certain arboreal ornaments did reach Egypt from other countries. At this time numerous Canaanitic words, names and worships begin to find their way into the language and life of Egypt; the griffin, it would seem, is now imported from the land of the Hittites in Northern Syria.*) Furtwängler has recently in his admirable study of the griffin**) exhibited these relations in the clearest light. It was he who, as long ago as 1879, in one of the notes in his "Bronzefunden von Olympia"***) called attention to the Egyptian elements in the Graeco-Phoenico-Kyprian decorative tree. He there expresses his dissent from the view of Helbig, who had, it may be too broadly, identified the Cyprian representations of trees with the holy trees on Assyrian reliefs; but, as the next section of this work will clearly show, Furtwängler has himself gone rather too far in stating emphatically (in the same Essay†) that the designs of trees on Kyprian antiquities have, as regards their ornamental elements, absolutely nothing to do with the Assyrian holy trees, but are Phoenician compositions built up out of purely Egyptian motives. We shall soon have occasion to see how the Kyprians is particular, the principal producers of the silver and bronze paterae with reliefs, found holy trees and a system of arboreal ornament existing not only in Egypt, but among the Mesopotamian peoples. Another hypothesis which the facts by no means exclude is that certain

---

*) Cp. E. Meyer. Geschichte des griechischen Alterthums, I, p. 257: A. Erman, Aegypten und aegyptisches Leben. (Tübingen 1885) I, p. 70. L von Sybel, Kritik des aegyptischen Ornaments (Marburg 1883).

**) A. Furtwängler's Essay "Gryps" in Roscher's Lexikon der griechischen und römischen Mythologie (Leipzig 1884) cols 1744 and 1751 et alibi.

***) Berlin 1880: (reprinted from the Abhandlungen der Königl. Akademie der Wissenschaften zu Berlin 1879.) p. 49, note 4.

†) Furtwängler very kindly tells me that at the present day he regards certain passages of the essay to which I have so frequently referred "Die Bronzefunde von Olympia" as antiquated, since superseded by a whole series of new archaeological discoveries. In 1891 the Imperial German Archaeological Institute brought out Furtwängler's magnificent illustrated work Olympia Bd. IV. " Die Bronzen." The text which accompanies the plates does not travel beyond brief explanations of these. Furtwängler, however, contemplates publishing a literary work dealing at large with the Olympian Bronzes. The work has been announced, and its speedy appearance is all the more to be desired in that Furtwängler is one of the best living connoisseurs of antique bronzes, and antique monuments generally.

of these motives found their way to Egypt from Kypros itself, or, if not from Kypros, from other adjacent regions in Syria or Asia Minor. There is much here which only further research can determine.*)

I open this section with the Tamarisk. While the Greeks and Romans regarded this tree as of evil omen,**) the Egyptians, like the Hebrews, reverenced it as holy. We may surmise that the tamarisk was also an object of adoration to the ancient inhabitants of Kypros. This cannot up to the present be de-
monstrated on the evidence of the monu- ments which have reached us; but the tree is reverenced by the modern Cypriots just as it is reverenced by the Arabs of to-day in Mesopotamia. A very beautiful example of a holy tree is given us by the Egyptian monument here il- lustrated***) in fig. 90. (Cp. Lepsius, Denk- mäler III 37a, 169). Ramses II is seated in front of the ancient holy tree, the tamarisk of Heliopolis, on which the gods are carving

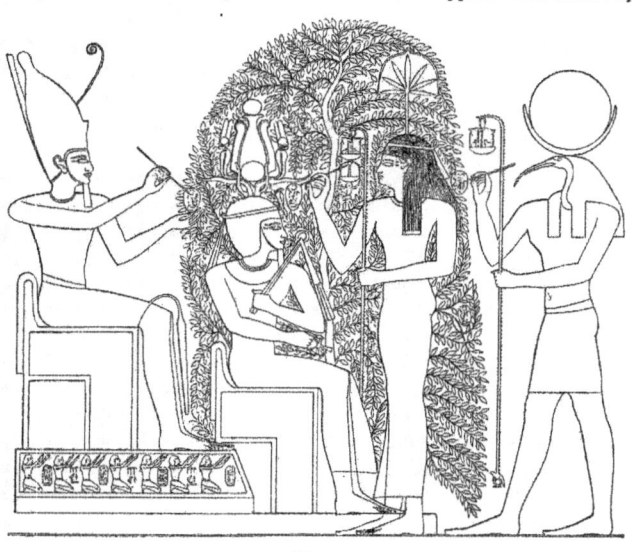

Fig. 90.

his name. Who can help recalling the wide-spread custom in northern and southern lands of cutting in the bark of a tree the name of a god or a beloved person?†) I am also reminded of a custom prevalent in Cyprus and the East (where the trees do not necessarily belong to the owner of the

---

*) Cp. especially L. von Sybel. Kritik des ägyptischen Ornaments.

**) Boetticher in his Baumkultus der Hellenen (Berlin 1856) p. 304, cites Pliny N. H. XVI, 108: XXIV 68 and Diodorus Fr. 12, 12. It may be worth-while mentioning (as perhaps tending to show that the tamarisk was a holy tree in Kypros, that Μυρίκη (tamarisk) seemingly took the place of Myrrha in one version of the Kinyras myth See Hesychins s v. μυρίκη.

***) Wilkinson's Manners and customs of the Ancient Egyptians, a new edition revised and corrected by Samuel Birch (London 1878), II, p. 164.

†) As is well known, the lover cuts his beloved's name in the bark of the May-tree which he sets up outside her door. As the custom of planting May-trees is already mentioned in documents of early medieval times (13th century), it is quite possible that it is not unconnected with the observances of ancient Oriental peoples. Cp. W. Mannhardt, Der Baumcultus der Germanen und ihrer Nachbarstämme (Berlin 1875) p. 160—163. For the custom of writing on trees among the Greeks and Romans, see Bötticher's Baumkultus, pages 52 and 53.

soil); every owner of a tree here puts his mark on it. The Egyptian wall-painting,*) fig. 90, comes from a small tomb at How (Diospolis Parva). The short hieroglyphic inscription attached to the picture tells us, as a fact, that the bird resting on the branches of the holy tamarisk means the soul of Osiris. The holy tree overshadows the tomb of Osiris, the bolted entrance-door of which is indicated on the picture. This holy bird of Osiris, the soul of Osiris, was called by the Egyptians

Benu and occurs in company with Osiris, as Benu-Osiris. This miraculous bird of fable, the Benu, with its strange myth, found its way into the Graeco-Roman world as the Phoenix.**) The worship of Osiris and Isis, carrying along

Fig. 90.   Fig. 91.

Fig. 92.

with it the worship of the tamarisk, migrated at an early date to Byblos and Kypros.

In the third volume of Wilkinson-Birch's work ***) a specimen is given of the series of sculptures in the sepulcral chamber dedicated to Osiris at Philae, representing the miraculous history of the god. The scene selected for illustration is the watering of the holy Osiris-Isis tamarisk (our fig. 91).

---

*) Wilkinson III, p. 349, No. 388.   Erman's Aegypten II, p. 368.
**) Riehm's Bibellexikon II, p. 1205.
***) III, p. 350, fig. 509.

On the left a priest holds a watering-can in each hand and pours their contents over the tree: the priest on the right is pouring water from one can only; his left hand grasps the Nile-key. At the foot of the tree a horned uraeus-snake darts forth. The picture in the tomb at How with the Dena-Osiris (fig. 90) and the picture in the tomb at Philae (fig. 91) are here placed side by side, and below them I have set the tracing, reduced from Plate XXI, of the paintings on a Cyprian vase. It looks as if the Cyprian vase-painter had combined both the Egyptian pictures into one. We see on the right two priests with cans in their hands, about to water the holy tree, on the left the phoenix-bird perched on the tree.

Flowers, bouquets, artificially composed trees, columns adorned with flowers or carved to resemble flowers played a great part in the religious and profane life of the Egyptians. Fig. 93 is taken from a painting of the nineteenth or twentieth Dynasty. We see a human figure (in our illustration only the two hands are given, the remainder of the figure being omitted owing to want of space) holding erect an enormous blossoming branch, the gigantic dimensions of which give it more the look of a tree. I take the engraving from Prisse d'Avenne's splendid work the Histoire de l'art Egyptienne, Tome II (Bouquets peints dans les hypogées). We have here before us evidently an object of worship or votive offering in the form of a huge artificial bouquet.*)

Such bouquets, sometimes of small size, sometimes larger, are very often seen in the hands of the figures on Cyprian vases. I will refer the reader for examples to the Vase-paintings on Plates XX (= XIX 2) and XIX 4, as well as to the relief on the Cyprian stone stele, Plate XXVI. 2.

The tree-column at the left edge of our figure 94 bears a still closer resemblance to the tree on the stone relief (Pl. XXVI, 2) to which reference has just been made. We see how the bouquet is gradually transformed into a tree, and this, in its turn, into a column. The picture with

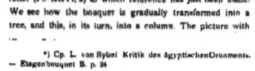

*) Cp. L. von Sybel Kritik des ägyptischenOrnaments. — Etagenbouquet S. p. 34

the holy Nile-boat of which fig. 94 is an illustration dates from the reign of King Amenophis III, who is now placed circa 1440—1400 B. C.*)

Fig. 95 shows a mural painting of an Egyptian house and its garden.**) We shall have occasion to discuss this house in greater detail when we come to deal with Cyprian architecture. The roof of the house is supported by columns, which seem in form to imitate growing trees. In the garden, visible to the left, we see first, in the upper section, a vine trained on a trellis supported by columns, flanked on either side by a cypress. In the lower sections of the garden stand two fruit-trees, one of which is clearly characterized as a pomegranate. In fig. 96 I reproduce this pome-

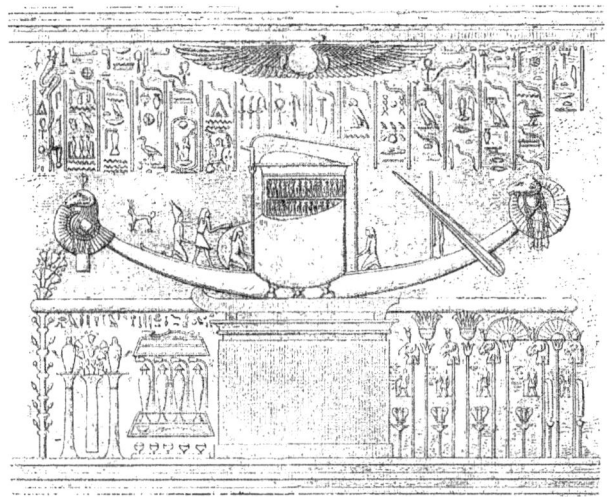

Fig. 94

granate tree***) from the mural painting, placing by its side for purposes of comparison (fig. 97) the relief in stone of a pomegranate tree taken from one of the numerous Carthaginian votive stelae now in the Bibliothéque Nationale in Paris. We see at the first glance that the Carthaginian sculptor must have worked directly from Egyptian models, the hypothesis of any transmission through other peoples of peculiarities of motive or style being here obviously inadmissible. The Carthaginian tree is a formal copy of the Egyptian original. Perrot, who in his Histoire de l'Art†) was the first to

---

*) For the correct dating of this and other Egyptian and Oriental monuments I am indebted to Herr G. Steindorff managing-assistant in the Egyptian and Oriental Department of the Royal Museum, Berlin. I have already in the Introduction expressed my thanks to this excellent and very amiable scholar for his kind cooperation.

**) Rosellini. I monumenti dell' Egitto e della Nubia. Pisa 1832. M. C. Plate LXVIII. = Erman's Aegypten I. p. 250 = Perrot et Chipiez II, p. 453, fig. 256.

***) A separate cut of it is given also in Wilkinson-Birch I, p. 376, No. 148.

†) Vol. III, p. 460, fig. 335: hence our figure 94.

publish this Carthaginian stele, is of opinion that the pomegranate here is not copied from a foreign model but drawn from nature.

It was only necessary for him to turn over the leaves of the first volume of his own monumental work, the Histoire de l'Art, to find on page 453 (fig. 256) this very wall-painting and in it, attracting the eye by the charm of its design, the pomegranate tree, the original, earlier by many centuries, of the Carthaginian imitation. The contours so delicately drawn by the Egyptian artist have met with a relatively rude and stiff rendering at the hands of the Carthaginian stone-mason. It is true that the leaves, roughly added on the Carthaginian relief, are absent from the Egyptian original, but the Egyptian artist has shown how well and truly he could draw leaves and tendrils by his rendering of the trellissed vine on the same picture, which is as graceful as it is full of realistic detail. Probably the Carthaginian imitator had before him other Egyptian pictures of pomegranate trees in leaf. What I would particularly call attention to is the different use made of the pomegranate tree in the two cases. On the Egyptian painting it is an accessory of the landscape, one of the objects which combine to form the picture of the garden attached to a mansion, while on the Cartha-

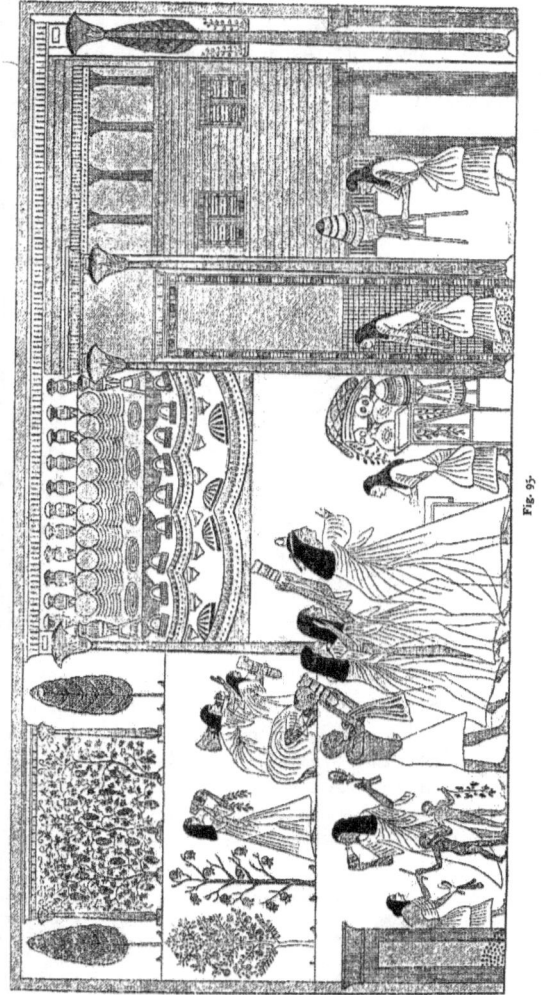

Fig. 95.

ginian relief it stands alone. Though, perhaps, even here, the decorative impulse is a factor which we should take into some account, we must yet understand this tree to be a symbol charged with that

11*

deep religious significance which it carried among the peoples of the East. In Cyprus it was Aphrodite herself who planted the pomegranate (according to the comic poet Antiphanes quoted by Athenaeus III, p. 84 c.); it was sacred to Adonis, and it is interwoven in the theogonic myths of Phrygia.*)   In the temenos of Aphrodite at Dali described above on page 5 (No. 3 in my

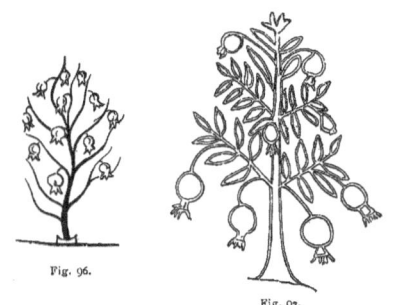

Fig. 96.

Fig. 97.

list**), I found, among thousands of other votive offerings,***) a model of a pomegranate, about the size of a real one, in terracotta, with which the terracotta pomegranates found in tombs at Nola in Campania and first published by Gerhard†) may be instructively compared. And many of the crouching figures of the youthful Tammuz-Adonis-Kinyras which were dedicated in such very great numbers in the Kyprian shrines both of Astarte-Aphrodite and of Rešef-Apollo hold in their hands, not only flowers, doves and pine-cones, but, among other fruits, the pomegranate.

After the lotus, papyrus, tamarisk, and pomegranate, the cypress is the tree most prominent on Egyptian monuments.   It seems to have been the sacred tree of the god Min, the god of luxu-

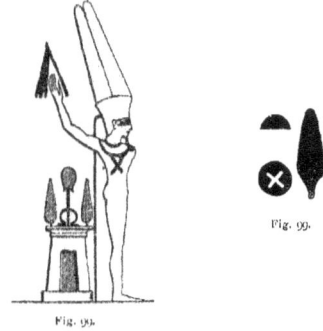

Fig. 99.

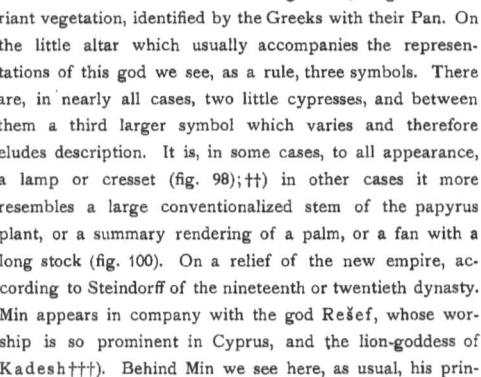

Fig. 99.

riant vegetation, identified by the Greeks with their Pan. On the little altar which usually accompanies the representations of this god we see, as a rule, three symbols. There are, in nearly all cases, two little cypresses, and between them a third larger symbol which varies and therefore eludes description. It is, in some cases, to all appearance, a lamp or cresset (fig. 98);††) in other cases it more resembles a large conventionalized stem of the papyrus plant, or a summary rendering of a palm, or a fan with a long stock (fig. 100). On a relief of the new empire, according to Steindorff of the nineteenth or twentieth dynasty. Min appears in company with the god Rešef, whose worship is so prominent in Cyprus, and the lion-goddess of Kadesh†††).   Behind Min we see here, as usual, his principal attribute, a little altar with its symbols (as in fig. 98), the two little cypresses and between them

---

*) Cp. Engel, Kypros, I, p. 62: Hehn, Kulturpflanzen und Hausthiere (Berlin 1883), p. 193.   For the pomegranate see also "Journal Asiatique" X, (Paris 1877), pages 224—225 and 236. Clermont-Ganneau. "Le dieu Satrape".

**) Cp. the Explanations of Plates II 36, VII, X 7, XIII, XVI &c.

***) The catalogue, comprising only specimens in good preservation, extends to 575 numbers.

†) Denkmäler und Forschungen (1850) No 5. 14. 15.

††) Wilkinson. Vol. I, p. 405, fig. 174. In Vol. III. p. 24 &c. the cult of this god is full described.

†††) Of the Goddess of Kadesh I will speak in the section of this work dealing with that Hittite influence through which so many strange elements in Art, Civilisation, and Worship (e. g. the griffin) reached both

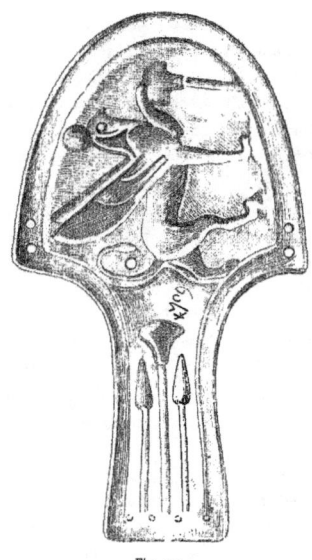

Fig. 101.

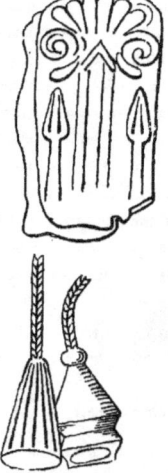

Fig. 102.

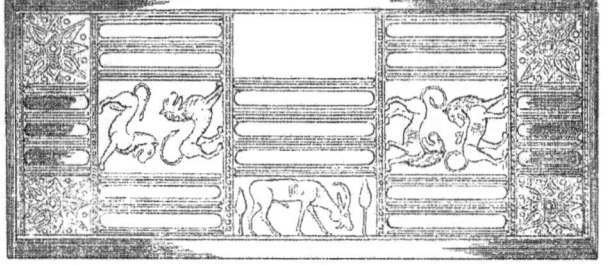

Fig. 100.

Fig. 103.

the taller tree which I should in this case describe either as a gigantic papyrus-stalk, or, more probably, a conventionalized palm. I have (fig. 99) placed close to fig. 98 a group of hieroglyphs taken from Wilkinson-Birch. The symbol on the right is a tree (possibly representative of Min's two cypresses); the two symbols on the left represent a cup viewed in the one case from above, in the other from the side. This cup is supposed to signify "Land", and the whole group of hieroglyphs is thus interpreted as "Land of trees," "Land of Egypt". When I come to discuss the custom of dedicating vessels in the Cyprian holy groves, I will, in dealing with the very instructive Egyptian parallels to this custom, recur to the question of the real significance to be attached to this group of hieroglyphs.

Fig. 101 shows us the portion of a cuirass which I have already mentioned above on p. 14 in my discription of the sites of worship. Even without the presence of the griffin, who is conceived quite in accordance with Egyptian canons of taste*), the group of trees, simply copied, as it is, from the groups which surmount the altars of Min, would not admit of our doubting that Egyptian influence is here very strong. The cuirass-fragment is Kyprio-Graeco-Phoenician, and comes from the sanctuary of the Anat-Athene of Idalion. Very instructive also are the fragments of a woman's girdle of metal, unearthed by me in 1889 for the Berlin Museum from a tomb at Tamassos the date of which can be fixed in the 6th century B.C. I have already described this girdle above on page 52 and I here (fig. 10?) reproduce, in the size of the originals, three of the most important fragments. We see (1) two of the little silver bells which hang from the girdle by chainlets of electron and (2) a portion of gilded silver-foil on which a high column with its capital, the whole suggested by the palm-tree, stands between two little cypresses. The Cyprian artist has slavishly adhered to the form and style of his originals, the tree groups of the Min worship as rendered in Egyptian art. Fig. 103 shows, also in the dimensions of the original, one of the gilded silver plaques belonging to the clasp of the silver girdle from Poli tis Khrysokhou discussed above on pages 50—52. The whole has been restored as far as possible, one of the fields being purposely left unoccupied, as it was impossible to make sure from the existing fragments that this field contained the same design as that opposite to it, viz. a quadruped feeding between two cypresses. With these cypresses the reader should compare the two cypresses to the right and left of the vine in the garden of the Egyptian house on our figure 95.**)

We shall see in another place how much the Cyprian goldsmiths and silversmiths have learnt from their Egyptian fellow-craftsmen. Here, in fig. 104, I give an illustratian of the beautiful golden bracelet of the Egyptian prince Psar. It is worked in cloisonné enamel of many hues and we are captivated by the marvellous colour-effect. But in drawing, style and delicacy of execution this

Egypt and Kypros. In Roscher's Mythol. Lexikon (Art. Astarte col. 653) the middle part of our figure 100 is reproduced and interpreted as Astarte.

*) That griffins in particular, either alone or with trees, appear on cuirasses and other pieces of mail both in Egypt and Kypros, is not without its special reason See Oscar Montelius, Bronsåldern i Egypten (1888) p. 21, fig. 3. Cp. also Furtwänglers essay "Gryps" in Roscher's Lexikon der griechischen und römischen Mythologie, col. 1744. We are reminded of the dragons on the cuirass which Agamemnon received as a gift from the Kyprian King Kinyras.

**) Dümmler in the Jahrbuch of 1888—89 pointed out the Egyptian origin of the star-rosettes in the corners of these plaques. The same is true of the cypresses and groups of trees (on figs. 101—102).

gorgeous product of Egyptian goldsmith's art falls considerably below the standard of older works.*) Indeed it almost seems as if the Egyptian craftsman, anxious to strengthen his own hackneyed repertory by the introduction of some novelty or to produce an imitation of popular imported wares, had worked from foreign models. It is even possible that he may have counterfeited the rude style and rough workmanship of these imported articles of adornment. Steindorff would place the Egyptian bracelet in the 19ᵗʰ Dynasty, which is now taken to cover the period between circa 1400 and circa 1270 B. C. In the illustration I have had the red colour indicated by dots, the green by horizontal and the blue by vertical lines. Two griffins are heraldically seated on either side of a holy tree of more or less pronouncedly conventional form. The bracelet consists of two portions connected by hinged fastenings constructed on the same principle as those which unite the plates of our Cyprian girdle from Poli tis Khrysokhou. In order that the reader may have before his eyes the means of instituting between these

Fig. 104.

Fig 105

two objects a comparison which cannot fail to throw light on the history of Art and Worship, I here reproduce once more, in the size of the original, a portion of the silver girdle as restored (fig. 105).

*) Maspero has recognized this and expressed himself to this effect in his Egyptian Archaeology (p. 322 of Miss Edward's translation). The Theban bracelet in the Louvre, figured by Perrot III fig. 598, where the style of the work is similar, belongs to the same period. The holy trees here, although somewhat more elaborate, are composed of similar members, and one of them is adored by a griffin of the same thick-set form. Perrot correctly compares the cloisonnés enamels of the Egyptian goldsmiths with Cyprian work in the same technique. On one of the Plates of the present work I reproduce a splendid specimen of Kyprio-Hellenic work, a bracelet inlaid with cloisonné enamel which I unearthed in 1886 in the same necropolis whence comes the silver girdle, fig. 105. The original is in the Clerq collection in Paris.

In Maspero's Egyptian Archaeology p. 322 fig. 299 will be found another view of Prince Psar's bracelet showing the hinges. The bracelet is composed of two pieces of unequal lengths. On the longer piece (about two thirds of the whole circle) here shown (after Prisse d'Avenne) in figure 104, stands the holy tree, as above described, between the two griffins*); on the shorter piece (about one third of the circle) one griffin only sits in front of the tree. The two narrow terminal

plaques of the Cyprian silver girdle, to which the long plaques forming the clasp (fig. 102 shows us one of these) were attached, bear, it is true, not winged griffins but winged sphinxes; but the manner in which these sphinxes sit on either side of the holy tree**) is full of interest when we place them side by side with the design on the larger and principal piece of the Egyptian bracelet, and griffins occur on other parts of our Cyprian jewel***)

Fig. 106

Fig. 106 represents a painted and inlaid casket from a Theban tomb.†) On the narrow face we see a tree treated in the same conventional fashion

Fig. 52 a

Fig. 52 b

as those on the Egyptian and Cyprian pieces of jewellery, figures 103 and 104. Two goats standing on their hind-legs are browsing on its leaves. Compare the goats which are clambering up the holy

---

*) The same tree is summarily described as a "Phoenician bouquet" by von Sybel, Aegyptisches Ornament, p. 25 and Plate III E.

**) I had only so much of the holy tree drawn as is well preserved and clear in outline; and in the drawing of all the other details of the girdle I have followed the same rule. It is evident that the pairs of griffins, in all the cases in which they occur, were identically formed, and not unlike the griffins on our Plate XXV. i. e. with beaks agape and knobs on their foreheads. In some places the silver-oxide and earthy matter had so closely coagulated with the metal, that, in spite of the most diligent and careful cleaning, the exudations and foreign substances could not be removed. The plaques were on the whole in relatively good preservation, but in some places the outlines had been destroyed and were no longer determinable. The illustration in the text is directly reproduced by the photo-zincographic process from the original drawing made with the most conscientious care by Mr. E Foot, a very skilled draughtsman. We see (beginning from the right) the first pair of griffins in its entirety and half of the second. The first griffin of the first couple is drawn as if its beak were closed. In the case of this plate and its griffins it was impossible to detect accurately the original outlines, and here the artist has drawn simply what he could see. For all details as to the griffin and his kinds I would refer the reader to Furtwängler's admirable article "Gryps" in Roscher's Lexikon der griechischen und römischen Mythologie, cols 1742—1777.

***) The style of these Cyprian griffins on my silver girdle certainly comes nearer to the archaic-Greek type established for all time by Furtwängler's industry and insight. They have knobs on their foreheads.

†) After Wilkinson-Birch II, p. 200, No. 399, fig. B.

Fig. 107.

Fig. 103.

12

tree on the Kurion silver patera, fig. 52, and the goats standing on either side of the tree on the vase-paintings Plate XIX, 1 and Plate LXI.

Related in some measure to the design on the Theban basket and still more nearly approaching the corresponding Cyprian designs are the paintings·on a little gold basket, already often described and figured in archaeological works.*) It comes from the tomb of Ramses III, and its date is accordingly the middle of the 13th century B. C. In figures 107 and 108 I reproduce from Prisse d'Avenne the engravings of two sides ʹof this remarkable basket and repeat on the opposite page (fig. 52a and b) two portions of the engraving of the Kurion patera given above in fig. 52. In spite of diversities in style, we detect at a glance the striking relationship which subsists between the groups of two goats with the holy tree between them on the Egyptian (fig. 107) and· Cyprian (fig. 52a) works respectively. No less obvious is the relationship between the Egyptian picture of the griffin among realistically formed trees and plants, and Cyprian pictures of the same creature now engaged in combat with men under the shadow of cypresses,**) now ranged in heraldic attitude on either

Fig. 109

side of the holy tree (fig. 52b).***) While the griffins on the left are by their position characterized as armorial animals, symbolical of something, the griffin on the right is a real wild beast dwelling in a forest of cypress-trees and meeting his doom there at the hands of the man or hero his antagonist: Of his kindred is the griffin whom on the golden basket from Ramses III's tomb, we see careering through the forest dells, but the great amulet which is hung round this monster's neck points to the possibility that he bears, in part at least, some sacral significance. The griffins on the Cyprian silver bowls, with their top-knots. betray a perhaps not very pronounced Egyptian influence; certainly, if we come to classify them, they fall under Furtwängler's Egyptian griffin-type.

The silver patera, fig. 52, apart from ʹthe subject of the man fighting with a beast, is perfectly free from the direct agency of Assyrian influences. It belongs to that sub-class of Cyprian work in silver, which, were not the designation too long, one might best style Kyprio-Graeco-Egyptian (the Phoenician element being comprised in the Kyprian.)

On other Egyptian monuments the manner in which conventional trees or groups of plants and schemes of animals heraldically posed on either side of such trees are introduced leaves no doubt that their useʹ is a purelyʹ decorative one. A short description of two examples will suffice. In Wilkinson-Birch, vol. I, .p. 383, fig 159 we see a picture of a vintage. On the left are two baskets full of grapes, one above the other; next is a group of two men, ʹone of whom (the taller) is lifting

---

*) L. von Sybel (Aegypt. Ornament, p. 25 and III D) and Furtwängler (in the article "Gryps" to which repeated reference has been made) cite the decorations on this gold basket (they are, it is to be presumed, in low relief.)

**) Cited and figured by Furtwängler in Roscher's Lexikon col. 1757.

***) Described by Furtwängler (ibid.) who styles the holy tree an Egyptian vegetable ornament. In the section on Mesopotamia I hope to give further proof of the holy character of some of those Cyprian groups to which Furtwängler assigns a purely decorative significance. At present I simply call attention to Plates XIX 1, XXI and LXI and figures 89, 90, 97—99.

from the head of the other shorter man on the right another basket. To the right we see a vine the clusters of which have been plucked, and on either side of it a goat, standing on its hind-legs tries to nibble the topmost twigs. The two goats are in heraldic position, just like those which stand on either side of the holy tree in fig. 109.

In the second volumne of the same work (p. 102, no. 361)*) we find an illustration of a mural painting comprising two scenes. On the left the artist has represented the capture of winged game, on the right that of fish. He has separated the two scenes by a compound tree the conventional construction of which resembles that of many of those compound trees which seem to serve purposes of worship or are to be directly explained as mystic holy trees like the holy tree of the Assyrians.

We have certainly found sufficient ground for asserting that Tree-worship played a not unimportant part in Egyptian life, and that favourite subjects of Egyptian religious Art, such as, for example, the groups of trees on the altars of Min, were carried to Cyprus. But all that the material already adduced enables us to conclude is that the Egyptian motive was adopted, with slight local modifications, by Cyprian artists and decorators, on account of its ornamental value, its religious significance being neglected and finally lost. In the chapter on the Ashera and the relation of the Hebrew and Canaanitic worships to the Cyprian I shall be able to show that tree-idols of indisputably religious nature were fabricated in Cyprus and set up in its holy groves. It is not advisable, unless urgent proof be forthcoming, to follow von Sybel (Kritik des aegyptischen Ornamentes) in styling as Phoenician diverse objects found at Mykenae and in Egypt. (See Note 1 on the following page.)

4. The holy and profane tree on Babylonian and Assyrian monuments compared with the Kyprian.

Now that we know at how early a period cuneiform characters and Babylonio-Assyrian idioms formed even in Egypt the recognised medium through which diplomatic intercourse with foreign nations was held, we must make up our minds that much more than was suspected in Egyptian Art and Civilization will be found to be not original but borrowed, retraceable to forms and ideas matured in a world far from the banks of the Nile. As Erman in the Introduction to his admirable work "Aegypten und ägyptisches Leben im Alterthum"*) had already hinted, it would indeed seem that ancient Babylonia can furnish us with monuments of a higher antiquity than any which Egypt has produced.**)

---

*) Prisse d'Avenne, hist. de l'art égypt. 2 pl. 84; Wilkinson, manners and customs 3² 312; Erman, Aegypten I, p. 329; Gerhard hist. acad disc. Atlas pl. 9, 1.

**) P. 4.

***) Taking as a basis the famous Turin Papyrus (see Erman's Aegypten p 62) we must, according as we follow Erman, E. Meyer, Lepsius, or Brugsch place king Snefru, the first ruler of the Old Kingdom in Egypt of whose deeds we have any record, circa 2800, 2830, 3124 or 3766 B. C. Within the two extremes the arguments for one date are neither more nor less plausible than for another The oldest known fact of Babylonian history, the reign of Sargon (of Akkad) would seem, since the publication by Pinches in the Proceedings of the Society of Biblical Archaeology Nov 7th 1882) of the cylinder of Nabûnâhid to remount to circa 3800 B. C. This king as we know, reigned in Babylon from 555 to 539 B. C., and in the inscription on the cylinder he places the date of Naram-Sin son of Sargon I 3200 years before his own reign i. e. circa 3750 B. C. (See E. Meyer Geschichte des Alterthum's I, p. 161).

Under these circumstances we may look forward to detecting traces of a primitive intercourse between the two civilizations dating from times we know not how remote. Egypt gave to Babylon and received in return. At times it will be beyond the bounds of possibility to decide which was first the giver or the receiver of the gift; to which of the two lands the original parentage of much that meets us both must finally to be assigned. A closer treatment of these questions lies outside the plan of the present work. More than this, comparative Ethnography continues to teach us ever more convincingly from day to day how different peoples may indenpedently arrive at modes of expression, for which in the past, and until quite lately, we have been inclined to assume a common source. For this or other reasons it may never be possible to point to the origin of certain ideas, ritual usages, and artistic types. In other cases it may be only the fragmentary character of the monumental tradition now at our disposal which makes it impossible to attain to certainty at the present day. To take one instance from many. The still disputed question "What is properly speaking Phoenician, specifically Phoenician, pure old Phoenician?" can never receive a satisfactory or final answer until we have excavated in Phoenicia itself Phoenician tombs of undisputed antiquity and, if possible, capable of being exactly dated within certain limits.*) In the course of the last few decades archaeological research in the countries watered by the Euphrates and Tigris has made vast progress. But much is still unexplored, especially in the matter of Glyptic, that great world of craftsmanship which has not only of late, but for many years previous to the dawn of the new epoch initiated by Sir Henry Layard's discoveries, continued to furnish to our public and private collections such great numbers of the products of its successive stages of development. It is in the main the little stone seal-cylinders which are the objects of our immediate concern here. On most of them designs alone are incised; in some rare cases inscriptions are added. Accurate classification, chronological or otherwise, of the whole mass will only be rendered possible by further comprehensive excavations. In the case of many cylinders we unfortunately do not know under what circumstances or where they were found.**)

I open the series with Fig. 110, the design (magnified to rather more than twice the actual size) on a black jasper cylinder-seal in the British Museum.***) It would appear to belong to that class of archaic Babylonian cylinders which is, for the present at least, assigned to the 3rd millen-

---

*) The expedition for the exploration of Phoenicia conducted by Renan, brought to light for the most part only empty tombs or tombs of late date. Such finds as can be dated scarcely reach further back than the middle of the fourth century B. C. In Phoenicia everything is yet to do. A rich and hitherto quite unknown civilization, extending over a period of 1000 years or more, and attaining to a high stage of early development awaits the hand of the lucky excavator. As I first found in Cyprus whole series of Graeco-Phoenician tombs reaching back to the 10th century B. C. or earlier, tombs the date and character of which I was able to establish, I might be in a position to reach similar results over in Syria.

**) G. Perrot (Hist. de l'art II, pages 676 and 677) discusses Ménant's Recherches sur la Glyptique Orientale, and condemns Ménants classification as, in his own opinion, too detailed. Since then Ménant has, partly in articles scattered in various Periodicals (e. g. the American Journal of Archaeology) and partly in Clercq's magnificent and exemplary volume (see next page), recorded his latests results, which, in view of the very unsatisfactory character of much of our information as to "provenance," must be styled far the best work yet done in the difficult province of Oriental and Babylonio-Assyrian glyptic. Many matters of detail will doubtless have to be corrrected by the light of accurate information as to finds and of fresh excavation, but Ménant's work will always retain its value as the foundation of an enduring structure.

***) F. Lajard, Recherches sur le culte du cyprès. Paris 1854. Pl. IX, 2.

nium B. C. We see in the middle a cypress. To the left Eabani, the Chaldaean hero, is engaged in combat with an erect lion*); to the right are two man-headed horned bulls facing each other armorially in a half-erect position.

In fig. 111 I give in the dimensions of the original the impression of a concave cylinder of light-green jasper found in Cyprus. I was unable to learn with any certainty from what site in the island it comes, but we should be perhaps right in stating its "provenance" to be probably the necropolis of Ayia Paraskevi near Nicosia, in which I unearthed the cylinder (later it is true by several centuries) with cuneiform inscription figured above on p. 35 (Fig. 35). This rare specimen still remains at Nicosia in the collection (to which frequent reference has already been made) of my learned friend Mr. Evstathios Konstantinides, Director of schools. To the left is placed

Fig. 110

Fig. 111.

the single line of script. In the centre a branch seems to issue from a winged sun-disc. Above this, as well as in the corners to the rear of the groups, other branches are introduced. At two thirds of the height of the cylinder an arboreal ornament intersects the whole design. The two lions springing at each other are held back by two heroes. The two groups are symmetrically placed in regard to each other and to the tree on the one hand and the column or band containing the inscription on the other. The hero on the right is Izdubar, he on the left Eabani; they are the Herakles and Theseus of Chaldaean mythology. Mr. Sayce to whom I sent impressions of this cylinder in 1886 read on it the name of the royal scribe of King Sargon I of Accad, whom he places in 3800 B. C.**) Whether Sayce's reading and dating be accepted by other Assyriologists or not, we have in any case before us a very old Babylonian monument, certainly not later than the third millennium B. C. Fig. 110 obviously belongs to the same period. This is evinced by the style, arrangement, subject and treatment. The beautiful marble or porphyry cylinder of the Metropolitan Museum of Art in New York which Perrot publishes in the second volume of his History of Art,***) and rightly appraises so highly, although of a much more finished technique than these two, yet furnishes an

---

*) Eabani, Izdubar's companion has, as we know, the lower extremities of a bull, the body and head of a man with long horns.

**) Sayce wrote to me on the 29th of December 1886 as follows: "We know now that Naram-Sin and his father Sargon of Accad reigned B. C. 3800 instead of in the 16th century B. C. . our cylinder with the name of the royal scribe, which the society of Biblical Archaeology is going to publish, is of the age of Sargon (B. C. 3800) — Unfortunately a fire subsequently broke out in Queens' College Oxford, where Mr. Sayce resides. The impressions of this cylinder and Mr Sayce's manuscript on the subject perished, as well as an illustrated report of excavations which I had forwarded to him and the loss of which cannot be supplied.

***) p. 675 fig. 332.

instructive parallel to them as regards mythological matter and motive and is not, in all probability, very far removed from them in point of time.*)

In old Babylonian times the part played by the cypress as a holy tree seems to have been as important as subsequently among the Phoenicians, Syrians and Kyprians, and among the people of Palmyra even in Roman times. As I devote a special section to the cypress, I reserve the Chaldaean examples of this tree for that place.

Next in point of importance to the cypress comes the palm, of which we find isolated examples on old-Babylonian cylinders. I here reproduce (fig. 112) the impression of a cylinder (of

Fig. 112.

talc or haematite) which F. Lajard has by mistake inserted among his cypress-designs.**) The original is in the British Museum. The manner in which the trunk is drawn shows that the tree is meant for a palm. The coronal too, although too small for a normal palm, bears much more resemblance to a palm-top than to a cypress-top, and instances of palms in nature with small coronals are by no means uncommon. We see a priest or god seated by the holy tree before a columnar altar or other object of worship from the summit which wing-like appendages issue. In his left hand he holds up a bowl. The crescent in the field above the bowl is part of the ordinary sacral apparatus of Chaldaea. On the other side of the column, opposite the seated figure, stands a man. In front of the column lies an ox, perhaps the victim. Both figures grasp a long garland of twisted twigs or a myrtle-rope like those still plaited in the East and used to string together the buckets of draw-wells. The seated figure holds one end of the rope fast with one hand, while the standing figure has both hands employed in twisting the other end,***) perhaps, as his attitude would indicate, with the intention of passing it round the altar, column, or gate (?). This is just the way in which myrtle-ropes are now plaited in the East. Palm-branches richly decorated and plaited with extraordinary art, the single fronds being passed through each other and coloured ribbons inserted, play at the present day, as of old, a great part in oriental festivals, e. g. among the orthodox Greeks. Indeed

--- ------

*) Cp. also Clercq-Ménant, Antiquités Assyriennes Nos 41—81. On No. 51 there, also concave (like our fig. 111) and with a similar archaic Babylonian inscription giving the name of a scribe of the same royal house of Accad (Agade), Eabani and a lion are represented in the same position as the two heroes and lions on fig. 111. Eabani there grasps the rearing lion under the belly with one hand and by the tail with the other. Cp. also Ménant, Recherches sur la Glyptique Orientale I, p. 71—91.

**) Plate IX, fig. 5 = the same authors "Culte de Mithra," Plate XVIII, 2.

***) We have to do with the representation of an act of worship of frequent recurrence in Old Babylon. On a cylinder of the same age in Lajards' Mithra (Pl. XVIII, 1) we see the same motive slightly re-cast. Here the throned figure already grasps the ox of sacrifice by one horn. The ministrant on the other sides is in a squatting position, a favourite attitude at the present day in which to twist myrtle-ropes The winged object of worship in the centre and the myrtle-rope are here again; but the tree is absent. Instead of the crescent moon the sun-disc floats above the group. On later Assyrian cylinders (e. g. Perrot II fig. 343) we frequently see ropes descending from the winged sun-disc on to the holy tree and grasped by the figures who stand beneath. At the present day it is a custom among the Greeks of the island of Cyprus to twist a long rope of cotton and pass it several times round the roof and tower of the church. It is left there for months, and then removed by the priests and their acolytes, with the same ceremony which accompanied its attachment. This holy cotton is then made into wicks for the church candles.

many of these plaited Easter palm-branches very much resemble the mystic trees on Assyrian monuments. To judge from its style, technique, and design, this specimen also belongs to the group of archaic Babylonian cylinders.

Fig. 113 exhibits the impression of a cylinder in the Cabinet des médailles at The Hague (Cat. 139—109) considered by Ménant to be archaic-Assyrian.*) Two griffins stand as if in

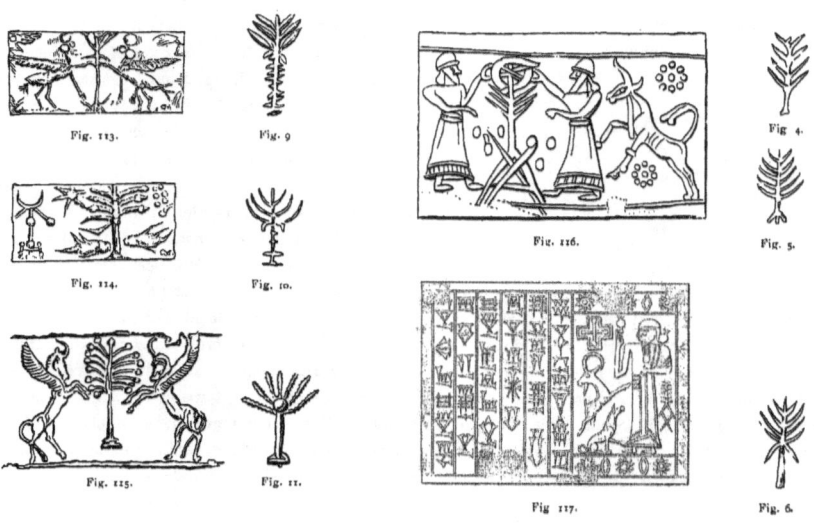

Fig. 113.   Fig. 9.

Fig. 116.   Fig. 4.

Fig. 114.   Fig. 10.

Fig. 5.

Fig. 115.   Fig. 11.

Fig. 117.   Fig. 6.

an attitude of adoration before the holy tree, each holding up one of his fore-paws towards it. The tree resembles in outline those of the Cyprian cylinders of our type a (figs. 4—11), from which, however, griffins are absent (cp. also figs. 1 and 2 on p. 28). Beside fig. 113 I have placed (fig. 9, repeated from p. 30) the design of a tree on the cylinder Cesnola-Stern Pl. LXXVI No. 15. On the other hand griffins occur frequently on Cyprian cylinders with trees of our type b. (fig. 14—21). I give in figs. 122 and 123 cuts of the impressions of two such cylinders.**) Fig. 122 shows a man (perhaps a priest), or god in human form, between the holy tree (the idol of the Paphian goddess according to Sayce and Ménant) and a gigantic seated griffin (Hence fig. 20). Fig. 123 shows a gigantic griffin sitting by itself before the holy tree and raising one paw in sign of adoration (Hence the tree in fig. 16). Ménant lays stress on the remarkable rudeness of the workmanship, the round graver alone having been employed. In fig. 124 I reproduce the impression of another Cyprian

*) Recherches sur la glyptique orientale II, 34, fig. 16 (hence our fig. 113). It is regrettable that the provenance seems to be doubtful. The cylinder may well be of Cyprian manufacture.

**) After A. P. di Cesnola, Salaminia, Pl. XII, 2 and 5. A bad reproduction of the first is given by Ménant II, 250, fig. 254

seal-cylinder,*) executed in very much the same technique. Sayce**) pronounces its style to be Babylonian. The great goddess of Cyprus stands in the middle, holding two quadrupeds by their hind-legs. To her right are two bulls' heads, a bird, and a winged quadruped (griffin or sphinx?); to her left two men and the holy tree. The man stand between the tree (hence fig. 14 above) and the bulls' heads, and seem to be performing a .sacrifice. There is a star on one side of the goddess'es head and two discs on the other side.

Fig. 114 exhibits the impression of another cylinder in the Cabinet des médailles at the Hague (Cat. 134-28)***) the technique of which is very similar to that of fig. 113. The holy tree is here adored by two fish, above which float a six-rayed star and a rude rosette formed of seven pellets. At the side of the tree we see set up on an altar-table the holy post sourmounted by the crescent.†) For purpose of comparison I have here repeated our fig. 10.

On the cylinder fig. 115 we see two winged goats rampant supporting the holy-tree. I place beside this the tree fig. 11 (repeated from p. 30), and here reproduce in fig. 125 the whole design of the seal from which fig. 11 is borrowed. On this Cyprian specimen we see three goats, antelopes or moufflons grouped in adoration round the holy tree, two of them lifting up their right fore-paws. A horned head, two discs with single tails, a four-rayed star, the symbol compounded of sun-disc and crescent, and other less district signs fill the spaces between the tree and the beasts. The tree, in this case, may be meant to represent a palm.

The cylinder fig. 116 is or was in England††) in the collection of Mr. Jarman. Two priests in long cloaks are engaged in performing some ceremony in regard to a holy tree of peculiar appearance, its crown having the form of a star, disc, or wheel. The priests seem to be turning this object round. To the right is the victim, a goat, careering towards the tree. Two rosettes or stars formed by dots and six pellets occupy the interstices. The tree is evidently meant for a young conifer of some kind, felled and set up like our Chistmas-trees on a stand placed on a table. We may compare figs. 4 and 5. In the latter case we clearly see the stand which serves to support the felled tree†††) in the erect position, and we again notice a similar device in fig. 11.

The inscribed cylinder of fine black obsidian, fig. 117, was, when Lajard published it, in the collection of the Duc de Luynes, and now belongs to the Bibliothèque nationale in Paris.

It is here a single priest, king or royal servant, who officiates, raising his arm, as it seems, in adoration in the direction of the cross suspended in the air before him, a holy object with which we often meet on Assyrian and Babylonian monuments. (e. g. fig. 73 above). The goat which is springing towards the priest, and the little animal, like a dog, which sits at his feet seem to represent

---

*) From Salaminia Pl. XII, 1.

**) Ibid. p 121.

***) From Ménant II, 34, fig. 18.

†) I will discuss this post when I come to deal with the Post-worship and Asher-worship.

††) From Lajard, Mithra, Pl. XVI, 6.

†††) The existence of the custom in Kypros is confirmed from a literary source. Engel (Kypros II, p. 558) cites a statement of Hesychius, according to which trees were felled, consecrated to Aphrodite, and set up at the entrances of sanctuaries.

the victims about to be offered. Behind the priest the holy tree fixed on a stand which we saw in fig. 116 is again introduced on a smaller scale.*)

In Fig. 118 we meet with two priests of whom the one on the left raises one arm, his fellow on the right both arms in prayer to the holy tree (= fig. 4). Four discs and a lance, sword, or dagger are introduced in the interstices.

The design on the next cylinder fig. 119 (from which I have taken the tree fig. 6) shows us an anthropomorphic being seated on a throne in front of the holy tree under the branches of which

Fig. 118.   Fig. 119.   Fig. 120.

Fig. 121.   Fig. 122.

Fig. 123.   Fig. 124.   Fig. 125.

two symbols resembling pairs of wings are visible, one on each side. Two large sun-discs or light-discs, loosely connected by a branch, float in the air beside the tree. The rest of the space is occupied by two bulls' heads and a lance-point or small dagger. Figs. 118 and 119 are Cyprian.**)

Fig. 120 (Cesnola-Stern LXXVI, 20) exhibits a single priest or sacrificant standing with uplifted arms by a holy tree of the simplest form. Arms and sacrificial utensils, a dagger or knife and a double axe are scattered round. Above the roughly indicated altar-table at his side hangs a bull's head. We have here a specimen identical in style, motive, and technique with the cylinder illustrated above on p. 28, fig. 7. The cylinders figs. 118 and 119 as well as figs. 1 and 2

---

*) For the dog in Assyrio-Chaldaean texts and on the monuments cp. Ménant's remarks in Collection Clercq, pages 154—5. A closely corresponding cylinder is there figured and described on Plate XXVI, 4. Both belong to one period and show one style; both bear Akkadian inscriptions. The god Marduk is mentioned on both.

**) Salaminia XIII, 20 and 17.

on p. 28 belong to the same period, and exhibit the same style and technique.*) (Cp. p. 28 above, Type a).

In fig. 121 I reproduce the design on a cylinder in the Louvre,**) in which it has been sought to see an act of homage rendered by women to the goddess Istar. The holy tree in front of which the action takes place, is here exceedingly similar to the Kyprian trees of our group a (figs. 4-11). But nevertheless it is quite possible that the engraver had in his mind a palm loaded with date-clusters. We shall see, in a little, how general is the tendency of the different tree-types to pass into each other.

With the series of figures which now follows (126—147 and 15, 50, 52, 53, 54, 55, 89, 92, 106, 109 repeated from above) we pass out of the dark, and find ourselves in an age where many dates can be accurately fixed, the age of the kings Asurnasirpal (884—860), Sargon II (722—705), San- herib (705—681), Asarhaddon (681—668), and Asurbanipal 668—626). The points of connection now become more numerous. We are led back to the groups of monuments we quitted not long

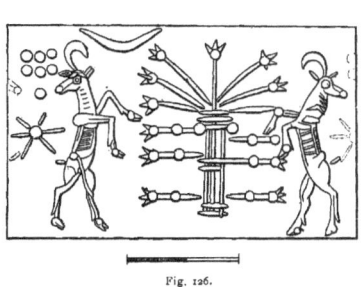 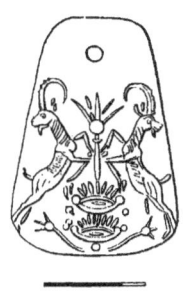

Fig. 126.   Fig. 127.

ago, southwards to Egypt in the days of Ramses III (about 1250 B. C.) and westwards to Mykenai. The latest specimens link themselves to the contemporary or nearly contemporary pottery of the Dipylon class, to that of Melos, Rhodes, Boeotia, Etruria and Attica, the similarity in the motives enduring through all the changes of style. Here again Kypros furnishes us with all kinds of connecting threads and links, with bridges frail or substantial, between the East and West. I refrain in this place from noticing, in so far as it is worthy of notice, the material bearing on this subject of Tree-worship contributed by the Hebrews, Aramaeans, Hittites, and other Syrian

---

*) When I come to deal with pillar-worship and the transition from tree-worship to pillar-worship, I will adduce a number of Kyprian cylinders of the same technique. Ménant calls them Hittite, but there is no proof that they are so. (E. g. Pl. XXXII, 6 = American Journal of Archaeology II, Pl. VI, 10 and Collection Clercq IV, 30). Were there any such, we should have to assume either the existence in Cyprus of a stratum of Hittite civilization differing as widely from other deposits called Hittite as they differ from each other, or of a very extensive importation of Hittite seals during the Copper-Bronze Period. We may style such cylinders as figs. 13, 122, 123, 148—50 Hittite with much more claim to probability. These belong to that group of Kyprian cylinders in which Furtwängler detects Hittite influence. (Roscher's mythol. Lexikon, col. 1753).

**) From Perrot II, p. 679, fig. 334.

and Anatolian races, and I also defer the consideration of allied phenomena in Homeric Greece, in Crete and other places. We shall have occasion to point out in subsequent sections dealing with the cypress, the snake, the trees of Knowledge and Life &c., how in Hellenistic and Graeco-Roman times, in the times of the Ptolemies and the Roman Emperors old Tree-worships and Snake-worships assumed new forms. Not unoften indeed we shall be justified in calling in the help of these later monuments to enable us to draw conclusions as to their older originals still resting in the bosom of the earth. As we descend we again meet in the New Testament with a powerful link between Palestine, Kypros and Rome. It was at Paphos that the Apostles Paul and Barnabas vindicated themselves before the Roman governor Sergius Paulus from the slanders of Elymas the sorcerer.*)

We pass on to our fig. 126.**) Two goats, rampant regardant, are here the supporters of the holy tree. Round the group we see the star of the sun, the crescent moon, and the seven Pleiads indicated by as many pellets. I give below an illustration of a quite similar design, in the same style and of the same period. We there see an identical tree supported by goats in the same position, the only difference being that behind the goats stands the holy post surmounted by the crescent and sun-star. The drawing and modelling of the holy tree, and the form of the figures of men and beasts leave no doubt that both our cylinder fig. 126 and the stele figured below (fig. 148) belong to the period of the Sargonidae. An Assyrian relief (Perrot II, p. 513, fig. 235***) represents Sargon II adoring a holy tree, which is drawn and stylised in quite the same manner as the trees on the two cylinders with goats just described. This very Sargon had a statue of himself erected on the coast of the island of Cyprus at Kition, the famous Phoenician port and trading station (fig. 138).†) The town, called Kition by the Greeks, was known to the Assyrians by the name Karti-hadas(š)ti, as Schrader has demonstrated by the help of two Phoenician inscriptions.††) The stele helps us also to date not merely a whole class of Cyprian vases, but a particular stratum of Cyprian civilization. Schrader assigns this work to an Assyrian artist of about 707 B.C.†††) In the rich series of products of ancient glyptic collected by Lajard§) will be found an enlarged view of the five engraved sides of a pierced chalcedony weight of irregular conic form. The provenance and present ownership of this remarkable specimen are unknown. It was formerly in the collection of the Abbé de Persan. Whenever this cone was found — whether in Assyria, Syria, Asia Minor,

*) Acts 13, 4—13.

**) Lajard, Mithra XXVI, 8, present possessor unknown.

***) Perrot also gives an illustration in the same work (p. 685, fig. 343) of the impression of a very beautiful cylinder in the British Museum, which he correctly assigns to the epoch of the Sargonidae. We see priests and demons assembled round a tree of the same form as that under consideration. The style is identical. Cp. also for the Sargonidae Clercq-Ménant, Antiquités Assyriennes, Cylindres orientaux pages 187 ff.

†) After the illustration in Riehm's Bibellexikon, p. 1374.

††) Zur Geographie des assyrischen Reiches, in the Sitzungsberichte der Königlichen Akademie der Wissenschaften zu Berlin 1890, p. 337 ff. In my paper in the Ausland (1891) "Cypern, die Bibel und Homer." I have adduced further material. This Assyrian town-name Karti-hadas(š)ti of the cuneiform texts, appears in the Phoenician texts of Cyprus (C. I. Sem. 5 and 86 B) under the form Kart-hadast, and must be identified with the Cyprian New-town-Karthago (Καρχηδὼν).

†††) "Die Sargon-stele des Berliner Museum," extract from the Abhandlungen der Königlichen Akademie der Wissenschaften zu Berlin 1881 (Berlin 1882).

§) Mithra, Plate XVI, 7, 7a—7d.

Cyprus*) or elsewhere—it is evident that the design on the side which I reproduce in fig. 127 forms a striking parallel to the cylinder-design, fig. 126. The chief difference lies in the divergent form of the holy tree, which here shows a tendency to approach the type of tree we have met with on the Cyprian silver paterae, figs. 50—52, and on the Cyprian silver girdles, fig. 105 and Plate XXV. I would in this place re-direct the attention of the reader to fig. 107, the painting on one side of the gold basket from the tomb of Ramses III. He will be at once clearly convinced· of the striking similarity which exists between these different representations, coming respectively from the banks of the Nile and those of the Euphrates and Tigris, of the adoration of holy trees by rearing animals. And yet between the engraved designs (figs. 126 and 127) and the painted design (fig. 107)**) lies a period of more than four centuries. I also repeat here from previous pages four other illustrations, figs. 115, 106, 109, and 52a; and in fig. 128 I give once more on a reduced scale the painting on a Cyprian vase reproduced in colours on Plate LXI and discussed above.

We have in fig. 115 an Archaic-Assyrian design, in figs. 106 and 109 two Egyptian designs,

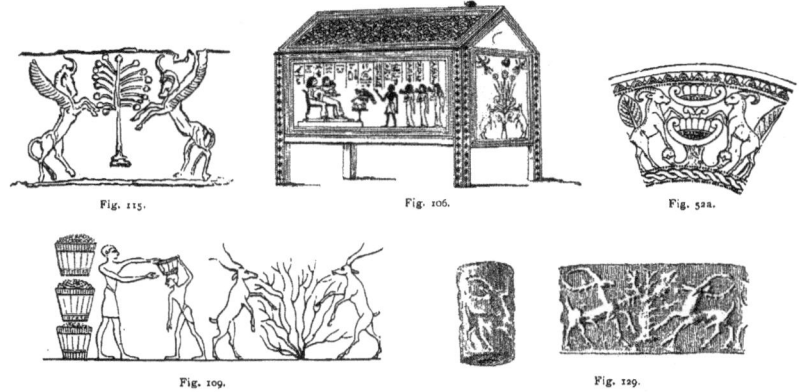

Fig. 115.   Fig. 106.   Fig. 52a.

Fig. 109.   Fig. 129.

in fig. 129 a design of unknown origin. This cylinder (fig. 129) is in the Asiatic Department of the Royal Berlin Museum, where it bears the Catalogue-number V. A. 2116. Two antelopes or kids jump up against a tree.***) A common vein permeates this series of tree-designs from Egypt, Western Asia, and Cyprus.

Several of our Assyrian examples have brought us into contact with the period of the

*) The chances are in favour of its Cyprian origin. Style, form and subject suggest Cyprus, and similar objects have not unfrequently been found here. A conic weight of the same period and style, with engraved designs in which the palm played some part, was found at Kition in 1884, and secured by me for Mr. Lander (now in Constantinople). The drawings I then made from the original are not at hand at the time I write.

**) Perhaps in course of time versions of this subject will be found in Mesopotamia which are older than the Egyptian.

***) There is a very similar cylinder in Ménant, II, 90.

Sargonidae and of the great Sargon II himself (fig. 138); our next illustration fig. 130, takes us back a century and a half to the age of King Aśurnaśirpal. Although we already possess in the large monumental works (e. g. Layard's) numerous illustrations of these scenes of trees adored by demons which recur so frequently on the alabaster plaques from the North-east Palace at Nimroud, I thought it would not be labour lost to take a photograph of one of the originals in the Berlin Museum, and have a good autotypic illustration prepared for insertion in the text here. Two winged eagle-

Fig. 128.

headed demons stand before the holy tree, which is decorated with ribbons and other ornaments, and perform some ceremonial act. In their left hands they carry holy baskets; with their right hands they seem to be plucking fruit off the tree, or rather (as Mr. Tylor interprets the gesture) artificially fertilizing a female palm with the pollen of male palm-flowers. To facilitate direct comparison I repeat here our figures 90, 91, 92, 53, 54 and a portion of fig. 50, and I append the designs of three additional cylinders, two of them (figs. 131 and 133) probably of Asiatic, the third (fig. 132) of Cyprian origin. Figures 90—92 showed us that Cyprian vase-painters seem to have a predilection for rude imitations of Egyptian mural paintings and their subjects, and now we see an allied motive in Assurnasirpal's palace at Nimroud. In fig. 131, a cylinder of green jasper in the Museum at the Hague,

Fig. 131.

Fig. 91.

we find the subject of the Cyprian vase-painting fig. 91 treated in a not dissimilar manner. In a cartouche visible on the right a few cuneiform characters are rudely and quite summarily engraved by a stone-cutter evidently ignorant of the cuneiform script. As on our Cyprian vase, several varieties of trees are represented. The principal tree is a lofty conventional palm, from which two men appear to be plucking date-clusters. They hold in their other hands clusters already plucked, while a third man standing on the left is receiving the fruit from their hands. Above the figures

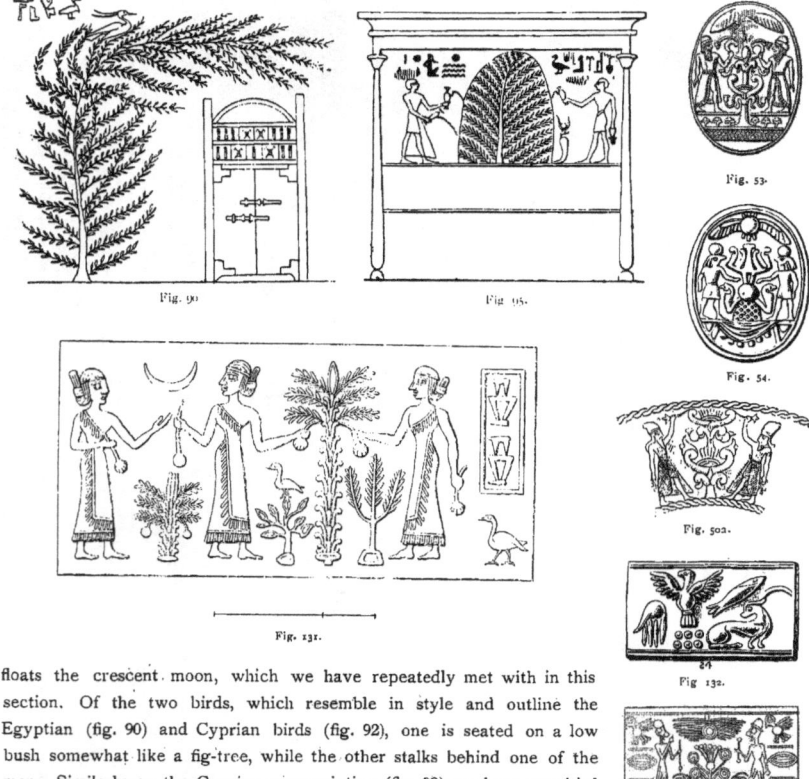

Fig. 90.

Fig. 95.

Fig. 53.

Fig. 54.

Fig. 50a.

Fig. 132.

Fig. 133.

Fig. 131.

floats the crescent moon, which we have repeatedly met with in this section. Of the two birds, which resemble in style and outline the Egyptian (fig. 90) and Cyprian birds (fig. 92), one is seated on a low bush somewhat like a fig-tree, while the other stalks behind one of the men. Similarly on the Cyprian vase-painting (fig. 92) we have one bird sitting on a low tree and two others standing on the ground. The "coiffure" of the figures consisting of a peculiar kind of "chignon" is also very similar on the Hague cylinder and on the Cyprian vase, and the long priestly robes, with their edgings, worn by the men on the cylinder correspond to those worn by the men on the vase. In fig. 50a I reproduce from fig. 50 the scene of tree-adoration on the silver patera of Amathus. The two priestly celebrants are robed in the Assyrian fashion and wear beards and caps of Assyrian shape. While the costume and style of the figures points to Assyrian influence, only the emblems of life in their hands being traceable to Egypt (the priest on the right in the Egyptian painting, fig. 91, carries the same symbol in the same way), the elements out of which the tree is built up are in part Egyptian and in part Assyrian, and are modified in the Kyprio-Graeco-Phoenician manner. The version of the same design on a gem, here again figured (fig. 54) and described above, is decidedly Egyptian in form matter and style. Fig. 183 exhibits another curious cylinder on which, apart from a slight difference

Fig. 134.

in the pose of the figures, the two halves on each side of the median line of the holy tree are absolutely symmetrical. In the middle stands a tree or fantastic object which we might either describe as a man whose extremities terminate in tree-twigs, or a tree formed like a rude anthropomorphic idol. It is quite Cyprian in style. Above the tree-agalma floats the winged globe of the sun. The men who are adoring the tree hold sticks in their hands. In front of them, beneath the tree, lie two antelopes or goats, behind and above which on each side are an bird, a eye (?) and a human hand. For the sake of comparison I reproduce from Cesnola-Stern*) the engraving on a Cyprian cylinder (fig. 132). In the lower right hand corner lies a horned quadruped in the same position as the quadrupeds on fig. 133. A hand and fish

and a bird (eagle), hovering with expanded wings above six small globes, complete the design of this cylinder.

While with Sargon we again a foothold in the end of the 8th, with Asurnasirpal in the middle of the 9th century B. C. the Hiram inscriptions mentioned above on pages 19 and 36 carry us back as far as the middle of the 10th century. Such vases as our Plate XXI, fig. 2 may very well be products of the 9th or 10th centuries, the general circumstances of their discovery favouring this early date.**) With the illustrations which follow, figs. 137—145 we descend to the first half of the

---

*) Pl. LXXVII, 24.

**) While the Cyprian tombs of the 6th century B. C. can be accurately dated by the occurrence in particular cases of large quantities of Attic pottery, we are not at present enabled to fix so exactly the date

7ᵗʰ century, the age of Sargon's successor King Sanherib who reigned 705—681 B. C. We begin with fig. 137,*) the impression of a fine cylinder of transparent fold-spar, now in the British Museum, discovered by Layard at the principal entrance of Sanherib's palace. It is supposed to be Sanherib's own seal. Above the mystic tree, to the right, hovers no longer the simple winged sun-disc in its primitive Egyptian form. Instead of the disc we see between the two great wings the bust of

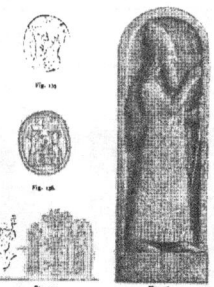

Fig. 137.

Fig. 138.

Fig. 139.

a god terminating beneath in a feather-fan or bird's tail.**) While this tree on the right, evidently the holy tree in the form prescribed by public worship in Sanherib's time, retains the shape it bore in his father's time, we see on the left another group of tree and flower, which somewhat recalls the sacrificial bouquets and flower-columns of Egypt (fig. 92 and 93), and directly suggests the lotus-flowers on Cyprian vases e. g. fig. 41. On the summits of the uppermost petals of this flower-tree stands a goat or buck "passant".***) Between the two trees two further figures are inserted. To the right of the holy tree, evidently within the holy precinct, the statue of King Sanherib is erected as an "anathema." It is a stele of the same form and kind as that erected in Cyprus by Sargon, Sanherib's father, to perpetuate his memory. No doubt the Cyprian stele, like this one, stood in a holy precinct beneath the shadow of a holy tree. For purposes of comparison I give here an illustration (fig. 139) of this Cyprian Sargon-stele.† The design on the seal-cylinder (fig. 137) should correctly have been so reproduced that the lotus-flower

of tombs belonging to the preceding four centuries. The absence of certain objects and the occurrence of others indicate (1) that a certain class of tombs are older than 600 B. C., and (2) that in some cases they cannot be much later than 1000 B. C. Certain types of pottery and certain early fibula-types are the determining factors.

*) First figured in Layard's Nineveh and Babylon p. 160 = Ménant Glyptique II, p. 79, fig. 65 = Perrot II, p. 204, fig. 69 = Riehm's Bibellexikon II, p. 1567.

**) For this Assyrian symbol of deity and the cuneiform character resembling it in shape cp. Ménant Glyptique II, 17—19 = Perrot II. 89.

***) As is well known, the motive of quadrupeds, such as bucks, goats and oxen standing on palmettes, rosettes and flowers is a favourite one in Assyrian decorative Art during several centuries. Cp. e. g. Perrot II, p. 793—3, figs. 140—142.

†) The custom of erecting such royal stelae among the Babylonians and Assyrians dates from early times and can be retraced with certainty far back into the second millennium B. C. Cp. Ménant, Glyptique II, p. 80.

14

tree stood not on the left, but on the right behind the Sanherib-stele. The impression of the cylinder from which our illustration is taken, was so made that in the group as now transferred to a plane surface the subordinate person, Sanherib's servant or court official*), who is adoring the holy tree (and perhaps the stele of his lord and master as well), comes to stand in the place of honour between the two trees.

Figs. 135 and 136 are the engravings on two conic stone seals. In both cases two demons who remind us of Izdubar and Eabani (cp. figs. 110 and 111 supra) stand before the holy tree, and uphold the bust (here of gigantic dimensions) of the great local divinity (Assur? Il? Marduk?) This symbol of the supreme godhead occupies, like a canopy or aedicula, the whole breadth of the design. The cone, fig. 136**), was found by Layard in Sanherib's palace at Kouyounjik. Fig. 135, reproduced from Lajard's Mithra***) is a better rendering of the same scene. The holy tree here no longer adheres to the type familiar to us since Sargon II, the type which we have observed on Sanherib's cylinder (fig. 137), and can still trace on the cone, fig. 136. It bears a much greater resemblance to the lotus-tree on Sanherib's cylinder. This type of tree guides the course of our enquiry to the very curious Cyprian vase here illustrated in fig. 134. †) Of this unique two-handled amphora, found near Ormidhia in the Famagusta district, we possess unhappily only a fragment. Large Graeco-Phoenician necropoleis of high antiquity, the oldest tombs, however, not being much earlier than the year 1000 B. C., extend around and between the modern villages of Ormidhia, Xylo-tymbo, Akhna, Makrastika, Kalopsida, Askhyritou, Avgorou and Liopetri. As will be seen from the Map (Plate 1) I have myself undertaken extensive, but, apart from Akhna,††) somewhat unpro-ductive excavations in this eastern corner of the island lying to the South and South-West of Salamis and to the North-East of Kition. To the North of Xylolymbo, however, I excavated in 1882 three architecturally very remarkable tombs, which I will publish when the opportunity presents itself. These widely stretching necropoleis testify to the existence of a numerous population here in the first half or first two-thirds of the first millennium B. C. In spite of the extensive excavations in the neighbourhood made by the peasants, by the brothers Cesnola, by Mr. Lang, Mr. G. Hake (for the South-Kensington Museum, in 1882), Messrs Munro and Tubbs (for the Cyprus Exploration Fund), and myself (for Sir Charles Newton acting for the British Museum), such Early-Graeco-Phoenician necropoleis have not been discovered there, and will probably never be discovered on any large scale. I believe that old Salamis, the city founded by Teukros after the Trojan war, did not lie to the South-East of the modern village of Ayios Seryios, the position usually assigned to it and in which I have provisionally placed it. It is probably to be sought further inland, and, if I mistake not, up in this very district where so many early and valuable tombs have been opened (unhappily not under the eye of a practised archaeologist) and where I have been able to demonstrate the existence of so many holy groves of Artemis-Kybele.†††) From this ancient centre of civilization and religion comes the vase illustrated in fig. 134. On the shoulder is drawn a scene of sacrifice and tree-adoration, perhaps one

---

*) Cp. e. g. the servant standing behind Sargon II in Perrot II, p. 99; fig. 22.
**) Our illustration is taken from Ménant Glyptique II, fig. 57.
***) Ibid. II, fig. 56.
†) From Perrot III, p. 711, fig. 523.
††) See above p 1.
†††) Cp. above p. 1, site 1; pp. 11 and 12, Nos. 10—15.

of those tree and flower festivals held in Kypros as at Byblos in honour of Tammuz-Adonis and Astarte-Aphrodite. We see from each end a pair of men in long robes with flowers, branches, and trees hurrying towards the centre of the scene Here rises the massive holy flower-tree. Beside it (to right and left) are two men, gods or images, seated or lying on large, richly decorated throne-chairs. Each holds a flower to his nose with one hand, while with his other hand he reaches back behind the chair and clutches or holds a blossoming branch. All the figures are so rudely and summarily drawn that it is difficult to tell their sex. Behind the throned figure on the right we see the crane-like magic bird of which we have repeatedly spoken. The geometric decorations of this vase, consisting of tresses, rows and groups of rosettes, and parallel and contiguous zigzag lines are peculiarly rich. These elements of ornament, with which the illustrations to which I refer back the reader in the note*) have already made as sufficiently familiar, are employed by Cyprian Art in the first half of the first millennium just as frequently as, or even more frequently than, lotus-flowers, branches, trees and palmettes. That many forms came straight from Egypt to Cyprus is as certain as that others found their way to the island from Assyria.**) This holy tree on our Cyprian vase from Ormidhia (fig. 134) bears to the holy tree on the Assyrian stone seal (fig. 143) a formal and stylistic resemblance so close, that, even in the absence of epigraphical evidence, we should be obliged to concede the existence between the two lands of far-reaching relationships, of a deeply rooted reciprocity not in industrial art alone but in the wider sphere of civilization as a whole.***) But if we require any confirmation, it is at hand in the shape of the historical facts recorded on bronze and stone and in the pages, now through the cuneiform inscriptions re-invested with their full authority and significance, of the Sacred Writings. Of a value for our enquiry no less great than the Hiram-inscriptions and the Sargon-inscription of Kypros, are the Tribute-lists of the Assyrian King Asarhaddon (681—668) and Asurbanipal (668—626). In these weighty documents 22 kings of the Chatti are entered as forming one large group. Together with twelve kings of the Land by the Sea (Syria), among whom appears Manasse, King of Judah, ten kings of the Land in the Sea, Kypros, are named †) Need we be surprised to find that numerous elements of Art, Civilization and Religion came to the island from Assyria in the course of the years 1000—500 B C.? — Phoenicians, Canaanites, Aramaeans Hebrews and other Syrian peoples may have played the part of mediators; but the supposition that Kyprians, were trained in the Assyrian and Babylonian capitals is every bit as legitimate, while, on the other hand, Kyprian craftsmen, especially copper-smiths and workers in bronze,

---

*) Fig 39, rosettes. Figs. 49 and 50, tresses and rosettes Fig 52, tresses. Pl. XIX 1. — Pl. LXI. — Fig. 128, rosettes and zigzags. Pl. XIX 2. — Pl. XX, tresses. — Pl. XIX 3. — Pl. XXI, tresses. — Pl. XIX 4, rosettes, zigzags &c.

**) Perrot II, p. 200, fig 116, rosettes and zigzag or herring-bone pattern. P. 308, fig. 124, rosettes. P. 310, fig. 126 and p. 311, fig. 127, tress. P. 320, fig. 136, rosettes &c.

***) Mr. A. S Murray has in his very good article on Cyprian pottery in Cesnola's Cyprus (Cesnola-Stern p 355—366) called attention in a general way to both the Assyrian and Egyptian elements in Cyprian Art. But he follows Helbig (Annali dell Inst Arch. 1876, p. 6, ff.) in assigning too important a place to the Phoenicians. If we substitute "Kyprians" for "Phoenicians" things are all right. The Phoenician element is therewith not excluded but included. Both Murray and Helbig allow that holy trees are represented both on Cyprian silver paterae and on Cyprian vases. In discussing fig. 159, a relief of the time of Asurnasirpal, I will recur to this vase in another connection.

†) Eb. Schrader. "Zur Kritik der Inschriften Tiglat-Pileser's, des Asarhaddon und Asurbanipal', extract from the "Abhandlungen der Königl Akademie der Wissenschaften zu Berlin 1879 (Berlin 1880,.

producing for the Assyrian governing classes or for the market of Assyria itself, may have conveyed to Syria and Mesopotamia either peculiar and original designs and elements of style or technical and artistic inventions and motives derived from Asia Minor, Greece, the Greek islands and Egypt. The process of discovery and excavation*) continues to teach us that between Kypros and the countries mentioned, a traffic was carried on not only in the products of Nature and raw materials, but in works of art. Side by side with this commercial intercourse, with the exchange of wares and the crossing of styles, went an exchange of ideas, of religious beliefs and ritual usages. Not only the products of Art as Art but her products as the handmaid of Religion travelled backwards and forwards. There is another reason already briefly hinted at for dealing at such length with the relations to Assyria and Babylonia. In view of the aniconic and iconoclastic character of the Jewish state monotheism on the one hand, and the nature, on the other hand, of the polytheistic image-worships to which the Jewish people gave themselves up whenever they abandoned their God, the Assyrian, Aramaean and Phoenician monuments are more indispensable for the elucidation of the Bible and the establishment of points of contact with Kypros than those of Egypt. For what worship played a greater part among the peoples of the Bible, the chosen people Israel and their heathen neighbours, than this very worship of trees, of high-places and groves? Did not Yahve himself originally not only permit but ordain that sacrifice should be paid to him on rude altars of earth or stone beneath the green trees of the heights and hills? Since the monotheistic iconoclasts among the Jews tolerated no images, and every time they got the upper hand, destroyed afresh the idols and pillars erected by the party which had abandoned itself to the heathen polytheistic rites, scarcely a single Jewish monument or idol has reached us. Jewish Religion was as killing to the practice and growth of a peculiarly religious Art as were subsequently Mahomedanism and Protestantism. Judging from the Phoenician monuments known to us up to the present day, and until fresh discoveries teach us the contrary, we pronounce the Phoenician traders to have been sterile as regards Art, lacking artistic genius and powerless to create new things. And yet they were Phoenician artists and workmen to whom, as the bearers of an art derived from abroad, the task of building and adorning Solomon's temple was committed. And the Bible tells us other things which make us fain to linger long with the representations of holy trees and arboreal ornament among the Assyrians. The Assyrian monuments take the place of the missing Jewish documents in the illustration and interpretation of the text of the Hebrew Bible.

Let us for example take the 17th chapter of the 2d Book of Kings, the period of Hosea and Sargon II. Sargon**) captured Samaria in 722, carried the Israelites away, assigned to them other dwellings (v. 6) and settled Babylonians and other peoples in Samaria (v. 24). The Assyrian colonists

---

*) The bronze paterae found in Assyrian towns, some of which are figured by Perrot (II (Assyrie), p. 736, fig. 398; p. 739, fig. 399; p. 741, fig. 405; p. 742, fig. 406; p. 743, fig. 407; p. 751, fig. 408) were manufactured in Cyprus, and the same applies to most if not all of the bronzes found by Halbherr and Orsi in Crete (Museo Italiano II, Antichità dell' Antro di Zeus Ideo in Creta descritte ed illustrate da F. Halbherr e P. Orsi) — The great mass of the pottery found at Samal-Senjerli by L. v. Luschan and Koldewey, comprising all the specimens of finer workmanship and turned on the wheel, was also made in Cyprus and exported during antiquity.

**) In the Bible the capture of Samaria is wrongly attributed to Salmanassar Eb. Schader in his „Keilinschriften und das Alte Testament" (Giessen 1883), p. 272 ff. has corrected the scriptural statement from cuneiform texts.

were tormented by lions and saw in this visitation a proof of the displeasure of the god of the country i. e. Yahve (v. 26). The King of Assyria, on learning of this, sent them one of the Jewish priests who had been carried away captive to "teach them the law of the god of the land. Then one of the priests whom they had carried away from Samaria came and dwelt in Bethel and taught them how they should fear Yahve"*) (vv. 27 and 28). This narrative shows how easy it was for Babylonio-Assyrian colonists at Bethel to adopt the Yahve-worship, and consequently for the religions of Assyria and Babylonia to amalgamate with that of Judaea. The following chapters are even more instructive from our point of view. Hezekiah, the King of Judah rebels against the King of Assyria (ch. XVIII, v. 7). He indeed sends tribute to Sargon's successor on the throne of Assyria, Sanherib (v. 14—16) but he succesfully defends Jerusalem against the assault of the Assyrians (v. 17—34 and ch. XIX). Schrader cites four cuneiform inscriptions in illustration of this narrative. From the fourth of these cuneiform texts we learn how Elulaeus, King of Sidon, was, unlike Hezekiah, seized with terror at the approach of the Assyrian monarch and fled to the Island in the Sea, i. e. Cyprus. Shorthy afterwards under King Manasseh a "graven image of the grove" (A. V.) an "idol of Ashera" (Zuntz and Kautsch) was set up in the House of God, the temple at Jerusalem (II. Kings XXI, 7), and remained there until King Josiah removed it, burnt it at the brook Kidron, and stamped it to powder. Of the inscribed monuments hitherto brought to light only one, a Phoenician inscription, mentions by name these Ashera which play such a great part in the writings of the Old Testament. This important document, as late, however, as the 4th century B. C., comes again from Kition in Cyprus. The goddess Ashera seems to be called in it the "mother of the sacred pole".**) Thus we have everywhere evidences of a lively political and religious intercourse between Assyria, Israel, Phoenicia and Cyprus during that very period to which belong our series of monuments of Sargon, Sanherib, Asarhaddon and Asurbanipal in Assyria and their Cyprian parallels. They stand in the closest relationship to the Tree-, Ashera- and Grove-worships of the Bible.

Count Baudissin***) believes that the Assyrian holy tree was nothing more nor less than an idol of the god Assur, while Schlottmann sees in it the representation of Nature or the World, which, personified as Ashera or Astarte, is the feminine counterpart of Baal, the Lord of the World. The winged ring or the bust of the god supported by pinions above the tree he believes to be the symbol of the Lord of the World, the supreme God.†) Tylor's interpretation is certainly right for a particular type during a certain period at least, viz. the brilliant epoch of Asurnasirpal. He rightly sees in scenes such as fig. 130 (supra) the artificial fertilization, performed by winged demons as a solemn religious act, of the female palm-tree and its flowers by the pollen of the male tree. At the present day the fertilization of the female palm is, among the Arabs of Mesopotamia, attended by ceremonies of a religious nature.††) The first to publish a study accompanied by good illustrations

---

*) Cp. A. Kuenen. "Volksreligion und Weltreligion" (Berlin 1883), p 81. I recur to this matter in discussing Post-worship and Ashera-worship.

**) R. Smith, Religion of the Semites, p. 173, note.

***) Studien zur semitischen Religionsgeschichte. (Leipzig 1878) II, p. 189.

†) In Riehm's Bibellexikon p. 112, where Schrader gives an illustration showing the Assyrian holy tree with the winged globe of the sun above it.

††) During the correction of the proofs my attention has been called to E. B. Tylor's most valuable study "The winged figures of the Assyrian and other ancient monuments" which appeared in the number for June 1890 of the Proceedings of the Society of Biblical Archaeology and had escaped me. Mr. Tylor was so kind as to send me a copy of his admirable illustrated paper. It is of abiding value.

of the palm as a holy tree on Babylonio-Assyrian monuments was Schrader. He has pointed out some cases in which it is tolerably clear that the tree is meant for a palm, and others (belonging especially to the time of Asurnasirpal) where a cross between a palm and some variety of pine is represented. I am, however, no longer of opinion that, as Schrader has sought to prove and as I believed until quite recently, the palm is the sole prototype of the so-called holy tree of the Assyrians and Babylonians. We have seen above (p. 29, ff. Type a) how on Cyprian monuments a coniferous tree of some kind was, long before the introduction of the palm, the prototype on which the holy tree was modelled, and in despite of the fact that the palm was indigenous in Babylonia, the same or something similar may there have been the case.*) It appears to me that we shall be nearest to the truth if we accept the view first enunciated by A. W. Sayce,**) viz., that in one district of Babylonia a conifer (cedar, fir, or cypress) became at an early date the prototype of the holy tree, in another district the palm, and that in later times the two types may have been crossed, and a hybrid type thus produced.***)

As adding something to what I have tried to convey by word and picture in the present section and in section 1, I would refer the reader to Plate XXIX and the remarks explanatory of it at the end of this work. It is, if not quite certain, at least highly probable that, in the beginning, both the ancient Kyprians and the ancient Babylonians, independently of each other, represented on their monuments holy trees (conifers) of very much the same rude form. The presence on the earliest Babylonian monuments with holy trees of wild beasts and monsters, winged figures and figures compounded either of man and beast or of distinct beasts, and the absence of such creatures from the earliest Kyprian monuments with trees of our type a (see p. 28) speak decisively for the independent origin among both peoples of primitive tree-idols When, subsequently, the Babylonian monuments with trees and monsters (chiefly in the form of the easily transportable products of the lesser arts) came to the island (Type b p. 29), it was easy for all kinds of further modifications to arise, taking at first the form of crosses between conifers and palms, and afterwards, as time went on, of fantastic-ally formed and elaborately conventionalized trees making no longer any pretence to reality, and, by their very nature, forbidding the attempt to identify them with any natural species. Other varieties of tree and flower, especially the lotus-tree, lotus-branch and lotus-flower†) (cp. figs. 134, 135 and 137) were also employed by the Assyrians in their representations of holy trees.

*) "Ladanum und Palme" in the Monatsberichte der Königl. Akademie der Wissenschaften zu Berlin 1891, p. 413—428 with 9 illustrations. Fig. 4 ibid. is an illustration of the central group of our fig. 131 and fig. 7 of the tree in our fig. 137.

**) The Religion of the Ancient Babylonians, pages 241 and 242

***) Cp. p. 32 supra, where I have referred to the present passage. Cp. also p. 84.

†) While these sheets are passing through the press, Mr. W. H. Goodyear's elaborately illustrated work "The Grammar of the Lotus. A new History of Classic Ornament as a Development of Sun-worship," and several press notices of it (among which I would signal Mr. Tylor's in the Academy 1892, p. 498) have appeared. Next to Egypt the largest share of space in this work is assigned to Cyprus, but much matter for comparison has been drawn from the Babylonio-Assyrian monuments. I shall have frequent opportunity of recurring to this book and the illustrations which adorn it. The previous section (p 66—81) "Representations of trees, holy and profane, in Egypt and Cyprus" had been printed off before Goodyear's book appeared; otherwise I should have already had occasion to cite its text and illustrations. It is a pity that the author has at times let his fancy run away with him, and persists in finding lotus-flowers or lotus-bushes or their derivatives, where, as in the case of Tylor's and in part of Schrader's instances, the palm was certainly the

One question remains. Mannhardt suggests that the holy tree of the Assyrians may correspond to the German May-tree. Apart from the very considerable difference in size, those oriental Easter-palms of which we have spoken above on p. 84, elaborately plaited into the shape of highly ornamental trees and decorated with coloured ribbons passed in and out, form a striking parallel to our tall German May-trees with ribbons and garlands of leaves and flowers wound about them. Both the oriental Easter-palms and the German May-trees again resemble those strange Assyrian shapes which, originally representing the holy tree, afterwards went on their travels, undergoing all kinds of changes and becoming part of the current coin of ornament in other countries, especially in Greece. The island of Kypros stands in the focus of these movements, of this process of formation and transformation of the religious and profane forms through which the Art of the ancient peoples dwelling on the shores of the Mediterranean found expression. The next chapter will make this clearer to us.*)

III. Trees and Tree-gods, dendromorphic and anthropomorphic idols, their transitions and transformations.

When motives of religious Art pass from one people to another, the myth often accompanies the type on its travels from the outset. In most cases, however, the religious symbol is first naturalized, its mythological significance following it at a later date. Elsewhere the type alone is adopted, and not the myth, and, when this happens, if a religious meaning can be perceived at all, it is often totally different from that which the symbol bore to its creators.

On the following Plates (LXXI—LXXXVI) I have collected from various countries a number of designs which will enable us to institute in the first place typological and, secondarily, mythological comparisons.

1. Divinities dwelling in trees or issuing from trees.

We see on plates LXXI and LXXII (figs. 1 and 2) three Egyptian monuments, one Palmyrene monument of Roman times and the fragment of a Roman monument found on German soil. On the Egyptian mural paintings it is in two cases (Pl. LXXI, 1 and Pl. LXXII, 2) the goddess Nut, the mother of Osiris who grows out of the holy tree; in the third case (Pl. LXXII 1) it is Hathor. The hieroglyphic inscriptions appended to the pictures (that of Pl. LXXII, fig. 2 would be visible on our illustration, but has been purposely omitted) style both goddesses "Lady of the

---

prototype. But that need not prevent us from availing ourselves of Goodyear's numerous correct comparisons and, even where we cannot accept his views, of utilizing his very extensive pictorial material collected at the cost of so much labour.

*) Other particulars concerning the holy trees on Cyprian, Babylonian, Assyrian, Hittite, other Asiatic, and also Mykenaean seals will be gleaned from Plates XXVIII—XXXII and the elucidations thereof at the end of this work

Sycamore*) who bringeth bread, fruit, and water." We have therefore before us tree-goddesses dwelling in the sycamore, and, as one of the monuments (Pl. LXXI, 1) is certainly of the 19th Dynasty this kind of Tree-worship is certified as having been practised in Egypt at some time at least during the period 1400—1270 B. C.**)

The Roman monuments (Pl. LXXI, fig. 2 and LXXII, 3) are separated from the Egyptian by an interval of fifteen centuries. Although only a few links from each end of this long chain of typological tradition remain to us***), we can surely enough catch, on the Palmyrene altar and on the relief of Heddernheim with its representation of a sacrifice to Mithra, the echo of the old Egyptian motive. The transformation is of a character which does not allow us to forget the original. The child Mithra rises from the cypress, like Nut from the sycamore, to descend into the theatre of his miraculous and heroic deeds.

In most other cases Mithra, at the period of this relief, is pictured as issuing from a rock, the circumstances of his birth coming to be interpreted as an imitation of the prophecy of Daniel ("the stone cut from the great mountain without the aid of men's hands") and of Isaiah (XXIII, 13—19. "He will dwell in the hollow places of the rocks.") See Justin's dialogue with Trypho (160 A. D.); Windischmann "Mithra" in the Abhandl. f. d. Kunde des Morgenlandes I, p. 61.

The only difference is that, in the one case, the birth of the god from a tree is intended, in the other, the indwelling energy of the goddess in the tree. This representation of the birth of Mithra might stand very well for the birth of Adonis. One of the many Adonis legends, as we know, tells us, how Smyrna, the daughter of the Kyprian King Kinyras and of Kenchreis was changed into a myrhh-tree, which after ten months opened and gave birth to Adonis. The fact that, of all the Roman emperors, it was Heliogabalus (218—222 A. D.) who favoured and propagated most the worship of Adonis as well as that of the sun-god Elagabal would lead us to suppose that what our other illustration (Pl. LXXII, 3) represents is, in fact, the birth of Adonis. Although this Palmyrene altar is more than three centuries later than the Emperor Heliogabalus (its date is 547 A. D.), it appears, from the bilingual (Latin and Palmyrene) inscriptions (not here reproduced) and from the reliefs on its other sides, that it was dedicated to the Sun-god Malachbel and Moon-god Aglibol. We can thus quite well conceive of a trinity Aglibol-Malachbel-Adonis. In this case the cypress represents Smyrna, the daughter of Kinyras, transformed into a tree and giving birth to Adonis. Bötticher (Baumkultus p. 141 ff.) sees here the pine of Attis to the summit of which the waxen image of Attis is attached. As the monument dates from Roman times, as Attis-worship was at this period

---

*) Pl LXXI, 1 from Roselini III, CXXXIV; 2 from Lajard, Mithra XC, the well-known relief found at Heddernheim in 1832; LXXII, 1 from Wilkinson-Birch III, XXVIII; 2 from XXIV ibid ; 3 from Lajard, Le culte du cyprés I, 2 = Bötticher, Baumkultus, fig. 47.

**) Cp. Frazer, Golden Bough I, 308. The cypress is still a holy tree in Cyprus, although not indigenous to the island. We often meet with it beside Turkish mosques or the tombs of Turkish saints. Brugsch in several passages of his book (Religion und Mythologie der alten Aegypter) calls attention to the high antiquity of Nut and Hathor (for the former see in particular p. 129). He also lays stress in the fact that in the New Empire the representations of Nut growing out of the sycamore are of frequent occurrence on the monuments.

***) The designs on the coins of Gortyna in Crete (Bötticher, fig. 46 and Imhoof-Blumer, Thier- und Pflanzenbilder X, 40) which show Europa seated on the holy plane-tree, and those on coins of Myra in Lycia where we see the seated figure of the Mother of the Gods (Gerhard. Akadem. Abhandlungen IX, 8) supply further parallels to the Egyptian tree-goddesses.

especially prominent in Rome, and as the existence of Adonis-worship at Palmyra is an established fact, we must see in this representation an amalgamation of the two cults. Evidences of such an amalgamation of Attis and Adonis have been frequently pointed out (see e. g. Roscher's Lexikon col. 717). On Plate XXXIII, 1—5 will be found some of those figures of crouching temple boys, of which such great quantities were set up in the votive areas of Cyprian holy groves, several thousand examples (including fragments) having been found in the course of excavation. These temple sacrificants or herd-boys hold sometimes a box of incense or oitment, sometimes a flower, fruit or fir-cone, sometimes an animal of sacrifice (usually a dove, but in other cases a quadruped, either a kid ram, lamb, calf, or ox.*) This figure of a youthful temple-servant, which it was the custom to dedicate both in the precincts of Rešef-Apollo and in those of Astarte-Aphrodite, resolves itself into a mixed type combining the attributes of Tammuz-Adon-Adonis, Pygmaion-Pygmalion, Kinyras-Kirys-Kyris, Gingras-Linos and Attis. Dionysiac elements too are present to some extent. In the next section we will discuss these worships, which have left their traces in the Homeric Poems and the Bible, and of which Kypros was one of the most active seats, if not indeed the chief focus. The Palmyrene altar-relief also recalls an inscription recently discovered at Magnesia in Asia Minor. We are told therein how in the trunk of a plane-tree blown down in a storm an image of Dionysus was found, and how, in consequence, after the Delphic oracle had been questioned, the worship of Dionysus was introduced.**) The inflammability of trees, the occurrence of forest fires, and the custom at religious festivals of deliberately setting fire to trees, early resulted, among the most widely different peoples, in a relation being established between Tree-worship and Star- or Fire-worship or in the amalgamation of both. We need not therefore be surprised to find Tree-worship, Sun-worship and Fire-worship interwelded in the case of the Sun-god Mithra, whose cultus, of Persian origin and already appearing on the cuneiform inscriptions of Artaxerxes II, was in later times so highly developed among the Romans and played so particularly important a part in Roman military quarters on German soil.***) Like Nut and Hathor in Egypt, Mithra in Persia and Rome, Adonis at Palmyra at Byblos and in Cyprus, Istar and her lover Dusi dwelt in a tree at Babylon†) and Jehovah, the god of the Hebrews is seated in the burning bush.††) In dealing with the mythological aspect of certain figures we must distinguish the process of metamorphosis of the dendromorphic into the anthropomorphic from the reverse process to which the births from trees belong. It was at times beyond the power of Art to picture the two processes in any but a similar or identical manner.

A following section will make us acqainted with a Babylonian parallel, perhaps a Corn-spirit (Pl. LXXV, 6 and 8 and Pl. XXX, 2), to our Egyptian Lady of the sycamore (Pl. LXXI, 1 and LXXII,

---

*) For further details see Section IV, 7. Three similar ram-carriers occur among the stone statuettes found by Cesnola (Atlas XVI, 21—23) in the groves of Apollo at Athiaenou (22 and 23) and Hyle (21), and meet us in company with the crouching temple-boys as servants of Apollo. In 1880 I unearthed in a Hellenistic necropolis at Salamis a terracotta figurine of a youth carrying a ram on his shoulder.

**) Mittheilungen des deutschen Inst. Athen XV, 1890, p. 330; Revue des Études grecques 1890, p. 349.

***) Bötticher in his Baumcultus (p. 512) points out how intimately Fire-worship and Tree-worship are connected among the Parsees. On numbers of the older Persian tomb-stones the figure of lion as a symbol of the sun, (Mithra) is found in juxtaposition with the cypress (Anahita). Mithra is the god of light and of the sun, but also the god of chasms, who has a thousand eyes and a thousand ears (Spiegel, Eranische Alterthumskunde II, pages 77—87'. Below, in speaking of the cypress we shall meet with Old-Babylonian parallels.

†) Sayce, Religion of the Babylonians, p. 238.

††) Deuteronomy 33, 16. Smith, Religion of the Semites, p. 177.

1 and 2), which can perhaps lay claim to a higher antiquity. I would here recall a later masculine variety of the Egyptian type, the Ampelos with which we meet on a marble found in Italy and now in the British Museum. Dionysus clasps his beloved, whose head, trunk and arms retain their human shape, while her lower extremities have already been transformed into a vine.*) The sight of the Egyptian goddess growing out of the trunk of the sycamore makes us think again of the poetical fairy-tale of the grape-girls so divertingly narrated by Lucian. They were women down to the hips and vines below. Mannhardt sees therein the parody of a Hellenistic Egyptian legend, and, once on Alexandrian soil, we can scarcely be wrong in deriving this grape-girl story from the goddesses of the sycamore. Below we shall find further counterparts on Biblical soil in the Asheroth, cypress-gods, and palm-gods of Canaanitic and Jewish religion, and the Greek parallels, Dryads, Hamadryads, Drymides, Thyades, Maenads, Nymphs, Nereids and Kyparissoi-maidens, are both very numerous, and have left traces, however faint, in the Homeric poems. In the Tree-, Wood- and Corn-spirits, the Wood-ladies and Moor-ladies of Northern Europe we have a series of remarkable analogies, of which, as Mannhardt**) speculates, the Southern or Oriental origin will one day be established.***) In this region of Tree-gods, Tree-spirits and Tree-souls, of modifications and trans-formations of dendromorphic and anthropomorphic images, as in other regions, a rough connecting thread penetrates the typology and mythology of the peoples of the ancient world, and can be traced home to our native Germany.†)

2. Images of gods of vegetation and their compendia.

The eight figures united on Plate LXXIII bring another movement before our eyes. The image of an Egyptian god of fertility and vegetable growth, the Nile-god Hapi (figs. 1 and 2), and his Egyptian compendium (fig. 4) are adopted by the Kyprians as early as the first third of the first millennium B. C., and (figs. 3 and 6) come to occupy the significant position on the vases of the period reserved as a rule for the holy tree of the Assyrians and other mythological representations, such a figures of divinities and demons of human or animal form or the holy bundle of wands. The circumstance that the Cyprian vase-painters in many cases treated this motive in purely empirical and decorative fashion, and grew finally either forgetful, or neglectful, or entirely ignorant of the religious meaning of the representation, does not affect the character of its origin as a fact in the history of religion. On the contrary this very utilization of such cultus-images in the profane and decorative Arts goes far to demonstrate that their worship was extensively practised and that its figured ex-pressions were widely known. Although, as Brugsch and others tell us, Nile-worship is one of the oldest forms of religous observance in Egypt, the representations of the Nile-god Hapi here pictured††)

---

*) Cp. Roscher's Mythologisches Lexikon, col. 292.

**) On a stone relief in the Egyptian Department of the Berlin Museum the arm of Nut grows out of a palm (see Plate XXXIX), just in the same way as the bust of Nut out of the sycamore. I recur to this representation below in speaking of the palm.

***) Cp. his Antike Wald- und Feldculte, ch. I, and various passages of his Baumcultus.

†) See below the section headed "Oriental festivals attached to vegetation-spirits compared with those of Southern and Northern Europe.

††) Plate LXXIII, 1 from Rosellini III, XXV; 2 from ibid. LXXIV upper left-hand corner; 4 ibid. XXI lower left-hand corner.

date from late Hellenistic or Roman times. Fig. 2 alone may belong to the twentieth dinasty. In the first picture (fig. 1) the androgynous Nile-god is fertilizing with his own milk and with water the plants growing in a pot. As in the case of the pictures of the Lady of the sycamore, the soul of Osiris, in the form of a human-headed bird perched on the plant, points to the dead as partakers in the rite. In the second picture (fig. 2) the same androgynous god, Hapi, is carrying plants, flowers and fruits. The god's head is always surmounted by the tuft of papyrus or lotus which becomes in the hieroglyphic script the siglum for lower Egypt. Figure 4 on the Plate shows us the same tuft borne aloft as a standard by the hieroglyph of Life with a pair of human arms added.

The Cyprian vase-paintings figs. 3, 6 and 7 (on Pl. LXXIII) easily explain themselves with the help of the Egyptian designs, while figs. 5, 7 and 8 (ibid.) clearly show how the tree and bird are ousted from their place on the vases by this new thing, which we should describe in the one case as a cone-idol or post-idol with human arms, in the other as an anthropomorphic figure, wearing, in place of a human head, a flower or tuft of foliage. We may regard it as demonstrated that, in the period (1000—600 B. C.) during which these Cyprian vases were manufactured, Egyptian as well as Babylonio-Assyrian and other influences affected Cyprian ceramics. Hapi himself is introduced, in quite Egyptian fashion, on the Palestrina patera (Perrot III, p. 97, fig. 36) with its Phoenician inscription and unmistakeable Egyptian tendencies, it is, as I have stated,*)  exceedingly probable that this patera is of Cyprian manufacture. The circumstances of the discovery of the Cyprian vases figured on Pl. LXXIII, the quality of the clay and the method of manufacture, make it further certain that, precisely in that portion of the island where the oldest Graeco-Phoenician towns were situated, the representations here adduced are indissociable from a class of vases strictly limited by both form and technique. Although it so happens that few specimens of the class have been as yet unearthed, the particulars of their discovery indicate that we have not to do with commissions executed to the order

Fig. 139

of a single wealthy client, but with the extensive manufacture of a particular kind of vases of red clay with decorations peculiar to them. The two vases figs. 3 and 5, to which the designs figs. 6 and 8 belong, were found at Idalion and passed into the Lawrence-Cesnola collection. The third vase, that from which the design fig. 7 is taken, was excavated by me at T.amassos in 1885. It is of the same black-glazed clay as the others, and has the same geometrical patterns painted in dull black. It comes from the very tomb which produced the Tamassos crater already figured from more than one point of view (fig. 37, p. 36; fig. 38, p. 37; fig. 71, p. 62; fig. 75, p. 63). They were accompanied by a third vase meant to be filled from beneath on the system illustrated in Cesnola's Salaminia fig. 269 (p. 275)**) and with an aquatic bird (like those on our figs. 42, 43 and 84 (p. 67) painted on it. The form and ornament of the vase with which we are here concerned are similar to those of Perrot's fig. 497 (III, p. 691); the form is shown in the annexed cut (fig. 139) On the shoulder,

_____

*) Cp. p. 98 above, and the Section on ring-dances and metal paterae
**) In the January Session of the Berlin Archaeological Society (1892) Hiller von Gärthringen exhibited a Greek vase of the 6th century B. C., evidently manufactured in Boeotia, the system of which is the same as that of these ancient and modern Cyprian vases (the ancient specimens are of about 600 B. C.) I was enabled to enlighten him as to its mechanism. Cp. Sitzungsberichte der Archäologischen Gesellschaft zu Berlin 1892, p. 33.

opposite the handle, where the large circles intersecting horizontally and vertically (see Perrot fig. 497) leave an approximately quadrangular space, the figure of an idol of conical or columnar form was painted and is here (Pl. LXXIII, 7) imperfectly reproduced from a hasty sketch. The same circumstances which I have narrated in full in the Note on p. 37, in speaking of the great Tamassos crater, unhappily resulted in the ultimate loss (as it would seem) of this further valuable specimen, which could only be extracted in fragments and was then found to be not quite complete. In any case there can be no doubt that on the Idalion vase (Pl. LXXIII, fig. 3) an Egyptian original, the image of the god Hapi, has been imperfectly imitated by the Cyprian potter, and that the painter of the headless idol of the Tamassos vase (ibid. fig. 7) had in his mind's eye Egyptian designs resembling the standard with the tuft of papyrus (fig. 4). In dealing, in the next chapter, with Snake-worship and hermaphrodite. gods, 1 will recur to the subject of the Nile-god, and the analogies he presents to various Semitic, Carthaginian, Moabitic, Canaanitic, Kyprian, Anatolian and Greek androgynous deities. One of these analogies may be anticipated here. The Egyptian god Hapi is nothing else than a form of Osiris*) who, in the capacity of Nile-god, is conceived as androgynous. Now the practice of Osiris-Adonis-worship, at Amathus in Cyprus is certified. It was in this same city that the bearded Aphrodite and the Hermaphrodite had their origin.**) We need not then be surprised to find the Cyprian painter decorating his vases with figures of Hapi-Osiris-Adonis or aniconic agalmata representative of this god.

8. From trees, posts and planks anthropomorphic idols gradually originate: these are at first shaped like posts or plank.

The design on a Cyprian cylinder (Pl. LXXIV, 1) shows us yet again two sacrificants and two victims between two holy trees.***) The interstices are occupied by little globes and by what seem to be twirl-sticks or lopped portions of branches. These objects, representing either rough-dressed poles or artificially composed crosses, appear in the following figure (LXXIV, 2), also taken from a Cyprian cylinder, as aniconic wooden agalmata taking the place of the dendromorphic image. Two men here swear by and adore these symbols of the godhead. A sacrificial table or altar stands beside them and above it hangs the bull's head.

On a third Cyprian cylinder (LXXIV, 3) the divine symbol takes the form of a post with appendages resembling eyes and perhaps really intended for a pair of human eyes. Two quadrupeds in heraldic attitude look up at the tree. A priest advances towards it. The fourth figure (LXXIV, 3), also from a Cyprian cylinder, shows in a clearer light the transition from the aniconic post-idol to the post-idol with anthropomorphic organs. The idol's body is a simple wooden post. Two bent sticks placed at right angles to the body indicate the arms; two straight sticks placed at acute angles the legs, while the eyes (as in fig. 3) are represented by two circles. Beside the idol is a human figure seated on a throne. A trifoliate object on the opposite side is difficult to define.

The large figure (5) in the centre of the Plate gives an unpublished and very accurate view

---

*) Cp. Brugsch, Religion und Mythologie der alten Aegypter, p. 638.

**) Roscher's mythol. Lexikon, col. 2314.

***) Cp. Section IV, 6 "The Asheroth."

of the Kyprian vase now in Oxford which I once published in the Journal of Hellenic Studies, and of which I have already, in fig. 41, given another view taken from above.*) Two stags and two birds stand in adoration fronting an agalma which brings before our eyes the moment of transition from the dendromorphic image into the anthromorphic, or vice versa. I have placed beneath it in fig. 6 the outline of the lower portion and in fig. 8 that of the upper. From the mother tree above (fig. 8) the child tree below (fig. 6) seems to issue. The lines and composition of the vase-design should be carefully compared with those of the cylinder-designs (especially figs. 3 and 4). A rudely formed plank-idol (Pl. LXXIV, fig. 7)**) of red polished clay, the incised designs filled in with a white substance, was found on the Northern range of Cyprus near Lapithos and purchased from myself by the Antiquarium of the Berlin Museum. It is impossible to tell if the head be meant for a human one or not; the little indentations on the mouth or muzzle seem to indicate the nostrils, the large round holes, bored right through the tablet, the eyes. The idol is quite intact and is meant to be feminine and draped. The ridges which pass down from the head to the breasts and arm-stumps seem to be intended for locks of hair. The form of the head of this, in its way, unique idol resembles that of the image on the Cyprian cylinder, Pl. XXXI, 13. While the vase (figs. 5, 6 and 8) belongs to the Graeco-Phoenician Iron Period (somewhere between 1000 and 600 B. C.), the cylinders (figs. 1—4) and the plank-idol (fig. 7) belong to the Pre-Graeco-Phoenician Copper-Bronze Age and are probably as early as, or earlier than, the third millennium B. C.

On Plate XXVIII (see the Explanation of the Plates) the designs on three vases and 21 cylinders are given. Among the latter (fig. 17) is a better rendering of Pl. LXXIV, 3. Next it (fig. 16) is a cylinder (taken from Clercq, Plate LXXIV, 29) clearly of the same age, country and school of art. In this case, however, the holy post with its pair of eyes has become a purely decorative embellishment, and, in this respect, the cylinder must be classed with Nos. 9—14 on the same Plate. One of these latter, no. 9, can be approximately dated. It comes from the tomb in which the bull-crater (p. 33, fig. 33) and the idol ibid. fig. 31, as well as the idol fig. 7, Plate LXXV were found. Among the other objects in the tomb was an Egyptian scarab, pronounced by Erman and Steindorff to be certainly not older than the New Empire. The character of the numerous Mykenaean vases of this tomb points also to a date between 1500 and 1000 B. C., and a third testimony to the date of the cylinder is rendered by the contents of another tomb described in detail on pages 33 and 34. Two cylinders were found in this tomb. One of these (v and v^l = fig. 34) belongs certainly to the same group as that under discussion. This is evinced both by the style and by the material, an artificial substance resembling porcelain. The other, that with cuneiform inscription (w w^l = figs. 34 and 35), dates according to Bezold and Sayce, from the second millennium B. C. From the above brief statement, taken together with what is said in the explanatory remarks to Plate XXVIII, it appears that the cylinders in M. de Clercq's collection, Nos. 11, 13 and 16 of our Plate XXVIII, may not be older than our Cyprian cylinders (ibid. 9, 10, 12, 14 and 16), and, that, as their provenience is unknown, we may feel ourselves considerable justified in attributing them to Cyprus. M. de Clerq himself places these three cylinders at the beginning of his work among the oldest of the archaic specimens. Ménant, his collaborator, places them, as it seems, in the time of Sargon I and the still older Hammourabi i. e.

---

*) Cp. what has been said above on pages 36 and 37 regarding this vase.
**) = Pl. XXXVI, 3a and b. Cp. generally the board-idols on this phototypic plate as well as those illustrated on Plate LXXXVI.

before 3800 or, roughly speaking, in the fifth millennium B. C. Ménant's deserts as the initiator of a system of classification of Babylonio-Assyrian cylinders are, of course, beyond question, but, as regards these particular specimens, his attempted classification has proved quite untenable and called for correction.*)

We have already (p. 61, fig. 68 and p. 65, fig. 77) made the acquaintance of two Mykenaean amphorae, found in Cyprus, with holy trees and an anthropomorphic idol of a highly primitive kind depicted on them. The men who adore the tree on the first vase (fig. 68) have no vestiges of arms; the feminine idol on the second vase (fig. 7*l*) has arms of a kind, and the flowering plants on this vase show some progress as compared with the holy tree or post on the other. If we place side by side the drawings of trees and plants on these two vases, those on other Mykenaean vases, figs. 76, 82 and 83, the Cyprian drawings of similar objects, and the designs figured on our Plate LXXV, we have an unbroken cycle of types, illustrating the development of religious imagery as regards the tree and of the various forms of Tree-gods. The dendromorphic fetish becomes an agalma of columnar or tabular form, at the first aniconic, then wholly or in part iconic, then finally passing into the true image, the complete semblance, rude though it may often be, of man. I do not think it can be set down to chance that the same necropolis of Haliki which yielded the Mykenaean vases, figs. 76 and 82, gave us the cup the paintings on one side of the shoulder of which I reproduce on Plate LXXV, fig. 1.**) Furtwängler and Löschke regard the central object as a shrub and pronounce the objects which flank it to be unusual motives. It appears to me, however, that there can be no doubt that the painter desired to represent in the centre a columnar or tabular trunk and growing out if it a fantastically formed human head adorned with a crown. The "unusual motives" at the sides must be meant for wooden planks or posts with human heads. The plank-idol, Pl. LXXIV, 7 has scarcely more resemblance to human form than the central object on the Haliki vase (LXXV, 1), while the plank-idol, fig. 29 (p. 32), in spite of its rudeness, gives a fairly complete and correct idea of a human figure wearing a crown. The very remarkable painted terracotta idol, Pl. LXXV, 7, is undoubtedly meant to be human. It bears more resemblance to a wooden post than any other post-idol laying claim to humanity hitherto excavated, but a terracotta idol in Schliemann's Tyrins (Plate XXV k) runs it very close. We see, executed in clay, a little forked tree-trunk, retaining the knags and stumps of its lateral branches, carved into the semblance of an idol of human form. The legs are formed by the fork of the trunk, the knags become stumps of arms, and three twirling branches were so trained or pruned as to assume the form of a human head with two pierced ears, a nose, and holes for the eyes. The idol was supposed to the draped, and the dress and ornaments are indicated by bands and lines painted in reddish-brown colour. Our illustration in taken from a sketch of the original made by Mr. Carletti at Nicosia.***) The idol was found in two pieces, the breakage, visible in the illustration, being just above the arm-stumps. The upper portion has unfortunately (as it would seem) been mislaid in the course of transport to Berlin. The still existing lower portion is 12.3 cm (= 5 in.) in height. Seven further plank-idols, all of which have something to tell us, are figured on Plate LXXXVI and will receive further notice in the Section dealing

---

*) For further detail I must refer to the Explanation of Plates XXVIII - XXXI, at the end of this work.

**) From Furtwängler and Löschke, Mykenische Vasen p. 39, fig. 23.

***) First published by me in the Journal of Cyprian Studies, Pl. I, 43a and b.

with the Ashera. All the seven (as I write they are all in my possession) were found in the Pre-Graeco-Phoenician necropolis (already so often referred to) of Ayia Paraskevi near Nicosia. One (no. 2) demands our particular attention here. The idol is broken below, and the arm-stumps and ears are damaged. The coarse, uncoloured clay of which it is formed has received a coating of fine, washed clay of a reddish-brown tinge, and we are hence enabled to put it beyond doubt that this plank-idol, though of the rudest, is meant to be a representation of a human form. We see the body with its indications of drapery, the attachments of arms, human ears with their earrings and a human head with its crown. But the human face has been purposely omitted. Where one expects to see mouth, nose, eyes and cheeks, all that one sees is an oblong depression produced by pressure with the finger and round about it an aureole produced by incised lines. Here there is no doubt that the artist desired to replace the human face of a human idol by the sun in his glory.

A step further. Two designs on Conze's Melos vases (our Plate LXXV 2 and 3)*) show figures that of our Kition vase (LXXIV, 5). Especially in the case of the latter does the question suggest itself. — Did not the vase-painter desire to represent a thing half tree, plant, or creeper and half man, and stamp it as feminine by introducing the organ of sex?**) The portion of the well known Rhodian Euphorbos plate reproduced Pl. LXXV fig. 4***) shows also between the combatants a twining plant with terminal palmettes under which human eyes are inserted. The apotropaic character of these eyes has been generally acknowledged. For this very reason†) we must regard the object to which the eyes belong as the compendium of a divinity who was conceived as something half way between tree and man. I add (ibid. fig. 5) for purposes of comparison, and as representative of the myths and types of Greece itself, the figure of an idol of the bearded Dionysus on a Volcentine stamnos first published by Panofka.††) On a draped post are suspended two cymbals or basins and the mask of the god with a bunch of ivy branches springing from it. In front of this post-idol to which, although it lacks arms, the drapery and the suspended mask give a human appearance, stands the sacrificial table with the sacred vessels.

Dionysus *ἔνδενδρος*, the Boeotian numen dwelling in the tree (Hesychius), and the images of Dionysus in the market-place at Corinth, carved from the wood of a tree reverenced as Dionysus†††), form important literary analoga to our illustrations. F. A. Voigt, the author of the admirable study "Dionysus" reaches the conclusion that the god was first venerated as immanent in the fir-tree, and that then the erection in the sanctuary of felled fir-trees brought about the transition from dendro-

---

*) Melische Thongefässe V, 1 and the vignette at the end of the Notes.
**) Cp. in the Section on the Ashera below figs. 145—148 and Plates XXX 11, 12, LXXIX, 12, 16, 17.
***) Salzmann Necropole de Camirus, LIII.
†) As regards Cyprus I have material to show how in very early times, from the Pre-Graeco-Phoenician Copper-Bronze Period onwards, one or more divinities of human or animal form, to whom an apotropaic character must be assigned, or parts of these divinities, appear on the vases. We see sometimes whole figures, sometimes only heads or portions of heads, sometimes merely eyes or horns. The variants are of such diverse kinds and the material at my disposal so vast, that detailed treatment of the typological and mythological developments and transformations of these artistic counter-agents to the evil eye can only be undertaken in a comprehensive study of this single subject. I shall incidentally, have occasion to mention a few examples.
††) Dionysus und die Thyiaden p. 28 ff. and Pl. II, 1 = Bötticher, Baumcultus 43b. Cp. also Pl. LXXIX, 2 below.
†††) Pansanias II, 2, 5.

morphic to anthropomorphic form in the worship of the Spirit of Vegetation.*) The analogy is astonishingly close between our Cyprian vase painting (LXXIV, 5) and the cylinder design fig. 133 p. 93 and 94); where the agalma in the centre, the object of devotion, has an approximately human

Fig. 133.   Fig. 140.

form, wears a massive crown and terminates in tendrils. The whole composition beneath the winged sun-globe reminds us on the. one hand of cylinder designs with the holy tree like our figs. 135 and 136 (p. 95), and on the other of those representations, in which, while the scheme of the whole is similar, the place of the tree or hybrid compound of man and tree worshipped by two men and surmounted by the winged globe is taken by the Egyptian god Bes with his high crown of feathers, straddling legs and grotesque forms. I hear repeat fig. 133 and place beside it (fig. 140) a cylinder design from Lajard's Mithra XXXII, 1. The Persian cuneiform inscription on this carneol cylinder (formerly in Col. Stewart's collection) takes us into the fuller light of the age of the Achaemenidae, the 6th and 5th centuries B. C..**) A step further and we reach the picture on the Melian vase (Pl. LXXV, 3).***) A comparison of the designs speaks for itself.†)

The same idea, that of the god dwelling in the tree, meets us among the Abrahamites in Palestine before the Egyptian bondage. For it is said of Abraham††) "And he planted a tamarisk (grove A. V.) in Beer-sheba and called there on the name of Jehovah, the everlasting God." It need not then cause us any surprise, when, at the time of the Exodus, after the Israelites had sojourned in Egypt and become acquainted with Egyptian Tree-worship, Jehovah reveals himself to Moses from among the branches of a tree; when we read.†††) "Let the good will of Him that dwelt in the bush come upon the head of Joseph and upon the top of the head of him that was crowned among his brethren." Do we not here actually figure Jehovah in the position of Nut or Hathor whom we saw (Pl. LXXI, 1 and LXXII, 1 and 2) giving their elect food and drink from the midst of trees? Sinai with its holy mountain-forest of Jehovah recalls to us the Elysian fields of Arou with the holy sycamore grove of Nut§) and the holy hill-forests of Tammuz-Adonis on the Lebanon and at Idalion in Kypros. Still at the present day the valley descending on the South from the Idalian hill-forest is called by the people „ Tò παραδίσι ".

4. Plants grow from gods of human form: gods create plants.

Fig. 6 and 8 of Plate LXXV show us the impression of two archaic-Babylonian seal cylinders, the first of which (6) is figured in Clercq-Ménant's collection (No. 140), the second, a serpentine

---

*) In Roscher's mythol. Lexikon, col. 1061.

**) The date I owe to Schrader's verbal communication. He also recognises the Egyptian influence.

***) The Persian seal, later by a century or more than the Melos vase, goes back to an older original.

†) A similar cylinder with Bes in the British Museum is figured by Ménant II, p. 171, fig. 149.

††) Genesis 21, 33.

†††) Deuter. 33, 16.

§) For fuller details see Brugsch, Religion und Mythologie der alten Aegypter, p. 175.

cylinder now in the Cabinet des Médailles, Paris, in Lajard's Mithra (LIV, B. 12). Ward*) interpreting the plants or branches growing out of the figures or held by them as ears of wheat**) sees in these and similar representations a god of Agriculture or Corn-spirit. As he is almost certainly right in pronouncing an object occurring on some of the specimens to be a plough, his interpretation has much in its favour. Be this as it may, at all events we may take it for certain that the engravers of these designs attempted to represent gods, demons and priests, the objects or renderers of a peculiar plant-worship in which the metamorphosis of the dendromorphic into the arthropomorphic idol was, and was meant to be, conspicuous. We have here coming from Old Babylon one of the oldest of the primitive types from which descend those numerous and varied legends and rites where demons, heroes and gods are changed from human form into that of trees, plants, or flowers.***) Another no less interesting motive, also, it would seem, of fairly early Babylonian times, is supplied by the seal device Pl. XXIX, 3.†) Two beings of human form are confronted by two monsters whose lower limbs are anthropomorphic, their upper extremities clearly dendromorphic — tree-branches.

As the island of Kypros is the central point of the present work, it is of double interest for us to note how large a number of the legends of this cycle are localised in Kypros. I here collect the most prominent examples. I remarked above on the origin of the myrrh or myrtle††) from the Cyprian princess, Smyrna King Kinyras' daughter, transformed by Aphrodite who was envious of her beauty. Another legend tells us how Aphrodite transforms Myrrha, the priestess of her temple in Kypros, into the holy myrtle tree, that she may eternally enjoy the company of her beloved.†††) The oft quoted passage of Polymachus (Athenaeus XV, 8§) once more adduced by E. Gardner in the second volume of his Naukratis§§) traces back the origin of the Naukratitic garland to an adventure which befell a certain merchant Herostratus on the passage from Kypros to Egypt. Herostratus on his voyage had touched at Paphos and bought there a quaint idol of Aphrodite a span long. The ship, on nearing the coast of Egypt, was overtaken by a storm, and the sailors offered prayers for deliverance to the Kyprian idol. Aphrodite stilled the storm, and caused myrtle to grow up all around herself. Herostratus, on reaching home in safety, dedicated the image in the already

---

*) "A god of agriculture" in the American Journal of Archaeology 1886, p. 261—266. The two cylinders are there figured (29 and 32). On Plate XXX, 2 of the present work a further good phototype of the one cylinder (Clerq 140 = Ward 32 = Plate LXXV, 6) is given.

**) One of the scenes painted on the walls of one of the Osiris chambers at Dendera, the ancient Philae, should be compared. Sheaves of corn spring from the dead body of Osiris and are watered from a can by a priest. The accompanying inscription contains the words "This is the shape of him who may not be known, Osiris of the mysteries, who grows from the returning water" in other words "the periodical revivification of Nature whose productive power is derived from moisture." (Brugsch, Religion der Aegypter p. 621).

***) In Panofka's Dionysos und die Thyiaden, pl. I, 1 we see on an Attic vase a post-idol of Dionysus dressed up in a similar manner to our Pl. LXXV, 5. The manner in which tree-branches grow from the foot of the post and from the shoulders of the anthropomorphic part of the idol directly recalls to us these Babylonian cylinder designs LXXV, 6 and 8.

†) American Journal of Archaeology II, Pl. V, 2.

††) Baudissin (Semitische Religionsgeschichte I, 199) has already pointed out how apt the myrtle and the myrrh are to pass into each other.

†††) Bötticher, Baumkultus, pages 262 and 415.

§) Ibid., p. 446.

§§) P. 55.

existing sanctuary of Aphrodite at Naukratis, sacrificed to the goddess and, at the sacrificial feast, presented each of his friends with a wreath of the myrtle of such miraculous growth. These myrtle-wreaths continued henceforward to be ceremonially employed and were styled Naukratitic.*) Just as the myrtle tree springs from the Kyprian princess the priestess of Aphrodite, so the apple tree springs from Melos foster-father of Adonis and priest of Aphrodite, while Pelia, the wife of Melos, is transformed into a dove. Doves**) and apples are among the most frequent attributes in the hands of the cultus-images of Adonis excavated by myself and others. As many of these images date from the 6th century B. C., the tales of transformation into myrtle tree, apple tree and dove, reaching us only through late literary tradition, are invested with a higher significance as evidently the survivals of more ancient legends known to us from no literary source. Adonis, who, according to a local Cyprian fable, is pursued and slain by Apollo, is found again by Aphrodite in the temple of Apollo at Argos in Kypros.***) Apollo from being the foe of Adonis becomes his friend. For this reason we find images of Adonis in the holy groves of Apollo, as well as in those of Aphrodite. The statues and statuettes of priests of Apollo from our excavations often enough carry, just like the priestesses of Aphrodite (and like the Jews at the feast of booths: see Nehemiah 8, 15), not only holy-water sprinklers made of laurel-leaves strung together in rows, but also branches of myrtle. Apollo in Kypros even bears the name $Mυρτάτης$, myrtle-god, as the inscription found by Hogarth tells us.†) The rose too in Kypros first blossoms from the blood of Adonis slain by the boar, and the anemone from the tears shed for his sake by Aphrodite.††) On the hills of Cyprus quantities of wild or semi-wild roses grow, and in summer the fields are richly carpeted with the countless blossoms of the anemone. A son of the Kyprian Kinyras (the father of Myrrha and priest of Aphrodite) is Amarakos. He is changed into the fragrant herb sampsychon, henceforth bearing his name, the plant from an extract of which he had prepared the precious ointment to be used in the ritual of Aphrodite.

With the worship of Kybele and Attis, of which I shall have more to say in the following section, there came to Kypros that of the sexless being Agdistis, from whose excised male organ

---

*) U. Köhler ("Die Zeit der Herrschaft des Pisistratos in der $πολιτεία \,Ἀϑηναίων$" in the Sitzungs-berichte der Akademie der Wissenschaften zu Berlin XX and XXI, April 7th, 1892, p 341) has recently shown that Solon traded in Naukratis and founded a town (Soloi) in Cyprus. So that earlier than the time of Amasis (569—526) a Greek commercial settlement must have existed in Naukratis, and must have been in active inter-course with Cyprus, all which lends additional value to this story of the Cyprian Myrtle-Aphrodite, the counterpart of the Myrtle-Apollo whose worship is attested by an inscription. Flinders-Petrie's discoveries (Naukratis I and II) teach us further how the designs and the technique of the sculptured votive images of Naukratis were influenced by Cyprian work, although, on the other hand, the Cyprian sculptors of this period took many lessons in style and the use of the chisel from their Egyptian fellow craftsmen.

**) Cp. Pl XXXIII 2 and 4. For the Cyprian legends as to the origins of apple, dove &c, see especially Engel, Kypros II.

***) Ibid , II, p. 268.

†) Pages 22 and 23 above. Another counterpart to the Myrtle-Aphrodite of Kypros and Naukratis and the Myrtle-Apollo of Kypros is the Myrtle-Artemis at Boeae.

††) See the passages quoted by Engel (Kypros II. Similarly in Asia Minor from the blood of Attis spring violets, and in Crete from the blood of Dionysus pomegranates. According to another legend, of which further mention is made below, Attis in the form of a pomegranate-tree springs from the blood shed by Agdistis when mutilated. We have in Kypros additional combinations, such as those of Aphrodite-Kybele' Artemis-Kybele and a $μήτηρ \, ϑεῶν$. The presence of the latter was first demonstrated by an inscription found by myself. Cp No. 5 in my list (p. 10 supra).

grew the almond-tree. Just as Kybele and Agdistis are confounded and even become one being in Asia Minor, so does Aphrodite amalgamate with Agdistis in Kypros. The bearded Aphrodite of Amathus seems to be connected with this Aphrodite-Agdistis. When therefore the goddess of Melousha*) is distinguished from other Kyprian Aphroditae as the Aphrodite of the almond, Ἀφροδίτη Μυκηρόδις, we have a right to attribute to her the character of an Aphrodite-Agdistis.

5. Some further Holy Trees and Tree-gods of the Kyprians and Hebrews.

Various other legends of trees, flowers and fruits with which we again meet in the Bible are especially connected with Kypros. I here select some of the most important. In the following sections of this chapter and in chapter III I deal with the cypress, fir, cedar and palm.

a) The pomegranate tree.

The pomegranate, with its countless seeds, is still at the present day, as in antiquity, a symbol of fertility among the Kyprians. Still at the moment when, after the completion of the marriage ceremonies, the bride and bride-groom are about to enter the dower-house, a pomegranate is thrown against the door-post so that it splits in two and scatters its seeds about. The wish is thus symbolically conveyed that as the seeds of the pomegranate are many, so may the young pair be blessed with numerous offspring.**)

In Homer's Iliad we do not hear of the pomegranate tree, but in the Odyssey it is once mentioned among the fruits in the garden of the Phaeacian King.***) It is of Semitic origin.†) Although the tree is not a native of Cyprus, the fruit ripens admirably, is more highly prized by the Cypriots than any other, and is one of the most favourite and welcome presents. The people of the Karpas still carve in relief on the capitals of their stone columns either female nipples or pomegranates. Above on p. 74 we spoke of the occurrence of the pomegranate in excavation, either as a separate votive offering or in the hands of the crouching boy-priests. In the same place I discussed and gave illustrations of pictures of pomegranate trees from Egypt and Carthage. Below, on Plate LXXVII we see yet another of those Carthagenian stelae with Phoenician dedicatory inscription to Tanit, Face of Baal, and Baal Hammon. On the column of Ionic form in the centre stands a pomegranate.

The pomegranate in the Old Testament has been exhaustively discussed by Riehm (Bibel-lexikon p. 539 ff.) We know that the tree played a prominent part in the religious and secular life of the Hebrews, that its fruits were employed both in the decoration of the crowns of the columns which stood before Solomon's temple††) and in that of Aaron's priestly robes. In Exodus XXVIII, 33 it is described how from the hem of the blue and purple stole of the high-priest golden bells hang, alternating with pomegranates of twisted thread. Above on p. 50 ff. I showed how the silver girdles

---

*) The inscription is published in Cesnola-Stern p. 377, No. 23.

**) Cp. Hehn, Culturpflanzen, p. 486 who narrates the story of Darius after Herodotus (IV, 123) and that of King Otto after Fiedler (Reisen I, 625) In both cases, the ancient and the modern, a similar symbolical conception of the pomegranate, as full of the promise of fertility, is insisted upon.

***) Hehn p. 192.

†) Ibid. p. 193.

††) Cp. also Perrot IV, p. 321.

figured on Plate XXV and figs. 105 (p. 77) and 102 (p. 75) illustrate the Homeric girdle of Hera with its hundred little bells. In fig. 102 we saw how on the Tamassos girdle two varieties of bell alternate. These flower-bells bear a remarkable resemblance to pomegranate flowers, and recall therefore the fringe of the Jewish high-priest's robe just described, which we may regard as composed of the alternating flower and fruit of the pomegranate. It is remarkable that on one of the oldest Hebrew seals we possess (Pl. LXVII, 7*)—a specimen which, in point of rarity, yields to few of the treasures in the Berlin collection of gems—such a continuous border of pomegranates recurs as a frame enclosing the inscription. In the Song of Solomon (4,3 and 6,7) Sulamith's cheeks glisten like pomegranates beneath her veil. In a modern Cyprian love-song we hear "Thy mother gathered pomegranates, roses, and flowers of Paradise, and built thy body out of them."

It has long been believed, and is stated e g. by Movers (Die Phönizier, I, 197) that the divinities mentioned in the Bible, Rimmon and Hadad-Rimmon were connected with the pomegranate, the Hebrew name for which is "rimmon." This is not, however, so, as Schrader has exhaustively proved, first in the Jahrbuch für protestantische Theologie I (1875) p. 33 ff. and p. 342, later in Riehm's Bibellexikon p. 549 and p 1294 and in his work "Die Keilschriften und das alte Testament," p. 454. As one still sees from the Septuagint (i. e. 300 B. C.) the original form of the name was Ramman or Remman, and the Aramaean and Judaean god is identical with the homonymous Assyrian god—a god of lightning, storm, rain and the sky. The Syrian god Hadad has the same character, and the Babylonio-Assyrian gods Bin and Martu are also of the ' same order. Ramman, who appears more than once in Cyprus, was evidently there identified ͺin certain local cults with the Cyprio-Aramaean god Rešef and the Cyprio-Hellenic Apollo. The stone colossus excavated by Luschan and Koldewey at the modern Senjerli in the ancient land of Samal, the old Biblical Kingdom of Hamath, bears the oldest known Aramaic inscription. Carved in the reign of Tiglatpileser II. (circa 730 B. C. according to Sachau), it is dedicated, as the inscription tells us, by King Panammu to the gods Hadad and Rešef. Rešef-Apollo appears in Cyprus now (as we have seen) as a god of trees and forests, now as a pardoner and cleanser from guilt, now as a god of war and the chase (an archer, as his name implies, or spearman), now, like Hadad, Ramman, Bin or Martu, as a god of light, the sun and the weather. He at times unites with Baal-Zeus to form one divinity and bears, as may be seen on our Plate LVI, the attributes of Apollo (holy-water sprinkler) or of Zeus (roll of writing, thunderbolt, Nike or eagle). Rešef-Apollo, just like Ešmun-Hephaistos unites at times with Izdubar-Melqart-Herakles, at times with Tammuz-Adonis, at times with Osiris-Adonis, at times with Bes-Pygmaion. The stone colossus now in Constantinople which Schröder ("Phönizische Miscellen" in the Zeitschrift der morgenländischen Gesellschaft XXXV) pronounces to be Asur, appears to represent this solar and martial, vegetative and meteorological divinity, the product of so many cross-currents of mythology but standing in the closest relationship to the Hadad-Ramman and Hadad-Rešef of the Hittite country. The two colossi, that from the kingdom of Hamath in Northern Syria and that from the kingdom of Amathus in Kypros (Hamath-Amathus) approach each other very closely in size, style, and rendering of form, and belong to the same period. I shall have to speak of their resemblances elsewhere. Now, as the post-exilic prophet Zachariah (12, 11) in his description of the approaching Last Judgment compares the great wailing at Jerusalem with the wailing for Hadad-Rimmon in the valley of Megiddo, we need not, in spite of the fact that the Hebrew god Remman is distinct from "rimmon" the pomegranate, exclude the possibility of his association in Jerusalem with Tammuz-Adonis. (Ezech. 8. 14.) In Kypros Ramman (I have twice found and made known epigraphical evidence of his presence here, (1) through Bezold, Zeitschrift für Keilschriftforschung II, 1885 p. 191, (2) by a communication made to Erman) does, in fact seem to amalgamate with Rešef-Apollo and Tammuz-Adonis. Inscriptions testify to Rešef-Apollo being locally worshipped in the island as a forest-, myrtle- or ivy-god. The Tammuz-Adonis temple-boys in sanctuaries of Rešef-Apollo carry, in numerous instances, apples; and (as we have already hinted and will show at greater length in the section dealing with the Aoia) the tree of Attis enjoyed in the Artemis-Kybele groves of Cyprus the same honours as the tree of Adonis in Astarte-Aphrodite groves. Adonis and Attis unite to form one god. According to a local legend transmitted by Arnobius, Attis was born, in the shape of a pomegranate tree, from the blood of Agdistis when Dionysus mutilated him. In Amathus, the chief seat of Adonis-Attis worship, the androgynous Agdistis appears in the shape of a bearded Aphrodite, that very Aphrodite who planted the pomegranate tree in Cyprus and plucked its loveliest

---

*) Clermont-Ganneau, Sceaux et cachets israélites, phéniciens et syriens No. 2.

fruits hard by Amathus at Tamassos. The pomegranate was also in Cyprus in a special sense the holy plant of Adonis, just as in Crete it was pecularly consecrate to Dionysus (cp. the Note on p. 112). Under these circumstances was it not possible that Rimmon should be identified with Tammuz-Adonis, and that the pomegranate, as symbolizing vegetable fertility, should be set in the hands of that god who by his gifts of light, warmth and rain brought its fruit to perfection. In Egyptian mythology the god of light and sunshine, Osiris, becomes alike a harvest-god and a Nile-god (Hapi), the fructifier of the earth and the father of its products. Osiris indeed unites at Gebal in Phoenicia, as at Amathus in Kypros, with the god Tammuz-Adonis

Fig 141.

and becomes a spirit of vegetation who comes and goes. True, it is only at a period almost a thousand years after the completion of the translation of the LXX, in 600—700 A. D., that later copyists, such as the Masoretes, confused the Hebrew word for pomegranate "rimmon" with the originally Assyrian god Remman or Ramman and made of the weather-god a tree god, a god of the pomegranate; but, nevertheless, it is always possible that in the times of Ezekiel, (and earlier), in the times when the women still mourned for Tammuz in the court of the temple at Jerusalem, this same confusion and identification may have been made. Baudissin, who at the end of the first volume of his Semitische Religionsgeschichte devotes a long section (p. 296—325) to the mourning for Hadad-Rimmon, concedes the possibility that the wailing for Hadad-Rimmon mentioned by Zachariah may be in some way an allusion to the wailing for Tammuz-Adonis; and Eb. Schrader (Riehm p. 1610) supposes that the two gods Hadad-Rimmon and Tammuz-Adonis may have been identified in a secondary manner. When we find pomegranates attached to the vestments of the high-priest and to the columns of the temple at Jerusalem, and observe on Carthaginian stelae (cp. Pl. LXXVII) the seated figure of the boy Adonis in the very place elsewhere occupied by the column surmounted by a pomegranate, we may be sure that, both here and there, Adonis-Attis-Tammuz was worshipped as a pomegranate-god· It was an easy step to identify this tree-god Tammuz, to whom the "rimmon" was sacred, with the weather-god Ramman, whose name was so similar, and to call him Rimmon. What was, as a fact, the origin of the name of the Greek spirit of vegetation Linos, the beautiful singer too early claimed by Death, whom we meet first on Homer's shield? Simply this — that the Phoenician and Hebrew cry "ai lenu" i. e. "alack" used in the lament for Tammuz-Adonis was misunderstood, and the word "Linos" formed from this half-articulate voice of sorrow. If authorities such as Preller in his "Griechische Mythologie" (I, p. 377) and Baudissin in his Semitische Religionsgeschichte (I, p. 303) hold that this word and the accompanying myth were certainly thus produced in Homer's time or yet earlier, why should not "rimmon" have been associated with Ramman, why should not Hadad-Ramman and his dirges have come thus into contact with Tammuz-Adonis and his songs of sorrow? Why in the religion of the closely related Semitic peoples should not the familiar name of a tree and fruit (the pomegranate) have created this bridge, if the Aryan Greeks formed from the unfamiliar Semitic interjection "Ai lenu" the word Linos, and made this word part of the vocabulary of their native tongue; if they derived thus their Linos-song from the lamentation for Tammuz?—I recur to this question in another connection in dealing with Linos. In conclusion I may be allowed to point out in the light of another Babylonian monument (fig. 141) how the sun- and weather-god there represented (a combination of Samas, Ramman Bin and Martu) becomes a god of husbandry and a bearer of the plough-share. I rely, herein, on Sayce and Lenormant and on Ward's remarks on this cylinder (American Journal of Archaeology 1886, p. 264, fig. 31). See what I have said above on p. 112 in regard to the cylinders Pl. LXXV 6 and 8. Pinches, who reads in the inscription accompanying the design the name Amur-Shamash (i. e. "I have seen the sun-god") places the gem circa 1800 B. C. We possess in Berlin (Vorderasiatische Abtheilung No. 243) an Old Babylonian cylinder which belongs to the class of cylinders with the Sun-god Samas figured on Pl. LXXXIV). There, too the god holds the plough and is therefore Sun-god, Lord of Heaven and Earth-god in one.

b) The Terebinth.

This tree played also, as is well known, a very great part in the religious and secular life of the Hebrews. The cavities of old trees were sacred dwelling-places. Already do we find Abraham building an altar to Yahve beside the terebinths of Mamre.*) The terebinth never came into pro-

---

*) Gen. 13, 18. The whole material is collected in Bötticher's Baumcultus p. 519 ff. and in Riehm's Bibellexikon, p. 1648. Cp. also Hehn, Culturpflanzen, p. 337.

minence among the Greeks, but has from all time been a tree of note among the Cyprians. This may be owing to the fact that this tree does not grow in Greece, while more than one species of the Pistacia Family grows wild in Cyprus.*) Up to quite recent years a particular kind of turpentine-oil of high quality and price was known to the trade as "Cyprian", whether produced in Cyprus or not; in such high esteem was the balsam obtained in Cyprus from the Pistacia Terebinthus held. And in antiquity also the terebinth had acquired among the Kyprians an importance no less than was attached to it by the Hebrews. An ancient town situated in the great plain of Mesaurea and lying N. of Kition, S. of Chytroi, S. E. of Ledrai and S. W. of Salamis was called in ancient times Tremithus i. e. "Terebinth-town". The place was still of importance and the seat of a bishop in early Byzantine times.**) The small village occupying the site of the ancient town still bears the name Tremithousha, In 1883 I opened for the Cyprus Museum several tombs in the vicinity of the ruins and with good results (the finds are in Nicosia); and before our time many tombs (chiefly Hellenistic and Phoenician), containing much fine glass and gold jewellery, had been rifled.***) On the other side of Nicosia (Ledrai), 8½ miles to the West, there is another little modern village called Kotshini Trimithia i. e. "Red Terebinth",†) the adjective being added to distinguish this village from several others of the same name. A third place Ayiai Trimithiais (Ἅγιος Τριμιθίας according to Sakellarios) lies about 9 miles from Nicosia in a south-westerly direction. We have in this case a direct testimony to the present or former existence of several holy terebinths or terebinth-sanctuaries, and we see how the traditional reverence paid to this holy tree of the Semites and ancient Kyprians has survived among the Christians of the island up to the present day.††) At Ayios Yannis, a few miles south of this place, I also opened a few Hellenistic tombs in 1883 and found some fine gold ornaments now exhibited in the Cyprus Museum at Nicosia. Finally, a little to the North of Ktima (Neapaphos), we find a fourth place again called Tremithousa, where one can still rest under the shadow of enormous terebinth-trees. The modern Cypriots (Greeks as well as Turks) regard the terebinth as a febrifuge, and reverence it accordingly. An example is the terebinth at Neapaphos on the tomb of Solomoni (Pl. XVIII, 2).

c) The Oak and Olive.

Quercus Ilex, the familiar ever-green oak of the Mediterranean countries is entirely wanting in Cyprus. Nature has here replaced it by a variety of ever-green oak (Quercus alnifolia) peculiar to the island. As this oak is entirely different from other oaks in size, habitus and appearance (the leaves being of quite another form), it is scarcely probably that the ancients reckoned it among the

---

*) Cp. Unger u. Kortschy, Die Insel Cypern.
**) Cp. D. Pieridis "The early bishops of Cyprus" in the Owl 1888, p. 58. The earliest bishop is St. Spiridion (325—44 A. D.); the last mentioned in these early lists Georgios (circ. 787).
***) Cp. Cesnola-Stern, p. 216; Reinach, Chroniques d'Orient p. 197 (5², 362).
†) The village is one of the so-called "red villages" (κόκκινα χωρία) of the island. Villages built on red ferruginous soil are so called. They do actually look red, as the air-dried bricks of which the houses are built are formed of this red clay.
††) Here, then, in Cyprus we find the same regard paid by the Christian Church to the terebinth as on the opposite coasts of Syria and Palestine. Constantine the Great, at the urgent request of his mother, St. Helena, ordered the bishop·of Jerusalem, Makarios, to fell Abraham's terebinth at Mamre (to which pagan observances still attached) and to build a Christian chapel on the spot where the tree had stood. Cp. Bötticher, Baumcultus, p. 529.

oaks. Several other deciduous varieties of oak (catalogued in Unger and Kortschy's work) also occur in Cyprus; and among them is again a variety peculiar to Cyprus.*) It is often difficult to discriminate the words used in the Old Testament for oak and terebinth.**) Both trees were equally sacred. I will content myself with mentioning the oak of Ophra, under which the angel of the Eternal sits and appears to Gideon.***) The oak, as we know, has alway been a tree of especial import in the mythology of different races. Here I will merely call attention to some interesting Cyprian parallels to beliefs and usages found elsewhere. Above on p. 20 (No. 50) I mentioned the grove of a woodland Apollo (Apollo Hylates) near the modern village of Drymou. Oaks abound in the neighbourhood. A holy oak-copse (δρῦς the oak) at this spot may have given birth to an ancient place-name Δρύμω, which, though ignored by our literary sources, survives in the modern name of the place.†) A holy wood of oaks in the neighbourhood of Evrykou on the northern slope of the Troodos range, close to the modern Turkish hamlet of Ayii Aliphotes (not on the Map), has become the means of making this spot a place of pilgrimage for Christians. I once, in company with some Greek pilgrims, spent the vigil of the saint's festival in the house of a Turk here. Not far from Drymou, a little to the South, between the villages of Letymvou and Polemi is the monarch of the Cyprian oaks, the largest tree in the island. Its branches extend to a distance of 118 feet and its trunk at a height of 5 feet measures 23½ feet in circumference. Beneath its boughs lie the remains of a ruined church. Pilgrimages are still made to this oak, and on one day in the year mass is read on a rude altar, and a fête is held. This oak in called Δρῖς Σταυρολιβόνου††) i. e. the oak of "the cross and frankincense" a formula frequently recurring in the worship of the Orthodox Church and stamping this tree with the character of especial sanctity. Of the other modern Cyprian tree-worships and tree-legends of religious significance which carry us back to antiquity two examples, one Mahometan the other Christian, may here be briefly mentioned.

In the middle of one of the Bazar-streets of the capital Nicosia, at a place where the street is very narrow and much crowded on weekly market-days, stands an Olive regarded by the Turks as holy and inviolable—as the town-tree. A Turkish saint lies buried beneath it, and the English Government respect this saint, his tree and his grave. On the trunk hangs a lamp which is always kept burning. Who can help thinking of the old sacred olive-tree in the agora at Megara? As an oracle had foretold, the town fell in ruins when the tree was felled.†††) As regards the olive, this one striking instance may suffice. The importance of this tree in the general and religious life of the Hebrews, Greeks and Romans (to mention only the three chief nations of antiquity) is so well known, that it is unnecessary to give further examples.

The most famous Madonna of the island of Cyprus, the Panagia tou Kikkou, whose picture is said to be the work of St. Luke, has assumed the functions of a pagan rain-spirit. The name of

*) Cp. also my paper in the Ausland (1881, p. 777 ff.) "Cypern's Wälder und Waldwirthschaft.
**) Cp. Riehm's Bibellexikon, p. 342.
***) Judges 6, 11.
†) Cp. Pape's Wörterbuch der griechischen Eigennamen, p. 324, when a whole series is collected of Greek names of persons, towns, places and regions connected with the word δρῦς.
††) Hogarth, Devia Cypria, p. 30. In 1882 I took part, near Kyperoundha up in the mountains, in the festival yearly celebrated in honour of a clump of plane-trees (the largest I have seen in the island) and their protecting saint. The little church there looks like a toy beside the gigantic trees.
†††) Plinius, N. H. 16, 72; Bötticher, Baumcultus, p. 167.

this Virgin and the foundation of her monastery are connected by legend with the seed of a plant. Once when the monastery was burnt, the image took refuge under a tree. When the rains are delayed, the Panayia is carried down from the monastery up in the hills to the plain, as it is believed that the image has the power of causing rain. The chief legends concerning this Panayia, whose sway over the popular religion in Cyprus is as powerful as was the Paphian Aphrodite's of old, have been collected by me and published in the "Owl". I have myself witnessed how in a time of great drought*) the Panayia was brought down from the hills to Nicosia, and how, when the image had entered the town, the longed-for rain did as a fact, by a curious coincidence, begin to fall.

....

IV. Tammuz, Adonis, Osiris, Linos, and allied gods of the Babylonians, Hebrews, Egytians, Kyprians, and Greeks.***)
The Asheroth, the Masseboth and Chammanim.

Ištar descends into Hell, to seek the water of life, that she may sprinkle it on the beloved of her soul, Dusi (or Dumusi) and awaken him from death.**) The roots of the legend seem to pierce deep into Pre-Chaldean times, the times of the Accadians or of still earlier inhabitants. Dusi or Dumusi is an Old-Accadian word and means "Son of life".

The same legend of an awakening from death meets us in the ritual of the Babylonians and Assyrians and of the Semitic peoples of Syria and Palestine. In the court of the temple at Jerusalem***) the Jewish women chant the same dirges and carols for Tammuz, as the daughters of Canaan and Phoenicia for Adonis in the temple at Gebal.†) In Egypt the death and resurrection of Osiris are bewept and celebrated in like fashion. ††) The passion of Attis was solemnized in Asia Minor and afterwards with renewed fervour in Rome.†††) The Cretans and Delphians lament and exult for Dionysos§) in the same notes as Homer's hinds and herds for Linos.§§) Everywhere we find the same alternation of passionate sorrow and exuberant joy in these festivals where gods very different in

---

*) Rain-charms must have always played a great part in Cyprus. Both the climatic conditions of the island, and the testimony of inscriptions and other literary sources tell us as much. Besides this Rain-Madonna, the Cypriots still venerate at a place up in the hills and not far from the Panayia tou Kikkou, in the district of Marathoussa (i. e. fenuel-land) a rain-stone. In times of drought, supplicatory processions headed by priests are made to this stone, and on and around the stone curious rites are performed.

Cp. what I say above, in the section on the pomegranate, on the subject of Rimmon, Hadad-Rimmon, and Ramman

**) See Sayce, Religion of the ancient Babylonians, p. 221 ff.; Lenormant in the Memoires du Congrès intern. des Orientalistes; Eb. Schrader, Keilinschriften und das alte Testament, p. 425; Mannhardt, Wald und Feldculte, p. 275; Frazer, Golden Bough, I, p. 287; Roscher's mythol. Lexikon col. 76.

***) Ezekiel 8, 14.

†) Lucian de Syria Dea 6 ff.; Roscher's Lexikon col. 73.

††) Brugsch, Religion &c., p. 623 ff.

†††) The most complete references to the literature of the subject will be found in Roscher's Lexikon, cols. 715 ff.

§) Frazer, The Golden Bough I, 322.

§§) Iliad XVIII, 570.

name, but very near akin in fact die and rise from the dead either at yearly or longer intervals. Everywhere the decay and renewal of vegetation is represented in this dramatic form. Men, trees, or dolls represent the Spirit of Vegetation, the god of the tree. The forms under which he appears are very different in different places and among different peoples, but the main act of the drama is always, more or less, the same. It is the same thought which underlies all these ceremonies, although differences of need, taste and circumstance may modify the form under which it finds expression. Owing to variations of locality and climate, the earlyness or lateness, as the case may be, of seed-time and harvest, and specific peculiarities of race, there arise all manner of local cults, and local names for one and the same thing. The festivals are mostly held either in spring or in late summer and autumn. These local worships and local gods, have a tendency to intermingle. Linos unites with Attis or Adonis, Dusi with Tammuz, Adonis and Osiris with Kinyras, Pygmalion &c. No other country of equally small area supplies such evidences as the island of Cyprus of keen and energetic participation in the process of giving form and name to these spirits and gods of vegetation and in the development of their worships. I must here content myself with referring the reader to some of the principal modern works dealing with the subject and to the stores of literary, monumental and epigraphical testimony which their authors have gathered. The following list makes no pretence to completeness: 1. Engel, Kypros, 2. Movers, Die Phönizier, 3. Mannhardt, (a) Baumcultus, (b) Wald-und Feldculte, 4. Berger, La Phénicie, 5. Baudissin, Semitische Religionsgeschichte, 6. Ermann, Aegypten und ägyptisches Leben, 7. Brugsch, Religion und Mythologie der alten Aegypter, 8. Smith, Religion of the Semites, 9. Frazer, The Golden Bough, 10. Sayce, Religion of the ancient Babylonians, 11. Perrot, Histoire de l'Art dans l'antiquité (I–V), 12. Roscher's Mythologisches Lexikon. As we shall soon see, certain local religious usages, unquestionably derived from antiquity and practised at the present day in Cyprus, more especially by the orthodox Christians, but to some extent by the Mahometans, acquire, in their relation to the annual birth and death of the spirit of Vegetation, and to field-worship, tree-worship and fire-worship, an enhanced significance.

1. Adonis and Tammuz.

I begin with the festival of St. Lazarus, celebrated on the Saturday preceding Palm-Sunday throughout the whole island, but nowhere with such pomp as at Larnaka, where, according to the legend, Lázarus died for the second time and lies buried.*) Mary Magdalen is also said to have come to Cyprus with Lazarus and to have died there. A stone sarcophagus, now empty, in the church of St. Lazarus, is pointed out as the saint's tomb. We are not here so much interested in the festival-mass celebrated inside the church, which is decorated with flowers and branches for the occasion, as in the subsequent procession, which, starting from the church porch, traverses the whole town and has not completed its rounds before a late hour in the night. The death of Lazarus and his awakening from the dead by Christ are dramatically represented. The principal actor is the Lazarus boy (τὸ παιδὶ τοῦ Λαζάρου.) The church-wardens and priests of Lazarus (ἐπίτροποι καὶ παππάδες τοῦ Λαζάρου,) select for this honourable service the most intelligent and beautiful boy in the town. From the flowers of a long-stalked yellow compositum, the Chrysanthemum coronarium,**) which grows in abun-

---

*) Cp. also Riehm's Bibellexikon, p 896.
**) Cp. Unger und Kortschy's Insel Cypern, p. 239.

dance round Larnaka at the time of the festival, and is called by the Cypriots Lazarus-flower (λουλλούδι τοῦ Λαζάρου,) a regular flower-dress is woven, and donned by the Lazarus-boy. The priests, church-attendants, choir-boys and musicians attend him on his progress from house to house through the town. The same ceremony is repeated at each house. The Lazarus-boy throws himself on the ground. People of the higher classes prepare a mattrass decorated with flowers and covered with rugs for him to fall upon. One of the priests or deacons*) then reads the eleventh chapter of St. John's gospel, in which the raising of Lazarus is narrated. When he comes to the words (verse 43) " Lazarus come forth (Λάζαρε ἔξελθε,) the priest of highest ecclesiastical rank among those present sprinkles the Lazarus-boy, who is all the while counterfeiting death, with the holy water which he has at hand. A branch of myrtle is used as a sprinkler. Lazarus comes to life, jumps up, and the carolling begins, flute, guitar, fiddle and tamboutshi**) strike up. The householders throw fragrant rose-water or lemon-water over Lazarus, make presents to the performers, and treat them with wine, brandy, preserved fruits, and fine bread and rolls specially baked for the occasion. The ceremony is hurried over as rapidly as possible, so that the procession may get on to the next house. A longer time is spent in rich houses, while the dwellings of the very poor are left unvisited. So they go on until they have made the round of the whole town. As is known, the word Lazarus is a contraction of the longer Hebrew word " Elasar " (God-help). The raising of Lazarus was viewed as the highest revelation of the splendour and life-giving power of Christ's divinity.***) We think at once of Dumusi, the Akkadian " Son of Life " whom Istar raises from the dead by the virtue of the water of life from the world below; we think of the Adonia, the festival celebrated in diverse fashions in honour of Aphrodite and Adonis, of Astarte and Tammuz, divinities the two chief centres of whose worship were Kypros (Amathus and Idalion especially) in the first place and, next to Kypros, Byblos, the Gebal of the Phoenicians†) on the opposite coast of Syria. The Lazarus ceremony further reminds us of a rite practised in the worship of Ariadne at Amathus, a worship here secondary to or connected with that of Aphrodite. At her festival, which once more fell in the month Gorpiaios, already so frequently referred to, a youth in woman's clothes played the part of Ariadne and lay down in the position of a woman who is in labour and cannot bring forth.

Five weeks previous, however, to the Lazarus-festival—which in Cyprus, where the harvest is early, falls a little before or at the commencement of reaping—comes another spring festival, which we must describe. It falls in the hey-day of the spring, when the corn is well in ear, but still green and the whole country is for a brief time one magic carpet of rich and varied colour. Then, on the first day of Lent, in the early morning. the people of the towns and villages flock out to the corn-

---

*) The deacon in the Greek church is something in the nature of an aspirant to the priesthood. He participates in the performance of the service and wears priest's clothes, but may not himself read mass.

**) The modern Cyprian name for the tambourine.

***) Riehm's Bibellexikon, p. 896.

†) Theocritus (Id. XV) expressly states that King Ptolemy Philadelphus and his wife Arsinoe (probably circa 277 B. C.) instituted the celebration of the Adonia after the Kyprian fashion at their court in Alexandria. Cp. Engel, Kypros II, 538. We shall have frequent occasion to see how old-Kyprian cults most strongly impregnated with Phoenician elements show the closest relationship to the particular cults of Byblos Gebal. Pl. X of this work with its Explanation p. 39 in Dissertation is in itself a sufficiently eloquent witness to this.

fields, taking with them all kinds of Lenten fare, abundance of wine and brandy, and instruments of music. Parties of relatives or friends are made up for the picnic, and those who can afford it hire musicians. Some pretty spot, always in among the green corn where it is most luxuriant, and usually beside a bush or tree, is found. Here all lie down, and the feasting, toasting, singing, playing and dancing begin. The proprietors readily allow the people on this day to lie about in their fields and tread down the corn. Everybody eats too much, gets tipsy, rests at full length in the corn, dances, plays, sings and makes rhymes. Some decorate themselves with anemones and narcissi and other beautiful and fragrant flowers gathered in the corn-fields. Often a youthful couple will steal away for a time from the rest of the company. So the whole day is spent among the loveliness of nature, and glorious weather rarely fails to make enjoyment complete. Then in the evening we see the holiday-makers trooping back home in merry mood, often dancing and leaping for part of the way to the accompaniment of music and song. If there be no other instrument at hand, the tamboutshi, answering to the ancient tympanon, is scarcely ever missing, and nearly always there are pipes or flutes, either brought from home or roughly cut in the fields. They call this spring-festival— a festival of banqueting, singing and dancing—the nose of Lent, and will say when proposing to start on the outing:

Να πᾶμεν νὰ κόψωμεν τὴν μούτι τοῦ σαρακοστιοῦ.

"Let us go and cut Lent's nose off."

That is as much as to say that they desire to celebrate, by an outburst of merriment the beginning of the long fast, and to say good-bye to the flesh (" Carne vale " as they put it in Roman-Catholic countries.) But they also, by this turn of expression, show that they regard Lent itself as a demon or saint—as a person, like the Prince Carneval of the Roman-Catholics.

Another Cyprian festival, in which the month of May is conceived as a person—a male god, hero or demon—is regularly celebrated on the 1st of May. The ceremonies are in this case performed by women and maidens alone, and are met with in a slightly different form elsewhere, chiefly in other parts of the modern Greek world. While the Greeks outside Cyprus call the festival Κλείδονας, *) the Cyprian name for it is "τὸ τραγοῦδι τοῦ Μά" **). On the first of May the girls only of the towns and villages go out into the fields in large parties, lie down in a circle, eat, drink, sing and dance. At the end "Βάζουν τὸν Μᾶν" i. e. they set up the Ma. A vessel of some kind, as good as can be had, is taken, and into it the girls cast their rings, together with pomegranate blossoms afterwards covering it with a red cloth. The vase is left out in the field for three days, and on the third day the girls reassemble on the spot. They preface the ceremony which follows by singing a song, the first words of which are:

The May comes in, the May goes out,

The first of June comes in,

May with its roses,

---

*) Foy described to me this Klidhonas-festival as often witnessed by him in Greece. The word κλήδων should, according to Foy, be connected with κλείειν "to shut" and with the fact that after the vase has been tied up with cord or tape a padlock is always attached to it and locked.

**) Sakellarios Τὰ Κυπριακά. Athen 1890 p. 709.

June with its apples,

August with its warm showers

And with its cool grapes.*)

They then seat themselves on the ground in a circle with the vase in the centre, and it is opened by the youngest of the party. The other girls sing each in turn a couplet either impromptu or from memory, which may be either of serious or of comical, satirical, equivocal, or improper import. As each couplet is recited, the young girl takes out one ring from the vase without looking. The others applaud in proportion as the lines are to the point and appropriate to the girl to whom the ring belongs. It is believed that what the verses say to the owner of the ring will be accomplished, and the whole ceremony is regarded as a kind of fortune-telling or oracle. Friends who were not present will ask the girls who took part in the ceremony what the May foretold to them. The core of this modern festival is certainly ancient, although later accretions have obscured much. We should also in such a case bear in mind that many ancient usages are known to us from the monuments or from modern survivals alone, and not from literary sources. The word Mas here is certainly a contracted form of *Μάϊος*, the month of May. But one thinks involuntarily of the Anatolian goddess Ma (identified with Kybele) of the Greek Maia, the mother of Hermes, of the old Italian goddess of the Spring, Maia and of the Deus Maius at Tusculum. At all events in the silver patera of Kurion (fig. 141) and the bronze patera of Idalion (fig. 40) we have splendid illustrations both of the ancient festival of Adonis on the one hand, and of the modern Ma-festival on the other.

I have above, and it may be correctly, surmised that the paintings of the vase represented p. 94 (fig. 134) may represent a scene from the Adonia, Aphrodite and Adonis being present. We may with complete certainty pronounce the relief on the Kurion silver patera in the Metropolitan Museum of Art in New York (fig. 142) to represent an Adonis festival, rightly recognised as such by the first publisher A. Marquard.**) I am in the agreeable position of being able to supplement his interpretation of the scene. At the altar-table lie two divinities, or two person representing divinities, to the right on the low couch Adonis with the apple, to the left on the higher bed Aphrodite. The vessel on the altar is filled with fruit, flowers or viands. To the left is the corps of female musicians represented by three dancing figures. A fourth female figure behind them carries in her right hand a jug, in her left hand what is either a cake set on a trencher, or one of those "gardens of Adonis" described by ancient writers, and still prepared by the modern Cypriots for use in the Eastern ceremonies. Then follow first a gigantic amphora, and next the altar-table with a vase set on it and decorated with flowers or foliage. The worshippers approach it with measured steps. The first bears in her extended palms dishes of fruit or flowers or "gardens of Adonis," the second carries two bags and the third two domestic fowls.

---

*) *Καὶ 'μπαίνν' ὁ Μᾶς καὶ βκαίνν' ὁ Μᾶς*

καὶ 'μπαίνν' ὁ Πρωτογιούνης,

καὶ ὁ Μᾶς μὲ τὰ τραντάφυλλα

καὶ ὁ Γιούνης μὲ τὰ μῆλα

καὶ ὁ Άουστος μὲ τὰ χλιὰ νερὰ

καὶ τὰ κρύα σταφύλια.

**) American Journal of Archaelogy. 1888. P. 169—171 with plate VII. An archaic patera from Kourion.

A bird, perhaps a dove, is flying behind these three figures and in the same direction. The leader of the choric procession seems to be about to empty into the vase standing on the table the flowers she holds in her extended left hand. The rest of the outer zone is missing, the fragment of a figure still visible behind the recumbent Adonis being difficult to make out. Of the middle zone also only a part remains. An archer, perhaps the god Resef-Apollo aims at one of the quadrupeds. Two other quadrupeds, one of which would seem to be a lion, the other a winged griffin, look up at the holy tree which one would think, is intentionally placed immediately under Aphrodite. Of the innermost zone only the ends of two lotus-flowers or papyrus-stalks are preserved. All the figures in the outer zone are, it is to be noted, with the exception of Adonis, female.

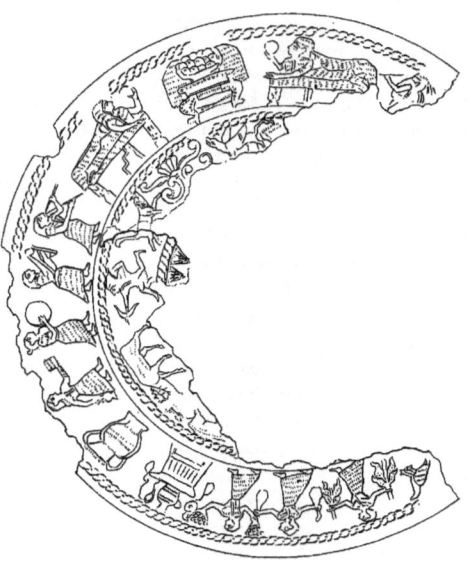

Fig. 142.

On the Idalion bronze charger (p. 46, fig. 49) they are again only women (dancing-girls and musicians) who, beneath the trees of a holy grove, dance in a circle round the seated image of Aphrodite, her altar and church-plate. The leader of the dance reaches out the hand which is free to grasp the neck of one of the two vases standing on the four-footed altar-table. The priestess who performs the sacrifice stands between this table and the large tripod of altar form so obviously analogous to the altar loaded with fruit on the other patera. The seated goddess or her locum tenens, a priestess invested with her attributes, holds a flower and a fruit. We cannot help thinking of the Adonia, and the festivals of Aphrodite in which only women took part. The vessel towards which the "première danseuse" is reaching out her hand reminds us directly of the vessel round which the Cyprian girls dance, into which they throw their rings and the blossoms of the pomegranate, and from which after three days they receive the oracular confirmation of the rhymes they rehearse with their own lips, singing and dancing the while.

Below on Plate LXXXIII, 6 will be found a relief on which is represented the celebration on a hill-side of a similar festival in honour of Apollo.*) The lime-stone votive slab, was, as the two holes near the upper edge show, suspended, like other Cyprian inscribed slabs (e. g. the Phoenician temple-tariffs from the sanctuary of Astarte on the Akropolis of Kition = C. I. S. 86 A and B: I

*) Cesnola-Stern XXVI, 3.

discuss them below), suspended in a grove—here the grove of Apollo at Athiaenou. Below to the right we see first the pilgrims reclining in a circle, just like a group of modern Cypriots lying at their case out in the fields, They are feasting and drinking. Immediately to the left is a second scene, that of the ring-dance. Above this three pairs of worshippers ascend the hill in procession to the mountain-altar, which has the form of a large omphalos. On it is seated either Apollo with the lyre or the high-priest as the god's representative. Although this votive slab is dedicated to Apollo, the scenes here depicted are, as it were, the complements of those on our two previous illustrations, and throw light not only on the worship of Apollo, but on the allied ceremonies of the Aphrodite and Adonis cult. Feasting, it may be remarked, has always played a great part in Cyprian life. In a Greek inscription of late date found at Larnaka the memory of a cook is perpetuated,[*]) and at the present day Cyprian cooks are in especial demand among the Embassies, Consulates and other foreign families of distinction in the East. I can indeed myself testify to their skill. The early Autumn, the months of August and September, is still a season of especial sanctity in Kypros, and it is noteworthy that an inscription, found in the Apollo-temenos at Voni and reproduced in uncial and cursive above on p. 5, chronicles the performance by certain societies of a series of sacrifices (presumably to Apollo) in the month of Gorpiaeos, which fell at this very season. (I there inadvertently stated Gorpiaeos to be a Cyprian month. It is, of course, originally a Macedonian month, and only secondarily Cyprian. Of the old Cyprian calendar, expelled by the Macedonian, we know very little.) The inscription should, perhaps, be written as follows:

LF *Γορπίο(υ) θίασος*
τῆς ἀποσκευῆς
ἔθυσεν τὸ ἱερέον.
LΔ *τὸ ἱερέον ὁ θία-*
σος τῶν Ἡδυλλίων.
LE *ὁ θίασος τῶ[ν]*
Κισάων τὸ ἱερέον.

The form of the letters points to a time before the Christian Era, and possibly as early as the 2nd century B. C.

The sign L before a number is commonly used at this time to indicate either the year of an era or the year of a king's reign. It would seem that in three successive years of a certain king's reign sacrifices of sheep (*ἱερέον* usually means a sheep) were performed in the month Gorpiaeos, each time by a different society. The *θίασος τῆς ἀποσκευῆς* may be the "society of temple-scavengers." In the names of the second and third thiasi the *Ἡδύλλιοι* and *Κίσαοι* it is scarcely possible to recognize anything but proper names The readings are certain, and the word *Κισάων* is complete in itself, as nothing beyond the final of the article *τῶν* can have been lost in. One would rather desire to find in the names of these two thiasi some indication of services performed by them in the temple analogous to the services performed by the thiasus *τῆς ἀποσκευῆς* Among the modern Cypriots many strange usages and beliefs are attached to the months of August and September. The first five days of August are thought to be unlucky. On the night of the 5th of August it is believed that heaven

---

*) Cesnola-Stern, p. 387, No. 45 (read by D. Pierides).

opens, and it is the custom to keep vigil for this night.*) On the fifteenth of August falls the great festival of the Panayia, the Assumption called " Photou " at Ayios Andronikos. A little later comes the festival of St. Andrew at the monastery of the same name in the extreme North-East of the island, not far from Cape Andrea.**) Among ourselves, as we know, all kinds of heathen Old-Germanic survivals cluster about this very festival of St. Andrew. In modern Cyprian festivals we find similar traces

Fig. 143.

of old-world heathendom. The rites practised by Greeks and Phoenicians thousands of years ago, at the festivals of Resef-Apollo, of Astarte and Tammuz, of Aphrodite and Adonis still live before our eyes.

On the outer zone of a hitherto too little noticed bronze patera, we see a series of scenes which may well belong to that voluptuous ritual of Aphrodite-Adonis, the religious elements in which were too apt to be merged in the profane. While on the patera (fig. 142) of which we have just been speaking there is nothing to remind us of Egypt or to suggest an Egyptian original but the papyrus and lotus ornaments on the central medallion***), the Egyptian influence in the present case

---

*) Cp. Sakellarios, *Τὰ Κυπριακά*, p. 770.

**) See above p. 27.

***) The central medallion is occupied by a scene borrowed by Oriental Art, with which it is a favourite, from Egyptian Art, viz. the scourging of prisoners by an Egyptian king. We have already observed this scene on the Kurion bowl (fig. 52, p. 53) and we shall find it again on the Praeneste bowl (Plate LXXIX, 1). Birch perhaps correctly identifies the god Ra on the right with the Cyprian Rešef of whom, however, we have a further and more obvious equivalent in the Egyptian god Raspu. I think that both assimilations are possible and in a high degree probable,

is tolerably pronounced. The patera was published in A. P. di Cesnola's Salaminia. To the detailed and very admirable description of its chasings there given (p. 51 ff.) by Mr. Birch I am able to contribute one or two addenda. The principal scene of the outer zone is directly above the medallion. In front of an object which is too much damaged to be described we see seated on a throne a goddess with a child.*) It is either Isis with Osiris, Istar with Tammuz or Aphrodite κουροτρόφος with the babe Adonis.

A priest approaches her with a jug which he has just filled with water or wine from the sacred vessel set upon the tripod behind him.**) The goddess is approached from behind by a procession led by a priestess in an attitude of adoration, and closed by a waitress who carries a basin and ewer containing the libations. A third female personage plays the tambourine. On the Cyprian monuments, as in the Old Testament narrative, the office of playing on this instrument is nearly always performed by women or girls. We see it here, as we often hear it in Cyprus and the East at the present day, unaccompanied by any other instrument. Between the leader of the procession and the musician two men advance, the first raising one arm, but carrying, it would seem, nothing, the second bearing aloft with both hands a votive offering of some kind. This group is separated from the following by a small tree.

We here see on a bed in the centre a figure obviously meant for one of those hieroduli or hetaerae who played so great a part in the festivals of Aphrodite. She is approached by two men carrying between them, suspended from a pole resting on their shoulders, a large amphora. Behind the recumbent female, who invites to dalliance, a man is carrying off in his arms a woman whom he has selected for himself in the grove of Aphrodite. This group is again shut off from the next by a tree or candelabrum. We here see first a man seated on a chair and drinking from a kylix. Next follows one of those love scenes which must almost universally have been associated with festivals of Aphrodite in Kypros. A couple on a couch are engaged in amorous converse.***) It is difficult here in some cases to distinguish what is religious from what is profane, and the same confusion must have pervaded the festivals of Aphrodite and Adonis. Often religious ceremonies were only a cloak for the satisfaction of the grosser appetites.

In the third section of this chapter we shall concern ourselves with the figured anthropomorphic representations of Adonis-Tammuz, himself of the temple-boys who represent this god, and of allied beings such as Attis and Kinyras, while the fourth section will deal with the various names and functions of this family of heroic, demonic or divine children. It will there be necessary to say something as to their mother. Before treating of the anthropomorphic images, it will be best in the following section (2) to complete our review of the holy posts, columns, trees and gardens which characterize or symbolize the various divinities, serving sometimes as their attributes or the gifts they receive, sometimes as aniconic representations of their persons.

---

*) Cp. the same goddess on the Olympia bowl (Pl. CXXIX, 2).

**) Cp. the water-vessels on the cups fig. 142 and 49.

***) These scenes of figures on a bed are not uncomm onon a certain class of Cyprian sepulchral reliefs, where they are frequently surmounted by either one or two lions, sphinxes &c. A fine specimen of the class was found in 1884, while I was in Cyprus, in a tomb at Athiainou. I acquired it, and it is now in the Antiquarium of the Royal Berlin Museum.

2. Aoïa-Adonis-Aphrodite Trees; Attis-Artemis Trees. Gardens of Adonis. The Asheroth, Masseboth and Chammanim

a) Trees in the groves of Aphrodite and Artemis.

The day succeeding the Cyprian festival of St. Lazarus described above is Palm-Sunday. I regret that I neglected to acquire, draw or photograph any examples of those ornamental "palm-branches," plaited into all kinds of fantastical and elegant forms, which are carried into church to be blessed on this occasion. We have in them the original types, still surviving after thousands of years, of certain Tree-agalmata of the Babylonians and Assyrians and of much of that arboreal ornament which passed into the Art of Greece. These types, consecrated by their use in Pagan festivals, have been handed down from year to year, perhaps unchanged as regards both form and material, to the festivals of the Christian church at the present day.*)

Holwerda in his paper on Corinthian and Attic vases**) attemps to show how certain arboreal ornaments and motives on Corinthian vases and Assyrian cylinders and reliefs are derived from work in metal. The smith produced such designs from wire, and these designs were imitated in other materials by the sculptors, stone-cutters and painters. I cannot assent to this view. However plausible the hypothesis may seem, it is as little tenable as the assertion frequently made that the incised ornaments of geometric style employed by Ceramic Art—a technique which reached the highest perfection in ancient Cyprus—are borrowed from the art of engraving on metal. There are whole find-strata in which, while rectilinear geometrical patterns occur on the pottery and convolute patterns on the clay or stone cylinders the stone reliefs and the pottery, yet no trace of a metal vase or of work in wire has been met with. These ancient series of tombs are in part earlier than the use of copper, in part they fall within the limits of the Copper and Bronze Periods; but from the discovery of the arts of smelting copper and mixing bronze to the fabrication of metal wire and metal vessels the way is a long one. All such early essays in decoration are originally borrowed by workers in clay and stone from the still more primitive techniques of wood-work, rush-work or palm-plaiting. For further details see the Descriptions of Plates XXXIV and XXXV.***) Even assuming that, at the date of the Corinthian vases, and at the earlier date of Asurnasirpals tree-designs, metal wire and engraved vases of metal could have been fabricated; even regarding it as established that at a certain period the forms and technique of the metal vases did influence Ceramics, we must with certainty pronounce the early Greek ornaments adduced by Holwerda (cp. the illustrations scattered through the text on p. 240 of the Jahrbuch) to be imitated not from plaited wire, but from palm-plaiting, or other plaited work composed of leaves, rushes or twigs. They are derived from the Assyrian repertory, from the conventional plaited work of the holy trees and the profane decoration which sprung therefrom. Photographs of the Cyprian Easter palms plaited by the women and girls for the approaching holiday would distinctly rank as illustrations of the holy trees represented on Assyrian monuments,†) and would illustrate almost as strikingly the holy trees of the reliefs on Cyprian silver paterae††) and those on Egyptian paintings.†††)

While this conventional holy tree, produced by the crossing and combination of coniferous trees, palms and various forms of the lotus, is represented for us by the numerous trees on the Cyprian silver patera (fig. 52) and silver girdle (Pl. XXV) and by the modern Cyprian Easter palms, the twelve terracottas figured on Plate LXXVI§) bring before us trees of more realistic form answering to those Aoia (Ἀοῖα) or Eoa (Ἠῶα) which, according to Hesychius, (s. v. Ἀοῖα) were felled for Aphro-

---

*) Cp. above pages 84 and 99.
**) Jahrbuch V. p. 240.
***) Cp. my Address: "Parallelen in den Gebräuchen der alten und der jetzigen Bevölkerung von Cypern" in the Proceedings of the Berliner Anthropologische Gesellschaft 1891. p. 34—44.
†) Figs. 130, 136 and 137.
††) Figs. 50—52.
†††) Figs. 106 and 107.
§) Pl. LXXVI 7 = Pl. XVII, 1.

18

dite and set up at the entrances to her temples.*) Ao (᾿Αῶ) is also another name of the god Adonis
and Aoos ("Αωος) the name of a Cyprian king and of a Cyprian river. The mythical Cyprian kings
are called Aooi (Ἄωοι).**) When we find trees, rivers, gods and kings called by the same name, we
may look upon this as tolerably clear evidence of some transition from dendromorphic to anthropomorphic worships or of the reverse process. More than fifty years ago, Engel, relying exclusively on
literary sources, distinguished two kinds of holy trees, viz. Attis-trees and Adonis-trees, the pine being
proper to Attis, the cedar to Adonis. I have excavated in various sanctuaries tree-idols and groups
of figures dancing round such idols, and at a time when I had not yet read Engel's remarks, I had
already distinguished two kinds of such tree-idols. G. Colonna Ceccaldi also mentions the discovery
by Lang at Pyla of limestone groups of priestesses dancing round a cypress (?)***) My enquiries
have established that both in Artemis-groves and in Aphrodite-groves little tree-idols of clay (imitations
of real trees of large size, not growing but felled, like our May trees and Christmas trees)†) were set
up near altars, at the entrances of the sanctuary, and in the votive areas. Owing to the rudeness of
the workmanship it is rarely possible to decide what kind of tree is meant to be represented, but it
is certain that the idols which were dedicated in the groves of Artemis differ essentially, as regards
both form and colouring, from those dedicated to Aphrodite. Of the twelve specimens figured on
Plate LXXVI, Nos. 1 and 2 come from the sanctuary of Artemis-Kybele at Akhna excavated by me
in 1882.††) I found here the fragments of at least 80 such tree-idols, their height averaging about
13 cm. (= 5 in.). On Plate LXVIII 7 the upper portion of No. 1 is again reproduced in colours; all
the fragments bore traces of similar black and red colouring. We are to understand the tree to be
of dark, almost black, colour with brownish-red trunk and branches. These tree-idols were all
deposited at the north-west end of the votive area (see Pl. IV, 1). The largest pile of them lay at
the spot marked SAC. It was the custom in all the older Cyprian places of worship to make, in
addition to the great burnt-offerings on the high altar, minor burnt-offerings in the votive area beside
the votive images there erected. Here also incense was burnt, lamps were lighted, and numerous
little vessels found in these spaces may have contained consecrated water or salt. These dark-brown
and red tree-idols were found some of them close to such a place of sacrifice, the rest actually within
it.†††) As the tree-idols in the groves of Aphrodite-Astarte are of quite another character and have
not this dark colouring, or indeed any colouring at all, we can not be far wrong in saying that these
Artemis-Kybele trees are fir-idols, idols of Attis. In spite of their rudeness I think I can detect in
these images the attempt to represent the Caramanian black fir (Pinius Laricio) §) the tree of which
the Cyprian mountain-forests, at an altitude of about 1500 metres and upwards, mainly consist—glorious

---

*) Engel, Kypros II p. 558. Cp. p. 86 above.
**) Pape's Wörterbuch der griechischen Eigennamen, p. 188.
***) Monuments antiques de Chypre, de Syrie et d'Égypte, p. 21.
    †) Cp. p. 86 above and figs. 4, 5 and 116.
   ††) Cp. p. 1 above.
  †††) On the plan (Plate IV) the sites of such little burnt-offerings in the votive area, recognizable by
the layers of charred matter and ashes found there, are indicated by dotted circles. FL are places where fires
and lamps (always of the old shell shape) were kept burning. As spots marked TG small vessels stood, Ph
signifies phalli or phallus-shaped vases. The tree-idols therefore lay close to the lamps, vessels and phalli
Coloured illustrations of some of these phallic vases are given on Plate LXVIII, 8—10.
    §) Cp. my paper "Cyperns Wälder- und Waldwirthschaft" in the Ausland 1881, p. 744.

forests where one can well imagine oneself present at festivals of Attis and Kybele. In the neighbourhood of these tree-idols numbers of phalli, represented as abscised, were deposited.*) These objects have not been found in precincts of Aphrodite-Astarte, and their occurrence here points to a ritual specifically belonging to Artemis-Kybele-Attis, a ritual in which not only the tree and its erection but the organ of generation and the act of emasculation were symbolised in these little, easily handled clay images. Fragments of trees and very numerous fragments of phalli were found by me in nearly all the Artemis-Kybele groves (Nos. 10—14) described above on pages 11 and 12. Phalli and vases of phallic form were especially numerous at Pharangas (No. 14 on p. 12). Plate LXVIII, 9 shows the upper end of a hand-made phallus the form, size and colouring of which are tolerably realistic (this portion of the Plate has been printed a little too dark). In Plate LXVIII, 10 we see an adaptation of this form. It is a little wheel-made vase still bearing a distinct resemblance to the extremity of a phallus. No. 8, on the same plate is a vase the form of which would scarcely suggest the phallus, did not the numerous variants representative of intermediary stages found at the same spot determine the true significance of the form. These phallic emblems are, as I have said, attached exclusively to the groves of Artemis-Kybele; they do not occur in groves consecrated to other deities, and are likewise entirely absent from the tombs. They are cultus-objects of the Artemis-Kybele worship in Kypros. If (as is sure some day to be the case) yet another grove of Artemis-Kybele be excavated in the Eastern half of the island, in that grove other specimens of these black-fir or pine idols, of these phalli and phallic vases, will inevitably be unearthed. They attest the myth of Attis, who unsexed himself under a pine, and bring before our eyes in an emblematic and gentler form the savage and sanguinary ritual of Asia Minor and especially of Phrygia.**) While in the Kyprian groves of Astarte-Aphrodite anthropomorphic images of Adonis invariably occur, such images of Attis or of his temple-ministrants are quite absent from the groves of Tanit-Artemis-Kybele-Hekate-Agdistis. The god is always here conceived as a tree***)- a pine—, as in early Phrygian religion. It is no matter of surprise that out of Kybele, whose worship was indeed orgiastic but at the same time inculcated sexual restraint and even the sacrifice of sex, the island Greeks made their chaste and pure Artemis with all her virginal charm. Yet it is none the less instructive to come across in an island so permeated by Aphroditic elements as Kypros clear proof, supplied by numerous monuments and by the excavation of entire temene, of the existence of a worship of Artemis-Kybele, clearly deriving its origin from Salamis and the royal house of Salamis,†) and, in its sublimated and pure Hellenic form, linked during the first half of the fourth century B. C. with the name of the hero-king and reformer Euagoras I. The style of the monuments fixes their date at this period.††) But in the second half of the fourth century, not long after the death of Euagoras, these groves of Artemis-Kybele-Attis, with their pine-idols of

---

*) A similar custom prevailed in the sanctuary of one of the Kyprian Apollos, Apollo Melathios or Melanthios (= Opaon-Melanthios), at Amaryetti. See Hogarth, "Excavations in Cyprus" in the Journal of Hellenic Studies VIII (1885), p. 173. For the deposition of phalli in Kyprian sanctuaries of Aphrodite see Engel Kypros II. p. 141.

**) Cp. Ramsay's article "Phrygia" in the Encyclopaedia Britannica XVIII, 835; Frazer, The Golden Bough I, 300; Roscher's Mythologisches Lexikon, col. 715 ff.

***) Cp. Smith, Religion of the Semites, p. 174.

†) Traces also occur elsewhere, e. g. in Kition. Cp. No. 7 above on p. 11.

††) Cp. the Plates illustrating the Artemis-Kybele temenos I, 1.

Attis and their images of a goddess attended by a stag, buck or dog, cease to be. It would seem that the Kinyrads, in their devotion to the voluptuous rites of Astarte-Aphrodite, expended their iconoclastic fury on these groves of Artemis and swept them away. The imperfect character of the reports on the excavation make it difficult to pronounce at the present day who was the goddess venerated in the grove where, according to the passage cited above from Ceccaldi, Lang dug up the group of women dancing round a holy tree. In general it would seem that, where Artemis is, there we meet with the pine or black-fir, the cypress, cedar and palm being associated with Astarte-Aphrodite. Did not the black colouring of the Akhna idols point to their being black-firs, we might recognise in them Cyprian cypresses (Cupressus horizontalis).

The remaining ten specimens (3—12) on Plate LXXVI all come from groves of Astarte-Aphrodite. Figs. 5 and 9 are from the sanctuary of this goddess near Idalion excavated in 1885 (No. 3 in my list; see p. 5). These seem to be two tree-idols which have never belonged to a ring-dance, but were separately moulded and are complete in themselves, as is the rule with the Attis-trees in the temene of Artemis. The other specimens on the plate (3, 4, 6—8, 10—12) are all taken from the sanctuary of Astarte at Chytroi described above on p. 14 (No. 24). I myself dug up nos. 3, 4, 6, 10—12; the originals are now in the Cyprus Museum at Nicosia. No. 8 I pieced together from several fragments. No. 7, now in the University Museum at Bonn, was found on the same spot by the peasants. Four of the idols, figs. 4, 10, 11, 12, are so much damaged that all conjecture as to the kind of tree represented is useless. Nos. 5 (Idalion) and 6 (Chytroi) rather suggest a palm, Nos. 9 (Idalion) and 3 (Chytroi) a sprouting cedar, No. 7 (Chytroi) a young Cyprian cypress (Cupressus horizontalis). In the last case the identification seems tolerably certain. All the tree-idols from Chytroi here figured are broken off ring-dance groups consisting of three women dancing round the tree, as shown in the reconstruction, fig. 8. Fig. 9, again from Chytroi, would appear also to represent a palm. Figs. 4 and 6 resemble the palm-columns of the shrine or dovecote of Astarte (with the figure of the goddess, half bird half woman, standing in the doorway) found at Idalion and figured above on Plate X, No. 3. The Idalion idol with the point chipped off, fig. 5, is also not dissimilar, although the branches are here more pendant. Two other Idalion tree-idols, figs. 5 and 9, (now in the Antiquarium of the Royal Berlin Museum) were found, together with the censer of columnar form figured on Pl. XVII (fig. 4), in the layer of ashes and charred matter which marked the site of the altar of burnt-offering (S on Plate IV) at the spot *ta*.

In these ten tree-images, with and without figures dancing round them, (Pl. LXXVI 3—12) we must certainly see representations of holy trees or at least of trees which played some part in the worship of Astarte-Aphrodite and Tammuz-Adonis. They are copies in clay of the 'Αοΐα or 'Ηῶα, as described by Hesychius, felled trees erected at the entrances of temples. The locality of their discovery speaks for this. In the holy precinct excavated at Idalion the open space where stood the altar of burnt-offering (Pl. IV S) is flanked by a space (Pl. VIII, H) in which we must conceive a primitive roofed sanctuary to have once stood.*) The tree-idols lay therefore on the spot where

---

*) Cp. also Plate X. The foundation-walls of the elongated space on the south, H, are stronger than the other foundation walls. Wherever a heavier load had to be supported or increased lateral pressure came into play, especially at the corners, the builders, who elsewhere used sun-dried bricks, employed lime-mortar, which still remains. The same method of building is still in vogue in Cyprus even in towns). The spots in

Hensychius tells us that the felled trees were erected and (let us add) burnt, viz. at the entrance to the sanctuary. At Akhna also (Pl. IV) most of the tree-idols were lying in a heap at the North-west corner of the votive area*) (at points *SAC)* in the layer of ashes and charred material.

This Cyprian custom of erecting trees beside the altar of burnt-offering in the courtyard of a temple, or in unroofed holy places of the nature of groves, and burning these trees as offerings to the deity**) stands in the closest conceivable connection with the Ashera-worship of the Bible. As however, both in literary and monumental tradition, it is often difficult to separate the Ashera from the Masseba and Chammanim—the holy wooden posts, wooden columns, wooden crosses and wooden cones from their counterparts in stone—we must (in Section c) survey from a common point of view the various objects of worship so frequently set up near altars on hills and under green trees be the material of these objects stone or wood. Before proceeding to do so, we shall gain (in Section b) a closer acquaintanceship with the Gardens of Adonis and the offerings of flowers, fruit and viands which accompanied the celebration of the Adonia.

b) Gardens of Adonis, Offerings of flowers, fruit and viands.

At the splendid festival of Adonis, celebrated, according to Kyprian usage, at Alexandria by Ptolemy Philadelphus***) and his queen Arsinoe, the images of Aphrodite and Adonis were laid side by side on a couch. Beside and around them lay fruits of all kinds, gardens in silver baskets, cakes

---

question are distinguished on the plan by the letters *ce* and a divergent technique. (For further details see the explanations appended to Pl. VII). Walls of sun-dried bricks were superimposed on the stone foundation walls of the southern space *H*, but these upper courses of brick are absent from the walls of the two spaces on the North, *S* and *V*. As the land, rich garden-land, has been for long under cultivation, the soil had been disturbed down to the foundation-walls, and even some pieces of these walls removed in places where the cultivators had dug deeper than elsewhere. This was in fact the way in which the sanctuary was discovered by them in 1884 and its excavation in the following year rendered possible. It is no wonder therefore that I no longer found any bricks here. In other neighbouring places on the contrary, e. g. on the Eastern Akropolis of Idalion I found evidences of brick structure. The excavated area belongs to two different peasants; the lower northern portion (*S* and *V* on the Plan) is the property of one man, the higher southern portion (*H*) that of another. On the line of demarcation of the two properties, a bank with a northern slope of about one metre in height, trees are planted, as may be seen in the view, Pl. XVI. The layer of rubbish covering the actual primitive sanctuary (*H*) with its thesauri. priest's houses &c. was therefore of considerably greater depth that that covering the space in which stood the altar of burnt-offering (*S*), and the votive area (*V*). I consider it therefore to be an attested fact that the sanctuary had higher walls and was roofed, while the altar-space and votive space (the latter enclosed on two sides only by a light portico with wooden columns $= V^2$) remained unroofed.

*) The soil on the Northern side had been removed long ago in order to extend and provide the means of irrigating another garden lying at a lower level. I therefore cannot say where and what was the limit of the holy precinct at this spot. As the altar *A*, on which, as the excavation tells us, no burnt offerings, but only, it would seem, bloodless offerings of fruit &c. were made, stood before the Eastern entrance (*E*) the altar of burnt-offering must, I think, have been similarly situated on the North.

**) Lang unearthed in his Resef-Apollo sanctuary (see No. 30 on p. 10) a large charred tree-trunk now in the British Museum.

***) A Greek inscription from Kition of the time of Ptolemy Euergetes (first published by me in the Heimath 1881, p. 347) names also his parents Ptolemy Philadelphus and Arsinoe. Cp. Reinach, Chroniques d'Orient, p. 174 [5², 344—334]. It runs as follows.

Βασιλέα Πτολεμαῖον, θεὸν Εὐεργέτην τὸν ἐγ βασιλέων
Πτολεμαίου καὶ Ἀρσινόης θεῶν Φιλαδέλφων τὸν ἑαυτῶν προστάτην
οἱ ἀπὸ Γυμνασίου.

made of meal honey and oil, and all kinds of (baked?) animals flying and creeping. Such are almost the very words of Theocritus, a true witness*) The Kyprian worship of Adonis with all its apparatus found its way to Athens as to Alexandria. Beside the bier of Adonis stood the Adonis-gardens (Ἀδώνιδος κῆποι), baskets or pots filled with earth in which were growing all kinds of young plants (flowers, corn, fennel and lettuce) forced from seed by eight days' exposure to a strong sun. These gardens round the bier of Adonis were called at Athens ἐπιτάφιοι **)

I have above on p. 102 had occasion to indicate what great dimensions the worship of Adonis attained at Rome and Palmyra in late imperial times. Christianity was at this date a powerful force. The bishops resorted to tactics of two kinds in order to convert the heathen. One plan was to destroy the sites of pagan worships, to eradicate the pagan rites and replace them by those of the Christian church. The other policy was to permit such of the pagan usages as were not diametrically opposed to Christian doctrine to continue, absorbing them into the body of Christian ritual. Only when, as I have shown to be the case with the Cyprian Lazarus ceremony, old pagan myths and rites seemed as if specially created to supply the elements for the embodiment of Christian ideas, to make the miracles of the Saviour live before our eyes or to adorn the worship of the Saints, were the fathers of the church ready and anxious to transfer quite mechanically what they found among the pagans to the service of their own religion. Anyone who has lived long in the East among the people and kept his eyes open, knows to what an extent traditional usage there is ossified. The remark applies to all sects alike, to Islam as well as Christianity. Islam, as we know only reached Cyprus in the 16th century on the expulsion of the Venetians by the Turks (1570—1571); but the Greek Orthodox Churchs is here of great antiquity, dating back to the age of the Apostles the contemporaries of Christ. We learn this from the New Testament and from the traditions and legends of ecclesiastical writers.***) The numerous finds made in the island of early episcopal seals† and early Byzantine inscribed lamps, would, in the absence of other testimony, suffice to teach us the same lesson. Two very early and precious Byzantine gold rings, a pair of Byzantine ear-rings and a gold cross hung on a chain, found all together in a tomb at Kerynia (formerly a see), are now in the Museum at Nicosia. I have excavated quantities of poorer Byzantine tombs, and have constantly met with Byzantine antiquities of all kinds. Everything tends to show that Christianity was fastly rooted throughout the whole island, while the Christianisation of the surrounding coast of Asia and Afrika did not progress by any means so uniformly. The island at the present day is essentially Christian. The figures of the last English census††) tell us that of a total population of 186,173 souls, no fewer than 137,631 belong to the Greek orthodox church, 45,458 being Mahomedans (the small remaining fraction is composed of members of various Christian sects and 68 Jews)—While the Christian church could not but view with repugnance and unhesitatingly reject many of the usages connected with the worship of Astarte-Aphrodite, she found no difficulty in adopting such rites of the Adonis-worship as bore upon the pure and marital association (and this was the most prominent) of Aphrodite and Adonis. Though the cakes, the steeped corn made luscious with fruit—all the dainties laid on the table of Adonis and consumed by his devotees—are lost to us (for embalming was never the practice in Kypros), though his gardens, that withered even in less time than it took them to spring into life, have vanished into nought, yet the festival of Adonis with all its accessories still lives in the festivals of the Greek Church in Cyprus. Many of the practices which I now describe may be found existing by Oriental travellers elsewhere than in Cyprus; but many others, and among them some of the most characteristic, have either been peculiar to Cyprus from the beginning, or have here been preserved in a more or less unimpaired form, while in other Oriental localities they have either long

---

*) Idyll XV, 112. Cp. p. 128 above and Mannhardt, Wald- und Feldculte p. 278. See also Roscher's Mytholog. Lexikon, col. 74.

**) Mannhardt, p. 279.

***) The Apostle Barnabas, a Levite from Cyprus (Acts IV, 36) suffered martyrdom in his native island (Riehm, Bibellexikon p. 150). In the time of the emperor Zeno, the discovery at Constantia (Salamis) of the Apostle's body with the gospel of St. Matthew on its breast was the occasion for a synodic decree pronouncing the Greek church in Cyprus to be independent. Barnabas and Paul (Acts XIII, 4—13) traverse the island preaching the gospel. Lazarus and Mary Magdalene also ended their lives in Cyprus. (Riehm, Bibellexikon, p. 896).

†) Cp. D. Pierides, "The early bishops of Cyprus" in the Owl 1888, pages 58 and 59.

††) Cp. F. W. Barry's Report on the Census of Cyprus (London 1884.)

ago disappeared or, if they have survived, have survived as meagre rudiments of themselves. I must not here transgress the limits of space, and will content myself with refering to Schmidt's Volksleben der Neu-Griechen und des Hellenischen Alterthumes (Leipzig 1871) for all that concerns a comparison of Cyprian usage with that of the modern kingdom of Greece and of other modern Greek settlements.*)

It is still generally the custom in Cyprus, at many feasts, but especially at Easter, to sow wheat in pots, potsherds and baskets, and to make it sprout rapidly by means of frequent watering and constant exposure to the sun. These green Adonis-gardens are consecrated in the church by the priests. Many are allowed to remain in the church or monastery; others are brought back home, and placed in some position of honour in the house, either under the mirror in the best room or in the recess where the image of the Panayia stands. Here they are left until they fade, which usually happens very soon. The Lazarus-festival is representative of only one act of the Adonis-drama, the resurrection. In the ceremonies practised on Good Friday and Easter day the relics of both acts —the lamentation for the dead god and the exultation at his restoration to life—have survived. On the evening of Good Friday the procession of the ἐπιτάφιον passes through the streets by the light of torches and tapers. Large and wealthy churches possess a figure of the dead Christ which is placed at full length on a bier decorated with green branches and beautiful flowers. Sometimes the bier is surmounted by a baldachin of carved wood or reeds, all round which flowers are twined. Or a canopy composed entirely of branches and flowers may be built up for this occasion. When there is no image of Christ, it is replaced by a cross laid on the bier. Many of these Easter sepulchres, or ἐπιτάφια as they are called, may rank as master-pieces of the art of floral decoration such as the skilled gardeners of many an Europaean capital might well be proud of. Cakes made of meal honey and oil, many of them shaped like feathered or creeping things were baked, as Theocritus tells us, for those Alexandrine Adonia which King Ptolemy Philadelphus celebrated according to the Cyprian rite. Just such cakes are baked in our own day by the Cyprian women for the Easter festival. My cook would have given me warning and thought me no Christian to boot, had I ventured to forbid her baking the Easter cakes and Easter bread. She used to take the dough plentifully sprinkled with sesame and mould it into all kinds of figures, either rude doll-like men or beasts: of these birds, crabs, snakes and tortoises were her favourites.

Another custom current in a simple form in other parts of the Greek word, e. g. at Rhodes**) is more elaborately and more frequently observed in Cyprus. No church festival no Sunday is free from it. It is attached to people's name-day to and their patron saints. It is an intimate part of the worship of the dead which no Cyprian Greek could indeed conceive of as existing without it. One of the most terrible curses known to the Cyprian-Greek language is this—"Νὰ φάω τὰ κόλυβά σου,' —"May I eat your Kolyva," i. e. I wish you may perish, or, to be still plainer, I threaten you with

---

*) As Schmidt did not know Cyprus personally, he here relies on Sakellarios' Κυπριακά, a work in which a long series of interesting habits and customs is collected. Most of those described in the present work were either hitherto quite unknown or imperfectly described by Sakellarios. Some, however, of our descriptions, e. g. that of the Ma festival, will be found to correspond almost exactly with those of Sakellarios. The fact that so many highly interesting customs have escaped this observer, who spent many active years of his life in Cyprus as a village and town school-master, may serve as an excuse for my own oversights. Now that I am here at home again, I can see how I erred in attaching no value to and leaving unobserved many usages now current in Cyprus, which could throw a welcome light on some of the dark spots of Antiquity.

**) Newton, Travels and discoveries in the Levant I, p. 214.

death, I kill you, so that then when you have ceased to be I may in memory of your life eat your Kolyva, the Kolyva which are yours in the sense that they are representative of your corpse. In every village which boasts of a church one of the peasants on each Sunday has to make at his own expense fine wheaten loaves (usually five or ten) and the Kolyva. The loaves are sugared and made without yeast. He stamps each of them in the centre with the church seal lent to him for this purpose. According to the means of the sacrificant and the number of those who, it is expected, will attend church, a larger or smaller number of Kolyva is prepared at home. Wheat is steeped until it is soft enough to eat; then such fruit as may be in season and abundance of sesame-seed is mixed with it. The fruits used for the Kolyva are nuts, almonds, raisins, figs and pomegranate seeds by preference if they are to be had.*) If the peasant is minded to make a little extra display, he garnishes his Kolyva in the town manner with European preserves and sugar-plums. The sacrificant brings the loaves (also called παννυχίδα) and the Kolyva, together with a large gourd of wine, into church and sticks wax tapers on both Kolyva and loaves. They are laid on an altar-table in front of the high altar and near the image-screen or ikonostási, and are then sprinkled and incensed by the priest, who at the same time lights the tapers. At the end of the service the priest cuts up several of the loaves into small pieces, which are piled by the church-wardens on dishes belonging to the church. Priests, church-wardens and people now stream out into the courtyard or porch of the church, where seats are ready for them. Wealthy churches and monasteries have handsome stone benches for the purpose of this ceremony. Only the men seat themselves, the women and children remain standing at one side. The sacrificant, his wife, children and relations, wait on the others, handing round bread and Kolyva and filling the glasses. Sweet-scented rose-water or orange-water is poured over the head and hands of those whom it is particularly desired to honour. Everyone gets his or her portion, if there is enough to go round, but the men are helped first. All the bread that has been cut up and all the Kolyva is distributed and all the wine is drunk up. Sometimes a kind of sweet-meat, made of pressed grapes and flour and very pleasant to the taste is handed round. It is called soujouko and is made in the form of little sausages or cakes, the best kind having nuts inside.**) The loaves which were not cut up and distributed remain in the church and belong to the priest, or when, as is mostly the case, there are more priests than one, are divided among them. It often happens that several people combine to furnish this oblation of meat and drink. At times, especially on ordinary Sundays at small villages and the lesser affiliated monasteries, no one can be found to defray the expense. When this happens, the consequence very frequently is that no service is held in this church, and those who want to attend service must find a church in another village or another quarter of their own village where someone has provided the Kolyva. Those who love or pretend to love the memory or their dead relatives prepare the Kolyva for them on the anniversary of their death or on the feast-day of their patron saint, and dishes containing Kolyva with burning tapers stuck on them are left for a certain time on the grave. How often in Cyprus has it been my lot to participate after church-service in this distribution of Kolyva, bread and wine! The best morsels, sweetest fruits and

---

*) Pomegranates can be kept for several months.

**) The ancient Hebrews must have been acquainted with similar grape cakes, for we read in Isaiah chap. XVI, 7.

"Ye shall sigh for the grape-cakes of Kir Hareseth."

the nicest sugar-plums are offered to the stranger. Many persons do not eat the Kolyva on the spot, but wrap them up in a handkerchief and take them home to consume them there with their friends.

Osiris, as we know, was a god whose worship was intimately linked with that of the dead. The soul of the buried dead becomes one with that of Osiris. The souls of the mystic bird Benu and of Osiris, conceived as a bird, also amalgamate. Both at Byblos and at Amathus in Kypros Osiris and Adonis combine to form a composite divinity, endowed with the functions of both. Osiris-Adonis is therefore a god of the dead. These modern Cyprian customs recall not only the offerings of fruits and viands at the Adonia, but that worship of the dead over which Osiris-Adonis presided. We think also of the festival of the Pyanepsia and the Eiresione at Athens; of the cooking pots ($\chi \acute{v} \tau \varrho o \iota$)*, filled with brose or pulse and all kinds of fruits; of the sweetmeat made from raisins and the crushed kernels of stone fruits of which the ancients were as fond as the modern Cypriots. These sweet stuffs with which the ancients filled the "chytri" were called Panspermia. The old word survives in the modern Cyprian "Spernà" or "Spermá," another name for the Kolyva. The Kolyva or spernà are also offered by the Cyprians of to-day in performance of vows and at all kinds of consecrations, just as the ancient Athenians at the Thargelia and Pyanepsia offered their panspermia to Helios-Apollo, and made similar oblations at the consecration of altars and images.**) Above on figs. 49, 142 and 143 we saw on Cyprian silver and bronze paterae representations of vases and pots, with which we compared the oracular vase used by the Cyprian girls in the rites of their May festival. Perhaps these vessels may also stand in some connection with the Panspermia offered in pots at Kyprian festivals of Aphrodite and Adonis. We may suppose the vases filled with fruit on the altar-tables of the silver patera fig. 142 (p. 123) and the bronze patera fig. 49 (p. 46) to contain panspermia. The object carried by the leader of the procession of dancers on the silver patera (fig. 142) seems to be a garden of Adonis, while the woman who walks behind the musicians appears to carry in her left hand a garden of Adonis and in her right hand a panspermia.***) The Cypriots carrying with them to church their loaves, cakes, Kolyva, pots of green wheat and palm-branches are the exact counterparts of their fore-fathers advancing with their gifts, loaves, cakes, panspermia, gardens of Adonis-eiresione palm-branches†) and holy trees to the altars of their gods, or the biers on which the images of these gods were laid. The Epitaphion on which at ancient Athens, as in Kypros, the dead

---

*) Perhaps the name of the ancient town Chytroi has some connection with these $\chi \acute{v} \tau \varrho o \iota$, which were of such ceremonial importance. The numerous holy trees and groups dancing round these trees of which examples are figured on Plate LXXVI (figs. 3, 4, 6—8, 10—12) were unearthed here.

**) Cp. Schmidt, Das Volksleben der Neugriechen und das hellenische Alterthum, p. 59; Mannhardt Wald- und Feldculte, p. 214 ff.

***) Some, however, of the vases pictured on these metal paterae are certainly holy-water vessels, the use of which was common in the cultus of various divinities and especially common in that of Aphrodite. These receptacles, of varying dimensions, meant in some cases to contain in others in draw or ladle out water, were stamped with the seal or name of the god or goddess in whose ritual alone they might be used. Interesting details as to the urns and vases of Aphrodite are contributed by Plautus, (Rudens 1, 2, 45 ff.) I and others have found in Cyprus numerous holy-water bowls, the inscriptions on which testify that they belonged to the Paphia (see on p. 13 No 23 in my list of places of worship), to Apollo, see the inscription No. 7 on p. 4 site 7 and the description of site 4 on p. 9), to the Baal of Libanon (C. I. S. 9), to Ešmun-Melqart (C. I. S., 16, 24) and to other deities. We possess also a silver sacrifical ladle or scoop with a dedication in Kyprian writing to the Golgia, the ancient Kyprian Aphrodite. (Deecke 61.)

†) Cp. Pl XLI, 3.

Adonis lay strewn with flowers survives with unimpaired magnificence in the modern Epitaphion on which the dead Christ lies in the same fragrant floral pomp.

In the Antiquarium of the Royal Berlin Museum there is a fragment of a fine Cyprian terra-cotta which is represented on Plate CCVII, 7. It is, if not certainly attested, at least highly probable that it was found at Kition in the sanctuary on the salt lake (site No. 7 on p. 11). A priestess, or temple servant carries on her right shoulder a large flat basket or bowl full of cakes and fruit. I have myself found at various times and in various sanctuaries, e. g. at Idalion in 1883 (p. 17, site 31) and at Akhna in 1882 (p. 1 site 1) terracotta statuettes of priestesses, temple servants, or persons sacrificing with the skirts of their mantles gathered up and filled with fruit, flowers or cakes (Plate CCX, 6)*) These figures recall those bloodless offerings of flowers, fruit and cakes, those little gardens, which played so notable a part in the feasts of Tammuz-Adonis. Of feminine figures carrying flowers there is such an abundance in all Kyprian sanctuaries, that it would be scarcely necessary to call attention to them but for one remarkable fact. A motive of almost universal occurence, the prototype of the Roman Spes, has here been from very early times used to represent Aphrodite or at least one of her priestesses. I refer to those figures of a woman advancing in rhythmical step, grasping with the fingers of her left hand the edge of her uplifted skirt, and with her right hand holding a flower to her bosom. These dancing girls holding flowers appear in quantities in all Cyprian sanctuaries of female deities without exception.**)

The modern Cyprian religious customs above described are evidently modelled on customs practised by the Hebrews and other Semitic nations. Between the great candle-sticks, beneath the burning lamp, just in front of the central door, usually closed by a curtain, of the gilded and glitter-ing image-screen—the door which admits to the Holy of Holies and the high altar—stands, in the Cyprian churches, the table on which rest the dishes containing the flat loaves of unleavened bread and the Kolyva. It is the table of show-bread in the temple or tabernacle of the Hebrews.***) In the narthex, the pronaos of the Greek churches, or, where there is no such space, in the open air, close against the church wall or in the church-yard, the men alone seat themselves and partake of the show-bread cut into morsels, and the Kolyva. The women must remain standing in the back-ground and receive only a little of the sacrificial food, and that little only when the supply in sufficient. This custom too reminds us of corresponding Hebrew usages, and especially of the Minscha-ordinance in Leviticus.†)

The Tammuz-Adonis gardens are known to the prophets of the Old Testament, as we learn from the words of Isaiah (XVII, 10, 11):

*) Cp. Cesnola-Stern, Atlas, Pl. CVIII, No. 696.
**) I found them in sanctuaries of Artemis, Aphrodite and the Mother of Gods. This "danseuse" with a flower in her hand may be but a temple servant or, at most, a priestess, not Aphrodite at all. On the other hand, if a priestess, she may be a priestess in the guise of Aphrodite. But it is a great mistake to regard all figures of priestesses and priests as necessarily representative of the deities they serve. Cp. Plate CXCVI and our remarks on it.
***) Riehm, Bibellexikon, p. 1390
†) Cp. VI, 16—17. "And the remainder thereof shall Aaron and his sons eat, without leaven shall it be eaten in the holy place; in the court of the tabernacle of revelation shall they eat it. It shall not be baken with leaven, I have given it (them) as their portion of my offerings made by fire; it is most holy, as is the sin-offering, and as the trespass-offering. All the males among the children of Aaron shall eat it &c." Cp. also Riehm p. 1519.

" Because thou hast forgotten the God of thy salvation and hast not been mindful of the rock of thy strength, therefore thou plantest pleasant plants and settest them with strange slips. On the day thou plantest thou makest a hedge (around) and early makest thou thy seed to flourish."

These artificially forced " pleasant plants " which " flourish early " can scarcely be anything but the gardens of Adonis*) which meet us at Alexandria, at Athens, and in Kypros, and have been taken over by the Greek Church and incorporated in its ritual. The women who sat weeping for Tammuz at the door of the Lord's house (Ezekiel VIII, 14) were weeping round the bier of their god, and had loaded it with their offerings of fruit and cakes and their gardens of Adonis.

Another custom to which allusion is made in the 17th verse of the same chapter of Ezekiel must also be connected with the worship of Tammuz-Adonis. The passage is as follows in the A. V. " — for they have filled the land with violence and return to provoke me to anger, and lo, they put the branch to their nose." For "branch" Luthers version substitutes "grapes." Smend,**) who has made the passage the basis of an admirable study, renders the final words: "They hold the spray to their nose" and Cornill***) translates: "They hold to their nose the bundle of twigs. Smend's rendering corresponds most closely to that solemn ceremonial act which we have frequently seen represented on Cyprian monuments, the act of smelling a flower, flowering branch or spray, or the holy tree itself. Two of the best examples have been described and represented above on pages 38 and 39 and Plates XIX, 2 (= Pl. XX) and XIX 4†). In both cases we see a man standing between blossoming trees and holding a flower to his nose with his left hand. In the vision of Ezekiel (ch. VIII) the greatest abomination of all is the sun-worship practised by about twenty men in the inner court of the temple at Jerusalem. It is these sun-worshippers who hold the spray to their nose. They stand not far from the altar and the "image of jealousy" of the Ashera which Manasseh had set up at the same spot.††) And close by, in the outer court, are the women sitting and weeping for Tammuz. In the grove of Apollo-Hylates at Kurion (p. 19, site 48) where hundreds of votive images representing Tammuz-Adonis-Linos were erected (about 50 well preserved specimens are published by Cesnola alone), statues holding a flowering spray in their left hand were also dedicated. Among them is a very fine limestone statue of nearly life-size (it stands 3 ft. 5 in. high without the head and feet, which are missing), the careful workmanship of which shows it to be of significance (Cesnola-Stern's Atlas XC, 588). In the grove of Apollo Hylates, as at the temple of Jerusalem, one might listen to the dirges and carols sung for the flower god Tammuz-Adonis-Linos, and see at the same time groups of worshippers standing with their faces turned to the rising sun, which they venerate by this symbolical act of holding a flower-spray to the nose with the left hand. We have, in Ezekiel's vision, the description of a single and simultaneous performance by men and women in the two courts of the temple at Jerusalem of the rites of a composite sun-, tree- and flower-

---

*) Cp. also Kautzsch, p. 443.

**) Der Prophet Ezechiel (Leipzig 1880) p. 54.

***) Das Buch des Propheten Ezechiel (Leipzig 1886, p. 227. The Vulgate has "et isti naribus suis quasi anhelantes."

†) S. Reinach in describing this vase (Pl. XIX, 4) in his Chroniques d'Orient (p. 194—195) called attention to the motive of flower-smelling, and pointed out the occurrence of similar motives on black-figured Attic vases, the Xanthos Harpy monument and the situla from Watsch. He regards this Cyprian motive of holding a flower to the nose as being a simplified variant of the Assyrio-Babylonian design of a tree worshipped by two demons (like our fig. 130 p. 92 and others.

††) Cp. section d) Asheroth, Masseboth and Chammanim; Smend, Ezechiel, p. 50.

19*

worship. The deities they venerate are the Sun-god, Baal, the Ashera and Tammuz. Smend calls attention to a similar Persian usage (Spiegel, Eranische Alterthümer III, 571; Avesta II, p. LXVIII). While praying to the sun the Persians held in the left hand a bunch of tree-twings, by preference those of the date-palm, pomegranate, and tamarisk, called "bareçma".*) On the vase from Ormidhia (fig. 134, p. 94) Astarte-Aphrodite and Tammuz-Adonis, or the human representatives of these deities, recline on thrones in front of the Ashera tree. They have flowers in both hands and hold one bouquet to their nose. On the bronze patera from Idalion represented above on p. 46 (fig. 49) the throned goddess (Astarte-Aphrodite?) or priestess representing her, is smelling a flower which she holds to her nose. On the bronze patera with Phoenician inscription found in the Alpheios near Olympia, but manufactured in Cyprus, the same throned goddess holds the same lotus flower in her left hand. With this special characteristic of the Persian rite, the express rule that the spray must be held in the left hand (Vend. 19, 64) many of the Cyprian representations are in striking accord. On the two Cyprian vases Pl. XIX 2 and 4 the men hold the flowers to the nose with the left hand. Very remarkable is the pose of the figure standing between blossoming trees on the Cyprian vase represented on p. 40 (fig. 41). This personage looks to the left, and instead of grasping the holy tree with his right hand as he could quite conveniently have done, clutches at it over the right shoulder with his left hand. The priest of Apollo on Pl. XLI, 3 (the stone figure was found in the grove at Voni shown by epigraphical evidence to belong to Apollo)**) also holds the date-branch in the left hand, as was the Persian custom. It would seem that this custom of holding a spray of some plant in the left hand while sacrificing was adopted by the Persians from Assyria. As early as the time of Asurnasirpal, i. e. in the 9th century B. C. (884—860) priests engaged in sacrifice carry a spray in one hand, often in the left hand (cp. Perrot II, p. 108, fig. 29). On a relief from the palace of the same king now in the British Museum, the priest who performs the sacrifice grasps a stag with his right arm, while with his left hand he is raising the flower-spray to his face, evidently in order to enjoy its perfume. Ezekiel reckons the custom among the worst abominations practised by those of his countrymen who had renounced Yahve. It stands evidently in close relation to Tammuz-worship, the gardens of Adonis, and the sacrifices to him of fruit and flowers. Just as this sheet was about to be printed off I made a further very important discovery which I now communicate, adding on Plates LXX, XC and CXV illustrations of the objects on which my conclusions are based. On Plate LXX, 1 we see two of the plates, united by joints, of a bronze cuirass, which I excavated in 1889 for the Berlin Museum in an earth-tomb (Tomb 3, Section IV) at Tamassos. Other portions of the cuirass were found, and will shortly be published in my Report on the excavations. The tomb can be dated with tolerable accuracy, and belongs to the sixth or to the beginning of the seventh century—the time at which Sargon and Sanherib ruled over Assyria and received tribute from Cyprus. It is just the time at which one of the most pious monarchs, one deeply devoted to Yahve, Hezekiah,***) was succeeded on the throne of Judah by the notorious renegade Manasseh.†) On the upper plate an advancing

---

*) Further parallels will be found in Smend's work, p. 50.

**) Site No. 2 (p. 3).

***) 2nd Kings XVIII, 5. "He trusted in Yahve God of Israel, so that after him was none like him among the kings of Judah, nor any that were before him." and in verse 4 "He removed the high places, brake the boundary stones and cut down the Ashera.

†) 2nd Kings XXI, II. Manasseh "hath done wickedly above all that the Amorites did which were

female figure raises in her left hand to her nose a spray of the lotus; her right arm is idle and hangs at her side. Above this priestess or goddess (Astarte?) float a sun-globe and crescent moon of large dimensions. On the lower plate stands the holy tree, the Ashera. The whole ends in a kind of palmette. Here therefore we have the goddess Astarte or her priestess standing between the symbols of the sun and moon and the holy tree. She holds the spray to her nose with her left hand. The cuirass-plates are Cyprian work with marked Egyptian tendencies. The ivory relief from Nimroud reproduced, nearly in the dimensions of the original, on Pl. XC, 2 *) shows a female figure in the same pose, similarly draped and executed in the same style. Her head-dress is indeed different,**) but the rest of her costume nearly corresponds. She holds in her left hand an Ashera in the form of a fantastic lotus-tree, and plants it on a low altar shaped like the capital of a column and itself only a transformed lotus-flower***) much resembling the terminal ornament of the cuirass (Pl. LXX, 1). The Ashera on the ivory tablet from Nimroud and the bronze cuirass found in Cyprus bear such an extraordinary resemblance to each other in form, outline and style, and the style and motive of the figures on both afford so many points of comparison, that we can scarcely be wrong in supposing the Nimroud tablet to be also Cyprian work.†) The manner in which the Cyprian armourer has conceived Astarte as issuing from the Ashera, here a lotus-tree, reminds us vividly of an Egyptian theogonic myth represented on an inscribed picture at Tentyra. Pharaoh in handing a lotus-flower to the youthful sun-god, who himself emerges in his glory from another lotus flower, addresses these words to him: "I hand thee the flower that was in the beginning, the glorious lily of the great lake. Thou comest forth from the heart of its petals to the city Chmun, and thou givest light to the Earth that was veiled in darkness." We see here how close is the connection between the worship of a flower, the lotus, and that of the sun, and how the Kyprians

---

before him," and in verse 7 "And he set a graven image of the Ashera that he had made" in the temple.

*) Perrot II, p. 222, fig. 80.

**) Just the same head-dress is found in Cyprus at least as early as the beginning of the 6th century and perhaps earlier. It is only worn by women, and the evidence of my own researches up to the present date seems to show that it was peculiar to players on the tympanon. The head-dress consists of a peaked bonnet or hood, something like a helmet, and terminating, like our artillery helmets, in a knob, but seemingly not so much a covering as a net, through the meshes of which the hair is visible. Two terracottas (Pl. LI, 1, 2) with this head-dress, found by me in the precinct of Aštoret-Aphrodite at Idalion (site 3, p. 5), are now in the Antiquarium of the Royal Berlin Museum. Of the eleven figures on the silver patera described and represented above on p. 126 (fig. 142) only the player on the tambour wears this headdress. These peaked bonnets or hair-nets, and other lower bonnets similarly composed of plaited ribbons or threads, much affected in the Cyprian Artemis-worship (e. g. often at Akhna, site 1 p. 1, see Pl. CCIX, 2) but also worn elsewhere, e g. by the women on the Dali patera (fig. 50 p. 47 , remind us of the crowns of cord worn by the girls who sat outside the temples in lines and awaited the pleasure of the men. Herodotus 1 199, Strabo 6 745. The resemblance of this head-dress, characteristic, as it seems to be, of the tambour-players who accompany the ring-dance, to a basket recalls to us also the name of a certain dance, Καλαϑίσκος.

***) Cp. also the capitals on Plates LVIII and LIX which must be interpreted as Masseboth or Chammanim, and below Fig. 159—163

†) On the same plate (XC) figs. 1 and 3 (= Perrot III figs 283 and 316) are illustrations of two reliefs in stone, one from Amrit and one from Moab. The style of both is flatter and ruder than that of the two others, the Egyptian influence less apparent. Not the divinities of peace and love, but martial gods are here represented; but the family resemblance of these Phoenician and Moabite monuments to their fellows from Kypros and Nimroud is none the less striking.

borrowed their ideas from Egypt. The Amathus patera represented above on p. 47 (fig. 50) exhibits as the principal scene of its central zone the birth of Harpokrates. The child Horus sits naked on the outspread petals of a lotus-flower*), holding one finger to his lips as children often do. It is the gesture by which Egyptian religious Art characterized the morning sun conceived of as a child god. His mother Isis, here winged, holds bunches of flowers in both hands and offers them to her baby. To the right on a little altar-table we see the sacred scarab adored by hawk-headed deities; in the left is a scene of tree-adoration in the grand style. Two men, with the hieroglyph of life in their hands, are picking sprays of lotus from the holy tree here treated in a conventional style peculiar to Egypt and Kypros.**) Next comes a second group of Isis standing opposite her son Horus-Harpokrates.***) Although the god is, in this case, conceived as having attained to man's estate, he still has his finger in his mouth, like a baby. A highly interesting object from Phoenician soil supplies a further parallel to our Cyprian cuirass and the ivory tablet from Nimroud. I refer to a small ivory casket the remains of which were discovered in the same tomb at Sidon which gave us the well-known sarcophagus of Ešmunazar.†) Of the three best preserved sides, one has in relief a bundle of three staves, the central one surmounted by a kind of capital; on the second we see a star between two sun-globes or rosettes. The third side is given on Plate CXV (4). A woman is smelling a large lotus-flower which she holds in both hands. It is almost certain that this ivory casket was manufactered in Cyprus, where ivory, as my discoveries have demonstrated, was always a common material for works of art, but at no time more common than in the 6th century B. C.†††) The points of resemblance between this little ivory relief from Sidon and the bronze patera from Idalion are, to say the least, striking. Subject and style are the same. The shift worn by the woman on the ivory relief falls into the same folds as the shifts of the women on the Dali bowl, and in both cases is gathered together at the waist by a cord. The goddess on the bronze bowl is smelling, it is true, only at a single large lotus-flower which she holds in her right hand; in her left hand she bears a fruit. But the arrangement of the woman's hair on the Sidonian relief is the same as on that the Idalian patera, and on many other specimens of ancient Cyprian art. The hair is gathered up in a knot and confined in a kind of net.

The monuments here adduced are not illustrative alone of the time of the prophet Ezekiel (i. e. the first half of the 6th century B. C.). When we find the act of "holding the spray to the

---

*) Cp. the groups of two stags or lions seated on the lotus flower on golden fibulae from Mykenae, two of which are figured on Plate LXXXIX (figs. 4 and 5).

**) Cp. on pages 78 and 79 above, figs. 52 a and b, 106, 107. On p. 46 I incorrectly spoke of a tree conventionalized after Assyrian models. The design of two men adoring a tree is certainly of Assyrian origin (cp. p. 95 fig. 135), but the style is divergent and non-Assyrian.

***) Horus and Harpokrates, themselves frequently amalgamated with Osiris, combine with Tammuz, Adonis and Ptah-Pataecus to form other composite beings some of whom we shall encounter below. Harpokrates, as is known, is the only form under which Horus was worshipped by the Greeks outside Egypt. Harpokrates was also venerated by the Phoenicians. Cp. Roscher's Mythol. Lexikon, col 2747.

†) C. I. S. 3

††) Renan, Mission p. 100 = Perrot, p 847, figs. 611—613.

†††) In 1889 I dug up some swords and knives of local-Cyprian fabric, the hilts of which were ornamented with ivory insertions. The ivory casket exported from Cyprus to Sidon may be of just the same date as the Cyprian bronze cuirass and the iron swords decorated with ivory. We know the sarcophagus in which the Sidonian King Ešmunazar was buried about the time of Alexander the Great, to be of Egyptian workmanship and several centuries earlier than the Phoenician inscriptions cut on it.

nose represented on Cyprian and Assyrian monuments coeval with the building of the temple, we may safely assert that Ezekiel pictures to us a pagan rite practised as early as the days of Solomon, David and Hiram. We thus indirectly gain some justification for referring back the worship of Tammuz with all its accessories — its chants of joy and sorrow, its gardens of Adonis, its sacrifices of fruit, flowers, and viands — to a date much earlier than that of Ezekiel. The Old-Babylonian legend of Ištar and Duzi narrated above, a legend which must have been the original or the Aštoret-Tammuz mythe carries us back into far earlier times. It must however be noted, in conclusion, that the Cyprian monuments which literally illustrate the rite of holding the spray to the nose bespeak Egyptian rather than Assyrian influence.

c) The Asheroth, Masseboth and Chammanim of the Bible: holy staves and lances in the Bible and Homer.

Much has already been written on the subject of these things, which play so great a part in the religions of the Hebrews and other allied Semitic peoples. The literature on the Asheroth especially is now most extensive. Notwithstanding all the paper that has been blackened, the views of the learned on this subject seem to be as divergent as ever.

Must we conceive of the Ashera as a deity to whom human form was occasionally attributed, or not? Is Ashera to be unconditionally identified with Aštoret or not; and if we affirm this in whole or in part, when and how did the identification arise? I hope with the help of the results of previous workers to demonstrate that discoveries made in Cyprus put us in a position to unify the divergent views of different enquirers, and to lift, at least in part, the veil which still rests on the Ashera. Ashera-worship has passed through successive phases, and assumed different forms among the different peoples who adopted it. All kinds of similar religious conceptions and similar external forms crossed and intermingled. Even within the borders of a single people, differences in local cultus were the cause of the same deity being conceived and spoken of under numerous and often very divergent forms and by many different names. It must be stated at the outset that the Ashera, as a symbol, attribute, or utensil of worship meets us, generally speaking, only in the cultus of feminine divinities.[*]) In Kypros we take note at once of the distinction between the wooden Ashera-tree or Ashera-post, which was burnt in the votive area close beside almost all the larger statues on the day of their consecration, and the plastic imitations of these Asheroth, the Ashera-idols.[**]) While these trees and

---

[*]) Count Baudissin (Semitische Religionsgeschichte II, p. 219 and 220) has already properly recognised that originally the erect stone pillar was the emblem of the god, the tree or wooden post that of the goddess. In later times the Phoenicians ceased to differentiate strictly the two emblems; so that now the tree may occur as the emblem of the male, the conic stone as that of the female deity (as in the case of Astarte-Aphrodite at Paphos, Byblos &c.) We shall soon see that Baudissin is, in part, right.

[**]) I have as yet only found tree-idols of clay in Cyprian τεμένη, while some of stone were found by Lang. But just as at Gades in the temple of Melqart (Movers p. 613) there stood a golden olive tree of the Cyprian hero Pygmalion (who is only another form of Adonis), so in Cyprian sanctuaries golden Ashera and Adonis-Pygmalion trees must have been dedicated. In a tomb at Poli tis Khrysokhou (1882) I found a golden flower of some size and of very delicate work, which had been worn as an ornament on the breast. The contents of the tomb and the circumstances of the discovery fixed the date at the end of the 6th or beginning of the 5th century B. C. The practised Cyprian diggers know quite well that in the holy precincts the spot must be found on which the major burnt-offerings were performed. As I have already said on p. 20, they speak of this place as the βωμός. They also are well aware that in the votive area, beside all the larger statues, and often on spots where heaps of smaller idols lie packed together, minor burnt offerings took place.

sticks were burnt in the groves and holy precincts of all divinities without distinction of sex or character, the Ashera-idols of clay, stone, bronze, silver or gold were, as the preceding Section has told us, dedicated only in the votive areas of those precincts in which a female divinity was worshipped. We have in the first place, as the most original form, a single object*), the emblem of this feminine deity, soon however appearing in conjunction with that of her male correlative. Two symbols, two similar or dissimilar trees, posts, pillars, columns or cones, two aniconic agalmata**) are now erected. These two objects either express the presence and joint rule in the holy place of a god and goddess, or they signify that the single deity is conceived as of a double nature, a being both male and female at once.***) To these rude symbols were added heads, extremities and other parts of the human figure,†) until at length the transition to true anthropomorphic images was completed.††) The process thus summarily sketched was, like most processes, subject to interruptions and reversions. The god who has attained human form is regarded as dwelling in the tree, cone or post, and is himself represented under these forms †††) The aniconic emblems and agalmata which are supposed to incorporate the essence of the deity survive, side by side with the iconic anthropomorphic agalmata, until the decline of paganism.§) The aniconic agalmata accompany the true images§§) or continue to be separately reverenced in the holy places. Or the tree, post or column is the principal idol of the sanctuary, the anthropomorphic votive offerings being grouped around it or suspended from its branches. Above on pages 18 and 19, under nos. 36 and 42, two places of worship are described, one (no. 36) at Idalion, the other at Lithrodonda. At the first I was able to determine that divine honours were paid to a single holy tree, on whose branches numerous human masks and one mask of an animal were suspended, while lamps and all kinds of votive images, among

---

A workman who knows his business will, on coming across ashes or charcoal in laying bare the votive area exercise the greatest care, as he may otherwise destroy with the next stroke of his pick or spade some valuable statue or inscription. He begins at once to work cautiously with hand and knife alone, and his care is usually rewarded in a quarter of an hour's time by the discovery of some fine votive offering. Lamps and small vases also often stand within the area of the place of burnt offering.

*) A single tree, shrub, branch, pole, trunk or cone, a simple triangle, quadrangle, cross &c., sometimes intended to be masculine, sometimes feminine or androgynous: Plate LXXVII, 6, 8, 9, 10, 13—21. LXXVIII, 1, 3, 4, 5, 6.   LXXIX, 2, 3, 7, 8, 11, 18, 21.   LXXX, 1, 2, 3, 4, 5, 7.   LXXXII, 2, 3, 4, 5, 6.   LXXXIII 1—7.   XVII, 1.   XXIX, 6, 7, 9, 10, 11, 12, 13, 14, 16, 17.   XXX, 1, 4 8, 10.   XXXI, 3, 4, 9, 11, 14.   Cp. also the preceding sections and Plate LXXVI.

**) LXXVII, 12.   LXXVIII, 8, 11, 12.   LXXIX, 1, 4, 6, 12, 14.   LXXXIII, 17.   XXIX, 1, 5, 8.   XXX, 5, 9, 14, 15.

***) The two great monoliths on the sea-shore at Paphos (Pl. XVIII) were also doubtless meant to indicate the androgynous character of the Cyprian Astarte-Aphrodite. In the sanctuary at Idalion (site 3, p 6) tree-idols (Asheroth) of clay (Plate LXXVI 5 and 9) and a copy in clay of a sun-pillar (Pl. LVII, 4) were deposited next each other. The pairs of columns and cones which we meet with throughout the whole Phoenician world, which we find alike in Solomon's temple in Greece and in ancient Babylon, perhaps also point to a similar symbolization of the androgynous nature.

†) LXXVII, 2, 3, 4.   LXXXII, 1 (at the foot).   LXXXIII, 4, 5, 9, 11, 14, 19.   Cp. also the preceding sections.

††) Pl. LXXVIII, 10.   LXXXIII, 15.   LXXXV, 3.   LXXXVI, 1—7.   Vide supra.

†††) Cp. especially Plates XVII, 2, 3, 4 and XVIII with their descriptions.   Also LXXXIII, 8, 16.

§) As one example among many I mention the idol of the temple at Paphos.

§§) The coins on Plates LXXXIII with aniconic agalmata (3—5, 8—20, 22) are all of late Greek or of Roman times.

them some of Aphrodite κουροτρόφος and Adonis, were set up under its shadow. The latest images are not more recent than the fourth century B. C. Though there is no inscription giving us the name, the deity here venerated can be no other than an Ashera. At the holy place of Lithrodonda there was evidence that beside a spring and underneath a little platform of rock, an aniconic worship, consisting in keeping lamps alight and dedicating small coins, was still practised in Roman times. There is now a tree close to the spring, and the same was doubtless the case in ancient times. In other cases it would appear that the male and female elements were united in one holy symbol*) from which, when gods came to be worshipped under human form, the androgynous deity took his birth.**) In other cases a third symbol appears beside the male and female ones.***) This third symbol is in some cases representative of something conceived as the child of a father and mother; elsewhere it symbolises not the offspring of the male and female, but their absorption in a being which has something of both. In this case, as well as in the other, it comes to be regarded as a separate entity, and thus divine triads originate. Lastly, these sacred symbols and their combinations may be still further multiplied. The monuments here to be adduced bear, generally speaking, no inscriptions, but on such as are inscribed, with three exceptions, the name Ashera is mentioned. These three exceptions are certainly, as will be seen, very significant. Although as a rule the monuments themselves are silent witnesses, the repeated and detailed descriptions of the Asheroth in the Bible, especially when they occur in conjunction with altars of Baal and Masseboth,††) leave no doubt that in a preponderating number of cases we must recognise the presence beside the Baal-pillar, the Masseba or Chamman, of the Ashera-tree or wooden Ashera-post briefly styled 'Ashera'.†††) Our Biblical

---

*) E. g. in the cone of the bearded Aphrodite in Kypros.

**) Axieros is the product of Axiokersos and Axiokersa. Baal-Zeus and Tammuz-Adonis unite with Astoret-Aphrodite and Aśrat-Ashera to form bisexual beings. Iśtar in Babylon, Astor-Kamos in Moab, Aphrodite and Aphroditos in Kypros, Tanit, face of Baal, in Carthage, Hermaphroditos in Greece are some examples of androgynous deities. A very unequivocal and early example of a hermaphrodite deity, a terracotta from Cyprus now in the Berlin Museum, is given on Pl. XXXVI, 1. This is evidently the oldest known representation of such a being (though the imperfect notices of the circumstances under which it was found do not give us a clear clue to its date) and it is significant that it comes from Cyprus, the home of Aphroditos. The quality of the clay, the modelling, and a comparison with other allied figurines, would induce me to assign this important specimen to the years 1200—1000 B. C., the period of transition from Bronze to Iron. Figs. 4a and b and 10 on the same Plate are two board-idols of polished red clay also obtained by me for the Berlin Museum. They are meant to be draped, the ornaments and the details of the dress and anatomy being incised and filled with a white compound. From a single trunk issue two busts, one male, the other female. These three figures, dating from the last half of the second millennium B. C. at least and perhaps still older, are the earliest monumental evidences of the union in one person of the two sexes, and Roscher's Mythologisches Lexikon (col. 654; Astarte-Hermaphroditos) should be corrected accordingly. The Greek Hermaphroditos, who is mythologically and typologically identical with the Aphroditos and bearded Aphrodite of Cyprus, is thus carried back to pre-Hellenic times. We have also in these figures parallels to the Egyptian images of Hapi. See Riehm's Bibellexikon, p. 112.

***) Three symbols: Plate LXXVII, 1a, 5. LXXIX, 15. LXXXII, 1, 8. LXXXIII, 18, 19, 20, 21, 22.

†) Pl. LXXIX, 9, 10 LXXXII, 1.

††) As early as in Exodus (XXXIV, 13)· it is commanded that the stone monuments (Masseboth) shall be destroyed and the holy trees (Asheroth) cut down. See Kautzsch's translation of the Bible p. 94. Cp. also Deuteronomy VII, 5, where together with the Ashera graven-images are mentioned; Judges VI, 25—30; 1st Kings XIV, 23; 2nd Kings XXIII, 14; 2nd Chronicles XIV, 3.

†††) I direct attention only to some of the clearest representations of the juxtaposition of the stone Masseba, which we hear of always in the Old Testament as being broken, or hacked in pieces, and the wooden Ashera, which is always hewn down, felled, burnt with fire, or used to feed the fire of sacrifice.

sources also clearly show that any Baal, the owner of this or that sanctuary, the local god of this or that place, may have as his 'paredros' an Ashera, just as he may have an Aštoret. In the 2ⁿᵈ chapter of Judges (v. 13) we hear of the renegade Hebrews worshipping Baal and Ashtarot; in the 3ʳᵈ chapter (v. 7) it is the Baalim and Asheroth. In 1ˢᵗ Kings XVIII and XIX we read of 450 prophets of Baal and 400 prophets of Ashera being assembled on Mount Carmel with the people of Israel.

Stade had attempted to oust the Ashera from the Semitic pantheon, in part because there is, he says, a confusion somewhere, in part because the passages in which the Ashera is mentioned as a goddess in company with Baal occur in Deuteronomy, and are therefore not older than the 7ᵗʰ century B. C. But H. Winckler and Eb. Schrader*) have shown that already on one of the tablets of Tell-el-Amarna (i. e. in the 15ᵗʰ century B. C.) the cult of the Phoenician and Assyrian goddess Ašrat-Ashera is referred to. The tree-goddess Ashera is only another form of Aštoret or Astarte, who herself was often conceived of as a tree. As a fact, the planting and felling of Asheroth is, as Schrader states, quite compatible with the assumption of a goddess Ashera venerated under the form of a natural object.

In Kypros the worship of both Ashtoret and Ashera is attested by inscriptions and images at the Phoenician commercial town Chittim, the Kition of the Greeks, the Karti-hadas(š)ti of the Assyrian cuneiform texts (Karthadast in Phoenician, Carthago in Latin). On the acropolis of this city stood a sanctuary of Aštoret and Mikal, and on the hill-side by the shore of the salt lake both Artemis Paralia and Ashera as Mother of the holy Post or Mother of the Gods were worshipped together in the same grove. Although the Ashera inscription, found, during my stay at Larnaka, close to the spot which yielded the Artemis inscriptions, must, like most of the Phoenician inscriptions of Cyprus and those of Kition in particular, be assigned to a comparatively recent date, viz. the commencement of the fourth century B. C., we are yet, in view of the early intercourse between Mesopotamia and Cyprus of which we have above found evidence, justified in carrying back the cult of Ashera in Cyprus to a date at least as early as the Ašrat inscription on the Tell-el-Amarna tablet. Cyprian monuments indeed permit us to carry back to a far earlier date the worship in the island of holy trees and posts, pillars, or columns of wood as well as that of stone monoliths. Whatever may have been the primitive names of these different fetishes, from which anthropomorphic deities and idols were developed, the cult of a goddess named Ashera existed among the peoples of the Old Testament at as early a date as the cults of the various Baals and Astartes. The Ashera is nothing but a primitive local Aštoret, who has preserved, in a purer form and for a longer time, her fundamental character of a tree or wooden post, the vegetative ground-work of her nature. In the case of other Astartes, on the other hand, the sidereal (lunar or solar) the telluric or meteorolithic principles come more to the front. That, however, Aštoret-Aphrodite too was for long conceived as a tree, more especially as a cypress or palm, we know from our literary authorities, as well as from epigraphical and other

---

Pl. LXXVII, 1b Ashera on the left, Masseba on the right; LXXIX 16 Masseba on the left, Ashera on the right; ibid. 17 Ashera on the left, Masseba on the right. XXX, 12 Ashera on the left, Masseba on the right; ibid. 14 Masseba on the left, Ashera on the right. On Pl. LXXVII 1a we seem to see first on the left the Ashera and Masseba united to form a single object of worship, next the Masseba, and finally on the right the Ashera.

*) Eb. Schrader " Die Göttin Ištar als malkatu und šarratu, " in the Zeitschrift für Assyriologie III (1888), p. 353—364

monumental sources.*) The 'provenance' of the inscriptions seems to show that the Semitic Ashera in Kypros combined more readily with that goddèss from whom the island Greeks made their Artemis-Kybele-Hekate, Aštoret on the other hand combining with Aphrodite.**) All the Canaanitic and Kyprian goddesses who attained to anthropomorphic form derive from a single feminine divinity, the primitive Babylonian goddess.***) Similarly when a male anthropomorphic idol was first substituted by the Canaanites and Kyprians for the pillar representative of the male deity, it was in both cases Bel-Baal, the husband of Belit-Balat, who was taken as a model. The pair are Lord and Lady,†) owners of some holy place, from which in most cases they derive their appellative titles. The present is the most appropriate place to lay before the reader the text of the Cyprian Ashera inscription and the beginning of the text of the Ašrat inscription from Tell-el-Amarna. The Ashera inscription from the salt lake at Kition runs, according to Schröder's restoration and translation, as follows:—"On the twentieth day of the month Sebasemesh in the year of the rule of Pumiyathon, King of Kition and Idalion, erected (this) Abdosir son of Bodo, son of Ikunshella (son of Eshmunadon, son of — — — —, son of) Bodo to his Lady the Mother Ashera because she heard (his prayer and blessed him)."†††) Eb. Schrader§) reads as follows the passage with which we are here concerned at the beginning of the Tell-el-Amarna tablet. "To the King of the Sun my Lord, thy servant Abad-Asratu." Schrader adds that the name Abad-Asratu is written with the ideogram of the god, and concludes his explanation with the remark that this inscription demonstrates the existence of a god Ašrat-Ashera in the 15th century B. C. As this cuneiform inscription was found in Egypt, our eyes turn almost involuntarily to the parallel phenomena in the Egyptian pantheon. Ptah-Sokari-Osiris and

---

*) To prove that Astarte Aphrodite was worshipped as a cypress-goddess, we need only recall the Baalat-Berut, i. e. the lady of the cypress, from which tree the ancient city of Berytus (the modern Beyrout) derived its name (Baudissin, Semitische Religionsgeschichte II p. 196.) Cp. the remarks offered above in discussing Pl. LXXVI. Among the graffiti in the grotto near Tyre (Corpus Inscriptionum Semiticarum p. 27—28, No. 6 Pl. III = figs. 142—145 below) we see palm branches and a distinctly characterised palm-tree, side by side with the vulva. Astarte-Aphrodite there is a palm goddess, a goddess not only of human but of vegetable fertility.

**) Cp. site 7 (p 11. This does not exclude the possibility of Aphrodite and Kybele uniting to form a single goddess.

***) Many years ago Curtius in his essay: "Die griechische Götterlehre vom geschichtlichen Standpunkte" attempted to demonstrate that all Greek feminine deities were derived from a single Semitic deity. This is doubtless true as far as Cyprus is concerned.

†) Cp. in Roscher's Mythologisches Lexikon, Ed. Meyer's two very instructive articles Astarte (cols. 645—655) and Baal (cols. 2867—2880). It is there shown in detail how the gods Melek, Moloch, Melqart, Merodach, Yahve, Tammuz, Adon, Adonis &c. and the goddesses Ištar, Aštoret, Atar, Atargatis, Zarpanit, Mylitta &c, (let us add Ashrat and Ashera) are nothing but differentiations, originally attached to particular localities, races or peoples, of a single primitive divine pair. Cp. also Schrader, "Keilinschriften und das alte Testament," p. 173—176, where, relying chiefly on the evidence of Assyrian and Babylonian monuments he distinguishes two Bels, an older and a younger, each with his feminine counterpart.

††) Zeitschrift der deutschen morgenländischen Gesellschaft XXXV, p. 423—431. "Phoenizische Miscellen."

†††) The editors of the Corpus Inscriptionum Semiticarum translate (p. 43): Die XX° mensis sacrificiorum solis, anno II° . . . . regis Melekyatonis, regis Citii et Idalii. [Statua haec (est) quam dedit et erexit.] Abdosir, filius Bodonis, filii Jak [unsillemi pro uxore sua . . . . . ., filia . . . ., filii . . . ., filii] Bodonis, dominae suae, Em-Haazurot (vel. Em- Haazoret); quia audiit [vocem; benedicat]. Ed. Meyer (Roscher's Lexikon, col, 2870) renders the name of the goddess "the Lady-mother of the Asherat."

§) "Die Göttin Ištar als malkatu und šarratu" in Zeitschrift für Assyriologie III (1888), p. 353—364.

Hathor-Isis are received into the theognosy of Canaan, Phoenicia and Cyprus. The myths of Hor-Harpokrates too have their significance in this connection. The Egyptian notion of Osiris as a column, and the festival celebrating the erection of this Tatou-column, this Osiris once more standing on his feet and upright, are of great antiquity.*) We think of the Baal-columns and Sun-columns of Assyria and Babylonia of Judaea and Kypros; but at what time these Egyptian conceptions were transported to other lands we are not in a position to state. The amalgamation at Gebal and Amathus of the worship of Osiris and Isis with that of Astarte and Adonis is, in the form we meet with it, certainly of no very high antiquity, but nevertheless seems to point to the confluence, in much more ancient times, of currents which may either have originated on the banks of the Nile or on those of the Euphrates, or on both. The myth of the sacred Erica at Byblos, hewn down by Isis, is however admirably suited to the conception of the Ashera which prevailed during a certain period at least, the period when the book of Deuteronomy was composed. According to Plutarch's narrative,**) Isis extracts from the tree-trunk the bier of Osiris. She wraps linen bandages about the stump itself, and anoints it with precious ointment, and in Plutarch's day this erica was still worshipped like an Ashera in the temple at Gebal.***)

Another peculiar feature in the worship of Astoret and Ashera as we find it among the Geblites, Hebrews and, as the Ashera inscription enables us to add, among the Kyprians, is its obscene

symbolism. Twice in sacred writ we read that the queen-mother Maacha had erected to Ashera a " horror ", something unusually terrible and monstrous.†) It is cut down and burnt by Asa. Movers††) has interpreted the word used in the Hebrew text (mipleseth) as the 'pudendum'. But he erred in following the interpretation of Jerome, who makes it a 'simulacrum Priapi' i. e. a phallus. Schlottmann,†††) following the Vulgate, which talks of "sacra Priapi," fell into the same error. In many cases where Masseboth and Asheroth stand side by side, where a "horror" is set up to Ashera, or where the male hieroduli, the Kedeschim of the Hebrews render their shameful service to Ashera in houses at the gate of Yahve's temple,§)

Fig. 144

not the male but the female pudendum is intended. On the stone masseboth of Baal was set often a huge phallus, on the wooden Asteroth a representation of the vulva equally conspicuous. I give here (fig. 144) a small cut of one of the large phalli of trachyte, of which a considerable number has been found near the tomb of Tantalus at old Smyrna.§§) On a Babylonian or Assyrian cylinder in the Western Asiatic Department of the Berlin

---

*) Brugsch, Religion und Mythologie der alten Aegypter p. 627 ff. Ermann, Aegypten und aegyptisches Leben p. 377. Frazer, Golden Bough I, 303.

**) De Iside et Osiride, 16.

***) Smith, Religion of the Semites, p. 175 note.

†) 1st Kings XV, 13. 2nd Chron. XV, 16.

††) Die Phoenizier I, 571.

†††) Riehm's Bibellexikon, p. 113.

§) 2nd Kings XXIII, 7.

§§) Weber, Le Sipylos II = Perrot V, p. 54, fig. 18. This phallus resembles in form our little terracotta phalli from the sanctuary of Artemis-Kybele at Akhna (Plate LXVIII, 8), while a second example given, ibid. by Weber and Perrot, rather resembles no. 9 on our Plate. I would recall attention here to the Old-Babylonian terracotta phalli described above which, originally quite realistic in form, gradually lost their primitive characterisation and finally passed into the pure cylinder. Eb. Schrader was the first to point

Museum (Pl. XXX, 12) we see an Ashera and Masseba erected on a common stand. On the left is the wooden Ashera, on which the representation of the vulva is not quite distinct; on the right the Masseba, the summit of which is obviously that of a phallus. The crescent moon above the Ashera, and the radiate sun above the Masseba, are significant of the sidereal aspect of the worship, the fish and the rhomboid at the sides symbolize its relations to human and animal fertility. The priest at the altar, which is surmounted by the winged globe of the sun, adores the two divinities. These rhomboids, often, as in the present cases, with a line bisecting them, occur frequently as emblems of fertility on Mesopotamian, Hittite and other cylinder-seals. Sometimes two of the corners are rounded off, thereby heightening the resemblance to the vulva.[*] The representation is very unequivocal on Cylinder 11 of the same plate (XXX), and on Pl. LXIX in the third row I have collected a series of such symbols from various gems, including therein those on these two cylinders (Pl. XXX, figs. 11 and 12. For further details see the explanation of Plate LXIX.) Figs. 145—148 show us four of the graffiti

Fig. 145.   Fig. 146.   Fig. 147.   Fig. 148.

on the walls of a grotto near the river now known as Al-Kaamie not far from the ancient Tyre.[**] These graffiti, which represent the vulva in a triangular form are, some of them, accompanied by inscriptions in Greek, Aramaic and Phoenician (No. 145 has a Greek and Phoenician bilingual), as well as by all kinds of ornamental appendages, such as palm-branches, a palm-tree, a bird and a hand. Among the Greek inscriptions one is a dedication to Aphrodite. There can be little doubt that this grotto

this out and to show how the later, pure cylindrical form of the Babylonian inscribed cylinders was gradually developed from the phallus. These large inscribed cylinders of terracotta must not be confused with the small seal-cylinders and amulets, to the testimony of which we have had so often to appeal in the course of the present work.

*) A similar rhomboid in Menant, Glyptique II, figs. 47, 51. Cp. Plates LXIX, 33, 39, 41, 96, 101; LXXXVII, 13. Above the gigantic figures of the deities on the Old-Cappadocian rock-reliefs of Boghaz-Kieui we see little aediculae. In one case the deity holds the aedicula in his hand (Perrot IV p. 639, fig. 314 = our Plate LXIX, 61) and stands on an object resembling a gigantic fir-cone or an omphalos (cp. pl. LXXXIII, 1, 2, 3). Two columns with primitive ionic capitals support the roof, which consists of a large winged sun-globe. The (female?) divinity in the centre seems to grow out of a cone or omphalos; she reaches not one hand to grasp one of the gigantic symbols between which she is placed. They are not, as Perrot incorrectly surmises, oxen, but are representations of the vulva. On a second relief (Perrot IV, p. 643, fig. 331 = our Plate LXIX, 81) the deity in the centre is replaced by a huge phallus, which Perrot has rightly recognised as such. It appears to me that we have here the Asheroth and Masseboth of Syria and Babylonia, adopted and differently rendered by the Hittite art of Cappadocia.

**) Corpus Inscriptionum Semiticarum Pl. III, 6 .: our fig. 145; ibid. p. 28 =. our figs. 146 -148.

has been correctly styled an ancient holy place of Astarte-Aphrodite. The Arabs at the present day still call it "specus pudendorum." The editors of the Corpus Inscriptionum Semiticarum cite very aptly the passage of Herodotus, where he recounts how in Syria and Palestine he saw stelae with *γυναικός αἰδοῖα* incised on them. The story of the gesture by which Baubo made Demeter laugh

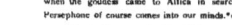
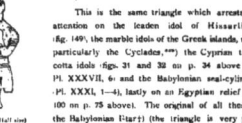

when the goddess came to Attica in search of Persephone of course comes into our minds.[*]

This is the same triangle which arrests our attention on the leaden idol of Hissarlik[**] (fig. 149), the marble idols of the Greek islands, more particularly the Cyclades,[***] the Cyprian terra-cotta idols (figs. 31 and 32 on p. 34 above and Pl. XXXVII, 6) and the Babylonian seal-cylinders (Pl. XXXI, 1—4), lastly on an Egyptian relief (fig. 100 on p. 75 above). The original of all these is the Babylonian Istar† (the triangle is very plain on Pl. XXXI, 1): her type is borrowed by that

(Fig. 149 (half size))

goddess of Kadesh whom the Egyptians adopted (fig. 100) and by the Istar-Astarte-Aphrodite of Hissarlik, Cyprus and the Greek islands. To the same cycle belongs a coloured idol of Astarte-Aphrodite found by me in an early Graeco-Phoenician tomb at Kurion (fig. 150).†† Although this idol belongs to the period circa 1000—700 B.C., both the form and the svastikas, painted in black colour on the fore-arms and shoulder, establish an analogy between it and Schliemann's leaden idol, many centuries older; and the outlines, especially that of the head, serve to remind us of the marble idols of the Cyclades. In the graffiti of the Tyrian grottoes of Aphrodite we see only the compendium of this nude goddess, the vulva represented by an almost equilateral triangle with its apex (in one instance, fig. 149 rounded off) pointing downwards. On the Babylonian cylinder, Pl. XXX, 15, we see a precisely similar triangle, and issuing from it a staff, on the top of which is set a star. This symbol occupies a position

Fig. 150
(From the site of the original.)

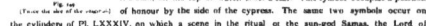

of honour by the side of the cypress. The same two symbols occur on the cylinders of Pl. LXXXIV, on which a scene in the ritual of the sun-god Samas, the Lord of

---

*) Movers, Phönizier I, p. 595.

**) Schliemann, Ilios, p. 380, no. 226.

***) One is given by Perrot V., p. 385, fig. 343 and by Collignon, Histoire de la sculpture Grecque, p. 18, fig. 5.

†) Cp. Lenormant, Les Antiquités de la Troade p. 46; Schliemann, Ilios p. 381.

††) Cp. my essay "La croix gammée et la croix cantonnée à Chypre" in the Bulletin de la Société d'Anthropologie de Paris, 1899. There is a far-reaching similarity, as regards the general mien and form, the round elevated head, the short and cylindrical legs, between my idol and the figure playing the double flute from the Greek island of Keros (near Amorgos in the Cyclades), first published in Mittheilungen des Kaiserl. Deutschen Archaeol. Institutes zu Athen for 1884 and reproduced by Collignon (p. 19, fig. 6).

Heaven, Baalshama, perhaps himself rising through the sun-door*) between the two sun-pillars (Chammanim), is represented. A comparison of figs. 3 and 7 on this plate shows vividly how the cypress may take the place of the Ashera (Aṣrat) and vice versa. On both cylinders we see the same act being performed in the sun-gate between the two sun-pillars. The cypress in one case stands in the same relative position to the fire-temple as the Ashera in the other. We have only to insert the vulva-triangle to get the cone, the well known symbol of the goddess of Paphos (Pl. X, 2 = LXXXII, 7) Byblos (LXXX, 1), Sidon (LXXXIII, 16) and Carthage (LXXVII 2—4 and LXXXV 2 and 3). By the side of the stone pillar of Baal, the Masseba or Chamman surmounted or not, as the case may be, by the phallus, stands the tree or wooden pillar (of Aštoret-Ashera?) with or without the female triangle at its summit. On the seal with Phoenician inscription, Pl. LXXVII 1a and b, this post of Ashera, the " horror " of the Bible, is twice repeated. We meet with it again in union with the pillar of Baal on the late Babylonian cylinders, LXXIX, 16 and 17, and on no. 15 of the same plate we see the Masseba and the Ashera post, from which flames, it would seem, are issuing, in company with the tree. The symbols are usually surmounted by the radiate sun and crescent moon.°*) On the cylinder LXXIX, 14 the stone Masseba is absent. Two stags, beside whom rises the Ashera, here adore the holy tree. The sun and crescent rest on the triangle or cone which surmounts the post. The deity here seems to be conceived as androgynous. The Ashera of post form surmounted by a triangle or cone appears in company with the stone pillar of Baal (just as on Pl. LXXIX 15—17) on a very fine cylinder in the Berlin Museum (Pl. XXX, 14). They there perform the office of symbols of Istar malkatu and šarratu***), the Atar-Samain of the Aramaeans, the Queen of Heaven of Jeremiah.†) Round her head is a radiate crown resembling the glory of Catholic saints.

The scene of a victim lying or standing at or upon an altar (which may be absent but must always be supplied with the two symbols Masseba and Ashera standing or suspended behind it (e. g. Plates XXX, 14; LXIX, 44; LXXVII, 16) is one of the favourite subjects of Oriental Glyptic.††) Very often we see either a Masseba behind the animal, while the Ashera either stands beside it or is absent, or an Ashera behind it and a Masseba beside it (Pl. XXX, 9), or no Masseba at all.†††) On cylinders of the late Babylonian empire, the altar on which the animal (a dog) stands or lies is often of equal height with and as richly decorated as the two sacred symbols, which have now, however, dropped their distinctive forms of Masseba and Ashera, and appear as almost similar stones of rather irregular oval form slightly voided at the edges. On one of the holy stones rests often the radiate sun, on the other the crescent moon. On Pl. LXXXVII, 16 I have given a late Babylonian cylinder of this class, showing the two holy stones with a priest standing before them, the dog being absent; on Pl. LXIX, 30

*) Cp. Ward "The rising sun on Babylonian cylinders" in the American Journal of Archaeology III (1887), p. 50—56.

**) Cp. also Pl. XXX, 12.

***) At the end of the scene we see the dragon Thiamat. On the cylinder Pl. XXIX. 4 Masseba and Ashera are absent. Here Marduk in fighting with a dragon, and divine honours are being paid to Ištar. On Pl. XXXIX, 326 of Clercq's work on cylinders we see the adoration of Ištar with Masseba and Ashera beside her, but with no Marduk and Thiamat. Cp. our Pl. LXXXVII, 113. A similar cylinder in the Louvre is given by Ménant (II, Pl. VII, 5).

†) VII, 18, XLIV, 17—19.

††) Cp. Ménant's Glyptique II p 70, fig. 67; p. 71, fig. 70; p. 139, fig. 132; p. 226, fig. 223.

†††) Cp. Ménant II p. 70, fig. 68.

another showing the two stones and dog, but no priest.*) The design on Pl. LXXXVII, 13 **) is very distinct. A priest is performing his devotions before the stone Masseba, the wooden Ashera and the image of the Queen of Heaven. Behind the priest we see first the rhomboid representing the vulva, above it the crescent, and above this the radiate sun. Asheras of other forms surmounted by crescents will be found on Pl. LXXIX, 11 and 12 and Pl. XXX, 11. The cylinder of the Royal Berlin Museum represented Pl. XXX, 7 shows in the centre the holy tree with the winged sun-globe above it, to the right the Ashera with the crescent, and to the left the Masseba with the radiate sun.***) In the case of many of the mythological designs on these gems it is difficult to say wheter a stone Masseba, a wooden Ashera, or an aniconic agalma formed by combining both is intended. The object or objects, whatever they be, are at all events symbols of peculiar sanctity adored by gods, demons, men and animals, and many of them belong, or belonged before they passed into ornaments, to the cycle of the Masseboth and Asheroth, the idols of Baal or Baalat. Even in the simple palmette which appears on one of the oldest known inscribed Hebrew seals (LXXVII, 8 now in the Berlin Museum)†) we may assuredly detect the rudiment of a holy tree, an Ashera. The same palmette forms the top of the holy tree on a cylinder with Phoenician inscription (LXXVII, 6): the tree is here adored by men and animals, among the latter a bearded sphinx, and above it hover the winged sun-globe and the symbol compounded of sun and crescent moon. The "provenance" of this specimen is unknown, but it is highly probable that it comes from Cyprus. We find the same "Phoenician palmette" as the topmost member of the holy tree on a Graeco-Phoenician scarab from the necropolis of Tharros (Pl. LXXVII, 21) ††), on Cyprian silver paterae (p. 47, fig. 50; p. 48, fig. 51; p. 53, fig. 52 &c.) A holy tree composed of superimposed palmettes of this form is found on Cyprian stelae (Pl. XXVI, 1 and 2) and silver paterae (p. 53, fig. 52) and on a Phoenician gem (Pl. LXXVII, 17),†††) where it is adored by two rampant animals, a winged goat and a sphinx. Both this gem and the marble slab with relief (0,50 m. = 20 in. in height) found in the neighbourhood of Arados and represented on Plate LXXXVII, 10§) are, it is highly probable, Kyprian works. The holy tree, the griffins clambering up it, the tress above the group, the pattern composed of palmettes stamped with the character of textile work, the style and the subject—all are quite Kyprian.

---

*) LXXXVII, 16 = Ménant II, p. 133, fig. 120; LXIX, 30 = ibid p. 135, fig. 124. Cp. fig. 152 on the next page.

**) Ménant II, p. 56, fig 47, a cylinder in the Montigny collection.

***) Cp. especially the third row from the top on Pl. LXIX, and our description of the plate.

†) Clermont-Ganneau "Le sceau d'Obadyahou, fonctionnaire royale israélite" in the Recueil d'archéologie orientale, 1885, p. 33—38 = Sceaux et cachets israélites, phéniciens et syriens, No. 1 = Perrot IV, p. 439, fig. 226 = our Plate LXXVII, 8. For the sake of completeness I place beside it (no. 7 on the same Plate) another old Hebrew seal = Clermont-Ganneau 2 = Perrot 227. I have already alluded to this seal and its border of pomegranates above on p. 114.

††) Spano, Bulletino Sardo I, p. 149 = Perrot III p. 237, fig. 180. Style, motive, technique and execution bear so great a resemblance to those of Cyprian gems and silver work (cp. the scene of tree-adoration on the Amathus patera, p. 47 fig. 50), that one is inclined to regard this intaglio as a work of Kyprian Art exported to Sardinia in ancient times.

†††) Lajard, Mithra LVII, 1 = Perrot II, p. 689, fig. 348. Conic Chalcedony cylinder (No. 948 in the Bibliothèque Nationale at Paris) here magnified to 1½ times the size of the original.

§) Perrot III p. 131, fig. 76 = Longpérier, Musée Napoléon III., Pl XVIII, 3.

On Mykenaean (Pl. LXXVIII, 3 and 6)*) or Graeco-Phoenician gems (for further examples see Pl. LXXVII, 13, 19**) LXXVIII, 5, 13) we find savage or fabulous animals in a heraldic attitude before a branch, pillar tree, or nondescript object partaking of the character of all three. This object, in its origin a symbol of high sanctity, embodying (as a Masseba? Ashera? &c.) the god or goddess, declined in time to the level of a mere ornament, and was finally altogether discarded. On a Phoenician seal (Pl. LXXVIII, 9) nothing is left but the two griffins facing each other.***) That Kypros very materially contributed to the formation of these types and myths is evinced by the gem with the goats†) LXXVIII, 13, found at Kurion, and evidently manufactured in the island, as well as by the Kurion bronze patera (Plates XXXII, 41, and LXXVIII, 7) on which we meet with the same pair of erect lions holding pitchers in their paws, and clothed in the skins of fish, that we see on the gem from the Vaphio tomb (Pl. LXVIII, 6). The octagonal seal Pl. LXXVII, 13 (after Lajard's Mithra XLIII, 26) must certainly, [three other octagonal seals, Pl. LXVIII 5 and 9 (= Lajard Mithra LXVII, 9 and XXVI, 6) almost certainly, have been made in Cyprus, and belong quite to that class of Cyprio-Graeco-Phoenician artistic products which has so many points of connection with the possibly contemporaneous industry of Mykenae. The winged lions on this cylinder (LXXVII, 13) join paws over an Ashera. Above is a short Phoenician inscription. Knoll in his pamphlet "Studien zur ältesten Kunst in Griechenland" regards the design of two lions on the bronze vessel from Kition (Plan LXXVIII, 7) as having the best claims to originality, but he is right only in part.††) The chief difference is this—that the pair of lions on the Mykenaean gem stand in a religious attitude on opposite sides of the holy tree (Ashera) issuing from a stand shaped like an altar; while the three similar pairs of lions on the handle of the Cyprian bronze vessel are grouped in more decorative fashion, and have neither tree nor post between them. The form of the Masseba expanding as it rises (e. g. LXIX 33, 34, 36, 43) recurs on the Lion-gate of Mykenae (LXIX, 41 and fig. 151, p. 155.) The lions rest their fore-paws on the base of a Masseba, Baal-pillar, Sun-pillar (Chamman) or some such holy symbol, like the lions on the Phrygian relief J. H. S. 1888, p. 368, fig. 10. On another Phrygian monument, the rock tomb of Arslau Kaya, two lions rest their paws on the shoulders of

---

*) 3 = Furtwängler und Löschke, Mykenische Vasen, Pl E. 16.　6 = Τσούντας, ʻΕρευναί ἐν τῇ Λακωνικῇ καὶ ὁ τάφος τοῦ Βαφείου', in the ʻΕφημερὶς Ἀρχαιολογικὴ' 1889, Pl. 10, 35.

**) LXXVII, 19 = Perrot III, p. 641, fig. 435. Perrot compares the design on this seal with the relief on the lion-gate at Mykene (our Plate LXIX, 41 and p. 155, fig. 151). Furtwängler also (Mykenische Vasen p. 67) cites the intaglio as illustrating the Mykenaean fragment from Charvati (fig. 83 on p, 65 of the present work). He compares the style of the trees on the seal with that of Mykenaean palms. In addition to the material for comparison adduced above in discussing the tree-designs collected on p. 65, I would call attention to the holy trees of Cyprian τεμένη (Pl. LXXVI) and the column of the Idalion chapel (Pl. X, 3). Furtwängler also cites the Dipylon vase, Cesnola-Stern Pl. LXVIII (= our Plate LXXXIX, 1) with its pairs of goats and kids facing the holy tree.

***) Octagonal seal in the Bibliothèque Nationale, Paris.

†) Cesnola-Stern, Pl. LXXXI, 23 (from Kurion).

††) Knoll considers the bronze vessel to be pure Phoenician work, and pronounces the gems collected in Milchhöfer's "Anfänge der Kunst in Griechenland" to be the product of an invention made in some seat of Phoenician industry, probably in Cyprus. This assertion, thus formulated, is, it seems to me untenable. Böhlau, in his notice of Knoll's pamphlet in the Berl. Philologische Wochenschrift, classes this bronze vessel as Mykenaean. I believe that the Cyprian bronze vessel in question, the Cyprian gem LXXVIII, 13, and the gems LXXVIII, 5 and 9, LXXVII, 13 belong all of them to a definite early-Graeco-Phoenician style nearly related to the Mykenaean (LXXVIII, 3, 6; LXXXIX, 3).

the idol of Kybele (Pl. LXXVIII, 1)*)] and on the façade of the same tomb we see two sphinxes with the sacred pillar between them (LXXVIII, 1 much reduced)**); on a gem of unknown provenance LXXVIII, 3***) two lions are the supporters of the sacred palm-column; on a later Persian cylinder (LXXVII, 9)†) a similar palm-column stands between two bearded sphinxes, who bear between them, resting on their crowns, the winged bust of the god. On a cone of the Louvre††) we again see bearded sphinxes underneath a winged sun-disc adoring a little column over which hovers a globe: the capital of the column resembles the heads of columns or tree-tops represented on Plate LXXVI and Plate LXXVII, 19. On LXXVII, 20,†††) a large stone seal, we have bearded sphinxes before a tall palm-tree, and a Cyprian gem (LXXVII, 18 = fig. 55 on p. 57 above) shows us two similar monsters raising their paws in adoration to a stylized post surmounted by a crescent (evidently an Ashera). The work is Cyprian, and shows clearly how from the straight post, by artificially curving branches left unlopped, or adding curved artificial branches, and by plaiting and arranging the twigs and leaves, those fantastic holy trees of which we have already seen so many, and four further examples of which we now encounter on Pl. LXXVII, 6, 13, 17, 21, were gradually produced. On another cylinder of the same Plate (no. 12)§) two bearded sphinxes in the same attitude are adoring a flower. Beside them stands a palm, and above them hover the crescent sun-globe and winged bust of the deity beneath which runs the inscription. This inscription is Aramaic, but the owner bears the Persian name Mithras. The cylinder no. 10, on the same plate§§), found in the Lebanon, likewise bears an Aramaic inscription, but is of Persian origin. A king or god is struggling with two lions beside a palm-column, above which floats the crescent. On no. 11§§§), a cylinder in the British Museum of the same epoch as the last two examples, but bearing the name of the Persian owner in Phoenician characters, we see a similar scene, but the holy tree is absent. The god or king here wrestles with a bearded sphinx and griffin. The cylinder no. 14,°) where the representation is more Assyrian in character, also bears an Aramaic inscription. Here two enormous winged demons, and a priest of diminutive stature, have met for the celebration of some act of worship under the shadow of the winged sun-disc, and before a holy symbol (burning tree or altar?). Nos. 15 and 16 on this Plate are the most important of all. The first (15),°°) a conic seal in the British Museum, shows us a man, possibly a priest, adoring the pillar of the sun or moon, the Chamman of the Hebrews, erected on an altar. Above his head floats the crescent moon. The Phoenician owner of the seal is called Pal-zir-Shamash, i. e. servant of the god Samas, who was the son of the Moon-god Sin, and was himself conceived sometimes as a Sun-god,

---

*) Journal of Hellenic Studies, 1884, p. 245 = Perrot V, p. 157, fig. 110.
**) Journal of Hellenic Studies 1884, Pl. XLIV = Perrot V, p. 156, fig. 109.
***) Lajard, Mithra XLV, 24.
†) Ibid., LVII, 2.
††) Ibid., LVII.
†††) Perrot III, p. 136.
§) In the Schlumberger collection published by Ph. Berger, "Cylindre perse avec legende araméenne," in the Gazette Archeologique, 1888, p. 143 = Perrot V, p. 853, Fig. 504.
§§) Ménant, Glyptique II, p. 220, fig. 213 = Perrot III, p. 635, fig. 426. See Proceedings of the Society of Biblical Archaeology, 1883—84, p. 16.
§§§) Lajard, Mithra L, 6 = Ménant II, 214.
°) Ménant II, 211 = Perrot III, 422.
°°) De Vogué, Mélanges, Pl. VI, 23 = Levy, Phöniz. Studien II, 30 = Ménant, Glyptique II, fig. 222 = Perrot III, p. 648, fig. 454.

sometimes as a Moon-god.*) On the second stone (16), a cone first published by Renan**) we see a priest standing before an altar, behind which a shorter Ashera of tree shape and a taller Baal-column surmounted by a phallus are clearly visible. On the accompanying Phoenician inscription we read the name Hinnom. In the valley of the children of Hinnom lay the fire-sanctuary so deeply loathed by the Hebrew prophets, that Tophet at which under the idolatous kings Ahaz, Manasseh and Amon, until its desecration by Josiah, sons and daughters were burnt in the fire to Baal-Moloch.***)

We pass to Plate XXXII, figs. 1—18. Here we see some of the designs on Plates LXXVII and LXXVIII repeated to facilitate a comparative survey. On 15 of these 18 designs it is a Masseba, Ashera, or combination of both, which is adored by a pair of animals or monsters confronting each other in a heraldic, and in most cases erect attitude. Figs. 1, 6, 10 are certainly, fig. 14 probably, Mykenaean. On figs. 22—24, of which 22 and 23 are Mykenaean, two couched or rampant animals face a tree which is clearly characterized as a palm; while in fig. 20 a small palm stands behind each of the two animals. On fig. 19 (now in Berlin: from Cyprus, but the style is Mykenaean) a tree stands behind the ox, and in front of him lies a branch resembling the branches and emblems of Cyprian cylinders (Plates LXXVIII, 12 and LXXIX, 1). The intaglio on the gold ring from the Vaphio tomb perhaps represents a festival of Adonis. The tree reared in a pot on the left may be a garden of Adonis. The nude man who is trying to pull the tree down may be Tammuz-Adonis, the female figure in the centre Astarte-Aphrodite. The figure reclining on a couch on the left may be intended for one of the images of Adonis laid out at the feast of mourning. The holy symbol (tree, pillar or flower?) visible on the gem, of which figs. 13 and 14 show the original and the impression (in the Berlin Museum: provenance unknown) resembles the symbols on figs. 15 (= Perrot p. 136) and fig. 16 (= Pl. LXXVII, 19) and the Cyprian holy trees (e. g. Pl. LXXVI). The Berlin gems 17, 18 and 24, here published for the first time, are evidently late Babylonian or Persian. On 18, the cylinder with the scorpion-man, the holy symbol has shrunk to a small post; on the cone with the two bearded sphinxes, a lofty palm stands in its place; this design resembles that of Pl. LXXVII, 20. We may now briefly discuss the Cyprian sculpture in stone, fig. 2 on Plate LXXVIII, †††) and in doing so we are again guided

---

*) Cp. Sayce, Religion of the Babylonians, p. 167—8.

**) Mission de Phénicie, p.144 = Levy, Siegel und Gemmen I, 14 = Ménant II, 223 = Perrot III, fig. 455

***) Riehm's Bibellexikon I, p. 615; 2nd Kings XXIII, 10; 2nd Chron. XXVIII, 3; XXXIII, 6. Jeremiah VII, 31, XIX, 6. Ménant in his description of these noteworthy seals, refers to other intaglios with similar designs figured on pages 139 and 140 of his work, and almost certainly dating from the reigns of Darius and Artaxerxes. He is doubtless right in assigning to the same date these two seals, in the one case with the name of the owner "servant of the god Samas" and in the other with the mention of Hinnom.

†) Nos. 7 and 16 here = Pl. LXXVII, 13, 19; Nos, 10, 11, 1, 12, 9 here = Pl. LXXVIII, 3, 5, 6, 9, 13; 15 here = Perrot III, p. 136 (reil de lampe); 8 here (the Mykenae gate) = fig. 151 over the page; 2 here = Tzountas, Vaphio tomb X, 36; 3 = Furtwängler and Löschke, Mykenische Vasen, Pl. E, 11; 4 = Tzountas, ibid. X, 13; 5 = Furtwängler and Löschke Pl. E, 6; 6 = ibid., Pl. E. 13; 13 and 14 are from photographs of a stone in the Western Asiatic Department of the Royal Berlin Museum (catalogued V. A. 2524, 13), and its impression; 17 from a stone in the same collection (No 512); 18 from another stone in the same collection (V. A. 2111); 19 = Furwängler and Löschke Pl. E, 18; 20 = Tzountas, X 40; 21 = Tzountas 39; 22 = Berlin V. A. 2520; 23 = Furtwängler and Löschke 30; 24 = Berlin V. A. 2520; fig. 41 (cp. Pl. LXXVIII, 7) = Perrot III, p. 795 fig. 556; For figs. 24—40 see the Description of the Plates at the end of the work.

†††) Found in 1890 by unauthorized excavators at Amathus, in a Graeco-Phoenician tomb of the beginning of the 6th or end of the 7th century B. C. and acquired by me for the University Museum in Bonn,

to the Lion-gate, at Mykenae and the allied representations in Mykenae itself, Phrygia, and Cyprus. A quadruped, unhappily headless, but, apparently, a dog*), rears up against a pillar. For purposes of comparison I give here (fig. 156) a cut of a late-Babylonian cylinder, with cuneiform inscription of very late date, obtained by L. Raymond in Babylon, and now in Count Woronzow's collection.**) Above an altar of columnar form float the radiate sun and crescent moon. Behind the priestly cele-

Fig. 156.

brant rises the holy palm, in front of which a dog appears to be devouring the offal from the victim. To the right of the altar a rampant winged sphinx rests its fore-paws against the first line of the inscription in just the same manner as the dog in the Cyprian group places his on the column.***) Now the presence of sacred dogs, the Kelabim of the Hebrews and Phoenicians, in the sanctuary of Aštoret and Mikal on the acropolis of Kition, is attested; two are mentioned in the temple-tariff (Corpus Inscriptionum Semiticarum Nos. 86 and 87). They were fed at the deity's expense, out of the revenues of the temple. They are holy animals like the dogs of Asklepios in his sanctuary at Epidaurus.†) On the cylinder Pl. LXIX, 44 (= Collection Clerq 373) we see a dog on the altar which supports the Ashera and Masseba, and a second Masseba standing beside this altar. The originals of these designs of animals, mostly themselves sacred, jumping up against sacred symbols trees, posts, and columns††) (the Masseboth, Asherot and Chammanim), were supplied by the countries of the Euphrates and Tigris. On Pl. XXIX, 1 Izdubar and Eabani appear in company

the director of which, Mr. Löschcke, writes to me as follows: "The column against which the quadruped rears is 13 cm. (a little over 5 in.) in height. The capital is red; on the shaft and on the beast's body some gray stripes are visible. I believe that this column answers to the Egyptian columnar altars on which the victim is laid. The animal, probably a dog, is, as the breakages show, dragging a longish object from the top of the altar. He must be one of the sacred dogs reared in Semtic sanctuaries and in those of Asklepios, and discussed by Reinach in the Revue Archéologique 1884, p, 129 ff. The dog is appropriating his part of the sacrifice".

*) Cp. the dog of Marduk-Merodach on fig. 117 (p. 85) and Ménant in Collection Clercq pages 154—5. See also the remarks on p. 149 of the present work.

**) Lajard, Mithra LII, 4.

***) Among the vases brought as presents by the Keta to the Egyptian king Thutmosis III, on the mural paintings of the tomb at Rekhmara, is one with two handles formed by dogs standing on their hind-legs (represented Pl. CXXXVI, 2). In an earth-tomb at Tamassos of the end of the Bronze Period, I unearthed (in 1889) a hand-made painted vase of similar form. The handles are formed by two quadrupeds (evidently dogs) rearing up against the vase. It would seem that this ceramic motive, which uncommonly resembles the motive of animals resting their fore paws on sacred pillars and trees, reached Egypt through the Keta, of whose territory Cyprus also formed part.

†) S. Reinach, Revue Archéologique 1884, p. 129—135. "Les chiens dans le culte d'Esculape et les Kelabim des stéles peintes de Citium." Cp. also, for dogs in Assyria since the reign of Asurbanipal, Collection Clerq pp. 154—55, No. 264 and fig. 117 on p. 85 above. For dogs in the ritual of the second Babylonian empire. Cp. Ménant, Glyptique, II, pp. 134—5, figs. 121—124; also our remarks on p. 150 and Pl. LXIX, 30 and 44.

††) Cp. above p. 65, fig. 83; p. 78, figs. 106 and 52a and b; p. 79, fig. 107; p. 80, fig. 109: p. 85, figs. 113 and 115; p. 87, fig. 125; p. 88, figs. 126 and 127; p. 90, fig. 129; p. 91, fig. 128.

Fig. 137. The Lion-gate of Mycenae

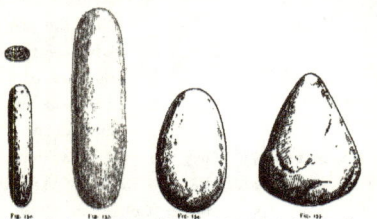

Fig. 130.   Fig. 131.   Fig. 132.   Fig. 133.

[Fig. 130-133. Rows find as sign at the lion-portion of Tirynthem (kupron). Average height about 1cm. Cp. p. 118.]

with two erect bulls and a lion grouped about a tree and post symbol resembling a balance (the holy symbol repeated Pl. LXIX, 4). The tree, evidently a cypress, (Cupressus horizontalis) is exactly like the tree on the Cyprian vase Pl. LXXIII, 5 and 8 (the tree is repeated Pl. LXIX, 3). On another cylinder (Pl. XXIX, 9)*) we see a similar scene; Izdubar, two bulls and a lion are here grouped round an artificial tree. On No. 5**) of the same Plate (XXIX) two goats are rearing up against a tree or post, while two men perform sacrifice before a cone or tripod.

On cylinder-designs of higher antiquity the god Merodach-Marduk is often represented, like the Cyprian and North-Syrian god Rešef, armed with bow and arrow. Between Merodach, the bowman about to release his arrow, and Thiamat, the winged or wingless dragon, there stands in most cases a natural or artificial tree (Pl. XXIX, 6***) and 7†); the tree of 6 is repeated on Pl. LXIX, No. 112); or at times the god stands between two holy trees or symbols (Pl. XXIX, 8††); the two holy symbols are repeated on Pl. LXIX, 3). The winged sun-globe, the radiate sun, the crescent moon, the seven Pleiads and the fish stand as sacred symbols of the sky, water, animal and vegetable life, plenty and fertility. Later when Marduk-Merodach becomes, like Izdubar-Asur-Melqart-Bes (Pl. LXXVII, 5) a subduer of animals, the palm stands beside him (Pl. XXIX, 16†††) and Pl. LXXVII, 10; the tree is repeated Pl. LXIX, 105). On the Persian cylinder, LXXVII, 5,§) we see the divine lord of animals standing on two sphinxes and hugging two antelopes in his arms. Two conventional trees (a cypress and a palm?) stand to right and left of him. On the right two lions are adoring a holy plant (the lotus?) surmounted by bust of the god with its four wings. A priest stands in the space between the two groups. (The three holy symbols are repeated LXIX, 12). The holy palm rises also behind Ištar, conceived as a martial goddess, armed with bow and arrow and standing on a lion's back (Pl. XXIX 14 §§) the tree repeated LXIX, 115. The same tree stands behind a throned divinity on a cylinder (Pl. XXX, 1)§§§) which belongs to one group with the cylinders XXX, 2 (= LXXV, 6) and LXXV, 8 (p. 110 above). The cylinder XXX, 4°) may be also regarded as a member of the same group. Here the throned deity is seated in a chamber or shrine at the entrance of which stands the holy tree (Ashera?) in the form of a palm-branch.

On three further cylinders we see representations of felled trees set up on stands, the Asheroth of the Bible, the Aoia of Kypros. The lower extremity of both the trees on the cylinder Pl. XXX, 5°°), one evidently natural the other artificial, consists of three apices or feet (cp. fig. 5, 6, 11, 115, 116, 117 on p. 85). On the second example (Pl. XXVIII, 18)°°°) an artificial pole (Ashera?),

---

*) Collection Clercq IX, 78.

**) Ménant, "Oriental cylinders of the Williamson collection " in the American Journal of Archaeology II, p V, 8.

***) Ménant Glyptique II, Pl. VII, 6.

†) American Journal II, Pl. VI, 9.

††) Ibid., Pl. VI, 16.

†††) From a photograph of the original, no. 563 in the Western Asiatic Department of the Royal Berlin Museum. Cp. our plates on the palm below CLV–CLVIII.

§) Chalcedony cylinder in the British Museum = Lajard, Mithra LIV, A. 13.

§§) Ménant, Glyptique II, Pl. VIII, 1. (in the British Museum).

§§§) Collection Clercq, Pl. XVI, 144.

°) Ibid. 143.

°°) Ibid., XVI, 145.

°°°) Ibid. XVII, 156.

rudely imitative of a human figure, is fixed upon a kind of table or stand. (The holy symbol is repeated, Pl. LXIX, 6). In the third case (Pl. XXIX, 13)*) a post (repeated Pl. LXIX, 14) with three pairs of arms, two pairs of legs and three protuberances, the uppermost of which may represent a head, stands between two deities in whom we must recognise the King and Queen of heaven. Above float the crescent moon and the seven Pleiads. In the centre a priest is adoring the Ashera. The one deity has an aureole, the rays of which terminate in stars; the rays of the aureole with which the other is invested terminate in discs. The interstices of the group are occupied by a bird, a fish, the radiate sun, and the symbol of the vulva (here very plain). On a Cyprian vase (Pl. LXXX, 6; the idol = no. 15 on Pl. LXIX) we meet with a very similar design. The body of the strange, rudely anthropomorphic idol is here formed by one of those concentric circles which were so much liked by the Graeco-Phoenician ceramic artists of Kypros.**) On Plate LXIX, A-H, I have grouped eight further Cyprian designs taken from Goodyear's "Grammar of the Lotus".***) Of these D is a Cyprian tomb-stone surmounted by an omphalos, or truncated pine-cone (or lotus-bud?).†) The re- maining seven designs are from vases; A and B certainly represent the emblem of a feminine deity, the feminine triangle, on a kind of stand (an Ashera?): C a holy emblem of more columnar form, with appendages rudely representative of human arms; E is the sacred triangle; on the vase two birds are perched upon it, another bird stands beside it, and to right and left of it are two other similar triangles surmounted by pillars; G is a holy symbol — a cross with rays on the shoulder of a vase the neck of which (see Goodyear) is summarily indicative of the human form; H seems to be a sacred symbol composed of the triangle, as representative of the feminine deity, and the sun-globe as re- presentative of the male — both set on a staff.††) The fact that on many of these Cyprian vase- designs the original mythological significance is no longer present, or present only in a shadowy form— being trivialised or nullified by a decorative instinct stronger than the religious—does not impair the pri- mitive value of these holy symbols. (Cp. also pages 104 and 106 above and Plates LXXIII and LXXIV.) Three trees, rendered in very realistic fashion, enliven the scenes on the remarkable cylinder which has until now been universally considered to be old Babylonian (Plate XXVIII, 1)†††). If we com- pare it with the Cyprian example (Plate XXXI, 13) §), we are immediately convinced of the close connection that exists between the technique, the style, the typology and the mythology of the two. The simpler representation on the Cyprian cylinder now at Nicosia is a reduction of that on

---

*) Ménant, "Glyptique" II, Pl. VII 4; the original is in the Louvre.

**) Cp. Goodyear, "Grammar of the Lotus," p. 305 and Pl. XLVIII, 9; p. 341 and Pl. LVII, 3.

***) A = ibid. p. 297, fig 157; B = fig 152; C = fig. 153; D = fig. 120; E = Pl. XLIX, 8; F = Pl. XLIX, 4; G = Pl. LX, 15; H = Pl. XLIX, 11.

†) The object resembles, more than anything else, the upper portion of a pine-cone. Entire pine- cones are met with in Cyprian tombs of Hellenistic and Roman, but generally not in those of much earlier date. I have myself dug up several, and in Cesnola's Atlas (CXXI, 882—885, 887, 889—891) eight examples are given.

††) A number of other interesting parallels from Cyprian myth and typology will be found scattered in Goodyear's book.

†††) Collection Clerq III, 26. The style and motive of the design on the well-known Caillou Michaux (Perrot II, p. 609—11, figs. 300 and 302) should be compared.

§) Cylinder of black jasper, found by unauthorised diggers in a rock tomb of the necropolis of Ayia Paraskevi near Nicosia, and now in the collection of Mr. E. Konstantinides at Nicosia; here given in the dimensions of the original. A sketch of the designs was published by S. Reinach, "Chroniques d'Orient" p. 420 [8,80].

the Parisian cylinder in the possession of M. de Clercq. In both instances we have a goddess with a pair of horns, or even as it appears with two pairs, to whom the Hebrew appellation of Astaroth-Karnaim*) is exactly suited. On the larger cylinder the goddess, enthroned and with two fishes and two trees on either side of her, is subduing two snakes. Beneath her are two horned quadrupeds disposed round a ring. Next to her a god is subduing wild beasts of the lion species, and in the field below him are two fantastic quadrupeds**) and a gigantic bird. A tree overshadows him.***) It may be considered certain that in this instance also we have before us sacred trees, which explain the frequently mentioned Asheroth of Holy Scripture.†)

With regard to Cyprus, the special object of our study, I would refer to what has been said in this and the preceding sections and to the numerous illustrations that have already been given††) of sacred trees, pillars, columns, triangles, torches, cones of wood and of stone. On Plate LXXXVII, 1—9†††) I give nine other cylinders from Cyprus, on each of which is figured a sacred tree, which is either worshipped or held by men, animals or fabulous beings (1—8). Very often on the Cyprian cylinders two figures or one,—with raised arms, as if taking an oath—stand near the sacred tree (LXXIX, 4, p. 29, fig. 1, p. 87, fig. 120)†††) the sacred column (LXXIX, 2 and 3, XXVIII, 21) or the sacred symbols (LXXIX, 1 = LXXIV, 2). Far more important in the life of the Hebrews than the ceremony of "holding the twig to the nose" described above shown upon the monuments, was "the planting of the Ashera, or holy tree" and "the erection of the Masseba or holy pillar."

The Abrahamites planted trees and erected pillars in memory of important events, according to a custom which, from time immemorial has been, and is still held in honour among peoples of widely different race, of different lands and independently of one another, and which we ourselves are wont to observe to the present day.§) Had we no other Biblical instances than, for example, that of the tamarisk, which Abraham planted at Beer-sheba in memory of the Covenant he made

---

*) Genesis XIV, 5.

**) The design and the hump of the quadrupeds should be noted. Compare also the design on the Cyprian cylinder, Pl. LXXXVII, 6. The humped ox of the Assyro-Babylonian monuments evidently appears also on Cyprian monuments at an early date. Cp. Goodyear, "The Grammar of the Lotus," p. 191, and Keller, "Thiere des klassischen Alterthums in kulturhist. Beziehung," p. 70.

***) For further details, see explanation of Plate XXVIII.

†) Other peculiarities connected with the numerous examples given of holy trees, pillars, poles, columns, crosses, cones, triangles of wood or stone, which illustrate the Asheroth and the Masseboth, will be best studied in the explanations of Plates XXVIII—XXXII, LXXVII—LXXXV. Plate LXIX, with its explanations affords a specially instructive survey.

††) P. 29-31, figs. 1—28; p. 36—38, figs. 37—39; p. 40—57, figs. 41—56; p. 61, figs. 68 and 69; p. 63, fig. 75; p. 65, figs 77-81; p. 67, fig. 84; p. 70, fig. 92; p. 75, figs. 101 and 102; p. 77, fig. 105; p. 87, figs. 118—120, 122—125; p. 91, fig. 128; p. 94, fig. 134. Plate XVIII, 1, XXVIII, 16, 17, 20, 21, 22; XXXI, 6—9, 11, 13 and 14; LXXIII, 3, 5—8; LXXIV, 1—8; LXXV, 7; LXXVI, 1—12; LXXVII, 6 and 17, possibly from Cyprus 18 = above p. 57, fig. 55; LXXVIII, 3, 12, (= LXXIV, 1) 13; LXXIX, 1 (= LXXIV, 2) 2, 3, 4 (= p. 87, fig. 118), 5, 6, 7, (= LXXIV, 4), 8 (= LXXIV, 3,) 10, 13, 20 (= p. 61, fig. 69); LXXX, 5; LXXXI, 3—6; LXXXII, 8; LXXXIII, 6, 7, 19, 22; LXXXVI, 1—7.

†††) It was from these and other figures, which occur more particularly on Cyprian and Asia Minor cylinders, that the Cypriotes, as will appear from a consideration of Plate LXIX, derived their Cyprian syllabary.

§) Count Arnim, Owner of the Barony of Muskau, inaugurated the annual meeting of the Society of Anthropology and primitive history held at Muskau in June 1892, by planting a young oak next to the celebrated Hermann oak. Cp. also the material collected by Bötticher in his Baumcultus ".

with Abimelech, we should not be justified in recognising a special cult of the Ashera in the sacred trees from the Cyprian and Western Semitic fields of discovery. If Abraham planted the tree, and called there on the name of the Everlasting God,*) and Isaac on the renewal of the covenant with the King of the Philistines built an altar in the same place, and pitched his tent there,**) there was nothing in these acts to clash with the commands of Jahwe. Even in the times of Moses Jehovah still has his seat in the bush.***) But as early as the time of Moses, or at any rate at the time when the third and fifth books of Moses were written, it appears that the limits of simple honour paid to the tree had been transgressed, and that the trees and pillars by the altar of the Lord were placed there as divinities themselves, that is, as images of the goddess Ashera or Aštoret and of Baal, simultaneously with Jahwe.†)   In order to combat this abomination, which was connected with the idolatrous worship of the Sun, Moon, and Stars ††), the law of justice (Deuteronomy XVI, 21 and 22) decreed: 'Thou shalt not plant for thyself any Ashera (sacred tree, according to Kautsch) of any kind of wood near to the altar of Jahwe thy God, which thou makest for thee.   Neither shalt thou set thee up any pillar (Masseba) since Jahwe thy God hateth it."   And further we read (XVII, 5): "Then shalt thou bring forth that man or woman, which hath committed that wicked thing .... and shalt stone them with stones till they die."†††)   When the rebellious children of Israel, therefore, erected pillars hewn into unmistakable shape, Baal columns of the shape and kind which Jahwe abhors, they also planted next to the altar of Jahwe Asheroth of various kinds of wood, but of a quite distinct character and shape, which from Moses down to the latest Prophets was an abomination in the eyes of Jahwe. Sometimes they planted real trees with their roots, sometimes hewn trees without roots, which soon withered up. Sometimes the hewn trees were placed on stands or tables like our Christmas trees. This solemn act of the setting up or planting of the Ashera sealed treaties of peace between peoples and kings, it marked the covenant between God and man. Just as I was able to exemplify by monuments the idolatrous practice of holding twigs to the nose, so now I am able to point to a series of monuments which represent the solemn act of the planting of the Ashera, and particularly in the case of two peoples, the Cyprians and the Hittites. I have given on Plate LXIX, 120—125, six cylinders which reproduce the scene in question. Four of them certainly belong to Cyprus (120—123) §) although in the case of two only can it be certified that they are of Cypriote production (120—121). §§) Two further cylinders, the figured portions of which I reproduce in figs. 124 and 125,§§§) may belong to Cyprus, but they may also have been made and found in Western Asia. They bear no trace of the genuine Assyro-Babylonian style. On five of the six

---

*) Genesis XXI, 31—33.
**) Genesis XXVI, 25.
***) Cp. above, p. 110.
†) Cp. Movers I, p. 581.

††) Above the Masseba or Chamman, and above the Baal image we have the sun star, above the Ashera or the Aštoret cone the crescent of the moon, Plate LXXIX, 16 = LXIX, 33, or the globe of the sun surrounded by the half moon above the divinity conceived as androgynous.

†††) Deuteronomy, XVII, 5.

§) 120 was given on p. 65 fig. 81, 121 on p. 61, fig. 69 and Plate LXXIX, 20, 122 and 123 are reproduced on Plate XXVIII 19 and 27 (= de Clercq-Ménant IV, 32 and 39).

§§) Cp. below the explanation of Plate XXVIII.

§§§) 124, 125 = Clercq-Ménant IV, 37 and 38.

figures (120—122, 124 and 125) the ceremony of the planting of one (121, 122 and 124) or of two Asheroth (120 and 125) is represented. In 125 the accompanying symbols (omitted in the illustration) of the sun, star and the half moon indicate that of the two sacred trees the one is to be regarded as male, the other as female. In 120 and 121 (cf. p. 65 fig. 81 and p. 61 fig. 69) the burnt offerings in honour of the ceremony of the planting of the Ashera are indicated by the heads of oxen near to the altar. In the scenes of oath-taking in front of the Ashera, when the covenants are being sworn to (e. g., p. 29 fig. 1; p. 87 fig. 120, Plate LXXIV, 2) the head of the sacrificial ox often lies on the altar, or is represented suspended in the field of the design. (Plate LXXXVII, 1 and 2). In other cases the sacrificial animals either stand or are suspended near to the scenes of oath-taking or of worshipping the sacred symbols (Plate LXXIV, 1 = LXXVIII, 12, LXXIX, 2 and 3). In addition to the Cyprian scenes already mentioned enacted in front of the sacred emblems, similar swearings of covenants between men, or compacts between men and divinities, or between divinities and demons with the accompaniment of sacrifices, appear to be represented on Plate LXXVII in figs. 1 and 6 (with Phoenician inscriptions) and in fig. 14 (with an Aramaic inscription), on Plate LXXIX, 11, 12, 15, and on in LXXX, 1 and 2 (Hittite cylinder). The cylinder found in Cyprus and given on Plate XXXI, 9 (No.736 in the department of Western Asia of the Royal Museums in Berlin) although found in Cyprus (from Cesnola's collection), fully agrees in character with another cylinder which Ménant considered to be Hittite (see Plate XXXI, 10 = Ménant II, Plate X, 1; Cesnola-Stern LXXV, 6 and others, and my Plate LXXX, 1 and 2). I consider it quite probable that this example also may eventually be claimed for Cyprus. The sacred symbol may be an Ashera, a Masseba, or a symbol arising from a combination of both, with the star surmounting a pillar that recalls the anthropomorphic shape (with head, breast, arms). Two figures, presumably a man and a woman, are worshipping or taking an oath in front of it. The twisted band characteristic of this group of cylinders separates the winged sphinx from the winged lion, before the mouth of which is the head of an animal. If the Hittite hieroglyphic inscriptions before us be alternately considered it will be seen that the group of hieroglyphics of which I give three different examples on Plate LXXIX, 19 (Hamath), 21 (Aleppo), 18 (Jerabis) recurs frequently.*) If this group of hieroglyphics be further compared with the scene on the Cyprian cylinder, Plate LXXIX, 20, it will be noticed that the Hittite group of hieroglyphics in all its variants is only an abbreviation of the scene on the Cyprian cylinder. It is well known that these Hittite hieroglyphic inscriptions have not been deciphered, yet it cannot be doubted that many are documents important to the history of the world and of civilisation. After what we read in the cuneiform inscriptions, in the Egyptian hieroglyphic inscriptions, in the Aramaic, Hebraic and Phoenician inscribed monuments, and after what the Bible teaches us, we may venture to see in these Hittite inscriptions similar political or religous documents, and records of the most important events of the history of the time. Many of these inscriptions begin or end — according as one begins to read backwards or forwards — with the hieroglyphic group of which we have given three instances. However the text may sound phonetically, the sense in each case would be identical, namely, that the event recorded begins or ends with a religious ceremony, the planting of an Ashera (or the erection of a Masseba) accompanied by the sacrifice of animals, four footed beasts and birds. On

---

*) Cp. Plate LXIX, 118 and 119 and W. Wright, The Empire of the Hittites, London 1884, and also: Transactions of the Society of Biblical Archaeology, Vol. VI and VII.

the Aleppo inscription (LXXIX, 21 = LXIX, 119) we again have a human figure setting up the sacred symbol. On the inscription from Hamath (LXXIX, 19 = LXIX, 118) the Ashera pillar is being planted by a human arm, while the female symbol is seen above it, and the male symbol below. On the inscription from Jerabis (LXXIX, 18) the human arm can no longer be recognised, yet the same or a similar group of hieroglyphics is employed. Above the Ashera pillar floats the head of an animal, and the sign emblematic of humanity in its dual male and female element. From a combination of Genesis XXI and XXV with Leviticus I—VII it would seem that the Cyprian cylinder, Plate LXXIX, 20 (= p. 61, fig. 69) and the group of hieroglyphics 18, 19 and 21 on the Hittite Plates, bear the following meaning: "They made a covenant and planted an Ashera, and called there upon the name of God, and made sacrifice in that place." Equally interesting is the comparison of the sacrifice described in Genesis XV with the pictures of sacrifices on the Cyprian cylinders, figs. 2, 3 and 20 of Plate LXXIX.

When Jahwe made his covenant with Abraham, he demanded a heifer, a she-goat, a ram, a turtle-dove and a young pigeon. On cylinder 20 the couchant quadruped seems to be a goat, the ox head indicates the sacrificial kine; two birds are also represented. On cylinder 2 there are three four-footed sacrificial beasts, on 3 two quadrupeds and two birds engraved. One bird is larger than the other. On the Hittite hieroglyphic monuments the five animals of Abraham's sacrifice seem likewise to be represented in abbreviation. On fig. 18 of Plate LXXIX two birds are distinctly visible, a larger and a smaller one, two heads of animals, and a fifth less distinct object, which may, however, also be the head of an animal. (Cf. the better illustrations in W. Wright's Empire of the Hittites.)

Like the planting and the setting up of the Ashera, and of the Baal column or sun pillar, so too their cutting down and destruction was an important ceremonial rite. This annihilation of the emblems displeasing to Jahwe, this destruction of the forbidden pillars, this felling of the sacred trees and groves which were the objects of an idolatrous worship, was an iminently important political and religious act. From the days of the falling away from Jahwe, every king in Israel and Judah, who obtained the sovereignty and was faithful to Jahwe, inaugurated his reign with this ceremony. The Assyrian kings in like manner were wont to mark their victories by the felling of the sacred groves in the neighbourhood of the conquered city, and to represent this on their reliefs. The representation of this act in the chastisement of the conquered people also passed over into Cyprian art. On the silver cup from Amathus, p. 47 (fig. 50) men are cutting down palms and other trees, evidently a sacred grove, in front of the besieged city. Jahwe speaks this word concerning Sennacherib, King of Assyria: (Isaiah XXXVII, 24:)

---

*) Cp. "Beiträge zur kunde der indogermanischen sprachen," XL, 1886, p. 250 and 251; from a letter of Dr. Deecke, where he points out for the first time two additional signs previously unknown in the Cyprian alphabet, and yet attached to it as signs denoting syllables; these occur in precisely the same form among the Hittite hieroglyphics. One sign is formed by a vertical line with a half moon turned outwards; either on the right hand or the left: used singly it means "man", and doubled it means "people" and is the determinative for proper names; in Cyprian it reads "nos". The second sign, which Deecke reads "vos" in Cyprian, corresponds to a Hittite hieroglyphic, in the form of a hand holding a small pointed pillar surmounted by halfmoon, obviously with intent to plant it, the whole being emblematic in condensed form of the planting of the Ashera.

**) I may quote as an instance that of the accession of Hezekiah, King of Judah in 727 B.C., 2 Kings, XVIII, 4. "He removed the high places, and broke the statues and cut down the holy trees and broke in pieces the brazen serpent that Moses had made." Cp. also Movers on the Ashera in "Die Phönizier" p. 560—584.

> " By the multitude of my chariots am I come up to the heights of the mountains,
>   to the outermost parts of Lebanon;
> and I »out down« the tall growth of its cedars, and its choicest fir trees,
>   and »pushed« forward to its outermost height,
> within its thickest groves."   From Kautzch's version p. 463.

This signifies the sacred mountain grove of the mountain god, of Baal and of Lebanon. The worship of this Syrian local god penetrated at an early date into Cyprus, and the Phoenician inscriptions we possess (the oldest monuments with alphabetical characters that have come down to us) were not only found in Cyprus, but also made there. They are addressed to Baal Lebanon, on whose mountain altar on mount Muti Shinoas among the Cyprian highlands they were deposited. This cult of Baal Libanon in Cyprus is several hundred years older than the passage quoted from Isaiah, and considerably older even then the time of the Kings Sennacherib and Hezekiah, which is under consideration for us. J. Euting and other Phoenician scholars are now persuaded that these votive inscriptions to Baal Libanon belong to the time of King Hiram, who was the contemporary of Solomon and of David, and the architect of the temple of Solomon.*) Isaiah XIV, 8) in the song of triumph pronounced over the fallen king of Babylon, says:

> "Even the fir trees rejoice over thee, and the cedars of Lebanon,
>   Saying, Since thou art laid down no feller is come up against us."

The anointing of the Ashera by the priests appears, as Robertson Smith in his "Religion of the Semites" (p. 171) had already conjectured, to be represented on the relief from Khorsabad given on Plate LXXXVII, 14.**) It is well known that literary tradition confirms the pouring of ointment and of oil over the idol of the Paphian Astarte Aphrodite, that is over the conical stone, or navel of the earth, as it is also called. (Engel, Kypros II, p. 136.) The Masseboth or holy pillars seem further to have been anointed with oil by the Hebrews as well. When Jacob awoke after his wonderful dream of the ladder, he set up the stone which had served him for a pillow,***) poured oil over it, and gave to the spot the name Bethel.†) A similar anointing of the Masseba and of the Ashera on the cylinder reproduced on Plate LXXXVII, 13, appears to be performed by a priest. Similar scenes of anointing or of worship may be intended on the stones with Phoenician inscriptions on Plate LXXVII, 15 and 16. In both cases the priest holds the Ashera which may stand alone upon or close to the altar (perhaps an altar to Baal)††) as in fig. 15, or may be placed on (or next to) the altar along with the Baal column (16). In fig. 1 the officiating priest touches neither the Ashera nor the Masseba, but the androgynous symbol composed of the male and female emblems.†††) Possibly it is this same

---

* The editors of the Corpus Inscriptionum Semiticarum are mistaken in not giving under the section Cyprus, but under that of Phoenicia, these inscriptions to Baal-Libanon which were found in Cyprus, and in attributing them to Libanon under the impression that they were brought to Cyprus in antiquity. Further, they do not consider the King Hiram named in the inscriptions to be the Hiram of the Bible and of the Temple, and they assume several Kings of this name.

**) G. Rawlinson. "The five great monarchies of the ancient Eastern world," II, p. 273 (Botta, Plate 146, Layard II, second series, Plate 24.) Stade, "Geschichte des Volkes Israel," p. 461.

***) To this day the shepherds and labourers of Cyprus use stones to rest their heads on.

†) Genesis XI—XXI.

††) Judges VI, 25. "And it came to pass the same night that Jahwe said unto him (Gideon): Take ten men of they servants, and a bullock of seven years old, and throw down the altar of Baal that thy father hath, and cut down the Ashera that are by it." (From Kautzsch's version).

†††) When the chronicler (2nd Chronicles XXXIV, 4) made the extracts from his authorities (2nd Kings XXIII, 6—7) he placed three different kinds of idols together instead of two. (Cp. Movers I, p. 56). I fancy

androgynous emblem which is being anointed on the Assyrian sacrificial scenes, Plate LXXXVII, 14, where two holy symbols, exactly similar except for their different supports, stand on the altar table. Another sacred solemnity is the crowning or wreathing round of the Ashera tree with garlands, myrtle and palms which are generally suspended in pairs from the sun disc that hovers above. In addition to fig. 112, p. 84 which has already been described, I would point out fig. 14 on Plate LXXVII, figs. 8 and 11 on Plate LXXVIII, and fig. 1 on Plate LXXXIV. The conception aimed at seems to be to surround the tree with sun rays. It was probably soon observed that vegetation required the light and the sun in order to develop. It is well known that light is indispensable to the chlorophyl. Therefore, as no green plant or tree can prosper without sun, the connection between the cult of the sun and that of trees arose.

The cult of the Ashera as goddess, or rather the Phoenicised form of the Assyro-Babylonian goddess Ashrat or Asherat, can be proved by an inscription to have existed in Cyprus about B. C. 375. The inscription comes from Chittim-Kition, a city and kingdom, which, as the Bible tells us, was alone known to the Hebrews. The Phoenicians held constant intercourse with it after the supremacy of Amathus and Tamassos. The Assyrian great King Sargon II. likewise considered the city as of the highest importance. It was here that he erected as an everlasting memorial the great statue of himself (see p. 95 fig. 138) which was in reality only a figured Masseba. Further, if the alabaster vase in the Syrian department of the Berlin Museum was not brought from Assyria into Cyprus, Sargon must have had a palace built where his royal stele stood. Eb. Schrader reads the inscription on the vase that comes from Kition as: "Palace of Sargon, King of Assyria". Other Assyrian names appear in Chittim-Kition under a Phoenician form. The city itself was, as already noted, surnamed Kartihadas(š)ti, i, e., "the New city", by the Assyrians. From this form the Phoenicians of Cyprus derived their Kart-hadašt. So that this inscription to Asherat tells us on the one hand how this Assyrian goddess was adopted by the Phoenicians and Cyprians and really worshipped; when once this is proved, then it follows on the other hand that the Hebraic Ashera so often mentioned in the Bible, like Aštoret, in connection with Baal, must also have been worshipped as a goddess. We saw further that the Asheroth often appear as sacred trees and pillars in the places of worship of various Cyprian divinities, either alone or in combination with the sacred pillars, the Masseboth. We proved this also in the case of the monuments of other countries of Syria. We showed how the Greeks embodied the Asheroth and the Masseboth into their typology if not into their mythology; we find that the Mycenaeans adopted them at a time, which is partly previous to the period when the oldest portions of the Old Testament arose, and partly contemporaneous with the lifetime of the poet of the Song of Deborah, which is the oldest portion of those fragments of the Holy Scriptures that have come down to us unadulterated. On Plate LXXXVIII, figs. 1 and 2, I give as further illustrations of this a Persian relief*) and a Archaic Greek vase (the François vase). The similarity of the trees is quite startling.**) We see that both Persians and Greek borrowed the forms of the

---

that he wished to be more exact than his authority, and make his theogony complete by placing next to the sign for the god and the goddess the androgynous sign, to which the Lingam of the Indians would correspond. Cp. above, p. 143.

*) From Lajard, Mithra, XLVIII, a relief from Persepolis.

**) From Benndorf, "Wiener Vorlegeblätter," 1888. III. E. B. Tylor in an article quoted above (p. 99) entitled: "The winged figures of the Assyrian and other ancient monuments" has anticipated me in comparing

sacred tree of Ashrat, of the Ashera, from the Assyrians, and soon turned it from its religious impost to purely decorative and ornamental purposes. As with the Ashera, so it was with the Masseba, as we see from the Gate of the Lions at Mycenae, and from the numberless Mycenaean gems and Greek vase paintings, like those exhibited on Plate LXXX, 4. On Plate LXXXIX I have represented together two Dipylon vases (1 and 8) a Rhodian vase (2) two Egyptian chests (6 and 7, Fig. 6 = Mittheil. Athen. XIII, p. 302, fig. 9, Fig. 7 = above p. 78, fig. 106) two Mycenaean gold plates (4 = Schliemann, Mykenae p. 207, fig. 265, 5 = ibid. fig. 266) and a portion of a Cyprian silver bowl (3 = above p. 53, fig. 52 and p. 90, fig. 52a). On the Dipylon vase found in the Cyprian city of Kurion the holy tree of the Ashera is supported by two goats rampant,[*]) while young kids are sucking just as on the painting of the Egyptian chest (fig. 6).[**]) On the Dipylon vase belonging to the Berlin Museum, published by Boehlau

---

the Persepolis relief and the François vase (i. e. the griffins heraldically disposed on either side of the side of the sacred tree) to Assyrian monuments.

[*]) See above p. 99, note 5. Furtwängler compared the vase with the figured gem (Plate LXXVII, 19) when he described the Mycenaean vase fragment (p. 65, fig. 83) in " Mykenische Thongefässe " (p. 67, fig. 36.)

[**]) Dümmler, who was the first to call attention to this object in his: " Bemerkungen zum ältesten Kunsthandwerk auf griechischen Boden " (Athenische Mittheilungen XIII, p. 302) believes now that the Dipylon vase found in Cyprus (our Plate LXXXIX, 1.) was not manufactured in Cyprus but in Athen. Along with A. S Murray I have never doubted this Attic importation, only I cannot agree with Dümmler in thinking that the material correspondence between these Dipylon vases, and the old Cyprian Graeco-phoenician vases and silver bowls, is purely accidental. I could prove that at the beginning of the 6th century the Athenians manufactured, expressly for the Cyprian market, black-figured ware, in which although employing their own motive and technical methods, they introduced Cyprian shapes otherwise unknown in Greek ceramic art, and which I not only found in Cyprus, but was the first to recognise. I have exhibited these on Plate frontispiece, where further details will be found in the description. Some 150 years previously a Dipylon vase painter working for importation did something of the same kind. He had received from a distinguished and wealthy Cypriot of Kurion a command for a gala vase. Forthwith he selected a Dipylon shape, but of a kind that does not occur exactly in Cyprian pottery. In the decoration, however, the artist made some concessions to the Cyprian taste of the day, without yet giving up his style or his motives. We only have to compare this Dipylon vase from Kurion with the Ormidhia vase p. 94, fig. 134, in order to see that the whole system of decoration observed in the geometric pattern of the Dipylon vase is derived from the gala vase of the contemporary ceramic art of Cyprus. In like manner the motives from animal life were altered, and replaced by the sacred image of the heraldic goats supporting the sacred tree (the Ashera) a motive in which the Cypriots and other inhabitants of Western Asia took special delight. It is certain that the Dipylon painters of the 7th and 8th centuries made use of Egyptian adaptations of this motive (figs. 6 and 7) just as the Cyprian silversmiths did in the 6th century (fig. 3). But wherever these and similar motives appear in Egypt (see above p. 77, fig 104; p. 78, fig. 106; p. 79, 107 and 108; p. 80, fig 109) it is evident that they are due to the influence of the presents brought by tributary nations, especially the Kefa, and that the motive was previously unknown to Egyptian art. I have further shown, above p. 87—92, figs. 125—130 and p. 70, fig. 92 (repeated on p. 92) how Cyprian, Assyro-Babylonian and Egyptian influences intermingled. Even if every wave of the stream of art and civilization, as it surged to and fro, has not yet been accurately distinguished, and even though some of its component drops may ultimately defy analysis, it is still clear that Egypt received from Western Asia motives like those of the paintings on the wooden chest (LXXXIX 6 and 7). The Egyptian artist, as he took them over, naturally painted them after his own manner and sentiment, and gave to the contours the contemporary Egyptian style with which he was familiar. These imitations combine the qualities and faults of Egyptian art; on the one side we have its finicking and mannered technique, on the other the graceful conceptions and the strivings for realism that mark some of its productions. It is to be hoped, however, that further excavations will soon enable us to analyse further and to date the strata of civilisation in the island of Cyprus, which lie between the years 600 to 1500 B. C. Then it will perhaps be possible to show more accurately how it was that the Kefti, among whom were also Cyprian Kefti, brought motives from Syria to Egypt, in order to carry them back a little later in their Egyptising and Egyptianised dress to the North, North-East and North-West, till they reached Greece. Certain Egyptian contributions are unmistakable, e. g., that of the sucking

(Jahrbuch d. Archäolog. Instituts II. 1887, p. 54, fig. 16) two birds of the crane species are grouped about the Ashera, which is represented as a conventional tree.*) On the Rhodian vase of the same Museum (fig. 2, from Furtwängler) stags are kneeling before the sacred tree, which has become more purely decorative. They remind us of the stags on Cyprian vases (p. 38, fig. 39 and Plate LXXIV, 5). In the explanations of Plates CLIX to CLXIII I show more fully how Asiatic and Egyptian motives belonging to the cult of the tree, and to the system of ornamentation derived from it, migrated west-wards to Greece. In this process the great island of Kypros, which was visited from all parts of the world because of the wealth of its copper mines, necessarily performed an important part as "Middleman".

We still have to consider the third and most interesting Phoenician Ashera inscription, which was found on actual Phoenician soil at Ma'sûb, to the North of Akko. In spite of the ease with which it can be read phonetically, the interpretation (to quote Ed. Meyer) **) offered until now in-superable difficulties. I am fortunately able with the help of the Cyprian monuments which I have found or collected, and of a few types of coins collected by E. Gerhardt, to remove the difficulties both in this and other Phoenician inscriptions. The text of the inscription reads strangely, as follows, that on the command of Melki'ashtart and of his servant Ba'alchamman a building is erected for the Astarte in the Ashera of the Elchamman. This extraordinary statement loses all its strangeness, if we examine and study the representations on Plates XVII, 2—4, XVIII, 1, XXIX, 5, LXXX. 6, LXXXIII, 4, 5, 8, 9—11, 15 and 16. Moreover we shall have to extend our enquiry, and when the ancient myths, monuments and inscriptions are silent, follow up the traditions and customs of the modern Cypriotes with good results. We begin with the representations on Plate XVII, 2—4. The remarkable terra cotta object (2 and 3) also comes from Kition and was dug up in the grove of Artemis-Ashera (See above p. 11 No. 7) on the freehold land of a Larnakiote who sold the curious fragment to Mr. Pierides, in whose collection it was for many years. He allowed me to make a photograph and a drawing from the original. I show two sides of the object (2 and 3). We see a dove-cot in the form of a hollow and slightly conical column. About the upper portion round apertures are bored through the wall; these are intended for the doves, which are moulded on the intervening spaces outside. Within a great towerlike niche sits the dove-goddess, conceived in an-thropomorphic shape. The whole object served, like the column I excavated (XVII, 4), as an incense bowl. In the case of the column, a great square opening pierces the vertical hollow cylinder hori-

---

goat or cow near the lotus or papyrus grove. Goodyear in his "Grammar of the Lotus" Plate XXVII, p. 197, 1 (after Levy) gives a scarab with a Phoenician inscription, on which a cow is suckling her calf in front of a small lotus tree. On Plate XXXII, 29, I reproduce a scarab which I found at Marion-Arsinoe, where the same scene is taking place within a grove of lotus or papyri. Among the hunting and pasture scenes of the Kurion bowl (p. 53, fig. 52 and p. 55) the cow suckling her calf within a wood is also represented. In 1885 I excavated in a holy grove sacred to a goddess protectress of animals, groups of cows and suckling calves which had been placed there as votive offerings. (See above, p. 18, No. 39). For similar votive offerings from Athienou, see Cesnola's Atlas Plate XCVIII, 666 and 669. The Athenian artist of the Dipylon vase (LXXXIX, 1) need not therefore have borrowed the motive of the goats and kids that frame the holy tree direct from Egypt, but he probably, we may say certainly, received it through the mediation of others, in this case through his Cypriot employer.

*) Jahrbuch des Kaiserl. Deutsch. Instituts, 1886, Anzeiger p. 138.

**) In Roscher's Mythol. Lexikon p. 2870.

zontally from side to side.   At the top three triangular openings are disposed at equal distances.*)
I found this columnar incense bowl in 1885 at Idalion amongst the ashes and coals of the hearth of a
great fire altar built of earth and unhewn stones, and belonging to the sanctuary of Astarte Aphrodite
(above p. 5 No, 3, cf. also p. 131).   Just as the incense vessel of Kition (XVII, 2 and 3) represents a
cone, so this one (4) represents a pillar.   Now comparing it to the great pair of monoliths which
stand on the bay at Old [Paphos (Plate XVIII, 1 = LXIX, 77) it will readily be allowed **) that the
incense vessel from Idalion (= LXIX, 78) is only a diminutive terra cotta copy of these great stones
with their horizontal cavity.   To the terra cotta diminutive of the Masseboth or columns, correspond
terra cotta diminutives of the Asheroth or trees (Plate LXXVI, 5 and 7).   These monoliths, which only
taper very slightly towards the top, stand out to this day as impressive features on the Paphian coast.
These familiar beacons possibly helped the pilgrims who sailed or rowed up to the shrine of Astarte
to avoid the shallows, and to land in the bay without running aground.   Now the sandbanks run out
further into the sea, but in those days the bay must have afforded a fair enough harbour for the
ships of the time.   We need not consider the question whether the stones were originally beacons***)
for ships or sacred stones conceived as the habitation of the Paphian goddess.   In any case we must
consider them also to have been objects of ritual, Masseboth dedicated in this instance to Astarte
Aphrodite, just as the ambrosian stones in the harbour at Tyre might be Masseboth in honour of
Melqart-Herakles.   These Tyrian monoliths represented on Tyrian coins (one on Plate LXIX, 54, reproduced from Gerhardt LX, 9 = Rochette, Hercule, Assyrian III, 2) resemble in many respects the
Paphian and other monoliths scattered about the island. †)

     Form and dimensions correspond in both cases.   On the coin of Tyre the monoliths stand
under the shadow of a holy tree, an Ashera.   Beside the Paphian stones, at the present day stand
several trees††) doubtless on the spot where the holy Asheroth flourished in antiquity.   In the case of
another monolith, known as the pierced holy stone, ἡ ἅγια τρυπιμένη †††), which stands in the Paphian
district near the modern village of Yerovasa, the bushes and underwood round about are actually worshipped at the present day.   Each of the numberless shreds of clothing suspended here (as at Solomoni,
Plate XVIII, 2) signifies that its former owner has been cured of fever by the guardian-spirit or saint, who
dwells in the stone and trees.   Near the village of Ayios Photios, also in the Paphos district, are four such

---

     *) The Cypriots are accustomed to insert in their houses just such triangular openings, as ventilation
holes and apertures for the doves that nest in the houses.   The triangular space results naturally from dis-
posing three sun dried bricks of the ordinary size and shape in the most convenient manner.   Two are placed
at right angles to each other, and the third brick laid horizontally as a basis forms two angles of about 45°.
     **) Herr von Luschan conjectures that on this broken column a cup was placed, as on the censer
which he dug up in Senscherli (as on the censers which appear on Paphian coins, as in Plate LXXXII, 8.)
Even if this were so, the foot of the censer might be conceived as a holy Masseba, and formed like one.
     ***) The monoliths could no doubt only be seen from a very short distance, and are now too far from
the present line of shore to be used as beacons.   However, the extent to which the land has since then en-
croached on the sea, and the conditions of navigation in ancient times, must not be forgotten.
     †) Further particulars concerning these remarkable memorial stones are to be found in the explanation
of Plate XVIII, 1 where the theory of oil press stones put forward by Messrs. Guillemard and Hogarth is
also met.   In my dissertation "Ancient Places of Worship in Kypros" p. 57, I have already discussed
the matter.
     ††) Not visible on our illustration (Plate XVIII, 1) but visible on Hogarth's "Devia Cypria," Plate
facing p. 46).
     †††) A very apt designation.   Cf. the stone at Paralimni (our Plate LXIX, 99).

Masseboth called by the inhabitants the "holy stones" ($\mathring{A}\gamma\iota\alpha\iota\ \pi\acute{e}\iota\varrho\alpha\iota$). The Masseba, now thrown down, near a ruined church outside the village of Kolossi (between the ancient Kurion and the modern Limassol) was still venerated in my time. Ailing children were passed through the opening, lighted tapers and lamps were placed in the niches, coins were laid on the stone as offerings and allowed to accumulate in security until removed, from time to time, by the priests of the village. Hogarth narrates how the villagers told him that sick children were passed through the openings in the great Paphos monoliths in order to be restored to health; and barren women jump through the stone at Anoyira in the hope of afterwards conceiving. L. P. di Cesnola,*) who made many interesting observations, tells us how young girls, on their marriage or on being betrayed by their lovers, came and broke their glass ornaments at the colossal triangular Masseba illustrated on the Plate LXIX, fig. 99. Old women come and light tapers at the same stone in order to be cured of bodily ailments. The remarkable custom attached to our Paphian monoliths (Plate XVIII, 1 = LXIX, 77) expressly mentioned by Hogarth and described to me in almost similar terms by the villagers on the spot (without their being aware of the reason of my query) stands in direct relation to the ratification by oath of covenants and treaties in the presence of the Masseboth and Asheroth, a practice for which I have above adduced monumental evidence, and which Biblical tradition mentions as already existing in the days of Abraham. At this day troth is literally pledged before and in these stones, by joining hands through the orifice. Just as the stones at the harbour of Tyre appear on the coins of that city, so do the two monoliths of Paphos appear on Paphian coins, but ideally transferred from their site on the shore to the temple-hill. Thus the coin figured on Plate LXXXIII, 22, shows us, in all probability, the holy cone of the Paphian goddess in the centre of the great gate of the temple courtyard, and to right and left of it the two monoliths. A dove is perched on the idol of the goddess. The coin of Sidon, fig. 17 on the same Plate (= LXIX, 65) exhibits two similar cones or triangles on a processional car of Astarte—sufficient proof that identical cones, triangles, columns or pillars of stone or wood played identical parts at Tyre, Sidon and Paphos.

We return from this digression to our pigeon-house from Kition (Plate XVII, 2 and 3) in order to compare with it the design on a coin of Tarsos,**) figured Plate LXXXIII, 16 (= Plate LXIX, 79). In both cases the goddess is represented as dwelling in a cone or triangle. As the coin-types of a city reproduce in a compendious form its great holy places and the idols which stood in them, we may state as a fact that at Tarsos in a triangular (pyramidal or conic) building of wood or stone there was set up the image of a goddess standing on a lion's back. This goddess resembles the Assyrian Ištar (Riehm's Bibellexikon, pages 113 and 114) and the city goddess of Kadesh, whose image Ed. Meyer (in Roscher's Mythol. Lexikon, col. 653) reproduces as actually representing Astarte,***) although the relief from which his illustration is taken is of Egyptian origin (it is our fig. 100 on p. 75 above).†) We further notice that just as on the coin of Paphos we have a dove perched in the

---

*) Cesnola-Stern, ps. 157—158. Our cut (Plate LXIX. 99) is after Cesnola's sketch, ibid.

**) Gerhard, LIX, 15 = Rochette IV, 2.

***) This Egyptian monument bears certainly other traces of foreign influence. For to the left of the goddess stands the god Raspu-Rešef, whose worships seems to have been first introduced into Egypt by the wars with the Hyksos and Cheta. Rešef, as we now know, is next to Astarte, the most important divinity, in Kypros.

†) Cf. also the Egyptian votive pyramidion, Plate CXXV, 1, below (= Perrot I, p. 236 fig. 154). There

one case on the idol (Plate LXXXIII, 22) in the other on the roof of the sanctuary (Plate LXXXII, 8 and LXXXIII, 19) so on the Tarsian coin a dove sits on the apex of the triangular structure enclosing the idol of Astarte. In these two cases therefore a dove-goddess (Astoret-Aphrodite), conceived as anthropomorphic, dwells in a small wooden, stone or brick structure of somewhat conical form, which is itself again an aniconic agalma, an Ashera. Astarte dwells in her mother Ashera*) who is one with El-Chammân, the god of the sun-pillars, the god who was worshipped by the erection of Chammân-stones. This sun-pillar god, El-Chammân, is further identified by Ed. Meyer with the androgynous deity Melki-Ashtart of the Ma'sûb inscription and must therefore be regarded as a deity of like nature to the bearded Aphrodite or Aphroditos, the Venus duplex of Kypros. The citizens of Chittim-Karthadašt set up in one and the same grove, on the shore of the salt lake outside their gates, dedications to Artemis Paralia and to the lady, the Mother, Ashera and votive images of Astarte dwelling in the Ashera. Within the walls of the harbour-fortress, on the Acropolis, stood the principal sanctuary dedicated, as the inscriptions show, to Mikal and Astarte.**) This pair of divinities Mikal-Ashtart suggests at once the Melki-Ashtart of the Ma'sub inscription. In the inscription from the salt lake ot Chittim, Ashera is called "Lady" and "Mother". I found in 1889 at Tamassos an inscription (now in the Berlin Museum) mentioning a μήτηρ θεῶν. It is engraved round the edge of a holy-water vessel. The Assyrian Baaltis or Belit (the Mylitta of Herodotus) is also styled "Mother of the Gods" in Assyrian and Babylonian cuneiform texts, and the same title "Mother" recurs an a Carthaginian inscription.***) We find on a coin of Myra in Lycia (Plate LXXXIII, 8)†) an illustration of a legend belonging to this cycle. The anthropomorphic idol of the Mother of the gods grows out

---

two personages a male and a female, possibly divinities, are seated in the niche. It would appear that the votive column of Kition (Plate XVII, 2) is made after Egyptian models.

*) This Ma'sûb inscription seems to point to a better explanation of the remarkable designs on Plate LXXIV. Out of the mother goddess, conceived as a tree or post, as an Ashera, issues the anthropomorphic Astarte. On the cylinder designs, figs. 3 and 4 the presence of Astarte in human form in the Ashera post is only indicated by the eyes. On the vase designs 5, 6 and 8, Astarte assuming a form more anthropomorphic than dendromorphic (6) issues from an Ashera, in the forms of which the dendromorphic prevails (8). Clermont-Ganneau, the first editor of the Ma'sûb insciption (Revue Archéologique, 1885, I, p. 382), compares with the expression "Astarte in the Ashera" the Athenian Ἀφροδίτη ἐν Κήποις and the Aphrodite of Temnos, whose image was cut out of a living myrtle. It is possible, nay probable that these are but two other variants ot the same conception; but the best illustration of the strange phrase in the Ma'sûb inscription is supplied by our Astarte seated in the Ashera post and dove cage, from the grove of Ashera-Artemis by the salt lake ot Kition. This will become still more evident when I have dealt (in the following pages) with the Chammanim and the anthropomorphic Baal Hammon in his capacity of servant of the anthropomorphic Moloch-Astarte.

**) C. I. S. 86 A. and B. Mikal here appears as the name of a distinct divinity, while at Idalion it is an epithet of Rešef. In another Kition inscription (C. I. S. 10) Rešef bears the additional name "Hes" i. e., "he with the arrow". Coming from Idalion we possess Phoenician dedications to Rešef-Mikal (C. I. S. 89, 90, 91, 92). One of these Idalion inscriptions (90) is a bilinguis, and in the Cyprian-Greek text the Phoenician Rešef-Mikal is rendered by Ἀπόλλων Ἀμυκλος (not Ἀμυκλαῖος). I believe in opposition to W. Deecke ("Zwei bilingue Inschriften von Tamassos" in the Sitzungsberichte der Königl. Akademie der Wissenschaften, 1887, p. 115) and R. Meister ("Die griech. Dialekte" II, pages 147 and 149) and with Foucart (Bulletin de correspondance Hellenique, 1883, p. 513) that the Greek epithet Ἀμυκλος is formed from the Phoenician Mikal and not vice versa. Cf. my paper "Cypern, die Bibel und Homer" (Ausland, 1891).

***) Euting ("Punische Steine," p. 21) compares the Punic word "amma" in Plautus, Poen. 33, 22 and cites the gloss in the Etym. magnum Ἀμμὰ, ἡ τροφός καὶ ἡ μήτηρ κατὰ ἱποκόρισμα καὶ ἡ Ρέα λέγεται καὶ ἀμμὰς καὶ ἀμμά (Cf. also Hesychius d. V. ἀμμάς). See Schröder in the Zeitschrift d. deutschen morgenl. Gesellsch. XXXV. p. 423–431. "Phönizische Miscellen."

†) Gerhard, LX, 8.

of the summit ot a holy tree or Ashera. At the foot of the trees two Kabiri or Dactyls are brandishing double axes. On the two coins figured as 4 and 5 *) on the same plate the goddes, evidently Artemis, dwells in the Omphalos. No. 5 (Perge) shows, in an aedicule, the head of this goddess growing out of a stone covered with network, of quite the usual omphalos form; on No. 4 (Caesarea ad Libanum) the omphalos out of which the head of the goddess (probably again Artemis) grows or peeps, has taken rather the form of a woman's body wrapped in a large mantle.**) That the omphalos already appears in Assyrian religion and art, the Assyrian form being the prototype ot the Greek, is shown by a comparison of figs. 1—3 on the same Plate.***) Fig. 1, an Assyrian cylinder, unites the omphalos as masculine symbol with the vulva as feminine symbol. Fig. 2 is an omphalos from a black-figured vase on which it is accompanied by the legend $BOMO\Sigma$. On the coin of Emesa (3) we see in the Temple the omphalos-shaped idol of Elagabalus. The omphalos is in fact only a variety of monolithic monument intermediate between the cone and the column. Figs. 9—12 on the same plate (LXXXIII) are, like 4 and 5, illustrative of the conception expressed by the phrase "Astarte in the Ashera", the conception of the iconic living in the aniconic agalma, the anthropo-morphic deity living in the lithomorphic or dendromorphic idol.†) The snakes, ears of corn and poppies which at the same time grow out of the idols containing the anthropomorphic goddess, express the fertilizing energy of an Earth-god or god of Vegetation. On the coin of Iasos in Caria, struck in the reign of Commodus, (ibid 14) the human body of a veiled goddess (Artemis) grows out of a polished stone or wooden post of cylindrical form. On the next coin (fig. 15) which is of Hierapolis, the bust of Artemis, as in the case of her Ephesian idol, grows out of an inverted conic column or a triangle with the base uppermost, answering to the representations of the vulva mentioned by Herodotus and found in the Tyrian grotto. (Figs. 145—148 on p. 147 above.)††) On an imperial coin of Carthage (Fig. 18 on Plate LXXXIII)†††) three Asheroth (here cypresses) stand in the temple. Finally on the reverse (Fig. 20b) of a Jewish bronze coin (struck under Yaddous in the reign of Alexander the Great)§) a holy tree, an Ashera, stands between two little stone Masseboth, while on the obverse of the same coin (20a) are two pots (perhaps gardens of Adonis) with plants growing in them. Although with this single exception the designs on coins and gems here collected do not even go back to the period of the Diadochi, but belong to Roman times, they are none the less valuable witnesses to the existence, in far earlier times, of certain religious conceptions and representations.

The design in relief, Plate LXIX, 61 §§) carries us many centuries further back, to the period (the 8th or 9th century B.C.) when the later Hittite empire at Boghez Kieui attained its greatest splen-

---

*) Ibid LIX, 9 and 4.

**) In Greek religion myths of the omphalos, and idols and altars of omphalos shape, apparently come into play especially in the worships of Apollo and Artemis. Figs. 6 and 7 on Plate LXXXIII are examples of Apollonian omphalos-altars in Cyprus.

***) Fig. 1 = Lajard Mithra. XIII, 2; 2 = Gerhard LIX, 1; 3 = ibid 5.

†) Asheroth like fig. 16 on Plate LXXIX, show us an evacuated triangle or cone set upon a straight post. In the vacant central space one may well conceive the goddess Ashera or Astarte as dwelling.

††) Gerhard, LIX, 7.

†††) Ibid, XLIII, 19.

§) De Saulcy, "Numismatique Juive," I. 6 = Perrot IV, p. 308, fig. 154.

§§ = Puchstein, "Das ionische Capitell," p. 60 fig. 51 = Perrot IV, p. 639, fig. 314.

dour. Two Masseboth support by its wing-tips a winged sun-disc, which thus forms as it were the canopy of an aedicula, in the centre of which is an omphalos, and growing out of it a divinity of human form. Two large Asheroth, of a form suggesting the vulva, stand between the omphalos deity and the columns. The whole aedicula is supported on his right hand by a god standing on another omphalos. On the similar design fig. 81, on the same plate*) we see occupying the place of the omphalos god an enormous phallus, which extends upwards until it meets the sun-globe.**) We are now enabled to take in its literal sense, one point excepted, a remarkable passage of Jeremiah, which thus understood, is in admirable accord with the results of our researches on the Ashera and Masseba. Jeremiah says (chapter II, verse 27) "Saying to a stock, thou art my father, and to a stone, thou hast brougt me forth." The Hebrew word for stone is feminine, and in later times it did come to pass that, as at Paphos and Sidon, the wooden post became representative of the god, and the stone cone or column of the goddess; but if we are to make the passage of Jeremiah illustrative of the primitive conception according to which the wooden symbol belonged to the goddess, the stone symbol to the god, we must substitute "stone" for "stock" and vice versa. I think I have sufficiently proved that in many cases the masculine stone Masseba is, as a fact surmounted by the masculine phallus, while the wooden Ashera at its side carries a triangle or cone representative of the feminine equivalent of the phallus. The Masseba need not be, but is in some cases, an ἀνδρὸς αἰδοῖον and at the same time a cippus or monumental stone; the Ashera similarly may be at once a γυναικὸς αἰδοῖον and a post.***) When Jeremiah (III, 9) says: "She committed adultery with stones and with stocks," the meaning is that these obscene emblems and their cultus did actually sanction adultery, just as they demanded from maidens the sacrifice of their virginity.

I also believe I have proved that the hexagonal or octagonal star is often representative of the male sex and the sun, while the sickle represents the female sex and the moon.†) The composite

---

*) Perrot, p. 645, fig. 321.

**) Chr. Belger calls my attention to another similar aedicula from Pterion, figured (after Texier) in Layard's Nineveh and its remains, II, p, 449. The canopy in the form of a winged sun-globe is here supported by two pairs of gigantic male and female organs, while a further figure of phallic form seems to stand in the centre. This design has an even grosser look than the two others. These religious images and ritual usages, so repugnant to morality. are alluded to so often in the Bible, that I am obliged to do my best to explain and illustrate them by light of literary epigraphical and monumental evidence. Archaeologists and historians of civilisation must follow doctors in aiming at the full exposition of the natural causes of such phenomena, in so far as such exposition appears to be necessary for the proper comprehension of the life of ancient peoples. Cp. e. g., Prince Pückler-Muskau in his: "Aus Mehemed Ali's Reich," III, p. 305.

***) I believe, on the contrary, with Robertson-Smith ("Religion of the Semites," p. 437—438) that the two high columns at the temple of Jerusalem were not phalli. On the other hand, I consider that, in opposition to the view of the same writer (Additional note E. ibid. "The supposed phallic significance of sacred post and pillars") and in accordance with that of Perrot (IV, p. 385), I have been able to confirm and extend Movers' views as to the obscene significance of certain Asheroth and Masseboth.

†) In different publications Ménant interprets the sun star as invariably the symbol of Samas, and the crescent moon as symbol of the goddess Sin. In many cases he may be right. It is also certain, however, that the sun star in many cases merely denotes the male deity (whether Samas, Baal, Merodach, or any other), and the crescent moon the female (Ištar, Beeltis, Aštoret &c.) Baudissin, "Semitische Religionsgeschichte" II, p. 219, confirms this view. Eb. Schrader goes farther in his essay on "Die Abstammung der Chaldäer und die Ursitze der Semiten." After the elimination of the Babylonian moon-deity Sin, Ištar-Astarte became the grave and severe moon-deity. Here Schrader shows by the help of a syllabary (III Rawl. 53, No. 2, Z. 3 sq.)

figure showing the sun star or the sun-disc with the sickle of the moon either above or below it (Plate LXXX, 1 and 7; LXXXII, 8; LXXXIII, 21, &c.) is a genuine Phoenician symbol, which corresponds admirably to the mixed sex of the Cyprian Astarte-Aphrodite. It occurs in Phoenicia and is very common in Cyprus.*) (For an instance in Carthage, see Plate LXXXV, 9. The square is also a symbol of the female sex and of fertility. A similar meaning appears to attach to the frequent representations of the fish.**) On Cyprian (p. 93, fig. 132) and on Carthaginian (fig. 157) monuments, that is on monuments influenced by Phoenicia, the juxtaposition of the hand and the fish cannot be without significance. We shall find out later how and why. First with regard to the human hand:

Fig. 157.   Fig. 158.

W. Robertson Smith has shown that a further variety of holy Masseboth, cippi, stelae or pillars are surmounted by the human hand throughout antiquity, and by the correct interpretation of a verse in Isaiah***) has adduced biblical evidence for this custom.†) I give here another Carthaginian stele fig. 158,††) from which it is evident that the human hand by itself is merely symbolical of a human being raising his hand.†††) On Plates LXXVII, 4 and LXXXV, 3 and 9,§) we see a hand surmounting three Carthaginian stelae with votive inscriptions to Tanit and Baal Hammon.§§) The human hand stands as a holy symbol for the human individual who worships and makes oath to the divinity, in fact it is an abbreviation of the scenes of prayer and of oath taking such as appear on Plate LXXIX, figs. 1—4 and elsewhere.

If along with the Carthaginian stele (fig. 157) we consider the Cyprian cylinders, Plate

how Istar and Baaltis were differentiated out of the star of Venus, Istar being the star of Venus at the rising, and Baaltis of the setting sun.

*) Many hundred examples from Cyprus can be given. It appears in Egypt as an ornament for the head of the goddess of Kadesch, who was introduced from abroad, cp. p. 75, fig. 100.

**) See p. 93, fig. 133, Plate XXVIII, 1, 13 and XXIX, 6, 8, XXX, 7; LXXXVII, 3. In reference to the Dagon-worship and fish-worship, I shall mention and reproduce many other representations of fishes.

***) "And behind the door and the post didst thou set up thy memorial; for faithless to me thou hast discovered thy bed and art gone up, thou hast made it wide . . . . thou lovedst their bed, and lookedst forth on (every hand that beckoned)." (from Kautzsch's version.)

†) Religion of the Semites, p. 437. Robertson Smith is, however, mistaken, as we see, in thinking that by the correct interpretation of a group of holy Masseboth or stelae with the human hand he has proved that the phallus never surmounted Masseboth.

††) Perrot IV, p. 485, p. 329.

†††) The Roman method of talking with the fingers and hands is well known. To this very day the Jews in the East and in North Africa observe a custom which was once universal. The uplifted hand is still placed upon the gravestones of the priests (coheinim) (as in fig. 157 and Plate LXXXV, 3 and 9). This is the position of the hand usual with the priest when giving the blessing. I have to thank my friend Baron W. von Landau for this important observation.

§) C. I. S., No. 240, Fasciculus tertius, p. 281 and No. 183.

§§) In the Corpus Inscriptionum Semiticarum I can count 68 inscribed stelae from Carthage, on which as a rule one hand and occasionally two hands are represented. The religious character of the emblem is quite evident from the manner in which these hands are represented and combined with different other sacred signs and symbols.

LXXXVII 3 and 6, p. 93 fig. 132, we shall soon see that cosmogonic ideas underlie their designs. The most interesting of the two designs (fig. 132)°) is composed of a hand, a fish, a bird, the heavenly spheres and quadrupeds. It is as though Genesis I, 28 were written down in hiero-glyphics: "Have dominion over the fish in the sea and the birds in the air, and over all creatures that move upon the face of the earth". The same is signified by the cylinder Plate LXXXVII, 6, where indeed the two fishes below on the right are indistinctly given, but where in place of the hand the man himself is introduced, in a commanding attitude. The sun, moon and stars are also most clearly recognisable. On cylinder LXXXVII, 3, the man is as yet wanting in the creation, or is again left out. On the other hand there are given the sun and moon (two spheres) the birds of the air (two birds), the fish of the sea (one fish) and the animals on the earth (one quadruped) and in addition the fresh green (one tree) that the earth brought forth. (Ge-nesis I, 12). On the Carthaginian votive Masseba (fig. 157) the human hand and fish appear side by side.**) Tanit face of Baal und Baal-Hammon, the androgynous divinity, perhaps bearded like the bearded Astoret-Aphrodite-Venus of Cypros,***) is mistress of the earth and of man who dwells upon it, of the sea and the fish in the sea. So far we have observed ;the Masseba together with the Ashera.

On the Masseba standing alone much has already been written, and various efforts have been made to illustrate it by monuments which have come down to us. In addition to the numerous re-presentations of the Masseba both with and without the Ashera which have been already given, I would call attention to a number ot instances, most of which have never been explained. Plates LXXVII, 2—4, LXXX, 5 and 7. LXXXI, 1—6, LXXXV, 1—9. I begin with the most primitive

---

††) Menant, Glyptique II, p. 246, fig. 243, reproduces this cylinder, which he, with many others, takes to be Cyprian manufacture, and explains it correctly with reference to the corresponding repre-sentations of Hittite hieroglyphs. He also lays stress on the numerous other relations between the Cyprian cylinders and the Hittite ones from Asia Minor, and especially with Syrian cylinders. Cf. also Menant's essay "Intailles de l'Asie Mineure" in the Revue Archéologique, 1885. pp. 293—318. A. H Sayce, as is well known, first tried to derive the Cyprian syllabary from the Hittite hieroglyphs (e g. in W. Wright's Empire of the Hittites, "Decipherment of the Hittite inscriptions," pp. 168—170) W. Deecke, who at first wished to explain the Cyprian syllabary by means of the Assyrian cuneiform letters, has since followed Sayce (cf. "Beiträge zur kunde der indogermanischen sprachen," 1884, p. 250—251). The similarity of the designs engraved on Cyprian and Trojan antiquities has already been mentioned pp. 58—60. (Hissarlik and Cyprus). I have left the attempts made by A. H. Sayce to decipher them unnoticed, (Ilios, pp. 766—781) as they seemed to me too venturesome. On the other hand this indefatigable student seems to be right in recognising a Cyprian inscription on the whorl discovered by Schliemann at Hissarlik in 1890 (cf. also Richard Meister's article in the Berlin philol. Wochenschrift, 1891, No 21). We have here further relations between Troy, Cyprus and the country of the Hittites. (I use the word with reservations, in spite of Puchstein's essay on "Pseudohethitische Kunst.") The cylinders of Asia Minor and Cyprus form another link in this chain of comparison. It is astonishing to observe how many designs on our Cyprian cylinders find their counterparts in Hittite hieroglyphs. It almost seems as if certain motives had been fully expressed for the first time on the cylinders of Cyprus (and other parts of Asia Minor), and as if their grouping had already given rise to a kind of picture-writing. These groups of designs must then have been abbreviated and summarised, simplified and allied to the Hittite hieroglyphs. They must further have been considerably simplified in order to find expression in the Cyprian syllabary (and other alphabets of Asia Minor which have not as yet been deciphered: as writing signs for syllables. On Plate LXIX, fig. 118—119 this process can be followed in the case of the Cyprian syllable *to*. I must not go beyond th's explanation, as I have already laid myself open to the reproach of wandering too frequently away from my subject.

**) Perrot, IV. "La Judée" p. 384 also mentions the Masseba terminating in a hand.
***) This is also the opinion of Robertson Smith, Religion of the Semites, p. 459.

Masseboth which I excavated myself. They illustrate in a striking way the ancient custom of the Israelites, the original form of the Masseboth, as they are repeatedly described in Holy Scripture (p. 155 fig. 152—155 = Plate LXXXI, 3—6). These Masseboth are nothing but large natural stones from the bed of a river, shaped by natural forces. Many thousand years must have been necessary for the action of the water to give these hard stones their present shape. The men who erected Masseboth on graves before the year 1000 B. C. (this is about the date of my Masseboth) that is during the bronze age, must have sought for long in the neighbouring river beds, before they found stones of such regular shape as those drawn for this book by Mr. Luebke, the artist, partly from the originals (now in the Berlin Museum and partly from photographs. The height of these monumental stones from river beds is from 60 m.; (about 23½ in.) to 1 m. (39 in.). The stone in fig. 152 given in a side view and in section is 0,52 m. (20½ in.) high, with a maximum thickness of 0,12 m. (nearly 5 in.). In 1889 I excavated a large numbers of these stones for the Berlin Museums at Tamassos on a sand hill with limestone slopes, which was quite free from stones from river beds. It was almost impossible to find a grave which did not contain at least one memorial Masseba. In many graves there were several, either upright or horizontal. In some cases the ends projected above the surface of the earth. When my workmen had once thoroughly grasped this custom, they used these memorial stones or primitive grave stones as a quick and sure means of discovering graves which had not yet been opened. I have selected four of the most regularly shaped stones for the illustrations. Fig. 152 somewhat resembles a slender column, long in proportion to its thickness, and fig. 153 a thicker column. Fig. 154 is shaped like a gigantic egg, and Fig. 155 like a gigantic stone chisel. It seems certain that these shapes were chosen intentionally. These same graves yielded small stone chisels and hammers of the shape shown in fig. 155, and the egg shown in fig. 154. The egg plays a part in early Phoenician mythology as it does in Egypt[*]). As I gradually learnt in course of time to distinguish between the different Cypriote finds, I venture to express it as my conviction that the period 1200—1000 B. C. might be safely fixed upon as a terminus ante quem for these graves. The countless offerings consisting of pottery, milk cups, milking cups, stone implements, whetstones, millstones and spinning whorls can leave no doubt on this point. These finds take us back therefore exactly to the period when the song of Deborah, the oldest portion of the Old Testament, came into existence. We are fully justified in transporting ourselves back to a period several centuries older than that in which the five books of Moses were written. All those who have written on the subject of the Masseba, connected their origin with the stone of Jacob in Genesis XXVIII, 18.

"And Jacob rose up early in the morning, and took the stone on which he had laid his head, and set it up as a pillar and poured oil upon it."

In Genesis XXXI, 13, Jahwe acknowledges himself to be the God of this stone, which is called the 'house of God.'

"I am the God of Bethel, where thou anointedst the pillar, and where thou vowedst a vow unto me."

In Genesis XXXI. 44—53 Jacob and Laban made a covenant, set up a stone as a pillar, and

---

[*]) A terra-cotta votive egg of the size of a hen's egg, which I found in one of the early Phoenician graves at Kition in 1879, is given on Plate CIX, 5

gathered stones into a heap for the sacrificial meal, slaughtered the beasts for the sacrifice, and ate the meal.

In verse 52 Laban said "This heap shall be witness and this pillar shall be witness, &c."

In Genesis XXXV, 1, God commands Jacob to erect an altar at Bethel near the Masseba. In Genesis XXXV, 9—14 we are told how God gave to Jacob the name Israel, and how Jacob celebrated the change of name. In verse 14 it is said: — "And Jacob set up a pillar where he had talked with him—even a pillar of stone—and he poured a drink offering thereon, and he poured oil thereon." Soon after Rachel died (v. 20) "And Jacob set a pillar upon her grave, that is the pillar of Rachel's grave unto this day."

Exodus XXIV, 4, Moses wrote up all the commands of Jahwe there. And early on the next morning, he builded an altar under the hill, and twelve pillars, according to the twelve tribes of Israel. Therefore twelve pillars stood by the altar.

But most important are three other Old Testament passages (Deuteronomy XXVII, 1—8, and Joshua IV, 2—24, VIII, 30—32). Moses saw his end approach and commanded the people to erect memorial stones, on which the words of the law should be inscribed.

Deuteronomy XXVII, 2—8: "and when ye pass over Jordan into the land which Jahwe thy God giveth thee, thou shalt set up the great stones, and plaister them with plaister; and thou shalt write upon them all the words of this law when thou art passed over, that thou mayest, even as Jahwe the God of thy fathers has promised thee, go in into the land which Jahwe thy God giveth thee, a land that floweth with milk and honey. Therefore it shall be when ye be gone over Jordan that ye shall set up these stones (in accordance with that) which I command you this day, in mount Ebal, and thou shall plaister them with plaister. And there shalt thou build an altar to Jahwe thy God, (truly) an altar of stones which thou hast not prepared with any iron tools, — of unhewn stones shalt thou erect the altar of Jahwe thy God — and thou shalt bring to Jahwe thy God burnt offerings, and slaughter peace offerings, and shalt eat them there, and rejoice before Jahwe thy God. And thou shalt write upon the stones all the words of this law, very plainly."

When, after the death of Moses, the whole people of Israel had completed the passage over the Jordan (Joshua IV, 4 and 5) Joshua called upon the twelve men whom he had appointed from among the Israelites, out of every tribe a man. And Joshua commanded them: "Pass over before the ark of Jahwe your God, into the midst of Jordan, and take you up every man of you a stone upon his shoulder according unto the number of the tribes of Israel."

Further, in verse 9:—"And Joshua set up twelve stones in the midst of Jordan, in the place where the feet of the priests which bare the ark of the covenant stood; and they are there unto this day."

In verse 20 we are told: "And those twelve stones which they took out of Jordan, did Joshua pitch in Gilgal."

Joshua VIII, 30—32: "Joshua erected to Jahwe the God of Israel an altar of unhewn stones in Mount Ebal, as Moses had commanded. And he wrote there upon the stones a copy of the law of Moses."

What we are told here therefore, is how Joshua erected in the midst of the Jordan twelve stones, which were evidently twelve large ones of regular shape, from the river bed, and had them set upright on their ends, exactly as the ancient Cypriotes at Tamassos in the second millennium B. C. placed the pillars on the graves of the Lamberti hill (page 152, figs. 152—155) and as Jacob placed the pillar on the grave of Rachel (1st Moses XXXV, 20). We are next told of the size and weight of the twelve stones, which twelve Israelites, corresponding to the twelve tribes, carried on their shoulders from the Jordan to Gilgal and erected there. It was possible therefore for a strong man to carry one of these stones on his shoulders. The stones which the Cypriotes had carried from the neighbouring river Pidias near Tamassos up to the hill of Lamberti, were as a rule of this size and weight. Only a few were still heavier. I tested this by means of my workmen, as they carried these pillars for me on their shoulders to the convent of Hagios Heraklides at the foot of the hill.

In addition to these Masseba from the river bed, we heard of other pillars which were erected on Mount Ebal. They were to be covered with plaster, and to have all the words of the law of Moses very plainly written upon them. Moreover an altar of unhewn stones, which had not been prepared with iron tools, was erected.

We are thus able to learn precisely the nature of the Masseboth permitted in the worship of Yahve. They were either simple, unadorned stones, unhewn fragments, stones found in the river bed without any ornament or inscription, like the stones from Bethel, Gal'ed, Bethlehem and from the foot of Sinai, or they were simple hewn and inscribed stones, tablets (like the tables of the law of Moses in the ark) pillars or columns (like those erected by Joshua on Mount Ebal) without any figures or ornamental design.

It is a remarkable coincidence, that in the same year (1887) both Stade in his history of the people of Israel (I. p. 459) and Perrot in the fourth volume of his History of art "La Judée" (p. 385, Fig. 203) gave the same Cyprio-Phoenician inscribed monument (= my Plate LXXX, 5) in order to illustrate the Jewish Masseba of the Bible.*)

We have learnt from the books of Moses and from Joshua what were the Masseboth not only permitted but required by Yahve. We must now consider those which Yahve abhors. In Leviticus XXVI, 1, it is said: "Ye shall make you no idols, nor shall ye set up carven images and pillars, neither shall ye set up any figured stone in your land, to bow down to it; for I am Yahve your God".

In Deuteronomy VII, 5, Yahve commands: "Ye shall destroy their altars and break down their pillars, and cut down their holy trees and burn their carven images "

Along with the Masseba abhorred by Yahve, appear the Chammanim or sun-pillars. Already

---

*) Stade made use of the reconstruction in the „Zeitschrift der Morgenländischen Gesellschaft" (XXIV, p. 676) drawn for P. Schröder by J. Euting from my photographs, drawings and measurements. G. Perrot, on the other hand, took his illustration from C. I. S. (Vol. I) fig. 44, Plate VIII. The photogravure of C. I. S. was executed directly from my glass negative of the original. I was one of the first to hear of this monument. It was accidentally discovered in 1880, while a road was being made in front of the S. E. point of old Larnaka (Kition) in the immediate neighbourhood of what was then the Government School of Forestry. The position of the find does not point to a grave, nor consequently to a funeral inscription, but to a votive inscription in honour of Ešmun, or more correctly of Ešmun-Adonis (See above). The inscription is cut on the marble base which supports a marble Masseba, shaped like an obelisk.

in Leviticus (XXVI, 30) Yahve threatens: "And I will lay waste your (sacrificial) mounds, and destroy your sun pillars, and will cast your carcasses upon the carcasses of your idols."

In Isaiah XVII, 8 and XXI, 9 the Asheroth and the Chammanim are mentioned together, as previously the Asheroth and the Masseboth.

Yahve, the God of Israel, therefore permitted and required the erection of simple pillars, and originally also the planting of trees by the altar. It was likewise permissible, or even compulsory, to erect inscribed stones. We learnt further that both the Hebrews and the Cypriotes were in the habit of setting up simple stones from the river-bed. If we imagine two pillars like those which I excavated (Plate LXXXI, 6), set up side by side on the ground close to a tree rising above them, we shall exactly recover the motive of the ambrosian stone dedicated to Melqart on the Tyrian coin legend (Plate LXIX, 54). Another simple shape of Masseba which Yahve permitted, provided no tree worship or worship of the stone resulted from it, was the conical triangular stone. We can recover the shape of this Masseba by imagining the pillars taken from the river bed (fig. 155 = LXXXI, 4) to be fixed into the ground, as on Plate LXXXIII, 13.*) It has been a common error, whenever a conical stone was excavated in Cyprus, to believe that both it and the enclosure in which it was set up, must have been consecrated to Astarte Aphrodite, because the idol representing the Paphian Aphrodite happened to be a cone. This is, however, not the case, as I was able to prove by my excavations and observations. In the precincts of Rešef-Apollo, for instance, pillars whose conical shape was unmistakable, had been set up; e. g. in the grove of the Rešef-Apollo excavated by L. P. di Cesnola at Athiaenou**) and in another excavated by H. Lang in Idalion. Further, in the rough Phoenician temple on the little island of Gozzo, near Malta (See infra Plate CXXVI, 2)***) the holy cone was worshipped, just as in Paphos and Biblos. One of the most interesting cults connected with the cone was discovered by D. ·G. Hogarth in 1888 at Amargetti in the grove sacred (as is attested by inscriptions) to Apollo Μελάϑιος and to Opaon Μελάνϑιος (a Cyprian local god). He found a conical stone with a phallos attached to it, as good an instance therefore as can be adduced of those Baal pillars and sun-pillars repudiated by Yahve. (Some very realistic phalli had also been set up by themselves, as votive offerings; two of these were of bronze). Near to the conical stone lay a small cast image, a votive ox of bronze (cf. the similar votive bronze from Limnite Plate XLIII, fig. 1). Several of the numerous statues and statuettes of clay or of stone that had been set up, had stone phallic characteristics. Occasionally these obscene male figures were combined in groups of three, i. e. in a triad (cf. the three women from Kition Plate CCV, 2). Some carried a bunch of grapes, others doves. Several votive doves had also been dedicated separately. One votive image consisted of a pair of doves confronted heraldically (cf. Plate CV, fig. 10 from Marion-Arsinoe): other votive figures consisted of a well executed male head set on a hollow stand shaped like a foot, a further instructive example of the transition from the aniconic to the iconic-anthropomorphic cult.

As soon as cut, hewn, or cast images or idols of wood, stone or metal—either anthropomorphic or zoomorphic—agalmata were placed by the altar next to the Masseboth and Asheroth, or fastened

---

*) Gerhardt, Akademische Abhandlungen, LIX, 13.
**) Perrot, III, p. 273, figs. 205 and 206.
***) Perrot, III, p. 298, 299, figs. 221—223.

to it,[*]) the displeasure of Yahve arose. It was still worse when images of the gods in the shape of men, animals or fabulous beings, or phalli (as for instance in the case of Hogarth's cone at Amargetti) were introduced. As Ed. Meyer has already recognized,[**]) the pillars of the sun, the Chammanim,[***]) were in many respects very similar to the Masseboth, the sacred stones. On the other hand, in the votive tablet to Ba'alchammân from Lilybaeum (Plate LXXXII, 1)[†]) he also recognized a very characteristic form of the Chammanim in the group of three stones on the upper portion of the tablet. Such groups of three or four stones' of exactly the same or very similar shape, meet us in different countries of the basin of the Mediterranean, from Babylon to Sicily and Sardinia. Their appearance outside the boundaries of Syria seems always to be connected with the Canaanites and their near relations, the Phoenicians. These remarkable stones, these pillars of the sun, against which the faithful worshippers of Jahwe contend, can only be rightly understood if we follow Ed. Meyer in considering them with the help of inscriptions, and trying to determine the deities to whom these Chammanim were set up in any particular case, and who were served by these "divine servants" in the form of pillars. One or more gods who are supreme in one locality, appear in another as subordinate, as servants of a god that has the pre-eminence, and from this arise all manner of mixed characteristics and degrees of rank, which appear also in the inscriptions. In such cases the observations made during the excavation of a sacred grove often give the key for all time. From Cyprus we have amongst others Melqart-Herakles, Tammuz-Adonis, and Baal-Chamman-Zeus in the service of Mikal-Rešef-Apollo. Divinities like Baal-Chamman, the fire Baal or Baal of the sun pillars, and Baal-Schamem, and the Baal of the sun and heaven pass into another.[††])

We may begin with the Babylonian cylinder given above, p. 115, Fig. 141, the Chammanim on which, consisting of one single and two double cones are given again in Pl. LXIX, 49. The old Babylonian inscription on the cylinder, which cannot be placed later than the year 1800 B. C.[†††]) says 'Amur-Shamash' i. e. "I have seen the sun-god." Supposing a proper name to be also implied, the owner of the seal must still be a worshipper of the sun or moon god Samas,[§]) who in this case is standing in person before his Chammân or Samas stone as god of ploughing and of the field.[§§]) A

---

[*]) For copies in clay of primitive or very early carved images in wood, see p. 33, figs. 29 and 30. Plates XXXVI, LXXIV, 7 and LXXXVI. The oldest carved image of stone from Cyprus which is yet known, is of soap-stone, and is given in Plate CLXXII, 15a and b; it dates from the second half of the second millennium B.C. The oldest cast figure, XLIII,2, a four-footed animal of bronze or copper, found in Cyprus, cannot be much later.

[**]) Roscher's Mythologisches Lexikon, p. 2870.

[***]) For the Chammanim compare also Baethgen, " Beiträge zur Semitischen Religionsgeschichte," pages 28 and 29.

[†]) C. I. S. No. 138.

[††]) Cp. also Baethgen, p. 28.

[†††]) Cp. above, p. 115.

[§]) The crescent moon suspended above the scene seems here to point to the lunar side of Samas, the son of the moon-god. A. H. Sayce (Religion of the Babylonians, pp. 164—167) has shown that the worship of the moon-god of Ur and of the sun-god of Larsa were originally combined in the Babylonian worship of Samas. Later on, however, Samas becomes the mere sun-god, and it is with the worship of this sun-god, Baal Samas, that the Baalshamên of Phoenician inscriptions is connected. Cp. sup. p. 170, note 4.

[§§]) W. H. Ward (American Journal of Philology, 1888, " A God of Agriculture ") has already raised the question whether the deities of the plough, of corn and of trees which he has identified, (Plate LXXV, 6 and 8) are not further to be identified with the deity of the gate of heaven (Plate LXXXIV). Cylinder No. 243 in the Syrian Department of the Berlin Museum gives us a sufficient answer. If we must

priest appears to be pouring wine, oil, or water over the sacred stone. In the Cyprian Ashera inscription P. Schröder, its first interpreter, has already discovered a new month, Sebahshemesh, which
received its name from the sacrifices which were offered during its course to the god Shemesh.
Schröder identifies the god Shemesh, (who therefore as well as the god must be connected with the
Ashera) with the Assyro-Babylonian god Samas and Baal-Solaris.

He also points to two Phoenician inscriptions from Athens, on which worshippers of Shemesh appear.
A glance at these two bilingual Graeco-Phoenician gravestones set up at Athens (C. I. S. 116 and 117) and at
two corresponding Phoenician ones found at Kition (C. I. S 52 and 53) are convincing as to the uniformity of style
in the written characters and in the ornamental rosettes and palmettes. In addition, the one Sidonian buried in
Athens, to whose memory the gravestone (117) was set up, is described as a Kitian, an inhabitant of Cyprus
and a son of Abdmelqart (worshipper of Melquart). Presumably the man had lived formerly in Kition, and
together with his brothers had set up in honour of Abdasamus the gravestone No. 53 on which the dedicators
appears as sons of Abdmelqart.

Two of the Phoenician Cypriotes mentioned on the Athenian stelae are also related. The stele
No. 107 is dedicated by the sons of Abdsemesi to the son of Abdmelqart. One of them dies, and the stele
No. 106 is now set up and inscribed in his honour. A cultus of Shemesh Samas in Cyprus, and the
erection of the Athenian funeral stelae by Sidonians of Kition (= Phoenicians)[*] are thus
both confirmed. Even if these monuments are of comparatively late date, and do not go further back
then the third century B. C., they yet throw light on the customs and cults of a much older epoch.

I have taken the figure composed of two pair of double cones arranged symmetrically about
a snake (Plate LXIX, 50) from fig. 118, p. 128 of the Salaminia of A. P. di Cesnola. A quadruped and
a bull's head with a star between the horns, represented in the fourth field, signify the sacrifice
brought to these stone. When Dr. F. Dümmler visited Cyprus in 1885, we saw at an art dealer's of
Nikosia a cylinder of precisely the same technique, and reproducing the same picture. The only
difference was that in place of the snake, a man stood between the four double cones, the Chammanim.
The ambrosiac Melqart stones from the harbour of Tyre (Plate LXIX, 54) cited above give us another
representation of the Chammanim. Next to two stone columns rounded at the top stands a double
cone, which serves as a fire altar. An Ashera or tree spreads its sacred branches above the sun
pillar. The nearest approach to the Chammanim from Lilybaeum (Plate LXIX, 55 and LXXXII, 1)
are the groups of three stones set up in niches cut in the rock, which were discovered North of
Medina in Arabia. The sketch given on Plate LXIX, 56 (= Perrot IV, p. 391, fig. 205) gives the best
view. Next in order comes a Sardinian grave monument, taken from the necropolis of Tharsos
(Plate LXXXIII, 21). It undoubtedly represents a group of Chammanim-stones. The central pillar
bears a marked resemblance to the Cyprian monument already discussed as a type of the Masseba
Plate LXXX, 5). In the centre of the Sardinian Chammanim stones we have in addition the sun disc
enfolded by the crescent of the moon, that combination of sun and moon which is of such common
occurence on Graeco-Phoenician monuments. On several Cyprian coins from Paphos three Chammanim likewise appear. The central stone, the actual Astarte cone with the dove, stands within the taber-

recognise these varying forms of Baal and Samas deities who enter into all manner of connections with
Ramman, Bin, Martu, Hadad, Resef, Tammuz and Adonis, we need not be surprised if the fiery Baal of the
sun-pillars, Baal-Chamman of Carthage, &c., and the less fiery Baal, who still is the sun-god, the king of the
heavens, Ba'alshamen of Laodicea, the *Βεελσάμην* of Byblos, &c. pass one into another.

*) Count de Vogue has already pointed out fully, from inscriptions and from the shape of characters,
the numerous links between the Phoenicians of Cyprus and those of Sidon ("Mélanges d'Archéologie Orientale."
esp. p. 87) "Les inscriptions de Chypre appartiennent à la famille que nous avons appelée Sidonienne." The
Phoenicians of Cyprus liked to call themselves Sidonians (cp. also for example, C. I. S. No. 5).

nacle or pillared court, while two further cones are disposed on its right and left (Pl. LXXXIII, 22).*) In other cases when the pillared court has broader dimensions, two huge candelabra, presumably of bronze, are placed on either side of the stone cone of Astarte-Aphrodite. (Plate LXXXII, 8 and LXXXIII, 19). These candelabra, upon which the fire was kept burning, themselves became sun pillars or Chammanim. We can study them on Plate LXXXII, 1—6, on the votive stela from Lily-baeum (1) on two Graeco-Phoenician (probably Cyprian) scarabs (2 and 3)**) on the Carthaginian votive stelae (4 and 5)***) and on a bas-relief found near Tyre (in the neighbourhood of Adlum) which resembles Cyprian work so closely, that one is inclined to think of it as having been imported from Cyprus to Tyre in antiquity.†) Plate XLIII, 8—10, shews three bronze candelabra belonging to this group; they were manufactured in Cyprus, where I excavated two of them at Politis Chrysokou (9 and 10) the third had been sent in antiquity from Cyprus to Sidon, where it was found.

We must return to the Ashera inscriptions of Kition and Ma'sûb, and study along with them Plate XXXVIII, 12 (= Plate XVII, 2 and 3) and 8 (= Mycenae p. 306, No. 423). We are now for the first time able to offer a complete explanation of the remarkable Mycenaean gold plates, three examples of which were found. In the three niches stand Masseboth or Chammanim. These have the shape of columns that thicken towards the top, like the central column of the Gate of the Lions at Mycenae††), to which Schliemann himself has already drawn attention (Mycenae, p. 308). The three Chammanim are about the same size as those on the monument from Lilybaeum. (Plate LXIX, 55). These three Baal-Chamman pillars are the deputies representatives of the androgynous divinity Moloch-Astarte†††) and her servant Baal-Chammân. These fetishes dwell within another fetish, a sacred wooden pillar, the Ashera; on its angles adorned with waxing and waning moons perch the holy doves of Moloch-Astarte or of the bearded Aphrodite. The terracotta column from the Ashera grove near Kition (8) is the dwelling of the anthropomorphic Astarte, but the Chammanim pillars are not represented: in the case of the gold plates of Mycenae, on the other hand, the Chammanim pillars or aniconic emblems of the servants of the Chamman-god (who is himself a servant of the androgynous Astarte) dwell in the Ashera, while the anthropomorphic image is not represented. Ba'alchammân, Elchammân is therefore the divine being who dwells within the stones which are here imitated in gold; consequently he is also the male correlative of the mistress, the mother Ashera, just as in Cyprus Mikal Moloch, Melek Melqart, Malika, Eśmun, Adon Adonis, Reśef-Mikal and even Baal-Libanon himself stand by the side of the goddess Aśtoret.

---

*) On a Cyprian bronze mirror (Salaminia, p. 59. fig. 66) the entrance to the holy sanctuary of old Paphos is likewise represented. In the small cella, or entrance to the court, two smaller cones stand, one on either side of the great cone of the goddess; we have therefore a Chammanim group of three stones as on the votive stelae from Libybaeum.

**) Cp. what is said below about the cultus of spears and sceptres, when this bronze candelabrum will be mentioned again.

***) = Perrot, III, p 134, figs. 82 and 83.

†) These bronze candelabra, which originated in Cyprus and were manufactured there in great numbers, were exported and afterwards imitated in other countries; for further details see the section on the cultus of spears and sceptres, and Plate XLIII, 8—10, and its explanatory notes.

††) For this column supported by lions, see also Overbeck: "Ueber das Cultusobject bei den Griechen in seinen ältesten Gestaltungen," Berichte der sächs. Gesellschaft der Wissensch. 1864, p. 158.

†††) In Kition called Mikal-Astarte.

An explanation of the anchor-like projections at the base of these sun columns will naturally be demanded. I believe that they are intended for the sun's rays, which in other cases (p. 84, fig. 112, Plate LXXXIV, 1) hang downwards from the sun pillars and sun discs. Perhaps these sun fetishes indicate the rising sun (cf. below p. 182 for a description of the sunrises of Samas) so that the rays may be imagined to be shooting up from the earth, the sea, or the lower world. Further we learn that this anchor-like symbol existed in Cyprus as far back as the second or third millennium, from a potsherd (Plate XXVIII, 4) which I found in 1885 at Hagia Paraskevi in an early earth grave of the copper bronze period. It belongs to the class of hand-made pottery of red polished ware, on which all the ornaments, animals, or human figures (these for the first time observed) are rendered by very roughly modelled bits of clay laid on to the vase. Fig. 6 of the same Plate (XXVIII), with a decoration of stags, affords another very good instance of this ware. As this anchor-like symbol occurs in combination with other signs and images, like half-moons, discs, snakes, female nipples, the horns and heads of animals, and animals, it presumably had on the vases also not only a decorative but also a sacred meaning. Further, the same motive was found at Gurob in Egypt by Mr. Flinders Petrie[*]) on a vase which he dates at about 1300 B. C., and the anchor-like design of which he compares to the similar symbols on the little Mycenaean gold foil shrines which we have just described.

One of the votive stelae (our Plate LXXXV, 9 = C. I. S. 183) dedicated to Tanit, the countenance of Baal, and to the lord Baal Chammân, taken in connection with the image of the Idalian tabernacle (Plate XXXVIII, 13), affords another highly interesting counterpart to the monuments from Lilybaeum, Mycenae, and Kition. Within the door of the Idalian shrine, which resembles a dove-cot (see also Pl. X, 3) stands a goddess with a human head and the body of a bird. On the Carthaginian stele (Pl. LXXXV, 9) a winged woman stands or floats within the entrance to the shrine, above the strip that bears the inscription. She holds in her outstretched arms the half moon and the sun disc in the same position in which the winged woman on the Cyprian censer (Pl. CXCVII, 2) holds a winged sun disc. The human hand adorns the summit of the stele. Beneath the inscription two doves surround the familiar conical idol of Tanit. There, accordingly, dwell here, within the Chammân or cone fetish sacred to Tanit, a winged anthropomorphic goddess, two doves and a hand.

Those Ἀμμουνεῖς, those temple columns with secret inscriptions from which, according to Philo, Sanjunjathon drew his wisdom[**]), are in reality Holy Masseboth, Baal-Pillars sun and fire columns, holy Chammanim. A whole series of these Chammanim, these Baal-columns are now known, as may be seen from the Corpus of Semitic Inscriptions. They occur sometimes singly, often also in pairs. Some are also bilingual. I have given figures of nine of them (six from Carthage Plate LXXVII, 2–4, LXXXV, 1, 7 and 9, one from Cyprus LXXX, 5, one from Malta LXXXI, 1 and one from Lilybaeum LXXXII, 1). Two, the one from Malta and the one from Carthage (LXXXV, 1) have the shape of a column. The Carthaginian, which is 0,463 m. (18 in.) high, and shaped like a smooth Chammân pillar, is intended for a dwelling house or tower. A niche below signifies the door, the three niches above stand for windows. If we glance through the various plates, we shall be struck at once by the resemblance between the sun pillars described here and the terra-

---

*) W. M. Flinders-Petrie, Journal of Hellenic Studies, XII, 1891, p. 199, " The anchor-like design in the middle of the gold foil shrines is found on a jar of about 1300 B. C at Gurob."

**) Schroeder. " Die Phoenizische Sprache," p. 125.

cotta columns from Kition (Plate XXXVIII, 12 = XVII, 2 and 3) and Idalion (Plate XVII, 4.) The objects of cultus, the Chammân-pillars, the Ammon-columns, are identical. But in Egypt also the sanctuaries of Ammon were surrounded by stone obelisks. This amalgamation of the Ammon cult borrowed from Egypt, and of the cult of Samas-Baal-Schemesh and of Baal-Chammân, borrowed from Mesopotamia and Syria, did not take place as late as is generally supposed*). At any rate motives of sacred art which originated in the Egyptian cult of Ammon, had already found their way to Mycenae in the second millennium B. C., as may be seen from Plate XXXII, and below in Chapter III. Of the nine inscribed stones represented here, the six Carthaginian bear the name of the lord Baal-Chammân, inscribed next to that of Tanit. The Cyprian stone from Kition is dedicated to Ešmun or Ešmun-Adonis; the pillar from Malta, which is one of a pair, is dedicated to the Tyrian Melqart. The two next inscribed monuments from Malta (C. I. S. 123a and 123bis) afford two more very instructive instances of sun columns. The two first had been simply dedicated to one god, while here the dedication is more complicated; it is in honour of several divinities, and consequently recalls still more strongly the Ashera inscriptions from Ma'sûb. One of the columns is called the property of Malak-Baal and the other that of Malak-Osiris, yet each is also dedicated to Baal-Chammân. Therefore Malak-Baal and Malak-Osiris appear here as servants of Baal-Chammân.

We now pass to a brief consideration of another group of Chammân or Samas columns, (i. e. sun columns) which almost always appear in pairs, are dedicated to the god Samas, and represent the gate of the Sun. Sometimes the god emerges between these sun columns, — the prototype of the columns of Herakles,—from the depths of a mountain cleft.**) (Plate LXXXV, 2,)***) He has not yet received the wings of flame, because he personifies the sunrise whose beams have not yet attained full vigour. Only separate rays shoot up from behind the mountains. Two attendants open the folding door. At other times we see the god (cf. LXXXIV, 4)†) having already spread his wings of flame and reached the earth, setting his foot on the highest mountain that he may shed his light about it also. The symbols for the male and female sexes float about him.††) Lions sit upon the columns of the gates, which in this case also are being opened by attendants. A small tree sprouts up from the earth. A third servant awaits orders. The god holds in his left hand an instrument resembling a saw.

In another scene (5) †††) the gate of the sun is only indicated by a pillar, held by an attendant. An attendant of the god, with the horned priest's-cap, leads by a bare-headed man. In the centre the god is setting his foot on a heap of logs. He holds the saw raised in his left hand, while with the right hand he is swinging back his club for a blow. The grouping, drawing and conception of the figures tend to show that a human sacrifice is about to take place upon the pile of wood in front of the sun temple. Very similar are the scenes fig. 3 §) and 7 §§). In both cases the sun-god has perhaps

---

*) Cf. Ed. Meyer in Roscher's Lexicon of Mythology, p. 291.

** Cf. American Journal of Archaeology, III, 1889, p. 50—56 and Plate V and VI. W. H. Ward, "The rising sun on Babylonian cylinders."

***) Lajard, "Mithra," XVIII,'4.

†) American Journal, 1887 Taf. V.—VI. Fig. 1.

††) The symbol on the right is given again on the general Plate LXIX, 87.

†††) Lajard, "Mithra," XVIII, 4.

§) Lajard, "Mithra," XVIII, 3.

§§) Lajard, "Le culte du Cyprès," IX, 1.

just risen over the mountains, visible between the wings of the sun gate, which is being opened by the priests. In fig. 7 a cypress stands between the priests; in fig. 3 the sacred symbol, the sun-crowned staff *).

One of the priests holds the saw, the other an object resembling a sword. In fig. 6 finally the god is making his way down from the mountains. One priest stands by the temple denoted by the wing of a door, and the other reaches out the saw to the god. The last figure (1) **) is quite different, but evidently belongs to the same class. Below lie three goats. Above sit two divinities or priests in front of a sun-pillar, which has wings of flame, and a crown of light or fire attached to its summit, while behind it is a second pillar without any rays. A star floats on the left in front of the principal personage, probably the god, the king of heaven, Samas-Baal-Shemesh, while the figure on the right perhaps represents his female counterpart. If that be so, we must assume that the goddess is the queen of heaven, the Istar-Malkatu of the Babylonians, the Atar Samain of the Aramaeans, the Meleket-has-Samain of the Jewish prophets. Yet perhaps the figure might be male. Be that as it may, in any case, these throned deities are here either grasping at a ray of light or fire, or else they grasp a cord hanging from the fire pillar, as in the cylinder given above, p. 84, fig. 112, where we have this same pillar. Since there, however, we see the moon-crescent suspended above the throned god, Samas seems to be in this case conceived as the moon-god, like his father Sin. Almost every large museum possesses several of these representations of Samas, emerging as the rising sun between the folding gates held open by the priests.***) The representations of Samas in front of the winged sun-pillar are also common.†) It is quite evident from the representations that the pillars denote originally the folding gates, which turn upon their hinges. Gradually the notion of movable folding doors to the gate of the sun was lost, and only the fire-pillars, the sun-pillars, remained, at first usually in pairs. One sees at once from the whole technique and drawing, that the cylinders with the rising sun are of the same epoch and style as those with the winged sun-pillars. Further, a later Phoenician inscription from Umm el Awâmid (C. I. S. No. 7) proves definitely that a gate could be

---

*) Also figured on Plate LXIX, 86.

**) Lajard, "Mithra," LIV, 1.

***) The Berlin Museum has two examples, V. A. 248 and 257.

†) In the same Museum (Vorderasiatisch. Abth.) there is also an example of a sun column, which has winged projections attached to its upper extremity, like LXXXIV, 1. and above, p. 84, fig. 112 On the Berlin example we see two figures grouped about the winged column (in the Catalogue it is incorrectly described as a tree) in front of which lies the sacrificial four-footed beast. The persons represented further appear to be pulling at ropes, above the one on the left floats the crescent moon, as on our fig. 112. The cylinder represented Plate LXXXIV, 7, is very important for another reason. We have here a religious observance which was of the highest importance in the later Persian theology of Zoroaster, illustrated some two thousand years before on an old Babylonian monument; a fact which leads one to believe that primitive Babylonian (and perhaps even Akkadian) religious conceptions and types were preserved by tradition down to Zoroaster. Zoroaster planted in front of the gate of the fire temple (Atesh-ḡah) at Kishner in Korasan a cypress taken from Paradise, as the prototype for all subsequent dedications of such fire temples (Pyreia, Pyratheia), and on the bark of the cypress he cut as witness and seal of the doctrine which he had received from Gustasp the following words: — 'Gustasp has received the true faith." On the old Babylonian cylinder we see the cypress planted at the gate of the sun and the fire. On the cylinder Plate XXX, 4, a tree (palm or cypress) stands by the little temple, within which the god (Samas?) is sitting. The inscription on Zoroaster's cypress reminds one of the inscription on the Masseboth of Joshua and on our pairs of Phoenician Chammân columns.

dedicated by itself. It is addressed to the lord Ba'alshamêm, the Baal of heaven, to whom a gate with folding doors ("portam hanc et **valvas**") is solemnly dedicated. *)

The custom of erecting a pair of sun-pillars, Chammannin, and often also of dedicating them to a divinity by an inscription, is of frequent occurence in the various countries bordering on the Mediterranean. As a rule Phoenicians appear as the dedicators of these pairs of pillars, in which case they bear Phoenician or bilingual inscriptions. The form and size of the monuments of this kind which have come down to us, vary; but small monuments of the pillar and slab form preponderate. The greater number of these duplicate and bilingual inscriptions are engraved on the stone, and many are afterwards coloured; some are only written in colour upon the stone-slabs. We have already come across two dedications of two pairs of pillars. (C. I. S. 122 and 122 bis, 123 and 123 bis.) The most important inscription, which proves the wide-spread Chaldaeo-Phoenician use of the two pillars inscribed to Chamman or to Schamem, to Hammon or to Ammon, is the dedication found on Inasêm—the island of the hawks (' *Ιεραχῶν νῆσος*)—near Sulci in Sardinia; on it two pillars are erected to the lord Ba'aschshamem (another form of Ba'alschamem).**)

Now in Cyprus we meet with many of the same customs, as here among the Phoenicians of Cyprus and Greeks. Within the sacred grove of Rešef-Apollon at Frangiassa near Tamassos, I only found two Cyprio-Phoenician monuments with bilingual inscription (without counting the Greek inscription to Apollo on the holy water basin of the precinct). None were found elsewhere. Both inscriptions are dedication to Rešef-Apollo.***) In both cases there remains only the basis in shape of a pillar, upon which stood a small anthropomorphic statue, which have been lost. The fact that this dedication is expressly mentioned, that in both Greek texts the word *ἀνδριάς* is expressly chosen, indicates that elsewhere there stood upon these columns no human figures, but fetishes in the shape of a pillar or cone, as at Malta (C. I. S. 122 = our Plate LXXXI, 1).†) The Editors of the Corpus Inscriptionum Semiticarum have already called attention on p. 152 to this Phoenician custom of worshipping deities in the form of pillars, and of setting up two of these and dedicating them to deities. They mention in this connexion also the two pillars, so often quoted, in the temple of Melqart in Tyre.††)

---

*) For a votive inscription to the same god in Carthage, see C. I. S. 139. In Kition, Idalion and Lapithos (Larnaka-tou Lapithou) we meet repeatedly with another god, who appears five times in the same manner under the proper name Abdsasan, servant of Sasam. (C. I. S. 46, 49, 53, 93, 103). The fifth time on the Bilinguis from Larnaka tou Lapithou (C. I. S. 95) there occurs the proper name Sesmaos (*Σέσμαος*), formed from the name of a god. Gesenius and Levy (Cf. Beitrag. z. Semit. Religionsgeschichte p. 64) explained Abdsasam to mean "Servant of the holy sun flush". This god Sasam, who must have been in great honour at Kition, since there are four Phoenician inscriptions on which one or more dedicators call themselves "Servants of Sasam" or sons of the "servant Sasam", has been held by Clermont-Ganneau to be the Poseidon of Larnaka, whose worship is attested by inscriptions. (Waddington, No 2779). I believe that this god Sasam is to be identified with Samas-Schemesh. These gods Samas and Sasam would then have to be amalgamated as sun and storm gods with the gods Rešef, Mikal and Rešef-Mikal. *Ποσειδῶν Λαρνάκιο* would exactly suit this meteorologic divinity of the sea.

**) The shape of the inscribed stone agrees, in respect of height and breadth, with the inscribed stone of Anat from Idalion (See above p. 15)

***) The one refers to Rešef 'Elijjat-Apollo *'Ελείτας*, the second to Rešef 'Alahijotas-Apollo *'Αλυσιώτας*.

†) The inscribed bases of these two Maltese monuments correspond in shape and size with the two from Tamassos.

††) Just before going to press, I observe that Movers has already, more than 50 years ago, treated of this dualism from the mythological and typological point of view, as fully as the conditions of science in his

The cultus of the Hebrews, in which images were unknow, prohibited from the first the setting up of sun-pillars, which was a first step towards the worship of images. In place of the inscribed sun-pillars were introduced Masseboth, as that of Joshua, but above all inscribed tablets, like the two tables of the Law of Moses, "tables of stone, written with the finger of God".*)

They were thin and small tables, "written on both their sides; on the one side and on the other were they written."**) While Moses had gone up to Sinai, the hill of God, to receive these stone tables with the law and the commandments,***) and had remained upon the mountain forty days and forty nights,†) the people of Israel had made unto themselves a golden calf and worshipped it.††) When, therefore, Moses came down with the tables of the Law in his hand†††) and, drawing near to the camp, heard sounds of singing and beheld the calf and the circle of dancers, "his anger waxed hot, and he cast the tables out of his hands and brake them beneath the mount." The tables were renewed by Moses at the bidding of Yahve: "Hew thee two tables of stone like unto the first: and I will write upon these tables the words that were in the first tables, which thou brakest."§) And again Moses remained there with Jahwe forty days and forty nights, and "without eating bread or drinking water.§§) And he wrote upon the tables the words of the covenant, the ten commandments." Already during his first sojurn on the mountain Yahve had commanded Moses "to put into the ark what he should give him."§§§) When Moses erected the Tabernacle, he took the law and put it into the ark.°) We thus see in the Old Testament an express dualism.°°) Two tables of the law, written on both sides, and twice hewn. In later Judaic tradition it is even related that in the ark, side by side with the second pair, lay the fragments of the first pair of tables.°°°)

---

day, and the scanty number of monuments then discovered permitted it (Phoenizier I, p. 393 &c.). Much that was said by him has been superseded by later research; but a great deal that he put forward at the time as hypothesis has been brilliantly confirmed by discoveries, and has passed into the province of acknowledged fact.

　*) Exodus XXXI, 18.
　**) Exodus XXXII, 15.
　***) Exodus XXIV, 13 and 14.
　†) Ibid. 18.
　††) Exodus XXXII, 1—9.
　†††) Ibid. XXXII, 18.
　§) Ibid. XXXIV, 1.
　§§) Ibid. XXXIV, 28.
　§§§) Ibid. XXV, 16.
　°) Ibid. XL, 20.
　°°) It would appear accordingly that E. Knoll is incorrect ("Studien zur ältesten Kunst in Griechenland". Bamberg 1889. p. 68—69) and that Preller-Roberts' view ("Griechische Mythologie" I, p. 332, 2) should be put forward again. Knoll is of opinion that the divinity was originally represented double for mere decorative purposes, and variations afterwards introduced. It is precisely the fact that the divinities are represented double which emphasises the religious character of the representation, even though this might at the same time fulfil a decorative object The lion demons with fish scales, who carry jugs and are repeated in pairs on the bronze vase from Kition, (Plate XCVI, 12) are conceived exactly in the spirit of the Hebraeo-Semitic religion. We encounter the holy twofold and fourfold number on many other Cyprian as well as non-Cyprian Graeco-Phoenician monuments. We find them in Egypt, especially in the ritual of Ammon. I shall return to the subject in Chapter III, Section 2. Cf. also Movers, "Phönizier" I, p. 395.
　°°°) I owe this important observation to Herr G. Minden, who called my attention to two passages in print: Midrasch Tanchumak to 2nd Moses, XXXVII, 7, and Midrasch Rabba to 4th Moses. Paraschah Rabba, Leipzig, Otto Schulze, 1885, p. 71.

In Kypros we have the two inscribed tablets from the sanctuary of the dual divinity Aštoret-Mikal on the Akropolis of Kition. One has the characters painted in black on each side (C. I. S. 86 and 86 bis). The second tablet, which, owing to its bad state of preservation, only shows a portion of the inscription in red paint on one side, must also have been inscribed on both sides. Both tablets have holes for strings to suspend them by, just like the bronze tablet inscribed on both sides in Graeco-Cyprian characters, which hung within the Sanctuary of the warrior goddess Anat-Athene, on the chief Akropolis of Idalion. In 1883 I excavated in the Sanctuary of Apollo at Voni, near the ancient ·Chytroi, the torso of a votive statue, which held a similar tablet suspended by means of a string from its left hand that hung down its side; this tablet was also inscribed with the Graeco-Cypriote signs for syllables. The torso is given on Plate XLII, 8, with an enlarged reproduction, of the inscription.

While the couple of bilingual stones from Tamassos, just like the two columns from Malta, (Plate LXXXI, fig. 1) give information concerning the dedication of votive inscriptions, the erection of pillars and statues, the inscribed stones from Kition, like the tables of the Law of Moses, are concerned with important regulations for the service of the temple and its preservation. J. Halévy [*]) makes interesting comparisons between these temple ordinances from Kition and the celebrated temple tariff of Marseilles (C. I. S. 165). Thus the two tables of the Law of Moses with the ten commandments afford an excellent illustration of a practice of the Syrio-Semitic ritual which we can trace from Jerusalem and Tyre, through the Mediterranean, to Cyprus, Carthage and Malta as far as Sardinia. We find its most interesting analogies only on the most ancient Greek soil, on the most sacred spot of Attica and Athens at the entrance to the Hekatompedon, the Temple of Athena, burnt by the Persians in the 6th Century. There, in the entrance, was set up one of the most remarkable inscriptions of the age of the Peisistratids; it is inscribed on two marble slabs. By decree of the people the details of the temple ritual were regulated and inventoried. Both the marble slabs with the new temple regulations were then set up in the entrance to the temple, exactly like the marble slabs in the entrance of the Sanctuary of Astarte and of Mikal on the Akropolis of Kition. The details of the inscriptions from Athens and from Kition have many points of similarity. In both instances the various duties of the priests and priestesses, of the sacrificial servants of both sexes are minutely set out, together with the salary for the service performed, and the money fines imposed for violation of the temple ordinances, &c.[**])

We saw that the Semitic and Oriental custom of writing important religious laws, temple ordinances, tariffs and contracts, on two columns, pillars, slabs, &c., which were then set up in the temple, spread from Mount Sinai to the Hekatompedon on ·the Akropolis of Athens. We must now turn to consider the cultus of two columns on a mountain height when there is no temple. It can be illustrated by the primitive cult of Zeus in Arcadia, on Mount Lykaion (also called Olympos or

---

[*]) Revue des Etudes Juives, Paris, 1881. " Les inscriptions peintes de Citium; p. 173."
[**]) Cf. W. Dörpfeld, "Der alte Athena-Tempel auf der Akropolis." Mittheil. des Kaiserl. Deutschen archäol. Instituts, Athen 1890, XV, p. 420. H G. Lolling, Δελτίον 1890, p. 92, the Greek publication Ἀϑηνᾶ 1890, p. 627. E. Curtius ·in the Archäologische Gesellschaft, November 1890. Jahrbuch des Deutschen arch. Instituts, 1891. Anzeiger p. 163. I must be content with these brief indications, and refer the reader to the publications mentioned here and on the previous page, and to C. I. S. Nos. 86 and 87.

simple the "holy hill") which in so far as its type is concerned is certainly borrowed from the Semitic East. Pausanias*) has pictured for us in detail this imageless ritual such as he saw it still in practice. Before the Mound of earth which was the altar of Zeus stood two holy pillars facing East, upon which in former days two golden eagles had stood. Do not these two columns of Zeus correspond to the two Melqart columns in Tyre, the two Baal columns in Malta, the two pillars of 'Astarte-Aphrodite in old Paphos &c.?

We still have to study a group of sun columns with a specially beautiful and distinctive ornamentation which are found on the Akropoleis of Cyprus, I can show such columns to have stood on the Akropolis of Kition, Idalion, Amathus; they appear to be connected with the stelae which were set upon the Akropolis of Athens as individual architectonic features, and not as portions of a monument.**) I give on Plates LVIII, 1 and 2, LIX, 1 and 2, and p. 188 figs. 159—162 eight stelae or capitals belonging to this class. The symbol combined of the sun and the half moon occurs within a cone or a triangle on the lower portion of six of these examples. On a seventh (Fig. 162) the double symbol floats above the cone or triangle. Ornaments borrowed from plants fill, in six cases, the space between the volutes above the triangle, In the seventh example it is replaced by a head of Hathor, surmounting a semicircle (LXXXV, 4). Three of the examples are known to have been found on the Eastern Akropolis of Idalion, in the celebrated mountain grove of the Idalian Astarte-Aphrodite, (Plate XLIII, 1, 2, LIX, 1). The same provenance may be claimed for Stele LIX, 2 which was found by Dr. Dörpfeld and myself, built in the wall of a house in the modern village of Dali, and for a fifth fragment (not figured) from the same village. It is true that the votive stelae figured on p. 188 figs. 159 to 161 are said to have been found in Athiaenou. But their size and technique correspond so precisely to that of the examples found on the Eastern Akropolis of Idalion during my stay in Cyprus, that one feels inclined to assume that they come from the same place, namely the Temenos of Aphrodite on the Eastern Akropolis of Idalion (No. 29 in my list). It is certain that the sanctuary of the dual divinity Astarte-Mikal which I discovered on the Akropolis of Kition had no stone colonnade. On the other hand it is equally certain that a few columns with Ionizing capitals stood as holy columns in front of the sanctuary, like the columns in front of the temples of old Paphos, of Hierapolis, and the columns of Jachin (i. e., he stands firm) and Boaz (in him is strength) in front of the temple of Jerusalem. The two latter were symbols of Yahve. I saw one of the columns still standing upright at Kition; I have indicated it on my plan of the Akropolis (Plate CCI). When the Akropolis hill, on which stood the sanctuary of Astarte-Mikal stood, was removed in 1879, only one large Ionizing capital with rich ornamentation was found, which is imperfectly represented in Perrot III, 264, Fig. 198. A larger reproduction is accordingly given on Plate CXCVII, 1, from a photograph taken direct from the object by Dr. Dörpfeld. Further the fragments of a second similar capital were found. Therefore in the period to which the capital belongs, no stone colonnade with capitals of this kind can have existed on the spot, much less can a temple, in the Greek sense of the word, have stood there. The two columns either stood quite free, which seems the more probable from the disconnected notices of the find, or else they supported the projecting porch of a small shrine, as is the case in the small terra cotta imita-

---

*) Paus. VIII, 38, 2, 6—7.

**) Cf. R. Borrman, "Stelen für Weihgeschenke auf der Akropolis zu Athen." Jahrb. des Kaiserl. Deutschen Archäol. Instituts. 1888. pp. 269—285.

tions (Plate CXCVIII) of shrines from Amathus, and in the little shrine which surmounts the large stone capitals from Kition, which will be immediately described. (Plate CC, figs. 1 and 3). These two columns, which stood before the sanctuary of Astarte-Mikal, *) therefore belonged presumably to a couple of columns that stood free, like the two columns of bronze in front of the temple of Solomon. In that same place, however, must have stood many other single columns. On the spot marked r a column, a portion of whose shaft had been broken away, still stood in situ.

G. Perrot, who has drawn such scholarly and brilliant conclusions with regard to those Oriental, Syrian, and Egyptian monuments which are the objects of the present study, was the first to show Vol. IV. p. 291) that in the little Cyprian terra cotta shrine of which repeated representations are given in this book (X 3 = XXXVIII, 13 = CIX, 3 = CXXIV, 5), the two columns, which the potter leant, out of technical necessities, against the cornice of the door, must be conceived of as standing free. Otherwise the capitals shaped like blossoms would have no head. The two interesting Hathor capitals, which are free Cyprian imitations of their Egyptian models (Plate CC, 1—3), come from the same find in Kition or from one near by. I was the means of obtaining the largest and most interesting of these capitals for the Louvre **) in Paris; the smaller***) went to the Berlin Museum (Vorderasiat. Abtheil.) Both capitals have on each side the head of Hathor supported on a stand decorated with a pattern of opening lotus buds, but on both sides of the smaller capital the head of Hathor carries a little temple framed by a pattern of leaves, and with a divinity standing within its porch. This is only the case on one side of the larger capital. On the second side, above the head of Hathor, is a fantastic holy tree with thick branches rendered in the Egyptizing, Graeco-Phoenician-Cyprio style; within its upper branches is a heraldic group of Sphinxes facing outward and smelling flowers†). I discovered these capitals in two houses of old Larnaka, they must come from the city of Kition, and possibly from the citadel of the neighbouring harbour, which in Kition protected the Akropolis. I must leave undecided the question whether these capitals were set up as free votive stelae or columns in some holy enclosure, or whether they were architectural members supporting the porch of a shrine. On the head of Hathor, both in the Berlin and the Paris examples, we see pillars supporting the façade of a small shrine, within whose entrance stands an anthropomorphic divinity growing out of a pillar. On the specially richly ornamented Paris example, which has a winged sun disc, moons, and stars on its architrave, there are on each side of the door frame of the shrine what may be described as large cones tapering towards the top, or else as pillars or columns of the obelisk shape, on which heads of Hathor are set, and stumps of arms are clearly indicated. It is uncertain whether they are supposed

---

*) Unfortunately the workmen, before I could come up to the spot, had removed the remains of these columns and capitals from the actual place of the find, so that I have not been able to indicate this place on the ground plan Plate CCI. I was, however, able to learn, when I arrived, that they must have stood at about the same height as the enclosure for votive offerings E, on the North East side of the latter and towards the harbour.

**) The larger capital is 1. 33. m. high; it is imperfectly published by S. Reinach in his "Chroniques d'Orient", p. 178 (5. 347) from my communications and photographs. I give a letter publication, and show both its sides on Plate CC, 1 and 2.

***) The smaller capital-height 1,13 m. is represented on the side which is best preserved (both sides are alike) on Plate CC, 3. It is due to Mr. C. D. Cobham, Commissioner in Larnaka, that this interesting monument of Cyprio-Graeco Phoenician and Egyptizing architecture was obtained at a moderate cost for the Museum of Berlin. It arrived in Berlin in 1891, when I had already left the island.

†) Cf. with this representation the ivory relief, Plate CXVI, 5.

to stand free, or whether they carry the projecting beams of the little cella. The latter is the probable conclusion, as in the case of the Hathor pillar on the right, a projection for the attachment of some object can be seen above the roll of hair.

Of quite extraordinary interest is a Hathor capital, unfortunately in a very fragmentary condition, which Dr. Dörpfeld's keen eye discovered in my presence on the slopes of the Akropolis of Amathus at the beginning of 1890. Its present height is 1.45 m. It is one of the treasures of the Antiquarium of the Berlin Museum. While the Hathor capitals from Kition are still completely in

Fig. 159.   Fig. 160.

Fig. 161.   Fig. 162.

the Egyptizing style, we see here Assyrian and Persian motives, winged horses and the animal tamer, combined with the Egyptian motive of the head of Hathor, by Cyprian artists who were working under stylistic conditions that tended more and more towards the pure Greek.*) The group itself,— a naked man in profile, running to the right, with arms raised to hold the hands of the horses, and the two winged horses who raise themselves on their hind legs against the tamer,—just like well trained horses in front of a trainer in a modern circus,—betray at every point the peculiarities of the

*) Cp. for ex B. XCIX, 1, 4, 5, 6: CI, 1: CXI, 1

archaic Greek manner.*) It is better not to try to decide at present whether this Cyprian Hathor capital belonged to a monument, or stood free as a sun column. Figs. 159—162 show four other capitals which come from Cyprus.

We see at once that the capitals 159 and 160**) belong to the same period and to the same category, as the capitals from Idalion on Plate LVIII and LIX. Indeed, their resemblance is so great even in details of motives, shape and size, that one is inclined, as I have already hinted, to assume that they were all found in the same place, namely the sacred precinct of the Idalian Aphrodite on the Eastern Akropolis hill, p. 16, No. 29. If the capital snow in the Louvre (159 and 160) pass for having been found at Athiaenou, this may be due to an error which could perhaps be traced back to an intentional desire on the part of the vendor to deceive the buyer as to the real place of the find. From the investigations of Dörpfeld and Borrman it would appear that all these capitals (Plates LVIII and LIX and Figs. 159, 160 and 161 of the text, probably also Plate CXCVII, 1, and possibly Plate CC) do not belong to an architectural order, but represent votive monuments, which were set up in a holy enclosure, (in this case the Aphrodite grove on the Eastern Akropolis of Idalion) as sun pillars

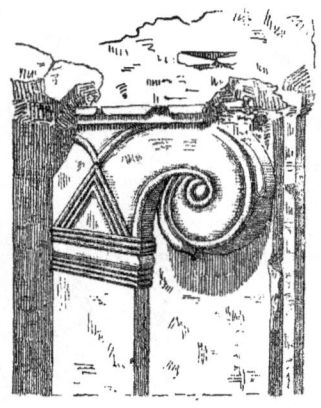

Fig. 163.

or Chammanim. It is doubtful whether these Cyprian votive columns carried statues like those found on the Akropolis of Athens. As among the Cyprian stelae, we find by the side of a very broad one, (e. g., LVIII. 2 has a surface breadth of 1,164 m.) a very narrow one (LVIII, has a thickness of only 20 cm.) and as the upper surfaces of the stelae bear no marks which could leave one to infer that either statues or any architectural member were attached to them, we may conclude that they most probably were set up as Masseboth, as Chammanim by the altar of the holy precinct, on the

---

*) In Cesnola's Atlas Plate XCIV, fig. 627, a slab carved in relief and unfortunately much mutilated is given, which comes from one of the precincts of Apollo at Athiaenou (Nos. 25 or 26 of our list). Two lions rise up against a naked man who is in the position of the tamer, is rendered in the same style, and is likewise turned to the right in the running scheme.

**) Longperier, Musée Napoléon III. XXXIII, 4 and 5 = Perrot III. p. 116, 52 and 53.

sacred mound. The dowel holes on the lower surface (in the example Plate LVIII, 2, the channel for the molten lead is preserved) prove that these stelae must have been set up on some object, possibly a little pedestal shaped like a pillar or column, &c. We must therefore imagine these sun columns to have been as tall as, or taller than, a man, and to have looked something like the cultus column on the Hittite cylinder, Plate LXXX, 1. They are shaped like tree columns, like those fantastic holy trees and Asherat now so familar to us, whose rich curling volutes grow out of the triangle, the cone of Astarte, and are decorated with the sun and moon. Fetishes of the Chamman god, of Ba'alchamman, of Zeus-Hammon, were dedicated to Astarte-Aphrodite on her holy mountain grove in Idalion. In the Hathor monuments of Kition, another pillar divinity, Hathor-Astoret-Aphrodite, with shrine and winged sphinxes dwell in the Chamman pillar which is shaped like an Ashera. Within the Chamman stones of Amathus dwell Hathor, Astoret Aphrodite, and a god with the beasts which he has subdued. On the Cyprian monument, given fig 161*) the head of Hathor on a semicircle is seen within the frame formed by the rising volutes. Hathor-Astarte-Aphrodite therefore dwells here within the Chamman-stone, in form like an Ashera. A passage in the second book of Kings, X, 26—27, illustrates exactly the connection of Baal columns and Ashera. When Jehu drove Baal out of Israel "they brought forth the Ashera out of the temple of Baal and burnt them, and they brake down the pillar of Baal."

Fig. 162**) shows a simpler capital, in which the upper volutes are more pressed downwards; the whole shape is transitional to that of the Ionic or Ionicizing capital.***) I found similar capitals on the pillars of two stone graves of kings, which I shall publish in my work upon Tamassos. I only give one in fig. 163 for purposes of comparison. Similar Ionicizing capitals have been roughly imitated by the potter on the small copy of a shrine (which I discovered in an old Graeco-Phoenician grave at Amathus in 1885, Plate CXCIX, Figs. 1 and 2). This time we certainly have architectural members and not independent votive stones. On the other hand the monuments given on Plate XXVI (= CXVII and described above p. 56—60) must be considered as separate votive stelae, either sacred or sepulchral, or both. The same Masseboth or Chammanim which were dedicated to divinities within the grove, were also given to the dead in the grove, particularly when the deceased had lived and moved in the service of divinities.†) On all these there is within the Chamman-stone, which resembles an Ashera and a fantastic holy tree, a second smaller Ashera, about which Sphinxes, and sacred fabulous beings are grouped heraldically. We must accordingly imagine the Ashera and the Sphinxes to be dwelling here within the fetish of Ba'alchamman.

The fragment of a slab sculptured in relief on Plate CXVI, 5, must have belonged to a still more richly ornamented object, which represented in reduced proportions a similar cultus column, a Chammanim; winged griffins have taken up their abode within the branches of the Ashera, which

---

     *) Perrot III, p 535. fig. 381.

     **) Perrot, p. 116, fig. 51.

     ***) Ibid. p. 264 Fig. 198.

     †) In Cyprus columns were sometimes placed on groves. In addition to the grave stones taken from river beds previously mentioned, larger limestone monoliths are found marking the site of rock cut graves; Hogarth discovered three of these at Kamarais in Karpaso. The natives call the site after the three monoliths "Thria Litharia," i. e , "the three stones."

is introduced on the column. This sculptured slab found in Nimroud was certainly manufactured in Cyprus.*)

To this same category of cultus columns, which seems to have originated from a Semitic Oriental practice that has its root in Babylon, (Plate LXXXIV, above p. 185) belong two groups of monuments, one from Kommagene**) (Plate CXCIII, 1—5) the other from Athens (Plate CXCIII, 6—9).***)

We shall consider first in the Kingdom of Kommagene the mound of graves at Sesönk and the sketch of its restoration (CXCIII, 2). Three couples of massive pillars were erected about this mound in the South, the North-East, and the South-West; they were connected by an architrave and carried sculpture (one pair of columns is given on a larger scale, fig. 1). The funeral monument which is situated on the almost horizontal crest of a hill, is visible from a great distance.

The colonnade of the tumulus of Kara-Kusch (Plate CXCIII, 5) likewise erected on a hill, consists of thrice three groups of columns. Sculptured figures in this case also adorn the columns which are not, however, as in Sesönk, connected by an architrave. Instead of sitting figures we have a slab carved in relief on the central column, and on the columns to the left and to the right figures of beasts, two lions, two bulls, and two eagles (CXCIII, 3 and 4). The characteristics of the animals could not have been better brought out. The colossal dimensions of the work 'are apparent from the plate.

Fig. 164

The following group brings us to the votive columns with sacred beasts which L. Ross has shown to have existed in Greece.†) These pairs of columns are not only palaestric symbols as on the Panathenaic prize amphora (CXCIII, 7), but also cultus columns. In Ross's time there were observed in the neighbourhood of the temple of Artemis-Brauronia and of Athena Ergane two small monolithic columns; I reproduce one of these on Plate CXCIII. 6; it is 5 feet 9 in height, on its shaft is an inscription to Athena in archaic characters. These little columns carried owls (CXCIII, 7). Ross compares them, among other instances, to the two columns surmounted with eagles that were on the summit of Mount Lykaion in Arcadia, and which were mentioned above. On a vase painting (Plate CXCIII, 8) we also have an eagle on the little cultus column which stands before a Zeus enthroned. These analogous instances from Kommagene and from Athens are all the more interesting

---

*) = Perrot II, p. 535, fig. 249. Perrot classifies the small carved ivory objects from Nimroud, to which the example given here belongs. Cp. also Plate CXIII, 1 = Perrot II, p, 534, fig. 248) and the Nimroud metal cups (Perrot II, p. 739, fig. 399 = Plate XCII, 4) as foreign (Phoenician?). They are the productions of a Graeco-Phoenician industry that had its origin in Cyprus, and attained there to a high degree of perfection. The King of Cyprus, as early as the reign of Thutmosis III, supplies Egypt with copper ore, blue spar, horses chariots, plated gold and silver, tusks of elephants (Brugsch, "Geschichte Aegyptens," p. 317 and 322). Objects of ivory actually appear in the stratum of the bronze age of Cyprus which corresponds to the reign of Thutmosis III. (For example CXLVI, 8 B is artificial blue spar, i. e., Kyanos.) Cp. also the explanatory notes to Plate CXVI. The ivory tablets quoted and described on p. 139 (Plate XC. 2) and p. 140 (CXV, 4) are productions of these same Cypriote industries.

**) K. Humann and P. Puchstein's "Reisen in Kleinasien und Nordsyrien," p. 211—234. Our fig. 1 = Humann-Puchstein, 34,2 = 37,3 = 40,4 = 41,5 = 43.

***) L. Ross, "Archäologische Aufsätze". Our fig. 6 = Ross, Plate XIV, 1, 7 = XIV, 5, 8, = XIV, 6. 9 = XIV, 4.

†) "Archäologische Aufsätze", pp. 201—209.

that on an old Babylonian cylinder (Plate LXXXIV, 4 = fig. 164) lions likewise crown the pillars of the folding gates which frame the sunrise of the god Samas. In Kommagene lions also appear on the columns of the gravestone. The parallels to eagles are equally striking. The couple of columns already described from the Temple of Athena Ergane, and the two inscribed slabs from the Hekatompedon of the Athenian Akropolis, afford further analogies to our Phoenician and Hebrew inscribed columns, and to the pairs of inscribed slabs from Tyre and Mount Sinai, from Cyprus, Malta, Carthage and Sardinia.

Finally the six and the nine columns which rise impressively at the foot of the tumuli at Kommagene, recall to us the altar with the six columns which Moses erected at the foot of Sinai.

The interpreters of the Holy Scriptures often make a further distinction between sun columns and sun images. The images, as opposed to the columns which we have hitherto been considering, probably attempted to give a more realistic representation of the sun as a star or a wheel (see Perrot II, p. 211, fig. 71°) like the wheel on the column, Plate LXXX, 1, or on the tree, p. 85, fig. 116. Next, the anthropomorphic conception of the sun and of the sun divinity strove to find artistic embodiment, a tendency which we shall be able to trace among the sun images. A fine instance of an attempt of this kind, which was made in Cyprus as early as the second or third millennium B. C., may be seen on Plate LXXXVI, 2; it is a fragment 14 cm. ($5^1/_2$ in) high, of a flat idol of the plank shape which is in my possession; together with the other plank idols of the same type, it comes from the Nekropolis of Hagia Paraskevi, the burial ground of the city Lider-Leerai, which has been so often mentioned. The drawing was most carefully executed by the painter Lübke from the original. The core of the idol is of rough clay, coated with a fine levigated brown clay; with the exception of the female breasts, which have been stuck on, and the roughly modelled human ears which are twice pierced, and are supposed to carry ear-rings, every detail has been obtained either by sinking, scratching, boring or impression. The lower portion of the body, which is intended as female, is broken off; the arm stumps have also disappeared, and the ears are injured. Otherwise the idol is intact, as shown by the preservation of the clay coating. The artist conceived of the goddess as a woman, but without human face, with the faces of the rayed sun. Instead of eyes, nose and mouth we see a great round depression for the sun globe, and all around the rays are given by incised lines. When the rough, carved, molten or hewn images are perfected, when figures in the round take the place of the plank or pillar idols, or at least appear alongside of them, the symbols of the sun columns get transferred to the sun images. We find that the double symbol of half moon and sun disc, which is so familiar on Cyprian monuments (cp. fig. 159, 160 and 162, as a few examples out of many) has been transferred from the column found at Tyre, fig. 165 (= Plate LXXX, 7) to the breast of the life size statue, whose torso is given in fig. 166**), and which was found between Tyre and Sidon near Sarfend (the ancient Sarepta). Out of the sun column grew the sun image. On the Cyprian censer or holy water bowl (fig. 167) the winged woman holds a winged sun disc. She stands by a sun column; the two together form the stand for the basin. This object comes from Chytroi.

---

*) The god Samas is enthroned in a shrine, before him on the altar table is a gigantic representation of the sun as a star. It is held by means of ropes by two bearded male busts which float above it on the façade of the shrine. Each holds a flowering twig in his left hand. Cp. the custom illustrated above p. 137 of holding a twig in the left hand in invocations to the sun.

**) = Longpérier, "Musée Napoléon III", XVIII, 1 = Perrot III, 428, Fig. 302.

I found in the excavations at Frangissa near Tamassos some statues of Rešef-Apollo (who is also often worshipped as a sun and light god) or of his priest, which carry the winged sun disc on their belt, as an indication of service to the sun.*) In the same manner the head of Hathor-Astarte-Aphrodite passes from the Hathor stelae to the dress of the priests, where it appears sometimes on the breast, sometimes on or beneath the girdle, in the centre of the apron, or below it. As an example of the

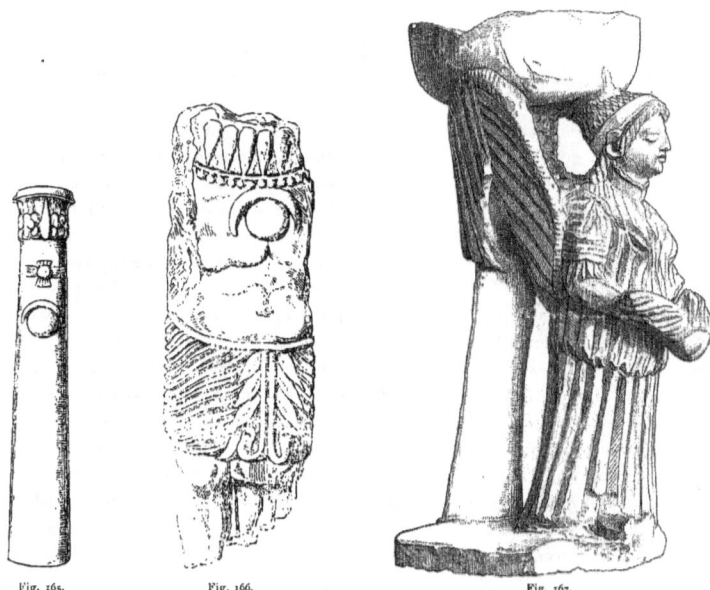

Fig. 165.   Fig. 166.   Fig. 167.

last variation, see fig. 168 on p. 195 a Cyprian statue now in the Museum of New York.**) The same head of Hathor occurs on bronze cuirasses, for instance on the cuirass from Tamassos Plate LXX, 12) which is unfortunately in such a fragmentary condition; it alternates with lions seated in pairs and a pattern of lotus flowers; a connection which again emphasises the link between the cults of the sun and of plants. Fig. 169, a terra cotta from the Louvre, which certainly comes from Cyprus, (although the provenance has up to now been unknown)***) taken together with other Cyprian stone and terra

---

*) Apollo corresponds to Horus. The Graeco-Phoenician god Rešef Apollo borrows from Horus the winged sun disc, which in the religious art of Egypt is symbolical of Horus himself. Cp. Meyer in Roscher's Mythol. Lexikon, Sp. 2744.

**) = Perrot III, p. 534, fig. 360. Cp. what is said below in section 3 about the heads of divinities in mythology and art typology. Cp. also Plate XCI, 4 and 5.

***) = Catalogue de la collection Barre No. 161 = Perrot III, p. 76, fig. 25. Perrot considers the provenace unknown. The object comes from Cyprus. In the first place a number of other Cyprian antiquities were sold at the same auction. Secondly these sitting figures are of frequent occurrence in Cyprus, and many bear the stamp of the same style.

cotta figures (three of which, excavated by myself, I reproduce on Plate XCI, 2 and 3, and XCI, 4)
affords a certain key to the interpretation already attempted on p. 165 of many forms in the Phoenician and Assyro-Babylonian inscriptions, and the Hebraic vocabulary of the old Testament, which
had until now seemed obscure. We now understand how Ba'alchamman can be servant of Rešef-
Apollo or of Astarte-Aphrodite, or of the androgynous divinity Melki'Ashtart, who is a combination
of the two former; we can understand also how images of this servant came to be dedicated in the
groves and on the heights sacred to his lord. We further learnt how a divinity conceived as
anthropomorphic can dwell within another divinity conceived as a fetish, so that the Ashera
became the dwelling place of Astarte, &c. If any are still inclined to doubt the assertion I have just
made that Ba'alchamman, Baal-Hammon-Zeus must literally be conceived of as the servant and attendant of
Melki'Ashtart, they will be convinced by the following observation. These seated images of the bearded
and horned god, accompanied by two rams, are found in almost every sanctuary of Rešef-Apollo
but never of a large size. They are votive offerings. Believers dedicate images of the Chamman god, of
the servant in the grove at the altar of the lord Rešef-Apollo or Mikal. They likewise dedicate, though more
rarely, these images of the Chamman god in the groves of Astarte-Aphrodite. Plate XCI, figs. 2 and 3 show
two very roughly executed stone figures, which I excavated in 1885 in the grove of Astarte-Aphrodite at
Idalion. Among several thousands of female votive images, it was possible to distinguish the remains of
some few male bearded masks, and the two images reproduced here of the god Chamman-Ammon. For
it is certain that in all these images we have a fusion of the Syrio-Semitic god Chamman with the Egyptian
god Ammon. In fig. 2 the god stands in human form, but with the head of a ram, and holding one of those
pouches or little baskets which are carried by the Assyrian demons.[*] In fig. 3 a figure that sits very low,
and whose human shape is almost entirely confined to the lower part of the body, supports a ram's
head in place of the human head. A ram stands on each side of the throne. The execution and
style of the stone statuette of a god enthroned on Plate CXCI, 4, are much superior, and bear a
thoroughly Greek stamp. Zeus-Baal-Hammon holds in his left hand a large horn of abundance.
Rams' horn grow from the temples of the god, and the two rams stand at his side. The god places
his hand on the head of the ram on the right hand side, just as in the stone statuette, (Fig. 169) he
holds the two rams by the head with both hands.[**]

These images of the god Chamman-Ammon were therefore dedicated to Rešef-Mikal-Apollo
and to Astarte-Ashera-Aphrodite. The images of the subordinated god, conceived of as servant and
attendant, are dedicated in the grove of the lord or mistress, who are also worshipped together on
the Akropolis of Kition as Mikal and Astarte. In Cyprus Rešef and Astarte were the lords, and ruled
over the servant Baal-Hammon. In North Africa, Malta and Sardinia the reverse was the case.
Accordingly there stelae of Malak Baal and of Malak Osiris, i. e., stelae of the serving divinities, were
dedicated either to the lord Ba'alchamman alone or to the pair of ruling divinities, Tanit, face of
Baal and Ba'alchamman.[***]

---

[*] A similar basket of somewhat larger dimensions was found with the figure, and is given on
Plate XCI, 1.

[**] Precisely the same motive of Baal-Zeus-Ammon enthroned, holding the rams, is repeated three times
in three stone statuettes, in a bad state of preservation, but still clear enough to admit of recognition. (Cesnola-Atlas Plate LXXXVII, figs. 582—584). One of these was found in the precinct of Rešef-Apollo at Athiaenou,
(No. 25 or 26 in the list).

[***] Cp. E. Meyer, Roscher's Mythol. Lexikon, Sp. 2871.

We now pass from the cultus of the actual Asherat, Masseboth and Chammanim to that of staves, spears and sceptres. These, however, will be found to be only small Asherat and Masseboth.

Robertson Smith (Religion of the Semites, p. 179) is right in comparing the staff in Hosea IV, 12 to a small Ashera: "My people ask counsel at their stocks, and their staff declareth unto them . . . . ."

In Numbers XVII we have the exact description of the worship of a staff. Of the twelve staves (rods in the A. V.) inscribed with the names of the twelve tribes of Israal, which Moses had laid up before the Eternal in the Tabernacle of witness, the staff of Aaron was budded, and brought forth buds and bloomed blossoms and yielded almonds (vv. 22 and 23). And this wonderful staff, a small Ashera, was by the command of Jahwe kept by Moses in front of the tabernacle in the tent of dedication, as a token against the rebels. This was therefore an

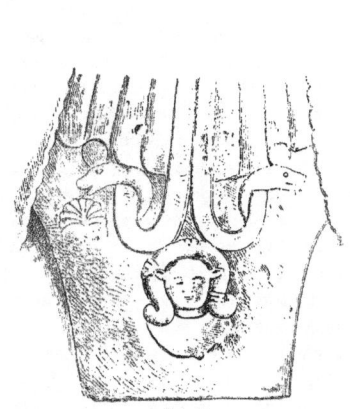

Fig. 168.   Fig. 169.

Ashera of the staff shape, like those we have so often seen on altars (cp. Plate LXIX) and which became, through a miracle, a living and fruit-bearing little tree. This is the gist of the passage in Isaiah XVII, 10, which has already been quoted more fully in connection with the little gardens of Adonis: "thou plantest pleasant plantings and settest them with layers from foreign parts." The Phoenician custom, of which Philon of Byblos has preserved the tradition for the Roman epoch, goes back to a much older period. Staves and columns were dedicated by the Phoenicians and honoured every year in a special feast. This custom is also illustrated by our monuments. To return to the staves of Moses and of Aaron. The staff of Aaron which had become a serpent swallowed the serpent staves of the Egyptian sorcerers.[*] Moses raised his staff and divided the sea,[**] so that the waters separated. He struck the rock, so that water gushed forth from

---

[*] Exodus VII, 11 and 12.
[**] Exodus XIV, 16 to 21

it. To this day the legend of snake staves exists among the Cypriotes, and the shepherds like to cut themselves staves which terminate in one or two heads of snakes. The upper portion of a similar snake staff, which I have long had in my possession is given Plate CXXI, 3 (Chapter III, Section 7.) The end of the stick has a natural curve, carved to represent two heads of snakes supposed to be growing together, one of which is provided with a horn. The vase from Cyprus repeated on Fig. 12 of the same plate, shows a Cypriote sorcerer of the period previous to 500 B. C. armed with the magic staff.*) He stands**) before a small Ashera resembling that staff of Aaron which brought forth buds and blossoms. The left hand is raised above the Ashera in the attitude of prayer or of oath taking, the right carries a spear shaped staff. He stretches his left leg forward to touch the foot of the Ashera, and places his right foot upon a snake coiled twice upon itself.

The herald's staff and the staff of Hermes are apparently derived from the Egyptian and Semitic snake staves.***) On the Carthaginian monuments these staves are introduced in such a manner, that their sacred character is quite clearly recognisable in spite of the decorative use they are put to. Two examples will suffice. On the Carthaginian stele Plate LXXXV, 2 two of these herald's snake staves are growing out of palm stems, and bear on each side of them the familiar conical idol of Tanit, face of Baal. The same herald's staff appears together with the idol of the Carthaginian goddess, and with the ox head on a counter or die, which was found in Carthage in the same precinct of the ex-voto to Tanit, face of Baal and of Baal-Hammon. (Plate XCIV, fig 8; ch. III, section I.†) Finally similar staves, closed, however, at the top and surmounted by a formal spear-point, are seen to the left and the right of a conventional palm or palm column on a Carthaginian votive stele (below Plate CLX, fig. 3).††)

Plain or carved staves terminating in balls, fruit, &c. (i. e., more richly decorated sceptres), simple spears and lances of wood tipped with copper, bronze or iron, have from time immemorial been given as tokens of honour and symbols of power and sovereignty to gods and to kings.†††) It is well known how wide-spread the worship of the spear was among the Romans.§) In the heroic period of the Trojan War, the sceptre was also universally reverenced. In the quarrel between Aga-memnon and Achilles for the sake of Chryseis, Atreides swears his mighty oath: (Iliad I, 233–236) "Verily by this staff that shall no more put forth leaf or twig" &c. In the Homeric Epic the weapons of Achilles and of Agamemnon are the richest and the most artistic.

The greater number of them are described as guest-gifts from the King Kinyras of Kypros, and are therefore the products of Kyprian workshops. §§) And even those, which are described as the work of Hephaistos and not especially as Kyprian gifts, may just as well (as

---

*) To this day the sorcerers and snake conjurors, generally Greek Catholic or Turkish Mohammedan priests, play an important part in Cyprus.

**) The shape and the technique of the vase convince me that it cannot be dated later.

***) Perrot (III, p. 463) raises the question as to the origin of the Greek herald's staff and staff of Hermes, without, however, deciding it.

†) = Perrot III, p. 463. Fig. 339.

††) = Ibid. p. 461. 336.

†††) Cf. Boetticher, "Baumkultus," p. 232, XVI, § 5.

§) The most ancient agalma of Mars in Rome was a spear; cp. Varro, quoted by Clem. Alex. Protrept. IV, 46.

§§) Cf. Plate CXL—CXLII and explanatory notes.

probably they were) have been executed on Kypros, the island of copper. We are, therefore, justified in surmising that Agamemnon's sceptre came from Kypros. The sceptre of the sceptre-bearing Kings of Homer might be used at one time as a lance for thrusting; at another, like the sceptre of the Egyptian Kings,*) as a club for striking. Agamemnon's sceptre, which Hephaistos had artistically worked, is called golden, i. e., it was either plated with gold, or had a golden head, while the sceptre of Achilles was adorned with golden nails. These divine sceptres of kings were wooden parade-spears terminated in a knob of some form or other, while the indispensable feature of the very similar heralds' staves were the twining snakes at the end. An eagle sits upon the sceptre of Zeus, as upon that of Agamemnon at Chaeronea, a cuckoo upon that of Hera, a fir-cone crowns that of Dionysos, a deadly spearpoint the sceptre of Ares. Not only Athena but also Aphrodite, where she is conceived as war-goddess, carries the lance. This warlike Aphrodite**) thus resembles the kindred Semitic goddesses in their warlike function. The spear is, therefore, sacred to Astoret among the Kyprians, Canaanites and Hebrews, as to I'tar among the Assyrians and Babylonians. In Plate XXXI, 3 I give an impression taken from an ancient Babylonian cylinder, which is in the Syrian Departement of the Berlin Museum (Catal. V.-A. 526). Ištar stands naked, facing the spectator, with her hands on her breast. On her left, two heads of animals indicate the sacrifice. On the right stands a dog above the spear, which is larger and more distinctly rendered than usual; it is set up here, like an Ashera, as a sacred symbol. (The lance appears again on Plate LXIX, 88). The cylinder may date from about 2000 B. C. or even earlier, but is certainly not much later. To the same early period belong the representations of that worship of the sacred staff and lance, which I abundantly proved for Kypros from numerous instances on early cylinders of local Kyprian manufacture (Plate XXXI, 7 = LXIX 91***) LXXIX, 4 = above p. 87, fig. 118 = LXIX 90†), LXXIX, 5.††) = LXIX, 89, above p. 87, fig. 119 &c. The sacrifice by the sacred lance is represented on three figures (Plate XXXI, 7). In the topmost field stand the two persons sacrificing the victim, a quadruped, and the lance, side by side. In the central field the men surround the animal in whose breast is plunged the lance, and above the scene is suspended the snake. Below the sacrifice is accomplished. The high priest is enthroned with the lance in his right hand. In front of him stands the assistant, between them is suspended, beside a little tree, the head of the ox, which together with the lance recalls the sacrifice now accomplished. Upon Cylinder, Plate LXXIX, 4, stand two men praying or taking an oath, between the sacred tree and the sacred lance. On LXXIX, 5, the priest sits and holds the lance before the sacred symbols, the sacred snake, two sacred staves (one of which is crowned with a half moon), the sacred tree and a sun disc with hairy appendages. Another variant of the same subject is seen Fig. 119, p. 87. The divinity enthroned is surrounded by two sacred trees, two ox-heads, the lance and other symbols. On Fig. 120, the priest

----

*) Egyptian spear throws can be seen, for example, on the figured medallion of the Palestrina silver cup. (Perrot III, p. 97. fig. 36 = our plate CXXIX, 1.) Behind the King, who is chastising his prisoners with the club spear, stands his lance bearer, who carries another sceptre of the staff kind crowned by a massive apple.

**) When writers mention an armed Aphrodite in Kypros, it seems that not Astarte, but another Baalat, namely Anat-Athene is intended. I shall return to this point below in the section an Astarte Aphrodite.

***) = Salaminia XIII, 27.

†) = Ibid. XIII, 20.

††) = XIII, 22.

stands, his arms raised in prayer, between the sacred trees, the ox-heads upon the altar, the spear-point and the double-axe. The sacred tree, conceived as a branch, with the ox-heads and two snakes above it, is seen on Plate CXXI, 6, between the standing sacrificial assistant and the high priest, who sits enthroned, grasping in his left hand the lance, in his right the tree. In the following very similar scene the high priest is enthroned in front of the snake and of the sacred tree, which is suspended over a sun disc with hairy appendages; he grasps the lance with his left hand, and with his right the quadruped for the sacrifice. Behind him approaches the sacrificial attendant, who also lays hold of the animal.· The completion of the sacrifice is indicated by the ox-head suspended above the group. On a cylinder not reproduced here, (Salaminia XIII, 28) the sacrificial attendant is in the act of thrusting the lance into the back of the quadruped, at which a dog is barking.

Among the other symbols floats a human hand.[*] Especially important is a cylinder of the collection De Clercq. No. 30 [**] repeated on Plate XXVIII, 20 of provenance unknown[***]) up to now, but which I can claim as having been made in Cyprus. The high priest enthroned holds in his right hand the ox-head, beneath which floats the half moon, and in his right the sceptre, upon which perches a bird, thus recalling the sceptres of Zeus and Agamemnon, for which it may have served as model. Behind him stands the sacrificial assistant. With one hand he touches the chief priest's spear, while in his left hand he holds a second spear. Two stones — one of them quite evidently a dagger of the copper-bronze period (shape as on Plate CXLVI, fig. 3 B. a and b, 4 B., and Plate CLXXIII, 20 and 21 a and b)—and what is presumably a bird, fill up the space. The gesture of the attendant priest between the two spears is suggestive of the planting of the two Asherat on fig. 81, p. 65 (= Plate LXIX, 120) or of the budding stems (Asherat? Plate XXVIII, 27 = LXIX, 123). On Plate CLI, 35, I have further given, in its natural size, a very heavy ring of electrum excavated in Cyprus. God and goddess sit on chairs and hold staves in their hands. This finger ring, which the late Mr. S. Birch also held to be archaic Babylonian, was found in the South of the island by a peasant in an early grave of the copper-bronze period, near Zarukas. The motive of the throning and seated divinities, and of their representative, the high priest, with the outstretched spear passed from the pre-Graeco-Phoenician copper-bronze period into the Graeco-Phoenician iron epoch. Figs. 2 and 3 of Plate LXXXII are, according to Lajard (Mithra. LXVIII, 26 and 24), evidently Graeco-Phoeni-cian seals; moreover they are shaped like scarabs, which adds to the probability of their having been made in Cyprus.[†] On the seal (2) the god or the priest stands before a blazing candelabrum, like those so commonly manufactured in Cyprus, (where I have often excavated them,[††]) three examples are given Plate XLIII, 8—10) and exported to Sidon and other countries, and afterwards also imitated elsewhere (in Phoenicia, Carthage, Etruria). While he raises his right hand in the attitude of bene-diction, he holds in his outstretched left hand a spear and budding twig. On fig. 3 the same god or high priest sits with his arms in the same position, before the candelabrum; only the budding twig

---

[*] Cp. above p. 171. For similar scenes with the lance, see Salaminia, XIII, 21 and 22.

[**] Cp. below the explanatory notes to Plate XXVIII.

[***] Cp. XXVIII, 21 and 22. LXXIX, 1—5 &c.

[†] Further examples in Lajard, "Mithra" LXVIII, 25 and 27. A Sardinian scarab (Perrot III, p. 658. fig. 477) must belong to the same class. The god sits before the candelabrum

[††] See Cesnola-Stern, Plate LXX, for three further examples also Perrot III, p. 863, fig. 630, cp. below the explanatory notes to Plate XLIII, 8 – 10.

is not represented. The winged female sphinx stands at his side, and the winged sun disc floats above him. If we turn now to the images of divinities in the Corpus of Semitic inscriptions (Vol. I, p. 38) *) said to represent the god Rešef-Raspu, they will serve as instances for the Cyprian Rešef. We notice the same spear-bearing god on the Egyptian monument given above on p. 75, fig. 100 grouped with the Egyptian god Min and the goddess of Kadesch who recurs in precisely the same form in Cyprus and is identical with Astarte. Further in 1885, I excavated numerous votive images**) in the precinct proved by two bilingual inscriptions in Phoenician and in Greek to have been that of Rešef-Apollo. **A whole row of these images like the colossal figures held in their right hand, and in front of them a wooden spear. It had naturally rotted away long ago, but it can be proved that these cultus statues held the spear from the round hole, which the potter had bored in the hands of his statues; these holes are preserved and in the case of the life size and colossal statues are just large enough to hold a stout wooden spear.** The sphinx, who appears next to the spear-bearing god on the seal of Plate LXXXII, 3 (and on several similar seals) belongs to the ritual of Rešef-Apollo on the Island, and I excavated several images of sphinxes on the same spot at Frangissa (one is given Plate CXCVII, 4). These sphinxes are just as common in the groves of Rešef-Apollo***) as the images of Melqart-Herakles, the right hand of Apollo and of Apollo's servant Baal-Hammon-Zeus (cf. above p. 194). The gods Rešef and Mikal, or Rešef-Mikal, who are so highly honoured in Kypros, are nothing but localised Kyprian Baals. They are, as already stated, most closely connected to the local gods Hadad, Ramman, Marfu and Bin (in a lesser degree also to Samas, Baal-Schamen and others). The several regions of Cyprus in their turn had their own special Rešef-Apollo, and just as he was honoured in one place (Kition) under the form of Rešef-Hes or Rešef with the arrow, so in another he was the spear-god (Frangissa). The same god with the spear evidently on the point of thrusting it into the sacrificial beast appears to be represented on the relief from Moab, Plate XC, 3 (= Longpérier, Musée Napoléon III., Plate XXVIII). †) The best parallel from Greek mythology is afforded by a Boeotian local cult which Pausanias saw in all its primitiveness, and which as he quite correctly remarked, could be traced back to a very ancient source. I append a literal translation of this interesting passage (Paus. IX, 40, 11 and 12).

"Of all their gods the people of Chaeronea venerate most the sceptre, which Homer says Hephaistos made for Zeus, and which Hermes received from Zeus to give to Pelops: Pelops left it to Atreus, Atreus to Thyestes, and Agamemnon got it from Thyestes. This sceptre therefore ($\sigma\varkappa\tilde{\eta}\pi\tau\varrho o\nu$) do they worship and they call it the spear ($\delta\acute{o}\varrho\nu$); that it has something divine about it is sufficiently shown by the brightness which emanates from it on to the spectators. They say that it was found on the borderland between their territory and that of the Panopeans in Phokis; and that the Phokaians also found gold with it, but that they preferred the sceptre to the gold. It was brought to Phokis, I believe, by Elektra, the daughter of Agamemnon. It has no public temple, but every year the priest places it in a shrine; and sacrifices are made to it daily, and a table is set in front of it, covered with all sorts of meats and cakes." ††)

The finds in the interesting Kyprian layer belonging to the Graeco-Phoenician period (from the end of the seventh to the beginning of the 6th century B. C.) have up to now thrown more light than the finds of any other layer upon the Homeric age which, however, was several centuries older·

---

*) Cp. also Perrot III, p. 71, fig. 24.
**) Cp. above p. 6 No. 4.
***) Also found by Cesnola in groves of Rešef-Apollo.
†) = Perrot III, p. 443, fig. 316.
††) Perrot III, p. 799, fig. 563.

This same layer has now also yielded a number of sceptre heads, to which the Homeric sceptre has already been compared. In the case of the finest example, which was found at Achat, C. W. King (in Cesnola Stern p. 327) and ·C. T. Newton (ibid. p. 417 and Plate LIV, 3)*) have already drawn the obvious parallels. King quotes the custom of the Babylonians, recorded by Herodotus, according to which each carried a sceptre resembling a long staff, surmounted by an apple, a rose, a lily, an eagle, or some similar object. On Etruscan reliefs men and centaurs very commonly carry staves and spears. Generally they are plain lances, but in other cases they are evidently staves surmounted by flowers. (Cf. Plates CIV, 2 and CV, 9).**) King also quotes the "thousand guards" of Xerxes who carried an apple as a badge on their spears, and were therefore surnamed μηλοφόϱοι. I have found several similar sceptre ends in the shape of apples, in different parts of the island, both at Kurion and again in 1889 at Tamassos. In one case it was plain from the position in which the sceptre end was found, that it belonged to a staff of command. It lay on the right side of the corpse, within the sarcophagus, in the small stone King's grave, which can be approximately dated, within which the iron sword of Homeric type, Plate CXXXVII, 7, quoted below was discovered***). Althogether I have already discovered three such bronze sceptre ends of the same apple shape, and I have seen several at the art dealers' in the island. We are therefore confronted here with a quite distinct type of Apple-bearers (not unlike the μηλοΦόϱοι at the court of the Persian King) which, considering the Persian influence in Kypros, is not astonish-ing. The shape of the sceptre end is always the same, a round apple with plain, small round lumps upon it.†) Its shape resembles that of the somewhat more angular agate sceptre from Kurion, about which Sir Charles Newton says (quoted by Stern in Cesnola's p. 417): "If that gold sceptre with which Odysseus inflicted on Thersites his well deserved punishment was like this one, then we can imagine how the meddler bent under the blow," A sceptre end also of bronze was found in the rich grave of Kurion (Cesnola-Stern, LXV = Perrot III. p. 799, fig. 564 = our plate CVI, 8). These ox-heads are disposed about the end of the staff. The most interesting sceptre end we have, however, also of bronze, was found in Idalion on the Western Akropolis within the precinct sacred to Anat-Athena (cf. above p. 16 — No. 28).††) It is figured in Perrot III, p. 494, fig. 348. No more suitable votive

---

*) Cf. also Overbeck. "Ber. der Sächsischen Gesellschaft der Wissenschaften", 1864.

**) These Etruscan staves surmounted by flowers are also borrowed from the East.

***) Cf. below, Plate CXL = CXLII, and my article in the Berliner Philologische Wochenschrift 1892, Sp. 900 and 925 on "Die Homerischen Schwerter auf Kypros."

†) I am publishing in my work on Tamassos one of these apple shaped sceptre ends. Further the staff crowned with an apple which the King's spear-bearer is holding on the silver cup with a Phoenician inscription from Praeneste, (which I claim it to have been manufactured in Cyprus) affords a typological parallel which is not to be overlooked. In the Cyprian graves are found quite smooth round ivory balls or buttons which have a deep boring. They must certainly have surmounted sceptres. One which I found in 1886 at Poli tis Chrysokhou (Marion Arsinoe Nekr. I. Grave LXIV) has a diameter of 2,5 cm. In another, an ivory button 2,7 cm. in diameter, shaped like a pointed felt hat (from the same excavation), the bronze pin by which it was fastened to the staff may still be seen in the middle of the flat side. It is perhaps no mere coincidence that the Archbishop of Cyprus (which forms a separate church independent of Constantinople) does not carry a crozier but a long staff crowned by a round Imperial globe. When this Cypriote dignitary visits his diocese, he takes the apple crowned staff in his hand as he enters a place. He unites imperial to high priestly rights and dignities.

††) Where I also mentioned this bronze implement, though I did not decide whether it was to be looked upon as a sceptre end, a club, or some portion of a chariot. Meanwhile I have come to the conviction that in reality we have here the end of a lance of the sceptre category. Shape, length (18 cm) diameter (3 cm. clear width) suit exactly.

offering could be offered to the Idalion war goddess than an exquisitely decorated spear. The inscription on the spear runs thus:*) *Τᾶ ᾿Αθάνα τᾶ ἰν ᾿Ηδαλίοι βάϰϱα δέϰα* (If by *βάϰϱα* we must understand *τύμπανα*, these 10 tambourines had been dedicated at the same time for the service of Athena, the spear-bearer). It has already been fully stated above pp. 48 to 50 that an imageless cult in honour of Athena must have certainly taken place at the spot where the find was made, similar to the imageless cult of Athena introduced at Teumessos in Boeotia by the Telchinians (Paus. IX, 19,1). The strangeness of the cult had so struck the traveller Pausanias, that he made special mention of it as of the Boeotian spear cult at Chaeronea.   Now since Homer pictures nearly all the offensive and defensive weapons of Agamamnon, with the exception of the sceptre, as guest-gifts from Kinyras, King of Kypros, and since Pausanias asserts that the imageless cult of Athena was brought from Kypros to Boeotia in very ancient times, we may fairly conjecture that the imageless spear cult also travelled the same road from Kypros to Boeotia.   As the spear idol of Chaeronea was reputed to be the lance of Agamemnon, our deduction with regard to the Athena sceptre of Idalion found on the Akropolis of the city amounts to certainty, We can very well conceive a small tabernacle or tent of dedication in the holy grove of the Idalian Athena under the green trees upon the hill, within which as at Chaeronea stood the holy sceptre idol, while on the walls of the little shrine or tent and on the trees round about would be suspended the swords, the cuirasses,**) the double axe***) the shield p. 869 Fig. 636, the little bronze tablets†) inscribed on both sides, the twelve gilt silver dishes††), all of which objects were found, on the same spot.   No sort of iconic agalmata was found, such as are found elsewhere in such abundance on the sites of ancient sacred precincts.   On the other hand we can also imagine a sort of trophy tree in the precinct of the warrior goddess, Anat-Athena, on which the captured arms could be hung after a victory.†††) This would quite well suit the contents of the agreement on the bronze tablets in which there is mention of a blockade of Idalion by the Medes and the Kitians, during which the Physician Qusilos is to tend the wounded in battle without payment, and receive in return a state indemnity in money or land or freedom from taxes.§)

This remarkable cult of the spear Anat-Athena, taken together with the oppression of the Idalians at the hands of their besiegers the Medes and Kitians, reminds us in conclusion of the cult of the war-like Astarte (i. e, Anat) among the Philistines, on the downfall of Israel and the death of Saul. When the Philistines found Saul lying on Mount Gilboa, they cut of his head, stript him of his armour, and dedicated it in the temple of Astarte.

---

*) Cf. R. Meister. "Die griechischen Dialekte," p. 156.

**) The one preserved is figured above, p. 75 Fig. 101 = Plate CXLI, 4.

***) Perrot, III, p. 867, fig. 634 = below Plate CXXXVI, 5.

†) W. Deecke's "Griechisch-Kyprische Inschriften" p. 27, No. 60. R. Meister "Griechische Dialekte," II, pp. 150—151.

††) One given on p. 48, fig. 51, where I compare with these twelve votive gilt silver dishes from Cyprus, the detailed description of the offerings brought by the princes of Israel on the occasion of the dedication of the tabernacle, of the tent of manifestation at Jerusalem (Numbers VII). The twelve gilt silver cups from Idalion possibly came from the similar dedication of a tent of manifestation. The ten or twelve tambourines would also suit this theory.

†††) Cf. Bötticher, "Baumcultus" VI, § 6, p. 71 and fol.

§) R. Meister. "Die griechische Dialekte" II, p. 155.

Be this as it may, it is at any rate certain that Anat-Athena was worshipped on the Akropolis of Idalion, in an imageless cult by the dedication of metal armour and dishes, among which the holy lance also had an important part. We also saw from the numerous designs on the earlier Kyprian cylinders that the cultus of the lance and the staff is of the highest antiquity on the Island, and can be traced back to the second or third millennium B. C. Further the god Rešef-Apollo in the sacred precinct at Frangissa was, we saw, of special importance.

3. Anthropomorphic images of the Youthful God of Vegetation and Plants, and of his Mother.

The child-god, the Flower-child, the nursling that appears either naked (Plate XXXVII 2, 5, 6 and 9; CXXIX, 2)*) or wrapped in swaddling clothes (XXXVII, 1, 4, 7, 8)**) on his mother's breast, is Dusi, Tammuz, Adonis, Osiris on the bosom of Istar, Astarte, Aphrodite or Isis. The child grows up, learns to run and eat all manner of meats, to drink, and yet continues to suck (as is customary now-a-days in the East) its mothers breast (Horus-Osiris-Harpokrates, on the cup from Praeneste, Plate CXXIX, 1).

And when the child no longer sucks, it gets all sorts of tricks. Instead of the nipple or of its bottle it sucks its fingers, like the Horus child who passed into Graeco-Phoenician—Phoenician-Greek mythology under the name of Harpokrates. The naked child Harpokrates sits like a flower spirit on the lotus bud,***) from which he sprang. The mother stands in front of him as flower goddess. As he cannot take the breast he sucks his finger (above p. 47, fig. 50, centre of the cup from Amathus). He is approaching adolescence; but the habit of sucking his finger has not left him (see the same cup on the left) Harpokrates always sucks.†)

Sometimes the goddess Mother has two children about her. She nurses the smaller while the bigger stands at her side (Plate XXXVII, 4).††) This stone figure now only 1,18 m. high and broken at the top was excavated with the capitals figured on Plate LVIII, 1 and 2, and LIX, 1, on the Eastern Akropolis of Idalion (at *n* No. 8, Plate III) which terminates that celebrated Idalian mountain

---

*) XXXVII, 2 a terra cotta = Perrot, p. 202, fig. 144. There is a similar one in Berlin. Other similar Egyptizing images, with or without the child, were found in great numbers in the sanctuary of the divinities Astarte Mikal on the Akropolis of Kition. This is a Cypriote type of the motherless goddess peculiar to Kition. Fig. 3 is a terra cotta which I found at Idalion, in temenos, No. 3, p. 5 of my list. Fig. 5 is a fragment of a terra cotta of pure Greek style from the salt lake at Larnaka. Fig. 6 is a terra cotta of the bronze periode from a grave at Hagia Paraskevi. The goddess is intended to have a bird's beak (cf. above, p. 34, Fig. 32). Either she is naked, in which case the vulva is strongly emphasised, or else she is supposed to wear a short tunic: the first supposition is the more probable. Fig. 9 = Perrot III, p. 553, fig. 376, is Graeco-Phoenician and cannot belong to the copper bronze period of Alambra. This terra cotta is in the Louvre.

**) XXXVII, 1. a stone image = Perrot III, p. 554, fig. 377. Fig. 7 is a very primitive plank idol, from the copper bronze period, found in a grave at Hagia Paraskevi. It is of red polished clay, details are scratched in. Mother and child are clothed; the latter is wrapped in swaddling clothes; originally both ends of the pillow on which the child's head rested could be seen. Fig. 8 is a stone image which I discovered in a grave at Poli tis Chrysokhou (Marion Arsinoe) in 1886.

***) Cf. Mariette, "Description de l'Agypte," A. I. 78, 24 = Goodyear, "Grammer of the Lotus," p. 21, I. 2.

†) Roscher, "Mythologisches Lexikon," Sp. 2747; a Phoenician inscribed bronze in Madrid.

††) For a similar representation treated more in the Greek manner, see Cesnola's Atlas, LXVI, 436 from Athiaenou.

grove, the scene, according to other legends, of the loves of Aphrodite and Adonis, but where Adonis, was slain by Apollo transformed into a boar.*) In no other grove of Idalion, perhaps in no other grove of the island, did the group of mother and child, find such a fervent worship as on a hill west of the City of Idalion (Plate II, 15 and p. 14 No. 24 of our list, cf. also Plate I). I proved that a sanctuary dedicated to the mother goddess, i. e, to an Aphrodite κουροτρόφος had existed here. Among the votive offerings were swarms of images of this goddess and child. The latter often wears a high, pointed, so-called Phrygian cap. In two cases I found two children grouped with the goddess, the nursling on her lap, the bigger child leaning upon her on the left,**) one group is from the above mentioned spot, No. 24 of the list, the other (Plate XXXVII, 4) from the grave No. 8 on Plates II and III (p. 13 No. 19 of the list).

It is very seldom that the history of the development of a religious art type extending over 2000 years allows itself to be traced in one country as completely as I can show from monuments to have been the case in Kypros. The roughest beginnings (XXXVII, 7) show us the earliest type, a primitive carven image imitated in clay. A vertical scratch ending in a round depression indicates nose and mouth, horizontal scratches on each side stand for the eyes. The idol may belong to a stratum previous to the oldest period of Chaldaean influence, it may, however, also belong to the time of the first introduction of Babylonian cylinders. The next type (XXXVII, 6) belongs to that period in the middle of the second millennium B. C. in which began the importation of Mycenaean vases, of the products of the minor Egyptian arts, and also in great measure the importation of the Assyro-Babylonian cylinders with cuneiform inscriptions (which, however, also appear in the older categories.***) The maker has intentionally given to the goddess a bird's head,†) and the head of the child has something of the same appearance The two first types are both previous to the iron age. Nana Ištar elements are mixed up in them. The third type comes in the iron period and introduces into the island a powerful Egyptian influence with elements of Hathor-Isis. We find it in terra cottas (ab. 20 cm. high) which were especially dedicated to Astarte-Aphrodite in Kittim-Kition. The fourth type (perhaps quite contemporary with the third type in the 6ᵗʰ century B. C.) of the Cyprio-Graeco-Phoenician potters, executed like a xoanon with the lower part columnar (i. e. as children make a "snow man"), is often black and painted red. (Black and red stripes employed at first with great reserve begin to appear at the close of the bronze period in the type p. 34, fig. 31††) of which, however, up to now I have only found images of the goddess without the child (Plate XXXVII, 3 and 9).) Next there appears as fifth type the stone image of the goddess enthroned (XXXVII, 1 and 8) which is imitated in terra cotta. Gradually these stone and terra cotta images pass into the pure Greek style, first of the archaic and then of the fine period. These Greek terra cottas of the fourth and beginning of the third century B. C. (CCV, 4, 5, 7—9) were all manufactured in Kition, and were found partly in graves, partly in sacred groves on the salt Lake of Larnaka. These mother goddesses (or else divine or deified mothers) also appear to have been found in the temenos of Artemis-Paralia-Ashera. Sometimes the child sits on his mother's shoulder, sometimes

---

*) Cf. above p. 112.

**) Sketches in the Owl, 1888, p 63, Plate V, 6 and 7. In No. 7 the nursling wears a high Phrygian cap, while the bigger child who leans against his mother has no head covering. The Cyprus Museum also possesses a big goddess mother enthroned, with two children, one on her lap, the other at her side; the group is roughly executed in Greek fourth century style: it comes from Tremithus (See Plate I). Further in Cesnola's Atlas (LXVI, 436) may be seen a similar group, somewhat better executed, of the mother and two children, belonging to about the same period. Athiaenou is mentioned as the place where it was found.

***) Cf. above p. 83, fig 111.

†) Above p. 34, fig. 31 and 32. I show for comparison on the left the type with male head, on the right that with the bird head. Both types occur side by side.

††) The human type (31) is sometimes discretely painted with black and red wings, I believe it is the oldest Kyprian idol painted in two colours. In the same layer, when the brilliant technique of the Mycenaean vases is adopted by the Cyprian potters for Cyprian vases, it is also imitated on the idols, which are painted in one colour with brilliant lustrous paint.

he is kicking for joy on his mother's bosom. The period stretching between the primitive plank idol, (XXXVII, 7) perhaps belonging to the third millennium B. C., and the image in pure Greek style (XXXVII, 5) covers some 2000 years.

Another type of the Duzi-Tammuz-Adonis-Osiris-Harpokrates child common in Cyprus, shows him naked and with both arms and legs bent in a crouching attitude, which is hardly aesthetic: it is figured on Plate XCII, 3 from a terracotta which I bought in 1883 from a peasant in Dali, and which is said to have been found on the northern slope of the Western Akropolis (see Plate III), called Ambilleri. The same type, also from Cyprus, with further attempts at amalgamation with Ptah-Pattäko, Ptah-Embryo, Pygmaios and Bes, may be seen in Perrot III, p. 78, fig. 27.*)

We pass to the most usual type. The boy god, now conceived as somewhat older and bigger, generally appears clothed (Plate XXXIII, 1—5 and XCII, 4, 5) seldom naked (XCII, 1 and 2); in most graves he is without any head covering, at times, however, (and then often) he wears a round cap, the crown of which projects like the cap of a modern sailor (XCII, 6). He sits on the ground and generally has one leg partly or totally drawn under him. When the figure is clothed the dress is purposely drawn back so as to disclose the membrum virile. The boys with caps were common in the sanctuary of the mother of the gods at Tamassos (mentioned again p. 10, No. 5 on our list). The head (Plate XCII, 6) also comes from the same place.**) This votive boy appears as a constant attendant figure as much in the groves of Rešef-Apollo as of Astarte-Aphrodite, whereas in other cases a strict division of the sexes is observed in the votive offerings. As a rule male figures were dedicated in the groves sacred to gods, and female figures in those sacred to goddesses. The innocent child Tammuz-Adonis forms an exception. Pursued and slain by Apollo, he is found again by Aphrodite after a long, fruitless search in Kypros, in the temple of Apollo in Argos.***) The relation of hostility is turned into one of intimate friendship. Henceforth Adonis performs the duties of grove or temple guardian, of sacrificial attendant boy for Apollo as much as for Aphrodite. The nude terracotta figure, Plate XCII, 2, also from Idalion and purchased by me, is also said to come from the grove of Aphrodite κουροτρόφος Taf. II, 15 (p. 18, No. 33 on my list) which is quite possible seeing that I excavated there for Sir Charles Newton a rough small stone of a naked reclining Adonis. (Plate XCII, 7.)

In this Aphrodite grove hundreds of images of the clothed and seated type (Plate XCII, 4) had been dedicated. Although the site had been thoroughly,—and unfortunately quite unsystematically — excavated before my time, I still found fragments of more than a hundred replicas. The Astarte-Aphrodite grove (p. 5, No. 3 of our list) contained only isolated representations of the mother and child. The stone examples of this group, enthroned, so numerous in grove No. 24, were entirely absent. In Plate XXXVII, 3, I have given the one standing stone idol of the mother and child which was dedicated there. Consequently only isolated instances of the crouching Adonis-youths were found.†)

---

*) Cf. Perrot III. p. 420, figs. 293 and 294.

**) There is a whole series of these figures in other Museums, in London, Paris; in New York alone are 50 in good preservation (Cesnola, Atlas, 937—987), there are also five in the Cyprian collection of the Constantinople Museum. (S. Reinach, "Catalogue du Musée Impérial d'antiquités," Constantinople, 1882. No. 436—441. Grotesques accroupis orné chacun d'un collier.

***) Engel, "Kypros", p. 668.

†) In the groves of Tanit-Artemis-Kybele (as at Achna No. 1 in the list) not even a fragment was found that could lead one to suppose that any images of the crouching temple boy had been dedicated there.

Still I discovered a very interesting though unfortunately headless fragment of a stone statuette, clothed in a short sleeved tunic and painted red.   The upper part of the arms was decorated with hooked crosses 卐 (svastika).*)   In an Aphrodite grove (p. 13, No. 24 of our list) belonging to Chytroi, a large number of such images of sacrificial youths, some of large dimensions, were likewise excavated by me for the Cyprus Museum.**)   I have republished two of the most interesting fragments on Plate XXXIII, 3 and 4.   In both cases a chain composed of a row of signet rings hangs over the breast of the youth.   In fig. 3 there is suspended as centre-piece a bearded and hideous head, in No. 4 a rectangular ornament composed of tassels.   The boy holds up a large dove by the wings.   Two stone figures which I excavated in the Apollo grove at Voni (above p. 2, No. 2 in our list), and now in the Cyprus Museum, — one with (XXXIII, 1) and the other without a head (XXXIII, 2) — wear a triangular amulet suspended from a neck or breast band.   The same triangular amulet is worn by one of the boys of Cesnola's Atlas from the sanctuary of Apollo Hylates at Hyle (No. 48 of our list) (Plate XXXIII, 5 = Cesnola Atlas CXXXII, 985). — The same shaped amulet, made of silver, is worn to this day by both Greek and Turkish Cypriotes.   Fig. 8 of Plate XXXIII shows a modern amulet of this kind in my possession; it is shown again in fig. 6 round the neck of a pretty Greek girl. These triangular objects, which appear on our Adonis-boys as early as the fifth and sixth Century B. C. indicate plainly the cone, the triangle of the Paphian Astarte Aphrodite, the Paphian as she is called on inscriptions from Chytroi. ***) On Plate XXXIII, 16 I have given a golden amulet of tubular shape found at Poli tis Chrysokhou (Marion Arsinoe) †), which from the conditions of the find can be attributed to the 5th Century.   Like the modern triangle, this ancient tubular amulet is hollow.   All sorts of talismans are stuck into the modern instances, a bit of the real Cross or some talisman given by priest, if the wearer be a Christian; some little relic of a Turkish saint or the talisman of a Chodshah's, if he be a Turk.   The triangular amulets worn by our Tammuz-Adonis boys or by the sacrificial boys who represent him must have been used in precisely the same manner.   Another of these figures, which are usually of stone, (Plate XCII, 4) is taken from Cesnola's Atlas, and like fig. 5, Pl. XXXIII, comes from the Apollo-Hylates grove (p. 19, No 48).   The amulet consists of a tubular piece, from which a round object is suspended.   In Cesnola's Atlas no fewer than 50 of these sitting statuettes of boys are figured, (Plate CXXX—CXXXII of the Atlas, No. 937—987); among them may be seen all kinds of variants.††)   Three of them (No. 945—948) come from one of the Apollo groves at Athiaenou (No. 25 or 26 of our list, above p. 14).   The remaining 47 and three others (Cesnola-Stern LXXIII, 3) were found in the sanctuary of Apollo-Hylates (No. 48 of our list).   A fourth instance (Plate XXXII, 4 of Cesnola-Stern) from one of the Apollo temples at Athiaenou like the three of the

---

*) Cp. above p. 148, figs. 149 and 150.

**) Cp. explanations of Plates XXXIII, XCII and XCIII.

***) P. 13, No 14.

†) Ibid., sect. I, grave XLII and sect. II, grave LXXXII of the Journal of Excavations have yielded similar, although more richly decorated silver amulets which exactly resemble those which we see on the breast of Cyprian statues, especially of the crouching boys.   The Englishmen who excavated after me on the Akropolis of Marion Arsinoe which I had first discovered, have published on Pl. V. 4 of the Journal of Hellenic Studies a tubular golden breast amulet similar to the one on our plate XXXIII, 16.

††) In one case (No. 978) the sculptor has placed the boy so that he looks as if he wanted to stretch himself full length, or as if he had been lying down and was now preparing to get up.

Atlas 945—948) is already executed in the pure Greek style. A head of Medusa[*]) is suspended from the necklace. The right hand holds a bird (a dove?), the left an apple.

A characteristic and interesting boy's statuette was excavated by H. Lang in the sanctuary of Rešef-Mikal-Apollo-Amyklos at Idalion (p. 16, No. 30 of our list). A chain composed of signet rings crosses the body from the left shoulder to the right hip. The short sleveless shift is open in front to disclose the membrum virile. Thick rings adorn wrists and ankles. The right hand is broken, the left holds a small, four-footed sacrificial beast. We accordingly have here a priesthood of boys peculiar to the Cyprian ritual, where they formed a distinct caste; when they grow older they could join the Kynirades (the priesthood connected with the worship of Aphrodite Astarte) or the Karyeis (the priests of Apollo Rešef both in the Apollo grove at Voni, and in another Apollo grove at Athiaenou) or some other priestly college. Possibly these young servants of Tammuz-Adonis who passed on to form a separate priestly caste, should be recognized as the priesthood of the prophetic Tamyrads, just as in Tamassos we recognize the city of Tammuz. Be that as it may, we certainly have in these thousands of boys' figures proof positive of a local custom that extented to all Cyprus, and of a ritual practice which had its origin in Cyprus itself, the home of Adonis. The younger sitting boys develop into older standing boys, and these in turn into youths. On Plate XLI, I give the much multilated fragments of a life size votive statue which I found in the Apollo temple at Voni (No. 2 on the list). Next to the god – or the deified priest of Apollo the Purifier,—stands Apollo's servant, the young Adonis or the priestly boy who represents him. Figs. 1, 5 and 8 of Plate XCII show us how this ritual of Tammuz-Adonis with its specially trained and accoutred caste of priestly boys migrated through the greater part of the coastland of the Mediterranean till it reached Malta, Carthage and Etruria.

The crouching attitude, like the necklace worn by the boys, was of the highest sacred import. The Art type accordingly penetrated into the countries of the Mediterranean along with the myth.

In the antechapel of the very irregular temple of Hagiar Kim (Perrot III, p. 301, fig. 223) were found seven shapeless sitting or crouching stone statuettes; so far as the bad state of their preservation permits us to judge they were naked. Two are given by (Perrot III, p. 305, figs. 230 and 231 = our fig. 8, Plate XCII). However primitive these representations may be, this set appear to reproduce our sitting sacrificial boys. Even if these Maltese instances seem doubtful imitations of the Adonis boys, no hesitation can be felt in the case of the Carthaginian stele (XCII, 5) or the Etruscan stone statuette with an Etruscan inscription on the left arm. On the conical summit[**]) of the Carthaginian stele we see a sitting figure of Tammuz-Adonis clothed exactly similar to the Kyprian sacrificial boys (cp. e. g. the next fig. below XCII, 4). The naked Etrurian Tamuz-Adonis boy who also wears an amulet ring on his necklace, likewise affords an instructive comparison to the naked sacrificial boys from Idalion. (Cp. fig. 2 immediately below on Plate XCII). Even the facial expression is the same

---

[*]) These amulets, in the shape of heads, at one time unbearded and less repulsive and of a type feminine rather than masculine, at another bearded, often occur on these necklaces worn by the boys and Adonis. A figure I found in the grove of Aphrodite κουροτρόφος in Idalion (p. 18, No. 33 of the list) also wore one.

[**]) Tanit face of Baal, or one of her priestesses, is seen in this same position on a Carthaginian stele Pl. LXXXV, fig. 8.

in both boys. We have already pointed out more than once the numerous connections between Etruria and Cyprus, and shall frequently have occasion to do so again. We can scarcely feel astonished if Etruria where H e r a was surnamed K u p r a and was represented exactly like a Cyprian or Mycenaean Astarte-Aphrodite with a dove on her head (Cp. the explanations to Plate XXXIII, 6 and CV, 2—5) also welcomed Tamuz-Adonis and his cultus images. The reverse would indeed have been surprising.

As Cyprus, with all its wealth of monuments, has until now only yielded a miserable fragment of a reclining Adonis, and one example of him standing up (Cesnola's Atlas CXXXI, 978) and as no instance of the dead Tammuz-Adonis laid out in state and surrounded with flowers has yet been found there, we must adduce the corresponding figure of Osiris from the Egyptian monuments of Philae. (Goodyear, "Grammar of the Lotus", p. 19, fig. 1). As already noted it is precisely in Byblos and in Amathus in Cyprus that Adonis and Osiris were blended into one divinity.

The heads, which we noted as breast ornaments on the Cyprian temple boys, oblige us at this point to collect some few types of these amulets in shape of heads as well, as some of the myths concerning the severed heads of divinities, without, however, laying any claim to a complete classification. I shall attempt more especially to bring forward Cyprian material, particularly those portions of it which are unedited, or which up to now have either been incorrectly or insufficiently explained, in so far as they seem likely to throw a light on the cult of Tammuz-Osiris-Adonis and of his mother. In the Cyprian Hathor capitals of Kition, the head of Hathor sprang from the lotus flower, as described in the Book of the Dead.[*] We saw Hathor heads in the volutes of a Cyprian capital, under the apron of a Cyprian statue, on a Cyprian bronze image. This same head of Hathor and other male and female heads borrowed from Egyptian art and religion reappear as amulets and chain ornaments. The same grave, dating from the beginning of the 6th century B. C., which contained the remarkable silver girdle (Plate XXV, 1—4), also yielded the fragments of the threaded chain (XXV, 7 = fig. 170).

An eye drawn in the Egyptian manner, and three small heads or masks in the Graeco-Cyprian Egyptising style, each alternate with a fruit-shaped bead (three of these are preserved). One of the heads resembles that of Hathor.[**] For purposes of comparison I show next to it a head of Hathor (after Prisse d'Avenne) taken from an Egyptian monument, which was worn as an amulet

---

[*] Cp. Pierret, "Livre des Morts", chap. LXXXI, fig.: A head springing from a lotus flower. "I am a pure lotus coming up between the shining ones. I keep watch over the nostril of Ra, who keeps watch over the nostril of Hathor. I give the commands which Horus fulfils, I am a pure lotus, sprung from the field of the sun."

[**] Cp. in Perrot III, p. 237, fig. 179 the glass paste from Sardinia (after Crispi, catalogi pl. B., fig. 15). Ibid. fig. 182 a square amulet of white glazed clay, on the one side of which is the Egyptian eye, on the other the lotus flower, cow and suckling calf (cp. above p. 164 and Plate LXXXIX, 1 and 6, XXXII, 29). F. Dümmler mentions in "Jahrbuch" II. p. 88 a number of analogous objects to these small gold mask-amulets, which on the authority of A. Furtwängler ("Bronzefunde in Olympia" p. 71 and Arch. Ztg., 1884, p. 111) he says are very common on Greek soil. My belief is, that in the process of formation of these heads and their conversion into the Gorgoneion within the archaic Greek period, Greek artists working in Cyprus and trained in Cyprian methods played a prominent part, and possibly even transmitted the Oriental and Egyptizing types to Greece. Both smaller and larger Egyptizing Greek-Archaic terra-cotta masks, which resemble the corresponding masks found in Rhodes and at Tanagra, were also excavated by me in groves at Poli tis Chrysokhou; one is given, Plate CLXXXVI, 6. The same archaic Greek style appears in the almost life size terra-cotta statues from Limniti (Pl. XLV) which are certainly of Kyprian production. This and other considerations lead us to assume that there was in Kypros a native Archaic-Greek terra-cotta industry and goldsmith's art.

or ornament on the breast. Very important, though only dating as far back as the end of the fifth, or beginning of the fourth century B. C., is the gold chain (plate XXXIII, 15) found in grave No. 24, Sect. I in 1886 at Poli tis Chrysokhou along with other ornaments &c. (Cp. the explanation

Fig. 170.   Fig. 171.

to Plate XXXIII). From each of the seventeen rosettes mounted on a bar, and intended to be threaded together, hang, suspended by delicate chains, plates stamped with all sorts of patterns, like the lotus flower, grapes, owls—full face and in profile—and finally bearded masks of the Silenus type. The same excavation (sect. II, grave CXLII) also yielded fragments of a similar ornament, where in place of the hideous bearded face, a youthful mask, possibly that of Medusa, was suspended from the little chain. (The same grave again contained a large gold flower some 0,4 m. long, intended to be worn on the breast.)

Another necklace amulet worn like the Egyptian eye to avert the evil eye*) is given fig. 171 (= Plate XXXIII, 17 **). It likewise was found at Poli tis Chrysokhou. The famous Metope of Selinos offers the nearest analogy to this small gold Gorgoneion, as P. Herrmann has already noted.***)

———————

*) We see for instance a similar apotropaeic eye hung around the neck of the griffin on the golden basket in the grave of Ramses III (above). The amulet in shape of a hooked cross painted on the neck of the horse of a roughly modelled Graeco-Phoenician horseman on a Cyprian terra-cotta in the Louvre, (Henzey, "Catalogue des figurines antiques de terre cuite du Musée du Louvre," p. 153) in likewise intended to avert the evil eye. To this day in the East, the Mussulmans hang half moons as talismans round their horses, while the Cyprian camel drivers prefer the gaily painted many coloured eyes, adorned with tassels. Apotropaeic virtue was ascribed in ancient times in Cyprus to the heads or skulls of oxen, cows and calves, or to the whole animal; hence their appearance on Cyprian vases, earrings, chains (Plate LIII, 4, 19, 24, 33 from terracotta figures, XXXIII, 22 a calf's head of gold). The same is the case nowadays when the dowry of a bride is being carried through the streets, the apotropaeic ox skull is displayed aloft on the cart. Children have crosses and coins hung round them against the evil eye &c.

**) = P. Herrmann, "Das Gräberfeld von Marion." p. 19, fig. 9.

***) A similar, though somewhat later, Gorgoneion from Vulci, worn as a prophylactic apotropeion, is given on Plate XCIII, 10 from Micali, Mon. ined. Pl 51, 4. On the reverse is a lion mask. I discovered an exceedingly interesting and still unpublished Greek cylinder in the Berlin Museum (Vorderasiat. Abtheil. Cat. 2145) which I give on Plate XXXI, 16. Perseus in profile is striding to the right, but turns his head round, so that it appears in profile to the left, while his body fronts the spectator. With his left hand he is seizing the Gorgon by the wrist, whilst with the right he holds the sickle shaped weapon ready to strike. The Gorgon is turned to the left, in the kneeling posture indicative of running, the upper portion of her body and her head are seen to the front; her head and breasts are roughly drawn and are in feminine form. The influence of the newly introduced Greek archaic style is evident, yet the facial expression, the contours of the head, and ends of the locks suggest as model the head of Hathor, from which, however, the Gorgon head varies in the introduction of snakes into the hair, which dart in all directions like the nimbus of a saint. Subject and style show that the work belongs to the beginning of the sixth (or perhaps end of the seventh, century B. C. This instance of the Perseus and Medusa myth may pass as unique in ancient Greek glyptique art, while amongst other representations of the same subject it is remarkable for interest and truth to life. accompanied by an undeniable charm. Its nearest analogy (as in the case of the Marion-Arsinoe gold ornaments (Pl. XXXIII, 17) is the much less beautiful Perseus and Gorgon Metope from Selinos. Unfortunately the place where the cylinder was found cannot be ascertained; the cylinder most nearly connected with it is the Cyprian (Pl. XXXI, 8 = above p. 31, fig. 28). It should be noted that the latter is taken from a rough sketch and not from a photograph of the original, as was possible in the case of the Berlin example.

The Greek goldsmith working in Kypros in the seventh century B. C. used, combined and trans-formed all kinds of heads of divinities, which he saw as ornaments of dress, or on sun columns and stelae, and derived from them the Gorgoneion. At any rate the supposition that the Gorgoneion came to the Greeks from Kypros, or more correctly, that it was created by the Greek themselves in Kypros*) cannot be decided on the spur of the moment, even if in the description of Agamemnon's armour the lines II. XI, 36 and 37 be considered a later interpolation. **) It is not necessary to lay the main stress on the fact that the whole armour was a guest present from King Kinyras to Agamemnon; for that would prove little with regard to the Gorgoneion on the shield. Purely decorative designs can be combined with figures. The shield was adorned with twenty bosses of tin (ὀμφαλοί) and the centre with one of dark blue glass paste (smalt). " And the grim Gorgon of terrible aspect was set around it (ἐστεφάνωτο), and about her (περὶ δὲ) were Dread and Fear (Λεῖμος and Φόβος)." In the Gorgon we have here not the Gorgon's face but her whole figure as we know it from archaic art; Deimos and Phobos are similar figures of terror. The arrange-ment of these figures would than have to be conceived of in continuous rows without any variation. The expressions ἐσι κρἀνωιο and περὶ δέ points to a composition in rows. With regard to the whole representation we have a parallel to it in the fragments of a shield casing from Tamassos in the Berlin Museum (Pl. LXX, 12) which, as the small round holes show, was nailed on to a solid core; its shape exacts corresponds to the κίκλοι, which apparently composed the Homeric shield; it is a circular strip of metal. On the outer and inner periphery is a continuous decoration of Lotus buds and Lotus flowers. In the angles formed by the. stems are round buttons which remind one of the twenty bosses of the Homeric shield. In the midst of the strip with the lotus decorations, heads of Hathor alternate with winged lions or pairs of lions. The centre of the Cyprian, as of the Homeric, shield was formed by a large, prominent shield buckle nailed on separately, which has been preserved. Not only in technique but also in decoration the analogies between the two shields are striking. In the case of the Cyprian example, however, the connection between figures and decoration is closer than we have any reason to assume was the case on the Homeric shield, and consequently represents a more advanced stage of art. The conditions of the find show that the shield belongs to the beginning of the sixth or end of the seventh century B. C. Certainly the decoration of the Cyprian shield is far removed from the genuine Greek method of presentation of the Homeric shield, but that can cause no astonishment in Cyprus.

The Graeco-Cyprian designer of the beautiful decorative archaic Gorgoneion (fig. 171), one of the finest and oldest of ancient Greek art, made use in addition to the heads of Hathor-Isis of heads of Bes, as we see it on the Egyptian mirror handle (XCIII. 8) or in its Cypriote form on the necklaces of the boy Adonis (XXXIII. 3 = XCIII. 2) of Chytroi. In Cyprus Bes further contributed to form the very complicated type of the husband of Astarte-Aphrodite.***)

Heads of Bes, singly or arranged in rows (Pl. XXXVIII, 16 = LIII, 6, XXXVIII, 20 = LIII, 39) adorn the crown of Aphrodite or one of her priestesses found in the sanctuary of Idalion excavated in 1885 (No. 3 on our list). A terra-cotta sarkophagus which I excavated in 1886 at Marion-Arsinoe (Poli tis Chrysokhou) had a decoration formed of cow's heads (Hathor-Isis) alternating with bearded male masks (Osiris-Adonis-Bes &c.) (Plate XXXVIII, 19). Further the artists who in Cyprus gradually composed the Greek Gorgoneion, were aided by very ancient stone Gorgoneia, like the stone mask

---

*) This was first suppested by Six, "De Gorgone", p. 94.

**) On this point I adopt the view of W. Helbig ("Homerisches Epos," p. 388) in opposition to that of Furtwängler (Roscher's " Mythol. Lexikon," Sp. 1702 and 1703) who holds the well known verses of Iliad XI, 36 and 37 to be a later interpolation.

***) Compare a small group representing Hathor-Isis-Aphrodite carrying Bes-Osiris-Tammuz-Adonis on her shoulders, and herself sitting on a capital formed by lotus flowers, given on Pl. CI, 4 (= Perrot III, p. 408, fig. 279). The ends of the sarkophagus from Amathus are occupied respectively with four figures of Astarte-Aphrodite, and with four figures of her husband Rešef-Apollo-Melqart-Herakles-Bes-Pygmaios. The colossus of Amathus, who is made up of various divinities (Pl. CIII fig. 4 = Perrot 561 fig. 386) has also absorbed Bes elements like the Cyprian beast tamer with four beasts (silver girdle Pl. C, 7, gem C, 2, CI, 8, 9), like the Cyprian horned centaurs (Pl. XLVII, 10 and 16, terra-cottas) and apparently also like the winged centaurs, tamers of animals which also come from Cyprus (gems Pl. CIV figs. 11 and 12).

from a Greek grave belonging to the same Nekropolis of the end of the seventh or the beginning of the sixth century B. C (Plate XCIII, 7). The style, the form and the general character of this stone mask recall the Mycenaean gold masks. Perhaps the marble head of the Medusa in Argos, which passed as the work of the Cyclops, resembled it somewhat. We are continually reminded of those far reaching connections between Kypros and Argos, which have now received linguistic confirmation. Is it merely a coincidence that it was precisely next to the head of Medusa that stood the shrine in front of which the wives of the Argives sang their laments to Adonis? (Paus. II, 9, 6) The passage in Pausanias suggests irresistibly the heads of the Medusa and Bes type, which hang on the breast of our Kyprian Adonis images. (Cf. also Paus. IX, 41, 2.)

The limestone head with two faces (11,5 cm. high) which is still in my possession (given from three sides Pl. XCIII, 4—6) further shows excellently other and early Cyprian adaptations of these ancient Oriental Syrian and Egyptian heads of gods, which, rough though they might be, could inspire the Greek artists of the Gorgoneion. One of the two faces has two additional eyes in the forehead, above the two deep-set natural eyes, so that in these images we have not only the model for the Gorgoneion, but also the model for Argus, the watchman of the Io-cow. This limestone double faced head, bearded on both sides, of the six-eyed Argos, was placed as a votive offering in the grove of Artemis-Paralia-Ashera on the salt lake of Larnaka (No. 7 on our list). I have given on Pl. XCIII, 3 a sixth century Aryballos, with double head of greenish white glazed clay, found in Cyprus in a grave by the village of Parasolia (now in the Berlin Museum). Here also the heads are bearded. We see that in Cyprus these representations of Argus, which here also could easily arise from figures of andro-gynous divinities,*) early haunted the imaginations of artist and poets. A whole, early Phoenician terra-cotta figure of Argus (now in the Cyprus-museum of Kurion) has the second pair of eyes on the breast (Pl. CCVI, fig. 5). — An interesting Etruscan parallel to the gold and bronze heads and masks of Cyprian breast ornaments is given Plate XCIII, 9.**) The horned, bearded head reminds us further of the four Carthaginian heads of Jupiter-Ammon on a lead tablet (Perrot III, p. 815, fig. 568) though these only come from Roman times. As a pendant we have four bronze heads of youths with long hair (but without braid or horns) intended to hang on a chain; they were found at Idalion in 1883, and were for some time in the collection of Mr. Jul. Naue, to whom I ceded them. The beautiful Etruscan gold ornament (Plate CXLIII, 3) which can be compared with our Cyprian gold ornament (Pl. XXXII, 15) has, next to rows of winged figures of the harpy type, naked crouching women, lotus flowers, and egg shaped ornaments a row of horned, bearded heads. They closely resemble the Cyprian bearded heads with or without horns and the Etruscan gold head (Martha, "l'art étrusque", title plate). These bearded heads and masks with or without horns bring us also to the type of Acheloos and other river gods (cf. below in the case of Dionysos what is said of the Cyprian river god Bokaros). The very ancient silver amulet shaped like a horned head (Pl. LXVII, 9) was found in the same grave as the Gorgoneion, fig. 171 (= LXVII, 12), and thus forms on Cyprian ground a further point of contact.

---

*) Double heads of glass, also found in Kypros, which are obviously not earlier than Hellenistic times, but are therefore all the more interesting because they lead us step by step up to or down to the Roman head of Janus. A similar glass double head from Cyprus was obtained through me, for the collection of Herr Ritter von Lanna in Prague.

**) = J. Martha, "l'art étrusque", title plate.

The actual model for the Gorgoneion seems to be a terra-cotta disk of rough clay, coated with a finer red clay and polished, which was found in Cyprus at Hagia Paraskevi, in a grave of the copper bronze period. I give this remarkable object, which is much older than the Mycenaean vase whose design is reproduced on Pl. LXXV, 1, on Plate XCIII, 1. This primitive human face reminds one irresistibly of the moon and sun faces of our modern calendars. It can also be seen at a glance that the artist of the Mycenaean vase intended to place a similar sun or moon face on the summit of a sun column or Ashera pillar. On Pl. XCI (lower row) I give in addition the torso and the upper portion of a Cyprian statue. It shows how the apotropaeic head passed from the breast to the apron or to the tunic, and how further adaptations of the Uraeus-snakes led to the Greek Gorgoneion with its fantastic wreath of snakes.[*])

Finally heads of cows by themselves represented Hathor-Isis-Astarte-Aphrodite; they were set up as ex-votos by the altars in the sacred precincts. I give an example of one on Plate XCIV, 4. It is 0,11 m. high. Several of these cow head idols were set up in the room for votive offerings of the Astarte sanctuary on the Akropolis of Kition.

The head which the boy Adonis, the young temple attendant, wears on his breast, the head which Kinyras Adonis, when he has reached adolescence and manhood and become priest of Apollo and Kinyras, wears below on the apron of his apparel; reminds us of the **Osiris-Tammuz-Adonis head which swam from Alexandria to Byblos.**[**]) Although this myth of the swimming Adonis head in the form in which we have it is late, and belongs to the Alexandrian and late Ptolemaic period, yet it points back to much older legends.[***])

In Abydos the head of the murdered Osiris was preserved as a relic of high sanctity.[†]) Isis finds the body in Byblos.

Dionysos is mutilated like Osiris and Adonis. As the Osiris-Adonis head swims to Byblos, so the Dionysos head swims to Lesbos. There can be no longer be any doubt that the Tammuz-Adonis-Osiris cult on Cyprus is very old, for we have succeeded in pointing to very old cultus images of this god and of his mother, and of the head severed from the body of the god. The images, the gardens the laments for the young flower god, for Dusi-Tammuz-Adonis-Osiris-Linos, existed everywhere, in

---

[*]) Cp. above p. 195, fig. 168 the head of Hathor under the apron on a Cyprian statue. A great number of other Cyprian adaptations and variations of the head with or without snakes on the apron of the robe are best studied in Cesnola's Atlas. In Kypros, at a time probably anterior to that of Homer, Anat-Athena arises under Phoenician and Greek influence from the armed Baalat-Astarte, i. e. from the warlike aspect of Aphrodite. Since Istar, and her naked images in Cyprus, wear on their breast a great round disc (e. g. Perrot III. p. 553 fig. 375), it was quite easy, with the help of the breast amulets in shape of heads, of the Uraeus snakes, and of the realistic snakes about the heads on the apron of Rešef-Horus-Apollo and of his priest, to form the Gorgoneion, and to place the aegis of Anat-Athena on the breast (cp. Pl, CCVI).

[**]) Engel, "Kypros", II, p. 594.

[***]) I was able, for instance, to trace the horned race of centaurs in Kypros through numerous votive offerings in different parts of the island back to the sixth century and even earlier, while the only literary authority on the subject (Nonnus) is several hundred years later. The same must hold good with the swimming head of Osiris-Tammuz-Adonis. We shall also become acquainted in the next section with two legends of modern Cyprus, one Turkish Mohammedan, and the other orthodox Greek, which both point back to the old myth of the swimming Adonis head.

[†]) Brugsch, "Religion der Aegypter," p. 620.

Egypt, in Babylon, in Palestine, in Syria, in Kypros, in Greece, in Malta, in Etruria and in Sardinia. The Egyptian and the Babylonian hymns, like the Old Testament and the poems of Homer, announce the same youthful god of vegetation. Everywhere in legend, cultus and cultus image, the young flower spirit-genius of plants and sun-god cannot be separated from the goddess, who appears at one time as his mother, at another as his beloved.

4. Names and Local Cults of the youthful God.

We have shewn that Egyptians and Babylonians, Assyrians and Hebrews, Phoenicians and Aramaeans, Syrians and Asiatics of Asia-Minor, Kyprians and Greeks, Carthaginians and Etruscans, even the Romans during Pagan times, worshipped substantially the same youthful god of spring and reviving vegetation. The name and the ritual of this god vary in different places, but he is always pure and beautiful, often young and unwed. Everywhere it is his fate to wage continual war with an evil demon, the war of Summer and Winter, Light and Darkness, Bloom and Decay. When the autumnal storms strip the trees, or the fiery glow of an Oriental Midsummer scorches the fields, the evil demon overcomes the good spirit and slays him. But in spring (which in the East appears considerably before the end of our European winter), when nature awakes, the good Spirit rises to new life, and with his sunshine, flowers and fruit, chases away the evil malicious demon of death and destruction.

In the Kyprian Lazarus-festival, as I have already said, I recognize in modern shape the resurrection of the "good spirit" of the ancients, and before proceeding to discuss the myth of Busiris-Osiris-Set-Typhon, I wish to give some account of a rite still practised by Greeks of Kypros and other parts of the East, to typify the destruction of the evil one. This popular ecclesiastical festival takes place with special solemnity at Larnaka, because the absence of the Turkish Pasha (who till 1878 resided in Nicosia), and the protection of their own consuls, have allowed the Greeks in that town an unusual measure of freedom. It is celebrated in the court of St. Lazarus', the principal church of the richest parish in the town, on Easter Monday afternoon, and is repeated on the remaining afternoons of the same week in other parishes. It consists of two ceremonies, of which one is enacted within the church, and the other outside, in the porch if there is space enough, and if not, in the church square. It is the latter of these two ceremonies with which we are concerned at this point. A life-size effigy, filled with inflammable materials and fire-works, represents Judas and is destroyed in a variety of ways. The people of the various parishes vie with each other from year to year in the invention of new costumes for Judas, and new ways of putting him to death. In 1879 the parish of Hagios Giannis at Larnaka bore the palm for invention. The effigy of Judas was first hanged, than shot at as it hung, then blown in pieces by fireworks wrapped up inside, and finally burned to ashes. When Judas is burned, the custom is that all, young and old, leap through the glowing embers.

The effigies are often made of wooden shavings, either that they may burn easily, or possibly in order to represent the Demon of Vegetation. A stranger must often serve as model for the effigy, a custom which perhaps points to a survival of traditional human sacrifices, such as were offered to Osiris-Busiris in Egypt and Kypros. According to the legend, Phrasios, the soothsayer of Kypros, went to Egypt, and advised Busiris to institute human sacrifice in order to appease Zeus. Busiris

followed the advice of Phrasios and made him the first victim.*) This unhappy soothsayer is sometimes called a kinsman of Pygmalion, mythical King of Kypros, and sometimes priest of the Hero-
God Pygmalion, one of the favourites of Aphrodite.

To show how firm a hold this Easter rite of Judas-burning has taken of Oriental Greeks, I may here
cite the narrative communicated to me by an eye-witness, Dr. Foy, Docent at the Seminary for Oriental
Languages, Berlin. In Terapia, the well-known suburb of Constantinople, there lived some years ago a poor
Greek, who earned a scanty livelihood as a porter or messenger or boatsman. Every Easter this man made
a Judas-effigy, and burned it on his own behalf and that of his co-religionists. The necessary money was
got by begging. The Turkish authorities objected to this proceedings on the grounds of public safety, as the
burning always took place in a small square in the workmen's quarter, quite close to some wooden barracks.
Therefore every year, just before Easter, the goodnatured Lieutenant of Police would send for the Greek, who
was well known to be ringleader in the affair, and threaten him with severe punishment if he should burn
a Judas-effigy. The Greek always gave the same reply. "Even if you kill me, I will burn Judas." The next
year, before Easter, the Turkish Bimbaschi would send for the Greek again, and strictly enjoin him that this
time no Judas was to be burned. But all the same, the Greek would get a "Judas" ready and burn him. It
happened once on Easter-eve that the Greek had to row over the Bosphoros to the Asiatic coast. He hesitated
for some time, in view of the approaching festival, but finally consented on the promise of a good fee, his
money being at a low ebb. When he had done his business on the Asiatic side and was getting ready to
return, a storm arose, so that it was impossible for him to risk crossing in his little boat. He gazed eagerly
at the sky, but there was no cessation of wind and tempest. The day of the festival broke, and the Greek,
taking off his clothes, made them into an effigy, stuffed them with leaves and twigs, and there on the lonely
shore burned his Judas according to his usual custom. As soon as the storm was over, Georgi, for that was
his name, returned naked in his boat to Terapia, and told what he had done. The Turkish Bimbaschi, delighted
that for once there was no Judas-burning among the wooden sheds of Terapia, gave Georgi new clothes and
a present of money.

This burning of the Judas-image**) recalls the "passing through the Fire to Moloch" of the
Old Testament, and the fire-rites at the festivals of Melqart at Tyre and of Dido at Carthage. We
may also mention in this connection the pictures of Sandon-Herakles, who was burned in women's
garments at Tarsus. Similar rites must have been performed in Kypros, and particularly at Amathus,
where Osiris and Adonis were worshipped together, where human victims were offered to Baal Zeus
$\xi\acute{\epsilon}\nu\iota\sigma\varsigma$ and where, in the festivals of the bearded Aphrodite-Ariadne, men appeared dressed as women
and women as men. The hanging of the Judas-effigy recalls the rite practised by the Thyiades in
the Dionysia at Delphi, viz. the burying of the Charila-doll (which we must interpret as a corn-
spirit), with a rushrope round its neck.***)

From among the numerous Egyptian Osiris-myths I may here instance the tale of the floating
chest in which Set-Typhon had shut up the body of Osiris. The chest was committed to the sea,
floated to the coast of Phoenicia, and being cast ashore by the waves near Byblos, came to rest at
the foot of a tree which grew on the beach. The tree grew round the chest so as to inclose it
completely. The king of the country, admiring the huge tree, caused it to be felled, and made it a
pillar of his palace. There Osiris was found by Isis†) &c.

A Mahommedan legend, still current in Kypros, connected with a Graeco-Phoenician megalithic

---

*) Engel, "Kypros" II, 90. These Busiris-Pygmalion fables from Kypros can be traced to the middle
of the 4th century B. C., being in one of Isocrates' orations attributed to the Kyprian Kings of Salamis: but
they are most certainly derived from still older sources.

**) Cp. p. 119.

***) Cp. Roscher's "Mythol. Lexikon," p. 872.

†) A. Erman, ("Aegypten und ägyptisches Leben") relates this myth from Plutarch in full.

structure, reproduces almost exactly the Osiris-fable which I have just related. This ancient Egypto-Phoenician fable, preserved by tradition, has only been slightly altered to make it appropriate to the Moslem faith. On the shore of the Salt-Lake near Larnaka-Kition, at a picturesque spot occupied in antiquity by the sacred groves of the Mother Ashera-Artemis-Paralia (No. 7 of our list) and of Ešmun-Melqart-Herakles (No. 8 on the list), there is still to be seen a megalithic building of early Graeco-Phoenician period, almost intact, consisting of three large stones and belonging to the same category as the Hagia Phaneromein monuments near Kition and the Hagia Katharina monuments near Salamis, published by me in Berlin *) and London **) respectively. The Hagia Phaneromein of Larnaka lies not far from the coast, and east of the Ashera-Astarte grove on the east side of the salt lake. The third structure (still unpublished) with which the Turkish legend is connected, lies west of the Salt Lake and south of the hill-grove of Ešmun Melqart. This ancient building perhaps a grave, a sanctuary or a wellhouse, perhaps used for various purposes, is now known as the monument of Mahomet's nurse. It is hung with scarves and a chapel has been built over it. Other buildings stand near, a Mosque, a Turkish Monastery with a garden of palms, and the house of a Scheik. The Monastery, called Um-al-Harem or Halité Sultan Teké, enjoys at the present time extensive privileges, which the English government respects. These privileges, and the frequent pilgrimages of the Turks to the place, are connected with the following legend. The three colossal stones of which the building consists floated over the sea, like the coffin of Osiris, from Ramleh in Egypt, first to Jaffa on the coast of Syria, and then, still self-propelled, to Kypros, where they stopped of their own accord at their present resting place near the Salt-Lake. In the magnificent-structure formed by these stones the Prophet's nurse, who was living on the island at that time, and died there, was buried. It is quite evident that a legend similar to that of the Osiris-coffin in Byblos, and a cultus of the same kind, were connected with these stones in ancient Graeco-Phoenician times. In course of time one religion was supplanted by another. But the stones remained, and with them survived the cultus and the legend. ***)

The numerous points of contact between Byblos and Kypros in written characters, language, art, and religion, make it not improbable that a legend existed in which the Osiris-coffin floated to Kypros. Aphrodite, too, hid Adonis in a chest and disputed his possession with Persephone.†) At Amathus in Kypros, as at Byblos, Osiris and Adonis are merged in one. True, the only authority for this Kyprian fusion of deities is Stephanus of Byzantium, a comparatively late source. But on the sarkophagus of Amathus, opposite the four pictures of Astarte-Aphrodite, are four pictures of a god who is compounded of many various elements and types, Osiris and Adonis, Set and Typhon, Bes and Patäke, Isdubar-Melqart and Herakles, Rešef and Apollo, Baal-Libanon and Zeus-Labranios.

---

*) Max Ohnefalsch-Richter. "Ein altes Bauwerk bei Larnaka," Archäologische Zeitung, 1881, p. 311 and Pl. XVIII = Perrot III, p. 278 and 279. Fig. 209 and 210,

**) Journal of Hellenic Studies, 1883, p. 111—116, Pl. XXXIII and XXXIV.

***) Mr. C. D. Cobham first gave this legend in his short introduction to my paper in the "Journal of Hellenic Studies" on the Hagia Phaneromein of Salamis. G. Perrot III, p. 898, quoted my work and gave the legend in a French translation. Greek legend and cultus has taken possession of the other two colossal structures, the Hagia Phaneromein of Kition and the Hagia Katharina of Salamis. Close to the latter there is a sacred grove of old trees, respected by Greeks and Turks alike. Cp. "Journal of Hellenic Studies," 1883, p. 115. S. Reinach, "Chroniques d'Orient," p. 157 and 179 [5³, 107 - 8 and 5², 347—8].

†) Cp. also Brugsch, "Adonisklage und Linoslied".

The name Osiris occurs among the Phoenician proper names on Kyprian inscriptions, and again at Kition, where on Stele No. 46 *) (C. I. Sem) the dedicator is called Abdosiris, Servant of Osiris.

A similar or identical ancient legend of a floating head of Adonis must be the origin of a modern fable which the orthodox Greeks of the Island believe. It is said that if an oil-flask be dedicated to Saint Andrew and then thrown into the sea on the shore of Varoschia (near Famagusta south of Salamis), it will swim up to the sacred grotto of Saint Andrew, a modern shrine which lies at the north-eastern extremity of the Peninsula of Karpasia close by the ancient height formerly dedicated to Aphrodite Akraia (No. 70 in the list, cf. p. 27). This modern legend of Saint Andrew is also very like another Adonis-myth known to the Christian Fathers. The women of Alexandria, so it runs, take a vessel, and place in it a letter on Byblus or Papyrus leaves containing the news that Adonis is found again. This letter swims of itself to Byblos, and is received by the women of the place, who begin the Adonis lament as soon as they have read it.

We have already entered pretty fully into the subject of Adonis. "Adon" was at first a name of reverence for various gods, among them the Jehovah of the old Testament.**) But it seems certain that there was also an individual Phoenician god Adoni***) (the name appears in Hebrew as Adonai, in Greek as Adonis). As we meet with Ešmun-Melqart in Kition†) and Adonis-Osiris in Amathus, Renan is probably right in reading "Ešmun-Adonis" and not "Ešmun the Lord" on the inscribed Stele of Kition††), cited above as an example of a Hebrew Massebe. Additional evidence for this reading†††) is found in the fact that Ešmun in the same manner as Adonis§) was worshipped in Kypros, and bore the same relation to Astarte-Aphrodite. Ešmun-Asklepios (spoken of above p. 154 in connection with the dog-cultus of Kition) bore, like Apollo, the surname Παιάν. The Kyprian Opaon of Kition and Amargetti, who merges in Apollo, and together with him bears the surname Melanthios, may very well have been identified with this Healer and Physician Παιών on account of the similar sound of the two names, although the word Opaon has really no connection with Παιάν, and means companion, shepherd &c.§§) Movers §§§) in his turn identified this Ešmun-Paian with Phaon, the most beautiful of men, a hero like Adonis, happy and unhappy like him, whom Aphrodite hid in the lettuce. Festivals like those of Adonis seem to have

---

*. So much has already been written on Adonis (for references see Roscher's Mytholog. Lexikon Sp. 76) that I only mention here what is connected with Kypros, and especially any points which may be elucidated by new discoveries of monuments and inscriptions.

**) cf. Roscher's Mythol. Lexikon Sp. 72.

***) Baethgen, "Semitische Religionsgeschichte" S. 42.

†) C. I. Sem 16—39.

††) ibidem No. 44.

†††) Baethgen, "Semitische Religionsgeschichte", S. 43.

§) On page 28, by an oversight, I stated that the Ešmun-Melqart inscriptions were found in the same place as those of Ešmun-Adonis. The fact is that only the marble cups and votive inscriptions dedicated to Ešmun-Melqart (C. I. Sem. No. 16—39) were found in the sacred grave on the hill near the salt lake, while the Ešnum-Adonis inscriptions (No. 42—44) were all found in or near Larnaka. No. 44 is the only one whose provenance can be exactly fixed, and this has no connection with the Ešmun-Melqart grave (cf. p. 179 and plate LXXX, 5). I was therefore in error when I spoke of a Phoenician Triad Ešmun-Melqart-Adonis in the same grave.

§§) Similar confusion occurs in the names Rimmon and Ramman, Chamman and Amon.

§§§) C. I. S. 227.

29

been celebrated in his honour, and Adonis gardens of lettuce and fennel laid out for him. Among the ancients μελάνθιον was the name of the coriander plant, which is still used in the East and in Kypros because of its spicy taste and smell. This Opaon-Melanthos *) then, a spice-god like Amarakos, is the attendant of Apollo Melanthios, his shepherd, temple-servant, sacrificer, incense-bearer.**) Ešmun-Adonis must have stood in the same subordinate relation to Rešef-Apollo and Astarte-Aphrodite, as Melqart-Herakles,***) Baal-Chamman-Zeus, Adonis-Osiris and others. I should not be surprised if an inscription were discovered in Kypros, such as has been already found in Cirta (C. I. Sem. 332) describing Baal-Hamman and Baal-Adonis as equal in rank, both servants of Rešef-Apollo or Astarte-Aphrodite.

Tammuz, as such, appears on no known Kyprian inscription, but the name Tamassos can only mean the city of Tammuz, and to this reference has been made by A. H. Sayce †) and D. G. Hogarth ††). In the tribute-lists of the Assyrian kings Asarhaddon (681—668) and Asurbanipal (668—626), two Kyprian kings of Kurion (Kuri) and Kition (Karti hadas(s)ti) bear names which seem to be compounded with Tammuz. In both lists the king of Kurion is called Damasušar, and the king of Kition Damusišar (in the case of Asarhaddon) and Damusušar (in the case of Asurbanipal) †††). On the Phoenician funeral stele at Kition dedicated by Abdosiris, servant of Osiris (C. I. S. 46) a woman, daughter of Tamuz, appears. Thus we have the god's name as a personal appellative.

We now come to Kinyras, whose name is supposed to be derived from a Phoenician-Hebrew musical instrument, the kinuar or harp. This instrument is often referred to in the Bible, but seems only to have been used for secular purposes, never for worship.§) Kinyras appears, not only as a mythical king, but also as a temple-attendant of Aphrodite and Apollo. In the numerous represent-ations of standing or crouching attendants we may recognize Kinyras as well as Tammuz, Adonis as well as Linos, Amarakos as well as Pygmalion. Kinyras also appears as the favorite of Aphrodite. When we hear that Adonis was called Κύρις, Κίρις and Κίῤῥις by Lakonians and Kyprians, the derivation from Κύριος may seem nearest to hand, but there is also a possible connection with the attendant and king Kinyras, and with the priestly race of Κάρις in Kypros, to whom I was the first to call attention. Movers has already remarked on the probable Karian origin of the name Kinyras. My Karys-inscription which shews in one case (see p. 6 No. 4) the name Κάρυς in the nominative on the garment of a life-size statue of a priest, make this origin a certainty (cf. Section on Apollo). While Adonis and Linos are purely mythological figures, Kinyras stands at the beginning of

---

*) I take the view of Hogarth ("Devia Cypria" p. 24) and not that of Reinach (Revue des Etudes Grecques, 1889, p. 232, "Apollon Opaon à Chypre").

**) Or possibly this Opaon-Melanthios is a rural form of Dionysos, worshipped by herdsmen (cf. the section on Dionysus in Kypros).

***) Baethgen, "Semitische Religionsgeschichte" p. 42. The numerous Phoenician votive inscriptions point to an important cultus of Ešmun-Melqart at Kition.

†) "Religion of the Babylonians" p. 234 note.

††) "Devia Cypria" p. 27.

†††) Eb. Schrader, "Zur Kritik der Inschriften Piglath-Pileser II., des Asarhaddon und des Asurbanipal." Schrader says that the god Tammuz is proved by the Calendar to be essentially Assyrian and secondarily Babylonian ("Die Keilinschriften und das alte Testament" p. 425).

§) Riehm, Bibellexikon II. p 1039.

History.*) True, he is himself no more a historical personage than the Homeric heroes, but his doings and the masterpieces of his artists are proved by the recent discovery to have had a foundation in fact. We have before our eyes the sword, helmets, cuirasses, shields, cups and goblets which the age of Kinyras produced in Kypros, that is, we have either the actual objects themselves or traditional representations of their types, purposes and workmanship. In Amathus, the royal city of Kinyras, clay ships have been found, buried in the grave with the dead (cf. Plate CXLV 3 and 6). This gives a kind of historical foundation to the tale that Kinyras, to evade his promise and mock the Greeks, sent clay ships instead of real ones to the Trojan expedition. Kinyras is called the first king of Kypros and the first priest of Aphrodite. He composes Adonis hymns and festal songs for the service of Aphrodite. He is of marvellous beauty, fragrant with spices like Sardanapalus, rich as Gyges and Midas. He enters upon a musical contest with Apollo. He institutes sheep-rearing and wool-weaving, mining and forging, he invents anvil, hammer and tiles for the roof. This "Fortunatus" of the ancients lives to the great age of 160 years, and in death he and his race still rest in the temple of Venus.**)

This Daemon of flowers and vegetation, this attendant and favorite of Aphrodite, whom we know best as Adonis, appears yet again as Gingras, who resembles Adonis on the one hand, and Kinyras on the other. This hero takes his name from the flutes, and the dance which formed part of the cultus of Aphrodite and Adonis. The Gingras-dance, the Gingris-flutes were personified, and the dancers, players and singers who excelled in their art became heroes. Gingras, type of the flute-music with song and dance, is one with Kinyras and Adonis. Linos, another form of the same god, is known to Homer, and figures on the shield of Achilles. As Agamemnon's arms came from Kypros, we may reasonably conclude that the shield of Achilles, called the work of Hephaistos, came from the same place, as also the Sidonian gala vessels.***) This conclusion seems the more probable, because the subjects, composition and arrangement of the shield of Achilles as described by Homer correspond more nearly up to how (this will probably always be the case) to the designs on Kyprian Graeco-Phoenician bowls than to any others. It is not impossible that shields may yet be found in Kypros, decorated like those bowls given on p. 46 fig. 49, p. 47 fig. 50, p. 48 fig. 51, p. 53 fig. 52, and also Plate CXXVIII—CXXX. In the meantime the shields most like the Homeric description are those from the Zeus-grotto at Gortyna, Crete (Plate CXXXI 1, 2). Kyprian bowls have been found among these Kretan votive offerings, and therefore we may possibly succeed at some future time in tracing the shields dedicated to the Kretan Zeus back to Kypros as their place of manufacture, perhaps even to Tamassos and Amathus, in whose environs copper was cast from the ore.

But to return to the lament, to the mourning flutes, to Gingras, Linos, Kinyras, Tammuz and Adonis. Just as the Greeks misinterpreted the cry "ai lenu" (woe to us) of the Phoenician and Hebrew mourners, as "Linos",†) the name of a hero, whose mythology and type are the same as those of Tammuz-Adonis, so they formed from the word of lament "Gri" and the mournful song "Gingri" (reduplicated)††) a hero Gingras, identical with the former two. There may have been

*) cf. Engel, "Kypros" II, p. 105.
**) Preller, "Mythologie" I. p 292.
***) cf. p. 178 for the identification of the Sidonians and Kyprian Phoenicians.
†) cf. p. 115.
††) Engel, „Kypros" II. p. 110 and 612. A. H. Sayce, in his Religion of the Babylonians, p. 236 explains

28*

at different places on the island forms of the Tammuz-Adonis god localized under different names; we know at least that the forms of Rešef-Apollo and Astarte-Aphrodite in Kypros alone varied as much as do the modern Madonnas of the orthodox Greek Church. As I stated above (p. 20 No. 53) there was found in 1883 on the banks of a river near the villages of Katydata and Linu a sacred precinct dedicated to Astarte-Aphrodite. Among the votive offerings, representations of a group of dancers round a flute player were very frequent. One of these, a Gingras-dance in fact, is reproduced on Plate XVII fig. 5. Three men (of these figures only one is complete, while one has been quite broken away) with high conical caps and long pointed beards, dance round a flute player of similar appearance, who blows a short double flute.*) In the Kyprian τεμένη of Rešef-Apollo, flute-players are much more commonly represented than players on stringed instruments, indeed stringed instruments and the kettle-drum are often absent altogether. In the worship of Astarte-Aphrodite the kettle-drum holds the first place, stringed instruments the second, and flutes the third. But in some few Astarte-Aphrodite groves, such as that near Linu, the double flute is the chief instrument. In the groves of Panit-Artemis stringed instruments predominate; there are few kettle-drums and no flutes. "Linu", the name of the modern village, may very well be a reminiscence of Linos, the ancient hero who was worshipped there. I was first led to the discovery of this place of worship by some votive offerings brought me nine years ago by a shepherd who pastured his flocks among the copses on the river-bank near the village, and, like Linos and his priests, played wonderful airs on his flute. Thrusting his staff into the ground, he had uncovered one of the dancing groups with flute-player which I have reproduced on Plate XVII, 5.

It has been rightly assumed that the Adonis worship came from Kypros to Athens, Argos**) and Bœotia***). The same is true of Linos, who is akin to Adonis in name and meaning. The Kyprian metal-workers of the age of Kinyras represented on the shield of Achilles boys singing the Linos song.†)

Kyprians transplanted the Linos cultus to Bœotia††), Argos and Greece, as they did the imageless worship of Anat-Athene†††). Linos and Adonis meet at Argos, whither they both come from Kypros§). The ceremonies and songs which were customary in Greece in the cultus o Linos, corresponded even in very late times with those in Kypros. Herodotus §§) finds the Linos cultus and the Linos song in Kypros.

Hitherto no signs of a separate worship of Rhea-Kybele in groves dedicated to her have been found in Kypros. That she influenced other cults is shown by the presence of her image,

the word Gingras by the Akkadian equivalent for Istar, viz. Gingira or Gingiri. W. A. I. II, 48, 29; K. 170, Rev. 7. Baudissin in his "Semitische Religionsgeschichte" p. 200 refers to Hyginus, according to whom Kinyras was an Assyrian king.

 *) For this essentially Syrian Gingras flute, with which the Karian-Lydian flute is connected cf. Riehm's Bibellexikon II p. 1037.
 **) Pausanias II, 20, 6.
 ***) Roscher's Mythol. Lexikon Sp. 73.
 †) Iliad XVIII, 569, 570.
 ·††) Pausanias IX, 29, 7 and 8.
 †††) Pausanias IX, 19, 1. cf. p. 17.
 §) Engel, "Kypros" II, 614.
 §§) 2, 79.

enthroned between two lions and wearing a mural crown (Plate CCVI, 6) in the Tanit-Artemis grove at Achna (No. 1 on the list). Wherever Kybele appears, she is co-ordinated with Tanit-Artemis or Astarte-Aphrodite, or she is absorbed by the mother of the gods, μήτηρ θεῶν (as for instance in Tamassos (No. 5 of the list). The same is true of Attis, as we have seen; Attis tree-images were found in great numbers in the Tanit-Artemis-Kybele grove at Achna (No. 1). It is possible that some of the representations which have been connected with Tammuz-Adonis-Osiris may have some reference to Attis, whose characteristics merge in theirs. No examples have as yet been found in Kypros of iconic anthropomorphic images of Attis. The Phrygian cap is common to Attis and Tammuz-Adonis. We cannot assume that Attis was a late eastern importation in Kypros as he was in Greece, a stranger who forced his way into the circle of the gods. The disguises practised at the Kyprian festivals (cf. below, Dionysos) the worship of the man-woman and of Semiramis-Atargatis, the well-known connection between Kypros and Hierapolis (not to mention Thrace and Asia Minor, (cf. below, Dionysos) point to a North-Syrian origin for Attis. He was worshipped between Zeus-Hadad and Atargatis-Rhea *) and was represented as Eunuch or Hermaphrodite with a golden dove perched on his head (cf. below, the Dove-deities). It seems certain that in Kypros Attis was very early fused with Adonis**) and other similar divinities, just as Rhea-Kybele, Semiramis, Atargatis, Derketo and others were identified with the female divinities of the island.

Pygmalion has been already referred to in connection with Busiris. In Kypros the form Pygmaion also occurs. This king, hero or god, an important figure in the myth and ritual of Kypros, is a favorite of Aphrodite, and his name is used, as in Tyre and Gades, as a personal appellative, especially for royal persons. The legend of the ivory image of Aphrodite is well known. Pygmalion himself wrought it, and on her festival day implored the goddess to give it life. Aphrodite heard his prayer, and the image glowed into life in his embrace. The offspring of this union was the beautiful boy Paphos.***)

Pygmaion-Pygmalion of Kypros brings us to the fabled race of the Pygmies, and with them to the Egyptian divinities Bes, Ptah and Patäke who passed over to Kypros (spoken of above in connection with the myth of the floating heads) and to the Graeco-Carthaginian gods Pumi and Pa'am.†)

On this vexed question I share the views of the French investigators Perrot, Berger and Henzey, and I think that the representations given in Plates XXXIII, 1—5, XXXVIII, 16, 18—20, XCII and XCIII and treated of in the previous section, offer material for the elucidation of this portion of the subject. In these Kyprian types and other monuments we can trace how the Egyptian types became hellenized after their arrival in Kypros, how Bes, Ptah, Patäke were remodelled as Adonis-Pygmaion, and how the mask of Hathor developed into the Greek Gorgoneion. The Pygmy image (Plate XCII, 2 and 3) may be as reasonably referred to the dwarf-race of Greek fable as to the Pygmaion or Pygmalion child.††) As for the Carthagian-Kyprian gods Pumi and Pa'am, we are the more

---

*) cf. Baethgen, "Beiträge zur semitischen Religionsgeschichte" p. 71. The late authors whom he cites certainly obtained their information from earlier sources. (For Hadad-Rešef cf. below Rešef-Apollo.)

**) cf. Roscher's Mythol. Lexikon sp. 723.

***) Ovid, Metam. 10, 245. Engel, "Kypros" II, p. 376.

†) cf. Baethgen, "Beiträge zur semitischen Religionsgeschichte" p. 53.

††) Ed. Meyer in Roscher's Mythol. Lexikon, Abschn. Bes, sp. 2894—2898. Ph Berger, "Le Mythe de Pygmalion et le Dieu Pygmée". Comptes rendus de l'Ac. des Inscript. et b. l. 1880, p. 60—68.

justified in identifying them with the hero Pygmalion, because hitherto they have only been inferred from personal appellatives on Kyprian-Phoenician and Carthaginian inscriptions *). The names of these gods in their full form have a closer phonetic connection with the hero-name Pygmaion than the contractions which up to now have been detected in personal names.

In conclusion, a word must be said on Eros. **) At Thespiae in Boeotia, from the most ancient times, Eros was worshipped in the form of a very primitive symbol, an unhewn stone, but

in Kypros these was no room for such a cultus, for Aphrodite***) was worshipped at Paphos under the same symbol and was predominant there, instances in Kypros of the worship of Rešef-Apollo under the symbol, being few and small. Anthropomorphic images of Eros are not of earlier date in Kypros than elsewhere, i. e. do not appear before the 5.th century B. C. To this period belongs the bronze mirror-handle representing a winged Eros, crouching, front view, probably made in Kypros, although purely Greek in style (Plate CXCVIII, 1).†) The base on which the Eros rests is shaped like an Ionic capital and ornamented with conventional foliage. The style is that of about 400 B. C. A very beautiful Eros-head in marble, still of the good Hellenistic period, was found by the English excavators in Old Paphos in 1888.††)

The marble Graeco-Roman fountain-statue of a reclining Eros was found early in the year 1884 among the débris at Neapaphos, when the ground was being ploughed (Pl. CXCVIII, 2.). Eros is represented asleep on a wine skin, over which a garment is spread. There are various replicas of this motive in different Museums, but this one, at present in the Kypros Museum at Nicosia, and here published for the first time, may claim to be the most valuable of all from an artistic point of view.

Fig. 165.

It is not impossible that Kypros had some influence on the formation of the archaic Eros-type, but this is as yet not proved. On the other hand it seems almost certain that the origin of the Group-type, Eros and Psyche, is to be sought for in Kypros or its immediate neighbourhood. The proof is that Eros and Psyche groups frequently occur on the shoulders of Kyprian bathing-vessels which are older than the 4th century (see Plates LXIV and CLXXIX—CLXXXI, repeated for convenience of reference in Fig. 165). These amply shew how the ornamental ox or lion-head, seated

---

*) Collected by Baethgen p. 53 and 54.

**) Cp. Furtwängler's "Eros" in Roscher's Mytholog. Lexikon, Sp. 1339 – 1373.

***) Pausanias 9, 27, 1. Since the aniconic Eroscultus is found in Boeotia, whither the imageless worship of Athena was introduced from Kypros, it is not improbable that this stone-cultus, proper to Eros and other gods, was derived from the Semitic lands of the East.

†) First published in the Jahrbuch des arch. Inst., 1888, III, 246; at present in the Antiquarium of the Royal Museum at Berlin.

††) Published in the Journal of Hellenic Studies, 1888, Plate X.

winged ox, woman carrying pitcher, woman alone, &c., are replaced by the standing group of Eros and Psyche. At first only Eros is winged. We can trace in Kypros also how these groups detach themselves from the vase. The Kiss of Eros and Psyche is a late Hellenistic motive, and does not appear in early art. In proof of this I may refer to Plate CCVIII, reproduced from my own Kyprian excavations, or from other discoveries on the same island, hitherto unpublished. Plate CCVIII, 2 represents a richly painted terra-cotta group discovered by Mr. J. W. Williamson in 1883 in a tomb at Kurion. Unfortunately, the workmen were not superintended at the time, so that no reliable record of the circumstances of the discovery exists. After examining the site and the tomb, I came to the conclusion that the group is older than the Roman period. Psyche is un-winged, and is enveloped from neck to foot in a long thin garment. Eros is winged, and his garment has slipped during the embrace. The terra-cotta which I found at Marion-Arsinoe in 1886 (CCVIII, 3) is of Roman period. In it both the figures are nude and winged. The two terra-cotta groups on the same plate (no. 1 from Kurion and no. 4 from Kition) seem to be caricatures of Eros and Psyche. A comparison of the group of Kition with the comic terra-cottas found at the same place seems to prove that the former belongs to the 4th century B. C.*)

With this we close our examination of tree-worship and its development into anthropomorphic image-worship as illustrated by monuments. "Per varios casus, per tot discrimina rerum tendimus in Latium" (Virgil). "Treu dem Zweck auch auf dem schiefen Wege" (Goethe). We have seen what an important place Kypros holds in this investigation, and how Kyprian antiquities or surviving Kyprian customs throw light on many obscure points in ancient Hebrew or Greek Culture, Art, and Religion, not only in the Old Testament and Homeric times, but in the period before and after them.

---

*) Cp. the explanation of Plate CCVIII.

CHAPTER 3

Worship of Divinities and fabulous beings.

I. Imageless worship of the divinities of Kypros and other countries.

1. Imageless Rites, especially to Mountain and Storm divinities.
Imageless Altar-rites.

The period in which the gods were worshipped under the form of aniconic symbols such as unhewn stones, tree-trunks and posts, was preceded by a time when worship was carried on without images of any kind. When the worship of images had had its way for some time, a great reaction against it arose. Jews, Christians and Mohammedans waged war on images, and tried to restore an imageless worship.

As Yahve appears on Sinai from the midst of a thick cloud, with thunder and lightning, fire and smoke,*) so Zeus sits on Ida in the thundercloud and hurls his thunderbolts.**) As when Moses set a bound round Sinai by command of Yahve, and any one who approache must die,***) so, at the summit of the Arkadian Olympos, any one who entered the sacred precinct of Zeus Lykaios must die within the year. †) As Hebrew belief identified Sinai with Yahve, so did Pelasgic belief identify the Arkadian Olympos with Zeus. Even in Tacitus' times Mount Carmel was accounted a god worshipped without a temple or image. ††) Similarly we must conclude (see p. 16, no. 28) that the Anat-Athena-Idalia on the Akropolis of Idalion was worshipped, like the Athena Telchinia who came from Kypros to Teumessos in Boeotia, either entirely without images, or with unhewn stone or wood symbols. Curtius says of Zeus Lykaios. §) "He lived

*) Exodus XIX, 16—20.
**) Iliad VIII, 47 ff. and XIV, 292 ff.
***) Exodus XIX, 12 and 13.
†) Pausanias VIII, 38, 6.
††) Hist. II, 78.
†††) Pausanias IX, 19, 1.
§) E. Curtius, "Peloponnes" I, 308, R. Beer, "Heilige Höhen," p. 11.

and moved as nature spirit without form on his sacred mountain, like Yahve on his holy hill of Sinaï, like Baal on the Syrian or Kyprian Lebanon,*) or like Zeus Labranios on the same Kyprian Lebanon.**)

To Yahve on Sinaï,***) to Zeus on Ida, to Aphrodite on the hill of Paphos, are dedicated sacred precincts and altars of incense, but no temple, image, or even aniconic symbol. For the twelve stones on the altar of Sinaï were not symbols of Yahve, but of the twelve tribes. There is a bilingual inscription in Kypros whose importance has not been sufficiently realized. It is written in Phoenician and Greek, and is a dedication of an altar to Anat-Athena and to King Ptolemaeus.†††) In the Phoenician the Anat is called the life-force (robur vitae); in the Greek, Athene is called *Σωτείρα* and *Νίκη*, the healer and conqueror (Salutaris et Victoria). This double inscription is cut into a flat perpendicular wall of rock on the southern slope of a steep and rugged peak of the northern range near the modern village of Larnaka tou Lapithou (p. 23, No. 61). There is no trace here of a cultus with images. If such had existed, the very thorough examination to which the ground has been subjected must have brought some fragments to light. Remains of narrow walls seem to belong to a peribolos, which further excavation would probably reveal more completely. A sacred enclosure round the altar is dedicated to Anat-Athene, as the enclosures on Sinai to Yahve, on Ida to Zeus, and on the hill of Paphos to Aphrodite. While, however, we have only literary tradition for the dedication to the last three divinities, we have in the present instance the votive inscription itself cut on the living rock of the wild mountain district, the rock which may well have been the symbol of the goddess, as Mount Carmel and the Arkadian Olympos were symbols of Yahve and Zeus. We can scarcely conceive of a more poetical idea than to present Anat-Athene, the vigour of life, the victorious goddess of Peace, wounding, but healing the wounds she makes, by a mighty peak of rock which lifts its summit to Heaven.

This is perhaps the only known example of a purely imageless cultus attested by a bi lingual inscription, and practised in the open air on a mountain.§) Probably the cultus of Anat-Athene on

---

*) "The Trodos Mountain," p. 21, No 47, C. I. Sem No. 5.

**) P. 19, No. 46.

***) Exodus XXIV, 4.

†) Iliad VIII, 47.

††) Odyssey VIII, 363.

†††) C. I. Sem. No. 95. The Greek text is:

> Ἀθηνᾷ Σωτείρᾳ Νίκη
> καὶ βασιλέως Πτολεμαίου
> Πραξίδημος Σέσμαος τὸν
> βω[μὸ]ν ἀνέϑ[ηκ]εν.
> Ἀγα[ϑ]ῇ τύχῃ.

The Phoenician text transcribed into Latin is:

> Anatae, robori vitae,
> et domino regum Ptolemaeo,
> Baalsillemus, filius [Ses]maei,
> Consecravit altare.
> Fortunae bonae.

§) An instructive parallel is found in a modern stone-cultus practised at a place further East on the same coast near the Monastery of St. Chrysostom, a barren precipice about 1 kilometre west of the monastery there is a fossil stratum of rock which forms clefts and jagged points. I visited the place in 1890 with the brothers Bergeal, one of whom, being a geologist, collected some of the fossils, and found among them

the Acropolis of Idalion (p. 15, No. 28, cf. cultus of the lance p. 201), was anikonic, like that attested by this rocky wall of Larnaka Lapithou; but whether entirely imageless is doubtful, when we consider the sceptre-lance point, and the arms and votive tablets found on that site.

In 1885 I showed that there was at Lithrodon (p. 19, No. 42) a true imageless cultus not less interesting than these, viz. the worship of a spring I communicated my discovery to Helbig at once, and he admitted that it remarkably confirmed the description of the Well of the Nymphs at Ithaka.[*]) (Od. XVII, 205):

> "Around it was a thicket of alders that grow by the waters, all circlewise, and down the cold stream fell from a rock on high, and above was reared an altar to the Nymphs, whereat all wayfarers made offering."

This sacred grove, consisting of a few trees, must have been without temple, image or enclosure, else surely some allusion to them must have been made. In Kypros, many if not all of the sacred groves indicated by the excavations seem to have been unenclosed. It is true that these cultus sites when excavated are found to be surrounded by low walls, but I have never yet come on a piece of wall which was not partly composed of older images and inscriptions. We may therefore conclude that in very ancient times these sites were unenclosed, and that images and inscriptions used to be dedicated long before fences were thought of. When at length walls were built around the sanctuary, the older inscriptions and gifts were used as part of the material.

The scene at Lithrodonda reminded me of Homer's description, only the water flows out from under a wall of rock in a glen. Bushes grow luxuriantly around, while between the spring and the cliff is a flat table-like rock, not extensive enough to support any structure larger than a small shrine.

Excavation failed to bring to light any traces of a wall, and this makes it impossible to assume the existence of any kind of burial place. The stratum of soil on the adjoining rock was at many points only half a metre thick, or less, and its presence there could only be accounted for by a wash of earth in rainy weather from the cliff immediately above. A shepherd, who guided me to the spot, told me that shortly before my arrival (May 1885) he had been resting one day at the spring with his flock to take his meal. To amuse himself he had scratched with his iron-pointed stick in the ground, and had struck against some ancient copper coins and lamps. Beginning to dig, he had soon found more lamps and coins, but no other remains. These he sold to me, when I came to the village armed with spade and shovel, and ready to examine the ground for myself. I too found only lamps and coins. Two or three of the copper coins, and a clay lamp adhering to them through the rust, belong to the same period. The coins, as far as I can discover, belong either to the later Ptolemaic or to

---

bones of bears and other wild beasts. The Greeks believe that the bones are human, and that the place is the scene of a Christian martyrdom, and therefore sacred and possessed of miraculous powers. They come and roll on the rocks in order to cure themselves of disease, they light candles, as if in a church, and pray to the saints to whom the district is dedicated. Their altar is a small flat surface of rock among the rugged boulders and peaks. Once a year, on the name-day of the Saint, a church festival is celebrated there, and the Mass is sung in the open air before the rocky altar. Pilgrims from the surrounding villages flock to the place. Near the monastery of St. Chrysostom is a well, to which healing powers are attributed, especially in cases of skin-disease. It is said that several rich mule-drivers of the village of Athiaenou were healed in this manner quite lately, and that they proved their gratitude by a donation, recorded in an inscription, and by restoring and enlarging part of the monastery. We are irresistibly reminded of the votive inscriptions of the ancients.

[*]) Od. XVII, 205—211. Helbig "Das homerische Epos," p. 420, who quotes me, and who could find no instances among the monuments discovered, except those cited by me.

the early Imperial Roman period, except a very few which were of the later Empire. The form and ornamentation of the lamps shewed them to be late Hellenistic and Roman. A few bore the stamp of late Roman and early Byzantine times.

Removing part of the silt from the small rock platform above the spring, we found below 20 to 30 centim. of ashes and cinders, imbedded in which the lamps and coins lay. Many are left on the spot, so that anyone who wishes to verify my report may do so. It was evidently customary for travellers who took a cooling draught at the spring to offer a lighted lamp and a few coins, besides a small burnt offering of dried twigs. Can a better illustration of the Nymphs' fountain and grove at Ithaka be imagined than this sacred spring hidden among the trees on the face of the rocks at Lithrodonda? *)

Sacred heights**) shaded by green trees were favourite spots for sacrifice and burning of incense. A natural rock, one or more rough unhewn stones,***) or a heap of earth, †) formed the simple altar of such a high place. In primitive times this is the only kind of sanctuary well pleasing to the gods. ††)

These altars of earth, where sojourns the god of light who rules the mountain, became centres of miraculous legend. Even in the time of Pausanias it was commonly believed that no shadow was cast in the Adytum of Zeus Lykaios.†††) When in times of drought the priest of Zeus touched with his oak-branch the spring within the precinct, Zeus completed the rain-charm, and was poured forth in the form of reviving showers over the fields of Arkadia.

Yahve sent down fire from heaven upon his altar, which consumed the burnt-offering and licked up the water that was in the trench. §) On the chief altar before the cone of Astarte-Aphrodite at Paphos no rain ever fell, although it stood in the open air.

Zeus Lykaios of the Arkadian Olympos is worshipped as the god of storm and rain, and his

---

*) I am informed by M Lander, of the Ottoman Bank, that a similar cultus, in which the votive offerings entirely consisted of coins, lamps and small vessels was anciently practised on a promontory near Constantinople. These votive lamps and vessels are many of them in possession of English families living on the Bosporos. The objects were found closely packed together like fish in a barrel.

**) Sacred hills and upland groves are not rare in Kypros. The Mountain grove of the Idalian Aphrodite, often mentioned by later writers, (cp. E. Oberhummer, "Ancient Idalion," in the Owl, 1888, p. 67, also above p. 16, No. 29 of the list) and the sacred hill of Aphrodite on Cape Pedalion (Strabo IV, 682, p. 12, No. 16) have both been discovered by me (cp. "Berliner Philologische Wochenschrift," 1891, pp. 962, 963, "Ein heiliger Hügel auf Cypern.") — D. G. Hogarth discovered the precinct of Aphrodite Akraia on the Kyprian Olympos, often mentioned by Strabo, whose Adytum women were forbidden to enter (p. 27, No. 70 of the list).

***) For instance, the altar of earth and unhewn stones in the burning space of the precinct of Astarte-Aphrodite at Idalion (p. 5, No. 3, Pl. VII,A, and Pl. LVII, 2, also numerous references in the Old Testament.)

†) For instance, the earth altar of Zeus Hypatos on the Arkadian Olympos. (Curtius, "Peloponnes," I, p. 308.) The altar which Yahve commanded Moses to make (Exod. 20, 24 and 25. Joshua 8, 31.)

††) From the prohibition of Yahve (Exodus XX, 24—26) we gather that the custom had arisen of making altars of hewn stone, and that some were supported by pedestals on steps. In the Rešef-Apollo grove at Frangissa a single square-hewn block served as altarstone on which to offer burnt sacrifices (p. 6 No. 4 and outline Plate VI, A) steps led from the level of the ground to the altar, either downwards (Plate VI) or upwards (Plate VIII and above p. 16, No. 30. Rešef-Apollo sanctuary in Idalion. cf. also on Plate X coin of Byblos &c.)

†††) Pausanias VIII, 38, 6.

§) 1st Kings XVIII, and many other examples.

cultus is imageless. In these points he resembles the divinities Baal-Libanon*) (attested by an inscription in Kypros), Zeus κεραύνιος,**) also in Kypros, the Hebrew Jehovah on his mountains and other mountain Baalim, such as Báalshamen called Ζεὺς κεραύνιος on a bi-lingual inscription of Palmyra. We have already spoken of Baálshamen in connection with the sun-pillars, and of the inscription found on the " Hawk Island " in the gulf of Cagliari, Sardinia, and dedicated to Ba'alshamen as god of heaven on the " Hawk Island ". I have called special attention to the two pillars which in that inscription were dedicated to the god, and pointed out the analogy with the two eagle-crowned pillars on the earth-altar of the Lykaian Zeus. Now as this Ba'alshamen to whom two cultus-pillars are erected must be identified with Zeus κεραύνιος, it is evident that the Arkadian cultus of Zeus Lykaios, at first probably imageless and then aniconic, was also of Semitic origin. The Semitic influence is quite as likely to have come to Greece through Kypros as through Asia Minor,***) because in the pre-Dorian period there must have been a Greek emigration to Kypros from the Peloponnesus, in which Arkadians probably took part.†) As Baudissin has already shown, we may perhaps identify this Palmyrene and Kyprian mountain god Zeus κεραύνιος with the mountain god Zeus κάσιος specially honoured on two hills named Kasios, which lie, one on the coast of Syria near Antiochia, the other near Pelusion between Syria and Egypt. Coins of Peleukia in Pieria bear the legend Ζεὺς κάσιος, and symbolize the god by a stone (sometimes interpreted as a representation of the mountain) standing (like the cone of Paphos) in a tetrastyle or distyle temple. An eagle with spread wings is often represented above.††)

There were two other mountain divinities in Kypros who had a wider reputation for rain-making than Zeus-Keraunios. Astarte-Aphrodite, in addition to her other attributes, was a rain and storm divinity, as I have already shown.†††) But in this region her power was not supreme. That Rešef-Apollo was the chief storm-god and giver of rain, and enjoyed by far the highest reputation as such, is amply proved by the discoveries of Phoenician-Kyprian inscriptions, and by my own and R. Meister's investigations. This god is really only another form of Baal, in whose return we have already found Melqart-Herakles, Baal-Chamman and Tammuz-Adonis. We have seen (p. 114) how this Kyprian god

*) On Muti Schinoar, No. 47 of the list.

**) This Kyprian Zeus Keraunios of Kition is probably one and the same as the Kyprian Zeus Labranios at Pharsulla (No. 46 of the list).

***) R. Meister says in his " Griechische Dialekte " II p. 128: " The Homeric poems represent Kypros as a home of Greeks and Greek culture, therefore the colonization of Kypros must have taken place long before the earliest of the poems were composed." It is assumed by W. Deecke and R. Meister, both authorities on Kypros, that the first Greek colonists of the island were Achaians, and this hypothesis would explain the relations with Arkadia and Lakonia which are to be traced in the Graeco-Kyprian religious history. The Arkadian dialect is the one which most resembles the Kyprian.

†) Cf. p. 191 on the monuments of Commagene and also Pl. CXCIII.

††) cf. our Apollo-Zeus images with the eagle or Nike of Chytroi as attribute (Pl. XL, 1, 2 and 4, 5). On the site of the Zeus-Labranios mountain grove (p. 19 No. 46) fragments of statues with the eagle have been found. (Account of Major Chard, also Cesnola-Stern p. 241.) Baudissin identifies this Zeus Kasios with the god Ramas or Raman of the Syrian Laodicea, whom again he makes one with the Rimmon of the old Testament and the Assyrian Raman (I. S. 306 and ff.). But when, later on, Zeus is represented at Pelusion (Baudissin II p. 242) as a youth similar to Apollo and holding a pomegranate, surely Baudissin must acknowledge in this instance a correspondence which he elsewhere denies, viz. that between the Rimmon of the old Testament with the pomegranate, and the pomegranate god Tammuz-Adonis (cf. p. 113—116).

†††) For affiliation of the gods see Welcker "Götterlehre" I, 492, 637, II, 43—45.

Rešef becomes more or less fused with similar rain lightning and storm divinities of Syria and Assyria, with Bin, Ramman, Martu and Hadad. Ἀπόλλων ὁ Ἄμυκλος of Idalion was invoked for help in time of drought, as Zeus Lykaios was invoked in Arcadia. The festival of the Hyacinthia was celebrated in honour of the Laconian Apollo of Amyklai, in order that he might protect growing things from the burning heat of summer. Meister proves this by a new reading of the bilingual Phoenician-Kyprian votive inscription in the sanctuary of Rešef-Mikal-Apollo-Amyklos, and by his essay published in my periodical "The Owl" (Nicosia 1888 No. 5 p. 33).*)

Most of the sacred precincts lately excavated in Kypros do not give evidence of aniconic cultus, still less of worship entirely without images, but it is not unreasonable to suppose that such cults existed on these sites in primitive times, especially since the discovery of the three striking examples which I have just adduced, and which give additional value to the numerous literary references to imageless and aniconic cultus, as collected by Overbeck.**)

2. Hebrew and Kyprian cults connected with mountains, valleys, springs, rivers, the sea and caves.

In the primitive stages of all nations we find many places set apart for the ritual of sacrifice. Such are mountains, slopes, valleys, plains, fountains, brooks and rivers, or subterranean caves. This kind of worship, arising as it does from the ideas and natural environment common to humanity. does not necessarily imply any race-kinship between the peoples who practise it.

But among the Hebrews and Kyprians worship had reached a later stage of development, i. e. gods of the mountains had been differentiated from those of the valleys, and, what is more important, artificial heights for worship had been constructed in valleys and in towns, at city gates and by the waysides, and even sometimes at the summits of lateral hills.***)

"Their gods are gods of the hills, therefore they are stronger than we," is the excuse offered by the Aramaeans to their king Benhadad after their defeat by the Israelites.†) A year later the Israelites were victorious in the plain. Yahve will prove that He is Almighty, because the Aramaeans said that he was a god of the mountains and not of the plains.††) Yahve is definitely a mountain god.

a) The Bâmôt.

As late as the eighth century B. C., and under the pious king Jotham, who did what was well pleasing to Yahve (740—735) the mountain cultus existed side by side with the service in the temple of Jerusalem.

---

*) Cf. also Meister's "Griechische Dialekte" II p. 149 and 150. He thus reads the inscription: "In the fourth year of the reign of king Milikjaton over Ketion and Edalion. and on the last of the five days inserted into the Calendar, Baalram, son of Abidmilikos, dedicated this pillar to Apollo Amyklos, because he had answered his prayer in time of drought."

**) For objects of Greek worship in their oldest forms see "Berichte der sächsischen Gesellschaft der Wissenschaften" 1864, p. 121—172.

***) Baudissin, in his admirable history of Semitic religion (p. 232—267) has collected a large mass of material on the subject of hill-worship among the Hebrews and heathen Semites, which I have used largely in my work. The object of the present work is to present fresh information gained from newly discovered monuments and inscriptions.

†) 1st Kings XX, 23

††) Idem XX, 28.

" Save that the high places were not removed, the people sacrificed and burned incense still upon the high places." *)

After the idolatry of Manasseh, Josiah for the first time thoroughly purified the worship of Yahve.

" And all the houses also of the high places that were in the cities of Samaria, which the kings of Israel had made to provoke the Lord to anger, Josiah took away, and did to them according to all the acts that he had done in Bethel." **)

It seems then that even king Hezekiah, who is said to have " removed the high places ",***) (727—699) did not make a thorough abolition, for between his death and the accession of Josiah only one reign intervenes, that of Manasseh. It was reserved for Josiah to destroy those high places erected by former kings which Hezekiah had spared, as it would appear, in considerable numbers.

From the frequent descriptions in the Old Testament we gather further that the Bâmôt or high places gradually conformed to a definite type displeasing to Yahve, viz. that of an idolatrous sacred precinct.

The Bâma, sacred high place, corresponds to the Temenos, sacred grove.†) It is a place for sacrifice (originally on a mountain, later in other places) whose essential part is the altar for burnt offerings and incense. These simple Bâmôt with imageless cultus were well pleasing to Yahve. But when they were defiled by idolatry, either by the aniconic cultus of Asherôt, Baal-pillars and Sun-pillars, or by the iconic worship of carved, hewn or molten images, they became displeasing to him. The simple unenclosed Bamâ with its altar became a sacred fenced high place, a precinct; the Baal-mountain top become a grove. Around such sanctuaries other small enclosures grew up. The introduction of aniconic and iconic worship made a treasure-chamber a necessity, in order that the votive Asherôt, Massebôt and Chammanim, the anthropomorphic and zoomorphic images and the representations of fabulous beings, might have safe keeping. Outside of these unroofed enclosures were erected roofed and pillared arcades open on one side (sun-halls, ἡλιακοί, still found in primitive places of pilgrimage) to serve as secure store rooms, Thesauroi, for valuable gifts, dwellings for the priests, sacristies, chapels or temples. It was thus that the "houses of high places" of the Old Testament grew up. (1st Kings XII, 31; XIII, 32. 2nd Kings XXIII, 19.

These sacred Bâmôt were originally real heights, ††) to which the worshippers had to ascend, just as the sacred groves were originally real groves. In process of time the name Bâmôt was applied to places of worship not upon hills but in valleys †††) and towns §), by the wayside and at street corners.§§) In such cases we must suppose either that artificial hills were constructed at these places, or that the name had come to mean " place for worship " in general. We have a parallel in the use of the term "grove", which became merely a name for a sacred precinct without a temple

*) 2nd Kings XV, 3 and 4.
**) Idem XXIII, 19.
***) Idem XVIII, 4.
†) Cf. also Riehm's Bibellexikon 625—627.•
††) Isaiah XV, 2. Jeremiah XLVIII, 35. 1. Samuel IX, 13 ff. 19 &c. cf. Baudissin, " Semitische Religions-geschichte ", II p. 257.
†††) Jeremiah VII, 31; XIX, 5; XXXIII, 35. Ezekiel VI, 3.
§) 2nd Kings XVII, 9; XXIII, 5.
§§) Ezekiel XVI, 24 ff.; XXXI.

fenced round and used for sacrifice, incense and votive gifts, but not necessarily enclosing trees. The frequent reference to a Bâma on a hill*) can only mean a place of worship situated on a hill. The burning of a Bâma (2nd Kings XXIII, 15), like that of an Ashera, implies that the materials of which it was made were combustible, perhaps wood, cloth or the like. Ezekiel (XVI, 16) speaks of Bamôt decked with "divers colours" and "garments"; expressions which seem to imply a tent-like structure. The Bâmôt must sometimes have been very small, as they were placed under trees.**) We hear also of a high place at one of the city gates of Jerusalem.***) The Bâmôt which Solomon erected in honour of the Canaanitish gods whom his wives worshipped can only have been places for worship.†) My Kyprian investigations will throw fresh light on these Hebrew-Aramaic-Canaanite-Moabitish Bâmôt, and on the Bâmôt-cultus.

In the Old Testament the high places of Baal, like the pillars of Baal, mark sites of worship and we meet with Bâmôt-Baal in Moabitish territory. Balaam and Balak, before proceeding to Pisgah and Peor, built seven altars on the high place of Baal, and sacrificed on them.††)

A Bâmôt-Baal of the same kind is in existence in Kypros, I mean the Acropolis of Chittim-Kition, the harbour-mountain, near the closed harbour mentioned by Strabo. There is another sanctuary on this height dedicated to Astarte and Mikal. This hill of Kition, now called in the popular dialect Bambula, a contraction of Bama-Baal,†††) is a natural elevation enlarged by art.

Of the 72 cultus-sites enumerated in the first chapter, 32 were on mountains (many of them being promontories visible from a long distance) and 36 in valleys and plains, mostly near fountains, brooks or rivers. In four instances the situation could not exactly be determined. Among the number were four cave sanctuaries. One of these is in a formidable ancient mountain fortress Urania (modern τὸ ῥάνι) (No. 71) almost at the extreme north-eastern point of the peninsula Karpasis, but still south-west of the sanctuary to Aphrodite ἀκραία (No. 70) on the promontory. The other cave sanctuary, near Neapaphos, is dedicated to Apollo Hylates (of the woods) (No. 56). The cultus of this divinity began at Hyle, the fortress of the coast table-land (No. 48 and 49) and spread principally towards the west. We find it again at a fountain near the modern village of Drymou where the soil is favourable to the growth of oaks (No. 50). The high places in and around the town of Idalion (cf. Map, Plate II with plan of the town, Plate III, and views Plate LX) were occupied alternately by precincts of Aphrodite and of Apollo. Aloupophournos, the most conspicuous hill in the near environs, was dedicated, as the discoveries shew, to Apollo (cf. Plate II). The prospect from this splendid height, this Bâmôt-Baal or Bambula as it may be called, is enchantingly beautiful. The view given on

---

††) Ezekiel VI, 3. 1st Kings XI, 7: XIV, 23. 2nd Kings XVII, 10 ff. 2nd Chronicles XXI, 11.

†††) 1st Kings XIV, 23.

§) 2nd Kings XXIII, 8.

§§) 1st Kings XI, 7 ff.; 2nd Kings XXIII, 13.

§§§) Numbers XXII, 41; XXIII, 1 ff.

*) The word Bambula, which the Kyprian Greeks used to designate any hill, can not be traced to a Greek word. In Larnaka and the neighbourhood Bambula is the name of this special hill, with its town-ruins, and of no other. The hill has been partly removed by the English since 1879, in order to fill up a swamp lying near the sea, and formed by the silting up of the ancient harbour. Even Dr. Pierides, a reliable authority on ancient and modern Kyprian Greek, and on Kyprian and Phoenician inscriptions, could not explain the word Bambula. The penetration of Herr Eb. Schrader in Berlin at once interpreted it as Bambala, a contracted form of Bama-Baal, the sacred height of Baal. The vowel change a—u occurs also in modern Greek, as M. Foy assures me.

Plate LX is taken from a point some distance below the summit,[*]) and yet the famous sacred mountain-wood of Aphrodite, so often sung[**]) by the later poets, lies far below. I was able to shew (cf. Plate III) how this famous grove of Aphrodite (8) formerly lay quite outside the town fortification, which originally ended at point *a* with a kind of tower of defence. In later times the great mountain wood must have over-spread the whole of the Apollo hill Aloupophournos, and it was probably only then that the western portion of the wood, which immediately adjoined the fortified tower and the eastern side of the old ring wall, was marked off as a sacred precinct and included in the system of fortification. By this means there grew up a second, eastern Acropolis almost as important as the original western one, on which stood the Anat-Athene high place and the theatre (1, 2, 3). At a weak point of this eastern Acropolis (*o*) where the Aphrodite height (monti tou Arvili, 8) was over-topped by the Apollo height (Alopophournos 16) a strong stone bulwark [***]) was built, and a double ditch dug (ditch *o* Plate III and LX, 1 and 2). In the construction of this fortress-precinct (8) some

---

[*]) The numbers and letters on Plate II correspond to the map of Idalion, on Plate III to the plan of the town, and on Plate LX to the views of Idalion. For further details see the explanations of the plates.

[**]) My investigations have once more shewn what false conclusions are drawn by blindly adhering to literary sources, without studying the excavations on the spot. References to the Paphos-sanctuary are found in ancient literature from Homer onwards, but the Idalion sanctuary only appears in later writers of the Roman period. The accounts of the worship of Adonis and the death of Adonis in the mountain grove of Idalion are comparatively recent. Now the excavations give a directly contrary result, i. e. they point to a cultus in and near Idalion which was of more ancient standing than that of Palaepaphos. The capitals found at the southern edge of the principal precinct of Aphrodite, which have an important bearing on the question (see on Plate III and Plates LVII and LIX), can not be dated later than the beginning of the 7th century B. C., but the excavations in and near Palaepaphos have yielded nothing so early. The oldest architectural fragments found in the precinct of old Paphos which can be approximately dated, are probably not (with the exception of one fragment overlooked by the English) earlier than the Hellenistic period. The age of the upright remains of megalithic walls cannot as yet be determined (Journal of Hellenic Studies, 1888, Plate IX, 1). As they resemble the walls of the temple of Baalbek in their lower foundations of smaller stones, they may possibly belong to the same period. Excavations in the burying grounds around both towns, a complete record of which has been kept, point to the probability that Idalion was older than Palaepaphos. In the immediate neighbourhood of Idalion early settlements have been found which go back as far as the copper-bronze period. Passing over Alambra, so frequently mentioned in modern literature, I wish to call attention to the copper-bronze town of Nikolides, indicated just beyond the margin of my map of Idalion (Plate II) with its accompanying burying-grounds (29 and 30). Now in old Paphos no trace has as yet been found of the true copper-bronze period. The oldest graves hitherto discovered in the neighbourhood belong to the end of the transition period between the copper and the iron age. They lie eastward of Kuklia and the great Tumulus (Journal of Hellenic Studies, 1888, Plate VII) near orides (J. H. S., p. 170). In these graves of the early iron period, iron vessels preponderate, but a few late Mycenean "Bügelkannen" were also found. I visited the sites with one of the pioneers appointed by the English, and verified the information I had received by the fragments dug up or found lying on the ground. D. G. Hogarth and M. R. James admit that they found in Paphos no tombs of the true bronze period (J. H. S., 1888, p. 264). They say: "Tombs of all periods" (this is incorrect, for they did not come on the oldest Strata of all) "have been opened during the past season, a few Archaic ones at Leontari Vouno" (cf. Plate CLXVII) "which have been described by W. James in his account of that site, and others of all subsequent ages down to the very latest." Now these Leontari-Vouno graves belong to the later bronze period, hence it is evident that the English excavators did not touch on strata belonging to the early bronze or copper periods. I hope to offer conclusive proofs hitherto wanting of this statement, by examination of separate instances. The English investigators also admit that everything found in the Paphos graves is more recent than these "Archaic tombs at Leontari Vouno." In spite of these facts, D. G. Hogarth makes on his own map (Plate VII, J. H. S., 1888) the astonishing statement: "**The whole of this plateau is a vast Nekropolis containing tombs of all dates.**" (Sic!)

[***]) This was pulled down in the time of Cesnola and built into the Turkish mosque of Dali (cf. Cesnola-Stern).

of the older statues and pillars were used. Plate XXXVII, 4, and Plate LVIII, 1 and 2, LIX, 1. They were found at *n*. (Plate III). *)

In the depression between the two Acropolis hills at the southern gate of the lower city (G. I., Plate III, No. 6, Plate II, 6, Plate LX, 2 and 4 No. 6), in the glen at the entrance of the town gate, was built the Bâma of Rešef-Mikal (outline Plate 8, p. 16, No. 30 of our list). As shown by the plan (Plate III), the lower town seems to have had three gates, one on the north side which there comes to an abrupt end (G. II), and two on the south side, viz. the principal gate (G. I) in the depression where the lower town runs between the two citadels, another at the south-west point of the lower town (G. III), where a small flattened round hill is marked. The Bâma of Rešef-Mikal-Apollo-Amyklos at the city gate (G. I) seems to have been placed on a small artificial height, which was also strongly fortified. (This was a second weak point in case of siege.) The tumulus-like knoll at the gate (G. III) in the south-west corner of the low ring wall, which I have not yet dug through, may be the remains of a sacred Bâma like those which the Hebrews built in the time of Ezekiel.**) At least the undisputed Rešef-Apollo-Bâma at the principal gate of Idalion (G. I, 6) corresponds very closely to Ezekiel's words:

" Thou hast also built unto thee an eminent place, and hast made thee a high place in every street. Thou hast built thy high place at every head of the way. and hast made thy beauty to be abhorred."
(Ezekiel XVI, 24 and 25)

This Bâma-Baal (Rešef is only a form of Baal) at the gate of Idalion corresponds also to the

"High places of the gates ('Bâmôt der Bocksgestalten', Kautzsch) that were in the entering in of the gate of Joshua the governor of the city, which were on a man's left hand at the gate of the city."***)
(2 Kings XXIII, 8.)

b) Fountains, Brooks and Rivers.

One must have lived long in the East fully to realize the value of water, the preciousness of a spring. When, after journeying for hours, perhaps days, over sun burnt steppes, where not a tree, bush or blade of grass is to be seen, the traveller, almost dropping from his beast, comes on a village by springs of water, with its busy going mills, groves of fruit, and flowering trees, and thick carpet of green vegetation kept alive and fresh by running streams, the sight is an unspeakable joy to him, and as he rides into the shade over the roots of giant trees, among greenery, flowers and water birds, the exquisite beauty of the oasis seems at once to give him life and vigour. Is it strange that Eastern nations should pay special rererence to fountains, and that in the Old Testament the fountain is used as an emblem of the life-giving power of God?†) Jeremiah calls God Himself a Fountain of Living Water.

There can be no human habitation without a fountain or a well, and therefore almost all sanctuaries are near springs.

Cultus sites on bare hill-tops, like the Bâmôt of Rešef-Apollo on Aloupophournos near Idalion, (No. 16, Plate II) in default of brooks or wells, were supplied with water by artificial cisterns, one of which I discovered and have marked on the map. (Plate II, cistern). We have already discussed the

---

*) For further particulars see explanations of Plates.

**) Cp. Baudissin II, p. 259 where he quotes Gesenius (in Gramberg p. XX) and Ewald.

***) For further details about the complicated Bâmôt, with all its idolatrous survounding, cp. chapter IV, on the subject of sanctuaries, groves, heights and the ceremonies connected with them.

†) Baudissin, " Religionsgeschichte " II, p. 149.

imageless fountain cultus at Lithrodonda (No. 42 on the list) and the fountain in the grove of Apollo-Hylates at Drymou (No. 50 on the list). In the sanctuary at the town-gate of Idalion a small spring gushed out, and in Plate III this spring, and the brook flowing from it, now dried up, are indicated. The Rešef-Apollo groves or high places at Frangissa (No. 4) as at Voni, (No. 2) were situated on springs.

On the most important stream of the island, the Pidias (ancient Pedaios) there are two precincts, both sacred to Rešef-Apollo. One lies at the source near Tamassos, the other at the mouth near Salamis. The pebbles from brooks or rivers had important functions in secular and religous life. They were used for building houses and for marking off sacred precincts ($\tau\epsilon\mu\acute{\epsilon}\nu\eta$), sacred groves ($\ddot{\alpha}\lambda\sigma\eta$) and sacred high places (Bâmôt). On many sites of towns, as for example at Idalion and Tamassos, the boundary of the town buildings can be distinctly made out without excavation by observing the position of the pebbles lying on the ground among the other débris. Many of the modern Kypriote earth houses, made of unburnt bricks, have foundations of pebbles. It seems that pebbles from the brook had a special sacred meaning, as in the Old Testament. (Cf. the section on Boundary Stones, above). It is possible that the use of pebbles for the peribolos-walls of sacred groves and high places, as well as for altars, was enjoined, and if so the reason may have been that they were more easily distinguished from stones hewn by the hand of man than any other rough stones could be.

A most interesting passage in the Prophecy of Isaiah illustrates the worship of trees, altars pebbles, mountains and valleys, and also the Moloch cultus in a river valley, aniconic cultus in a sacred precinct.

"Are ye not children of transgression, a seed of falsehood, enflaming yourselves with idols under every green tree, slaying the children in the valleys under the cliffs of the rocks? Among the smooth stones of the stream is thy portion; they, they are thy lot: even to them hast thou poured a drink-offering, thou hast offered a meat offering. Should I receive comfort in these? Upon a lofty and high mountain hast thou set up thy bed; even thither wentest thou up to offer sacrifice. Behind the doors also and the posts hast thou set up thy remembrance: for thou hast discovered thyself to another than me."

We note that the offerings of meat and drink were brought to the pebbles of the brook. This must surely imply an altar built of pebbles, i. e. of unhewn stones and earth, (cf. Plate VII, A & LVII) in a valley and on the bank of a brook. They slay children in the valleys under the cliffs, hence in a scene similar to that around the fountain at Lithrodonda described above (No. 42 on the list). We are at once reminded of Tophet, the place of sacrifice in the valley of Ben Hinnom. They enflame themselves under the green trees (which are here sacred), as in the cultus of Astarte-Aphrodite and of Moloch. Then the prophet in his vision ascends a high mountain, on which animals are slain for sacrifice. On the Bâma is either a sacred precinct with a door, or the house of the high place. The "remembrance" behind the door evidently means an aniconic Agalma, a Masseba or Chammam. It is evident that the prophet is giving a brief enumeration of the different heathen practices carried on on mountains and in valleys, under trees and rocks, by brook-sides, on altars and in sacred precincts, consisting of human and animal sacrifices, dedication of symbolic boundary-stones, and sensual religious rites.

c) The Sea.

The worship of the Sea, while not traceable in the religion of the Hebrews, who were an inland people, necessarily held an important place on the island of Kypros. Aphrodite herself, the Kypris of the Iliad, is born of the sea, and her first footfall is on the strand of Paphos. The myth of the foam-born goddess was known to the author of the Homeric Hymn and to Hesiod.*) We have seen that sacred high places (Bâmôt) groves, (ἄλση) and altars (βωμόι) of Kyprogeneia are frequent on the sea-coast and promontories of Kypros. But Artemis too (Artemis-Paralia No. 7) and Apollo (Apollo Hylates Nos. 48 and 49) loved the sea-coast. From the rock of Phrurion, a bold promontory still easily distinguished near the Apollo precincts on the coast, human beings were thrown as expiatory offerings, Aphrodite herself was said to have leaped from this rock into the sea, that she might have rest from her love and longing for Adonis, slain by Apollo.**) In the supplement on Oriental festivals compared with those of northern and southern Europe, I have given a description of a popular ceremony which is still performed every year on the sea-shore, and which seems to be the survival of an Aphrodite festival handed down by tradition. Some of the customs, modern as well as ancient, connected with the myth of Adonis and the floating heads, seem to shew that an extensive sea cultus existed in Kypros, although not always independently of other rites. In the narrative of the merchant's voyage from Kypros to Naucratis given above (p. 111) we noticed, in connection with the myrtle, that Aphrodite was regarded as goddess of flowers and mistress of the sea. Like Poseidon, she can lull the winds and spread calm over the waters, or she can bring thunder, lightning and storm.

d) Caves.

The cultus of caves, unknown among the Hebrews, demands a few words of explanation. In Kypros, caves were generally used as burial-places for the nobles.***) It is true that in a few scattered instances the Kyprians enlarged caves and adopted them to cultus purposes. Such are the grotto at Neapaphos (No. 56 on the list) dedicated in Kyprian syllabic characters to Apollo Hylates; and a hypoethral cave sanctuary which I have myself examined, discovered on the hill of the town Urania †) by P. Schröder, and outlined and described by him. But these instances of ancient cave worship in Kypros bear, as far as we can judge from the monuments hitherto discovered, a very small proportion to those in Krete, Asia Minor and Greece. On the other hand, the modern cave-worship ††) of Kypros has various striking characteristics which, when thoroughly investigated, may throw light on antiquity. Engel has collected extant information on the Kyprian Aphrodite as cave-goddess, Morpho-Zerynthia.†††) That the only known cave sanctuary in Kypros is dedicated by an inscription to Apollo Hylates, can be no mere chance. This Apollo of Hyle, god of woods, rocks, sea and caves, must have a close connection with the Magnesian Apollo, who had a cave-sanctuary at Hylai, and was worshipped in festivals near Aenos similar to those of the Kyprian Apollo at the rock Phrurion. The Zerynthian caves on the Thracian coast, near Aenos and Drys, the worship at

---

*) On the subject of the Greek Aphrodite and her genesis from a fusion of Greek and Oriental-Semitic religions I can add nothing to the accounts of Roscher and A. Furtwängler in Roscher's "Mytholog. Lexikon," sp. 390—419, where a complete collection of the literary sources and the newest discoveries may be found.

**) At this part of the coast the sea has been silting up sand, till it has formed under the cliff a small strip of beach which did not exist in antiquity. Sacrifices thrown from the cliff would not now fall into the sea.

***) For the rock-graves of Kypros cf. the explanations of the plates.

†) No. 71 of our list. Cf. p. 27.

††) Space and time forbid detailed description, even of the most important.

†††) Kypros II p. 247 and 256.

the same place of Apollo Zerynthios, directly opposite Samothrace with its Zerynthian cave of Hekate, seem also to shew some kinship with the Apollo Hylates worshipped in caves in Kypros.*) We know that there was a precinct of Apollo Hylates at Drymou in Kypros (No. 50 of our list). The modern geographical name Dryum, which I discussed above in connection with the oak (p. 117), recalls the ancient Thracian region Drys, with its Zerynthian cave. The Zerynthian Aphrodite of the same Thracian coast, and the Kyprian Aphrodite Morpho-Zerynthia, strengthen that evidence for the kinship of cave-worship in Thrace and Kypros.

e) Fire, Sky, Sun, Moon and Stars.

In speaking of the cultus of mountains I mentioned fire-worship, and in the section on Asherôt, boundary stones, and sun pillars, I showed by numerous illustrations and explanations, how important was the cultus of Sun, Moon and Stars. In Deuteronomy (IV, 19) Yahve warns the Hebrews not to be seduced to worship "the Sun, the Moon, the Stars, even all the host of Heaven."**) In 2nd Kings (23, 5 and 11) we read that in the time of King Josiah (640—609) the idolatrous priests offered incense to Baal, to the Sun, to the Moon, to the constellations and to the whole Host of Heaven, and how the kings of Judah had set up horses and chariots, in honour of the Sun at the entrance to the temple. I myself excavated hundreds of these sun-horses and sun-chariots, in the form of small painted terra-cotta images, at the entrance of the sanctuary of Rešef-Apollo at Frangissa near Tamassos (No. 4 on the list). They were principally four-horse chariots, and represented various periods of arts. Most of them were in the rough Graeco-Phoenician style, which has been happily called the "snow-man-technique," but there were also images of horsemen, and some of these shewed better workmanship on a larger scale. Most of these figures lay in the stratum of ashes around the sacrificial stone (A. on the outline plate VI.) Some fragments of a chariot and four horses in lime-join-stone, about half life-size, were found in the Rešef-Apollo precinct on the river Pedaios at Tamassos (No. 6 on the list). These fragments were very much defaced by friction and the action of water. Yet it was the opinion of Dr. Furtwängler that the figures were executed in the severe, purely Greek style of the school of Pheidias. Plate XCVI represents chariots made of lime-stone. Two-horse chariots usually belong to secular, and four-horse chariots to religious life. It is interesting to note that all four examples were found on the same spot, in the same series of graves at Amathus, and belong partly to the sixth and partly to the fifth century (cf. the explanation of the Plate).

Examples of these Sun-horses and Sun-chariots and riders are almost to be found in the groves of Rešef-Apollo, and I discovered a few dedicated in the sanctuary of Astarte-Aphrodite near Idalion (No. 3 on the list).***) Ezekiel (VIII, 16) relates that the five and twenty idolatrous worshippers †) turned "their backs towards the temple of the Lord and their faces to the East, and they worshipped the Sun towards the East." If we examine the large ground plan (Plate VII) of the Astarte-Aphrodite precinct

---

*) The sanctuary of Apollo at Delos is said to have been originally a cave. Robertson Smith ("Religion of the Semites" p. 183 note) is of opinion that the Greeks found it a cultus site and took it over from the Phoenicians.

**) Cf. p. 159.

***) To suppose that the discovery in a grove of votive representations of four- or two-horse chariots proves a cultus of Apollo-Helios, is as great an error as to imagine that all cones or doves belong to Aphrodite.

†) See p. 137.

(No. 3 on the list) we shall see by the position of the extant bases, which are carefully marked, that almost all the larger statue-pillars faced the east, irrespective of the direction of the walls. This fact is also illustrated by Plate LVII, which gives a reproduction of a photographic view of the precinct. In my restoration (Plate LVI), I have drawn some of the larger statue-pillars, which are reconstructed from fragments, with their faces towards the spectator, although they, like the others, must have looked towards the east. Several of these figures hold in the left hand a twig or a flower. While this work was in the press, the translation of the Book of Ezekiel by Kaütsch appeared. The passage to which I referred on page 137 is rendered as follows: "Nun sieh, wie sie den Reiserbüschel an die Nase halten." The editor adds that by the word "Reiserbüschel" he understands a bunch of green boughs, such as the worshippers of the Sun used to hold before their faces when they prayed. We have here a striking example of Sun cultus in practice, which exactly corresponds to Ezekiel's description of the idolatrous worship in the court of the Temple at Jerusalem. As men, when they prayed to the Sun, must turn their faces to the east, so all the statue-pillars must be placed facing the east. It seems that a Sun-cultus of this fashion was frequently practised in the precincts of other divinities, male as well as female. Although Rešef-Apollo is the divinity above all others in Kypros who incorporates the idea of the Sun, and is worshipped most frequently with sun rites (in proof of which I would adduce the winged sun-disc on the girdles of his images or those of his priest) *) yet, as I have shown above, the Sun was worshipped on certain occasions even in the groves of Astarte-Aphrodite.

Among the symbols of Astarte-Aphrodite occurs that remarkable double emblem, so frequent in Kypros, which consists of a round sun-disc with a large half-moon above or below it, and which therefore presents the solar and lunar aspects of this goddess, the combined male and female nature of the bearded Venus. I have already given (p. 186 and ff., fig. 159—162, Plates LVIII and LIX) examples of Kyprian sun-pillars, with the sun-disc and the half-moon enclosed in the cone or placed over it. In many antiquities of Kypros and other places (Plate LXXX, 7, LXXXIII, 19, 21, CI, 5, LXX, 1) these combined emblems of sun and moon occur, and are probably the origin of the modern Turkish Crescent and Star. The tutelar goddess of Kadesh (p. 75, fig. 100), the tamer of wild beasts, who is represented nude, standing on a lion, with a snake in the left hand a flower in the right, wears as a head-dress a sun and a half-moon. The same emblem occurs on the golden breast-plate of Amathus (Plate CI, 5) above the chariot of the Sun, and again over the door of a small terra-cotta shrine found in the same place (Plate CXIX, fig. 1 and 2). On a coin of Sidon is to be seen the processional chariot of Astarte with a shrine resting upon it, and over the chariot and shrine float the sacred symbols of sun and half-moon. Other Sidonian coin-types show instead two cones within the shrine (Plate LXXXIII, fig. 17).

The same double emblem alternates with stars and rosettes on the crown or diadem of a life size terra-cotta figure, a fragment of which is shown on Plate LIII (fig. 43). This statue, which was found near Idalion (No. 3 on the list), represents Astarte-Aphrodite or her priestess.

In the next section, when I come to discuss divinities with ox- or cow-heads, I shall offer some explanation of the horned sun-disc.

---

*) Hitherto I have found girdles of this kind only on figures of Rešef-Apollo at Frangissa near Tamassos, (No. 4 of the list) but there many of them.

In the god Samas-Shemesh,[*]) whose cultus was borrowed from Mesopotamia, there is, as I have said, a union of lunar and solar functions, and in course of time the solar element becomes dominant over the lunar.

Before speaking of the worship of the Moon and constellations [**]), I must say a few words about the worship of the sky as a whole. On the one hand this worship is connected with the fire-cultus of the Sun and Stars, called in the Bible "all the host of Heaven," and on the other hand this cultus, when it appears as the worship of the Lord of Heaven and his female correlative the Queen of Heaven, is connected at many points with the worship of the Father of Fathers (i. e. the Father of the Gods) and the Mother of Mothers (i. e. the Mother of the Gods). Even the Creation of the World has a place in this religious system.

The worship of the sky, as it appears by day and by night, must have been originally practised entirely without images and with very simple rites. But the very fact that such worship is independent of dogma and of artistic representation, makes it very difficult to bring logical proof of its existence.

In the religion of Egypt, on which our information is admittedly vague, the god Nunu, the original Chaos, appears as Father of Beginnings, Creator of the World-Egg, of the Sun and of the Moon. As Creator he is Father of Fathers and Mother of Mothers.[***]) In a papyrus of Greek origin the goddess Nut,[†] the feminine correlative of the god Nunu, says: "I am the Mother of Gods, and my name is Heaven" (ἐγώ εἰμι μήτηρ θεῶν ἡ καλουμένη οὐρανός). Isis too, appears in Egyptian writings as mistress of the sky.[††]) I have already spoken of Baal-Shamem, Βεελσάμην, the god of the sun-heat, the Fire-Baal, Baal-Chammam,[†††]) in conjunction with the cultus-pillars of Bel Samin the Lord of Heaven. To these I have to associate another form of the same divinity, who, according to a Syrian cuneiform inscription, seems to have been worshipped at the time of Asurbanipal by a tribe of northern Arabia, I mean the Adar of the sky, Adar Samin. Now there is a female divinity with a similar name, Adar Samain, queen of heaven, who holds an important place among the Aramaeans and Hebrews, and corresponds to the Ištar malkatu and šarratu of the Assyrians.[§]) She is called by the prophets of Judah Meleket-has-samim. To this heavenly divinity are subject all the Host of heaven, sun, moon and stars, the sea, the earth and all that is therein. Both these divinities of heaven appear on Babylonian-Assyrian cylinders, sometimes separately, sometimes together (Plate XXIX, 4 and 13, XXX, 14, LXXXVII, 13). They are surrounded by a crown of rays similar to the halo of christian saints. Sometimes the divinity of heaven is represented with a priest in adoration before him and surrounded by the sun, the winged sun-disc, the crescent, the constellation of the seven stars and other of the Host of heaven. Sometimes figures of fish are added, or heads of oxen and four footed animals as symbols of the sacrifices which were offered before the Masseba and Asherôt. The evil spirit or power of darkness is represented by the man-scorpion, an upright, walking

---

[*]) Cp. p. 177.

[**]) A more detailed discussion of this and other vexed questions concerning sun-worship and sun-divinities would be outside the scope of this work. In fact much of the material is as yet undigested.

[***]) H. Brugsch, "Religion der Aegypter," p. 111—113.

[†]) Cp. Brugsch, p. 646.

[††]) Roscher's "Mythol. Lexikon" II, Sp. 362. Cp. Section 3.

[†††]) Cp. p. 115 and 177.

[§]) Eb. Schrader, Zeitschrift für Assyriologie, III, 1888, pp. 353—364, "The goddess Ištar as malkatu and šarratu."

figure. The arrangement of these star, animal, and plant pictures, with the human element in addition leads us to the belief that they were intended to express religious ideas on cosmogony and astronomy. (For further details see page 171.)

In the prophecy of Jeremiah we find the queen of heaven reigning alone and we read that she was approached with offerings of cakes and incense.*) She thus resembles Astarte-Aphrodite, who is usually worshipped alone in Kypros, and who, as we have seen, is fused with the mother Ashera, who became a goddess.

This queen of heaven sometimes appears as a powerful ruler, like the tutelary goddess of Gebal and Kition,**) sometimes as a mother, like the Carthaginian Amma ***) (Tanit) or the Rhea of Asia Minor. In the section on Adonis and similar divinities I spoke of the goddess as the mother, with one or two children. With these queens of heaven and mothers of gods from Egypt, Babylonia, and Assyria, Rhea-Kybele, the Mother of the Gods from Asia Minor, associates herself, and is found in Kypros fused not only with Astarte-Aphrodite, but also with Tanit-Artemis. The cultus of the Mother of the Gods, proved by inscriptions (at Tamassos, No. 5 on the list), bears the stamp of an admixture of the worship of Aphrodite and of Kybele, in whose service Adonis-Attis is to be found.†) On the other hand Rhea-Kybele is found in conjunction with Tanit-Artemis and Hecate in groves, as for example in No. 1, 10—14 of our list. We see Tanis-Artemis-Kybele of Achna enthroned between two lions (Plate CCVI, 8, No. 1 of the list). A connection must also be noted between these cults and that of the Kyprian Aphrodite-Urania, whose worship like that of Aphrodite ἐν κήποις was transplanted to Athens, and exercised a double function as Queen of Heaven and goddess of animal and vegetable fertility.††) The Aphrodite of the Mountain and of the Promontory, whom we have described above, also mingles her characteristics with those of Aphrodite-Urania in Kypros.†††) In Sicily on an inscription of Egesta the mountain Aphrodite of Eryx is called Urania.§) The heavenly Aphrodite is as difficult to distinguish from the Moon-Aphrodite as is Tanit-Artemis-Urania. Aphrodite as goddess of the moon and Mistress of the Heavenly Host appears in Kypros to be similar to Venus, Juno, Virgo Caelestis or Tanit of Carthage, for these goddesses all command moon and stars, rain and lightning.§§) Astarte-Aphrodite and Tanit-Artemis, among their other functions and mythical genealogies, have in Kypros this in common, that they are both goddesses of the moon and both related to Iŝtar. Their points of likeness and difference are discussed in the section on Tanit-Artemis. But we may note here that the Venus-stars, the Morning Star and the Evening Star, form part of the circle. From Iŝtar, the Venus of the morning, is developed in Kypros the nude, pleasure-loving Astarte-Aphrodite-Ashera. From Iŝtar, the Venus of the evening, is developed the chaste draped goddess Tanit-Artemis-Kybele.§§§)

*) Jeremiah VII, 18, XIV, 17 ff.
**) C. I. Sem., 1 and 11.
***) Euting, "Römische Steine," p. 21, cp. p. 172 note *)
†) Cp. p. 172 and the description of the images of temple-attendants. Plate XCII, 6.
††) Preller, "Griechische Mythologie," I³, p. 277.
†††) Ibid., p. 278.
§) Ibid. p. 278.
§§) Ibid., p. 279.
§§§) Cp. Eb, Schrader, "On the origin of the Chaldeans and the earliest home of the Semites", and Rawlinson III, 53, No. 2 Z. 36, ff. At sunrise the planet Venus is the Iŝtar among the gods, and at sunset she is the Baaltis among the gods. Schrader says besides, that the goddess of the morning star, in course of time,

About the period when the Kyprian religion, originally a monotheism *) of Nanai-Ištar-Astarte, was developing through bitheism,**) into polytheism, another goddess, also Egyptian, a divinity of the sky and of the moon, makes her influence felt. I mean Hathor-Isis. This Egyptian divinity, when she comes to Kypros, is co-ordinated only with the moon goddess Aphrodite, and she transmits to her the cow head and cow horns.***) But the Kyprian moon goddess Tanit-Artemis, who, like Astarte-Aphrodite, is of Babylonian-Assyrian origin, does not adopt these Egyptian-Syrian elements. She becomes instead the graceful maidenly goddess of Greece who plays on the lyre, tends flowers and animals, and is represented holding a torch, caressing a dog or a roe, or hunting with bow, arrows and quiver.†)

II. The Ox and the Horse in Cultus.

1. Representation of the Ox.

The ox holds an important place as sacrificial animal among nations of the most differing characteristics, who seem to have adopted independently of each other the practice of sacrificing bulls, oxen, cows and calves. I must here confine myself to a few instances of customs and rites connected with oxen, illustrated by the Bible, Homer, and the discoveries in Kypros. We shall find that in this island, as a centre, threads of connection will lead us down to Egypt and up to North Syria, Asia Minor, Crete and Mykenae. As our principal evidence is to be sought for in monuments, and as comparative mythology at its present stage will hardly suffice to explain the complex religious history which underlies them, I shall only adduce, here and in the following sections, a few types similar in their outward aspect, and possibly indicating organic relationships. And although we can no fully examine these organic relationships, we may at least obtain some material towards their elucidation. In Plates XCIV and XCV I have represented (with the exception of three pictures in XCIV viz. 7 from Mykenae, 8 from Carthage and 24 probably, but not quite certainly, from Kypros) only Kyprian discoveries.

Heads of oxen, cows or calves appear very frequently as a symbol of sacrifice among the monuments of the copper-bronze period. We find the bull- or ox-head on ten cylindrical stone seals found in Kypros (XCIV, 3, 5, 6, 10, 14—19), and also on a stone bead of cubical form (XCIV, 12).

---

after the elimination of the Babylonian moon-god Sin, became the serious, severe moon-goddess, while the goddess of the evening star became the effeminate Mylitha-Ashera. Schrader's explanation, with slight modifications, corresponds to the discoveries in the Kyprian sacred precincts.

*) In the oldest strata of remains the earliest iconic divine symbol is always the same, viz. a female form in clay, first clothed, afterwards nude: see p. 33, 34, Fig. 29—32.

**) Then follow hermaphrodite man and woman in one image. Plate XXXVI, 1, 6, 11 and 12 and then a pair of gods, viz. god and goddess. Plate CLXX, 13e.

***) Plate XCIV, 4, and XXXI, 13.

†) Images of Tanit-Artemis-Kybele or her priestess.—Players on the lyre. Plate XII and CCXI, 7 and 8. (Achna-Grove No. 1 of the list). Grave figure of Kurion, Plate CCII, 3—women carrying flowers and animals XI, 12—14, CCX, 1—7, CCXI, 1—5, (Achna-grove). Women carrying torches, Plate CCXII, 10 (Achna-grove) CCII, 4 (grave figure from Kurion).—Goddess with dog CCXII, 11 (Achna-grove), with dog and quiver CCII, 2, (grave-figure from Kurion). Goddess with stag or roe. Plate CCXII, 4 and 5. (Achna-grove).

The usual position for the ox head is over the altar or beside a sacred tree. In Fig. 14 it is held by two men grouped in heraldic fashion, and the spaces are filled up by Sun and Moon, two four-footed animals, and two snake symbols. On the cylinder (Fig. 10), which is more in the Hittite style, there are, besides other figures, on the right a man kneeling, in front of whom are a small pillar resembling an altar and an ox ready for the sacrifice, and on the left two figures heraldically grouped round an ox-head in an attitude as if taking an oath (cf. Fig. 17).*) In Fig. 80, p. 65, three women perform a ring-dance round sacred symbols, viz. the double emblem of sun and half-moon, flanked by two sun-stars, and the sacred tree flanked by two ox-heads.

We meet the ox-head everywhere. It occurs on a vase found in a grave (XCIV, Fig. 9) of the copper-bronze period near Psema tismeno, on the southern side of the island between Kition and Amathus.**) Plate XCIV, 25 shews a calf's head carved on a small bead made of glazed clay of a dirty greenish-blue colour. I found it in 1883 at Phönitschäs between Lidir-Lidrai-Nicosia and Idalion along with other beads shaped like fruit or balls, in a grave of the bronze period, which may be dated early in the second century B. C. These beads must have been worn on a string with the calf's head as centre. A small bronze votive tablet (XCIV, 1) in the form of cow's head, with horns resembling a half-moon (now in the Antiquarium of the Royal Museum at Berlin) seems to belong to Kypros, where it came into my possession. The circumstances of its discovery are not recorded.

In speaking of heads worn as amulets, I pointed out the apotropaeic character of ox-heads and ox-skulls, adducing as instances the centre pieces on the necklaces of large terra-cotta statues, which often take the form of an ox-head, a calf-head or that of the animal (Plate LIII, 4, 19 and 24). I also called attention to the golden amulet in the form of a calf-head I found in my excavation of a grave at Poli (Plate XXXIII, 22). On a sarcophagus of the same Nekropolis masks of the cow and the human face alternate (Plate XXXVIII, 19). In an early Graeco-Phoenician grave at Kurion I dug out, besides numerous other silver ornaments, a small particoloured amulet of glazed clay, with gilding on the mouth.

·Ox- and cow-heads are very frequent on Kyprian terra-cotta vessels, especially bathing-vessels. of the 6th, 5th and 4th centuries B. C. (Plate XXIV, 2, 5 and 6, CLXXVII, 3, LXIV, 4 and 7, pitchers from Marion-Arsinoë). Sometimes a female figure is seated on the overturned vessel, holding an ox-head by one of its horns (Plate CLXXIX, 1 = LXIV, 5, also from Marion-Arsinoë). On the shoulder, opposite the handle, of a vase of the same class and from the same place, there is a female figure in relief holding a small pitcher (cf. p. 43 and ff. and Fig. 46 and 48) while on each side right and left, a bull, walking and feeding, is painted. (For a similar painting of bulls in colour see Plate LXIII, 2) Another vase of the same class (bathing vessel), found by me in a grave of Kurion (Plate XCIV, 21 = Plate CLXXXI, 3), shews, in place of the ox-head or female figure, the fore-part of a seated winged

---

*) Plate XCIV, 3 = p. 61, fig. 69; 5 = p. 29, fig. 1; 6 = p. 29, 2; 8 = Plate LXXXVII, 2; 15 = LXXXVII, 8; 16 = p. 31, fig. 27; 17 = LXXIV, 2; 19 = LXXXVII, 4. Cp. also p. 65, fig. 81; p. 87, fig. 120 and 125.

**) The vase passed into the possession of a Greek of Nicosia, M. Nikolaides, Director of the Anglo-Egyptian Bank. The drawings were done by me from photographs. It is a large and ornate Hydria, probably for festival domestic use, and on its shoulder are represented in relief the fountain itself from which the Hydria is filled, the trough for the water to run into, and the drinking-cup into which the water is poured from the Hydria. Fig. 9a represents the whole vase, 9b the best view of the ox-head on one of the handles, and 9c the fountain on the vase on an enlarged scale.

bull. Under the two double handles of the great Tamassos vase (p. 37, Fig. 38 and p. 63, Fig. 75) cow-heads are introduced, and their horns branch off into the double handles. Cow- or calf-heads are applied in the same way to the great warrior vase of Mykenae (p. 63, Fig. 74).

An ox-head of ill-baked terra-cotta with a red polish, broken from a large figure, is reproduced in outline on Plate XCIV, 2 and in photograph on Plate CXCI, 3. It comes from a grave of the bronze-period of Hagia Paraskevi (Lidir-Ledrai). The ox from Cappadocia (Plate CXCI, 1 and 2 front and side view) in the Syrian department of the Berlin Museum resembles it very closely not only in style and technique, but in the quality of the clay and the glazed slip. The detail of eyes, mouth and forehead are incised, cut, or pierced. Both the Kyprian and the Cappadocian ox-heads recall the large silver ox-head from Mykenae belonging to the same period, and the Kyprian example is not far below it in style and execution. A smaller votive ox made of bright red-polished terra-cotta (Plate XXXVI, 3) from a bronze grave of the same Nekropolis near Lapithos is, like the plank-images (XXXVI, 4—6 and 9—12), richly ornamented in intaglio filled in with a dazzling white. The grave at Hagia Paraskevi (Ledrai-Lidir), in which the Mykenaean ox-krater (p. 34, Fig. 33) and the Ištar-Astarte image (Fig. 31) were discovered, also contained the figure of an ox, treated partly as statuette, partly as vase, which I reproduce (XCIV, 20). It is painted over with a ground of dull dark grey, and on this lines of white are applied. These votive ox-images in graves are, as far as we know, entirely absent from the strata of the earlier, Copper-period, but after they appear they are extremely numerous. In each of the four crescent-shaped niches formed by the curve of the handles on the colossal stone vase of Amathus (now in the Louvre) is placed an ox (Plate XCIV, 23).*)

A bronze votive ox from the Apollo precinct at Limniti (No. 52 of the list) is represented on Plate XLIII. On the same Plate (Fig. 6 and 7), are given two views of a votive offering of bronze, found near Arsos (No. 18 of the list) and now in the Louvre. The style is true Kyprian, i. e. early Graeco-Phoenician, and the effect ugly and unpleasing. The subject is a man leading an ox.

A striking analogy to our Kyprian ox-, cow-, and calf-head amulets and bronze votive tablets in form of an ox-head, is found in the gold-leaf Mykenean ornaments in the shape of ox-heads with double-axes**) between the horns, and also in a terra-cotta votive plaque from Carthage, flanked by a coneshaped idol of Tanit image and a herald's staff (XCIV, 8).

On Plate CXCI, 5 is represented the upper part of a vase of spherical form, not surmounted, as is usual in this kind of Kyprian vase, by a female head such as that of Astarte-Aphrodite***) (as for instance on Plate XIX, 2 = p. 39, Fig. 40) but by the head of a cow excellently modelled and painted.

---

*) = Perrot III, p. 282, fig. 213. In Plate CXXXIV, 3 (= Perrot III, p. 280, fig. 211) is a reproduction of the whole gigantic vessel, which Perrot compared to the Brazen Sea of the Temple of Jerusalem. Cp. Explanation of Plate CXXXIV.

**) Cp. below, for the double axe of Dionysos and Zeus Labranios. Cp. also Plate CXXXVI and p. 62, fig. 71.

***) Cp. Plate XIX, 2, and Perrot III, Plate IV &c. On a Kyprian monument Plate CVI, 2, we see on the left the springs of the Nile. The water, represented as a snake, darts out of the rock. The Nile-god Hapi sits among the coils of the snake. In front of him stands Isis of Philae with a cow-head, and waters an artificial Osiris and Adonis-garden planted in a vase. On one of the tiny plants of the garden stands the soul of Osiris, Lord of the Underworld.

2. The goddess with head and horns of a cow.

On Plate XCIV, Fig. 4, I reproduce one of these numerous cow-head figures which, with many other votive gifts, were set up in the treasure chamber (Plate CCI) of the sacred Bâma on the Akropolis of Kition (No. 9 of the list). The Hathor capitals found at Kition prove, as we have already seen, that there, as at Gebal-Byblos, the influence of Hathor-Isis, transmitted from Egypt,*) was prominent. The terra-cotta figures of Astarte-Aphrodite with the child (Plate XXXVII, 7) seem to be copies of some Egyptian original,**) probably Isis and Horus. We may conclude then, that the cow-heads dedicated in the precinct sacred to Astarte and Mikal are meant for images of divinities. The head of the cow-goddess Hathor has been passed on to the Kyprian Astarte-Aphrodite.***)

Wherever we find the head of a cow (Plate CXCI, 5) in place of the head or bust of the anthropomorphic Astarte-Aphrodite (Plate XIX, 2) we may be sure that it represents the goddess. A small votive figure of a cow-headed goddess ending in a pillar basis, which represents Hathor-Isis-Astarte-Aphrodite was found by Cesnola-Stern near Kition.†) This same Kyprian goddess, cow-headed or horned, occurs in a very instructive combination of forms and symbols on the cylinder mentioned above (Plate XXXI, 13). The goddess is in human form, but her head, of which the under part is more youthful than the upper, is that of an animal rather than a woman. Thick, tangled hair hangs from it, and it is surmounted by the sun-ball flanked by two mighty curved cow-horns. At some distance is a cow-head looking in another direction, and surmounted by horns which form a crescent. Around this head three balls are placed, — one between the horns, two right and left of the mouth.††)

In this figure we recognise the tutelar goddess of Biblos, who is seated on the stele of King Jechaumelek, holding in her left hand the sceptre in form of a lotus flower. She is the same goddess whom the Hebrews call Ashtaroth Karnaim, Astarte with the horns or the two horned goddess, which is only another name for the Queen of Heaven.

I have already called attention to the ox- and cow-masks hung upon trees, the existence of which was proved by me near Idalion (No. 36 on the list, and by Munro and Tubbs in Salamis) (the daemonastasium and cistern No. 66 on the list, p. 25).

We saw in Kypros the cow-headed goddess with the sundisc and the horns. We also saw

---

*) Plate LXXII. 1, (cp. p. 101) a picture borrowed from the work of Wilkinson Birch, is a combination of various monuments, intended to show four different Hathors. (In the Egyptian Pantheon their number grew gradually greater). To the left stands Hathor of the island of Pigae near Phylae, next is placed Hathor, called the ruler of the gods, next Hathor the goddess of the Sycamore (the same, who sits to the right in the tree,) and last Hathor goddess of the West. For information on this point I have to thank Messrs. E. Ermann and Steindorff.

**) Cp. above, the section on "Anthropomorphic images of the youthful god of vegetation and flowers and of his Mother", p. 202, ff.

***) Brugsch, "Religion der Aegypter," p. 314.

†) L. Stern draws attention to a similar terra-cotta in the Berlin Museum (No. 185¹, to a bronze head of a cow from Kurion, (Plate LXXI) and to the cow-headed figures in Mykenai. Schliemann ("Mykenae", p. 117) interpreted the cow-headed female figures, and the figures of cows as idola of Hera, and his opinion has been much controverted. Cp. the silver cow-head with golden horns (Schliemann, "Mykenae," p. 250 and 251, fig. 327 and 328) and the cow- and ox-heads with double axe (ibid. p. 252, fig. 329 and 330) 330 = our Plate XCIV, 4.

††) Herr F. Dümmler and I found some of these cylindrical seals in the market. They bore ox-heads with a star between the horns, which recall the design on the silver ox-heads of Mykenae.

31*

separate images of cow-heads images, deposited as votive gifts in the sanctuary dedicated to Astarte-Hathor-Isis, and to Mikal-Apollo-Horus on the Bâma-Baal, the Akropolis of Kition. The name "Servant of Isis" *) appears in Phoenician inscriptions, and these inscriptions are only found in Carthage and Kypros. The name of Horus,**) too, who is identified with Apollo, is found in Kypros as a male appellative.***) Now since Apollo, Rešef and Mikal appear together in Kyprian inscriptions (the word Mikal is a contraction of the name Resef-Mikal) we may consider it proved that Horus and Isis were worshipped equally with Rešef-Mikal-Apollo and Astarte-Aphrodite on the sacred height of the Akropolis of Kition. In two late Greek inscriptions of Arsos we meet with the triad Serapis, Isis and Anubis.†)

We know from Ovid (Metam. 10, 372) that offerings of young cows to Aphrodite were frequent in Kypros, particularly at Amathus. These sacrifices of cows and calves (Himerios, Oration 1, 5, mentions the sacrifice of a calf) in honour of Aphrodite have some analogy to the worship of Isis, who had a temple near Soloi in Kypros. Bulls also were sacrificed to Aphrodite in Amathus, as in Lemnos.

8. Bulls and Calves. The Man-Bull and the Man-headed Bull as Divinities. Horned Divinities.

As in the Greek inscription at Kition (No. 2739, Waddington††) by the side of Keraunia goddess of thunder and lightning (her full name is Aphrodite-Keraunia) the masculine correlative, the King of Heaven, god of thunder and lightning, Keraunios (who in another inscription of Kition, C. I. Gr. 2641 is called Zeus Keraunios†††) appears; as, again, we see Horus by the side of Isis, so from the presence of the cow of Heaven, the cow-headed goddess or the horned goddess with the sun-disc, we may assume the worship of the bull of Heaven, the bull-headed god whom the Hebrews developed into the idea of Yahve, or whom at least they were accustomed to represent either as a bull or as a bull-headed divinity, like Moloch the dark God of Evil.

Indeed we find in Kypros this bull-god besides other Greek, Cretan and Naxian kindred divinities, for instance Ariadne with her Minotaur, Europa with her bull who came from Tyre to Crete, and finally her kinswoman Harmonia of the famous necklace.

---

*) For quotations see Baethgen. "Beiträge zur semitischen Religionsgeschichte," p. 64. Many of the personal appellatives formed from the names of gods which appear in Phoenician inscriptions only occur in Kypros and Carthage, and there are other kinds of monuments which are found almost exclusively at these two places. As an example I may mention the shelj-formed lamps which occur in thousands in Carthage and Kypros (Plate CCX, 16.) I discovered a few of these lamps among old Graeco-Phoenician remains from Phoenician territory in the collections at Beirut (American and French Colleges). It is therefore evident that the Phoenicians in Kypros and at Carthage must have been in constant communication from very early times. The discoveries even give a kind of historical background to the legend, according to which Phoenicians from Kypros had a share in the founding of the Tyrian colony Carthage.

**) In Kypros, as I shall show when I come to speak of Rešef Apollo, Horus as a youth is identified with Rešef Apollo, while Horus as a child and his well-known Graeco-Phoenician double Harpokrates becomes fused with Osiris, Tammuz and Adonis.

***) Baethgen, p. 64.

†) Waddington, 2837 and 2838.

††) Le Bas and Waddington, "Voyage Arch". III, 1.

†††) "To Zeus Keraunios, to Aphrodite, to the City, to the People, and to Harmony, Aur. Anius and Aur. Ania dedicated this portico and everything in it."

Let us first examine Yahve*), the bull-god or bull-headed god, and Adrammelech, the winged bull with human head from whom the Kyprians derived their river god Bokaros.

The Hebrew worship of bulls and calves, which Josiah abolished at Bethel**) about 640—609 B. C., was borrowed from Egypt, and it is generally supposed that the Golden Calf represented the Black Apis-Bull of Osiris or Ptah, or the White Mnevis-Bull of Horus. The peculiarity of the Hebrew form of worship seems to have been the adoration of a calf instead of a bull. The small calf-heads made of gold or glazed terra-cotta,***) which are so frequently found in Kypros and were used as amulets, as well as other representations of calves, seem to imply, that the animal was not only sacrificed, but that it was also worshipped. The large statue from one of the Rešef-Apollo groves near Athiaenou (25 and 26 on the list) (Cesnola-Stern XXXVI = Cesnola-Atlas CXXIII) appears to hold in its hand the head of an ox. We must suppose that this ox-head was intended for a votive gift, like the cow-heads in the Akropolis Sanctuary of Kition. On Plate XCIV, 22 a stone statuette†) from the same place is reproduced. It represents a man in a long close garment who has an animal's head, but whether, as Perrot believes, it is the head of an ox, cannot be determined, because of the faulty execution. It is quite possible that it is intended for Anubis, the god with a jackal- or dog-head. Another statuette from the same precinct (Cesnola-Atlas Plate XXIV, 59) almost certainly represents an ox-head. Here the god or demon places both hands on his mouth. Cesnola's opinion that the head is that of a stag seems to me unfounded, and I agree with Perrot in supposing it to be the head of an ox.

The calf idols of the Hebrews, which they intended as representations of Yahve, are always called "molten" in the Old Testament. The small gold amulets of Kypros are molten, and so are many of the votive bronzes in ox form, as for example the ox of Liminiti (Plate XLIII, 1, No. 52 on the list) and a very beautiful little votive bronze of the good Greek period representing a bull, which I found in the Rešef-Apollo precinct (No. 4 on the list) in the stratum of ashes near the altar for burnt-offerings.

The colossal capital††) with bull-heads found by the English in Salamis in 1880, near which was discovered a votive inscription to Zeus, must have been the head of a cultus pillar, a Baal-Zeus pillar, and recalls the Zeus-Bull which carried Europa from Tyre to Crete, or the bull-headed monster Minotaur. We are reminded here of the wide-spread cultus of Zeus himself, and of the legend that

---

*) Yahve himself was symbolised by an upright post like the Ashera. Schrader (Zeitschrift für Assyriologie III, 1888, p. 363) quotes Hoffmann as follows: "Ich spreche hier ohne Begründung aus, dass der Pfahl den Gott Yahve oder Baal selbst bedeute." For the cultus of Yahve cp. Baudissin, "Semitische Religionsgeschichte," Baethgen, "Beiträge zur Religionsgeschichte," and Stade, "Geschichte des Volkes Israel." For the Golden Calf cp. Delitzsch in Riehm's Bibellexikon, p. 807, and for the worship of images ibid. p. 188. Movers should also be read, but I do not entirely agree with his view.

**) 2nd Kings XXIII, 15.

***) I have spoken of the calf-head of gold (Plate XXXIII, 22) and of two made of glazed terra-cotta. (One of them is given on Plate XCIV, 25.) A golden calf-head Plate VI, Cesnola-Stern. Terra-cotta imitations of a necklace centre-piece, in the form of a calf-head, belonging to large terra-cotta statues of Idalion. Plate LIII, 19 and 24. The quadrupeds on the same Plate, Fig. 15 seem to be calves, but the faulty execution makes judgment difficult. Among the gold amulets which Cesnola mentions among the discoveries in the tomb at (Kurion (he discovered no Templetreasure there) he enumerates some in the form of lion-bull- and calf-heads. I found several gold amulets shaped like calf-heads in the markets in Kypros, which certainly had a sacred and apotropaeic character.

†) = Perrot III, p. 606, fig. 414, = Cesnola, Atlas, Pl. XXIV, 57.

††) Journal of Hellenic Studies, 1891, p. 132.

human sacrifice was offered to him here and in Amathus as late as the time of the Emperor Hadrian, although Engel's assumption, that it was probably abolished earlier, is more likely to be correct. In Kypros a considerable number of small golden statuettes a few inches long have been found. They are hollow inside, and intended to contain a charm or a small relic. These were worn as amulets, and have a hook for hanging up. Most of them show Egyptian influence; and some have ox- or bull-heads.

We shall see presently how the worship of Dionysos was united with that of Aphrodite in the fruitful plain surrounding old Paphos, in the district watered by the river Bokaros. This river-god Bokaros appears on the coins of Paphos as a man-headed bull, and on many of these coins the legend in the Kyprian syllabic characters gives the name Bokaros.*) The god is represented sometimes as a man-headed bull (Plate CXCII, Fig. 9 = Six VII, 14), sometimes as a complete bull lying down, and turning his head round (Plate CXCII, Fig. 5 = Six VII, 15). He represents one particular kind of bull-god. Euagoras I. of Salamis issued coins which bore on the obverse the head of the tutelary goddess Athene, on the reverse the fore-part of the sacred reclining bull (Plate CXCII, Fig. 4 = Six VI, 16). Other coins of Kypros, attributed probably correctly by Six to Paphos, are provided with an ox-head. The coin reproduced on Plate CXCII, Fig. 8 = Six VI, 20 is very ancient and beautiful, but nothing is known of its origin.**) On the obverse is a lion leaping forwards, on the reverse a bull with head lowered in the attitude of defence.

Divinities with ox-heads, male as well as female, often merge into human divinities with ox-horns. A good instance of this is the bull-headed god of Kypros, who only retains the horns or the stumps of horns. Another is the Colossus of Amathus (Plate CIII, Fig. 4) where we have evidence of very ancient cults of different male and female divinities. I have already pointed out that the oldest Graeco-Phoenician cultus is to be traced to the district of Amathus and Tamassos, which extends as far as Idalion. This is proved by discovery as well as tradition. From literary sources we have obtained information about the worship of Adon, Adonis and Osiris, Baal and Zeus, Melqart Malika and Herakles. In fact from all these gods a mingled type has been formed, to which the functions of Iolaos-Ešmun, Set-Typhon, Besa-Ptah-Patäke and especially of Dionysos***) are added. This complex divinity is a monster like Moloch and the Minotaur, a god who demands human sacrifice, or rather an evil demon, whose power cannot be escaped and who can only be propitiated by the slaughter of men. He is well represented by a wild bull or by a creature half man half bull.

In front of the Temple sacred to Adonis and Amathusia Duplex (i. e. the bearded Aphrodite) who was worshipped with sensual rites, stood the altar of Zeus ξένιος or Malika (i. e. Moloch-Melqart) in whose honour men's blood was shed, just as in Byblos Malkandar or Adarmelech†) was worshipped

---

*) J. P. Six, "Du classement des séries Cypriotes." Paris, 1883. Extrait de la Revue numismatique, p. 249—374.

**) Perhaps it comes from Amathus. Among coins of uncertain origin there must be some Amathusian For a long time Amathus was by far the most important town of the island, but hitherto Six has not been able to trace any coins to the town.

***) For the Bull-Dionysos cp. p. 253.

†) Movers, "Die Phönizier," p. 382. The Palmyrene Malachbel, whose companion is Adlibol, belongs to the circle of the Moloch-gods. Baethgen ("Semitische Religionsgeschichte," p. 85) draws an analogy between the amalgamation in Palmyra of the native Molach with the foreign Bel, and the fusion in Kypros of Adonis, (the native god) with Osiris (the foreign god). These complex divinities, of Palmyra and of Kypros, are

in conjunction with Adonis and Baaltis. The Hebrews used to devote their first-born children to a fiery death in order to appease Moloch, the God of the Valley, and the same child-sacrifices were offered to Milkom,*) the Mountain-god, the "Abomination of the Ammonites", and to Kamos, the "Abomination of the Moabites",**) but the Kyprian rites were even more horrible than this. It is well known that the virtue of hospitality was always highly esteemed in the East. The Jew of the Old Testament ***) would sacrifice his own children rather than be wanting in his duties to a guest. In Kypros the guest was sacrificed for the god; the old Kyprians sacrificed to Malika this horned divinity, at Amathus, their highest and dearest possessions, viz. their guests, a fanatical observance almost as revolting as the ancient Kyprian custom, not, it is true, indigenous to the Island, of offering the virginity of their daughters to Astarte-Aphrodite.

I feel quite convinced that the custom of human sacrifice came directly from Kypros to Carthage, and in proof of this we have only to compare the antiquities and votive inscriptions found in both places with the literary evidence. The myth, that Carthage was founded by Dido-Elissa and a noble race from Tyre, as well as the part which Kypros was said to have taken in the colonization, are probably founded on a historical occurrence. The story is that the fleet on its way to Carthage was moored at Kypros, that the eighty men of Tyre there seized eighty maidens of Kypros, and that their marriage rites were celebrated on the shore. A Kyprian priest of Zeus†) (Justin 18, 5 ff.), or

connected with similar religions rites and ideas. The sun-god Elagabal of Emesa, who has become so notorious through the Emperor Heliogabalus, demanded human sacrifices in order that he might prophecy from the entrails of the children. (Cp. p. 102 and Plate LXXII, 3). He belongs to the same circle. The suggestion which I made on page 102 towards a Palmyrene Trilogie, Malachbel-Aglibol-Adonis, occurred to me before I had read Baethgen's admirable book.

*) Kautzsch has "Melech."

**) 1st Kings, XI, 5 and 7. On the hill east of Jerusalem Solomon erected sacrificial mounts for his foreign wives and their gods.

***) Genesis XIX, 8; Richter XIX, 24; Movers I, p. 304.

†) The Tyrians must have taken Kyprian Phoenicians with them to Carthage, and, as is universally admitted, from the oldest and most important Phoenician settlements on the south coast. At the time of this colonization Chittim was known as an island, but not yet as an important city and kingdom, and above all other towns, even above Paphos, stood Amathus and Tamassos. Even without the literary notices and legends of Amathus vetustissima (Tacitus) and ἀρχαιοτάτη (Stephen of Byzantium), even without the evidence of Skylax that the Amathusians were considered to be the original Autochthonous inhabitants of the town, the monuments alone would prove that both towns have associations reaching far back into antiquity. Meltzer, in his Essay on Dido-Elissa, (Roscher's Mythol. Lexikon, p. 1012) assumes that the priest of Jupiter, supposed to have been taken from Kypros, must in reality have been a priest of Juno or Astarte. I see no reason for this view, and I rather incline to think that the priest from Amathus introduced a religion and rites similar to those of Amathus, viz. the worship of several principal gods and of subordinate demons. Besides the worship of Moloch he transplanted the worship of the warlike Baalat, of Anat-Athene, of the maiden Baalat, Tanit-Artemis, of the bearded male and female Amathusia Duplex, of Tanit, and of the countenance of Baal. Since, as R. Meister conclusively shows, the Greeks had colonized Kypros several centuries before the Homeric wars, it follows that at the time of the foundation of Carthage (9th century B. C.) the Phoenician Anat Cultus had been fused with elements of the Greek Athene cultus, and become a Kyprian Graeco-Phoenician, goddess of War and Peace, Anat-Athene. This goddess, like the Tanit-Artemis and the bearded Aphrodite of Kypros, like Aphroditos and the Kyprian Baal-Hammon, who is also a horned god, were transplanted to Carthage. (Engel, II, 67). An image of Astarte worshipped in Carthage was said to have been brought thither by Dido. (Herodian 5, 6). As Dido's high-priest was a Kyprian, this Astarte-image probably came from Kypros. Even Dido herself, who belongs more to legend than to history, has been identified with Astarte. Images of Tammuz-Adonis also must have been brought from Kypros at the time of the colonization of Carthage or later, for how else could the young Kyprian flower-god and temple attendant, the crouching

of Hera (Servius on Vergil Aen. 1, 443) followed them of his own accord by command of the god, and obtained the promise that he and his posterity (like the descendants of Kinyras in Kypros) should hold the priesthood in the city which was to be founded. The meaning of this myth is the transmission to Carthage of the cultus of Baal-Moloch-Malika-Melqart, originally brought from the mother-city, Tyre, to Amathus.

Horned demons and horned gods occur frequently in the religion of different ancient nations, the Egyptians, the Babylonians, the Assyrians (p. 83, Fig. 110 and 111, Plate XXX, Fig. 1, 2, 4 and 5) and, as we have already seen, many other Semitic and Aryan peoples. The horn was used as a symbol of super-human or divine power,[*] and as such is frequently associated with the kings beginning with Alexander the Great, whose head on coins is adorned with the Ammon's horn like the God Baal-Zeus-Hammon.[**] Demetrios Poliorketes is represented with bull's horns,[***] and the same symbol occurs in the coin portraits of the Seleukidae.[†] Even Michael Angelo represented his famous "Moses" with horns.[††] The horns of the Colossus of Amathus (Plate CIII, 4) are very small and seem to be intended for those of a young ox. It is certain that the centaurs are represented in Kypros with bull's horns (Plate XLVII). In conclusion, we may compare this Colossus with another which was found by von Luschan and Koldewey in Samal, a Hittite region in north Syria. The Colossus of Amathus is entirely nude, the body is hairy, the legs resemble those of an animal, and remind one of the images of the god Eabani, the companion of Izdubar in the Assyrian-Babylonian mythology. The Colossus of Samal has the upper part of the body nude, while the under part is covered by a

---

boy of the Carthaginian votive stele, have come thither? (Plate XCII, 5). The same is true of the sheep-cultus connected with Baal-Hammon (more correctly Baal-Ammon). Robertson Smith's Study, "Sacrifice of a sheep to the Cyprian Aphrodite," ("Religion of the Semites," p. 450 and ff.) should be read for information on this point. The legends of the Kyprian priest who introduces the worship of the gods into Carthage, and of Dido, who brings an image of Astarte, recalls the other story, already quoted (p. 111) of the merchant Herostratos, and the bringing of an Aphrodite image from Kypros to Naukratis. All these and other fables contain a germ of truth, with reference to the history of states, art, culture or ritual. From Kypros, the seat of early Graeco-Phoenician culture, ritual and images for worship were transplanted to other countries, and this is confirmed by research. The discoveries at Naucratis (cp. Plate CCXIV) show that Kyprian works of art, whose style is influenced by Egypt, were brought to Naukratis, and the discoveries at Carthage show the same thing. Besides the objects already mentioned there are two Carthaginian pillars, which lead us to infer an artistic and ritual connection between the different aspects of the female divinity. In Plate LXXXV, 8, the pillar shews a throned goddess with the Lotus-flower, quite as in Kyprian monuments. The goddess on the Carthaginian stele, (Plate LXXXV, 9) who is half bird half human, besides the pair of doves around the cone-symbol of Tanit, exactly recall Kyprian images. (Cp. Plate XXXVIII, 12, CII, 1, CV, 10 and below, the passage on the Etrurian Kypra.)

*) The following narrative will illustrate the survival to the present time in Egypt and the East of legends about bulls: (Pückler-Muskau: "Aus Mehemed Ali's Reiche," I, Unterägypten, p. 223.) "The Defterdar was talking of the inconceivable obstinacy of the Bedouins: "Only think," he said, what happened to me lately. Two fellows boasted about their father to me, and said he was a bull. Well, I answered, if your father was a bull, your mother must have been a cow. But I could not make the obstinate fellows in this plain argument. The dogs would stick to it, that their father was a bull, but their mother was not a cow."

**) Immhoof, "Portraitköpfe aus antiken Münzen," I, 1, II, 1—4.

***) Ibid. II, 7 and 8.

†) Ibid. III, 8.

††) Herr G. Minden calls my attention to the "Moses" of Michel Angelo, whose horns are the result of a misreading of Exodus 34, 29, 30 and 35. It is said of Moses that the skin of his face was bright or shining. Instead of "shining" the Vulgate has "horned." In old illustrated Bibles Moses is sometimes represented horned, and for the same reason.

long rich garment. On this garment is inscribed the oldest known Aramaic inscription. In the Kyprian Colossus the horns grow out of the hair, but in the Colossus at Samal they appear on the cap which the god wears, and which is also an attribute of the Assyrian Babylonian demons. But the two Colossi resemble each other strongly in the characteristics of the head, the prominent cheek bones, the wide compressed mouth, the thin lips, the square cut curled beard, the treatment of the hair and the form of the shoulders. I have already pointed out that on both these sites are found clay images of the female goddess, and many other works of art on a smaller scale, which show a strong resemblance, and it is well known that there was a constant import trade in primitive weapons, vessels &c., from Kypros to Samal. We are thus amply justified in assuming an analogy between the Hamath district of Syria (Samal-Sendsherli lies near Hamath and probably belonged to it) and the region of Amathus. The Colossus of Samal, as the inscription tells us, is dedicated first to the god Hadad and then to the god Rešef. The dedication, according to Sachau, took place in the reign of Tiglatpileser II. about the year 730 B. C., and the giver was King Panammu.

Sacred herds of cattle occur frequently in the religion of different races belonging to the Aryan and Semitic families. Detail would be here out of place. But I may mention an ancient custom still surviving in Kypros. which is described by Herodotus,[*] quoted by Movers (the Phoenicians, p. 375) and referred to lately by Robertson Smith in his "Religion of the Semites" (p. 280). The Phoenicians and Egyptians, like the inhabitants of the coasts of Lybia, would rather die than eat the flesh of an ox. Before the English occupation of Kypros in 1878, oxen were hardly ever slaughtered, because it was considered a sin to put them to death for purposes of food. Sometimes an ox would break a bone by accident, and would have to be, killed, and then some of the flesh was given to the Europeans on the island as a great delicacy. Even cows' milk was avoided in the same manner. This custom has lasted for thousands of years, and the consequence is that the native cow gives so little milk, that the English families who have resided in Kypros since 1878 and require milk for their children, have been obliged to send for cows from other places. An enterprising Englishman has devoted himself to the introduction and rearing of cattle and to the crossing of the breeds, but even at the present day none of the distinguished Greeks of the Island can be induced to taste a morsel of beef. I had in my service for several years an intelligent Greek peasant lad from Dali, who had learned from me how to clean the antiquities which were excavated, to restore them, and to make photographic copies. It sometimes happened that the beef supply was in excess of the demand, since it was only eaten by the Europeans, and a few natives who had overcome the prejudices usual in their countrymen. At such times only beef was used in my household, and the servant would regularly receive from the cook, who was proud of her enlightened views, his daily ration and would consume it, so that I flattered myself I had made a convert among the Kypriotes. The Greek left my service, and went back to help his father in gardening and field labour, and on one occasion he had to kill a weakly but perfectly sound ox belonging to his father. The carcase of the ox was entirely consumed by the village dogs! Neither Loizo, my former servant, nor any of his relations, nor indeed anyone in the whole village, would taste the beef.

4. Horned Men and Horned Centaurs. Winged Centaurs and Winged Horses.

We come now to the horned men and horned centaurs of Kyprian legend, and we shall find that both are connected with Amathus. When Aphrodite could no longer bear the human sacrifices which took place in honour of Kronos (i. e. Moloch), she changed the servants of Kronos at Amathus into horned men, or, according to another version, into bulls.[**] Can we find a better parallel to this myth than the Colossus of Amathus (Plate CIII, 4), the horned god who holds the lion?

[*] IV, 186. Movers quotes in addition Porphyrius (de abstin. II, p. 120, cp. Hieronym. adv. Jovinum pag. 201, Martianay.)

[**] Engel, "Kypros" I, p. 171. In the Rešef-Apollo grove at Limniti (No. 52 on the list, the best of the remains are at Berlin, Plate XLIV—XLVII) the English excavators found a terra-cotta head belonging to

Nonnos has another version of the genealogy of the race of horned Centaurs. Zeus, the father of Kypris, fell in love with his new-born daughter on account of her beauty. The goddess escaped his pursuit, Zeus fell to the earth in the form of rain, and Gaia, the All-mother, brought forth a monstrous race with horns, called the Centaurs, who are afterwards form part of the retinue of Bacchus.*)

I was fortunate enough to find at five different sites in Kypros, numerous images of Centaurs, certainly as old as the seventh century B. C., and perhaps in one example (Plate CIV, 6 repeated in Fig. 173) even older. On three of these sites I found images of Centaurs showing evident traces of horns. Those represented on Plate XLVII (8—10, 12, 13—16 and 18) all come from the grove of Rešef-Apollo at Limniti**) (No. 52 on the list) (No. 10, repeated at Fig. 175). Plate XLVII, 11 represents the head of a horned Centaur which was acquired by Cesnola, and seems to have been found at Papho.***) It is at present in the Antiquarium of the Royal Museum at Berlin. Plate XLVII, 17 which gives the upper part of a painted terra-cotta statuette representing a Centaur, comes from Amathus, and was acquired by me at Limassol from the excavator. It is now in the Berlin Museum. Heuzey, in his "Catalogue des figurines antiques" (p. 155), mentions two Kyprian terra-cotta Centaurs. One of these, which almost certainly comes from the neighbourhood of Idalion, is reproduced in Fig. 174†) (= CIV, 9.).††) Finally there is a terra-cotta which I myself found in a grave near Kurion, and which, though not horned, is extremely interesting. From the evidence of the site, the technique and the style, it is clear that this figure must belong either to the seventh century B. C. or to an earlier period. The painting corresponds to that on the vases found in the oldest Graeco-Phoenician strata

---

a female statue evidently horned. Cp. Journal of Hellenic Studies, 1890, p. 93, fig. 11). The horns project from under the head-dress, which is in the form of a flat coif or Kyprian kerchief, and, as H. A. Tubbs has shewn, do not belong to the head dress. His explanation seems to me correct; the figure, is either the horned Aphrodite herself, or one of those mythical horned beings into which she transformed the Amathusians.

*) Nonnos 5 sub fin., and 14, 187. Here I have followed Engel II, p. 72, almost word for word.

**) Hundreds of images representing horned centaurs, who here appear in the retinue of Rešef-Apollo instead of that of Dionysos, must have been deposited on the altar as votive gifts of worshippers. I have had fragments of at least 60 or 80 such rude, partially painted figures in my hand (cp. No. 12). Some are coloured yellow on the body, and hair is indicated by black brush-strokes. Most of the figures protrude a fiery-red tongue. Although the site had been secretly rifled by the peasants to a great extent, yet when the English made a hasty search in 1890 (see Journal of Hellenic Studies, 1890, p. 87 and ff.) they found a number of such figures of Centaurs (p. 93). They describe the arms of these Centaurs, spread out "to suggest a crescent"; but the passage in Nonnos has escaped their notice. When the peasants had begun to dig there, I bought in large quantities the objects which had been brought to Nicosia, and gave information to the Government of the island, so that further depredations were stopped. I then induced Mr. C. Watkins, for whom I had repeatedly conducted excavations, to hire the site from the proprietor, and this was arranged through Mr. J. W. Williamson. Messrs. Munro and Tubbs, who were sent out by the Cyprus Exploration Fund, took the work over in 1890 but the time of year was not favourable for their operations, and they soon came upon water, as the site is a river-valley near the sea. They did not even succeed in systematically digging out what the peasants had left, and after a few days work with a very small party of labourers, they gave it up.

***) Cp. Explanation of Plate XLVII. The name Papho, as used by the modern islanders, designates quite a large district, reaching almost to Limniti. The figure must come from some Rešef-Apollo sanctuary of the Papho district.

†) Perrot III, p. 600, fig. 411.

††) Perrot has "Alambra." As Alambra is only a mile and a half from Dali, the error could easily creep in. The information as to the site of the discovery may be correct, only we must understand, not the Nekropolis of the Copper-bronze period over or near the village of Alambra, but the Graeco-Phoenician burying-grounds of the Iron period in Idalion.

of the Iron Period. The Centaur carries a small figure of an ox under his left arm and is treated as a shepherd or a sacrificial attendant.

On the right shoulder is painted a barbed cross. This, besides the style and the formation and position of the head, recalls the small figure of Astarte given on page 148, (Fig. 150). Both figures come from the same Necropolis and from the same stratum of excavation, and, although made of terracotta, have a certain analogy in method and style to the nude marble figurines of the Kyklades. It is evident that Kypros had a large share in the formation of the centaur type.

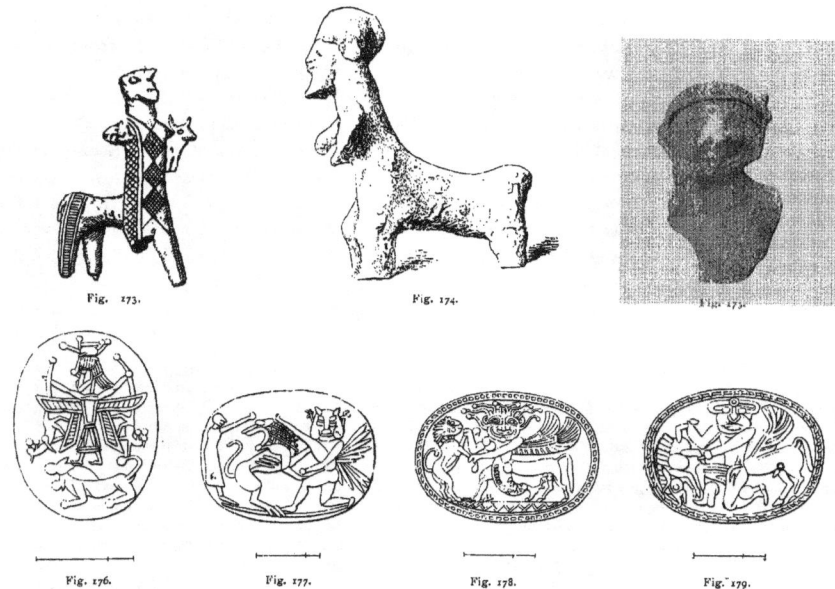

Fig. 173. Fig. 174. Fig. 175.

Fig. 176. Fig. 177. Fig. 178. Fig. 179.

As soon as the horse-type was introduced, the man-headed bull was changed into a man-headed horse,*) whose front legs, however, were at first not human. Attempts to form centaurs by adding to

---

*) Into the myth of the founding of Carthage an episode has been woven, which illustrates the substitution of the sacred horse for the sacred ox. When the colonists from Tyre and Kypros were about to begin building, and struck their spades for the first time into the earth, they came upon the head of an ox. As they took this for an evil omen, they broke ground at another spot. This time they found a horse's head buried at the foot of a palm, and as they considered this to be a favourable omen, signifying strength and excellence in war (they built the city there. The horse and the palm became symbols of Carthage, and appear as such on the coins of the town. (Cp. Meltzer's Essay on Dido-Elissa in Roscher's Mythol. Lexikon.) Kyprian priests had a share in this colonization. The transition from ox-cultus to horse-cultus, from the sun- or sky-bull to the sun-horse) justifies further analogies in Kypros. From the man-headed bull, Adrammelech, is developed the man-headed horse, the Centaur, from the winged ox (Plate XCIV, 21 = CXI, 4) the winged horse. (CXI, 1 and 5, Plate CC, 4). This change of cultus takes place in Assyria after the introduction of

the winged or unwinged demon in human form the middle and hinder parts of a horse, may be very plainly seen in Figures 176—179.[*]) These instances are all taken from scarabs, which may very possibly have come from Kypros. If so, they may belong to the Graeco-Phoenician circle of animal-gods or animal-demons, such as the Colossus of Amathus, the animal-taming god on the Kyprian scarab (Plate C, 2) or on the Kyprian silver girdle (C, 7 = p. 77 Fig. 105). In all these types (and also in that of the Kyprian Centaurs) is mingled a Bes-type borrowed from Egypt. (Bes on an Egyptian monument, Plate CI. 10, on a Kyprian monument, Bes riding on the nude Astarte-Aphrodite, Plate CI, 4) A comparison of the winged demons (Fig. 176 & 177), who show no trace of the centaur type with the same demons who have become Centaurs by the addition of parts of a horse (Fig. 178 & 179), will show that these are conceptions of contemporary artists, who were trying to give shape to ideas common at the time in which they lived. The winged demon who stands on two beasts and holds two, (Fig. 176), is another attempt of a similar kind and falls within the series of types which we shall have to examine in the section about the gods and goddesses represented as taming animals. From the type of the Centaur with snaky hair (Fig. 178) to that of the archaic Greek Gorgon (Plate XXXI, 16) is no violent transition. We have on a cylinder made of agate (Berlin Museum Vorderasiat. Abth. No. 673 of the Catalogue, Plate XXXI, 15) of Assyrian style, possibly even made in Assyria, an attempt to compose a fabulous monster from a human being and a four-footed animal. A demon in the position of Marduk bending his bow and shooting his arrow (Plate XXIX, 4 & 7) is wrestling with the dragon Thiamat represented as a gigantic bird. The demon has the upper part of a winged man, the legs of a bird, and the body of a four-footed animal, which again finishes in birds' legs.

The Centaur in Fig. 178 has a horse's body and hind legs, and in front, at the end of his human legs, there are distinct traces of birds' claws. The Centaur images on the monuments of Rhodes, on the golden Hormos (Plate CII, 3) of Kameiros[**]), and on vases in relief (Plate CIV, 1) together with the Etruscan friezes in relief of the Bucchero vases (Plate CIV, 2, & CIII, 2), form a transition to the bronze relief of Olympia (Ol. IV, Plate XXXVIII, 696), to the Melian and Corinthian gold bands (Plate XXV, 9 & 8), and to the Centaurs as they appear on Greek vases of various styles. From the early Attic Dipilon vases and from the Corinthian vases, we may follow the Centaurs type step by step, until it reaches its highest development in the Attic vases of the finest and most severe period. Homer probably knew Pegasus, but not the Centaur. I hope I have shewn clearly what an important part Kypros must have taken in the formation of the Centaur type. Asia Minor must also

---

the horse. The Greeks made use of the Oriental winged horse to form the type of Pegasos, as we see him springing from the neck of the Gorgon on the Kyprian sarcophagus of Athiaenou (Cesnola-Stern Plate XVIII) cp. the man between winged horses. (Plate CC, 4).

[*]) 176 = CIV, 7 = Lajard Mithra LXVIII, 21. An agate scarab of unknown provenance, now in the Bibliothèque Nationale, Paris. 177 = Lajard Mithra, LXVIII, 22. 178 = CIV, 12 = Lajard Mithra LXVIII, 20. Plaster cast (No. 212) Cades in Rome, taken from a scarab 179 = CIV, 11 = Lajard Mithra LXVIII, 19 like the former, Cades No. 213.

[**]) The Centaurs here carry hares, and recall the "Centaurs carrying an ox" of Kurion, fig. 173. The winged female figures carry lions, and recall the figures carrying animals on the silver girdle. The best analogy to these representations hitherto is to be found in the golden Hormos of Kameiros, and the silver girdle with gilt clasp, of Marion-Arsinoë, with which may be associated the fragments found in Spain and reproduced on Plate CII 4 and 5. Cp. also F. Dümmler, Jahrbuch des kaiserl. deutschen Archäol. Instituts, 1887, p. 93.

have had some share in it.[*]) In spite of this, the Greek Centaur myth may belong to the original Aryan stem, and be connected with the Indian myth of Gandarvah, for the words come from similar roots.[**])

Through Zeus and Aphrodite, Malika and Astarte, who with the help of the earth produced the horned race of Centaurs in Kypros, we have come to the horse and horse-types[***]). We must now return to the bull-type.

5. Minotauros, Ariadne, Dionysos and Europa.

The demon Minotauros, the bull-man type adopted by the Greeks, is not found in Kypros, but belongs to Crete. And yet the myth of Theseus and Ariadne has as much connection with Kypros as with Naxos, and the two versions show a close analogy. The Kyprian version brings us again to the old original colony of Amathus, where Greek and Phoenician elements were mingled in very early times. Theseus, sailing from Crete, was thrown by a storm on Kypros, and there he abandoned Ariadne, great with child. She died at Amathus. When Theseus came again to Kypros to mourn for Ariadne, he dedicated to her at Amathus two images[†]), one of silver and one of brass, and in his grief, he instituted a festival in her memory. Ariadne is said to be buried in a sacred grove, now called by the inhabitants of Amathus the Grove of Aphrodite-Ariadne. The ritual in honour of this double goddess of life, love and death is divided into a festival of mourning and a festival of joy, thus resembling the Adonis-Osiris cultus, which flourished in Amathus more than in any other part of Kypros. The custom which I have already mentioned, of disguising a youth like a woman and making him represent a woman in childbed, points to the fusion with Adonis. We know too that this festival took place in the same month, Gorpiaios, in which the Adonia and the Feast of Kora fell.[††])

I have excavated from an early Graeco-Phoenician grave a monument made of clay, which seems, to judge by its form and contents, to be extremely ancient. The walls of the simple square rough grave-chamber were hewn out of the conglomerate which lay on the spot, and a huge shapeless mass of stone formed the covering. In this grave were found only early Graeco-Phoenician vessels (the oldest of these vases may easily have been of a date as early as 1000 or 1200 B. C., but the date of the newer ones cannot be determined. Besides the monument (8 cm high) represented on CXCIX, 1 and 2, were found two small roughly painted terra-cotta figures of a goddess ending in a pillar, and holding a large round disc in front of her. (Cp. Plate CCVI, 5 from Kurion.)

The interesting monument on Plate CXCIX., 1 & 2 represents a small shrine, formed, as it seems, half of wood and half of cloth, like a tent. The whole forms a niche in which is seated a mourning figure, veiled, and holding her right hand to her face, according to the scheme of a woman

---

[*]) Böhlau regards this figure of a Centaur as a creation of the Greek art of Asia Minor. (Jahrbuch des kaiserl. deutsch. Arch. Instituts, 1887, p. 41.)

[**]) In Assyrian Art we find all kinds of fabulous beings, composed of parts of men and animals in different combinations (Plate XXXI, 15) but not the Centaur properly so called. The type which approaches it most nearly, is the monster archer, a compound of man, goat, winged horse and scorpion, already adduced by G. Perrot (III. p. 664, fig. 412). The Centaur is a specific Graeco-Phoenician conception, adapted by the Greeks.

[***]) For the horse-headed demons see below.

[†]) This is an instance of the dualism which I see Movers has already noticed in Phoenicia. ("Die Phönizier", I. p. 393).

[††]) Stoll in Roscher's Mythol. Lexikon, Sp. 543. Engel, "Kypros" II, p. 656, cp. p. 5, the Gorpiaios inscription and p. 120.

lamenting (cf. Plate CLXXIII, 23a). Two Ionic wooden pillars carry a small three cornered gable, in which may be seen our Kyprian double symbol of sun and half-moon. These Ionic pillars have their broader side away from the spectator, and towards the opening of the cella, and close to them are pillars, which bear on their front surfaces twelve discs in the form of seals, six on each side. It is my opinion that this veiled mourning form in the sanctuary is Aphrodite-Ariadne-Amathusia, fused with Persephone as with Adonis.*)

Another legend of Ariadne brings us to her husband Dionysos and to Thracian-Phrygian cults, some of which must certainly have come to Kypros in very early times. The literary sources and the monuments discovered leave no doubt, although at present we possess fewer antiquities from Thrace and Phrygia than from Kypros.

The oldest population of Kypros seems to have been not Semitic, but European, and indeed Phrygian-Thracian. Helbig ("Homerisches Epos," p. 6—12) has explained fully how the Thracians of the Homeric period are the equals of the Achaians. In the funeral games for Patroklos, Achilles exhibits as prizes for the contests the sword and coat of mail of Asteropaios the Paionian, and praises the marvellous workmanship of both. (Il. XXIII, 560, 807.) According to the Iliad there were Thracians on the island of Lemnos, therefore they may well have been in Kypros also. Even the Lemnian Thracians themselves, whose trade was piracy, (Il. I, 594, Od. VIII. 294) and who very early had connections with the Phoenicians (Il. XXIII, 745), might have gone round to Kypros in their voyages. Other Thracian-Phrygian hordes of hunters and nomads could march through Asia Minor, and after mingling with other Syrian tribes, Karians, Lydians and Lykians, could easily row over to Kypros in a few hours, On Plates CXLVI—CXLIX I illustrate the striking similarity between the civilization of Trojan Hissarlik and that of the early Kyprian copper bronze period. Dümmler ("Aelteste Nekropolen auf Cypern", 260, Mitth. d. Arch. Inst. Athen XI, p. 209 and ff.) has even gone so far as to assume a complete identity of population on these two sites, an opinion with which I cannot agree (cf. my lecture, "Cyperns Cultur im Alterthume". Mittheilungen der Anthropologischen Gesellschaft in Wien, 1890, p. 90—95). It is then extremely probable that in Homeric times Thracians (Paionians) were settled in Kypros. The Thracian arms which Achilles gave as a prize in the games, are as likely to have been made in Kypros as his own, or those of Agamemnon which Kinyras sent him from Kypros. The costly mixing-cup, which had been given to the Thracian King Thoas of Lemnos by Phoenician merchants, may have been made in Kypros. Kyprian Phoenicians probably brought the Tyrian Melqart cultus from Kypros to Lemnos, just as they brought Kyprian-Phoenican cults to Carthage, where, from the very foundation of the city, they regulated state worship and possessed the rights of a hereditary priesthood. It is probably no mere chance, that the Thracian Minstrel of the Iliad (II 595—600) is called Thamyris, for the name is very closely connected with the Kilikian sooth-sayer Tamiras, who comes to Kypros and becomes the ancestor of the priestly race of Tamiradai, who held the office contemporaneously with the Kinyradai. Let us now compare the account given in the Iliad of the Thracian prince Rhesos (X, 436—441) with the account, centuries older, of the Kyprian princes on the Egyptian hieroglyphic records.**) In the Iliad Dolon says of King Rhesos:

"His be the fairest horses that ever I beheld, and the greatest, whiter than snow, and for speed like the winds. And his chariot is fashioned well with gold and silver, and golden is his armour that he brought with him, marvellous, a wonder to behold; such as it is in no wise fit for mortal men to bear, but for the deathless gods."

On the great tablet of victory from the 34th year of the reign of King Thutmosis III we read:

"These were their horses taken as booty, their golden and silver chariots, which were made in the country of Asebi." (Kypros)***)

In another part of the tablet, among the tributary offerings of the King of Asebi (Kypros), are mentioned copper ore and mules.

At the present day in Kypros there exists a small but useful breed of horses, and the mules, which

---

*) Cp. Engel, " Kypros," II, p. 306.

**) Brugsch, "Geschichte Aegyptens unter den Pharaonen," pp. 301, 317, 320, 322, 341, 355.

***) A. Erman has recently tried to prove in my periodical, " The Owl " (1888, p. 23) that Asebi is not to be identified with Kypros. H. Brugsch, Ed. Meyer and others consider the identification established, and the contrary evidence insufficient.

are a cross between these horses and Kyprian asses, are so famous, that they are bought up for military purpose by the Austrian, Greek and English governments. *)

If these analogies between the Homeric Achaians, Kyprians (Kinyras) and Thracians are established, we need not be surprised to find that Dionysos-Sabazios cults emigrate to Kypros with Ariadne and that Dionysos appears in the retinue of Rešef-Apollo and of Astarte-Aphrodite-Ariadne. We have also proved the fusion of the Thracian and Phrygian Dionysos cults.

We now know in how many ways the orgiastic festivals celebrated in honour of Dionysos, Rhea-Kybele, and Attis, were mingled and identified with each other. The Phrygian-Thracian, as well as the Argive and Delphian, elements are all thrown into this Kyprian mixing vessel of cultus. I have repeatedly referred to the numerous analogies to Argos. With Delphi too, Kypros was early connected; King Euelthon of Salamis dedicated a vase for incense there. So it happens that in Amathus we find a confused heterogeneous crowd of rites and festivals.

Dionysos has some points of contact even with Malika and his kindred divinities. The physiognomy of the Colossus of Amathus, the rude, animal expression and the horns answer exactly to a Bull-Bacchus according to the religion of old Thrace. And when the Sabai, priests of Kybele, Attis and Sabazios-Dionysos, utter the lament εὐοῖ σαβοῖ, ὕης ἄττης, we are reminded of the corresponding cry αἴλινον in the service of Astarte-Aphrodite, and of Tammuz-Adonis Linos. The Zagreus-Dionysos child too, the offspring of Zeus and Persephone, torn in pieces by the Titans, had the form of a bull. In Argos the women called on the Bull-Bacchus βουγενής, and according to a Greek legend Dionysos himself comes to Kypros and falls in love with Adonis. The head of Dionysos, (mentioned above) which swims to Lesbos, is an imitation of the Adonis head which swims to Byblos and to Kypros. Adonis is also a river-god; the Syrian river Adonis takes its name from him. The Kyprian river-god Bokaros, in the form of a man-headed bull, seems to represent a modification of the Assyrian Hebrew Adarmelek. The Moloch sacrifices, like the Adonia, took place in valleys, on rivers and brooks, and on the sea-coast. As Adonis is slain by Apollo, and Osiris by Set-Typhon, so here Adonis falls a victim to Moloch. When the sacrifice of children as representatives of Adonis to Malika-Moloch ceased, the children dedicated their lives to the service of the god. Thus the head of Moloch came to be represented on the breast of Adonis or the temple-attendants (cp p. 207). Perhaps it is by this or a similar process, that river-gods like the Kyprian Bokaros**) became manheaded bulls like Dionysos. For many a man and many a bull must have been offered, not only at the rock Phrurion to Apollo Hylates and his retinue, on the coast near Amathus to Malika, Zeus-Xenios and his kin, but also on the Paphian shore at the mouth of the Bokaros, where the two cultus pillars still tower, to the dark Moloch. The enthusiasm of the Maenads, and the union of the orgiastic Dionysos cultus with the sensual rites of Aphrodite, have been associated by Euripides with the mouth of the Bokaros.***) (Cf Engel, Kypros II, p. 654.) From the abundant information and explanations collected

---

*) For horse, chariot and rider in antiquities of Kypros, see Plate CXCVI.

**) In Kypros the maidens actually sacrifice their virginity on the shore or in the sanctuary of the Paphian Aphrodite, in Troy symbolically, by bathing in the river Skamandros.

***) Bakchai, v. 375. "Would that I could come to Cyprus, island of Aphrodite, where the witching Loves wait for mortals, and to Paphos, where the hundred-mouthed streams of the wild river make fruitful the land, though showers there are none. Thither, where is the most lovely Pierian dwelling of the Muses, the sacred slope of Olympos, thither bring me, o Bromios. Bromios, divine Leader of the Bacchic dance. There are the Graces, there is Love-longing, there may the Bacchantes revel in sacred frenzy."—The description corresponds closely with the actual spot. The river, which flows all the year round, although less abundantly in summer than in winter,

by Movers (Vol. I cp. the Index, sub v. Dionysos) it is quite evident that Dionysos was by the various Syrian tribes in later times identified with the Fire-god Moloch. The discoveries in Kypros, and the early appearance of the Greeks on the scene, go far to prove that Kypros was largely concerned in the formation of this composite Aryan and Semitic divine type, perhaps even originated it.

The Adonia, the festivals of Aphrodite, Ariadne and Persephone, as they were celebrated at Amathus in an orgiastic and sensual manner, are as much akin to Dionysos and Kybele as to Aphrodite. The Kyprian festivals to Rešef-Apollo too, contain as many Dionysiac and Aphrodisiac elements as the festivals in the Aphrodite groves. As in Delphi, Apollo is fused with Dionysos, becomes Kisseus or Kyssaios.°) It is true that in the groves a division of sexes takes place, as we learn from the

is dammed at a considerable distance from the mouth, and its waters are used to irrigate and fertilize a large extent of country belonging to villagers or larger proprietors (mostly rich Turks), so that the epithet "hundred-mouthed," may really be understood literally. The βάρβαρος ποταμός of Euripides (Kirchhoff's edition) can only mean the river Bokaros, (so too in the older editions of Euripides) which rises on Mount Troodos, the Olympos and Helikon of the Kyprian Greeks, and flows into the sea near Paphos. In this well watered corn-land by the sea were celebrated Dionysia, Aphrodisia and Adonia; the orgiastic fury of Dionysos was blended with the sensual observances of Aphrodite. Even the name Bokaros is significant, and is easily explained by local and climatic conditions. Βώκαρος is, I think, a form of Βοΐκαιρος i. e. ox-time. In winter or spring the river became a raging bull, causing the most dreadful devastation, and is still dreaded at the present day, for often after a sudden fall of rain the stream becomes so swollen that horses cannot ford it even by swimming, or if it is passable at all, the large boulders in the bed make the crossing dangerous. Herr W. Dörpfeld and I can testify to these facts from personal experience, for in the winter at the beginning of 1890, on our journey from New Paphos to Old Paphos, we had to ride through the Bokaros in flood. At that time of year, when the river becomes a raging bull, now tearing down pieces of soil, now throwing them up, many of the most fruitful fields are laid waste by the mud and pebbles, which are washed up over them, while other tracts are completely carried away. At the mouth of the Bokaros and other streams, broad yellow streams are distinguishable in the sea to some considerable distance. But the benefits conferred by the river far outweigh the destruction it brings. Hence this Bull-season is a καλός καιρός, a good season, in which sheep and cattle bring forth their young. It is the time of abundance, of green grass and bright flowers, of young lambs and calves. It is possible that this Bokaros, this river-god, is to be regarded as the personification of vegetable and animal fertility, i. e. as a god of spring, like the Adonis river of Byblos when it ran red, at the time of the spring Adonia. Βώκαρος, the spring, among the Troezenians, was probably thus named for a similar reason. (Cp. Pape, "Wörterbuch griechischer Eigennamen"). For the Bull-Dionysos cp. F. Wieseler's paper (Nachrichten v. d. Königl. Gesellsch. d. Wissenschaften zu Göttingen, 1891, p. 367–388).

°) On p. 5 we learn from Inscription no. 9 that there was a three-yearly festival in the Apollo grove at Voni (no. 2 on the list). A Dionysiac Thiasos was celebrated in three consecutive years, and in it the chief function consisted in the slaughter of animals (sheep). The first Thiasos took place in the month of feasting, Gorpiaios (in which fell also in Amathus the feasts of Ariadne, Aphrodite, Persephone and Adonis (cf. p. 127). The third Thiasos seems to have been peculiarly orgiastic in character; possibly there were ivy-wreaths, or ivy-men (τῶν Κισάων). The ivy-wreaths and myrtle-twigs were called, like them, Βάκχοι. The divinity himself was present in the ivy. The ivy-men, Κισάοι, would form an analogy to the Διόνυσος Κίσσος in Acharnai.—In one and the same precinct at Voni, Apollo appears first as soothsayer and purifier (Plate XL, 3), then with a roe or a young stag as protector of wild animals (Plate XLII, 1 and 2), and lastly with Zeus, in combination with the roll of writing, the Eagle and the Nike (XL, 1, 2, 4 and 5). In his retinue inspired as by Dionysos, appear Maenads and Satyrs blowing the double flute (XLII, 3 and 6). The god leans on a sacred pillar, which is ornamented with a Silenus' head (no illustration). Among the numerous votive inscriptions to Apollo there is one dedicated by a woman to Artemis (p. 5 no. 8) who must therefore have been worshipped there in a subsidiary degree. Among hundreds of votive gifts from men alone, there was found a small terracotta representing Artemis. The only votive bronze, which lay in the stratum of ashes and bones near the Thiasos inscription, represents a stag. A draped goddess with her hands on her breast, who might be Artemis or Aphrodite, was found among the fragment of large statues, and probably had been applied as ornament to one of the pillars on which the statues, which are more than life-size, rested. A piece of a lion's claw from a nearly life-size stone image, and a fragment of a Sphinx statue are, with the exception

excavation.°) The Apollo cults assume local peculiarities in different places. Aphrodite groves could be roughly distinguished from Artemis or Athene groves or heights. But there were some precincts, in which the compound male-female divinity of his own accord called Rešef-Apollo and his retinue to share the honours of the Astarte-Aphrodite grove, and vice versa**); or both divinities, alone or in conjunction with others, appear from the beginning as σύμβωμοι in a large precinct. Although human sacrifice was no longer practised here in Kypros, yet animals were torn asunder in the orgiastic dances, and their flesh was swallowed raw. The Korybantes danced their special Kyprian armed dance,***) called here not Pyrrhric, but Prylis. All kinds of indecent dances were performed, mostly ring-dances,†) and a special dance in honour of Aphrodite, called Ἀφροδίτης γοναί. These festivals were usually celebrated at night, and the maidens used to offer their virginity to the goddess by giving themselves up to strangers, and thus earn a wedding dowry from the goddess. This custom was transmitted from the Kyprians to the Carthaginians and Etrurians. As in the rural Dionysia at Argos and in Rhodes, the Phallos was carried round, the procession being called φαλλοφορία, the accompanying dance ᾀλλικὸν ἐπὶ Διονύσῳ, and the songs φαλλικά, so in Kypros their were similar feasts and processions, holding an even more important place. The Phallos-cultus in connection with the Kyprian Aphrodite is well known from literary sources, although by a strange accident no evidence of it is as yet to be found in the Aphrodite groves. We have already seen that in the Tanit-Artemis-Kybele-Attis groves (cf. p. 128 and 129) the amputated Phalloi (Pl. LXVIII, 8—10) held an important place in cultus. I pointed out that this practice is connected with the myth of the castration of Attis. Hogarth found at Amargetti (no. 58 of our list), a wide-spread Dionysiac Phallos-cultus, combined with obscene gesture and vine worship. It is true that according to the evidence of some inscriptions, Apollo was worshipped there in the special aspect of Apollo Melanthios, but in the votive inscriptions here and in Kition the name of a god or hero, Opaon, or Opaon Melanthios, occurs much more frequently. It is not impossible that this Opaon is merely Dionysos in disguise.†) Where could the mummeries in which men appeared in women's garments

of the votive stag, the only traces of animals or fabulous beings. In conjunction with Apollo Adonis was specially worshipped. We found not only a number of figures of the crouching temple-attendant (Pl. XXXIII, figs. 1 and 2), but also a large statue, at the left side, of which stands the Adonis-child. The head of the latter figure is missing (Plate XLI, fig. 8). (For details cf. Plates XL—XLII.)

*) In the Tanit-Artemis-Kybele grove at Achna (No. 1) are found female draped figures almost exclusively. The only exception is a draped figure of Apollo or his priest (motive as in Plate XL, 3). In the Rešef-Apollo grove at Voni (No. 2) are only male figures with two exceptions, for which compare the preceding note. In the Astarte-Aphrodite precinct at Dali are only female figures, with one exception, a small male bearded mask (Plate LII, 20) &c.

**) Rešef-Apollo and Astarte Aphrodite as appear as Paredroi in Amathus, (No. 43 on the list), in Limniti, (No. 52 on the list, Plate XLIV—XLVII).

***) Bearded men dance round a bearded flute-player in the precinct of Astarte-Aphrodite near Katydata-Linu (No. 53 on the list, Plate XVII, 5).

†) In Plate CXXVIII, 4, 5, 6 we see on Kyprian cylinders belonging to the second, or, more probably the third century B. C., three female (?) figures, one (No. 5) nude, two, (Nos. 4 and 6), draped, dancing round the sacred symbols or sacrificial animals, the constellations, the sacred tree and ox-heads. Two bronze Kylikes, found in the cave of Zeus at Gortyna in Crete and at Olympia, and probably manufactured in Kypros, are decorated with a representation of the rhythmic dance, like the bronze kylix of Idalion. (CXXX = p. 50, fig. 49). On the last-named cup, the dance is performed in a sacred grove; I have added (Pl. CXXX, 2) the picture of an Attic kylix. Here Maenads are dancing round Dionysos Dendrites and his altar. (Cp. Plates CXXVII—CXXXII).

††) Cp. pp. 129 and 215.

and women in men's have originated, if not at Amathus in the cultus of the bearded Aphrodite, Dionysos, and Aphrodite-Ariadne? The custom must have first come to Argos and Athens, from Amathus, but it is doubtful whether this is its oldest source, or whether it came originally from the worship of Kybele and Sandon in Asia Minor, or of Atargatis and Hadad in Heliopolis.

Amathus may have originated the custom, or have been the first place which received it from the East. Or again the custom may have arisen independently in different places. The terra-cotta from Kition seems to have reference to such a disguise (Plate CCVIII, 4.) It may possibly have come from the precinct of Tanit-Artemis, Kybele-Paralia (No. 7 on the list), where the Ashera inscription (cf. p. 148) was found, and where Demeter-Persephone elements are not to be traced. A man and a woman, half nude and with a grin on their faces, walk along arm in arm and imitate Eros and Psyche or Adonis and Aphrodite. As a pendant to this we may mention a small group of rather obscene character (Fig. 180), of Etruscan origin. It represents a nude couple seated side by side, a bearded man or god, and a goddess. Both wear crowns (cp. the crouching Bes-Ptah-

Fig. 180.

Patäke figure made of parti-coloured glazed clay*) (Plate LXVII, 1 a and b) (cf. Plate CCVIII, 2 and 3). A similar comic group, representing a small satyr-like man attempting to seize a veiled woman, who repulses him (Figure from a grave at Kurion CCVIII, 1) seems to have reference to a similar custom. The terra-cotta statuettes of comic actors (CCVIII, 5--8) were found, it seems, on the sacred wooded height dedicated by inscriptions to Artemis-Paralia, on the shore between the salt lake and the sea (No 7 on the list). These caricatures, comic figures of actors and groups, belong to the musical and dramatic aspects of Dionysos, who no doubt shared in this cultus. The remarkable fusion on this site (at least in later times) of Artemis-Kybele, Demeter-Persephone and Astarte-Aphrodite is shewn by a votive offering bearing in late Greek characters a dedication to Artemis-Paralia, which must certainly have been deposited in this precinct. It is a truncated cone, bearing in relief representations of the female pudendum and of a closed sea-shell. The votive inscription is written on the lower part of the cone, to left and right.**)

We have already seen Dionysus, his Satyrs and Sileni, in the rout of Apollo, and more than once we have given some description of the horned family of Centaurs. According to the same authority, Nonnus, it is from the country of Apollo Hylates that these horned recruits come to join the army of Bacchus. Once more therefore do we find the Centaurs linked with Zeus Aphrodite, Dionysus and Apollo. The images of these Centaurs, together with those of Dionysus, Herakles Baal-Hammon, Adonis, the Satyrs and Sileni, are deposited in the groves, on the heights and by the altars, where Rešef-Apollo is venerated as the supreme God. In countless holy places, all those gods heroes, and demons combine to form the train of this supreme god, their lord and master.

Above***) I touched upon the tree Dionysus, the Dionysus ἔνδενδρος of the Boeotians. It would

---

*) From these groups which combine the two sexes we must distinguish the groups of two women which must be interpreted as Demeter and Persephone. (Plate CCV, 1 and A). In the next section, on the goddesses, I shall return to this subject.

**) *ΑΡΤΕΜΙΔΙ ΠΑΡΑΛΙΑ ΑΠΕΛΛΗϹ ΑΝΕΘΗΚΕ* A. P. di Cesnola, "Salaminia," p. 95, 96 and Fig. 80.

***) Cp. p. 109 above and Pl. LXXV, 5.

seem that this tree god also, worshipped like the Hebrew Ashera*) under the form of a post, was provided with a mask and with drapery. To hang masks on trees or posts was a favourite act of homage to Dionysus. These primitive Greek worships came face to face in Cyprus with the equally primitive worships of the Hebrews. In the course of my own excavations I found in two instances (Sites 3 and 36, both at Idalion) evidences of this custom of hanging up masks. In the latter case there seems to have been no sanctuary apart from the tree to which the masks were attached. Tubbs found numbers of human masks of life size and under (once, in all probability, suspended from trees) in the grove of Apollo and Aphrodite at Limniti (site 52), the same grove, in the votive area of which hundreds of figures of horned centaurs had stood. On one of the Salamis sites (No. 66) were found numerous masks of oxen or cows, also, doubtless, once hung on trees. The principal deities worshipped as σύμβωμοι in this temenos must have been Artemis and Apollo, Dionysus occupying the third place. The warriors with shields and peaked caps, the chariots and cars unearthed here, occur as a rule in sanctuaries of Apollo; the female figures which came to light, some holding stags and others wearing crowns adorned with rows of griffins and rosettes, are in Kypros the property of a deity, whom we find to be a combination of Artemis-Kybele and Demeter-Persephone. The masks of animals point to Dionysus. The same triad, Apollo, Artemis and Dionysus, meet us again at Pyla (site 27), and here again Apollo under the title of Magilios (this we learn from the inscribed dedications) occupies the place of honour. By the side of figures of Apollo and one of Artemis there were here found figures of Pan, one ithyphallic, and numerous groups of women dancing round cypresses &c.**) A large number of the figures were acquired from the discoverer, H. Lang, by A. P. di Cesnola, and seven of them are represented in his Atlas.***)

The double axe, the civic arms of Tenedos, is peculiarly associated with the worship of Dionysus. We see this double axe on the gold foil with the bull's head from Mykenae (Pl. XCIV, 7).†) On the fragment of a vase from Rhodus (Pl. CIV, 1) the men who alternate with the Centaurs hold double axes. We find them in Cyprus as implements of war and peace (p. 47, fig. 50; p. 62, fig. 71). One of the Cyprian examples is a real double axe of bronze, and had been dedicated to the Idalian Anat-Athene in her sanctuary on the Akropolis of Idalion. From the Cyprian Zeus Labranios,††) the counterpart of the Carian Zeus Labrandeus, his daughter Athene and his many sons, the horned Centaurs, and the companions and ministers of Dionysus and Apollo, receive the double axe. It is Furtwängler's opinion ("Bronzefunde von Olympia", p. 35) that numerous small votive axes of bronze found at Olympia beside the altars of the gods, and at a great depth, point to a connection with the

---

*) Voigt in Roscher's Lexikon I, 1047. He explains the Theban Dionysos Perikionios as the ivy climbing round a column. Cp. the Thiasos inscription p. 254 above. The Theban image of Dionysos Kadmos was a piece of wood (Pausanias IX, 12, 4.)

**) "Ceccaldi", "Monuments antiques de Chypre", p. 21.

***) Pl. CXVII, 848—854. In style, technique, design size and execution they so exactly resemble our figures from Akhna and Pharangas (sites 3 and 14), that all must have been produced at the same time in the same factory. This factory must also have produced a large number of the figures from the Salamis cistern site (No. 66 in the list). For Tubbs, in his mention of there latter, cites as exact parallels to them certain Cyprian figures in the British Museum which can only be those I excavated for Sir C. Newton in 1882 and saw exhibited in the Museum in 1884.

†) Cp. also, for the double axe, Plates CXXVII. 3; CXXXVI; CXXXVII, 6 and the description.

††) Cp. p. 19, site 46.

East and possibly with Cyprus. The sole parallel, at least, which he was able to cite for this usage of dedicating bronze axes was a Cyprian one. The thirteen small double axes which Döll saw in Cyprus in the Cesnola collection (nos. 7685—7697), erroneously (like the terra-cotta horsemen) stated to come from Alambra, come, almost certainly, from the neighbouring Idalion, and may very well, like the large double axe (CXXXVI, 4), have been found with in the precinct of Anat-Athene.

The Naxian Ariadne myth carried us from Naxos to Amathus in Cyprus. Another link is the dolphin, still in southern seas the welcome companion of weary mariners, and in ancient times the symbol of divine escort and of happy voyage. When the Tyrrhenian pirates, who had charged them-selves to carry to Naxos the youthful Dinoysus, violated their trust, the angry god changed them into dolphins. On Kyprian coins the dolphin is by no means rare (e. g. Pl. CXCII, 7 = Six VI, 12 a coin of King Nikokles of Salamis, about 374—368 B. C.). Two Cyprian monuments representing dolphins exist in the collection of E. Konstantinides at Nicosia. One is a small votive bronze dolphin. The other, a large work in marble, was procured by me in Larnaka where it had been found in the neighbourhood of the salt lake (i. e. in the neighbourhood of the Artemis grove, no. 7 in my list). The steps leading up to a sanctuary (the sanctuary itself is missing) are here represented. The steps are flanked by two huge dolphins, the symbols of Dionysus, the god to whom the little sanctuary was consecrated.

Lastly, I have to mention two Greek inscriptions, one from Salamis, the other from Old-Paphos.*) In both we find mention of the Dionysiac artists, ·companies of actors who were in the service of the god and performed at his festivals. Taken together with the passage of Euripides and other literary evidence, these inscriptions show that, from the 5ᵗʰ century B. C. onwards until Roman times, the worship of Dionysus, associated always with that of Aphrodite, was widely diffused in the island; and we are justified in dating back its origins to times coeval with its birth in Greece and other regions where it gained as strong a foothold. But we have no example from Cyprus of old anthropomorphic cultus-images, representing Dionysus as such in character and costume, uncontaminated by the individualities of other gods. It would seem that for long he was worshipped here in the form of an undraped post or pillar; and it is at the same time certain that his worship never here came to be so prominent as those of Aphrodite and Apollo. It is only in Hellenistic and Roman times that we first meet in Cyprus with the god of the vine in anthropomorphic form, either alone or as the nursling of a Satyr. A terra-cotta group of the Satyr holding the young Dionysus was found by me in a tomb at Kurion. Hard by, in a Graeco-Roman tomb of the same necropolis, I found the very

*) 1) Engel, "Kypros" I, p. 97 = CI b. 2619, from Salamis.

'Ολυμπιάδα τ[ὴν τοῦ δεῖνος, γυναῖκα δὲ
Θεοδώρου τοῦ [δεῖνος, τοῦ συγγενοῦς τοῦ
βασιλέως τοῦ στ[ρατηγοῦ καὶ ναυάρχου
καὶ ἀρχιερέως το[ῦ] κ[α]τ[ὰ
Κύπρον, γραμματ[έως τῶν περὶ τὸν Διόνυσον
τεχνιτ[ῶ]ν.

2) Ibid. p. 134 = CIG, 2620, from Paphos.

Ἀφροδίτη Παφίᾳ ἡ πόλις Παφίων Κάλλιππον Καλλίπ[π]ου δὶς γραμματεύσαντα τῆς βουλῆς καὶ τοῦ δήμου καὶ ἀρχι[ερεύ]οντα τῆς πόλεως καὶ τῶν περὶ τὸν Δ[ι]όνυσον καὶ θεοὺς Εὐερ[γέ]τας τεχνιτῶν, τ[ὸν] γραμματέα τῆς π[όλεως] γ[υμνασι]αρχήσαντα καλῶς τὸ . . sc. ἔτος

interesting glass covers with hand paintings which are reproduced in colours on Pl. LXVI, 1—6.*) They show how strong was the tendency in this late period, as in an earlier, to combine the Aphroditic and Erotic with the Dionysiac. On nos. 1 and 3 stands Aphrodite in the well-known attitude of the Medicean Venus. On no. 4 is painted a winged Eros, holding, like Dionysus, a bunch of grapes. On no. 6 a draped figure (perhaps the youthful Dionysus) holds such a bunch in either hand. The figure on no. 5, the most graceful of all, may be either a child Bacchus or a Psyche of tender years. The Eros of Plate CXCVIII, 2 (p. 220 above) also combines Erotic and Dionysiac elements Drunk with wine and love, he has cushioned himself on a wine-skin, the proper couch of the child Dionysus. After a certain date Love had no privilege denied to him; and he has allowed himself this particular liberty with all the easier conscience, in that his trade has always required the cooperation of the wine god. As I have above indicated, there is no trace of the Greek Minotaur in Kypros. Below I reproduce, word for word, a brief study communicated to me by Herr Hubert Schmidt on this subject. It would appear from this that, at least, the Minotaur was adopted at an early date by Oriental Ionic Art.

One word on the Europa myth and the Zeus-bull which link Crete with Tyre. Certain Cyprian coins show a female figure riding on a bull, and Luynes has recognised Europa. Another type shows a female figure (regarded by Six as Aphrodite) riding on a ram. Among the prochoi excavated by me at Poli tis Khrysokhou, are some which have spouts attached, consisting of figures of women grasping a bull's head by one or both of the horns (Pl. LXIV, 5 = CLXXIX, 1). Are these rudiments of the figures of Europa, holding on to the horns of the bull Zeus as he bears her from Tyre to Crete or not? It is possibly but not necessarily so. "Prochoi" of this kind have usually for spouts either bulls' head alone or a seated, (on later examples erect) figure of a woman pouring water from a miniature "prochus" **). It is excessively probable that some potter combined the two motives, giving the seated feminine figure a bull's head to hold in the place of her water-can.

Europa picking flowers on the shore of Sidon or Tyre encounters Zeus under the form of a bull; in Crete their nuptial couch is spread under a plane tree. Besides the bull type on the Cretan coins we have the type of Europa sitting up in the plane tree. One of these Gortynian coins is figured on Pl. LXXXIII, 8, and described above in our chapter on tree-worship. Europa in Crete is therefore not only a moon-goddess, but is at the same time a goddess of the earth and of vegetation.***) She also, like Io, has been interpreted as a Demeter heroine.†)

The myth of Io-Argos must also have been carried to Kypros by the Argives at an early date. On the other hand, as I have had already occasion to point out, the Greeks employed, for their Argos type, oriental representations of many-headed, many-faced or many-eyed demons. In view of the extent to which moon-worship prevailed in Kypros, where more than one feminine divinity represents the moon, it is by no means beyond the bounds of possibility that we shall some day come across clearer traces here of the Argive Io.

---

*) A much more perfect glass cover, from a Salaminian tomb similar to Pl. LXVI 1 and 3, is represented in Cesnola's "Salaminia", p. 173, fig. 159; a glass cover from a tomb at Old Paphos resembling LXVI, 4 is represented in the Journal of Hellenic Studies, 1888. p. 271.

**) Cp. Pl. LXIV, 4—7; CLXXVII, 3; CLXXIX, 2 and 3; CLXXX, 4; CLXXXI.

***) Cp. Roscher's Mythol. Lexikon; col. 1418.

†) Ibidem.

For the following remarks on the Greek Minotaur I am indebted to the kindness of Mr. H. Schmidt, "The figure of the Minotaur, as a type, must be stripped of its mythical import, and classed among the most ancient compound forms of Greek Art". Furtwängler (Olympia IV, "Die Bronzen", p. 89) stated the general significance of this type, and O. Wulff ("Zur Theseussage", Dorpat 1892, p. 8 ff. and 159) has subsequently, but independently, attempted to justify in detail a like conception. The history of the Minotaur is very much the same as that of other compound beings in Greek art, e. g. the Centaurs and Gorgons; originally they carried to the popular mind the significance of demonic powers; then, as the epos, springing into vigorous life, began to exercise its influence on the arts of design, the artists, in order to find appropriate graphic expression for the productions of poetic fancy, or for those creations of popular fancy which had passed into epic poetry, went naturally to that repertory of design which had descended to them from pre-epic times. As a fact, we find not only Centaurs and their variants apart from Herakles or the Lapithae, and Gorgons apart from Perseus; but Minotaurs standing in no connection with the Theseus legend. Wulff cites as examples two Etruscan bronzes (Inghirami Mon. Etr. III plates 31 and 35 = Micali "Storia" pl. XXXI). I have grave doubts whether the figure on the well-known Etruscans bucchero vase (Micali pl. XXII = Mus Chius. 1 pl. 34) is, as Wulff thinks, really a bull-man. The head bears no resemblance to a bull's, the most characteristic feature, the horns, being absent. The appendages on the upper part of the head can only be ears, Wulff rightly mentions as analogous the ass-headed figures on Mykenaean mural paintings (Ἐφ. ἀρχ. 1887, pl. 10) and other compound creatures on island stones (Furtwängler and Löschke, Myk. vas. Pl. E, nos. 25 and 32; Ἐφ. ἀρχ. 1888, pl. 10, nos. 33*), 41) and on older classes of vases (Longperier Mus. Nap. III. pl. IX).

The original significance of the Minotaur has also survived on the oldest coins of Knossos in Crete (of the period 600—431 B. C : cp. Wulff p. 10) where it had the value of a kind of cultus-symbol. It is of course impossible to fix the date at which it first came to be regarded as the bull of Minos in the sense of the myth.

Whether this type, like other compound creatures, already formed part of the Mykenaean repertory, would seem, from what I have said, to be doubtful. It had certainly established for itself a position in oriental Ionic Art. Both the Etruscan bronzes and the oldest representations of the exploit of Theseus on products of oriental-Greek art point to this (see Wulff p. 15)".

---

*) "I cannot, however, agree with Wulff (p. 9) in interpreting the design on this Mykenaean stone as a man-bull. There is no analogy for what he styles horns; the upper part of the skull is too round, the eyes are placed too close together. The stone no. 8 shows in admirable execution the look of a bull's head when viewed en face. We cannot make an exception, for the very reason that bull's heads and bulls are very common in Mykenaean art, and are always depicted with great truth to nature. Besides this, the claws are those of a beast of prey, and as a fact the head is more like that of a tiger or panther (not a lion; cp. the animals' heads on the Polledrara hydria, Micali, Mon. ined., Pl. IV). The figure on the gem is therefore a creature half man and half a beast of prey.

III. The principal feminine deities and demons of Cyprus, and some of their counterparts in other lands.

In this section I will deal with the principal feminine, in the section which follows with the principal masculine divinities. I give the goddesses the precedence, because from the outset their power is greater than that of the gods, as regards both the cults and the mythical history of the island. Astarte-Aphrodite is their sovereign. While in Greece the establishment of the idea of a senate of deities resulted in each deity being differentiated with some precision, in Kypros the different deities become merged with a facility unexampled in the non-Hellenic East and Egypt. Originally the state of matters on the island was very simple. When the transition from aniconic worship to anthropomorphic image-worship took place (a transition never, however, fully accomplished until the introduction of Christianity) the only idols carved or worshipped were the columnar or tabular idols of a single goddess. (Pl. LXXXVI, p. 33, fig. 29, and others.) On the first appearance of idols of true human form we can distinguish two types, both feminine and nude (p. 34, figs. 31 and 32), but one always bird-faced (fig. 32).[e]) Next, by the side of these two types, we encounter the idol of the Hermaphrodite god (Pl. XXXVI, 1, 4, 10), and that of the pair of deities male and female, the latter still of very rare occurrence in the Copper-Bronze Period. (Pl. CLXX, 13e.) From the one original type of the feminine deity, with both hands on her breasts, three distinct goddesses, worshipped (as inscriptions testify) under distinct names and in separate sanctuaries, are derived. There is first and foremost Astarte-Aphrodite; then comes Tanit-Artemis, and then Anat-Athene.[**]) All the deities, both male and female, venerated in Cyprus, have grown by process of differentiation from one original goddess. Of course this statement does not reckon with the importations from other lands, in very early times, of idols of deities of either sex. Together with the goddesses I will discuss (without any hope, however, of approaching to comprehensive treatment) the principal demons, winged creatures, and monsters of female sex.

Polydaemonism and polytheism are things almost indissociable from each other.

1. Astarte-Aphrodite.

a) The stone cylinder of this goddess, and her oldest anthropomorphic idols in the Copper-Bronze Period.

Let us, in our treatment of this question, start from Aphrodite, the golden-haired goddess of love. No two things can be, it seems, more diverse than the Cnidian Aphrodite of Praxiteles and the stone fetish in the form of a meteoric cone,[***]) which still in Roman times was, in the sanctuary of Paphos, venerated as the embodiment of Aphrodite-Astarte. At first the object of worship, the

---

*) Cp. the *Κουροτρόφος*, p. 203 above.

**) I do not of course mean by this that no other goddesses (e. g. Hera, Demeter &c.) were worshipped in Kypros, or are mentioned in inscriptions. I am here giving a general outline sketch, and adhering, as far as possible, to my design of limiting my review to the oldest periods.

***) Roscher's Mythol. Lexikon, col. 395.

symbol of the goddess, was a meteoric stone of irregular shape, fallen from heaven. In process of time the original aërolith was either cut into a regular conic form, or replaced by a conic stone. The head-like appendage and the rudimentary arms, which we see on certain Paphian coins, are symptoms of still further modification, dating from a time when iconic worship was strong enough to demand concessions to its spirit *).

The English excavations at Paphos (1888) did not result in the discovery of the celebrated cone of Aphrodite. **) But in the South chamber (see Pl. IX) a little marble cone was discovered, evidently a small dedicatory copy of the great cone. In no Cyprian Aphrodite sanctuary has a large stone cone yet been discovered. But I think that both in the sanctuary of the divine couple Astarte-Mikal on the acropolis of Kition (no. 9 in my list; plan on Pl. CCI) and in that of Aphrodite-Astarte at Idalion (no. 3 in my list, plan on Pl. VII d¹—d²) I have been successful in determining the spot on which the large cone stood. To one approaching the temenos from the North (Idalion, no. 3) or from the North-East (Kition no. 9) the cone of the goddess was visible through the gate, standing on a large stone substructure in the court of votive offerings.***) Accordingly on Pl. LVI, I have had drawn standing on this existing substructure a conic pillar of the form known to us from the coins of Byblos and Paphos (Pl. LXXXII, 7, 8 and Pl. LXXXIII, 22) and resembling the Esmun-Adonis stele (Pl. LXXX, 5). Above on p. 29 in discussing the designs of holy trees on Cyprian seal cylinders, figs. 14—21, I stated that both Sayce and Ménant regard them as idols of the Paphian goddess (cp. also pages 65 and 85, Pl. LXXIX,10 &c), that is to say stone cones of the goddess. On pages 140 ff, in the section on the Ashera, I showed that there is better reason for seeing in these idols the holy post or tree, the Ashera. It is far more probable that on the scarab figured on p. 57 (fig. 54) we see a representation of the conic stone idol of the goddess, here of omphalos form and surmounted by the sun-disc, uraeus &c. From the facts (1) that old Paphos is a younger settlement than Amathus —both literary evidence and the comparative dates of the deposits excavated testify to this—(2) that at Amathus there is no demonstrable tract of stone worship, (3) that while designs of the holy tree are common on the cylinders and vases of the Copper-Bronze age, we find no examples of conic images at this early date, we may reasonably conclude that the stone cone was not the oldest form under which the national divinity was worshipped in Kypros. Homer speaks of the altar of Aphrodite at Paphos, but makes no mention of a cone, and Hesiod is already familiar with the goddess of love, the child of the surf. It would seem that the worship of the stone cone was introduced into Kypros in post-Homeric times by the agency of Phoenician-Semitic influence, and at a time when anthropomorphic idols had for long been carved, moulded and adored. While quantities of terracotta board-idols and cylindrical idols (including some post-idols) are found together with the cylinders, no conic fetish occurs at this early date, and even at the end of the Bronze Period it is impossible to point to a single anthropomorphic idol, which has in it anything of the elements of a

---

*) I have dealt with this subject in extenso above, in discussing the Masseboth and Chammanim.

**) Journal of Hellenic Studies, 1888, pp. 22 and 194.

***) Such was also the case at Old Paphos, as the coins and the plan of the temple, as determined by the English excavators, show (cp. our Pl. IX). In Roman times the entrance was certainly from the East, facing the rising sun. The substructures supporting the great pillars of the door were also found. Through the door, as we see on the coins of Paphos and Byblos, the cone of Aphrodite was visible. For further details see the description of the Plates.

cone. As nothing can be easier to form than a simple cone, we should certainly, had the cone been then an object of worship, have found representations of it in the course of our very extensive excavations in strata of the Pre-Graeco-Phoenician Copper-Bronze Period. The only seeming attempts to represent cones meet us on two seal-cylinders. One is a cylinder found during my residence in Cypros, and seen by Dümmler and myself; the other (Salaminia p 128, fig. 118 = our Plates LXIX, 50 and CXXI, 4) had been previously acquired by A. P. di Cesnola. In both cases we see an object resembling an hour-glass, composed of two cones, placed in inverse positions. The horizontal line traversing the point of contact of the two cones shows that we have here to do with representations of wooden erections—Asheroth. In the Graeco-Phoenician period the case is quite different.

To return to the temenos of Astarte-Aphrodite at Idalion (No. 3 in the list)—it is true that I found no simple cone here, but among the anthropomorphic terracotta statuettes were not a few consisting of cones or columns with the head, breasts, and arms, of a woman attached. (Pl. L, 6; LI, 6, 8, 9). The most carefully executed example (L, 6) represents either the goddess herself in the act of conferring blessing, or the high-priestess of the sanctuary as her representative. °) Another terracotta, Pl. XXXVII, 9, shows us again an Astarte-Aphrodite composed of an anthropomorphic bust rising from a cone. The goddess is in this case characterised as the fruitful mother and nurse by the child she clasps to her bosom, and as the water-goddess, the source of fertility, by the pitcher she carries on her head. The adoration of Aphrodite under the form of a stone cone, is, except in Cyprus, localised only among Semitic peoples (especially the Phoenicians at Byblos, Pl. LXXII, 7), and no example of a conic Aphrodite occurs in Greece. We find, however, in Athens a certain Aphrodite, the "oldest of the Moirae" represented under the form of a quadrangular term. The cultus of this Aphrodite is as certainly of Cyprian origin as those of the Aphrodite ἐν κήποις, the Aphrodite ἐν Καλάμοις, the Aphrodite πάνδημος. The worship of Eros at Thespiae under the form of an old unhewn stone may also be derived from Cyprus. The existence of many other close relationships between Boeotian and Kyprian worships would seem to favour the hypothesis that in this case the stone fetish of the mother has been transferred to her son.

The oldest anthropomorphic idols of Astarte-Aphrodite were carved wooden idols of tabular form. Terracotta copies of such, dating from a very remote period, are represented on Pl. XXXVI, 3 °°), Pl. XXXVII, 7 (here with the child) and Pl. LXXXVI ***). These board-idols, which are in very nearly all cases draped,†) seem, in part at least, to date from a period anterior to Babylonio-Assyrian influence. It is not yet known with any certainly how the type reached Kypros. My own opinion is that it originated in the island.

---

*) Cp. with this an almost identical terracotta figure in Perrot III, p. 563, fig. 384. The terracotta LI, 9 is repeated on Pl. XXXVII, no. 3. The mother holds the child (Adonis-Pygmalion?). Pl. LI, 8 is a figure beating the tympanon, Pl. LI, 6 a woman with uplifted arms, of very rude workmanship.

**) Pl. LXXIV, 7. Cp. Cp. also section on the Κουροτρόφος p. 203 above.

***) For details see the Description of the Plates. As regards the idol LXXXVI, 2, cp. what I have said on p. 192 regarding the images of the sun.

†) A solitary apparent exception is the idol LXXXVI, 4, possibly undraped. All the others have indications of drapery. Cp. fig. 29 and 30 on p. 33. Fig. 30 is a back view of the idol of which Pl. LXXXVI, 7 gives us a front view. Below in dealing of Tanit-Artemis I will speak of an ancient Babylonian goddess, always represented as draped, whom Ed. Meyer figures and describes in Roscher's Mythol. Lexikon, col. 647 as the "draped Babylonian Astarte." Tanit-Artemis is an outgrowth of the Baalit, the armed Anat-Athene an outgrowth of the nude Astarte-Aphrodite.

We have contrasted the stone fetish adored at Paphos until paganism was finally extinguished by Christianity with the developed Greek type of Aphrodite. Scarcely less striking is the contrast between the oldest Kyprian nude idols of the goddess (p. 34 figs. 31 and 32 and Pl. XXXVII, 6) and the beautiful nude statues of Aphrodite chiselled by the hands of Praxiteles and Scopas. But nevertheless, there can be no doubt that a historical connexion here subsists. The type of the nude Aphrodite was derived by the Greeks from the East through Kypros. The process of development took nearly 2000 years to accomplish, but most of these Kyprian idols of Nana-Ištar-Astarte-Aphrodite belong to the period 1500—1000 B C and are found in company with Mykenaean vases*). In the same strata of discovery occur imported Egyptian scarabs of the New Empire, and what is most important, Babylonio-Assyrian inscribed cylinders, which must belong to this period. The oldest examples of these nude idols belong to finds of a later date, than the finds comprising the oldest imported Babylonian inscribed cylinders. A comparison of the idols with the nude, full-face representations of Ištar on Old-Babylonian seal cylinders leaves no room for doubt that the nude Ištar was the prototype of these early Kyprian idols, as well as of the Cycladean idols and the leaden idol from Hissarlik **) (Cp. the Old-Babylonian cylinders on Pl. XXXI, 1—4) ***). Ištar is here represented (Cp. also Pl. CXV, 5) as we read of her in the well-known hymn celebrating her descent into hell. She has put off all her clothing, and all her jewellery, except her necklaces and earrings, that she may start on her mission to the underworld to fetch the water of life, which will arouse her beloved Dusi from death. We see her as she was before she came to that last gate, at which she had to strip herself of her necklaces and earrings too. To write a history of the development of the Astarte-Aphrodite type in Cyprus is far beyond the scope of the present work. The sketch of this goddess in her capacity of a mother and of her place and progress as such in the history of Art given above on p. 203 may be taken as standing good for Kypros. Here we must content ourselves with noticing some few very marked Hebrew and Phoenician types.

In discussing these types we will also attempt to define, which anthropomorphic figures represent the immortal gods and which must be taken to be the portraits of ordinary mortals.

b) Mortals and Immortals; images of Astarte-Aphrodite and her priestess, servant, or sacrificant.

While it is particularly difficult in the older Graeco-Phoenician deposits to distinguish the images of the gods from those of ordinary mortals, this can be done with great ease in the Pre-Graeco-Phoenician Copper-Bronze period. In the oldest strata of all, as I have said, there are no representations of the human form at all, and anthropomorphic figures are quite the exception on the Old-Kyprian hand-made vases of red clay with reliefs, vases which are of much higher antiquity than the oldest relief-vases with human or quasi-human figures found in Rhodes and on Italian soil. The reliefs on the Kyprian vases consist on the one hand of symbols such as sun-discs, crescents, globules, rings, anchor-like figures, tree-branches, snakes, on the other of all kinds of quadrupeds and

---

*) The idol fig. 31 (p. 34) was found in the same tomb with the Mykenaean crater fig. 33. Cp. my observation in Furtwängler and Löschke's "Mykenische Vasen," p. 26, as to the occurrence of these idols of the Kyprian goddess in company with Mykenaean vases.

**) Cp. p. 147.

***) See the Description of this Plate.

the heads and horns of quadrupeds. During an experience of twelve years I have only met with one instance in which on a vase of this class a man-like demon (sex undeterminable) holding two animals heraldically grouped, is figured in relief. Unfortunately I can give no sketch of the fragment in question, which was found at Ayia Paraskevi, and is now in the possession of Mr. E. Konstantinides (Nicosia). The anthropomorphic images of the Copper-Bronze Period, board-shaped, post-shaped, or cylindrical, represent, with a few exceptions, divinities (p. 33—34, figs. 29—31; Plates XXXVI, 3, 4, 8, 10; XXXVII, 6, 7; LXXIV, 7; LXXXVI; CXLIX, 15 e (= CLXX, 13 e; CLXXII, 15 a and b, 18 a, 17 t; CLXXIII, 20 and 21 e, f, 23 b). Only one example excavated by myself, Pl. CLXXIII, 23 a, seems to represent a wailing woman, and this explains itself by the fact that female mourners formed part of the apparatus of the worship of the dead from the earliest times onwards. The figure seated on the jug (Pl. XXXVI, 6) will be regarded by many as non-sacral; but I see in it the Kyprian goddess set as a talisman on the vase, and bearing the same sacral significance as the pairs of doves and gods perched on the tetrapod Pl. CLXX, 13 e. All the images which appear before the transition to the Iron Period is accomplished, certainly represent not men, but gods conceived as anthropomorphic. But with the establishment of the Iron Age the circumstances change. We now meet with genre subjects, single figures and groups mingled indiscriminately with the idols and images of divinities. As we have seen, aniconic worships survived in Kypros down to the introduction of Christianity; we even saw how the orthodox church has adopted various fetish-worships, and kept them alive in all their individuality down to the present day. But a comprehensive review of the results of the excavations hitherto made in Cyprus warns us that we must be careful not to accentuate too much the prevalence and importance of aniconic worships here.*) It is just as much a mistake to pronounce off-hand all the draped and undraped anthropomorphic figures to be representations of ordinary men, as it is to see an Aphrodite in every figure of a woman lifting her skirt and pressing a flower to her breast.°**) A closer view tells us, as regards the figures found in the groves and on the holy hills of the Graeco-Phoenician Iron age, that although the votive statues, large and small, of private people, form the great majority, yet pronounced examples of the images of gods are not wanting. In the preceding Copper-Bronze Period, such images occur in quantities, and the representation of the human form in Kyprian Art starts from them. Figures like Pl. L, 4 are nothing but Graeco-Phoenician images of the Kyprian goddess. As the disciples of the Kyprian Schools of Art developed truer artistic feeling, and were empowered by their progress in technical ability to express better what they felt, they began to attempt to represent their chief goddess, the Kypris, in a more artistic manner, their essays, at first purely realistic and often actually hideous, ever gaining in grace. They started from the motive which had descended to them from the Bronze Age, the nude erect goddess with both hands pressed to her breasts. From figures like our 29, 31 and 32 (pages 33, 34) and Pl. CLXXII, 17 t grew figures like Pl. LV, 5, 6 and L, 4.°***) I scarcely think that any one will be bold enough to pronounce these

*) Cp. Renan, Revue archéol. 1879, (1), p. 321 ff.; Chanot, Gazette archéol., 1879, p. 187 ff.; Furtwängler "Bronzefunde in Olympia" (1880) p. 29.

**) Cp. Pl. XLIX, 1 and 6. Pl. CCIII and the Description. I recur to this question under the head of Tanit-Artemis.

***) This terracotta (L, 4) would, however, appear to be draped in some very light stuff. (Cp. the Description of the Plate). The edge of the dress seems to be visible on the neck. But the impression it gives when one first looks at it, is that it is nude.

statuettes, entirely nude, or clothed only with the rings and necklaces which some of them wear, to be votive statues of private women. Although at the Aphrodisia license was carried to some excess, yet things cannot have gone so far as to sanction or ordain the consecration to the goddess by women of nude statues of themselves. Literary and monumental tradition alike forbid us to entertain such an idea. In cases where private persons dedicate their own statues to a god, and describe them as such in the inscribed dedication, not only are the statues of women always draped, but in Cyprus those of men also. We must therefore absolutely concede that the nude female figures deposited in the holy places are representations of a goddess. This nude goddess is, in Cyprus, always Astarte-Aphrodite; for in the sanctuaries of Tanit-Artemis which I have excavated, or at least personally examined, I have scarcely found a single undraped figure. When the Kyprian figures are draped the question becomes more complicated, at times indeed quite insoluble.*) Very often it is only by means of certain attributes, which are never borne by private persons, and by means of the inscriptions that we can pronounce a particular statue to be either that of an immortal or of a mortal, as the case may be. Since the very beginnings of portraiture in Kypros, it was the custom to depict priests or priestesses, male or female sacrificants or temple-servants, in the costume and in the attitude of the god. Of this I can give convincing proof. Pl. XL, 1 and 4 are certainly representations of a deity who is a combination of Apollo and Zeus. In his right hand he holds the Apollinine holy-water sprinkler in the form of a bunch of myrtle, and the head is that of Apollo. On his left hand sits in the one case (no. 1 the figure grasping a roll of writing) the eagle, in the other the Nike of Zeus. I think no one will deny that in these life-size votive statues, excavated by myself, we must recognize divinities. But in the same sanctuary a whole number of priests of Apollo have dedicated their own portrait-statues, which represent them in the pose and costume, and with the attributes, of Apollo as a purifying god. The heads of these portrait-statues have not the features of Apollo, nor is the mode of dressing the hair his (as on Pl. XL, 1 and XLII, 1). They do not carry (like XL, 4 and 5) the Nike, nor the eagle (like XL, 2) nor the facon (like XLII, 1 and 2). The high priest wears, it is true, a laurel crown, like Apollo, and on the fourth finger of the left hand the temple signet-ring (Pl. XL, 3); in his left hand he carries the box of incense (Cesnola-Stern Pl. XXV)**), in his right hand the holy-water sprinkler (Pl. XL, 3). The inscription scratched on the dress of one of these statues is clear evidence that they represent priests and not the god. The name of the high priest whose statue is inscribed was Karys.***) He sat for his portrait to the sculptor in the attribute he took and the vestments he wore when he occupied Apollo's place in ritual functions. What this inscription demonstrates in the case of Rešef-Apollo holds good also for Astarte-

---

*) Cp. Furtwängler in Roscher's Mythol. Lexikon, cols. 408 and 409.

**) The motive of the draped statue XL, 3, the right hand holding a sprinkler, the drapery falling in identical folds, was an exceedingly favourite one among the Greek sculptors at Voni. I found numerous replicas of all dimensions, as well as several variants. But similar statues were also dedicated in one of the Apollo groves of Athiaenou (either 25 or 26 in our list, probably the latter, see Cesnola-Stern, pl. XXV). Cesnola also represents (ibid. XLII, 2) under Lapithus-Leucosia, a statuette of the same motive and in the same style, and Lang found another in the Rešef-Apollo grove at Idalion, no. 30 in our list (Transactions of the Royal Society of Literature, XI, Pl. III). Finally in the Artemis grove at Akhna (no. 1 in the list) among hundreds of female figures I found one fragment of a draped male statue. It was once more the same Apollo with the sprinkler.

***) Cp. p. 3, no. 4.

Aphrodite. Although in her case we chance to possess no similar epigraphical testimony, we have in the results of excavation which lie before us, other criteria which enable as to assert that a certain statue is that of a priestess, just as the nudity of a statue is a sure index of its representing the goddess herself. In the next paragraphs I shall speak of some of the nude types of the goddess. Here I will content myself with bringing before the notice of the reader a particularity which enables us to determine that such statues as Pl. XXXVIII, 3—5 (= Pl. LII, 19, 15, 12), Pl. LII, 13, 17, 18 and the colossal statue, put together from fragments, which stands in the foreground of Pl. LVI, represent priestesses in the service of Kypris. Just as the priestess of Tanit-Artemis (Pl. XXXVIII, 15 = LXVIII, 6) wears a crown decorated with lotus flowers and winged griffins,*) and thus proclaims herself to be the servant of Artemis, so do the priestesses of Astarte-Aphrodite wear crowns encircled by rows of beads and ornamented with little figures of the goddess, nude or draped, pressing her hands to her breasts.

c) Some of the most important types of the Astarte-Aphrodite images.

I open the series with a type which is nude, and at the same time (and this is very singular) wears the nose-ring. I have been the first to succeed in demonstrating that the nose-ring is worn first by Astarte-Aphrodite and then by her priestesses, and to point out the significance of this fact for the Nezem, the nose-ring of the Bible. Nos. 5 and 6 on Pl. LV are views of a statuette which is the most archaic figure wearing the nose-ring hitherto found, and can only represent the Paphian goddess. The arms and legs are broken away at the elbows and knees. I dug up this interesting terracotta in 1883 for the Cyprus Museum at Nicosia, where it still remains. The goddess in this case does not hold her breasts with her hands, but has her arms hanging at her sides. The breasts are, however, exceedingly prominent, and are conceived as distended by abundance of milk. The navel and pudendum are clearly indicated, and the manner of their indication reminds us of the terracottas of the Bronze Age (e. g. Pl. CLXXII, 17t). Although the coroplast has succeeded in liberating his style from Egyptian influences, and has produced a figure of a woman as hideous as it is repulsively true to nature, we are yet reminded of Egyptian fashions by the form of her wig-like head-dress. She wears no necklaces, no ear-rings, no jewellery on her breast or on her head. Her only article of adornment is a huge nose-ring inserted in a hole pierced through the membrane which separates the two nostrils. I found this remarkably characteristic terracotta to the West of Chytris in the temenos discribed as no. 23 in my list (p. 13: the number has fallen out of the text), a temenos, the ownership of which is determined by 14 dedications to the Paphia in Kyprian syllabary found there. From the same place comes the colossal female head given on Pl. XLVIII, 4. It was surmounted by a very high modius, but unluckily fell into so many pieces that restoration or reconstruction was impossible. It is then certain that this nude figure with the nose-ring from Chitroi represents Astarte-Aphrodite.

An image of the same goddess, of somewhat more advanced style, but still very archaic and of flat work, is figured on Pl. L, 4. She here wears quantities of jewellery on her head, neck and bosom. She is either conceived as nude or draped in some very light material. This terracotta, also of great interest for the characterisation of Kyprian art, was found by me in the grove of Astarte-

---

*) In Kypros the griffin appears as the attribute and companion of Tanit-Artemis.

Aphrodite, described in our list as no. 3 (p. 5). Although I found no inscriptions here, the character of the very abundant votive images made it evident that the grove was consecrated to Astarte-Aphrodite. Here the goddess grasps her breasts with both hands, like Nana-Ištar on Chaldaean seal-cylinders, and like the Kyprian terracottas of the Bronze Period (Pl. CLXXII, 17t). In addition to her numerous other ornaments she wears a large nose-ring passing through the septum of the nose at the same spot as that worn by the last figure. Her head is adorned with a crown; two wig-like flaps of hair hang down as far as her shoulders. Her ears are covered by the same kind of "epaulette" that we see on the heads (Pl. LV, 1, 4, 7) and many others. Close round her neck is set a richly ornamented chain, and a still heavier chain from which depends a locket hangs on her bosom. Either we are to conceive that an expanded piece of drapery, resembling a wide veil thrown back, is hung behind the figure, or else we have here an imitation of relief-technique, and the figure is supposed to be cut out of a relief or moulded from a portion of the mould of a relief. The last possibility is the most probable, in that the two most analogous figures are in relief. The closest analogy is found in the four identical figures of Astarte on one of the narrow sides of that Amathus sarcophagus which we have had so much occasion to cite (Cesnola-Stern XIV = Perrot III, p. 610, fig. 417). The resemblance is striking, but the goddess on the sarcophagus wears no nose-ring, and our figure is ruder and more archaic. Only somewhat less analogous are the two identical figures on each of the two narrow sides of the stone box from Amathus, given on Pl. CXCIX, 5—7. They appear to be nude; they wear an elevated head-dress resembling a modius, and raise their arms in the attitude of the "adorante" [9]).

Plate LV, 7 evinces the occurrence of the nose-ring in yet another sanctuary of Astarte-Aphrodite. We here see the head alone of a terracotta statue of nearly life size. The provenance of this specimen, as of the heads on Pl. XV also, like this, forming part of the Cesnola collection, is stated to be "Paphos" simply; but it is clear from the quality of the clay, and from the technique when compared with those of the objects which I either found myself on the spot or acquired from the peasants in the village, that this head (as well as the heads on Pl. XV) come from the sanctuary of Aphrodite at Boumo (no. 51 in our list). I myself possess a head of the same technique (but without nose-ring), which I bought from a peasant on the spot. (It was photographed by Dörpfeld, and photographs can be obtained. See Jahrbuch des kais. Deutschen Archäol. Instituts 1891, Anzeiger p. 90, no. 40.) While our first two figures wearing nose-rings certainly represent the goddess Astarte-Aphrodite herself, this head from Boumo may belong to a statue of a mortal, a priestess or other private individual, who wore a nose-ring.

The three terracotta heads with nose-rings, Pl. LV, 1 and 2 (two views of the same specimen) 3, 4, also belong to whole statues which may just as well have represented the goddess as a private person. It is at least certain that all these women loaded with jewellery, even if they are not the goddess herself, stand in the closest relation to the cultus of Aphrodite. Their advanced style is, if they are portraits, a striking evidence to the maintenance, in times when the Greek spirit had found

---

*) On Pl. CXXXIII, figs. 5—8 I give illustrations of some further Cyprian stone boxes, one of which (figs. 5a and b) found in Idalion is an abbreviated version of our Tamassos box (Pl. CXCIX, 5—7). We see on it an extract from the larger design (cp. the Description of the Plate.) The figure of the goddess is repeated twice only instead of four times. I attach the highest importance to this deliberate repetition of the same figure four times or twice. Cp. p. 184 note 11) above, and what I say below on Ezechiel's four faces and four cherubim chariots in the Description of Plate XCVI: also Pl. XXXII, 35, 36, 39—41.

real artistic expression, of this barbarous custom of wearing nose-rings. These heads also come from temenos no. 3.

The fourth place in which I found proof of this custom is the site near Idalion where a single holy tree was worshipped (no. 36 in our list, p. 18). Here I unearthed fragments of a large terracotta head or mask with a nose-ring.

Lastly there falls to be mentioned the temenos at Limniti, in which Rešef-Apollo was venerated together with Astarte-Aphrodite (no. 52 in our list). Tubbs says in his report (Journal of Hellenic Studies, XI (1890) p. 90, note 3) "in at least one case the nose-ring is added".

The Greek Aphrodite with all her full womanly beauty, the Aphrodite of Homer and Hesiod, the Aphrodite of whom the Medicean Venus is a type, is the child of the Kyprian Astarte and the Babylonian Ištar, with their hideously realistic forms. Perrot has attacked Curtius' article "Das phönikische Urbild der mediceischen Venus" (Arch Zeit. 1869, p. 63), but unjustly as regards the main fact. The motive of the nude goddess, who lays her right hand on her left breast and with her right hand shadows her secret parts is, as a fact, familiar in Kypros at an early date, long before the 4th century B. C. We can, even without quitting Cyprus, trace it back to the second·millennium B. C. A terracotta figure in this attitude, of this very early indeed perhaps of earlier date, the hands and features being indicated by incised lines, was acquired by me in 1883 from a source which leaves no doubt that it is from the necropolis of Ayia Paraskevi. It is now in the collection of Herr Schaaffhausen at Bonn. The Astarte of Phoenicia, no less than the Hebrew Astarte of the Old Testament, is indissociably linked with Kypros and the works of Kyprian Art. Often the spirit of enquiry, which is the spirit of progress, is forced by the testimony of monuments just dug out of the earth to destroy ruthlessly ideals which are dear to us. But not too often, for the destruction or correction of familiar conceptions, however beautiful they may be in themselves, is a good work, when new discoveries show them to be false. So is it with the beautiful Rebecca, who is wooed for Jacob from her parents by Abraham's slave. "He took a golden ear-ring of half a shekel weight and put it upon her face" says the Authorised Version (Genesis XXIV, 22 and 47). Our Kyprian finds show only that modern Biblical enquiry is right. The fair Rebecca actually wore a heavy nose-ring like Astarte-Aphrodite, the goddess of love' and her priestesses in Kypros.

We have met Astarte-Aphrodite under the form of a goddess of trees and flowers. In Amathus a flower festival called κάρπωσις was celebrated in her honour and in that of her beloved Adonis. At Tamassos golden apples grew for her to pluck. She was a garden goddess. The modern name of a village "Holy gardens" perpetuates the memory of her holy gardens between Old and New Paphos. This village of Hieroskipo is on a rock above the fertile garden-land, watered by a perennial spring gushing from the rock. We have met with Astarte-Aphrodite as a goddess of hills and rocky promontories as the Aphrodite of the sea, of rain and thunder. We have seen her as the Queen of Heaven, as the celestial cow, as the goddess with the sun-disc and cow's horns, or with even the head of a cow. We have learnt to understand her sidereal and lunar character where she wears on her forehead this sun-disc, or these moon-horns. This double nature was the bridge which led to our conception of her as an androgynous being, the bearded Aphrodite-Hermaphroditus. We found her to be at the same time a goddess of vegetable, animal and human fertility, of wanton growth. At one time she was the pure Urania, at another the Pandemus, giving her divine sanction to unchastity. We have learnt how maidens offered their virginity to her, how the male organ of generation, the phallus, was venerated at her festivals. We saw her assume the character of the infernal goddesses Ariadne and Persephone, and of the cave goddess Hekate. In the orgiastic Aphrodisia, celebrated after nightfall, we found an intermixture of elements borrowed from the Anatolian worship of Rhea-Kybele and from the various cults of Dionysus-Bacchus-Sabazius of Phrygia, Thrace and Greece; just as, on the other hand, elements of the Kyprian Aphrodite worship have introduced themselves into the Dionysiac rites of those lands. These rites and mythes of Dionysus led us to the dolphin, which we found recurring in Kypros, and will lead us to the consideration of fish-worship and the fish-goddess, who is again a Baalat, a kind of Astarte-Aphrodite bearing the names Derketo and Semiramis. Of this form of the goddess we shall speak below.

2. The dove, and other animals sacrificed by the Kyprians and Hebrews to Astarte-Aphrodite and other deities.

There is scarcely any point in oriental mythology as to which such erroneous notions have hitherto been entertained as the significance of the dove in cultus, and when borne as an attribute by votive statues. The English excavators who were at work during my residence on Cyprus did not avoid the errors into which nearly all their predecessors, who have written about dove-bearing figures and doves in the votive areas of holy precincts, have fallen.[*]) Hogarth found, in the temenos which inscriptions tell us was that of Apollo Melanthios and Opaon Melanthios, [**]) statuettes carrying doves, and considers the doves here to be, like the cone previously found, emblems due to the influence of the worship of the neighbouring Aphrodite Paphia. Tubbs, in his description of the Limniti finds, has given expression to similar views. [***]) He is certainly right in concluding that Rešef-Apollo and Astarte-Aphrodite were worshipped as σύμβωμοι in this interesting grove (cp. Plates XLIII—XLVII), but the reasons on which he bases his conclusion, are, as far the goddess is concerned, quite invalid. He considers that he has demonstrated the practice here of Aphrodite worship by the pod-like ear-covering worn by certain figures, and by the doves which others carry. This is a serious error. As the nose-ring only occurs in connection with Aphrodite-worship, and as the nude female figures pressing their breasts with both hands invariably represent Astarte-Aphrodite, the occurrence of both at Limniti sufficiently establishes the practice of the worship of Astarte-Aphrodite; but neither the ear-tire adduced by Tubbs nor the female figures carrying doves have any weight as proofs. In the sixth century B. C. (and, in all probability in the fifth as well) this peculiar ear-tire was in fashion throughout the whole island. We find it, worn by women playing on the lyre (Pl. XII, 5), by women carrying doves and poultry in the Artemis grove at Akhna (No. 1 in our list; see Plate CCX, 2—4) and by women carrying tympana or flowers in the grove of Aphrodite at Dali (no. 3 in the list; see Plates XLIX 3, 5, L, 3) &c. Both Astarte-Aphrodite and her female ministrants may wear it, but the ears of the priestesses of Artemis

---

[*]) The only person, as far as I know, who, basing his treatment on my communications, has made an initial attempt to present these confused relations in their proper light is A. Furtwängler (Roscher's Mythol. Lexikon col. 406 · 409).

[**]) Journal of Hellenic Studies, 1888, p. 173.

[***]) Journal of Hellenic Studies, 1890, p. 90.

(Pl. XLVIII 2—4, where the ear-tire is very clear) and of the archaic Artemis herself (Pl. XI, 4) may be similarly adorned.

The doves and dove-sacrifices with which we meet in Kypros differ in no way from the doves and dove-sacrifices of the old Testament, and are in perfect conformity with the ordinances of Leviticus. I will show by innumerable examples that the sacrifices prescribed by the Mosaic law were habitually practised in Kypros. It is impossible to excavate one of those holy places, whose courts were packed with votive statues of various sizes and kinds, without finding evidences of the observance of these ancient Hebrew or Semitic sacrificial ordinances. In the oldest strata of Olympia and in the sanctuary of the Kabiri at Thebes *), we find similar sacrificial and ritual usages derived from Kypros and the Semitic East, adopted by the Greeks. Both Curtius **) and Furtwängler ***) have drawn attention to this origin, and to the Kyprian parallels, but it has not hitherto been given to anyone to demonstrate by means of numerous single discoveries the general observance of these Mosaic ritual laws, and from the results of comprehensive excavation to satisfactorily explain and vividly illustrate the actual words of many Old Testament passages. If I wished to give an approximately complete list of the thousands of votive figures which, in many different manners, mirror to us the observance of these rules of sacrifice, I should have to cite almost all the works, illustrated or not, which have in recent years been written on the subject of Kyprian antiquities. It will suffice for my purpose if I take the illustrations of the present work, and show from them how in the votive areas of four different holy groves, many varieties of statues of men or women carrying different animals to sacrifice were dedicated. Most are representations of ordinary mortals, but in one or two instances we must suppose the figure to be that of a deity. Any reader wishing to make a more detailed study of the subject will easily find more abundant material, both in my own works and in those of others.

Site 1 (p. 1). Temenos of Tanit-Artemis-Kybele at Akhna.

a) Female figures carrying doves, Pl. CCX, 3 and 4, probably also 6 and 7.

b) Female figures carrying poultry, Pl. CCX, 1 and 2.

c) Female figures carrying lambs, Pl. CCXI, 2 and 3.

Site 2 (p. 2). Temenos of Rešef-Apollo at Voni.

a) Erect male figures carrying doves, Pl. XLI, 1, 2, 7 and 9.

b) Crouching boy with dove, Pl. XXXIII, 2.

c) Male figures (perhaps Apollo) carrying deer-calf or fawn, Pl. XLII, 1 and 2.

d) Male figures (perhaps Apollo-Zeus) carrying eagle or Nike, Pl. XL, 1, 2, 4, 5.

e) A small votive bronze stag.

f) In the layer of ashes (Os, Pl. V, 1) bones of many sacrificed animals, both birds and quadrupeds, were found.

---

*) Mitth. d. kaiserl. deutsch. arch. Inst. Athen XIII (1888) p. 82—102, 412—428, XV (1890) p. 355—419.
**) "Die Altäre von Olympia", p. 29 ff.
***) "Die Bronzefunde von Olympia". Cp. p. 1 above. Recently similar customs, the deposition in a temple of terracotta votive offerings of indifferent character, which only attain sacral significance by the fact of their dedication to a god, have been proved to exist elsewhere. See Pierre, "Elatée, la ville et le temple d'Athéna Crania". Paris, 1892, and Baumgarten's critique in the Berl. Phil. Wochenschrift, 1892, col. 1334.

Site 3 (p. 5). Temenos of Astarte-Aphrodite at Dali.

a) Only a single terracotta dove, of large size (8.5 cm = $3^1/_4$ in. in height), was found here
(no. 108 in the Report on the excavation; not figured). As it has no legs, but terminates
beneath in a single round, somewhat pointed pin, at would appear certain that it was
carried in the hand of a large terracotta statue (cp. Cesnola-Stern, Pl. XXII = Perrot,
p. 511, fig. 349). No female figures carrying doves were unearthed; but I found here
the fragment of the corner of a casket-shaped dove-house represented Pl. XXXVIII, 11.
A dove (the head is now missing) is perched upon it.

b) Female figure carrying an ox (fragmentary) Pl. LII, 11.

c) Female figure carrying goat (fragmentary) Pl. LIII, 50.

d) Female figure carrying a rude quadruped (ox, calf or sheep?), Pl. LIII, 15.

There was also found a considerable number of terracotta fragments of oxen (cp. Pl. LII,
21, 28, LIII), which may have either stood alone or been borne by statues. The central
amulets of chains in the form of ox-heads, oxen, and goats, also testify to the frequency
with which quadrupeds were sacrificed to Aphrodite.

e) The skull of a hare which had been sacrificed, was also found in the votive court.[*]

Site 4 (p. 6). Temenos of Rešef-Apollo at Tamassos (Plates representing the objects discovered
and here cited will be given in my work on Tamassos).

a) Male figures carrying doves.

b) Male figures carrying oxen.

c) Male figures carrying goats.

d) A votive bronze bull of pure Greek style.

e) Quantities of quadrigal and equestrian figures.

It is clear that in the temene of Rešef-Apollo, Astarte-Aphrodite, and Tanit-Artemis, the same
quadrupeds and birds were sacrificed. It even so happens that the groves of Apollo at Vouni and
of Artemis at Akhna have given us more doves and dove-carriers than the groves of Aphrodite. As
in the case in the Bible, rich men sacrificed larger and more costly victims, if possible oxen
goats, or sheep, while the victims offered by the poor man were smaller and cheaper. His sacrifices of
doves or even, in some cases, of fine meal [**] were accepted as graciously by Yahve as the great
animal-sacrifices of the rich. In order that the theory that the different animals which it was
permissible to sacrifice, were all of equal value in God's eyes, Abraham sealed his covenant with
Yahve by the sacrifice of a cow, a ram, a turtle-dove and a young dove [***]

In the purificatory sacrifices of the Kyprian, as in the those of the Hebrews, the victim was
always a small animal. As these purificatory offerings were in Kypros made to Rešef-Apollo (the

---

[*) Cp. Bötticher, "Baumkultus," fig. 20. Two hares-heads are hung as votive offerings from a branch
of the holy tree of Pan; fig. 23, a faun about to dedicate a hare he has captured in the chase at the holy tree
of the rural god. (More about the hare will be found below in Paragraph 4).

[**) Leviticus V, 7. "And if he be not able to bring a lamb, then he shall bring for his trespass,
which he hath committed, two turtledoves or two young pigeons unto the Lord, one for a sin-offering, and the
other for a burnt-offering." V, 11: "But if he be not able to bring two turtle-doves or two young pigeons,
then he that sinned shall bring for his offering the tenth part of an ephat of fine flour for a sin-offering."
Cp. also the rules for the cleansing of lepers. (Leviticus XIV, 10, 21 –23.)

[***) Cp. p. 161 above.

purifying god par excellence) far oftener than to Astarte-Aphrodite, the fact is explained that the votive figures of mortals carrying doves for sacrifice are of more frequent occurrence in the groves of Rešef Apollo than in those of Astarte-Aphrodite. It is also clear from the ordinances of Leviticus XV, 14 and 29 that men and women alike had to deliver to the priest at the door of the tent of revelation the same purificatory offerings, two turtle-doves or two young pigeons. In Kypros we even find a probable testimony to the sacrifice of a **pair of doves** in a lime-stone group of two billing doves (Pl. CV, 10: the bills are broken off). I found this specimen in 1886 among the sepulchral offerings in a tomb at Marion-Arsinoë, but similar groups have been found by others in temené. Thus, for example, in the temenos of Apollo at Amaryetti, to which such frequent reference has been made, Hogarth found a limestone group of two doves sitting next each other (Journal of Hellenic Studies, 1888, p. 172). Further, since the employment as symbols in the ritual of the dead, or as simple offerings to the dead, of certain votive offerings, such as ring-dances, chariots, equestrian figures &c., originally peculiar to the holy places and altars, can be demonstrated, we may, but with due caution, adduce sepulchral offerings to supplement the lessons taught by the votive offerings of the temené. It would appear that in the Cyprian collection at New York there exist several similar groups of two billing doves, one of them being figured in Cesnola's Atlas (Pl. LXXX, 527 = Perrot III, p. 598, fig. 409),

The same old Mosaic sacrifice is mentioned in the gospel of Luke (II, 24) as having been celebrated on the occasion of the circumcision of Christ "And to offer a sacrifice according to that which is said in the law of the Lord, (Lev. XII, 8) a pair of turtle doves or two young pigeons. Richer women than Mary had to bring to the priest for a burnt offering a lamb of the first year and a young pigeon or turtle-dove for a sin-offering. "But if she be not able to bring a lamb, then she shall bring two turtles or two young pigeons, the one for a burnt offering the other for a sin-offering".*) At Poli tis Khrysokhou (Marion-Arsinoë) I found (in 1886) in a tomb a limestone votive group, in which we see standing beside each other the lamb of the first year and the young pigeon which wealthy women had to offer on the occasion of the circumcision of a son (Pl. CX, 1).**)

3. Doves and dove-goddesses in Kypros and Mykenae.

Our enquiry has taught us that the simple presence of doves as animals of sacrifice speaks neither for nor against the practice of Astarte-Aphrodite worship. On the other hand, we should be committing an equally serious error, did we underrate the importance of a specific dove-worship attached to Astarte-Aphrodite, and allied Baalats, such as the Semiramis of Askalon. In this last connection the island of Kypros supplies us again with abundance of instructive matter showing us

---

*) Cp. the article "Taube" in Riehm's Bibellexikon, p. 1616—1619. He also alludes to the sellers of doves, who had their stalls in the outer court of the temple at Jerusalem in the time of Christ. The demand for these birds so commonly sacrificed must have been great. (See Matth. XXI, 12; Mark. XI, 15; John II, 14—16).

**) Nos. 4 and 6 on the same plate are two votive terracotta ducks and one hen from the same necropolis. No. 5 is a limestone statue of a broad-tailed sheep (cp. Exodus XXIX, 22) coloured red and admirably characterized, in the possession of the Agricultural Institute of the University of Halle. It and a dove were obtained from a peasant who had found both specimens in a tomb at Amathus.

how this worship found its way from Kypros not only to Mykenae but to Etruria, and how close must have been the relation between the cultus of Askalon, and that of this island.

Before proceeding to institute these comparisons, I wish to say something as to a number of Kyprian cultus-images, cultus-utensils, and vessels with representations of doves, in which the divine character in some cases either prevails over the decorative or is exclusively dominant, while in others it is tempered or mastered by the latter. In the crouching temple-boys, the Tammuz-Adonis boys, with whom we have met above, the sacral element is preponderant. In support of this statement I will once again cite the large and very interesting replica of a stone statuette found by me at Chytroi in the grove of Astarte-Aphrodite (No. 24 in our list), and represented Pl. XXXIII, 4. We see in this fragment the temple-boy holding a huge dove by its wings. The throned female figure with the dove (Perrot III, p. 64) may also be certainly pronounced to be purely sacral. This terracotta, now in the Louvre, was found on Phoenician soil, and must decidedly be taken to represent Astarte-Aphrodite. True, none of these images are older than the sixth century B. C. while some are more recent.

I now come to discuss a form of dove-worship, to which our monuments testify as being attached to the Baalat, who in Askalon is known as Semiramis, in Kypros as Astarte-Aphrodite. We meet with it only in the holy places of Astarte, never in those of any other deity in Kypros. Offerings of doves, either one or two pigeons or turtle-doves, were made to all deities, but only in the groves (ἄλση), precincts (τεμένη) and high places (bâmôt) of Aphrodite were flocks of pigeons kept in dove-cots of peculiar form close to the altar. Had these appliances existed in the holy places of other deities, we should have had some record of them in literary sources, or we should have found some traces of them. The dove, as a bird of sacrifice, is made welcome by all deities, but it is specially sacred to, the peculiar property of a group of goddesses represented by Astarte-Aphrodite Semiramis, and Kypra.[*] From the same root grew the dove-worship of Dodona, where the doves, as at Askalon and Paphos, enjoyed peculiar sanctity. In later times the art of pigeon-breeding practised in the temple of Paphos must have reached a high degree of perfection. The beauty of the white and coloured doves of the Urania in Paphos is celebrated by ancient authors.[**] Above on the cylinders[***] we saw a number of drawings of birds, which in many cases must have been meant for doves. The doves on the remarkable terracotta tetrapod (fig. 182 = Pl. CXLIX 15e = CLXX 13e) found by me (1886) in an early tomb of the Copper-Bronze Period at Ayia Paraskevi must also be regarded as bearing some sacral character, either as victims or as sacred tame doves. On a large ring supported by four feet are set at equal intervals four caldron-shaped vessels, two groups of a god and goddess of board or post form, and two single doves. On the same Plates (d = fig. 181) there is an illustration of a tripod of similar construction, and coming from the same stratum of tombs. In this case two jugs, two vases, and a dove are set on the ring. Fig. a ibid. is a bird-shaped vase with three legs. From these utensils of worship with representations of doves, are derived the terracotta dove cups (b and c = figs. 185, 186) also belonging to the same stratum of discovery. These dove-cups are the prototypes of Nestors dove-cup, and the silver dove-

---

[*] In Etruria. See the next paragraph.
[**] Cp. Movers, "Phönizier" I, p. 632 where the principal works on the subject are cited.
[***] Cp. Pl. LXXIX, 3; Pl. LXXXVII, 3 and 6; p. 93, figs. 132, 133.

cup found by Schliemann at Mykenae. Here the decorative already outweighs or replaces the sacral character. On the rims of the small semi-spherical, footless bowls also we find set doves alternating with little saucers or perpendicular handles on which the thumb could rest in drinking. Pl. CLXXIII 22 g shows a bowl from Ayia Paraskevi with such a dove and handle.

In the same necropolis was found a painted dove-cylix, on the rim of which four doves alternate with four of these perpendicular handles (it was acquired by Col. Warren). These Cyprian pre - Homeric dove-bowls throw more light than any other monuments on Nestor's cup in Homer. The much-discussed passage in the Iliad (XI, 632 ff.) runs as follows. "And by them she set a cup very beautiful, that the old man had brought with him from home. It was studded with nails of gold and had four ears, and at either side of each ear a golden dove was picking, and under were two $\pi\upsilon\vartheta\mu\acute{\epsilon}\nu\epsilon\varsigma$. No other man could take it full from off the table without putting forth all his might, but old Nestor lifted it with no labour". I will, to begin with, show by help of the vast numbers of dove-bowls and analogous bowls found in Cyprus and of the annexed illustrations (figs. 183 - 186, cp. the Owl (1888) Pl. IV, figs. 4—8) that Helbig ("Hom. Epos", p. 372 ff.) in explaining the two $\pi\upsilon\vartheta\mu\acute{\epsilon}\nu\epsilon\varsigma$ (bottoms) as supports is wrong, and that Schliemann, who discovered the Mykenaean silver bowl, and first saw its significance (Mykenae, p. 273—275), was right. Schliemann believed that by the two bottoms the poet meant (1) the bottom of the cup itself and (2) the bottom of the foot on which it stood. Had my Kyprian discoveries never been made, Schliemann's view would have little in its favour, and Helbig's interpretation would strike a reader as being much the more plausible. For, as he rightly

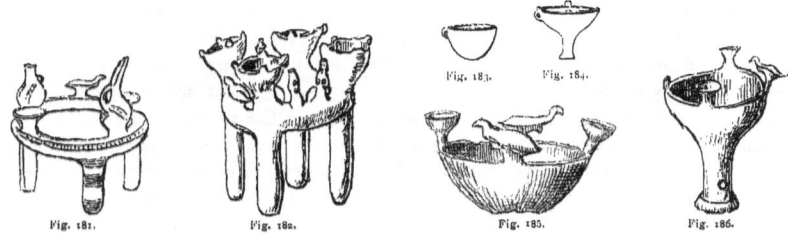

Fig. 181.   Fig. 182.   Fig. 183.   Fig. 184.   Fig. 185.   Fig. 186.

remarks, it seems to be a matter of course that a cup consisting of a wide receptacle resting on a tall narrow and hollow foot must have a double bottom. In Epic pictures, he continues, there is no analogy for any such insistence on a fact so unessential and so little obvious to the eye. With this opinion we should have to cordially agree, had we only to deal with Schliemann's Mykenae cup, the Etruscan cup (Helbig, p. 74, fig. 158 = our Pl. CXXIII, 6) and our own Kyprian dove-cup (figs. 185, 931). But our verdict is reversed at a stroke when we come to review the thousands and thousands of drinking-vessels, bowls and cups, of the Kyprian Copper-Bronze Age. We find that the ordinary form of drinking vessel used by ordinary men of all classes is a simple semispherical bowl. In its simplest form it has one simple pierced handle (fig. 183 and Pl. CLXIX, 8b). Next, it is made more pointed at the bottom (CLXIX, 8a). Then all kinds of excrescences, knobs, or little saucers, or such like, are set upon its rim (CLXVIII, 5b). Then its outer surface is adorned immediately below the rim with continous reliefs, e. g. snakes (Pl. CLXXI, 11 and 12h), Then the excrescences on the rim take the form of little vertical handles, set at equal distances from each other, and varying in number from one to eight. Lastly, doves are introduced between these prominences, now walking along the rim (fig. 185), now standing on the rim looking into the cavity (fig. 186).

The larger number of these bowls are semispherical (fig. 183) or pointed at the bottom (CLXIX, 8a). They are imitated from bowls made of gourds (cp. Plates XXXIV and XXXV). Of every 1000 or 2000 examples of these semi-spherical, pointed, or cylindrical bowls, about one has a foot. The idea of giving feet to these bowls, which cannot stand, and had to be drunk out of before they were set down, arose only after some lapse of time (figs. 184—186 and CLXVIII, 2a; the foot of fig. 185 is broken off). Attempts were even made in some cases, after the bowl had been painted and baked, to cement on to it a foot, which easily became detached. I myself found an example of such an attempt. It is the bowl, Pl. CLXXIII, 22 f (now in the Cyprus Museum at Nicosia). It had been moulded, baked, painted and in all probability used, when its owner conceived the notion of having a foot made for it, thus converting it into a cup. This foot was of course only cemented on and became detached, so that, when I found the vessel, it was once more footless, but still showed traces and remains of the attached foot on its under surface. The rule therefore is that the vast majority of drinking vessels are bowls with **only one bottom** (fig. 183); cups formed by adding to these bowls a foot and **second bottom** (fig. 184) are of the utmost rarity. In Homeric times, as in the Kyprian bronze period, every one had footless drinking-bowls with a single bottom *). Only grandees like Nestor and his companions drank from cups with a foot and double bottom. This novel device would naturally arrest the eye of a poet who saw it for the first time. He would compare the drinking-cup standing full of wine erect on the table with the less practical and humbler drinking-bowls he had been accustomed to, into which one could only pour just as much wine as one could drink off. Therefore Homer could not avoid mentioning that Nestor's drinking-vessel was a cup with a foot and two bottoms.

Now as to the handles, of which Nestor's cup had four, with two doves pecking at each (i. e. eight doves in all). The little saucer-shaped vertical handles set on the rim of the bowl (one Pl. CLXXII, 22g. two CLXVIII, 4c, four on Col. Warren's vase, six CLXXIII, 22 f) are not meant merely as ornaments, part served to assist the drinker in grasping and steadying the vessel. This is obvious in those cases where a large bowl is provided with only two of these perpendicular handles, placed exactly opposite each other. By placing the two thumbs on the concave upper surfaces of the two handles, we get a far better grasp of the vessel in raising it to the lips. As the bowls have a very smooth polish and their surface becomes still more slippery when moist, they are very apt to slip from the hand in drinking. Even where (as on Pl. CLXXIII, 22 g) there is only one of these saucer-topped handles on which to rest the thumb, our hold is far more secure, and we can raise the vessel to our lips with one hand without any apprehension of spilling the contents or dropping the bowl itself. Helbig ("Hom. Epos", pp. 376 and 447) discusses my dove-cups (figs. 185, 186) and explains the concave objects on the rim as not being handles at all, but saucers for the doves to drink from. This is not so. Very many drinking-bowls have these little handles on the rim, but no doves. The painted drinking-vessel (also from my own excavations), Pl. CLXXIII, 22 f, has six of these little handles surmounted by saucer-like cavities, and exactly resembling those of the dove-cups (as well as one pierced handle), but it has no doves. On the vase in Col. Warren's collection, sold by auction in Paris **), were four doves alternating with four similar handles. On one of our vases, Pl. CLXXIII, 22 g, one dove and one such handle are set on the rim, on the vases figs. 185 and 186, two doves and two handles. The projections were originally simple handles. The addition of the doves gave them another meaning. While retaining their function as handles, they came to be regarded as saucers out of which the doves sipped water. The transformation of the bowl, with a vertical support for the thumb, into the dove-cup, is an evidence that the artistic spirit is already awake, the spirit which makes all the parts of an object of utility into living members of an organism, and not content with the more satisfaction of the needs of to day, gives life to dead things. Helbig is essentially right, but he has failed to recognise the origin of this particular form. Technical necessities are clothed by fancy with her own garment; the more practically useful the form, the greater her triumph in veiling its merely practical aspect. The Egyptians were full of this spirit when they transformed their spoons and boxes into swimming girls, birds &c.

The painted terra-cotta figure of a three-legged dove carrying its young on its wings (Pl. CLXXIII, 20 and 21 h) was also found by me at Phoenitshais in 1883 during excavations made for Sir C. Newton. It also belongs to the Bronze Period, and may be dated early in the second millennium B. C. I have in my possession a small dove belonging to an early dove-cup tripod or tetrapod, and the fragment of a large terra-cotta dove (measuring from tail to neck 0,225 m. = 9 in.). This last is also of very early date; it is of red polished clay with incised ornaments, and, like the small one, comes from the necropolis of the Copper-Bronze Period at Ayia-Paraskevi, the ancient site which I have identified with the Lidir of the Assyrians, the Ledrai of the Greeks. Cyprus, like Greece, is rich in wild species of the dove tribe, ring-doves, turtle-doves, rock-pigeons. Hehn, who devotes a whole sections of his admirable work "Culturpflanzen und Hausthiere" to the dove

---

*) A similar form of cup, with the foot open at the bottom, occurs at Hissarlik (Schliemann's "Ilios," p. 605, no. 1121).

**) Catalogue des Antiquités de M. Hoffmann, Paris, 1885, Avril, no. 245 ("Antiquités chypriotes premier envoi").

(pages 273—285), believes, doubtless rightly, that the domestic pigeon reached Greece from Babylon by way of Syria and Kypros, coming in the wake of the worship of Aphrodite. But it appears to me that, relying too exclusively on linguistic evidence, he puts the arrival of the domestic pigeon in Greece at too late a date, viz. the fifth century B. C. It is true that the rudeness of the figures of doves which date from early times does not admit of our pronouncing them to belong to any particular species or variety; but the way in which doves, in the pre-Graeco-Phoenician Copper-Bronze Period, appear on tripods, tetrapods, cups and bowls (of the cylinder designs I say nothing) renders it a matter of certainly that they lived with mankind in a state of domestication. This was only possible in the case of the domestic pigeon, the tame variety of the Columba Livia. Pairs of turtle-doves still visit the gardens of the capital Nicosia and rear their young there, but they are shy of man, and cannot, like the Columba Livia, be permanently tamed.*) The domestic pigeons do actually live with man. The dovecots in the villages are often constructed on the roofs of the box-shaped houses, just as is the case in the little aediculae of Astarte-Aphrodite (Pl. CXXIV, 4, 5, and CXXVI, 1). Hehn is also right when he says that the amalgamation of the Astarte and Ashera worships with that of Semiramis gave a new impulse to dove-worship and pigeon-breeding. But the Kyprian finds make it evident that the domestic pigeon was introduced into Kypros long before Semiramis worship struck root there, and did not, as Hehn believes, first reach the island with this goddess. As some of the tripods, tetrapods, cups and bowls with representations of doves are certainly as early as the third millennium B. C., the domestic pigeon must already at this remote period have been introduced into Kypros from Babylon by trade, intercourse, conquest or immigration.**) If Pinches is right in dating King Sargon I. 3800 B. C. and if this King really included Cyprus in his dominions, then there is nothing to surprise us in the fact that tame pigeons were bred in the island so long ago as the third or even the fourth millennium B. C.***) Archaeological discovery further seems to tell us that in pre-Homeric or heroic times, in those times which Homer pictured in the clothing of his own time, the tame pigeon accompanying the cultus of the dove-goddess Astarte Aphrodite, came from Kypros to Mykenae. There is, I believe, general agreement among the learned, that the stamped ornaments of gold foil, of which several replicas were found at Mykenae, (see Pl. XXXVIII, 9, 10 = CV, 2, 3) represent the dove-goddess Astarte-Aphrodite; and it is also generally acknowledged that these little gold figures of the dove-goddess, together with the little

---

*) Hehn ("Culturpflanzen und Hausthiere," p. 283) describes, from literary sources, a halfbreed pigeon produced by crossing the wild grey pigeon with the quite domesticated white pigeon of Cyprus and Syria, to which countries it came from Babylon. He thinks this cross between the wild and domestic pigeon is of great antiquity not only in Asia Minor (where Galen saw and described it,) but in the whole East and in Egypt. He remarks further with great truth that the Mosaic law forbad the sacrifice of wild animals. When therefore we find in the sacrificial ordinances directions for the sacrifice of both pigeons and turtle-doves, we must suppose that both species (including the turtle-doves) were, to some extent, tame. The distinction in the Bible between pigeons and turtle-doves leads us in fact to suppose that the two varieties of domesticated wild-pigeons, i. e. the domestic pigeon proper and the half-domesticated turtle-dove, existed then as now in Judaea and Cyprus. As the dove which Noah sent out returned to the ark, the domestication of the wild-pigeon and the development of the domestic pigeon of which so many varieties now exist, must have made some progress at the time when this story originated.

**) For the dating of the Cyprian finds, cp. the Explanations of Plates CXLVI—CLII.

***) The first domestic pigeons probably reached Greece together with the first idols of Istar. Cp. Knoll, "Studien zur ältesten Kunst in Griechenland," p. 77, note 1.

Mykenaean aediculae of Astarte (one on Pl. XXXVIII, 8 = CV, 6) point to an early connection between the worships and art of Kypros and those of Mykenae. In one case (3) a single dove is perched on Astarte's head, in the second (2) two additional doves sit on her shoulders. On the corners of the little gold aedicula sit likewise two doves.*) We must either admit that these gold ornaments are native productions (this is the view which now finds most favour), or if not, we must pronounce them to be imported from Kypros or the East. If we accept the first alternative, we must believe that both the worship of Astarte-Aphrodite and the domestic pigeon reached Mykenae and Greece from Kypros in pre-Homeric times. In admirable accord with this conclusion are those derived by Richard Meister from the facts of language and from mythological traditions. The Greeks, he says, must have had strong and populous settlements in

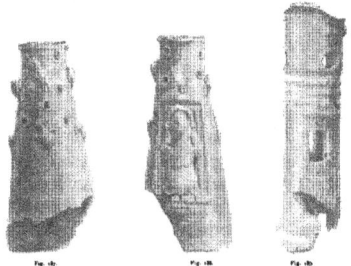

Fig. 1b.   Fig. 1a.   Fig. 1b.

Kypros at a date several centuries before Homer.**) If (as is not probable) these gold ornaments were brought to Mykenae from the East, then their presence here does not cease to testify to the introduction into Greece from Kypros of the worship of Astarte-Aphrodite. The golden Astarte idols from the royal tomb at Mykenae have doves on their heads. It is by a pure chance that we have no idols of the goddess from Kypros showing this particular motive. The intimacy

---

*) Cp. p. 179 above.

**) "Die griechischen Dialekte," II, p. 128: "This tradition (of an Arcadian immigration) is belied by the fact that Hellenes and Hellenic letters are already at home at Kypros at the period of the poem, i. e. that the earliest Greek colonisation of Kypros must in some centuries older than the originator of the Homeric poems. The titax actually calls Aphrodite Κύπρις after her principal seat of worship (3, 330, 433, 446, 725, 865); the Odyssey is acquainted with the worship of the Paphian goddess (8,362), and this Homeric Aphrodite of Kypros is the daughter of the Babylonian Zeus and Diona."

which subsisted between the goddess and her house pets here is shown by the cylindrical or columnar censers (figs. 187 and 188 = Pl. LXIX, 80 = XVII, 2 and 3 = XXXVIII, 12) and by the aediculae (Pl. X, 3 = XXXVIII, 13 = CIX, 3 = CXXIV, 5; Pl. CXXIV, 4 = CXCIX, 4). On coins of Roman times we do actually see the dove perched on the conical idol of the Paphia (Pl. LXXXIII, 22). The two doves on the corners of the golden aedicula of Mykenae have their counterparts in the two which, on Roman coins, sit on the roof of the colonnade of the Paphian sanctuary.

Schliemann (Mykenae pages 210 and 308) has called attention to the Kyprian parallels for his little Astarte idols, and aediculae.*) Of the annexed illustrations, figs. 187 and 188 (cp. pages 165—169 above) represent the conic dove-cote from Kition, fig. 189 (= Pl. XVII, 4 = Pl. LXIX, 78 = Pl. CXXXV, 3) is the columnar censer excavated by myself, and with it should be compared the votive column from Carthage Pl. LXXXV, 1 (cp. p. 165 above). Both examples evidently represent those dove-towers, which still at the present day, as in the days of Herod the Great (Josephus, Bell. Iud. 5, 4, 4), exist in Palestine (cp. Riehm's Bibellexikon II, p. 1616). Dove-cots, as is well known, are first mentioned by the prophet Isaiah (LX, 8):

" Who are these that fly as a cloud and as doves to their cots ".

The small golden Astarte figures with doves from Mykenae were ornaments, and on the crowns worn by the colossal terra-cotta statues of priestesses from our Dali sanctuary (no. 3 in the list) we see numbers of quite similar little idols of Astarte (Pl XXXVIII, 3 = LII, 19; Pl. XXXVIII, 4 = LII, 15; Pl. XXXVIII, 5 = LII, 12, 13, 18). In an early Graeco-Phoenician tomb at Kurion I found (in 1884) eighteen rectangular plaques of silver, which had formed part of an ornament. On Pl. XXV, 7 I give an illustration of one. On each of these plaques the same design, the busts of two women, is stamped. Tiny little gold idols, which were strung on necklaces as amulets, have been found in Cyprus in not inconsiderable numbers. The resemblance is quite surprising between the little (imperfect) image of Astarte (found by myself and belonging to one of the great crowns of the colossal statues) fig. 4 on Pl. XXXVIII and figs. 9 and 10 of the same plate, Mykenaean golden images of the goddess. The Kyprian terra-cotta is several centuries later than these, but a comparison shows how motive and style remained unchanged during this whole period. Were we not acquainted with the exact circumstances under which these three specimens were found, we would not venture to assume a difference in date of six to eight hundred years between the Mykenaean and Kyprian figures. Yet this is so; the Kyprian figure cannot be assigned to an earlier date than the end of the 7th century B. C.

I have already repeatedly been enabled to explain ancient manners and customs by those still surviving in Cyprus. The method enables me to demonstrate that in ancient Kypros not only the priestesses of Aphrodite, but the whole female sex in the character of her devotees, wore in their hair large pins of gold or silver surmounted by figures of doves. The Cyprian women still wear such pins just over the forehead (see Pl. XXXIII, 6). Before leaving Cyprus I bought from a goldsmith at Nicosia one of these pins, but it was stolen from me on the journey; so that I can only give a poor illustration after a small photograph.**) The more fact that such pins are worn would

---

*) Cp. also Milchhöfer, " Die Anfänge der Kunst in Griechenland," p. 8, figs. 1 and 2; Lenormant Gazette Archéol., IV (1878) p. 78—81; Helbig, " Homerisches Epos," p. 33, fig. 3; Schuchardt, " Schliemann's Ausgrabungen," p. 230—333.

**) In constructing this phototypic plate, the phototyper has unfortunately placed the head of the pin in a too slanting position. Cp XXXIII, 6).

not be in itself sufficient to prove that the custom was a general one in antiquity. The proof is made complete by the following circumstance. The heads of most of the modern pins do not represent doves, but all kinds of fantastic figures. Very often the head of the pin resembles a lyre, at other times it is a rosette, or has some geometric, grotesque, or conventional form suggested by modern Syrian or Arabian, and in recent years even more, by modern European designs. The Cyprian village belle (from the village of Politikou) whose portrait is given on Pl. XXXIII, 6, wears in the centre a pin of this kind in which, do all we can, we can detect no resemblance to a dove. When she sat to me, I stuck my own dove-pin, the one I bought in Nicosia, into her hair, to the left of the other. Now although their large hair-pins, which are always worn in front, stuck into the kerchief covering the hair, have their heads only in exceptional cases shaped like doves, they are everywhere called "πεσοίνια" i. e. young doves. "I have lost my little dove", my cook used to say, when she had mislaid her hair-pin, which was an ornamental hair-pin of quite modern European design. Oral tradition has kept alive among the people the memory of the "dove of Aphrodite", which the women of ancient Kypros wore as part of their head-tire. Therefore golden figures of Astarte with a dove on her head similar to those found at Mykenae must have existed in Kypros. How else could it have come to pass that the Cyprian women of to day call their hair-pins, be they like doves or not, "πεσούνια" "little doves"? *)

The dove-worship of Dodona, the prophetic women there called "Doves", and Dione herself, who is either the mother of the Kyprian Aphrodite or identical with this goddess—all these point also to Kypros. These legends were known to Homer who used them in his Iliad (5, 312, 330, 370, 422) **). This story of the birth of Aphrodite is older than the daughter of the foam.

4. The Cyprian Astarte-Aphrodite and the Etruscan Hera-Kypra. Hare goddesses, Bird-goddesses, and Potniae Theron.

The dove-goddess did not arrest her progress at Mykenae, but continued her wanderings westwards to Italy, and found a home among the Etruscans. When we hear that the Etruscans called their Hera by the name Kypra ***), we now know (thanks to the finds and results of excavation here adduced in support of my assertion) that this Hera can only have been Astarte-Aphrodite We are further told that the Etruscans represented their Hera under the form of Aphrodite, and I am in a position to prove the literal truth of this assertion by the evidence of Etruscan antiquities known to me. †) Lastly in the passage of Silius Italicus (8, 432).

Et quis litoreae fumant altaria Cyprae

we must see in Cypra a goddess who coincides with the Kypris of Kypros. The copious material supplied

---

*) The motive of carrying a bird on the head seems to have originated in Egypt, like so much else: or, by means of early Syrian or early Babylonian influence, it may have been introduced into Egypt at a very remote time. We saw that certain types of the holy tree (e. g. p. 79, fig. 107) were originally carried to Egypt by foreign peoples, were then modified by Egyptian artists and returned to their originators, the artists of the east, as Egyptian novelties, and the like may have befallen this motive of a bird on the head of an anthropomorphic idol. Below, in speaking of Rešef-Apollo-Horus and the god Qeb, we shall come across other Egyptian parallels to this motive.

**) Cp. Roscher's Mythol. Lexikon, col. 1028; also R. Meister, "Griech. Dialekte," p. 286, note.

***) Strabo 5, p. 241. See Engel, "Kypros," II, p. 63.

†) Gerhard, "Prodromus", p. 35, note 87 and Pl. II; p. 64, note 115.

by recent excavation or chance discovery enables us draw closer the ties which link this shore-goddess Kypra with the Kypris the protectress of harbours, than was possible for Engel, who, though he surmised that the two were one, had not at his disposal the facts for verifying this surmise. At cape Andrea in Kypros (site 70 in the list, p. 27) we found Aphrodite Akraia on her sacred mount, and again at Cape Pedalion (site 16, p. 12) we saw Aphrodite throned on a holy hill by the sea. The Romans gave the name of Juno to the principal goddess of the Etruscans, just as to the principal goddess of the Carthaginians.

Of the highest importance is the notice that the Etruscan images of Hera bore a resemblance to Aphrodite. This was so, because the Etruscan Kypra was a Kypris, an Astarte-Aphrodite, both in name and nature, because her worship and her images had come to Etruria from Kypros. This statement requires support. We have seen above how the Adonis worship of Etruria was at an early state typologically influenced by Kyprian images of that god. Objects illustrative of this are collected on Pl. XCII. The influence on Etruria both of the types and myths of Kypros was far stronger in the case of the goddess, who in both lands had her hieroduli, to whom in both lands maidens sacri-ficed their virginity. From a vast number of illustrations of this connection I select two peculiarly striking examples (Pl. CV, 4 and 5) The first (4) is an image of a two-winged goddess; her bust is naked, from the waist downwards she is draped in a tightly-fitting skirt, while on her head, as on those of the Mykenaean idols, and of the Cyprian women, sits a dove. The second image is that of a goddess with four wings, entirely draped, wearing on her head a tutulus, and holding a dove to her bosom. She stands on a kind of palmette-ornament of very frequent occurrence in Etruria. The connection with Kypros, where female figures of goddesses, priestesses, &c. are so exceedingly numerous, is obvious. The high pointed cap also is in Kypros a favourite head-dress not only for men, but for women. The winged woman on the Kyprian censer (Pl. CII, 1 = CXXXIV, 2 = p. 195 fig. 169 = Pl. CXCVII, 2) wears it. This Kyprian winged figure, however, carries in front of her not a dove, but a winged sun-disc. In Etruria similar censers supported by figures of the Kypra have been found. On Pl. CXXXIV, 1, I give an illustration of one example. The Kypra images of Etruria, our winged woman on the Cyprian censer, and the dove-goddesses of both lands are connected by a further thread with Carthage. Compare for a moment our images of the dove-goddess, our Cyprian dove-cots, and the Cyprian monsters, half bird, half man (Pl. CV, 8, XXXVIII, 13, &c.), with the Carthaginian inscribed votive stele (Pl. LXXXV, 9) which we have already more than once cited. At the summit of the stele is an outstreched hand uplifted in prayer; beneath it, under a semicircular canopy flanked by two Ionic colonnettes, hovers a goddess half woman, half bird. Her human body, to which huge pinions are attached, ends in a feather-dress. She carries in the Cyprian fashion the sun-globe, and crescent. Beneath the inscription stands the cone of Tanit Face of Baal. Two doves, heraldically grouped, hover round the idol.

On the well-known Bucchero vases Kypra appears accompanied by her holy bird, which here however takes the form of a goose or swan (Pl. CIII, 2). She is often escorted by wild beasts, such as lions, panthers, by Chimaerae, and by Centaurs. Do not these last point again to Kypros? And the swan, is it not in Kypros the bird of Astarte-Aphrodite, the giant bird which bears the goddess on its back across sea and land?[*] Noteworthy parallels to these images of Kypra and Kypris, although

---

[*] Such an Aphrodite on the swan is figured by A. P. di Cesnola, who found several replicas in

the art which produced them is essentially other, are the feminine figures grasping brutes, such as the winged goddess holding birds by their necks on the Theban terracotta casket*) (Pl. C, fig. 8), the winged goddess on the Rhodian necklace (CII, 3, again accompanied by Centaurs), and lastly the winged goddess on the celebrated bronze hydria of Grachwyl (Pl. XCIX, 3). She has about her four lions, two snakes, and two hares, and like the Kyprian, Mykenaean, and Etruscan images, a bird on her head. Hares are associated with Astarte-Aphrodite. I found evidences of a hare-sacrifice in a Kyprian holy grove (No. 3 in the list); and in 1881 I excavated at Salamis a terracotta figure (not older, however, than early Hellenistic times) representing Aphrodite or one of her priestesses carrying a hare. The Centaurs who alternate with the winged goddesses on the Rhodian necklace also hold hares. The hare must at a very early date have become an Aphrodisiac animal, and must also in quite early times have been numbered among the characteristic attributes of the goddesses from whom Astarte-Aphrodite derived her origin. Male figures carrying hares would appear to be a creation of Babylonio-Assyrian art, and occur, it seems, in earlier examples than female figures carrying this animal (Layard, Niniveh II, 9).

On the cylinder of unhappily doubtful date, and of uncertain origin (but probably Hittite) Pl. CXV, 2, already adduced by Milchhöfer in his discussion of the "Island" stones**), we see two demons with the heads of beasts bearing, hung from a pole, a dead stag. One is winged, the other, who is wingless, carries also a hare. On the cylinder Pl. XCVI, 5 (= Pl. CXXVII, 1)***), which, if I am not mistaken, is either Hittite or shows Hittite influence, we see at the top figures dancing round a sun-god or a flower-god. Beneath is a scene of tree-adoration, and three demons with animal heads, one without wings and with animal legs, the other two with human legs and wings, carry each a hare, it would seem designed for sacrifice. Demonic figures of this kind are the prototypes of centaurs carrying hares. The winged or unwinged feminine demon grasping animals is a later conception than her male counterpart; the hare is among the animals she inherits from him. If (in default of access to the original) we may trust the illustration, a cylinder found in Cyprus, and most probably of native manufacture, supplies the oldest example of a winged female figure holding a hare. This cylinder was in Cesnola's possession, and an illustration is given in Cesnola-Stern, Pl. LXXV, 7. A winged feminine demon holding a hare, and with a dove hovering at her feet, is adored by a man. A second smaller figure of a worshipper is introduced above three human heads. Next comes a male deity holding a staff, and standing on the back of an ox, while a little altar signifies that a sacrifice is being performed. This Cyprian representation of the winged goddess with the hare certainly belongs to the pre-Graeco-Phoenician period.

Of the eight Cyprian cylinders here represented (figs. 190—197†) six at least (190, 191, 193—196)

Salaminian tombs, in his "Salaminia" (to face p. 204). I also found a replica, now in the British Museum, in a tomb at the same place. These terracottas are of the 4th or 3rd centuries B. C., but the motive has its origin in older myths and religious imagery.

*) Knoll ("Studien zur ältesten Kunst in Griechenland") while believing that the type of the winged female figure with the dove is originally proper to Ištar-Astarte, regards the figure on the Theban terracotta box as the representation of a pure Greek archaic Artemis. We shall see below how Aphrodite and Artemis pass into and out of each other in Kypros.

**) "Anfänge der Kunst in Griechenland," p. 55, note; Lajard, Mithra XXXVI, 13.

***) Lajard, "Mithra," XXIX, 1; Milchhöfer, ibid. p. 55.

†) Fig. 190 = Pl. CXVI, 1 = A. P. di Cesnola, "Salaminia" XIV, 38.—Fig. 191 = "Salaminia" XIV, 40.—Fig. 192 = "Salaminia" XII, 3 —Fig. 193 = Pl. LXXIX, 6 = "Salaminia" XIII, 29.—Fig. 194 = CXVI, 8 = "Salaminia"

seems to represent feminine figures grasping animals. One of the figures on 192 is winged, but their
sex is in this case doubtful, and more probably male than female. On 195 two figures, one male and
one female, appear to carry a bird between them on their hands. The animal held by one of the
women on 193 looks very like a hare. The other quadrupeds of the determinable species subjected
by these anthropomorphic goddesses or she-demons are lions, griffins, goats, and moufflons. Lions
and griffins, held by their tails, are particularly common. On the cylinder, fig. 196, three winged
goddesses with the heads of animals are dancing in a circle round the holy tree. The one on the left
grasps the tree alone, the one on the right grasps the tree with one hand, and an animal with the other,

Fig. 190.   Fig. 191.   Fig. 192.

Fig. 193.   Fig. 194.   Fig. 195.

Fig. 196.   Fig. 197.

while the central one grasps with one hand a similar animal, and holds aloft a branch in her other
hand.*) The cylinder 197 illustrates those dove-cots, dove-cups, tripods, and tetrapods with doves
perched on them, of which we spoke above. We see two divinities with short staves in their hands
seated before a tripod, on which is set a small structure resembling a dove-cot; on its roof sits a bird

p. 130 Fig. 122.—Fig. 195 = Pl. CXVI, 4 = "Salaminia" p. 121 Fig. 115.—Cp. also p. 87, Fig. 122 and 124 and
Pl. CXXVIII, 5, "Salaminia" XIV, 41 and 42—Fig. 196 = Pl. LXXXVII, 9 = "Salaminia" p. 121, Fig. 116.—
Fig. 197 = Pl. XXVIII, 25 = "Salaminia" XIV, 45.

*) None of these cylinder-seals, indeed no cylinder-seals at all, have been hitherto found in Graeco-
Phoenician tombs of the Iron Age in Cyprus. The hundreds of seal-cylinders which have come to light were
all (like those I myself excavated (cp. p. 34, fig. 34, v, w, = Pl. CLXXI, 14, where see the Description) in
tombs of the Copper Bronze Age. L. P. di Cesnola did not find in Graeco-Phoenician tombs of the Iron Age
at Kurion (still less in a temple-treasure) the cylinders he publishes (Cesnola-Stern, Pl. LXXV—LXXVII) as
part of his Kurion find, and A. P. di Cesnola did not find at Salamis the cylinders he publishes as coming
from Salamis ("Salaminia," Plates XIII—XV, 51 and figs. 113—123). As all the cylinders, relating to the discovery,
of which we have trustworthy information, were discovered in Pre-Graeco-Phoenician tombs of the Copper-
Bronze Period, we are justified in assigning those published by the two Cesnolas to this early date. The
latest specimens can scarcely be later than 1000 B. C.

which may be meant for a dove. This cylinder is repeated on Pl. XXVIII as fig. 25, and I there place beside it (Fig. 24) a cylinder of unknown provenance from the Clerq collection. A comparison shows us that both specimens come from the same fabric, or are productions of the same school of art. In this case a goddess is seated before a tetrapod, on the edge of which sit two birds (doves?) Other birds amid other symbols flutter and hover around. The cylinder Pl. XXX, 3, although of distinct style may belong to the same cycle of myths. We see, perched on a structure like a dove-cot, a bird, resembling a swan, to which two figures, one seated, and one erect, offer prayers or sacrifice.

The fact that we have no other examples from deposits of the early Kyprian Graeco-Phoenician period of winged she-demons holding hares or birds may, as in the case of the figures with doves on their heads, be due to chance. Of a small steatite relief, found while I was in Cyprus, I can unhappily only give an imperfect description. It was for sale at Nicosia in 1886. The square I took of the relief was lost, and I possess only a very imperfect sketch. The goddess, nude, stands on two animals; her arms are extended, and each hand grasps a goat by its horns and ears and raises it aloft, the whole being strictly symmetrical. This nude figure is an instructive counterpart to the draped figure of a winged female on the Rhodian hormos (CII, 3). Still more strikingly parallel, however, to the Cyprian steatite relief is the nude "πότνια Θηρῶν" on a shield from the grotto of Zeus Idaeus in Crete (Pl. CII, 2 and Pl. CXXXI, 4). This shield is almost certainly of Cyprian manufacture; the goddess bears an extraordinary resemblance to the national goddess of Kypros under that form (a modification of the Babylonian Istar; see the Babylonio-Assyrian seal-cylinders, Pl. XXXI, 1—4) which we already meet with in the Bronze Age (see p. 34, figs. 31 and 32) and which Schliemann's leaden idol from Hissarlik (p. 148, fig. 149)*) again reproduces**). The type of the nude "πότνια Θηρῶν" holding lions by their ears °°°) on the Cretan bronze shield is intermediate between this early Kyprian type and our nude idols of Astarte-Aphrodite (Pl. LV, 5 and CXCIX, 6).

We also possess coming from Cyprus a nude bronze figure of Astarte-Aphrodite (Pl. CVII, 2)†) which must be described in this connection. Although the exact circumstances of its discovery are unknown, there is no doubt that it was found in the island. This interesting specimen formed the handle of a mirror, meant to be either grasped in the hand or set upon a table. The lofty

---

*) Schliemann Ilios p. 381) rightly recognised in this idol an Aphrodite with goat's horns, and Sir C. Newton agrees. Both these scholars compare Cyprian idols of Astarte-Aphrodite with ram's or cow's horns (Lenormant, "Les Antiquités de la Troade," p. 23 and Cesnola-Stern, Pl. I, 7). Knoll ("Studien zur ältesten Kunst in Griechenland," p. 81) believes that this species of Istar had wings given her for no particular reason. I think the wings of the female figure holding animals are simply transferred to her from her male counterpart, cp. e. g. Pl. XCIX, 1 (Assyria), Pl. CLV, 2 (hither Asia) &c.

**) Cp. the figure of the same nude goddess in the centre of the cylinder CXV. 5 = Lajard, "Mithra," XXX, 1. It is, unfortunately, difficult to date this specimen. The group of Izdubar and Eabani on the left, as well as the style, would speak for somewhat early Babylonian times, while the god on the right standing on a humped ox points rather to Hittite, or perhaps we should say North-Syrian or Cappadocian influence.

***) A. L. Frothingham (American Journal of Archaeology, IV, 1888, p. 431—449), in his article on the early Cretan bronzes, maintains that the nude goddess on the shield is not Istar, but the only reason he gives is that Istar as a goddess of war is always clothed and armed. But in this case we have the Graeco-Phoenician modification of the nude Istar. Frothingham gives, as illustrative of this nude feminine divinity holding lions by the ears, a drawing of a Persian cylinder of the British Museum, on which a demon holds two winged bulls by the ears, but this proves nothing. Demonic beings at all periods frequently hold monsters or wild beasts by the ears or horns (e. g. Pl. XCIX, 4; Pl. CIV, 4 and 13).

†) After Perrot III, p. 862, fig. 629.

headdress of the goddess is composed of a flower, as in the images of that deity, who is formed by the union of Aphrodite and Isis *); she carries a pair of cymbals **) and stands on a frog. She wears, in addition to the chain on her neck, a strap passing from the right shoulder to the left hip, like the quiver-strap of Artemis, but hung from it. In place of the quiver is a massive signet-ring. On the two shoulders and fore-arms we still see the fore-paws of the two lions which clung in an inverse position to the figure of the goddess and formed the attachment to the missing disc of the mirror. As pendants to this bronze we can again adduce two Italian works, the one of early date and Etruscan (CVII, 3), the other considerably later and probably Roman (CVII, 1). The first shows us a draped female figure standing on a tortoise,***) an animal sacred to Aphrodite. Her left hand grasps her skirt; her right hand is raised as if to pronounce a blessing. The himation hanging from the right shoulder is gathered up on the left hip, its raised edge recalling, by its form and direction, the quiver-strap worn usually by Artemis. The second (CVII, 1) is a colossal female form supported by two equestrian figures, with two sphinxes and two lions seated on her head and shoulders. Her right hand rests on her bosom; with her left hand she also grasps her skirt; it is that familiar and very ancient hieratic attitude in which women, both mortal and immortal, are so often portrayed.†) Next to this figure I have placed (CVII, 4) a nude figure of Harpokrates, of Ptolemaic times, which shows how in Egypt the youthful Horus also became a lord of animals. Behind him, over his head, peers the grinning god Bes, his head and hands alone visible.

To return to the hare, I still have to note that Kypros took some part in the development of a non-mythical motive, the hare-hunt.††) The bronze patera from Nineveh (Layard, "Monuments of Nineveh" L^d series LXI A) on which are depicted in concentric zones hounds in cry, and hares, has already been held by others to be a Phoenician work, and must, in my opinion, have been made in Cyprus. An abbreviation of the hare-hunt, a group of a grey-hound tearing a hare to pieces, occurs in Kypros executed in limestone with a frequency quite surprising. The example given on Pl. CCVI, 9 comes from a tomb of the 6th century B. C. at Amathus, a site which has given us several replicas of the group.†††) Cesnola in his Atlas (Pl. LXXX, figs. 523 and 525) gives illustrations of two similar groups. which must come from the same stratum of discovery as our more perfect specimen, with which they are identical in style. §)

---

*) Cp. Roscher's Mythol. Lexikon II, col. 495.

**) I found at Tamassos in 1889 a pair of bronze cymbals.

***) Tortoises of terracotta are frequently found in Cyprus; small bronze ones also occur, but less frequently. I myself, for example, met with several in tombs at Marion Arsinoë in 1886. The English excavators also found one of these terracotta tortoises (together with doves) in a tomb at Old Paphos. They also found there, within the precincts of the celebrated temple of Aphrodite, a limestone block with dedicatory inscription, on the upper surface of which a tortoise is carved in relief. This votive offering of a tortoise to Aphrodite was unfortunately found in a very fragmentary condition See for the terracotta tortoise Journal of Hellenic Studies, 1888, p. 270, for the stone one, ibid. p. 253, no. 117.

†) Cp. Plates XLIX, 1--3 and 6, LI, 11, 12 &c.

††) Cp. Löschke, Archaeol. Zeitung, 1881, col. 33; Knoll, "Studien zur ältesten Kunst in Griechenland," p. 96.

†††) The hare is coloured grass-green all but its eyes, which are outlined in red, the basis and the background are red, the dog stands out white against this red background. The other replicas were similarly coloured.

§) On the Boeotian box a hound is chasing a hare (Pl. CXXXIII, 3) A proto-Corinthian vase found in Cyprus near Limassol (Pl CLII, 18, a, b, c) shows us a hare with a pack of hounds at its heels.

This section has taught us how Kyprian worship and Kyprian idols were carried to Etruria *) no less than to Naucratis and Carthage. We have traced also the direction of many other threads of culture passing from Asia Minor and Syria through Kypros to the countries of the West, to Rhodes, Crete, Greece and Italy, and even to Switzerland.

It would require a thick book, specially dealing with these questions, to treat at proper length the history of the numerous and far-reaching relationships and consonances between Kypros on the one hand, and Etruria and Sardinia on the other. I must here content myself with the examples I have given.

Before concluding this section, however, I would say something as to the Kyprian Hera. Just as the Romans at a later period identified the Etruscan Kypra or Kupra with their own Juno, so it would appear that the Kyprian Hera is no other than Aphrodite. There are no traces in Kypros of any ancient widespread worship of Hera. But in later times, as the process of decomposition advances, one original divinity being in her different functions resolved into a number of new divinities with distinct names, and as more and more foreign gods take their places in the Kyprian pantheon, the shrines of Hera in Kypros become more numerous. Thus we find dedications to her or mention of her at Niso near Idalion (Bull. de Corr. Hell. III, 166—167) at Amathus (C. I. G. 2640 = Wadd, 2822, a Heraion) and at Paphos (C. I. G. 2640 = Wadd, 2795, Aphrodite, Zeus Polieus, and Hera in this order). °°) If Hogarth, despite Deecke's and Meister's doubts, is right in reading the name of Hera on an inscription ("Devia Cypria", p. 33; cp. site no. 60 in our list, p. 23 above), Nikokles, King of Paphos and high-priest of Aphrodite dedicated an offering to this goddess. If this is so, this inscription of the 4th century B. C. affords the earliest mention of Hera in Kypros.

What I have said in the preceding paragraphs on the subject of the feminine deities or demons grasping animals must here suffice; further notice of these beings will be found in the Description of the Plates. Before concluding, I would, however, state my emphatic opinion that in

---

*) Enmann in his voluminous study, "Kypros und der Ursprung des Aphroditecultus" (Mémoires de l'Academie imperiale des sciences de St. Pétersbourg XXXIV, 1886, no. 13, 1—85) unhappily develops views which we cannot but regard as in the main erroneous. His object is to prove that Aphrodite is an Aryan goddess, and he maintains (p. 62) that the island of Kypros had nothing to do with the origin of Aphrodite-worship. According to him, all ancient authors from Homer and Hesiod onwards were wrong in understanding Κύπρις, the ancient epithet of the goddess to refer to her origin or birth in the island. Consequently Enmann proceeds to criticise Engel's statements as to the Etruscan Kypra, and the introduction into Etruria from Kypros of the worship of Astarte-Aphrodite and Adonis. E. Curtius comes off worst of all. We read (p. 85) "Seltsam muss es erscheinen, wenn ein so gefeierter Forscher, wie E. Curtius, unter vielem Beifall der Mit-forscher, die banalen Irrthümer der Alten" (i. e. the ancient authors Homer, Hesiod. &c.) "noch übertreffen konnte, indem er nicht blos Aphrodite, sondern auch fast alle übrigen weiblichen Gottheiten der Hellenen in den unbekannten und unbestimmten Orient hinüber spielte." Since then, Curtius has published two further important studies "Studien zur Geschichte der Artemis" (Sitzungsber. d. preuss. Akad. d. Wissensch., Berlin 1887, p. 1169—1183) and "Studien zur Geschichte des griechischen Olymp" (ibid. 1890. p. 1141—1156). It is marvellous with what insight Curtius has analysed those elements of Greek mythology which are derived from the Semitic East not by actual transference of myths, but by the suggestive power of transferred types and motives. The results of this quite new treatment, which my discoveries in Cyprus amply support and justify, are of course inconvenient not only to Mr. Enmann, but to others also. What Curtius maintains as regards the feminine deities, holds good for some of the male also. That Herakles, for instance, takes his origin both typologically and mythologically from Izdubar-Eabani, may now be regarded as established. That he is a primitive Greek deity is out of the question (cp. also the article Izdubar in Roscher's Lexikon).

°°) Cp. also Drexler in Roscher's Lexikon, col. 2086.

doubtful cases it is far better to give these goddesses or demons no names. We saw how certain types
of figures, male or female, carrying flowers or animals, are employed solely to represent mortals, and
so may meet us in the holy places of all gods alike. We saw
how in some cases it was easy, in others difficult or impossible,
to distinguish the statues of mortals from those of the immortals.
We saw further, and shall again see in following sections dealing
with Athene and Artemis, how one and the same type, one and
the same motive, may be used to represent distinct goddesses.
The same applies to the winged and unwinged female figures
grasping animals. Often the attributes which are added and
other circumstances tell us that the artist wished to portray
Artemis (e. g. the winged females on the François vase and the
Olympian bronze plaque). In other cases it is no less certain
that the winged female with beasts is Astarte-Aphrodite (e. g. the
Cretan shield). Elsewhere the characters of both goddesses are
combined. I give here a cut of a statue which shows us such a
combination of Tanit-Artemis and Rhea Kybele (fig. 198 =

Fig. 198.

CCVI, 6). The goddess is seated on a throne between two lions, and wears the mural crown.
This limestone statue was one of votive offerings in the sanctuary of Tanit-Artemis at Akhna
(no. 1 in our list).

5. Astarte-Aphrodite, Atargatis, Derketo and Semiramis, Fishes and Fish-demons. Ornithomorphic deities. The Harpies and Sirens.

The fish-goddess Derketo was, according to legend, the mother of the dove-goddess Semiramis.
Both are then interfused with each other, and with Atargatis and Astarte-Aphrodite. The
legends as they reach us are not of great antiquity, but, as a nude figure of Astarte-Aphrodite from
Amaryetti *) shows, rest upon older traditions.

The sanctity attached to certain fish, animals which also belong to the ritual apparatus of Astarte-
Aphrodite in Kypros, is mentioned by ancient authors, and is illustrated by archaeological discovery.
Above (p. 93, fig. 132; p. 171 fig. 157, pp. 172–3 and Pl. LXXXVII 3 = XCVIII 5) I made mention of
the holy fish of Kypros and Carthage, and in the sections on Dionysus I said a few words about the
dolphin. Here I would call the reader's attention to certain other illustrations collected on Plates
XCVII and XCVIII, which show how the fish was sacred in Kypros, and from being a symbol became
an ornament. XCVII, 4 shows one side of a small tripod of terracotta, intended to support a small
caldron-shaped vessel **). On Plate CLVI, 4 we see the design of the three sides of this tripod
transferred to a plane surface, as well as a cut of the tripod itself. One of the three sides is
geometrically ornamented; on the second (CLVI, 4) stands a figure, holding a small plant of palmettes

*) Journal of Hellenic Studies, 1888, p. 172.
**) I found in 1883 at Kurion three of these tripods, with the caldron-shaped vessels still standing on
them. They are now in the Cyprus Museum at Nicosia.

form, between two quadrupeds; on the third side XCVII, 4 a similar figure between two fish. We must see in this figure either the male correlative to Derketo, Dagon, or the Philistine god of the Bible (of whom more anon), or some similar fish-demon. On Plate XCVIII, 2, 3 and 8 three vases are reproduced, an Egyptian plate with green glaze (2), a Boeotian plate with dull-black ornamentation (8) and an oenochoe found by me in 1883 at Salamis in Cyprus (3). On 2 we see a design, adapted to the circle of the plate, of three fish alternating with as many lotus-flowers; the fish being so grouped that one head serves for all three. On 8 is a design of two lotus-flowers and two ribbons also adapted to the circle. I give this Boeotian plate here, because in 1886 I found at Marion Arsinoë a cylix on which were painted four lotus-flowers alternating with as many buds, the whole design being strikingly parallel to that on the Egyptian as well as to that on the Boeotian plate. On 3 the shoulder of the vase is decorated with three fishes.

We see the sacral significance of the fish*) already superseded by the decorative. In October 1892 the Berlin Museum acquired from the Lawrence-Cesnola collection an early-Graeco-Phoenician vase from Cyprus, on which two quadrupeds and two fishes are heraldically grouped round a holy or decorative tree**). Very similar, but more nearly influenced by the Mykenaean ceramic style, or perhaps actually belonging to this style, are the decorations on the porringer from Cyprus of the Metropolitan Museum of New York, represented Pl. XCVIII 4. Here four fishes, whose tails terminate in concentric circles from which issue snakes' heads, are heraldically posed round about an arboreal ornament. The terracotta duck and boat (Plate XCVIII, 6 and 9) were found in a tomb at Lapithos, together with the objects represented Plate XCVII 1a—f. The amphora with stag and tree (a and b) and the two false-necked vases (c and e) belong to the late Mykenaean class. The vase d, of Cyprian clay, with an animal's head on the double handle, is a local Kyprian variant of the ordinary Mykenaean false-necked vase or "Bügelkanne". f, also of Cyprian clay, is an ointment pot in the form of a fish***). The duck (6) served the same purpose, while the boat (9) is solid. The ornamentation of these vases although Kyprian, is under the direct influence of the Mykenaean style. On a vase from Kalymnos, published by W. R. Paton†), we see grouped together the various ornamented motives, which are, dispersed among the vases of our Cyprian tomb, i. e. the arboreal ornament terminating in spirals, (as on 1 b), fishes (cp. 1 f) and aquatic birds (cp. 6)††).

The ornamental designs incised on the seal-cylinders from Cyprus (Pl. XXVIII, 9, 10 and 12), consist of trellises, spirals, &c. alternating with rows of fish. The cylinder, ibid. No. 13, bears rows of fish alone, bearing, as regards both their style and the manner of their arrangement, a close family

---

*) The artifical reservoir faced with regular courses of hewn stones at the foot of the sycamore of Nut is also alive with ducks and fish swimming among aquatic plants.

** With this the far older cylinder, Cesnola-Stern, Pl. LXXV, 8 (Cyprian work influenced by Hittite) should be compared. We there see a group composed of an anthropomorphic deity (who takes the place of the holy tree), and two quadrupeds, a moufflon and a winged griffin. Again, there was found in a tomb at Old Paphos (Journal of Hellenic Studies, 1888, p. 270) an archaic Graeco-Phoenician vase (now in the Ashmolean Museum at Oxford) on which are painted in black and red, trees, fishes, and stars, symbolizing Heaven, Earth and Sea, or, if in this case mere ornaments, yet pointing back to such early symbolisation.

***) Vases in the form of fish are very frequent during the second and longer half of the Copper-Bronze Period in Cyprus. An engraving of one is given by Cesnola-Stern, XV.

†) Journal of Hellenic Studies, 1887, Pl. LXXXIII, 5.

††) Cp. above p. 67, figs. 42, 43 and 84, (Cyprus.; 85–88 (Mykenae).

resemblance to those on the Cyprian cylinders. The provenance of this cylinder is uncertain, and it may very well have been made in Cyprus. On Babylonio-Assyrian cylinders we not seldom find fish introduced, either as symbols or as ornaments, or in both capacities at once (Pl. XXVIII, 1, XXIX, 6, 8, 13, XXX, 7, 12).[*] The fish as the symbol of fertility played, among the peoples of Western Asia, and among the Cyprians, a leading part in the cultus of feminine deities, and sacred fish were kept in tanks, ponds, and lakes. Xenophon (Anabasis 1, 4, 9) saw such fish, which were regarded as gods, in the Chalus near Aleppo[**]. Pausanias (VII, 22, 4) mentions the rites of a fish-worship evidently transplanted from the East[***] to Pherai. Fish (boiled or roasted), or gold and silver imitations of fish, were laid on the altar of Atargatis. A magnificent specimen of such a gold votive fish is that from the Vettersfeld gold-find (fig. 199 = XCVII, 7)[†]. I have already mentioned the discovery in Cyprus of a bronze dolphin. This custom of dedicating fish travelled at an early date from Egypt[††] and the East to Greece.

Fig. 199.

The feminine fish-goddess, who is at one time and at one place styled Atargatis, at another Derketo, and amalgamated even with the dove-goddess Semiramis, has a male counterpart in Dagon, the Philistian fish-god. Representations of this god are figs. 1—3, 5, 6, and 8 on Plate XCVII, and also, as I have above surmised, fig. 4, the painting on the Cyprian tripod. Like the analogous Derketo of Askalon he is half-man, half-fish. Dagon must be identified with Anammelech (Anu-Malik), the god of the Nepharvites[†††], and like Adrammelech (Adar-Malik) is to be regarded as another form of Moloch-Milkom produced by the conjunction of two divinities. Just as the bull-Dionysus, the Greek Minotaur§, and the Greek and Kyprian river-gods, such as Bokaros, derive their origin from the bull-headed anthropomorphic god Moloch, and the man-headed bull-god Adrammelech,

*) Movers ("Die Phönizier", 1, p. 308), in discussing a similar Babylonian seal-cylinder with fish engraved on it, refers us to Lucian's "De Dea Syria", where (chap. 49) it is narrated that pilgrims carried home with them pictures of similar scenes of worship.

**) Smith, "Religion of the Semites", p. 160

***) Even at the present day in the East both Turks and Orthodox Christians keep fish in tanks, regarding them as holy, attributing miraculous powers to them, and deriving oracular responses from them.

†) Furtwängler, "Winckelmannsprogramme", 1883, Pl. 1, 1.

††) For holy fish among the Egyptians, cp. Wilkinson-Birch, "Manners and Customs", p. 330—344. Votive bronze fish are not rare in Egypt.

†††) Cp. Riehm's Bibellexikon p. 61 and p. 330; Baethgen, "Semitische Religionsgeschichte", p. 56 and p. 265.

§) For the Greek Minotaur, see above p. 260.

so these forms of Moloch with the fishes tail, Dagon and Anu (Anu Malik), have given birth to those fish-tailed demonic beings of Greece, one of whom we see represented on the Vettersfelde gold fish, and who occur with especial frequency on black-figured vases. Pl. CX, 7 shows part of the design on an Attic kylix discovered by myself in 1886 at Poli tis Khrysokhou (Marion-Arsinoë). We here see a fish-tailed demon holding a fish in each hand between two human-headed birds. Just as these Greek mermen are derived from Dagon-Anammelech, so are the Sirens derived from the allied dove-goddess Semiramis-Derketo.

Hogarth found in or near the grove of Apollo-Opaon-Melanthios at Amargetti (No. 58 in our list) a terracotta statuette of a nude goddess holding a fish, whom he rightly styles Aphrodite. We see her here as a fish-goddess corresponding to Derketo-Atargatis. That Isis was also at times con-ceived as a fish-goddess by the Egyptians is shown by a bronze now in Liverpool, and reproduced (after Inman, "Ancient Symbol Worship," p. 68) by Goodyear in his handsome volume "The grammar of the lotus" (Pl. XLII, 7; hence our fig. 236 below). On p. 266 of his work Goodyear cites two further Egyptian parallels. We see the nude seated figure of Isis with the baby Horus, on her head the goddess wears a large fish. A terracotta of late Hellenistic times found in a tomb at Salamis ("Salaminia", facing p, 203) shows us once more the Cyprian fish-goddess, or sea-goddess in her later development, as an Aphrodite. She seems to have just emerged from the sea, and is arranging her hair, still wet from the waves, beneath her crescent shaped coronet. Two huge dolphins play about her feet, and one of them veils her nudity with its tail-fin. On the other dolphin sits an Eros playing upon a shell-shaped instrument, while a second Eros stands on the right, and beats time with a pair of clappers. The group is exceedingly graceful; the artist doubtless was not thinking of the old fish-goddess, but merely desired to portray the Greek Aphrodite.

As an appendix to these remarks on bird, and fish-Aphrodites, I may be allowed to say a word or two about the egg, which occupies an important place in the mythology of Egypt, Western Asia, and Kypros, and is also an attribute of Aphrodite.[*]) According to a local myth which reaches us in a very late form, Atargatis was hatched from an egg which the sacred fish of the Euphrates found in the stream and pushed out on to the bank [**]).

In Egypt the egg has a place in the myths of several deities. The earth-god Zeb is called in an Egyptian text the great gold-finch. He lays on the ground the egg, from which the sun-bird

issues like a phoenix.[***]) Ra, Chnum, and Ptah are often in our text called "Creator of the great egg which sprung from chaos."[†]) Ptah is said to have turned this cosmic egg on his wheel, like a potter.[††]) In an Old-Graeco-Phoenician grave at Kition I found in 1879, in the presence of Professor Sayce, a votive egg of terracotta turned on the wheel. The other objects found in the tomb fix circa 600 as the terminus ante quem. Fig. 200

Fig. 200.   (= Pl. CIX, 5) is from a photograph of this remarkable egg, which is about the size of a goose's egg, is hollow, and has a small hole communicating with the cavity. The

*) Preller, "Griech. Mythologie," [3] I, p. 305.
**) Smith, "Religion of the Semites," p. 160.
***) Brugsch, "Religion der Aegypter, p. 175.
†) Ibid. p. 169.
††) Cp. also Erman, "Aegypten und ägyptisches Leben," II, p. 352.

Etruscan finds of decorative ostrich eggs show that in those times the eggs of the gigantic bird were treasured and reverenced no less than at the present day in the East, where we see richly ornamented ostrich eggs hanging in Turkish Mosques and Christian churches. The ostrich was a holy bird in Assyria also, as appears especially from the bird-cylinders (e. g. Perrot II, p. 566, fig. 266). In Kypros aquatic birds (Pl. CVIII, 2), in Etruria sometimes aquatic birds, and sometimes cocks (CVIII, 4) took the place of the ostrich (CVIII, 1 and 3).

Pausanias (III, 16, 1) tells us that from the roof of the sanctuary of Hilaeira and Phoibe at Sparta hung an egg with ribbons tied round it. It was said to be Leda's egg. At the present day in Cyprus not only are, as I have said, large eggs, especially ostrich eggs, hung from the ceilings of mosques and churches, but the country people hang certain eggs as bringers of good luck, and as natural marvels from the ceilings of their houses. If one asks them the reason, one is gravely assured that this egg is no ordinary hen's egg, but was laid by a cock. But I have never come across any one who actually saw the cock lay the egg.

6. Astarte, Semiramis. The winged sun-globe and winged bust of a god.

The fish-goddess Derketo is the mother of the dove-goddess Semiramis. Derketo's beautiful baby is exposed by her heartless mother, and fed by doves, until found by the herdsman Senimas and named Semiramis. Semiramis at the end of her days changed into a dove.°) An idol with a dove on its head was, so Lucian tells us, said to be that of Semiramis.**) The idols found at Mykenae (fig. 201 = Pl. CV, 3) and in Etruria (202
= CV, 4) answer admirably to this description. Like Astarte-
Aphrodite in Kypros (fig. 210 = Pl. CV, 8), Semiramis becomes
herself a dove. This goddess, as we know, was, like the bearded
Aphrodite of Kypros, conceived as bisexual. Such a being, half
dove and half human, with breasts like a woman and a beard
like a man, is represented below (fig. 210).***) The creature is
playing on Pan's pipes. It comes, like the aedicula with the
doves (Pl. XXXVIII, 13), from the neighbourhood of Idalion,
where also were found the fragment of a dove-cote (Pl. XXXVIII,
11) and the dove-tower (p. 278, fig. 189), the latter in the temenos
of Aphrodite (no. 3 of our list). The aedicula (XXXVIII, 13) is
inhabited by three feminine monsters half woman, half bird

Fig. 201.   Fig. 202.

(we should presumably say half-dove). One of these bird-women stands in the door, the two others at the windows. A little dove-house with no door and only one window, out of which peers a human-headed bird, is represented on Pl. CXCIX, 4.†) The conical dove-tower in which the goddess, here in human form, sits with her doves flattering round her, ††) has been more than

*) Movers, " Die Phönizier," p. 632—633.

**) Ibid. p. 633.

***) Perrot III, p. 600, fig. 410.

†) Ibid. p. 897, fig. 641.

††) The Carthaginian votive stele (Pl. LXXXV, 1) with its doors and windows also represents a dove-tower. With these towers should be compared a modern Syrian dove-tower in Riehm's Bibellexikon, p. 1616.

once represented and discussed in the present work (e. g. p. 278, figs. 187 and 188). Both the winged sun-globe of Egypt (e. g. p. 72, fig. 94), Western-Asia (e. g. Pl. LXXX, 2), Cyprus (e. g. p. 57, figs. 53 and 54) and other countries in which we meet with the production of Graeco-Phoenician art (Pl. LXXVII, 21) and the winged bust or busts of one or more divinities, belong to this cycle of types, although the myths suggested by, rather than suggesting, the type differed materially in different ands. It is at least clear in many cases that the pinions and tail both of the sun-disc and of the busts are those of doves.

I here give (fig. 204) an illustration of one of those satchels which the Assyrian winged demons are accustomed to hold in their hands.*) Inwoven or embroidered on this satchel, which

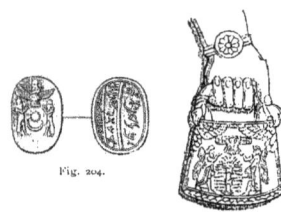

Fig. 204.

Fig. 203.

undoubtedly served some ritual purpose, is one of those scenes of tree-adoration which recur on all parts of their dress furniture and arms, and which we have above dealt with at such length. Above the tree hovers the winged solar globe, and the two upper angles of the field are occupied by two huge dove's wings. Side by side with the satchel I give (fig. 203) the two engravings of an ellipsoid gem with Phoenician inscription. We here see, quite in accordance with Kypro-Phoenician conceptions, the sun and crescent moon adored by two men, while above hovers the bust of the supreme god ending in a dove's tail and supported by dove's wings. These are the symbols in which the god of gods, or the divine triad or trinity, was thought to be embodied.

7. The soul of Osiris. The dove as Holy Ghost.

(Plate LXXII, 1, 2 = CIX, 9; LXXIII, 1 = CIX, 4; CVI, 2).

Riehm's Bibellexikon (p. 1616—1618) has dealt with the relations which subsist between these symbols (dove, winged-disc &c.) of the religions of Mesopotamia, Syria and Egypt, and the conceptions prevailing in the Old and New Testaments. The soul of Osiris, which Egyptian eschatology regarded as the soul of all the dead, is another of the threads running through that gorgeous tapestry of oriental symbolism, which kindled and fed the imagination of the Greeks, and which has furnished the religion which has conquered the world with nearly all its imagery.

In my work on Tamassos I shall publish an interesting scarabaeoid paste, set in a gold swivel. A dead man, bewailed by two winged genii, lies on a bed. Above hovers his soul on its way to heaven, under the semblance of a dove. The winged genii of this Graeco-Phoenician gem of the early sixth century B. C. precisely resemble angels. Old symbols have imperishable power, and forms which belong in their origins to another world of thought, become, in the hands of new generations, the exponents of new ideals, and survive as such. The dove, the bird of Astarte-Aphrodite and Semiramis, became the symbol of the Holy Ghost.

---

*) De Vogüé, Mélanges, Pl. VII = Perrot III, p. 631, fig. 423.

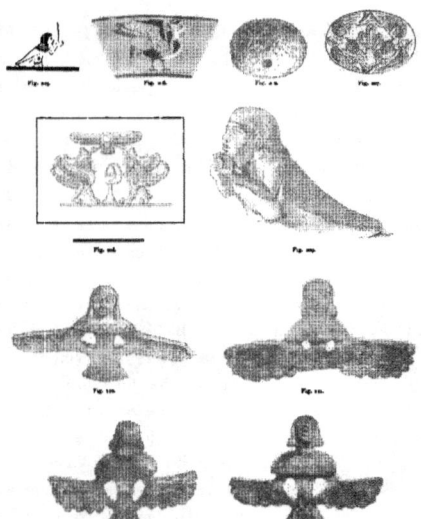

Fig. 303. Fig. 304. Fig. 305. Fig. 306.

Fig. 308. Fig. 309.

Fig. 310. Fig. 311.

Fig. 312. Fig. 313.

8. Harpies, Sirens and Erinyes.

Hausey[*] and Perrot[**] are, if I am not mistaken, the first who have made any serious attempt to refer back these Greek monsters to their Egyptian and Oriental originals[***] and to point out the influence exercise on the development of these types by motives and conceptions of which the Cyprian dove-cotes, Pl. CIX, 3 and CXCIX, 4 and the Cyprian human-headed bird, Fig. 209, are

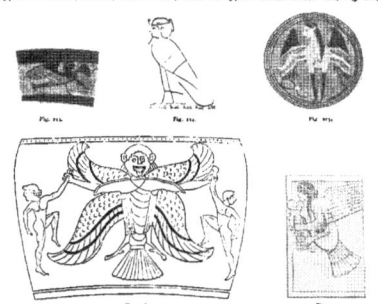

Fig. 214.   Fig. 211.   Fig. 213.

Fig. 216.   Fig. 217

examples. The Louvre possesses a terracotta figure from Cyprus of a similar monster, half bird, half woman, carrying in its arms, which are human, a child or adult. Even in Greek mythology Harpies, Sirens and Erinyes[†] pass into each other, and in the more fluid medium of typology they can rarely be distinguished.

*) Catalogue des figurines antiques de terre cuite du Musée du Louvre, p. 135.

**) Perrot II, p. 594, fig. 391; III, p. 599—600.

***) All that I aspire to here is to make some slight contribution to the history of the types of Harpies and Sirens. The task of tracking out the essential nature of these monsters, and of resolving the myths in which they are inwoven is foreign to the plan of this work. Langbehn (" Flügelgestalten der älterten griechischen Kunst," Munich 1880), Milchhöfer (" Die Anfänge der Kunst in Griechenland, Leipzig 1883) and Knoll (Studien zur ältesten Künste in Griechenland, Bamberg, 1890) have dealt with the subject in detail. Compare also the reviews of Knoll's work by Milchhöfer in the Wochenschr. für klass. Phil., 1891, no. 16 and by Böhlau in the Berl. Phil. Wochenschr., 1892, no. 4, p. 119.

†) For Erinyes and Harpies, cp. Roscher's Mythol. Lexikon cols. 1310—1336 and 1842—1847.

I therefore abstain from pronouncing to which class of Greek mythical beings a particular figure should be stated to belong. As in the case of the fish-tailed demons, which are all derived from the fish-gods of Mesopotamia and Syria (Anu, Anammelech, Dagon, Anat, Astargalis, Derketo) we must start here from the general type of a demonic being with the body of a bird. Our illustrations, figs. 205 - 217, convincingly show that the Greeks, in conceiving these monstrous forms, with which Homer was already familiar, had present to them various Oriental and Egyptian representations of gods or monsters. We must briefly discuss the process of which these Greek conceptions are the result; for, on the one hand, Kyprian Greeks participated in their creation, and on the other hand the artists were influenced by the representations of Astarte-Aphrodite as a dove-goddess. It would be highly erroneous to describe these half anthropomorphic, half ornithomorphic Kyprian images as Harpies or Sirens, even when, like the Harpies on the Xanthos monument, they carry a human figure in their arms (as in the case with the Kyprian terracotta referred to above and described by Heuzey Catalogue, p. 155) or play on instruments of music. The Kyprian artists desired, doubtless,

Fig. 218.

to portray in these cases their national goddess who, like Semiramis, is at times conceived as in whole or part a dove. From this Kyprian type of Astarte-Aphrodite with the body and legs of a dove arise the types of the Harpies, Sirens and Erinyes. Kypros is our best starting point, if we would trace this Astarte-Aphrodite-Semiramis type throughout its successive developments, and clearly establish its influence on the formation of these creatures of Greek fable. The first thing to strike us is the use made of the originally Egyptian type of the soul of Osiris (fig. 205 = Pl. CIX, 9 = LXXII, 2; fig. 214 = LXXIII, 1 = CIX, 4; Pl. LXXII, 1; Pl. CVI, 2; Pl. XXXIX, 4). A glance at the Kyprian bird-women who dwell in the dove-house (fig. 218 = CIX, 3 et alibi) will compel us to concede that Egyptian forms have here been imitated in Kypros.[*]) These Egyptian Osiris-souls have sometimes human heads, busts and arms (Fig. 205); sometimes the head alone is human, the whole body that of a bird (fig. 214). The Greeks, it would appear, used to give the Harpies, who had to

---

*) Not only the winged goddesses, but the houses, chapels and columns follow Egyptian models. On Pl. CXXIV, 2 and CLX, 6 we see Egyptian chapels, aediculae and houses, on Plates CXXIV, 4, 5 and CXXV, 3, 4 Kyprian. The capitals of the columns of the Kyprian chapels (fig. 218 = CXXIV, 5 = X, 3), Pl. XXXVIII, 13 and Pl. CIX, 3 are peculiarly Egyptian in form. (Cp. e. g. Pl. CLX, 6 and fig. 95 on p. 73).

raise weights, human breasts and human arms in addition to the human head (figs. 207, engraved gold-ring from Cyprus; 216, Greek vase; 217, Xanthian monument), while the Sirens, who had only to sing, were conceived and pictured as mere human-headed birds (figs. 206, 213, 215, from Attic vases found in Cyprus). The originals of both types are to be found in the Osiris-souls, which sometimes have arms (205) and sometimes not (214). It is of course quite possible that Sirens may in some cases have been portrayed with arms, just as, in very early times, the Harpies were represented by Greek vase painters as human beings with wings and claws (Pl. CX, 2). In the same tomb which gave us the Attic vase with a fish-tailed demon and two human-headed birds, (Pl. CX, 7 = fig. 206) was found the cylix figured on the same plate (CX, 7), on which is painted a winged demon running with extended arms. This demon need not be a Harpy and might very well pass for Eris (cp. the vase painting, Gerhard, "Akad. Abh." X, 5 = Roscher's "Mythol. Lexikon", col. 1338).*)

These fabulous creatures are usually represented as feminine by Greek mythology and art. In some exceptional cases we meet with analogous male forms (fig. 210, Cyprus; 212, Olympia). We shall very soon see that both these male characteristics (such as the beard), and the double head (Perrot II, p. 735, fig. 397) were intruders, here and that their reign was quite transient. This element we will discuss together with another, viz. egg-shaped bodies of some demons who are styled Harpies, and in this latter connection we must study the Xanthus monument (fig. 217).

I have in fig. 208 (= CIX, 1), figs. 7 and 8 of Pl. CIX and figs. 18 and 33 of Pl. XXXII given a series of illustrations of scorpion-men from Assyrian monuments. Four of the five are engravings of cylinders, and in each case we have a holy tree or post (Ashera?) with two scorpion-men in each side of it. In two cases the crescent moon, in another the winged sun-globe floats above the scene. No. 33, an Assyrian conic seal of the Berlin Museum, is of peculiar interest. Here we see a scorpion man in the centre of the circle with three birds (one bearing a great resemblance to a dove) and a fish about him. All these scorpion demons have human heads, with long beards and peaked caps, the bodies and tails of scorpions, and the legs of large birds of prey. The significance of the Berlin example lies in the fact that the demon is accompanied by the fish, the sacred animal of Atargatis-Derketo, and the dove, the sacred animal of Semiramis. When we consider also those busts of gods, terminating in dove's tails and furnished with long dove's pinions, which hover over the scenes of countless monuments either Assyrian or Babylonian, or influenced by the arts of these countries (cp. p. 95, figs. 135—137 and p. 292, fig. 204), we find a ready explanation of the occurrence of winged beings with beards (e. g. 210 Kypros, 212 Olympia); with the characteristics of the two sexes (210) or with two heads (Perrot II, fig. 397). No less do the egg-shaped bodies of the Harpies on the Xanthian monument and the Cyprian gems (figs. 217 and 207) betray the influence of the terminal forms of the winged busts of gods and of the bodies of the scorpion-men. It is, however, quite conceivable that the sculptor of the Xanthos monument did in fact (as has been asserted by earlier students of this work, but subsequently disputed)**) wish to signify that these Harpies were produced, like Semiramis beside the

---

*) The Assyrian relief, Pl. CX, 3 (= Perrot II, p. 774, fig. 446) shows an eagle-headed, four-winged demon in courant attitude catching by the leg a bearded sphinx. Beneath is a palmette. The design shows how Greek vase-painters were not alone influenced by Assyrian models in their choice of figure subject, such as the courant winged figure, but drew their incidental ornaments from the same source. The palmette in the Assyrian relief is the original of those beneath the handles of Attic cylices.

**) Cp. Overbeck, "Geschichte der griechischen Plastik." I, p. 170—172.

Euphrates and the Egyptian gods beside the Nile, from the egg, the imprisoned and motionless seed of life. The third of the women who on the upper zone of the Xanthos monument approach the throned Astarte-Aphrodite does in fact bring an egg as an offering.*) Had the artists of both the Xanthian relief and the Cyprian ring not desired for some reason to give the Harpies egg-shaped bodies, they would not have thus drawn then. All the other details of the two works show that the artists possessed enough power of observation and technical skill to produce, had they wished, a much more perfect and realistic picture of a bird Observe on the Xanthos relief how excellent is the drawing and modelling of the birds, a dove and cock, which are brought as offerings to the goddess, and with what a high degree of skill the other details are carried out. And the same may be said of the artist who engraved the Cyprian gold ring; he knew excellently well how to draw the heads and arms of his figures.**) These harpies, then, we may be sure, were meant to have egg-shaped bodies.

It remains for as to consider those bronze winged figures attached (or meant to be attached) to caldrons which have been found at various places, but of which the greatest number of examples come from Olympia, and of which admirable drawings have been published by Furtwängler***) (Pl. XXXIX, 3 a and b = fig. 211 = Olympia 784 and 784 a; figs. 212 and 212 a = Olympia 783 and 783 a; fig. 209 = Pl. CV, 7 [from Lake Van] = Perrot II, fig. 281). The fact, emphasized by Furtwängler, that the wings and tails of these figures stand in no organic connection with the human bust, at once directs our attention to the possibility of their being imitated from the winged and tailed busts of the Assyrian monuments (e. g. p. 95, figs. 135—137). Side by side with caldron-appendages in the form of winged human busts, we find others in the form of demi-eagles and winged bulls' heads, which recall still more vividly the winged sun-globes and hovering birds of victory that we meet with so often in Egypt and Assyria. The bearded winged figure, with shorn upper lip, from Olympia (fig. 212) is in this respect analogous to the human-headed bird from Cyprus (210). Another specimen coming, like fig. 209, from Lake Van (Perrot II, fig. 399) has two heads (a male and a female) and thus reminds us (1) of oriental Hermaphroditic forms such as Semiramis and the bearded Venus of Cyprus, (2) of Kyprian plank-idols with the two heads distincts but the bodies merged in one, such as Pl. XXXVI, 4 and 10, (3) of the Rhodian double-headed terra-cotta Pl. CVII, 5, and finally (4) of the Kyprian double heads or heads in the two faces, such as Pl. XCIII, 3—6. The first of these latter (XCIII, 3), a glazed aryballus composed of two heads, resembles in style and feature the bearded human head of the bird-demon who plays on Pan's pipes (fig. 210). The two faces have beards and whiskers, but shorn upper lips.

---

*) Cp. ibid. p. 171, fig. 37 (upper zone).

** The Cyprian gold ring, admirably wrought as it is, is yet not, I think, later than the sixth century. Here the Harpies or Sirens flutter round the holy tree, which is, as King (Cesnola-Stern p. 323) has pointed out, a modified form of that of Assyria. As one of these demonic beings carries two garlands, the other a garland and a lyre, they would seem to be meant for Sirens rather than Harpies. The similarity of the designs on this Kurion ring and on the Xanthos monument is no matter of chance, but has its roots in the relationship between Kyprian and Lykian art. We find also, for example, that figures smelling flowers are frequent on Lykian monuments. Another important archaic monument from Xanthos, the frieze of a sepulchral chamber, has, as is universally recognised, remarkable points of resemblance, as regards subject, composition and style, to the Cyprian sarcophagus of Amathus (cp. Overbeck, I, p. 176; Cesnola-Stern, Plates XLV—XLVIII and pages 414 and 415; Perrot III, p. 611). In both these works the employment of Assyrian motives and the Assyrian manner has been detected.

***) Olympia, Vol. IV. Die Bronzen, p 114—118, no 783—790.

We see then how in the case of these winged figures of demons with the bodies of birds and human-headed bird-deities, Cyprian forms, not unrelated to Astarte-Aphrodite, acquire peculiar significance in the typology of Eastern art, and, like other oriental types, suggest to the Greeks their mythical monsters such as Harpies, Sirens and Erinyes.

9. The martial Astarte-Aphrodite and Anat-Athene in Kypros.

We saw how Astarte-Aphrodite in Kypros takes her origin from Ištar as the queen of sensual love, the mother of gods and men. As such she is represented as nude, and nowhere did this view of her functions take stronger root than in this island, where in extensive deposits of the Bronze age we find no other idols but those of this nude goddess. At times as we saw, she presses her breasts, like the Egyptian hermaphroditic god Hapi, calling to her children to come and drink her milk; at times she holds a suckling child in her arms. We then saw how this national goddess assumed in Kypros all kinds of functions and forms. Not the least important of her epiphanies is as that martial goddess whom the Greeks identified with their Athene. Under this form we already meet with Ištar in Babylon and Assyria. A. Jeremias, in his article "Izdubar" in Roscher's Lexikon*), has given as a picture of this Ištar, the patroness of war and the chase, which is so complete that it exempts me from dealing here at length with her. Among the illustrations to his article Jeremias includes the cylinder which I publish as fig. 14 on Pl. XXIX.**) We here see Ištar in the form of an oriental Valkyr. At the foot of her holy palm she stands, clothed in splendid armour, on the back of a tiger or lion. Like the Greek Athene, she sounds the note of battle and leads on to victory or defeat.

We met with Derketo-Atargatis as a fish-goddess or fish, with Semiramis as a dove-goddess or dove. These goddesses also, as they mature, become warriors and conquerors. Semiramis amalgamates with Derketo and Anat. This Baalat of the Philistines and the martial Astarte-Aphrodite become one and the same goddess. By the side of the fish-god and war-god Dagon-Anu stands the martial Baalat Astarte-Anat. Schrader, in Riehm's Bibellexikon I, p. 61 has given an enlargement of our cylinder Pl. XXIX, 14, and quite rightly styled this form of Ištar Anat-Astarte.

Ancient authors often mention a Cyprian martial Aphrodite, an Aphrodite of the lance. But of this armed Aphrodite I have hitherto found no trace in Cyprus. Of the countless votive offerings we possess from groves of Astarte-Aphrodite, some one at least should have suggested this conception, were the armed Cyprian goddess an Aphrodite. When our ancient authorities speak of an armed Aphrodite, I believe they allude to a particular manifestation of the Baalat as a goddess of war and arms, a goddess differentiated, perhaps, from Ištar at as early a date as Astarte-Aphrodite herself; and whose local Greek and Phoenician title, namely Anat-Athene, they have neglected to transmit. This war-goddess was called Astarte, simply because this name was most familiar. The very passage of Scripture, which is usually cited in support of the assertion that these was an armed Astarte goes rather to prove that the name of the armed goddess was not Astarte but Anat. We read in

---

*) Mythologisches Lexikon. Bd. II, Sp. 811 and ff.

**) Cf. in Riehm's Lexikon (p. 113 A and 114 B) the goddesses standing on lions, whom Schlottmann calls sometimes the Assyrian Ištar, and sometimes the Assyrian Astarte.

1ˢᵗ Samuel XXXI, 10 how the Philistines hung up Saul's armour in the temple of their Astarte. Now the divine couple worshipped by the Philistines are a Baal called Anu-Dagon, and a Baalat called Anat-Astarte. The Philistines suspend Saul's armour in the temple of their war-goddess Anat-Astarte, just as the Idalians suspended in the temple of their Anat-Athene (with whose primitive aniconic worship we are acquainted, see p. 15) the weapons and armour of the vanquished Median Persian and Kitian princes. Some of these trophies together with an inscription recording the siege of Idalion by Medes and Persians have reached us. This Venus hastata this Cyprian Aphrodite ʾ Ἐγχειος (Hesychius) is Anat-Athene*), the Strength of Life, the goddess of war, who wounds, the goddess of peace, who heals. We found evidences of her worship in two places in the island, where it is not attested by ancient authors, at Idalion and a little south of Lapathos at the modern Larnaka tou Lapithou**) while literary authorities testify to the worship of Athene at Salamis***). Here the temples of Athene Agraulos and Dionysus stood within a single enclosure. One of the few figures of Athene we possess from Cyprus, a very charming terracotta, was found by me in 1880 in a tomb at Salamis. It has been already twice published, first by Percy Gardner in the Journal of Hellenic Studies for 1881, Pl. XV and secondly by A. S. Murray in his "History of Greek Sculpture", vol. II, Pl. XVII. On Pl. CCII, 1 I give for the first time a good reproduction in phototype of this interesting figure, which shows us Athene as a goddess of peace rather than of war with power to heal the wounds she or others have inflicted. Bareheaded and without her lance, the warrior goddess stands before us, her eyes cast up in thought, as if tired of the tumult of war. Her left hand reposes on her shield, and in her right she holds her helmet. The terracotta is a work of the latter end of the fourth or beginning of the third century. We must not expect to find in Cyprus iconic agalmata of Athene of very early date. Her worship was doubtless aniconic all over the island, as in the kingdoms of Idalion and Lapithos. But we have plenty of evidence that this worship was of early date. Laodike, daughter of Agapenor, sent from Kypros to the sanctuary of Athene-Alea at Tegea a votive offering of a peplos, the inscription concerning which was seen by Pausanias. Kyprian Telchines transplanted the imageless worship of Athene-Telchinia to Teumessos in Boeotia. No doubt the worship of this Athene Telchinia is to be localised in Tamassos and Idalion, the two places in Cyprus where the descendants of the mythical Telchines, the copper-miners in the one case and the bronze-casters in the other, worked. The similarity even of the two names Tamassos and Teumessos may not be accidental, but this is a matter upon which I cannot form an independent opinion. Further, if we consider that (as Meister first had the courage to assert) the Greeks had been settled in Cyprus for several centuries at the date of the Homeric poems, the still moot question "where was the Temese of the Odyssey?" can only be decided in favour of the Kyprian town Tamassos. Athene, then, in the person of Mentes, narrates how she went to exchange iron for bronze in Kypros, the copper country. That Kypros was a familiar land to the author of the Odyssey we know. Not only the Agamemnon of the Iliad had relations with the kingdom of Amathus, from which, according to a later tradition

---

*) Cf. the Lance-Athene in Idalion (p. 201).

**) On p. 223 I gave the Greek text and the Phoenician in a Latin translation, according to C. I. Sem. 95. The male correlative to this Anat, robur vitae, this Athene Σωτείρα Νίκη is the Baalmeraf or Baal Sanator who appears at Kition (C. I. Sem. 41) and is probably to be identified with Eśmun (C. I. Sem 42—43) and Eśmun Melqart (C. I. Sem. 16, 23, and 24).

***) Engel, Kypros II, p. 664.

he is said to have expelled Kinyras. But the Menelaos of the Odyssey reached Cyprus in his wanderings, and Odysseus, disguised as a beggar in his own house, pretends he had been in the service of Dinetor the Jasid in Cyprus*), and is sent back there by Antinoos with a curse.

I have made mention of all these details in order to show that the Greek Athene-worship in Cyprus can, and must, be of great antiquity. I have shown how the typology of the Kyprian Athene-worship is dependent on that of the Canaanitic and Philistian Anat-worship. But, of course, I do not deny the possibility of the independent development in Kypros of the cultus and myths of the Hellenic Athene. The name Anat, as that of a goddess, is found only in Phoenician inscriptions from Cyprus, and therefore it may seem hazardous to talk of a "Philistian Anat-worship", but the place-names Beth-Anat (Joshua XIX, 38, Judges I, 33) and Beth-Anôth (Joshua XV, 59) signify the "House (or sanctuary) of Anat", just as surely as Bethel means the "House of God", and Beth-Dagon the "House of Dagon". Of this Anat of the Kyprians, Canaanites and Philistines the Persians subsequently made their Anâhita**).

About a millenium before, or even earlier, after the period of the Hyksos, two divinities which have a wide influence in Kypros, i. e. Rešef and Anat, appear in Egypt. As I remarked before, E. Meyer represents as Astarte the goddess Qadesch who came from Creta to Egypt (Roscher, Mythol. Lexikon sp. 653, cf. p. 75, fig. 100). On this Egyptian relief Anat-Astarte is represented with the god Rešef, and the Kypros-god Min is the third in the group. It seems that the island of Kypros had a large share in the transition of the Anat-cultus, and the Anat cultus images to Egypt.***)

One word about the Gorgoneion of Athene and certain carved seated images of Athene with the Gorgoneion on the breast.†) If we compare the terra-cottas from Athens and Agrigentum (Pl. CCVI, 1—4) with the terra-cottas of the Artemis-Kybele-Paralia-groves in Kypros (Pl. CCIV, 1—3), with the heads on amulets, and the images of Adonis (Pl. XXXII, 1—5, and 17, XXXVIII, 16—20, XCII, 4, XCIII, 2, 9—11), and with the snake-surrounded heads on the garments of Rešef-Apollo, and his priests, we see many allied representations which might very easily have been adapted in the formation of the Greek gorgoneion worn by Athene on her breast. The gorgoneion on the shield of Athene has a Kyprian counterpart in the shield of Tamassos (Pl. LXX, 12), on which heads of Hathor resembling the Medusa alternate with winged lions.

In the formation of the gorgoneion it is quite possible that round sun and moon discs, sun and moon faces were combined with heads of Hathor-Bes-Osiris and Adonis. In the Kyprian Ištar figures of the bronze period, and in the early Graeco-Phoenician Astarte figures of the iron period, we find a large round disc under the breast.††)

*) Odyssey, XVII, 443 and 448.

**) For Anu, Anu-Malik, Anat and Anâhita cf. also Schrader "Die Abstammung der Chaldäer und die Ursitze der Semiten."

***) For Anat and Rešef in Egypt, cf. E. Meyer's "Geschichte des Alterthums", I, p. 133. I shall refer to this again when I speak of Rešef.

†) CCVI, 1 = Gerhard, Akad. Abhandlungen, Taf. XXII, 2, clay figure from Agrigentum and 2 = Gerhard, XXII, 4. - 3 = Gerh. XXII, 1.—4 = Gerh. XXII, 5.

††) Perrot III, p. 555, fig. 375. In the Graeco-Phoenician tomb at Amathus which contained the small clay model of a temple (Plate CXCIX, 1 and 2), were found two small rude Astarte figures with the round disc (sun? moon?) on the breast. In Plate CCVI, 5 is represented an early Graeco-Phoenician terra-cotta figure 5²/₃ inches = 14,34 cm in length, with a pillar base, from a tomb at Kurion. (Now in the Cyprus Museum.) Astarte-Aphrodite holds a large round disc in front of her. On the breasts are painted two large eyes. In 1879 I photographed a corresponding figure, (at that time in the collection of Dr. Castan) with a disc in the same position, and I still have a copy. These instances seem to prove the existence of a definite type.

These breast-discs were also found by me on nude images of Aphrodite in a grove on the plain of Salamis (No. 17 on the list). Draped images of the goddess or priestess show the same disc (Idalion No. 3 in the list, Pl. L, 4 and 5). These breast-discs are developed in a peculiar fashion in the cultus of Tanit-Artemis-Kybele, so that after a little practice it is very easy to determine whether any given votive image comes from the Artemis groves of the island, or not. I shall treat of this point more fully below.

8. Astarte-Aphrodite and Tanit-Artemis-Kybele. Demeter and Persephone.

The name of Tanit, which occurs more than two thousand times in the votive inscriptions of Carthage, has up to the present time not been found as a name of a divinity on Kyprian-Phoenician inscriptions. The few traces of the name hitherto found elsewhere than in Carthage have been collected by Baethgen on p. 55 of his "Religionsgeschichte." Among these there is a personal appellative formed with the name Tanit, which points us to Kypros, and in conjunction with artistic representations and literary sources seems to prove that there was a cultus of Tanit in Kypros. The Sidonian Abtanit, who set up a monument in Athens during his lifetime, belonged, as I showed on p. 176, to a family of Kyprian Sidonians i. e. Phoenicians, who came from Chittim-Kition. Although, as we saw, the Kyprian materials of cultus were transplanted to Carthage, a differentiation and transformation of the adopted divinities, their names, images, and rites soon took place in the newly founded city. The Carthaginian Tanit with her surname "countenance of Baal", and with her companion Baal-Chammam represents a divine pair of a

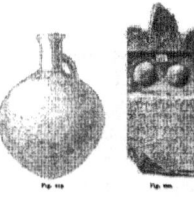

peculiar sort. But it is the female divinity who presents the greatest peculiarity on inscriptions and monuments, so that we can well understand why Polybius spoke of her as a θεῖον ἄγαλμα. A comparison of the Kyprian and Carthaginian monuments yields on the one hand similarities so striking that they must arise from identical conceptions. But from another point of view there are equally striking differences.

We have already seen that the principal image of the Carthaginian goddess and also of the Paphian goddess, is a cone (Pl. LXXVII, 3, 4, LXXXV, 2, 3, 5, 6 and 9). We found the Kyprian dove-goddess, and the doves on the cone images, recurring in Carthage (LXXXV, 9). We saw on a Carthaginian stele (Pl. LXXXV, 8) the motive of the same enthroned goddess which we have found so constantly recurring in Kypros. In early Kyprian vases of the copper-bronze period two female breasts

*) C. I. S. no. 116. Baethgen, „Religionsgeschichte," p. 55.

(Fig. 219)*) are represented as a symbol of the female divinity, and the same occurs on votive stelai of Carthage. (Fig. 220 = Plate LXXXV, 7). We saw also that the child of the goddess, Tammuz-Adonis as crouching temple attendant, came in Kyprian form to Carthage (Pl. XCII, 5).

We constantly notice on Carthaginian inscriptions that Tanit is called "Countenance of Baal". We may therefore assume a combined male and female divinity for Carthage, the bearded goddess, a conception similar to that of the Kyprian Amathusia.**) As from the combined male and female divinity, the bearded Aphrodite in Kypros, a Hermaphrodite and an Aphroditos are developed, so the Carthaginian Tanit, also of double sex, bears on the pillars the title Dominus instead of the usual title Domina ᶜ**) This double divinity was in most cases chiefly female, and less frequently chiefly male. The sexual parts were sometimes male and sometimes female.†) So far I have shewn the similarities between Kypros and Carthage. The differences are not less striking. The form of the cone which is the symbol of Tanit in Carthage is different from that of the Kyprian Astarte. The cults in Carthage are developed in a one-sided manner, and the forms of them stiffen under the influence of the conservative Punic race. The Greek spirit, Greek culture, and Greek art do not influence Carthage until a later period, and then not extensively. But in Kypros Greeks had settled as early as the Phoenicians, and it even seems, from the investigations of R. Meister, that the Greeks were more powerful than the Phoenicians in the heroic period before Homer.

As in Kypros the armed Astarte-Aphrodite merges in the Anat-Athene, it also appears that Anat and Tanit were combined. Perrot (III, p. 73) has already shown the great similarity of the names. As to Artemis, she is combined in Kypros not only with Aphrodite but also with Kybele and Hekate. We cannot yet determine how old the Artemis cultus is in Kypros, but as far as excavation is a guide, it seems to have been introduced long after the Astarte-Aphrodite cultus, and to have been confined to the Greek divisions of the island, especially the kingdom of Salamis, and within this kingdom peculiarly to Kition and Chytroi. We have seen that centuries before Homer the Greeks were very numerous in Kypros. In the Homeric period most of the Greek divinities have taken definite shape, and have each their own sphere, their own characteristics, and their own attributes. Since the Greeks borrowed a great deal from other Oriental peoples, and from the Egyptians.

---

*) Hand-made vase of red clay 0,536 m. in height, from a tomb of the copper-bronze period in Alambra.

**) Cf. p. 242, note 1 p. 245, note 4, p 249, note.

***) C. I. S. 401 and 402.

†) The cultus of a divinity of double sex, the act of which is established in Cyprus, (cf. the Explanation of Plate XXXVI, 1) is easily accounted for by natural circumstances. As Dr. Heidestam, Physician to the English government in Cyprus, proved by investigation, there are at the present time more double-sexed persons in Cyprus than in other countries. Most of these are women with undeveloped male sexual organs. I myself saw a man-woman of this kind in the village Episkopi (near Kurion). In the middle of the Turkish quarter there lived for many years a Greek woman who carried on the trade of a butcher close to the Turkish Mosque. She wore woman's clothes and had a woman's name, had fully developed breasts, a beard which many men would have envied her, and a male voice. She was of great bodily strength, and no one dared to attack her. She lived in the very midst of a Turkish population, and her stall was exactly opposite the much frequented Turkish Café. An ordinary woman would have found it impossible to live alone and keep a shop in a Turkish village. I saw other man-women showing themselves at church festivals as the female Hercules. I was present in the Monastery of Hagios Heraklides on the name-day of the saint, when a gigantic bearded woman performed feats of strength, lifting and carrying huge stones which strong men had tried in vain to move.

their influence upon the island must have had a tendency to introduce instead of monotheism, i. e. the worship of a single feminine goddess of nature who was practically omnipotent, the worship of several divinities i. e. polytheism. As I have shewn above (p. 237 and 261) the Kyprian artist, whose task it was to give shape to the religious conceptions of the priestly caste, utilised the various myths, forms and types of the goddess Ištar in his representations of the most important goddesses, which, according to the spirit of the time, he must differentiate. His object was to present to the people, by symbols and images which they could understand, the various divinities who were worshipped in separate groves and heights with special altars and sanctuaries.

As the Kyprian artists made use of the type of the nude Ištar for certain cultus images of Astarte-Aphrodite, and the type of the armed Ištar for the images of Anat-Athene, similarly they reserved a peculiar draped type of Ištar for the archaic Artemis.[*]) I do not mean that every draped goddess who holds her hands to her breast must represent Artemis, but only that the Artemis images at this time are distinguished by a special priestly garb, and that Kyprian images of divinities represented nude, in whatever position, cannot possibly represent Artemis.

After about twelve years' study of the antiquities of Kypros in the island itself, and visits (in 1885 and since my return) to all the great European museums, I have come to the conclusion that the principal type of the archaic Graeco-Phoenician Artemis as of also the purely Greek Artemis is to be found in Kypros. And I can show that certain definite ritual practices were carried on only in these groves of Artemis-Kybele, and that they were there never lacking. I would refer here to the custom which I have described above (p. 128 and 129) of depositing small painted tree-images, phalloi, and phallos-shaped vessels. I can point to no fewer than ten sacred groves or heights (No. 1, 2, 7, 10—14, 27 and 66 in the list), in which Artemis was worshipped. In seven of these sanctuaries she is either the sole goddess, or is mingled only with such elements as the goddesses Kybele, Hekate, Persephone, and Demeter (1, 7, 10—14). We must notice, first, in all these groves of Artemis that very ancient statues, with one exception, (fig CCXII, 6 and 7) are entirely wanting. Many give the impression of being archaistic rather than archaic, and belong probably to the 5.th century B. C. (Pl. XI, 4—6, XII, 5, L, 1 CCX, 2—4, 8). The fact that the images of Astarte-Aphrodite are mostly older proves that Artemis is a younger conception than Aphrodite in Kypros. Another circumstance struck me, and after exact measurements and examination of historic events I have been able to explain it. There is a large gap in the discoveries of the Artemis sanctuaries, which occurs about the middle of the 4.th century B. C. The sanctuary of Artemis-Paralia on the Salt Lake (No. 7 in the list) appears to be the only one to which an earlier date can be assigned. It is the only one which is situated in the kingdom of Kition, and it is directly in front of the capital city. It differs very materially in its votive offerings from the other six sanctuaries, which all lie within the kingdom of Salamis (1, 10—14). Of the remaining three sanctuaries,

---

*) Ed. Meyer, in his Essay on Astarte (Roscher's Mythol. Lexikon, I, Sp. 647) has already distinguished between a draped and an undraped Babylonian Astarte. The figures which he reproduces, are it is true, not very old, but they take their origin from earlier types of the same kind. Ed. Meyer's nude Astarte-type is certainly the one which was adapted in Cyprus along with other elements to the cultus-images of Astarte-Aphrodite, but it is not found as an element of the cultus-statues of Artemis in Cyprus. On the other hand Ed. Meyer's illustration of the goddess whom he calls "the draped Babylonian Astarte", is strikingly like the definitely developed type of the archaic Artemis or her priestess (as in Plate XI, 4--6, XII, 5, L, 1, CCX, 2--4, and 8).

where Artemis appears combined with other divinities, two (27 and 66) are in the kingdom of Salamis and the third (Voni No. 2) is in the kingdom of Chytroi. The last sanctuary is dedicated by inscriptions principally to Apollo, and he is represented in all the images. There is only one exception, viz a small figure which represents Artemis, and to which a votive inscription is dedicated (cf. p. 4 inscription No 8). The sanctuary on the Salt Lake (No. 7 on the list), is the only one situated in a kingdom known to be Phoenician, and not Greek, viz. the kingdom of Kition. And yet in this sacred grove there are many votive images executed in a purely Greek style (Pl. CCIV, CCV, and CCVII), a style too which is peculiar to Kypros, and is only found in Kition, and in this sanctuary (Heuzey's "Beau style hieratique", "Catalogue des figurines antiques" p. 184), all the other groves of Artemis lie within the Greek kingdoms, most of them in Salamis (No. 1, 10—14, 27 and 66). It is evident that this Artemis cultus arose in the 6th century in Salamis, after being fully developed there spread to Kition, where it inspired the highest works of art (Pl. LXVIII, 4—6, CCIII, 5, CCIV, CCV, CCVII), and then suddenly disappeared in the 4th century. In Kition it appears to have survived longer. In other sanctuaries of other divinities the votive gifts may be dated as late as the period of the Ptolemies and the Roman period. The excavation of the Artemis grove at Achna, which was accomplished with the greatest care, (No. 1 on the list outline Pl. IV, Pl. XI, XII, CCIX—CCXII) showed that the archaic and archaistic works of art which strongly resemble images of Aphrodite-Astarte, and therefore belong to the earlier date, are in better preservation, and are usually found complete with the heads, while the images of pure Greek style, accompanied by stag, dog or torch, are as a rule terribly mutilated and have lost the head (Pl. CCXII, 4, 5, 10 and 11). One might have thought that the Artemis images with the dog or the torch, made as they are of limestone and not of clay, were likely to last longer. But most of these purely Greek Artemis pictures were not found in situ in the treasure chamber as the archaic and archaistic images were, but thrown out of the temple and lying outside the peribolos wall. On Pl. IV I have shown an excavation of this kind (EL) outside of the precinct. From all these circumstances we may conclude that about the middle or in the second half of the 4th century B. C. there was a general and sudden destruction of the sanctuaries of Artemis. The iconoclasts wreaked their vengeance especially on those types of Artemis which differed from the types of Astarte-Aphrodite and represented the pure chaste Greek Artemis, the maiden huntress. The evidence of excavation is confirmed by the evidence of history. The Greek dynasty of the Salaminian kings, beginning with Euelthon (560—525 B. C.), sympathised with the Greeks of Greece, and Euelthon himself dedicated a costly vase for incense in the sanctuary of Apollo at Delphi. King Euagoras I., who seized the lordship over the other Kyprian princes and kept it for a short time, is known to history as the fosterer of Greek manners and culture. It appears that these Salaminian kings purposely introduced the cultus of the chaste and severe Artemis in order to counteract the influence of the effeminate worship of Aphrodite. But the successors of the great Euagoras on the throne of Salamis returned to the allegiance of the licentious and immoral worship of Aphrodite. The Kinyrades, who had long looked with envious eyes on the growing influence of the Artemis cultus, seized the occasion, and urged the Salaminian kings to order the destruction of the Artemis sanctuaries. Images were broken all over the island in the groves of Artemis, and especially, as I have shewn, those representing the purely Greek Artemis with the stag, the dog or the torch (CCXII, 4, 5, 10, and 11). Those on the other hand which were more like the images of Astarte-Aphrodite, or her priestess were left untouched (Pl. XI and XII, CCX, 1—4, 8, 18—20 and 23, CXII, 6 and 7) as were also portraits and images representing pilgrims or persons offering gifts (Pl. CCXI, &c.) because these were equally well adapted to the groves of other divinities.

I will now give a short description of the types which are peculiar to the Artemis-Kybele groves of the island.

a) The Kyprian-Artemis type with arm-stumps.
(Plate CCX, 18 - 20 and 23.)

The hands are missing, and the stumps of the arms are sometimes longer and sometimes shorter. Occasionally a rough indication of fingers is to be seen at the ends of the stumps. We must therefore suppose that the image of the goddess of which these small clay images are copies, was represented with arm-stumps like the image of the Carthaginian Tanit. Since many of these images are purely Greek in the formation of the head and execution of the drapery, and betray a certain skill on the part of the artist, the supposition that the arm-stumps are accidental must be left out of the question. These Artemis images with arm-stumps are essentially different from the image of the worshipper in the Astarte-Aphrodite sanctuary (No. 3 on the list, Pl. LI, 6), which is represented with complete arms and hands, only very roughly executed. They must also be carefully distinguished from the fragments representing a ring-dance (Pl. XLVII, 1 and 5), in which the horizontal roughly represented arms of the dancers are intended to show how they stood round in a circle and held each others' hands (Pl. XVII, 5, LXXVI, 8 = CXXVII, 4, CXXVI, 6). The Artemis images with arm-stumps, which are all made of clay, show distinct traces of painting in yellow and red (Pl. LXVII, polychromy seems to have been specially developed in the votive images of the groves of Artemis. Cf. Pl. XLVIII, 4 — 15).[*]) These images have not yet been found in any groves of Astarte-Aphrodite, but one of the coins of Paphos distinctly shows arm-stumps on the cone-symbol of the Paphian goddess (Pl. LXXXIII, 13), and therefore it is possible that this type, which occurs in hundreds of examples connected with Artemis, may at some future time be found among the votive images of the groves and heights of Aphrodite. But even if this should be the case, we shall probably find that the type was never so widely known in connection with Aphrodite as it was in connection with Artemis, and besides the island has already been so thoroughly excavated that it is not likely that anything essentially different will now be found.

The Ephesian Artemis type with the many breasts has not been found in Kypros, because the sensual and licentious aspect of the female goddess of nature was represented by Astarte-Aphrodite. And yet these Kyprian images of Artemis which end now in a block and now in a pillar are not unlike the Ephesian type (Pl LXXXIII, 15). How far the winged female figures and tamers of animals to which I referred when I spoke of Astarte-Aphrodite, may be identified with Artemis is difficult, if not impossible, to decide. We have seen that in Kypros Astarte-Aphrodite as well as Ištar might appear as the goddess who protects or tames animals and therefore it would be erroneous to

---

[*]) The delicate Polychromic of the good Greek Praxitelean period is shewn in Cyprus at its highest point in the Artemis of Kition. (Plate CCIII, 5) cp. the Explanation. Coloured images were manufactured in great numbers in Cyprus, as the clay was very well suited to such work. The painting of images was derived from the terracotta technique. The Cyprian limestone was less suitable for painting, hence the stone images of Cyprus were only painted with red and black stripes and spots. The fine-grained marble, which is more suitable for polychromy, is not found in Cyprus, and, in the case of the rare and expensive works of art, like the Artemis of Kition and the Sarcophagus of Amathus, must have been imported.

interpret all such images without further proof as representing Artemis. With reference to the aniconic cultus of Artemis out of Kypros I have already said what is necessary in speaking of the cultus of Ashera and Masseba (p. 169). I have also treated exhaustively of the tree images in the groves of Artemis-Kybele (p. 127) which I have shewn to represent the aniconic cultus of the Kyprian Artemis and to be identical with the trees of Attis (Pl. LXVII, 7, LXXVI, 1 and 2).*)

b) The Archaic drapery and attitude of the Kyprian Artemis and her priestess.

(The coloured picture on Plate LXVII, 13, and the black and white pictures on Plate XII, 4—6, XII, 5, L, 1, CCX 4, 12—14 give us very clear examples of the two variants of this type).**)

The attitude and dress is originally that of the great Babylonian Iśtar-Astarte (Roscher's Mythol. Lexikon p. 647). The goddess stands stiff erect, the legs pressed close together and the hands held to the breast (LXVIII, 13, XI, 4—6). This goddess or priestess representing the goddess holds sometimes a lyre (XII, 5) and sometimes a bird (L, 1, CCX, 4), i. e. a dove or a hen. She wears a long under-garment which hangs down to her ankles, and above that a shorter over-garment cut off horizontally and lying close to the figure. Between the under and the over garment appear the ends of two broad fringed bands which are not unlike the ends of the stole worn by priests of the Greek Church. The upper garment is square cut on the breast (cf. especially Pl. CCX, 13). The women of Kypros still wear their dresses and jackets cut in the same way (cf. Pl. III, 6). They call this front square cut part of the garment κόλπος or κόρφος and they conceal in it all sorts of things such as hand-kerchiefs, jewellery, money, perfumed leaves and flowers. Sometimes, when they go into a frequented place or when they ride, they put the ends of their long neck chains into this bosom of their garment. It is evident that the κόλπος of the women of Homer was exactly of this kind, and such too was the κόλπος in which Hera hid the magic cestus which she had received from Aphrodite.***) The various head-coverings and modes of dressing the hair in these archaic and archaistic images of Artemis and her priestesses can be best seen from the illustrations. Although I have only represented the peculiarities to be found in the groves of Artemis, such as low crowns made of woven basket work or ribbons, kalathoi (Pl. CCIX, 2 and CCX, 4), yet similar headdresses are to be found in many other places. The head dress which covers the ears and hangs down over them (Pl. CCIX, 2 &c.) and wigs of hair were evidently in fashion at that time all over the island for human beings and divinities alike (Pl. L, 4 &c.). On the other hand the priestesses of Artemis, like the goddess, seem to have been distinguished by wearing one or two veils. In the oldest fashion a veil reaches from the head down to about the middle of the body (Pl. XI, 4 and 8). Afterwards the veils become longer (Pl. XI, 6) and thinner, and as costume becomes Hellenized the one thick veil is replaced by two long thin veils which reach to the ground (Pl. XII, 9). There are single examples of long veils in the representations of Aphrodite but not so frequently as in those of Artemis. The most interesting detail of the costume

---

*) An equally good example of an archaic Artemis-figure of the same type, from the place Pharangas (No. 14 on the list) in A. P. di Cesnola's Salaminia, p. 202, fig. 206.

**) A more detailed account of Artemis is not within the scope of this work. In Roscher's Mytho-logisches Lexikon there is an admirable and exhaustive treatise on Artemis by Th. Schreiber. On this subject also we must bring new Cyprian material to bear.

***) Helbig, "Homerisches Epos," p. 243. Iliad XIV, 214.

of the archaic Kyprian Artemis and her priestess is an ornament which appears to be essential and consists of a group of insignia hanging on an embroidered strap, a twisted cord. In representations of Aphrodite and her priestesses we find a round disc ornamented with tassels and hanging down from a little strap or chain between the breasts. But it is only in images of Artemis and her priestesses that these insignia are shewn hanging lower down from the disc (Pl. CCX, 12, 13 and 14). Two forms occur.

In the older form these archaic insignia hang in a row directly under the breast plate. On the left, there is a fantastically shaped human image, in the middle, two double rings and on the right, a long bent seal (in Pl. CCX, 14 it is represented somewhat too pointed). In the newer form (Pl. XI, 5, 6, XII, 5, CCX, 4 and 12, cf. A. P. di Cesnola, Salaminia, p. 202, Fig. 206) the form and arrangement of the insignia differ considerably and yet show clearly that they are only the old sacred symbols in another shape. From the breast-plate hangs, by a small double chain, a simple flat ring and to this two flat double rings are attached. To the latter rings are made fast, on the left, a small dwarfish anthropomorphic image,[*) and on the right, a temple seal ring. These insignia, which are peculiar to the figures of the Kyprian Artemis and her priestess, have a striking parallel in the insignia symbols and foreshortened human images which we see on the hands of the Hittite divinities (cf. Perrot IV, p. 637, fig. 313 and p. 645, fig. 321). Although these insignia belong in Kypros to Artemis and not to Aphrodite, they recall the κεστός ἱμάς, embossed strap, of Homer, that magic girdle which Aphrodite loosed from her bosom and gave to Hera.

There is a possibility that this magic girdle of Aphrodite only represents the shortened form of the Kyprian breast ornament, i. e. the chain with the breast plate, but without the insignia attached, like the breast chains and round discs which we see in the images of the grove of Astarte-Aphrodite (No. 3 on the list) (Pl. L, 4 and 5) or like the amulets shaped like a triangle (Pl. XXXIII, 1, 2, 5, 6, 8, cf. p. 205), or like a cylinder (Pl. XXXIII, 16 and CLXXXII, 26). We have seen that in the centre-piece of these chains, which in the worship of Tammuz-Adonis became official chains, a charm was often enclosed. This charm is known not only in antiquity, but in modern times among the Kypriote women, whether they are Turks or Greeks, and to it is often ascribed the same effect as to that of Aphrodite. Girls who wear these talismans (represented on Pl. XXXIII, 6) believe that by their help they can entangle the hearts of men and win husbands.

I must here mention another group of clay votive offerings belonging to the Artemis grove in the Kingdom of Salamis, a group which is as numerous as it is rich in various forms and colours. The style is definite and decided, but very rude, and forms a class by itself, which is only found in these groves (No. 1, 10—14), but there in immense quantities. On Plate IV I have marked with the letters PHT the place in which these rough bizarre coloured doll-like images were found lying packed close together in hundreds. On the coloured Plate LXVII, 11, 12, 14 and 15 four of the most interesting examples are reproduced from my original water-colour drawings; on Plate XI, 1—3, XII, 1—4 seven more of the images are reproduced (cf. the explanations of these plates). These rude images are possibly older than those of purely Greek style, as for example XI, 12 and 13, XII, 8—14 and are probably contemporary with the archaic and archaistic figures of better artistic execution,

---

*) This seems to recall the earlier human sacrifices offered to the goddess.

such as those represented in Pl. XI, 4—6, 8—10, XII, 5, LXVIII, 13. It is evident that the image dealers who offered their wares at the entrances of the Artemis groves had to make provision both for rich and poor. Hence the workmen who made the images for them produced for the monied classes better executed wares (XI, 4—6, 8—10, XII, 5, LXVIII, 13) and for the poor cheap and common ware (XI, 1—3, XII, 1—4, LXVIII, 11, 12, 14, 15). Even the uneducated excavators in Kypros recognized this fact and at the present day at the feast of Panagiris sell pictures of saints of different prices according to the execution. We have evidences of the same procedure at Kition, where a kind of rough clay figure without paint and of strongly pronounced Egyptian style was produced in masses for the poor. These rude puppets, whose makers did not even always take the trouble to represent the arms, are called by the Kyprian excavators *Φτωχοί* "the poor". They are ruder and radically different from the images of the goddess with arm-stumps (Pl. CCX, 18—20). These images may, in many instances, represent the goddess Artemis, but they are just as likely to be portraits of priestesses and female pilgrims.

c) Greek standing figures of Artemis in Kypros with veil, modius and seal.

(Pl. XI., 13, 14; XII., 10, 14; CCX., 1; CCXI., 1, 4 and 6)

This type c arose out of the former type b, when the stiff priestly costume and the magic string of rings, images and seals were given up. In their stead the female figure carried the temple seal in her hand (Pl. CCX., 7 and 22). The wig of hair disappeared and the Greek ear-ring took the place of the large barbarous ear-coverings. In the place of the stiff priestly cap or of the low kalathos, which was shaped like a small basket we find a modius, which becomes gradually higher, and is decorated with rows of rosettes flowers, suns, half moons (CCIV, 1—3; CCVII, 2; CCIX, 6—7; CXC, 2 and 3; CCXI, 1 und 2), and vultures (LXVIII, 6 = CCIX, 8; CCXI, 3) (cf. also Cesnola-Salaminia p. 223 fig. 213 and p. 224 fig. 214 from Pharangas No. 14 on the list). We find that the Aphrodite of Kypros*) also wears high tower-like crowns, or modii, but they are much rarer. They are never ornamented with rows of vultures. These vulture or eagle crowns**) belong to the ritual of the Kyprian Artemis (Pl. XXXVII, 15) as the crowns with puppets or heads of Bes belong to the ritual of Aphrodite (XXXVIII, 3, 5, 20). When the chain with the insignia of divine or priestly power disappeared from the Greek images of Artemis, the temple seal held in the hand survived in many of them (CCX, 7). In the precinct dedicated in common to Apollo and Artemis I found a fragment of a limestone statue. It is a female hand holding a large seal on a ring (PL. CCX., 22).***) The very high modius from which a long veil often hangs down to the ground, is worn by the players on the lyre and tambourine, and by those who carry offerings of animals or flowers (Pl. XI., 9, 13, 14; XII., 10—14; CCX., 7, CCXI., 1-5, 7) i. e. by those who officiate in the festivals and sacrifices to Artemis. Here we find a fusion of Artemis and Kybele. The goddess with the towered crown is sometimes represented seated between lions (p. 287 fig. 198).

*) Cp. the Owl, Nicosia, 1889 p. 72 and 77. (Plate IX, 7 - 12).

**) Cp. the detail of an eagle-crown of Artemis-Kybele, Salaminia, p. 224, fig. 214.

***) A. H. Sayce thought he could recognize in the marks on the seal-plate a rough decorative imitation of Kyprian-Hittite characters. I have reproduced the seal-plate on a large scale in the Owl, 1889, p. 76 and 77. Plate IX, 16.

d) Artemis more freely represented.

The goddess as huntress accompanied by stag, deer or dog. Artemis Kybele with the lion. The goddess as maiden.

A stag, a deer or a dog (Pl. CCXII, 4 and 5 CCII, 2) stands close to the side of the goddess. She also carries the torch (CCII, 4, CCXII, 10). Sometimes she stands with her garment girt up and holding a bow and a quiver full of arrows, ready to take her course over mountain and through valley (Pl. CCII, 2). Sometimes she seized her garment and her quiver with a hasty movement (CCXII, 8). Sometimes she stands with or without quiver, bow, stag or long garment, in an attitude of dreamy contemplation (CCIII, 5; CCXII 2, 3 and 5). Her hair is sometimes gathered into a knot at the back of her head and the veil falls down from it (CXXII, 2 and 3) but she is often represented entirely without ornament and adorned only by her chaste maidenly dignity and beauty (Pl. CCIX, 9 = 10 and CCIII, 5),

e) The Artemis group from Kition belonging to the school of Praxiteles.

This splendid marble group (CCIII., 5) 80 cm. high, and delicately painted in various colours, was found by some quarry-men in a garden at Larnaka Skala belonging to a Greek named Saparillas, in April 1880. At that time I had just begun my first excavations for Sir Charles Newton and therefore the discoverers and the buyers feared to shew me this costly discovery at Kypros. But as I was one of the first to whom the photographs became accessible, I published in illustrated magazines an account of the work of art, which I enthusiastically admired*). In 1884, when I was making a journey from Kypros to Europe, I found, that the statuette was in Paris and still unsold, because Friedländer had declared that it was a Roman copy.**) It had stood since 1880 almost forgotten in the dark corner of a room belonging to a Kyprian merchant of Larnaka, who was related to the possessor. This room is so dark, that this beautiful work of art could not be seen even in the daytime without the aid of artificial light. Longpérier had seen the statue, which is undoubtedly a Greek work of the 4th century B,. C. and is now considered by many archaeologists, in spite of its small dimensions, to be an original, and had simply passed it by without notice. Feuardent, the well known dealer in works of art, told me that he knew the statuette. He pointed to the Roman statues full of mannerism which he has just aquired from Italy and summed up his judgment in the words, "Moi je veux de belles choses comme celles-ci, la statuette de Larnaca n'est pas pour moi." Fröhner and Hoffmann had not seen the work and were first introduced to it by me, otherwise they must have been struck by it. After trying in vain in 1880 in Berlin, Paris and London to gain a hearing for the merit of the work I succeeded at last in 1884 in bringing it in notice in Vienna. At the present time the statuette occupies the place of honour in the new Kunsthistorisches Museum in the Ringstrasse in Vienna, and its artistic value is prized more highly then ever. In fact Vienna does not possess a more beautiful Greek work of art. R. von Schneider, to whom I am indebted for the photographs from which my illustrations (Pl. CCIII., 5a and b) are taken, published this statuette of

---

*) L'Illustration (Paris, 4th Sept.); Neue Illustrirte Zeitung, (Wien, 26th Sept.); Illustrirte Zeitung, (Leipzig, 5th Okt.); Graphic (London, 20th Nov. 1880); Heimath (Wien, 1881, No. 22). Cp. also S. Reinach "Chroniques d'Orient," p. 174 [5², 344—345.]

**) Archäologische Zeitung, 1880, p. 184 and Plate 17. To Friedländer belongs the credit of having first recognized in the group a representation of Artemis.

Artemis in the 5th volume of the "Jahrbuches der kunsthistorischen Sammlungen des österreichischen Kaiserhauses" (Vienna 1899 p. 1—11 with Pl. I and II) and I wish to draw special attention to his admirable work. I made excavations at the place where it was found within in the town circle of Kition, and I can testify that the statuette stood in a large building, which was covered with stucco and frescoes, perhaps a palace of the first Ptolemaic kings. Adjoining the ruins of this building, there are on the east the remains of another building, proved by inscriptions and monuments to have been a gymnasium.

The inscription found here and first published by me, which was set up by the scholars of the Gymnasium, dates from the time of Ptolemy Euergetes (246—221).[*] The group is executed in the style of the Praxitelean school. The principal figure represents Artemis in a long garment. As I communicated to Herr von Schneider, she holds in her right hands a torch and in her left a bow.

Fig. 171.

The stag, such as we see on the coins of Eucarpis, is absent. A quiver made of marble or bronze, formerly hung at her back. The maiden goddess leans against the older image of her own divinity, which is executed in good archaic style. This older Artemis is formed after the so-called "Spes" type, holds the edge of her garment with the left hand, and with the right presses a flower to her breast. This motive is familiar to us in numerous images of Aphrodite (cf. p. 136 and 263) and we found it also in the Artemis grove of Achna (No. 1 on the list, Plate XI. 13).

*) Cp. S. Reinach, "Chroniques d'Orient," p. 174 (II, 344—345).

In the present work are represented a number of female images from different localities and sanctuaries of Kypros, holding the edge of the robe with the left hand. Some of these also hold in the right hand a flower pressed against the breast. The pre-Persian statues of priestesses on the Acropolis of Athens hold with one hand a fold of the garment, and in the other a Kylix or other object.

The motive in itself, therefore, argues neither for nor against a representation of Artemis. The Etruscan figures repeated in fig. 221 and 223 (= Plate CVII, 3 and CCIII. 4) and the animal taming goddess , fig. 222 = CVII, 1) hold the garment in the same manner and certainly do not represent Artemis. But on the other hand if we compare the small archaistic figure of our Artemis-group, (Plate CCIII, 5) with the female figure holding the robe and a flower in the Artemis grove of Achna (Plate XI, 13) and with other images of Artemis (Plate CCXII, 10 and 11), we notice a peculiarity which only occurs in sanctuaries of Artemis. The folds run from the middle line symmetrically to both sides.

In some cases it seems as if the garment opened in the middle, a style of costume which may be seen at the present day worn by the women of Kypros°). The resemblance in style and mode of dressing the hair between the principal representations of the beautiful Artemis of the 4th century B. C. (CCIII, 5a and b), and the small limestone head which I found at Achna in the sanctuary of Artemis (Plate CCIX, 9 and 10), is very remarkable. They belong to the same period, the same art, and the same stage of culture. In Figs 225 (= Plate CCIII, 1) and 226 (= CCIII, 2) I have represented, after Gerhard, ("Akademische Abhandlungen" XXIX, 6 and 5) two groups resembling that of Kition, of which the first was in Paris in the Rollin collection and the second is in Berlin**), and comes from Tarquinii. The latter of the two is considered to be a good Greek work of the 4th century B. C. Interpretation is undecided between the goddess leaning on her own image and an priestess or worshipper leaning on the image of the goddess.***) R. von Schneider is probably quite right in his interpretation of the work of art at present in his keeping at Vienna (CCIII, 5 = Fig. 227 and 228), as Artemis Paralia, whose worship spread with the rise of Greek influence. If it is so, we must admit the possibility that the work of art was made in Cyprus.

In addition to this we must notice that the place where the marble group of Kition was found is only about a mile from the grove of Artemis-Paralia on the Salt Lake. It is quite possible that this cultus of Artemis-Paralia, and with it the cultus image, came first from Kypros into the Phrygian towns of Eukorpia and Tiberiopolis. When we consider the constant intercourse between Kypros and Phrygia, which we had occasion to notice in considering Dionysos and Ariadne (p. 252), we shall not be surprised to find that the cultus of Artemis is transplanted to a later period, even to Roman times. With the aid of our illustrations we shall now examine more closely the cultus of Artemis-Paralia on the Salt Lake near Kition (no. 7 on the list). Demeter and Persephone, as well as Kybele, powerfully influence this cultus.

---

*) Cp. especially the figure on Plate XII, 6 from the grove of Achna-Artemis. A garment of this kind, which meets down the middle of the front and which was often worn open, seems to have been worn by Aphrodite, when she tried to cover Aeneas with her Peplos, (Iliad V, 315. Helbig, " Homerisches Epos," page 204).

**) Berlin Museum, No 586 ("Beschreibung d. antiken Skulptur", 1891, p. 226).

***) A similar group, representing Aphrodite, was found at Pompeii.

Fig. 221.

Fig. 173.

f) The grove of Artemis-Paralia on the Salt Lake near Kition.

a. The principal divisions of style.

On the heaps of earth, which look like gigantic mole-hills, numerous fragments are lying. I made an attempt to excavate this heaped up soil in an orderly manner for Sir Charles Newton, but I was soon obliged to give up the undertaking as hopeless. The sacred height of Artemis occupies a most beautiful situation on the slope of a hill on the eastern shore of the Salt Lake, between it and the sea. From this spot one can see sun and moon rise from the sea in the east and set behind the mountains in the west, while their image is reflected on the right in the sea and on the left in

Fig. 224.   Fig. 225.   Fig. 226.

Fig. 227.   Fig. 228.   Fig. 229.   Fig. 230.   Fig. 231.   Fig. 232.

the lake. The objects found on this cultus site fall naturally into two divisions as to style, the purely Greek and the not purely Greek. They are almost all terra-cottas. Among those which are not purely Greek we may classify such of the Graeco-Phoenician works as are older than the purely Greek, and also those which are contemporaneous with earlier Greek works of art. As an example of this older Graeco-Pheonician division I can here only refer to a group of two goddesses probably nude, standing in a niche (Pl. CCV, 3 = XXXVIII, 6). Some purely Greek images from this site are reproduced on plates CCIV, CCV, CCVII, and CCVIII, 4—8. Among the rude Graeco-Phoenician terra-cottas of Kition we may notice some which show a strong Egyptian influence and have as yet not been found on other sites. These are Πτωχοί, "the poor", i. e. votive gifts which were brought by the poor, similar to those in Achna and the Artemis groves of the kingdom of Salamis. The character of these images in Kition is somewhat different. They are never painted, the clay is of a different quality, and in spite of their rough execution it is easy to trace a different style and a more Egyptian costume. I have reproduced only one of these clay images (XXXVII, 2), of somewhat better execution. Others are much more primitive, and some hardly indicate the mouth at all. In the sanctuary of Astarte-Mikal on the Acropolis of Kition (No. 9 on the list) a number of these πτωχοί, images of the poor, were set up in honour of Astarte, the mother with the child. There were also many of these in the grove of Artemis-Paralia. They were manufactured en masse in the following manner. The rudely formed heads could be fastened to the still ruder pillar—or tube—shaped torsos according to the wish of the purchaser. Hence the heads were made separately, baked and fitted with pegs underneath, in order that they might be easily attached to the bodies. The pilgrim who wished to buy a votive offering at the image shop in order to lay it down before the altar of Artemis-Paralia chose out a head and a body according to taste, and then the image maker quickly fastened the two together. This custom explains the numerous heads of Πτωχοί found on the site of the former treasure chamber, and provided with these pegs.

In remarkable contrast to these images stand the beautiful Greek terra-cottas made in Kypros and found in this sanctuary on the Salt Lake. The artists of these images seem to have tried to fuse into one type Artemis-Kybele, Demeter and Kore. I select here only the types of the enthroned goddesses and the veiled woman, and refer for further information to the explanations of Plates CCIV, CCV, CCVII, and CCVIII, 1.[*] The chief image of the goddess of the Salt Lake must certainly have been for a long time an enthroned figure. Heuzey has already called attention to the fact that these enthroned divinities may be dated as early as the 5th century B C, the time of Pericles, when a Kyprian sculptor and caster in bronze, named Styppax, gained honour and fame by his masterly productions. On Pl. CCIV, 1 and 3, I give two replicas (photographs) of this single throned goddess, i. e. two hitherto not completely published terra-cottas of the Berlin Museum. In Pl. CCIV, 1 the whole figure is shrouded in a long veil-like garment, which seems to fall down from the high modius. The arms and hands are hidden under the veil, but the head is free. In Fig. 3 we see the same goddess seated on a chair of state in a similar position, having the right leg somewhat more advanced than the left. The posture of the arms is also similar, but the veil is absent, so that arms and hands are free. The left hand, which is placed on the breast, holds a fruit. While this work is going through the press I find among my collection of photographs from originals some copies of beautiful terra-cottas, which were found in the sanctuary of Artemis-Paralia, and were in 1879 in the collection of D. Pierides. I cannot resist giving two of these (Fig. 233 and 234). In Fig. 233 we see one of the most beautiful examples of a supreme goddess enthroned, and in Fig. 234 one of the most beautiful of the inferior divinities, standing and holding a mysterious cista, which ever were produced in the workshops of the clay modellers of Kition.[**]

---

*) Cp. also Heuzey's "Catalogue des figurines antiques," p, 184—196.

**) Fig. 233 measures 0,28 m. in the "Bulletin de correspondence hellenique" III, p. 86, this figure is briefly described by Potier, No. 4 (head missing) 0,21 m. high. The head which is at present on the figure may belong to it, but this is not certain. The head (Potier p. 87, No. 17) is 0,07 m. high. At the request of

The second type (Pl. CCIV, 2) shows us the enthroned goddess wrapped in a veil like that in Fig. 1. Only in this instance the feet are placed evenly together. Two small female figures in similar costume and carrying little baskets in their left hands (cf. Fig. 234), stand as independent figures to the right and left of the large enthroned centre figure.

The third type (Pl. CCIV, 1 = XXXVIII, 7) shows us two goddesses similarly robed, throned together upon a wide chair. Their upper garments, which resemble veils, are arranged in the same way as in Pl. CCIV, 3, and fall down over the shoulders and the back part of the arms, so that the front part of the arms, hands and breast are left free and the under garment is visible. In addition to this one large veil seems to be wrapped around the heads and crowns of both figures. The goddess

Fig. 131   Fig. 132

seated to the right seems to be the older of the two, perhaps the mother, and has placed her left arm round the younger goddess, perhaps her daughter, who sits to her left. The left hand of the mother may be seen on the left shoulder of the daughter, who with her left hand presses a fruit or a flower to her breast. I interpret the goddess throned alone (CCIV, 1 and 3) as the chief goddess, Artemis-Kybele, or Artemis-Paralia, to whom the precinct is dedicated. The two small figures which

D. Pierides I myself placed the head on the body, and marked the measurements in the catalogue which I handed over to him. Fig. 234 is in Potier (p. 87, fig. 281 0,2 m. high.

sometimes stand by the side of this Artemis-Kybele (as in Pl. CCIV, 2), may be priestesses or secondary divinities (perhaps Demeter and Kore?). The two enthroned goddesses may be two sisters or (Pl. CCV, Fig. 1) mother and daughter. If they are sisters we may perhaps identify them as Artemis and Kybele or Artemis and Persephone, if mother and daughter they may represent Demeter and Kore. These goddesses appear in the retinue of the principal divinity Artemis, whom they serve and in conjunction with whom they are worshipped.

In our third type of the two enthroned goddesses (Pl. CCV, 3 = XXXVIII, 6) we have taken as model an archaic Graeco-Phoenician image, which is, so far as I know, the only instance of a nude image found in a grove of Artemis. But the provenance is not quite certain, although the proprietor, D. Pierides, told me that it was found in the grove of Artemis-Paralia. Two nude goddesses stand upright and press their arms to their breasts. They either stand in a niche, or are surrounded by a piece of stuff like a veil which forms a kind of tent or cloak. There are two holes above, in order that the group might be hung up as a votive offering.

In Etruria this pair of goddesses occurs as frequently, if not more frequently than in Kypros. I have represented one of these in Pl. XXXVIII, 14. Behind the goddess who sits on the left is the sacred palm tree, and beside the goddess, who is seated on the right, a roe stands, while a small nude male genius flies above and arranges her veil. This Etrurian group strongly resembles the Kyprian in attitude and drapery.*)

To this throned Artemis, attended by two smaller figures of goddesses or mortal women, there is an interesting pendant in the throned Athene, also attended by two standing female figures (Pl. CCVI, 3).

These enthroned goddesses of the grove of Artemis-Paralia near the Kyprian Salt Lake are always on a small scale, but the execution is on the whole good. Technique and style point without doubt to a Greek manufactory established in Kition. A very instructive analogy may be found in the larger terra-cotta figures of about half life size representing divinities enthroned, which I excavated in the dromoi of Greek tombs at Marion-Arsinoë. On Pls. CLXXXVI, 2 and CLXXXV, 3, I reproduced five of these large enthroned figures, which are connected with the cultus of the dead. The influence of Phidias and his school was distinctly to be seen in them. Two of them, CLXXXV, 3 and CLXXXVII, 2 represent mourning women. CLXXXVII, 3 also bears the stamp of a veiled figure mourning for the dead. The most effective are CLXXXVII, 1 and 4. The first figure wears the upper garment in such a manner as to conceal the mouth and the lower part of the face. A small female figure, of which the head is missing, holding a kerchief in the right hand, stands to the right of the principal seated figure. In Fig. 4 small images of mourning women ornament the arms of the throne, and form a remarkable parallel to the genius on the Etrurian terra-cotta (Pl. XXXVIII, 14).

After this digression we must return to the sanctuary of Artemis-Paralia and glance at two of the images of veiled women, which probably represent Artemis-Persephone (Pl. CCVII, 2 and 5). The Kyprian Ariadne myth (see p. 251 ff.) may have also had some influence on these representations. Both show a closely veiled woman, of whose face only eyes and nose are visible. In the figure on Pl. CCVII, 5 the veil lies closely to the head, while in Pl. CCVII, 2 a richly decorated crown is worn

----

*) The Antiquarium of the Berlin Museum possesses several groups representing a pair of goddesses from Etruria in various styles and motives, which form an instructive parallel to the terracottas of Kypros.

over the veil. The grove of Artemis-Paralia near Kition, in which the Ashera inscription (cf. p. 144) was laid down, contained, like the Artemis grove in the kingdom of Salamis, a great number of interesting objects.

Next to the cultus of Ištar-Astarte-Aphrodite, who had the supremacy from the earliest times and held sway until the introduction of Christianity, the cultus of Artemis in later times, i. e. perhaps from the 5th century B. C. or even earlier, exercised the strongest influence throughout the island. We must now turn from the goddesses and consider the male divinities.

—

IV. The most important male divinities and daemons of Kypros compared with some of non-Kyprian origin.

As I shall consider in my work on Tamassos several sanctuaries of Kyprian gods, and as space in this work is limited, I must treat of this part of the subject briefly. Many details will be found in the explanations of the plates. Much has also been said in the foregoing sections about the gods of Kypros. The index will guide the reader in this somewhat scattered mass of material.

It is impossible to say with certainty what was the name of the most ancient god, whose cultus can be traced in Kypros in remains of the Copper Bronze Period. As I have shewn on p. 269, when anthropomorphic images first began to be used in Kypros along with imageless, anikonic and fetish-worship, there was only one divinity, viz. a goddess. The first development was to make from this divinity a complex deity of double sex, a man-woman.*) Afterwards this double existence was differentiated into man and woman During the Copper Bronze Period in Kypros this change is only to be traced in its first feeble beginnings. Most of the clay images belonging to the transition to the Iron Period are female, and either entirely human in form, or human with a bird's head. During this transition period images of mortals, with the exception of some few representations of mourning women (Pl. CLXXIII, 23a), are not found. It is only at the culmination of the Graeco-Phoenician Iron Period that images of gods begins to appear beside those of goddesses.

In the art of engraving a different course of development is followed. On the well-known cylindrical seals, both those imported into Kypros and those manufactured there, we saw a variety of divinities, both male and female, daemons and mixed monsters, animals native and foreign. As far as we can judge from Babylonian-Assyrian cylinders with cuneiform inscriptions found in Kypros, and bearing the names or cartouches of divinities, the most influential god appears to be Ramman-Martu, the Babylonian-Assyrian god of rain, lightning, thunder and storm, who was afterwards identified with Hadad and Rešef.**) We have also met with the Babylonian-Assyrian daemons and heroes Izdubar and Eabani.***)

---

*) Cp. Pl. XXXVI, 1, 4 and 10.
**) Cp. p. 114
***) P. 83 &c.

1. Baal and Zeus.

In the oldest known Phoenician inscription on the island of Kypros we have evidence that in the times of King Solomon and King David, Baal of Lebanon was introduced into the island of Kypros. We saw that a servant of King Hiram of the Old Testament, the builder of the temple of Solomon, had offered bronze vessels on the altar of this Libanon-Baal, to whom a high place or bambula was dedicated in the Kyprian mountain range.*) We also meet with Baal-Sanator**) in inscriptions at Kition. To these Baalim different forms of Zeus correspond, Zeus Labranios***) to Baal-Libanon, Zeus-Xenios†) to the Baal of Amathus, and Zeus Keraunios††) to the Baal of Larnaka who appears there to have undergone fusion with Rešef. Baal-Hammon-Zeus, the god with ram's horns, throned, and attended by rams,†††) is proved by numerous monuments and images to have been one of the most distinguished servants and attendants in the groves of Rešef-Apollo, although he does not appear on inscriptions. He frequently carries a huge horn of plenty§) filled with fruit and flowers.

2. Melqart-Herakles and Marduk-Merodach.

Melqart-Herakles also may carry the cornucopia.§§) Images of this god are set up in Cyprian groves of Rešef-Apollo even more frequently and in greater numbers than images of Baal-Hammon-Zeus. Melqart-Herakles appears on the right hand of Rešef-Apollo. As his servant we meet him everywhere e. g. in Hamilton Lang's§§§) grove of Rešef-Apollo at Idalion (No. 30 of the list), in Cesnola's°) groves of Rešef-Apollo at Athiaenou (No. 25 and 26 of the list), in the groves of Rešef-Apollo at Voni°°) which I myself excavated or rather examined more closely (No. 2 of the list), and at Frangissa°°°) (No. 4 on the list). In the superficial supplementary excavations that I made in the high place of Rešef-Apollo at Goschi (No. 20 of the list), which had been roughly rummaged out before my time, I found, together with some fragments of small stone images of Baal-Hammon-Zeus, remnants of a colossus of Melqart-Herakles, which in conception and style was exactly similar to that found at Athiaenou (Cesnola-Stern, Pl. XXIII).†*)

Just as certain particular Baalim like Baal-Libanon and Baalmerach could be worshipped, independently of Rešef-Apollo, in groves which are known from inscriptions to have been dedicated

---

*) Cp. p. 19, 161 and 223.
**) P. 299, C. I. Sem. 41.
***) P. 19, No. 46.
†) P. 244 and 253.
††) P. 242.
†††) P. 129, fig. 169.
§) P. CXCI, 4, from the sanctuary at Frangissa, where, as usual, Baal-Hammon-Zeus appears as the servant of Rešef-Apollo.
§§) Pl. XLII, 5.
§§§) Transactions of the Royal Society of Literature, Pl. IV.
°) Cesnola-Stern, Pl. XXIII.
°°) Pl. XLII, 5.
°°°) To be published in my book on Tamassos.
†*) One of the photographs I took.

particularly to them, so also Melqart-Herakles enjoyed the distinction of being worshipped in special groves either alone or as the principal and especial divinity. We have already repeatedly seen how the animal-taming god was fused into all sorts of compound forms by contamination with Izdubar, Eabani, Marduk·Merodach,· Melqart-Herakles and Hadad, with Osiris, Adonis, Adon-Baal, Zeus Moloch, Dionysos, Ešmun, and Bes-Ptah-Patäke. In Amathus this form of Baal was called Malika instead of Melqart. We noted the colossus of Amathus, which represented this divinity compounded of all sorts of elements (Pl. CIII, 4). We observed how this god, just as in Amathus, united himself with Astarte-Aphrodite, and thus made up a divinity of double sex, the bearded Venus, from which the Greeks developed their Hermaphroditos. *) In Plates XCIX—CIV the ' male and female animal - tamers, especially those of oriental style, are placed together. If we put together the pictures scattered over Plates XXIX---XXXI and CLV, 2, we clearly see how the animal-tamers, who bear the name of Izdubar and Eabani came under Graeco-Phoenician influences to be developed into the animal-tamer Melqart-Herakles, under Syrio-Persian influences into Marduk-Merodach. The palm-Baal of the Bible and Baal-Tamar follow the same rule. These Graeco-Phoenician and Perso-late-Babylonian types, originally perhaps distinct, passed one into the other and formed compounds so complex that it is a difficult task to analyse their construction. Many of these animal-tamers perform their herculean deeds at the foot of a palm that stands near. The same animal-tamer on a cylinder, who, according to the inscription of the date of the first Persian Kings, is called Marduk (Pl. CLV, 2), appears at exactly the same date and in the same fashion on a Cyprian silver ornament (C, 7) and Cyprian gems (C, 2). Whereas, however, no instance of Marduk-Merodach is demonstrable by indigenous inscriptions, we frequently meet with the name of Melqart. Phoenician inscriptions from Idalion and Kition testify to the cult of Melqart, either alone, or in conjunction with Ešmun and Adonis. Cyprus has the cult of Melqart in common with Tyre, Carthage and Malta. In Kition Ešmun appears some-times with Adonis, sometimes with Melqart. Ešmun and Melqart fuse at Chittim into a new and peculiar divinity, who, as he is not known elsewhere, must be originally proper to Cyprus. No less than six examples testify to this. **) It seems that in Chittim Ešmun was highly reverenced as Melqart, i. e. as King of the city. Next we must adduce as evidence coin-types and coin mythology, always of great importance to local cults. The figure or simply the head of Melqart-Herakles, in many positions and variously conceived, plays on Cyprian coins, especially those of Kition and Salamis, almost a more important part than Astarte-Aphrodite. It may suffice to refer to coin-types accidentally published together in Pl. CXCII. We meet, for example, on the coins of Euagoras, some-times the head of Herakles (Pl. CXCII, 3), sometimes the whole figure of the hero, seated on a rock with club and cornucopia (Pl. CXCII, 6). Even supposing phil-Hellenic scholars, who are determined, in the case of Herakles, to make out that all the elements of his mythology and typology are originally Aryan and Greek, are in a certain sense right, yet it can scarcely be denied that the Cyprian Greeks found their Herakles with an anti-type that had taken its rise from the animal-taming figures of Oriental,

---

*) The very primitive images of gods of the Bronze Period (in Pl. XXXVI, 4 and 10) of double sex with two heads and one body have nothing to do with these representations of the Iron Age. On the other hand the androgynous image in Pl. XXXVI, 1, seems to belong here, or at all events to the transition between the bronze and iron ages. Unfortunately accurate information as to the provenance of this unique specimen of Cyprian terracotta work is lacking.

**) Baethgen, " Beiträge zur semitischen Religionsgeschichte," p. 46.

Syrian and Egyptian art and religion. Egyptian as well as Babylonian, Assyrian, Hittite, Canaanitish and Aramaic elements, forms, myths and images all went in Cyprus to make up the inspiration of Greek artists and poets, and to influence the condition of Greek priests and teachers of religion. The Cypriot Greek artist created his Herakles out of a repulsive image like the colossus of Amathus, which in its turn had borrowed elements from the Egyptian Bes (Cl. 10), the Aramaic Hadad-Relief of Sendscherli, from the Istubar and Eabani of Babylonia and Assyria (p. 87, fig. 110 and 111), the gloomy Moloch of the Bible &c., &c. And as Phoenicians and Greeks lived together in so small a space of ground, and as complex blood-relationship arose, there came into existence here also those Graeco-Phoenician compounds which we meet with in the temple-images of religious art. On a Cyprian scarabaeus (Pl. CIV, 3) we have Herakles-Melqart plunging a long dagger into the body of a lion, which stands on a mountain in front of him. Both the motive and the execution show a preponderance of Greek influence. We have the Graeco-Phoenician Melqart-Herakles as an animal-tamer, who might just as well be called Marduk-Merodach (Pl. XXIX, 16 and CLV, 2). He appears in another Cyprian scarabaeus (Pl. XXV, 6 = C, 3), and holds four wild animals, a motive borrowed from Assyrian art (XCIX, 1, Cl, 1). Phoenician and Greek influence here seem to hold the balance even, whereas in the scarabaei in Pl. Cl, 8 and 9, which are also evidently made in Cyprus, and in the silver belt from Marion-Arsinoë (reproduced, e. g. XCIX, 8, and C, 7) the scale inclines towards Phoenicia. Lastly, the engraved design from a cylinder found in Cyprus and published by me for the first time on Pl. XXIX, 15 is a clear revelation of Cappadocian-Hittite art and religion. The seated image of the god stands on the heads of two lions, while on their bodies daemons with animals' heads, together with human figures standing side-ways, adore the animal-taming god.

Fig. 235

The Greeks borrowed from these foreign representatives what they could utilize for their own hero. In Cyprus too, we find a Herakles in pure Greek style. Fig. 235 is the head of a stone Cyprian figure of Herakles. We find also in Perrot III, p. 577 and 578, Fig. 389—391 three variations of the same type, which belong to the same order, and these best demonstrate what efforts the Greek artists made to develope the type of their Greek hero from the Oriental idol. But Melqart-Herakles was conceived of, not only as an animal tamer or an archer, a sword-holder, a club-wielder. He appears also as a god of peace, or dispenser of good fortune and plenty. He can pour out upon us the cornucopia of plenty like Baal-Hammon-Zeus, as I mentioned at the beginning of this paragraph.

In the place for votive offerings of certain sanctuaries of Nuïet-Apollo, we find dozens and hundreds of stone figures deposited, which are replicas of a well defined Herakles type. Motive, style and treatment are in favour of a late-Greek, Hellenistic date, or even of one as late as the Roman Emperors. In Pl. XLII, 5 we have one of these Herakles statuettes, which are now in the Berlin Museum; they are almost uniformly of the same size and are very carefully and mechanically executed. This statuette was purchased from a peasant at Voni (No. 2 of our list) whose house adjoined the excavations, and against whose house-wall I set up my little forest of statues. The Greek's house also appears in the background in Pl. V, 2. I myself have dug up several replicas of this same Herakles type. I have seen a still greater number from time to time for sale. In Cesnola's time, on this same spot, which later yielded me such rich results, some superficial scrapings were made.*) We must reckon the number of these perfectly similar Herakles statuettes, which this precinct yielded, as over a hundred. The hero is represented as having thrown back the lion's skin that hangs down from the head, so that the nude body is visible. The right hand leans with the club upon the ground, the left holds the cornucopia, which is only occasionally clearly to be recognised, but without doubt is present.

Many other divinities have been previously discussed in full. In speaking of the cult of Adonis, we were able to dismiss a whole group of gods, heroes, and daemons. In that connection we became acquainted with Egyptian gods, like Osiris and Harpocrates, Babylonish divinities, and those of Canaan and Israel, e. g. Dusi-Tammuz, also Homeric heroes, like Linos and Kinyras. Nearly all of these heroes are found again in Cyprus. It remains to summarize briefly and supplement the many points about Rešef-Apollo that have been dealt with in the course of the discussion.

3. Rešef-Apollo.

We have intentionally reserved this, the most important of the Cyprian gods, to the close or this section. It is true the chief goddess Astarte-Aphrodite, on the island of Kyprogeneia, surpasses the first and most distinguished god, both in power and influence, even down to Christian days. But, after her, in the second place, Rešef-Apollo towers mightily aloft among the assembly of Cyprian divinities. Indeed there must once have been a time in which this god was worshipped side by side with Astarte-Aphrodite, as almost equal in rank, and by all the Cypriots, of whatever race they came. It is well known that, as has been previously emphasized, Cyprus was in evil repute, even in anti-quity, on account of its licentious cult of Venus, which necessitated impurity. For religion served as the pretext for the indulgence of sensual appetite. Corruption of manners must in fact have spread over the island in the time of the later Ptolemies and Roman Emperors to a terrific extent. On this account the champions of the Christian faith, with its purity of manners, i. e. the Apostles and Fathers of the Church, always persistently waged zealous war against the Oriental Venus, and especially the Cyprian and Syro-Phoenician goddess. But, spite of all this, we saw, from the vast quantities of images that had been deposited in places for votive offering in the sanctuaries, that, as a rule, there was separation of the sexes (cf. supra p. 201). The men offered the images that they dedicated, e. g. images of gods, heroes, daemons, animals, or finally their own portraits, in the precincts of male divinities, the women in those of female. In exceptional cases, a god (Rešef-Apollo) and a goddess (Astarte-Aphrodite) at Limniti (No. 52) or Tanit-Artemis (No. 12 of the list) were worshipped together as σύμβωμοι. Even more rarely it happened, that side by side with hundreds and thousands of male images in the places for votive offerings for gods, a single image of a woman occurs, lost in the crowd (Voni No. 2 of the list, in the Temenos of Apollo, a single female figurine side by side with

---

*) In Cesnola's ' Album of Gleanings," Pl. LXIV, three such stone statuettes of Herakles are figured, whose provenance I feel able to state was this same place, Voni.

hundreds of male statues'), or in that of the goddess a male image (Achna No. 1 of the list, Temenos of Artemis, Dali No. 3, Temenos of Aphrodite, side by side with more than a thousand female figures, one male). If this custom was but once naturalized, from that time there must also have been set apart sacred groves, high places, and altars, peculiar to the male sex alone, and dedicated to male divinities. Moreover since in ancient days, much the same as at the present time, woman in the East occupies a very subordinate place and never plays an equal part with man, so in many cases, even in Cyprus, the worship and priestly families of the male gods must have had a more powerful influence both in public and private than that of the goddesses.

We see then, in fact, that Rešef-Apollo and, in the same way, Melqart-Herakles were honoured by mighty Colossi, by richly furnished groves and high places in hill and valley, by spring and river, and that in far more magnificent fashion than even Astarte-Aphrodite. Sanctuaries like those excavated by Cesnola, near Athiaenou (Nos. 25 and 26) by Lang at Idalion (No. 30) and by me near Chytroi at Voni (No. 2) and near Tamassos at Frangissa (No. 4 in the list) far surpass, both in important finds, in their large size, and in their statues made of hewn stone and in standing position, all the sanctuaries of Astarte-Aphrodite hitherto discovered, not excepting even that at Old-Paphos.*) They are all dedicated to Apollo, as is testified by inscriptions, and two of them to his Phoenician correlative, Rešef. In general, if Colossi occur at all in the precincts of goddesses (Achna No. 1, a fragment of a Colossus, Dali No. 3 fragments of several colossi cf. Pl. LVI), they are for the most part of clay. The mass of life-size and more than life-size stone statues in the two groves of Apollo at Athiaenou (25 and 26) and in the grove of Apollo at Voni, was positively oppressive in effect. The reader may get a very good impression of it from the view in Pl. V, 2, as a whole row of the better preserved stone statues can be seen set up against the wall of the house behind the tents.

What we have already brought into notice about Astarte-Aphrodite is even more true of the Cyprian Rešef-Apollo. This chief god is equipped for any function. He is a divine hero, and as such is called Baal. He represents, and is the king; and as such his name is Melek or Moloch. He can take on all shapes, have local cults of every kind, which were as carefully distinguished by the Cypriots of antiquity, as are the two S. Georges, the Long and the Short, by the Larnakiots of to-day. Moreover, this Rešef-Apollo can suffer other gods within his kingdom, and can fuse himself with all manner of other divinities. To make use of a phrase by Schopenhauer**), he does not only live, but lets others live. He tolerates his colleagues in the precincts dedicated to him. For the most part, as we have seen, he utilizes them as slaves and servants to his own gratification. For the god whom other gods serve must be especially great and powerful. It may indeed come to pass that thereby

---

*) It is evident from the numerous inscribed bases of statues that have been found in Old Paphos that a great number of bronze statues had been set up there. But these are all of late date. Excavations carried on in the temple of Apollo at Hyle (No. 49 in the list) would yield as many, if not more, bases of bronze statues. But in ancient times, e. g. from the 7th to the 5th century B. C, even in the precinct of Astarte-Aphrodite at Old Paphos, there could not have been as many and as important stone images set up as there were in the groves of Rešef-Apollo that have been excavated and mentioned above. Even if one bears in mind that the Romans, when they took possession of the island, carried off to Rome for their triumphal processions all the remarkable statues that were still available from the most famous sanctuaries of Venus, still, when subsequently the English carried out their excavations, they must have found many more fragments of important statues, if such had ever been as a general practice dedicated there.

**) "Ueber Religion" Parerga and Paralipomena II, (vol. V, Griesebach) p. 376.

one who originally acted as servant and temple guardian, like Herakles-Melqart, may suddenly soar aloft from the status of vassal to be lord himself, and depress his former lord and master Rešef-Apollo to the position of servant. It seems, e. g., that at Kition Ešmun-Melqart over-stepped the rank of Rešef-Bes and Rešef Mikal.*) Rešef must be a very ancient divinity of Mesopotamia. I have already shown (supra p. 300) how he, in very early days, passed with Anat into Egypt. I have also (supra 75) introduced Rešef in company with the Anat Astarte of Qadesch and the god Min in an Egyptian relief of the 13th century B. C. In other passages (p. 113—119 and 218) it has been already shown how this god Rešef had relations to other Syrian gods, Ramman, Bin, Martu, Hadad, the Baalim of lightning, rain and storm, Schamm and Samas, and in the country of Samal appears also with the god Hadad in Aramaic inscriptions, that are the oldest so far known.

a) Rešef-Apollo as Spear-god.

If the cult of Rešef first came southwards to Egypt**) through the medium of Syrian peoples, among whom we must count the Cyprians, later on the god returned back northwards in Egyptianized form, after he had got fused with Horus into one and the same divinity. In figs. 236—239 there are our scarabaei reproduced from Lajard, Mithra (fig. 236 = Pl. LXXXII, 2, fig. 237 = LXXXII, 3)***). Their provenance is unknown, and they must have been made in Cyprus (as is very probably the case with 238 and 239, cf. 326 infra). To the same class belong two scarabaei found in Sardinia

Fig. 236.   Fig. 237.   Fig. 238.   Fig. 239.

(Perrot III, p. 656, fig. 467, and p. 658, fig. 477). To these must be added a seventh scarabaeus, published Menant II, p. 235, fig. 232. All the seven specimens are so alike that they must have been the work of the same artistic school, yes, and must have been made in the same place. On each of the seven examples the god Rešef is represented as a spear-god, sometimes seated, sometimes standing

*) At the present day among the Greek Christians of Larnaka. and indeed of the whole island, Saint George the Short, ('Ο Ἅγιος Γιόργιος ὁ Κοντός) ranks higher than Saint George the Long, (ὁ Μακρός), and higher than Saint Lazarus who died in Larnaka (cp supra p 119), higher indeed than any other Saint. Only the Panagia of Kikku (cp. supra p. 118) is held in higher esteem.

**) Cp. supra p. 300.

***) Both these scarabaei have been described supra p. 199.

Also we find everywhere the same sort of candelabrum as that so commonly made in Cyprus (Pl. XLIII, 9 and 10). In two cases Rešef is combined with Horus; for the god has a hawk's head (fig. 238 and Perrot III, fig. 467). In three cases the sphinx stands near the seated gods*) (fig. 237—238 and Ménant II, fig. 236) where the one is hawk-headed. In three the sun-disc hovers over the scene (on fig. 237 and Perrot III, fig. 468 and 477). In the fourth case a star (fig. 236), in the fifth a sun-disc and a half-moon, are entirely Cyprian conceptions. In five cases out of the seven instances the exergue below the scene is filled up with the same wicker-work pattern that appears on the coins of Paphos below the temples, and that is so common in other Cyprian and in non-Cyprian Graeco-Phoenician gems. The editors of the Corpus Inscriptionum Semiticarum (I, p. 38) give a picture of this same spear-god Rešef from the treasury of Egyptian monuments, to illustrate the Cyprian Rešef. I dug out a whole series of such spear-god images of Rešef-Apollo, or of his priest in the Frangissa sanctuary (no. 4 of the list)**). We see there (Pl. CXCVII, 4), as in other sanctuaries of Rešef-Apollo, countless sphinx-figures made either on their own account, or as incense holders***) The winged sun-disc, so characteristic of Horus†), is taken over by that Rešef-Apollo who has developed out of Rešef-Horus, and in Apollo's sanctuary at Frangissa many instances of it can be shown

Fig. 240. Fig. 241. Fig. 242. Fig. 243. Fig. 244. Fig. 245. Fig. 246.

in statues and their girdles. The helmet-shaped caps, with or without a globular point, which are sometimes of leather, sometimes of metal, also come from Egypt and were transferred to Cyprus, especially in the cult of Rešef-Apollo, the images of the god and of his priests and servants (cf. fig. 243 = Pl. XLVI, 1 and XLI, 5 and 6) from the sanctuaries of Rešef-Apollo at Limniti (No. 52) ††), and at

*) Cp. also Journal of Hellenic Studies, 1890, p. 54, fig. 1; and infra p. 326.

**) Cp. p. 119.

***) Pl. CXCVII, 5, purchased from a peasant from Athiaenou, must certainly have come from one of Cesnola's Rešef-Apollo groves (No. 25 or 26). An isolated example of a sphinx also occurs, to be sure, in a grove of Astarte-Aphrodite at Idalion (No. 3 of the list) (Pl. LIII, 13).

†) Cp. E. Meyer in Roscher's Mythol Lex., p, 2744.

††) Cp. also Cesnola-Stern, Pl. XXVIII, 1 from one of the groves of Rešef-Apollo at Athiaenou (25 and 26) and many others. To be sure, it was the fashion throughout the whole island to wear this sort of helmet made of stuff, leather, or metal, and with or without a round ball at the topmost part In 1889, I dug up just such a helmet made of bronze from a grave at Tamassos of the 6th century B. C. These caps, bonnets and

Voni (No. 2 of the list). Moreover there are found in the sanctuaries of Rešef-Apollo terracotta figures, numerous if of very small size, which wear a gigantic cap elongated far beyond the dimensions customary in Egypt, and either with or without a globular termination (e. g. from Limniti figs. 241, 246, and Pl. XLVII, 7). This head covering, which, in this particular form, is peculiar to Cyprus, has so far been frequently found in sanctuaries of Rešef-Apollo, but nowhere else. Again, there is a helmet or cap-like covering, that, so far, has only been found in Cyprus and among the votive offerings in the precincts of Rešef-Apollo. It ends in a large ball (Fig. 241 from Limniti) or in a hemisphere open at the top (Fig. 244).*) The heads that appear in this connection are distinguished by a short cropped whisker, and shaved upper lip (Fig. 242 from Limniti = XLVI, 10). Whenever these warriors in the service of Rešef-Apollo carry swords, they are long, pointed, thrusting swords,

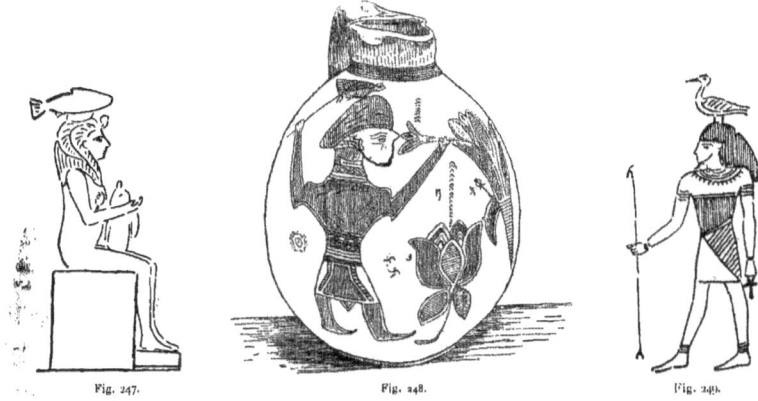

Fig. 247.   Fig. 248.   Fig. 249.

as in the case of Herakles-Melqart (Pl. CIV, 3). In addition they carry small round shields, spears, bow and arrows.*) In the τιμένη of the war-like Rešef-Apollo, as he is seen in the specially ornate and

helmets were studded with one, two, four or more knob-shaped bosses, and finally this decoration was continued all round. Hence these Cyprian helmets correctly illustrate for the first time the κυνέη τετράφαλος and όμφίφαλος of Homer (Iliad V, 743, XI, 41, XII, 384, cp. Helbig, "Homerisches Epos," p. 301) i. e. the helmet with four studs or studded all round. A helmet of this sort, made of leather, and from the grove of Rešef-Apollo at Limniti, is published in Pl. XLVI, 2. It is decorated with no less than twelve bosses in four rows and at regular intervals. On the other hand, the small head of a warrior in Fig. 246 wears a leather or metal helmet studded with four bosses, hence analogous to the helmet of Achilles. Iliad XXII, 314. The band round the top does not indicate a phalos, but is certainly the remains of a metal ring set round horizontally for strength.

       *) Cp. also Cesnola-Stern, Pl. XXXVIII, 2; XXXI, 1 = Perrot III, p. 533, fig. 359 = Pls. XCI, 5 and CXL, 7.

       **) If in these Cyprian warriors, who people the graves of Rešef-Apollo, we have not actual representatives of the Sardana who served in the Egyptian army under Rameses II in the war against the Chetites (Helbig, "Homerisches Epos," p. 323) still these images do illustrate the Sardana costume and type. It might very easily happen that these mercenaries, who lived by and made a business of war, and who held themselves to be Peloponnesian Greeks and Arcadians (as the Agadata believed themselves to be Achaeans and the Sakarusa Laconians) came in the course of their expeditions to Cyprus and settled there, and that their influence left on the country traces visible for centuries, in customs, language, dress and type of face.

well-defined fashion again at Frangissa near Tamassos (No. 4) but also e. g. in the sacred high place of Apollo at Goschi (No. 20). I have excavated images of all kinds, warlike folk on foot, on horseback, and in war-chariots. The warriors wear the same clothing and armour as that described, and in which they appear in the ancient Tamassos vase (CXXXVII, 6). And at Tamassos itself numbers of these long, thrusting swords were found (handle in Pl. CXXXVII, 7). We must return once more to the images of the spear-bearing Rešef-Apollo, and of the hawk-headed Horus, and to the hybrid figures compounded of both (i. e. Figs. 236—239). I have reproduced Fig. 249 from Goodyear*) — it is a figure of the god Qeb, father of Horus, from the Egyptian treasury of types. Instead of having a bird's head, he carries the bird on his head, as do the Astarte-Aphrodite figures of Mykenae (Fig. 201) and Etruria (Fig. 202). On the Cyprian vase Fig. 248 (Pl. XIX, 4) the man who is smelling at a flower holds a bird over his head. His dress, his peaked shoes with turned-up toes, the apron, the whole air of the figure, in spite of the Egyptian adjuncts, remind one of Hittite influence.**) As clearly we have here a sun-worshipper who holds the spray to his nose, he might quite well stand in relation to the cult of Rešef-Apollo, among whose many characteristics were also those of light and sun-god. The Hathor seated on a throne, with the fish on her head, (Fig. 247) was discussed above p. 290, and could have been better reproduced in the same place. But be that as it may, the picture may not be unwelcome here, for comparison side by side with the figure of Qeb and the sun-worshipper with the bird and the flowers, and may serve as a typological counterpart to these.

As I was going to the press with this part of the book, my eye caught, as I was turning over the leaves of the Hellenic Journal, 1890, the engraving on p. 54, of a dark green scarabaeus, set in a gilt bronze ring. This same ring was excavated in 1889 in the cemetery, first discovered by me at Marion-Arsinoë (Poli tis Chrysokhou). The representation is so exactly like an illustration in Lajard's book on p. 334, that our picture (setting aside the more oval shape of the stone on it) at the first glance would be taken by many to be an enlargement of the one published by Munro and Tubbs (J. H. S. 1890, p. 54, Fig. 1). This discovery dispels every doubt, and is a brilliant confirmation of what I laid stress on in reference to the candelabra, and repeated here. All the four gems published p. 324 (obviously all scarabaei) were made in Cyprus and represent the Cypriote Rešef (Rešef-Horus).

b. Rešef-Apollo as god of trees and groves, of incense and healing. His attributes are the asperges, the fawn, the eagle, Nike. Apollo and Zeus. The god of music.

The great importance in itself of the sprig of flowers in the left hand of Rešef-Apollo follows from the representation in Fig. 236. The god stands before a blazing candelabrum or torch-holder, and elevates his right hand in token of benediction or supplication, while in the left, together with a lance, he holds a bunch of flowers. I have already drawn attention (p. 137 and 266) to the flower-sprigs in the hands of Rešef-Apollo and his priests. On Pl. XLI, 3 and XLII, 7 may be seen

---

*) "Grammar of the Lotus," XLIII, 1 = Randhuisen, "History of Ancient Egypt," I, p. 375.

**) Early in 1885, when the vase was discovered, I had correctly identified this influence as Hittite and expressed my opinion in my pamphlet on the vase. Unfortunately the passage was struck out by Herr F. Dümmler, who was so good as to look over what I had written. Shortly after G. Perrot reproduced this same vase from S. Reinach's publication (= Fig. 248) Chroniques d'Orient [5², 359—360] and referred to the Hittite influence. Cp. p. 190, Pl. XIX, 4, and for the peaked shoes Pl. IV, 2, LII, 3, LXXXVII, 9 and p. 87, fig. 122.

figures of priests from the sanctuary of Rešef-Apollo at Voni. They hold in the right hand the incense box, in the left the spray or twig. Apollo as Hylates played a conspicuous part in Cyprus, as has already partially been shown (p. 229 and 232). Hylates was a wind, rock, sea and cave-god, and at the same time an avenging deity, a Moloch, whose anger and general malevolence men sought with ever increasing earnestness to avert by human sacrifices, like those offered at Amathus to Baal-Malika-Zeus (p. 244). The principal expiatory cultus practised in relation to the worship of this Apollo Hylates has been already described (p. 232). It took place close to the chief seat of his cult in the wood at Hyle at the cliff Phrurion, from which the victims were cast headlong down into the sea.

Mention has already been made of the myrtle-god Apollo-Myrtates (No. 59 of the list, cf. p. 112). We recognised the god of spices at Amargetti (in the grove No. 58 of the list) in Apollo Melanthios, who is the same as the god Opaon Melanthios (cf. p. 215 and 255), and whom we found again at Kition. This god was at once a god of herds and herdsmen and a *Παιάν*, and seems to have stood in some relation to Ešmun-Asklepios of Kition (p. 215). We also saw that his cult had in it very many Dionysiac and Priapian elements. We noted that to this very god offerings were made which exactly illustrate those male columns of Baal, and Massebas in contradistinction to the female Asherôt, which the old Testament prophets so detested. We also found Phalloi dedicated in great numbers, and some even made of bronze; some also we noted fastened to pillars and cones. Incense, without end. Surely to no god in all antiquity was ever so much incense burnt as to Apollo, i. e. Rešef. I drew attention just now to two incense-carriers of the Apollo sanctuary at Voni (No. 2 of the list Pl. XLI, 3 and XLII, 7). I have published three more on the two plates devoted to the Voni sanctuary (XLI, 1, 2, and 7). All three figures carry sacrificial incense in the right hand—the sacrificial dove in the left. Incense is the link, even early in the 6th century B. C., between Salamis in Cyprus and Delphi, both centres of Apollo-worship. We know that King Euelthon of Salamis (560—525 B. C.) dedicated a censer in the temple of Apollo at Delphi. I believe it to be practically impossible to excavate any precinct of Rešef-Apollo, that is rich in votive offerings, without coming on images of worshippers holding incense boxes. *)

Incense and purification are in antiquity, as to-day, inseparable. To this day censing serves as a means of disinfection against contagious epidemics and evil of all kinds. The Cypriot of to-day censes men and beasts against the evil eye. My cook used to cense the camera when she saw that a negative was a failure. She censed my antiquities when they had to be put together, me and my horse when I started on a ride, and so on. All the censers which I have published were, with but two exceptions, excavated in groves of Apollo or Artemis. **) If the men employed incense mostly in the worship of Rešef-Apollo, the women did the same for Tanit-Artemis, into whose worship had

---

*) H. Lang found them at Idalion (No. 30 of the list: Transactions of the Royal Society of Literature XI, pl. III and coll. in Brit. Mus.) L. P. di Cesnola at Athiaenou (no. 25 and 26 of the list. Cesnola-Stern (Pl. XXV, XVI, 1, 2 &c.).

**) Pl. XVII, 6, CCX, 21. Censers abounded in the cult of Artemis at Achna (No. 1). Cp. the censer Pl. CXCVII, 2 with the winged woman, presumably from a grove of Artemis Chytroi Pl. CXCVII, 4. Censers from the grove of Rešef-Apollo at Frangissa (No. 4 on the list), where a whole series were found. Also in the Voni sanctuary a fragment of a censer was discovered. Indeed censing went on in all sorts of cults; enormous quantities of incense were burnt to Astarte Aphrodite. Incense vessels from the cultus of this deity have appeared in Pl. XXXVIII, 11—13.

crept many elements from that of Kybele and of Hecate. Both divinities, Apollo and Artemis, who were sister and brother, were accounted divinities of magic and incantation.

Under No. 27 of the list (p. 15) I introduce a sanctuary, in which Artemis appears as Paredros of Apollo Magirios. The brother and sister are worshipped as σύμβωμοι. *) The inscription on the altar found there is to Apollo Magirios, the Apollo of magic. **)

Incense and holy water are near akin. So it was in antiquity, so to-day. To Rešef-Apollo the asperges were as indispensable as the incense box. Here again it is impossible to find a temenos of Rešef-Apollo, if it be one well supplied with votive offerings, without finding representations of the asperges set up. ***) We find them also e. g. in the precincts of Apollo mentioned by H. Lang (Transactions Royal Society of Literature XI, Pl. III), at Idalion (No. 30) mentioned by L. P. Cesnola (Cesnola-Stern, Pl. XXV), at Athiaenou (No. 25 and 26) &c. The statue published by Cesnola-Stern (XXV) is doubly interesting, because the laurel-crowned priest of Apollo there instanced holds in the left the incense box, and in the right a bunch of alternate myrtle and laurel leaves for asperging with holy water. The Cypriote Papas to this day make use of just such bunches, when they make their monthly house-to-house circuit to asperge the dwellings.

There were certain sanctuaries in which this aspect of Rešef-Apollo was specially emphasized, and in these possibly the principal cultus-image represented the god as himself holding the asperges in his capacity of purifier. Such a sanctuary is the one I excavated at Voni (No. 2 on the list). From the collection of life-size statues that I have put together on Plates XL, XLI, 8 and XLII, 1 and 2, it is evident that these asperge-carriers represent, in fact, not merely priests but the god himself. The statue No. 3, XL is open to some doubt. Possibly we have to see in it, as in another (Cesnola-Stern Pl. XXV), a priest who had himself portrayed in the aspect of the god, but statues No. 1 and 4 can only represent the god, and indeed they both bear in their hand the asperges. The attributes settle the question that these are undoubtedly statues of divinities. The statue in fig. 1 holds in the left a manuscript roll, while on the forearm perches an eagle, given full size in fig. 2. Add to this that the head of the statue is thoroughly Apolline in character, with the large lines of its features, the hair arranged in long curls, and the impressive laurel wreath; all this shows that the intention of the sculptor was to represent a god. In the small curls that frame the face, holes are bored, which once served to hold some sort of metal decorative adjuncts, possibly stars or rays of gold, gold-bronze or bronze. An exactly similar coiffure characterises the representation in Pl. XLII, 1, unfortunately much damaged, in which the god holds a young roe or fawn. Here, as the head is published in

---

*) Even where we are supposed to have a trinity, Apollo-Artemis-Dionysos, Apollo Magirios always holds the first rank. For Rešef-Apollo as paredros of Astarte-Aphrodite, cp. supra p. 263.

**) To this day in Cyprus priest and magician are one and the same. In Cyprus Turco-Mohammedan and Greco-Christian priests, mosque- and church-attendants, practice alike this detrimental business of magic snake-charming, and incantations for healing. A written charm from a Cyprian snake-charmer is supposed to be an infallible cure for the sometimes fatal bite of the Mauritanian viper (Kufi) met with on the island. The magicians (who are either Turkish or Greek priests) need not even see the sufferers. They employ a secret formulary of incantation, which remains the property of the initiated only. The people call them Μάγοι. Possibly the word is connected with the Magirios title of Apollo.

***) Ceremonies of aspersion naturally occur in the cult of the most diverse divinities. On Pl. XVI, is a holy water stoup put together out of fragments. It was set up in the sanctuary of Astarte-Aphrodite (no. 3 on the list). In the sanctuary also on the Acropolis of Kition, that was in the first instance dedicated to Astarte, when the hillock was dug away, a stone stoup was found in situ at the entrance of the precinct.

profile, the rows of curls falling on the back of the neck in vertical lines are more clearly seen. I excavated two considerable fragments of a second similar large sized image, in which the eagle is perched on the hand that holds the roll, like the Zeus type. So far as one can judge from the fragmentary character of statue 4, XL, it seems as if in this instance there was the same short curled coiffure as in statue 3, from which we may conclude that statue No. 3 also represents a god. On the other hand, in the case of another inscribed statue, which it is true is somewhat differently draped, and is unfortunately headless and much mutilated, it is certain, as I showed above p. 266, that a priest is represented whose name was Karys (cf. also Mittheilungen des deutschen archäologischen Instituts, Athen 1884, p. 136, also supra p. 6 No. 4).

It is clear that here attributes of Apollo and Zeus are united in one representation. The statues belong to the 4th century B. C. and possibly to its second half when in Cyprus the whole of art was Graecized. It is equally clear that in the statues that carry the young roe (XLII, 1 and 2) we have representations of Apollo. These statues also carry in the right hand the bunch of leaves. Common to priests and gods alike is the signet ring of the temple worn on the fourth finger of the left hand (Pl. XLI, 1 and 2). The priestly family of Karys, whose existence I have proved; in this sanctuary (Mittheil., Athen 1884, p. 136), together with the god who carries the young roe and the god who is a combination of Apollo and Zeus, these all point to Caria and the Branchidae sanctuary of the Didymaean Apollo at Miletus.*) There too Zeus was worshipped side by side with Apollo. The whole motive of the asperges-carrier (as on Pl. XL, 3) can be shown through the length and breadth of the island to be the common possession of the sanctuaries of Apollo and of Greek art in Cyprus. Attitude and costume, the arrangement of the drapery and its folds, the very style and approximately the date are uniformly the same. We rarely miss (as in XL, 1) the terminal fold of drapery that as a rule hangs from the left shoulder (XL, 3 and 4, XLI, 8 XLII, 1 and 2). The execution only varies. The right hand uniformly holds the asperges in almost exactly the same position, hanging down just to the upper thigh of the advanced right leg. The more important variations are for the most part confined to the position of the left hand, which in the main hangs like a pendulum close to the body; some-times reaching a little higher, sometimes a little lower, and which in some cases rests on a column which is either square (XLII, 2), or round (XL, 4, XLII, 1). This left hand sometimes holds an attribute e. g. an incense-box (Cesnola-Stern, Pl. XXV), the young roe or fawn (XLII, 1 and 2), the eagle (XL, 1), the Nike· (XL, 4), sometimes nothing at all (XL, 3). In very rare cases a boy stands near the full grown figure, and this represents either a boy attendant near a priest, or Tammuz-Adonis near Rešef-Apollo. **) This motive of Apollo the Purifier with the bunch of leaves occurs in Cesnola-Stern (besides Pl. XXV, Athiaenou) Pl. XLII, 2 (possibly from Lapathos?), also in H. Lang (Transactions Pl. III). All these figures come from groves of Apollo. I also find the same type at Voni (No. 2 of the list) in precincts of Rešef-Apollo at Goschi (No. 20 of the list) and at Frangissa. The single fragment of a male statue found in the Artemis-Kybele grove at Achna (No. 1) belongs to just such an asperges-carrier, and represents either Apollo or one of his priests.

A word as to the Cyprian Rešef-Apollo as god of music in Cyprus. Traces of the god as god of stringed instrumental music are excessively rare. On the two reliefs found in the grove at

---

*) Cp., remarks to Pl. XL—XLII.
**) For Apollo and Adonis cp. especially supra pp. 112 and 204.

Athiaenou the god seated appears to be playing the cithara (Pl. LXXXIII, 7), or holding it (Pl. LXXXIII, 6). I myself have only once dug up a figure of a god playing on a stringed instrument, in the grove of Rešef-Apollo at Frangissa. The lyre and the cithara are, on the other hand, prominent objects in the cult of Artemis, while they appear, though rarely, in connection with Aphrodite. In the cult of Rešef-Apollo just the opposite has been found to be the case to what one would have expected. Flute music was always present, and was just as prominent a feature in the Cyprian feasts of Apollo (Pl. XLII, 3 and 6) as in those of Aphrodite. Evidently from this, the flayer of Marsyas, the opponent of the flute, is nowise at home here. On the other hand, the tympanon which was sounded at the festivals of Astarte-Aphrodite (L, 5), as well as at those of Tanit-Artemis-Kybele (XI, 10), does not appear at Apolline festivals. No trace of a tympanon player has been found in any precinct of Apollo. As with the Hebrews of the Bible, it seems that to play on cymbals was a prerogative of women, and only customary at the festivals of female divinities.

c. Further particulars of Rešef-Apollo as war-god, sun-god, weather-god again Rešef-Mikal and other analogous divinities.

Under a) we have already learnt to know our chief Cyprian god as a god of the spear, and of light and the sun. There are, however, groves of Rešef-Apollo, in which his warlike aspect is wholly absent; e. g. at Voni where no trace can be shown either of an armed warrior figure or of a war-chariot. In other groves, as in that at Frangissa, the warlike aspect entirely preponderated, and the aspect of the Purifier only found expression in quite subordinate fashion, in a few small figures. The horses of the sun in the Bible, which Ezekiel (cf. supra p. 231, and infra Pl. CXCVI with commentary) saw in the temple court at Jerusalem, these and the sun worshippers accord admirably with the cult of Rešef-Apollo. And moreover, if the women lamented for Tammuz, we saw that Tammuz-Adonis was servant and friend of Apollo-Rešef.

Rešef-Apollo, the archer, appears to have been represented in the stone pyxis of Amathus (Pl. CXCIX, 7), and he appears as a statue in one of the sanctuaries at Athiaenou (no. 25 and 26) (Cesnola-Stern Pl.XXXIII, 1). Among the scenes with a number of figures forming chariot groups*) that had been deposited in hundreds on the altar and sacrifice-place of the grove of Rešef-Apollo at Frangissa, one notes among the armed men a number of votive offerings representing archers in various attitudes, like that on the Cyprian vase (Pl. CXVIII, 1). Here again the type of Rešef-Apollo approaches that of Melqart-Herakles, and vice versa. One is also reminded of Marduk-Merodach as archer (Pl XXIX, 4, 6—8), before he turned into the type of animal-tamer. We have often considered Rešef-Apollo as storm- and weather-god, specially on p. 235. It seems that prayers were addressed to Rešef-Mikal-Apollo-Amyklos in time of drought as a rain-sender, like Zeus Lykaios in Arcadia.

In fact, all possible powers were attributed to the principal god of a place, even when these same powers were attributed in another place to another principal god. The powers proper to Zeus in Greece, or to Yahve in Judaea, became in Cyprus the prerogative of Apollo.

It only remains to institute a comparison between the cult of Rešef-Mikal-Apollo-Amyklos and that of the Greek Apollo of Amyklae. It is not the Cyprian god that has copied the Greek but

---

*) I shall describe these in detail in my work on Tamassos, cp. also Pl. CXCVI.

vice versa. The Greek titles of Apollo are not the original ones, but, as Foucard has already stated, the Cypriot Greeks graecised the Phoenician word Mikal, and made out of it their Amyklos. But Foucard stopped half way when he asserted that this Cyprian Apollo-Amyklos had nothing to do with the Hellenic Apollo Amyklaios. Again, Clermont Ganneau has treated the subject of these divinities in detail in his "Le Dieu Satrape et les Phéniciens dans le Péloponèse". *) Pausanias has, of course, left us a fairly close description of the archaic cultus-image at Amyklae. The figure consisted of an iron column with the addition of feet, hands, and a helmeted head. The hands held bow and spear.

Such a column-image is represented in many of the votive terra-cotta figures I excavated in 1885 at Tamassos and Frangissa. The god even holds in most cases the spear in his hand. The feet stick out beneath the column, which increases in size towards the top. The legs are not indicated, but on the other hand, in most cases, besides head and arms the breast is given, growing out of the column. In Cyprus, then, we have the prototype of the image seen by Pausanias at Amyklae. For, as the art of modelling in stone or terra-cotta was developed earlier in Cyprus than in the Peloponnese, it is much less probable that the cultus-image of the Laconian Amyklae served as model for the votive image in Cyprus. We know now that there were Greeks settled in Cyprus in pre-Dorian days several centuries before Homer. We also know from the Cyprian dialect that they were Peloponnesian Greeks, and were a race made up of Arcadian, Achaean and Laconian elements. In the time of Thutmosis III. and his successors, these Peloponnesian Greeks (Sardana, Aqaivasa, Sakarusa) passed over to Egypt. On their way they had touched at Cyprus, and some of them had stayed behind on the island. Their descendants had lived for centuries there, and had mixed with other races who peopled the island, races of Asia Minor, Chetites, Phoenicians and other Syrian tribes. It seems that at one time the tide turned back to the old motherland, and that the half orientalized Greeks carried their idols back with them to the Peloponnese; we may conjecture that they founded a town and called it Amyklae in honour of the god who in their Cyprian home bore the name of Amyklos.

Many things yet remain to be said about Resef-Apollo in Cyprus, but time presses. By the help of the index the reader may easily refer to much information scattered about in previous portions of the book and not resumed here — information about the god who dominated the religion of the ancient Cypriots almost as much as Astarte-Aphrodite. Even in the famous sanctuary at Old-Paphos, Resef-Apollo seems to have been present as Paredros by the side of Astarte-Aphrodite. We gather this from an inscription to Apollo in the Greek language written in the syllabic Cyprian alphabet, which Herr E. Dörpfeld and I found in 1890 built into a dilapidated turretted wall close to the sacred precincts of Astarte-Aphrodite.**)

---

*) Journal Asiatique, X, Paris, 1877.
**) A. Meister in the Berliner Philologische Wochenschrift. The inscribed stone is in the Berlin Museum.

Appendix I.

A comparison of the festivals of Oriental vegetation-divinities with those of southern and northern Europe.

If we compare the oriental festivals here instanced, both in antiquity and the present time, with analogous popular ceremonies going on now in the north of Europe, the result is exceedingly surprising. Although, in the case of many festivals, a clear connection is not yet made out, and possibly never will be, there are others in which countless very peculiar details of ceremonial in various places and of various dates are so absolutely identical, that to speak of a psychical unity for mankind, as Peschel*) would have it, is now out of the question. In face of the proofs which we have already adduced and are about to adduce, I hold it to be simply impossible that in Egypt, Asia Minor, Cyprus, Southern and Northern Europe, the same spring and summer customs, due to a temper of mind substantially the same, should have originated in these various peoples independently one of the other.**) It is just these Cyprian popular customs, which subsist to-day, which prove incontestably that certain modern customs of Northern and Southern Europe took their rise in the ancient East. We saw how the Cypriot of to-day, especially the orthodox Greek Christian, has preserved, in tolerable purity, the festivals celebrated in antiquity to the Babylonian Dusi and the Hebraic Tammuz of the Bible, to the Egyptian Osiris and the Greek Adonis, the Phrygian Attis and the Homeric Linos, and that through a tradition that runs unbroken through thousands of years.

We became acquainted in Cyprus with the child Lazarus covered with yellow flowers, and raised by Christ from the dead by the water of life, as Dusi is raised by Ištar in the ancient Babylonish hymn. At Rauschenberg in Hessen it was customary to wrap a man from head to foot thickly round in yellow flowers. At Lausitz, the Johannis-King is completely covered with blue cornflowers. At Buschweiler a lad called the Pfingstklötzel (Whitsun fool or stock) is covered with flowers and greenery, and led about the town.***) In Russian Lithuania "Green George", in the shape of a doll

---

*) "Völkerkunde", p. 22—27.
**) Cp. Mannhardt, "Baum- und Feldculte," p. 301.
***) Cp. cit. 312, 313.

covered over with green birch twigs, is thrown into the water. In Ruhla the children choose one of themselves as "Little Leaf-man", and take him about from house to house collecting presents and food; then they sprinkle him with water, like the Cyprian Lazarus or the Babylonian Dusi.*)

In Cyprus the great popular festival in which the islanders of all classes take part is celebrated in Whitsun-week. All who possibly can make the journey to Larnaka or Limassol. To Larnaka especially the inhabitants stream in thousands for this day. The memory is still preserved among the people that this water festival, now called Katakeismos, was an ancient festival of Aphrodite. The festival in its fullest significance can only be celebrated at the sea and in the largest sea-ports. The people bathe in the sea on the sea shore, which for this day is called the sacred shore.**) They sail along the shore in boats and crafts of all sizes, decked out with flowers, bright streamers, and flags. Music, singing, and dancing goes on on land wherever space can be found, and also on board ship. Piercing flutes, cymbals, and big drums are the favourite instruments. The people in the various boats chaff each other and throw water, sometimes even upset each other into the water. Fire-balls and firework figures are sent off.

Even in well-to-do middle-class families it is the custom on this day, when two people first meet and greet, that each should pour a glass of water over the other—a custom I myself have taken part in. Inland the same ceremonies go on, on a small scale, with rivers, streams, wells, and fountains. Everywhere feasting and drinking goes on valiantly. The Turks are often even more jovial than the Christians. The festival is no ecclesiastical one; it begins in the afternoon and goes on far into the night, Link-lights, torches, lanterns, and coloured candles illuminate both the shore which is all alive with people in picturesque attire, and also the countless and no less picturesquely crowded crafts upon the sea. Rockets, Catherine wheels, blazing globes, Bengal fire all cast their particoloured reflections on the thousands that make up a festal throng, wholly given up to enjoyment. Dancing, drinking, singing on the ships as well as in front of the cafés on land, culminate in some places in what is practically an orgiastic rout.

I took part also in an exactly similar festival in Santa Lucia at Naples in August 1878. It is the festa of the Madonna della catena. The Neapolitans formed themselves into curious processions, they were for the most part hung about with flowers and fruit and provided with fireworks. Many of the men were disguised as women. Some carried boughs and poles, which were hung with fruits, flowers, comestibles, and fireworks. A band with the big drum and flute accompanied them. Whoever possibly could, threw some one else into the sea. Hundreds could be seen swimming about, snatching and grabbing at the fruit and flowers which had fallen off the dresses or had been intentionally thrown into the sea. It was a great public bath, under a fire of the most crazy jests, and accompanied by the letting off of the noisiest possible fireworks. This festival of the chain Madonna ended with a vast illumination in the evening, a magnificent pyrotechnic display, at which the Neapolitans are noted as adepts, and a universal drinking, feasting, dancing and singing. It reminds one absolutely of the festival of the Thracian Kotyto, whose cult had spread to Corinth, Athens and Sicily***), at which

---

*) Cp. cit. p. 320.

**) τὸ ἅγιον γιαλόν.

***) Mannhardt, " Wald und Feldculte," p. 258.

young men assisted dressed in women's clothes (as in Cyprus at the festival of Aphrodite Amathusia), in which people threw themselves into the water, and branches of trees hung with cakes and tree fruits were given up to the crowd to despoil. These Cyprian and Neapolitan water and sea festivals show on a large scale what is represented in miniature by the sousing with water, or the immersion of the German tree-mannikin, the Whitsun-man or the Green George.[*]

These festivals go back to the Dusi and Tammuz, to Adonis and Osiris and the festivals in honour of Dionysos. The sea festivals I have described have their counterparts in the Adonia which were celebrated both at Amathus in Cyprus and at Alexandria and Byblos in which sometimes an image of Adonis was thrown into the sea, sometimes a head of Adonis swam from Alexandria to Byblos or a whole chest with the dead body of Osiris strangled by Seti. They remind one of Dionysiac mysteries of the head of Dionysos which the waves carried to the coast of Lesbos. The festival at Naples, however, corresponds in a surprising way to the festival of Kotyto. We noted above, Pl. XCIII, how one was reminded of the myths of the floating heads of gods. The crouching boy-attendant of the Temple of Adonis bore on a chain across his breast a large human head (Pl. XXXIII, 3).

A full description has been given above of how during Easter week from the first day of the festival each afternoon in a fresh diocese a Judas variously dressed is put to death in various ways, but the end of it uniformly is that the puppet is blown to pieces and burnt up by fire-works with which it is stuffed and which are set off. Once we saw a Judas, made entirely out of shavings, burnt before the church. In Upper Bavaria a wooden figure of Judas was burnt in the Easter-fire which was prescribed by the Church. In other districts a straw puppet (which occurs in Cyprus also) was decked out as Judas, stretched on a wooden cross on some rising place and burnt. Mannhardt[**] lays special stress on the loud rejoicings that took place when this was done, as though the betrayer of the Saviour was punished in person. There is exactly the same down-right fanatical rejoicing in Cyprus at each fresh burning of the Judas.

We find the counterpart of the water festivals mentioned above and these fire festivals in the Roman festival of the Argeiri, in which 24 figures made of rushes were thrown by the Vestals into river Tiber for the 24 quarters of Rome.[***] At Larnarka in Cyprus in just the same way each quarter of the city has its Judas-puppet.

Mannhardt has also described in detail[†] from the classical sources (Caesar, Bellum Gallicum VI, 16 Strabo IV, C. 198 and Diodor V, 32) an ancient Gallic festival of a yearly bonfire in which images of human shape made of willow and over life-size, in which were concealed living human beings, were burnt. Criminals, prisoners of war, and also foreigners were utilized for these sacrifices. In Gaul, then, in Caesar's time human sacrifices still took place. At Rome at that time rush figures had already been substituted for throwing into the Tiber. The burning of the Judas puppet points also to previous human sacrifices and indeed to the Moloch offerings among the Hebrews and Canaanites. Human sacrifice is attested for Cyprus in the case of several divinities. Foreigners were offered to Osiris at Amathus, and even in the present day the Cypriots like to make up their Judas puppet as

---

[*] Mannhardt, "Baumcultus," pp. 327—355.
[**] Mannhardt, "Baumcultus," p. 504.
[***] Cp. cit. p. 505.
[†] Cp. cit. p. 525 &c.

a foreigner. When the English came to Cyprus in 1878 in one diocese at Larnaka at the Easter festival of 1879 there was a Judas dressed as an Englishman. Criminals were hurled down into the sea from the rock Phrurion, which stands near to the temple of Apollo Hylates at Hyle, west of Kurion.*) At Salamis, in very early days, each year a human being was killed and burnt.**) In the course of my excavations in Cyprus I have not succeeded in proving the existence of human sacrifice. But H. Lang reports that in his excavation of the sanctuary of Rešef-Apollo at Idalion the skull of a child was found. Had it only been accurately shown that the provenance of the skull was from the layer of ashes of the place of sacrifice, then anyhow the practise of human sacrifice would have been evidenced.

---

*) The rock actually exists. Cp. supra p. 232.
**) Engel, " Kypros", II. p. 664.

Appendix II.

Gold objects discovered in Cyprus.

V. Pl. CCXVII.

By Herr Direktor Frauberger (Düsseldorf).

The island of Cyprus was highly esteemed even in ancient times for its productive copper-mines, and its situation was favorable to commerce with the whole known world. Of late years, for some decades archaeologists have come to hold it in special esteem also for the rich discoveries they have made of gold ornaments which have come to light in the various religious centres that have been excavated. From its situation the possession of the island was extremely important to such powerful peoples as left their own shores for commercial purposes. We therefore find Assyrians, Egyptians, Persians, Phoenicians, Greeks, Romans, Venetians and English as successively masters of this mountainous island which yet is by no means wanting in fruitful spots. It is further owing to this situation that not only articles of commerce, but that manners, customs, habits of life of the peoples who successively ruled it are to be found on the island, and that its native population could not free itself from the influence of foreign culture: this has left its mark in the remains of ancient architecture, and is very clearly evidenced in the diverse contents of the various graves that have been opened.

From the contents of these graves, which form the starting point and basis of the conclusions arrived at in this book, I shall select the gold ornaments, although they have been frequently commented on before, and I shall say a few words about them more especially with reference to the ornaments in the industrial Museum at Düsseldorf which are published in plate CCXVII.

In most of the ancient graves of Cyprus gold ornaments are found; but in each grave the quantity found varies and so does the artistic merit. In Cyprus the old law about treasure trove is still in force. The third of the find belongs to the government of Cyprus, and already it has obtained possession of a goodly number of specially lovely gold ornaments, which in time will adorn the Cyprian Museum at Nikosia, as soon as a spacious building has been got ready for their reception and an archaeologist, who has a thorough acquaintance with the ancient art of Cyprus, has been appointed excavator. One third of the find belongs to the excavators and as the funds for excavating

44*

come for the most part from abroad it follows that in Germany, France, England and Italy, both in public museums and in possession of rich amateurs, there are fine collections formed of gold ornaments, the largest of which, in the Metropolitan Museum of New York, was formed by the late American Consul Cesnola in the many years during which he was at work in Cyprus. A third of the find belongs to the owner of the land in which the excavation is made. This third part forms the fluctuating amount of ancient gold ornaments which exists collectively on the island including such pieces as are filched by the workmen while at work. By degrees these pieces go the round of the collections which are formed from single acquisitions by well-to do bankers, officials, wine merchants and the like and from these sources I myself when on my travels through Cyprus have got together for the Düsseldorf Museum more than 200 pieces, of which twenty characteristic examples are published.

The topmost piece (Fig. 1,) the clay bead set both sides in gold betrays a Cypriot maker to whom a difference in the value of the raw material was unknown. We no longer feel the symbolical significance of the earth but the material power of gold is meanwhile made vividly clear to us. In the second row there came next two oval buttons with border of ·seed-gold and adorned with figurines.

On the one is a figure of Abundantia (Fig. 2) on the other a naked goddess (Fig. 3). These gold buttons occur frequently in some graves in large quantities but the dresses to which presumably they belonged have perished. The damp climate of the island was bad for the preservation of delicate textile stuffs, whereas the dry sand of Egypt has preserved for us purple textures, linens of cobweb delicacy, fine embroideries and the most minute network. Egyptian rule over Cyprus is shown by the figurine in Fig. 4, a specimen of delicate turning which contains in the hollow core a small roll of parchment which gives information about the original possessor. A wide-bellied vase with opal enamel and a delicate acorn, a fruit that is very common in Cyprus, are ornaments that often occur as pendants to chains and earrings. Both are burned work, the vase has been laboriously worked out in one piece and is of the finest period of Greek art, the acorn is of archaic date and made up of two plates soldered together in the middle.

A delicate little chain (Fig. 7) has as pendant a gold bead with gold seeds, smelted on in a beautiful pattern. Lower down on the plate (Fig. 12) comes another delicate but fragmentary chain from the best period of Greek art. Between two remarkable finely turned rosettes there are placed alternately bored beads of ruby and emerald (the first are nearly all, the last in part broken off) and between the little rosettes are simple chain links. The catch at the end has a dog's head as fastener. The whole is of great charm.

Between the two chains are two masks, an ornament for the breast, and a sepulchral earring. The two masks, worked in fine beaten gold leaf, show very different degrees of artistic ability. The top one (Fig. 8) is the work of a Greek artist, the lower one (Fig. 11) the work of a goldsmith who was not able to model the human head properly. The ornament for the breast (Fig. 9) is beautiful in effect.

Between two centric circles made of small and granulated filigree is a dull disc of flat hammered work. The inner disk is highly polished, it almost looks as if there had formerly been some figure upon it in very low relief which had disappeared through rough handling. At least the industrial Museum at Düsseldorf contains, but more frequently on frontlets, similar representations with figures in relief that rise very little above the surface. We have a very early and remarkable piece of work in the large earring given in Fig. 10; it probably points to Syria (Assyria). In shape, size and in the tint of the gold it presents a considerable difference to the others.

Among the great mass of ear- and also hair-rings decorated with beast's heads, which are to be found in the collection five specimens in the last row but one are characteristic. The ear-ring (Fig. 13) with a beast's head is of great beauty, both in conception and execution. It may have been a copy of the beautiful wild-goat of which there we had several examples e. g. in the monastery of Kikku. It is wrought work of a specially skilful sort: the turned horns and granulated streamers are added on and the ring is wrought of twisted gold thread with careful finish. The next piece is cast entire but has filigree work soldered on, it is decorated with a lion's head and represents a type too that is very frequent on the island. The bull's head (Fig. 7) is also evidently the work of an indigenous artist and in the choice of the head betrays Assyrian influences. The next ear-ring (Fig. 16) with the head of a ram whose horns are made of minute thinly beaten thread now much bent and · spoilt, is a remarkably fine, though much damaged, piece of work. It may belong to the best period of Greek art in which the noblest style of work in gold was executed. The dog's head on the last ring (Fig. 17), which is scarcely a centimetre in diameter, is very fresh and lifelike in conception.

In the last row come three types of ear-ring which also occur very frequently in graves and with many variations. The first piece (Fig. 18) reminds one, as to shape, of the leather pillows found in ancient graves in upper Egypt, but in the elegant arrangement, gold granulations that are smelted on, in the able concealment of the junctions and in fact in the general effect it reminds one of best period of Greek art.

This shape is often found quite flat without impression consisting of two beaten leaves of different sizes. The second piece of later date (Fig. 19) also inclines to the more archaic forms only that in this case a vase already serves as pendant, whereas those simple massive rings which, however decrease in size towards the ends are, some of them, without an appendage. Some have cases in which precious stones or beautiful glass composition is set. Sometimes one also finds pendants which consist of several gold beads soldered together and are in shape just like the ear ornaments on the figures in the alabaster reliefs of the Assyrian palaces.

Starting from the simple smooth hoops diminishing towards the ends and ending with the last shape (Fig. 20), at which the thicker middle part of the hoof is beaten out to thin foil, there are to be found in Cyprus many transition stages which are for the most part simple, either quite smooth or with edges bent up, or granulated on the surface, sometimes with gold grain, sometimes haphazard sometimes in a fixed pattern. The final development that this shape takes in the way of rich treatment has the inner plate flat, and on the outside, which when the ring was in the ear was in sight, has an outer rim of gold thread soldered on, a row of golden grains in the form of a triangle and two circles adorned with gold grains as well as two ivy leaves made of the thinnest gold thread. It looks as if this wire had served for the making of the cells for the cellular smalt which so often occurs in Cyprian gold ornaments. That delight in colour which the Greeks of antiquity possessed and which still has a traditional influence in their national embroideries, is manifested also in their goldsmith's work, already celebrated for its form, for artistic skill of metal work, for minute treatment of gold filigree and for richness of symbolical and decorative and always stylistically fine ornament.

For example the eyes of all ear-rings made of animals' heads which are found in Cyprus are made of enamel, of which there are traces left in the specimens in the last row but one, except on the lion's head.

These few examples show clearly how instructive and inspiring both from the point of view of the history of culture and of style as well as ornament and technique, these treasures of gold ornament dug from the graves of Cyprus are. The rich collections in New York have been utilized by Tiffany for the education of American goldsmiths, Castellani has made the like use of what was found in Italy; for German craftsmen there still remains much that is new to be learnt from the sources.

Explanation of the Plates.

The illustrations marked ⚲ belong to my excavations in Kypros. Those marked † are antiquities first appraised and brought into the market by me. The descriptions marked H. S. were written by Dr. Hubert Schmidt and supervised by me.

Plate I.

The ancient cultus-places of Kypros, arranged by Max Ohnefalsch-Richter.

I attach special value to this map, because in it the newest topographic observations have been used, and it is founded on the admirable map of E. Oberhummer, which he published along with his Essay on Kypros in the "Zeitschrift für Erdkunde" (Berlin).*) For the situation E. Oberhummer had made use of the new English map by Captain (now Colonel) H. Kitchener, published in 1885 by Edward Stanford, and for the letter press, of Kiepert's map. Oberhummer also added some corrections, by the help of his investigations and my own. Oberhummer has verified or corrected the situation of some other ancient towns, and has altered the phonetic German orthography of Kiepert's map. I have continued the work on the same method, so that my map, in spite of its small scale, may be considered as the most complete topographical representation of the island which has as yet been published.

Plate II.

Map of the ancient town of Idalion and its environs, made from the observations of E. A. Carletti, Surveyor for the Government in Kypros. Archaeological details added by Max Ohnefalsch-Richter, 1887.

This map, which was first published in "The Owl, Science, Literature and Art", No. 6, is repeated here for various reasons. **) As my attempt to keep up an illustrated periodical in Kypros failed, this admirable map is very little known. A study of this map together with Plate III, the town plan of Idalion, will give us a very complete picture of the civilization and cultus of ancient Kypros. For the details a magnifying glass will be found very useful. Unfortunately E. A. Carletti's original drawing has been lost, and my own reproduction, being too much reduced in scale, almost gives the impression of careless measurements, whereas the exact contrary is the truth. We began by drawing in the town plan of Idalion as it had been made by E. A. Carletti and myself from trigonometric measurements with the theodolite. We also worked in the newest English surveys on a large scale (4 in. to a mile) which were begun after the appearance of Kitchener's map, and are still in progress. These new survey results are entitled "The Revised Revenue Survey". The map was prepared for me without charge in the office of E. A. Carletti by permission of Sir Henry Bulwer, the Governor General of the island, who has always shown a deep interest in scientific investigation, and great assistance was given by Mr. A. P. G. Law, who had charge of the Survey Department. In the map I have filled in all the archaeological details on the spot, using for the purpose chain, measuring-line, pole and prismatic compass. The most reliable villagers were questioned about the discoveries, the information obtained from one being checked by that given by another, in order to get the nearest approach to the truth. Several of the oldest excavators, particularly Abraami Charlambou, a Daliot, the finder of the Resef-Apollo Temenos (H. Lang's), and Gregori Antonion, whom I have, since 1883, repeatedly employed as pioneers and overseers, accompanied me in these topographic labours for several weeks and were, with me all day. In most cases I was able to check the information of the villagers by the fragments lying around the spot, or by the ruins still in situ. Where an examination of the surface was not sufficient, I made my pioneers dig with their pickaxes and spades.

No. 1—10. Idalion, reduced from Pl. III (Pl. I. of "The Owl").

No. 11. Provenance of the vase with the woman's head. (cf. p. 39 Fig. 40, Pl. XIX, 2, XX and CCXVI = Cesnola-Stern Pl. LXXXV, 1 = G. Perrot "Histoire de l'Art" III, Fig. 522.)

No. 12. Provenance of the well known bronze dish with representations in relief. P. 46 Fig. 49 = Pl. CXXX, i. G. Perrot XIII, Fig. 482.

*) Berlin 1890, XXV. p. 183—240. "Aus Cypern." Tagebuchblätter und Studien von E. Oberhummer.
**) Edited by Max Ohnefalsch-Richter. 10. November. p. 44, Plate II.

No. 13. Hellenistic Necropolis with many glass vessels, similar to those found in Soliais and Kurion, Pl. LXV. Here I excavated in 1883 for Sir Charles Newton.

No. 14. A stone tomb long since destroyed, with a pointed roof formed of stone slabs. Imitation in stone of a wooden building (cf. No. 19, 21 and 22).

No. 15. Temenos of Aphrodite *Κουροτρόφος.* I made excavations here in 1883 for Sir Charles Newton. (No. 33 of Pl. I.) (cf. p. 14 No. 24 and p. 208).

No. 16. Temenos of a male divinity, perhaps Apollo (No. 35, Pl. I and p. 18).

No. 17. Temenos of a god, Apollo (?) (No. 34, Pl. I and p. 18).

No. 18. Hellenistic Necropolis containing many transparent glass vessels. (Similar to No. 13.)

No. 19. Stone tomb with pointed roof, part of which was well preserved and of which I made a drawing. I published a section of a similar grave at Kition in the Journal of Hellenic Studies, 1883, Pl. XXXIV, 6.

No. 20. Part of a large necropolis in the ancient part of the town. Here I made excavations in 1885 for C. Watkins and F. Dümmler.

No. 21. Four large stone tombs, now destroyed, with pointed roofs, situated on a low hill. Four other tombs, somewhat smaller and without pointed roof, situated north-east on a still lower hill.

No. 22. Site of a stone tomb now destroyed, with a pointed roof.

No. 23. Hellenistic necropolis of uncertain extent, containing many glass vessels.

No. 24. Necropolis. Graeco-Phoenician influence is to be seen here, but there is no trace of the pre-Phoenician period, nor of the Hellenistic (transparent glass).

No. 25. Large necropolis of uncertain extent. Most of the tombs show Graeco-Phoenician influence, and some few Hellenistic.

No. 26. From one of these Hellenistic tombs came the aryballos made of transparent glass, in the form of a human head, in the Greek style and with a Greek inscription, now in the British Museum.

No. 27. Pre-Graeco-Phoenician tombs, which were laid bare by a winter torrent. They resemble those in the necropolis of Phoenidschas, after the period of the people whom I call the "Race of Shepherds". (The larger dishes, intended for milk and cheese, with long double perpendicular holes in the shape of tubes, as on Pl. CLXVIII, 1, b, c, 4b, 5a, do not occur.)

No. 28. Temenos where in conjunction with Apollo (Rešef), Heracles (Melquart) was worshipped. (No. 40 Pl. I and p. 18).

No. 29. Necropolis of one of the races belonging to the pre-Graeco-Phoenician Bronze Period. No trace is here to be found of the existence of the early "Race of Shepherds". A large number of clay vessels like the Kyprian vessel found in Thera[*]), were found here, and a few varnished Mykenai-vases.

No. 30. Settlement or town of the race to which necropolis No. 29 belongs.

No. 31. Temenos dedicated to a divinity as protector of animals. I made excavations here in 1885 for C. Watkins (No. 39 on Pl. I and p. 18).

No. 32. Remains of ancient masonry. I made excavations here in 1885 for C. Watkins.

No. 33. Remains of a Temenos on a hill, evidently dedicated to Apollo. In 1885, when I was excavating here for C. Watkins, I found this temenos already destroyed. It was omitted in the map Pl. I. It is therefore not mentioned in the list of 72 examples.

No. 34. (Top left hand) Tombs at Lithosurus. The number only and not the name of the district is indicated. Graeco-Phoenician influence is present A field of débris in the neighbourhood, which gave its modern name to the district, seems to prove the existence of a settlement corresponding to the necropolis.

No. 35. Graeco-Phoenician tombs. The district is called Hassaveri.

No. 36. Temenos and roofed sanctuary of Aphrodite, which I excavated in 1885 for C. Watkins No. 3 on Pl. I and p. 5.) Outline on Pl. VII, perspective views of the excavation on Pl. XVI and LVII, conjectural restoration of the treasure chamber with the statues in situ Pl. LVI, illustrations of the votive offerings Pl. XIII and Pl. XVII, 4, also Pl. XLVIII, 3, LIV—LV, 1—4).

No. 37. Small temenos and sacred grove, in which many masks were found hung up on trees. On p. 18, No. 36 (also 36, Pl. I) I described the place and adduce here only one single sacred tree. I made excavations here for C. Watkins. One of the masks is represented on Pl. CXCVIII. 4.

No. 38. Necropolis on the left bank of the river Dali (Satrachos). Here about twenty tombs were opened, some of which contained transparent glass vessels, and others black glazed clay Athenian ware. The modern name of the place is Angonides.

No. 39. Necropolis on the Dali-Nicosia road. Graeco-Phoenician influence.

No. 40. Tombs on the right bank of the River Dali.

No. 41. This I described in the English text as an ancient well or cistern near the house of Abrnami, filled with images. I have since become convinced that this is a most instructive Kyprian example of a sacred gallery or underground tunnel, specially connected with the cultus of heroes (No. 37, Pl. I and p. 20).

No. 42. An ancient marl-pit. The marl is strewed upon the roofs, and, with the beams and thatch of rushes and twigs, forms a water-tight covering.

No. 43. An ancient lime-stone quarry still used. Marked on the map "quarries." It is situated east of No. 16, and to the right of it, but the number is not marked on the map.

---

[*] A. Furtwängler and G. Löschcke, "Mykenische Vasen." Berlin 1886. Plate XII 80, and p. 22.

No. 44. Sandstone quarry used in antiquity and also at the present time. This is not marked on the map. It is situated near Nicolides, No. 29 and 30, near the middle of the upper edge of the map.

τ = temenos.

ͻ˘ͻ ˄ = tombs showing Graeco-Phoenician influence.

˄ ˅ = tombs which contained not only numerous Kyprian Graeco-Phoenician vases, but also Attic vases, both black and red-figured.

▲ = large stone tombs with pointed roofs.

ͻ ͻ ˄ = Hellenistic tombs.

◦ ◦ ◦ = pre-Graeco-Phoenician tombs of the Bronze-Period, but later than the early "Race of Shepherds".

d b = pre-Graeco-Phoenician tombs of the Bronze-Period, containing some varnished Mykenai vases

�˘˄ = pre-Graeco-Phoenician tombs of the Bronze-Period, with many drinking vessels similar to those found under the in Thera. (Furtwängler and Löschcke. "Mykenische Vasen" Pl. XII, 80. Also our illustrations Pl. CLII, 6, CLXII 16a, CLXIII, 23c).

˘˘˘ = settlement of the people who were buried in the above mentioned tombs.

R = ruins.

Plate III.

Plan of the town of Idalion. Measured and drawn by E. A. Carletti. Archaeological additions by Max Ohnefalsch-Richter 1887. (From "The Owl", Pl. I p. 42.)

Part of the trigonometrical measurement and drawing i. e. the south eastern part with the large temenos of Aphrodite, No. 8 (No. 29 on Pl. I, p. 16), was added by me after Carletti had completed his work and returned to Nicosia, for it was only then that I clearly recognised the cultus site with its fortifications. The plan which Carletti and I had made was prepared by the kind permission and assistance of Sir Henry Bulwer and Mr. A. P. G. Law. On my recommendation Carletti received from the Government of the Island the necessary leave, in order that he might have time to make trigonometrical observations on the spot, and to complete the drawings. Pls. II and III were prepared from photographs taken directly from Carletti's drawings. Future excavations will probably make it possible to improve and correct this plan. The measurement of the hills may also be made more accurate by taking the altitudes, for which process we had no time, but a solid foundation has been laid in the actual recorded discoveries, i. e. the proportions in size and shape, the circular formation of the town, the situation and character of the burial places, cultus-sites etc. The triangulation taken with the theodolite and the chain may be considered correct, since the end of the measurements tallied accurately with the starting point. In addition to this we drew a base-line diagonally through the whole town, and by this we tested all the measurements and found them correct.

▬ = stone walls found in situ.

▪▪▪▪▪ = ramparts of the town.

▬▬▬ = streets made since the English occupation.

▪▪▪▪▪▪ = ordinary roads and footpaths.

= brooks or natural water-courses.

No. 1. Place where the iron swords were found, similar to those excavated in Tamassos in 1889 (Pl. CXXXVII, 7).

No. 2. Provenance of the Idalion silver dishes, two of which are now in the Louvre. G. Perrot[3], P. III. Fig 566 and 548 (= our Fig. 51 p. 48).

No. 3. Provenance of the small bronze tablet known as "Tablette du Duc de Luynes".

No. 1—3 lie at the highest point of the principal Acropolis, where was the cultus-site of the Anat-Athene of Idalion. Further details on this point are to be found on pp. 15 and 16, No. 28 also in "The Owl" 1888, pp. 46—47 and on p. 47 of this work. (Cf. also p. 201).

No. 4. Remains of an ancient building, probably part of an olive mill, found by me in 1887, of which I made measurements and drawings.

No. 5. Ruins of an ancient fortress, in shape somewhat like a castle, which I uncovered in 1888 for Sir Charles Newton, and of which I took an exact outline and section.

Between 4 and 5 on the slope of the principal Acropolis, which gradually falls northwards down to the lower part of the town, a temenos dedicated to Aphrodite, represented and described on Pl. I and p. 17 No. 32. (Cf. also "The Owl", p. 54).

No. 6. Temenos of Rešef-Mikal-Apollo-Amyklos, still recognizable as a foundation dug out of the ground and represented in correct proportions in the illustration. This was discovered by H. Lang in 1868. (No. 30 on Pl. 1 and p. 16, outlines on Pl. VIII. "The Owl", pp. 55 and 56, also p. 281 of this work.)

No. 7. A site excavated by me in 1888 for Sir Charles Newton (at that time of the British Museum), which I suppose to have been a place dedicated to the worship of Aphrodite, and which I represent on p. 17, No 31 (also 31 of Pl. I.).

No 8. The great chief sanctuary of the Idalion Aphrodite, the grove so well known in literary tradition, shortly described under No. 29, pp. 16 and 17 (also 29 on Pl. I). For further details see "The Owl" 1888, p. 56—64, in my essay "New Discoveries at the most celebrated temenos of Aphrodite". P. 54. "Ancient Idalion and Neighbourhood", and in the same volume, p. 67 E. Oberhummer's "Historical Studies in Cyprus" (Ancient Idalion), in which he agrees with me, and acknowledges me as the first discoverer of this important point bearing on the religious history of Kypros. Cf Pl. LVIII—LX).

No. 9. The Greek Church, in which the Phoenician votive inscription dedicated to the goddess Anat was found (p. 15—16).

No. 10. Tombs which are older than the town of Idalion as drawn on this map. They lie within the circle of the town rampart at the northern end.

G I—G IV. The town gates. Cf. p. 231.

Pls. II and III may be supplemented by the perspective views on LX, and by the explanation

Plates IV, V and VI.

Representing the outlines of the following cultus sites: of Artemis, found in 1882 at Achna (No. 1, pp. 1 and 2, and Pl. I, 1), of Apollo, found in 1888 at Voni (No. 2, p. 2—5 and Pl. I, 2), of Rešef-Apollo, found in 1885 at Frangissa (No. 4, p. 6—10 and Pl. I, 4). By Max Ohnefalsch-Richter.

As I have used the same letters in these plates for corresponding details, I shall consider the three sites together. The explanation of Pl. X. offers an opportunity for comparing the different outlines of Kyprian cultus-sites, not only with each other but, also with the Temple of Byblos. For the Achna discoveries (outline Pl. IV) cf. Pl. XI, XII, CCIX—CCXII, for the Voni discoveries (outline Pl. V) cf. Pl. XL—XLII and CCXV. The Frangissa discoveries (outline Pl. VI) are reserved for my work on Tamassos. Only two images from this place are represented, i. e. on Pl. CXCI, 4, and CXCVII, 4.

P. Peribolos walls. These are low walls of rough execution, made of broken stones, river pebbles or débris, put together either entirely without mortar, or with a kind of mixture of earth and slime, never with limestone.

E. Entrances, doors &c. In the outline Plate of Voni (Pl. V), the door which leads from the arcade into the space containing the altar has, by a fault of the draughtsman and of the photographer come out too light. As a fact, there is at that place only a space in the wall; the threshold of the door is formed of masonry, similar to that at Achna (Pl. IV. E).

Col. Basis of pillars in situ. These were observed by me in Voni (Pl. V), also in Dali (Pl. VII) and in Idalion by H. Lang (Pl. VIII.) Apparently there were two of these bases in one of the temené at Athienou (L. P. di Cesnola). (G. C. Ceccaldi, "Monuments antiques de Chypre" &c., p. 42.) Some of the pillars belonged to the Temple of Astarte at Kition, which I was the first to point ont (No. 9 p. 12). (cf. Pl. CCI.)

Although these are missing at Achna (Pl. IV), and at Frangissa (Pl. VI). yet it is not impossible that they were formerly to be found on the spot in larger or smaller numbers, since in both cases, from want of time or money, the excavations have not been completed. In Achna I had intended to excavate farther to the east and south-east, and in Frangissa to the north (See the outline plates.)

Ce. = Mortar made of limestone. This is not marked on Pls. V and VI, but on Pl. IV we see in the left top corner, above the treasure chamber, the remains of a more regular and stronger piece of masonry, about 2,4 m, wide, and enclosing a space paved with small stones and mortar.

Mortar was used in Achna, Voni and Frangissa in order to strengthen the bases of the larger statues. In Pl. IV, 2, I have represented on a magnified scale the large clay statue Te, which was erected opposite the principal entrance NE. It is an archaic female figure, wearing shoes with pointed and turned up ends, such as occur so frequently in Hittite works of art, and are also found in certain places in Kypros. This large clay statue was set up on the trampled earth of the treasure chamber, but, in order to fix it firmly, a small square wall of stone fastened with lime mortar had been built round the clay basis.

A = altar.	**BA** = bases for statues.
L and **LA** = places with many lamps.	**BA. ST** = stone bases.
F = places for fire.	**C** = colossi.
AS = layers of ashes.	**NA** = life-size statues.
CO = layers of charcoal.	**B** = votive bronzes.
OS = heaps of bones.	**GR** = statues in Greek style.
HY = vessels for holy water.	**AR** = works of art in the archaic style.
IM = places where the principal inscriptions were found.	**EG** = works of art showing Egyptian influence.
AP. IN = Apollo inscription.	**TE** = clay images.
AP. IN = Artemis inscription.	

PHT = places where very rough images of clay, probably manufactured for the poor, were found. The Cypriotes call them nowadays Φτωχοί *) i. e. the poor. Cf. Pl. XI, 1—8, XII, 1—8, LXVIII, 12.

TY = places where female figures of tambourine players were found.

---

*) So in modern Cypriote Greek; other Greek dialects write πτωχοί.

PH = places where Phalloi and vessels in the form of phalloi were found (cf. p. 129 and Pl. LXVIII, 8—10).

SAC = places where heaps of sacred tree images made of clay were found (cf. p. 128, and Pl. LXXVI, 1 and 2, LXVIII, 7). These images are in their form. workmanship and painting peculiar to the groves of Tanit-Artemis-Kybele.

EL = places where images of Artemis-Kybele with the stag or dog were found (cf. Pl. CCXII, 4, 5, 10 and 11).

OR. = places where I found silver and glass chains contained in small clay pitchers (lekythoi). (Pl. CCX, 9—11).

TG = places where clay vessels, especially small kylikes, were found.

PO = also clay ware in the shape of pots and lekythoi.

N = nothing, i. e. places where nothing was found. It is important to mark the places in these treasure houses which are destitute of votive gifts, for they give us a clue to the situation of doors and passages. A series of the marks just explained will be found in Pl. IV in the precinct of Achna. (Cf. "The Owl", January 1889, p. 76—80, and March 1889, p. 81—86, Pl. IX and X. Excavations for Sir Charles Newton, September and October 1882. Temenos of Artemis-Kybele at Achna.) Pl IV, 3 gives a perspective view of the altar (A'), formed of earth and marked out with stones (on Pl. V, 2, is the perspective view of the excavation at Voni, described on p. 3).

Plate VII.

Outline of the sanctuary at Dali (Idalion) on the island of Kypros, excavated and recorded by Max Ohnefalsch-Richter, Superintendent of Excavations in Kypros. (February—April.) Mr. Sotherland, Royal English Engineer and Surveyor to the Government, assisted.

The reader will find a full explanation on the plate; p. 5 No. 3 and Pl. I, 3 should be compared with it.

On Pl. VII, I have represented three of the six hooks which were found on the altar of burnt offering. Four of these hooks lay close together, and, pointing in the same direction, the fifth and sixth were not far off (cf. Pl. CCXIII, 1 and 5). From this and other circumstances we may conclude that the sanctuary was suddenly destroyed by a catastrophe, such as fire or earthquake, which happened during or shortly after the completion of a sacrifice, in the 4th century B. C.

Pl. VII, a—f. Objects from the sanctuary formed of limestone.

a) The fragment of a head belonging to a lifesize statue in the Egyptian style. This head was afterwards used as a basis for a statuette, and was cut for the purpose. Part of the face has been cut away, and on the flat surface thus left the marks may still be seen where the small statuette was fastened on.

b) Life-size head of a statue in Egyptian style, much damaged. The side of the head has been similarly hewn away to serve as a basis for a statuette.

c) Pillar basis, much damaged, found in situ at Col. Pl. VII, 1, here represented on a large scale.

d) An enlargement of the basis of one of the larger statuettes (st. ba 9 on the outline pl. VII₁). On the base is still to be seen the fractured lower part of the statuette in situ, the feet with shoes on, and the lower part of the robe, which consists of folds of stuff, evidently pressed with an iron and resembling the plaited and frilled edge of a modern lady's skirt.

e¹ and e² show two sides of the lower part of a lifesize archaic statue which had also been cut to form a basis for a statuette.

f) A rude statuette-basis hewn out of the middle part of an ancient statue. It is still possible to make out that the larger statue held a twig in the left hand which hung down by its side.

Hardly any Kyprian temenos containing works of art can be examined without bringing to light similar objects. The place near the altar reserved for the exhibition of votive gifts soon became so full that after a few generations the older images were removed. They were thrown away, broken or used up as bases for the new images, or as part of the material of the walls.

Plate VIII.

1. By H. Lang.

2. The plan of the same sanctuary at Rešef-Mikal-Apollo-Amyklos at Idalion, published by G. Colonna-Ceccaldi, see p. 16 No. 30, and Pl. I, 30.

1. In the Transactions of the Royal Society of Literature in London, 1878 p. 35—42, Lang gives an instructive explanation of this outline; and he describes how the objects were found during the excavation.

2. Ceccaldi's explanations of his outline are printed on the plate. A few errors must be corrected, for, as I have already shewn, the "Monuments antiques de Chypre, de Syrie et d'Egypte" was only published after the death of Ceccaldi. Point W. (left hand top), 14 metres in front of the south-eastern corner of the precinct, represents an underground passage. On p. 291 and in Pl. XXI, 4 and 5 I have assumed that the drawings found among the papers of the author after his death, and representing a section of such a passage, without explanation attached, correspond to this one (W). Unfortunately I had not Ceccaldi's book in Kypros with me. But as I found, south-east of the sanctuary at exactly the same distance, a water cistern plastered with lime mortar (marked as a black square in the town plan of

45°

Idalion, Pl. III, and called "tank"), I think that the editor of Ceccaldi's book must here have committed an error. If so, the "conduit souterrain" would correspond to this tank, which was in connection with the precinct of Apollo.

Plate IX.

This plate reproduces the outline of the Aphrodite-precinct found by the English in 1888 at Palai-paphos, and published in the Journal of Hellenic Studies 1888, p. 47. (Cf. Pl. I and p. 21, No. 54.)

Plate X.

Pl. X, Fig. 1—10. Kypros and Byblos.

Fig. 1 = Pl. LXXXII, 7, = CXXVI, 3 coin of Byblos from Chipiez "Histoire de l'art d'anti-quité" III, p. 60 Fig. 19. (Cf. p. 167, 179, 262 etc.)

Fig. 2 = Pl. LXXXII, 8 = CXXVI, 4, coin of Kypros. Perrot III, p. 120, Fig. 58. (Cf. p. 149, 167, 171, 262, 279 etc.)

Fig. 3 = XXXVIII, 13 = CIX, 3 = CXXIV, 5 = Fig. 218, p. 295. Clay representation of a small chapel fuom Idalion. Perrot III p. 277, Fig. 308, variouly described and illustrated in this work.

Fig. 4—9. Reduced reproductions of the outlines of Kyprian cultus sites represented on Pls. IV—IX.

Fig. 10. Outline of the Zeus temenos from the Journal of Hellenic Studies 1891, Pl. VI, which was excavated in Salamis by the English in 1890. (See p. 23—25 and Pl. I, No. 64.)

We have seen how the smaller cultus sites in the more level parts of the island, where the villagers and inhabitants of the small towns performed their worship, were arranged, how from primitive erections in the open air they became roofed buildings, how treasure chambers grew up around the altars, and how in certain periods definite arrangements of buildings around these altars and treasure chambers became custo-mary. The coin of Byblos, No. 1, is the best possible illustration of this fact.

We have first the altar (A. on the outline) in the open air (Nos. 1 and 6) or in a covered space resembling a chapel (Nos. 5 and 7) the altar is sometimes made of earth, pebbles or other unhewn stones (No. 7), sometimes of hewn stones (No. 5), and sometimes of a single cube of stone (No. 6) on which burnt sacrifices were offered (cf. the passage on altar cultus p. 223—226). It seems that originally the votive gifts were simply laid down near the altar, and that there was no special treasure-chamber. In the surrounding walls we almost always find fragments of older works of art, and inscribed stones with the inscription towards the inside (cf. Pl. VI, In.). There must therefore have been a time when there were no stone walls. If there was an enclosure at all, it probably consisted of tiles or a thorny hedge. At the present day in Kypros, churches, mosques and cemeteries are to be seen thus fenced in. The space for the votive gifts remained in the open air long after it was the custom to make buildings with roofs inside the sacred precinct. In outlines 4—10 is represented the large principal court for the votive gifts, and we see it also on the coin of Byblos. At first, the space for the votive gifts is marked off by rude low stone peribolos walls ($\gamma\varrho\acute{o}\gamma\mu\alpha$) without pillars or arcades, but possibly surmounted, as in modern times, by a thorn hedge (Nos. 4 and 6). In later times arcades are built round the space for the votive offerings, first on one side only (No. 5), then on two sides (No. 7), then on three or four sides (Nos. 9 and 10). The principal entrance is frequently, as in the Bible, on the north (Nos. 7 and 8, as also Cesnola-Athiaenou). According to the account in the Bible, a person entering the court would see opposite him in the middle of the courtyard either one of the principal votive statues (as also here Nos. 4 and 8) the large cone or the cultus pillar (cf below the excursus on Pl. LVI, "Jerusalem's Götzendienst zur Zeit Ezechiels") of the god or goddess (No. 7 $\vartheta^2 - \vartheta^7$ Idalion, Nr. 1 Byblos). Sometimes in important cultus sites one of the outer sides of the arcade surrounding the treasure space was more richly decorated than the others, and in later times several sides used to be decorated, as in the façade of the court of Byblos on the coin No. 1.

The coin of Paphos, No 2, as indeed all the surviving Paphos coins which represent buildings, reproduces not the temple itself, but the principal entrance to the court of offerings. The gateway and the porch are represented with their rich adornments, and correspond closely to the entrance buildings in the temple courts at Jerusalem described by Ezekiel, and to those in the town of Samal (the modern Sendscherli). Hittite buildings in the neighbourhood of Samal seem, according to Puchstein and Koldewey to have had a similar formation to those in Assyria. The large stone royal tomb at Tamassos, excavated in 1889 for the royal museums, represents a building of this kind, which may have served as a gate, a temple, a palace or a tomb. The outline of this royal burial place corresponds to the outline of the three gate-outworks in the town Samal (Sendscherli) which, according to Koldewey's investigations, seem to have been situated between the first and second circular concentric walls of the lower town, and at almost equal distances from the gates of the town. The principal difference (besides that in material and dimensions) consists in this, that in the Kyprian royal grave the back wall is complete, while in the gateways of Samal it is broken through. In the same manner, instead of the side doors to be found at Samal, we have at Kypros false or walled-up doors. The gateways of the present day in Kypros correspond in many other points to the description of Ezekiel. On our coin and on other coins of Paphos we see, behind the gate, the cone set up in the middle of the Court of offerings.

Close to the Court of offerings there is very often a space, partly or wholly covered, for the fire of the hearth, the sacrificial fire for incense, the burnt offerings, the altar, or at least one of the altars

(Nos. 5 and 7 Kypros. No. 1 Byblos). The outline of Idalion (No. 7) is specially interesting. Here a small space of semi-circular form, intended for burnt offerings, seems to have adjoined the south side of the court of offerings. When the court proved too small for the multitude of gifts, the place of burnt offering was removed from the north west corner of the precinct to the large sacrificial stone A, and its old site was used as an additional place for offerings (op. the explanation of Pl. LVI and LVII). Such sacrificial chambers sometimes have a flat roof, sometimes a pointed one (No. 1 Byblos). On the monumental freestone tombs at Kition, Idalion and Tamassos I observed the same flat and pointed roofs, and at Amathus on the megalithic early Graeco-Phoenician graves I found flat or horizontal roofs (cf. Pl. CLXXV.).

These sacrificial chambers develop into chapels, sanctuaries or primitive temples (cf. Pl. CXXIV-CXXVI). In our representation (Fig. III) of the clay image, 21 cm. high, the projecting door covering is supported by pillars with palm capitals (cf. the description of the windows of the Temple in Ezekiel). The windows are to be found in this example. (In the royal grave at Tamassos the niches for the windows are over the doors, as on the coins of Paphos.) A divinity, half Ashtoreth, half dove, stands in the entrance. The chapel is used as a dove-cote, where the birds sacred to the goddess have their dwelling (cf. Pl. XVII, 2—4). On the coin of Byblos No. 1 there are steps up to the court of offerings, and also to the sacrificial chamber. H. Lang discovered this (No. 8). A small staircase on the northern side brings us up to the court for offerings which he discovered, and a second leads to the south-east corner of the sacrificial chamber. In Frangissa (No. 6), as in Athiaenou (Cesnola), steps led down to the court of offerings or to the sacrificial chamber. That such steps and stair-cases led up to the altars of the Hebrews, even in very early times, may be concluded from Exodus XX—XXV, where steps to the altars are distinctly forbidden.

Plates XI and XII.

28 terra-cottas from the temenos of Tanit-Artemis-Kybele at Achna, which I excavated for Sir Charles Newton in 1882 (p. 1 and Pl. I).

The size of the terra-cottas represented here varies between 6 inches (= 15,3 cm) on Pl. XII, Fig. 9, to 15¹/₄ inches (= 38,5 cm) on Pl. XII, Fig. 5. For the intervening measurements I may give as examples Fig. 13 Pl. XII, height 11³/₄ inches (= 29,8 cm); and Fig. 6 Pl. XI, height 12 inches (= 30,4 cm). The equality of size in the figures on our plates is only apparent. I have enlarged the smaller objects and reduced the larger ones. The principal spots where the objects were found have been indicated on the outline, and the requisite explanations have been added. Most of the 28 clay figures represented here, some of which showed more or less well preserved remains of painting, were discovered by myself, and are now in the British Museum. A few which I bought in Larnaka (see p. 2) found their way into other collections. (For the painting cf. Pl. LXVIII.) We are concerned here with terra-cottas which in type and execution belong peculiarly to Tanit-Artemis-Kybele. They are confined to a definite district, viz. the Kingdom of Salamis and its neighbourhood. In the section on Artemis I have treated of these discoveries in full. All the figures, even those with the hands on the breasts, are draped. While other motives, carrying a flower for instance or a tambourine (Pl. XI, 8—14), although originally Oriental, were adopted by the Greeks and developed in the time of Praxiteles and even later, the motive of the hands on the breasts was not developed in the same way (XI, 1—7). This stiff attitude, combined with the symmetry of the legs and arms on both sides, offended the Gre∖k instinct for beauty. Pl. XI, 7 (the original was sent by me to London) shows the only attempt, and that an unsuccessful one, to bring this symmetrical stiff oriental motive into Greek art. Whilst of other images, such as 1—6, a large number of repliquas were found in all the Artemis groves of Achna and its neighbourhood, I could only find a single example (No. 7) which seemed to show an attempt to bring this motive into the domain of Greek art. I have grouped the figures in such a manner as to begin with the rudest, and end with the most perfect and most purely Greek. It would however be an error to suppose that a ruder image must necessarily be older than a more perfect one. On the contrary, the reverse may easily be the case, and instances of it are given here. The same artificers who sold the better executed and more expensive figures to the rich at the sacred groves (Pl. XI, 4—6), also kept cheaper and rougher specimens for the poor (1—3). A comparison, however, between Fig. 4, Pl. XI and the image found by Schliemann in Mykenae, and illustrated in Fig. 112 of his "Mykenae," will show that the development of the art of terra-cotta image followed in its general lines the course indicated by my illustrations. We may see too, from the development of costume and of the divine and priestly insignia, that these images represent an actual historical growth in art and religion. Fig. 11, Pl. XI is particularly instructive. When the artist modelled this image, he at first gave it the stiff priestly apron, such as we see on Fig. 4—6 Pl. XI, but he afterwards painted over it in colour an upper garment more in Greek fashion. Pl. XII gives 14 different representations of the motive of the female lute or lyre player. We can see here how attitude, costume, and insignia vary with the style. The last four figures, 12—14, are good examples of the Graeco-Kyprian local art of the 4th century B. C.

Pl. CCIX—CCXII represent other discoveries from this temenos.

Plate XIII.

1—4. Heads from the Astarte-Aphrodite sanctuary at Dali (Idalion) 1885. I, 3.

1 and 2 female head of a large clay statue. Berl. Mus. Antiquarium M. J. 8015, 63.

Only the mask survives, and is formed of several parts. The strong eyebrows are very characteristic; they are given in relief and decorated with incised lines grouped into triangles. There is also on the eyebrows a trace of black paint. The eyes are very large, the upper eyelid curving over the lower, which is represented by a straight line; the edges of the eyes are given by strong lines in relief, and show traces of black paint. The eyes are somewhat sloped towards the inside. The mouth is very small; the lips are closely pressed together, and show traces of red colour. The upper lip is divided, as in nature, by two lines. From the corners of the mouth two wrinkles descend to the jaws; they mark off the pointed chin, and emphasize the plump cheeks. The nose is usually large and prominent. The hair, which falls over the forehead without a parting, is only modelled where it touches the forehead by incised perpendicular parallel lines, between which at the outer edge are lines of cross hatching.

3. Female head of a large lime stone statue. Berl. Mus. Antiquarium M. J. 8015, 382.

The face is the only in part preserved. The back part of the head is cut away in front of the ears. The nose is knocked off. The hair surrounds the forehead in a thick roll, and is confined by a diadem in the form of a ribbon; there is no parting, but strands of hair fall from the centre to right and left, and hang around the temples in thick masses. The eyes are strikingly small, almond shaped, and set in on a slope. On the left pupil there are traces of red paint. The upper edge of the eyebrows is given by a fine incised line. The lips, which show traces of red colour, are sharply cut and closely pressed together; the upper lip, the chin and the cheeks are finely modelled throughout.

4. Fragment of a female head in limestone, life size. Berl. Mus. Antiquarium M. J. 8015, 390.

Only the front part of the face remains. Most of the left cheek, the left temple, part of the left eye and most of the right side are destroyed. The firmly closed mouth gives a stern expression to the face. The forehead is not modelled at all, but shows a smooth surface, slightly curved towards the temples. The axes of the eyes are not on a horizontal line and protrude out of the eye-sockets. The head gives a better effect in profile (H. S.).

The three heads represented here were excavated in the same sanctuary, (1, 3) dedicated to Astarte-Aphrodite. The clay head (1—2) illustrates the Kyprian Graeco-Phoenician style of the end of the 7th or beginning of the 6h. century B. C., the stone head (3) illustrates the Greek archaic style, and the later stone head (4), 200 years later in date, shows the advanced free Greek style of the 4th century.

Plate XIV.

1 and 2. Bearded head, the hair dressed in rolls, belonging to a large clay statue from Dali. From the collection Cesnola, Berl. Mus. Antiquarium T. C. 6682, 31.

The head is intact as far as the head-dress, which consists of two rolls lying one over the other of which the upper one has partly disappeared. The painting is unusually rich. In order to indicate the colour of flesh, the yellowish clay is covered with a dark red paint, distinctly traceable on the right cheek and on the ears. The hair on the forehead is represented by a narrow band in relief, with tooth like cuttings, and painted black. The hair falls on the neck in a short bunch spreading out to the sides and painted black. On the curls, which fall over the shoulders, lie two strings which are connected with the head ribbon. The pointed beard is given in relief, hatched with incised parallel lines and painted black; a small triangular beard under the mouth is also indicated by black paint. Moustache and eye-brows are also painted black. The edges of the eyes are, according to local custom, represented in relief; the eyes are in proportion to the small size of the face, remarkably large, the mouth is wide and clumsy. The ear is only modelled at the edge, not within, but the ear-lobe is represented correctly.

3 and 4. Bearded head wearing helmet, life size, (clay) from Dali. From the collection Cesnola. Berl. Mus. Antiquarium. T. C. 6682, 30.

The colour of the clay is light grey. The hair, beard, eyebrows, eyelids and pupils are painted black. The helmet consists of four pieces which meet on the crown of the head and the junction of which is indicated by incised grooves; on the top is a hoop like a handle. The beard is, as in the preceding head, given in relief; the conventional locks of hair are separated from each other by parallel grooves. The upper lip is clean shaven. The formation is similar to that of the preceding head. The eyebrows are formed in a peculiar manner; the inner side is strongly marked by means of several parallel vertical grooves; while wavy horizontal lines are drawn from these towards the temples. The ears are modelled inside in a superficial but fairly natural manner.   (1—4 H. S.)

Both heads are broken off from life-size clay statues, which must have been set up in some temenos dedicated to a male divinity, perhaps Resef-Apollo. The upper head, (1 = 2) is here published for the first time. Cesnola (3 = 4 = Cesnola's "Cyprus" p. 207, = Cesnola-Stern Pl. XL, 1, = Holwerda "Die alten Kyprier" I, 4,) gives Papho as the provenance of the lower head, and states (Cyprus p. 207) that it was afterwards lost. Holwerda, who illustrates the head and describes it, did not know where it was to be found. L. Stern, who was studying the Kyprian collections of the Royal Museum at Berlin during the preparation of Cesnola's "Cyprus," did not recognize the head, although it was at that time in the Museum. It is now placed in the Kyprian division of the Antiquarium (Gallery in the Great Staircase of the New Museum, West side), and is marked, like head 1, (= 2) as coming from Dali. I think it more likely that both heads are from Dali and not from Papho (cf. Pl. XV.) (The name of a whole district.)

Head 1 (= 2) is perhaps the most interesting of those hitherto found in Kypros. The style, although local Kyprian, is so similar to that of the heads on ancient Greek monuments, that we are justified in classifying it as archaic Greek. It immediately precedes the period of art which is illustrated by the ancient marble figures of Orchomenos, Thera, and Tenea, and by other works, for instance a marble torso (Pl. **XXVII**, 2 from Marion-Arsinoe) discovered by me. Here we note the origin of the broad grin of Kyprian art, still to be traced on old Greek vase paintings. This developed into the archaic Kyprian laugh and smile, which passed over into Greek archaic art, and was there refined and softened down. The resemblances in the form of the face, the arrangement of the hair and pointed beard, the shaven upper lip, and the head dress, are very striking especially on a profile view. Our Kyprian head should be compared with the following heads: Apollo on the great Melos vase, (Conze, Melische Thongefässe Pl. IV.), Zeus and Hermes on the François vase (Fig. 250 and 251, Wiener Vorlegeblätter 1888 Pls. II. and III.) ancient bronze plate from Krete (Annali 1880 p. 213 ff. Tav. d'agg. T), Typhon-head from the pediment of the Acropolis of Athens (Poros-Sculpturen, A. Bruckner, Mittheilungen in Athen 1889, p. 67, Pls. 2, 3 &c.). The idea that Kyprian art was a caricature of ancient Greek art is now no longer tenable.

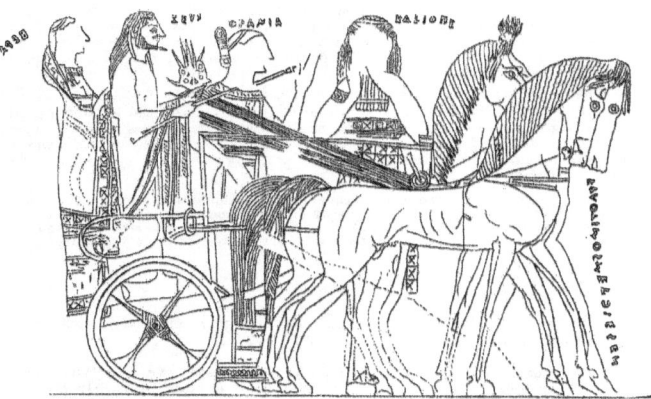

Fig. 250.

We have seen, then, that the Kyprian Greeks and races akin to them have a large share in the process of development of ancient Greek art. Their influence is made plainly to be seen in the early period of archaic Greek art. After the Persian wars, there was a pause in the development, which we may almost call a retrogressive movement. There are no original works of purely Greek art to be found in Kypros which can be compared with the masterpieces of Greek sculpture or vase-painting.

Although Greek art in Kypros does not rise to the highest point of beauty and perfection, it has a grace and individuality of its own which I was in great part the first to discover.[*]) I was also able to point out how Kyprian art undergoes an organic development, as proved by the works of art found in all the newly excavated sacred precincts. There are many examples, as I have shown, of archaic Greek works of art made of clay or the native limestone (cf. for instance Pl. XIII. 3, and many others), and of others which precede these or follow them. (Cf. Pl. CCXV.)

The lower head (3 = 4), which is of more advanced style than the upper one (1 = 2), belongs, as is evident from the kind of clay, and from my other observations at Frangissa in 1885 during excavation, to the same sanctuary. This helmeted head is executed in a more purely Kyprian archaic Greek style, and the proportions are better than those of the former head. The smile has given place to a quiet meditative expression. The profile is different, and approaches more nearly to the outline which we call classic Greek.

This head is a striking example of the analogy in technique between the Poros sculptures of the Acropolis, and the discoveries in Krete which seem to belong to the "School of Daedalus," and to be imitations in stone or clay of well known wooden statues.

Fig. 251.

---

*) Cf. my papers "Das Museum und die Ausgrabungen auf Cypern seit 1876." Also extracts from lectures on my works by A. Furtwängler and P. Hermann (Repertorium für Kunstwissenschaft 1886, Berliner Philologische Wochenschrift, Wochenschrift für klassische Philologie.)

Plate XV.

1. and 2.   Female head of a large clay statue supposed to come from Paphos. From the collection Cesnola. Berl. Mus. Antiquarium T. C. 6683, 9.

The clay is dark red in colour. The head is hollow, the back part having been broken away. A large hole is in the upper part. The high diadem has been broken away in front of the right side.

This head is a good example of the fine Greek style, perhaps about the beginning of the 4th. century B. C ; the profile view is specially good. The proportions are faultless, but there is a certain severity in the expression which may possibly be ascribed to local artistic tradition.

The hair is parted on the forehead, and comes out from under the diadem in curls indicated by spiral grooves. The ear is decorated with a disc hung round with small prisms; this is wanting in the right ear. A large double chain decorates the neck. A kerchief is drawn over the head, and its edge is visible at both sides of the neck.

3. Female head of the same type, supposed to be from Paphos. From the collection Cesnola. Berl. Mus. Antiquarium T. C. 6683, 10.

The upper edge of the diadem has been broken off in the middle. The head belongs to the same period, the same style, and, perhaps the same place of manufacture. The modelling is more refined. The necklace consists of a string of beads. The dark red clay has still been painted red.

4. Female head of the same type, supposed to be from Paphos. From the collection Cesnola. Berl. Mus. Antiquarium T. C. 6683, 8.

This head corresponds in all its details to the two preceding heads. The diadem is in better preservation; the ear-ring is wanting in the right ear. The clay is dark red.   (1—4 H. S.)

I discovered these heads, I may almost say, afresh, in the Antiquarium of the Royal Museum, for after repeated investigations on the spot I was able to assign their provenance to Bumo. Louis Palma di Cesnola, to whom we owe these master pieces of Kyprian Greek local art, assigned them to Paphos. The difference is not important, for Bumo is situated in the district of Papho, and the Kypriotes of the present day call the whole region Papho. When they say "We are going to Papho", they may mean Bumo, Poli or any other place in the Papho district. I heard from the old peasants in Bumo that Cesnola's people actually excavated in the sacred grove there and took away with them a number of statues, head &c. This however proves nothing. It would be necessary to know the motives, the local style, the dimensions and more especially the colour of the clay and its preparation, the method of baking, the geological substances found in the clay and the quality of the clay as adjudged by experts. I have in my possession one of these heads, which I bought on the spot in 1890 from the peasants. It represents a female clay figure and I have given no illustration of it simply because the surface was so much worn. Dr. Dörpfeld photographed the head in 1890 when he was in Kypros, and anyone who is interested in the subject may obtain a copy from the Imperial German Archaeological Institute. (Jahrbuch des Kaiserlich deutschen Archäologisches Institutes vol. VI 1891. Heft 2, Anzeiger p. 90 No. 40.) The soil around Bumo is red in colour, owing to the oxide of iron which it contains, and the coarse clay found in the neighbourhood is coloured by the same substance. The votive gifts for the altar of Aphrodite. which range from lilliputian to colossal size, are numerous at present on the spot. (cf. p. 268.) The productions of this local manufactory at Bumo are very similar to those of Poli. (cf. Pl. CLXXV, 3, CLXXVI and CLXXXVII.) But there are differences, of which I may mention some. First, the figures hitherto found in Bumo were intended as votive gifts for the altar, while those found at Poli were meant for the cultus of Bumo, for racecourses and for tombs. In spite of the fact that they both belong to the same period of Greek art, and in spite of the similarity in the mode of dressing the hair, the motives are different. Second, the clay differs in quality. In Poli it resembles marl, is of a light grey colour, sometimes almost white, and contains some limestone, while in Bumo it is dark red. occasionally very brilliant. Both classes of examples belong to the purely Greek style of the 4th century, and date from about the time of Praxiteles. In the conception and execution there is a magnificence and dignity which can only be traced to the influence of Pheidias. When A. Furtwängler gave information on the subject of these votive images of Bumo and Poli, which are so closely similar (in the Archäologische Gesellschaft Nov. 2, 1885) he laid special stress on their artistic value. (Wochenschrift für klassische Philologie 1885 Sp. 1593.) These beautiful large Greek monumental figures of Poli, like the temenos figures at Bumo, will probably never be found out of the western part of the island and most likely nowhere but in the north-western coast region of Poli-Marion-Arsinoë, up to Karavastosi-Soloi. This highly developed Graeco-Kyprian art. belonging to the fine period with reminiscences of more severe style, is explained like the Greek archaic Kyprian local art, which had already produced figures of Apollo and Tanagra masks*), by the topographical peculiarities of the island, by its marit ime connections and by the wealth of its copper mines. It was on the principal line of communication by sea from Athens. (cf. Pl. LV, 7.)

Plate XVI.

Perspective view of the excavation in the Aphrodite temenos at Dali, described above, p. 6 and Pl. I, No. 3.

The outline is given on Pls. VII and X, 7. This admirable view, drawn by Herr Lübke (to whom I am indebted for almost all the new illustrations) was prepared from photographs which I took, from a sketch and from the outline. It is taken from the south-east corner, so that we see in the fore-ground and middle distance the masonry which is marked on the outline as H, s a n c t u a r y p r o p e r. The draughtsman has however committed the error of bringing the three foremost limestone blocks of the peribolos walls too far out by the width of one block. This mistake was only discovered after the printing. The only conjectural restoration in the whole picture is the vessel for holy water, nearest on the

---

*) Cp. the clay mask. excavated by me at Marion-Arsinoë (Pl. CLXXXVI. 6) and similar to those of Tanagra and Rhodes, with the clay heads from Limniti (Pl. XLV).

outline. The size of the vessel may be considered as ascertained, but not the shape. Almost exactly in the middle of the picture, behind the labourer with a barrow, we see the limestone slabs in their vertical position, marked on the outline as x^1 and x^2. This is a most peculiar piece of masonry which corresponds in a remarkable manner to the architecture illustrated by the flat ring of Mykenae. K. Schuchardt's view, published in his book on Schliemann's excavations (p. 185, No. 142), is much less exact than that of A. Milchhöfer, given in his essay on "Heinrich Schliemann und die Bedeutung seiner Ausgrabungen" (Westermann's Monatshefte, 1891 p. 169, cf. also p. 130 Note 1).

Plate XVII, 1—6.

5. Votive Gifts from cultus-sites, 1—5 four pieces in clay, 6 one piece in stone.

Fig. 1 = LXXVI, 7 and CLIV, 3. Clay image of a sacred tree from the Aphrodite temenos at Chytroi, described and illustrated on p. 14 and Pl. I, No. 24. Bonn, Universitäts-Museum. The provenance is certain. Herr G. Löschcke, to whom I am indebted for the photograph from which the illustration is made, wrote to me that the image was complete in itself, but this is not the case, for the breakage shews that this sacred tree (cf. p. 165) was fastened on to a round disc of clay, similar to that which is to be seen in Fig. 5, representing a ring dance round a flute player. Here three women were performing a dance round the sacred tree. In the Kypros Museum is a whole series of fragments and replicas of such ring-dances around a sacred tree, found by me in this precinct (cf. p. 133).

Figs. 2 and 3 = p. 278, Fig. 187 and 188 = Pl. XXXVIII, 12 give two views of the same extraordinary objects of worship about 13 cm. high and made of clay. The only materials which the artist had for this illustration consisted in a sketch made from the original on the same scale at the house of Mr. D. Pierides at Larnaka. The object is a hollow cone. In a large square niche in the cone is seated a female figure, Astarte-Aphrodite. A number of small round holes represent the entrances to the dove-cote. There is a rude representation of birds, which sit on the sacred cone or fly around it. Here the goddess and her doves dwell together. In the same Aphrodite temenos, where I found at the foot of the altar of burnt offering the sacred pillar which I shall shortly describe (G Fig. 4 of this Pl. Idalion 1885 at point No. 3 Pl. I p. 5), I also dug up a fragment of a pigeon-house similar to that on Pl. X, 3. In this latter example a dove is perched on the corner of the projecting roof. It seems that these cones, pillars and square chests shaped like shrines were used in acts of ritual as vessels for incense and for charcoal, like the stone vessels of the Artemis grove, one of which was represented on Fig. 6 of this Plate (cf. p. 164 and 165, 179—180, 277 and Pl. LXIX, No. 80).

Fig. 4 = p. 278, Fig. 189, = CXXV, 3. The clay pillar broken above and below, at present in the Antiquarium of the Royal Berlin Museum, 32 cm high in its present condition, had been turned upon a potter's wheel, so that we may conclude that these objects were produced in large quantities for cultus use. This example is probably an Astoreth pillar on a small scale. If it had been found in a grove of Baal, we should have to call it a Baal pillar. There is a large square opening, which passes diagonally and in a horizontal direction through the whole pillar, and also, higher up, are three small triangular holes, at equal distances from each other (cf. p. 130, 164—165, 180, 277 and Pl. LXIX, No. 178)

Fig. 5. A ring-dance of clay about 14 cm. high, found by me with many other works of art near the villages Katydata and Linu in 1883, and excavated for the Cyprus Museum. Although Aphrodite was the principal goddess worshipped there, the dancers are represented by three bearded men around a bearded flute-player. Like the Astarte cone, Figs. 2 and 3, this ring dance is executed in the fashion to which Dümmler and I first gave the name "Snow-man technique." This rude workmanship,[*] which consists in kneading parts separately and then fastening them together, must be dated at least as early as the 6th century B. C., for these rude terra-cotta images are entirely wanting in the precincts of Achna (I, 1) and at Voni (I, 2). One of the three dancers is completely broken away, and the head of the second is wanting. This is evidently a votive offering, representing the dance which was so commonly performed at festivals of the gods by Aryans, Semites, Greeks and Hebrews. The object was not intended to be used as a vessel for incense or for any other practical purpose. Cf. p. 218 and 255 Note 3.

Fig 6 = CXXXV, 5. A vessel for charcoal or incense in the shape of a ring-dance. The upper part of the figures was missing, and has been restored from a comparison of numerous replicas and fragments. Stone vessels or utensils of this form were found by me in large numbers in the temenos of Artemis-Kybele at Achna, where I excavated in 1882 for Sir Charles Newton (p. 1 and Pl. I, No. 1) and in several groves of Artemis-Kybele, but nowhere else (cf. the explanation and remarks on Pl. CXXXV.). There are always three female figures executed in rude Egyptian style, holding each others hands for the dance. Only in one example are there four women in the circle. From fragments found in all the remaining groves of Artemis-Kybele in the district (pp. 11 and 12 and Pl. I. Nos. 10—14), we may conclude that these vessels were used for incense. We are here concerned, therefore, with a very common cultus object, and one which is specially connected with the worship of Artemis-Kybele. For in precincts dedicated to other divinities, not a single fragment of vessels of this kind has ever been found. It is true that incense might be offered to any divinity, but probably each divinity had his own special type of vessel, which was used for this purpose. The artificers who made these vessels for the festivals of Artemis-Kybele either did not take the trouble to form the hands of the figures, or omitted them on purpose. The three large square openings, widened at the top, of which only one is shewn in our illustration, are always present. The pans for charcoal which the Kypriotes use at the present day, although of larger dimensions, correspond

---

*) Called so first by Dümmler & myself. This term is a very suitable one, and has been adopted by French and English archaeologists. This technique gradually disappears in the 5th. century B. C.

to these in shape, but are not decorated with figures. On the three projections are placed the vessels for cooking. We see from these discoveries at Achna that the ancient ring dance practised in the service of Artemis-Kybele was adapted to cultus vessels.

PLATE XVIII.

Fig. 1. A Roman burial place hewn out in the rock, afterwards made into a Christian chapel, and now dedicated to Hagia Solomoni. It is near the modern village of Baffo, the ancient Neapaphos (Pl. I).

It is said that in this vault the early Christians carried on their worship in secret while there was still a Roman pro-consul at Neapaphos. A sacred spring in one of the caves of this burial-place adds even at the present time to the sanctity of the place. A terebinth tree, which has struck its roots into the clefts of the rock near the entrance, is regarded with great reverence by Greeks as well as Turks, who hang on its branches ribbons and shreds of clothing, in order to obtain healing from various diseases, especially fever (cf. p. 116 and 166).

Fig. 2. Two monoliths from Palaipaphos which I have already illustrated on p. 23 and Pl. I. No. 57.

The theory originated by the English investigators, F. M. H. Guillemard (Athenaeum. London, 14th April 1888) and D. G. Hogarth ("Devia Kypria" p. 47—52), i. e. that these and other monoliths found in various places on the island are stones belonging to oil presses, seems to me untenable. It is of course possible that, among the fifty stones which they collected with great trouble from all parts of the island, some may have belonged to primitive oil-presses, but it is certain that the two huge monoliths from Paphos here represented, were objects of worship. On some of the Kyprian coins of the Roman period, which show the so-called Paphos Temple, we see two stones in the form of obelisks or cones. I think that a glance at Pls. XVII. and XVIII. will be enough to settle this point for the monoliths of Paphos. The clay pillar (Pl. XVII, 4) 32 cm. high, from the sacrificial chamber of the Aphrodite sanctuary at Dali (Pl. I, 3) is a reduced image of a large stone monolith of this kind. The goddess is supposed to reside within the open space in the stone, and this conception is pictorially represented in the cone of Kition 2 and 3, Pl. XVII. The above remarks are intended to supplement the explanation given on p. 165—166. (Cf. also Pl. LXIX, 77.)

Plate XIX.

1. Cesnola-Stern IV, 1 = Perrot III p. 706, Fig. 518, = Goodyear "Lotus" Pl. XXXVII, 7. Oinochoë with short neck from Larnaka (Cesnola-Stern p. 403) or Dali (Berl. Spezialinventar). Berl. Mus. Antiquarium. Furtwängler Vas. Cat. No. 70.

In the centre of the representation a decorative tree against which two stags are rampant; the whole arranged in an heraldic scheme. At the edge of the mouth are geometrical ornaments in the form of concentric circles and semi-circles, with a svastika on each side. From the each side of the junction of the handle a primitive conventional branch is carried downwards, similar to those in the geometric style. The representation on the body of the vase is described more in detail on Pl. LXI. Cf. text p. 38 and nofe pp. 78—80, also p. 91, Fig. 128.

2. = CCXVI, 23 = Cesnola-Stern LXXXV, 1, = Perrot III, p. 710, Fig. 522. Oinochoë with thick body from Dali. From the collection Cesnola. Berl. Mus. Antiquarium. Furtwängler, Vas. Cat. No. 72.

On the neck of the vase is a female head in high relief; the hair is modelled, and two thick curls fall down on the right and left over the body of the vase. The neck is ornamented with a painted necklace, to which is hung a round ornament also painted. (On p. 39 Fig 40 the head alone is represented.)

In order to emphasize the imitation of the human figure, two nipples are modelled on the body of the vase beneath the curls.

The body of the vase is richly painted. In front, underneath the female head stands a woman in long robes, holding in her left hand a lotus flower; this figure is reproduced and described on Pl. XX. Around the right and left sides of the vase are drawn vertical circular stripes; and the centre of the round design is filled up by a white rosette made of concentric circles. There are also other stripes of ornament, some narrower, some wider; one of them is filled up with zigzag ornaments; another broad stripe nearer the edge shows a row of lotus flowers, while the stripe next it is formed by a plaited band painted white; on the outmost edge there are two wide black stripes. (Cf. text 38 ff.)

3. = Cesnola-Stern LXXXVI, 2 Oinochoë with a double handle and a tube at one side for pouring out the liquid. Dali. Berl. Mus. Furtwängler, No. 71.

In the centre of the shoulder a decorative tree, on each side a human figure and a bird. The principal representation is more exactly described on Pl. XXI. Underneath are three red stripes with black edges. The painting is applied to the background of reddish clay, and the colours are red and black, as on the geometrical vases of Kypros. The reverse is decorated with geometrical ornaments and plants; at the top a large lotus flower hangs downwards; underneath are horizontal stripes filled in with vertical lines, zigzag patterns or plaited bands. The tube and the neck of the vase are also painted with stripes and lines, while an ornamental stripe consisting of several members connects the two. The same pattern is painted close to the handle to form a connection between the neck and the ornamental stripes of the reverse. (Cf text p 39 f.)

4. Oinochoë with oval body and short neck from Athienou. Now in the collection Konstantinides (Nicosia).

The painting is executed in black and two shades of red. Neck, handle and foot are decorated with vertical and horizontal stripes, the spaces being filled in with the following ornaments: 4 svastikas;

groups of ornaments consisting of lines, such as also occur on the Mykenae and Dipylon vases; a rosette, formed of concentric circles and a circular row of dots, which has analogies in the pottery of Mykenae, but has nothing to do with the groups of concentric circles belonging to the geometric style of Kypros. The principal design shows a man in Egyptian costume in front of two large flowers; in the left hand he holds a flower to his nose as if he were smelling it. His right hand is raised and seems to hold a strap or cord attached to a bird which is flying over his head. Cf. text p. 40 f. and p. 71, 187 and 138. (1—4, H. S.)

On p. 336, Fig. 248, I have repeated a sketch of vase No. 4 which was first published by S. Reinach in "Chroniques d'Orient" p. 194 [5², 859, 60]. I myself described the vase fully in the Jahrb. d. Archaelogischen Instituts 1886, I, 79—82, and gave a coloured illustration. Herr F Dümmler had undertaken to edit my Essay, but did not send me the proof sheets. In consequence of this some passages are omitted which I wished to publish, and others appear which I wished to suppress. (Cf. p. 40 and Note 2.)

Plate XX.

Representation on the vase Pl. XIX, 2.

On the obverse of the vase, below the female head, is painted a figure in long robes. The profile is turned towards the right, the garment, which seems to have been painted white, spreads out below, and shows a stripe of maeander pattern in the centre down its whole length. The face of the figure is the colour of the clay; the thick bunch of hair is black; in the raised left hand the figure holds a flower with a long stalk, and seems to smell it; in the right hand, which hangs down, is some object outlined in black. On p. 41 this object is indicated as a bird, the lower ends resembling a bird's claws. On the right of the figure grows out of the ground a plant with leaves and one large blossom similar to a lotus flower. On the other side is a similar flower, but on its blossom is placed an ornament consisting of two upright volutes and a kind of scroll of several members. This ornament is repeated on the reverse of the vase, and will be treated of more fully in the next plate. Over the breast falls an upper garment resembling a shawl. (Cf. p. 38—89, 71, 187—188.)   (H. S.)

Plate XXI. = p. 74, Fig. 92.

Representation on the vase Pl. XIX, 8.

In the centre of the shoulder stands a conventional decorative tree, consisting of four parts. The two first parts, which are duplicates, consist of two upright volutes converging at the top, and connected by a pattern in form of a bow; this last is supported by a vertical band. On the upper pair of volutes lies an abacus of several members, and on this again lies a horizontal plaited band. The essential part of this ornament. the volutes and the abacus, we have already seen on the vase Pl. XIX, 2. But while in that instance it is purely ornamental, here it evidently has significance as a sacred tree. On each side is a bird on the ground, and this type, as the connection shows, is very important in connection with the sacred tree. On each side also are long-robed figures, who stand touching with one hand the sacred tree, while in the other they hold a pitcher. The type of these figures is exactly the same as that on Pl. XX. The drapery is the same, having the same border in the centre, and the same shawl hanging over the breast. Face and hair are also exactly the same. On the left side the volute ornament is repeated, but on it is seated a large bird, which proves that the conception of the sacred tree is present. The spaces are filled in with designs of flowers and trees. Cf. p. 39 ff, 56—57, 71 and 94. (H. S.)

A comparison of the four vases reproduced on Pls. XIX, XXI and LXI, and others, gives an instructive result. They all belong to the same class of Kyprian ceramic art and to the same class of vases, which may again be divided into different types and subordinate groups. As I proved on Pl. CCXVI, we must call them neither Greek*) nor Phoenician, but rather Graeco-Phoenician. Although in vase XIX, 1 the human figure is wanting, yet this vase most resembles XIX, 4, for the size and form of the two are alike. This shape came into use in Kypros, when the Kyprians adopted the potter's wheel from the Mykenaeans.**) The hand-made vases of the Bronze Period, CLXXVIII, 5e, CLXII, 17e, 18b) gave place to those of the Iron Period, which were made on a wheel, (CLXXII, 17g, CLXXIII, 19n), and thus vases XIX, 1 and 4***) took this form.

The clay and the painting are the same in the two instances. Both are made of the same fine-ground clay, of a dull yellowish-white colour, which is characteristic of this vase type.†) Both are painted

---

*) Dümmler, after his residence in Kypros, when he was editing my Essay on vase XIX, 4, in the Jahrbuch, I, p. 81 and 82, ascribed to the Phoenicians far too wide an influence, but soon after this he altered his view, and sought for the origin of the Kyprian vase style which he had in 1886 ascribed to the Phoenicians, among the Arcadians of Peloponnesus, supposing that they had brought this kind of art to Kypros when they first emigrated from Greece. ("Bemerkungen zum Aeltesten Kunsthandwerk auf griechischem Boden," p. 291). Both these theories had to be given up, as untenable in view of the facts which came to light in consequence of my excavations and observations on the island. In 1880 I had already formed the opinion that there had never been a purely Phoenician art in Kypros, but that Greeks and Phoenicians, from the very beginning, had merely had a share in the formation of the Kyprian art, in its departments of painting, engraving and metal work. When in the spring of 1883 by my excavations in Phönetschas (port of Dali, Pl. I) I made discoveries connected with the pre-Graeco-Phoenician Copper-Bronze Period, (which I immediately communicated by letter to A. George Julius Naue, (A. H. Sayce and others) I had always opposed the theory of the non-Semitic, non-Phoenician, Indo-Germanic-Aryan origin of the geometric style, without being able to give conclusive proofs of my opinion. But after being warned by letters from Conze in 1883 (who was opposed in 1885 by W. Helbig in his "Osservazionisopra la provenienza della decorazione geometrica." Annali 1875 p. 221) and after I had been almost involuntarily influenced by the exact penetration of F. Dümmler, I inclined more towards the Philo-Phoenician opinion. But I only extended the influence of this dens ex machina of Helbig to a certain extent in the formation of the Iron Period and Kyprian ceramic art, represented by the vases on Pl. XIX. From the beginning of the discoveries I always held firmly to the theory of the non-Phoenician and non-Semitic origin of the pre-Graeco-Phoenician ceramic art of the Copper Bronze Period (which Dümmler ascribes, along with the other departments of sculpture to a Semitic non-Phoenician inland race). In the essays which I wrote in 1885, and published in 1886 in the Repertorium für Kunstwissenschaften I spoke not of a Phoenician style, but of a style showing Phoenician influence, and in spite of all opposition I steadily maintained the importance of the Greek element in Kyprian art. **) Cf. below Pl. CLXXII, 17e and g. ***) Cf. also p. 40—41, Fig. 41—43.
†) The cask-shaped vase on Pl. LXXIV, 5, (cf. p. 38, Fig. 39) is formed of the same material.

(like LXXIV, 5) with the same black and red colours.*) This painting in two colours came into use gradually in Kypros at the end of the Bronze Period, and the first traces of it are to be found on the images of the island goddess in the stratum of remains which contains the numerous Mykenae vases, i. e. about the middle of the 2nd. millenium B. C. The image (p. 34, Fig. 31) which was found in the tomb of the Mykenaean ox-krater (Fig. 33) is painted mostly black, and of the three bands round the neck only the centre one is red. The flowers and trees on vases XIX, 1 and 4 differ considerably from each other, but the lotus bud, which the man on vase 4 is smelling, is exactly like the one which in vase 1 crowns the fantastic tree. The arrow pattern, peculiar to Kypros, is applied to both vases; we find it for example on a large scale on the vase with the chariot, which is of the same shape, style and size.**) (Pl. CLVIII, 1a and 1b.) On both vases XIX, 1 and 4 (as well as on the vase with the chariot CLVIII, 1) we find the stripes, or cartouches formed of ornaments in the shape of the letter W. This motive belongs in common to our Kyprian vases, and to the vases of Mykenae and the Dipylon tombs.

The Svastika (cf. p. 148, Fig. 149 and 150) 卐 appears also on the neck of vase XIX, 1, beside concentric circles and semi-circles, and on vase XIX, 4 introduced four times into the pictorial scene.***) The Svastika is entirely wanting in Kypros in the pre-Graeco-Phoenician Copper-Bronze Period. It appears in the Graeco-Phoenician Iron Period, and disappears in the 6th. century B.C; how it came to Kypros cannot as yet be ascertained.†) In the class of vases to which XIX, 1 and 4 belong, eyes are often painted on the snout-shaped vase mouth, and concentric circles and half circles constantly occur; in vase 1 they are still to be seen, and in vase 4 they must have been present. (Cf. also p. 40, Fig. 41 Pl. CLVIII, I, CLXII, 19e and 1).

The concentric circles, which hold such an important place in the ornamentation of Kyprian pottery were not brought to Kypros by the Phoenicians, Syrians or inhabitants of Asia Minor, nor did they come through the Greeks of Hellas or the islands. A glance at Pl. CCXVI and its explanation will show us how they were developed from the groups of incised concentric circles. We have just as little reason to suppose that the concentric semi-circles of Kyprian pottery (cf. p 67 Fig 84), (also combined with the Svastika), which occur singly or in pairs, and are attached to horizontal or vertical straight bands or lines, were borrowed from Mykenae.††) On Pl. CCXVI I have shewn that these semi-circular ornaments were indigenous to Kypros, that they were invented on the island in the Copper-Bronze Period, and that like the concentric circles, they were at first incised.†††) The introduction of the potter's wheel and the compass into Kyprian pottery brought about an increase in regularity of execution, and many variations of the original type. The custom so much in vogue among the Kyprian potters of Graeco-Phoenician Iron Period, of painting human eyes (as an indication of the human head) on the mouths the of vases of certain kinds, was derived from a custom which was already practised in the pre-Graeco-Phoenician Bronze Period. §) The same is true of the representations of the female breasts, an instance of which is to be seen on vase XIX, 2 (cf. p. 39 Fig. 40). This custom is also derived from the Copper-Bronze Period (cf. CCXVI, 15, 16 and 28).

On the other hand the scale pattern, which occurs in Kypros at the same time, and consists of a row of segments of a circle, sometimes overlapping, certainly has its origin in Mykenae. It first occurs on Mykenaean vases (p. 61, Fig 68) where it is very frequent. Afterwards we find it on Kyprian vases, but more rarely. It is then transferred to the Graeco-Phoenician vases. On our four vases of Pl. XIX it is wanting, but it is to be seen on a vase in the form of a duck, Pl. XCVIII, 6, which was found in the same tomb as p. 38 Fig 39 (= Pl. LXXIV, 5). It is also on the vase Pl. CLXIII, 1. The Kyprian vase painter imitated the chariot scenes so common on the Mykenaean amphorae found in Kypros (p. 61 Fig. 68, p. 65 Fig. 77) and applied them to his oinochoë (CLXVIII, 1), while he used the Mykenaean scale pattern as an ornament for the body of the chariot. Cf. also the scale pattern painted on the very ancient clay statues of Joumpa near Salamis (Journal of Hellenic Studies, 1891, Pl X). The Tamassos vase (p. 37 Fig. 38, p. 63 Fig. 75), excavated by me, shows on the shoulder a continuous decoration of this scale pattern. The last named vase was found in 1885 in a necropolis, where I opened a number of graves again in 1889 for the Royal Museum at Berlin. The discoveries show that the graves are probably Graeco-Phoenician, but that they extend to the end of the Bronze Period. §§) The rosette with concentric

---

*) In Pl. XIX, 4 the blood-red colour of the lower part of the figure, and its contrast with the rusty red used on the rest of the vase, was marked by me in the coloured Pl. (Jahrbuch 1888, Pl. 8). These contrasts of colour are, I think, purely accidental. The painter intended to use black and red, but not two shades of red.

**) Cf. p. 41, Fig. 42.

***) Cf. also the svastikas on the Kyprian vases p. 71, Fig. 84 CXLV, 9 CLXXIII, 19e, k. n, CCXVI, 26. on the clay figure p. 148, Fig. 150, and on the stone figure Pl. CCIII, 3. I published an exhaustive study on the appearance of the svastika in Kypros in "La croix gammée et la croix couronnée à Chypre." par M. Max Ohnefalsch-Richter (read by M. A. de Mortellet) in the Bulletins de la Société d'anthropologie de Paris XI, 1888. P. 669—680.

†) In the paper quoted I tried to show that the svastikas came to Kypros from India, but unfortunately it is impossible to find in India information of a date early enough to make this credible. Cf. also CCXVI, 26 and explanation.

††) In 1886, after the publication of my article on the Athienon vase Pl. XIX, 4 (Jahrbuch I p. 80). Dümmler formed the opinion that these semi-circles could be traced to Mykenaean influence, because a vase from Tiryns (Schliemann, Tiryns, p. 144. No. 42) and other vases of Mykenaean style show this ornament. Two years later, in speaking of this ornament on vases of Halikarnassos. (W. R. Paton's discoveries) he asserted that because it appeared in a purely geometric style, it could not have spring from the ceramic art of Mykenae. He added that Kyprian and that very old Rhodian vases offered the nearest analogy.

†††) Cf. on Pl. CLXVIII, 3d. the incised semi-circular ornaments on the lower edge of the conical surface of a clay whorl shaped ornament. See also the painted semi-circular ornaments on the vases, Pl. CLXXIII, 19ka and n.

§) For details see Pl. CCXVI.

§§) Here I excavated two clay imitations of the Mykenaean Bügelkanne, and I mentioned them in my Essay in the Repertorium. Dümmler (in the Mittheilungen Athen XII, p. 280; note 1) is wrong on this point.

circles and rows of dots which we saw on the Athiaenou vase XIX, 4 and which sometimes occurs on Kyprian vases of this style, finds its analogy in Mykenaean pottery*), but also appears, e. g. on the Rhodian vase, (LXXVIX, 2), and seems to have come to Cyprus from this island.

The star-rosette formed of eight rays, which occurs on the bodies of the goats along with car-touches and W. ornaments XIX, 1, happens to be missing on the other three vases of the same plate, but is to be seen arranged in rows on the vase of the same class (p. 38 Fig. 39), at present in Oxford, which resembles the Ormidhia vase (p. 94 Fig. 134). The same rosette forms in the Kyprian vase, Pl. CVIII, 2, the centre of a sacred tree surrounded by birds. Over one of the birds there is a semi-circle attached to the horizontal band, while behind the other is a dotted rosette. On p. 67 Fig. 42, 43, 84—88 I have shown that the painted water-birds were transferred from the Mykenaean pottery of the Bronze Period to the Kyprian pottery of the Iron Period. While these birds are to be seen on the hand-made ball-shaped vases of Mykenae (Fig. 88), they are entirely wanting on the corresponding Kyprian vases of the Bronze Period, and first appear on the wheel-made vases of the Iron Period, especially with oinochoës with spouts (Fig. 42 and 43). To the Kyprian vases with eight-rayed stars or rosettes, often arranged in rows correspond remarkably in shape and arrangement some late Mykenaean vases (cf. Furtwängler-Löschcke Myk. Vasen. Pl. XXXVIII, 393, and the present work p. 94 Fig. 134).

Although the flowers and trees on vases XIX, 1 and 4 are very various, yet they are closely related in style, technique, arrangement of colours and patterns. On vase 4, two goats are adoring the sacred tree, on vase 4 a man is represented performing an act of worship. (Cf. p. 187.) The manner in which the face of the man and the front part of his head are merely outlined is a remarkable peculiarity in style. The unwinged goats of vase 1 resemble the winged goat of Pl. CXI, 3 (= Perrot III. p. 706 Fig. 517) in contour, rosettes and cartouche with W. ornament. Between the representations of 1 und 4 Pl. XIX, comes the Kyprian vase representing a winged four-footed animal with a human head (Pl. CXIII, 3). On the body of the last figure is to be seen a semi-circular ornament. The vase picture Pl. CXVIII, 5 (repeated from Goodyear Pl. XXXVII, 12), which represents a winged stag, is also very instructive in this connection. In style and design it resembles the animals just mentioned, and like the goats, winged and unwinged, it bears the two rosettes and the cartouche on its body. Besides this there is a towering lotus flower, behind it which bears a strong analogy to the principal flower on the vase picture Pl. XIX, 4.

The figure on vase XIX, 4 has another analogy in the figures of vases XIX, 1 and 3 and p. 62 Fig 71, in the Bronze Kylix p. 46 Fig. 49, and in the cylinder p. 31 Fig. 28 (= Pl. XXXI, 8). Although the costume varies, all these representations show the same type, and a style which is in its essentials the same. Vases XIX, 2 and 3, (= XX and XXI) in spite of their variety of form and decoration, show remarkable points of resemblance. As vase 3 happened to be baked a very dark red, the painter coun-teracted this effect by a white slip **), which is absent on vase 3. The painter of vase 2 worked with black and white on a red ground, the painter of vase 3 with red and black on a light grey ground. On, both vases the painted band is very frequent; while plants, trees and flowers are very similar in motiveve design and execution. But the strongest resemblances are to be found in the figures, which show the same drapery and dressing of the hair, and the same formation of the nose and eyes. Other striking analogies are to be found in the figures of the Bronze Kylix of Idalion (p. 46 Fig. 49), which is, like vase 2, surrounded by a plaited band, and in the cylinder, p. 31 Fig. 28, on which is a representation of a nude goddess with the same type of face and hair seated in front of a branch and an animal. The animal is very similar to those represented on the class of vases under consideration. This cylinder comes from the Necropolis of the Bronze Period at Hagia Paraskevi, and is undoubtedly older than the vases. How much older cannot be determined, as the cylinder, now in possession of Colonel Warren, was excavated in secret, and the circumstances of its discovery are unknown. Vase XIX, 2 is in general formation similar to vases 1 and 4, but the body more nearly resembles a bull, and instead of the snout-shaped mouth there is, on the neck of the vase, a large female head fully modelled, from the mouth of which the liquid is poured. The style of the head and the long thick plaits of hair form a striking ana-logy to the types of female figures on the well-known silver dish of Kypros. The figures and decorations of the Ormidhia vase (p. 94 Fig. 134) belong to the same set of types. A comparison between the ornaments on this Kyprian vase of Ormidhia, consisting of rows of rosettes and segments of plaited bands, with the corresponding decorations in relief on the robe of the king, Pl. XCIX, 1, will lead to a conclu-sion that Assyrian motives were borrowed, just as Egyptian influence is plainly to be traced in vases XIX, 4 p. 40 Fig. 41 &c. From these Assyrian analogies (cf. p. 94 ff.), we are able to assign an approximate date, which corresponds admirably with other Kyprian discoveries and more recent observations. We may place the vases and the Bronze Kylix of Idalion in a period of time beginning about the reign of Asurna-sirpal (884—860), reaching its highest point in the reigns of Sargon II and Sanherib and ending with Asarhaddon and Asurbanipal (681—626). The most recent vases belonging to this period are older than the 6th century B.C. Another criterion, which also corresponds with our dating, is offered by the bronze fibulae of Kypros. These are entirely wanting in the Bronze Period, and are associated with the older part of the Iron Period which we are at present discussing. In all my excavations hitherto I only found one fibula in a grave dating from the beginning of the 6th century B.C. (1889 at Tamassos); the others were all older, and disappear from the graves about 600 B.C., buttons being used in their place to hold the garments together (cf. Pl. LXVII, 19 and CLXXXVII, 4). The most usual kind is the well-known

---

*) Jahrbuch 1887 p. 90. Together with F. Dümmler I was wrong to declare this dotted rosette to be an exclusive peculiarity of Mykenaean and Cyprian pottery.
**) A white slip was constantly used in Kypros during the Bronze Period. There is a class of vases of this period which has a blackish or dark brown ground with decoration exclusively in white, for example Pl. CI., 3—6. For a vase of the Iron Period painted with black and white ornaments, and belonging to the 6th century B.C. see p. 47, Fig. 46.

bow-shaped fibula (a Kyprian instance made of gold, Perrot III p. 831, Fig. 595), known from Greek and Italian discoveries, and more recently from discoveries at Halikarnassus and Sendscherli, and belonging to the period from the 7th to the 9th century B. C.*)

In my excavations at Marion Arsinoë (1886) and at Tamassos (1889) I wa able to classify the stratum of tombs of the 6th century by means of an examination of the imported vases and other details, and I also know fairly exactly the Graeco-Phoenician vases of this century. Vases like Fig. XIX, 1—4 LXXIV, 5 are older than this period, and are therefore not to be found in the graves. The use and manufacture of the cask-shaped vases (Pl. LXXIV, 5. CCXVI, 26) ends about 600 B. C. For in graves known to be of the 6th century no trace of them is to be found. The newer series of vases with concentric circles, in which human figures are absent and representations of animals rare**), belong to the 5th and 6th centuries, and some of them are even as late as the 4th century. The illustration on the title page gives some of these more recent varieties, and in my work on Tamassos I shall say more about them.

In general we may state that all the vase styles of the Graeco-Phoenician Iron Period have their predecessors and prototypes in the Bronze Period, from which they are developed. Thus the Graeco-Phoenician wheel-turned vases of the Iron Period, with a spout in the shape of a female head, (as on Pl. CCXVI, 23), are developed from the pre-Graeco-Phoenician hand-made vases of the Bronze Period (as on Pl. CCXVI, 21 and 22).

How far the pottery of Mykenae influenced that of Kypros has been seen on Pls. CL—CLII and CCXVI. I will only call attention here to the form of vase 3 Pl. XIX, which also occurs in Mykenae (cf. Furtwängler and Löschcke "Mykenische Vasen," Pl XLIV, 67).

An oinochoë with a long straight tube for pouring in the middle of the body opposite the handle. This is the shape which the potter of the Iron Period chose for vase 3 Pl. XIX, and which he had adopted from the Bronze Period. A similar shape, in which the handle does not go from the edge to the shoulder of the vase, but is carried across the mouth in a curve somewhat resembling that of a stirrup, is still more frequent in Mykenae (Furtwängler·Löschcke, "Myk. Vasen" Pl. XLIX, 68) This shape is met with as often, if not oftener, in Kypros, especially in tombs belonging to the transition between the Bronze and the Iron Period. In the Antiquarium of the Royal Museum at Berlin are exhibited the contents of the tombs which I opened at Katydata Linu in 1885. On Pl. CLXXII, 16—18 three of these tombs are represented in outline and section, and the objects found in them are illustrated. 16b and 17p, representing two vases of the shape described above, are repeated in Furtwängler and Löschcke XLIV, 68.***) In this early stratum there was found for the first time traces of iron or rust, and some fragments of an ornamental chain (CLXXII. 16c). This Mykenaean class of vases, with the stirrup-shaped handle, was also transferred to the Graeco-Phoenician Iron Period. The transition period between Bronze and Iron may be dated between 1200 and 1000 B. C. About 1000 B. C the new Graeco-Phoenician Era, the Iron Period, came to a close, and the time from 1000 to 600 B. C embraces the highest ceramic period of Kyprian Graeco-Phoenician art, as is well shewn by the illustrations. (Pl. XIX—XXI and LXI, p. 36 Fig. 37, p. 37 Fig. 38, p. 40—41, Fig. 41—43, p. 62 Fig. 71, p. 63, Fig. 75, p. 94, Fig. 134, Pl CLVIII, 1). The Tamassos vase on p. 37 Fig. 38 (parts of it on p. 36 Fig. 37, p. 62, Fig. 71, p. 63 Fig. 75, Pl. CXXVII, 6) illustrates the similarity between this class of vases and the large warrior vases of Mykenae (Furtwängler and Löschcke, „Myk. Vasen" Pl. XLII, and XLIII), although it is uncertain which class most influenced the other. The concentric circles of the vases of Mykenae seem to point to a probability that the art of Mykenae was influenced by Kypros. On p. 63 Fig. 74 and 75 is shown one of the double handles of a Mykenae vase, beside a similar one of Kypros (cf p. 65).

Plate XXII.

° 1a.   A clay pitcher from Marion-Arsinoë 0,352 m high (13⁷/₈ in.) — b and e. The paintings are from my water colour tracings of the shoulder of the vase.

The ornamentation is black and white on a dull blood-red ground. All the colours are low in tone. Round the body of the vase in a horizontal direction run wide bands of black and white lines and trellis-pattern. while round the neck is a narrow beading. The mouth is bordered by a stripe consisting of black and white curved triangles. Round the middle of the neck runs a wreath of white leaves. On the widest band round the body of the vase trees are represented, under which four water-birds walk in a row, one behind the other. Under each bird, which is coloured black, is a white star formed of dots. At, the root of the handle are two horn-shaped ornaments, executed in black with white dots, in a design resembling beads. Opposite the handle is a plastic representation of a woman holding a small pitcher on her lap. This pitcher serves as a spout or pouring tube for the large vase (cf. p. 40—44).

The head of the figure is stamped, and only the face has been fashioned with a tool. The rest of the figure is thrown together in the rude "snowman" style. The face and the forehead are painted with a thin coating of white, the lips and the rest of the figure with the same red as the background of the vase. The woman wears a high pointed cap. The modelling of the head is in the archaic Greek style. The vase certainly belongs to the first half of the 6th century.

In the same tomb (Nekr. II, 118) were found Attic black-figured vases of the beginning of th 6th century. For the site of the Necropolis I and II and the formation of the tombs see Pl. CLXXIV and CLXXV.

---

*) If Studniczka's theory of the Greek fibulae („Mittheilungen", Athen 1887 p. 19) is correct, in spite of the discovery of the fibulae in Sendscherli and in Kypros, we must conclude that Greek influence in Kypros during the first half of the first millennum B. C. was much greater than has hitherto been supposed.
**) The animals found on painted Kyprian vases of the 6th or beginning of the 5th century are executed in a style which is quite peculiar. Cf. Pl. XXII—XXIV and LXII and LXIV.
***) Cf. F. Dümmler, „Mittheilungen", Athen. 1888, p. 289.

° 2. The same provenance. Fragments of a similar bathing vessel of better execution, but the same in technique, clay and colouring.

It was impossible to reconstruct the whole vessel. But the most important parts of it have been preserved, viz. neck (2a) shoulder (2b and 2c) and seated female figure holding a vase. This is described in detail on p. 42 (2c = Fig. 45 = Pl. CLV, 6).

The style and the circumstances of discovery allow us to date these prochus in the same period as No. 1, i. e. in the first half of the 6th century B. C.

Plate XXIII.

° 1. Hydria from the same place.

Height of this hydria, which is broken at the top, from the upper handle-junction to the ground 0,355 m = 14 in. The same provenance, clay, colours, technique, style and period as the vases on Pl. XXII. Most of the seated female figure is broken away. Of the six painted birds five are walking one behind the other, while the sixth walks to meet them. It is evident that the trees growing up in the centre and branching out to either side are palms (cf. Pl. CLV, 6, = XXII, 2c, and CLV, 4 = XXIII, 1c = Fig. 44) (cf. p. 39 and 41—42).

On p. 43 hydriae XXII 1 and XXIII, 2 are erroneously given as XXI, 1 and XXII, 2.

° 2. From the same excavation a similar hydria 0,333 m (= 13¹/₄ in.)

Handle, part of neck and female figure broken away. A row of six water-birds walking under trees, decoration of dotted stars (cf. p. 39 and 43).

Plate XXIV.

° 1. The same excavation at Marion-Arsinoë. Shoulder of a hydria about 0,30 m high.

The spout is formed by a crude ox-head. The technique is similar to that of the former vases; the dull black and white design being applied on a ground of dim red. On each side is a black and white branching design with ornaments between consisting of concentric circles (cf. the explanation of 3—6 and 9).

This vase also belongs to the beginning of the 6th century B. C. The grave (Nekr. II No. 62) contained an early black-figured Attic vase. As a rule concentric circles are not found on this class of vases. On this Plate and on Pl. LXII 1, I have given some exceptions to this rule.

° 2. Provenance, nekropolis, clay, colours and technique are the same.

Shoulder of a bathing vessel, 0,305 m high, with an ox-head (cf. p. 240) which is painted black, with horns, forehead, and ears white. Between the well-known ornaments in the shape of trees, branches and stars is to be found a flower spray in white dots or a peculiarly formed shrub.

This tomb was rich in bathing vessels with figures of seated women, in terra-cottas and in bronzes. There were also some Attic black-figured vases. The golden perforated ring with Karneol-scarab described on Pl. CLXXXII. 44, was also found here.

° 3. = p. 44 Fig. 47, the same provenance. Shoulder of a bathing vessel 0,537 m high. A seated female figure, (not shown in the drawing) roughly kneaded together without any attempt at the use of a mould. Between a vertical row of black concentric circles and white dotted stars rises a peculiar ornament like a palm or a flower, resting on a curved basis somewhat like a table (cf. p. 44).

° 4. The same provenance, technique, &c. The broken hydria, to which the piece here reproduced belongs, is decorated with one of the best seated female figures of the archaic Greek style. (Omitted in the drawing).

On the shoulder of the vase on each side of the figure a dotted ornament is applied, consisting of two spirals in white, one over the other. Between a black and a white branch is a row of simple black concentric circles and also a row of black circles with white dots.

It is evident that the concentric circles did not please the Greek taste of the artist, and that he tried to vary their monotony and stiffness by adding a design in white. (Cf. Pl. LXII, 1.) I have noticed similar attempts on vases from Kurion which I photographed (1883—84).

° 5. The same Nekropolis. Shoulder of a bathing-vessel 0,25 m high; clay and colouring the same.

The large ox-head, about 0,08 m high, is conceived and executed with real artistic vigour and, along with the ram's head vase (Pl. LXIV, 6), belongs to the best modelled animal heads of this class.

Whilst as a rule concentric circles are drawn with the compasses, and have no dot in the centre, in this case the vase painter has drawn without compasses wide irregular concentric circles with a dot in the centre.

° 6. Shoulder of a pitcher, 0,285 m high, from the same Nekropolis.

An ox-head carelessly modelled and concentric circles correctly drawn &c.

In the same tomb was found the fragment of a bathing vessel illustrated in Pl. CLXXVII, 1, on which we notice that a lion's head has taken the place of the ox-head as a spout. This is the only piece of the kind from Kypros which I know of. The tomb was also rich in early Attic black-figured vases.

° 7. The same provenance. Bathing vessel of the same kind.

This vessel is 0,275 m high, and is surmounted by a goat's head. The ornamentation consists of a rudely executed white palm-tree and two white dotted rosettes enclosed in vertical black double lines.

? 8. The same excavation. Fragments of a painted shoulder belonging to the bathing-vessel from Nekropolis I, No. 13 (marked on the Plate wrongly II instead of I). Technique and clay like the former examples. Described on p. 44.

? 9. Nekropolis II, grave 126. The painted shoulder of a pitcher 0,328 m high.

? 10. In the Kylix from the same place, Nekropolis II, No. 82, several rows of water birds are introduced on the neck between black and white stripes, while on the shoulder of the vase a tree formed of dotted rosettes is surrounded by birds. These birds look like storks or pelicans.

Three concentric circles, a shrub and peculiar ornament like a palmette, which spreads out above and below (cf. 3 and Pl. XXII, 2). Also Pl. LXII—LXIV, CLXXVII, 1 and 3, CLXXIX—CLXXXI.) On the later plates we see that in the 4th century B. C. there was a peculiar class of pottery, beautiful in its own way, which reached its highest perfection in the vases such as Pl. LXIV, 1—8 (= CLXXXI, 1 and 2) and CLXXXI, 4 and 5, but it holds a very subordinate place beside the Greek ceramic art represented by figures which the discoveries of Flinders Petrie have proved to come from Rhodes and Egypt. The Kyprian Greeks had a large share in the development of the forms of vases, and of the geometric vase-style, even as early as the pre-Mykenaean time. At the time when the civilisation and art known as the Mykenaean arose in Greece, the Kyprian artists received more from the potters of Mykenae, (among other things the potter's wheel), than they gave to them. But the Mykenaean artists also learned something from the artists of Kypros and, as sculptured stones show, in other departments besides the ceramic art. The Rhodian vases from Ialysos and Kamiros were no more fabricated in Kypros than were those called Melian because they were first found in Melos. But the artificers of these vases[*]) borrowed, like the potters of Mykenae, shapes and ornamental motives from the Kyprian artists. For the development of the Dipylon style, of the proto-Corinthian, Corinthian, old Ionian and other black-and red-figured styles there was no scope in Kypros. Most of the vases discovered in Kypros were imported[**]), and many of them were made in Attica for the Kyprian market.[***])

Kypros also had a large share in the first beginnings of figure painting on vases. The Peloponnesian Greeks who brought to Kypros the first vase-paintings representing human beings (the Mykenae amphorae p. 61, Fig. 68, p. 65, Fig. 77), inspired the Kyprians and the Greek and Phoenician settlers to similar attempts, and they in their turn for a long time fostered the art of figure painting. The principal subjects painted on vases gold breast-plates by these Kyprians in the period between 1000 and 600 B. C. (p. 62, Fig. 71, Pl. CLVIII, 1 and Pl. XXV, 11, CXCIX, 3) were chariots for war, hunting or processions. But all these attempts to paint human beings on vases (cf. Pl. XIX—XXI) came to an end in the 7th century B. C. In the stratum of discovery belonging to the 6th century B. C, thoroughly investigated by me, every trace of the human in representation has disappeared from Kyprian vase-painting. While the Greeks of the mainland and of the various colonies were painting men and divinities in human shape on their clay vessels, and thus producing the finest masterpieces of vase-painting, there was a sudden pause in Kypros, during which human representation ceased, and this fact is the best proof that in the 6th century B. C. the Greek-Aryan characteristics of ceramic art were overpowered by Phoenician-Semitic influence. Similar effects may be noticed in sculpture, modelling in clay, and metal work, but in these arts the date is somewhat later.

Plate XXV.

1 and 2 = p. 75, Fig. 103, p. 77, Fig. 105, Pl. XCIX, 8, C, 7, CLIX, 6). Two of the best preserved pieces of a silver woman's girdle from a grave in ·the Necropolis of Marion-Arsinoë near Poli tis Chrysokhou (Jahrbuch d. Archäol. Instituts II. 1887, Pl. VIII).

Of the whole ornament there remain one piece consisting of four plates, one piece of two plates, (illustrated in No. 2) fragments of smaller plates with a design of seated sphinxes, and several other small fragments. ¡ This girdle is discussed in detail by F. Dümmler in the Jahrbuch d. Archäol. Instituts, 1887, II, 85—56, (cf. p. 50 ff, 55—56, 78, 92, 114 &c.).

3 and 4. Reconstruction of the girdle corresponding to the original pieces, after a watercolour by Foot. Dümmler thinks it probable that the plates were made in sets of four, and that two rectangular plates with different ornamentation (No. 1 in its original state, No. 4 reconstructed) formed the front clasp of the girdle.

---

[*]) The shape of the pinax of Rhodes is borrowed from Kypros. I shall give in my work on Tamassos some of the oldest Kyprian examples in this kind, which disappears from the tombs about the beginning of the 7th century. Meanwhile cf. Cesnola-Stern Pl. VII. in the middle. For later Kyprian variations of this early plate form from the 6th century see Pl. CLXXVIII, 1, and from the 4th century Pl. CXXVIII, 3. The plate found in Marion-Arsinoë (Journal of Hellenic Studies 1890, p. 41. Fig. 7) on which a sphinx and bird are painted, seems to occupy in technique and colouring a place between the pottery of Rhodes and that of Naukratis, and to represent one of the most interesting original attempts of a potter working in Kypros. The Rhodians (Pl. LXXXIX, 2) borrowed from the Kyprians the shape of the oinochoë with a spout (cf. title page and Pl. CCXVI), which they developed. They also borrowed the plaited band XXIX, 2 and 3, p. 94. Fig. 134: very ancient plaited ornaments on Kyprian vases which were found along with vase XIX, 4) and the ornament consisting of concentric circles or semi-circles, and afterwards developed into a twist (Pl. CCXVI, 9 from Kypros). The amphora shape of Melos, and the double handle, at whose junction with the vase are placed animal heads or painted eyes (Pl. CXI, 2, CXVIII, 8), were also copied from Kyprian originals (p. 37, Fig. 38, p. 63. Fig. 75, p. 94, Fig. 134).

[**]) Cf. p. 164 note 2. and the explanation of the title page.

[***]) With the exception of the Dipylon vase given on Pl. LXXXIX, I only know a single Dipylon kylix which was found in Kypros and excavated by me. I discovered it together with a rudely executed vase surmounted by a female head, in an early Graeco-Phoenician grave between Larnaka and Goschi. Type like that of XIX, 2. On the shoulder are concentric circles with dots in the middle connected by tangents. A proto-Corinthian vase found in Kypros in an early Graeco-Phoenician grave near Limassol is given on Pl. CLII, 18. At Tamassos in 1889 I excavated in tombs of the 6th century B. C. Corinthian vases and Ionic-Attic vases made in Asia Minor, together with black figured Attic vases.

5. Golden ear-ring from the same tomb.

6. = C, 2 = CXLII, 2. Chalcedony-scarab from Kypros, obtained by Dümmler. (Cf. Jahrb. &c., p. 91.) From this we may complete the representation of the girdle. (Cf. p. 209, Note 8 and 250.)

7. = p. 208, Fig. 170. Parts of a gold necklace in Egyptian style from the same tomb as Nos. 1, 2, 5.

From an examination of the contents of the tomb, given in full in the Jahrbuch, p. 87, Dümmler dates the grave not later than the middle of the 6th century B. C. This girdle is discussed more fully on p. 50 ff. of the text. On p. 50, l. 28, for Pl. XXIV read Pl. XXV.

In Fig. 252 I repeat the outline and section of the tomb in which I found the objects illustrated in Nos. 1—7. The entrance to the grave evidently was in the form of a sloping dromos I like those in graves 140 and 92 (cf. Pl. CLXXIV).

In Fig. 253 I repeat (from the Jahrbuch) the drawings of vases which were found in the tomb. These drawings were prepared from sketches made in correct proportion, and by the aid of a prism. Of these 1—5 are Kyprian, 6 is an Attic Kylix of the oldest shape.

8. Thin gold leaf with stamped figures from a grave near Corinth (original size). Berl. Mus. Antiquarium. The style is throughout similar to that of the Dipylon-vases. From Furtwängler, Arch. Zeit. 1884, p. 99, Pl. 8, 1 (cf. p. 250).

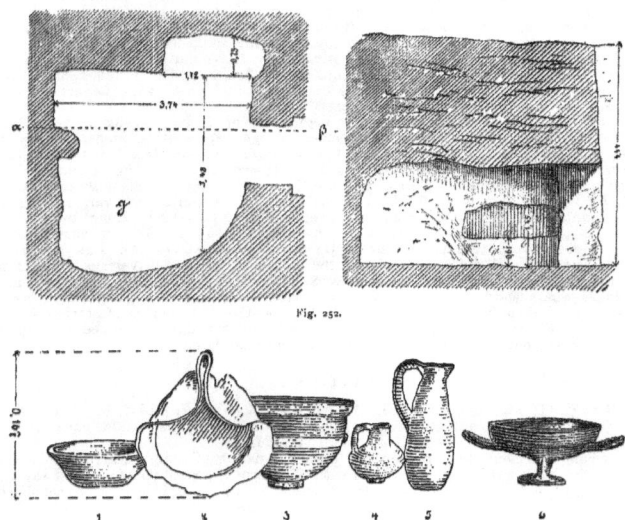

Fig. 252.

Fig. 253.

9. Thin strip of pale gold from a Dipylon tomb in Athens. Copenhagen Museum. The style is similar to that of the preceding. Both must have come from the same workshop. From Furtwängler, Arch. Zeit. 1884, p. 191, Pl. 9, 1 (cf. p. 250).

10. Thin embossed gold-leaf from Amathus. Berl. Mus. Antiquarium.

On a two wheeled gold chariot, drawn by one horse, stand two figures, one of them holding the reins, the other the whip. In the right hand top corner are the symbols of sun and half moon. In the upper smaller field are two female figures in long robes, walking towards the right, each holding a flower; they are exactly alike, both wearing long hair and a headdress like a modius The style of the figures is very similar to that of the bronze Kylix of Idalion (see p. 46, Fig. 49). The illustration on our plate is a repetition of the publication in the Jahrb. d. Arch. Inst. 1891, VI. Anzeiger, p. 126, 1a (Furtwängler, who considers the style to be old Syrian). Repeated on Pl. CI, 5, CXXXVIII, 8, cf. p. 235.

11. Model of a temple in clay painted in stripes. From Dali. Inside is a male figure wearing a pointed hat and pounding with a pestle in a mortar (from Perrot-Schipiez "Histoire de l'art", IIIp. 579. Fig. 392 = Heuzey, "Figurines antiques", Pl. X, 1).

47

12. Gold leaf of the same kind and from the same place as No. 10. Berl. Mus. Antiquarium.

This represents a nude goddess facing, with the arms hanging down. On the ground to the left a cypress is distinctly to be seen. The object on the right is interpreted by Furtwängler and others as a two-handled vase. If this were so, we should be surprised to find the foot and the handle formed as they are, for we should expect the right side to correspond exactly with the left. The form of the object is exactly the same as that on the right, and might be a cypress. The pattern of the inner design is very lightly impressed. As to the supposed handle, there are on the original no volutes corresponding to those on the drawing, but to the right and left round projections, shaped like buttons, are inserted. If these belong to the original design, their meaning is not clear. No one has made any observation on the two sprays which grow out to right and left from the ankles of the figure, and appear to float in the air. They might be brought it into connection with the lower hands of the goddess, and be considered as her attributes. These sprays bear upright flowers. It is noticeable that while the figure is facing, the legs are represented in profile turned to the right.

This is published in the Anzeiger des Jahrbuches d. Arch. Inst. &c., No. 1b. It is repeated on Pl. C, 3 and CXXXVIII, 9.

13. Gold leaf of the same kind and from the same place. Berl. Mus. Antiquarium. A nude goddess wearing a necklace and holding both arms up. Published in the Anzeiger des Jahrb. &c., No. 1c. It is to be noticed that the feet of the figure are turned outwards. This type is often found in Kypros (cf. Pl. CXXXIII, 5b, 6, 8, CXCIX, 6). In the oldest clay modelling the same type is represented; an example is shewn on Pl. LI, 6.

14. Small embossed silver-leaf (original size) from an old Graeco-Phoenician grave of Kurion, which in 1884 was in the possession of Captain Sinclair. Busts of two nude female divinities. This small plate belongs to a discovery of 18 similar objects. (Cf. p. 278.)

15. Thin gold-leaf from a tomb near Corinth, like No. 8. Berl. Mus. Antiquarium. From Arch. Zeit. 1884, Pl. 8, 2 (p. 108 Furtwängler). A dance of women is represented.

16. Thin gold-leaf belonging to the same discovery. Berl. Mus. Antiquarium.

From Arch. Ztg. &c., Pl. 8, 4. This represents a two-horse chariot with a charioteer and a warrior.

17. The same. Berl. Mus. Antiquarium.

From Arch. Ztg. &c. Pl. 8, 3 (p. 106). This represents the slaying of the Minotaur by Theseus in the presence of Ariadne. The scheme is essentially different from that of the Chalkidian and arly Attic vases.

18. The same. Berl. Mus. Antiquarium.

From Arch. Ztg. &c. Pl. 8, 5 (p. 108). This represents a man taming two lions, in heraldic scheme.

19. Large breast ornament with rich embossed ornamentation. From Etruria. Berl. Mus. Antiquarium.

From Arch. Ztg. &c. Pl. 10, 2 (p. 112 ff. Furtwängler). 1—19. H. S.

On this plate are collected together illustrations of various kinds. Some, such as 8—9, were inserted here in order to make use of the space. I have placed the rectangular gold and silver plates and the clay model of a temple beside the silver girdle, because we are here speaking of breast-plates or objects which we may profitably compare with them. Cf. Pl. CXXXVIII, CXXXIX and CXCIX.

Plate XXVI.

1 = CXVII, 4, = CLIX, 1. Stone pillar from Atheniou 1,450 m high, from Cesnola's Atlas Pl. XCIX, 671 = Perrot III, p. 217, Fig. 752.

2 = CXVII, 7, = CLIX, 3. Capital of a similar pillar from Athiaeniou. 0,655 m. high, from Cesnola's Atlas, Pl. C, 676.

3. = CXVII, 2 = CLIX, 2. Capital of a similar column from Athiaeniou. 0,762 m high, from Cesnola's Atlas Pl. C, 678.

These three pillars are fully discussed in the text p. 55—61; the oldest is number 3, perhaps from the end of the 7th century B. C. No. 1 belongs to the middle of the first half of the 6th century B. C. No. 2 is the most recent, and perhaps belongs to the end of the 6th or beginning of the 5th century. According to this explanation, the passage in the text, p. 56, ll. 22—25, should be corrected.

For the development of the capitals from the type of the sacred tree see Pl. XIX, 1, = Pl. LXI. (Cf. also p. 71—72, 150 and 190. Similar capitals are collected on Pls. LVIII, LIX (cf. p. 189), (1—3, H. S.)

Plate XXVII.

? 1. Fragment of a sphinx (limestone) from Marion. Berl. Mus. Antiquarium.

The only remains are the breast, the junction of the wings, the upper part of the fore legs and a small part of the body. The figure is smoothed off at the back. The body is in profile, turned towards the left. Three curls fall down from the head on each side of the breast. The fragment corresponds with the following, which is in the Louvre and in better preservation. Both were found in the dromos of a tomb (Nekr. II tomb 140), and therefore must be supposed to be monumental figures.

? 2. Fragments of a figure of a sphinx (limestone) from the same tomb as No. 1. Louvre.

There remain the front part of the body with the head, a small piece of the fore legs, about half of the torso, and almost all the wings. The head is facing, and is in the pure archaic style of the 6th century B. C. The feathers are modelled.

Both these figures have been discussed by P. Herrmann (48 Berl. Winckelmannsprogr. p. 22 f) and he also makes some remarks on the sepulchral signification of the sphinx. As to the position which the figures occupied, the smoothing off of the back shows that they must have been placed in front of a background. They cannot be pendants, for both have the profile towards the left. In the Berlin fragment it is certain that the face was full, for it comes between the falling curls of hair. Hence the figures cannot have been applied as on the Xanthos relief (Cesnola-Stern Pl. XLVII), and we may consider it certain that they were set up as guardians at the door of the tomb. (1—2, H. S.)

It would be very desirable to obtain particulars of these explorations, and a description of the tomb. Fragments of three sphinxes were found on the 22nd of May 1886 in the road leading to a tomb, which at first bore the number 128 On the 29th of May a tomb-entrance was discovered about 15,20 m south of the place where the sphinx was found, and to this I gave the number 140. While the road to the tomb was being cleared out I discovered a Dromos dug in a slanting direction into the earth, and ending at the surface of the earth just over the place where the sphinx was found. This Dromos was about 17,65 m long. About 2,45 m from the end lay the first fragments of the lime-stone sphinx, which were discovered 0,5 m under the earth. Their position at the end of the Dromos, here about 2,5 m. wide, in a row one behind the other, makes it probable that they originally stood upright. They formed the ornament to the entrance like the rows of sphinxes on the roads leading to the royal graves and temples in Egypt, or like the seated statues on the sacred way leading to the Didymaean sanctuary of the Branchidae. These sepulchral sphinx-statues appear to have stood somewhat higher than the surface of the earth, and this explains their fragmentary condition. Of one of them only a piece of a wing was found. Perhaps after the interment the end of the Dromos may have been only partly filled up with earth. As it was important to excavate these rare works of archaic Greek art in as perfect a condition as possible, and to obtain information about the architecture of the tomb, most of the Dromos and the tomb itself were very carefully cleared out. Unfortunately the grave chamber, which was shaped like a cave, had fallen in, so that it was impossible to obtain a good idea of its shape. The flooring of the grave lay about 3.5—4 m under the surface of the earth. The height of the chamber was approximately calculated to be 1.75 2 m The depth was about 2,10 - 2,77 m, and the breadth perhaps a little more. As is the case in most of the Kyprian graves, it was found that interment had taken place. Several corpses were found, but it was impossible to determine what position they had occupied before the grave fell in. Fourteen bronze nails, about 10 cm long and 2 cm wide, showed that there must have been a wooden coffin. Funeral gifts made of bronze were also found, for instance the remains of a strigil, a bronze mirror with a handle, a bronze shell lamp with a palmette on the handle (in shape like the clay lamp on Pl. CCX, 16), and one-edged knives made of iron, (shape like Pl. CLXIII, 19 f), one of them 0,247 m, the other 0,20 m long. Among the objects made of clay were a lamp of the same shape as the bronze Kyprian Graeco-Phoenician vessels, a bathing vessel decorated with black concentric rings and two white cocks (Pl. LXII, 1), and Attic varnished clay ware, including a very ancient black figured Amphora about 0.215 m high. On each side of this last is represented Dionysos accompanied by a Maenad and holding the horn of plenty and sprays of ivy. There were also found a green glass alabastron about 9 cm long without figures, (a kind of vase which is much more rare in Kypros than in Rhodes) and a very beautiful Kyprian onyx scaraboid (Pl. XXXII, 25) with Kyprian syllabic inscription written boustrophedon, and belonging to the first half of the 6th century B. C. The stone was set in a silver perforated ring, which fell to dust as it was taken out. The only gold objects found were three small beads resembling Pl. CLXXXII, 37 in shape and technique, but more delicately and finely worked. An ivory button, measuring about 0.023 m in diameter, showed that the use of the fibula had been given up. This grave, with grave XCII, in which the marble torso Fig. 2 Pl. XXVII was found, belongs to the most interesting of those discovered at Marion-Arsinoe in 1886. Both graves belong to the first half of the 6th century.

? 3a and b. Torso of a nude male figue in marble (front and side view), now in the British Museum (Jahrbuch d. Arch. Inst. III 243).

The figure is represented in the so-called Apollo type. The head, arms and legs from the knees are missing. According to Furtwängler's account the workmanship is imperfect, and bears a provincial character. This figure is important because its provenance is exactly known. It was found in the Dromos of tomb 92 Necr. II.[*]

The tomb (Pl. CLXXIV, 2[**]) deserves a brief description. As in the case of the preceding grave a Dromos of earth 22,80 m long (of which only 11,40 m is given in the illustration) leads in a slanting direction into the sepulchral chamber, which is about 8 m long, and consists of four irregularly shaped caves communicating with each other. A section shows the height to be about 2,28 m, of which 1 82 cm belong to the opening of the door of the tomb. The distance from the tomb door to the surface of the earth is about 2,28 m.

Like the sphinxes in the former tomb, and like the large enthroned or recumbent clay statues on other tombs (Pl. CXXXVII), the archaic Greek marble figure (given on Pl. XXVII, 3a and 3b) was here set like up a stele in front and over the door of the tomb. In spite of the closest observation ont

---

[*] As soon as I saw the statue I recognised it as a figure for a tomb, and I communicated my opinion to Furtwängler and Herrmann. This is therefore the first absolutely certain example of the truth of Milchhöfer's assertion about the figure of Tenea (Arch. Zeit. 1881. p. 54). I was the first to discover and interpret this example. (Cf. Herrmann. „D. Gräberfeld von Marion" p. 22).

[**] Cf. Herrmann's Winckelmannsprogramm 1888. p. 9 and 22. In this work will be found the outline and section of the tomb which I make use of on Pl. CLXXIV Unfortunately the measurements which accompanied my drawings have not been given. It will be therefore necessary to insert them here from my Journal of Excavation. My excavations at Tamassos in 1889 for the Royal Museum at Berlin afford a striking analogy to the long dromoi belonging to the earth-tombs of the 6th century B. C. at Marion-Arsinoe. Unfortunately the large outline of the tomb, in which I indicated its different divisions and the place of the various objects found, and of which Hermann made use, has been lost. However. I still possess the full description.

47*

a splinter of marble besides the torso was found. Hence the statue must have been destroyed in very ancient times. This intentional destruction and mutilation of statues has been constantly observed in the numerous clay statues of the tombs of Marion Arsinoë and other places.*)

The following sepulchral gifts were found in the tomb:

A silver coin, obverse a winged sphinx, reverse a square die stamp. Six ("Classement" p. 315) dates corresponding silver coins about 525—500 B. C., but they may easily be some decades older.

Two small bells shaped like pomegranate-blossoms**) 0,025 m long belonging to a silver girdle similar to that from tomb 205, Pl. XXV, 1—4.

A small silver buckle, about 0,05 m in diameter, perhaps from a shield.

A finger-ring of pale gold, on which is a design Egyptian in character, representing a Nile-boat.

Part of a very solid and heavy kylix of pure gold, (given on Pl. CXCVIII, 3) on which are represented in relief rows of acorns and lotus flowers.

A large flat bronze caldron 0,69 m in diameter (similar to the one found in 1889 at Tamassos in the same stratum of discovery.)

Heavy sarcophagus ornament made of bronze 0,70 m and 0,61 m long.

Part of a heavy bronze staff 0,247 m long.

Besides native pottery, a whole series of early black-figured Attic vases.

Several alabastra made of Egyptian alabaster, an ivory button and fragments of a small ivory box without ornamentation.

As the covering of the tomb had partly fallen in. I was obliged for the purposes of excavation to make a shaft through it. While doing so, I came upon the remains of a poor Roman grave containing a gladiator's lamp, I mention this in passing, because it often happens that a burial ground has been thus made use of at two different periods. This must be remembered, otherwise the discovery of objects in the same tomb whose dates lie perhaps 600 or 700 years apart is apt to be misleading. There was an instance in this nekropolis of a Roman grave having been dug from another direction under a Graeco-Phoenician tomb of the 6th century B C., so that the excavator came first on Kyprian and Attic clay vessels of the 6th century, and afterwards, far below, on a mass of Roman lamps and Imperial coins.

Plate XXVIII.

1—27 (2 is missing). 22 cylinders of different provenance are here compared with each other and with three Kyprian clay vessels, and a whorl-shaped ornament from Hissarlik.

1. Cylinder. Collection of Clercq, Catalogue Tome I, Cylindres orientaux Pl. III, 26. Described p. 157 of the present work. Cf. p. 111, 174 and 297.

? 3. (2 is missing). Red polished vase from Hagia Paraskevi.

? 4. Fragment of a red clay polished hand-made vase, with relief ornaments of anchors and four-footed animals. From a tomb of Hagia-Paraskevi. Cf. p. 179.

5. Clay whorl from Hissarlik with engraved stags. Berlin. Original drawing. Cf. Schliemann Ilios p. 639, Fig. 280.

? 6. = p. 59, Fig. 58e. = Pl. CLXXI, 11 and 12e. Red clay polished hand-made vase with relief ornaments representing stags. For this vase, which was found by me, and compared with Trojan whorls of the pre-Graeco-Phoenician Bronze Period see, p. 57 and 179.

7. Cylinder. Coll. de Clercq Pl. I, 1. Procession of four-footed animals. The old gravers' technique found on very early archaic (also on early Babylonian) cylinders, which consists in forming the figures by incised lines and stripes with punctured designs was transferred by the Kyprian potters to their vases with designs in relief (see No. 6).

8 Do. Col. de Clercq. II, 18 Man with animals. Cf. with 3 and 5.

† 9. = CLI, 2 and 4. Cylinders formed of a composition resembling porcelain. From the ox-krater tomb of Hagia-Paraskevi. Berlin. A pattern of fishes and geometric design. Cf. p. 111 and 297.

† 10 = CLI, 11. Cylinder of the same material. From a grave of Hagia-Paraskevi. Spiral pattern surrounded by two rows of fishes. Cf. p.

11. Cylinder. Coll. de Clercq. I, 4. Trellis-pattern and row of scorpions. Cf. p. 107.

12. Cylinder. A. P. di Cesnola, "Salaminia", XIV, 57 = Menant, "Recherches sur la glyptique orientale" II p. 249 Fig. 253 Row of fishes surrounded by trellis pattern. Cf. p. 107.

14. Cylinder. Cesnola, "Salaminia", XIV, 34 = Menant II p. 249 Fig. 252. Rows of concentric circles, half moons, stars and other ornaments. Cylinders 9—14 appear to belong to the same cycle.

15. Cylinder. Coll. de Clercq. IV. 35. Rude representations of the human figure. Cf. the Kyprian cylinders p. 59—60 Fig. 59—63.

16. Cylinder. Coll. de Clercq. IV, 29. Ornaments adapted from symbols. Cf. p. 107. Certainly of Kyprian origin. Cf. 17.

---

*) Cf. S. Reinach "Chroniques d'Orient". p. 303 [7, 84, 85].

**) I have spoken of fragments of such girdles found in Kurion (1884) and Tamassos (1889).

17. = LXXIV, 3 = LXXIX, 8 cylinders. Cesn. Salam. XIV, 33. A man and two four-footed animals in front of the sacred post on which two eyes. (see p. 171 note 3), are represented as a reminiscence of the divinity. cf. p. 106—107 and Pl. LXIX, 70.

18. Cylinder. Coll. de Clercq. XVII, 156. Figures before the Ashera. Cf. p. 156 and Pl. LXIX, 6.

19. Cylinder. Coll. de Clercq. IV, 32. A man holding in his right hand the Ashera, and in his left a four-footed animal by its hind leg. In the middle is an ox-head upside down, with a star between the horns. Cf. 158—159 and Pl. LXIX, 122. Certainly from Kypros Cf. the Kyprian cylinder p. 61 Fig. 69.

20 Cylinder. Coll. de Clercq. IV, 30. Certainly made in Kypros.

21. Cylinder. American Journal of Archaeology 1886. Pl. VI, 10. The scene represents taking an oath in front of the sacred pillar. Cf. p. 157. Certainly from Kypros. Cf. 22.

22. = LXXIX, 3. Kyprian cylinder. Cesn. Salam. XII, 10. Analogous oath-taking scene. Cf. p. 157—160, 198, note 3, and LXIX, 47.

23. Cylinder. Coll. de Clercq. IV, 34. Man, seated four-footed animal, ox-head, star and sun disc with appendages. This cylinder corresponds so closely to those of Kypros that we may assume the same origin. Menant considers it to be Hittite.

24. Cylinder. Coll. de Clercq. IV, 31. Enthroned figure in front of a four-footed seat with birds and other symbols. Cf. p. 284. Manufactured either in Kypros or the same workshop as No. 25, which was also found in Kypros.

25. = p. 283, Fig. 197. Kyprian cylinder. Cesn. Salam XIV, 45. Two enthroned figures around a dove-cote, on which a bird is seated. Cf. p. 284.

26. Cylinder. Coll. de Clercq. IV, 37. An enthroned figure in front of a sacrificial table over which a bird flies. Three figures are bringing gifts. A fourth figure to the right is planting an ashera. The space over the figures is filled up by animals (four-footed animals and scorpions?) Cf. p. 162 and 163 and Pl. LXIX, 124.

27. Cylinder. Coll. de Clercq. IV, 39. A figure plants two asherôt in the form of staves ending in flowers. On one side is a large sacred tree consisting of many branches, and similar to the Kyprian type (p. 30). (Cf. p. 158, 198 and Pl. LXIX, 123.

Menant, in De Clercq's work, asserts that cylinders 1, 7, 8, 11, 13, 16, 19, 20, 23, 24 and 27 are archaic Chaldaean, while 16, 19, 20, 24 and 27 certainly, and 23 probably are Kyprian. He suggests that cylinder 21 may possibly be Kyprian. (Americ. Journ. II p. 259.) I think there can be no doubt of this from the analogy of cylinder 22.

Plate XXIX.

1—17. 17 seal-cylinders, four of which viz. 11, 12, 15 and 16. are here edited for the first time.

1. Coll. de Clercq. VII, 61. Described on p. 154. Cf. Pl. LXIX, 4.

2. American Journal of Archaeology II. Pl. VI, 14. Rude representation of a daemon or divinity between animals. Cf. Cesn. Salam, p. 120, Fig. 114.

3. A. J. Arch. II. Pl. V, 2. Described on p. 111.

4. Do. Pl. V, 8. On the left a priest is praying to a divinity who is surrounded by a crown of rays (Ištar-Anat?) On the right Marduk-Merodach, standing on a winged lion, is aiming with a bow and arrow at the dragon Ihiamat. Cf. p. 149 note 3, 236, 250.

5. Coll. de Clercq. II, 15. Two figures standing at a tripod-shaped caldron. Two goats springing up to the ashera. Cf. p. 156 (where note 2 gives the citation which properly belongs to Fig. 4).

6. Menant. Glypt. Orient II. Pl. VII, 6. Marduk-Merodach as an archer aiming at the dragon Ihiamat. Between them the ashera. Above them sun, moon and star, below them a fish. Cf. p. 156 171 Pl. LXIX, 112.

7. American Journal II, Pl. VI, 9. Similar representation. Cf. p. 250.

8. Do. VI, 16. Similar representation with two asherôt. Cf. Pl. LXIX, 111.

9. Coll. de Clercq. IX, 78. Similar representation to No. 1. Izdubar, without Eabani. In front of the god is a small kneeling figure, behind him the ashera. Cf. p. 156.

10. Coll. de Clercq. XXXII, 342. = Menant II. Pl. VIII, 3. Two winged daemons.

11. An Assyrian cylinder in the Berlin Museum as yet unpublished. (Syrian Section No. 2047. H. 0,035 Dm. 0,013 blackish-green stone.) A sacred tree, over which floats a winged sun disk, and in front of which kneel a priest and a winged daemon. Each of these figures holds in one hand fruits with long stalks. (Dates?)

12. Unpublished Assyrian cylinder. Berlin Museum, V. A. 2055. H. 0,023, Dm. 0,012. Ironstone. Two winged daemons with eagle heads stand round the sacred tree Cuneiform inscription.

13. Menant II. Pl. VII, 4. Described on p. 157. Cf. p 236—5 and Pl LXIX, 14.

14. Menant II, Pl. VIII, 1. The armed Ištar-Anat-Astarte standing on a lion in front of her palm, is adored by a priest. Behind the latter are two goats rampant. Cf. p. 156, 298.

15. Unpublished cylinder found in Kypros Berl. Mus. V. A. 738. H. 0,026, Dm. 0,013. Ironstone. Col. Cesn. Hittite in character. Two lions in a couchant position are fighting with their fore-paws. On their heads a chair is supported on which a divinity is enthroned. On their bodies stand winged daemons with animal heads, each placing one outstretched foot on the lions' necks. The two daemons on the lions and two mortals who approach behind them, are adoring the divinity.

16. Unpublished Persian cylinder. Berl. Mus. V. A. 563. H. 0,027, Dm. 0,014 Chalcedony. Marduk-Merodach stands in front of his palm on two winged, bearded, and crowned sphinxes, and holds two lions up by their hind legs. Cf. p. 251.

17. Menant II. Pl. IX, 1 = Perrot V, p. 851 Fig. 498. The Persian king is stabbing a prisoner in front of the sacred palm. Behind are four other prisoners in chains.

Plate XXX.

1—15. Fifteen cylinders from different periods and countries.

1. Coll. de Clercq. XVI, 144. On the sacred palm is enthroned a god towards whom four persons are walking. Beside the god is a star. Cf. p. 156, 246.

2. = LXXV, 6. Coll. de Clercq. XVI, 140. A corn-divinity from whose shoulders ears of corn grow out, is seated on a throne, and hands over an ear of corn to a corn-daemon of similar form who stands before him. Three mortals are approaching in order to receive the gift from the mediator. Cf. p. 103, 110—111, 156, 177 note and Ward, Americ. Journ. 1886. p. 265, Fig. 32.

3. Menant. II, Pl. VII, 3. On an erection resembling a dove-cote sits a bird like a swan, which is adored by two figures, one enthroned and one standing. The space is filled by a number of stars. Cf. p. 283 and also Pl. XXVIII, 24 and 25.

4. Coll. de Clercq. XVI, 143. In a shrine beside the sacred tree a divinity (perhaps Samas) is enthroned. Three mortals approach. Cf. p. 156, 182 note 4.

5. Coll. de Clercq. XVI, 145. Two standing figures and one enthroned. Two sacred trees beside them, supported by small tripods. Cf. p. 157.

6. Unpublished cylinder of the Berl. Mus. V. A. 296. At an altar a standing figure and a seated one are performing an act of sacrifice. Behind the seated figure is a small crouching figure and indistinct marks.

7. Unpublished cylinder of the Berl. Mus. V. A. 732. A sacred tree over which the winged sun-disk floats. On the right the symbol for the female pudendum, and the ashera crowned by the crescent moon. On the left a fish and the masseba with the sun-star. Cf. p. 150, 171 and 289.

8. Menant II. Pl. IX, 2. Act of worship in presence of an ashera or a masseba.

9. Menant II. Pl. IX, 3. The ashera behind an altar on which lies a sacrificial animal. On the left the masseba and a worshipper. On the right an animal-tamer with two lions. Cf. p. 149.

10. Menant II. Pl. X, 2. A sacred tree, over which floats a winged sun-disk of peculiar shape; two figures beside the tree in an attitude of worship.

11. Americ. Journ. II. Pl. V, 5. An ashera made of wood, crowned by the crescent moon, and indicated as female by the presence of the symbol for the female pudendum, together with a small masseba probably of stone, are adored by two mortals. At the side under a stone is a third symbol, perhaps a combination of the male and female, of masseba and ashera. Cf. p. 147, 150, Pl. LXIX, 40.

12. Unpublished cylinder of the Berl. Mus. V. A. 682. Here are arranged in a series the ashera under the crescent moon, the masseba under the sun star, the female pudendum over a fish, an altar under a winged sun-disc, and the figure of a worshipper. Cf. p. 143 note 6, 147, 289 and Pl. LXIX, 42.

13. Menant II. Pl. X, 3. Side by side are ashera, masseba, sacred tree with sun-disc, cone and egg-shaped object (perhaps a fish) rudely executed. Cf. Pl. LXIX, 13.

14 Unpublished cylinder of the Berl. Mus. V. A. 508. The dragon Thiamat or a scorpion-daemon is represented rampant under the winged sun-disk. A longer cuneiform inscription with a star over it. Masseba and ashera behind a sacrificial animal and a fish, together with several other symbols such as cows' heads, human figures &c On the right, on a small altar, stands the Queen of Heaven surrounded by a crown of rays, by the sun, the moon and the seven stars, and is worshipped by a bearded man. Other symbols more or less indistinctly rendered are present. Cf. p. 143, note 6, 149, 236—237.

15. Coll de Clercq. XVI, 150. In the lowest band is an animal-tamer with four animals. and the symbol described on p. 149. On the upper band is an enthroned divinity between three standing figures. A cypress at the side. Cf. LXIX, 92.

Plate XXXI.

1—16 Sixteen cylinders of various periods and from various places.

1. Coll. de Clercq. XXII, 219. Nude Ištar worshipped by a mortal. Beside them a cuneiform inscription, in which the owner is designated as handmaid of Marduk and Zarpanit. Cf. p. 148, 264 and 284.

2. Unpublished Babylonian cylinder of the Berl. Mus V. A. 651. H. 0,08 m. Dm. 0,015 m. A green spotted stone. The nude Ištar stands upon a low altar, and receives the worship of two mortals. Beside her is a cuneiform inscription with the name of the owner, who calls himself servant of a goddess of Babylon.

3. Unpublished cylinder of the Berl. Mus. V. A. 526, H. 0,023 Dm., 0, 013. Ironstone. Nude Ištar between animals' heads, a lance and a dog Worshippers at the side. Cf. p. 148, 197, 264, 287 and Pl. LXIX, 88.

4. Coll. de Clercq XXIII, 233. The nude Ištar and two worshippers, with a longer cuneiform inscription, in which appear the names of the divinities Marduk and Bin.

5. Unpublished cylinder of the Berl. Mus. V. A. 524, H. 0,026 m. Dm. 0,015 m. Ironstone In front of a cuneiform inscription are placed opposite each other Izdubar and a lion rampant, while behind the inscription is a worshipper represented on the same scale. The rest of the space is filled by two smaller human figures, various symbols and stars. This should be compared with the following cylinder found in Kypros.

† 6. = CLI, 28. A cylinder found in Kypros in the nekropolis Hagia Paraskevi. Coll. Konstantinides, Nicosia. Lion and goat standing upright, and two standing figures beside them. Between the animals are a masseba and two disks, while around the figures are continuous spiral ornaments and objects resembling disks.

7. A. P. di Cesnola, „Salaminia". Pl. XIII, 27. Described p. 97. Cf. Pl. LXIX, 91.

† 8. = p. 31, Fig. 28. From Hagia Paraskevi. Coll. of Colonel Warren. Sacred tree between a human figure and a stag. Cf. p. 33, 208, Note 3.

9. Unpublished cylinder of the Berl. Mus. V. A. 736. H. 0,023 m, Dm 0,009 m. Ironstone. Found in Kypros, from the Coll. Cesnola. Described p. 163. Cf. Pl. LXIX, 5.

10. Menant. II. Pl. X, 1. By the side of two larger figures is a double scene (two lions above, four men walking below), separated by the same band of plaiting which we have seen used in the same manner on the former cylinder. Cf. p. 160.

† 11. From Hagia Paraskevi, Coll. Konstantinides. Two figures in the attitude of prayer on each side of an ox-head. On the right is a double scene as in 9 and 10. Below a kneeling human figure and an ox on each side of the sacred symbol (similar to ʰ). Above are two four-footed animals, an anthropomorphic goddess, and a figure resembling an ape.

12. Coll. de Clercq. IV, 40. Griffin between a stag and a kneeling figure.

? 13. Kyprian cylinder from Hagia Paraskevi. In the lower band of ornament, in a slanting position, is the goddess fully described on p. 242. On the upper band two animals. Cf. p. 107, 157—158 and 245; see also Reinach, Chron. d'Orient, p. 420 [8,80].

? 14 = p. 33, Fig. 13. Kyprian cylinder from Hagia Paraskevi. Made of a composition resembling glass. Now in the Syrian division of the Berl. Mus. 2590. Described on p. 30. Cf. p. 88, Note 1 and Pl. LXIX, 102.

15. Unpublished cylinder of the Berl. Mus. V. A. 673. H. 0,021 m. Dm. 0,008 m. A greyish-yellow stone with streaks. Described on p. 250. Cf. p. 251, Note 2.

16. Unpublished Greek cylinder of the Berl. Mus. V. A. 2145. H. 0,021. Dm. 0,01 m. A yellowish-brown stone, which came from Bagdad (Simon). Described on p. 208, Note 3. Cf. p. 250.

Plate XXXII.

1—41. Antiquities of Mykenae, Kypros and other countries. Principally engraved stones.

1 = LXXVIII, 6. Gem in the Mykenaean style from the Vafio tomb. Tzuntas, Ἐφημερὶς Ἀρχαιολογική 1889. Pl. X, 35. On each side of the sacred tree is a daemon resembling a lion and holding an oinochoë.

2. Do. X, 36. Similar daemon without oinochoë.

3. Gem in the Mykenaean style from Krete. Furtwängler and Löschcke Myk. Vasen. Pl. E, 11. Two lions heraldically arranged with the forelegs on a basis. A sun above.

4. Similar to 1. Pl. X, 13. Two animals fighting on each side of an object resembling an omphalos.

5. Gem in the Mykenaean style from Ialysos. Furtwängler and Löschke, Pl. E, 6. Two animals resembling dogs stand to the right and left of a burning pillar in an attitude resembling that of the lions on the fortress gate of Mykenae.

6 Gem in the Mykenaean style, now in the British Museum. Furtwängler and Löschcke, Pl. E, 13 Two goats in heraldic arrangement with the heads turned round.

7. = LXXVII, 13. = CXLII, 4. Gem in octagon form. Lajard "Culte de Mithra" XLIII, 26. Two winged lions join their fore-paws over an ashera; above this is a short Phoenician inscription; this was probably made in Kypros. Cf. p. 151.

8. The relief of the Lion Gate of Mykenae, given here for the sake of comparison with similar representations on the gems.

9. = LXXVIII, 18. = CXLII, 3. Kyprian scaraboid made of chalcedony. (Kurion?) Cesnola-Stern LXXXI, 23. Goats in a rampant attitude, the bodies turned outwards and the heads inwards. Leaves or shrubs between them. Cf. p. 151.

10. = LXXVIII, 3. Gem from Argos. Furtwängler and Löschcke, Pl. E, 16. Two goats springing up and butting each other; a shrub between them. Cf. p. 151.

11. = LXXVIII, 5. = Lajard, Mithra, XXVI, 26. A seal in the shape of an octagonal cone. On each side of a shrub are two lions rampant with the heads turned backwards. This, like Fig. 7, was probably made in Kypros. Cf. p. 151.

12. = LXXVIII, 9. = Lajard LVII, 9. Seal similar to the last, probably also from Kypros. Two griffins rampant, facing each other. If we compare these octagonal cone seals, 7, 11 and 12, of which one (7) bears a Phoenician inscription, with the Kyprian scaraboid (9), the bronze vessel (41) and analogous representations on other Kyprian gems and vases of clay and silver, we shall reach the conclusion that the former were also manufactured in Kypros. This result is confirmed by the discovery in Kypros of conical seals of a similar form. Particulars on p. 151. Cf. also C. W. King in Cesnola-Stern p. 342.

13 and 14. Unpublished gem and impression from the Berlin Museum. V. A. 2524. A yellowish stone in the form of a pyramid, through which a hole is bored. H. 0,02, breadth of the basis 0,014, height of the basis 0,018. Two goats stand upright on their hind legs on each side of a pillar crowned with flowers.

15. Conical seal in the Bibliothèque Nationale, Paris. Perrot III, p. 136. Two bearded sphinxes sit on either side of a small pillar over which are represented a globe and a winged sun disk.

16. = LXXVII, 19. Conical seal. Perrot III, p. 641, Fig. 435. Two goats are springing up to a pillar which ends in a kind of lotus flower. This pillar (like that in 13) resembles the pillars in the small dove-temple of Idalion, Pl. X, 3. which also appear on the bronze kylikes of Idalion, Pl. CXXX, 1 and of Olympia, CXXIX, 2. Cf. p. 151—152, 161, Note 1 and Pl. LXIX, 103.

17. Late Babylonian-Persian cylinder of the Berl. Mus. V. A. 512. A yellowish grey stone with white streaks H. 0,04. Dm. 0,014. Published for the first time from the plaster cast. Two bearded winged sphinxes in a rampant attitude on either side of the sacred tree, their heads turned round. Cf. p. 153—154.

18. Unpublished late Babylonian cylinder of the Berl. Mus. V. A. 2111. Lapis-lazuli. From Bagdad. H. 0,032, Dm. 0,014. Two scorpion-men grouped round a sacred pillar, over them the crescent of the moon. Cf. p. 151 and 296.

19. Gem in the Mykenaean style from Kypros. In Berlin (Coll. Cesnola). Furtwängler and Löschcke, Pl. E. 18. A bull. below and in front of him a branch, behind and over him a tree with foliage. Cf. p. 153.

20. Similar to 1. Tzuntas, Pl. X, 40. A lion tears an animal to pieces. To the right and behind the group a palm tree. Cf. p. 154.

21. Do. Pl. X, 39. Described on p. 153 and interpreted in connection with the Adonis festival.

22. Unpublished gem of scaraboid form. Berl. Mus. V. A. 1640. Variegated agate. Length 0,031, breadth 0,018, depth 0,009. From the plaster cast. Two fourfooted animals are lying couched facing on either side of a palm tree. Cf. p. 153.

23. Scarab from Ialysos (?) in the Brit. Mus. Furtwängler and Löschcke, Pl. E, 39. Tree between two oxen, under which is the svastika. The scarab form and the style of the star indicate, as in the former instance, a later Mykenaean period which influenced and was influenced by Graeco-Phoenician art. The frequent occurrence of the svastika in Kypros, the stone, No. 18, found in Kypros and other examples make it probable that the gem-cutters of Kypros had no little share in the development of engraving of this kind.

24. Unpublished conical gem of the Berl. Mus. V. A. 2520. Chalcedony. H. 0,023, Dm. 0,018. From the plaster cast. Two bearded winged sphinxes are seated on either side of the sacred palm. See Pl LXXVII, 20.

? 25. Graeco-Phoenician topaz scaraboid. About half as large again as the original. Excavated at Marion-Arsinoe in 1886.

The Kyprian boustrophedon inscription ἈριστοϜόναξ published by Deecke and Meister ("Griechische Dialekte" II. p. 176, No. 25 m). Drawn from the impression. A lion is tearing a four-footed animal to pieces. (A deer?) Found in the tomb of the sphinx, No. 140, necr. II; cf. the explanation and the account of the discovery belonging to Pl. XXVII, 1 and 2.

26 Carneol gem in the Mykenaean style from Athens. In Berlin. Furtwängler and Löschcke; Pl. E, 10. A lion tearing a stag.

No. 25 shows how the Kyprian gem-cutter of the 6th century worked with motives from Mykenae such as No. 26. Cf. No. 37.

27. Similar to 1. Tzuntas. Pl. X, 2. Two dolphins.

28. The same. X, 18. A lion seizing a bull by the neck.

? 29. Kyprian scarab from Karniol, from Marion-Arsinoë, excavated in 1886. Enlarged about a quarter from the original impression. A cow suckling a calf, behind them lotus or papyrus shrubs. Cf. p. 168, Note and p. 207 Note 2.

The tomb in which this scarab, and also the ornaments given on Pl. CLXXXII, 20, 21, 27 and 28 were found, is represented in outline and section on Pl. CLXXXIV, 3. This discovery, which also included a silver coin from the period of the first Ptolemies, considered in connection with what was not found on the site, make it quite certain that the tomb belongs to the second half of the fourth century. Nevertheless this scarab may be older than that date.

? 30. Do from the same nekropolis. Tomb 86, Nekr. II. Scarab from Karneol. Enlarged about a quarter from the original impression. A breakage in the centre is not shewn in the drawing. When this scarab was broken, the owner, who evidently prized it highly, had it enclosed in a perforated pale gold ring and set by a case of pale gold, so that only the surface actually used for sealing remained free. This metal casing follows the shape of the scarab.

A goat lying down. Graeco-Phoenician work of the 6th century. In the same tomb was found a good Greek archaic gem in the form of a flat scaraboid enclosed in a silver perforated ring, and showing an engraved representation of a nude female figure kneeling. The discovery in this tomb of black figured Attic clay vases, beautifully painted with subjects of horsemen, and other circumstances connected with the excavation, justify us in dating the tomb about the first half of the 6th century B. C.

?31. Engraving on the gold ring (represented on Pl. CLXXXII, 39) from the same nekropolis as 29—30. Tomb 98, Nekr. II. Enlarged rather more than a quarter. A nude human figure with outspread wings, holding a branch and a fillet.*)

Early Graeco-Phoenician-Kyprian work. This tomb, like the preceding, certainly belongs to the early part of the 6th century, as is proved by the Attic black figured vases found in it. The style of the work also corresponds exactly to that of the period in question.

?32. Also excavated at Marion-Arsinoë in 1886. Scarab from Carneol set in a very beautifully worked perforated gold ring. Enlarged about a third from the original impression. Now in the Coll. Konstantinides at Nicosia. A fabulous monster somewhat resembling a chimaera, a lion on the left, a boar on the right (?) This gold ring, which from its workmanship and the style of the stone within it must be ascribed to the 6th century. was stolen during the excavation by one of my workmen, and finally founds its way into the market at Nicosia.

33. An unpublished conical seal made of a translucent pale blue stone. V. A. 754. Berl. Mus. H. 0,028 m, Dm. 0,025 m. A scorpion-däemon described on p. 296.

34. Similar to 1. Tzuntas. Pl. X, 37. This representation is difficult to interpret. It is explained by Tzuntas as a pilos. In the centre is an object like an omphalos, from which two rams' horns grow out.

35. Upper part of a bronze pin, gilt, with a popular Greek inscription dedicating it to Aphrodite Paphia. From the famous temple-precinct at Old Paphos. Journal of Hellenic Studies 1888 Pl. XI, p. 222—223. Four goats heads grow out of acanthus leaves among blossoms. At the end is a large head of glazed clay, surmounted by a small bead.

36. = XCVI, 8 Cesnola-Stern Pl. LXV, = Perrot III p. 799, Fig. 564. The upper end of a bronze sceptre ending in three ox-heads. From Kurion. Cf. p. 201.

37. Chalcedony gem with a Kyprian inscription. Coll. Damicourt. Perrot III, p. 652, Fig. 462 A griffin tears a stag. Underneath is the head of a Gorgon.

38. Island-stone made of mountain crystal from Phigalia. In Berlin. Milchhöfer, "Die Anfänge der Kunst in Griechenland" p. 55, Fig. 44a. Two daemons similar to Fig. 1—2 stand upright on either side of a figure which is apparently human.

39. = XCVI, 7. From a larger Egyptian representation (Rosellini "Monumenti dell'Egitto" IV Pl. XLI, 1a). The four-headed ram, conceived of sometimes as a wind god, sometimes as a sun god.

40. Similar to 1. Tzuntas. X, 25. Four rams' heads.

It is evident that the gem-cutter of Mykenae imitated Egyptian models in his four sacred rams heads. Cf. 39. It was at this time that Peloponnesian Greeks emigrated to Egypt. Cf. p. 367.

41. = XCVI, 12. Cf. LXXVIII, 7 and CLVII, 4. Parts of a bron e vase from Kition. Perrot III, p. 795 Fig. 556 Two pairs of lion-daemons like Fig. 1, holding each an oinochoë. Three ox-heads, cf. p. 151 and 184. Note 11.

For images with three or four animals' heads, or with fabulous monsters and divinities four times repeated, see Fig. 35, 36, 39—41, and cf. Pl. XCVI.

Plate XXXIII.

1—5, 9—23. Kyprian antiquities either representing ornaments, or themselves showing ornamentation.

6—8. Illustrations of how modern Kyprian ornaments are worn.

24. From Riehm (Bibellexikon p. 387) reconstruction of the figure of a Jewish high priest with the ephod and the breastplate of Aaron and his sons. I discuss the breastplate on Pl. CXXXVIII and CXXXIX.

?1. Tammuz-Adonis temple attendant. Limestone figure about 0,25 m high.

This figure shows remains of red paint on the garment, lips and eye pupils. From the precinct of Apollo at Voni (I, 2). On the breast of the crouching boy hangs a three cornered amulet. Cf. 2, 5, 6 and 8 and p. 205 of the text. Cf. also p. 103 and for Figs. 1—5, cf. p. 74, 113, 204, 219 and 300. The original is well preserved, and is now in the Cyprus Museum at Nicosia. The collodium film on the stereotype-plate used for the illustration had a flaw on the left side.

?2. From the same excavation as 1. A similar limestone figure about 0,20 m high, the head missing, holding a dove in the right hand. On the breast the same amulet as in 1. Cf. also p. 111, 255, 271.

?3. = Pl. XCIII, 2. Found in the temenos of Aphrodite at Chytroi (No. 24 on the list) together with No. 4 and the representations of dances round the sacred tree, Pl. LXXVI, 3, 4, 7, 8, 10—12. While 1 and 2, like most Kyprian images, are finished flat at the back, this large limestone figure,

---

*) Cf. similar rings from the same nekropolis. Journal of Hellenic Studies. 1890. Pl. V. 9 and 10.

about 0,60—0,80 m high, is treated like a statue in the round, only the front side shows better workmanship. A boy's figure similar to the other (1 and 2) preserved in fragments. The figure wears a chain of seal-rings, with a centre piece representing a bearded head. Cf. 205 and 209.

? 4. Fragment of a similar smaller limestone figure, found with No. 3. The right hand holds a dove. A kind of square tassel ornament forms the centre-piece of the chain. Cf. p. 205.

5. Similar small stone figure, better preserved than 1 and 2, from the precinct of Apollo-Hylates (No. 48 on the list). From Cesnola's Atlas, Pl. CXXXII, Fig. 985. Cf. p. 205. For 1—5 cf. also Pl. XCII.

6—8. Kyprian girl from the village Politiko, rich ornaments on her neck and head. On her head is the dove shaped pin ($\tau\acute{o}$ $\pi\varepsilon\sigma\sigma o\acute{v}\nu\iota$) 7, on her breast the three-cornered amulet, 8.

For the last cf. 1, 2 and .5, for the first, the pin in the form of a dove, cf. Pl. CV, 2—4 and p. 280.

? 9—15. Gold ornaments all from the same tomb, No. 24, section I, Marion-Arsinoë.

Excavated March 5th 1886. This illustration only gives a very faint idea of these splendid ornaments, which are equal to the best Greek and Etruscan goldsmiths' work. Most of them are now in the possession of de Clercq (Paris). They belong to the end of the 5th or the beginning of the 4th century.[*])

9. Front view of one of the two bracelets, 0,073 m long, 0,012 m high, 0,061 m in diameter. Breadth of the opening 0,004 m. The other objects, 10—15 are given on the same scale. They are made of bronze thickly plated with gold, and are smooth within, but fluted on the outside. Their principal and most beautiful feature is the ornamentation of the clasp-shaped ends 0,018 m long. This ornamentation is carried out in granulated work, and a raised cellular pattern combined with enamel. The cells are formed of wires soldered on, and to these wires again are soldered small particles of metal which give them a granulated appearance. The cells are filled alternately with a glazed enamel in two shades of blue. The principal design consists of ornate stars framed in continuous spirals and egg-pattern.

10 11. Two small gold wheels, one front view, and one side-view. Diam. 0,024 m thickness 0,014 m. On Pl. CLXXXII, 48—52 five similar wheels made of gold and silver and found in the same nekropolis are represented.

These wheels are always found in pairs, and only with the corpses of women. It was not till 1889 that I discovered their meaning by examining a modern Kyprian loom. On the upper beam of the wooden frame of the loom two small wheels are fastened, through which run thin cords supporting the principal apparatus for holding the web. Without this pair of wooden wheels a Kyprian loom cannot work. These modern wheels of wood are very similar to the metal wheels excavated in the graves of Marion-Arsinoë, so that an illustration of the former, of which I possess several examples, is not necessary. Those of the ancient wheels, which are not ornamented, are as like the modern as one egg to another. Anyone who goes to Kypros may see them on the looms, or in the turners' shops in the streets. Just as the distaff and spindle were often buried with women in graves of the pre-Graeco-Phoenician Copper-Bronze Period (cf. Pl. CCXIII, 10—25) so from the 7th to the 4th century B. C. the custom of burying a pair of weavers' wheels in a woman's grave can be traced.

12 and 14. Two Karneol gems set in gold and hanging to gold rings, the larger in the form of a scaraboid, the smaller in the form of a scarab without an engraving.

13. A beautiful pendant shaped like a fruit, delicately and richly worked in a very finished style of granulation. It is formed of bronze plated thickly with gold, the upper end is broken, so that the bronze foundation (as in the bracelets) is visible.

15. This necklace, consisting of seventeen small chains of gold, surpasses all the other ornaments of the tomb. The small images which hang to the chains are formed of two stamped plates soldered to each other. Hence the representations are executed in the same manner on both sides.

On the seventeen small chains a lotus flower occurs once, a lotus bud twice, an ornament shaped somewhat like a bud five times, a winged sphinx once, a winged griffin once, a bearded mask twice, oval plates with a design representing the front view of an owl with outstretched legs and wings twice, and square plates, representing an owl in profile with very large eyes, three times. The latter example seems to point to a modification of the Egyptian Eye. There is a large plate of metal with an Eye shewing Egyptian influence in Tombs 181 and 205 of Nekropolis II. Pl. XXV, 7 LXVII, 12[**]). Cf. p. 208 and 210.

From these and other gold ornaments from engravings on Kyprian gold rings and from scarabs, either imported from Egypt or imitated in the Kyprian-Egyptian style, we must conclude that the Kyprians were very dependent on Egypt both with regard to technique and to the choice of subject. The Kyprian cellular enamel which often occurs in spirals (like XXXIII, 23) and ear-rings (like CLXXXII, 9) is borrowed from the Egyptian. p. 77 Fig. 104.[***])

---

*) Among the objects found were black-varnished Attic vessels with Graffiti in the Cypriote syllabary, which are a far surer criterion for fixing the date. The construction of the grave was peculiar. An irregular oblong, from 3,6 to 4,8 m. was dug to the depth of 2,9 m, in which two stone sarcophagi for two female corpses, had been placed. After the burial the grave was filled in again. One of the corpses had been plundered, the other not. On the latter a number of rich ornaments were found, of which I can only describe those represented here.

**) I am sorry to say that Herr Dümmler only restored to me at the beginning of November 1892 the full account of the excavations, the drawings, water colours and photographs which I had sent to him in 1886, and for which I had been asking for six years In fact I had given up as lost these materials, which I could not replace. If I had had them in my hands a year earlier, I could have accomplished my task better and given many other illustrations. As time now presses, I am obliged to leave much out of the explanations of the plates which I should have wished to insert. I cannot therefore add more details concerning the interesting contents of tomb 24. Necr. I and the circumstances of their discovery.

***) Up to the beginning of this century coloured cellular enamel was applied to ornaments of gold, silver and copper, and after that time the process fell into disuse. The prevailing colours were blue and brown, although others occur in exceptional cases. In 1890 it

How much the Assyrians learned from the Egyptians both in metal work and in ivory carving (Kyprian gold- and silver-smiths and ivory cutters being often the means of communication) is evident from the discoveries (cf. Pl. XC, 2, CXV, 4, CXVI, 5, CXXXI, 5 etc.). I have already shewn in speaking of the Kyprian silver vessels and the silver girdle from Marion-Arsinoë (Pl. XXV) how Assyrian motives found their way into Kyprian gold and silver technique.

? 16. Gold amulet formed like a tube, open on one side. Tomb 48 Necr. I in the same excavation as 9—15*). Technique the same as bracelet 9.

The same period as 9—15, end of the 5th or beginning of the 4th century B. C.

?17—20. = LXVII, 12. CXLIV, 2, 3, 5 and 17, also = p. 208, Fig. 171. Gold ornaments from the first half of the 6th century B. C. Tomb 131 Nekr. II of the same excavation as 9—16.**)

From the same tomb came the Attic clay vases represented on Pl. XC, 7 and the beautiful bronze candelabra-foot, in the form of a griffin's claw (Pl. CLXXVIII, 4). The same tomb also contained a very beautiful Greek bronze mirror with a palmette in purely Greek style on the handle, huge iron swords of the Kyprian type (like Pl. CXXXVII, 7 from Tamassos) and many other objects which shew Greek influence. This tomb belongs to that series, now considerable, which can be accurately dated at the beginning of the 6th century, and which manifestly belonged to the Kyprian Greeks. In Tomb 140 Necr. II (Pl. XXXII. 5) we saw a Kyprian Greek inscription written "boustrophedon".

? 21 - 23. From the same excavation II. These three articles of jewellery belong to a very rich mass of objects found with the skeleton of a woman in a niche of Tomb 88 Necr. II.

21. Sphinx of gold cut out of a piece of gold plate. H. 0.028 m. The face is pressed flat.***) At the back there is a small handle by which it was hung on a string or chain.

22. A calf-head of gold 0,018 m. long from the mouth to the end of the handle. The eyes are of glass, the pupils black with white edges.†) Cf. p. 208, 239, :43. Note 3.

From the objects found in this earth-grave, which was 4,82 m deep and 4,27 m broad, and consisted of four roughly made niches in the form of caves, it is evident that it was repeatedly used as a burial-place, first probably at the beginning of the 6th century, again early in the 5th, yet again early in the 4th century.

23. One of two spirals made of bronze plated with gold leaf, of which the front is shaped like a griffin's head, and the other end like a kind of flower-bud.

24. Jewish high priest with the breast plate, from Riehm's Bibellexikon p. 387. Cf. Pl. XXV remarks at the end, and Pl. CXXXVIII, CXXXIX and CXCIX.

Plates XXXIV, XXXV.

Parallels to be found in the customs, utensils, and apparatus of the ancient and modern population of Kypros.

XXXIV. 1, 5 and 6 Modern vessels shaped like gourds.

? 2, ? 3, ? 4. Antique clay vessels of the pre-Graeco-Phoenician Copper-Bronze Period. From the Necropolis of Hagia Paraskevi.

XXXV. 1, ? 2, ? 3, ? 5, ? 7, ? 9, ? 10. Antique clay vessels of the Pre-Graeco-Phoenician Copper-Bronze Period.

1. From Murray's "Handbook of Greek Archaeology" Pl. I, 15; 2, 3, 5, 7, 9, from Hagia Paraskevi, 10 from Tamassos.

4, 6. Modern imitations of straw plaiting.

8 Part of a modern wooden loom.

Cf. p. 127 and 275 and Pl. CCXIII, also my essay: "Parallelen in den Gebräuchen der Alten und der jetzigen Bevölkerung von Cypern". In the Verhandlungen der Berliner Anthropologischen Gesellschaft 1891 p. 34—44.

It is evident that the potters of the most ancient times applied to their vases and pots the shapes, decoration, and technique familiar to them on gourds, plaited straw and wood.

---

was through me that Herr Direktor Frauberger was enabled to acquire from the ecclesiastical authorities of the village of Millikuri, for his museum in Düsseldorf, a most interesting pair of clasps made of copper. They belonged to a priestly girdle, and are covered in large portions with this enamel in the brightest colours. At the present day the metal ornaments of the Kypriotes show in great part the antique shapes and styles of decoration, although these are sometimes overpowered and supplanted by later importations of Byzantine, Mediaeval, Gothic, Grotesque and Arabic-Turkish elements. We occasionally come upon a modern example executed in a purely antique style.

*) A similar amulet made of gold and shaped like a tube. from a grave of Marion-Arsinoë. Journal of Hellenic Studies XI (1890) Pl. V, 4.

**) I am sorry that in the present work I can give no fuller account of this tomb, which is so rich in discoveries and with reference to which I possess a detailed journal, plan. sections, drawings and photographs. A short abstract of the contents of this grave would fill a volume.

***) A similar sphinx in Cesnola-Stern Pl. LVIII, = Perrot III p. 830, Fig. 593. The English investigators, Tubbs and Munro, who followed on the track of my discoveries in Kypros, excavated after me in the nekropolis of Marion-Arsinoë, which I discovered, and found there two small gold figures of sphinxes. One of these is illustrated in the Journal of Hellenic Studies XI (1890) Pl. V, 7. It hangs on a chain. and recalls the links of the chain shown on Pl. XXXIII. 15. The second of these figures is in the J. H. S. XII, (1890) Pl. XV.

†) In the grave at Kurion in which I found the ornaments of hammered silver (one illustrated on Pl. XXV, 14), I also found a calf-head of about the same size made of coloured porcelain, the mouth gilt. These calf-heads should be compared with the calf or ox-heads which occur as centre-pieces of the chains worn by the large clay statues. (Pl. LIII, 19, 24 and 29).

††) The description of the excavation, although very important, must here be omitted.

The hand-made vase (XXXIV, 2) is formed principally of red varnished clay, but there is also some black varnish on the mouth, which on the neck of the vase shades off into the red. This technique is peculiar to many kylikes in the shape of a hemisphere (Pl. CLXIX, 8b). They are varnished red on the outside and black within, and the black varnish continues over the edge and shades off into the red. On this kind of vase (XXXIV, 2), which consists of a ball-shaped body with a straight thin neck widening towards the top, a handle does not occur, but instead two small holes are bored through the edge of the mouth. These vases occur very frequently in the Copper-Bronze period. A second example, which I found in a very early earth-grave, is given on Pl. CLXVIII, 2e. (For the illustration of the grave, see the same plate No. 2, outline and section). The shape is an exact imitation of the gourd bottle (XXXIV, 1) still used as a wine flask, one of which is in my possession.

Pl. XXXIV, 4 shows a peculiar shape of vase with a remarkably arched and curved neck and a handle resembling a string. The gourd-bottle XXXIV, 5 which is in my possession and which served as a powder flask such as the Kyprian hunters use, gives the key to this shape. The small thin handle of the bottle shows the origin of the clay handles twisted to imitate string. The V form of the small handle explains the origin of the corresponding double handle, which very early became a peculiarity of Kyprian pottery (see Pl. CLXVIII, 5g, h).*)

Pl. XXXIV, 3 = (CLXXI, 11 and 12b) represents a large hydria. It is evident that the potter placed small straps and strings round the neck, handle and body of the vase as if they were to be passed through wooden cross-pieces. The same arrangement is to be seen in the pottery of the present day.

The gourd-vase XXXIV, 6 (now in the Ethnographic division of the Royal and Imperial Court Museum at Vienna) was found by me hanging to the wooden beam, which formed the centre of the principal room in a peasant's house. It was used to keep the yeast for baking. Such modern gourd-vessels with four holes at equal distances for hanging up, and sometimes with a lid in addition, correspond to the ancient clay vessels with a cover (XXXV, 7, 2 and 5). The vase (XXXV, 7) which I excavated, was found in situ with the lid (XXXV, 5).

The modern gourd XXXIV, 6 resembles in shape a gourd cut off rather above the middle. This explains the kylikes of the same form both painted and unpainted, so frequent in the Copper-Bronze period, (see Pl. CLXIX, 8b, CLXXII, 16a, CLXXIII, 28c). The geometric style, which consisted of intaglio work and incised drawing, originated in the practice of ornamenting gourd vessels by carving the rind. The peasants are in the habit of filling up these designs in the bright yellow gourds with a pigment formed of soot, or gunpowder mixed with oil. Some very old gourd-vessels are of a deep red colour. Dust and lime stone get rubbed in to the cut designs, so that they stand out light on the dark background. The practice of covering clay vessels with a brilliant smooth varnish, and filling up the cut out portions with a white substance (see Pl. CCXVI), are also imitations of the treatment of gourd-vases. The Kypriote often squeezes his gourd-bottles by squeezing blue glass beads into the rind (e. g. XXXIV, 5). I excavated a clay vessel in Hagia Paraskevi, into which small bluish beads made of Agalmolite had been pressed into the clay before the firing.

Another important feature is shown in the ornaments carved in wood in the shape of concentric circles, fillets in relief, cross-bar, lunette ornaments &c. The huge milking dish (Pl. XXXV, 10) 0,315 m high and 0,535 m in diameter, now in the Antiquarium of the Royal Museum at Berlin, is an imitation of a wooden vessel. This is evident from the tube for pouring, the large clumsy handle opposite to it, the concentric circles stamped in, and the appliqué ornament in the shape of lunettes. The illustration above it, representing a piece of a peasant's chair (Fig. 8), shews workmanship and ornamentation similar to this vase, belonging to the period 1500—2000 B. C. Baskets and plates woven out of straw, palm leaves, and other materials gave the potter ideas for the creation of new forms and new ornaments. Pl. XXXV, 4 shews a plate made of woven wheat-straw, which I obtained from a peasant woman in Politiko, and which is now in my possession. Fig. 9, underneath it, represents a plate made of clay which I excavated at Hagia Paraskevi. About 2000 B. C. a potter must have pressed a straw plate into a clay plate, and then baked them both in the oven.***) The impression of the straw is only to be seen on the outside of the clay plate. Pl. XXXV, 6 shows a small basket woven of palm leaves, with a lid made to be tied on. Is it not at once evident that the vessels shaped like a foot with their lids (XXXV, 1 and 3 CLXXI, 11 and 12 i, CCXVI, 32) are imitations of such woven vessels? In the vases shewn on Pl. XXXV, 1 and 3 the whole weaving technique, consisting of horizontal layers of straw or leaves which are wound together, plaited or passed through from one side to the other, is reproduced in a design formed by incised lines.

Many shapes and decorations, which we now see to have been borrowed by the potters from the makers of gourd-vessels, have hitherto been held to be imitations of metal work. Those who held this opinion seem to have forgotten that many of these clay vessels are older than those made of metal, and that there was a fully developed geometric style consisting in hollowed ornament, before the first metal vessel was made, or even before the process of mingling copper with brass was invented.

---

*) Cf. F. Dümmler, "Mittheilungen" Athen XIII, p. 290.

**) Pl. XXXV, 7 and 5 = Pl. CLXXI, 14s = p. 31. Fig. 34s. For an exact description of the grave and its contents, among them a Babylonian-Assyrian cylinder with cuneiform inscription, see pp. 34 and 35. Cf. also Pl. CXLVII, 6a, the same Kyprian vase, with 5a from Hissarlik-Troy.

***) Professor Hitschfeld of Königsberg possesses a Dipylon vase which is formed of a small willow-woven basket, similar to those still used in Greece and Kypros, which has been pressed into a clay pot. In A. P. di cesnola, "Salaminia" p. 270, Fig. 263, is a representation in clay of one of the ordinary palm leaf baskets with a flask inside. (Bimbili).

Plate XXXVI.

1. Rude clay image supposed to be from Paphos (Coll. Cesnola) Berl. Mus. Antiquarium, T. C. 6688, 57. H. 0,185 m. The clay is greyish-brown, and is covered by a dull red slip.

The form still resembles a plank, but approaches the human shape. The face is rendered by a slight projection; holes are bored at the side for eyes; and the nostrils are shewn in the form of smaller holes made with some pointed object. A horizontal cut represents the mouth. There are clumsy vertical grooves in the cheeks. Instead of an ear is a kind of long projection (only preserved on the left side) with a hole bored underneath. The shoulders are very sloping, and there is no representation of arms. The trunk is unmodelled, and the legs hang stiffly down. Female breasts and the membrum virile shew that the being represented is of double sex.

To make the feet, the clay has been simply pressed somewhat closer together, while the toes are represented by four rough parallel grooves. A rudely executed groove also runs down the middle of the back. As both male and female organs are present, the figure probably represents a divinity of double sex.

For the divinity of double sex cf. p. 143, Note 2, 238, Note 2, 261, 297, 302, also Note 4.

‡ 2. Clay fragment in the form of a pinax, from Hagia Paraskevi. This pinax should be compared with fragment 9 on the same plate, which was subjected to a special examination. As far as the illustration can be understood, the surface of the pinax is divided into several portions by parallel and crossing lines, which, like those of the following objects, are incised. The various divisions are decorated with incisions in the form of eyes.

‡ 3a. Front view of a clay plank-shaped image, from the nekropolis at Lapiphos (Krini-karava, Kypros). Berl. Mus. Antiquarium, Misc. - Inv. 7, 8105, 14. H. 0,250 m. Br. 0,120 m. The illustration (Pl. LXXIV, 7) is from a drawing.

The clay, itself of a reddish colour, is covered with a red slip and varnished. The plank-like figure form is divided into three parts by two oblong holes. The upper part or head of the image, which is only 10 cm wide, shews on both sides large round perforations, whose meaning is obscure. At about the same height from the under edges of these holes, and in the middle of the surface, is a projection in the form of a cone about 1 cm high, on the sides of which small grooves are bored; while there is a horizontal cutting near its point. The signification of this projection is clear from a comparison with the clay image No. 1. It represents the face, the holes at the side are the eyes, the point is the nose, and the slit near it represents the mouth. The neck and the trunk seem to be connected by the three perpendicular divisions formed by the oblong holes. On the right and left, the divisions are representations of breasts, while beside these the figure widens, and forms projections which may be regarded as arm stumps. The lower part of the image is simply a flat plank only apparently divided.

The separate parts of the body are indicated by incised decoration. On the three divisions which run lengthwise a pattern of lozenges is applied, the inner drawing consisting of parallel hatched lines. The technique is very primitive. Under the right breast is a square mark, also hatched, whose surface is divided into two parts by a line through the centre. The lower part of the image shows two horizontal stripes ornamented with cross hatching, and under each of these there is a wavy incised line.

3b. Back view of the same image.

The surface is here smoother and more even than in front. The upper part or head is adorned by three slanting rows of lozenge-pattern, which probably are intended to represent hair. As in front, the perpendicular stripes at the back are filled up with lozenge-pattern; only below the holes the patterns, which run downwards are connected by horizontal waved lines. The lower part also shows two horizontal stripes, but without the waved lines. Cf. p. 107—108, 240, 263, 265.

‡ 4a. Plank-shaped image of clay from the same nekropolis as No. 3. Berl. Mus. Antiquarium. Misc.-Inv. 8105,16. H. 0,264 m Br. 0,11 m. Technique is the same as in No. 3. The head is missing. It was formerly joined to the upper end, where a small bored hole is still visible at the edge. On the upper horizontal division are no traces of a projection. But in the centre of the two perpendicular divisions projections are found. They may represent the nose or the breast according as the image represented a single or a double form. Projections at the sides of the trunk are probably stumps of arms, as in No. 2. The decoration is formed of incised lines. The upper holes are connected by horizontal groups of strokes in the shape of ∧, and by stripes with a pattern in lines. On the two perpendicular divisions are small groups of horizontal parallel strokes. Between the projections are also curved strokes. On the part broken off there is a horizontal stripe. On the trunk are to be seen circles which touch each other, and which are continued in a slanting direction from the shoulders to the waist. They may represent some kind of garment, possibly a cloak. The decoration finishes in several horizontal stripes filled up with strokes.

4b. The back of this figure is noticeable because in both parts of the head the hair is indicated by long rows of zigzags. The trunk is distinguished by several groups of small horizontal strokes to which the horizontal stripes form a continuation.

If we are right in supposing that the slanting lines and stripes on the trunk represent a cloak, we must also suppose that the projections are intended for a face. In that case the image would be a double one, with two heads and one body. Hence on p. 261 it is placed with No. 1 as a divinity of double sex. Cf. No 10 and p. 143, Note 2, 238, Note 2 (for 1, 6, 11 and 12, read 1, 4a and b, 10), 240, 265, 297.

5. = CCXVI, 8. Horned animal from Hagia Paraskevi. Formerly in the possession of Major Seager.

The clay is red, varnished and decorated with concentric circles, filled out with a white substance. The technique is the same as in the plank-images. Cf. p. 240, but the illustration on Pl. CCXVI, 8 is much better.

6. = CCXVI, 27 oinochoë with handles and the figure of a woman, nude, seated on the shoulder. From Kypros. Berl. Mus. Antiquarium. Vas.-Inv. 3197 (from the Coll. Gréau. Cat. No. 22) H. 0,182 m.

The shape is similar to that of a wine-bag with a short neck and a beak-shaped spout. The origin of this shape is a pair of vases together, such as are found in the Trojan and Kyprian pottery. In the present vase one of the necks has been supplanted by the female figure. This figure is independent of the painted ornamentation of the vase, which is continued over her body. The figure is very roughly executed, the face being indicated by the usual projection with two holes for eyes and no mouth. At the back, wavy lines on the head represent the hair. The breasts are strongly marked. The left arm is shaped like a bow, is placed on the breast and is painted. The right arm is broken where it joins the body. Both arms were made separately and joined on. The legs hang down from the shoulder of the vase, and the toes are indicated by incised lines. In shape and technique this figure resembles the rude clay idol No. 1.

The design consists of straight lines and wavy lines combined in various groups, which divide the surface of the vase into stripes and lozenges. Cf. p. 265.

† 7. Head of a stag (clay) from Hagia Paraskevi. Now in the Museum at Karlsruhe. Clay and technique are the same as in the plank images. The antlers, 0,010 m thick are covered with a pattern of incised lines. The head is represented by a projection in the round raised about 0,032 m above the back. Nostrils are indicated in front, and on each side are large eyes. The stag is about 0,064 m wide. It is hollow inside. The stag either formed a vase or was applied as ornament to a vase. The round hole in front of the neck served as a spout. The height of the whole fragment is 0,166 m.

Repeated on Pl. CXLIX, 9.

† 8. Upper part of a plank image from Hagia Paraskevi. Head, neck and breast are preserved. Holes are bored at the corners of the upper edge as in Nos. 3 and 4.

Under these in the centre is a projection for the face with two holes bored below it, which probably represent the nostrils The neck and breast are adorned with engraved lines, and female breasts are represented. The size may be reckoned from No. 9, which was photographed with it; cf. p. 265.

† Clay fragment in the form of a pinax from Hagia Paraskevi. In my possession. H. 0,137 m. B. 0,113 m.

This fragment must be interpreted like No. 2. The surface is divided into several portions by means of horizontal stripes, which are decorated with an incised pattern resembling eyes. At the upper edge between the two eye-shaped ornaments is a projection with a concave upper surface, of which the edges are broken. It is probably part of a small vase. Fragment No. 2 shows the same projections, but the illustration does not reproduce them clearly. At the lower and upper edges between the so-called eyes traces of them may be seen. The back of No. 9 also shows horizontal stripes, but the eyes are lacking.

As to the meaning of the two fragments (2 and 9), those projections, which resemble bowls, lead us to suppose that they were vessels of some kind. Their technique brings them into connection with the vases with incised ornaments, and the fragments perhaps belong to the lids of such vessels. If so, the vessels were probably cask-shaped, and had flat covers. Examples of these are given on Pl. CXLIX, 1, CLXXI, 11 and 12i. The small bowl-shaped projections may have served as handles, and have their analogies in the drinking-cups and goblets on p. 275, Fig. 181, 182, 185, 186.

† 10. Clay plank-image (front view) from the same nekropolis as Nos. 3 and 4. Berl. Mus. Antiquarium. Misc.-Inv. 8015, 15, H. 0,280 m, Br. 0,140 m.

The technique is the same as in the other images. The clay is more grey than red. This image certainly represents a double figure, but the upper part of one is broken away. On the inner side of the figure which remains (11 or 12 cm long), and on the upper edge, is a breakage, which shows that a cross bar connected the two upper parts. But this connecting portion was not an essential part of the design, as in No. 3, where it formed the head of a single figure. For the faces properly so called are placed below this cross-beam on the perpendicular divisions, and the holes which are bored through the flat portion are not found on the upper edge as in Nos. 3, 4 and 8, but on two projections at the sides of the perpendicular divisions. This shows that they cannot have been holes for hanging the image up, and a comparison with image No. 1 makes it evident that these holes are where the ears usually are. The projections must therefore represent ears, although the prominence for the nose and the holes representing eyes are found at some distance below. There is no indication of a mouth.

The ornamentation consists of incised lines. The upper edge shows a pattern in strokes of $\wedge$ form, which was probably continued over the cross beam. The head is crowned with a horizontal stripe shewing cross lines. A similar stripe passes between the ears. Then follow groups of small horizontal strokes. From the nose to the trunk runs a vertical stripe with pierced dots at both sides. The ornamentation of the trunk begins with three horizontal stripes, which are continued over the whole length of the image. Then the division into two begins again, the breast being adorned on the right with a curved ornament and on the left with an angular one composed of stripes. These evidently represent jewellery. Between them are four circular grooves in the surface to indicate the four breasts of the double shape. The trunk under the breast is filled up with various groups of patterns in stripes. From each shoulder a stripe runs slanting downwards towards the middle, and at the ends of these are seen three circular grooves. These marks certainly represent the arms and hands (cf. Pl. LXXXVI, 4, 6, 7). The under part of the trunk shows three horizontal stripes close together and separated into lozenges by groups of vertical strokes. We have here as in No. 4. a double figure with two heads and one body. The double character is shewn clearly in the region of the breast. Cf. Nos. 1 and 4 on the same plate. The engraving of incised lines is in this example much less aimless and is evidently intended to emphasize the separate parts of the body. The back, here not illustrated, corresponds to the front. The hair is indicated by two rows of zigzags. A vertical central line with eight small parallel strokes at the end divides the body into two parts, each of which is separately engraved, while the lower part of the body is distinguished by a row of zigzags bordered by a series of double strokes (cf. p. 148 Note 2, 288 Note 2, 261 297. (1—10 H. S.)

For the plank images cf. p. 83 Figs. 29 and 30. The large holes in the clay plank image, here fully described, evidently served the same practical purpose as in No. 3, i. e. to hang up the images which could not be set up. See also terra-cotta group on Pl XXXVIII, 6 = CCV, 3, the clay idol of Amathus*) published by Froehner in the Katalog Hoffmann, Paris 1891, 15 and 16 June 1891, Pl. II. On Pl. XXXIV, 2 we saw an example of two holes in a vase serving the same purpose**) (cf. also Pl. CXIX, 3).***)

If Pinches is even approximately correct in his dating of King Sargon I, the beginning of the appearance of the Kyprian clay plank images must be as early as the beginning of the 4th millennium B. C. Cf. p. 83 Fig. 111.†) It is true that the plank images were manufactured also in the second half of the Copper-Bronze period, i. e. the true Bronze Period. The plank image on p. 33, Fig 29 (= CLXXIII 20 and 21†) was found by me at Phoenidschaes in 1883 with the other objects illustrated on Pl. CLXXIII, 20 and 21, where two of the tombs are given in ground-plan and section. The two vases given on Pl. CLII, 8 a Mykenae vase to the right and a Kyprian vase made of clay like that of the Dipylon pottery to the left come from the same series of tombs. Hence this plank image is much more recent. The image itself shows very distinctly that it is a modification of the early plank image type, and belongs to about the middle of the 2nd millennium B. C., the whole conception execution and style of the image showing a definite advance. The material too is different, a dull rough grey having replaced the red varnished clay. One step farther and we come to the rude image in the round of Artemis-Kybele (Pl. CCXII, 6 and 7).

Plate XXXVII.

1—9. Development of of the type of the mother goddess out of which arises the Aphrodite *Κουροτρόφος*.

I shall speak briefly of the nine illustrations in the order of their development, 7, 6, 3, 9, 2, 1, 8, 4 and 5, and for further particulars I refer the reader to pp. 202—204

? 7. A red varnished clay image about 0,10 m high from Hagia Paraskevi now in the Museum at Karlsruhe. The mother, who is draped, holds the child in swaddling bands. A corner of the pillow on which the child's head rests has been broken since the discovery. The artist could only use a photograph which did not reproduce completely the head of child which was formed like the head of the mother. Cf. also p. 241 263, 265.

? 6. An image about 0,20 m high described on p. 203, from Hagia Paraskevi. From the collection of C. Watkins Larnaka. A very similar one is in the Louvre, see Heuzey, "Figurines antiques de terre cuite du Louvre." Pl. IV, 5 (cf. also p. 148, 264, 265).

? 3. = Pl. LI, 9 where it is exactly described. From the Astarte-Aphrodite sanctuary. No. 3 on the list.

9. Clay figure from Dali 0,18 m high, painted black. This figure, like the former, illustrates the "snowman technique" and ends in a spreading conical foot. Heuzey, "Figurines antiques" Pl. IX, 2 = Perrot III, p. 553 Fig. 376. It is doubtful whether this figure, which represents a mother, holding in her left arm a child which she is suckling and with the right hand balancing a vase on her head, represents a goddess or a mortal. In my opinion it is a goddess. A similar clay figure better executed which represents the goddess holding the pitcher on her head with both hands and shows the svastika occurring four times on her body, is to be found in Cesnola-Stern Pl. LXIX, 1) ††)

2. A clay figure 0,18 m high from sanctuary of Astarte-Aphrodite not yet identified, near the Salt Lake (not the Artemis-Paralia temenos No. 7 of the list). In the Kyprian Egyptian style.†††) Our illustration is somewhat imperfect. Heuzey, "Figurines", VI, 6 = Perrot, III p. 202. Fig. 144. A very similar figure found at the same place is in the Antiquarium of the Royal Museum at Berlin, T. C. 6289,

---

*) Now in the Louvre. Fröhner gives Kypros as the provenance. I discovered the real provenance by communication with those who excavated in secret and sold the remarkable statuette to a merchant in Limassol, through whose means it was brought to Paris.

**) The Kypriotes are still in the habit of hanging up all their household vessels, such as bottles &c. by strings or ribbons on the walls of their houses.

***) In Kyprian-Graeco-Phoenician plates without handles it is not unusual to find two holes for hanging up.

†) Further excavations in the burial places of the Copper-Bronze period in Kypros are much to be desired.

††) Cf. my Essay on "La Croix gammée et la croix cantonnée à Chypre" (Bulletin de la Société d'Anthropologie de Paris 1888 p. 669—680.)

†††) The type shown in 3 and 4 may be partly contemporaneous with this, which shows Egyptian influence, but it is certainly partly older, as is proved on p. 203, where I showed also that the type shewing Egyptian influence was older than the so-called "snowman technique".

from the Coll. Pierides. In 1879 I called attention to nine similar statuettes about 0,20 m high in the chamber for votive offerings of the Astarte-Mikal sanctuary on the acropolis of Kition (No. 9 on the list Pl. CCI, in the space to the right of S.) They had been set up along with other votive gifts, e. g. images of cow-heads (Pl. XCIV, 4).*)

1 and 8. represent a limestone type which exists contemporaneously with the clay "snowman type". 1 is more Phoenician, 8 more archaic Greek.

1. The artist's illustration is more beautiful than the orginal, Perrot's rendering (III p. 554, Fig. 377) from which this is taken, is more faithful. Kyprian limestone statuette, now in New-York.

? 8. A limestone statuette found in 1886 by me at Marion-Arsinoe in a tomb which can be exactly dated in the first half of the 6ᵗʰ century B. C. Its style resembles that of the preceding. The upper part of the child is broken off. Hitherto this type has occurred most frequently in Idalion on the hill west of the town. (No. 33 on the list).

4. A limestone group 1,117 m high in its present condition. From the Astarte-Aphrodite sanctuary on the eastern Acropolis of Idalion (No. 29 on the list). There are remains of a red colour. In front of the stand was written in colours an inscription, either Phoenician or bilingual Phoenician-Kyprian. Of this inscription unfortunately there are very few traces. In spite of the stiffness we see an advance and can trace Greek influence much more strongly tham in the preceding figure. This was found with the capitals LVIII and LIX, 1 p. 231 (cf. "The Owl", No. 8, Pl. V).

5. = CCV, 5 where it is fully described. This terra-cotta fragment belongs to the purely Greek style of the 4ᵗʰ century. It comes either from the Artemis-Paralia sanctuary on the Salt Lake near Kition (No. 7 on the list) or from the neighbouring necropolis which belonged to this sanctuary. Cf. Pl. CCV, 4, 7 - 9.

Plate XXXVIII.

1 and 2. Two small pieces of beaten gold from Delos. Berl. Mus. Antiquarium M. J. 3473, 3474. Both are published and discussed by Furtwängler Arch. Ztg. 1884 p. 111 Pl. IX, 11, 12. Both are made of beaten yellow gold the heads are embossed. Details are given by means of fine grains soldered on, a process which reached the highest point of perfection among the Etruscans. The rosettes in the form of stars are made separately and fastened on, so are the edges, which consist of fine wire. No. 1 belongs to a pendant as is shewn by a small ring for hanging. remains of a small chain on the lower edge and a tassel hidden as the back. With this should be compared the magnificent pendants from the oldest part of the necropolis of Kamiros in the Rev. Arch. 1863 VIII N. S. Pl. X. No. 2 is a link of a chain somewhat like No. 18 of the same Plate which is associated with it. = Pl. XXV, 7. Both represent the female mask in Egyptian style which occurs so frequently and which in later times was supplanted by the Gorgoneion. Cf. Furtwängler. Bronzefunde von Olympia p. 71 and p. 208 of the present work.

? 3. Fragment of terra-cotta. See Pl. LII, 19; cf. p. 278.

? 4. Do. See Pl. LII, 15. Cf. p. 231 and 278

? 5. Reconstruction of a diadem from the fragment Pl. LII, 12; cf. p. 278.

6. Group in terra-cotta. See Pl. CCV, 3; p. 314.

7. Group in terra-cotta; see Pl. CCV, 1; cf. p. 315.

8. = CV, 6 Façade of a small temple of beaten gold in the original size, from Mykenae. From Schliemann, Mykenae p 306, Fig. 423. This is generally supposed to be the temple of the Kyprian Aphrodite, coins of Paphos of the Imperial period should be compared with it (Perrot and Chipiez III, 120, Fig. 156. The objects which are visible in the three openings have hitherto not been satisfactorily explained. They cannot be pillars (as von Luschan lately proved in the Zeitschrift für Ethnologie 1892 p. 207) because they have no basis or connection with the ground whatever. Cf. also Schuchhardt, Schliemanns Ausgrabungen 2ⁿᵈ Ed. p. 232, Fig. 191 (cf. p. 179 and 277).

9. = CV, 3 = Fig. 201, p. 291. Small figure made of beaten gold with perforations for sewing it on to a garment. From Mykenae. See Schliemann, Mykenae p. 209, Fig. 267. This is one of the oldest types of Aphrodite. Cf. Furtwängler in Roscher Myth. Lex. I, 407. Schuchhardt, Ausgrabungen Schliemanns p. 230, Fig. 188. Helbig, Hom. Ep² p. 33, Fig. 3 also p. 279f, and p. 292 of the present work.

10. = CV, 2. Small figure of beaten gold found at Mykenae. From Schliemann, Mykenae p. 209, Fig. 268. The type is similar to the preceding, but besides the dove on the head there are two fastened to the elbows. There are no perforations. Schliemann says that the figure with small pegs or nails the heads of which are to be seen on the trunk and between the legs, was not intended like the preceding figure to be fastened to a garment. Schuchhardt, on the other hand, maintains (Schliemanns Ausgrabungen p. 231, Fig. 189) that the figure consists of two pieces of beaten gold worked in the same

*) Cf. my essay "Die Akropolis von Kition und das Heiligthum der Syrischen Astarte" in Ausland 1879 p. 970. S. Reinach Chroniques d'Orient p. 176 [3,2, 946], see p. 12. Henzey Pl. VI, 1—4, gives an illustration of four terra-cottas of the same style from Phoenicia. Until we have further information from excavations in Phoenicia, we must assume that the few figures found there were imports made in Kition.

manner and held together by two rivets. He therefore supposes that the figure formed the end of a hairpin. This opinion seems to me to be founded on a mistake; cf. p. 278f.

° 11 = CXXVI, 1. Clay fragment from the precinct of Astarte-Aphrodite at Dali (No. 3 on the list). Berl. Mus. Antiquarium M. J. 8015, 240. This is the corner of some object shaped like a box, and edged with a battlemented pattern. The sides are perforated. At the corner are some fragments of a dove, the head missing. H. 0,110. Evidently a fragment of a pigeon-house. See p. 272, 277, 278, 291.

‡ 12. = Pl. XVII, 2, 3 (with explanation) = p. 278, Fig. 187, 188; cf. p. 164 ff.

13. = Pl. X, 3 = CIX, 3 = CXXIV, 5 from Perrot Chiepiez III, 277, Fig. 208.

Inside the shrine at the door stands a composite monster, which has the body of a bird and the breast and head of a woman. Similar heads are looking out of the small windows in the sides of the shrine. These details can be better seen in Heuzey's illustration, "Terre cuites du Louvre". Pl. 9 no. 6. H. 0,210 m. Br. 0,200 m cf. p. 278.

14. = CLVIII, 4 Group of two enthroned goddesses from Caere. Berl. Mus. Antiquarium. T. C. 8218. Published by Furtwängler, Jahrb. des Arch. Inst. 1891. VI. Anzeiger p. 119 f. The group comes from a large series of votive terra-cottas said to have been found at Caere. The two goddesses are similar; each holds in her right hand a drinking cup. On the right stands an altar, behind which a palm is seen; on the left below, a deer. On the left above floats an unwinged boy, holding in his right hand an alabastron in and his left the mantle of the goddess. Cf. p. 316.

‡ 15. Part of a crown (clay) from a head found at Achna. In the Louvre. Cf. Pl. LXVIII, 6.

It belonged to the head (Pl. LXVIII, 6), which is given in profile in Pl. CCIX, 8. This head bears a close analogy to the fragmentary head in Pl. CCIX, 7 (London Brit. Mus.). The decoration of the crown is very peculiar; it consists of alternate lotus blossoms and eagles with outspread wings: these last are very indistinct in the reproduction. Specimens of similar work are to be found in Cesnola, "Salaminia" p. 223, Fig. 213, p. 224, Fig. 214. Crowns of this pattern are peculiar to Artemis, cf. Text pp. 267 and 308.

? 16. Terra-cotta mask (clay) cf. LIII, 6 from the Sanctuary of Astarte-Aphrodite, No. 3 in the list.

? 17. Lion couchant. v. Pl. LIII, 5, same provenance.

? 18. Gold ornament of Egyptian style v. Pl. XXV, 7.

? 19. Ornamental portions of a Sarcophagus (terra-cotta) from Marion-Arsinoé. Heads of oxen and heads of the Bes type cf. Text p. 209, 219, 239.

? 20. Terra-cotta fragment v. Pl. LIII, 39, from the Sanctuary of Astarte-Aphrodite No. 3 in the list.

(1—20 H. S.)

The plates were first arranged on the principle of the similarity of the ornamental objects. Next I wished to show how in the ornaments for the breast and in the necklaces as well as in the crowns, frequently the same heads, (1 & 19, 20) figures (2, 5) and animals (3, 10—15) are repeated, or different heads, figures or animals alternate either among themselves or with other objects. I wanted to demonstrate how in fact doves are a favourite subject for the head-gear of Astarte or her priestesses (9, 10, cf. Pl. XXXIII, 6, 7) or how, on the crowns of the priestesses, there often occur rows of miniature images of Astarte herself. Moreover I wanted further to show that doves and dovecots uniformly belong to the cultus and to the sanctuaries of Astarte-Aphrodite (8, 12, 13) cf. p. 275, 278, 284. Again, attention had to be drawn to Bes-Ptah-Patäke as paredros of the Cyprian Astarte-Aphrodite (cf. Pl. CI, 4) cf. also p. 209, 219. On the crowns of the Astarte priestesses are ranged small Bes heads (16), or groups of them (20).

In contrast to this, the crowns of the priestesses of Artemis-Kybele are decorated with rows of vultures alternating with lotus blossoms (cf. p. 308).

Finally, it seemed to me desirable, to facilitate a condensed view of the whole in the case of those representations of the same type which are repeated several times close together, to place certain pairs of gods side by side, two from Kition (6 & 7) and one from Caere (14). While, without more exact information as to provenance, it is doubtful in the case of group 6 whether it belongs to the cult of Aphrodite or of Artemis, it is evident that in the other two groups (7 Kition and 14 Caere), we have Demeter and Persephone. These groups, which abound alike in Cyprus and Etruria, occur in the island only in the sanctuary of Artemis-Paralia. Demeter and Persephone, to whom Kybele allies herself, there became fused with Artemis. In the text p. 252—256, in discussing the Tanit-Artemis-Kybele cult, I have spoken of this before and referred to the relation with Etruria. It seems that this type of the pair of goddesses passed with many another thing from Cyprus to Etruria, but not vice versa.

Plate XXXIX.

1. Egyptian relief from the Berlin Museum. Egyptian Department 7322.

Fragment of the wall of a grave published for the first time. Nicai, priest of Sechmet, kneels before a palm, from which the goddess Nut pours down upon him water and food 1400—1150 B. C.

Nothig of the goddess is to be seen except a human arm, which grows out of the palm; cf. Pl. LXXI 2 v. p. 104, note 2.

2. Egyptian throne of bronze supported by two lions, published for the first time. On the arms stand two winged figures. Discussed under Plate CXXXVIII.

3 & 3a, = p. 293, Fig. 212 & 212a — front and back view of bronze winged figures, from Olympia. A. Furtwängler, "Olympia" IV. No. 783 & 783a, cf. above p. 297.

4. Egyptian wood tablet. Berlin Museum, Egyptian Department — belongs to the period 600 — 300 B. C. Can however still be Saite. Above is seated the soul of Osiris.

The vase painters who worked at Naukratis and other Greek colonies seem early to have made use of the representation of the soul of Osiris for their representations of Harpies, Sirens and the like. When the custom set in of depicting these Greek fabulous creatures in sculpture, the artists who were at work in Cyprus seem by dint of further utilizing Egyptian models to have substantially aided that development of types, cf. p. 292 ff, and Fig. 205—218, Pl. CVI, CIX & CX. By means of Greek artists in Egypt, Cyprus, Rhodes, and Asia Minor these fabulous creatures, half bird half human, passed into the art of the mainland of Greece.

Plate XL—XLII.

With the exception of XL, 8 all these are from the Temenos at Voni, known from inscriptions to belong to Apollo (I, 2).

XL, 8. Votive arm in terra-cotta. From a grave at Hagia Paraskevi. Berlin Museum Antiquarium. Made of red terra-cotta with a fine glaze. The arm, in the form of a tube closed at the lower end, terminates in a very rudely modelled hand, which holds a cup-shaped vessel. As this vessel has a hole at the bottom which is connected with the hollow channel in the arm, it has been thought that this curious and rare object was a vessel for incense. This is the only instance so far known of an attempt made during the copper-bronze period to model a portion of the human body in dimensions of large size.

XL, 6 and 7. Votive arm in calcareous stone from the sanctuary of Apollo at Voni (L, 2).

No. 6 holds the incense box, No. 7, a round apple. As these arms are rounded off at the upper part, they have never belonged to statues, but must have been modelled as votive offerings.

XL, 1—5. Statues of calcareous stone, full life-size, described p. 266—267 and 330—331, cf. p. 113, 114, 227, 271 and 254—255.

Cf. also my report III, Sanctuary of Apollo at Voni, Mittheilungen des Kaiserl. Deutschen Archäologischen Instituts, Athen 1884, p. 133—135, No. 10. 11 and 14. Statue of Apollo or of a priest of Apollo (3), head of the same, full face and profile Pl. CCXV 4a and b. Statues of a divinity compounded of Apollo and Zeus (1 = 2, 4 = 5).

XLI, 1—9. These nine statues I describe in the following order 5, 6, 4, 2, 7, 1, 3, 8, 9.

5. Belongs to that class of sculpture of mixed Cypriot and Egyptian style in which the proportions of the body are excessively long. The figure is over nine head-lengths. Both arms hang straight down at the side of the body without holding anything. Described fully in the Mittheilungen p. 129.

6. Mittheilungen p. 130, 3.

4. Mittheilungen p. 130, 2. Whereas in 5 and 6 the intention was only to represent one closely clinging garment, here an over-garment is added. The head also is better executed, and shows more Greek influence. Otherwise the treatment is the same; the body is only slightly rounded in front, at the back it is perfectly flat in one vertical plane.

2. Mittheilungen p. 132, 7. A priest wearing a crown and shirt-like garment of fine stuff which falls in small crinkled folds; he holds a dove and an incense box. Cf. above p. 328 ff. This figure had been broken and roughly repaired before its discovery in modern times. A piece of stone had been inserted at the breakage, and left without any modelling, and the red colour (invisible in the Plate), carried over the broken place.

7. Headless statuette of priest with dove and incense box in similar attitude. The figure again of excessively long proportions. Over the under-garment, which falls in long vertical folds, an over-garment is passed several times. Execution careless.

1. A priest wearing crown with same attributes as 2 and 7 (Mittheilungen p. 132, 8). Over the shirt crinkled as in 2 an over-garment is arranged, falling from the left shoulder. Ample remains of red colouring.

3. A priest wearing crown and shirt-like garment, as in 2, with incense-box and palm-sprig (Mittheilungen p. 132 and 133, 9).

8. Statue of Apollo fully life-size, with the Adonis as child by his side. Greek work. The boy Adonis is completely wrapped in a garment with many folds; the head is missing. The head of Apollo was found separate from the torso in a damaged condition. Cf. p. 206, 255 note 1 and 271.

9. Bearded priest wearing crown, with dove. Style mixed Cypriot and Graeco-Phoenician. Head full size on Pl. CCXV, 1.

XLII, 1—8. Eight more pieces of sculpture.

1 and 2. Greek style. Statues of Apollo with fawn or young roe. (Mittheilungen p. 134, 12 and 13, cf. p. 254, 266, 271, 330—331).

3. Statuette of flute player. Head with face and ears like a satyr. The double-flute is held in front of the body, which consists of a thin flat slab slightly convex to the front, but without modelling (like XLI, 4—6). The over-garment coloured red.

4. Statuette showing increase of Greek influence. Broken off at the arms. The priest, of Graeco-Phoenician style (Pl. XLI, 3), shows more freedom in the expression of movement by the advance of the right leg. Here the left leg is advanced and in a freer, more natural fashion. The modelling of face and head, the angle of the technique of the eyes and hair show more decided Greek influence. (Cf. the archaic Greek head from the same excavations Pl. CCXV, 2a, and 2b).

5. Statuette of Herakles, late Greek, roughly executed. The garment (or skin) is knotted over the breast and thrown back, leaving the nude figure exposed. With the right hand he leans with his club on the ground. The left holds a cornucopia (indistinct). He wears the lion-skin on his head.

6. A player on the double flute. The customary Cyprus type style copied from the Egyptian, with the Egyptian head-cloth and close clinging short sleeved garment. The body is stiff and meagre, flat behind, carved in front (like Pl. XLI, 4—6).

7. Statuette of priest wearing crown, holding in right hand incense-box, in the left lustration-twig (cf. p. 328). Over the finely folded under-garment hangs an over-garment similar to that in 4. Style also Greek, but less pure than and inferior to 4. 8a and 8b. Torso, or an archaic statue of mixed Greek and Cypriot style. with upper and under garment similar to 4. The left hand hangs down and is broken off. It holds a tablet with Cypriot inscription which is preserved and is given enlarged in 8b Cf. p 5 and 184 also Mittheilungen 1884, p. 188, 9 and R. Meister, "Die Griechischen Dialekte" II, p. 169 14c &c. Meister gives the inscription as follows.

Γλ(λ)ίκα ἀμὲ | κὰτ ἔστασι | ὁ Στασικ | ϱέτεος

A number of other heads of various styles, among them some Roman ones, and all of the same provenance, are given in Pl. CCXV, and on plate V the ground plan of the sanctuary and perspective view of the place of excavation.

Plate XLIII.

† 1. Bronze bull from the grove of Apollo at Limniti No 52 in the list. Obtained by Ohnefalsch-Richter. Berlin Mus. Antiquarium T. C. 8211, 163.

The two forelegs are for the most part broken off: also the front part of the muzzle. Within the core for casting is still preserved. Cf. Text p. 176, 240, 243.

2. Primitive bronze horse from Paraskevi. Obtained by Ohnefalsch-Richter. Berl. Mus. Antiquarium M. J. 8105.

The body of the horse is not fully cast, but shaped like a bent plate. The legs also have been cast plate-fashion. On the back is a round hole about the size of a pea. Small depressions in the upper part of the head serve as eyes. The muzzle is beak shaped. Cf. p. 189.

3. Two small figures on a bronze basis from Karpaso. The arms hang down. The modelling of the faces very rude. A pointed cap serves as headgear. On the back of each of the figures is an eyelet with a hole.

These figures have been published and discussed by Furtwängler in the Jahrb. des arch. Inst. 1890, V, Anzeiger p. 91. He considered them to be "two daemonic figures of the type that later developed into the Dioscuri."

4. Primitive bronze figure from Tamassos. Obtained by Ohnefalsch-Richter. Found in the river Pidias near to the Temenos of Apollo (No. 6 in the list). Berl. Mus. Antiquarium. M. J. 8105.

The figure is male and nude. The left arm broken off. The right holds a small axe against the shoulder. The penis is erect but close to the body; the modelling of the face is even ruder than that of the previous figurines. Nose and chin are only divided by a rough slit, the eyes are barely recognizable. The ears are mere rough stumps. Published by Furtwängler, Jahrb. d. arch. Inst. a—a. O. S. 92.

5. Fragments of a crown of foliage in bronze from the Limniti Temenos (No. 52). Obtained by Ohnefalsch-Richter. Berl Mus. Antiquarium T. C. 8211, 166—168. The crown is divided into three pieces. The maximum diameter is 0,190 m. The whole no doubt served to adorn the head of a large statue.

6 and 7. Primitive bronze group found near Arsos (No. 18 in the list). Height 0,06 m breadth, 0,06 now in the Louvre.

Man leading an ox to sacrifice. Early Graeco-Phoenician Style. Cf. Text, p. 12 and 240.

8. Bronze candelabrum from Sidon in Brit. Mus., Syrian department. No 2518.

The candelabrum (h. 0,733) consists of a tripod support and a globe-shaped tube, originally filled with wood, and decreasing in size at the upper part, and a place for the light or the torch to be inserted into. This upper portion of the chandelier is distinguished by two umbrella-shaped structures, which hang suspended. Above these are three volute-shaped supports held together by a ring. The ritual purpose served by these candlesticks of clearly marked type is evident by the representations on Pl. LXXXII. cf. Text p. 179 and Note 4,

9 and 10.   Upper parts of two bronze candelabra, cf. the same kind as 8.   From Marion-Arsinoë in Cyprus.

No. 9 from Nec. II, grave 139. H. 0,385 m.   No. 10 from Necr. II, grave 96, H. 0,234 m from the excavation 1886.   Two similar examples from Tamassos are in the Antiquarium of the Royal Museum at Berlin.

Plate XLIV.

1. Male bearded colossal head (terra-cotta) from the temenos of Limniti No. 52 in the list. Obtained by Ohnefalsch-Richter.   Berl. Mus. Antiquarium.   T. C. 8211, 102.

The head is in the main well preserved; a portion only of the hair on the forehead to the right side, with corresponding hair-ribbon, is missing. The clay is covered with a coating of dull red. The shape of the head is round and broad, but not defective in expression. The eyes are wide open, the eye-lids are modelled like a skin drawn round the eye-ball. The lips are fast closed, the corners of the mouth a little drawn up, which tells especially in profile. The face is on the whole well proportioned, the nose very prominent. The shell of the ear is a shapeless mass without any internal modelling. The eyebrows and the hair of the beard are indicated by slight depressions in the surface, and this is intended to give the effect of curls. They are finished with black colour. The beard reaches from the chin to the under-lip. The hair on the forehead also is painted black, and the hair here has been put on in relief separately. The main mass of the hair, on the other hand, which falls in a thick short roll on to the back of the neck, is given by incised undulatory lines. An inadequate sketch appeared in the Jahrb. d. Arch. Inst. IV. Anzeiger p. 88.

2. Male bearded head (terra-cotta) from the same sanctuary. Obtained by Ohnefalsch-Richter. Berl. Mus. Antiquarium.   T. C. 8211, 103.

The lower part of the nose is broken off, also portions from the edge of the cap; for the rest the head is well preserved. The shape of the head is a long oval and shows individual expression. On the head is the pointed cap so usual in Cyprus. Its lower end hangs down to the back of the neck, and its borders are broken off at either side. Over the forehead the edge of the cap forms a crown-shaped band. The cap must have been of leather. The hair on the forehead and beard are rendered plastically, and painted over with a dark brown tint. The curling of the hair on the forehead and whiskers is indicated by small circles, which had been impressed in rows by some cylindrical object. The eye-brows are painted in in a dark brown, the pupil of the eye is rendered plastically, but not painted, while the eyelids are given in colour The shell of the ears is left a formless mass. The profile shows a retreating forehead and prominent nose. Published inadequately Jahrb. d. Arch. Inst. IV, Anzeiger p. 88.

3. Colossal youthful male head (terra-cotta) from the same sanctuary. Obtained by Ohnefalsch-Richter. Berl. Mus. Antiquarium.   T. C. 8211, 101.

The head is well preserved, but for the nose, which is missing. The proportions are on the whole broad. The clay is of a dull red colour, but painted over entirely with a deep red tint; certain special details are coloured black, e. g. eyebrows, pupils and eyelids. There is no trace of any attempt to render the hair either plastically or by colour. The eyes are set abnormally inward and are wide from corner to corner. The eyelids are rendered plastically. The mouth is exceptionally small, the lips somewhat prominent and open. In the profile the chin is prominent. The ears are formless, without modelling, and show a concave surface. Throat and back of the neck are, like the rest of the modelling, very much emphasized.
                                                                                                     (1—3 H. S.)

Plate XLV.

1a and b.   Female head with wreath (terra-cotta), from the same sanctuary as the head in Pl. XLIV. Obtained by Ohnefalsch-Richter. Berl. Mus. Antiquarium.   T. C. 8211, 103. The head is well preserved, only a small portion of the wreath is missing. The clay is rather yellow than red. Traces of paint are visible on the ears (bright red), and on the hair on the forehead (black). Eyebrows, eyelids, and eyeballs are rendered by surface modelling but somewhat vaguely and with no force. The cheeks too evidence some attempt to give life by modelling, also the mouth and chin. The mouth is somewhat drawn together at the corners, and gives the face a kindly expression. The shape of the face is oval, widening to the chin, and the back part of the head is too large for the delicacy of the face. The nose also is too prominent and too thick. The shell of the ear is of very peculiar modelling. The hair on the forehead, in a thick coil, has its small curls plastically rendered by small lumps. The head runs into the back of the neck without any break. On the front hair rests a wreath of leaves, in the middle of which are flowers and fruit. The artist has clearly attempted to give individual expression to the head.

2. Youthful male head (terra-cotta) with a large cap or helmet, from the same sanctuary. Obtained by Ohnefalsch-Richter. Berl. Mus. Antiquarium. T. C. 2811, 106.

The head is intact. The extreme point of the cap is broken off. Originally the hole for firing was at the top, and its edge is still visible. The whole face is painted a dull red. The cap, too large in proportion to the face, is yellow. Moreover traces of black colour are still perceptible in the locks of hair. that fall down sideways. The cap shows a border in front, which however is lost at either side. Behind, the clay is smooth. Below this border a roll of hair encircles the forehead. Eyebrows, eyelids and eyeballs are more clearly modelled than the rest of the head. The face turns to a point at the chin. The nose is pointed and very prominent The mouth small and delicate. The lips drawn together, and compressed into a smile. The shell of the ear has no inner modelling. The neck is exceptionally long. At either side a lock of hair falls on to the shoulders.

3. Youthful male head (terra-cotta) with a large cap, from the same sanctuary. Obtained by Ohnefalsch-Richter. Berl. Mus. Antiquarium. T. C. 8211, 107.

The state of preservation is very good. The point of the nose is broken off, as well as part of the border of the cap and of the right ear. The head is in outline and expression very like the female head No 1. The hair on the forehead shows the same technique in the rendering of the curls. The shape of the eyes, mouth, cheeks and chin is the same. The nose too is exceptionally broad. Neck and back of the neck are rendered with great emphasis This head is more closely analogous to No. 1 than to No. 2. Still all three heads show strong Greek influence, which cannot be detected in the heads in Pl. XLIV. Published "The Owl" Pl. III, 5.　　　　　　(1—3 H. S.)

Plate XLVI.

† 1. Youthful head with cap or helmet (terra-cotta), from the same sanctuary of Limniti. Obtained by Ohnefalsch-Richter. Berl. Mus. Antiquarium. T. C. 8211, 112. The chin and the locks of hair on the right side are somewhat damaged. The left ear is missing. The cap or helmet ends in a round ball. There are no traces of painting. On the back of the neck a lock of hair falls down on the shoulders to either side. The ear that is preserved has attached to it, as an ornament, a small disk. The modelling of the face, specially the eyes, is very superficial—the eyelids have evidently been originally rendered in paint. The nose is sharply cut and pointed, the lips are abruptly open. Cf. Fig. 245 p. 325.

† 2. Youthful head with pointed cap (terra-cotta) from the same sanctuary. Obtained by Ohnefalsch-Richter. Berl. Mus. Antiquarium. T. C. 8211, 117.

No traces of painting. The cap runs to a point, and has three little knobs on either side. (2 of them are missing). The ears are decorated with the same disc-like objects. On the neck was a round locket, but the chain is missing, having probably been painted on. On either shoulder fall two thick locks of hair. The superficial modelling of the eyes is a characteristic of the style of this head. The apple of the eye is given plastically, but there is no rendering of the eyelids. That has been made clear respecting the head in No 1, and occurs again in the following instances. The right corners of the eyelids are originally painted as they are in the bearded head in Pl. XLIV, 2, which also shews the same superficial modelling of the eye. Published "The Owl" III, 7. Cf. Text p. 325. Note 5.

† 3. Youthful head with cap (terra-cotta) from the same sanctuary. Obtained by Ohnefalsch-Richter. Berl. Mus. Antiquarium. T. C. 8211, 113.

The entire head and cap are painted over with a violet red. The eyes, which are only superficially modelled, are picked out in black. The left lock of hair also, which alone shows traces of paint, is coloured black. The face is narrow, and painted in as if the cheeks were pressed together. The cheek bones are very prominent. The mouth is but slightly modelled, and is rendered by a line dividing the lips and incised with a graving tool. To the ear a small disk is separately attached as an ornament The cap is like that in No. 1. At the top is an opening which served as the fixing hole. Cf. Fig. 244, p. 325.

4. Small female head (terra-cotta) with wreath. From Idalion. Obtained by L. Ross. Berl. Mus. Antiquarium. The left side is broken off up to the outside corner of the eye. The back is simply worked. On the skull is a firing hole. Otherwise the head is intact to the front of the nose. The face was painted with red colour, of which slight traces remain on the forehead and at the spring of the nose. The hair on the head and forehead is painted black, so are the eyebrows and eyelids. The wreath of leaves shows traces of green paint, while the large earring is yellow. In fact, everywhere the effort to obtain natural effect is manifested. The style is somewhat like that of other heads e. g. Pl. XLVIII, 3 (also from Dali) Pl. L, 6 (Dali) Pl. LV, 1 (Dali). These heads also have the large ear-coverings.

† 5. Very rude head with cap (terra-cotta) from Limniti. Obtained by Ohnefalsch-Richter. Berl. Antiquarium. T. C. 8211, 122

No traces of colour. The modelling of the face very rude. The eyeballs are very prominent and, as elsewhere is so often the case, are surmounted by no plastically rendered eyelids. Cheeks and chin are nearly a flat smooth surface coming to a sharp point at the lower end. The cap ends in a round point, and is surrounded by a double wreath of leaves damaged in front. Over the nose occurs some adjunct that seems connected with the cap. The ears are very simply modelled and have in the middle a deep hole probably intended for the aural passage. To the left ear a disc is fastened as an ornament. Below the ears are remains of locks of hair on either side of the shoulders. In profile the nose shows a marked arch of the ridge.

† 6. Head with pointed cap (terra-cotta) from the same sanctuary. Obtained by Ohnefalsch-Richter, Berl. Mus. Antiquarium. T. C. 8211, 105.

In good preservation. The end of the nose only is somewhat damaged. A portion of the shoulders also is preserved. The clay is painted red, the eyebrows, the hair on the skull and the neck ornament are given in black, the locks of hair, rendered plastically, are also painted black. The style of the head is related to Nos. 1, 2, 3, 5. The expression is very characteristic; the rendering of the features gives an impression of leanness. The muscles of the mouth are sharply separated off from the cheek. The neck-ornament consists of a ribbon, on which hangs a circular ornament.

‡ 7. Youthful head from the same sanctuary. Obtained by Ohnefalsch-Richter. Berl. Mus. Antiquarium. T. C. 8211, 118.

Use of paint only certain on the head. The front of the nose is somewhat damaged, the back of the head shows a broad firing-hole. The separate border over the forehead seems to have belonged to a fillet. One need not suppose that there was a cap with a border, because of the painting on the head. The eyelids are rendered plastically. The left ear, not visible in the plate, is in this case decorated with a spiral, instead of, as usually, a disc-shaped ornament.

‡ 8. Head with low painted cap (terra-cotta) from the same sanctuary. Obtained by Ohnefalsch-Richter. Berl. Mus. Antiquarium. T. C. 8211, 123.

The point of the cap and the left side are damaged. The ears are missing. The cap is decorated in front with a wreath of leaves and fruit, only preserved on the right. Below this the forehead is encircled with little snail-shaped curls which are painted black. So are the eyebrows, eyelids and pupils. The nose is somewhat tilted, and has deep nostrils. The mouth is small and distorted to a smile. The execution is careless, but compared to that of the preceding heads from Limniti shows marked progress.

‡ 9. Head with cap (terra-cotta) from same sanctuary. Obtained by Ohnefalsch-Richter. Berl. Mus. Antiquarium. T. C. 8211, 124. The point of the cap is missing—its place is taken by a firing-hole. That the point was originally there is certain from the border, which comes out clearly at the back. Over the forehead the border is damaged. With this exception only, a few locks of hair and the left side of the nose have suffered somewhat. There are abundant traces of colouring. The face was painted reddish. Eyes, hair, both on the forehead and the locks that fall on the shoulders, are black The modelling is very rude, specially the ears, of which the right one protrudes unduly forward and upward.

‡ 10. Fragment of a bearded head (terra-cotta) from same sanctuary. Obtained by Ohnefalsch-Richter. Berl. Mus. Antiquarium. T. C. 8211, 110.

A portion only of the face is preserved, with eyes, nose, mouth and chin and the right side of the neck. There are no traces of colour. The eyes show the familiar superficial modelling. Forehead and nose form in profile a straight line. The sides of the nose are markedly protrusive, the nostrils deep sunk. The mouth very expressionless. the lips pouting. The technique of the whiskers is interesting. It consists of a succession of twists made up of a little knob with a ring round it. The eyes are executed in this fashion in very early terra-cotta idols. Cf. Fig 242. p. 325.

11. Fragment of female head (terra-cotta) from the sanctuary of Astarte-Aphrodite at Dali (Idalion) No. 3 in the list. Berl. Mus. Antiquarium. T. C. 8015 64.

The front portion of the skull, the face without ears, a portion of the neck with fragments of neck-chain, these are all that is preserved. The nose has suffered somewhat on the right side. Clear traces of original colour remain. The face was painted red, eyebrows, eyelids, pupils and the hair on the skull are black, the portions preserved of the chain seem to have been painted alternately red and black. The coiffure is interesting. The hair is parted in the middle and lies to either side in close strands which are rendered plastically. In front of the ear at either side a small lock of hair hangs down. On the forehead, where the skull ends, is a sculptured knob probably of ahair pin. The eyebrows and eyelids are rendered plastically, besides being painted. The shape of the eyes is a pronounced almond. The nostrils are deep cut, and so is the line which bounds the nose from the cheek. The mouth is rather expressionless. The neck ornament consists of a series of discs, but with no connecting link. In style and technique the head is markedly different from those found at Limniti; it is unique also as compared with the Idalion heads.[*])

12. Rude head with painted cap (terra-cotta) from Cyprus. Obtained by Schönborn. Berl. Mus. Antiquarium. T. C. 5099.

The point of the cap is damaged behind; the right eye also is fragmentary. The cap is surrounded by a peculiar notched border which may indicate a wreath. The eyes are extremely primitive. They consist of a knob with a hole bored in the middle, surrounded by a circle. The nose is put on separately, and has an arched profile. The nostrils are deep cut. The mouth is indicated by a deep round hole. Below is a long painted object. set on, and indicating probably a pointed beard.

13. Rude head and neck (terra-cotta) from Cyprus. Obtained by Schönborn. Berl. Mus. Antiquarium. T. C. 51, 100. The back part of the head is nearly flat and roughly worked. It shows traces of colour. Eyebrows and eyelids are also painted black. The chin is broken away on the lower side. The profile is very characteristic. The forehead lies far back, the nose is a pronounced arch. The transition from nose and mouth is marked by a deep incision, which is carried on into the cheek on both sides. The ears stick out. Behind, stuck on to the neck, is a puzzling object painted black at the sides and showing a breakage above. Probably this marks the lower continuation of the hair; then the whole of the back part of the head must have been broken away. The broken edge of the neck also shows traces of painting, which probably belong to a necklet. For the sanctuary of Limniti cf. Text p. 270.

(1—18 H. S.)

---

*) Nos. 4, 11 and 13 appear here to economize space.

Plate XLVII.

‡ 1. Rude clay figure from the temenos of Apollo at Limniti, obtained by Ohnefalsch-Richter. Berl. Mus. Antiquarium. T. C. 8211, 46.

The clay is red coloured. Black is perceptible round the top of the head to the front, also round the lower part of the figure. The arms are stretched out sideways, the right is missing. The technique is extremely primitive. The face is a convex plane, on which the nose is stuck, consisting of a long vertical strip of clay. The mouth is also put on separately, and is made like that of an animal. The back of the head is depressed. On the right outstretched arm there are traces that look like the remains of something not belonging to the figure itself. Probably these are the remains of the arms of another figure close by, which would make the original figure be taking part in a choric dance. Cf. No. 5.

‡ 2. Upper part of a terra-cotta figure with pointed cap from the same sanctuary at Limniti. Obtained by Ohnefalsch-Richter. Berl. Mus. Antiquarium. T. C. 8211, 20.

The top-most point of the cap is broken off. The figure belongs to the type that stands upright with hands hanging down at the side, instances of which were given in Nos. 6 and 7. This one, like 6 is profusely coloured. The cap is coated over with dull red, and has a black border. Eyebrows, eyelids, pupils and whiskers are black. Besides, on the trunk of the body, there are traces of black and red stripes which form a sort of dress pattern. Nose and ears are indicated, by little pieces stuck on. The chin protrudes.

‡ 3. Female figure (terra-cotta) from Limniti. Obtained by Ohnefalsch-Richter. Berl. Mus. Antiquarium. T. C. 8211, 70.

The figure had been squeezed out of the mould, but the border, which shows wavelike inward curves, remains and also serves the figure as a background. The lower part is broken off. About the height of the navel there are two side pieces stuck on. A better example for this method of procedure is the Idol No. 8211, 60, which has 4 arms, two standing out at the side, two folded over the breast.*) The figure is draped in a long-sleeved chiton, in which both the vertical and cross folds are rendered sculpturally. On the breast is a chain, to which is attached a boss-shaped pendant. The rendering of the hair on the forehead and the face gives clear evidence of the style being archaic Greek.

‡ 4. Female figure (terra-cotta). The hands lying on the breast. From Limniti. Obtained by Ohnefalsch-Richter. Berl. Mus. Antiquarium. T. C. 8211, 61.

The lower part of the figure is broken off. The nose is damaged. The clay is of a dull red colour. The head is cast in a mould. The coiffure rises above the forehead, but is only modelled in front by means of slightly incised lines. Locks of hair fall sideways down on to the shoulders, and in these there are deeply incised lines. The drawing of the face is soft and effeminate, the eyes are only superficially indicated. The breasts are strongly emphasized; the rest of the body is entirely without modelling.

‡ 5. Female figure (terra-cotta) from Limniti. Obtained by Ohnefalsch-Richter. Berl. Mus. Antiquarium. T. C. 8211, 52.

The lower part of the figure and the right arm are broken off. The face, is simply cast and shows archaic Greek style. On the left eye are traces of black colour. The figure belongs to the same type as No. 1 of this plate, and must be considered as having formed part of a choros. At the end of the left out-stretched arm are traces of the figure that stood next. On the neck is a double neck-chain. One of these clings to the neck, the other has pendants. The female breasts are indicated by raised planes. The lower part of the figure and the arms are quite rudely shaped.

‡ 6. Male figure with long pendant arms, from Limniti. Obtained by Ohnefalsch-Richter. Berl. Mus. Antiquarium. T. C. 8211, 4.

The head is missing. The front of the figure is richly painted, whereas the back is of the rough dull red of the original clay. The breast is covered with a short over garment, which is painted wicker pattern with red and black cross lines. The colour is continued on the arms, where red and black horizontal lines alternate. The long chiton has a broad red vertical stripe down the middle, near to which in the middle are traces of a black stripe. The actual trunk of the figure is round and column-shaped. For the dress cf. the representations on vases on Pl. XX and XXI.

‡ 7. Male figure with pointed cap and long pendant arms from Limniti. Acquired by Ohnefalsch-Richter. Berl. Mus. Antiquarium. T. C. 8211, 1.

The figure shows the perfectly preserved type to which Nos. 2 and 6 also belong. It also has slight but evident traces of black and red colour, which seem to have been applied as in No. 2; also on the back. Style and technique of ears, nose and chin are also the same.

‡ 8. Horned bearded Centaur from Limniti (front view No. 13). Acquired by Ohnefalsch-Richter. Berl. Mus. Antiquarium. T. C. 8211, 79.

---

*) Many of the figurines now in the Cyprus Museum. e. g. 3 and 5, which I excavated at one o the sanctuaries of Chytroi (No. 24 in the list) had 4 arms. They all belonged to choric dances. The potter employed any chance mould, e. g. a mould representing women who held flowers or clasped their breasts &c., &c. and he then quite unconcernedly added further arms, so as to unite several women together in a circular dance. These he fastened on to a clay plate, and stuck the sacred tree in the middle. (Cf. Pl. LXXVI, 8 &c., of supra p. 43 — note 1.)

The arms and the back legs are entirely missing; of the front legs only the upper thighs remain. The left breast and shoulder are damaged. Further, the tail is broken off, but the lowest join is certain. The membrum virile is broken off, but the portion left is sufficient to prove its former existence. The horns are proved to have been there by the round breakages over the ears. : The style as rude as anything found in Cyprus. Published Jahrb. d. arch. Inst. IV. Anzeiger p. 80.

‡ 9. Front portion of a horned centaur in profile, from Limniti. Acquired by Ohnefalsch-Richter. Berl. Mus. Antiquarium. T. C. 8211, 81.

The figure is much broken. The horse-body is altogether missing. Of the human portion the legs are missing and the right arm, of the left arm only a small stump is left. The face is bearded, roughly modelled, and with the nose broken off. Of the right horn the place of junction is preserved.

‡ 10. Fig. 175, p. 249. Head and upper part of the body of a horned centaur from Limniti. Acquired by Ohnefalsch-Richter. Berl. Mus. Antiquarium. T. C. 8211, 84.

The figure is squeezed quite flat. The arms are missing. The face is large featured, and the expression animal. The wide mouth is open, and holds something tight in the middle. By the analogy of Nos. 16 and 18 this must be regarded as the remains of a tongue hanging out. The nose is very broad, and the nostrils large. The eyeball is scarcely indicated at all plastically, on the other hand the cheek bones are emphasized. The hair on the forehead ends with an abrupt line. The ears are made of pieces roughly stuck on. Of the left horn a small bit remains. A rudely shaped lock of hair falls on the right side of the shoulder.

11. Head of a horned Centaur from Paphos. From the Cesnola collection. Berl. Mus. Antiquarium. T. C. 6683, 38.

The technique of this head is somewhat different from the rest, but the style is of the same class. The hair which covers the forehead is parted in the middle by an incised line, and combed to the side. The hair thus combed to the side is in its turn indicated by incised lines, and the same method is adopted with the separate hairs of the beard, which collectively is rendered plastically. The face has the same animal expression; the nose is broad and snub. The ears also are animal. The left horn is in part preserved. The locks of hair hang down on the neck sideways. The back of the head is roughly worked. Cf. p. 248.

‡ 12. Upper part of a horned, bearded Centaur (terra-cotta), from Limniti. Acquired by Ohnefalsch-Richter. Berl. Mus. Antiquarium. T. C. 8211, 89.

The stumps only of the arms are preserved. The uppermost part of the skull is broken off. The figure differs from the ordinary type, in that the face is human, but the horns and the hanging out tongue have left traces that make the attribution certain. Use of colour is conspicuous here. The hair both of the head and beard, the eyebrows, eyelids and pupils are given in black colour or painted. Lips and tongue show traces of red colour. On the body there are vertical stripes in black. This was intended to indicate the shaggy skin. Short locks of hair hang down on both sides.

‡ 13. Front view of the Centaur No. 8.

The face is very roughly executed and the expression animal. The nose is wide and thick, and has deep depressions for nostrils. The mouth is large, and represented by a horizontal depression. The beard frames in the whole face, and is rendered plastically. Two short thick locks of hair hang down sideways. The back of the head shows traces of black colour.

‡ 14. Upper part of horned bearded Centaur (terra-cotta) from Limniti. Acquired by Ohnefalsch-Richter. Berl. Mus. Antiquarium. T. C. 8211, 85.

The left arm is entirely gone, the right has only the stump left; the horns also are broken away. The whiskers and hair are painted black. The face is animal like No. 11. The ears are rough separate pieces put on.

‡ 15. Head and breast of horned bearded Centaur (terra-cotta) from Limniti. Acquired by Ohnefalsch-Richter. Berl. Mus. Antiquarium. T. C. 8211, 88.

A large piece of the left horn is preserved. The ears are broken off at the points. The beard also has suffered. The arms are missing. The flesh parts have a coat of dull green. The face in this specimen is more animal than in any of the others. The eyebrows are arched high. The bridge of the nose is depressed. The lip is tilted upwards, so that the nostrils are visible, which may be observed in less degree in Nos. 10, 11 and 14. The cheek bones are very prominent. The ears are of animal shape. The hair rises abruptly from the forehead, and there are vertical incisions at the edge. The whole face has individual characteristics.

‡ 16. Head of a bearded horned Centaur from Limniti. Acquired by Ohnefalsch-Richter. Berl. Mus. Antiquarium. T. C. 8211, 87.

Only the stumps of the horns are preserved, otherwise the head is intact. The modelling is flat. The eyes are set deep, but without any modelling. There are no traces of colour. The head is specially interesting on account of the long tongue hanging out. Of this in Nos. 10 and 12 there were only slight traces. As the craftsman was not able to make the mouth correspond, he simply attached the tongue to the underlip. This technical peculiarity is observable also in Nos. 10 and 12. The hair is not rendered plastically, but indicated by a line which bounds the forehead, and another perpendicular to it incised along the back of the head. Published Jahrb. d. arch. Inst. IV. Anzeiger p. 88.

‡ 17. Upper part of horned Centaur (terra cotta) from Amathus. Acquired by Ohnefalsch-Richter. Berl. Mus. Antiquarium. T. C. 8305.

The right side is broken off. The horns are preserved, of their original length. Style and technique of this figure are ruder than of those preceding. Nose, mouth, ears and locks of hair are all put on separately. Moreover, traces of rich colouring are perceptible. The hair, whiskers, eyes and some details on the trunk are painted black. The ears, which are simply stuck on, and the mouth, are painted red. On the trunk also there are traces of stripes of red. On the left side of the breast are two objects stuck on, which may belong to some attribute. Cf. p. 248.

‡ 18. Head of a bearded horned Centaur (terra cotta) from Limniti. Acquired by Ohnefalsch-Richter. Berl. Mus. Antiquarium. T. C. 8211, 86.

The horns and the right side locks of hair are broken off. Style and technique similar to No. 16. The expression of the face is just the same. In this case too, the tongue hangs out, but is broken off at the lower end. The hair is rendered more plastically, but here too the bounding incised line divides it from the forehead.

For figures 1—7, cf. in general Text p. 270. For the horned Centaurs v. Text p. 247 ff.

(1—18. H. S.)

Plate XLVIII.

1. Youthful male head, (calcareous) stone from Kition. From the collection left by L Ross. Berl. Mus. Antiquarium. The preservation is excellent. Only the end of the nose and the left side of the hair over the ears is somewhat damaged. The head is of the first archaic period of Cyprian sculpture in stone. The eyebrows are rendered plastically, and arch gracefully from the plane of the forehead. The eyelids rise sharply from the plane of the eyeballs. The inner and outer corners of the eyes are closely copied from nature. The sides of the nose are carefully wrought, and the mouth too is freely modelled and has the archaic smile. The profile is regular. The forehead and nose are in one line, which tends to be vertical. There is an attempt at modelling, though rude, in the interior of the ears, which are partly covered by locks of hair. The coiffure is specially interesting The forehead is surrounded by a double row of small locks, and this is continued towards the back, though the work is less careful. Above these rows of locks rests a double flower-wreath, the flowers being turned alternately up and down. Possibly the sculptor conceived of this wreath as in gold. It is left unworked behind. The hair is divided on the skull, and falls to the side in thick strands.

2. Female head in life size (limestone) from Kition or Idalion. Obtained by means of L. Ross. Berl Mus. Antiquarium. The back of the head is cut short off, the point of the nose is broken, but in other respects the head is perfect. The style is archaic, but not purely Greek like the preceding head, the profile being sloping and less regular. The eyebrows are rendered in relief. The eye-ball is rendered by an almond-shaped prominence, and the edges of the eyelids are not defined. This formation of the eye occurs very frequently in the heads from Dali (Idalion), and we shall meet with more examples of it. The mouth is small and formed in a smile, but not so delicately cut as the preceding example. The nostrils are modelled in detail, the hair is given in relief, but not in detail, forming on the forehead a kind of rolled edge. A fillet with small buttons surmounts this. The ears are covered with rich ornament, which however does not illustrate the specifically Kyprian form of which we are shortly to treat. Round the neck is a double chain with tassels and a centre-piece.

3. Head of a female statuette in clay, half life-size, in fragments, from the Astarte-Aphrodite sanctuary near Dali (No. 3 on the list). Berl. Mus. Antiquarium. M. J. 8015, 60.

By a mistake of the photographer the illustration has come out reversed right and left. The description applies not to the photograph but to the original. The head is broken off at the neck, on the left side a piece of the neck is still to be seen with curls falling over the shoulder in front. The whole is made up of various pieces, the face being quite perfect. On the top of the head is a large hole, which must have been made for the purpose of burning. The technique and style of the head are very important, and the dressing of the hair is interesting. It is evidently intended to represent a coiffure of curls, and for this purpose a hanging spiral pattern has been impressed on the clay with a stamp. At the back of the head and on the neck there is no indication of hair. Curls hang down on the shoulders, one only, on the left, being in a state of preservation. This curl is rendered by incised lines, which cause it to resemble a lancet-shaped leaf with ribs. The eyebrows are rendered in relief, with an addition of hatched incised lines. It was evidently intended to give the impression of a luxuriant growth of hair. The eyes are specially large, and the edges of the eyelid modelled in sharp lines. The upper eyelid rises in a high arch from the inner angle of the eye, and is bounded by an incised line intended to represent the wrinkle caused by the opening of the eye. The nose is specially prominent, and, seen in profile, is somewhat aquiline, with a rounded end. It is interesting to note that the ears are completely covered by a large ornament in the shape of a pod and consisting of two divisions. The modelling of this recalls metal work. I was the first to point out the significance of this peculiarly Kyprian ear decoration (in the Repertorium f. Kunstwissenschaft IX, 320; cf. p. 270). The fragments on Pl. LIII, 36, 41, 43, 48, with explanations are instructive on the point. This characteristic decoration is very rare out of Kypros. The Berlin Antiquarium possesses a terra-cotta head from Rhodes (T. C. 7987; Jahrb. d. Arch. Inst. 1886 I Anzeiger p. 154); underneath the pod-shaped ear decoration there is a pendant in the form of a bow-knot, such as occurs very frequently in Kypros. I may also mention a small head from Athens, also in the Berlin Antiquarium (T. C. 6931), which is very similar, especially in the formation of the eyes, to the sculptures of Dali. In such cases there must have been communication with Kypros. Just under the chin on a the small piece of the neck which remains is a bow-knot belonging to a necklace. The Berlin Museum possesses a whole series of heads, which in style and technique may be compared with those adduced in the present work. Among them a special interest attaches to those which wear the nose ring: No. 8105, 54 = Pl. LV, 1, 2; 8015, 55, = Pl. LV, 4; and the first of these shows the same treatment of the hair. The head of figure No. 8105, 12 (= Pl. L, 6) has no nose-ring but is otherwise exactly the same. Fragment No. 8015, 56 (= Pl. LV, 3), shows the same treatment of hair. The same may be stated of heads Nos. 8015, 12 and 59. Nos. 8015, 12, 22 (= Pl. LI, 7), 23 (= Pl. L, 5); 8015, 61 have the same ear decoration. So far the examples given all come from Dali (Idalion), and represent a definite division of style, examples of which occur also in other places A head from Paphos, No. 6683, 40 shows the same hair technique, and I may also mention the head, also from Paphos, No. 6683, 16 = Pl. LV, 7). This eardecoration may also be seen in another group of figures, which represent a style more approaching the Egyptian, e. g. a fragment from Idalion Pl. XLIX, 5; also No. 8015, 298 = Pl. L, 3; and Nos. 8015, 291, 299, 331, 343, 353, all from Idalion. The following example also belongs to this series.

4. Female head, full life size, with crown from the sanctuary shewn by inscriptions to be that of Paphia (No. 23 on the list). Cyprus Museum, Nicosia.

In my absence this head was excavated and was so much injured that the crown can only be partly pieced together. It is certain that this ornament must have been unusually large and quite smoothly finished. The head belongs to the same style and technique as the former one. The face shows a remarkably thick and bulgy contour. Cf. p. 267.   (1—4 H. S.)

Plate XLIX.

1. Female statuette (limestone). Idalion. From an older discovery. Berl. Mus. Antiquarium.

The lower part of the figure with the feet and a good part of the left side are broken off, while the right is better preserved. A restoration with plaster has been made. The figure is finished flat at the back. This example belongs to the more developed archaic Kyprian style, in which Hellenic influence was already at work, and it is a good illustration of the Hellenic element. The artistic motive, i. e. a figure holding the garment in one hand and a flower in the other, is borrowed from archaic Greek prototypes. The clothing is Greek, the figure being dressed in a long chiton and himation. The latter is laid over the right shoulder; one end is passed under the left arm and thrown over the breast and right shoulder; the other end hangs down from the arm on the right side, and falls in regular folds at the edge, as in archaic Greek sculptures. The himation has been painted red. While the folds of the mantle are given in the regular scheme of sculpture, the artist has left the chiton, according to older fashion, unmodelled. The dressing of the hair is Greek, the three shoulder curls on each side, particularly being borrowed from Greek models. The hair on the forehead is arranged in three wavy lines, one over the other. The hair on the head is unmodelled, the ear, rudely modelled, wears an ornament like a disc. The wrists are adorned with bracelets. The type of the face is more Oriental than Greek. The eyes are almond-shaped elevations, such as so constantly occur in Idalion sculpture in stone. Cf. Pl. XLVIII, 2.

° 2. Female statuette (limestone). From the Astarte-Aphrodite temple near Dali (Idalion). No. 3 on the list. Berl. Mus. Antiquarium. M. J. 8015, 347.

This figure belongs to the transition style, and is much more rudely executed than the preceding. There is no plastic modelling, only the outlines being indicated by the carving. The face is treated in the same superficial manner as the other parts. Cloak, shoes, lips, nostrils necklace and head-fillet are painted red. The dress is Greek, consisting of a mantle and chiton, but without any plastic representation of folds. The motive of the figure is the same as the preceding. The flower in the left hand is a rude lump without any detail at all. The back part of the figure is unmodelled, and it is evident that the front view was the only important consideration.

° 3. Female statuette (limestone). From Dali (Idalion). Berl. Mus. Antiquarium. M. J. 8015, 343.

The head has been broken away and fastened on again, the nose is somewhat injured, but the other parts of the figure are well preserved. The back is again finished flat. The type is the same as that of the preceding figures, including the motive of holding the garment, but while the other showed Greek influence in the clothing but a still barbarous taste in the type of face, this figure shows exactly the reverse, a relation which is not uncommon in the transition period. The left hand holds in front of the breast a flower carefully rendered. The right hand, which hangs down, is slightly animated by a bend in the elbow. The dress consists of a long Kyprian garment without folds, such as we saw on vases Pl. XX, XXI. On the right side, from the breast to the lower edge of the garment, a red band is carried, on the left side; this band only reaches to the left wrist, and seems not to correspond (cf. Pl. L, 1). The edges of the sleeves have a red border. A broad band of colour, somewhat resembling a square opening, is to be seen on the breast. This mode of cutting the garment is frequent in Kyprian figures, e. g. Pl. L, 6. The hair radiates from the crown of the head, and is modelled, while on the forehead it falls down over the face in small volute shaped curls, corresponding to the spiral curls on the terra-cotta head Pl. XLVIII, 3.

On each side a separate curl hangs down beside the ear. Rich curls, divided in stages, fall on the shoulders. The head is surrounded by an ornament consisting of a series of small bosses or balls. The ornament of the ear is specially remarkable, and, as in Pl. XLVIII, 2—4, covers the whole ear; it also has the double division. To the ear-lobe a special hanging ornament seems to have been fastened. The ornaments on the breast and neck are very rich. On the neck is a band in three divisions, with vertical, cuts across it, and painted with vertical red stripes. This is probably intended for a triple row of beads. On the breast falls a double chain, each part of which has centrepiece, the upper one being painted red. The type of the face shows stronger Hellenic influence than the preceding examples. The mouth shows the archaic smile of Greek sculpture. The lips are painted red. The modelling of the muscles of the mouth gives animation to the contour of the cheek. The eyebrows are given in low relief. The eyes have the typical almond curve. The nostrils are painted red. The formation of the face forms a striking contrast to the rude treatment of the rest of the figure. The feet with the toes are very roughly modelled, some red stripes painted over the feet probably indicating the sandal-straps.

?4. Fragment of a female statue (limestone). From the same sanctuary near Dali (Idalion) as 2 and 3. Berl. Mus. Antiquarium. M. J. 8015, 801.

The lower part of the figure, from the knees and the right hand, are missing; the figure is broken in various places, such as the nose, the left elbow and the right side of the head. At the back it is finished flat, but the arms are separated from the trunk by deep grooves. Traces of red paint are numerous, but too indistinct to be systematically grouped. This figure differs very much in type and style from the preceding. The style is entirely non-Hellenic, and seems to be a mixture of ancient Kyprian with Egyptian elements. The attitude is one which is common to a number of Idalian stone sculptures of the same style. The right hand hangs straight down, while the left is bent, and holds in front of the breast a cup or a bowl. The figure is dressed like the preceding one, in a long garment without folds, through which are indicated the separation of the legs, the line of the thigh, the navel and the breasts; the edge of the sleeve is distinctly to be seen on the left arm. The shape of the head is remarkable; it is contracted at the top, and abnormally extended behind. Around the head is a kerchief, which frames the forehead, and of which the ends fall in front of the shoulder. Above this, on the surface of the head, are remains of an ornament resembling a crown. The form of the face shows a contrast to the treatment of the rest of the figure; it is evidently executed from Egyptian proto-types, but with some considerable amount of skill. The eyes show a kind of realism. The eyebrows are indicated by a sharp edge. The eyeball somewhat projects, but is partly covered by the upper lid, so that the impression of a half open eye is given. The eye is almond-shaped, but more like a slit. The pupils are rendered in fine plastic lines. The mouth and forehead are finished with care. The outer ear (only preserved on the left side) is modelled on the edge with small projecting bosses. This evidently represents the edge of an ornament covering the whole of the ear, such as we found on the other heads. A hanging ear-ring of peculiarly Kyprian form is fastened to the ear lobe. Of this I shall speak again, since this figure does not show it completely. At the right side remains of an ornament can still be seen. The neck is adorned by a chain with a long centre-piece.

5. Fragment of a female statuette (limestone) Idalion. Obtained in 1845 through L. Ross. Berl. Mus. Antiquarium.

The lower part of the figure and the right hand are broken away. The under edge is restored in plaster. The figure is finished smooth behind. In type and style it resembles the preceding. The attitude is the same, only that a lotus flower is held in the left hand. The dress consists of the long-sleeved garment without folds. Over the under garment there seems to be a short upper garment reaching to the waist. The head is covered by a kerchief. The ears are cased in the well-known sheath-like ornament, while a separate pendant hangs down below. This is shaped like the pendant in the preceding figure, but is more distinct. The Berlin Museum possesses two examples made of gold, which may illustrate by their shapes the prototypes used by sculptors in stone. They both come from Melos, and have been published by Furtwängler (Arch. Ztg. 1884 Pl. IX, 9, 10; text p. 110). This type in its simple form is known in Rhodes (Salzmann, "Necrop. de Camirus" Pl. I), and is one of the many indications that in ancient times there was communication between Rhodes and Kypros. The examples in Berlin show that in this intercourse Melos had a share. The Kyprian figures of stone and terra-cotta only reproduce the peculiar shape. The Berlin examples are richly adorned, and represent the highest point of perfection of archaic goldsmiths' work. These heavy pendents could not have been fastened to the lobes of the ear, but were either attached to the large pod-shaped ear decoration (cf. Pl. LIII, 11), or tied to the ear. The neck of the figure is adorned with a triple row of beads, while on the breast is a chain with a centre-piece. The expression of the face is somewhat peculiar, and resembles that of the terra-cottas (e. g. Pl. XLVIII, 4, 5, L, 1, 5, 9). The formation of the eyes corresponds with the terra-cottas.

?6. Fragment of a female statuette (limestone). From Dali (Idalion). Berl. Mus. Antiquarium. M. J. 8015, 361.

This figure is put together out of various pieces; the lower part from the knees is wanting. The back is not entirely flat as in the other figures, nor is it fully modelled. This figure is a typical example of the archaic Greek style in Kypros. The attitude of the figure is that of a development of a so-called Spes type. The dress, which is purely Greek, consists of a long chiton falling in fine folds, and a cloak in larger folds, worn like the himation in Nos. 1 and 2. The dressing of the hair is purely Greek; it is parted in the middle, and falls over the face in two thick rolls, while three curls fall on the shoulders on each side. A hoop-shaped diadem adorns the head. The ears, which are only super-ficially modelled, wear a disc-shaped ornament. There is a chain on the neck, and bracelets on the arms. The type of the face is purely Greek, but the eyes, as is usual in the Idalian figures, are represented by

50*

almond-shaped prominences. The object in the left hand is a fruit, perhaps an apple. Cf. Pl. LI, 12 LIV, 3 and 5. This figure does not correspond in height to Pl. XLVIII, 1.   (1—6 H. S.)

Plate L.

1. Female statuette (clay) with a dove, from Paphos. Coll. Barre. Froener, Catalogue Barre 151. Berl. Mus. Antiquarium. T. C. 7599. By a mistake of the photographer the illustration is reversed, but the description applies to the original. The lower part of the garment with the feet, and the left corner, are broken off. The modelling is somewhat worn away. Behind there is a round hole for burning. This figure is richly painted, the whole being covered over with a yellowish colour. The clothing is remarkable, and consists of a long coat with a square opening on the breast indicated by modelling, unlike the example on Pl. XLIX, 3. The breast is covered by the garment, but is indicated through it. Besides, this long garment, the figure wears an upper drapery reaching the knee, the edge of which is plastically rendered, and can be seen in the illustration. This upper drapery has a larger square opening, leaving the breast free; the edge of this opening can be distinctly seen in the illustration. The upper garment covers the arms but on the right side is a slit through which the right arm comes. This is evident from the fact that the groove which indicates this slit is continued over the fore-arm. There seems to have been a similar slit on the left side. At the left elbow the garment stops suddenly, and from there the grooved line passes along; the fore-arm was uncovered. In figure Pl. XLIX, 3 the red stripe on the left side, which only reaches the wrist, may be clearly seen. Probably the garment was drawn over the head. Other details are worthy of notice. On the neck is a narrow chain with a large centre-piece. A double chain hangs down on the breast, and is distinguished by a very large centre-piece in the form of a cylinder. Below this is a second chain to which a disc is fastened, with a small boss. This disk hangs down exactly between the breasts. Under the edge of the upper garment appear the ends of two wide fringed bands which hang down from the shoulders; these are not plastically rendered on the breast but, are indicated by red stripes which pass over the breasts and the edge of the square opening in the garment. This band must have belonged to a priestly costume, and seems to show that the figure represents a priestess. The hair is dressed in the usual manner with long and wide shoulder curls, and is painted black. It is adorned by a diadem rendered in relief and painted red. In the original the ear decoration cannot be distinguished; it resembles that of the figures Pl. XLVIII, 3, 4, XLIX, 3, 5; on the right side remains of an ear pendant, such as is described on Pl. XLIX, 5 are to be seen. The type of face is the well-known one (cf. Pl. XLVIII, 3 and the following plates) the eyebrows are strongly marked. Portions of the figure are quite contrary to nature. The line of the belly, which. as in figure Pl XLIX, 4, is given in relief, is placed much too low. Hence the left arm is much too long.   (H. S.)

This figure certainly comes from an Artemis sanctuary like those on Pl. IX, 5, XII, 5, CCX, 2 and 4. probably not from the Papho district but from Salamis. There is a wonderful correspondence in the quality of clay, painting, style, costume, decoration, jewellery and other details. I illustrate this terra-cotta here because of its correspondence with my discoveries at Achna (No. 1 on the list) and with all the other discoveries in the Artemis sanctuaries near Achna (No. 10—14 on the list). Here doubt or eror was impossible. Cf. p. 303 and 306.   M. O.—R.

2. Female statuette. (limestone) from Idalion. Obtained by means of Ross. Berl. Mus. Antiquarium.

The left side of the figure is broken off, but the head is preserved, although broken in various places. The figure belongs to the same category as the preceding. Traces of red paint are to be seen on the edges of the garment. The statuette evidently represents a priestess with the attribute of the goddess; she has seized by the legs with both hands a horned animal, perhaps a goat. The form of the face suggests an Egyptian woman. The dress consists of a stiff long sleeved garment, decorated with a broad border plastically rendered and painted red. The garment is cut in the same fashion as that of the preceding figure, and the opening on the breast has a broad border. The upper garment is shorter than the lower and only reaches over the hips. Here the bands are crossed in front. This is evidently the costume of the priestess as it would be shown in a standing attitude.*) The hair is dressed in the same manner, but does not look the same, because it is finished smooth. By the analogy of the other figures we must conclude that there was no kerchief on the head. Beside the ear a roll of hair is indicated, but this could not possibly represent a kerchief. A simple chain is round the neck. The face is carefully modelled in relief, and the outer ear approaches the natural shape.

? 3. Upper part of a female statuette (limestone). From the sanctuary near Dali (Idalion), No. 3 on the list. Berl. Mus. Antiquarium. M. J. 8015, 298. The figure is broken off at the height of the elbow, but the left arm, which is bent, is so far preserved. Nose, mouth and chin are somewhat injured. The figure represents the type of a woman holding a flower, but in the ancient Kyprian style like Pl. XLIX, 5. The face is narrower, and in the formation of the eyes it is noticeable that the lower eyelid is not indicated at all, while the upper is very strongly marked. This shows progress in comparison to the almond-shaped protuberance commoner to the ruder style of Idalion. The nose, mouth and chin are delicately modelled, but the other forms are carelessly rendered. The ornament of the ear is the usual one peculiar to Kypros, but it seems to have no pendant. Besides the chain the figure wears a broad necklace closely fastened round the neck.

---

*) I found a fragment representing a priestess dressed in the same manner in the Astarte-Aphrodite sanctuary (No. 3 on the list). which may be the origin of the figures illustrated on Pl. L., 3—6.

? 4. Female figure, the hands laid on the breast (clay), from Dali (Idalion) Berl. Mus. Antiquarium. M. J. 8015, 41. The head has been broken off and the nose somewhat injured. This figure has been made in a mould, and at the back it is stamped somewhat in the form of a tray. It belongs to the type of terra-cottas which occur so frequently in Dali, but it represents, not the most primitive stage of this type, but a stage corresponding to the female figure holding a dove (Pl. L, 1), and similar figures, There are traces of paint on the hair. At the first glance the figure appears to be nude, for the muscles of the trunk and the legs are indicated in sharp contours, but the square cut garment is shown on the breast, and its edges may be seen at the sides. There is a crown on the head ornamented with projections like bosses. The hair falls from under this crown on the forehead; while, at the sides, curls indicated by incised lines fall on the shoulders (cf. Pl. XLVIII, 3). The necklace consists of a double row of objects shaped like shells, and a large centre-piece.

An ornament somewhat like a disc (cf. 1 and 5 of the same Plate) hangs to the large chain. The ears are covered by the well-known ornament. Figures of this type must be identified as representations of Aphrodite, although in other cases, e. g. Nos. 1, 5. 6 of the same Plate, priestesses may be intended (cf. Holwerda). "Die alten Kyprier in Kunst und Kultur," p. 33, 34). Text p. 265—267, 270, 300, and 306.

? 5. Female figure with tympanum (clay) from Dali (Idalion), from the same sanctuary. Berl. Mus. Antiquarium. M. J. 8015, 23.

The figure was broken across the middle, the mouth was injured and, the nose broken off. Like the preceding figure, this was made in a mould, and the back is stamped in the form of a tray. There are numerous traces of red and black colouring. The type is Kyprian. (cf. Pl. XLVIII, 2; L, 1, 6.) The drapery is similar to that of Nos. 1 and 2; on the left side are the two red stripes. The left arm appears through the slit in the garment as in No. 1; the garment is indicated in relief. There is no reason to suppose that the sleeves were wide, as such a peculiarity would have no analogy among the numerous types. The dressing of the hair is that which is usual in figures of this kind. The head is ornamented by a high diadem with vertical flutings; in front and on the sides are small buttons painted black. The shoulder curls and the strongly marked eyebrows are painted black; the opening at the neck is also edged with black. The ornaments on the breast are similar to those on the preceding figure; the fringe-like appendage is painted black. The ear-ornament is of the usual kind, and there are traces of pendants such as are described on Pl. XLIX, 5. The tambourine-player is represented as at rest, her instrument hanging by a ribbon from her arm. It is well known that the tambourine players form a very important feature in Kyprian worship, and belonged to the temple retinue of Aphrodite (cf the copper vessel of Idalion p. 46, Fig. 49, and terra-cotta figures like Pl. LI, 1, 2, 8). Text p 139, 270, 300 and 306.

? 6. Female figure in the attitude of adoration (clay) from Dali (Idalion). Found in the same sanctuary as 3—5. Berl. Mus. Antiquarium. M. J. 8015, 12.

The figure was broken through below the arms, the left hand is missing, the right is injured and has lost the thumb. In other respects the figure is intact. Among the types of worshipping figures this one occupies a peculiar place. Most of them belong to the so-called "snow-man technique", as for example Pl. LI, 6; and in most cases both arms are raised in prayer. In this case however the left arm is held before the breast, and the gesture of adoration is made with the right alone. There is a striking contrast between the upper and lower parts of the body; the figure ends in a kind of pillar-shaped pedestal, the form of which is borrowed from the "snow-man technique", finished in a smooth round shape, probably by means of the potter's wheel. The head is carefully made in a mould, while the trunk and arms are superficially modelled with the hand. The head is a specially good example of the Kyprian type (cf. Pl. XLVIII, 3) and the technique is also Kyprian; the hair on the head and the curls on the shoulders are formed in the same manner as they are in the heads to which I have just referred. The hair and eyebrows are painted black. The ear-ornament is of the well-known form, but remarkably large. The breast. which is left free by the opening in the garment, is ornamented by a peculiarly twisted chain or string. (cf. p. 263).

Plate LI.

? 1 and 2. Woman playing tympanum (clay) from Dali (Idalion). Berl. Mus. Antiquarium. M. J. 8015, 20.

The figure was broken off at the waist, but has been pieced together again. Only half of the tambourine is preserved. The head is made in a mould, the trunk superficially modelled (cf. Pl. L, 6). Like the figure of the worshipper, this tambourine player belongs to the "snow-man technique", an example of which is illustrated on the same Plate No. 8. The head of this figure belongs to the Kyprian types of which I have already spoken. The covering of the head is interesting; it is a thick rolled cap with a rounded point, a shape which we have already seen on Pl. XLVI, 1, 3, but the material is in this case different, and shows a net-like pattern. The cap consists of four divisions, the edges of which are distinctly marked.

Ribbons with tassels are fastened to the end and hang down behind. The dressing of the hair and the jewellery are of the usual kind. The hair and eyebrows are painted black. The hands, rudely modelled, lie on the surface of the tympanum, which is painted red. The dress seems to be the same as in Figs. Pl. L, 1, 5. The slit in the garment, through which the right arm appears, is plastically rendered. Text p. 139, Note 2.

⁰3. Upper part of a draped female figure (clay) from Dali (Idalion). Berl. Mus. Antiquarium. M. J. 8015, 32.

This figure is complete to about the waist. It is made in a mould, and has the tray shaped impression at the back. The expression of the face is Semitic, and the dressing of the hair resembles that of the head on Pl. XLVIII. 3, showing also black paint. The figure stands upright with the arms hanging stiffly down, and has no attribute. A garment may be inferred from the edge which appears in relief above the breast.

⁰4. Upper part of a female figure (clay). From Dali (Idalion). Found in the same sanctuary. Berl. Mus. Antiquarium. M. J. 8015, 49.

The figure is broken off under the shoulders. An object resembling a roll or bundle was carried under the right arm, and extended to the middle of the back. The head is made in a mould. The eyebrows are prominent and characteristic, hatched lines being employed as on the heads on Pl. XLVIII, 3, 4. In respect of style the head belongs to the same series. In the centre of the forehead is a small protuberance like a button, and a similar one, only larger, is to be seen behind the right ear, which is itself not given in relief; at the left side the button has been broken off, but the fractured surface can be plainly seen. Cf. the similar buttons which serve to ornament the figure on Pl. L, 5. The drapery which covers the head and the chin is peculiarly modelled and painted black. A thick bunch of hair falls on the neck behind.

5. Rude clay figure from Dali. Coll. Cesnola. Berl. Mus. Antiquarium. T. C. 6682, 40.

This figure is quite intact. The clay is of a yellowish red colour, and is covered with a white slip. Eyebrows, eyes, mouth and beard are painted black. The pillar-like formation of the body is a feature which this figure has in common with the most primitive terra-cottas of Idalion, e. g. Nos. 6, 8, 9 of the same Plate. The nose is abnormally large. The ears, mere rude lumps, are made separately and fastened on. The man holds in his arms a horned sacrificial animal, the eyes of which are painted black.

⁰6. Rude female figure (clay) from Dali (Idalion). Found in the same sanctuary as 1—4. Berl. Mus. Antiquarium. M. J. 1805, 7.

The technique is extremely primitive; the body is shaped like a pillar; the breasts, the ears, the hair on the forehead and the curls on the shoulders, as well as the thick fillet, which is carried partly round the head, are made separately and fastened on. Black paint is laid on abundantly. Hair, eyeballs and parts of the drapery are painted. From the waist slanting stripes are carried downwards, being probably intended to represent the folds of the garment, while over the breasts the edge of the garment is painted black. On the arms three black rings are painted. On the side next the spectator the fingers are indicated by black strokes. The raising of the arms must be regarded as a gesture of adoration. cf. p. 263 and 305.

⁰7. Woman holding tympanum (clay) from Dali. Found in the same sanctuary. Berl. Mus. Antiquarium. M. J. 8015, 22. The lower part of the figure from the arm, which is bent at a right angle, is missing. The nose has been broken off. The type belongs to the series of figures representing temple attendants. (Pl. L, 1, 5, 6.) The tambourine is not slung on a ribbon as in Pl. L, 1 but is held in the hand close to the body. The woman wears on her head a broad decoration like a diadem, entirely covering the hair on the forehead. From under this fall the shoulder-curls. The dress is the same as that of the figures on Pl. L, 1 and 5, the opening of the garment being edged by a broad dark red border. The engraved lines in the curls, eyebrows, and right wrist, are worthy of notice.

⁰8. Woman playing tympanum (clay) from Dali. Berl. Mus. Antiquarium. M. J. 8015, 19.

This figure is in perfect preservation. The technique is of the most primitive kind and shows no plastic modelling whatever, being in fact a characteristic example of the "snow man" style. The body is in the form of a pillar decorated with black and red horizontal stripes. The arms are adorned with black rings. The edges of the eyelids, the eye-balls, the shoulder-curls, and the edge of the tambourine are black, while the diadem, the bridge of the nose, the mouth and the surface of the tambourine are red. The diadem and the shoulder-curls are made out of a continuous band of clay, which forms a cross at the back of the head. The left hand holds the tambourine by the lower edge, while the right lies against the surface. This attitude must indicate the action of playing.

⁰9. = XXXVII, 3. Woman with child (clay) from Dali. Berl. Mus. Antiquarium. M. J. 8015, 47.

In shape and technique this figure resembles the preceding. The edges of the eyelids, the eye-balls and the curls are painted black; the garment shows wide black vertical stripes, and the sleeves are ornamented with black strokes. The mouth, bridge of the nose, and ears are painted red. On her left arm the woman holds a child. The head of this figure has been broken off, but the arms can be distinctly recognized. Cf. p. 205, 263.

⁰10. Rude female figure (clay). From Dali (Idalion). From the same sanctuary. Berl. Mus. Antiquarium. M. J. 8015, 4.

The lower part of the body is broken away, and of the arms only stumps remain, which however show that they were represented raised. This figure therefore belongs to the type of worshippers, Pl. LI, 7. The style and technique belong to a very early stage, and may be compared with the figure just referred to. The so-called "snowman technique" as in Nos. 8 and 9 does not appear in this example. The form of the face recalls that of a bird. The eye-brows are strongly arched, the eyes protrude, the nose is large and curved, and the chin very pointed. There is no indication of mouth. The breasts are prominent and pointed.

?11. Woman with fruit (limestone) from Dali (Idalion). Berl. Mus. Antiquarium. M. J. 8015, 348.

This figure is in excellent preservation, and may be compared with similar ones on Pl. XLIX, 2. It belongs, like these, to the Transition Period, being Greek in motive and drapery, and foreign in type of face. The cloak and the shoes are painted red. The back is left flat as usual.

? 12. Fragment of a female draped figure (limestone) from Dali. Found in the same sanctuary. Berl. Mus. Antiquarium. M. J. 8015, 370.

The lower part from the thighs, as well as the right hand and the left fore-arm, are broken away. The head was also broken off, but has been replaced. There are many traces of painting. The back is roughly finished. The style is pure archaic Greek, and may be compared to that of Pl. XLIX, 6. It evidently represents the well-known motive of a woman carrying a blossom or a fruit. On the breast, just at the edge of the garment, is a fractured surface showing the original place of this attribute. The dressing of the hair is interesting. The bunch of hair at the back is tied up in a kerchief which is painted red, as in the heads Pl. LIV, 2, 3. Above the hair on the forehead appears a row of rosettes, which seem to represent metal ornaments fastened on a fillet. The lips are painted red. The ornament on the breast consists of a row of tassel-shaped pendants. A red streak painted on the neck above this probably indicates a chain. On the neck itself a pattern of red lines is visible.

(1—12 H. S.)

Plate LII.

All the objects represented on this Plate come from the Astarte-Aphrodite sanctuary at Dali (No. 3 on the list) and are now in the Antiquarium of the Berlin Museum.

1. Pedestal of a small statue (clay). M. J. 8015, 188.
The feet are represented in shoes with pointed turned-up ends. The heels are broken off. On the instep there is tied a bow, and it shows traces of black paint.

2. Fragment of a right foot from a pedestal (clay). M. J. 8015, 191b.
The left side with the point of the shoe, and most of the sole, is broken away. The clay is of a grey colour covered with a purplish-red slip. On the instep may be seen shoe-straps crossing, and a bow-knot. 0,160 m long; 0,110 m high.

3. Pedestal (clay) from Dali. M. J. 8015, 186.
The heels are broken off. The shoes are pointed and turned-up. On each instep is a bow covered by a three-cornered flap. Above this the edge of the garment, falling in folds, is preserved. The clay is light grey. Breadth of the lower surface 0,180 m.

4. Fragment of a right hand (clay). M. J. 8015, 164.
The back of the hand is rudely executed, as only the inner side was intended to be seen. The fore-fingers are decked each with three rings with imitations in clay of jewels, all turned towards the inner part of the hand. The clay is light grey. L. 0,160 m; Br. 0,098 m.

5. Right fore-arm and hand of a clay statue, M. J. 8015, 90.
This arm had been bent at the elbow and raised, so that the palm of the hand was turned outwards. The bend of elbow may still be seen. At the back is visible the broken edge of the garment to which the arm was joined. The motive must be explained as a gesture of adoration. The fore-arm is ornamented with a long bracelet in four divisions, connected by a broad centre-band. L. 0,265 m. The clay is light grey.

6. Fragment of a right foot from a pedestal (clay). M. J. 8015, 193a.
The right side and most of the sole are broken away. Between the great and the second toes pass sandal-straps, which are fastened together on the instep by a kind of buckle. The clay is light grey, the surface being burned to a reddish shade. Length of the lower surface, 0,158 m.

7. Fragment of a foot which corresponds to the preceding. M. J. 8015, 193b. Length of the lower edge 0,125 m.

8 and 9. A pair of feet with the edges of the basis (clay). M. J. 8015, 192a, b.
The feet are naked, and the fifth toe of the right foot is missing. All the smaller toes are decked with rings in three or four divisions. A spiral bangle is represented as an ornament of the ankle. The clay is light grey. L. 0,155 m.

10. Pedestal of a large clay statue. M. J. 8015, 1884.
On each foot is a kind of half-shoe, which leaves the instep and the toes free. The two side-flaps of these shoes are fastened together at the top to a strap, which passes between the great toe and the second toe. These flaps are painted red, and their rounded ends are coloured purplish-black. Nos. 6 and 7 probably wore similar half-shoes. The three centre toes are adorned each with four rings; the nails are marked by impressions in the clay. A broken edge passes from one ankle to another, probably the remains of the hem of the drapery. It is painted red. At the back the feet are connected with the garment by a thick bar, remains of which are to be seen on the left foot. Breadth of the lower surface, 0214 m.

11. Fragment of a left fore-arm, holding a small bull by the fore-legs. From a limestone statue M. J. 8015, 436.

The mouth of the bull is broken off. The arm of the figure lies close to the garment, part of the edge of which is preserved. There is a bracelet on the arm, adorned with horizontal stripes. The edge of the garment is to be seen close by it. The workmanship of the bull shows close observation of nature.

12. Fragment of a large cylindrical crown (clay). 8015, 147.

The design on this crown represents a series of female draped figures with the hands placed on the breasts; one of these is preserved. This figure wears long shoulder-curls, and a necklace with a long centre-piece. The upper and lower edges of the crown are provided with strings, to which small buttons are fastened, while broad tassels hang down from the lower edge. The head of the figure projects over the edge On the background of the crown and its lower edge are traces of purplish-red colour. The clay is light grey. H. 0,085 m. Cf. Pl. XXXVIII. 5.

13 Small figure of a woman holding the breasts (clay). M. J. 8015, 39.

This figure corresponds exactly to the one on the crown (No. 12); but is only 0,071 m high. It belongs, if not to the same, certainly to a similar crown. At the back of the head the clay shows where the little figure was fastened to the upper edge of the crown. The clay is light grey.

14. Female figure holding the breasts (clay). M. J. 8015, 42.

The feet are broken off, and part of the head is injured. What remains is composed of three divisions. This nude figure is made in a mould, the back being impressed in the form of a tray. Long shoulder-curls fall down in front. A chain is fastened closely round the neck, and on the breast falls a second chain with large ornamental pieces in the shape of rings. The ears are covered with the Kyprian ornamental sheath. The style is that peculiar to Kypros, H. 0,128 m. The clay is light grey.

15. Upper part of a female figure in a kind of relief, holding the breasts. (Clay). M. J. 8015, 40.

The head is in profile to the left. Three plaited strands of hair fall down on the right shoulder. The style is that of the preceding figures. This figure has also been fastened to some other object. H. 0,050 m.

16. Upper part of a female figure holding a dove (clay). M. J. 8015, 37.

This figure is made in a mould, and the back is finished off flat. A comparison with such figures as Pl. L, 1, shows that the object in the right hand must be a dove. The ornaments on the neck and ears are those which are usual in these figures of the Kyprian style. On each shoulder fall three long curls in conventional form. The clay is a dull grey, with traces of black and red paint. H. 0,100 m.

17. Fragment of a crown like No. 12. M. J. 8015, 149.

Part of the upper edge is preserved, with the head of a female figure which was fastened to it. The clay is light grey. H 0,036 m.

18. Nude female figure holding the breasts (clay). M. J. 8015, 45.

The type corresponds to No. 14. The ornaments consist of necklace, breast chain, ear ornaments and bracelets both on the upper and lower parts of the arm. The navel is abnormally large.

The style is that peculiar to Kypros. At the back the figure is finished off smooth. A lump of clay at the back of the head shows that this figure, like Nos. 13 and 15, belonged to a crown. H. 0,080 m.

19. Two fragments of a crown like No. 12, which fit together. M. J. 8015, 148.

To each fragment is attached a female figure holding the breasts. The workmanship is careless and the style that peculiar to Kypros. The clay is light grey, with a reddish yellow surface, and no traces of additional colour. H. 0,047 m; Br. 0 070 m. Cf. Pl. XXXVIII. 3

20. Fragment of a bearded head (clay). M. J. 8015, 65.

Only the face is formed in a mould, the back part of the head showing an impression in the form of a tray. There is a slanting breakage at the right side of the forehead. Traces of black may be seen on the hair of the head and beard. The upper lip is clean shaven. The beard is very long, the separate strands of hair being indicated by flat parallel impressed stripes. Cf. Holwerda, "Die alten Kyprier", p. 14. The large eyes, the edges of which are indicated in relief, and the large nose, are noticeable features. The head was made separately. H. 0,067 m. The clay is reddish brown. Cf. p. 255, Note 1.

21. Small head of a bull (clay). M. J. 8015, 210.

The left ear is almost all broken away, and the right is injured at the point. The details are given by engraved lines and punctured dots, the mouth and on the forehead between the horns. There are traces of black paint on the right side on the horn, ear, eye and mouth. The workmanship shows careful observation of nature. The clay is light grey. L. 0,071 m.

22. Upper part of a nude female figure holding the breasts (clay). M. J. 8015, 43.

The type is the usual one, like No. 14; the style local Kyprian. The figure is finished flat at the back. The painting is very abundant; the hair on the head, the shoulder curls and the edges of the eyelids being black, the flesh bright pink, and the necklace and chain dark red. The proportions are unusually long, and the workmanship very careless. The clay is light grey. H. 0,088 m.

23. Lower part of a nude female figure holding the breasts (clay). M. J. 8015, 44.

The figure is in good preservation from the shoulders downwards; the back is finished smooth. The type is the usual one. The navel is indicated. The legs are modelled quite flat; a section would be approximately triangular. The fore-arms are decorated with wide bracelets. The whole body shows traces of a pink colour. The ends of the shoulder curls are painted black. The clay is light grey. H. 0,117 m.

24. A female figure in long drapery with a dove (clay). M. J. 8015, 36.

This figure is broken across at the thighs. The back is finished smooth. Drapery may be inferred from the mark of the opening on the breast, although the outline of the body is quite visible (Cf. Pl. L, 1). The right hand hangs stiffly down, in the left hand a dove is held in front of the breast. Style and technique show the peculiarities of ancient Kyprian modelling in clay. The dressing of the hair is the same as in Pl. L, 6. The sheath-like ornament of the ear, with pendants in the form of bow-knots, are distinctly to be seen. There are traces of black colouring on the hair. The clay is light grey, the surface being burnt of a reddish hue. H. 0,195 m.

25. Female figure in long drapery (clay) M. J· 8015, 26. The feet are broken off. The left hand is chipped, the figure represents the type without any attributes. The right hand hangs down stiffly, the left is raised and lies close to the body. The dress consists of a long Chiton and of a shorter upper garment with broad bordered opening in front; the upper garment distinctly terminates below the waist. The deeply-chiselled line in the lower part of the body which marks off the legs, is worth noticing. The head and type of face may be best compared with Pl. LXVIII, 3 and L, 6. To represent the curls of the hair, drooping spirals are moulded in the clay, but more roughly than in the above mentioned figures. By way of ear-ornaments it has, besides the ordinary shells, the easily recognisable pendants of the form described in Plate XLIX, 5. Bracelets on the fore-arm. The clay is reddish. Height 0,226 m.

26. Female figure in long drapery (clay) M. J. 8015, 25. The head of the figure has been fastened on, but belongs to it. The reverse side is flat. The type of the figure corresponds to the former, and the style is the same. There is a thick coating of black paint on the hair of the head (even on the reverse side), on the curls falling on the shoulders, the eyebrows and round the eyes. The long robe is painted yellow with black seams; the broad border of the opening at the throat is painted dark red. The face presents heavy bloated features. The clay is bright grey. Height 0,178 m.

27. Female figure with flowers or fruit (clay), M. J. 8015, 76. This figure except the face is very well preserved; the reverse side has been left flat. Whilst all the previous figures in this Plate displayed the peculiar Cyprian style, the present one represents the old Greek style of clay-modelling. Drapery, hair, and type are in the well known Greek style, cf. Pl. XLIX, 6 The left foot is planted forward. But still we seem to see obvious traces of the influence of the stone sculpture of Idalion; the eyes, as is frequently seen in the Idalion limestone sculptures, are fashioned in the form of an almond-shaped protuberance. The small pedestal too has the form of the limestone figures. The hair with the three ringlets falling on each shoulder is painted black and adorned with a head band as in other Greek figures. The face and the drapery are of a dark rose colour. In spite of Greek influence the figure wears the characteristic Cyprian ear-pods which must have remained in fashion for several centuries. It has thick rings for bracelets. The clay is bright grey. Height 0,162 m.

28. Fragment of an ox (clay) M. J. 8015, 209.

The head, breast, and part of the trunk, with the upper part of the left fore leg, are preserved; the ears and horns are damaged. There are obvious traces of black paint. The details of the head and of the pendent dewlap are represented by engraved lines. The workmanship is much ruder than in the head No. 21; the upper part of the left fore leg is very unnatural. The work appears to have been meant only to show the left side. The clay is bright grey, with surface baked red. Height 0,080 m.

°Plate LIII.

All the specimens in this Plate come from Dali and belong to the antiquarian of the Berlin Museum, from the sanctuary of Astarte-Aphrodite at Dali, excavated in 1885 (No. 3 in the list).

1a and b. Umbellate flowers (limestone) M. J. 8015, 452.

The umbel consists of a number of small star-like blossoms, which we have to imagine attached to separate stalks. The thick stem of the whole umbel is grooved. On one side the tip of the finger of the hand which held the flower is preserved. Height 0,053 m. Similar flowers are to be seen in Cesnola's Atlas, Pl. 29, No. 162 ff.

2. Four leaved flower in limestone. M. J. 8015, 454.

The petals are painted red and are bow-shaped. The sepals are pointed and have a dentelated edge. Height 0,037 m.

3. Four leaved flower in clay. M. J. 8015, 258.

Two petals opposite each other are broken off. The petals are lancet-shaped and slope downwards. The thick pyramidal stem is painted green. The petals are dark red. The whole has been broken off from somewhere. 0,045 m.

4. Bosom of a female figure in clay. M. J. 8015, 88 (Twice represented).

One breast with the adjoining portions is preserved On the upper edge of the fragment the end of an ornament which hung down on the breast is preserved. It consists of ten tassels or tufts, which are divided into separate portions by horizontal stripes; and there is, in fact, an alternation of smooth and grooved ones. On the tassels there are abundant traces of green, red and yellow paint, but without any definite system being recognisable. Close to the breast, which is very projecting, are seen two pairs of strings hanging down. Their meaning cannot be made out. A small horned-animal, standing on the right and wearing a collar, seems to be connected with these, though this cannot be made out from the casts; it is to be regarded as an ornament. Right across the breast passes a streak of dark violet paint, which is bordered below by a black streak. The drapery below the breast is painted yellow. The meaning of the violet streak is clear, if we compare other figures, as Pl. XLIX, 3 and L, 6. In the case of the first the square cut of the dress at the neck is represented by a similar streak, in the case of the other figure, the opening at the neck is represented plastically, and all round a broad seam or broad border is painted in red. The row of tassels falling on the breast is not to be regarded as a specific breast-ornament, but is connected, as No. 9 and 20 of the same plate show, with the pendent plaits of hair. We have, then, before us the left side of the bosom. But the horned animal belongs to the luxurious ornament which hangs down upon the breast; other ornaments seem to be broken off higher up, to judge by the uneven surface of the clay. The clay is bright-grey. Height 0,157 m. Breadth 0,210 m.

5. A four-footed animal in clay. lying down M. J. 8015, 235.

The face is turned towards the spectator; the body in profile, to the right. The details of the bodily structure are suggested by rudely-sculptured lines. The workmanship is exceedingly rude. The clay is deep red. Length 0,047 m. Height 0,082 m.

6. Round mask in clay M. J. 8015, 236.

The expression of the face is animalish, especially the broad flattened nose. The forehead makes a kind of arched frame. Either it is actually an animal-mask, or intended to represent a demon with a brutish expression, perhaps a Silenus. The clay is bright-grey. Diameter 0,028, cf. XXXVI, 16 and p. 209.

7. Rosette in clay. M. J. 8015, 223.

The star in the middle is raised, and divided by incised lines; the separate rays are painted alternately red and yellow. The central streak is black. The edge is marked with a zig-zag line; the inner triangles thereby produced are painted red, the outer ones yellow. The clay is bright grey. Diameter 0,052.

8. Palmette in clay. M. J. 8015, 245.

The edge is damaged on the right side and at the top. The central part, on which the rosette rests, is not represented. The volutes with the acute-angled triangle from which the Palmette springs, is very common in Cyprian monuments, especially in representations of the sacred tree. The clay is reddish-brown. Height 0,120 m.

9. Fragment of a large female statue in clay. M. J. 8013, 80.

The bent right arm is preserved, also the right breast with the neighbouring parts, and a corresponding portion of the back. On the back and shoulders falls a plastically raised, rounded mass, which presumably is a tuft of hair Besides this, a series of narrow plaits painted black falls on the shoulders in front, to which are attached tassels reaching to the breast (cf. No. 4 of the same Plate). The drapery ends distinctly at the arm. The figure also wears a bracelet, consisting of four rings and a broad clasp (vid. No. 37 of the same Plate), and also a peculiar arm-ring. The drapery is uniformly painted over with violet-coloured paint. Near the breast can be seen traces of the breast-ornament. The clay is bright-grey. Height 0,335 m.

10. Left hand of a statuette in limestone M. J. 8015, 440.

The hand is clenched and is holding three lily-like flowers, which are gathered into a bunch. On the wrist a bracelet in the form of a ring. The workmanship is careful. Even the finger nails are represented. Height 0,095 m.

11. Fragment of a clay vessel M. J. 8015, 244.

On the lower border which is 0,070 m long, is an elliptical broken surface 0,045 m long, at which the fragment appears to have been connected with another object. It is probably only a portion of a larger vessel. The clay is bright-grey. Diagonal 0,113 m.

12. Fragment of a hand in clay. M. J. 8015, 174.

Three fingers of the right hand have been preserved, the thumb, the fore-finger, and the middle-finger, which are holding a bud. The middle-finger is adorned with a double ring; only the first joint of the thumb and the two first of the fore-finger are preserved. The other fingers have never been divided. The bud, which is just opening, shows traces of green paint on the sepals. The clay is bright greyish-brown. Height 0,108 m.

13. Fragment of a Sphinx in limestone M. J. 8015, 451.

The fore-legs and the lower extremities of the hind legs are broken off, and also the extremities of the wings. The face is damaged. The workmanship of the reverse side is rude. The type of face may perhaps be compared with that of Figs. 3 and 6 Pl. XLIX. The carefully executed feathers of the wings are painted red. Length 0,073 m.

14. Fragment of a large clay statue M. J. 8015, 118.

A piece of the drooping head and a part of the breast with remains of ornamental articles are preserved. The braid of hair twisted in two plaits and painted black. The parts of the breast are painted bright red and so are the ornaments; but the latter are also painted in other colours; they are mussel-shaped beads, some violet-red, the others green. The clay is bright grey. Height 0,105 m, Breadth 0,115 m.

15. Fragment of a hand with horned-animal. M. J. 8015, 167.

The animal lies on the palm of the hand. The back of the hand is quite roughly executed. There are the remains of a bracelet on the wrist. The animal's tail is broken off. The clay is bright-grey. Length 0,105 m, Height 0,075 m.

16. Star-rosette in clay. M. J. 8015, 226.

The pattern is represented by engraved lines. The clay is bright greyish-brown. Diameter 0,049 m.

17. Star-rosette in clay. M. J. 8015, 225.

The centre is represented by a plastic head, the separate rays are also modelled. There are traces of yellow paint on them. The clay is bright grey. Diameter 0,032 m.

18. Fragment of a female figure in clay. M. J. 8015, 97.

The neck with the appertaining ornament, the left breast, a part of the shoulder with the thick clusters of curls, are preserved. These are hatched on the system of opposite triangles with incised lines and painted black. Across the upper part of the breast the engraved edge of the throat-opening passes upwards. On the neck are preserved traces of a close double string of beads, on which a star-like ornament hangs (only small portions remain, which are painted black). On the breast hang down two distinct chains with pendants. The clay is bright-grey. Height 0,183 m. Breadth 0,183 m.

19. Fragment of a female statue in clay. M. J. 8015, 101.

A portion of the neck and of the breast with its rich ornament is preserved. The neck is adorned with a necklace consisting of a triple row of closely-fitting mussel-shaped beads; of the appertaining centre-piece only the lower portion is preserved. Then follow five breast-chains of different lengths, the three upper ones consist of tassel-like portions which hang with the thick ends downwards (similar to the gold ornaments in Cesnola "Salaminia" p. 19). The centre-pieces are of different kinds; the upper chain has for its centre-piece a pendant running to a point, and with traces of violet-red paint. The second bears a cylindrical cross-piece, to which a small ox's head is attached; the third a mussel-shaped bead. The two next chains have only been fragmentarily preserved, they consisted of thick cords which are figured by engraved lines. On the left side the remains of the braids of hair coloured black are preserved. On the right, however, we see two black locks not engraved, the ends of which are twisted. The clay is bright-brown. Height 0,155 m, Breadth 0,107 m.

20. Fragment of a large female statue in clay M. J. 8015, 116.

A portion of the left shoulder, with the hair plaits falling on it, is preserved. The hair is arranged in ten thin plaits, represented by engraved lines and painted black. The ends are inserted into cylindrical ornaments. It is the same fashion as in No. 4 and 9 on the same Plate. On the left side of the fragment (from the spectator) a portion of the breast is preserved on which is fastened a portion of a chain (similar to the former figure) with traces of green paint. The extant portions of the breast on the right side of the fragment show a zig-zag pattern in engraved lines. Probably this pattern belongs to the border of the throat-opening. The clay is bright-grey. Height 0,145 m, Breadth 0,200 m.

21. Fragment of a female statue in clay. M. J. 8015, 99.

A portion of the breast with the ornament is preserved. This is similar to that of No. 19. Above the protuberance on the left breast a combination of spiral-curls is preserved which no doubt belongs to the locks which fall over the shoulder.

The clay is bright-grey. Height 0,136 m, Breadth 0,135 m.

22. Fragment of a female statue in clay M. J. 8015, 102.

A portion of the right side of the breast is perserved. Remains of three chains falling on the breast are preserved. The links are similar to those of Nos. 19 and 21, but better executed. They are large beads which have somewhat the form of whorls; they are arranged on a string at intervals of about a finger's breadth and painted alternately red and black. A cylindrical pendant hangs from the shortest chain. On the right side of the breast is preserved a portion of the closely-grooved shoulder-lock, painted black. The clay is bright-grey. Height 0.140 m, Breadth 0,085 m.

23. Fragment of a clay statue M. J. 8015, 113.

All that remains is a piece of clay on which hangs a large ring with a small stone, fastened to two chains. The Berlin Museum contains several such fragments with similar ornaments; cf. infr. No. 29 and 30. Perhaps the ring is a badge of office. The clay is bright-grey. Height 0,054 m, Breadth 0,070 m.

24. Ox's head in clay M. J. 8015, 211.

The right horn is damaged. In the middle of the forehead a triangle is engraved. The eyelids are painted black; the head has many traces of yellow on it. Round the neck runs a ruff-shaped fracture-surface. The head belonged, as in the case of No. 19, to the large breast-ornament of a statue. The clay is bright-grey. Height 0,050 m.

51*

25. Fragment of a female statue in clay M. J. 8015, 103.

A part of the breast is preserved. The ornaments correspond to those in Nos. 19, 21 and 22. From a thin necklace hangs an acorn-shaped pendant. Of the right shoulder-lock the cylindrical cases painted yellow are preserved. The clay is reddish. Height 0,095 m, Breadth 0,178 m.

26. Fragment of a female statue in clay M. J. 8015, 98.

The portion between the breasts is preserved; of the left breast something like half remains; of the right only a slight trace. The breast-ornamentation is similar to the previous specimens; the links of the chains are painted alternately red and black. The shorter schain bears two smaller, and the longer one large pendant, which all bear traces of green paint. Besides this a broad grooved band hangs down over the breast. The dress is cut low and painted violet-red. The narrow border of the throat-opening is dentelated and represented by engraved lines painted black. The clay is reddish. Height 0,108 m, Breadth 0,170 m.

27. Clay fragment M. J. 8015, 264.

The object is composed of a number of individual similar parts, which are somewhat like a lancet-shaped leaf and which are standing up in a tuft; on the summit of these leaves is placed a four-leaved flower with bud-like centre-piece; two leaves of the flower are broken off. With the lens the details in the figure become plainer.

28. Fragment of a clay statue M. J. 8015, 108.

A portion of the neck is preserved with the broad necklace. The necklace is divided into lozenge-shaped fields by scratched lines, showing traces of violet-red, yellow and green paint. The large centre-piece is painted yellow. The clay is reddish. Height 0,078 m; Diagonal Breadth 0,100 m.

29. Fragment of a clay statue M. J. 8015, 111·

As in No. 28 a large ring, which is only half preserved, hangs to two small chains. The stone is particularly large. The clay is reddish. Height 0,065 m; Breadth 0,072 m.

30. Fragment of a clay statue M. J. 8015, 112.

A similar piece is preserved; the ring provided with a small stone, hangs by means of a small chain to a cord running across. Behind the fragment is preserved a protuberance running obliquely downwards, which was no doubt connected with the inner structure of the statue. The clay is dark red. Height including the protuberance 0,120 m, Breadth 0,045 m.

31. Right fore-arm of a large clay statue M. J. 8015, 81.

The arm is bent. The elbow, together with the greater part of the forearm, is enveloped in the drapery; the original position of the arm can be seen by the bracelet. The form of the bracelet may be compard with No. 37 of this Plate; it consists of several rings and a broad clasp in two parts. The clasp is composed of exactly the same parts as in No. 37 and painted the same. The eye of the spectator is directed towards it; the opposite side of the arm is rudely executed. The arm cannot then as represented in the figure be hanging downwards, but, on the contrary, must be raised, and in such a manner that the palm is turned outwards. The idea of the attitude is the same as in Plate LII, 5. We have before us the arm of a worshipping figure. Besides the bracelet, a spiral ring situated higher up adorns the arm. The dress in front is cut in a waving line. The painting is particularly well preserved. The drapery is painted yellow, and has a black edge about 2 cm broad. The flesh-colouring is rose. The arm-ring is yellow; the rings of the bracelet is also yellow. We have already spoken of the clasp. The clay is bright grey. Length 0,235 m.

32. Fragment of a clay statue. M. J. 8015, 117.

A piece above the left breast, with the ends of the shoulder-lock (similar to No. 20), is preserved. The locks are again inserted in cylindrical cases, which show traces of yellow paint; the ends of the locks appear below and are painted black. The small remains of the drapery are painted dark violet-red. On the right side of the fragment, there is, as in No. 20, a piece of similar pattern; the triangles produced by the zig-zag lines, are painted alternately green and violet-red. On the vertical edge of this pattern also traces of green paint can be seen. The clay is bright grey. Height 0,078 m; Breadth 0,140 m.

33. Small head of ox already depicted and discussed at Pl. LII, 21.

34. Fragment of a clay statue M. J. 8015, 82.

Part of a fore-arm with elbow is preserved. The motive is the same as in No. 31. We must imagine the picture reversed. Only the spiral-shaped ring of the bracelet is preserved, which terminates in a snake-like head; it is painted yellow. The drapery too, which is cut out in a curve at the elbow, as in No. 31, is painted yellow, but has a broad violet-red edge. It is no longer possible to make out the colouring of the flesh. The clay is bright green. Height 0,135 m.

35. Fragment of a large crown (clay) M· J. 8015, 144.

The parts preserved are those of two superposed strips and beneath a small protuberance with black paint, which doubtless represents the hair of the head. The upper strip consists of square spaces, which are marked out by thin strips of clay, and filled-in with small rosettes (2 preserved); on the edge of the strip hang lozenge-shaped pendants (2 preserved whole, 1 in fragment); a cup-shaped knob is fastened on. The parts of the crown are painted violet-red. At the lower fracture one sees the traces where a round object has been, probably the ear-pods, of which the following number offers a specimen. The clay is bright-grey. Height 0,083 m; Average breadth 0,060 m.

36. Pod-shaped ear-ornament (clay). M. J. 8015, 154.

From the upper pod, which has a jagged edge, hang seven pendants; every pendant has underneath a button-shaped appendage. The pod has still its red paint well preserved, while the pendants seem to have been painted yellow. The clay is bright grey. Height 0,075 m; Breadth 0,063 m.

37. Fragment of a large bracelet (clay). M. J. 8015, 158.

The bracelet consits of a hoop 0,085 m broad, furnished with incised parallel lines, lying close to one another, and a broad clasp in the middle. The latter is divided into two longitudinal strips by means of incised lines, which in their turn are divided into five isosceles triangles by means of zig-zag lines. These triangles are painted alternately red, yellow and green. The clay is bright grey and yellow. Length 0,055 m.

38. Fragment of an arm with bracelet (clay) M. J. 8015, 157.

The bracelet consists of a spiral in the from of a snake. The eyes are pressed in; in the same way the scales on the back and the outlines of the body are represented by incised lines. The clay is bright-grey. Height 0,050 m; Breadth 0,060 m

39. Fragment of a crown (clay) M. J. 8015, 139.

The rim of the crown is composed of separately laid-on strips of clay. The rounding was divided into square fields; on the right we see the remains of diagonally laid strips of clay; on the left the field is adorned with grotesque heads, probably representing Bes, which are printed with a stamp on a plastically raised surface. The whole is covered with yellow paint. The clay is bright grey. Height 0,087 m; Breadth 0,105 m. cf. XXXVIII, 20 p. 209.

40. Fragment of a large head (clay) M. J. 8015, 133.

The piece seems to come from the left side of the forehead. The locks are preserved, the diadem resting on them and a small portion of the skin of the head. The forelocks are represented in relief on them as hanging curls, hatched with parallel lines and painted black. The diadem is painted red and has stars left in the natural colour of the clay, which have in the middle pierced red beads (one of this kind is preserved). The clay is greyish-yellow. Height 0,090 m; Breadth 0,110 m. Coloured reprodution at Plate LXVII, 3.

41. Fragment of a female head (clay) M. J. 8015, 150.

The fragment comes from the left ear. The pod-shaped ear-ornament is preserved, also a part of the hair on the forehead, and a part of the locks which fall on the shoulder. The ear-ornament is here in three parts; on it at one corner is fastened a loop-shaped appendage. The colour is bright-grey. Greatest length 0,135 m.

42. Fragment of a head (clay) M. J. 8015, 121.

Remains of the hair of the head preserved, which is arranged in separate plaits and painted black. The plaits are so engraved with lines, that we might compare the pattern with a branch of a fir-tree. On the upper edge a row of lotus flowers and buds fall down on the hair, which appear to be painted yellow. We must imagine these to be fastened to a rim of a crown, of which a small portion is preserved on the left corner of the fragment painted dark-violet. The hair appears to be the upper ends of the shoulder locks, so that the fragment, to judge by the inclination of the separate hair-plaits, must be supposed to come from behind the right ear; cf. Pl. XLVIII, 3. The colour of the clay is as usual. Breadth of the pper ring 0,075 m. Length of the longest side 0,100 m.

43. Fragment of a female head (clay) M. J. 8015, 134.

The left ear-ornament of the well-known form, with the adjoining portions of the hair, and a piece of the richly ornamented crown open at the top are preserved. On this are three rows of ornament mingled together: the two outer are similar and consist of flowers, rosettes and a subject that occurs frequently on the tomb-stones and sacred monuments of Cyprus: this consists of the combined symbols of the Sun and Half-moon. Between the two similar rows of ornaments are placed cone-shaped knobs with flutings. The hair is marked out by rudely engraved lines. The hair shows traces of black, the crown and ear-ornament of yellow paint, the latter no doubt to imitate the gleam of gold. The clay is reddish. Height 0,140 m. Breadth of the upper rim 0,103 m.

44. Fragment of a head (clay) M. J. 8015, 71.

The right eye and a portion of the crown are preserved. The latter is ornamented with a sort of lattice made of strips of clay stuck on, and provided at the rim with pendants hanging down. The crown itself is painted dark violet-red, the pendants yellow. Below the pendants appears the hair of the forehead made with black paint and engraved lines. The eye, as is usual in this group, is large and provided with modelled lids painted black; the pupil of the eye is painted black, while the ball of the eye shows traces of red. The flesh portions above the eye are painted bright-red. The clay is bright-grey. Height 0,115 m, Breadth 0,068 m.

45. Fragment of a head (clay) M. J. 8015, 72.

The left side of the face is preserved, with the nose, eye and forehead; the hair, eyebrows, the edges of the eyes and the pupils are all painted black. The forehead band which lies flat and is marked out by engraved lines is painted violet-red. The flesh is bright-red, tho ball of the eye is the natural colour of the clay. The technique of the eyebrows is as in Pl. XIII, 1 &c. The technique of the hair has not yet been noticed. On the plastically raised surface which represents the hair, little circles are imprinted with some reed-shaped article of about the diameter of a pea, and in such a manner that there remains a small raised spot in the centre. The nose is strikingly pointed. The clay is bright-grey. Height 0,110 m, Breadth 0,080 m.

46. Fragment of a head (clay) M. J. 8015, 73.

The left eye with a portion of the forehead is preserved. Traces of black paint are found on the hair of the head, eyebrows, lids and pupils of the eye; the flesh is painted reddish. The eyebrows are not, as usual, plastically raised, but represented in the shape of a twig by means of engraved lines. The hair of the forehead is divided by parallel vertical lines. The clay is bright grey. Height 0,060 m. Breadth 0,085 m.

47. Fragment of a bracelet (clay) M. J. 8015, 159.

The one end, which has been preserved, consists of the head of some beast of prey, on which traces of green and red paint are preserved. Width 0,090 m. The clay is reddish.

48. Under-part of a pod-like ear-ornament. M. J. 8015, 156.

The fragment shows an arrangement in successive horizontal divisions. The individual longitudinal portions (7 have been preserved) are furnished with engraved vertical lines, which at the lower edges are cut by horizontal lines. The clay is reddish. Height 0,054 m; Breadth 0,080 m.

49. Fragment of a crown (clay) M. J. 8015, 135.

The top-surface is divided into right-angular fields by strips of clay laid on, the angles and centres of which are studded with knobs. The clay is bright-grey. Height 0,093 m, Breadth 0,128 m.

50. Fragment of a statue (clay) M. J. 8015, 169.

The left arm is preserved with a part of the drapery beneath. The hand is holding a horned animal, which to judge by the head is clearly to be distinguished as a he-goat. The arm is decorated with a broad complex bracelet. The contour of the drapery can also be made out. The clay is bright-grey. Height 0,080 m, Breadth 0,093 m.

51. Fragment of a crown (clay). M. J. 8015, 145.

In the upper broad strips rosettes are stamped; underneath hang fruit-like pendants (three preserved) and also a sun and half-moon. The sun is painted violet, the half-moon green, the rest yellow. The clay is bright-grey. Height 0,050 m; Breadth 0,055 m.

52. Fragment of a crown (clay) M. J. 8015. 145.

Apparently a crown of leaves is intended, the leaves are arranged cross-wise in three rows. The upper rim is composed of small knobs lying flat, on which are indented lines crossing each other. The clay is bright-grey. Height 0,035 m, Breadth 0,060 m.

53. Fragment of a statue (clay) M. J. 8015, 119.

There remains a piece on which lies a hair-plait composed of two strands twisted together, the ends of which are spirally curled. On the portion of drapery which is preserved are traces of green and dark red paint. The clay is bright-grey. Height 0,150 m, Breadth 0,88 m.   (1—53. H. S.)

°Plate LIV.

All the objects in this Plate come, like those of Pl. LII and LIII, from the same sanctuary of Dali and are in the Antiquarium of the Berlin Museums.

1. Female head (limestone). M. J. 8015, 318.

The style is the ancient Cyprian, mingled with elements of an Egyptian tendency. The representation of the hair is that commonly formed in the sculpture of Idalion. We are not to assume in these cases a kerchief, as was described above; cf. Pl. XLVIII, 2; XLIX, 4, 5; 4, 2, 3. We must, of course, explain such a treatment of the hair on the grounds of the technical difficulties which were presented by the working of the stone. The following heads show how a freer treatment of the hair only established itself with the introduction of Greek influence. So far that peculiar style of dressing the hair has also a stylistic significance. It is worth noticing that the ear-ornament is exactly the same as in the figure of the same style Pl. XLIX, 4.

2. Small female head (limestone). (Profile in the lower row.) M. J. 8015, 378.

The head is an excellent representative of the Archaic Greek style in Cyprian sculpture, both in regard to the type of face and of the dressing of the hair. The formation of the eyes is still the characteristic Cyprian, the hair is parted in the middle in front and falls in thick bulging masses sideways over the temples; the back hair is gathered up and tied in a knot on the top of the skull. This knot is fastened with a ribbon the ends of which are carried forwards cross-wise and are connected with another which keeps together the hair of the forehead with the hair of the neck. The ears are still smoothly modelled. In the place of the peculiar Cyprian ear-ornament there is only a disc-shaped ornament fastened to the lobe of the ear, another influence of the Greek fashion. But still the Cyprian ear-ornament does occur in heads of Greek style.

3. Small female head (limestone). (Profile in the lower row.) M. J. 8015, 374.

On the right side the hair of the forehead is somewhat damaged. Traces of paint on the kerchief and on the lips. The head belongs to the same class as the former as regards style. The workmanship is still finer and more advanced. The bands which are wound round the hair are broader; of the arrangement of the hair only a few details on the upper side of the head are visible. The disc-shaped ear-ornament is here carefully and fully modelled. The necklace is not plastically formed or represented by paintings but the mere outlines are scratched in.

4. Small female head (limestone) M. J. 8015, 380.

The nose is somewhat damaged. The style is again Greek; but the forms are not so perfected as in the preceding head; head No. 2 represents a somewhat similar stage. The treatment of the hair is particularly interesting. It is parted in the middle, but the plaits are so chiselled that they appear to be composed of square patterns. A peculiar lock is shown near the ear. We see how various are the ways in which the sculptor seeks to master the difficulty. Nos. 5 and 6 show the same technique. The diadem on the head is ornamented with a simple red meandering stripe. The lips are painted red, the broad necklace with a large central ornament also shows signs of red paint. The modelling of the ears is the same as in No. 2.

5. Small female head (limestone) M. J. 8015, 372.

The nose is somewhat damaged. The style is the same as in the preceding head. The hair is twisted into tresses; the ornamentation of the hair is similar to that of Pl. LI, 12. The ears are adorned with a small disc. The treatment of the hair as in No. 4. The expression of the face has individual character. The eyes, in contradistinction to the preceding head, are modelled with distinct lids and a fine almond shaped eye-ball. The red painted lips show a bolder curve. The chin is especially enlivened by a vertical middle-line. The concha of the ear is modelled as in head No. 3. It is in the same stage of art as the latter.

6. Small female head (limestone) M. J. 8015, 387.

The left side is somewhat damaged on the temple and cheek, likewise the back of the head and the left-shoulder lock. The style is the same. Treatment of hair as in Nos. 4 and 5; on the upper side of the head the plaits of hair are represented by simple lines. The hair is adorned with a wreath of leaves, with traces of red paint. The lips too are painted red. The modelling of the ears is natural; the disc-shaped ornament is represented only by an unmodelled brown surface. The workmanship is hasty.

7. Female head (limestone) M. J. 8015, 357. The back part is worked smooth, but the masses of hair falling on the sides are plastically modelled. The head also belongs to the Archaic-Greek style of Idalion, but the work is ruder or at all events more superficial. The profile has decidedly a rigidity which is very striking when compared with the previous heads. The treatment of the hair is very unskilful. It is parted in the middle and combed to the front in thick strands; there is no particular arrangement of the hair of the forehead; over the ears it falls down longer. The shoulder-locks have a zig-zag modelling. The whole head of hair is painted red; the lips and nostrils are also coloured red. The ear-ornament is peculiar; it covers the whole ear, but has an oval shape and is formed of four separate portions.

8. Small female head (limestone). M. J. 8015, 385.

Preservation excellent; only the lower rim of the crown is somewhat damaged. This head represents the zenith of the Archaic-Greek style in Idalion and stands on the same level with the large one on Plate XLVIII, 1. The profile is sharp but exceedingly fine. The modelling of the face is rounded. Nevertheless the eyes are formed in the way that was characteristic in Idalion. The locks of the forehead-hair are represented by wavy lines. A peculiar crown (cf. Pl. LV, 8) seems to represent a crown of leaves and flowers. Over the front of the forehead, between the rows of hair a red painted band is seen, which is doubtless meant to hold the hair together. The necklace is also painted red. The concha of the ear is modelled in conformity with nature.

9. Small female head in fragmentary condition (limestone). M. J. 8015, 391.

The back part of the head is cut off diagonally, so that more than the right half of the face is preserved than of the left. Nose and lips are much damaged. On the upper side the head shows an arched fracture, of which the edge arches more towards the right side of the head than towards the left. Between the preceding head No. 8 and the present one we must conceive a great interval of time. The symmetry here points to the best period of Greek sculpture, the fourth century B. C. The expression of the face is lovely, the contours of the body are animated and exquisitely modelled. The hair is parted in the middle and combed in wavy lines at the sides; from the right ear hangs a small curl. It is remarkable that the right side shows a different treatment to the left. The head is manifestly to be viewed neither en face nor in profile, but within a half turn to the left. This may also be inferred from the above-mentioned fracture-surface on the upper side of the head. The middle line of sight is the vertical line which we must conceive as drawn through the right eye somewhat to the right of the exterior corner of the eye (1—9 H. S.).

Plate LV.

♀ 1 and 2. Female head (clay) from Dali. The same shrine. Berl. Mus. Antiquarium M. J. 8015, 54.

The head represents the ancient Cyprian terra-cotta style and should be compared with Pl. XLVIII, 3; L, 6.

The hair of the head is rendered by hanging spirals stuck on, but only the forehead hair is indicated in this way; the whole head of hair, even the drooping shoulder locks, are painted black. The eyebrows are made, as in the examples referred to, by a plastic protuberance with triangular marks scratched in and also painted black. The plastic lids of the eye and the pupils also show signs of black paint; the face is painted red. The ornamentation of the ears is the characteristic Cyprian, but in one piece; peculiar pendants of a bow-knot shape hang from the lobes. The narrow necklace is set on plastically and adorned with a check-pattern. At the sides of the locks of hair we can see traces of a large breast-chain. The interesting point about the head is the nose-ring, about which we have spoken fully above. Cf. p. 267 ff.

? 3.   Fragment of a head (clay) from Dali.   From the same place as 1. Berl. Mus. Antiquarium M. J. 8015, 56.

Only the face is preserved, from which a piece is broken off on the left side of the forehead and the right jawbone. The nose is somewhat damaged. The head belongs to the same style and type as the preceding and is noticeable for the nose-ring; cf. p. 268.

? 4.   Fragmentary head (clay) from Dali.   Found in the same place.   Berl. Mus. Antiquarium M. J. 8015, 55.

The right cheek and the chin are broken off, the back broken out. The head belongs with its nose-ring to the same group as the preceding ones. Technique of the eyebrows similar. On the head is a cushion-shaped diadem, which has a pattern made by scratched lines, and is furnished with three knobs. The ear-ornaments are the characteristic Cyprian; cf. p. 268 and ff.

? 5 and 6. Nude female figure (clay) from Chytroi (List No. 23; from the shrine of Paphia which is confirmed by inscriptions) Cyprus Museum; (found along with the dedicatory inscriptions of 4 and 2 Pl. XLVIII, in Meister, "Die Griechischen Dialekte" p. 168, No. 14a and b).

The figure belongs to the type with drooping arms. The arrangement of then hair is very primitive; the hair of the forehead and shoulder-locks have scratched lines. The type of face is somewhat Phoenician. The large pointed breasts and the indication of navel and pubes are noticeable. This figure, like the preceding ones, wears a nose-ring. Cf. p. 263—267 and 284.

7.   Female head (clay) from Paphos.   From the Cesnola collection.   Berl. Mus. Antiquarium T. C. 6683, 16.

On the top is a large firing-hole, which extends over the whole upper surface of the head. The head has, it is true, the nose-ring and the Cyprian ear-rings, but the type of face is widely removed from that of the preceding head. The forehead and the ridge of the nose form a straight line. The nose runs to a point and the mouth is relaxed into a smile; the lips are sharply divided by an engraved line. The eyes are superficially modelled, the eyelids and eyebrows are represented with black paint. The technique resembles in its details heads from Limniti Pl. XLVI. The forehead is adorned with a cushion-shaped diadem covered with studs, on which at the side of the ears small locks are set. The neck is adorned with a narrow necklace consisting of several rows of small studs.

? 8.   Female head of a statuette (limestone) from Dali.   From our often mentioned shrine, No. 3 of the list, as 1—4. Berl. Mus. Antiquarium M. J. 8015, 386.

The back is, as usual, finished smooth; chin, mouth and nose somewhat damaged. The head belongs to a style different to those of the same Plate. The style is ancient Greek. The crown is particularly interesting, and is to be compared with Pl. LIV, 8. The crown itself is placed on a rim which is denticulated; on this comes a projecting row of small beads. Above these are two rows of flower-like discs, with small studs in the centre; the uppermost rim is composed of a row of upright bell-shaped flowers. The hair is arranged about the forehead in a triple row without parting, small ringlets fall about the ears. The ears are adorned with the characteristic Cyprian ornaments, besides, these there hang the loop-shaped pendants as in No. 1 of the same Plate.   (1—8 H. S.)

In the description of Pl. XV I have shown how the beautiful pure Greek life-sized terra cotta heads undoubtedly come from Bumo, and the Astarte-Aphrodite shrine which I have proved to have existed there (No. 51 of the list p 21).*) I have visited the place three times, once by myself. On the other two occasions I visited the place with E. Oberhummer (Munich) and W. Dorpfeld (Athens). In the course of my exploring expedition, undertaken in 1885 at my own expense, through a great part of Cyprus, I also went to Bumo. In this journey I learnt the importance of Tamassos, as well as the Greek settlement at Poli tis Chrysokhou (Marion-Arsinoë). There were at this altar, as at other altars, sculptures of different styles, as well as many of the old Graeco-Phoenico-Cyprian style, rude images in what is known as „Snow-man technique". In my illustrated book of travels which had been brought before the public on various occasions, as early as 1885, there is a copy of an old-Cyprian-style head (p. 137). It may be concluded with certainly, both from this head, from the explorations made on the spot, and above all from the specimens in my possession found on the same spot, that the head LV, 7 comes from Bumo. Our doubts are wholly set at rest by the style, treatment, motive, and above all by the clay and the mode of making the necklace with several rows of studs. Furthermore the nose-ring has hitherto only been proved to belong to sculptures from the grove of Astarte-Aphrodite. M. O.-R.

---

*) Of the previous discoveries in this spot a very fine head, of equal value to our Berlin head, having the same contours and produced by the same artists, came into the Piot Collection. Fröhner in Hoffmann's Catalogue. Paris 1890.

Plate LVI and LVII (cf. also Pl. VII and XVI).

The Shrine of Dali. No. 8 of the List.

1. Its situation.

It lies north of the town of Idalion, on the right bank of the river Satrachos, which flows from S. W. to N. E. through the fertile plains. The banks of the river, as far as the last drop of irrigation reaches, are fringed with cotton-fields, orchards and olive-groves, from whose verdure peep out here and there the houses of the present village of Dali. At the N W. end of the village our Temenos is engraved in the Map Pl. II as T. 36.*) In the floods caused by the heavy torrents the water comes up to the edge of our excavation-ground. In Pl. LX. 2 we looked down from the grove of Apollo on Mt. Alouphournos (Pl. II, T. 16) over the eastern Akropolis and the old town, on to the well-wooded river level, which stands out larger in the picture on Pl. XVI.

2. Disposal of the different spaces.

The excavation-ground covers a piece of land which belongs to two owners and forms an irregular oblong almost facing the four cardinal points. The larger piece, which faces northwards, lies lower and belongs to the peasant Philippi Michali; the smaller portion, which lies to the south, and is somewhat more elevated, is the property of Giorgi Pieri, the corner of whose house is seen in the large picture LVI behind the cactus. The boundary between the two arable patches is planted with figs and pomegranates (Pl. XVI, LVI, LVII). The view on Pl. XVI is taken from Giorgi's house at the S.E. corner of the temenos. We see in the fore-ground before the trees the narrower excavated strip with a considerable heap of rubbish and soil. In the views on Pls. LVI, LVII, which are photos taken from the N.E. corner (LVI and LVII, 2), or from the W. (LVII, 1), we see, on the contrary, first the broad Northern strip belonging to Philippi.**) The latter lies lower because the rubbish was less considerable. The bottom of the different excavated localites (H. V. and S.) is on one plane. Hence it is evident besides the other details sketched and explained in Pl. VII, that the long southern portion H. had on it a stout building with a roof.

Between this southern space, marked H, and the two northern uncovered spaces, viz. V¹, the space for the dedicatory offerings, and the sacrificial spaces (on the left) there ran a light colonnade, viz. V², supported on wooden pillars, which terminated at E., the principal entrance of the north side. The explanations upon Plate VII itself inform us on the further arrangement of the whole place of worship, which is highly instructive. The scale chosen for the plan is large enough to instruct the reader in the smallest details. The row of trees, which grew in an almost east-west direction across the holy precinct, did not need to be removed with the exception of a few trunks, because the sculptures all lay to the north of the trees and also because nothing of any architectural importance remained covered by masonry. Besides this (as may be seen from the plan) the peasants had been digging at this part when they planted the trees, and in 1883 on the accidental discovery of sculptures.

3. Our illustrations in general.

All the illustrations have been made with the most conscientious care from photographic views. For the large view on Plate LVI three stereotyped plates of 21 to 27 cm were taken from the same point of view and joined together. On plate LVII, 2 I have repeated the piece to the right of LVI with the space for the dedicatory offerings in the fore-ground, without the sculptures which stand upright and lie around. The large plan in which every stone of importance, every pedestal found in situ is entered, and the perspective views may be used to check each other. The reconstruction on Plate LVI is limited to the statues set up on correspondingly large pedestals. Some of the statues, even the colossal ones, have been reconstructed from the extant fragments. A few figures in the background which can only be shown in small dimensions were enlarged, amongst others the colossal statue pressing both hands on the breasts. Then I have turned several of the statues towards the spectator for the sake of clearness, whilst in reality almost all the pedestals found in situ (cf. the plan on Plate VII) are turned towards the rising sun (cf. supr. p. 235). Furthermore, I have placed on the quadrangle $\mathcal{I}^1 - \mathcal{I}^6$ (Plan) an obelisk-shaped stone not found in the excavation, similar to the Cyprian Masseba Plate LXXX, 5. Finally, I hung on one of the fig-trees, which just at the time of the excavations was budding into leaf, several of the large clay masks which I found in a heap lying further to the east (at the point 37 of Plate II, No. 36 in the List, supr. p. 18). One is portrayed on Plate CXCVIII, 4.***)

In order to give another standard of comparison, three male and one female native of Dali in the modern peasant-costume were drawn in the midst of the sculptures. The dress of the modern female peasant is instructive because it is so strangely similar to the ancient dress of the statues.

---

*) The lens should be used. Supr. p. 6 in Chap. 7, I promised to give a detailed account the of shrine. I have now neither time nor space to do this ; I therefore compress it here into the description of the Plate.

**) When I made the photographic views which formed the basis of our Pls. LVI, LVII, I had already been obliged to fill up the southern plot of Giorgi who immediately sowed a crop of beans on it. We do not therefore see in these pictures, behind and between the trees, the wall of the southern side which had already been removed and filled up, but a bright white higher plateau made of the earth that had been freshly filled in.

***) Our rich sanctuary only yielded the fragments of a single small mask which is portrayed and described on Plate LII.

4. The Arrangement of the Sculptures.

The expert will notice that most of the sculptures lying in the fore-ground and middle-distance are exactly copied from the discoveries on our plates and from the spot. Among them there is only one, not dug up on this spot. It is from Dali and was brought by L. Ross to Berlin (Plate XLIX, 5). I was justified in venturing upon this reconstruction of the space for the dedicatory-offerings in the fore-ground (Plate VII, V[1]) according to the experience which I had acquired in these and other excavations. At all events, I succeeded six months afterwards at Frangissa near Tamassos (No. 4 of the List) in excavating a place of worship of Rešef-Apollo in which whole rows of figures, of stone as well as of clay, were standing erect in situ, among them the largest colossus of clay, nearly double life-size.

5. The Pillared Hall and the Walls.

All the statues were set up in the space for the dedicatory offerings V[1]. The Pillared Hall V[2] on the west side had to be left free; towards the south the lower sculptures could not pass beyond the dotted line in the plan. On the south side too, where the space for the dedicatory offerings adjoined the building (Priests' dwellings and Shrine?) there appears to have existed a Pillared Hall. The building H had only a low stone foundation-wall carefully built of blocks and slabs, which did not exceed 1,5 m at the deepest point. But as the walls finish off horizontally, the walls were erected of pan-tiles. The modern house close by (Plate LVI) is built in the same manner.

The boundary walls of the space for the dedicatory offerings and of the space for the Sacrificial Altar lie much lower, scarcely 70—50 cm high. They are built of pebbles piled in layers on the top of each other and probably without mortar of any kind. In the case of the rest of the masonry, in some places (cf. the Plan on Plate VII and the explanations) where the building had to support more, lime-mortar was employed. This kind of masonry is shewn in Giorgi Pieri's house. In the interior of houses, where the ceiling is arched, the modern Cyprian mason is in the habit of fitting in a key-stone into the loam-wall with plenty of lime-mortar. These ancient small walls of river pebbles must however have carried some sort of superstructure, probably one made of thorn-bushes as in the modern house-yards and church-yards, in fact, an ancient φράγμα. Even the Cypriotes (for instance, Giorgi Pieri in the immediate neighbourhood) are accustomed to surround their house and yard with such thorn-hedges, for which rudely heaped-up layers of stone form the foundation. Even the ancient name has remained. They call their thorn-hedge τὸ φραμμό.

6. The Altar-Space.

The Altar-Space S., also lying to the north, appears to have been accessible to the priests only from the south. At the north-west angle were found in situ two slabs of stone 60 m high, set up on end. We have to imagine a plank laid over the stones. This is the slaughtering-table or slaughtering block for the preparation and carving of the flesh of the victim (in Achna probably the earth and stone table A, called an altar, corresponds to this arrangement, and over it we must also imagine that a plank was laid). More in the middle of the space I found the burnt-offering altar visible in the plan (Plate VII) and the perspective views (Plate LVI and LVII). In Plate LVII, 1 we get the best idea of its mode of building. It is about 0,80 m—0,90 m high and mainly composed of the very rich yellow loam, which clearly stood out from the mass of charcoal and ashes. As the Cypriotes of the present day are accustomed to build their fire-hearths of loam (often without any stone) my excavators burst into a cry expressing their astonishment: "Why that is a fire place (μία πεσούλα)!" Round the edge of the loam-built altar, which rose to the height of 0,9 m, a few fragments of stone were laid. In the middle the altar had a hole, which was filled up with masses of charcoal and ashes. I found huge pieces of charcoal, which I preserved as well as the loam; these still showed the structure of the stout logs of wood which had been burnt here. On the north side of this rude altar were found six pot-hooks, of which four lay on the top of each other, and two close by. I have copied and described these pot-hooks on Plate VII, 2. On Plate CCXII, 5 we also find one of them represented, where may be seen, from the Egyptian figure 1 which stands beside it, how these pot-hooks were used sometimes for poking the fire, sometimes for pulling the flesh out of the cauldron. South east of the Altar of Burnt-offerings in a layer of ashes and charcoal I found at ta the clay column (Plate XVII, 4) which has so often been mentioned and described, and also some few fragments of statuettes much blackened by the fire.[*]

7. Space for the Dedicatory-offerings of the Shrine at Dali.

It was open towards two sides, the North and East, and surrounded only by a φράγμα.[**]   On the West and South-West it was bounded by Pillared Halls, as may be seen from the stone pedestals

---

[*] For the fire-altars of other places of worship cf. the plans IV—VI.

[**] In the many village churches of the present day and especially in the holy places connected with cliffs, caves, springs and trees, which lie far from the villages a φραμμά marks off the holy space. When the church Hagios Giorgios mentioned at page 16 (cf. III No. 9) was restored (with the money raised by the sale of the Phoenician inscriptions to Sir Henry Bulwer) the space around the church was marked off by a Phrammo. Fragments of stone and river pebbles from the ruins of Idalion were laid in layers to the height of 0,40—0,60 m without any mortar, and thorns procured were of Poterium spinosum and other prickly shrubs, which shoot up so high, that neither man nor beast can get over them. A thorn-hedge of this kind makes a better obstacle than an earthen or stone wall, which can be easily climbed over.

and stone slabs that were met with. To this day the Cypriotes choose similar foundations for their Halls of Wooden Columns (there are also some of stone). Originally the space for the dedicatory-offerings may not have been walled in at all. If it was enclosed, this was doubtless done only by a thorn-hedge or a wooden fence. For only so can we explain the pieces of shattered old statues, which are regularly built into the circuit-walls. Our space for the dedicatory-offerings makes at the North-East angle a peculiar curve, as though the original walls which enclosed it more narrowly had been extended in order to make more room for the masses of sculptures.

8. Five Spaces for Dedicatory-offerings and the arrangement of them.

In these spaces it was customary to arrange the large statues close together in no particular order in groups similar to those which the working sculptor makes nowadays. Our Shrine of Dali so far forms an exception, that here the tendency was to put the dedicatory-statues towards the rising sun rather than towards the South-East and South.

In Voni (Plan on Plate V, 1) there was a low wall erected on which people placed their large dedicatory statues close to each other. In front of this principal mass, a row of larger statues, offerings of distinguished persons, was allowed to be set up in Voni. To this row, at the southern end, a very large full-sized statue was joined, to which a stronger support was given by means of stones built round it and cemented with mortar. This front row of the specially favoured statues in Voni (Plate V) as far as the row of Pillars of the hall which leads to the Altar-Space (A). In our shrine of Dali (Plan on Plate VII) there was a similar front row of favoured statues which were allowed to be brought right under the Pillared Hall built in front of the building H. In Frangissa (Plan VI) the large statues stood in close rows and all looked towards the west. Here the two more than life-sized images, badly mutilated, executed in pure Greek style, stood in situ at the entrance and on the same level as the circuit-wall which shuts off the western side. Here, at Frangissa, just at the entrance into the space for the dedicatory-offerings was a small and probably covered Chapel, in which one of the favoured stone colossal statues with a very ancient kind of beard*) was found in situ and erect upon the stone Na (Plate VI, now in the Cyprus museum). The sanctity of the chapel-like place was also shown by the Phoenico-Cyprian bilingual inscription stone, a small altar-shaped cube of marble, on which a bronze or marble figure must have stood. (Euting-Deecke No. 2, Sitzungsber. d. Preuss. Akad. d. Wissensch. Berlin 1887 p. 115.)

Here, in Frangissa, I believe, I found standing upright in situ an almost double life-size clay colossus almost exactly in the middle of the space for the dedicatory-offerings. Only the upper part of the body was somewhat jammed into the middle of the body.

The arrangement of the statues in the space for the dedicatory-offerings belonging to the Rešef-Apollo Shrine in Idalion and found by H. Lang (No. 30 of the List, on Plate II and III No. 6) may be seen from the plans on Plate VIII (cf. also Plate X). We see at the first glance an arrangement corresponding to ours. The holy-water vessels play a great part in all the spaces for dedicatory-offerings and enclosures. Even in the Frangissa-enclosure (VI) I found a broken one, made of stone, with a Greek dedicatory inscription to Apollo. The place where this was found is entered upon the plan. I have furthermore explained in the description of the plans that small walls and chambers were made round the larger statues for greater security. Lime-mortar was employed in these as in the foundations of the columns and pillars. All these places are accurately entered on the plan of our shrine of Dali (Plate VII). Furthermore a pedestal of a large archaic clay statue with the walls from the Achna-Shrine is represented on a larger scale on Plate IV, 2 (cf. Voni Plate V at C). On the same Plate IV, 1 one sees at T E¹ on a smaller scale the same pedestal with its little enclosing wall. This clay statue was one of the principal figures which worshippers would see as then came through the gate E. H. Lang also made the same observation. The eye of the visitor, who entered from the north, fell upon the water vessels (A and B Plate VIII, 1) and on the row of statues, in the midst of which at G stood a large important statue on a slab of stone. H. Lang conjectures that the beautiful stone statue, of which he has reproduced the upper part, on Plate 1 in the Transactions, stood on the same spot.

9. The Sacrificial Customs and Practices of Worship in the Space for the Dedicatory-offerings of these and other Shrines.

The worshippers, almost exclusively women, entered the enclosure from the north through the entrance E. On the threshold they stood still, lit their lamps, and laid them together with a small clay jug or a bowl on the spot Kr, 1 a (VII) where was a low seat built with small stones bound together with loam (in fact, another small Bezula such as are in use at the present day in the primitive shrines of the Greeks on the Archipelago). The number of the lamps lying here in one heap amounted, including the fragments, to over a hundred. They all of them had the shape of the ancient Mussel Lamps.**) Among the nume-

---

*) Furtwängler saw it in Nicosia and regarded it as one of the most important old-Cyprian statues, perhaps dating back to the 7th century B. C. It will be published in my work on Tamassos.

**) This form of lamp begins to appear in the 8th century, becomes common in the strata of the 6th century and reaches down into the 4th. One is depicted p. 359 Fig. 283, 2 (grave of the silver-girdle first half of the 6th century), and one from the grove of Artemis-Kybele (plan on Plate IV) on Plate CCX, 16. Whilst in this Artemis-grove, along with the mussel-shaped lamp, a few Greek lamps (Plate CCX, 15 and 17) were standing, and Roman lamps were wanting, whilst in the grove of Apollo in Voni (plan Plate V) the mussel-lamps were wholly wanting and a few Greek lamps occurred, but most were of the Roman type, I discovered only mussel-lamps here at Idalion (plan VII) in the grove of Aphrodite, as also at Frangissa (plan VI) in the grove of Apollo. There were at Achna (IV) and Voni

rous small vessels which lay near them and in which, as I imagine, salt was offered to Aphrodite there was especially a one-handled unpainted little jug, 0,09 m to 0,10 m of the technique, shape, and size shown at Figure 253,5 (Grave of the silver girdle).

When the pilgrim entered the Space for offerings, her eye fell upon the large quadrangle of masonry, on which probably an cone-shaped or pillar-shaped idol of the goddess stood, as in the reconstruction on Plate LVI. I have repeatedly and expressly remarked in my journal of the excavations that this walled-quadrangle was free from ashes and charcoal. On the other hand in the immediate neighbourhood of it the principal mass of small roughly executed clay images (at at Plate LI, 6, 8–10), larger statues and a layer of ashes and charcoal were found. It was, therefore, only to this holy symbol or image that people sacrificed and offered incense and smaller victims. At the shrine of Astarte and Mikal, (Plate CCI), which I have proved to have existed on the Akropolis of Kition, seems to have stood in the small space on the stone foundation N N¹ and N² the cone-shaped idol of the goddess, in a chamber (M) which had a projecting building supported by columns and facing the east, i. e. the rising sun. At S, and further to the east, lay the dedicatory-offerings before the statues, a stone vessel for Holy Water, still in situ, and the two often-mentioned Phoenician inscriptions, C. I. Sem 86 and 87. In the space for the dedicatory-offerings and. almost without exception, in the immediate neighbourood of every great statue small sacrificial fires were burnt and also lamps were frequently lighted and put down on the ground. This took place in all the spaces for offerings of all Cyprian Shrines, and so constantly that the Cyprian workman practised in the work of excavations always concludes from the appearance of charcoal ashes and lamps that he is close to a large statue or an inscription-stone. As soon as he hits upon such a place, he lays down his pickaxe and shovel, and carefully removes the earth with his hands and a knife.*)

Besides these large burnt-offerings on the altar in the sacrificial-space, small incense-offerings took place in the Dedicatory Space Dombined with the lighting of lamps and sprinkling of holy-water. All these peculiarities may best be seen from our Plans, in which the most important places showing these traces and remains of sacrifices in the dedicatory space, are drawn.

Time and circumstances did not allow me to enter the details in the Plans as fully as I now could wish. The plan of Achna (Pl. IV), which was first excavated in 1882, gives the clearest information. Anyhow I think that by means of careful photographic views and observations I have essentially increased our knowledge of these interesting details of Cyprian worship, and have done much more than others who have instituted excavations in Cyprus, either before me, with me or after me.

Excursus, Idol-worship in Jerusalem in the time of Ezekiel illustrated by details of Cyprian Worship.

The Book which the Prophet Ezekiel composed in exile, belongs to the beginning of the Sixth century B. C. i. e. exactly to the time in which our Dali-Shrine (No. 3 of the List) and our Frangissa-Shrine (No. 4 of the List) flourished. In the eighth chapter Ezekiel depicts to us in one of his visions the idol-worship in the fore-courts of the Temple at Jerusalem.

V. 5 "So I lifted up my eyes the way toward the **North** and behold **northward** at the Gate of the Altar, this **image of jealousy** in the entry" (Kautzsch). We see in our Dali-Shrine (No. 3 of the List), in Lang's Idalion-Shrine (30 of the List), and in one of the Athiaenou shrines of Cesnola (25, 26 of the List), the entrance from the north, and opposite the entrance an "image of jealousy" (also Achna 1, Voni 2, Frangissa 4) either an Ashera, Masseba, or an anthropomorphic image of worship.

V. 11 and 12. And there stood before them seventy men of the ancients of the house of Israel and in the midst of them stood Jaanaziah, the son of Shaphan, with every man his censer in his hand, and a thick cloud of incense went up: then he said unto me: Son of man, hast thou seen what the ancients of the House of Israel do in the dark, every man in the chambers of his imagery?" We describe fully the chambers of imagery in the space of the dedicatory-offerings which each individual built, and in which he burned his incense.

‡ Plate LVIII and LIX.

Four stone capitals of votive pillars from the shrine of Aphrodite on the eastern Akropolis of Idalion (No. 29 of the List), now in the Cyprus Museum. Plate LIX,2 was found, built into the wall of a house at Dali, by Dörpfeld and Ohnefalsch-Richter. The capitals may be compared with those of Plate XXVI but they are more important in the matter of style, because the development of ornamentation becomes more clear in them, from the representation of the sacred tree. . One may for the sake of comparison refer to the sacred tree on the silver bowl of Amathus (supr. P. 47 Fig. 50). It consists of a combination of two Cyprian palmettes placed each upon a column crowned with volutes (cf. the explana-

---

(V) no vessels with concentric circles, but they occured at Frangissa (VI) and Dali (VII). It is clear from these circumstances alone that the groves at Frangissa (VI) and Dali (VII) are of later origin, and fell out of use earlier than the groves of Achna (IV) and cf Voni (V). It is clear from other circumstances that the Dali and Frangissa shrines were certainly venerated almost as long as the Achna-shrine (IV). — Of the two groves Achna (IV) and Voni (V), the latter is decidedly of more recent origin, since all statues of the greatest antiquity and ancient lamps and vessels are wanting, even in built in and shattered fragments. Furthermore the Voni-shrine was excavated in a condition which clearly proved that it enjoyed a great repute in Roman times (cf. Plate CCXV). Nevertheless even the beginnings of the Voni-shrine date back to the 6th century (cf. Plate XLI, 9 and CCXV, 1 and 2).

*) Cf. supr. p. 141, note 2.

tion to Plates XXVI and LXI). The holy trees on the silver bowl, which belongs to the offerings to Anat-Athene (p. 48 Fig. 51), and on the Kurion Bowl (p. 53 Fig. 52), are in better style and more conventional.

On the stelae the volutes of the palmettes are arranged in three-fold order. They form to a certain extant the calyx of the flower but the filling-in, especially in the case of the second, third and fourth pillar corresponds completely with the representation of the abrue mentioned bowls. It is to a certain extent a tuft-like combination of pistils and stamens. The familiar Palmettes are freely added to this filling-in. The series of lotus flowers and lotus buds in Plate LVIII, 1 is borrowed from other pictures. Other examples of the same kind of Pillars may be seen above p. 188 Fig. 159 to 162 and Plate CLXXXVII, 1. Plate LVIII, 1 is also repeated on Plate CLXIII, 1. cf. text p. 186 ff., 202, 231 f., 235.

(H. S.)

As the drawings were prepared most accurately after the original photographs of Dörpfeld, it will suffice to give some of the principal measurements of the three first capitals according to the measurements which he has kindly placed at my disposal. The fourth capital (LIX, 2) walled-up in the village for centuries, is of similar proportions. Plate LVIII, 1, breadth of the lower surface 0.873 m, thickness 0,185 m. The quadrangular rivet-hole 69 to 40 m and 180 m deep LVIII, 2. Breadth of the upper surface 1,164 m, breadth of the under surface 0,425 m, thickness 0,200 m. On the lower surface two quadrangular rivet-holes 53 to 35 mm and 100 mm deep, with a channel behind to pour in the lead. LIX, I. Breadth of the upper surface 1,118 m, breadth of the under surface 0,810 m; thickness 0,173 m. Rivet-hole 33 to 70 mm, cf. supr. p. 188.

Plate LX.

Four Views of Idalion. The figures and letters marked on the pictures in small brackets correspond to the signs on Plates II and III.

1. The great enclosure of the Idalian Aphrodite on the Eastern hill of the Akropolis, taken from the east (No. 29 of the List).

(3) on Views 1 and 4 = 3. Pl. III. Place where the bronze tablet of the Duc de Luynes was found. Cf. Pl. III, 1—8 enclosure of the Anat-Athene No. 28 of the List. Western Akropolis.

(8) on 1—4 = 8 Pl. II and III. The large Aphrodite-Temenos (No. 29 of the List) from which the capitals Pl. LXVIII and LXIX, 1 and the limestone group Pl. XXXVII, 4 come.

(O) on 1—8 = O Pl. III. The earth wall lying between two moats (Ditch - Ditch Pl. III). Vid Fig. 2.

(P) on 1—8 = P. Pl. III. North-east angle of the strong fortifications of Temenos 8. At this spot so many large blocks had been dug out some years before Cesnola's time, that the Turkish mosque in the village of Idalion could be repaired from them. (Cesnola-Stern p. 77.)

Any one looking closely into the landscape can see three men, whom I included in the photograph to give a better appreciation of the distances. The first one is standing before the first low moat of the wall, the second on the first low earthern wall o. the third above o. on the ground of the Temenos 8 and its Northern side.

(2) The view is taken from Aloupophoumos (No. 35 of the List) facing the north (16 T. Plate II). One can see further behind the wooded river-level described on Plate LVI and LVII, with the modern village of Dali over which the chain of hills also visible on Plate II cuts the horizon.

(8), (O), (P) explained under View 1.

(a) on 2 and 3 = a Pl. III. Highest point of the oldest fortifications of the town, at (7) called Muti tu Arvili (cf. Fig. 3 and 7 Pl. III) before the sanctuary 8 was included within the circuit of the town. On this height a (cf. Fig. 3 and 4) we see the remains of a rudely-erected ancient building.

(10) = 10 Plate II and III. Low down in the plain at the North end of the Graeco-Phoenician town Idalion a group of graves, which originates from a small settlement of prae-Graeco-Phoenicians of the bronze age.

(6) on 2 and 4 = 6 Pl. II and III. H. Lang's Rešef-Apollo-Shrine (No. 30 of the List), situated at the Town gate G 1 of the lower town Idalion.

3. The photograph is taken from the plain, north of the point c. Pl. III.

(c) in the foreground = c Pl. III. A portion of the fortifications belonging to the ring-wall of the lower town, which I examined carefully in 1887. At a short distance from it in a north-west direction stands on the town-wall the church with the Phoenician dedicatory inscription to Anat given at Plate II and III, 9 (cf. P. 15—16).

(7) = 7 Pl. II and III. Small shrine of Aphrodite (No. 31 of the List). The other points explained under 1 and 2.

4. View of the pillared hall of the upper story in the house of Philippi Michaeli in the village of Dali. Both Akropolis hills of Idalion are seen on left at points (8) and (7), on the right at points (3), (2) and (1) = Pl. III, 1—3. The Anat-Athene enclosure with the places where the iron swords, the silver dishes, the bronze weapons and the bronze inscription-tablets were found.

(5) = 5 Pl. III, where I excavated in 1883 for Sir C. T. Newton a strong bastion which covered the approach of the western Akropolis from the west and north.

(15) = 15 Pl. II. Site of the Aphrodite-κουροτρόφος-grove (No. 33 of the List).

(6), (7) and (8) explained under 1—3*)

Plate LXI.

Principal explanation of the vases on Plate XIX, 1 cf. Fig. 128 p. 91.

In the midst is a tree, erected by way of ornament The lower part of it consists of a stem very broad below, and growing very thin towards the top, which is ornamented with black cross-streaks and rod-like ornaments stretching downwards, painted of a red brown colour on a back ground of the natural clay. On this stem rises a composite ornament; it consists in its characteristic parts of two opposite calykes of the peculiar Cyprian Palmettes, opening upwards or downwards, as we find them in similar combinations on the bronze bowls of Amathus (Perrot-Chipiez III, 775, Fig. 547) of Idalion (Perrot-Chipiez III, 779, Fig. 548), of Kurion (Perrot-Chipiez III, 789, Fig. 552), or in some cases on golden ornaments (Perrot-Chipiez III, 835 Fig. 603), or several united together on capitals (Perrot-Chipiez III, 116, Fig. 52, 53; 535, Fig. 361). As in the latter the proper centre of the Palmettes is wanting; instead of it on the upper part of the Palmette is inserted a latticed triangle, on the summit of which there is a flower which we have to imagine as on the bronze handle (Perrot-Chipiez III, 797 Fig. 557). Between the two Palmettes, which are held apart by a wedge forming the central point, there is on each side a horizontally placed leaf which is hatched by vertical stripes.

The he-goats which are climbing up this ornamental tree are adorned with two rosettes each and a zig-zag ornament lies between them enclosed in an oblong. This ornamentation is typical and also appears on the winged creature of a Cyprian Vase in New York (Perrot-Chipiez III, 706 Fig. 517); here too, a he-goat is meant and not, as Pierrot-Chipiez say, a cheval ailé. This is obvious from the whole structure of the body; even its horns are not wantings: for the long appendage on the head of the animal must be regarded as a horn, the short one as an ear. According to A. S. Murray in Cesnola-Stern p. 346, the oblong with the zig-zag ornament must be regarded as the imitation of an Assyrian inscription tablet.

Undoubtedly the ornament in the middle which I have described must represent the sacred tree; the vase painter has wished to bring out this meaning by means of the two leaves added on both sides. According to the above explanations this Assyrian heraldic figure must have been known and familiar to the vase painter. cf. Text p. 38, 78 and 90.   (H. S.)

Plate LXII.

? 1—8. Painted Vases of Marion-Arsinoë.

? 1 = CLXXX, 1. Part of the shoulder of a pitcher 0,273 high only partially preserved. The upper part of the woman, represented plastically as coming out of the jug, is wanting. She is holding, as is shown by the extant spout, the water-vessel before her on her knees. Found in the grave of the Sphinxes CXL Nekr. II, likewise supr. Pl. XXVII, 1 and 2. cf. also Plate XXIV especially on account of the black concentric circles with white points No. 4. It appears however that the white cocks which suddenly appear are painted on this Cyprian Vase after Attic black-figured models. There are two of them, one on each side of the modelled figure. The flower in front of the cock is very interesting.**) One can see plainly how the vase-painter made it by painting first with black a concentric circular ornament and then painting over it with white wash. Availing himself of the casual effects caused thereby he made out of them a flower-stalk, in which the concentric circles, faintly but clearly showing through, form the centre and the structure of the calyx, which must be imagined open, and on this he set the petals of the flower and the stalk. This vase assuredly belongs to the first half of the sixth century B. C.

? 2. Fragments of Vases from the Hermaios-bowl Grave, Grave LXX, Nekr. II. The vase is certainly only a few decades younger and shows clearly what progress the Cyprian vase-painters made in the interval. The concentric circles are entirely given up. Without any employment of concentric circles, a stalk of flowers of the pansy kind is painted on the shoulder of the vase, or perhaps the painter intended to paint a vine with grapes (cf. Plate LXIII, 1). Here we see for the first time a figure, painted red, white and black. no longer sitting, but standing on the vase. For the head a stamp of a fine type is employed which we are rather inclined in Cyprus to assign to the end than to the middle of the fifth century.

---

*) A glance at this Pl. LX and at Pl. II and III is sufficient to make it clear, how useless Cesnola's view (Cesnola-Stern p. 78) is, which to judge by the church, which lies in the middle distance on the left, must have been taken from a point of view, which, like our view 4, must be looked for in the village of Dali. Such a towering castle, such a steep precipice, as we have in Cesnola's picture, never can have existed. Just as little does the cleft, drawn by Cesnola between the two Akropoleis, exist, but the ground slopes away gradually and leaves a broad opening, in the form of a valley. Furthermore, only the western Akropolis is called Ambilleri, the eastern Muti tu Arvili. We must also regard as imaginary an artificial opening in the mountain-range to disclose the valley of Paradise (cf. Plate II and Cesnola-Stern p. 85 and 86).

**) Cf. Wilisch, "Altkorinth. Thonindustrie" Taf. V, 47. Cock with a star as a crest.

The much used Attic vessels which were laid in the grave, were black and red figured vases of severe style, which ought to be assigned to the second half of the sixth century. The most recent objects there might, at the latest, date from the beginning of the fifth century, to which our vase 2 should also be assigned.

3. Fragments of Vases from Grave 77, Nekr. II. of the same excavation.

In the illustration the bright-reddish ground has come out too rose-coloured. The colouring is generally inaccurate. Paintings in black, vermilion and sulphur-yellow. A similar attempt as in 2, to paint a tuft of flowers on the shoulder of the vase in a more realistic manner. The grave was large like the preceding one, and had been used for a long time. But while in the case of the former the most recent Attic vases belonged to the sixth century, and the other articles found served as a terminus a quo and proved the date to be about 450 B. C., the red-figured vases of the developed style, which occur abundantly here along with older Attic vessels, showing a more developed style (flat vessels with panthers and other animals), point us to the second half of the fifth and to the beginning of the fourth century. Cf. also Plate LXIV, 4 and 7, the two Vases from Grave 5, Sect. I, of the same excavation.

Plate LXIII.

? 1, and 2. The paintings on the shoulders of two washing-jugs, which certainly belonged to the second half of the fifth century B. C. Out of the same Necropolis as the vessels of the former plate.

1. Grave 160, Nekr. II. A washing-jug 0,434 m high.

2 = CLXXX, 3 and 4. Grave 72, Nekr. II. Water-jug 0,336 high. Both jugs have on them figures of women sitting on the spout (Cf. p. 239 and 259). Both betray a very different style of art and one more influenced by the Greek, both as regards the modelling and the painting.*) The one is reproduced at CLXXX 4. Both vessels are made of grey or greyish-brown clay, the paintings on them being in black and white. In 1 we see the same twig of flowers or berries as in Plate LXII, 2. A quadruped not easy to be recognised is leaping on each side between two crosses composed of squares, towards the spout with the woman (who is left out in the illustration).

The animals on vase 2 are more easy to make out. Here on both sides two oxen are walking one behind the other, of which the former one is 0,253 m, the hinder one 0,223 long (both measured from the tip of the horns to the tip of the tail); punctured rosettes and in front a four-petalled flower (cf. LXII, 1) serve to fill up the space. Ribbons, beads, necklaces and garlands of leaves, laid horizontally round the vase, complete the ornamentation, which is distributed over the whole vase from mouth to foot.

In the same grave (No. 72, Nekr. II) three pitchers were dug out, which have a pair of figures on the shoulder. The one, of which I am sorry to be unable to give an illustration, does not yet show the winged Eros with Psyche, but two beautiful unwinged female draped figures side by side, and at some distance from the spout with which they never were connected. The figures are executed in a pure Greek style, which must be assigned to the end of the fifth century. The same grave also yielded two very beautiful pure Greek terra-cottas of female draped figures, both of the fifth century, one from the first half, and the other from the second half. Furthermore, the grave yielded a pure Greek figure of a horseman from the second half of the fifth century. Unfortunately the head of the rider is broken off. The style, the attitude and the motive of the horse, which steps along solemnly and yet with a light and natural step, putting out and raising the left fore-foot and planting the right fore-foot behind, clearly points to the influence of the age of Phidias. For the fixing of the date we may merely mention a Cyprian ear-ring of gold, like one of precisely the same form, technique and ornamentation portrayed on Plate CLXXXII, 7 and which is quite characteristic of the 5th century.**)

Plate LXIV.

? 1—7. 7 Washing-jugs from the same excavation as the vessels illustrated on Plate LXII and LXIII. One can make out the colours and technique from the coloured illustrations. I shall describe the vessels 5, 6, 3, 1, 2, 4, 7, according to their period and development of their style.

5 = CLXXIX, 1. A washing-jug 0,37 m high. The seated woman is holding an ox-head. White and black paintings (here faded) on a brown ground, cf. p. 259.

In the same grave was found a second washing-jug with a figure holding an ox-head by both horns with both hands from behind. In the same grave-yard Englishmen following in my footsteps found a similar jug to No. 4, belouging to the sixth century, and to the first half of it.

6. On the jug, which is 0,36 m. high, is instead of the usual ox-head a ram's head 0,063 m. high. This is painted black and white and wears round its neck a ribbon with an amulet or little bell.

*) I found in 1886 in Poli tis Chrysokhou, besides the often mentioned alabastron of Pasiades, three bowls with artist's inscriptions, two with the signature of Hermaios, the third with that of Kachrylion.
**) I come again to the question of the date when discussing below Plates CLXXIV—CLXXXVII, in which only objects from Marion-Arsinoë are grouped.

Black concentric circles, black and white punctured stars and other simple ornaments on the reddish-brown ground. It belongs to the end of the 6th or quite the beginning of the 5th century.

Let us compare together both jugs 3 and 1. Jug 3 (Grave 78, Nekr. II) is some decades older than jug 1 (Grave 83, Nekr. II). The first (3) still belongs to the 5th century, the second (1) to the 4th century.

3 = CLXXXI, 2 = p. 220, fig. 165. A jug, 0,41 m. high, of elegant shape, fine bright yellowish-brown dull-glazed ground of unusually fine prepared clay. On this are the paintings, which cover the vessel.

The spiral and palmette pattern remind one of similar patterns in black on Rhodian vessels. On the shoulder of the vase for the first time we find the winged Eros and Psyche, while on a jug from Grave 72, Nekr. II (which is not accessible to me) were two more unwinged women. The wings, in this case shaped like a sickle and running to a point at the top*), have not been observed anywhere else, and are older than the wings which droop down (1 and 2),**) and more recent than those which are curved upwards and which do not occur in the figures on the washing-jugs. The unwinged female figure here is without its head. The winged male figure wears the pointed Cyprian cap.

With regard to the Eros cf. supra p. 220. A washing-jug portrayed on Plate CLXXXI, 3, excavated by me at Kurion in 1884, and belonging to the 6th century B. C., shows the upper part of a winged quadruped, horse or ox with similar sickle-shaped wings. The unwinged animals of the vase on Plate LXII, as well as the winged animal of the vase of Kurion (CLXXXI, 3) point to Assyrian models, which the Cyprians used and modified just as they borrowed from the Assyrians the animal-tamers of the silver-girdle and of the engraved stones on Plate XXV.***) It appears that in this way in the 5th and perhaps even in the 6th century the Greek Eros came to have wings in Cyprus (Plate CXCVIII, 1 bronze handle with Eros from the same Nekropolis, grave 94). Only once was a vase excavated with a figure of an Eros without Psyche. The grave No. 3, Nekropolis III) still belonged to the 4th century, as was manifest from the Attic vessels found in it. †)

In grave 78. Nekr. II, where our jug was found (Plate LXIV, 3) were found no less than eight sitting figures of the goddess with her hands in her lap in the style and clay of the Rhodian figures published by L. Heuzey.††) Also the terra-cotta on Plate CLXXXV, 1†††) of a woman lying down, wearing a pointed cap, comes from the same grave which has certainly been used several times.

1 = CLXXX, 1. This jug 0,388 m. high is painted on the yellow ground with brownish-red and black, and follows 3.

Here both the figures, which the potter left unpainted, are preserved. Eros wears a plate-shaped projecting headdress. Here also in the path of this grave, which had likewise been used for a long time, there were various small terra-cottas found, similar to the Rhodian. A sitting goddess like Heuzey's XIV, 2, and several standing draped statues holding flowers, or the skirts of their garments like Heuzey's XIV, 1, 4. and 5.§)

2. Upper part of a washing-jug 0,40 m. high. From the second half of the 4th century. From Grave 26, Nekr. I. The colour of the ground a richer reddish-brown and of a more decided glazing, which is also to some extent shared by the black painting. The group is painted in various colours. Our coloured plate only imperfectly renders the intensity of the colours. The figure of Eros, unfortunately headless, is painted purple like the jug. Only the wings have been left uncoloured in order to represent the outline of the feathers with purple lines. The woman, whose head remained unpainted, wears a purple chiton, while the himation, which has slipped down to the lower part of the body, shows traces of a deep blue.

4 and 7. Two jugs painted in the same technique and similarly. Both from the same Grave No. 5, Nekr. I, 4th century, No. 4 0,532 m. high, No. 7, 0,318 m. high.

---

*) The form of the wings is still like the wings of the griffin on the silver girdle of Plate XXV, which is some 150 years older like the harpies on the still older proto-korinthian vase of Plate CX, 2, like the winged horses of Assyrian monuments (CXI, 1 and 5) and like the winged goats of a Cyprian vase at Plate CXI, 3.

**) I. e. as in the Cyprian grave reliefs with pairs of sphinxes, Plate CXII, 1 and CXVII, 3 and in the Cyprian censer with winged woman Plate CII, 1.

***) Cf. also Plates XCIX—CIX.

†) Tubbs (Journal of Hellenic Studies, 1890) is equally in error in regard to the origin and disuse of washing-jugs with an ox-head and seated female figure. , On Plate CCXVI, 27—30 I show that this kind of jug was already found in the Copper-bronze-age in the second millennium B. C. (but not so late as the sixth century). Neither do they, as a rule, last beyond the fourth century B. C., whereas Tubbs thinks that they are very common in the Roman period and that precisely those which look the most primitive and ancient, might be the atest i. e. Roman It would seem that Messrs. Mounro and Tubbs have been deceived in their opinions about the graves by the repeated use of certain portions of the burial-field (cp. supra the explanation at Plate XXVII, 3). It is quite true that there are some water-jugs which come down to the period of the Ptolemies, and in quite isolated cases even to the Roman period; but all these few late objects bear in technique, form and ornamentation the traces of decline, and are essentially different from the vessels of the fourth, fifth, and sixth centuries. One of the latest specimens of the class with Eros and Psyche is portrayed in the Winckelmann-Programm, 1888, Plate III, 2 and is, together with the washing-basin that belongs to it (Plate CLXXVII, 3) in the Antiquarium of the Berlin Museum.

††) Figurines antiques Plate XIV, 3. Heuzey gives too early a date by some decades to these Rhodian figures, which are identical with the Cyprian. They belong to the middle of the fifth century.

†††) = Winckelmann-Programm, 1888, p. 37, Fig. 24. Hermann, on the other hand, appears inclined to make too young by some decades this figure, which belongs to the end of the fourth or the beginning of the fifth century.

§) These figures, both the standing and the enthroned ones, are much more common in Cyprus than in Rhodes. I found them also in other parts of the island. I bought several in 1883 from a peasant in Dali, who dug them up on the northern slope of the Akropolis-hill (No. 32 in the list). I brought these terra-cottas in 1884 to Heuzey in Paris, who bought them for the Louvre, but who at first would not allow that they could have come from Cyprus. Only after a long discussion would he believe me, in as much as he regarded it as impossible to find these terra-cotta anywhere but in Rhodes.

The technique is like that of the jug on Plate LXII, 3. Only here we find a ground-colouring of the jug with whitewash. No. 4 is only decorated with red and yellow and only with geometrical figures. No. 7 is painted red, yellow and black. A black garland of leaves with yellow flowers, made of groups of dots, runs between the horizontal bends and wavy lines round the belly of the jug.

Plate LXV.

Late Hellenistic and Roman glasses from Cyprus. From the Nekropoleis of Katydata (near Soloi in the Valley Soliais) and from Episkopi (Kurion). The photographs, almost in original size after water-colour drawings are prepared by myself from the original with the help of photographs. All of them are in the Cyprus Museum. Upper row from left to right.

? 1. A bowl with reliefs of semi-transparent purplish glass and milk-white strips melted in. From Kurion.

? 2 and 3. Two glass stems, a blue and a yellow one, of the the same form and size. One end is simply pointed, the other runs into a tapering bow-knot, around which a milk-white thread of glass is molten. From Katydata in the Valley of Soliais.

These glass stems were used for colouring the eyebrows, and more or less fluid colour could be employed according to one's wish, according as one dipped in the colour one or the other end. These stems so far as I know have not yet been found in any other place in Cyprus or anywhere else. On the other hand they were common in the graves at Katydata close to an old abandoned copper mine. On the slag hill is the convent called Skurgotissa on account of the slag (Skurgias).

As I have been informed by Herr Professor Weeren, of the Technical High School in Berlin, the ancient glass industry arose side by side with copper smelting. Evidently a glass manufactory existed in ancient times in the immediate neighbourhood of this copper mine. The ancient glass vessels, again, have in particular parts of the island a local character which differs here and there. Until my discovery of an ancient glass furnace (Tamassos 1885), the abundant ancient glasses found at Cyprus were regarded as goods imported by the Phoenicians. But that is not the case they were all made in Cyprus. The oldest glasses are the many coloured ones (as Perrot III Plate VII to IX) These I always excavated from such graves as showed a predominating Greek influence. The oldest opaque glasses were found in graves of the 6th century. The ferrettos, glass beads, glass rings and works of minute art of glazed clay were much older. Along with Egyptian imports may be noticed, nearly two thousand years B. C., the Cyprian local manufactured goods. I have myself dug out in graves of the bronze age (1200 to 1500 B. C.) beads of quite transparent glass, of the form seen on Plate CLXI. 6. The ring too of Hagia Paraskevi, drawn on Plate CLVI, 3, 8, 9, is transparent, almost colourless, glass. The whole manufactory of glass proves to be in Cyprus an art borrowed from Egypt. In the glass vessels and their forms one could see Graeco-Egyptian influence. In the case of the small vessels of clay, glazed over with green or white, the productions in greenish-blue cyanus*) and in many coloured glazed clay, the Graeco-Phoenician style is sometimes more employed. Thus e. g. in the case of the Aryballos**) made of clay glazed white or originally greenish blue (Plate XCIII) found in Cyprus. It belongs either still to the 7th or beginning of the 6th century. The little amulet figure (Plate LXVII, 1a and 1b) copied in colours of yellow, violet and blue glazed clay, representing the Egyptian god Bez in his Cyprian modification, is from a grave of the 5th century at Marion-Arsinoë, 1886. Among the ornamental objects of Grave 131, No. II, Plate LXVII is also a small necklace ornament of Kyanos which represents a lion couchant (14) and which forms the pendant to one made of Onyx (13).

4. A glass vessel of the shape of a modern ink-bottle found in a state of iridescence and so represented. Peculiar shape. From Katydata.

? 5. A glass tumbler decorated with folds made of glass of the thickness of paper and completely colourless and transparent, with the commencement of iridescence. For the water-colour sketch I poured wine into the glass in order to show the transparency. From Katydata..

? 6. Alabastron, composed of three pieces of glass. In the middle a milk-white piece, above and below a deep blue one. From Kurion.

Lower row.

? 7 and 8. Two round light rings of glass. Round the body of the rings, made of quite colour-less and transparent glass, are twisted threads of glass of the colour of a lemon and small plates of other colours melted on, in imitation of the stones of a ring. From Katydata.

? 9. A heavy ring of milk white glass. From Katydata.

The representation in glass of heavy gold rings, with and without jewels, and with and without inscriptions.***)

---

*) The Cyprian cyanus had a great reputation in ancient times side by side with the Egyptian, cf. Helbig, "Das homerische Epos," p. 101, ff. The excavations prove it.

**) First depicted in the Branteghem collection. Now in the Berlin Museum. A large vessel of cyanus 0,27 m. high found at Kurion 1883 is shown by the Greek inscription, scratched on before baking, to be the property of Ptolemaeus Philopator. (Collection W. Hoffmann, Paris, 1888, Pl. XII).

***) Cf. Pl. CLXXXII, 34: a gold ring of the same shape with Cyprian inscription. This shape of ring seems also to be the favourite one with the priests. The images of the gods and priests in the shrine of Apollo-Zeus at Voni wear such rings on the fourth finger of the left hand. Cf. Plate XI, 1 and 3.

A glass ring of the same size and shape, with a Cyprian inscription on the inner side, as our gold ring CLXXXII, 34 in A. P. di Cesnola's "Salaminia," p. 174, fig. 160, ibid. Pl. VII, 2, 6—8, four similarly formed rings made of ivory.

? 10. Marble-like transparent bowl of blue and milk-white glass. From Katydata.

? 11. A small glass bottle broken at the top. From Kurion. It is an imitation of opal by means of many-coloured threads of glass melted into each other. Our picture reproduces the colours of the water-colour sketch, and of the original, somewhat too coarsely.

? 12. Tiny bottle of black glass. From Katydata.

PLATE LXVI.

? 1—6. (There are no numbers on the Plate.) Six glass lids with hand-painting from Roman graves of Kurion. Partly in the Cyprus Museum, partly in the collection of Sir Thomas Brassey. Described p. 259.

2—5 coloured. One represented without colour, because the glass was too much iridised, and only allowed the contours to be seen. These glass lids were frequently manufactured in Cyprian antiquity. But as the colours are not burnt in, but only painted after the burning with sticky colours on the inner side, and were meant to be seen through from side to side, the paintings have for the most part not been preserved. Through damp in the ground, and the iridising of the glass, the coating of the paint is irrevocably dissolved. Nevertheless amongst the vast quantity of glass lids that have been found, a great many must have been excavated with the paintings preserved. But these were destroyed again by the excavators in the act of cleaning. Whatever colour then remained was mostly lost in packing and unpacking and in transport. I only succeeded in saving a large number by contriving arrangements· of my own to clean the glasses carefully and to pack them skilfully.

These remarkable glass lids, peculiar to Cyprus, are, in consequence of that fact, very rare in collections. Besides those represented here, the Cyprus Museum has two, dug up by myself, with the representation of a large full-face head of Apollo, and a quadruped running. A lid with Aphrodite, in the attitude of the Venus de Medici, i. e. like No. 1 here, only of great perfection in comparison with our sketch (if we may trust the copy) is represented in A. P. de Cesnola's "Salaminia," p. 173, fig. 159. A lid from a grave in Paphos dug up in 1886 at Old Paphos is given in the Journal of Hellenic Studies, 1888, p. 271, fig. 8 This is so similar in technique, drawing and painting to our lid No. 4, Plate LXVI, that both articles must originate from the hand of the same painter. We see a naked running Eros-boy with large wings and grapes.[*])

Plate LXVII.

°1a and 1b. Amulet of glazed clay, cf. on this subject what I have said in the small printed excursus to Plate LXV under 2 and 3 as well as p. 256.

° 2—14. Ornaments of gold, of silver of bronze overlaid with gold plate and of gilded earthenware (4) Onyx, Agate and blue lapislazuli (Cyanos). All objects found in Grave 131, Sect. II, Marion-Arsinoë. Cf. Plate XXXIII, 17—20. First half of the 6th century B. C.[**]) All pictures in original size. Single portions of these links of chains again produced on Pl. CXLIV, 1—10, 14—17.

2. Bronze head-band overlaid with gold plate. While most of those found in graves consist of thin gold leaf for the special use of graves (e. g. Pl. CXLIV, 11), this one is of strikingly solid metal and may have been worn a long time during life. Probably it was fixed upon and in cloth or leather. The holes or eye-holes elsewhere used for fastening are wanting.

3. Three small smooth gold rings found hanging together.

4. Fragment of a silver ornament in the form of an egg moulding, heavily gilded.

5. Silver spirals.

7. Five silver ornaments first arranged by me, three beads of the ordinary form and two in the shape of sitting lions, the latter formerly gilded. Granulated technique in silver.

8. Heavy gold spirals. At the extremities rosettes executed in granulated technique (cf. supra Pl. XXXIII, 9).

9. Amulet in the form of a silver mask. Cf. p. 210.

10. An Onyx set in gold, in the form of a non-engraved scarabaeoid, hanging to a ring.

---

[*]) O. Tischler, Königsberg, who unfortunately died too soon, in his time the best connoisseur of old glass, called my attention to the few specimens of such hand-paintings. A few such glass-lids of Roman times with dogs running, have been found in Denmark and are in the Copenhagen-Museum. That the better preserved lids of Cyprus, which I have here produced, (with which hundreds having slight remains of colour are associated) were manufactured in Cyprus, must be considered proved after the discovery of my glass-furnace, which contained masses of glass slag and glass beads. (Cf. my essay: "Das Museum und die Ausgrabungen auf Cypern." In the Repertorium für Kunstwissenschaft. 1886, 4.)

[**]) No. 6 is wanting in the numbering.

11. Spherical object of silver with a hole drilled into it; probably a button.

The grave contained two more buttons of a resinous material gilded. Buttons mostly manufactured of gypsum or earth, to be used for graves, richly ornamented and gilded, are frequently met with in the burial-fields of Marion-Arsinoë.*)

We also meet occasionally in this layer with solid buttons of ivory, bone and other materials, while brooches are wholly wanting.

12. A great number of ornaments found separately, which I first put on a string. One can easily distinguish on the coloured plate the objects of gold, cornelian, onyx, agate and blue lapis lazuli.

13—14 are the end-links of 12, represented again in a side view. 13 a couchant lion of onyx, 14 of cyanos.

The description of three of the objects represented in 12 was given supra Pl. XXXIII, 17—20, the rest are found infra. Pl. CXLIV, 1—10, described separately.

Plate LXVIII.

1—3. Fragments of painted colossal clay statues from the Astarte-Aphrodite Shrine No. 3 of the list; 3 = LIII, 40.

4—6, 11—15. Painted terra-cottas from Artemis-Kybele-Temenos No. 1 of the list.

7. End of a painted terra-cotta sacred tree from the same shrine = LXXVI, 1; cf. p. 131.

8—10. Painted vessels in the form of Phallos extremities, from the same place, cf. p. 131 and f. p. 150, note 1 and 263.

The colours of the plate have turned out somewhat too bright in some places only. For the most part the freshness of the colours of the drawing from which it is taken has not been attained. They were made in bright colours on the spot immediately after the excavation from the original with the help of photographs. Later on the colours faded. These older painted clay figures (cf. supra p. 312 and 315—317) which are finished off, some less (12 and 11) some more (13, 14 and 15), show us how the art of clay-modelling of the purely Greek style of the 4th century (4—6) came by its colours, The bright, peculiarly painted clay figures of the Artemis-Kybele Grove (11—15) are distinguished at a glance from the painted clay statues and smaller terra-cottas of the Grove of Astarte-Aphrodite (1—3) and Resef-Apollo. Time and space prevent our saying any more about them. (For the archaic costume of the priests cf. supra p. 315). The very beautiful head, fig. 4, portrayed here has the free style, the nobility, and all the grace of the school of Praxiteles. With this is combined magnificent colouring. A warm flesh-tint covers the face, (which in the copy has turned out too coarse), the lips were painted of a richer red, (in the copy too pale); a yellow blonde is used for the hair which falls in light, natural, wavy lines and is parted in the middle. The large crown adorned with a row of star rosettes appears to have been left unpainted. Fig. 5 represents the female lyre-player, already given on Pl. XII, 13 in a somewhat different position. This figure did not indeed show, as here represented, the painting of the purple himation, falling from under the high crown, but the purple colour had preserved itself in all its freshness in other headless replicas of the same type.

Even in many pure Greek painted terra-cottas of these Artemis shrines, which in other parts are painted in delicate colours, the lower dress is still very commonly of the saffron yellow which forms the ground colour in archaic and archaistic pictures (cf. p. 306—308, here fig. 11—15). It appears that saffron-yellow chitons (but sometimes also upper garments (13), or under and upper garments) were in favour with the priestesses, temple attendants and sacrificers to Artemis. Perhaps these saffron yellow garments in the Cyprian cult of Artemis are identical with the traditional custom of the Ἄρκτοι in Athens. It is well known that the youthful daughters of the Athenian citizens, between the age of five and ten, were presented to Artemis, the Moon-goddess of Brauron, in procession, clad in saffron-coloured garments. This took place at the Feast Brauronia, which was especially celebrated by women; and the girls so dedicated to the service of Artemis were called Ἄρκτοι.**) On the other hand the archaic, yellow clay figures point to the old Semitic and old Hebraic origin of the saffron-coloured garments which the Greeks first took from the East. In Homer the saffron coloured peplos of Eos, "gleaming bright as the morning-glow," is contrasted with the scarlet peplos of Aphrodite, which is "brighter than the glare of fire." We see in our figures here saffron-yellow and scarlet prevailing.***)

‡ 6. Represents in full face the same very beautiful head of the best period of the 4th century, 0,23 m. high, which was again copied in profile on Pl CCIX, 8. The head is somewhat severer than 4. It now belongs to the Louvre, but comes from the same shrine at Achna. It was found together with fig. 13, a row of rough clay idols like 11, 12, 14, 15 and the limestone figure p. 287, fig. 198 by the peasants in digging the holes for the destruction of the locusts in the spring of 1882.†) This very head and the goddess on her throne, with the tower crown and surrounded by lions, best show how Artemis and Kybele here coalesce into one. Here the head, the hair, and the forehead-band appear not to have been painted, except that the

---

*) Besides I can prove their existence all over the island in graves of the sixth century. We possess many similar objects found in Kameiros and Tharros, which were adapted to a similar costume to that for which the buttons were used. The statue depicted on Pl. CLXXXVII, 4, belongs, it is true, to the fourth century, but it is here very instructive, because it shows how the buttons served to open and shut the arm-holes.

**) Cf. Preller's "Mythologie," I, p. 246.

***) Cf. Hehn. "Culturpflanzen und Hausthiere," p. 210, and Helbig, "Das Homerische Epos," p. 205.

†) Vid. supra p. 2.

lips were coloured red. The upper part too of the towering head-dress was unpainted like the lower part; on the other hand the rich decorations in the middle (reproduced by themselves Pl. XXXVIII, 15, cf. p. 267) were painted purple. The hair, parted and open, is combed over a ring lying in the hair. This bulging ring passes into a low smooth crown which in the middle runs up into a point. From this low stephane, and connected with it, grows a huge crown in the shape of a bushel-measure. On this are lotus flowers and vultures or eagles*) in alternate rows, over delicately woven spirals. The wings of the birds are outspread (cf. supra page 309 and Plates CCIX, 6—8; CCXI, 1—4). This head-dress, consisting of one piece, was a metallic plate.

Plate LXIX.

Ashera. Masseba. Chamman. Konos. Omphalos. Stylos, &c.

Here I have collected in 134 illustrations (No. 1—126 and A—H) a large number of sacred symbols.

On the left recognisable by the kind of lines and the inscriptions underneath, a number of Cyprian syllabary-signs are written near each row, which are certainly borrowed from the Hittite hieroglyphics, and the pictures as we see them on the Cyprian cylinders (cf. Pl. LXXIX and p. 159—161). I have placed under the Cyprian syllabary-signs the customary Greek syllable-equivalents or vowels, as found in inscriptions which are now legible. It seems that the Cyprian Greeks who invented this syllabic-writing (why not in Cyprus itself?) began to lay down the most important signs for an abbreviated hieratic writing. They chose the initial sounds and the initial syllables of these most important Greek words similar to our modern initials and abbreviations. My further meaning will be easily understood by a few examples.

The signs 1 and 2 denote the syllable te (τε, θε or δε) and this syllable got the form of a twig or small tree, because the tree is called δένδρον, god θεός and because the godhead was originally wor-shipped in the form of a tree.

The syllable-sign pa (πα, φα, or βα) received the form of a double cross, of a vertical line (16) crossed by two parallel horizontal lines. It is a wooden Agalma, an Ashera, the sign for royalty and priesthood, for the Paphian goddess and the Paphian kingdom. The sign means pa, because king is called in Greek βασιλεύς, and because the chief sanctuary of the Cyprian goddess arose in Paphos, and the goddess herself is simply called Paphia. The sign plays an important part in the symbolic language of Cyprian coins. But we find it fifteen hundred to two thousand years before on Cyprian cylinders No. 18 and 19. In the same way the signs of the star (31) served the Greeks for the expression of their vowel alpha because they called a star ἀστήρ, and because the sun, which is a star, was the symbol of their sun god Apollo. The image of a sphere must serve for the syllable ko (κο, χο, γο). (No 45) because the Greeks called a cone κῶνος etc.

The simple numbers, as 116 (No. 8), signify the numbers of the illustrations in the Text.

The numbers with a comma, as 73,8 (No. 8) refer to the plates of our work.

G. O = Goodyear's "Grammar of the Lotus". Number of the page.

L = Lajard, "Mithra". Number of the Plates.

C = Collection de Clercq Cylindres Assyriens. Number of the illustration.

M at No. 80 and 116 = Menant, "Glyptique Orientale", Vol. 11. Pictures in the Text.

M at No. 41 = Schliemann, "Mykenae".

S = A. P. di Cesnola. "Saliminia". Figure

G = Gerhard. Akademische Abhandlungen. Numbers of the Plates and Figures.

P = Perrot, "histoire de l'art". Volume and Figure.

C. S = Cesnola-Stern. Cyprus. Number of page.

H. H = W. Wright. "Empire of the Hittites". Hamath-inscriptions.

H. A. = Do. Aleppo-inscriptions.

Plate LXX.

Fragments of bronze armour from Tamassos. Berl. Mus. Antiquarium M. J. 8142.

1, 2, 3 must, from their shape and structure, have had the same use on the coat of mail. They come from the same Grave (Sec. IV Gr. 4 Warrior 1) and are of nearly the same length. In No. 3 the part with the palmette is much bent out of shape, so that the whole length only amounts to 420 m. No. 1. shows itself by its fine engraving to be a masterpiece; No. 2 has a modelled ornamention, while in No. 3 only the palmette is visible. As far as regards the mode of fastening, the small holes on all the parts point to a leather lining; on this the bronze plates were fastened by means of stitches, and in such a way that the palmette hung down; for we can only imagine the Figure on No 1 as standing upright. The hinges must obviously have lain on parts capable of bending i. e. somewhere in the region of the navel, and behind in the loins. Thus the parts with the hanging palmettes on one side covered

---

*) The vultures and eagles here are no longer very clear. I dug up in the same shrine pieces of crowns and figures broken off from crowns and representing eagles, just as distinctly and realistically modelled as the fragments depicted on p. 233, fig. 213, and p. 234, fig. 214 of "Salaminia." These terra-cotta colossi of Achna, of which a piece was exhibited in 1885 in the British Museum, had, including the crown, a height of 2,70 m.—3 m. In Pharangas (No. 14), A. P. di Cesnola found the same figures. I have also depicted in "The Owl" p. 76, 77, Pl. IX, 7—12) several such figures of eagles from the crowns of these clay colossi.

the lower part of the body, on the other the buttocks. At the upper ends are hooks, as in No. 2, or round sockets (broken off in No. 1, turned to the back side in No. 3). These must have stood in connection with the upper part of the armour, and at the same time have been kept up in the same way, since at the upper end no hole is found for fastening them on the leather lining (For 1 cf. 138 to 139 and 235.

4—8 belong to another suit of armour (Warrior 2).

No. 7 has the same meaning as the preceding parts No. 1—3; it is the upper part of a corresponding plate with a hook broken off; but here the upper end has been stitched on, as the whole shows. It seems to be an important point that the proportions are different. The preserved fragment has a length of 0,095 m. so that for the whole plate we should have a length of 0.200 m. i. e. not half so much as for the preceding ones. Perhaps the presence of the similar plates No. 4, 5, 6 and 8 is connected with this difference (No. 5 is much bent at the left edge). These have been sewn on the leather only at the narrower ends, and in the middle, where the edge bends outwards. So the broad ends must have hung down free. The plates probably over-lapped each other as in the case of scale-armour.

9, 10 and 11 are smaller fragments, which, being ornaments, must have been fastened on by themselves; all three have lace-holes.

12. A number of fragments, which are not so thick as the former ones. The edge preserved points to a circular shape, so that one may conceive the whole as the plating of a shield. It is in this sense that we have treated the decoration more in detail above (cf. Text p. 193, 209, 300). (1—12 H. S).

With the armour-pieces 1—8 we may compare the object with a Phoenician Inscription described and discussed at p. 75 Fig. 101 = Pl. CXLI, 4, that seems to have belonged to a similar piece of armour. This was hung up on the Holy Hill of the Idalian Anat-Athene (No 28 of the List). The figure of a warrior, depicted on Plate CXLII, Fig 1, wears a coat of mail which perhaps had a similar arrangement to those of the coats of mail to which the pieces described here (p. 75 Fig 101) belonged. The same Nekropolis and layer in which I dug up these pieces of armour (Pl. CXLII) yielded a helmet which is like the one worn by the figure on Pl. CXLII. An accurate description of the objects found in the very interesting grave, in the long Dromos of which two warriors lay buried with their weapons and horses and to which our pieces of armour belonged, will be published in my work on Tamassos. The grave belongs to the first half of the sixth century B. C.

Plate LXXI.

1. Egyptian fresco of the nineteenth dynasty, with the goddess Nut. Rosellini, "Monumenti dell' Egitto" III Pl. CXXXIV, cf. p. 101, 110, 288 Note 1. and 295.

2. Part of the Mithras-Reliefs of Heddernheim more completely portrayed on Pl. CXIX. Lajard, "Culte de Mithra" Pl. XC. cf. p. 101—103.

Plate LXXII.

I. Group of four different images of Hathor, about which details have been given at p. 248 Note 3, taken from Egyptian monuments. Wilkinson-Birch, "Manners and Customs of the Ancient Egyptians" III p. 118 Pl. XXVIII. Underneath the Osiris-Soul, cf. p. 101—103, 110, 292—295.

2. Part of an Egyptian fresco with the goddess Nut and the Osiris-Soul. Wilkinson - Birch III p. 63, Pl. XXIV. The Osiris - Soul reproduced on Pl. CIX, 9 = Fig. 205, p. 293, cf. p. 101 to 103, 110 292—295.

3. Part of a later Roman altar from Palmyra. Lajard, "Culte du cyprès", Pl. I, 2; Bötticher, "Baumcultus", Fig 47. Discussed p. 101—103, cf. p. 244, Note 4.

Plate LXXIII.

1 = CIX, 4 = Fig. 214, p. 294. Egyptian Picture of late Hellenistic or Roman times. Rosellini, "Monumenti dell'Egitto" III. Pl. XXV, 2. The androgynous Nile God Hapi and the Osiris-Soul. cf. p. 104—105 and 295.

2. Egyptian fresco of the twentieth dynasty. Rosellini III, Pl. LXXIV. Hapi, carrying flowers and fruits, cf. p. 104.

3. Cyprian red clay vase from Idalion; Berlin. Cesnola, "Salaminia" Title-page and p. 249, Fig. 235. Discussed p. 104—105.

4 = CXXIII, 5. Rosellini III, Pl. XXI. Discussed p. 104—105.

5 = CLIII, 3a. Red clay Cyprian vase from Idalion. Cesnola "Salaminia", Title page and p. 248, Fig. 233. Discussed p. 104—105; cf. 156 and Pl. LXIX 3.

6 Picture on the shoulder of the vase Fig. 3.

7. Picture on the shoulder of a vase from Tamassos, discussed at p. 105, cf. Pl. LXIX, 68.

8 = CLII, 3b. Picture on the shoulder of the vase Fig. 5.

The Antiquarium of the Royal Museum at Berlin acquired in 1892 from the Lawrence-Cesnola-Collection the vessel depicted here 3 and 6, and at the same time a larger amphora, on the shoulder of which a similar rude figure is attempted. From a quadrangle project human limbs, rudely drawn. If we had not Egyptian models to go by (1, 2, 4), we should be inclined to regard these rude pictures on Cyprian vases (3, 6, 7 and the picture of the amphora which we have not reproduced) as mere unsuccessful attempts of a vase-painter who wished to paint a human being but did not know how. But as I dug up myself the vase with the picture 7 (together with the vase p. 37, Fig. 38) and can refer it to the period between 700 and 1000 B. C., in which for a long time past the human form had been better drawn in Cyprus, we see in these pictures, precisely as in the case of the Tanit of Carthage and the Paphian idols of Cyprus, the deliberate intention of representing aniconic Agalmata with the appendages of human limbs, or semi-anthropomorphic images with a flower in place of the human head &c. These Vase-pictures must not be regarded as purely decorative, but they also have at the same time a secondary or primary religious significance.

Plate LXXIV.

1 = LXXVIII, 12 Cesnola-Stern LXXVI, 14. Two Sacrificers and two victims between two sacred trees. Globes and verticillate pieces of wood (reproduced again LXIX, 19) fill up the space. Cf. p. 106—107, 158, Note 5, 160.

2 = LXXIX, 1 = XCIV, 17 Salaminia XIII, 19. Two Figures in an attitude of taking an oath or worshipping, on each side of two holy stakes, which show respectively two and three branches, as in Fig. 1. To the right an ox head on an altar-table. Cf. p. 106, 158, 160, 172, 239, LXIX, 18.

3 = XXVIII, 17—LXXIX, 8.

4 = LXXIX, 7, Salaminia XV, 54. A Figure is enthroned before a semi-anthropomorphic stake-shaped idol on which arms, legs, body and head are indicated by wooden staves and the eyes are put in, as in Fig 3, as great round discs. cf. p. 106—107, 168, Note 1, and Pl. LXIX, 71.

5 = p. 41 Fig. 39 Vase from Kition cf. Journal of Hellenistic Studies. 1889 p. 105 = Goodyear Pl. XXXVII, 5.

This illustration, prepared after an original photograph, is new.

At 6 and 8 I have again reproduced the outlines of this Agalma, formed in a fantastic fashion out of a tree and a human being.

Fig. 8. gives the contours of the upper principal figure (the Mother?) down from which hangs figure 6 (the Child?). If we compare these figures 6 and 8 with the Cyprian cylinder-pictures 3 and 4, with the Mykenaean Vase picture on the following plate LXXV, 1 and the Egyptian and Cyprian pictures of the preceding Pl. LXXIII. we become convinced that we have before us here attempts of Vase-painters to give expression upon vases to the fantastic religious ideas of their time. They wished to fix the Asheras, Massebas and Chammanim, which stood before their eyes, in the half aniconic half-iconic Agalmata of the Seats of Worship, cf. p. 37—38, 106—109, 164, 168 No. 1.

7 = XXXVI, 3. cf. p. 106—108.

Plate LXXV.

1. Mykenaean Vase-Picture from Haliki. Furtwängler-Löschcke, Myken. Vasen, p. 39, Fig. 23. Discussed p. 108, cf. LXIX, 74.

2. Melian Vase picture. Conze, "Melische Thongefässe" V, 1. Discussed p. 109.

3. The same. Conze, "Melische Thongefässe". Vignette under the notes. Discussed p. 109—110, cf. LXIX, 73.

4. Part of the Rhodian Euphorbos-Plate. Salzmann, "Nécropole de Camiros" Pl. LIII. Discussed page 109.

5. Vase-painting with red figures from a Stamnos from Vulci Panofka. Dionysos and the Thyads, Pl. II, 1, p. 28 ff. = Bötticher, Baumcultus Fig. 43b. Described p. 109, cf. p. 111. No. 3 and 257.

6 = XXX, 2.

7. Clay plank-idol from the Ox-crater Grave at Hagia Paraskevi. Berlin. Described in detail in p. 111 to 112.

8. Babylonian Cylinder. Lajard, "Culte de Mithra" Pl. LIV, B. 12. Two priests in a worshipping attitude between an enthroned and a standing Corn-demon cf. p. 103, 110—111, 115 and 177. No. 7.

N. to 1. There can be no doubt, I suppose, that on this Mykenaean vase-picture, at the summit of the medial stake-shaped decoration, it is a fantastic human face which projects, surrounded by a radiant crown. Plate XCIII, 1 a disc-shaped relief of red polished clay, coming from Hagia Paraskevi in Cyprus, gives us the definite key to this. This is considerably older than the Mycene vases. We see there a perfectly similarly painted and similarly crowned face.

N. to 2—4. Fantastic ideas floated in the minds of the painters of the vases of Melos and of the Euphorbus-Plate found in Rhodes, Similar to those which the painters of the Cyprian vases conceived (LXXIV, 5, 6 and 8).

5. The central vase-picture with red figures, showing Dionysus as a stake and Tree god, gives us a further typologically instructive parallel to our Cyprian vessel (Pl. LXXIV, 5), although it is some centuries later and belongs to a perfectly different medium of thought and art.

6 and 8 show how in Babylon the deities and demons make corn, plants and trees grow out of their bodies, and represent here too, along with the Egyptian (LXXIII, 1, 2, 4) the second source from which the Cyprians drew for their types and myth-formations.

Plate LXXVI.

? 1—13. Terra-cotta Tree-Agalmata from the groves of Astarte-Aphrodite and Tanit-Artemis-Cybele, all fully discussed and described supr. p. 127 to 131.

1 coloured on Pl. LXVIII, 7.

2 = Pl.—

8 = Pl. CXXVII, 4, where I have also treated of the Processional Dance.

Plate LXXVII.

1. Conical Seal with Phoenician incription and engraving on three sides. Ward, American Journal 1886, 11, p. 156, Fig. 17.

a) A priest is worshipping three holy symbols, viewed from right to left: the Ashera, the Masseba and the Union of the two, of which I have treated fully p. 143.

b) A Divine Trinity on the winged disc of the Sun. Underneath a kneeling man, behind him Ashera and Masseba, in front of him the inscription.

c) Group of human being and lion-headed deity, in an attitude of taking an oath and under a crescent moon cf. p. 143—144, 149, 160, 291 and Pl. LXIX, 36.

2. Stele from Carthage. Corpus Inscriptionum Semiticarum, Pl. XLVIII, 233. Dedicatory inscription to Tanit, Countenance of Baal and Baal-Hammon. Underneath, a column with a tendency to Ionic style, on which is a pomegranate, flanked by two columns shaped like herald's staves. Cf. p. 113 to 114, 149, 173, 180, 301.

3. Stele from Carthage C. I. S. Pl. XLVI, 235, cf. p. 149, 173, 180, 301 and Plate LXIX, 76.

4. Stele from Carthage C. I. S. Pl. XLIII, 240, cf. p. 149, 172, 180, 301.

5 = XCIX, 2. Persian Cylinder of the British Museum, Lajard, Mithra LIV, A, 13. Described p. 156, cf. also p. 291 and Pl. LXIX, 12.

6. Cylinder with Phoenician inscription. Lajard, Mithra LIV, A, 3.

Grouped round the Sacred Tree, over which hovers the winged Sun-disc, are goat-sphinxes and winged-sphinxes as well as two worshipping mortals. Underneath the Sun-disc is the combined symbol of the crescent moon and sun, cf. p. 150, 152 and 160.

The place where this came from is proved to be Cyprus by the details of the picture, the style and character, the dress and contours of the figures and of the bearded-sphinx, its wings running to a sword-like point, the double symbol composed of the Sun with the half moon lying round it, by the structure and the shape of the sacred tree, and lastly by the Phoenician inscription.

7 = CXVII, 6. Old Hebrew Gem with inscription from the Berlin Museum.

Clermont-Ganneau, Recueil d'archéologie orientale 1885, 1, p. 33—38 = Sceaux et cachets israélites, phéniciens et syriens No. 2 = Perrot IV, p. 439, Fig. 227. Continuous row of pomegranates as a border-decoration round the inscription cf. p. 113 and 150.

8 = CXIII, 6. Old Hebrew Gem with inscription, from the Berl. Mus.

Clermont-Ganneau, loc. cit No. 1 = Perrot IV, p. 439, Fig. 226. Over the inscription is a palmette as a rudiment of a sacred Tree cf. p. 150.

9. Persian Cylinder. Lajard, Mithra LVII, 2 = Goodyear Lotus XXXII, 6.

Above the Ashera hovers the winged bust of a god, crowned with palmettes. On both sides sit bearded, crowned, winged sphinxes cf. p. 152, 291 and LXIX, 104. A similar picture in Perrot III p 186.

10 = XCIX, 6. Persian Cylinder from Libanon. Menant, Glyptique II, p. 220, Fig. 213 = Perrot III, p, 635, Fig. 426. Close to a Palm-pillar a king or a god is wrestling with two lions. On the right, beneath a crescent moon, is an Aramaic inscription. Cf. p. 152, 156 and Plate LXIX, 105.

11. Persian Cylinder with Phoenician inscription and a Persian name.

Lajard, Mithra, Pl. L, 6 = Menant II, p. 221, Fig. 214.

Under a winged bust of a god, a king or god is wrestling with a bearded-sphinx and a griffin. Close by is a Phoenician inscription with a Persian name. Cf. p. 152, 291.

12. Persian Cylinder of the Schlumberger Collection.

Berger, Gazette Archéologique 1888, p. 143—144 = Perrot V, p. 853, Fig. 504.

Close to a palm are sitting two bearded sphinxes round a flower. Over it hover a winged bust of a god, a radiant sun and the crescent moon. In the middle an Aramaic inscription gives the name of the Persian possessor Mithras. Cf. p. 152 and 291 and Pl. LXIX, 113.

13 = XXXII, 7 = CXLII, 4.

14. Cylinder with Aramaic inscription.

Menant II, p. 218, Fig. 211 = Perrot III, p. 630, Fig. 422.

Between two - winged demons a priest is sacrificing under the winged disk of the sun in front of a tree or altar which is manifestly burning. An Aramaic inscription fills up the spaces. Cf. p. 152 and 163.

15. Phoenician conical seal of the British Museum.

De Vogue, Mélanges Pl. VI, 23 = Levy, Phönizische Studien II, 30 = Menant Glyptique II, p. 225, Fig. 222 = Perrot III, p. 648, Fig. 456. Described p. 152, 153 of our work. Cf. 163.

16. Phoenician octagonal cone.

Renan, Mission de Phénicie p. 144 = Levy. Siegel and Gemmen I, 14 = Menant II, p. 226, Fig. 223 = Perrot III, p. 648, Fig. 455. Described p. 156, cf. 152 and 166. But the symbol there hinted as Ashera appears rather to represent, in a rude fashion, a victim lying on the altar.

17 = CXIII, 5 = CLXIII, 8 Phoenician Gems.

Lajard, Mithra Pl. LVII, 1 = Perrot II, p. 689, Fig. 348.

A sphinx and a winged-goat, upright on their hind-legs, are standing by a sacred tree under the crescent Moon. For Cyprus as a probable place of manufactory vid. p. 150—151.

18 = p. 62, Fig 55. Cyprian Scarabaeus. Cesnola-Stern Pl. LXXX, 13. Described p. 61 to 62. Cf. p. 152 and LXIX, 27.

19 = XXXII, 16.

20. The image engraved on the under surface of a cone. Lajard Mithra XLIV, 24. Bearded-sphinxes are sitting about a palm; similar objects are described Pl. XXXII, 24 and Perrot III, p. 136, cf. p. 152 and LXIX, 114.

21 = CXVII, 5. Graco-Phoenician Scarabaeus from the Nekropoleis of Tharros. Spano Bulletino I, p. 149 = Perrot III, p. 237, Fig. 180.

The sacred tree under the winged disk of the sun, surrounded by two priests. Cf. p. 150, 152 and 291.

Besides the cylinder Fig. 6, proved at 6 to be Cyprian, the gems 13 and 17 appear to have come from Cyprus. The Scarabaeus (21) found in Sardinia is also so similar in style, motive, and conception, to the numerous kindred pictures on Cyprian stones, metal bowls, vases &c., that one asks one's self whether this Scarabaeus was not manufactured in Cyprus in ancient times, and transperred to Tharros through Cyprians. Whether the importers were Phoenician or Greek-Cyprians, or belonged to another non-Cyprian race, would not alter the question of provenance.

Plate LXXVIII.

1. Phrygian Rock - grave of Arslan - kaia. Perrot V, p. 156, Fig. 109 = Journal of Hellenic Studies 1884, Pl. XLIV. In the pediment two winged sphinxes stand on each side of the holy Pillar. Cf. p. 152.

? 2. Image of limestone. Found in 1890 in a Graeco-Phoenician earthern grave at Amathus. University of Bonn Museum. Described in detail p. 153 along with the Note 5.

3 = XXXII, 10.

4. Gems enlarged after Lajard, Mithra Pl. XLV, 24.

Two lions stand round the holy palm column. Crescent moons, stars, and small round discs (constellations?) systematically arranged, fill up the space, cf. 152 and LXIX, 107.

5 = XXXII, 11.

6 = XXXII, 1.

7 = XXXII, 41.

8. Cylinder. Menant, Glyptique Orientale II, p. 65, Fig. 60.

Two priests, standing one on each side of the Sacred Tree, are holding a kind of garland, which hangs down from the winged disc of the sun. On both sides a he-goat and a holy pillar, between a crescent moon and two stars. Of the meaning of the representation see p. 166. Cf. Pl. LXIX, 51.

9. = XXXII, 12.

10. Stone relief from the rock-grave of Arslan-kaia depicted Fig. 1. Perrot V, p. 157, Fig. 110 = Journal of Hellenic Studies 1884, p. 285.

Two lions are standing erect on their hind-legs on either side of the image of Cybele, cf. 152.

11. Cylinder. Lajard. Pl. LIV, B, 9.
Similar picture to that in the middle ground of Fig. 8. Over it is the crescent-moon and a star; close by a second sacred tree. Cf. p. 168, Pl. LXIX, 10.

12 = LXXIV, 1.

13 = XXXII, 9 = CXLII, 3.
The most interesting object of the Plate is the Cyprian No. 9. It shows how we have to imagine the holy animals to be symbolised in the holy trees, stakes, worship-pillars, altars, and statues. The pillar of the Mykenaean Gate, with the rampant lions, is also a worship Pillar as has been shown supr. p. 152.

Plate LXXIX.

1 = LXXIV. 2 = XCIV, 17. Cyprian cylinder, A, P. di Cesnola, "Salaminia" XIII, 19.
Two figures, in an attitude as if taking an oath or praying, on each side of a holy stake or post. On the left a similar post. On the right an ox-head on an altar table. Cf. p. 106, 158, 160, 172, 289.

2. Salaminia XII, 11.
A similar scene round the holy pillar; besides which there are three quadrupeds as victims. Cf. p. 158, 160—161, LXIX, 48.

3 = XXVIII, 22.

4 = p. 87, Fig. 118. Salaminia XIII, 20. Described p. 87. Cf. p. 158, 172, 197 and LXIX, 7 and 90.

5. Salaminia XIII, 22.
A priest with the lance is sitting in front of the Holy Symbols -- the serpent, two rods (one of which is crowned with a half-moon), the holy tree, and the sun-disc with a tail. Cf. p. 197—198 and LXIX, 89.

6. = Fig. 193, p. 288. Salaminia XIII, 29.
Two female animal-tamers with quadrupeds, one of which seems to be a hare, the other a he-goat. Besides, under sun and half-moon, the sacred tree, and furthermore the holy post, depicted similar to Fig. 1. On the upper part, sun and half-moon again, and an obscure symbol. Cf. p. 190 and Pl. LXIX, 22.

7 = LXXIV, 4.

8 = XXVIII, 17 = LXXIV, 3.

9. Cyprian Scarabaeoid, Salaminia XV, 53.
Holy Symbols, perhaps the Ashera, to the right under the crescent moon; the Masseba to the left. Cf. LXIX, 38.

10. Salaminia XII, 4. On the left the Sacred Tree. On the right perhaps a rudely indicated figure. On a level with her head the Cyprian combination of sun and half-moon. In the neighbourhood are obscure symbols. Cf. p. 262, LXIX, 39.

11. Lajard, Culte de Mithra, Pl. LIV A, 7 = Menant Glypt. II, p. 85, Fig. 19 = Perrot II, p. 647, Fig. 315
The Ashera crowned with a Crescent Moon, before which lies a fabulous animal, and the deity standing in a kind of halo in front of a horned quadruped, are being worshipped by a mortal. Cf. p. 150 and 160.

12. Menant II, p. 31, Fig. 13. Two mortals are worshipping the Ashera crowned with a crescent moon, near which the symbol of the female pudenda is indicated, and the Masseba is standing, drawn smaller; over the latter a star hovers. Cf. p. 150 and 160.

† 13. A conical seal found in Cyprus. Particulars unknown. Collection of E. Konstantinides, Nicosia. Perhaps an Ashera, evidently burning similar to Fig. 9, cf. p. LXIX, 37.

14. Lajard, Mithra LIV, B, 3. Two quadrupeds. he-goats or stags, are rearing up alongside the sacred Tree; close by stands the Ashera, who is probably conceived as androgynous, crowned with the radiant sun and the crescent moon. Cf. p. 149, LXIX, 35.

15. Lajard, Mithra XXXIII, 9.
A mortal is worshipping the deity in the halo, which is surrounded by sacred symbols. On the left, under a crescent moon, is a more realistic Sacred Tree, on the right the Masseba, and the stake-shaped Ashera evidently burning, as Fig. 1, cf. p. 149, 160, LXIX, 21.

16. Lajard, Mithra, XL, 5.
Under the radiant sun and the crescent moon Masseba and Ashera; close by on each side of an altar, a goddess enthroned, and a priest sacrificing. Cf. p. 143, Note 6, 119, 152, 159, Note 5, 169, Note 4, LXIX, 38.

17. Lajard, Mithra XXXIV, 10.

Ashera and Masseba, under a radiant sun and crescent moon, are surrounded by an enthroned goddess and a worshipping figure cf. p 143, Note 6, 149, LXIX, 25. Close to is a late cuneiform inscription.

18. A group of hieroglyphs, cut out of the second column, second division from the bottom, W. Wright. Empire of the Hittites. Jerabis-inscription 1, cf. p. 160—161.

19. Ditto, from the same work. Hamath II, inscription, lower row on the right, cf. 160—161, 172, No. LXIX, 118.

? 20 = p. 61, Fig. 69 = XCIV, 3.

From the copper-bronze age Nekropolis at Kephalovrisi at Kythraea. Collection of E. Konstantinides, Nicosia. Described p. 62, cf. 64, 159—161, 239, LXIX, 121.

21. Like 18 and 19. Aleppo-inscription I, 4. After G. Smith. Cf. p. 160—161, 172; No. LXIX, 19.

22. Lajard LIV, 3. A demon with four wings (two take the place of the arms), surrounded by two he-goats and two holy posts, which are like those on Figs. 1, 6, and 15, cf. LXIX, 28.

Plate LXXX.

1. Hittite cylinder. Lajard, Mithra, Pl. LII, 6 = Goodyear, Lotus Pl. XXXVI, 7.

About the holy pillar, on the volute-capital of which are resting the crescent-moon and the sun-disc, we see symetrically arranged two hares, two goats' heads and two demons, standing erect and having the head of a human being, the lower limbs of a lion, and wings instead of arms. Close by is a star and two quadrupeds (goat and lion) one on the top of the other, separated by a plaited band, as on Pl. XXXI, 9 and 10, cf. p. 160, 171, 190, 192 and LXIX, 109.

2. Hittite cylinder. Lajard, Pl. XXXVIII, 4.

On the right two mortals, grouped on each side of the holy pillar, in prayer, over them hovers the winged sun-disc. Close by, standing on a plaited band, Izdubar is taming an ox rearing up on his hind legs. Behind him another mortal, drawn smaller, above whom a lion is sitting, cf. p. 160, 292 and Pl. LXIX, 108.

3. Oriental cylinder. Lajard Pl. XXX, 3.

Two winged quadrupeds, with human heads and egg-shaped bodies, are climbing up a holy tree which is between them. Behind them a branch, over which hovers the winged sun-disc.

4. Greek vase-picture. From Cervetri. Conze, "Melische Thongefässe" Pl. V, 4.

Two lions and two sirens are standing on each side of a pillar, obviously borrowed from Assyrian models, cf. p. 164 and Pl. LXIX, 110.

? 5. Cypro-Phoenician obelisk, with dedicatory inscription to Ešmun - Adonis on the base. From Kition.

Illustrates the Jewish Masseba in the Bible. Cf. p. 173, 175, 178, 180, 215, 215, Note 7, 262; Pl. LVI.

6. Cyprian Graeco-Phoenician vase of the Metropolitan Museum in New York. Goodyear, "The Grammar of the Lotus", p. 305. Pl. XLVIII, 9 and p. 341, Pl. LVII, 3. At Pl. LXII, 1 we see a flower on a vase of the sixth century B. C, developed out of the concentric circle. Here we see an idol made from the concentric circle, one or more centuries earlier, with a rude indication of human members, the head, the arms, the legs and the phallos. Cf. p. 157 and Pl. LXIX, 15.

7 = p. 197, Fig. 165. Sun-column found at Tyre. Longpérier, Musée Napoléon, Pl. XVIII, 2 = Perrot III, p. 128, Fig. 72, cf. p. 171, 173, 192, 235 and Pl. LXIX, 52.

Plate LXXXI.

1. One of the Pillars of the well-known pair of Malta with bilingual dedicatory inscription to the Assyrian Melqart-Hercules. Perrot III, p. 79, Fig. 28. The inscription also C. I. G. 5753, I. G. Sic. et Ital. 600. Cf. p. 180 to 183.

2. Stone altar or holy-water font from the Phoenician shrine of Hagia Kim in Malta, 0,07 m high. Perrot III, p. 304, Fig. 228.

In front, in a niche that runs vertically underneath, is represented a holy tree, which grows out of a little box or vessel. Here a wooden frame on which a clay basin is placed and under which stands an Adonis-garden, is evidently imitated in stone. *)

What can the picture possibly mean, except one of those artificial Adonis-gardens of which we have treated in detail, p. 131? The monument was discovered, along with seven rude stone images of the nude Tammuz-Adonis-Boy (one pictured at Pl. XCII, 8), in the ante-chamber A of the shrine. This ante-

---

*) The Cypriotes have in the present day corresponding wooden frames for the reception of their water-vessels, under which they often place in pots the green corn grown for sacred uses, cf. p. 132, cf. also the frames depicted on bowls of Crete (CXXVII. 2), of Olympia (CXXIX, 2), of Cyprus (CXX, 1), p. 123, Fig. 142, p. 126, Fig. 143 on the Assyrian relief (LXXXVII, 11, 14 CXXIV, 1) and the cylinders (LXXXVII, 12 and 15).

EXPLANATION OF THE PLATES. 417

chamber A. seems then to have been the space for the dedicatory offerings and here it certainly would be in its right place. The Adonis-garden at the foot of the font would equally well suit the Adonis statuettes.

? 3—6 = p. 155, Fig. 152—155. River-pebble boundary stones from Tamassos. Berl. Museum p. 172—174.

Plate LXXXII.

1. Votive-tablet to Baalchamâmn, from Lilybaeum. C. I. S. Pl. XXIX, 188 = Perrot III, p. 309, Fig. 282 = Roscher, Mythologisches Lexikon I Col. 2869.

On the pediment Sun and half-moon, in the arrangement so much affected in Cyprus. Underneath, on an altar, the three Chamman-stones. In the middle Cone-idol of Tanit, flanked by the symbol of the herald's staff, presumably the symbol of the male deity, and the burning candelabra. In front is a mortal in worshipping attitude. Underneath is the Phoenician dedicatory inscription, cf. p. 177—180 and Pl. LXIX, 55 and 67.

2 = Fig. 236, p. 324. Graeco-Phoenician Scarabaeus. Lajard, Mithra Pl. LXVIII, 26.

A god or priest (in the left hand a lance and a bough, the right hand raised as if to give a blessing), stands before a burning candelabra; over him hovers a star. As at p. 197—198, presumably Cyprian workmanship. Cf. also p. 178 and 323 to 327.

3 = Fig. 237, p. 324. Graeco-Phoenician Scarabaeus. Lajard, Mithra Pl. LXVIII, 24.

Similar scene to the preceding, but the god is sitting and holds in his left hand only the lance. By his side stands a winged sphinx. A winged sun-disc takes the place of the star. Cf. p. 178, 197—198, 334.

4. Chandelier of a Carthaginian stele. Perrot III, p. 134, Fig. 83, cf. p. 178 and Pl. LXIX, 53.

5. Same subject. Perrot Fig. 82.

6 = CLIX, 8. Fragment of a relief from Adlum near Tyre. Perrot III, p. 133, Fig. 81.

As in Fig. 3, a god or a mortal sitting on a throne before a burning chandelier, the sphinx being by his side, cf. p. 178—179.

7 = X, 1 = CXXVI, 3.

8 = X, 2 = CXXVI, 4.

The Scarabaeus (mentioned p. 327 found in Cyprus in the burial fields of Marion-Arsinoë, proves that we have Cyprian workmanship in the Scarabaei 2 and 3. The Tyrian relief fragment must also have been made in Cyprus. The same Cyprian god Rešef appears to be sitting on a throne-chair before the candelabrum, and a sphinx to be standing by his side. The candelabra (4, 5 and 1) which appear on the Carthaginian and Sicilian relief pictures are imitated from the model found in Cyprus (Pl XLIII, 9 and 10). The large candelabra which stand in the side-spaces on the Paphos coin 8 differ, it is true, from the ordinary kind, but even for this form there are several varieties, dug up by me in Kurion, Marion-Arsinoë and Tamassos, made of bronze and iron, which originated in the same fundamental form There are also several Cyprian analogies for the steaming tripod, which stands (Coin Fig. 7) in the door-way of the chapel of the Biblos sanctuary.

Plate LXXXIII.

1. Assyrian cylinder of the British Museum. Lajard, Culte de Mithra. Pl. XIII, 2. A bearded demon with four wings is taming two winged, fabulous animals resembling' unicons. Between them the symbol of the female pudenda. On the left hovers over an omphalos the winged bust of a deity. Cf. P. 147 Note 1, 169, Pl. LXIX, 57.

2. Omphalos-altar of a vase-picture, with black figures. Gerhard, Akademische Abhandlungen Pl. LIX, 1, cf. p. 169.

3. Coin of Emesa. Gerhard, loc. cit. Pl. LIX, 5.

In a temple, the pediment of which is adorned by a half-moon, stands the Omphalos-idol of Elagabal, cf. p. 169 and Pl. LXIX, 58.

4. Coin of Caesarea in Syria. Gerhard, loc. cit. Pl. LIX, 20.

Under a round arch supported by pillars, stands the image of the goddess (Artemis) in omphalos-form, and wrapt in a cloak, cf. p. 169 and Pl. LXIX, 60.

5. Coin of Perge. Gerhard, loc. cit. Pl. LIX, 4.

In a temple stands the idol of Artemis Pergaia an Omphalos, from which the head of the goddess projects cf. p. 169.

6 = CXXVII, 2. Limestone votive-tablet, from a grove of Apollo of Athiaenou (No. 25, or 26 of the List).

Cesnola-Atlas Pl. LXXXV, 553; Cesnola-Stern Pl. XXVI, 3, described p. 124, cf. p. 169, 340 and Pl. LXIX 59.

7 = CXXVIII, 3. Same subject. Cesnola-Atlas Pl. LXXXV, 558. Cesnola-Stern XCVI, 6.

54*

Apollo with lyre and sceptre is seated on a throne, close to a tree and altar. On the right mortals engaged in the processional dance.

8. Coin of Myra. Gerhard, loc. cit. Pl. LX, 8, described p. 169, cf. p. 260.

9. Coin of Myra. Gerhard, loc. cit. Pl. LIX, 6.

In a Temple stands the same veiled statue of a god, which in Fig. 8 is projecting from the tree, cf. p. 172.

10. Red jasper of the Berlin Museum. Gerhard loc. cit. Pl. LIX, 10.

Aniconic idol between a star and the half-moon. Underneath a poppy and ears of corn are growing out.

11. Gem with an Agalma similar in outline to the former, but iconic. Gerhard loc. cit. Pl. LIX, 9.

12. Cornelian of the Berlin Museum. Gerhard, loc. cit. Pl. LIX, 12; similar idol to 10, but more in the shape of a house.

13. Coin of Mallos in Cilicia Gerhard, loc. cit. Pl. LIX, 13. Cone-idol, flanked by two grapes. cf. p. 176 and Pl. LXIX, 64.

14. Coin of Jasos. Gerhard, loc. cit. Pl. LXIX, 7. Described p. 169.

15. Coin of Hierapolis. Gerhard loc. cit. Pl. LIX, 18.

Idol of Artemis between two stags, cf. p. 169—170.

16. Coin of Tarsos. Gerhard, loc. cit. Pl. LIX, 15 = Rochette, Hercule Assyrien, Pl. IV, 2.

In a cone, on which a bird is sitting, the deity stands on an animal, cf. p. 166—167 and Pl. LXIX, 79.

17. Coin of Sidon. Gerhard, loc. cit. Pl. XLIII, 16.

On a procession-waggon stand two conical idols of Astarte, over which hovers the sun, cf. p. 152, 166, 235 and Pl. LXIX, 65.

18. Coins from Carthage. Gerhard, loc. cit. Pl. XLIII, 19.

In a temple, the pediment of which is ornamented with a bird, stand four cypresses, cf. p. 178.

19. Coin of Paphos. Guigniaut, Religions de l'antiquité, Pl. LIV, 206 = Perrot III p. 266, Fig. 199. Another copy of the coin represented at Pl. X, 2 and frequently, cf. p. 178, 235, 278, Pl. LXIX, 66.

20. Coin of the Jewish kingdom, at the time of Jaddus. De Saulcy, Numismatique juive I, 6 = Perrot IV, p. 308, Fig. 154. Described p. 170.

21. Tomb-stone from the Nekropolis of Tharros in Sardinia. Perrot III, p. 235, Fig. 174. Group of three Chamman-stones. On the middle one the well known symbol of sun and half-moon cf. p. 171, 178 and 235.

22. Coin of Paphos. Gerhard loc. cit. Pl. XLIII, 17 = Perrot III, p. 270, Fig. 202. In a peculiar tabernacle stands the Astarte-cone on which a dove is sitting. On both sides two more cones, cf. p. 166—167, 178, 262 and 278.

Plate LXXXIV.

1. Lajard, Mithra LIV, 1. Described p. 181—182. Cf. p. 163, 179, 182, Note 4.

2. Lajard XVLII, 4 = Menant Glypt. Orient, p. 122, Fig. 70 = Ward, Americ. Journ. of Archaeol. III, 1887, Pl. V—VI, Fig. 9. Inside the sun-gate, which is being opened by two attendants, the unwinged Samas steps out of a mountain ravine. Cf. p. 181.

3. Lajard, XVIII, 3 = Ward loc. cit. Fig. 6.

A similar scene, but Samas wears wings here, and on the left stands the holy star-crowned staff-symbol. Cf. p. 149, 181, LXIX, 86.

4 = p. 191, Fig. 164; after Ward. loc. cit. Fig. 1.

Similar picture. The winged Samas with the sword-shaped instrument is already placing his foot on the top of the mountain; around him hover the symbols for the male and female sex. On the pillars are seated lions, near one, a small tree seems to be indicated. On the right stands the third attendant. Cf. p. 181, 191, LXIX, 87.

5. Lajard, Mithra XXVII, 10 = Ward loc. cit. Fig. 2. Described p. 181.

6. Lajard, XXVIII, 15 = Ward loc. cit. Fig. 8. = Menant Glypt. Orient. I, p. 122, Fig. 69.

Similar representations as 2 and 3. Only one wing of the gate is given. On the right a priest is approaching the god with a saw. Cf. p. 181.

7. Lajard, Mithra XL, 8 = Lajard, Culte du Cyprès, LX, 1 = Ward loc. cit. Fig. 7.

Similar Scene to 3; but in the place of the staff-symbol there is a cypress. Cf. p. 119, 181, 182, Note 4.

On Samas cf. p. 115, 177—182, 191—192.

Plate LXXXV.

1. Votive-pillar in the form of a tower with gates and windows. From Carthage. H. 0,465 m, C. I. S. Pl. XLII, No. 181 A.
On it a dedicatory inscription to Tanit, face of Baal, and Baal Hammon. Cf. p. 278 and 291, Note 5.
2. Votive stele of Carthage. C. S. Sem. I. p. 281 = Perrot IV, p. 291, Fig. 150. Described p. 196.
3. The same, C. I. Sem. I. p. 281. Winged sun-disc and raised hand, above the cone-idol of Tanit cf. p. 172.
4. The same. C. I. Sem. I. p. 281 = Perrot III, p. 54, Fig. 16 = Goodyear XXIII, 6. Hathor-head on a column with volute-capitals, bearing an entablature.
5. The same, C. I. Sem. I. p. 281. Branches are growing out of a lotus-shaped flower, which end in the idol of Tanit.
6. The same, C. I. Sem. I. p. 281. A palm-shaped stem ends in the symbol called the herald's-staff, at the side branches project with the cone-idol of Tanit. Cf. Pl. LXIX, 69.
7 = Fig. 220, p. 301. The same. C. I. Sem. Pl. XLIII, 289. Breast-nipples, as abbreviated symbols of the goddess. Underneath the dedicatory inscription to Tamit and Baal Chammun.
8. The same, C. I. Sem. I. p. 281. A goddess enthroned, her right hand raised, in the left hand a lotus flower, cf. p. 206 Note 2 and 245 Note 4.
9. The same, C. I. Sem. Pl. XLV, 183. Described p. 281—282. Cf. p. 171—172, 171 and 245 Note 4. Cf. also p. 149, 173, ff, 180 and 301.

Plate LXXXVI.

♀ 1. Female idol (clay) from Hagia Paraskevi. H. 0,047 m.
The form is plank-shaped. We cannot quite make out the different parts of the head. On the other hand the breasts are plainly indicated. Stumps of arms are attached to the sides; they have the shape of small pegs hanging down; the left arm is broken off. The whole is covered with blood-red paint. The picture represents the actual size.
♀ 2. Female plank-idol (clay) from Hagia-Paraskevi. H. 0,146 m.
It has been fully discussed in the text p. 108 and 192. Particularly characteristic is the face which is explained as a radiant or sun-face. We should also notice that on the reverse side the hair hanging down is indicated by zig-zag lines, as on the idols of Pl. XXXVI.
♀ 3. Female plank-idol (clay) from the same Nekropolis. H. 0,180 m.
The under part is broken off. The clay is of a dirty yellow; the surface shows many traces of red paint.
The plastic raised surface in the middle, which broadens out downwards is characteristic; on the top is a plastic protuberance by way of face, situated on this strip, 1 cm distant from the upper end. Below, the female breasts are placed near the strip on both sides. This peculiarity may be explained perhaps from the connection between the shape of a post and a plank. The arms are, as in No. 4 and 7 of the same Plate, rudely indicated, and stand in direct connection with the plastic middle strip.
♀ 4. Female plank-idol (clay) from the same nekropolis. H. 0,185 m.
The right upper side of the head is broken off. The clay is grey in the middle of the fracture-surface, yellow at its edges. The surface is painted over bright brown. The face shows depressions, so far as it is preserved. The ears are furnished with three holes, as in the case of other idols (we should particularly compare the idol p. 34, Fig. 32). The necklace is here represented plastically, likewise the arms which lie upon the body; the hands are represented by engraved lines. The breasts have depressions to indicate the nipples. The indication of the female pudenda by rudely executed depression is particularly characteristic.
♀ 5. A similar one from the same Nekropolis. H. 0,180 m.
The clay is of a dirty yellow; the surface is painted over dark brown. The lower part is broken off, the left side and the upper rim much damaged. The details are represented by incised lines of which our picture shows the system. On the reverse side the hair is represented by zig-zag lines incised in. The arm-stumps are covered over in a very peculiar manner with small depressed lines in front as well as behind. On the back these groups of lines are not connected but are marked off separately by vertical lines. In form this idol is to be compared with No. 1 of the same Plate.
♀ 6. Fragment of a female plank-idol (clay) from the same nekropolis. H. 0,120 m, Br. 0,103 m.
The clay is of dirty yellow and painted over red. This fragment finds its best analogue in Plate XXXVI, 10. Only a single deity has been represented, to judge by the fracture-surface on the upper edge. With this fact the simple breast-ornament is connected. In other respects the details of the ornamentation are visible from our illustration.

? 7.   Upper part of a female plank-idol (clay) from the same nekropolis. H. 0,140 m.
The reverse side is depicted p. 33, Fig. 30. The clay is of a dirty grey and covered over with
bright red paint. The plastic protuberance on the head is clearly characterised as a nose by incised lines
in. Underneath the mouth is indicated. Neck-ornament and hair of the head on the reverse side are here
plastically represented, likewise the arms and the breasts. The other details are incised in. The
depressions made over the right arm and the corresponding part of the back of this idol are very peculiar.
Evidently a skin or an article of clothing is meant to be represented by them.

Cf. in general text p. 33, 261, 263, 265.   (1—7 H. S.)

All the idols illustrated on this Plate are in my possession M. O.-R.

Plate LXXXVII.

1. Cyprian cylinder. A. P. di Cesnola, "Salaminia" Pl. XIII, 18. The human figure is standing
before the Sacred Tree, surrounded by an ox's head and various sidereal signs. Cf. p. 157 and 160; the
treerepeated Fig. 8, p. 30.

2 = XCIV, 18. As Fig. 1. Salaminia Pl. XIII, 24. The representation agrees with Fig. 1 with
the exception of a single sign. Cf. p. 157—160 and 239.

3 = XCVIII, 5. The same. Cesnola-Stern Pl. LXXVII, 28. A fish, a bird, a quadruped, three
balls and a tree surround a bird spread out as in a coat-of-arms. As is shown p. 172—173 cosmogonical
ideas form the principal material of the picture. Cf. besides p. 157, 171, 274 No. 3 and 288.

4 = XCIV, 19. The same; Salaminia, Pl. XII, 6. Quadruped (lion or horse) before the sacred
tree (repeated Fig. 19, p. 30 and 65), the forelegs raised as if in prayer. Cf. p. 157 and 239.

5 = CXVI, 2. The same; Salaminia Pl. XII, 7. Similar Scene to 4. The animal must surely be a
lion. The tree is repeated Fig. 18, p. 30 and 65.

6. The Same; Cesnola-Stern Pl. LXXVI. 18.

A man in a commanding attitude close to a bird, a horned quadruped, two indistinctly
indicated fishes, sun, moon, and stars. The medium of ideas corresponds to Fig. 3, cf. p. 172—173
and 274, Note 3.

7 = CXVI, 3. The same; salaminia, Pl. XIV, 43. The holy tree (repeated Fig. 15, p. 30 and 65) is
being worshipped by a winged sphinx.

8 = XCIV, 15. The same; Salaminia Pl. XII, 8.

A quadruped is leaping up near the sacred tree, which is growing up under a crescent-moon and
a small star. Behind it is suspended an ox's head, and an obscure sign, cf. p. 158 and 239. The tree is
repeated Fig. 17, p. 30 and 65.

9 = p. 283, Fig. 196. The same as Salaminia p. 121, Fig. 11a. Described p. 283—284 of
our work.

10. Marble relief from Arados. Longpérier, Musée Napoléon III., Pl. XVIII, 3 = Perrot III,
p. 131, Fig. 76 = Goodyear Pl. LXXXVII, 4.

Two griffins are rearing themselves alongside the sacred tree. On the probability of Cyprus being
or the place of origin of this object see pp. 150—151.

11. Scene cut out of an Assyrian relief.

Two persons are sacrificing on a bowl, which is placed upon a frame. Cf. 12, 14 and 15.

12 = CLIII, 2 stone cylinder. Lajard, Mithra Pl. XXVII, 6 = Lajard Culte du Cyprès
Pl. IX, 3. Two cypresses on each side of a triangular symbol. Above them the cross-shaped star
peculiar to Babylonian-Assyrian cylinders (cf. p. 62, Fig. 73). Before them two mortals, in front a table-
like stand; while the one on the left holds bowl and axe, the one on the right is fanning with a straw
fan, evidently to kindle the fire*) which we must imagine to be in the triangle on the stand.

13. Babylonian stone cylinder. Menant Glyptique II, p. 56, Fig. 47. A priest is paying his
devotions before the stone Masseba, the wooden Ashera, and the heavenly deity in the halo. Behind him
the radiant sun, the crescent-moon, and the symbol of female pudenda. Cf. p. 147, 150, 162, 236—237 and
Pl. LXIX, 34.

14. Relief from Korsabad. Rawlinson, the five great monarchies of the ancient Greek world II,
p. 273 = Stade, History of Israel I, 461 = Menant Glyptique II, p. 70, Fig. 66. Two figures are anointing the holy symbol, perhaps regarded as androgynous, behind which an altar-table and two holy symbols
similarly formed except the pedestals. Cf. p. 162—163.

15. Assyrian cylinder. Lajard, Mithra Pl. LIV, A. 9. A priest is sacrificing before the enthroned
deity at a burning altar in the shape of a pillar. Behind him a stand with two vases, probably for the
holy water.

---

*) Cyprian women still in the present day universally use fans of this shape, made of palm leaves and fastened to a rod, to
blow up the fire.

16. Late Babylonian cylinder. Menant, "Glyptique" II, p. 113, Fig. 120. A priest is paying his devotions before two sacred stones of which one is crowned with the crescent moon, the other with the sun-wheel. Cf. p. 150.

Plate LXXXVIII.

1. Relief from Persepolis, Lajard, Mithra XLVIII; E. B. Tylor, Proceedings of the Society of Biblical Archaeology 1890. Pl. IV, 17; Goodyear, "The Grammar of the Lotus" p. 219, Fig. 182. Discussed p. 164.

2. = CXIII, 9. Part of the Francois-vase. Benndorf, Wiener Vorlegeblätter 1888 Pl. III; compare p. 164.

Plate LXXXIX.

1. Dipylon-vase from Kurion. Cesnola-Stern Pl. LXVIII = Perrot III, p. 708, Fig. 514. Discussed p. 164—165; cf. p. 151 Note 2 and 207 Note 2.

Oinochoë from Rhodes. Berlin Mus. Furtwängler, Jahrbuch des deutsch. archaeol. Instituts, 1886. Anzeiger p. 188 = Goodyear, "Grammar of the Lotus" Pl. XXXVII, 4. Discussed p 164—165.

3. = Fig. 52a p. 78 and 89. Part of the Silver bowl from Kurion (Fig. 52 p. 53).

4. Gold breast-pin with two stags, from Mykenae. Schliemann, "Mykenae" p. 207 Fig. 265, cf. p. 140 No. 1 and 164.

5. Do. with two lions. Schliemann, "Mykenae" p. 208, Fig. 266.

6. Side surface of an Egyptian wooden chest. Dümmler, Athen. Mittheilungen 1888 p. 302 Fig. 9. Discussed p. 164—165; cf. p. 207 Note 2.

7. = XCV, 3 = Fig. 106 p. 78 and 93. Painted and inlaid Egyptian chest from a grave at Thebes. Wilkinson-Birch, "Manners and Customs of the ancient Egyptians" II p. 200, Fig. 399, 8, cf. p. 78, 92, 140, 164—165.

8. Dipylon-vase from Thebes. Berl. Mus. Böhlau, Jahrbuch des Archaeol. Instituts 1887 p. 54, Fig. 16. Goodyear, "Grammar of the Lotus" Pl. XLVI, 4 cf. p. 164.

Plate XC.

1. Stone relief from Amrit. Perrot III p. 413 Fig. 288 cf. p. 139.

2. Ivory plate from Nimroud. Perrot II p. 222 Fig. 80 = Goodyear, "Gımmar of the Lotus" Pl. XXIV, 10. Discussed p. 189 and 191 Note 1 cf. also the ivory plate CXV, 4. Both objects may well have been made, like our coat of mail plates Pl. LXX, in Cyprus.

3. Stone relief from Moab. Longpérier Musée Napoléon III, Pl. XXVIII = Perrot III p. 433, Fig. 316 = Riehm's Bibellexikon, p. 1007. Discussed p. 189 and 197.

Plate XCI.

? 1. Clay basket, broken off an image, from the Grove of Astarte-Aphrodite at Idalion (No. 3 of the List) Berl. Mus. cf. p. 194 Note 1.

? 2. Rude figure in stone from the same place. Berl. Mus. H. 0,29 m. Discussed p. 194.

? 3. Do ; from the same place, but not in Berlin. H. 0,15 m. Discussed p. 194. A similar work in Cesnola, Atlas Pl. XXXVIII, Fig. 250.

4. = CXL, 2. Stone torso from Cyprus. Berl. Mus. Stark, Archaeol. Zeitung, Bd. XXI Pl. 171. Discussed p. 211.

5. = CXL, 7. Stone Figure from Cyprus. Perrot III, p. 533, Fig. 359. Discussed p. 211.

Plate XCII.

1—8. Crouching Tammuz-Adonis-figures, on the meaning of which I have spoken in detail p. 202 and ff.; cf. also p. 219, 258 and 281.

1. From Etruria. Micali, Storia Pl. XLIV, 1.

† 2. From Idalion, probably from the grove of Aphrodite-Kourotrophos No. 33.

† 3. From Idalion, presumably from the western Akropolis (Ambilleri).

4. From Hylae, Temenos of Apollo-Hylates No. 48 Cesnola, Atlas Pl. CXXXII, No. 987.

5.   Crown of a stele from Carthage; cf. also p. 301.
?6.   From Tamassos.   Shrine of the Mother of the Gods.   No. 5; cf. also p. 237.
?7.   From Idalion.   Temenos of Aphrodite-Kourotrophos No. 33.
8.   From the Phoenician Shrine of Malta called in the present day Hagia Kim.   Perrot III
p. 305 Fig. 231 cf. supr. LXXXI. 2.
9.   Osiris-picture from Philae.   Goodyear, "Grammar of the Lotus" p. 19.   Discussed p. 207.

Plate XCIII.

† 1.   Red polished clay disc from Hagia-Paraskevi.   Berl. Mus.   Diameter 0,032 m.   Discussed p. 210.
2.   = XXXIII, 3.
3.   Aryballos of greenish-white glazed clay.   From Parasolia.   H. 0,047 m.   Berl. Mus. cf. p. 210, 297.
† 4—6.   Limestone double-head from the Grove of Artemis-Paralia of Larnaka (No. 7 of the
List.)   H. 0,115 m.   Discussed p. 210; cf. p. 297.
7.   = CLXXX, 2.   Stone mask from Marion-Arsinoë.   Berl. Mus.   H.   cf. p. 209.
8.   Egyptian mirror with a head of Bes on the handle.   Wilkinson-Birch, "Manners and customs
of the ancient Egyptian".   II p. 251 Fig. 455, 1 cf. p. 209.
9.   Gold ornament from Etruria.   Martha, "L'Etrurie", Pl. I, 11 cf. p. 210, 300.
10.   Gold ornament from Vulci.   Micali, "Monumenti inediti", Pl. LI, 4.   Discussed p. 208, Note 3,
cf. 300.
11.   = CXLIII, 2   Egyptian gold ornament with the head of Hathor.   Prisse d'Avennes II.
Gold-ornament Plate.   cf. p. 300.

Plate XCIV.

† 1.   Bronze Votive Tablet in the form of an ox's head, from Cyprus.   Berl. Mus. cf. p. 239, 241.
† 2.   = CXCI, 3.   Ox-head of red polished clay.   Hagia Paraskevi.   cf. p. 240.
† 3.   = LXXIX, 20 = p. 61, Fig. 69.
† 4.   Ox-head from the Astarte Shrine from the Akropolis of Kition (No. 9).   H. 0,11 m cf. p. 211.
† 5.   = p. 29, Fig. 1.
† 6   = p. 29, Fig. 2.
7.   Gold plate from Mykenae.   Schliemann 'Mykenae" p. 252, Fig. 330.   Ox's head with a two-
headed axe between the horns.   cf. p. 239, 241, No. 6, and 257.
8.   Clay votive-disc from Carthage.   Perrot III p. 463, Fig. 335.   Described p. 241 cf. 196
and 239.
† 9a—c.   Vase from a grave of the copper-bronze age at Psematismeno.   Nikolaides Collection,
Nicosia.   Discussed p. 239.
? 10.   Cyprian cylinder from Hagia Paraskevi which bears a Hittite character.   A kneeling mortal
appears to be intending to slaughter an ox before an altar-stone.   Close to him two mortals standing are
raising their hands before an ox's head, which signifies that the sacrifice is complete.   Over the scene of
slaughter lie two quadrupeds, and one human figure is standing, whilst an ape-like figure is crouching.
cf. p. 239.
11a and 11b.   Cubical bead of stone, pierced, evidently a small weight.   11a, in its original size.   Two
stars and a man with outspread arms, twice repeated.   Found in Cyprus.   Collection of E. Konstantinides.
12a and 12b.   Similar cubical stone-bead (cf. p. 239).   From the same place and collection.
On two opposite sides, representations of an ox and an ox's head with a sphere between the horns.
? 13.   = p. 37, Fig. 88
? 14.   Cyprian stone cylinder from Hagia Paraskevi.   After my original drawing.   Described
p. 246.   Fine specimen of the Linear style.
15.   = LXXXVII, 8.
? 16   = p. 31, Fig. 27.
17.   = LXXIV, 2 = LXXIX, 1.
18.   = LXXXVII, 2.
19.   = LXXXVII, 4.
? 20.   Clay ox fashioned in the form of a vessel.   From the ox-crater grave at Hagia Paraskevi.
Discussed p. 240.
? 21.   = CXI, 4 = CLXXXI, 3 Kurion p. 240 and 249 Note 1.

22. Stone statuette from Athiaenou. Cesnola Atlas, Pl. XXIV, 57 = Perrot III, p. 606 Fig. 414. Described p. 243.

23. = CLX, 1 = CXXXIV, 5. Part of the large stone vase from Amathus CXXXIV, 3. Perrot III, p. 282 Fig. 213. Discussed p. 248.

24. = CXVIII, 7 c.

? 25. Glazed clay-bead. Nekropolis Phonitschas. 1882. p. 239.

Plate XCV.

1. Bronze ash-basket from the grave of the warrior of Vetulonia in Etruria. American Journal of Archaeology. 1888 Pl. XI cf. Notizie degli Scavi, December 1887.

2. Part of a gilded silver vessel from the same grave. American Journal of Arch. loc. cit. Pl. X, 1.

3. = LXXXIX, 7 = Fig. 106, p. 78 and 90.

Placed here in order to show that the form of the bronze casket Fig. 1, is borrowed from Egyptian models (cf. Frotingham in the Amer. Journ. of Arch. 1888 p. 179). A quite similar form is found frequently in stone caskets in Cyprus. (Pl. CXXXIII, 5, 7, 8, CXCIX, 5—?) and also occurs in sarcophagi (Pl. CXX), which also have a lid of the same roof-like shape. These Cyprian receptacles must however have also been influenced by Egypt.[*])

Fortingham, the American author of the article, refers the objects here depicted to the beginning of the seventh century, but regards them as Phoenician, and believes that they were exported from the east in ancient times and brought to Etruria. I regard both the bronze casket and the silver vessel as Graeco-Phoenico-Cyprian, and manufactured in Cyprus. In the same way, the bronze ship found with them, of which I give an illustration at Pl. CXLV, 5 (cf. the explanation of the Plate below) was very probably made in Cyprus.

Plate XCVI.

1. Engraving of a hemi-spherical gem. Paris Biblioth. Nation. Lajard, Mithra Pl. XLIV, 12. Three rams' or goats' heads, and one stag's head fastened together at their base at right angle.

2. Sardonyx jewel, more of the form of the Scarabaeoid, St. Petersburg. Lajard, Pl. XLIV, 13. Similar style and similar representation. The heads of a man, an ox, a ram and a stag are joined to one another.

3. Scarabaeoid of black agate. After a plaster cast of Cades. Lajard Pl. XLIV, 14. Present owner unknown.

A stag's head with two goats' heads, one on each side, with an inscription hard to make out (Persian?)

4. Gold hanging-ornament, semi-circular and broken in two, found in Lydia. H. 0,068 m. Perhaps a breast-ornament. Perrot V, p. 295, Fig. 203. Described in detail ibid. Below, in the middle, a Goddess with the upper part of the body nude. Around and above this are three ox-heads in the middle, on each side a vulture's and a ram's head represented.

The object is similar in its granulation and embossed technique, in motive, and in its style which has a tendency to the Egyptian, to the Cyprian gold and bronze works (Pl. XXXII, 35 and here Fig. 8 and 12). It may very easily have been brought in ancient times, from Cyprus to Lydia, along with the other gold objects found with it. The workmanship of this ornament completely agrees with that of the medallion Fig. 11. Then again we must compare with both, so far as regards the four heads, their arrangement, and style, the bronze bowl found in Assyria (Pl. CXXXI, 5). I regard all these works as Cyprian.

5 = CXXVII, 1. Hittite cylinder. Paris, Biblioth. Nationale. Lajard, Mithra, Pl. XXIX, 1 = Menant, "Glyptique Orientale" I, p. 113, Fig. 66 = Milchhöfer, "Anfänge der griechischen Kunst", p. 55. Described p. 282.

6. Jewel of Mykenaean style from Chalcedon. Lajard, Pl. XLIII, 19. After a plaster-cast of Cades (No. 220) = Milchhöfer, Anfänge der griechischen Kunst, p. 55, Fig. 44 e.

7 = XXXII, 39.

8 = XXXII, 36.

9—10. Egyptian porcelain group of the British Museum, represented from two sides. Wilkinson-Birch, Manners and customs of the ancient Egyptians III, p. 20, Fig. 499, 1 and 2.

Four deities, Ptah-Socharis-Osiris, Isis, Nephtis, and the Goddess Bast as a Soul (conceived in a similar manner to the Osiris-Soul), are standing beside each other on a round pedestal and holding two birds and a scarabaeus.

11. Golden ornament in the form of a medallion, from the island of Melos. Perrot III, p. 829, Fig. 591. Bibliothèque nationale, Paris.

---

[*]) I have been especially desirous of illustrating the bronze casket in order to collect under certain types the holy chests and boxes which occur among different nations, and to which the Hebrew Ark of the Covenant belongs. I shall therefore return below (Pl. CXXIII and CXCIX) to this casket found in Etruria.

Already regarded by Perrot as a piece of Phoenician and perhaps Cyprian work, which he thinks was brought in ancient times to the Aegean Sea. Round the periphery of a round open flower are distributed two oxen and two human heads opposite each other, while more towards the inside two bees are standing opposite each other on two petals of a flower, and appear to be sucking (the honey) from the pollen.

12 = XXXII, 41.

Perrot has very rightly compared with 11 a golden bee found in Kameiros in Rhodes. I dug out in 1886, at Marion-Arsinoë, along with the alabastron of Pasiades, since so frequently mentioned, in a grave of the sixth century B. C., a silver finger-ring, upon which there is a large fly, plastically represented, exactly in the same style and enamelled by the goldsmith in various colours. (It is now together with the Pasiades-Alabastron in the British Museum). The whole technique in regard to stamping, embossing, and granulation, was as we saw (cf. supr. Pl. XXV, 1—7, XXXIII. 9—15, 16—25 and LXVII), familiar in Cyprus from the sixth century, the same animal's heads, the same human heads, the same style borrowed from Egypt. These ornaments found in Lydia, in Melos and in Rhodes, were fashioned in Cyprus at this period, as well as the bronze bowl found in Assyria at the same period or somewhat earlier (Pl. CXXXI, 5), The Cyprian bronze vessel (here Fig. 12) belongs in style and period to a time before the bronze bowl with its Egyptian tendency, and reaches to the period of Mycenae, the island-stones (Fig. 6) and the allied Hittite cylinders (Fig. 5). But the bronze and gilded pin (Pl. XXXII, 35), belonging to the same style of religious decoration, points us back probably to the time of the Ptolemies. But the inscription of the Ptolemaic period made in dotted letters may be much younger than the pin on which it is placed. The manner in which flowers like water-lilies project over acanthus-leaves on the Cyprian pin, and alternate with four he-goats' heads, and the manner in which a bead of Egyptian porcelain is placed on it as a central ornament quite reminds us of the golden flower of Melos (11) with a sapphire in the centre. The style, too, and the technique of the Paph an pin, with all the fine qualities of Cyprian granulation and embossing, is similar to the style and technique of the golden flower of Melos Furthermore, the style, technique, and motive of the Paphian pin is so very similar to other Cyprian works of the goldsmith's art of the sixth century B. C, and to the bronze sceptre-handle of Kurion (8 = XXXII, 36), that I consider the Paphian pin as £00 years older than the inscription upon it. On the flower-medallion of Melos the oxen's heads have triangles on the forehead. We see the same triangles, which were filled up with molten glass, on the forehead of the three ox-heads of the bronze sceptre-handle of Kurion. An ox's head which forms the central object of a breast-chain of a life-sized clay statue in Idalion, has also the same triangle on the forehead. (Pl. LIII, 24).

The Egyptian illustrations 7, 9 and 10 also show us how the late Babylono-Persian jewels (1—3), the gold and bronze articles found in Lydia (4), Melos (12), Cyprus (8, 12 and XXXII, 35, Cesnola-Stern Pl. LXIX, 4), Kreta (CXII, 5) and Assyria CXII, 4 (CXXXI, 5), and the Mykenaean jewel (XXXII, 40), came to have their motives the grouping of three, four, and more similar or identical heads of animals and human beings. The repetitions, twice and four times over, of the same deities and demons (Fig. 11 Pl. CXXXIII, 5 and XXCIX, 6, cf. also the sarchophagus of Amathus, Cesnola-Stern XLV) arise from the same medium of types and myths which originated in Egypt and penetrated into the Graeco-Phoenician civilisation of the basin of the Mediterranean. The bronze bowls of Praeneste and Olympia depicted Pl. CXXIX, 1 and 2, for which I claim Cyprus also as the place of manufacture, belong entirely to the same Graeco-Phoenician group. It cannot either be regarded as a matter of chance that the single pure Egyptian specimen among the metal vessels, with the same four-fold articulation, viz. a silver bowl (Cesnola-Stern Pl. XIX), was excavated in Cyprus (Athiaenou). Cf. p. 430, Pl. CXII, 5.

We are now in a position, with the help of the fantastic shapes produced here, to give the correct explanation of the vision of E²echiel.

In Chap. 1, the Glory of the Lord is being described to us,*) the extraordinary cherubs' chariot, as we see hypothetically represented in a drawing in Riehm's Bibel-Lexikon, p. 231. Each of the four winged cherubim which stood between the wheels had four faces, in front was a man's face, on the right side the face of a lion, on the left side the face of an ox, and towards the inside the face of an eagle. (Ezechiel 1,10).

A glance at our plates XXXII, XCVI, and others shows us that Ezechiel in this vision was not merely giving the reins to his imagination, but was rather describing for the most part in a poetical and hyperbolical form the glory of the Lord as a fabulous being, for which numerous Egyptian, Asiatic, and Graeco-Phoenician worship-pictures of his time had served him as models.

Thus Ezechiel's vision of the Glory of the Lord here also rests on the foundation of the religious Art-symbolism of his age, as his vision about the worship of the apostates in the courts of the Temple of Jerusalem.

Plate XCVII.

Fish-gods and fish-demons, of which we have treated together p. 287—290.

1. Chalcedon-cone. Lajard, Mithra LXII, 2 = Menant, "Glyptique orientale" II, p. 50, Fig. 33.

2. Cornelian-cylinder. Lajard LI, 4 = Menant II, p. 50, Fig. 32.

3. Relief from Khorsabad. Menant II, p. 49, Fig. 31 = Riehm, Bibellexikon i. p. 320.

4 and CLVI, 4. Clay tripod from Cyprus. Cesnola-Stern Pl. XCII, 2. Fully described p. 288.

5. Assyrian cylinder. Menant II, p. 51, Fig. 36.

---

*) 593 B. C. suits exactly in point of time our illustrations of Graeco-Phoenician religious art borrowed from Egyptian models.

Here besides the priest two fish-bodied demons or gods, behind which is a procession of fishes, are drawing near to thn holy tree for worship. Near this a small sacred flower is growing. The priest and the fish-god are pulling at the cords which hang down from the winged sun-disc, which hovers over them.

6. Side-surface of a cone of Chalcedon. Lajard, Mithra Pl. XVI, 7a = Menant II, p. 52, Fig. 38.

7 = Fig. 199, p. 289. Gold votive-fish from Vettersfelde. Furtwängler, Der Goldfund von Vettersfelde; 43. Winckelmannsprogramm, Berlin 1883, Pl. I, 1. Cf. p. 290.

8. Assyrian relief from Nimroud. Menant II, p. 51, Fig. 35 = Perrot II, p. 65, Fig. 9 = E. B. Tylor, Proceedings of the Society of Biblical Archaeology 1890, Pl. I, 3 = Goodyear, "The grammar of the Lotus" Pl. XLII, 5.

Plate XCVIII.

? 1. Clay vessels from a grave at Lapithos. Described p. 289.

2. Green-glazed Egyptian clay plate. Berl. Mus. Wilkinson-Birch "Manners and Customs of the ancient Egyptians" II, p. 42, Fig. 306, 2 = Goodyear, "Grammar of the Lotus" XLII, 10, cf. p. 296.

? 3. Upper view of a oinochoë from Salamis in Cyprus. Cf. p. 288.

4. Vessel of Mykenaean style, from the Metropolitan Museum in New York, found in Cyprus, Goodyear, p. 299, Fig. 154. Discussed p. 288.

5 = LXXXVII, 3.

? 6. Clay vessel in the form of a duck. From the same grave in Lapithos as the vases grouped on the Fig. 1, cf. p. 288—289.

7. Clay vase from Kalymnos. W. R. Paton, Journal of Hellenic Studies 1887, Pl. LXXXIII, 5 = Goodyear, Pl. XLII, 6. Discussed p. 289.

8. Clay plate from Thebes. Böhlau, Jahrbuch des Deutsch. Archäol. Instituts, 1888, p. 330, Fig. 1 = Goodyear, p. 396, Fig. 198. Discussed p. 288.

? 9. Clay anointing-vessel in the form of a boat. From the same grave in Lapithos as the vessels grouped Fig. 1 and 6. Cf. p. 288—289.

Plate XCIX.

Group of monuments with animal-taming deities.

1. From the Assyrian relief of the period of Asurnasirpal (885—860, B. C.), Nimrud, North West palace. Perrot II, p. 771, Fig. 443. Upper portion of the embroidery of a royal robe.
In the middle of the external strip of embroidery stands in the four-winged animal-tamer and holds two lions by the hind-legs, which for their part are tearing to pieces two bullocks. The artist has therefore connected in one picture the motives of animal-tamer and animal-fights. On the plaited-bands and.

2 = LXXVII, 5.

3. Plating of a vessel from Grächwyl, Gerhard, Archäologische Zeitung, 1854, Pl. LXIII, 1, p. 185, cf. Friedrichs-Wolters, plaster-casts of ancient sculptures in Berlin; No. 237. Cf. p. 282.

4. Persian cylinder. Micali, Monumenti inediti Pl. I, 5 = Gerhard, Archäol. Zeitung, 1854, Pl. LXIV, 2. A bearded animal-tamer is seizing by the horns two winged animals. The god and the animals are standing on two bearded, winged sphinxes. On the right is enthroned a deity with bow and quiver, on a smaller scale.

5. Persian cylinder. Gerhard, loc. cit. Pl. LXIV, 4. Between two palms a bearded animal-tamer is holding up two lions by their tails.

6 = LXXVII, 10.

7. Jewel of the Museum at the Hague. Lajard, Mithra, Pl. XLIV, 11. Two winged sphinxes with peculiar heads are standing on each side of a sacred tree.

8 = Fig. 105, p. 77. Silver Girdle of Marion-Arsinoë. Cf. Pl. XXV, 1—14.

I have placed the gem, Fig. 7, over the end-plate of the girdle. The sphinxes, but still more the tree of the stone, are so similar to the sphinxes and the tree of the girdle, that we also venture to assume Cyprus as the place from which the former comes, and where it was made.

Plate C.

1. Mould for casting made of serpentine. From Lydia. In the Louvre. Perrot V = p. 300, Fig. 209. Probably used for casting gold. There are eight dies, viz, four stars, bosses, discs, amulets, a small shrine, a lion with a handle attached to the back and two small figures of divinities.
What most strikes us in the form of the nude goddess is the similarity to Kyprian idols. Cf. 4 of this plate, p. 84, Figs. 31 and 32, Pl. LV, 5, 6, and CXCIX, 6.

2 = XXV, 6 = CXLII, 2.
3 = XXV, 12.
4 = XXV, 13 = CXXVIII, 7.
5 and 6.   Gold bracelet from Corneto in Etruria, drawn from each side.   From Monumenti del Istituto 1854, p. 112, Pl. XXXIII, 1 and 2.

This bracelet should be compared with the Kyprian silver-gilt girdle (Fig. 7 and Pl. XCIX, 8) in respect of form decoration and shape of hinge, although the technique is different. (Cf. also the bronze pieces of a coat of mail on Pl. LXX, with respect to shape and hinges).   The band of plaited ornament, the macander pattern, the palmettes and the rosettes are common to both objects, as are also sphinxes and lions. But in the present instance instead of griffins we have figures resembling sirens.   As on the portions belonging to the buckle of the Kyprian girdle two pairs of sphinxes are worshipping the sacred tree so here two pairs of male figures.   On close examination many other important differences between the two objects will be detected.

7.   Part of XCIX, 8.

8 = CXX, 1, CXXXIII, 1—4.
Boeotian chest from Thebes.   Berlin Vase Collection No. 306.   Boehlau, Jahrb. des deutschen arch. Inst. 1888, p. 357.   Cf. p. 282, 285, Note 7.   This is described on Pl. CXXXIII.

Plate CI.

1 = CXXXIX, 4.   Assyrian relief.   Part of a royal mantle.   Above the medallion or crest, which represents the worship of a tree, appears an animal-taming figure with two winged sphinxes.   Perrot II, p. 772, Fig. 444.

It is evident that this is intended to represent embroidery as in XCIX, 1.   Rich Assyrian embroideries of this kind were often imitated and adapted by the artists of Kypros who combined them also with motives from Mykenae, e. g. the terra-cotta figures of the Apollo altar at Toumpa, No 67 on the list (Journ. of Hell. Stud. 1891, Pl. X).

2 = CXXXIII, 6.   Terra-cotta figure from Tanagra.   London, Boehlau, Jahrb. des deutschen arch. Inst. 1888, p. 344, Fig. 28.

3 = CXXXIX, 5.   The same from Thisbe.   Berlin, Boehlau, Jahrb. des deutschen arch. Inst., p. 343, Fig. 27.

This illustrates how the Greeks employed Oriental motives and adapted them in their own way. The ornaments on the breasts of the two figures are free renderings from breast-plates on which sacred trees were represented.   Cf. Fig. 1.   The plank images which were carved out of the wood of sacred trees were developed into clay images with sacred trees painted on them.

4.   Glazed terra-cotta figure from Kypros.   Perrot III, p. 408, Fig. 279.   Bes on the nude Astarte-Aphrodite, cf. p. 209, Note 3 and 250.   On purely Egyptian monuments (e. g. Wilkinson-Birch III, Pl. XXXIII) the divinity Bes is seated in a crouching position on Harpokrates.   In Kypros Astarte-Aphrodite, as here, takes the place of Harpokrates.   This figurine was certainly made in Kypros. Cf. LXVII, 1.

5.   XXV, 10 = CXXXVIII, 8.   Gold breast-plate from Amathus.   Berl. Mus. Furtwängler, Jahrb. 1891 Archaeol. Anzeiger, p. 126.

‡ 6.   Engraving of a silver wing from Lapithos in Kypros.   Coll. Konstantinides, Nicosia.   Two goats are springing up opposite to each other.   Under them is a flower.   Early Graeco-Phoenician-Kyprian work.

7. = CXXXIX, 3.   A seal in the form of a pyramid.   Lajard, Mithra, Pl. XLIX, 4.   Under the winged sun-disc and a star are seated two winged sphinxes facing each other.

Provenance unknown.   I consider the work Kyprian, like that on Pl. XCIX, 7.

8.   Scarab.   Lajard, Pl. LXIX, 5.   Under the winged sun-disc Bes is subduing four animals, two of which are quadrupeds and two birds.

9.   Do.   Berl. Mus. Lajard, Pl. LXIX, 1.   A similar representation.
Both these scarabs were certainly made in Kypros.   Cf. Pl. XXV, 6 = C, 2.

10 = CXXXVIII, 10.   Bes on an Egyptian monument.   Wilkinson-Birch, "Manners and Customs of the ancient Egyptians" III, p. 149, Fig. 533.   Cf. p. 250.

It is easy to see how the Kyprian silversmith made use of Assyrian and Egyptian prototypes for the decoration of his silver girdle (Pl. XXV, 1–3 = XCIX, 8 = C, 7).   The Bes type holds a very important place in Kypros.

Plate CII.

1. = CXXXIV, 2 = CXCVII, 2 = Fig. 167, p. 193.
Censer or vessel for holy water from Chytroi.   R. von Schneider, Jahrb. d. deutsch. arch. Inst. 1891. Anzeiger p. 171, Fig. 4.   Cf. p. 180, 192 and 281.

2.   CXXXI, 4.
Bronze shield from Gortyna in Krete.   Americ. Journ. of Arch. 1888, p. 442 and Pl. XVIII, 4. Museo Italiano II.   Atlas Pl. II.   Cf. p. 284.

The nude goddess who holds the lions by the ears, certainly represents Ištar-Astarte-Aphrodite. (Cf. Pl. XXXI, 1—4. Babylon; p. 84, Fig. 31 and 32 Kypros; p. 148, Fig. 149, Hissarlik.) This shield was certainly made in Kypros.

Fortingham (Amer. Journ. of Arch. 1888, p. 443) disputes Orsi's identification of this figure with Ištar. Yet this goddess is formed from a fusion of various types and may be called Ištar just as correctly as Astarte or Aphrodite. Figures represented as taming animals often grasp them by the horn, the fore-lock, the mane or the ear. (Cf. Pl. CIV, 4, 13, and p. 62, Fig. 71.)

3. Gold figure of Hormos from Kamiros. Salzmann. Nécropole de Camiros. Pl. I. Cf. p. 250, 282 and 284.

The male animal-tamer (e. g. on the Kyprian silver girdle) has been developed into a female figure. But the male type is still represented by the Centaurs. Cf. the winged Centaurs Pl. CIV, 11 and 12.

4 and 5. Gazette Archéologique 1885. Pl. II from Spain, quoted by Dümmler in discussing this silver girdle, Jahrb. 1887, p. 93. Cf. p. 250, Note 2.

6. Terra-cotta oinochoë from Kypros. Cesnola-Stern, Pl. LXIX, 2.

Figure of a rider before the sacred tree. Early Graeco-Phoenician vase.

The tail of the horse, spreading into several divisions at the end, is characteristic, and appears also on the gold-leaf designs 4 and 5 and in the horse on the Tamassos vase, p. 62, Fig. 71. Details like these point either to a manufacture in Kypros of gold leaf found in Spain, to technical and artistic intercourse with Kypros or to an actual imitation of Kyprian art.

Female figures in the animal-taming attitude occur in Kypros on Kyprian cylinders of the Copper-Bronze period in the 2nd or 3rd century B. C. (e. g. Pl. CXXVIII, 5 and LXXIX, 6). Graeco-Phoenician-Kyprian art had a share also in developing the type of a winged woman taming animals both in Etruria (Pl. CIII, 1 and 2) and in Greece (Rhodes CII, 3, Olympia Graechwyl XCIX, 8).

Plate CIII.

1. Micali Storia Pl. XXI, 2 = Arch. Zeit. 1854, Pl. LXIII, 8. Winged goddess holding by the legs two lions rampant. Etruscan terra-cotta relief of the 7th century.

2. Bands of relief from a bucchero vase found at Clusium. Micali, Storia, Pl. XX, 1. Kypra with her sacred bird among centaurs, human figures and animals. Cf. p. 250 and 282. Probably of the 7th century B. C.

3. A late terra-cotta relief, probably Roman. Berl. Mus. Arch. Zeit. 1854, Pl. LXIV, 1. This is interesting as shewing how the figure of a winged animal-tamer with a Phrygian cap was made use of even in late times. Cf. CXIX, 1, CXXII, 9.

4. Colossal figure of an animal-tamer from Amathus, shewing various elements. The head resembles the Bes type with the addition of horns. I have repeatedly referred in the present work to this extraordinary colossus, at present in Constantinople. Perrot III, p. 567, Fig. 386. Cf. p. 209, Note 8, 244—247, 253, 319.

Plate CIV.

1. Fragment of a vase from Rhodes. Milchhoefer, Anfänge der Kunst in Griechenland. p. 75, Fig. 48. A representation in relief of Centaurs and men holding double axes. Cf. p. 258 and 250.

2. Bands from a bucchero vase. Milchhoefer, p. 76, Fig. 49. Cf. p. 200 and 250.

3. Graeco - Phoenician scarab. of red jasper. Coll. Konstantinides, Nicosia. From Lapitho. See p. 320.

4. Persian cylinder. Lajard, Mithra, Pl. LVII, 6 = Micali, Mon. ined., Pl. I, 22. Cf. p. 293, Note 3.

5 = XLVII, 8.

?6 = p. 249, Fig. 173. Centaur of terra-cotta from a tomb near Kurion. Max Ohnefalsch-Richter, Bulletins de la.Société d'Anthropologie de Paris XI, 4. Série. 1888, p. 669—680, v. 248—250.

7 = p. 249, Fig. 176. Scarab. Bibliothèque Nationale, Paris. Lajard, Mithra, Pl. LXVIII, 21, v. p. 250.

8. Cylinder of chalcedony in the Bibl. Nation. Paris. Lajard, Mithra, Pl. LVII, 8. A bearded animal-tamer with four wings holding by the fore-legs two upright griffins. At the side a sacred tree under a winged sun disc.

9 = p. 249, Fig. 174. Centaur of terra - cotta. From the neighbourhood of Idalion, Perrot, III, p. 600, Fig. 411. Cf. p. 248.*)

10. Carneol - scarab. Lajard, Mithra. Pl. LXVIII, 23. I think that this gem also is of Kyprian origin.

---

*) But certainly not from a tomb of the Copper-Bronze Period at Alambra, as Hewsey and Perrod state, on the authority of Cesnola.

The animal-tamer, here probably Herakles, shows an originality in his attitude, which is probably a result of Greek influence. He is aiming a blow with his club at the lion, who is rampant on his hind legs. As the artist was familiar with the heraldic scheme of the figure holding up two animals (as in 7) he added a second animal figure behind the arm that holds the club.

11 = p. 249, Fig. 179. Do. Lajard, Pl. LXVIII, 19, cf. p. 209 Note 3 and 250.

12 = 249, Fig. 178. Do. Lajard, Pl. LXVIII, 20, cf. p. 209 Note 3 and 250. 11 and 12 may very well have been made in Kypros. The head of this Centaur shews the familiar Bes type.

13 = XCIX, 4.*) Persian cylinder in the British Museum. From Achat, Lajard, Pl. XIII, 8. Cf. 293, Note 1.

It is interesting to note that under the group representing Marduk as tamer of four animals appears an archer seated on a chair. We must suppose that this figure represents the older conception of Marduk as an archer (XXIX, 4, 6—8) supporting the later type of Marduk as an animal-tamer (Cf. also Pl. XXIX, 16, CLV, 2) just as the Artemis of the 4th century is represented in Kition and other places leaning on her own ancient image. (Pl. CCIII, 1, 2 and 4 and p. 314, Fig. 224—226, 231 and 232).

Plate CV.

1. Gold-leaf ornament from Mykenae, evidently representing Astarte. Schliemann, Mykenae p. 212, Fig. 273.

2 = XXXVIII, 10.

3 = XXXVIII, 9 = p. 291, Fig. 201.

4 = p. 291, Fig. 202. Etruscan bronze figure. Gerhard, Akadem. Abhandlungen Pl. XXVIII, 2. Cf. p. 207, 281, 291.

5. Do. Gerhard, Akadem. Abhandlungen, Pl. XXVIII, 1; Martha, L'Etrurie, p. 317, Fig. 213; Micali, Storia, Pl. XXIX, 2. Cf. p. 207, 281.

6 = XXXVIII, 8.

7 = Fig. 210, p. 293. Bronze winged figure from Wansee. Perrot II, p. 584, Fig. 281. Cf. p. 297 (where the Fig. is wrongly numbered 209).

8 = p. 309, Fig. 209. Perrot III, p. 600, Fig. 410. Cf. p. 281, 291—297. (On p. 291, 296—297 for Fig. 210 read Fig. 209.

9. Band from a bucchero vase; Micali, Storia. Pl. XX, 5. Cf. p. 200.

°10. Votive image of two doves (terra-cotta). From a tomb at Marion-Arsinoë. Nekr. I. Tomb 101. Cf. p. 176, 245, Note 4 and p. 273. Cf. also Cesnola-Atlas, Pl. LXXX 527, Hogarth, Journ. of Hell. Stud. 1888, p. 172.

Plate CVI.

1. Egyptian wall painting from Phylae. Rosellini, Monumenti del Egitto III, Pl. XXXVII. Isis and Nephtis with the god Rešef, The Nile-god kneels beside them.

2. From the same Plate (Rosellini). Provenance the same. The cow-headed Hathor is watering plants, which have been artificially grown in a vase, and which resemble a "garden of Adonis". The soul of Osiris appears above. Under a stone at the side is the source of the Nile in the form of a snake, beside which sits the Nile god Hapi pouring water out of Hydrias. Described on p. 240, Note 3, where by an annoying error of the compositor this Egyptian monument is called Kyprian. Cf. p. 295.

Plate CVII.

1 = Fig. 228, p. 314. Brass figure from the Troad. Gerhard, Akadem. Abhandl., Pl. LX, 3. Cf. p. 285 and 315.

2. Bronze mirror handle from Kypros. On the shoulders of the nude Astarte, who is playing the cymbals, are to be seen the remains of the paws of two lions. Perrot III, p. 862, Fig. 629. Cf. p. 285.

3 = Fig. 227, p. 314. Brass figure belonging to the stem of an Etruscan candelabrum. Gerhard as above Pl. XIX, 3. This probably represents the goddess Kypra, who was brought from Kypros to Etruria. Cf. Pl. CIII, 2, CV, 4 and 5. Cf. p. 285 and 315.

4. Relief representing Harpokrates and Bes. In Turin. Micali, Monumenti inediti, Pl. L, 1. Cf. p. 285.

5. Terra-cotta figure with double head from Rhodes. Salzmann, Nécropole de Camiros, Pl. XIV. Cf. p. 295.

---

*) Both Micali (= XCIX, 4) and Lajard (=CIV, 13) illustrate the same cylinder. The cylinder given in the American Journal, 1888, p. 443, Fig. 15, seems to represent the same original, but the archer, half moon, and sacred branch are mining.

6. Kylix from Kyrene, Studniczka, Kyrene, p. 1⁸, Fig. 10. In the centre is the goddess of Kyrene with two sacred trees and birds. Male and female winged daemons hover around her.

Plate CVIII.

1. Embroidery for a robe, from an Assyrian relief. Two ostriches stand on either side of the sacred tree. Behind them are cypresses. At the edge of the design are continuous patterns of rosettes. Layard, Nineveh Ser. I, Pl. XLVII = Perrot II, p. 566, Fig. 265.

2. Kyprian Graeco-Phoenician vase painted black and red. Perrot III, p. 700, Fig. 509 = Froehner, Catalogue Barre. Pl. I = Goodyear Lotus, Pl. XLV, 11.

3. Assyrian relief similar to 1. Conze, "Melische Thongefässe" Pl. V, 5 = Lajard, "Mon. of Nineveh" Pl. 43, 5.

4. Illustration of an Attic vase from Cervetri. Conze as above, Pl. V, 6 = Mon. d. Istit. 1858, Pl. XV.

5. Painted Attic funeral stele with representation of a cock, and over it a star (this interpretation has been disputed); cf. Brückner, "Attische Grabstelen", p. 89, also the device for a shield with cock and star on a Corinthian vase. v. Wilisch, "Die altkorinthische Thonindustrie" V, 47. Cf. Pl. LXII, 1. Attic funeral stelai.

6. Small illustration of a dipylon vase. Hirschfeld, Annali d. Ist. 1872 Tav. d' Agg. K, 6. These pairs of birds on a sacred or decorative tree show how the Kyprian and Greek vase painters adapted Assyrian motives.

Plate CIX.

1 = Fig. 208, p. 293. Persian cylinder of jasper. Lajard, Mithra, Pl. XLIX, 2, v. p. 295—296.

2 = Fig. 217, p. 294. Part of the so-called Harpy Tomb from Xanthos. Roscher, Mythol. Lexikon I, Sp. 1846.

3 = X, 3, &c.

4. LXXIII, 1 = Fig. 214, p. 294, The god Hapi and the soul of Osiris.

? 5 = Fig. 200, p. 290 and 293. Terra-cotta votive egg from an early Graeco-Phoenician tomb near Kition. Cf. p. 173, Note, 290 and ff.

6 = Fig. 207, p. 293. Cesnola-Stern Pl. LXXIV, 1. Cf. p. 304—305.

7. Cylinder from Achat. Lajard, Mithra, Pl. LIV, B, 2, v. Fig. 1, also cf. p. 295—296.

8 Cylinder of lapis-lazuli. Lajard, Mithra, Pl. XXVIII, 11 = Menant I, p. 97, Fig. 56. Similar to 1 and 7, p. 295—296.

9 = LXXII, 2 = Fig. 205, p. 293.

10 = LXXX, 4. Conze, "Melische Thongefässe", Pl. V, 4. A vase from Cervetri. Acad. des Inser. XVII, Pl. VIII. Around a pillar are grouped two lions or panters and two sirens.

? 11—12. An Attic Kylix found in 1886 at Marion-Arsinoë Nekr. II, Grave 91. Cf. Text p. 292 and ff. for the soul of Osiris, the Harpies, the Sirens and the Erinyes, also Pl. XXXIX, 3 and 4.

Plate CX.

? 1. Kyprian stone figures from Tomb 101, Nekr. I, Marion-Aosinoë 1886. These were found with the group of caressing doves Pl. CV, 10. On the left a sphinx. On the right a lamb and a bird. Cf. p. 273.

? 2. Figure of the Harpies from the Kylix of Aegina. In Berlin. Furtwängler, Arch. Zeit. 1882. Pl. LX. Berlin Vase Catalogue, 1682. Cf. p. 295.

3. Fragment of an Assyrian relief. Perrot II, p. 774, Fig. 446. Part of a garment with imitation of embroidery. A winged daemon with an eagle's head represented in the "running scheme" has seized upon a bearded winged sphinx. Underneath is a palmette, v. p. 296, Note 1.

? 4. Terra-cotta goose from Marion Arsinoë. Nekr. II. Tomb 88, found with the vase on Pl. LXIV, 1. Beginning of the 5th century. Cf. p. 273, Note 2.

‡ 5. Thick tailed variety of sheep, stone statuette. The head of this sheep, which belongs to a race still peculiar to Kypros, is painted black; the eyes and a ribbon by which hangs a bell or an amulet are red.

From Amathus, now in the collection of the Landwirthschaftliches Institut at Halle. Found in the same stratum of excavation as the four chariot scenes, v. Pl. CXCVI. The stone statuettes reproduced on Pl. CCVI, 7—9 viz. the recumbent male figure, the dog and the hare, the bird and the terra-cotta figure of the seated goddess, p. 273, Note 2.

? 6. Terra-cotta cock and duck from Marion, 1886. Tomb 20, Nekr. II. Cf. p. 273, Note 2.

? 7. Attic vases from the first half of the 6th century. Marion-Arsinoë 1886. Tomb 131, Nekr. II. Found with the ornaments (Pl. LXVII, 2—12) and the candelabrum foot in the form of a griffin's claw (Pl. CLXXVIII. 4). Cf. No. 1—6.

One figure of No. 4 repeats p. 293, Fig. 206. With No. 4 cf. p. 295. With No. 5 cf. p. 290.

This illustration shows how the Greek vase painter borrowed from Assyrian art the "running scheme" in which the bend of the knee was so exaggerated as almost to form a kneeling attitude. For this point cf. especially Figs. 3 and 7, No. 4. These illustrations also show how the Attic vase painters came by the palmettos which they painted around their handles. In this stone imitation of Assyrian embroidery (Fig. 3) we find along with the representation of a winged daemon and a sphinx a palmette used to decorate a fillet or ribbon, and it was this motive which the vase painter appropriated and modified in accordance with Greek taste.

Plate CXI.

1. Conze, Melische Thongefässe V, 8 = Lajard, Nineveh L, 6. Assyrian relief. Winged horses surrounding the sacred tree.

The palmettos springing from the soil, the dotted stars, the rosettes of eight and ten rays of this Assyrian monument served as prototypes in the ceramic and metal-working technique of Graeco-Phoenician and early Greek art. I can here only adduce a few examples taken almost at random. With the palmettos springing from the soil and the palmetto wreaths, cf. the Melos vase, Fig. 2 of this plate, the Kyprian silver girdle, Pl. XXV, 2 and 3, the ostrich egg from Polledrara in Etruria, Pl. CXVI, 12 and CLXII, 11, &c.*) With the stars formed of dots (often seven in a circle around an eighth in the centre) cf. the Kyprian vases Pl. XXII—XXIV, LXIII, 2.

The eight-rayed rosette so frequent in the pottery of Mykenae and Kypros, cf. p. 355 had an Assyrian origin. The rosettes of the Melos vases (Fig. 2) and of the Corinthian vases may be considered to be developments of the original Assyrian type. These decorative elements are applied at this period exactly in the same manner as they are in Assyria and in countries influenced by the art of Assyria, i. e. they are used to fill up odd spaces in the design.

2. Conze, as above. Title page = Goodyear, Lotus Pl. XIX, 1.

The shape of the vase and the double handle recall the Kyprian and Mykenaean vases of the same class. Cf. p. 356 and Pl. CXVIII, 8.

Some vases from Polledrara in Etruria (e. g. beautiful examples in the Antiquarium of the Royal Museum at Berlin) show the same shape and the same kind of handle. With regard to these features this class of vases seems to have originated in Kypros, but their decoration and technique are not Kyprian. They occur frequently on the island. An early richly decorated Graeco-Phoenician-Kyprian vase recently bought by the Berlin Museum shows the same shape and the same handle.

3. Perrot III, p. 706, Fig. 517.

A winged goat painted on a Kyprian vase, and mistaken by Perrot for a horse, is evidently an imitation of Assyrian winged horses and unwinged goats. Cf. Fig. 5 and CXII, 2, also explanation of Pl. LXI.

? 4 = XCIV, 21 = CLXXXI, 3.

5. Perrot II, p. 583, Fig. 279.

How the Assyrian winged horse and pair of horses arranged as an Egyptian motive on either side of an animal-tamer were modified by the Kyprian artists of the 6th century under increasingly Greek in-fluences is well illustrated by the capital of Amathus. (Pl. CC, 4, cf. also p. 249 f.)

Plate CXII.

Principally sphinxes and griffins.

1. Funeral stele of calcareous stone from Athiaenou. Cesnola, Atlas Pl. CIV, 679. Two winged sphinxes on either side of a palmette.

2. Assyrian relief. Perrot II, p. 321, Fig. 138. Two goats, each with a fore-leg bent, on either side of a palmette.

Even a part from the winged sphinxes, it is easy to see from these representations how closely the Kyprian sculptor of the 5th century imitated Assyrian prototypes.

3 = Fig. 52a, p. 78 and 90. Part of the silver Kylix of Kurion, Fig. 52, p. 53.

4 = CXCIV, 4. Bronze Kylix from Nimrud. Perrot II, p. 739, Fig. 399. Cf. p. 191, Note 1.

5. Part of a bronze Kylix from the Zeus Cave at Gortyna. Orsi-Halbherr, Museo Italiano II, Atlas Pl. VI, 1.

There can be no doubt that the two kylikes found in Nimrud (4) and in Krete (5) belong to the same period and the same artistic school and were made at the same place as the only silver kylix hitherto found (8) which shows purely Egyptian style (Cesnola-Stern Pl. XIX). This kylix, found at Athiaenou and illustrated on Pls. CXXVIII, and CXXXI may, in the judgment of Ermann and Steindorff, have been made in Egypt,

---

*) Cf. F. Dümmler in the Jahrb. 1888, p. 92, where the silver girdle (Pl. XXV) is discussed.

and I think that it probably was so. The style seems to belong to the period of Rameses III, i. e. to the 12th century B. C. This example illustrates the beginning of the Kyprian manufacture of silver and bronze kylikes and of shields, which began very early and gave rise to lively export trade with Assyria, Krete, Olympia, Etruria and other places. On the kylix from the Anat-Athene sanctuary in Idalion (Perrot III, p. 771, Fig. 546) illustrated below, we see a design of five sphinxes and five griffins alternately single and in pairs, holding human figures down on the ground. In the centre is a tree which we find again in still more strictly Egyptian form on the bronze kylikes of Nimroud and Krete and the whole scheme shows Egyptian influence in a slightly freer style.

6. Part of the decoration of the François vase. Benndorf, Wiener Vorlegeblätter 1888, Pl. III; also E. B. Tylor, Proceedings of the Society of Biblical Archaeology 1890, Pl. IV, Fig. 18. Cf. Pl. LXXXVIII, 1 and 2 and CXIII, 9.

It is clear that Persians (LXXXVIII, 1), Greeks (LXXXVIII, 2 and CXII, 6) and Kyprians (CXII, 1) in certain circumstances borrowed from the Assyrians branch and palmette motives which were derived from the sacred tree. The origin of these examples of Persian and Greek art are branches artificially woven together, and for this purpose palms were the most suited. Cf. p. 127. The other group of sacred trees and tree ornaments after having passed over to Egypt returned from thence strongly impressed with Egyptian influence and in this form found a place in Graeco-Phoenician and early Greek art. This second group of tree motives occurs frequently in Egypt (Pl. LXXXIX, 6 and 7, p. 78, Fig. 106, p 79, Fig. 107) and in Egyptian style on Graeco-Phoenician monuments found in Kypros and in many other places (e. g. Fig. 3 and Fig. 254, both illustrations from the silver kylix of Kurion, p. 53, Fig. 52). Assyrian and Egyptian motives were often mingled. So for example on the bronze chest of Vetulonia (XCV, 1 and 2) plants grow in the Assyrian manner but are Egyptian in shape and style. The same palmette branches slightly modified lend interest to the background of the early Attic vases in Eastern style. Cf. Pl. CXIII, 5 and 7.

Fig. 254.

Plate CXIII.

1. Ivory slab from Nimroud representing a sphinx. Perrot II, p. 534, Fig. 248. Evidently made in Kypros like the slab on Pl. CXVI, 5. Cf. p. 191, Note 1.

2. Stone funeral stele from Athiaenou in Kypros. Cesnola Atlas, Pl. CIV, 680.

3. Kyprian vase. A four-footed animal with human head. Perrot III, p. 707, Fig. 519.

4 = CLIX, 4. Greek head-fillet of silver from Amathus. Berl. Mus. Furtwängler. Jahrb. d. deutsch. arch. Inst. 1891, Anzeiger p. 126, Fig. 2 b.

5 = LXXVII, 17 = CLXIII, 8.

6 = LXXVII, 8.

7 = CLIX, 5. Graeco-Phoenician silver head-fillet from Amathus. Berl. Mus. Furtwängler, Jahrb. 1891, Anz. p. 126, Fig. 2 a.

8. Alabaster slab belonging to the same object as the slab Pl. CXIV, 8 (= LXXXVII, 10). Found in Arados (Syria). Longpérier, Musée Napoléon III, Pl. XVIII, 4 = Perrot III, p. 129, Fig. 73 = Goodyear, Lotos Pl. XLI, 12.

9 = LXXXVIII, 2.

On p. 150—151 (cf. also p. 414, LXXVII, 17) I tried to show that gem No. 5 was probably cut in Kypros. The alabaster slabs from Arados may also have been made in Kypros. The old Hebrew stone seal (6) shows over the inscription the same Graeco-Phoenician palmette. A comparison of the two head-fillets of silver found in Kypros in the same stratum of tombs at Amathus (perhaps even in the same tomb) and belonging to the 6th century B. C. shows us how the Kyprian Greeks borrowed Graeco-Phoenician ornaments, palmettes, rosettes and capitals derived from Egypt and Assyria and by placing them in combination formed a beautiful continuous decorative pattern which must be called purely Greek. We find spirals gracefully wreathed together with alternate palmettes and lotus flowers growing from them.

Plate CXIV.

Illustrations of griffins.

1. Part of an Assyrian alabaster relief. Perrot II, p. 474, Fig. 447. Two winged griffins are seizing a goat.

2. Perrot II, p. 583, Fig. 280. Assyrian representation similar to 1. From the Royal mantle of Asurnasirpal.

3 = XXXII, 37 = CXCIV, 5, Kyprian gem.

4 = CXCIV. 3. Coin from Teos. Furtwängler in Roscher's Mythol. Lex. I. Sp. 1763. Seated griffin with a bearded mask under its raised fore-paw.

5 = CXCIV, 7. Kyprian cylinder. Cesnola, Salaminia, 129, Fig. 121.

6 Part of the silver kylix of Kurion. Fig. 52, p. 53.

7. Wood-carving in relief from Egypt. Mykenaean style. In the Egyptian division of the Royal Museum at Berlin. Puchstein, Jahrb. des deutsch. arch. Inst. 1891, Anz. p. 41.

8 = LXXXVII, 10. Cf. Pl. CXIII, 8.

9. Part of a silver vase from Nikopol. From Roscher's Mythol. Lex. I. Sp. 1771. Two griffins tearting a stag to pieces.

10. Running griffin on a Mykenaean dagger. From Roscher's Myth. Lex. Sp. 1745.

Plate CXV.

1. Small tablet made of greenish talc. Bibl. Nation, Paris. Lajard, Mithra, Pl. XLVII, 6. On one side are two couching sphinxes arranged one above the other. On the other side in the lower part a couching goat and above two goats on either side of a sacred post. On the edges are human figures.

2. Hittite cylinder. Lajard, Mithra. Pl. XXXVI, 18 = Goodyear, Lotus, Pl. XXXVI, 5. Below a winged sun-disc appears a bearded figure handing the produce of the chase to a divinity enthroned. To the right two daemons with animal heads and two mortals offer slain animals. These figures are arranged in two series one over the other. Cf. p. 282.

3. Neck of a Kyprian amphora. Perrot III, p. 721, Fig. 531. Two men carry a wild goat on a pole. They wear shoes with pointed and turned up ends. Cf. the shoes of the man on vase XIX, 4.

4. Ivory slab from a casket found in Sidon. Perrot III, p. 847, Fig. 611. Discussed on p. 140. For the place of manufacture cf. p. 191, Note 1 and also XC, 2, CXIII, 1, CXVI, 5.

5. Babylonian (or Hittite?) cylinder in the Bibl. Nation, Paris. Lajard, Mithra, Pl. XXX, 1. In the centre on an elevation resembling a bench the nude Ištar. On the left Izdubar and Eabani. On the right a divinity on a bison. Cf. p. 264 and 284, Note 1.

6. Assyrian cylinder, Lajard, Mithra, Pl. XLIX, 9 = Menant II, p. 64, Fig. 58 = Goodyear, Pl. XXIV, 17. Two winged daemons stand on sphinxes in the attitude of adoration on either side of the sacred tree, over which floats a representation of the upper part of a divinity with wings.

Plate CXVI.

1 = Fig. 190, p. 283. Kyprian cylinder. Cesnola, Salaminia, Pl. XIV, 38 On either side of a sacred symbol stand two animals rampant, one winged, the other unwinged. A woman is holding the tail of the former in her right hand. At the side sidereal symbols. Cf. p. 283.

2 = LXXXVII, 5.

3 = LXXXVII, 7.

4 = Fig. 195, p. 283. Kyprian cylinder. Cesnola, Salaminia, p. 121, Fig. 115. Discussed on p. 283.

5. Ivory relief from Nimrud. Perrot II, p. 535, Fig. 249. Discussed on p. 186. Evidently made in Kypros. Cf. Pl. CX, 2, CXIII, 1, CXV, 4.

6. Kyprian cylinder. Two winged sphinxes seated opposite to each other. Three men walking one behind the other. Cesnola, Salaminia, Pl. XIV, 39.

7. Kyprian cylinder showing Egyptian influence. Two figures enthroned on either side of the symbol of life and a disc. Behind them are three men walking in Egyptian fashion. On a narrow band above are two winged sphinxes and a goat. Otherwise the style and arrangement are not Egyptian. Cf. 6.

8 = Fig. 194, p. 283. Similar to 1. Cesnola, Salaminia p. 130, Fig. 122. Here the woman holds in her left hand a sickle-shaped knife. In front of her is an ox-head, behind her a star. The animal which she holds by the tail is a winged griffin and opposite to it stands a lion. Between the animals is a kind of wreath with a star in the centre.

† 9. Fragment of a terra-cotta cylinder from Hagia Paraskevi. Coll. Konstantinides, Nicosia. The clay is imperfectly burnt and covered with a fine brilliant polished slip on which the figures are incised and filled in with some white substance. In front walks a man of colossal proportions followed by three small male figures, just as on Egyptian monuments, the king is represented of a huge size and ordinary mortals small. This is evidently a rude Kyprian imitation of an Egyptian subject and belongs to a period for which we must assign as terminus ante quem the reign of Thutmos III.

10 = Fig. 13, p. 80 = Pl. XXXI, 14.

11 = CXXXIX, 2. Bronze piece of armour in the Louvre. Longpérier, Musée, Napoléon III. Pl. XXXI, 4 = Lajard Mithra, Pl. XLVII, 1 = Perrot III, p. 813, Fig. 565. Perrot says that this belongs to a collection in Alexandria but comes from Phoenicia. That the breast plate is Kyprian work is, I think, almost proved by the band of plaiting at the edge, the lion and the panther seizing bulls, the winged griffin tearing a lion to pieces and throwing a goat on the ground, the form of the tree, the crest (cf. CXII, 1) and bunch of flowers (cf. Fig. 8) on the griffin's head, the wings of the griffin (cf. the wings of the sphinx CXII, 1), and in fact the whole style of the work. Furtwängler (Roscher's Mythol.

Lex. Sp. 1748) dates this bronze plate much earlier than Perrot (III, p. 813, Fig. 565). He separates it from the reliefs of Caere (e. g. Griffi Monumenti d. Cere antica I) by 500 years, places it in the period of the great Rameses and classifies it as a Syrio-Egyptian piece of work. Even if Furtwängler's dating should prove correct, this breastplate may have been made in Kypros, for we know that the oldest silver kylix of pure Egyptian style (which however corresponds to the numerous Kyprian kylikes in size, style and arrangement) was found in Kypros, cf. explanation of Pl. CXII, 5.

12. Perrot III, p. 857, fig. 625. Ostrich egg from Polledrara (cf. Pl. CLXIII, 11). On the right and left pairs of griffins stand facing each other, between these pairs are a bull walking and a huge bird which seizes one of the griffins from behind. The type of this griffin with curls hanging down and bunches of flowers on the head is similar to the griffin of the Kyprian cylinder (fig. 8.) The ostrich eggs of Polledrara were either decorated in Kypros or belong with other Kyprian productions to the same circle of Graeco-Phoenician art.

Plate CXVII.

1. Boeotian vase. Böhlau, Jahrb. d. arch. Inst., 1888, p. 389, fig. 15. This illustration is given here in order to show how the Boeotian potters had not yet developed the oriental palmette motive into a continuous decorative pattern such as we see on the silver leaf ornament of Amathus, (CXIII, 4) on the sarcophagus of Amathus (fig. 8) and on the silver girdle of Marion (C, 7). On the silver-leaf ornament of Amathus (CXIII, 7) the separate palmettes are arranged distinct from each other in fields resembling metopes.

2. = XXVI, 3.

3. Kyprian funeral stele from Athiaenou. Limestone. Two sphinxes are seated as guardians back to back on either side of a palmette in the centre. Each lays a fore-foot on a palmette at the corner. An egg and dart pattern runs round the foot. Style of the 5th century.

4. = XXVI, 1.

5. = LXXVII, 21.

6. = LXXVII, 7.

7. = XXVI, 2.

8. Part of the sarcophagus of Amathus. Cesnola-Stern, Pl. XLIV, = Perrot, p. 608—609. Fig. 415, 416.

Plate CXVIII.

? 1. Attic guttus (narrow-necked vase) of the 4th century. Found in 1886 in tomb 5, Nekr. I, at Marion-Arsinoë, together with the vases illustrated on Pl. LXV, 4 and 7. Two winged griffins are seated facing each other.

? 2. Similar guttus of rather more careful workmanship from the same excavation and the same nekropolis, Tomb 30.

3. Head of griffin from a caldron of Praeneste. From Roscher's Mythol. Lex. I, Sp. 1764.

4. Do. From Olympia. Roscher I, Sp. 1766.

5. Kyprian vase in New York. A winged stag feeding, a large lotus flower behind. Goodyear, Grammar of the Lotus, Pl. XXXVII, 12.

? 6. Illustration from an early Attic skyphos, perhaps belonging to the end of the 7th century. Two griffins are seated facing each other. Provenance same as 1 and 2 from nekropolis II, Tomb 51.

7a—c; c = XCIV, 24. Weight made of stone. Lajard, Mithra, Pl. XLVII, 5. Decorated on the four sides. 7a represents an animals taming figure, probably nude, with a lion; this figure resembles the Kyprian animal-tamer with the winged horses, (Pl. CC, 4).

7b. Shows two other sides of the weight. On one two goats are rampant back to back with their heads turned round as on the Kyprian gem (Pl. XXXII, 9 = LXXXVIII, 13 = CXLII, 3). On the other side is engraved the figure of a bearded and helmeted sphinx, which in style and drapery is characteristically Kyprian. The fourth side (7c) shows a daemon with animal head sacrificing in front of a tree or candelabrum. This was must probably made in Kypros.

8. Vase of Melos. Böhlau, Jahrb. d. arch. Inst. 1887, p. 211—215, Pl. XII.

A new discovery of vases, one of the most interesting, if not the most interesting, ever made in Kypros affords us a remarkable prototype for this Melos vase. The form of the vase is the same only somewhat more compressed and there is no lid. The handles are the same. The principal design on the shoulder of the vase is bounded, as in the Melos vase, by a strip of maeander pattern.[*] The principal design consists of a motive which occurs on both sides. Two oxen stand on either side of a conventional tree; over them are represented fish. At the top where the shoulder of the vase joins the neck is a strip formed of the same rosettes which we find on the vase of Ormidhia (CXLI, 3), the vase of Kition (p. 38, Fig. 39) and the

---

[*] Cf. the maeander pattern on the silver girdle of Marion Pl. XXV, 1 and 2 with the limestone vessel for incense, which is painted black and red and decorated with a winged sphinx. Pl. CXCVII, 5.

late Mykenaean pottery. (Furtwängler-Löschcke. Myk. Vasen, Pl. XXXVIII, 898). Around the neck of the vase runs a procession of eight birds. Svastikas and dotted rosettes consisting of concentric circles with a dotted wreath outside (as on the Kyprian vase Pl. XIX, 4, and the Rhodian vase Pl. LXXXIX, 2 &c.) correspond exactly, as do also c ay, style and colouring in red and black, to our early Kyprian class of vases. The ornaments which occur here and the manner in which they as well as the shapes of the vases justify us in giving this gala vase an intermediate place between the late Mykenae and Dipylon vases and the early Attic vases of Oriental style, between the Melian and the Rhodian vases. The question how far the Kyprian vase painter was the borrower and how far the lender is as yet undecided. This vase however seems to make it probable that the svastika was introduced into Kypros by means of the Dipylon vases an opinion which I have already expressed in the Jahrb. 1886, p. 80.[*]) It seems that Kyprian vase painters, clay modellers and armourers influenced the early Attic vase painters of the Oriental style to whom we attribute the so-called Phaleron vases (cf. Pl. LXXXIX, 8) which form a continuation of the purely geometric Dipylon vase style. When I visited Athens for the first time in 1884 I was struck with the contrast between these vases and the Dipylon vases, and I made a drawing of the oinochoë, at that time in the Polytechneion, which was published by Boehlau in the Jahrb. 1887, Pl 3 and 4. The band of plaiting, the W-shaped ornaments, the dotted stars, the flowers growing out of the ground, the animals feeding, the birds, the lions, and the ring-dance with palm branches recalled to me various works of Kyprian-Oriental-Graeco-Phoenician art, even before I had excavated the silver girdle (Pl. XXV). The Attic vase painter of Phaleron was evidently either directly or indirectly influenced by Kypros and not the least striking example of this fact is the instance of the centaurs. In an old Graeco-Phoenician tomb at Kurion I found a centaur (Pl. CIV, 6) certainly older than the early Attic vases of Oriental style. This centaur has on his right arm the mark of the svastika.

Excursus to Plates CXII—CXVIII.

Remarks on the griffin, the spinx and the cherubim of the Bible.

The types of the winged griffin and the male and female winged sphinx may, as A. Furtwängler shows in Roscher's Mythol. Lex. (Gryps, Sp. 1742 ff.), have originally come from Syria and the country of the Hittites. These types pass over to Egypt, are there modified (p. 79, Fig. 108), and return in their

Fig. 255.

Egyptian dress to pass through numerous other stages of development in the different countries of Asa Minor, and from thence to penetrate into Graeco-Phoenician and Greek art. The cylinders found by me in the Nekropolis at Hagia Paraskevi and formed of a kind of composition resembling glass (Pl. XXXI, 14 = CXVI, 10 = p. 80, Fig. 13) represents a griffin and a sphinx and is generally considered to be Hittite. Now in the Syrian division of the Museum. The cylinder may have been imported but it is equally possible that it was made in Kypros. I imagine that the culture of Northern Syrian and Cappadocia spread to Kypros. Furtwängler has already classified the griffins on Kyprian cylinders (as CXVI, 1, 38), with those of Kittite origin (as 10). One of the oldest known representations of griffins from Egyptian monuments (excluding the battle axe of King Ahmose) is to

be seen on a golden casket from the tomb of Rameses III (p. 79, Fig. 108). The Egyptian silver kylix found in Kypros (Cesnola-Stern, Pl. XIX) which forms the starting point for the group of bronze and silver Graeco-Phoenician kylikes, belongs to the same period.[**])

I must mention in passing the Greek griffin-type and its analogous form as we meet with them in Olympia (Pl. CXVIII, 4. To this cycle belongs the design on the ostrich-egg of Polledrara (CXVI, 1 12). The Kyprian cylinder, Fig. 8 shews a remarkably similar griffin with the same hanging locks of hair and the same ornament at the back of the head, which last also occurs in the figure of the griffin on the François vase CXII, 6). The griffins on the Kyprian silver girdle (Pl. XXV, 1, 2 = XCIX, 8) are more like those of Olympia. Both have the wide open beak, upright ears, and button-like projection on the head. (The last is also present in the griffin of the ostrich egg.)

The Graeco-Phoenician griffin-type, which has locks of hair on the forehead in common with the Egyptian type (CXIV, 6), is naturally more frequent in Kypros in the 7th and even perhaps in the 6th century than the Greek type. The presence of this Kyprian Graeco-Phoenician griffin-type justifies us in assigning Kypros as the place of manufacture of the bronze kylix of Olympia found, bearing a Phoenicia inscription which was found in the Alpheios. (CXXIX, 2, Fig. 255.)

The motive on the bronze kylix of Olympia is the same as that on the silver kylikes of Kurion (p. 53, Fig. 52) and of Idalion (p. 48, Fig. 51). On the last kylix it occurs five times.[*]) A man facing to the left stands in front of the griffin so as to partly conceal it. He seizes it with his left hand by the forelock and with his right hand stretches far back in order to thrust his long sword into its gaping jaws. The hind legs of the griffin are raised high in the air.

---

*) From this correct, p. 354, Note 4.

**) Time and space forbid further details on the griffin and sphinx types. We possess on the subject of the griffin the admirable study by A. Furtwängler in Roscher's Mythol. Lex.

***) The same motive on the second kylix of Idalion, Perrot III, p. 771, Fig. 546, illustrated also on p. 441, Fig. 257.

These and other Oriental elements are the chief features which were transferred from Kypros and Kyprian monuments to the early Attic Phaleron vases.

Archaic Greek sphinxes from Kypros, some of them reliefs on funeral stelai (Pl. XXVI), and some stone sculptures in the round (Pl. XXVII, 1) have been quoted in great numbers. On Pl. CXCVII, 4, 5 we see some stone vessels with sphinx-feet which were used for incense in the service of Rešef-Apollo. Cf. p. 199.

Representations of griffins in the Greek style both severe and free are not lacking in Kyprian art. There is no better counterpart to the splendid silver vase of Nikopol (CXIV, 9), than the gem with Kyprian inscription (CXIV, 3). The bristling mane which runs along the neck is a feature peculiar to these griffins and occurs in Kypros as early as the 6th century. The bronze spiral plated with gold leaf (Pl. XXXIII, 23) is adorned with a griffin whose mane is of this form.

The cherubim of the Bible, both those on the Ark of the Covenant and those who are represented as the guardians of the Gate of Paradise, have strong analogies with the griffin-type both mythologically, typologically, and linguistically. (Cf. Riehm's Bibellexikon I, p. 229 and 230.)

In consequence of a communication which Ed. Schrader was kind enough to make to me I have found it necessary to reject Lenormant's reading of the cuneiform inscription which was supposed to prove that the Hebrew cherubim corresponded to the Babylonian-Assyrian bull divinities. I see no reason to object to the earlier theory which identifies griffin, gryps and cherub.*)

Plate CXIX.

1. Mithras relief from Heddernheim; cf. Pl. LXXI. 2, from Lajard, Mithra, Pl. XC.

2. Cylinder in the Brit. Mus. Lajard, Mythra, Pl. XVI, 4 = Menant Glyptique I, Pl. III, 5 and p. 189, Fig. 120 = Perrot II, p. 97, Fig. 21.

3. Kyprian vase. Cesnola-Stern Pl. XIV, 5.

4. Persian cone in the Louvre. Lajard, Mithra Pl. XLVII, 4. A bearded male figure stands between a snake and a palm tree holding with his left hand by the horns a goat rampant and in his right a knife. Beside him is a half-moon and the symbol of the female sex.

? 5a and b. Vase of the Bronze period belonging to the Kyprian class which I describe on Pl. CLII, 13, CLXX, 9c and 10a—f. As to form and ornament it is an imitation of the Mykenaean glazed pottery, but is made without a wheel.

Plate CXX.

1 = C, 8 = CXXXIII, 1—4.

2 = Entrance to an Egyptian temple. From Prisse d'Avennes, I, Pl. X.

✝ 3. Limestone sarcophagus at Athiaenou published here for the first time.

Plate CCXXI.

1. Modern door-lock from Nicosia.

2. Kyprian vase. Perrot III, p. 708, Fig. 520. Discussed on p. 196.

3. Modern Kyprian shepherd's staff. Cf. p. 196.

4. Kyprian cylinder. Cesnola, Salaminia p. 128, Fig. 118. Four footed animal, ox-head, stars, snake and four double cones. Cf. p. 263 and Pl. LXIX, 50.

5. Do. Cesnola, Salaminia, Pl. XII, 15. A rude human figure among stars and sun-discs; at the side snake, four footed animal and stone pillar.

6. Do. Cesnola, Salaminia, Pl. XIII, 25 = Menant II, p. 249, Fig. 251. Described on p. 198.

7. Do. Cesnola, Salaminia, Pl. XIII, 23 In front of the snake and the tree is enthroned a divinity with a spear; beside him is a man standing, also four footed animal, ox-head and sun-disc with rays.

8. Do. Cesnola-Stern. Pl. LXXVI, 25. Various animals and symbols. On the left a snake.

9. Do. Cesnola, Salaminia, Pl. XIII, 30. Two rude human figures without arms; also two four-footed animals, a snake, stars, discs, etc.

10. A stone bead in the shape of a die, decorated with trees of two kinds. Cesnola, Salaminia Pl. XV, 61.

11. Similar bead. Cesnola, Salaminia, p. 145, Fig. 138.

---

*) Furtwängler's account in Roscher's Mythol. Lex. Sp. 472 requires some correction.

Plate CCXXII.

1 = Fig. 100, p. 75 Lajard, "Le culte du cyprès", Pl. XL. Egyptian relief from the 13th century illustrating, by the instance of the town goddess of Qadesch, who came from the kingdom of the Cheta how foreign cults penetrated into Egypt. This goddess, whom E. Meyer (Roscher's Mythol. Lex. Sp. 653) has correctly identified with Astarte-Aphrodite, stands as animal-tamer on the lion and holds a flower and a snake. On her head are sun and half-moon arranged in the Kyprian-Graeco-Phoenician manner. The god Rešef who very early fixed his abode in Syria and especially in Kypros stands as her lance bearer to her left, and the god Min, evidently a foreign importation, patron deity of fertility in the animal and vegetable world, to whom the cypress is sacred (cf. Pl. CLIII, 1 and CLIV, 1) is placed on her right. (Cf. p. 76, 148, 167, 199, 235, 300.)

2. The relief from a Kyprian vase of Hagia-Paraskevi, belonging to the later Bronze Period (Pl. CLXXII, 15g) which, together with fig. 3—5 belongs to the class of vases illustrated on Pl. CXXXVII, 4 and 5, comes like them from Egypt. Cf. also the excursus to Pl. CXIX—CXXIII. Two snakes are wound together in such a manner that at the first glance they give the impression of a horned animal's head.

‡ 3. Vase of the same class without reliefs. Provenance the same.

‡ 4. Vase of the same class and provenance. Fillets and serpentine lines.

‡ 5. = CLXXI, 11 and 12g. Vase of the same class and provenance. Two snakes; vertical fillets running perpendicularly down the vase. For a similar vase see Pl. CLXXXI, 149 (= p. 34, fig. 34, 9).

? 6. = CXLVIII, 11b = CLXXII, 18b. Vase belonging to the older Kyprian relief style with red or grey varnish. Under a horizontal fillet which surrounds the vase are two horns. This class of vase precedes the others (2—5) in date of invention, but the two styles run parallel for some time, for the vase illustrated here, now in the Antiquarium of the Royal Museum at Berlin, was found at Katydata in a tomb belonging to the transition between the Bronze and the Iron Period (18 Pl. CLXXII.)

? 7. = Fig. 3, p. 29. Relief ornament of the red terra-cotta hand-made vase sketched on p. 59, fig. 58c. cf. Pl. CLXXI, 11 and 12 a—f.

This was found in an early earth tomb at Hagia-Paraskevi and belongs to the period of the first appearance of large Hydrias with images in relief. Around the ball-shaped body of the vase are representations of stag, tree and snake placed one over the other.

8. = p. 57 and 93, fig. 54. Discussed on p. 57, 93, 262, 291.

9. Bronze plate in the Berlin Museum. Lajard, " Culte du Cyprès," Pl. VII, 6, Arch. Zeit. 1854 p. 210—217. Described in the excursus after Pl. CXXIII.

Plate CXXXIII.

1—2. Bronze shield from the cave at Gortyna. Orsi-Halbherr, Museo Italiano, 1888, II Atlas Pl. IV. 2 = the whole shield, so far as it is preserved. 1 represents a part of it. Cf. Pl. CXXXI, 1—4. (Cf. the excursus at the end of the explanation).

Most of the bronzes from Krete, as shields and kylikes, were made in Kypros. With the snakes and lions on this shield cf. the snakes and lions on the sarcophagus of Athiaenou, Pl. CXX, 3.

3. Part of a Greek vase painting representing the Hesperides. Gerhard, Akademische Abhandlungen, Pl. II.

4. From an Egyptian wall painting at Philae. Rosellini, "Monumenti del' Egitto," III. Pl. XXI (cf. the excursus).

5. LXXIII, 4. Part of the same wall-painting.

6. Bronze cup from a tomb at Caere. Helbig, "Homerisches Epos," p. 374, fig. 158. Cf. p. 275.

EXCURSUS.

Cultus of the Snake.

Snake-worship might easily arise independently at different times among the different nations of the globe, and we have evidence that this actually happened in the case of nations of antiquity both in the east and in the west. Besides these spontaneous independent developments there are others which are transferred from nation to nation by commercial intercourse by tribal migrations and by wars. It is often very difficult to distinguish independent from borrowed elements. I must here content myself with giving a series of types which give evidence for the existence of both. On the subject of the relations between one people and another and the transference of types and myths, which resulted from such relations I can here only speak very briefly. I must therefore leave out a number of quotations, which the reader might have a right to expect, but I hope at some future period to be able to collect under one view the religious and secular ideas, which belong to snake and tree cultus. The reader will find the illustrations very instructive, even in default of more exact information.

In the countries bordering on the rivers Euphrates, Tigris and Nile snake-myths and snake-representations are of great antiquity. In 1892 the authorties of the Berlin Museum had the opportunity of acquiring by purchase a piece of a Babylonian relief., which certainly belonged to a date at least as early as the middle of the 3rd millenium B. C. It represents two men, walking one behind the other, and two snakes. On the Babylonian cylinder (Pl. CXIX, 2) we see the tree-myth and the snake myth combined, and this although we cannot agree with the view of G. Smith, which identifies the enthroned figures stretching out their hands towards the dates as Adam and Eve of the Biblical Eden (cf. Perrot II, p 97). In Egypt we meet with similar conceptions and representations. In the wall-painting from Philae (p. 70, Fig. 91) a snake is darting out from under the sacred tree, which men are watering. Snakes are seated on the Egyptian pillars and staves (CXXIII, 4) and wreathe themselves round entrances to temples (CXX, 2). The Uraeus-snake is found everywhere and even adorns the heads and garments of human beings. In the hands of the goddess of Qadesch (Pl. CXXII, 1) we see the snake and the lotus flower. Snakes are found on the stelai of Sparta, on the handles of the Dipylon vases and on the lid of a Theban terra cotta casket (CXX, 1). They are also applied as ornament to the bronze cups of Caeré (CXXIII, 6). On a Persian gem (Pl. CXIX, 4) we find the snake rearing up behind the sacrificing figure. On the tree of the Hesperides (CXXIII, 3) a snake is hanging, and snakes may be seen in Greek vase paintings and on the tree of Mithras in the Roman relief from Heddernheim (CXIX, 1). On a Roman bronze plate where the principal design represents a Phrygian god on horseback (CXXII, 9) snakes grow out of the apex of the cypress trees.

In Kypros snake-worship as well as tree-worship is of great antiquity. It appears to have taken its own independent course at first and afterwards to have adopted Egyptian and other foreign elements, but it is found in all periods. Even at the present day snake-myths are popular and the snake exorciser is largely in request. The snake occurs frequently on early Kyprian cylinders of the Copper-Bronze Period (Pl. CXXI, 4—9). On the hand-made vases of the 3rd millenium B. C. or even of an earlier date, it is found represented in relief (CXXII, 7). In the 2nd millenium B. C. it is found painted (CXIX, 5). While the early vases of this kind with relief designs are either simply grey in colour (Fig. 256), or red with a brilliant glaze, in the 2nd millenium vases appear, which have a dull brown or black slip, but no glaze. On this latter group of Kyprian relief vases of the Bronze Period, numerous examples of which are found in Egypt (CXXXVII, 4), snakes frequently appear, often in pairs (CXXII, 5), or grown together (CXXII, 2). Graeco-Phoenician art represents snakes, now in slavish imitation of Egypt (e. g. on the scarab CXXII, 8), and again in a free, original and individual manner. An old Graeco-Phoenician Kyprian vase CXIX, 3), which may be dated before 600 B. C., shows a snake eating a tree. On another vase a man, holding in his hand a staff or a lance, treads with his right foot on a half unwound snake and with his left on the stem of a shrub. On the foot of the sarcophagus of Athiaenou, (CXX 8) is a design of four snakes radiating from the centre and stretching their heads over the fore-paws of the lions which are couched in the corners.

Fig. 256.

The lid, in a very fragmentary condition, is decorated with tendrils and sacred trees. On one of the bronze shields of Krete (CXXIII, 1 and 2) we see, by the side of a colossal bird, a sphinx and a goat, two huge snakes with half-moons on their heads under which are small lions. This shield appears, like most of the Kretan shields and kylikes of the Zeus Cave at Gortyna (cf. Pl. CXII, 5 CXXVIII, 1 and 2 and CXXXI 1—4) to have been made in Kypros. The snake-rods of the Egyptian charmers, the snake-rods of Moses and Aaron and the Brazen Serpent of the Temple at Jerusalem have their parallels in the manners, customs and legends of the Cypriots of to-day. On Pl. CXXI, 3 I illustrate the upper part of a black snake-rode now in my possession, which was given to me by a shepherd in the village of Dali. This staff ends in two snake's heads grown together, one of which is horned. The ancient myths of the horned snake and of many headed snakes are still current among the people. On Pl. CXXI, 1 I illustrate the iron lock of my house door at Nicosia. On this lock the house snake is represented as a talisman. Although the poisonous snake called Kukhi (vipara mauritanica) is regarded with disgust and enmity, it is considered a great sin to kill a black snake, for this kind is supposed to bring good luck and to devour the poisonous snake. The cultus of snakes and trees, about which I have already spoken so fully, made a great impression on the Island of Kypros at the earliest beginnings of civilization and seems to form a transition, not only to the Hebrew ideas of the snake in Paradise of the Tree of Knowledge of Good and Evil and of the Tree of Life, but also to the Greek myths of the Apples of the Hesperides and the snake, which guarded them.*)

Plate CXXIV.

1. Bronze relief from the time of Salmanassar II representing a portable shrine. Perrot II, p. 202, Fig. 68.

2 = CXXXVIII, 5 part of a sacred boat containing a small chapel or sanctuary resembling a tent. Two figures of the goddess of Truth, Isis or Nephtis, spread their wings out over scarab. Birch points out the analogy to the cherubim of the Hebrews and Perrot agrees with him. Wilkinson-Birch, "Manners of the Egyptians" III, p. 358, Fig. 594 = Perrot IV, p. 307, Fig. 153. Cf. p. 304, Note 1.

3. Sardinian votive pillar from Sulci, in the form of a small shrine in which the divinity is seated Perrot III, p. 253, Fig. 198.

4 = CXCIX, 4. Perrot III, p. 897, Fig. 641, cf. p. 277—278, 291—292 and 295, Note.

5 = X, 3 etc.

6. The same provenance as 3. Similar pillar in the form of a shrine, but older in style. In the niche stands the same divinity with the typanum, here in more archaic style. Perrot III, p. 310, Fig. 233.

*) These indications must suffice, although I am well aware of their fragmentary nature.

Plate CXXV.

1. Small Egyptian votive pyramid in stone. Perrot I, p. 236, Fig. 154. Cf. p. 167, Note 4. The Kyprian votive pillar, Pl. XVII, 2 and 3 (Kition) seems to have been copied from a stone Egyptian pillar of this kind or from something similar. The terra-cotta group from Kurion given on Pl. CLXXIII, 19 h belongs to the same period and to the same stratum as the votive pillar of Kition and is certainly a modification of an Egyptian motive. A woman is kneading dough while a second sifts meal.

2. A small granite votive shrine from the time and bearing the name of King Amasis. From Egypt. In the Louvre. Perrot I, p. 361, Fig. 211.

3—4. The megalithic Graeco-Phoenician building near Larnaka (Kition), at present dedicated by the Cypriots to Panagia Phaneromeni, is held in veneration by Greeks and Turks alike and especially by women. I published this under the title "Uraltes Bauwerk bei Larnaka" in the arch. Zeit. 1881, p. 311, Pl. XVIII, after I had thoroughly excavated and cleared out the walls and interior down to the foundations. Perrot's illustrations (III, p. 278—279, Fig. 209—210) were prepared from my drawings and illustrations, and I made use of his in my turn. In the innermost chamber I found a fountain with a wall round it. Even if the building, which is principally under the ground, only served as a tomb (in which case it would be difficult to account for the presence of a spring), we can draw important conclusions from it about buildings above the soil and small sanctuaries in the shape of shrines. Cf. Pl. CLXXV, and CXCIX.

Plate CXXVI.

1 = XXXVIII, 11.

2. Ground plan of a Phoenician temple. Gozzo near Malta. Perrot III, p. 298, Fig. 221.

The Kyprian sanctuaries (cf. Pl. X) correspond closely to this temple in ground plan architecture and material. Cf. p. 185.

3 = X, 1 = LXXXII, 7.

4 = X, 2 = LXXXII, 8.

The small Kyprian votive sanctuaries like Pl. XXV, 11, CXXIV, 4 and 5 (4 = CXCIX, 4), CXCIX, 1 and 2, to which also belong representations on small stone caskets like Pl. CXXXIII, 5 and 8, CXCIX, 6 and on golden breast-plates like Pl. XXV, 12 and 13, seem to have been in some cases tent-shaped shrines like CXXIV, (1 Assyrian, 2 Egyptian), and in others stone models like CXXIV, 3 and 6 from Sardinia, CXXV, 2 from Egypt and Phoenicia (Perrot III, p. 246, Fig. 188).

As late as the Roman Period the sanctuary at Byblos (CXXVI, 3) consisted of a similar small covered space like a shrine and of a pillared courtyard in which the cone of the goddess stood and to which the courtyard at Salamis (Pl. X, 10) forms an important counterpart. In old Paphos (CXXVI, 4) also even in the Roman period the cone of the goddess stood in the middle of the pillared courtyard. But in this case additional buildings for the priests and for holding the temple treasures were grouped around the pillared arcades (Pl. IX and X). The central building on the coin of Paphos (CXXVI, 4) certainly represents the decorated gate of the eastern entrance (Pl. IX and X) through which the worshipper could look into the court and see the cone of the goddess. The three square holes over the door represent windows belonging to a chamber built above. At the present day the same kind of architecture is found in monasteries and in the houses of rich peasants. Cf. explanations of Pls. IV—X LVI, LVII, and CCI.

Plate CXXVII.

1 = XCVI, 5 = Lajard, Recherches sur le Culte de Mithra, Pl. XXIX, 1 = Menant, Glypt. Orient I, 113, Fig. 66.

Cylinder of hematite. In the upper row of the design is a procession in front of an enthroned divinity. The figure of the daemon with the double head is specially worthy of notice. In the lower row are five daemons and one human figure. The daemons are represented as follows: to the left a horned figure in the running or kneeling attitude holding a tree in his left hand; next an upright figure draped and holding in the left hand a hare (the hind legs of this figure recall some beast of prey); in front of him walks a lion-daemon also holding a hare; again in front is an ass-daemon also with a hare. Cf. p. 282.

2 = LXXXIII, 6 = Cesnola, Atlas, Pl. 85, 553 = Cesnola-Stern, Pl. XXVI, 3.

Low relief (limestone) from Athienou. The representation is of a sacred festival. To the right above as if on a mountain is seated a divinity in long drapery, usually called Apollo, holding a cup in his outstretched right hand and in his left a lyre. Beside him is an altar shaped like an omphalos. The procession of men and women approaches him with votive offerings. To the left below a ring dance is being performed; to the right five figures are lying on couches round a festive meal; as far as we can judge from the reproduction this relief belongs to a later period.

3 = CXXXVI, 2. Gold seal-ring from Mykenae. From Schliemann, "Mykenae", p. 402, Fig. 530. Representation in the actual size from a cast. Arch. Zeit. 1883 p. 169 = Schuchardt, Schliemanns Ausgrabungen, p. 321, Fig. 295. Cf. Milchhöfer, "Anfänge der Kunst", p. 153 f, Arch. Zeit. 1883, p. 249, Rossbach, Arch. Zeit. 1888, p. 169 ff, 330 f.; Note 7.

As in the preceding examples, so here a solemn scene of worship is represented. Worshippers approach a seated goddess. The small figure to the left under the tree is generally supposed to be in the act of plucking the fruits of the tree. If this is so, the figure cannot have anything to do with the sacred function. I think it more likely that it represents a woman raising her arms in the attitude of adoration.

? 4 = LXXVI, 8. Ring dance of three figures in the "snowman" style around the sacred tree. This object has been put together from fragments such as are found in great numbers in Chytroi (No. 24 of the list).

5 = CXXXV, 6 = Perrot-Chipiez III, 587, Fig. 399 = Helbig, Hom. Ep. 2, 224, Fig. 67. Limestone group in the Louvre. Three female figures with headdresses resembling hoods, in the middle a flute-player.

6. Terra-cotta group from Levkosia. Coll. Cesnola. Berl. Mus. Antiquarium T. C. 6682, 38. H. 0,105. Ring dance of six figures with two tympanum players. One of the latter is broken off and the heads of both are missing. The outer figures are fastened on to a ring-shaped basis roughly kneaded together, while the inner ones stand on a cross-bar. The sex of the dancers and of the musicians is different: in the dance a man and a woman are placed alternately. This is to be seen from the breasts of the two figures still preserved; the third is missing. Of the musicians only one is female. There are many traces of black paint. The technique is very rude. We have here a mixed chorus of men and women or of youths and maidens, such as the singer of the shield of Achilles (Hom. II, XVIII, 590 ff.) had before his mind's eye, and which he developed into a kind of genre picture appropriate to the other scenes on the shield. The Dipylon vases too show this mixed chorus (illustrated on Pl. CXXXII, 1) and so does an early Attic vase of the class discussed by Böhlau, Jahrb. des Inst. II, p. 84 ff.; v. Pl. 3. This representation is specially interesting as showing us the partition of the ring dance into halves for the youths and the maidens (cf. Hom. II, XVIII, 602). In contrast to such representations we have the numerous metal kylikes to be discussed below on which the ring dance consists entirely of women.

(1—6 H. S.)

Plate CXXVIII.

1 = Mus. Ital. Pl. IX, 2. Fragment of a bronze kylix from the Zeus Grotto of Mount Ida in Krete. It represents a ring dance of women; other worshippers with sacrificial gifts walk in front. Cf. Orsi, Mus. Ital. 1888, II, 855. For the Zeus Grotto in general v. Fabricius, Athen. Mittheil. 1885, X, 59 ff.

2. Mus. Ital. Pl. IX, 3. Fragment of a similar kylix from the same place. An altar forms the centre of the design. Cf. Orsi, Mus. Ital. II, 855. In technique and treatment we may compare these kylikes with those of Idalion (p. 46, Fig. 49 = Pl. CXXX, 1), of Olympia in the Varvakeion (Pl. CXXIX, 2), and of Kurion in New York (Text p. 123, Fig. 142).

3 = LXXXIII, 7 = Cesnola, Atlas, Pl. 85, 558 = Cesnola-Stern, Pl. 96, 6. Votive tablet (limestone) with a Kyprian inscription from Athiaenou. A solemn scene of worship is represented, as on Pl. CXXVII, 1, 2, 3; under a tree is seated a divinity with a lance and another attribute; worshippers approach in procession.

4 = p. 65, Fig. 80 = Cesnola, "Salaminia", Pl. XII, 9. Seal impression of a steatite cylinder from Kypros.

Ring dance of three long-robed figures. Symbols: two ox-heads, sacred tree, half moon with stars, two dotted rosettes. The cylinder must belong to the Bronze Period in Kypros. Cf. p. 63—64, 239.

5. Impression from a cylinder used as a seal, found in Hagia-Paraskevi. Three figures, apparently nude, walking one behind the other; they appear to be holding each other's hands and performing a ring dance round a tree. Among them are representations of animals. The style of the figures is remarkably like the Dipylon style. Furtwängler called attention to this fact (Arch. Zeit. 1885, p. 140 f.) This cylinder is of the same period as the preceding.

6. Cesnola, "Salaminia", Pl. XIV, 37. Seal impression from a steatite cylinder. Ring dance of three long-robed figures. Symbols: ox-heads, sun and half moon, dotted rosettes. As the ring dance here is quite certain we may assume the same representation for the analogous cylinder No. 4.

(1—6 H. S.)

Plate CXXIX.

1 = Perrot-Chipiez III, 97, Fig. 36 = Helbig, Hom. Ep.², p. 28, Fig. 2. Silver kylix from Praeneste with Phoenician inscription (C. I. Sem. 164). The representations are in Egyptian style. Helbig ascribes this to Phoenician manufacture, cf. p. 441, Fig. 255.

2 = Olympia IV, Bronzen Pl. 52 = Perrot-Chipiez III, 783, Fig. 550. Bronze kylix found in the Alpheios near Olympia with engraved Aramaic inscription (C. I. Sem. 112.) From the 7th or 6th century

B. C. Syrian and Egyptian elements are mixed. Similar kylikes were found in Nineveh (Roscher's Lex. I, 1756). For further particulars about this kylix see Furtwängler, Bronzen von Olympia. Text, p. 110 and Note 2.

Plate CXXX.

1 = p. 46, Fig. 49 = Perrot-Chipiez III, 673, Fig. 482. Bronze kylix from Idalion. For literature on the subject see p. 45, Note 8.

This represents a dance of women with music before an enthroned goddess an altar and a sacrificial table.

2. Kylix by Hieron, from Panofka, Dionysos and the Thyades, Pl. I. Berl. Mus. Antiquarium. For particulars see Furtwängler. Vasenkatalog No. 2290. On the outside a feast of Dionysos is represented, celebrated by women with dances and flute music.   (1—2 H. S.)

The subject of the inspired dance of the Bacchantes around the Dionysos image, altar and sacrificial vessel has been adapted so as to fit into the circle of the Greek kylix.*) just as on the kylix of Idalion (Fig. 1) we find the ring dance grouped around the image of the goddess, her altar and all the apparatus of her ritual. We see in both cases that a similar subject fills the circle of the kylix. We may notice here the great difference between the beautiful conceptions of the highest period of Greek art and the ugly, though characteristic, representations of Graeco-Phoenician-Kyprian art.

Plate CXXXI.

1 = Mus. Ital. Pl. I = Amer. Journ. of Arch. IV, 1888, Pl. 16. Bronze shield from the same grotto as the kylikes, Pl. CXXVIII, 1, 2.

This represents the animal-taming god (Melqart? Isdubar?); beside him on either side a winged daemon. The style is strongly marked with Assyrian influence. Cf. Orsi. Mus. Ital. II, 782. Frothingham, Amer. Journ., p. 431 ff.

2. Mus. Ital., Pl. IX, 1 = Amer. Journ., Pl. 19, 1. Centre of a shield with lion's head and series of animals. Cf. Orsi, p. 831. Same provenance.

3 = Mus. Ital., Pl. VII = Amer. Journ., Pl. 20. Bronze Kylix with series of animals, from the same place. Cf. Orsi, p. 861.

4 = CII, 2 = Mus. Ital, Pl. II = Amer. Journ., Pl. 18. Fragment of shield with a representation of the animal-taming goddess (Astarte-Anaitis) and two couching sphinxes. Cf. Orsi, p. 794.

5 = Perrot-Chipiez II, 742, Fig. 406 = Lajard, Monuments II, Pl. 61, B. Bronze kylix from Nimroud in the Brit. Mus. cf. Furtwängler in Roscher's Lexikon I, 1756.

On p. 441, Fig. 257, I give the second bronze kylix of Idalion (= Perrot III, p. 771, Fig. 546) and in Fig. 258 the kylix of Athiaenou. Cf. Pl. CXII, p. 434, and Note 3.

Plate CXXXII.

1. Ring dance on a Dipylon vase, Mon. d. Inst. IX, Tav. 39, 2; cf. G. Hirschfeld, Annal. d. Inst. 1872, p. 142, No. 39; Kroker, Jahrb. d. Inst. 1886. I, 96, K.

This representation lacks continuity because several figures which naturally belong together are separated by ornaments. The male figures with bow-shaped objects, probably musical instruments, are most likely leaders of the chorus; two such leaders are to be found among the figures. There are also male figures among the dancers, as is shewn by the right side of the picture. Three of the men, the chorus leaders among them, are armed with short swords. This representation tallies very well with the Homeric description of a ring-dance (Hom. II, V, XVIII, 597).

Hirschfeld supposes that four or five figures are lacking on the right; the leg and the sword point belonging to one of these is preserved. Cf. explanation to Pl. CXXVII, 6.

2. Hydria with coloured figures from the Polledrara tomb near Vulci; from Micali, Mon. Ined. Tav. IV; cf. also O. Wulff, Zur Thesessage. Dorpat, 1892, p 3, No. 3. This represents the Geranos or ring-dance which, according to tradition, the Attic youths and maidens, led by Theseus, performed in honour of their rescuer Ariadne. The same vase shows one of the oldest and most interesting representations of Theseus' encounter with the Minotaur. Latterly critics have assigned the vase to the cycle of Ionic art. Cf. the Geranos on the François vase, Wien. Vorlegebl. 1888, Pl. III.

8. Bronze group from Olympia representing a ring-dance (Olympia IV, Pl. XVI, 263). Seven women stand on a ring-shaped pedestal with arms linked. Five similar ring-dances from the same place are also mentioned by Furtwängler in the text to the bronzes P. 41 ff. These, in form and content, offer the nearest analogies to the Kyprian ring-dances.

---

*) For the altar cf. Pl. CLXXVI, 1.

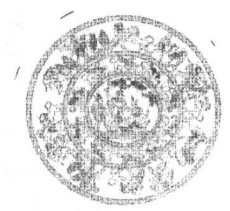

Fig. 157.

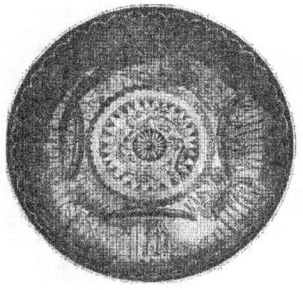

Fig. 158.

4   Part of a design from an Etruscan vase of the 7th or 6th century. Found at Tragliatella. From Annal. d. Inst. 1881. Tav. L. M. S.

The ornament, which resembles the winding track of a snail, bears the inscription Truia. Hence Benndorf ("Kunsthistorische Ergänzungen zum Trojaspiele". Sitzungsber. d. Wien. Akad. vol. 123, p. 47 ff.) interprets this as a representation of the Roman "Game of Troy". It is true that the ornament represents the place prepared for such a game, yet Benndorf's conclusion that this dancing place was also utilised as a picture of the Labyrinth for the dances in honour of Ariadne, and that it was represented on the Homeric shield beside the ring-dance seems to be incorrect. Pallat (De Fabula Ariadnea, Berlin, 1891, p. 2) is of Benndorf's opinion. Space and time forbid further discussion of this controversy.

(1—4 H. S.)

Excursus to Plates CXXVII—CXXXII.

The ring dance.

We have seen that the nearest analogy to the Kyprian ring dances (e. g. CXXVII, 4 and 6) is to be found in those of Olympia (e. g. CXXVI, 8). The two may be partly contemporaneous but Kyprian representations are found of an older date than any from Olympia. The ring dances represented on the Kyprian cylinders (CXXVIII, 4—6) go back to the pre-Homeric and pre-Mykenaean periods. It is a striking circumstance that the figures on the Dipylon vases, where the ring dance also occurs (CXXXII. 1), are very like the figures on Kyprian cylinders (cf. CXXVIII, 5), and yet the Kyprian cylinders are older by centuries than the Greek geometric vases of the Dipylon. On the cylinder (CXXVII, 1) evidently Hittite, the figures which approach a divinity in procession are so arranged that they suggest a pause in a ring dance. The Mykenaean gold ring (CXXVII, 3) is here illustrated because of its similarity in motive to a stone relief from an Apollo grove near Athiaenou in Kypros. Both represent an act of worship around a sacred tree in presence of a sacred divinity. The artist of the Kyprian monument, which is quite five hundred years later, evidently intended to represent a ring dance. On the Graeco-Phoenician bronze kylikes the ring dance appears very frequently. A good instance of this is the kylix of Idalion (CXXX, 1). From the same Kyprian manufactury must have come the bronze kylikes found in Krete which show, with small alteration, the same Idallian-Kyprian ring dance. On the bronze kylix of Olympia also, which was made in Kypros (CXXIX, 2, cf. p. 263, Note 4), the ring dance is indicated in a kind of short-hand by the presence of a group of women playing on musical instruments. The cymbal-player of this group is also dancing.

The painting from an Etruscan vase given on Pl. CXXXII, 4 has been connected, possibly without sufficient reason, with the Ariadne ring dance, but the other painting from the Poledrara vase, also Etrurian (CXXXII, 2), without any doubt refers to this subject. This Ariadne ring dance brings us to Amathus in Kypros, where such dances were often performed in honour of Aphrodite-Ariadne.

The silver kylix of Praeneste (CXXIX, 1) the bronze shield found in Krete (Pl. CXXXI, 1—4) and the bronze kylix found in Nimroud (CXXXI, 5) are here not given in full. Only the ring dance scenes on them are reproduced. The pieces themselves, however various in detail, evidently belong to a school of metal work which must have been active for several centuries and localized at a definite spot in Kypros. On these kylikes and shields, as on the Shield of Achilles, the ring dance very frequently occurs.

The ring dance is usually performed only by women, more seldom by men (e. g. Pl. XVII, 5) and still more rarely by women and men together. Like the old Kypriotes the Hebrews of the Old Testament and the Homeric Greeks were fond of the ring dance and practised it not only as an act of worship but also as an amusement of every-day life.

Plate CXXXIII.

1—4. Terra-cotta chest from Thebes. Berliner Vasensammml. 306 (Furtwängler). Boehlau, Jahrb. d. Arch. Inst. 1888, p. 357.

1 = C, 8. Front view. Cf. p. 282.

2 = CXX, 1. Lid.

8. Back view. Cf. p. 285, Note 1.

4. Narrow end, right hand.

4 a and b. Stone casket from Idalion. Cesnola, Atlas, Pl. LXXIX, 504. Cf. p. 268, Note 1.

6 and 8. Similar chests from Athiaenou. Cesnola, Atlas, Pl. LXXIX, 505.

7. Similar stone chest of more simple workmanship and about the same size. From Hagia-Paraskloev.

9. Figure of Erichthonios from a red-figured vase of the Brit. Mus. Roscher's Mythol. Lex. I, Sp. 1307.

(Add here Pl. CXCIX, 5—7, the casket of Tamassos.)

Excursus to Plates CXXXIII, and CXCIX, 5—7.

Sacred chests, boxes and baskets. The Hebrew "Ark of the Covenant".

The Boeotian painted terra-cotta casket (Pl. CXXXIII, 1—4) belongs to the same cycle of forms and types as the Kyprian stone caskets with incised ornamentation (5—8 and CXCIX, 5—7). Most of these show the svastika as trademark. The rudely incised designs on caskets CXXXIII, 6 and 8 seem to be imitations of other caskets like No. 5 which are of better workmanship although still extremely primitive. Casket No. 5 in its turn is only an imitation on a smaller scale in what we may call short-hand of the chest CXCIX, 5—7. On the smaller piece (CXXXIII, 5) on each of the narrow ends is a female divinity with arms raised as a worshipper. On he larger (CXCIX, 5—7) is on each side a pair of nude godesses in the same attitude. On one of the longer sides of the first piece (CXXXIII, 5a) are represented two chevril goats, male and female, in very rude relief, while on the long side of the last piece (CXCIX 5—7) is a complete hunting scene. In the archer who is kneeling above to the left I recognise the god Rešef-Bes, the Kyprian Apollo with the Dart, who is directly or indirectly analogous to the archer Merodach-Marduk (Pl. XXIX, 4, 6—8). Three animals are represented above, beside and below him, viz a chevril goat who is turning his head round towards the hunter, a larger female animal and a young one. The hunting scene is shut off on the right by a tree on which four birds are perched and around which is a design of four svastikas. The second long side of the casket is decorated with four stripes formed of contiguous triangles and filled in with trellis-shaped cross lines. The lid is missing but only accidentally as is the case with all the Kyprian caskets which we illustrate.

The oldest Kyprian stone casket from Hagia-Paraskevi (CXXXIII, 7), with pillar-shaped supports forming the only ornament on the long side, has holes bored through on the narrow sides.[*]) The painted Boeotian terra-cotta casket (CXXXIII, 1—4) is incomparably richer, even than the casket of Tamassos (CXCIX, 5—7). The svastikas, the hunting scenes and the mythological pictures are common to both. On the Boeotian casket on one long side a male figure armed with a battle-axe is looking after a hare which is being pursued by a dog. On the narrow sides an unwinged goddess is holding a horse by the bridle. On the second long side a winged goddess is killing two birds while a horse stands beside her tied to a pillar. The lid of this casket is preserved, and shows two snakes lying opposite each other and a pattern of svastikas and crosses. On the edge is a rude maeander pattern. The spaces are filled in with svastikas and the rosettes, crosses, gammas and flower sprays peculiar to Boeotian vases. The analogies between the Boeotian and the Kyprian caskets are undeniable.

The Tamassos vase, given on pp. 36, Fig. 37, 37, Fig. 38, 62, Fig. 71, 63, Fig. 75, and Pl. CXXVII, 6 belongs to the same cycle. On p. 37, Fig. 38 we see the side of the vase on which we have the hunt of the flock of goats in just the same stylo, exactly like the casket from Tamassos. One of the creatures also on the clay vase turns its head just in the same way as on the stone casket. Both objects come from the same layer in the same nekropolis.

The part which chests, caskets, coffins and baskets play in the myths of various people of Oriental antiquity is well krown, and cannot be further dealt with here. It is sufficient to recall from the sphere of Greek Mythology the Erichthonios Chest, which is given on Pl. CXXXIII, 9. The two snakes on the cover of the casket of Theano point to a similar symbolical significance.

The Ark of the covenant of the Hebrews, with the Tables of the law, belongs here. The gold plate which closed the ark of the covenant (according to Luther the Mercy Seat) was adorned at the ends with two Cherubim of fine gold. The Egyptian royal chair in Pl. XXXIX, 2, made of bronze, was supported by two lions. In front are couched two Spinxes. On the arm stand two winged figures, just as we may imagine the Cherubim. At the corners of the cover of the sarcophagus from Amathus (Cesnola-Stern Pl. XLVIII, 2) are seated four sphinxes, on our sarcophagus from Athiaenou (CXX, 3) are four lions and four snakes round a conventionalized tree. Plainly we have to do here with similar representations to those in Pl. XCVI, where there are figures that repeat themselves two, three and four times, only that is this case we have a casket of quite a special sanctity, in which was deposited a sacred token, like the tables of the law in the ark of the covenant. Further the funeral stelae in the form of a pair of lions or a sphinxes, which are so frequent in Cyprus, deserve attention. Together with the Hebrew ark of the covenant, these Cyprian chests, boxes, sarcophagi and funeral stelae, are all various modifications of one main type, which occurs again in Syria and Egypt. The Egyptian monuments given in Pl. CXXXVIII, 1—6, allow anyhow of the conjecture that this type took its origin rather on the banks of the Nile than of the Orontes, Euphrates or Tigris.

Plate CXXXIV.

1. Etruscan censer, representing Kypra, Bucchero vase. Micali Monumenti Inediti, Pl. XXVII, 1. Cf. p. 281.

2 = CII, 1 = CXCVII, 2 = Fig. 167, p. 193.

3 and 5. Stone vase from Amathus (Louvre) with handle (5 = XCIV, 23 = CLX, 1. Perrot III, p. 280 and 282, Fig. 211 and 213. Cf. p. 240.

4. Reconstruction of the brazen sea of Solomon's temple, after Riehm's Bibellexicon II, p. 969. Another reconstruction in Perrot IV. p. 327, Fig 172.

6 = CXCI, 6. See above for dimensions and description.

Plate CXXXV.

1a and b. Two different censers from Athens. Conze, Jahrbuch des Arch. Instituts, 1890, p. 134. 2. Section of the reconstruction from 1a and b. Conze op. cit. 135. 3 = XVII, 4 = Fig. 189, p. 278.

---

*) The holes have been omitted by the draughtsman.

4. From a drawing done in Syracuse. The original is now at Geneva in the coll. Fol. Conze op. cit. p. 187.

5 = XVII, 6.

6 = CXXVII, 5.

Excursus on certain ritual vessels of the old Testament.

(Brason, bazen-sea, censer, and incense holder, Pl. CXXXIV, CXCVII, 2, 4 and 5, CCX, 21).

Pl. CXXXIV, 3 and 5. The colossal stone vessel from Amathus is still the best illustration of the brazen sea of the temple of Jerusalem (Reconstruction Pl. CXXXIV, 4). The fragment in Fig. 4 of a small stone cylix belonged to a vessel that was evidently supported by several animals, in this case by rams, as the laver at Jerusalem was supported by bulls. Above the backs of the animals a human head is visible. We have here then, on a small scale, one of those curious types that floated before the mind of Ezekiel when he described his chariot of cherubim (cf. also Pl. XCVI). On the altar of Rešef-Apollo at Toumpa (No. 67 of the list) near Salamis, there had been deposited a great number of either incense or water vessels which were in the form of an ox on whose back was a cylix.*)

In the case of the vessels in Pl. CXCVII, 4 and 5, the foot is formed of a sphinx. No. 4 was excavated actually at Frangissa, in the grove of Rešef-Apollo (No. 4 of the list). In other cases the foot is formed by a winged female figure with a pillar (CXXXIV, 2 = CXCVII, 2). Related to them is an Etruscan vessel (CXXXIV, 1) In the case of the vessel given in Pl. CCX, 21, the foot takes the form of a columnar altar, and bears the inscription given above p. 2. The vessels that are large and deep, as well as the Etruscan specimen, CXXXIV, 1, were certainly nothing but small-sized holy-water stoups. Other small shallow ones may have served as water and incense vessels.

Holy water vessels, which are smaller than the colossal vessel from Amathus, but larger than the small ones in CXXXIV, 2, 6, CXCVII, 2, 4, 5, CCX, 21, and which would therefore correspond to the basons of the Hebrew tabernacle of the covenant, have been found in large numbers. An example, restored from a number of fragments, is given in Pl. XVI. I saw such a bason in situ (Pl. CCI. eastward of point S. and north of point K.) in the entrance to the place for votive offerings, in the sanctuary of Mikal on the Acropolis of Kition. It stood on a stone wall foundation, above the stone pavement, and was raised to such a level that a man could comfortably use it. The vessel was 0,72 m in diameter and was adorned at two opposite points with the same palmette ornament as is repeated four times beneath the handle of the colossal vase of Amathus. I am copying exactly from my diary of excavations. The vessel was only broken through in the middle, otherwise it was discovered intact, and in fact at the excavation of this interesting hillock. When I returned to the place, I found it smash d in pieces.

We pass back to the censers on Pl. CXXXV, 1—5. A comparison with Fig. 6 (= Pl. CXXVII, 5) shows us how censers were made of choros groups (Fig. 5).**) The transition from the choros (Fig. 6) to the censer, which must still count as a choros (Fig. 5) is plain to be seen. Further modifications of the type are seen in 1, 2 and 4. Among the votive offerings of the sanctuary of Astarte-Mikal on the Acropolis at Kition occurred this fragment of a censer, which Conze also mentioned in the Jahrbuch of the Institute, 1890, p. 121. His mention however, of the village Bambula is erroneous. He means the hill Bambula, i. e. the Acropolis of Kition. Fragments of a similar censer were found later on in Salamis.***)

I also excavated at Frangissa in 1885. in the grove of Rešef-Apollo, little clay shovels similar in form like the mussel-shaped lamps, but provided with an elongated protruding handle, stalk-shaped. What is said in the Old Testament of the incense shovels applies to them.

And last, reference must be made here to the terra-cotta tripod, which has already had several illustrations, and to the tetrapod (Pl. CLXX, 13 d and e) as well as to the terra-cotta cauldron of the bronze period, separately worked but found in situ on the tripods, which in 1882 I excavated in an iron period Graeco-Phoenician grave, together with the bow-fibulae (Fig. 260). They are the primitive models of the four vases and lavers which Solomon set round his temple (1 Kings VII, 19) "Such things as they offered for the burnt offerings they washed in them" (2 Chron. IV, 6.)†)

As the rule of the Hiram of the Bible is known certainly from inscriptions (cf. supra, p. 21, 39 and 98) to have extented over parts of Cypus, and, in particular, just over the most ancient copper-mine district between Amathus and Tamassos, we may assume with safety that the great bulk of the bronze and copper vessels for Solomon's temple were either actually made in Cyprus or made by Cyprian masters in Phoenicia or Jerusalem.

Plate CXXXVI.

1. Relief from Suksche-gösu. Perrot IV, p. 553, Fig. 279 = Humann and Puckstein, "Reisen in Kleinasien und Nordsyrien".

2 = CXXVII, 3. Repeated here on account of the double axe.

3 = Coin of Milasa. Perrot V, p. 386. A god with the double-axe and spear stands in a shrine which belongs to the type instanced in Pl. CXXIV.

4. Double-axe of bronze from Idalion. Perrot III, p. 867, Fig. 634, cf. p. 258.

---

*) The English mistook these vessels for lamps. (Journal of Hellenic Studies 1891, p. 159 Fig. 11.)

**) Cp. also above Pl. XVII, 5 and 6 and the Explanation p. 351.

***) Journal of Hellenic Studies 1891, p. 123.

†) Cf. F. Dümmler, Mittheilungen, Athen, 1886, p. 246.

I must add to Pl. CXXXVII, 6, one of the representations of the Tamassos vase shown on p. 37, Fig. 38. Given here on account of the double-axe which the man to the left brandishes in his right hand. Another version of the same vase, in which the double-axe comes out clearly, is given p. 62, Fig. 71. The double-axe again appears in the silver cup of Amathus brandished by the hands of the men who are felling the trees in front of the besieged city (cf. p. 47, Fig. 50 = Pl. CLVI, 3). Double-axes also appear on the Dipylon vase (Pl. LXXXIX, 1) which was made for the Cyprian market. Further thirteen double-axes of bronze have been found in Cyprus, not at Alambra, as has been stated, but at Idalion.*) The series of small votive double-axes, made of bronze-foil, form the lowest layer in the excavations at Olympia, and the double-axes of the Mykenae layer (Pl. XCIV, 7) point to conclusions as to a further historical relation between the civilization and ritual of Mykenae and Cyprus. For the double-axe cf. pp. 257—258.

Plate CXXXVII.

1. From Prisse d'Avennes. One of the painted vases of the Egyptian wall-fresco at Rehmarah.
2. Vases with two dogs on handles. Wilkinson-Birch, "Manners and customs of the ancient Egyptians" II, p. 5, Fig. 271, 2. From the great Egyptian wall-painting in Wilkinson-Birch I, Pl. II A. Cf. p. 154, Note 3.
3. Egyptian terra-cotta vase, from Wilkinson-Birch II, p. 4. Fig. 270, 1.
4. Do. Wilkinson-Birch II, p. 4, Fig. 270, 2.
5. Cyprian vases of the copper-bronze period from Hagia Paraskevi. These are just like those found in Egypt — i. e. 3 and 4. Cf. Pl. CXXII, 2—5.

The vases figured in 1 and 2, are instructive in other respects. They are brought as tributary offerings by the Kefti. Although the figures have been modified by Egyptian painters to Egyptian style, yet the foreign types are recognisable. They are Cypriotes, who are bringing the vases. With the vase in fig. 1 the Cyprian vases Pl. CLXXIII and CCXVI, 29 and 30 and others are to be compared. I also excavated in 1889, from a grave of the bronze period at Tamassos, a vase which was quite of the same shape as 2, and in which the handle was formed by two dogs represented as jumping up. This Cyprian vase is decisive evidence as to the origin of the Kefti. Kefti and Kapthor, moreover, must be identified. They are respectively the Cyprians and Cyprus.

? 6. One of the pictures of the vase from Tamassos, mentioned at the end of the description of the preceding plate. A hero, the hero Herakles, who already wears Greek dress and armour, is rushing to the left to attack the Hydra. He holds one of the heads he has hewn off in the right, while with his sword (of which only a small portion remains) in the left he gathers himself for another stroke or blow. Meanwhile, on the other side Iolaos is conceived of as preparing death for the Hydra in a different fashion from that traditional in Greek mythology. Originally Iolaos burnt the wounds on the trunk of the Hydra to prevent a double number of heads growing out. In this case Iolaos is striking with the double-axe on the head of a nail in order thus to kill the heads of the Hydra**) so that it is not necessary for Herakles to hew them from the trunk. This is the ancient Semitic fashion of killing a man, i. e. to drive the nail into his temples, just as in the song of Deborah (Judges) Jaël kills Sisera. Consequently we have in this case a curious fusion of early Greek and early Hebraic elements.

c7. The upper part of a long (0,71 m) iron sword found at Tamassos.

Excursus to Pl. CXXXVII, 7.

The Homeric swords in Cyprus.

If Agamemnon's coat of mail, the finest of all antiquity, came from Cyprus, it follows that in the time of Homer Cyprian manufactories of armour had a high reputation. Among the countless finds which I brought to light in making excavations at Tamassos for the Royal Museum at Berlin there were a number of iron swords in various states of preservation. From the circumstances in which these discoveries were made it can clearly be shown that the date of their origin was the 6th century B. C. If these iron swords are so late as post-Homeric, still it is clear from their shape, construction and material of the swords studs that they are copies in iron of older bronze and copper originals***) which belong to the group of Homeric swords studded with silver nails.†)

I reproduce in Pl. CXXXVII, reduced to one third, the upper end of the best preserved of these swords. It is now 0,71 m. long. Only the extreme point, which may be reckoned 0,05 m., was broken off so that the total length was 0,76 m. The blade, 0,62 m. long, increases 0,08 m. in breadth from the hilt, which is 0,14 m. long and extends out to a breadth of 0,118 m. The handle is thickest in that partin which the section was taken from the upper end and it has in that place a total thickness of 0,026 m. of which 0,006 m. consist of the iron case and 0,090 m. of the ivory shell. In the thickest place of all, the actual top piece, there is an excrescence of a total breadth of 0,37 m, After the bronze pegs of the six nails had been driven through both case and shell of the silver heads, shaped like a flat felt hat, were screwed and soldered on to

---

*) Cf. Furtwängler, "Die Bronzefunde von Olympia", p. 34.
**) A portion of this vase is in bad condition and the upper part of the Hydra is not quite correctly drawn by the artist.
***) Even before this I could point to very powerful and dangerous thrusting swords made of copper, which in consequence of their simple form and the circumstance of their discovery must be regarded as the starting point of this manufacture of swords which must be localized in Cyprus. (Cf. the Owl, p. 13 II, 1 and 6, and of the present work Pl. CLI, 27.)
†) Cf. Helbig Epos, pp. 333, 336, and 337, Fig. 130 and 131.

the hollow ends of the bronze bolts. In this way the shell of the handle (in this case of ivory) was held fast by the sword nails, which protruded 1 millim. on either side and at the same time was effected that beautiful scheme of ornamentation, which won for this sort of sword the epithet ξίφος ἀργυρόηλον. While the two lower nails, the heads included, were only 0,016 m. long the four nails on the thickened head piece had a length of from 0,036 to 0,039 m. Besides the extreme end of the blade only the handle was broken but, as the plate shows, could be put together again. The portion of the ivory shell that is preserved is given in the drawing in lighter tint and in higher relief. The sword lay, as most of those that were found, in a wooden sheath of which numerous fragments have been preserved, and one piece on the left side is given also in light tint The middle portion of the blade about the lower third of it, where there is a broadening up to 0,065 m. has a thickness of 0,019 m. I dug out a powerful two edged sword adapted alike for thrusting and hewing from one of the royal stone capitals with Iconic capitals. It lay not far from the bronze helmet at the end near the head of the buried corpse, outside of the sarcophagus. When the grave-despoilers of antiquity were seeking for gold, silver and engraved gems they had thrown the sword and helmet out of the sarcophagus. The prince who was buried here must have had on this tomb besides the ξίφος ἀργυρόηλον a sword which the grave-despoilers carried off on account of its great value. It must have been a show-sword like that which Agamemnon carried and which he very likely had received as a guerdon of hospitality, like his mail coat, helmet and shield, from King Kinyras who ruled over Amathus in Kyprus. Indeed I saw, as they were digging, something sparkle in the ground. Delighted, I drew out a bronze sword nail 0.028 m. long, on which to one side there was still fastened the nail-head of a shape like a felt hat, 0,004 m. thick and with a diameter of 0,017 m. the nail head was of pure gold. It seemed to have got loose from a sword which the grave-despoilers thought worth stealing. If my discovery brought before our eyes for the first time the ξίφος ἀργυρόηλον of Homer, this nail illustrates also for the first time the ξίφος ἐν δὲ οἱ ἧλοι χρύσειοι πάμφαινον (Pl. XI,29). The archaeologist will see at once from our reproduction that this sword, which, as I have shown, is wide spread through whole of Cyprus (from Tamassos and Idalion inland to Kurion in the South and Marion-Arsinoë in the West)*) is identical with the form of the bronze sword of the Acropolis of Mycenae**) It is the type from which are descended various types of Hungarian, central and north European swords of prehistoric date. The original type of these swords took its rise where copper was found and from whence it was carried by commerce to Greece, Hungary, central and nothern Europe, i. e. Cyprus. Indeed, it seems the sword in antiquity was the special invention of Cyprus. The oldest Cyprian swords are of copper and are nothing else but primitive daggers increased to colossal demensions.

Plate CXXXVIII.

1—2. Two bas-reliefs from the Memnonium at Thebes. Riehm's "Bibellexikon I, p. 229, 1 and 2.

3. The chest standing in the sacred ship. Riehm's "Bibellexikon," I. p. 229, 3.

4. Wall-painting from Thebes. The two goddesses of Truth and Justice. Wilkinson-Birch I, p. 296, fig. 102.

5. = CXXIV, 2.

6. Egyptian breastplate with the figure of the gods Re and Ma'at, who are seated round an obelisk and hold the Hieroglyph of life on their knees. Wilkinson-Birch III, p. 183, fig. 547. Riehm, Bibellexikon I, p. 916.

7 = XXV, 13 = C, 4,

8 = XXV, 10 = CI, 5.

9 = XXV, 12 = C, 3.

10 = CI, 10.

Plate CXXXIX.

1. Portion of an Assyrian relief which is a stone copy of an embroidered breastplate. In the midst the sacred tree. Perrot II, p. 773, fig. 445. The spaces bounded by quadrangular frames, which alternate with eight-rayed star rosettes and scale patterns, should be compared with the lower bands of the large Ormidhia vase from Cyprus (Pl. CXLI, 3) which have just the same scheme of decoration.

2 = CXVI, 11.

3 = CI, 7.

4 = CI, 1.

5 = CI, 3.

6 = CI, 2.

---

*) Cf. p. 368 the explanation of Pl. XXXIII, 17—20 and Pl. LXVII, 2—14. The grave no. 131 Nekr: II (Marion Arsinoë 1886) also yielded another bronze sword nail just like this with a gold head like the one described here side by side with the nails with silver heads. A heap of swords of the same type were found in the Western Acropolis of Idalion on the sacred high-place, of the Bâma, of Anat-Athene. Cf. p. 343, Pl. III, No.1.

**) The sword here described fell to the share of the landowner when the division was made of the objects discovered in the excavations made on behalf of the Berlin Museum. This was His Excellency the Archbishop of Cyprus, Sophronios. He sold it together with other finds made at the same time to the then General Governor, Sir Henry Bulwer. A report of this collection, since presented to the Museum at Cambridge, has appeared in the Academy, and at the end of it this sword and the golden sword nail is described. But the writer had not noticed its relations to the Homeric swords else he would certainly have mentioned them. The helmet with moveable side pieces from this grave as well as the very important pieces of mail armour with incised designs which came from a neighbouring grave of the same level (Pl. LXX) fell to the share of the Museum at Berlin.

Excursus on Plates CXXXVIII, CXXXIX, CXCIX, 1–3, XXV, 10–14 and XXXIII, 24.

Aaron's breastplate " with light and right. "

The breastplate of the Jewish high-priest, thus designated by Luther, that oracle by lot which contained Urim and Thummim, appears to have taken different forms at different epochs of the Old Testament. The materials also employed for it, do not seem to have been always the same. The breastplate belonged to the cassock i. e. the ephod, cf. pl. XXXIII, 24.

The breastplate of the high-priest appears to have played an important part in the rituals of various divinities and priests in the ancient East. With the same people it had different forms for each divinity. In many cases the breastplate, when it was of large size and quadrangular, was a copy on a small scale and only giving the main lines of the ark of the covenant, of the tabernacle of the covenant or of the sanctuary. In the Cyprian cults there occur small clay representations (e. g. in Pl. XXV, 11) which may equally well be taken as copies of small sanctuaries or as breastplates. Various real gold breastplates, as in XXV, 12 (= CXXXVIII, 9) and XXV, 13 (= CXXVIII, 7) represent, as the clay figures do, just such arks of the covenant and tabernacles and shrines, in the door of which a divinity stands. Other of these golden breastplates contain scenes with procession-chariots. The golden breastplate reproduced full size in Pl. CXCIX, 3 shows, behind the charioteer with a bird-face in profile, the goddess full face, with her hands on her breasts (cf. the stone procession-chariots CXCVI, 4). Above the group to the right, in the corner, a large window-shaped cartouche contains symbols and writing-marks which are difficult to make out, and which remind one of Hittite hieroglyphs. These breastplates, composed of two gold leaves lying on each other squeezed together, must have served as an ornament at either side of a pouch made of stuff or of a flat wooden case. To hold the gold leaves straight they were stretched on a frame made of bronze rods, which has been in part preserved. In our illustration we can see the place for it all round. In the second gold plate of Amathus, which is also rich in figures (XXV, 10 = CXXXVIII, 18) the chariot of the sun is represented as in the former plate, in the large lower space. Here both divinities are given in profile. Above, two goddesses of the same character are depicted walking one behind the other; they wear crowns, their hair falls in long nets and they press their breasts with their hands. They are sometimes represented full face, sometimes in profile. On the small gold breastplates of Amathus a nude goddess stands in a niche. In the clay copies there is seated in a little cell sometimes a god with a high cap who seems to be stamping in a cask (XXV, 11) sometimes a half-veiled goddess, who, as mourner, raises her hand to her face in an attitude of dejection.

Among the Egyptian monuments depicted together with these we see in Pl. CXXXVIII, 6 a breastplate which, in fact, is nothing else than the copy of an ark of the covenant (Fig. 5). The deities are present in pairs as they are in the Egyptian representations 1 and 2, and in the Cyprian gold-plates (Fig. 8 and CXCIX, 3). Finally the Egyptian picture in fig. 10 with the god Bes who is standing in a niche that is garlanded with flowers, is a further counterpart to the Cyprian gold plates (Fig. 7 & 9) with the Cyprian goddess who so often appears side by side with Bes and (e. g. in the group in pl. CI, 4), carries Bes on her shoulders. Even the frame of foliage that surrounds the plate where Bes is represented is repeated in the shrubs that sprout up around the goddess in the Cyprian gold plates, and in the garland of flowers of the frame. On the Assyrian breastplates CXXXIX, 1 and 4, the sacred trees play a yet greater part, in 1 the sacred tree alone fills the quadrangular breastplate, in 4 the circular space is surrounded by a frame of two sorts of sacred trees, conventionalized cypresses and palms. In the centre, beneath the winged sun-disc, two priests adore the sacred tree The bronze breastplate in CXXXIX, 2 (described above CXVI, 11) is adorned with combats between fabulous wild and tame animals; these combats take place over a sacred tree. The seal in Plate CXXXIX, possibly made in Cyprus, and clearly under Graeco-Phoenician and Hittite influence, gives us the reduction of a larger sized breastplate. The cord-like ornament forms the frame, as it does in the bronze-plate CXXXIX, 2 and in the Cyprian gold-plate CXCIX, 3, that I excavated. Here two winged figures are seated opposite each other while above them hovers a star and winged sun-disc. In the case of the Tanagra female idols which are related to the Boeotian vases the sacred breastplates are placed on the breast, and the artists have given to them the shape of phantastic conventionalized plants and trees. However various may be the forms, representations and artistic tendencies of these breastplates, yet one marked common trait runs through all of them. It is clear that the custom of these breastplates passed from country to country, and with them went the artistic types, the myths and superstitions that belonged to them.

We return to the Hebrew ephod with its "breastplate of judgment", with "cunning work". "After the work of the ephod shalt thou make it, of gold and of blue and of purple, of scarlet and of fine twined linen shalt thou make it." (Exodus XXVIII, 15.)

Note how in the Cyprian clay-image, XXV, 11, colour is imitated by various stripes in the woven garment. "Foursquare it shall be being doubled; a span shall be the length thereof, and a span shall be the breadth thereof." (Exodus XXVIII, 16.)

I mentioned before a breastplate I excavated myself, now in the Antiquarium of the Berlin Museum, which consists of two gold plates, both with the like decorations. The quadrangular form is the rule with these gold breastplates reproduced here. But from Cyprus there are many others, also round-shaped. I have reproduced on Plate CCXVII, 9, a very beautiful Cyprian one of gold, which gives us an original for the round breastplates copied in the various images (e. g. Pl. L, 1, 4, 5, CCX, 1–4, 12–14, &c.). (Cf. also Perrot III p. 819, Fig. 576, f. and 829, Fig. 590.)

In the "breastplate of judgment", the stones "shall be twelve. according to the names of the children of Israel". (Exodus XXVIII, 21.) The clay image that I excavated from an early Graeco-Phoenician grave (Pl. CLXXV, 2) was decorated with twelve round discs, six right and six left. The difference between this and the breastplate of Aaron is that on his the signet stones were set in four rows, each row with three stones. (Pl. XXXIII, 24.)

Exodus XXVIII, 22, goes on to say: "And thou shalt make upon the breastplate chains at the ends of wreathen work of pure gold."

One gold breast-pouch from Amathus (Plate CXCIX, 3) has the frame formed of a twisted gold cord. The breast-plate of judgment was fastened with gold cord. We see this on the round breast-plate (Plate CCX, 12—14, &c.).

Further Exodus XXVIII, 26 says "and thou shalt put two rings of gold on the two ends of the breastplate". The two upper rings we can see indicated as discs on the clay-image in Plate XXV, 11.

Next the breast-plate with the rings was to be fastened "into the rings of the ephod with a lace of blue", Exodus XXVVIII, 29. Each "lace of blue" we may see on the breast-plate of Artemis. Plate LXVIII, 13.

"And thou shalt put on the breast plate of judgment Urim and Thummim" (Exodus XXVIII, 30). Urim and Thummim mean a divine pair, divinities of light, personifications of the powers of light, sun and moon. In Cyprus this divine pair were called Rešef-Apollo, who personified the sun, and Astarte-Aphrodite, who personified the moon. The symbol of the disc of the sun with the half-moon round it, which represents the two divinities either singly or as a hermaphrodite deity, may be seen upon the golden breast-plate of Amathus CXXXVIII, 8 and in the clay breast-plates of Idalion (Plate XXV, 11) of Amathus CXCIX, 1 and 2.

Stade in his "Geschichte Israels" I, p. 466, believes that the breast-plate of judgment on the image was made of a core of hard clay or common metal over which was laid a coat of precious metal. The oracle itself (i. e., the "judgment") was called Urim and Thummim. The golden breastplate in Plate CXCIX, 3, which I found 'in situ' on the corpse, consisted of two gold leaves stretched on bronze rods; the core of wood or leather that had lain between had rotted away. Only the metal parts had been preserved.

"Breast-plates of Judgment" like these, of triangular shape, made of metal-foil and hollow within for the reception of the lot we have noted in the statuettes of the boy-attendants of temples of Adonis (Plate XXXIII, 1, 2 and 5). A large modern one of silver (that passed out of my hands to the Philadelphia Museum) is figured in Plate XXXIII, 8 and was hung round the Greek woman in figure 6. Below is a bar for opening it (cf. supra Text, p. 209). In these pouches (which are often made of leather or bright coloured cotton) Cypriote, Greek and Turkish women keep as talismans the charms, relics, sacred odds and ends they get from their priests. At the time of the kingdom of the ten tribes (Hosea III, 4) cassocks (i. e. Ephods) came into use in connection with the teraphim whereas before we only hear of teraphim and image in the private sanctuary of Micah with reference to what was subsequently the tribal sanctuary of Dan (Judges XVII, 5; XVIII, 30, 31). Their Ephods and teraphim were associated with an oracle cult*) from Micah's time down to Hosea. Stade thinks that in the time of Hosea two little teraphim images had taken the place of the Urim and Thummim and were employed for casting lots.

The breastplate made in a pouch form served to hold the divinities Urim and Thummim as well as the teraphim. Do not our Cyprian gold breastplates and the terra-cotta copies offer the best illustration of these?

The token of office of the Egyptian high priest (CXXXVIII, 6) makes us acquainted with one of the countless Egyptian types which the Jews as well as the Cyprians took over for the dress of their priests. The Graeco-Phoenician signet-stone (CXXXIX, 3) is a temple signet in which the same token of office is represented as in the breastplate. Two Sphinxes have taken the place of the Cherubim, of the goddesses of truth and justice, of the sun and moon deities and of Urim and Thummim.

I am now moreover in a position to prove that the teraphim was an oracle by lot and to show how it was worked. It corresponded with the one we noted in connection with the triangular oracle-pouch (Pl. XXXIII, 1, 2, and 5).

On Pl. CCXVII, 4 I give just such a teraphim image from Cyprus. It is of gold and hollow inside. It is executed in a style that imitates that of Egypt and still contains a small roll of parchment (cf. infra 337). These gold Teraphim for the breast which are imitated from an Egyptian and Jewish custom are not so very uncommon in Cyprus.**) The sphinx amulets, the heads of the Gorgons, of Bes, of oxen and calves, the bulls and rams used as ornaments for the breast belong to the same group, and so do the cylinder-shaped amulets of gold and silver (Pl. XXXIII, 16 and CLXXXII, 26). They are all lot-oracles like the teraphim of Micah in Judges XVII and later in Hosea III, and like the oracle-pouches they begin from the second book of Moses. Priests in those days, as now, placed their oracle utterances in the hollow space within these little pouches, these cases of all kinds, with or without ornament. Such was the Jewish lot-oracle of the Ephod, breast plate, Urim, Thummim and Teraphim. These Egypto-Jewish customs first forced their way in Cyprus into Graeco-Phoenician, then into Greek art and afterwards passed on westwards to Greece and Italy.

---

*) Cf. Riehm's Bibellexikon articles Bilderdienst, Ephod, Licht und Recht, Teraphim.
**) Cp. similar figures in Egyptian Style Cesnola-Stern, Plate IV middle of the upper row. A. P. di Cesnola, "Salaminia," p. 43, fig. 44.

Plate CXL.

1. The apron of King Ramses III, 20 Dynasty. From an Egyptian wall-painting in Prisse d'Avennes II, Pl. LXIX.

2 = XCI, 4. Torso of a Cyprian limestone statue in dress of Egyptian style.

3. Girdle of Ramses II. From an Egyptian wall-painting Prisse d'Avennes.II. Pl. XLIII.

4. Similar girdle. From Prisse d'Avennes.

5 = p. 195, Fig. 168. Fragment of a stone statue from Cyprus. New-York. Cesnola, Atlas, Pl. XXII, 50. Perrot III, p. 534, Fig. 360. Cf. p. 193 and 211, note 1.

6 = p. 193, Fig. 166. Stone torso of a colossal statue found between Tyre and Sidon. Longpérier Musée Napoléon, Pl. XVIII, 1, = Perrot III, 428, Fig. 302. Cf p. 192.

Plate CXLI.

1. Bronze breast corslet which was found at Olympia in the Alpheios. Murray, Handbook of Archaeol. p. 122, Fig. 52. = Furtwängler, „Bronzen von Olympia", p. 154, Pl. LIX, = Helbig, „Homerisches Epos", p. 175.

I believe the mail-coat to be an early Greek piece of work, in which there are still many traces of Graeco-Phoenician and Oriental-Cyprian tradition. But if the mail-coat was not made on Greek soil (as Murray, Handbook, p. 123, thinks), I believe it much more propably was made in Cyprus. Cf..2 and 5 and the following plates.

2 = Fig. 103, p. 75; cf. Pl. XXV, 1—4.

3 = Fig. 134, p. 94. Large amphora from Ormidhia. Perrot III, p. 711, Fig. 523. Cf. p. 96—100, 122, 158.

4 = Fig. 101, p. 75. Piece of mail-armour from the sanctuary of Anat-Athene at Idalion (No. 28 on the list). Perrot III, p. 867, Fig. 633. Cf. p. 15, 76, 201 and Pl. LXIX, 11.

5 = Graved design from a gold ring. From Cesnola-Stern, Pl. LXXIV, 2.

Plate CXLII.

1. (No number). Upper portion of the body of a warrior. Cyprian terra-cotta of the original size. Perrot III, p. 595, Fig. 406.

2 = XXV, 6 = C, 2.

3. XXXII, 9, = LXXVIII, 13.

4. XXXII, 7 = LXXVII, 13.

5a and b. Bronze shield from Kurion. Cesnola-Stern, Pl. LII = Perrot III, p. 871, Fig. 639.

6 = XCIX, 8. Cf. Pl. XXV, 1—4.

Excursus to Pl. CXL—CXLII.

The Cyprian shields*) CXXXVII, 6 and CXLII, 5, helmets CXXXVII, 6 and CXLII, 1**), mail coats (same Fig. CXLII, 1, cf. further CXLI, 4 and LXX) and girdles (CXLII, 6 possible women's girdles CXXXVII, 6, men's girdles with fringes), the swords (CIV, 3 CXXXVII, 6 and 7), spears (CXXXVII, 6) and battle axes (CXXXVI, 4, CXXXVII, 6), all these remind us by their shape and ornaments of the Homeric times (cf. the Excursus on the Homeric swords Pl. CXXXVII). We must briefly consider once more, though without going into detail, one coat of mail only, the most artistic of antiquity, i. e. that very mail coat of Agamemnon's which he received as a guest gift from King Kinyras of Cyprus.***) The mail coat was adorned on either side with three snakes worked in cyanos, which upreared their heads in the direction of the opening of the neck. We must conceive of this mail coat, manufactured as it was in Cyprus, as of a style that imitated that of Egypt, either like the coats and aprons in Pl. CXL, 1 (from Egypt), 2, 5, 7 (from Cyprus), 6 (from Phoenicia) or like the Cyprian mail coats (CXLII, 1) or made up of plates of mail in Egyptian style like the Cyprian specimens (Pl. CXLI, 4, LXX).

Plate CXLIII.

1. Egyptian signet ring. Prisse d'Avennes II (choix des bijoux) Analogous swivel-rings from Cyprus. Pl. CLXXXII, 41—43.

2 = XCIII, 11.

---

*) One of these I found at Tamassos in 1889.
**) A helmet of this same shape found at Tamassos in 1889.
***) Cf. Helbig. "Das Homerische Epos". p. 382,

3. Etruscan gold ornament from Monumenti inediti dell' Istituto 1854, Fig. 4, Pl. XXIV. Motive and technique of this curious and beautiful ornamental chain of Graeco-Phoenician style point as much to Egypt as to Cyprus.

4. Gold Etruscan fibula from Vulci taken from the same publication as 2.

5, 6. Two Egyptian earrings of gold. From same publication as 3 and 4.

7, 9. Egyptian ornament like 1. Prisse d'Avennes op. cit.

Note to Nos. 5—9. All these kinds of earrings make their appearance in Cyprus. The types 5—7 are very frequent, e. g. Pl. CLXXXII, 8 and 9 and CCXVII, Fig. 13—17. Akin to type 9 (which however appears in scarcely the same way in Cyprus) is the very early type which occurs so frequently in Cyprus, Pl. CLXXXII, 1. These earrings most forcibly call to mind Homer's epithet μορόεντα and challenge the comparison with mulberries or blackberries in an equal or even greater degree than the Etruscan earrings "orecchini a baule" (cf. "Helbig Homerisches Epos", p. 273. Fig. 95 and 96, and the specimens also Etruscan published in the same work, p. 274, Figs. 97 and 98) In Cesnola-Stern, Pl. VI an earring is figured, the decoration of which justifies, more than any other specimen I am acquainted with, a comparison with Homer. For the type with the Lotus flower (Fig. 8) cf. Salaminia Pl. I, 26.

Plate CXLIV.

°1—10. Separate portions of the necklace put together in Pl. LXVII; 2, 3 and 5 also = XXXIII, 18—20.

† 11. A gold forehead band hitherto unpublished from a Hellenistic grave in Tamassos. Coll. Nikolaides Nicosia. A drawing from the original by Mr. C. Konstantinides reproduced in zincophotography.

12. Etruscan bronze ornament from Corneto in the form of a fibula to which a pendant is attached.

With this should be compared the earrings from Hissarlik one of which is published in Ilios, p. 542, Fig. 822 and 823, p. 559, Fig. 920 and further the Cyprian ear and breast pendants from Kurion Pl. LXIV.

°13. Gold mouth from Marion-Arsinoë (cf. Pl. CLXXXII, 33).

The mouth here figured was excavated together with the gold ornaments that appear on Pl XXXIII, 9—15, from grave 24 Nekr. I. I was the first to discover these plates of gold and silver in the form of a mouth. So far they have only been found in the cemeteries of Marion-Arsinoë but there they have been discovered in numbers and several replicas have been found after my time in the same place by the English who were working for the Cyprus Exploration Fund.

°14—17. Like 1—10.

18—19. Egyptian ornaments. Prisse d'Avennes II, Choix des bijoux.

The only parallels so far known to me to these Egyptian gold chain links in the form of flies and bees are a gold bee found in Rhodes (Perrot III, p. 829, Fig. 592), a gold fly perched in a silver ring, which I excavated together with the Pasiades-Alabastron at Marion-Arsinoë, and the gold ornament from the Island of Melos (Pl. XCVI, 11).

20. Hands of a woman from an Egyptian mummy case in the British Museum. Wilkinson Birch II, 341. Fig. 447 = Riehm, Bibellexikon II, p. 1295. Besides the subject the technique is similar in all three objects and shows how the Graeco-Phoenician and Greek goldsmiths learnt from those of Egypt. The hands in Cyprian monuments e. g. the hand of the terra-cotta statue in Pl. LII, 4 should be compared with these hands covered with rings from the Egyptian monument.

The attire of Jewish women in the time of Isaiah, 740 B. C.

In Isaiah III, 18- 23, we read;

"In that day the Lord will take away the bravery of their tinkling ornaments about their feet, and their cauls, and their round tires like the moon, the chains and the bracelets and the mufflers, the bonnets and the ornaments of the legs, and the headbands, and the tablets and the earrings, the rings and nose jewels, the changeable suits of apparel, and the mantles and the wimples and the crisping pins, the glasses and the fine linen and the hoods and the vails."

The antiquities of Cyprus are so far the only ones that correspond with this description in all details and with ample completeness, and which show excessive wealth in ornaments for head, hair, ears, nose, neck, breast, arm, fingers, foot and toes. Toes as well as fingers are all covered with rings (e. g. Pl. LII, 8 - 10), Cf. for the nose rings, Pl. LV, for anklets Pl. CCIV, 1—3, g. 816, Fig. 233.

Plate CXLV.

1. Museo Italiano II, 1888, Sp. 730 and Atlas, Pl. XI, 1 and 5. Fragment of a curious piece of bronze work broken in two in which there is a ship with its crew and two genre scenes placed near it which comprise the human figure and animals as well as a palmette of the simplest sort.

Nothing like this has indeed been so far found in Cyprus, but the style of the figure is like the Cyprian ones (cf. the bronzes in Pl. XLIII, 4, 6 and 7 and Pl. CXXVII, 1—2, CXXXI, 1—4.

2. Sardinian votive boat of bronze. Perrot IV, p. 84, Fig. 83.

3 = XCVIII, 9.
4. Clay galley from Amathus, Perrot III, p. 517, Fig. 352.
5. Bronze ship from the grave of a warrior from Vetulonia. American Journal of Archaeology IV, 1888, Pl. X, A. Found together with the bronze casket and the silver vessel in Pl. XCV, 1 and 2. This object also may have come from Cyprus.
‡6. Clay boat from Amathus, cf. p. 218.
7. Clay galley from Cyprus. Presumably from Amathus. Catalogue Barre 1878, p. 20, Fig. 154.

Kinyras, the clay ships of Amathus and the Trojan war.

Heuzey (Figurines Antiques p. 116), being the first to follow Engel, again called attention to the commentary of Eustathios in Iliad XI, 20 (cf. also Perrot III, p. 516) where a story is narrated which, by means of the discovery of these archaic clay ships, gets a footing on real ground. Kinyras, King of Amathus, had promised ships to the Greeks for the siege of Troy. When he repented of his promise he sent in place of real ships a flotilla of little clay ships with warriors made of clay for crew. That these ships of clay have so far only been found in Amathus is all the more remarkable and seems to point to the fact that the making of clay figures was practised early in Cyprus and that these clay figures were famous. The clay ships seem to have drawn upon them the eyes of other nations in early days.

Plate CXLVI.

1A—9A. Objects from Troja-Hissarlik, all from Schliemann's Ilios. 4A from Schliemannn's Troja.
°1B—9B. From Kypros. From the nekropolis of Hagia Paraskevi, which belonged to the ancient town of Ledrai-Lidir, all from the Journal of Cyprian Studies.
1Aa. Ilios, p. 51, fig. 848. 1Ab. Ilios, p. 564, fig. 932.
1B. Kypros. Hagia Paraskevi.
Similar pins, made of copper or bronze with a slight alloy of tin from both places.
2A. Illios, p. 284, fig. 121.
2B. Kypros Hagia Paraskevi. In my possession.
The same pins or distaffs. Of silver in Troy, of bronze in Cyprus.
3Aa. Ilios p. 530, fig. 808; b, Ilios p. 531, fig. 810; c, p. 554, fig. 878; d, p. 588, fig. 811. The weapons of bronze, the spirals (c) of gold.
3B. Cyprus. a—l, Phönitschäs, a—d, g and l copper or bronze slightly alloyed with tin. e and f clay idols with incised ornaments, k and h, vase and bird with young, made of the same pale clay, with painted geometric patterns in dull black; i, vase with animal head and leaf-shaped spout of dull black clay. The vases and idols are only published together here because they were all found together at Phönitschäs. m and o, spirals from Hagia Paraskevi, made of silver and in my possession;*) p, two views of spirals of gold, q, made of fine, quite transparent glass, of greenish water-colour. The same provenance as m, o and p, from collection Konstantinides. q passed from my hands to the collection of Tischler (now dead) in Königsberg.
3Bn. Bronze pin with curious wire first wound up and then tied in a loop. Below another view of this pin head.
We observe the same arms and ornamental objects in gold, silver, copper and bronze, in Hissarlik as appear in Cyprus.
4A. Schliemann's Troja, p. 152, fig. 64. Copper and bronze.
4B, a and b. Kypros H. Par. (Cf. 3B/g from Phoenitschäs). Copper or bronze.
5A, a—d. Ilios 514, Figs. 705—708.
5B, a and b. Gold. In a, on the left side, is the gold setting on the cylinder with cuneiform inscriptions. H. Par. (Cf. p. 34 and 35, Figs. 34—36.)
At the time when I excavated the cylinder with the gold setting, both the hollow pegs of this mushroom-shaped gold setting were intact their whole length. The smaller tube of the one was inserted in the larger tube of the other, and both were in the perforation of the cylinder. Thus the owner of the cylinder, when he wanted to use the signet-cylinder merely as an ornament, could pass the gold setting over the cylinder ends into the hollow passage and push the two mushroom-shaped ornaments one inside the other. A thin cord was then passed through the stone cylinder and the gold setting, and if the owner wanted to affix his seal he first pulled pulled out the cord, then the gold ornaments, one inside the other, and then could make use of the cylinder for sealing.
5Bb also is a portion of half of the large gold setting of a seal. From this it is evident that the gold ornaments of Hissarlik (5A, a—d) are not earrings, as Schliemann and others suggest, but the settings of

---

*) Silver is rare in Cyprus during the copper-bronze period, but still much more frequent than gold, which is exceedingly rare. This silver is distinguished from that of the Graeco-Phoenician iron-period by its greater purity and the smaller amount of lead it contains. While the Graeco-Phoenician silver with its large content of lead oxydizes more homogeneously and is not so friable but takes on a grey, black or blue-black colour, the pre-Greek silver of the copper-bronze period oxydizes and crumbles away into layers and flakes but also takes on a very white colour. I am able from the external appearance of the oxydisation to distinguish between the two sorts of silver.

cylinders, which have also been found at Hissarlik in considerable numbers made of stone, clay and ivory.*) Or they may be the settings of clay beads, like the one figured in Pl. CLXXIII, 22, which belongs to the same early date and comes from the same nekropolis.

6 B, a - s (dimensions given below in English measure). Objects from Hagia Paraskevi in Bronze consisting of copper and a small proportion of tim.

1, q. r, s. Axe of the usual shape for stone axes, like 3 B, d. Phönitschäs, 3 A, b Hissarlik.

k, i. Small daggers with holes in the haft for fastening like 3 B, c Phönitschäs, exactly similar ones at Hissarlik. Also daggers with wedged-shaped points like 3 A, a, and not unfrequently in Cyprus.

d, e, H, Par. 3 B, a, b. Phönitschäs—also at Hissarlik 3 A, d.

f. Spear-heads with hollow tubes are not found at all in Hissarlik, nor in the older strata of the copper-bronze period; they also are never found in strata where the painted decoration of vases is absent. They appear in Cyprus, together with the Mykenae vases, which were imported about 1500 B. C. This is the case with the present examples. H. Par. In Mykenae, as is well known, they abound.

a, b. Portions of bronze and copper swords. In the oldest strata in Cyprus, as in Hissarlik, these do not occur at all. H. Par.

c. Cross Section of a dagger composed of two blades, melted and nailed together. H. Par.

g. Needle. H. Par. Just the same sort found at Hissarlik.

h. Upper part of a dagger of curious shape. H. Par.

m, n. Awls. H. Par. Same at Hissarlik.

p. Pincers for pulling out hair. H. Par. Not found in the earlier strata in Cyprus nor at all at Hissarlik. Often occur in the stratum in which are found imported vases from Mycenae. A silver specimen from Mycenae in Pl. CL, 2.

o. Pin, nail or hand-spindle (?) of peculiar shape, lower part broken away. The hold broadens out in the middle or in the upper third and is pierced through diametrically with a slit-shaped hole as in 4 A, Hissarlik. 4 B, a and b, Hagia Paraskevi. 3 B, g Phönitschäs**). Toy common in Cyprus. In the earliest strata of all this object never occurs. It appears first in Cyprus at the bronze period and goes right down to its end.***) It has besides been noted in Egypt and in the earlier bronze period of Italy.

7 A. Ivory tube from Hissarlik. Ilios p. 474, Fig. 525.

7 B, a, b, c. Ivory tubes from Cyprus. H. Par.

7 B, e. Terra-cotta seal of hemispherical shape. Similar ones at Hissarlik.

d. Clay bead with incised wickerwork pattern from a grave of the bronze period containing Mykenae vases. Identical beads from Ialysos, published by Furtwängler and Loeschcke, Myken. Vasen, Pl. A, 12.

8 A. Bone-awls from Hissarlik. Ilios 295, 123.

8 B, a—d, g—i. Small ivory objects found together with e in H. Par.

e. Lilliputian double-axe, Agalmatolithic, also from Hagia Paraskevi.†)

f. Small cylinder of blue glazed, but dull coloured clay. H. Par. later bronze period like 7 B, d.

9 A. Grindstone from Hissarlik. H. 281, 101.

9 B, a—d. Grindstones from Cyprus. H. Par. They are more frequent in Cyprus than in Hissarlik, but are absolutely confined to the bronze period.

For the whorls and vases with figures and ornaments partly incised, partly applied in relief, cf. supra p. 58—60, Fig. 57—66 and Pl. XXVIII, Fig. 3—6.

Plate CXLVII.

1, 3, 5, 7. Hissarlik-Troja from Schliemann's Ilios.

2, 4, 6, 8. Cyprus. With the exception of 7—8 clay vessels.

7a. Corn-grinder or hand-mill, made of Trachite from Hissarlik. Ilios 496, 678. Most of them are of green-stone.

8. Hand-mill from the town of the bronze period, near Psematismeno. Of green-stone. In shape and size indentical with the Trojan specimens. Cf. CLXIV, e—h hand-mills from the Acropolis of Lidir-Ledrai.

These hand-mills or corn-grinders were sometimes even placed with the dead in their graves. Every settlement in Cyprus of the bronze period is recognisable by the frequent presence of these stones. Sometimes the surface of the ruined place is simply strewn with them.

---

*) As with the silver, so the gold of the Cyprian copper-bronze period differs from that of the Graeco-Phoenician iron period by its greater softness and purity and by its red tint. Only the earliest Graeco-Phoenician objects in gold of the date 600 B. C. resemble the gold objects of the copper-bronze period in tint and chemical composition.

**) This place Phönikais, so-called from the palms that grew in the valley is pronounced Phönitschäs or Phönidsches by the Cypriotes.

***) Several of these in gold and silver were found by Flinders Petrie in Egypt and point to the 12th century B. C. But in Cyprus this object which is found so frequently goes back to a much earlier date.

†) Agalmatolithic ornaments occur in isolated instances in the bronze period. The early Graeco-Phoenician iron period tomb with the bronze fibula (Fig. 260) contained several agalmatolithic ornaments and seals.

1 h. Two-handled drinking cup from Hissarlik. Ilios 416, 320—not found in Cyprus.
2 b. Long one-handled cup which takes its place, not found at Hissarlik.
1 d. Hissarlik. Ilios 456, 470.
1 f. Similar. 457, 475.
2 a—g. Cyprus. H. Par. Crucibles, funnel-, trowel- and spoon-shaped vessels—same kinds found in both places.
2 k. Cyprus. H. Par. Tripod. At Hissarlik similar tripods not precisely identical. The Cyprian kind always have two large handles of unequal size.
1 i. Kylix from Hissarlik. Ilios 247, 38. Similar kylikes but varying in clay and technique in Pl. CXLVIII, 11 c.
2 l and m. Cyprus. H. Par. Kylikes which differ still more in shape.
5a. Tripod from Hissarlik. Ilios 251, 44. From the deepest stratum.
?6a. Kypros. H. Par. Identical in shape but of different clay. (Cf. the same vessel, p. 34, Fig. 34 = Pl. CLXXI, 14.)
3 b. Fragment of a milk vessel from Hissarlik, from the earliest stratum. Rare. Ilios, p. 245, Fig. 34.
4 a. Very rude, two-handled water-jug from Psemmatismeno, original model of the Greek amphora. Similar rude vessel also found at Hissarlik.
4 b, c. Fragment of a Cyprian milk-bowl from a grave of the copper-bronze period, from Psemmatismeno. Common throughout the whole island. From H. Paraskevi, Pl. CXLVIII, 7 a, 12 f, g, CXLVIII, 4 b, 5 a and a.
3 d. Jug from Hissarlik. II. 425, 345.
4 d. Similar one from Cyprus. Psemmatismeno.
2 i. From Hagia Paraskevi.
There are a quantity of vases from both places, identical in shape. They are also sometimes very similar in clay and technique. Spite of this, there remain certain local distinctions that show that the Hissarlik specimens are made at Hissarlik, those of Cyprus in Cyprus.
5 b. Animal-shaped vase from Hissarlik. Ilios 332, 160.
6 b. Same from Cyprus. H. Par. Red, polished clay, incised ornamentation. There are found at both places many of this sort that are very similar.
In Cyprus these animal-shaped vases went on being made down to the later bronze period. They were painted and taken over and modified by Graeco-Phoenician ceramography at the time of the Cyprian iron period. Cf. e. g. Pl. CXLVI, 3 B, h, XCVIII, 6, &c.

Plate CXLVIII.

1—6. Hissarlik. Ilios 432, 362; 438, 389; 486, 379; 332, 161; 603, 1110: 431, 359.
7 = CLXVIII, 5, 8 = CLXIX, 6, 9 = CLXXIII, 23; 10 = CLXX, 9; = CLXXII, 18; 12 = CLXIX, 8, f, g and b. Cyprus. Where ornamentation is present it is either deeply incised or laid on in relief; 9 c, 10 c and e are painted. These three vessels, together with 11 and 9 a, belong to the later bronze period. The great analogies, but also the differences, between the ceramic products of the two centres of civilisation are thus brought clearly into relief.
The vessel 9 c is a transition stage to Thera, where an identical or at least very similar vase was found beneath the pumice-stone *). Cf. CLII, 6.
The vessel 10 c is repeated in Pl. CLII, 23. It belongs to the group of Cyprian hand-made vases figured (with the exception of 10 g), in Pl. CLXX. These are covered with a glaze of bright red, and the ornament is geometric and consists only of bands, zig-zag, wicker and chess-board patterns. In this Cyprian style, which I was the first to call attention to, the Cyprian potter is imitating the coloured glaze of the Mykenae ware, but he has not taken on their patterns or their use of the wheel.
Thus we find in Cyprus, many earlier stages preliminary to those disclosed by the oldest strata at Hissarlik, and within the limits of the island we have come upon a continuous series of strata, which lead us on to the Mykenae, or an allied period, and from thence step by step downwards to Graeco-Phoenician days.

Plate CXLIX.

1—11, 13—22. Cyprus.
12. Hissarlik. Cask-shaped vessel II, 451, 489. Cf. Cyprus, Fig. 1 and supra Pl. XXXV, 1 and 3, infra Pl. CCXVI, 32. Schliemann has already called attention to the Cyprian analogies. The Graeco-Phoenician period maintains this cask-shape in Cyprus, and modifies it further. H. e. g. Pl. LXXIV, 5, CCXVI, 25.

---

*) Furtwängler and Löschcke. Mykenische Vasen p. 22 and Pl. XII, 80.

1. Cf. XXXV, 1 and 3 and CCXVI, 32. Incised ornament. H. Par.

2 and 7 = p. 275, Fig. 183 and 184. H. Par.

3, 4 and 8. Other frequently occurring Cyprian shapes of the copper-bronze period. H. Par.

5. Another clay spoon. Cf. Pl. CXLVII, 1 f and 2 f.

7 = p. 29, Fig. 3.

9 = XXXVI, 7.

10 = CXLVIII, 11 b. Similar vases with horns in relief, or with a symbol that has been taken for the Cyprian Ko are found at Hissarlik. (Ilios p. 386 and 387, Fig. 233 and a.)

11 = CCXIII, 7a. Clay whorl or distaff top. H. Par. Cf. similar cups strung together in compartments, formerly at Hissarlik, p. 598, Fig. 1083.

13. Above, a huge amphora of grey clay from the copper-bronze period. From Alambra. On either side, in the neck there is a horned quadruped of linear-style. Below, there runs round the vase in relief the spectacle or bead-string ornament. Cf. Pl. XXVIII, 6.

Below, a figure of a stag from similar vases with relief, the body is made of the spectacle ornament. A chevrenil in the linear style.

14c = XCIV, 9. The whole vase covered with red polish. H. 0,75 m—14a and b portions of the same on a larger scale.

15a. A vase in the shape of a three-legged, headless bird. Incised ornament. Cf. CXLVII, 5 b and 6 b.

b = p. 275, Fig. 186.

c = p. 275, Fig. 185.

d = ib. 177.

e = 178.

Described above p. 275.

16. Spheres of diorite highly polished and perforated, Diameter circ. 0,046—0,05 m. The perforation is wider at one side than at the other. These occur frequently in Cyprus in the second half of copper-bronze period. Common at Hissarlik. Not uncommon at Ialysos. Furtwängler-Löschcke, Myk. Vasen. Pl. B, 22.

17. Limestone hammer only, with small perforation 0,045 m long. H. Par. Similar ones at Hissarlik. Stone hammers with partial perforation occur in both places.

18. Similar hammer of green-stone 0,086 m long. H. Par.

19. Polished stone chisel from Karpaso 0,038 m long. Coll. E. Konstantinides, Nicosia.

20. Polished stone hammer of green-stone from H. Paraskevi. In my possession 0,08 m long, and up to 0,035 broad. Similar ones at Hissarlik.

Plate CL.

1, 3–9, 11—22. Cyprus.

2 and 10. Mykenae. All of clay, except 2 of silver.

For 2 cf. Pl. CXLVI, 6 B, p. Schliemann, "Mykenae". 352, 469.

? 1. Shoulder of a Graeco-Phoenician, Cyprian vase of red brown clay, painted in black and white body colour. Marion-Arsinoë 1886. Berl. Mus. The vase belongs to the 6th century B. C. The drawing of the palm still shows the influence of the palms of the Mykene style. Cf. CLI. 1.

‡ 3—6. Vases from the Cyprian bronze-period which were found together with genuine Mykenae vessels. H. Paraskevi. Made of black or black-brown clay with a dull glaze, decorated in geometric patterns with white body-colour. Horizontal, oblique, curved and zig-zag bands. Occasional dotted rosettes. While vase 5 is hand-made and of pure Cyprian shape, vases 3 and 4 and 6 have been incompletely turned on the wheel. Shapes 3 and 4 are genuine Mykenae. Shape 6 also occurs in Mykenae pottery (Furtwängler-Löschcke XLIV, 105.)

‡ 7. Example of a class of vase common at the same date. Grey-black pattern on red ground. H. Par.

? 8. Neck of vase with eyes in relief. Cf. Pl. CLXXII, 17q, and Pl. CCXVII, 17. From Katydata-Linu.

9. Flat-pressed, hand-made bottle. Technique like 3—6. H. Par.

10. Hand-made vase with dull coloured painting Mykenae. Furtwängler-Löschcke, Myk. Thongefässe, Pl IV, 13. Exactly the same class of vase and with the same geometric patterns occurs frequently in Cyprus.

‡ 11. Cyprian vase, now in Smyrna. Technique like CXLVIII, 9c.

? 12—15. Vases from Phoenitschäs. Now in the British Museum.

12. Cylix with horizontal, perforated ear-handles. A class which takes the place, in the later bronze-period of the milk-bowls with the vertical pairs of holes. (CLXVIII, 4 b.)

13. Like CXLVII, 2 h.

14. Small painted bottle, with ear-handles characteristic of the bronze-period of the island.*) (Cf. Pl. CLXXI, 14d.)
15. Another small cylix characteristic both in shape and painted decoration, divided into four spaces with four eyes.
16. Diminutive vessel, a greenish-grey clay, painted black in geometric style. Two necks. Hagia Paraskevi.
? 17. Vessel of red polished clay, closed at the top. At the side a small spout, broken off. Shape same as 20, with ear-handles ornament, and filled in with white. From a stratum that is much older than the ware known as Mykenaean. Clearly the transition stage to the "false-necked amphora". From an earthen grave in Hagia Paraskevi. Certainly belongs to the copper-period.
? 18. Flat bottle, with numerous ear-handles, and reed-shaped neck which is cut off where the larger handle joins in. A class of vase characteristic of the bronze-period. Phönitschäs.
19—20, belong to the close of the bronze-period. H. Par.
19 = Pl. CCXVI, 31.
20. Formerly painted.
21 and 22. Modern Cyprian vessels which show survival of ancient shapes.
21. Drawn in section to show the mechanism. A vessel closed at the top, which was filled from the bottom, and then suddenly turned over. Vessels with this same arrangement appear in Graeco-Phoenician pottery, in the period between 600 and 1000 B. C. One is figured in Salaminia p. 275, Fig. 269. I excavated a similar one, but with stirrup-shaped handles and painted water birds, at the same time as the Tamassos vase, p. 37, Fig. 88.

Plate CLI.

? 1. Shoulder of a vase like CL, 1, from Marion Arsinoë. Berl. Mus. Sixth century B. C.
† 2 = 4 = XXVIII, 9.
? 3 = p. 31. Fig. 34v = CLXXI, 14v.
† 5. Clay cylinder. H. Par.
† 6—10. 13—16. Beads, glazed and unglazed, from the bronze period. Similar to those discoveries at Ialysos, which fall within the same period. Mykenae pottery appears frequently at the same date.
? 11 = XXVIII, 10.
† 12. Stone cylinder. H. Par. With design of figures in linear style.
† 17. Bone object. H. Par.
† 18. Cyprian Stone cylinder with rude animals. H. Par.
† 19. Cyprian Stone cylinder, rude. H. Par.
† 20. Disc cut from a potsherd. H. Par. Similar discs at Hissarlik.
† 21. Curious flat stone bead with three perforations. H. Par.
† 22 Agalmatolite amulet. H. Par.
† 23. Fragment of recumbent figurine, of glass. Possibly a Sphinx? H. Par.
† 24. Upper part of a glass figurine, probably Egyptian. H. Par.
† 25 and 26. Rude Cyprian stone cylinders. H. Par.
† 27. Short bronze or copper thrusting sword.
† 28 = XXXI, 6.
† 29—31. Rude Cyprian stone cylinders.
† 32 = XXXI, 13.
† 33 = XXXI, 11.
† 34 = CXCIV, 4. Seal-impress of an ancient Babylonian cylinder made of onyx and found in Cyprus with the cylinder p. 83, Fig 111.
† 35. Engraved seal-plate of a heavy elektron ring. From an early bronze period grave of Hagia Paraskevi.

S. Birch. saw this ring, which belonged to me, in London in 1884 and he also believed it to be an ancient Babylonian one. His assistant, Budge, showed me analogous Babylonian gems. Two divinities, the sun-god Baal and the moon-goddess Baaltis, are seated on thrones and hold staves. Above is the moon disc, below the sun. Discussed p. 198 on CLI, 34.

Plate CLII.

As far as the Mykenae fragment Fig. 14 (from Furtwängler-Löschke Pl. XLI, 423) exclusively objects found in Cyprus.

*) According to the analyses which I owe to the kindness of Herr Prof. Weeren, Director of the metallurgical laboratory in the Technical High School, the Graeco-Phoenician copper-bronze period must without doubt be divided into a copper and a bronze period. In the cases here and later where I speak of a bronze period I mean the second great principal division of the time that precedes the iron period.

59

1, 2, 4, 5, 7, 8 (right), 16. Eight Mykenae vases from Cyprus. 8 (right) = CCXVI, 24. 16 = p. 34, Fig. 33. H. Par. and Phönitschäs.

3. Example of the latest bronze period vase style with reliefs. Dull-reddish brown clay. Different from the early relief-vases. H. Par.

6. Cf. CXLVIII, 9 c.

8. (Left.) Same technique and class of vase as CLXX, 10g. Hand-made Cyprian vases. Shape and ornament Cyprian. The clay which is apt to crack **is like that of the Dipylon vases.** Brown decoration .on light yellow ground. The vases have a moderate uniform glaze. Both vases 8, the Mykenae to the right, and the Cyprian to the left, are from the same grave at Phönitschäs. British Museum.

9. A ring-shaped clay vessel drawn from below. H. Par. Cyprian fabrique, but with polished glaze and colour like 13.

10. Lid with painted glaze. H. Par. Intended to be tied on to a vessel.

9—10. Show transition shapes from the stratum contemporaneous with Hissarlik to that contemporaneous with Mykenae in Cyprus. Two further examples are selected as representative of many.

11. Cyprian vase. H. Par. Reminiscences of Mykenae shapes and technique.

12. Cyprian vase. H. Par. Dull clay. In shape resembles vases of absolutely Mykenae style and bright clay, in painting resembles Mykenae vases of dull clay. Furtwängler and Löschcke, Myk. Vas. XLIV, 57 and 62, and our Plate CL, 10.

13 = CXLVIII, 10c.

15. Egyptian scarabaeus found in the ox-krater-grave 16 (16 = p. 34, Fig. 33) Berl. Mus.

17. Early Graeco-Phoenician Scarabaeus from Lapithos. Coll. E. Konstantinides.

18. Proto-Corinthian vase, found in an early Graeco-Phoenician grave at Limassol. Cyprus Museum.

19 = p. 38, Fig. 39.

Cf. the late Mykenae vases e. g. Furtwängler-Löschcke, Myk. Vas. Pl. XXXVIII, Fig. 393.

?20. Small cup (kyathos-shaped) excavated by me at Marion-Arsinoë. Nekr. II. Gr. 21. Sixth century B. C. The shape is influenced by Mykenaean tradition.

?21. Same provenance. Marion - Arsinoë 1886. Nekr. II, Gr. 194. H. 0,303 m. Here, too the triple ornament is borrowed form the Mykenae originals.*)

Plate CLIII—CLIV.

The cypress on the monuments of various peoples.

Plate CLIII.

1. Egyptian monument. Restored in Ptolemaic times, Rosellini, Monum. d. Egitto III, Pl. LVI, 3. Five small cypress trees on an altar near to the god Min, as in Fig. 98, p. 74 and Fig. 101, p. 75 = CXXII, 1. The king offers to the God two small cypresses i. e. small votive trees, such as are so often excavated in Cyprus. Pl. LXXVI, 1—12, 7 = CLIV, 3 = XVII, 1.

2 = LXXXVII, 12.

3a and b. Cyprian vase = LXXIII, 5 and 8.

4 = Fig. 110, p. 83. Babylonian cylinder of the British Museum. Lajard, "Culte du cyprès." Pl. IX, 2 = Lajard Mithra XV, 7. Described p. 82—83; cf. also p. 96 und 246.

5. Assyrian relief from Kujundschik. A little shrine in a park in which there are cypress trees and an undergrowth of leafy shrubs. Perrot II, p. 143, Fig. 42.

6. Babylonian cylinder. Lajard. "Culte du cyprès", Pl. IX, 4. Secret worship before a seated divinity behind whom towers a cypress.

Plate CLIV.

1. Egyptian wall-painting. Procession and ritual ceremonial. Wilkinson-Birch, "Manners and customs of the ancient Egyptians" III, p. 355, Pl. LX; the cypress-bearers alone op. cit. III, p. 404, Fig. 173.

---

*) Cf. Herrmann 48. Winkelmann programm, pp. 15 and 16.

It seems to have been the custom in Egypt to place a number of these little cypresses both natural and artificial on and beside the altar of Min as it was in Cyprian sanctuaries.

2. Later silver cylikes probably of Roman date. Lajard, "Culte du Cyprès." Pl. VI, 6a.

Two cypresses stand about an altar in the shape of a double sphere. Close at hand stands a cultus-pillar surmounted by a vase. Cf. the cylinder in Pl. CLIII, 2.

3 = XVII, 1 = LXXVI, 7.

The cult of cypress trees played an important part in the worship of antiquity. The name Beirut or Berut, still used to denote the well-known town on the coast of Syria, seems to come from the Hebrew word for cypress. On the other hand the Greek word for cypress κυπάρισσος which passes over into the Latin, German and other tongues is derived from the name of the island κύπος, evidence enough as to the great importance of the cypress groves in Cyprus from remote antiquity. The variety of the tree which is now indigenous to the island is not Cypressus Sempervirens but Cupressus Horizontalis. Hehn's statement ("Kulturpflanzen and Hausthiere" p. 228) is therefore incorrect.

Plate CLV—CLVIII.

Palms on the monuments of various peoples.

Plate CLV.

1 = Fig. 112, p. 88. Assyrian cylinder in the British Museum. Lajard, "Mithra", Pl. XVIII, 2 = Lajard, "Cyprès", IX, 5, described p. 88—89; cf. also p. 179 and 182.

2 Syrian cylinder probably Hittite. Menant Glyptique II, p. 115, Fig. 109 = American Journal of Arch. 1888, p. 133, Fig. 13. A winged animal-taming god (inscribed Marduk) stands on two winged animals. Close by three palms which grow out of a table. Cf. p. 284, Note 1 and 320—321.

3 Altar, tripod and palm from a red-figured Greek vase. Gerhard, Auserlesene Vasenbilder Pl. 224—226 centre design right.

4 = XXIII, 1c = Fig. 44, p. 42.

5. Palm from an Assyrian relief from Nineveh. "Layard, Monuments of Nineveh" Ser. I, Pl. XXIII = Perrot II, p. 617, Fig. 304.

6 = XXII, 2c = Fig. 45, p. 42.

7. Coin from Judaea, struck under Augustus Caesar; obverse palm; reverse palm-twig. Perrot IV, p. 308, Fig. 158.

8. Egyptian image from time of King Tuet' anchamun.

Lepsius, Denkmäler III, 118 = Erman, "Aegypten und ägyptisches Leben im Alterthum" II, p. 663.

°9. Painting on the portion of the neck of a large Cyprian Graeco-Phoenician Amphora which I excavated for Newton in 1880 from a grave at Kition. Now in British Museum.

A sketch has been already published in my pamphlet "La croix gammée et la croix cantonnée à Chypre" in the "Bulletins de la Société d'anthropologie de Paris" 1888, p. 669—680, Fig. 3, cf. LXIX, 126.

10. Punic coins of Carthage with horse and palm, Perrot III, p. 365, Fig. 253.

11. Bronze coins of Jaddus of the 4th century B. C., Perrot IV, p. 308, Fig. 154 = Riehm, Bibel-lexikon I, p. 141, Reverse, palm between two small altars.

Many of the representations of palms figured in this plate resemble each other is such a striking way that involuntarily one asks if there is not some sort of typological connection. The most similar of all are the designs of the Hittite cylinder (Fig. 2) and those of the Cyprian vase where birds conventionalized in just the same manner are hovering round the trees. The palm-group also of the Egyptian design (Fig. 8) is remarkably similar. Again the palm of the Assyrian relief (Fig. 5) are very like the palms of the Cyprian (Fig. 4 and 6) and Greek (Fig. 3) vases. The palm played an important part in the worship and in the deco-rative art of the people of Syria and the Mediterranean. We have a Palm-Baal, the Baal Jamar of the Bible and the Palm-Merodach-Marduk (Fig. 2) and as a counterpart to these we have the Palm-Astarte-Aphrodite (p. 147, Fig. 145—148). In Etruria (Pl. CLVIII, 4) too the sacred palm stands behind the pair of seated goddesses who are so nearly related to the Cyprian pair (Pl. CCV, 1—3).

Plate CLVI.

1. Assyrian relief with a banqueting scene of Assurbanipal beneath palms cypresses and a bower of vines. Perrot II, p. 106—107, Fig. 27—28.

2. Graeco-Phoenician silver bowl found in Etruria. From the Regulini-Galassi-tomb. Perrot III, p. 769, Fig. 544. Hunting scene under palm and cypresses. In the medallion design four pillars stand behind a bull attacked by two lions.

This vessel also must have been made in Cyprus like the Amathus bowl of which I place one row side by side with it. (Cf. also the Idaliou bowl, p. 48, Fig. 51.)

3. A portion cut out from the Amathus bowl. (Cf. p. 47, Fig. 50.) Perrot III, p. 775, Fig. 537.

4. Belongs to XCVII, 4. Clay tripod from an early Graeco-Phoenician stratum in Cyprus. Cesnola-Stern, Pl. XCII, 3, discussed p. 288.

A palm grows by the side of one of the feet. The rude figure between the quadrupeds also holds a palm. I excavated two similar tripods with their respective cauldrons still ·in situ and that in an early Graeco-Phoenician-Cyprian tomb at Kurion (1882) together with several bow-shaped fibulae. Cf. supra p. 449 Excursus to Pl. CXXXIV, CXXXV and CXCVII, 2, 4, and 5. The head of the figure should be noted. It closely resembles the heads in early Attic pottery of oriental tendency. (Cf. e. g. the heads of the women in the chorus on the jug from Analatos, Jahrb. 1887, Pl. III.)

Plate CLVII.

1. Portion of the well-known gold cup from the Vaphio tomb. Tzuntas, *'Εφημερις Αρχαιολογικη* 1889, Pl. IX, 1. The scene of the capture of the bulls has palm tree accessories.

2 = XCVIII, 1. Mykenaean and Cyprian pottery found together in a tomb at Lapithos, a, b, in Berlin, c, d, e. f in the Cyprus Museum at Nicosia.

3. Part of a wooden relief of the Egyptian Museum at Berlin. From Furtwängler in Roscher's Mythol. Lexikon, I, Sp. 1745. Griffin running, behind a conventionalized palm.

4. (No. 4 is missing from the plate.) Part of a bronze vessel from Kition. Perrott III, p. 794, Fig. 555. In Pl. XXXII, 41 and XCVI, 12 the handle of the vase which here is seen above the brim and foreshortened, is given in profile.

I have here turned the portion of the vase round so that the row of bulls running behind each other can the better be compared with the bull of the Vaphio cup. If the Kition ware is somewhat later and really belongs to the beginning of the Graeco-Phoenician post-Mykenaean period, the beginning of this period still shows the marked influence of Mykenaean art and metal technique, as we see them in the Vaphio cups. In Pl. XXXII I have already compared the gem found in the same Vaphio tomb (1) with the handle of our bronze vessel from Kition (41). We noted the same mythical creatures carrying jugs.

Plate CLVIII.

1a and b. Graeco-Phoenician vase from Cyprus, Perrot III, p. 716—717, Fig. 527—528 = Helbig Hom. Ep. p. 136, Fig. 29. War-chariot with charioteer and archer. To the right a twig (of palm), to the left arrow symbol or arrow-ornament, discussed p. 854. Cf. supra p. 854.

2 = CL, 1.
3 = CLI, 1.
4 = XXXVIII, 14.
5 = LXXXI, 2.

In Pl. CLVI = CLVIII I have placed together a number of other designs with palms, from Assyrian, Mykenaean, Cyprian, Etruscan, Graeco-Phoenician monuments and one from Malta.

Plates CLIX—CLXIII.

A collection of antiquities from various countries which go to show that capitals which arose from Egyptian and Oriental designs, were employed by the Greeks in the formation of the Ionic capital.

Plate CLIX

1 = XXVI, 1.
2 = XXVI, 3.
3 = XXVI, 2.
4 = CXIII, 4.
5 = CXIII, 7.
6. Belongs to XXV, 1—2.
7. Ivory tablets from the palace of Asurnasirpal at Nimroud, Perrot II, p. 214, Fig. 129.
8 = LXXXII, 6.

Plate CLX.

1 = XCIV, 23 = CXXXIV, 5. The whole vase CXXXIV. 3.

2. = CXVII, 8.

3. Votive stele from Carthage. Perrot III, p. 461, Fig 336. A stele surmounted by a palm, flanked by two heralds' wands, cf. p. 196.

°4. Fragment of a silver girdle coated over with thin gold-leaf, excavated at Tamassos in 1889. Two small cypresses to either side of a conventionalized palm-pillar.

5. Portion of an Egyptian wall painting from the tomb of Amenhotep I. Rosellini Pl. LXXIV.

6. Egyptian wall-painting. Wilkinson-Birch III, p. 469, Pl. LXXI. The pillars which support the baldachino, are surmounted by capitals, which are borrowed and modified from Graeco-Phoenician art. Cf. especially Pl. CLXIII, 2 and 3. (Cf. p. 295, note).

Plate CLXI.

1. Part of the decoration of a regal chair from an Egyptian wall-painting of the 18th —20th Dynasty. Prisse d'Avennes II.

2. Part of a later Egyptian monument, from Prisse d'Avennes.

3 = Fig. 93, p. 71. Bouquet of flowers from an Egyptian monument of the 19—20 Dynasty. From Prisse d'Avennes II, discussed p. 71.

Plate CLXII.

1. Gold armlet from Kurion. Perrot III, p. 835, Eig. 600.

2. Mykenaean gold ornament. Schliemann, "Mykenae", p. 213, Fig. 278.

3. Egyptian gold ear-ring, from Prisse d'Avennes.

4. Cyprian armlet of gold, from Kurion. Perrot III, p. 835. Fig. 603.

°5 = Fig. 163, p. 189. Pillar from a grave at Tamassos. Cf. p. 131 (where the reference to us is erroneously given as Fig. 159).

°6 and °7. Stone decorations of the window niche in the inside of a tomb at Tamassos.

8 = XCIII, 8.

9 = CXLIII, 9.

10 = CXLIII, 8.

11. The decoration of an ostrich-egg from Polledrara. Perrot III, page 859. Fig. 627. Cf. plate CXVI, 12.

Plate CLXIII.

1 = LVIII, 1.

2. Portion of LXX, 3.

3. Portion of a pillar, from an Egyptian wall-painting. From Prisse d'Avennes. Perrot I, p. 543, Fig. 317.

4—6. Fragments of plates of carved ivory, found in Assyria at Nimroud in the north-west palace. American Journal of Arch. 1886, p. 10.

7. Group of pillars of the date of Thutmosis III. Prisse d'Avennes, Goodyear, Lotus, Pl. VII, 6.

8 = LXXVII, 17 = CXIII, 5.

9. Drawing from the remains of Ceccaldi. Ceccaldi, "Monuments antiques de Chypre" etc. Pl. XXI, 6 = Goodyear Pl. XV. 10. Seems to be the design of a capital that was found by H. Lang in the sanctuary of Resef-Apollo.

10. Capital from an archaic vase. American Journ. of Arch. 1886 p. 6 Fig. 8.

11 = Fig. 162, p. 188. Perrot III, p. 264, Fig. 198. Cf. p. 190.

12. Taken from the same publication as 10. Reconstruction of conjectural original wooden capital.

A glance at the designs-suffices to make clear what an important place Cyprus occupied in this series of types, and also how the impulse came from Egypt.

Those that have been found in Assyria (Nimroud) are worked in a style that copied the Egyptian (e. g. CLIX, 7) and therefore also point to Cyprus. (The Neandria capitals also belong to the same series cf. infra pl. CXCVII).

Plate CLXIV—CLXXIII.

Sketches of Lidir-Ledrai, the Acropolis with the King's palace on Leontari Vouno and the Necropolis of the lower town at Hagia Paraskevi.

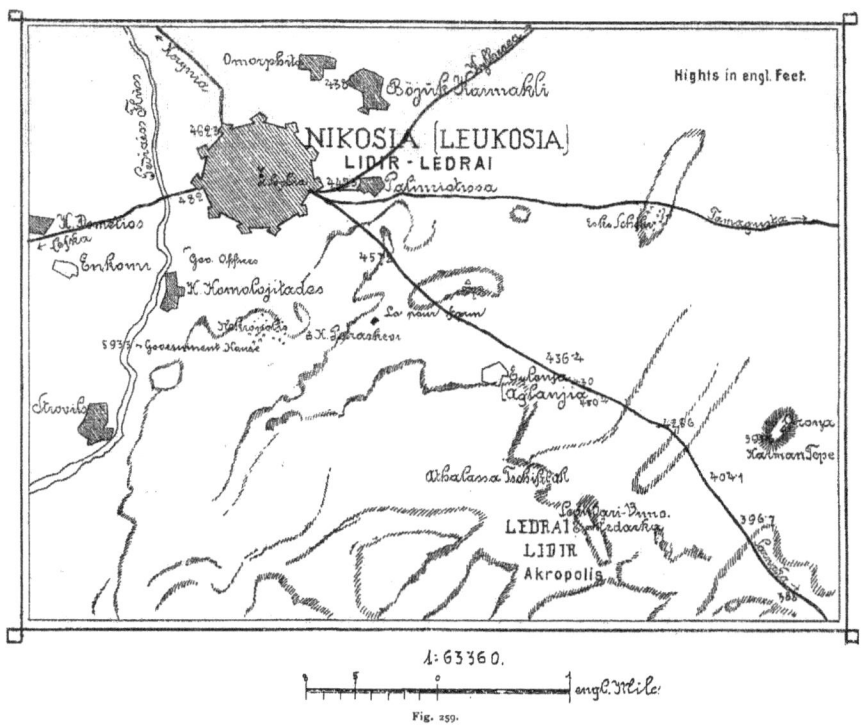

$1 : 63360.$

Fig. 259.

Plate CLXIV.

1. The plain with the table-land before the gates of the chief town of the island (cf. the map Fig. 259). The most prominent object in the view is the Akropolis of the town called by the Assyrians Lidir, by the Greeks Ledrai *) to the right. The mountain is now called by the Greeks Leontari Vouno or Drakendotopos. The view is taken from the North-west in the direction of Nicosia. The cutting in the long hill out-stretched behind the Akropolis is artificial and was made for the main road to Nicosia-Larnaka which runs through at that point.

---

*) In the plates which were prepared some time ago with the greatest care for my "Journal of Cyprian Studies" (alas! short lived!) I have preserved in part the English names and the English spelling. I accordingly write Leontari Vouno and Hagia Paraskevi, but in the small map, which has the names in English the form, Leontari Vuno appears again.

Engel (Kypros I, 152) cites Sophronios who (Descr. Eccles. in Meurs. p. 41) says: $Tριφύλιος \ Kύπρου \ Λήδρου \ ήτοι \ Λευτεώνος$ ἐπίσκοπος. Moreover Hieronymus (Script Eccles. Kap. 92 and d'Auville Histoire Eccles, 8, 12. Sozomenos 5, 10): Triphyllios, Cypri Ledrensis sive Λευτεώνος episcopus. Pape gives the form Λήδρα for the Cyprian town.

Engel, who with others and no doubt corretly places Ledron on the site of Nicosia or in its neighbourhood, concludes from the evidence given above that the two small towns Leuteon and Ledron, originally distinct were later fused into one place and became an episcopal seat. Only Engel would read Λευκεών or Λευκών for Λευτεώνος because that gave us the name Leukosia as Bishop of which Triphyllios is mentioned.

In early Byzantine times at all events there were two places. The one, Leuteon or Leontion lay behind our Lion-Mountain near the two modern villages of Athalassa-Tschifflik and Aglanjia where the remains of the settlement are still visible and from whence I took the photograph on which the view in Fig. 2 is based. The other and larger of the two lay to the north west about half an hour's distance from the first and occupied the site of the present chief town; it was called Ledrai or Ledron. At this same place, there is no doubt, there stood in ancient times the large border-town Lidir-Ledrai to which belonged the nekropolis of Hagia Paraskevi which almost adjoined the town to the south side. The Akropolis to this ancient town of Lidir-Ledrai lay half an hour from our Leontari Vouno i. e. the Lion-mountain. In the tribute lists of the Assyrian Kings Asarhaddon and Asurbanipal the town Lidir is mentioned. Under the new name Levkosia, which makes its appearance in Byzantine times, the two places were soon united the names also i. e. Leontion and Ledron or Ledrai. Levkosia means "shining" or "gleaming". The name Nicosia (Nikosia on the map) is of late origin and arose in the time of the House of Lusignan. Our map (Fig. 259) is in accordance with the most recent survey of the English Government. I have to thank the kindness of my friend, Herr Professor Dr. E. Oberhummer of Munich for the drawing on which it is based.

3—9 in Plate CLXV and CLXVI.

10   Section of the hill at the line F—G. CLXV, 4 the principal ruin is here somewhat restored. (Cf. CLXVI, 5 and 6.)

The section goes right through the shaft, which was sunk in the ground vertically and to a great depth.—S. H. 8 in Pl. CLXV, 4. In a—b I reproduce from the Journal of Hellenic Studies the several illustations that accompany the English Report of the Excavations; a. shows the section of the hill, b, and b₂ are two views of one of the stone hand-mills which were found in the tumulus H. 1. (CLXV).

c—k. Are reproductions of views which by the help of a drawing-prism I threw into correct perspective while the excavations were going on.—Above them the scale.

c—h. Hand-mills of the usual kind (like CXLVII, 7a from Hissarlik and 8 from Cyprus); e only has depressions (I found similar ones also at Alambra in 1888.)

i—k.   Stones with circular depressions.

1.   Vase fragment of a class of Cyprian pottery discovered by me, c—1 were all found together in tumulus H. 1 with many other vase fragments which all belong to the copper-bronze period. There is no trace of a vase-fragment or of any sort of object that could justify the supposition that the Acropolis was inhabited in the Graeco-Phoenician iron-period. The acropolis flourished during the Achaean days as did those of Mykenae and Tiryns. The acropolis of Tiryns is in size and shape just like ours, only that ours is much more precipitous and hence is in most places independent of fortification.

Fragment 1 belongs to a class of vases of quite peculiar character. The vase was made by the hand only without the potter's wheel and was covered with a dull black glaze. Then by means of the wheel fine bands of horizontal lines and parallel segments of lines were super-imposed in vermilion body colour. I found this class of vase also in three nekropoleis of the copper-bronze period at Phönitschäs (1883) at H. Paraskevi (1885) and at Tamassos (1889).

Plate CLXV.

Trigonometric surveys, 3 of the whole hill on a smaller scale, 4, of the northern part on a larger scale by E. Carletti.—Archaeological notes by Max Ohnefalsch-Richter.

The scales are in English chains. 100 chains = 66 English feet.

The acropolis is accessible only at two points and the top is levelled almost horizontal. Only the northern portion, which is the most precipitous, was inhabited. A high road leads on the west side up to the rocky plateau and there is a track, available only for foot passengers, asses and mules, on the east side. On the north side the rock is continued but it supports only 0,10 - 0,13 m of earth. Towards the south, where the nekropolis which was used exclusively by the inhabitants of the acropolis is situated the stratum of earth superimposed is more considerable. Hence some of the graves are entirely rock-hewn, others half rock, half earth, others entirely of earth. (Pl. CLXVII). The settlement on the north side of the akropolis, on account of the precipitous rocks all round, needed no wall. It was only towards the south that fortifications were necessary and there they comprised a large space and were very strongly built. At the southernmost point and, where the hill is most interlaced, a deep trench is sunk which utilizes a natural depression. On and in the earthern rampart here we first come upon a double wall. This is built of small quarried stones and consists of two lines of walls joined together by transverse bolts the space being filled in with earth and loose stones. Clay morter is the only binding material employed. Only the better preserved portions are indicated in thick black and of the breadth they were when discovered. The walls that lay north of the stone bastion, to be shortly discussed (cf Pl. CLXVI), I give in broken lines. They are in this condition or even worse. They are nothing but small low foundation walls built of little quarried stones and chance material and they were never cemented with lime mortar. Of the same sort are the remains of the foundation walls of houses, of which Carletti and I have included the better preserved portions so far as they could be measured and drawn. Clearly these small stone foundations supported walls of sun-baked clay the remains of which have long been blown away. These slighter fortifications to the north of the stone structure and which are given in a dotted line, consist of a simple wall drawn transverse over the plateau with an irregular quadrangular tower-shaped chamber in the west side. The actual stone-built akropolis with its fortifications south and north was a stronghold within a stronghold, and would be of use in times of revolt or when the remaining portion of the hill from one or other of the sides had fallen into the enemy's hand. On this account three cisterns (T. 1—3) had been constructed within these fortifications of the actual King's palace. For the inhabitants of the northern portion of the akropolis water was collected in the two collossal cisterns S. H. 1 and S. H. 2. That these five reservoirs were really cisterns there can be no doubt, as they are covered with a thick coating of lime-mortar. St. 1 and 2 are heaps of stones which came from these great cisterns and have lain there ever since their construction. The heap St. 1 is indeed so carefully piled up that it suggests the idea of a stone monument. H. 3 is a small stone heap. H. 2 a small tumulus of earth and stones which contained nothing.

H. 1 on the other hand is the interesting tumulus carefully constructed of courses of stone and earth which the English investigated. The portion of the trial trench which the English ran through the tumulus is given in dotted lines. Here too I have marked in thick black the piece of rude wall which runs north and south and which was found and noted by the English.*) The whole round tumulus consists of circular stone courses and is covered with a top layer of earth. The objects found in the tumulus were discussed à propos of the former plate.

South west of this tumulus is another egg-shaped elevation indicated by a dotted line. The dotted line to the west running past H. 8 and S. H. 1, shows that the mass of ruined dwellings only lay to the east, the narrow west strip was, it appears, never inhabited.

It remains to discuss the deep shaft S. H 8 which was not emptied out to the bottom by the English. They dug down as deep as 39 English feet without coming to the bottom. It is not cemented over. It is much to be desired that it shall be thoroughly cleared out for it is not impossible that it may be a shaft leading to some deep down royal tomb. All the objects found on the north side between the foundation wall of the primitive dwelling in tumulus H. 1, or in the principal fortifications, especially the fragments of pottery and stone implements, belong to the same time and to the same people who buried their dead to the south of the fortifications. The description of the finds and indeed the whole account in the Journal of this most interesting site is indeed very defective, but is sufficient to make me feel convinced that we are dealing here with a settlement of the Bronze-Period. Besides I paid frequent visits to the scene of excavations, saw a part of the discoveries myself and made sure of the rest from the fragments of pottery lying about. The describer and nominally the diretor of the excavations, R. James, alluded in his account to the discoveries made by me at Hagia Paraskevi. In fact we have here the same stage of civilization and the same people. On the east side of the inhabited northern portion of the plateau, near one of the primitive dwellings, a large and very beautiful spear-head was found which belongs to the Mykenaean stratum—as e. g. Pl. CXLVI, 6 B, f.

Plate CLXVI.

5—9. The stone main building.

It consists of two tower-like chambers joi.ed by a wall. Outside the walls are covered with blocks of "rustica", inside with smooth hewn masonry. Irregular blocks, quarried stone and lime mortar are all freely employed for filling up. Externally of symmetrical appearance, when looked at closer it presents in the space to the left certain irregularities. In the place marked "staircase"**) steps (given as 7) seem to have led up to the fortification walls. Towards the south (v. 6) the wall is much thicker (this cannot be seen in the outline 5) and as the section shows was fitted parapets for defence on the outside. The height given in the section (6) is certain and the dotted lines are correct. As in support of a date between the end of the 7th and the beginning of the 6th century B. C. I draw attention to the splendid hewn masonry of the royal tombs at Tamassos and the free use of lime mortar, and as lime mortar was certainly employed in the megalithic structures of Kition (Panagia Phaneromeni cf. Pl. CLXXV, 3, with description and Salamis CLXXV, 9) which are even earlier, ***) I have no hesitation in pronouncing this masonry to be antique, nor indeed, in attributing it to the end of the bronze-period, i. e. about 1000 B. C. In Idalion also I found a great deal of lime mortar below the layer of earth and used to fill up between the two lines of walls which are built into the town rampart and are of earth. The abundance of limestone in Cyprus soon brought about accidentally the practice of burning lime and hence of the use of lime as mortar. The quarry for the stone bastion work lay on the hill itself at its southern end near Z; unhewn blocks are still lying about which the stone mason had only just begun to hew.†)

---

*) Journ. of Hell. Stud. p. 154, 1888.

**) On the plate it is misprinted Straicnse.

***) Cf. especially Pl. CLXXV, 3—9.

†) Unfortunately time and space alike forbid me to enlarge further on this structure. Anyhow I have done immeasurably more than those who excavated the site; I hope later on to publish an extensive treatise on the subject. One word more I must add respecting the exceedingly defective publication of the English excavators Hogarth, James, Smith and Gardner. Although the report on Leontari Vouno was specially drawn up by James yet all four scholars who conducted the excavations for the Cyprus Exploration Fund hold themselves answerable for it. Mr. Ernest Gardner was director, A. Elsey Smith visited the place and took the measurements. Hogarth wrote to me from Paphos to say he had heard I was at work on a publication about Cyprus, Until he and Ernest Gardner were assured that I would not forestall them with the Leontari Vouno publication they said they could show me nothing of what they had found at Paphos. This was actually their answer to my request as to whether I might come to Old-Paphos to see the excavations and finds. I did not answer their letter nor did I go to Paphos and I kept back my first publication of the drawings of Leontari Vouno until the first issue of my "Cyprian Studies April 1889. I am bringing out now in 1893 my first description of the hill. But even if I had anticipated the English it would have been no blame to me. A year before I had in company with Prof. Dr. E. Oberhummer made a special study of the hill. Mr. S. Brown, then government engineer, was the first to pay attention to this important hill. He got W. Williams, an excellent draughtsman to make the first sketches which were placed at my disposal in the readiest manner and as can seen from our plates were made use of. I then with the help of another official of the English government, Mr. E. Carletti, surveyor and draughtsman to the survey and cataster made substantial improvements to these drawings and finally in conjunction with him I worked up all these discoveries, made indeed by the English, but of which the scientific gist had either wholly or partially escaped them. Moreover I had studied the excavations of the hill to much better purpose than the gentlemen of the Cyprus Exploration Fund. When these gentlemen arrived in Cyprus about New-Year 1888 they got their first information about the hill from Col. Warren (J. H. S. p. 152) who perfectly well knew that I had been at work for nine months studying in detail the archaeological and topographical conditions of the hill. Had the English published a model work on Leontari Vouno before me, then at the best they would have anticipated me not I them. As however the English publication about this hill, which seems to me quite as important as the whole of Old-Paphos, turned out contrary to expectation to be a mediocre and unsatisfactory production my publication which, — so far as the plates go —is a model. only gains in value. From an inspection of the pottery fragments corn-grinders and handmills that lay above the surface I had, long before the excavations took place, recognised the archaic and the end of the bronze period as the time to which the buidings of this acropolis in part belonged and that it formed the Acropolis to the lower town, to which in turn the Nekropolis of Hagia Paraskevi, half an hour away, belonged. Mr. J. R. James refers in his dilettante description of the objects found to the numerous antiquities that I discovered in the Nekropolis of Hagia Paraskevi — and this on account of their similarity. But Mr. James makes a mistake when he says Col. Warren and I found them. I have conducted numerous excavations for the Cyprus Museum for Mr. S. Brown and among others for Col. Warren I was, however, the first after the lamentable statements made by Cesnola-Stern to assign to the Hagia Paraskevi necropolis its right place. The Hagia Paraskevi type is now spoken of as a familiar matter. Duenmier and the English take their stand on what I was the first to Establish. I, too, was the first to decide the question about the nekropolis of Alambra. Duenmier, who gives vent to his views on the question in the Athenian Mittheilungen, (1886 pp. 209—282) again takes his stand on my statements and on what I brought him from Alambra, for he could not himself visit the place owing to indisposition. Moreover I have been the first to teach how to distinguish between and even assign dates to those different periods of Cyprian art and civilization which in Perrot (III) are still floating about in manifold confusion. In this I have often received help and encouragement from various learned friends to whom I in my turn

Plate CLXVII.

Figures 101—104*) give the outlines and sections of four graves on the akropolis. The graves lie for the most part to the south of the fortifications on the east edge of the hill, and begin close to the trench toward the south west where in Pl. CLXV, 3 the word "Nekropolis" stands. The one entirely rock-hewn grave (101) with an oblique dromos lay close to and beneath the structure of hewn masonry and is drawn in on a small scale in Pl. CLXVI, 5. A few graves, but only a few, lie on the slope to the east of the settlement south of grave F. Pl. CLXV, 4 and north of the track and of the rock given in Fig. 101.

Grave 105, a rock grave of Hagia Paraskevi, is figured side by side for comparison. This grave and all those figured in the subsequent plates up to CLXXIII together with their contents show that we are dealing at Hagia Paraskevi with one and the same civilization that lasted for centuries during the copper bronze period, and that the civilization clearly evidenced by the graves and other remains in the acropolis at Leontari-Vuono belongs to the end of the bronze-period, which forms the transition to the civilization of the iron period. I referred to evidences of this same period of civilization of the bronze period with transition to the iron at Tamassos in 1889. These Tamassos discoveries as well as those of Katydata-Linu (Pl. CLXXII, 16—18) and H. Paraskevi (Pl. CCXVI, 13—16) taken in conjunction with my present investigations give us not only the clearly defined pre-Graeco-Phoenician copper bronze period and the Graeco-Phoenician iron period but also the various transition stages from the one period to the other.

It is neccessary at this point to state definitely that the distinctions which F. Dümmler tries to draw (in the Athen. Mittheilungen XI, p. 209, Beilage 2) between the graves of the bronze and iron periods are inadequate and miss the point. The graves arranged together in Plates CLXVII - CLXXVII and their contents are for the most part taken from the diary of the excavation that was made during Dümmler's stay in Cyprus, in part the reports and sketches were all ready to hand. In many cases the early Graeco-Phoenician earth graves (e. g. CLXXII, 19 Kurion) cannot be distinguished at all from graves of the early copper-bronze period (e. g. CLXVIII, 1, Psematismeno 4 Hagia Paraskevi) either as regards their shape or the distribution of their accessories. They are shallow trenches widening towards the bottom, with the body in the middle, accessory objects hung on the walls. In all these cases distinctions can only be drawn by means of the accessory objects.

Plates CLXVIII—CLXXIII.

23 graves and their contents.

1—15, 20—22. Graves of the copper-bronze period. 1 from Psematismeno, 2—15 from Hagia Paraskevi. 20 and 21 from Phönitschäs (Phoenikiais).

With grave 5 (Hagia Paraskevi) I have figured (under h) a vessel found by me in 1883 in a bronze period grave at Katydata-Linu.

16—18. Graves of the transition to the iron period from Katydata-Linu.

19. Graeco-Phoenician iron period grave from Kurion.

For graves 11 and 12 only the plans of grave 12 are given and the contents of 11 and 12 are drawn together. Grave 12 corresponded exactly to grave 11.

Of grave 23 only the contents are published without plans. This grave corresponded to the regular rock tomb type of Hagia Paraskevi, like graves 10 and 14.

When in August 1885 a number of graves were opened during F. Dümmler's stay, it happened that no single skull was discovered in any of the earth graves. That it was the rule however, to bury the bodies and not to burn them is established by the previous and subsequent excavations. The damp clayey soil at Hagia Paraskevi, the constant use of cemeteries as cultivated land, the flat position of the bodies and the great age of the graves extending back to about 4000 years are the cause that so few bones are to be found. When in 1889 I excavated at Tamassos some bronze period graves in a sand-hill that had not been taken in for cultivation, I took out more than 20 skulls in a superior state of preservation from some 50 graves. I also in the presence of Dümmler discovered the rock grave No. 22 (CLXXIII) which presents the most interesting exeptional case in an experience of excavations that extend over 12 years. The door of the little chamber was closed by a slab of stone. In the middle of the grave itself cremation of the middle portions of the body had been carried out, and we found the

---

have unselfishly made over many of my most important discoveries for them to publish first. In such cases I may venture to claim my deserts as the chief. As to the classification of Cyprian ceramography and of the finds in the graves, long before R. S. Poole (Transactions R. Society of Literature XI) A. S. Murray (Cesnola-Stern p. 395) and G. Perrot. (Hist. de l'art III) Mr. T. R. Sandwith, their Consul, was on the right road. In his paper (read May 4, 1871). "On the different styles of pottery found in ancient tombs in the island of Cyprus" he had already by means of close observation separated the iron and the bronze period. He had further, and quite correctly, divided this Graeco-Phoenician iron-less period into two main divisions according to the finds in the graves, the earlier division having vases with incised geometric ornament, the later painted vases. Again he had already arrived at the distinction between the terra-cotta of the Graeco-Phoenician copper-bronze period (Pl. X, 4 of the transactions) and those of the Graeco-Phoenician iron period (Pl. X, 3 E op. cit.) Only Sandwith did not know how to draw the necessary deductions. Independently of him I had made the same observations, as unfortunately his excellent treatise did not come into my hands till afterwards. The distinction of priority belongs, therefore, in so far to Mr. Sandwith, whose treatise moreover is illustrated by very good coloured plates and deserves to be rescued from obscurity.

*) In my plate in the Journal of Cyprian Studies I began, on account of the other pictures, to number the graves from No. 101. The high number does not, therefore, mean that more than 100 graves were found in the akropolis. As may be seen from the Hellenic Journal 1888, p. 156 and from my investigations only a few graves (still not less than about 20) have been dug in the hill, hence only a portion of the population of the hill can have been buried in the akropolis. The rest were buried either in the nekropolis at Hagia Paraskevi or at the foot of the hill in some cemetery yet to be discovered. That in this akropolis we are dealing with a uniform population of the bronze period, of a Graeco-Cyprian heroic age, contemporaneous with heroic age of Greece as it appears in the hills of Mycenae and Tiryns, is shown by every vase-fragment, every piece of metal found, be it bronze copper or silver, and by the beautiful spear-head, which was found in the very site of the settlement at the east edge of the northern plateau. (J. H. S. 1889, p. 155).

remains of the burnt bones in a heap of charcoal and ashes. To the left of the door in the entrance were placed the skulls, to the right the bones of the extremities bearing no mark of fire, the accessory objects 22 h and f, were opposite the door.

Of the 28 graves figured 1—8, 13 and 19 are of earth, 6—18 and 20—21 graves of conglomerate,[*]) 9, 10, 14 and 15 (28 as well as 10 and 14), rock graves proper. Grave 12 corresponded to grave 11. Consequently plans are given of grave 11 only. Among the accessory objects in 11 and 12 there are included others which were found in graves of the same character as 11. Here may be seen quite shallow earth graves, trenches intended for several bodies, slabs of limestone built over and round the houses and the accessory objects round about, below and above.

Plate CLXVIII.

1—5. Five Earth graves. Vases with painted decoration still do not appear at all. Ornament when present is incised or in relief.

Accessory objects in metal only occur in 8. A bronze pin, which belongs to the whorl d.[**]) c. An animal of linear style in relief from a large globe-bellied polished red water jug (Shape of the vase in Pl. CLXXI, 11 and 12, a—f), 4 b and 5 a large milk cups. 1 b and c fragments of similar ones. Central diameter of the cups 0,45—0,55 m.[***])

The most primitive form of grave is that in No. 1. It is also the earliest and is peculiar to e. g. Alambra-Marragi. A stone slab stands upright at one side of the grave which is heaped up into a low hill. For the most part, however, the heaping up of the hillock is omitted. Often a few stones are put in near the surface when the trench is filled up (2). The graves have niches and little chambers at the side (3 and 5) or sometimes not (2 and 4) CLXVIII, 1 = CXLVII, 4, CLXVIII, 5 = CXLVIII, 7.

Plate CLXIX.

Graves 6—8. All earth graves. Contents of 6 = CXLVIII, 8, 7 = CXLVII, 2; 8, b, g. f = CXLVIII, 12.

In these also no trace of a painted fragment was discoverable. Ornament either incised or in relief. Except the fragment found in Alambra (8 g) all there came from Hagia Paraskevi.

In 8 the collective contents of grave 8 are figured and nothing else.

In 6 and 7 are figured the finds from Hagia Paraskevi (8 g only from Alambra) which were excavated from various graves of the same character and ground plan at Hagia Paraskevi.

The earth grave 7 differs in disposition and rather resembles the rock grave 9 (CLXX) and the conglomerate graves 16 and 17 (CLXXII).

Plate CLXX.

9 and 10. Rock graves, 13 earth grave.

Grave 9. Vessels coupled together from several similar graves are collected under No. 9. b. incised ornament, c and e painted (c = Pl. CLII, 13. Contents grave 9 = CXLVIII, 10.

Grave 10 a—f and 9 c, e. Hand made vessels with vivid glaze colour (cf. supra p. 458, Pl. CLII, 13).

9. Light brown clay, painted decoration in dull brown glaze. Clay like that of the Dipylon vases but hand made and the ornament Cyprian.

The tripod c was excavated with the Graeco-Phoenician vase CCXVI, 16 in an earth grave at Hagia Paraskevi of evidently late date, together with several bronze and copper daggers (now in the Cyprus Museum). The other objects come from rock graves, like grave 10.

Grave 13. The vases collected together under 13 = CXLIX, 15 were found together in early earth graves at Hagia Paraskevi which resembled No. 13 of this plate and No. 2 and 4 of Pl. CLXVIII.

a. Vase of bird shape, but with no head and three legs. Ornament incised and filled in with white pigment.

b = p. 275, Fig. 186; c = p. 275, Fig. 185; d = p. 275, Fig. 181; e = p. 275, Fig. 182.

Plate CLXXI.

Grave 11. Earth grave with stone slab. Cf. p. 463.

12 was a similar grave. The contents shown by the principal objects i. e. 11 and 12. The prevalent type here is that of the jugs that I first discovered with reliefs of animals, quadrupeds, snakes, trees, ribbons, ties, spectacle-ornaments, discs, lamps, wreaths (a—f). Cf. also Pl. XXVIII, 3, 4, 6, and CXXII, 7.

---

[*]) By conglomerate graves I understand the graves hewn out of the adjacent conglomerate quarries, hence a sort of mean between the earth and rock graves. It was just in this very bronze period that situations with adjacent conglomerate quarries were eagerly sought for cemeteries. But conglomerate graves occur also in other periods. Cf. 2 B a my report "Von den neuesten Ausgrabungen in der cyprischen Salamis", Athen, 1881, p. 192.
[**]) Cf. Pl. CCXIII, 9, c.
[***]) Athen, Mittheilungen XI, 1886. Beilage II, Figs 1 and 3, p. 209.

g = CXXII, 5, cf. 14, c, q and Pl. CXXII, 2—4.
h. Rude cup with four snakes in relief round the lip.
i. Cf. Pl. XXXV, 1 and 3. CXLIX, 1. CCXVI, 32.
Grave 14, = CLXVII, 105 cf. p. 34—35, Fig. 34—36.

Plates CLXXII and CLXXIII.

Grave 15. Rock grave of Hagia Paraskevi. This type, too, with the two doors occurs frequently. In all rock graves of very early date the entrance is in the form of a shaft. Under 15 the finds are placed together which occur from time to time in graves of this type.

a and b. An unusual sort of agalmatolite idol seen full face and profile.
c. Whorl = CCXIII, 7 a.
d. Painted dull black on ground of red clay. Six vessels and two vase-necks blended together into one.
e. Hammer of limestone. Cf. CXLIX, 17 and 18.
f. Diorite sphere. Cf. CXLIX. 16.
g. Vase with double snake in relief which is figured alone in Pl. CXXII.
h = CXIX, 5 b.
m = terra-cotta wheel.
k = clay bead.
l = Glazed terra-cotta bead in shape of a mussel.

Graves 20—23. Plate CLXXIII.

Graves of similar character to 15, 20—21 at Phönitschäs. 23 at Hagia Paraskevi. We are approaching the close of the bronze period. In graves of this sort vases of the Mykenae type like those in Pl. CLII, 1, 2, 4, 5, 7, 8 (right) 16 and others began to appear. At the same time also numerous idols. The appearance of the plank-idol in its later development as in 20, e, f, is exceptional. For the most part we find naked round idols of the Babylonian-Assyrian Ištar as in p. 34, Fig. 31 and 32. It is in this layer that we first find painted analogies to the pre-historic and pre-Carian civilization of the Greek islands and the Cyclades (attributed by Dümmler to the Leleges) (cf. our agalmatolite-idol Pl. CLXXIII, 15a and b with the idols from the Cyclades). More rarely we have idols like 23 a and b; 23a a female mourner or mourning goddess, cf. p. 251 and 265. In this stratum (to which grave 14, Pl. CLXXI also belongs) gold appears e. g. the gold cylinder setting Pl. CLXXI, 14 w, also a chain of gold beads, 22 m a clay bead set in gold, 221 (cf. Pl. CCXVII, 1). Agalmatolite clay and glazed terra-cotta beads set in silver (22a—e) are also now of more frequent occurrence. The number of silver spirals increases (22 k), gold spirals (CXLVI, 3 B, p) and glass ones (CXLVII, 3 B, q) make their appearance. In this stratum side by side with the Mykenae vases there now appear also the nails with slit pegs (e. g. CLXXIII, 20, 21 g) and also elegant though bizarre stump-painted vessels like 20 and 21 k, animals 20 and 21 h and hemispherical cylikes with white ground like CLXXIII, 23 and with decorations in reddish brown or black.

The graves 16—18, Pl. CLXXII from Katydata-Linu, their contents in the Antiquarium at Berlin, take us on to the iron period. In grave 16 was found a chain ornament of oxydized iron*), of which a few links are figured in 16 c.

The arrangements of the graves are strikingly and fundamentally different in individual cases. Grave 18 is the finest example. Our drawing does not show with sufficient exactitude that the grave was hemispherical in shape. The entrance is absolutely circular and almost identical with the roof.

In these graves we meet with the later stages of Mycenae art (17 c). The same images of Ištar still occur (17 t, 18 a). Clay whorls disappear and the stone ones become rarer and flatter in shape (17 b). The wheel has become the common property of all potters. In the same grave, 17, two vessels had been deposited (beaked-shape jugs) of which the one was hand-made, the other turned.

The small jugs, also, with bellies divided into partitions like fruit are now fully developed. Instead of indicating the depressed partition by incised lines (17 g) the raised portion are now rendered more plastically by modelling. The oinochoës with stirrup-shaped handles and spouts (16 b, 17 p) are of more delicate shape, turned on the wheel and painted with horizontal bands of colour. The hemispherical cylikes (16 a) were at first refined in style and then the making of them in quite coarse patterns went on for a while longer (17 m) only finally to be utterly abandoned. The Graeco-Phoenician wheel-turned plate (17 o) begins to make its appearance.

Grave 19. Plate CLXXIII.

By degrees the dominion of iron begins to be felt. The one-edged knife, mostly set in wood, is now rarely absent from a grave. The spouted jug (CLXXII, 17 d and e) is refined in shape and has painted decorations of waterbirds, sacred trees, and swastikas (CLXXIII, 19, n). Cups of graceful shape have feet added to them (e. g. 19 e). In place of the hemispherical terra-cotta cylix with ears (e. g. Pl. CLXIX, 8 b) we have the hemispherical bronze cylix without ears (CLXXXIII, 19 o). From the still

---

*) As Herr Prof. Weeren of the Technical High School Berlin informs me, before it was understood how to get iron in a pure state, objects of oxyde of iron were made and used.

clumsily shaped vase with fruit-shaped body (Pl. CLXXII, 17 g and l) hand made, or half hand, half wheel-made, is developed an elegant shaped jug carefully turned (CLXXIII, 19 b). The spouted jug with muzzle is over taken from the bronze and transition period (CLXXII, 16 b and 17 p) to the iron period and refined in the process (CLXXII, 19 a). The eyes in the liliputian vases, which are given in relief in those from grave CLXXII, 17 q, are now painted (CLXXXIII, 19 l).

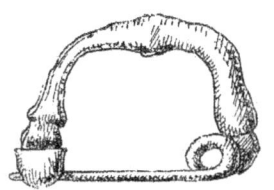

Fig. 260.

Gold earrings (like 19 i) silver rosettes (like 19 g) silver leaflets (like 19 c) with busts of divinities impressed now make their appearance. The art of figure writing in clay begins to apply itself to genre subjects (CLXXIII, 19 h).

Industries in metal and clay and sculpture in clay begin to flourish. Sculpture in stone sets in. By degrees we are led to the 9th, 8th and 7th centuries B. C. We have entered in the period of the Cyprian fibulae, which begin 1200—1100 B. C. and disappeared from the graves about 600 B. C. I figure here the ordinary type of the Cyprian Graeco-Phoenician fibula which appears just the same at Sendscherli or at Assarlik. This specimen in Fig. 260 belongs to the find of the three fibulae which was made in a grave at Kurion. Studniczka mentions these fibulae and my name as their discoverer on the occasion of a communication made to Dümmler and he ascribes them to the earliest Greek settlers (Athen. Mittheilungen 1887, p. 19). The fibulae are not found in the preceding copper bronze period and they disappear at the beginning of the 6th century B. C. Graves like CLXXIII, 19 represent the stratum of the bronze and gold fibulae in Cyprus.

Plates CLXXIV, CLXXV and CLXXXIX.

In these plates I publish plans and sections of the condition of Cyprian graves all of which belong to the iron period down to the plan of the lie of Marion-Arsinoë near to the modern town of Polis or Poli tis Chrysoku (Anglice Poli tis Khrysokhou), Pl. CLXXIV, 1 *). The earliest represented here go back to the beginning of the iron period (CLXXV, No. 2 of Amathus), the latest down to the time of the Ptolemies (CLXXIV, Marion-Arsinoë). Roman graves are omitted.**) In pl. CLXXIII, 19 I have already given an instance of the ordinary early Graeco-Phoenician iron period trench graves which may be quite similar to the pre-Graeco-Phoenician bronze period trenches, so that only the character of the accessory objects can be decisive.

In these early Graeco-Phoenician trench graves which belong to the period 1100—600 B. C. the graves of the rich are distinguished from those of the poor by their depth. As a rule all the rich graves are very deep. The graves of the Tamassos vase (p. 37, Fig. 38) and of the gold plate from Kurion (Pl. CXCIX) were about 12 m. deep. The trench developed by widening out into a rude chamber at the side which form again may be identical with the type of Greek and Graeco-Phoenician graves of the 6th century B. C. (Pl. CLXXV, 10—14).

We must first briefly consider the condition of graves that are built into the earth, either entirely of stone or partly stone, partly hewn out of the rock.

A. Plate CLXXV, 2. Grave with monolithic cover.

Excavated by me at my own expense at Amathus 1885. Beneath a crust of earth of about 0,65 m. deep stands the rock in which a long quadrangular space (scale in the pl.) has been hewn from above. This portion serves as entrance. Another, on which a huge block of stone is laid for a cover, serves as chamber. The interstices between the rudely hewn monolith which is only worked on the under side, and the equally rudely hewn rock basis are filled in with small stones.

In the grave I found the clay shrine mentioned above (p. 452) and figured on Pl. CXCIX, 1 and 2, also early Graeco-Phoenician clay vases and two painted clay-idols of the Cyprian goddess who holds a large disc in front of her. Style, painting and motive like CCVI, 5.

B. Pl. CLXXV, 1. Grave with the cover partly monolithic, partly driven into the rock.

From the same excavation. The grave had been used several times. The fragmentary finds and potsherds date from the same time as grave 1. The accessory objects, which are in better preservation and found near the bodies, are of Roman date. Roman lamps, glasses &c. Another grave close by showed the same structure.

C. The sections on Pl. CLXXV, 3—9 show the further development of the architecture of stone-graves.

The latest link in the chain, however, (No. 8) does not extend later than the first half of the 6th century B. C.

---

*) Excursus on Marion-Arsinoë at the end of this book according to the promise on the title-page.
**) Cf. as regards Graeco-Roman grave constructions my plans in the Mittheilungen of the K. Deutschen Archäologisches Institut Athen. 1881 and 1883.

3. Section through the inner chamber of the double-chambered grave at Kition (Panagia Phaneromeni) published in Pl. CXXV, 3 and 4. A colossal monolith hollowed out below dome-shaped serves as roof.

4. Front chamber of same grave (the back wall restored in accordance with graves 6 and 7).

5. Cross section through the inner chamber of the megalithic building at Salamis (Hagia Katharia). Vertical section of same chamber Fig. 9 The side and back walls of the chamber are hewn out of rock. The front wall and the door are made of megalithic blocks, which belong to the principal chamber. A monolith is superimposed as cover.

6. Section of the grave figured in grave 2 on Pl. CLXXIX. No. 2 from Xylotimbo excavated by me in 1882.

7. ibid. From Pl. CLXXXIX grave 1. Some provenance. The contents of both graves consist only of clay vases, which I figure together on Pl. CLXXIX, to the right below. From these it is evident that the graves were in continuous use for centuries. Similar graves are found at Kition. It is evident from the Kition stone-graves and those discovered in 1889 at Tamassos that these graves also at Xylotimbo must have been dug at the end of the 6th or beginning of the 7th century B. C. The section of a subter-ranean passage given here for comparison on Fig. 261 takes us to Pteria in Cappadocia (= Perrot IV, p. 620. Fig 804). But Etruscan tombs are still more similar to these Cyprian graves. Martha (L'Etrurie p. 140, Fig. 116) figures a grave chamb.r of Orvieto, which in the structure of its roof and the whole character of its masonry is the exact parallel of our Cyprian graves at Xylotimbo *).

Fig. 261.

Just such graves have been discovered in the Crimea (cf. Antiquites du Bosphore Cimmerien réedites par Salomon Reinach 1892, Pl. A and Ab).

8. Section of a stone-grave at Kition. The wood construction is imitated by stone slabs placed in a row one against the other, the protruding beams and the plank coverings are represented incised and in relief.

I excavated graves of similar construction only much richer both in their general appearance and in details in 1889 at Tamassos and these I was able to date accurately. They belong to the first half of the 6th century B. C.

9. Section of a megalithic building of the plain of Salamis (Hagia Katherina cf. 5) **). The steps added outside in dotted lines are in part conjectural and added in accordance with the remains.

Of the structures figured here 1--9; 1, 2, 7 and 8 are entirely subterranean; 3 (to which 4 belongs), 6 (cf. Pl. CLXXXIX) and 9 (to which 5 belongs) have their upper part above ground. In most cases lime-mortar was freely employed to fill up whatever was not meant to be seen by the spectator while the inner walls which were turned towards the visitor consisted of stone-cornices laid dry one over the other without mortar. I met with this sort of masonry also at Tamassos in 1889 in the stone graves of the beginning of the 6th century B. C..

At first I was inclined to overestimate the age of the megalithic buildings at Kition (Pl. CLXXV, 3) and 4) and Salamis (9), owing to the results of the excavations at Amathus (CLXXV, 1 and 2), Xylotimbo (CLXXXIX) and Tamassos, I find myself obliged to date the buildings at Kition and Salamis also as late as Graeco-Phoenician times. In any case Cypriots were the builders of all these stone structures, be they megalithic or mikrolithic.

D. The existence of Graeco-Phoenician, Greek and Hellenic graves in Cyprus proved by the evidence of the graves at Marion-Arsinoë.

The graves figured on Pls. CLXXIV, 2—4, CLXXV, 10—16 were all discovered in Marion-Arsinoë.

Of the two ancient towns near the modern village of Poli tis Chrysokou Marion is older than Arsinoë ***) But even the earliest graves of Marion cannot go back much further than 600 B. C. For one of the older kinds of vases are found there nor fibulae.

The customary small form of earth graves of the 6th and beginning of the 5th century B. C. is represented by the ordinary simple and rude quadrangular grave chambers of small size with rounded corners and steep sloping dromos (10 and 11) from nekropolis II (cf. CLXXIV, 1).

*) Martha believes this architecture was brought to Etruria by the Phoenicians from the east to Etruria. As in many departments of human activity and of religion we have come upon to many analogies between Cyprus and Etruria, this architecture may well have been brought to Etruria by Cypriots or Cyprian-Phoenicians. Martha also refers to analogous styles of building among the Egyptians (Perrot I., p. 113) and the Assyrians (Perrot II p. 262) but these analogies are but remote. Similarity of style is only met with in Cyprian sepulchral architecture.

**) Published in detail by me in the Journal of Hellenic Studies 1883, IV, 111—115 with two plates XXXIII and XXXIV, "A pre-historic building at Salamis". There are also to be found the sections reproduced here in pl. CLXXV, 3—8.

***) Op. Excursus on Marion-Arsinoë sub. fin.

12 and 13 are only slightly different in form from the previous graves and belong, as the contents show, to the 4th century B. C. But steps appear to have been cut in the passage. The terra-cotta statue (figured in Pl. CLXXXVII, 4) and the terra-cotta head (in CLXXXVI, 2) were found together with other fragments of seated and recumbent terra-cottas in the dromos.

The three graves that follow, 14—16, again belong to the 6th century B. C.

In grave 15, which like 12 I excavated on my own account in 1885, I found considerable remains of a sword of the same type as CXXXVII, 7 (from Tamassos). In this case we have a tolerably level dromos as the grave opens at a place where the ground sinks.

16. Shows how two graves lead one into the other. A grave of this sort is grave No. 131, Sect. II which yielded the gold ornaments Pl. LXVII, the black figured vases CX, 7, as well as the bronze claw of a griffin Pl. CLXXVIII, 4.

A good example of the earth grave of a rich man of the 6th century B. C., with an enormously long dromos, is given by grave No 92, Nekr. II, Pl. CLXXIV, 2, cf. p. 371, the grave which contained the marble torso figured in Pl. XXVII, 3a and b.

A grave of the 4th century B. C. with what was evidently a staircase is seen in the same plate, No. 4. In the dromos was found the upper part of a terra-cotta statue of the 4th century B. C. which is figured in Pl. CLXXXVI, 3.

The grave with steps, No. 41, Nekr. II, Fig. 3, in the same plate, is undoubtedly Hellenistic. Among other things I found a silver coin of one of the earlier Ptolemies. In this grave there were no Graeco-Phoenician vases, even of the later style, no fragment of a vase with concentric circles, but also no trace of any of Greek or Attic ones nor, even of impressed patterns. The vases were unpainted. The grave was rich in gold and silver ornaments and in small glass beads and figurines, but there was no indication of vases of transparent glass. On the other hand among the finds of this grave there was a pair of beautiful ear-rings with Erotes for pendants (Pl. CLXXXII, 21), the small glass head (28), the diminitive capital (27) and the tomb-ornament in the shape of a pair of snakes twined together in a knot and made of stucco-like composition gilt.

At Marion-Arsinoë so far no grave of the 6th century B. C has been discovered that has a regular staircase. But the excavations at Tamassos taught us in 1889 that the first stone stair-case had come in the 6th century B. C. in isolated cases for the rich and for princes. Before that none are found. Cf. also the staircase of the grave at Xylotimbo, Pl. CLXXXIX, grave II.

Plate CLXXVI.

° Stele in stone of pure Greek style from the finest period of the 4th century B. C. From grave No. 51, Nekr. III, Marion-Arsinoë, 1886. Cf. Pl CCVIII.

Made of the island limestone hence in Cyprus.

In the same grave, part of it in the grave-chamber itself part in the dromos with steps, a splendid attic rhyton in the shape of a ram's head was discovered (Pl CXCI, 7), also the silver ring in Pl. CLXXXII, 38, and a number of Attic vases of the 4th century B. C., one with graffiti in Cyprian writing, also a quantity of both large and small Cyprio-Greek terra-cottas of the 4th century B. C. &c.

° 2. Winkelmannsprogramm, 1888, p. 37, Fig. 23.

The original in Berlin 0,21 m high   Grave 35, Nekr. II, Marion-Arsinoë.

Cyprian imitation of the Attic Hydria. Very carelessly painted decorations in dull brown on the red clay ground. End of the 4th or beginning of the 3rd century B. C

° 3. = CLII, 21. = Winckelmannsprogramm, 1888, p. 16, Fig. 6. Berl. Mus. Nekr. II. Grave 194. H. 0,303 m. Same provenance.

Certainly from a Graeco-Phoenician grave with no imported Attic vase and dating early in the 6th century B. C. There were found together six early silver spirals, Cyprian vases with concentric circles (but not earlier than the beginning of the 6th or end of the 7th century B. C. like title page No. 2, not like CLXXVII, 2) and two Cyprian plates with double perforations.

But on the other hand, I believe that in 1886 I had already found at Marion-Arsinoë a larger number of these local Asia Minor, Ionic or Cyprian vases which imitate Attic ware. (Corresponding to those found in 1889 in the Tamassos graves of the first half of the 6th century B. C). Two rude painted terra-cottas representing Cyprian horsemen belong to the 6th century. In the "snowman" style. No imported Attic ware was found.*)

° 4 = Winckelmannsprogramm p. 17, fig. 8. Same provenance. Berlin. Museum. From grave 204, Nekropolis II.

Made either in Ionic Asia Minor or Cyprus. The clay and the colours are different from those of Attic vases. (Two vases made in the same place were found in 1889 at Tamassos).**)

---

*) As time went on I have learnt to recognize even in the clay figures of the "snow man" style various stages of development. The latest do not go down beyond the 5th century B. C. In the Kabeiroi Sanctuary the relations seem to have been otherwise. Cf. Pl. CXCII, 15.

**) Herr Professor Furtwängler drew my attention to these vases which I excavated at Marion-Arsinoë (1886) as well as at Tamassos (1889). The same kind has been found at Naukratis. It is indeed possible that Attic vase-painters who had settled in Cyprus made vases in Cyprus itself like the oinochoës 7 and 8 of the title-page. But even if this be the case, this Attic vase-painting by Attic vase-painters produced in Cyprus still remains an exotic, hot-house plant of short and feeble duration, and never became part of the organic life of the Cyprian island ceramography, as it did in Magna Graecia, or Rhodes, or Naukratis.

Plate CLXXVII.

? The antiquities figured on this and the following plates up to CLXXXI inclusive all came from the excavations at Marion-Arsinoë in 1886.

1. Fragment of a water-jug. In place of the frequently occurring bull or ram's head we have in this exceptional case a lion's head modelled as spout. Berlin Museum. Grave 145, Nekr. II. Of the 6th century B. C.

Ground of dark red clay painted in dull black.

F. Dümmler, in the Athenian Mittheilungen, advanced the theory that the Arcadians had brought the Cyprio-Graeco-Phoenician style of decoration with concentric circles from their home in the Peloponnese to Cyprus. Diametrically opposed to his view is that of P. Herrmann in the Winckelmannsprogramm for 1888, pp. 47 and 48. His view is that the original type of the water-jugs with animals heads and indeed the birth-place of the whole Cyprian geometric style of decoration is to be sought in North Syria among the Hittites. Both Dümmler and Herrmann would like to rob the Phoenician of all share in influencing this style and even in propagating it commercially. According to Dümmler, the Arcadians themselves brought their own style with them from the Peloponnese, as, according to Herrmann, the Hittites did from Northern Syria. Both are wrong. I show on Plate CCXVI that the concentric circle style was invented in Cyprus, taken up by ceramography and developed in that relation. In the same plate 29 and 30 (cf. also the bronze period vessels like those in Pl. CLXXIII, 20 and 21, 1) 27 and 28, 21–23, it is made clear that long before the date of the Hittite North Syria remains at Samal, the Cypriotes were in the habit of painting heads both animal and human and sometimes whole figures as spouts either on the shoulder or at the top of their vases. In company with Herr von Luschan I have examined the vases and fragments recently discovered at Sendscherli (Samal) since Herrmann's Programm appeared and I am convinced that the great bulk of the fragments in question were made in Cyprus and exported thence to North Syria. The few pieces that were made in the country of Samal itself are evidently helpless local imitations of Cyprian models. I believe that Herr von Luschan agrees with my view and the facts it is based upon. The matter seems to me to admit of no doubt.

2 = Winckelmannsprogramm, 1888, p. 14, fig. 5. Berlin Museum. Hight 0,495 m., Grave 8 Nekropolis II.

The vase belongs either to the 7th century B. C., and this is the more probable, or to the 1st decades of the 6th century B. C.

It belongs to the time when Attic ware was first imported. In this grave the only vases were of later Graeco-Phoenician style with concentric circles. But besides there was found in the grave a small blue-green Aryballos of glazed clay 0,04 m high which further helps to the determination of the date (quite apart from the other distinctive marks that I have arrived at in the course of twelve years of excavations). The belly of the vase is berry-shaped. Otherwise it belongs as regards shape size technique and date to the same class as the Rhodian vases of Aegina, Naukratis and Kameiros of which one is figured in Perrot III, Pl. V. (The centre one).

The ground of the vase is formed by the clay as far as the shoulder space, where there was a coating of vermilion. The stripes, bands and concentric circles are in black, the rude palm-trees in white slip. The manufacture of this style of vase went on for some hundreds of years during which period certain changes in technique and decoration took place. The expert can, however, distinguish between the earthen specimens and the later ones which show modifications in the clay painting and decoration. Then the rude trees disappeared in the later kinds.

3 = Winckelmannsprogramm 1888, p. 48, fig. 27. Berlin Museum. Hight 0,243 m., Grave 198, Nekropolis II.

Painted with coat of dull brown with white and black stripes and white rosettes of dots. On the forehead of the bull is the symbol made of the disc of the sun and the half-moon combined. Vase of the 6th century B. C. Cf. p. 240.

Plate CLXXVIII.

1 and 3. Washing basins or plates that belong to the water jugs; 1 is of the earlier style frequent in the 6th century B. C. 3 is one of the latest examples from the end of the 4th or the beginning of the 3rd century B. C.

No. 1. Dull red ground, in which the decoration is painted in dull black and in white slip. The ornament in the border is a well established type for that purpose i. e. a series of black triangles on a white ground, a form of decoration that frequently occurs also on the border of the lip of the earlier water-jugs (e. g. Pl. LXIV, 6 and p. 48, Fig. 46)*)

No. 3. The water jug that should stand in this washing basin and that is decorated with the same ornaments, wicker-work pattern, ivy wreath and egg ornament is published in the Winckelmannsprogramm 1886 in the right hand top corner of Pl. 3.

No. 2 = Winckelmannsprogramm 1888, p. 27, Fig. 17. Oinochoë H. 0,275. Grave 80. Nekr. II. Berl. Museum.

*) This particular kind of plates and bowls with two excrescences and pairs of holes, which appear at the beginning of the 6th or end of the 7th century B. C. was developed from an earlier kind with nozzle handles, which falls in the period between 600 and 1000 B. C. (below Fig. 268). The original type of these elegant vases, which are more like plates than bowls, is to be seen in the very primitive milk-bowls with two vertical reed-shaped pairs of holes like one I excavated. Athen, Mittheilungen, 1886 — p. 209 — Beilage II, 5.

I have given full particulars of the kind of oinochoë figured here which I first found at Marion-Arsinoë and of which I was the first to recognise the importance, in the description of the title-page. For the present I will only say that the vase has a coating of dark brown almost of black slip, on which are the decorations in white and violet body-colour. In the same grave were found Attic vases of the 5th and 4th centuries B. C.

No. 4. Foot of a bronze vessel. H. 0,182. Berl. Museum. Grave 181. Nekr. II. From the same grave Pl. LXVII, 2—14, CX, 7 and CXLIV, 1—10, 14—17.

Grave of the 6th century B. C. Good Greek work. (Cf. Herrmann in the Winckelmannsprogramm.)

Plate CLXXIX.

1 = LXIV, 5 = Winckelmannsprogramm, p. 55, Fig. 39, cf. p. 220, 240, 259.
2 = Winckelmannsprogramm, p 55, Fig. 38. Rude water-jug (Prochus) of the 5th century B. C. (Cf. Herrmann Winckelmannsprogramm, p. 55).
3 = Winckelmannsprogramm, p. 57, Fig. 40. Berl. Museum. H. 0,375 m. Grave 1. Nekr. III. Belongs to the class with polychrome technique which I was the first to discover and draw attention to. Painted decoration in white slip, sulphur yellow and dark red as in Pl. LXIV, 4.*) The countless other accessory deposits in this grave especially the Attic vases make the date (at the end of the 4th century B. C.) certain.

Plate CLXXX.

1 = LXII, 1 = Winckelmannsprogramm, p. 52, Fig. 35.
2 = Winckelmannsprogramm, p. 23, Fig. 16 Archaic mask of stone 0,180 m high. Berl. Mus. Grave 257. Nekr. II.
3 and 4 = LXIII, 2.

Plate CLXXXI.

1 = LXIV, 1 = Winckelmannsprogramm, p. 58, Fig. 42.
2 = LXIV, 3 = Winckelmannsprogramm, p. 58, Fig. 41.
3 = CXLI, 4, XCIV, 21 = Winckelmannsprogramm, p. 52, Fig. 34. Water-jug from Kurion (cf. p. 240, 415).

Two more vases from Kurion. The one has remains of a white ground and in it red ornaments and palmette (not visible in the plate). These vases are as late as the Hellenistic period, i. e. 3rd century B. C. This is shown by the style of the figure and by the things discovered with them. The terra-cotta groups, figured in Pl. CCVIII, 1 and 2, are Hellenistic and come from the same stratum of graves as the water-jugs figured here.

Plate CLXXXII.

Cyprian gold ornament described below in Pl. CCXVII (° 1—28, 30—52, † 29).
1. Tamassos. 2—4 Kurion. 10—11 Hagia Paraskevi. 16 Linu (near Soli in the valley now called Soliäs) 29. Idalion. Fragments also 5—9, 12—15, 17—28, 30—32. Marion-Arsinoë.

°Plates CLXXXIII—CLXXXIV.

Attic vases. Marion-Arsinoë; excavated by me in 1886.

Plate CLXXXIII.

1. Fragment of a vase. Grave 113. Nekr. II.
2. Grave 145. Nekr. II.
3. Grave 175. Nekr. II. (Possibly an Asia Minor, Ionian or Cyprian imitation of Attic ware.)

Fig. 262.

4. Grave 5. Nekr. I. Fig. 262 = Winckelmannsprogramm, p. 35, Eig. 22; a second guttus from the same grave.
5. Winckelmannsprogramm, p. 35. Fig. 21. Grave 30. Nekr. II.

*) Recognised later also by Munro. Cf. Journal of Hellenic Studies 1891, p 303. Our Necropolis III forms with Nekr. I a consecutive cemetery immediately encircling the village of Poli (Pl. CLXXIV, 1). I have called the northern portion only nekropolis III. My Nekropoleis I and III correspond therefore to the western nekropolis of Monro and my Nekr. II to his eastern one.

Plate CLXXXIV.

1. Grave 116. Nekr. II. Red figured lekythos of the fine period. Cf. A. Murray. Journal of Hellenic Studies 1887, p. 317 and Pl. LXXXI and LXXXII. Red and white figures in black ground with details hinted in relief and with gilding. The most splendid specimen that I excavated in 1886.

2. Grave 282. Nekr. II.

3. Grave 3. Nekr. I.

4 and 5 = Winckelmannsprogramm, Fig. 20. Grave 141. Nekr. II.

?Plates CLXXXV—CLXXXVI.

Terra-cotta statues and statuettes from the same excavation at Marion-Arsinoë.

Plate CLXXXV.

1. Terra-cotta now in Berlin. H. 0,130 m. From grave 78, Nekr. II, hence found in the same grave as the prochus figured in Pl. LXIV, 3 = CLXXXI, 2. Cf. supra, p. 406.

2. Terra-cotta now in Berlin. H. 0,100 m. From grave 83, Nekr. II, hence excavated with the water-jug figured above in Pl. LXIV, 1 (= CLXXXI, 1). Cf. p. 406.

3 = Winckelmannsprogramm; Greek terra-cotta statue of the fine style of the so-called "Mourning" type. (Cf. Pl. CLXXXVII, 2.) It is of pure Greek style inclining towards the Praxitelean manner. The portion preserved is 0,295 m H. Now in the Louvre. From the staircase dromos of grave 11, Nekr. III.

In the grave I found among other things 24 bronze copper coins of Alexander the Great, and Attic stamped ware of the 4th century B. C. but I also found one of the archaic mussel-shaped lamps (e. g. p. 359, Fig. 258, 2) which were so common in the 6th century and which go on down to the 4th century and then disappear from the graves altogether.

4 = Winckelmannsprogramm, p. 28, Fig. 18. H. 0,180. Grave 67, Nekr. II; terra-cotta.

Plate CLXXXVI.

Same provenance. 5 heads or upper parts of large terra-cotta statues (1—5) and one terra-cotta mask.

1. Head of a terra-cotta statue. H. 0,079 m. Grave 81. Nekr. I.

Good Greek work of the 4th B. C. and in the Praxitelean manner. The pupils are rendered by discs modelled into the eye-balls.

2. While Nos. 1, 3—6 were excavated by me in 1886, this beautiful bearded head, circa 0,095 m high, came from the 1885 excavations which I made in an exploration journey I undertook at my own expense. The pupils are indicated by slits.

The grave opened on the property of the then mayor of Poli, Kodschah Paschi, in the dromos of which this head was found together with a number of large broken recumbent terra-cotta statues, is situated not far from the grave in the territory of Negers, the dromos of which contained two very fine terra-cotta statues (one figured in Plate CLXXXVII, 4). The graves lay in the district between our cemetery-sections I and III of the excavation of 1886, which Monro[*]) in the Journal of Hellenic studies calls the west one in contradistinction to the east one in Nekropolis I. (Cf. Pl. CLXXIV, 1). As our sections I and II form one connected cemetery, I have marked this head as coming from Nekropolis I. The grave, a circular hole broader than it is deep with a steep dromos and rude staircase, is figured in Pl. CLXXV, 12 in a ground plan and section.

3. The upper part (portion preserved circa 0,198 m H.) of a fine female terra-cotta statue of the same Cyprio-Greek local style which I was the first to discover. In this case too the pupils are incised.

In Plate CLXXIV, 4 I figure the ground-plan and section of this grave which is of very irregular plan but cleanly hewn and dug. The staircase steps too were in this case very cleanly cut in the hard ground.

In the dromos I found no less than 12—15 (or even more) large terra-cotta statues packed together, some seated, some recumbent, but all purposely broken to atoms and with the heads knocked off.

Among the vases of local fabrique there were two water-jugs of polychrome technique with white body colour, sulpher yellow and dark red. The one had as spout an ox's head, the other a standing female figure carrying a jug.

Vases of black glazed Attic ware were to be found in large numbers and bore graffiti in the Cyprian syllabic writing. Among them one with four syllabic symbols ti-mo-ke-re = $T\iota\mu\omega\chi\varrho\varepsilon$ [$\tau\varepsilon o\varsigma$].[**])

---

*) Munro and Tubbs had an easy task, as they had only to follow up the traces of my discoveries. Cf. infra excursus at the end of this book.

**) Cf. Richard Meister "Griechische Dialekte" II, p. 177, No. 25 and the restoration by Deecke.

4. Head and breast of a clay statue preserved as far as the knee and now 0,425 m high. Of the same Graeco-Cyprian local style. The pupils are in this case also rendered by slight incisions. From grave 32, Nekr. I.

In the same grave was found a grave-stone with Kyprio-epichoric syllabic-inscription. The syllabic symbols were cut with the chisel and inlaid with strips of bronze.*)

5. Terra-cotta head. 0,11 m. Grave 130, Nekr. II.
6. Archaic-Greek terra-cotta mask H. 0,203 m. Grave 23, Nekr. II.

The face was painted vermilion. It was found in a side niche of the dromos of a grave in front of the door. In the same nekropolis I found a second, smaller terra-cotta mask of the same style. These masks resemble similar specimens found especially in Rhodes and Tanagra.

Plate CXXXVII.

Same provenance as previous plates.
1. Terra-cotta group. H. 0,596 m. Grave 122. Nekr. I.

The head of the large figure was found broken off, but belonging to it and stuck on again.**) The pupils in this case are neither given plastically as discs nor incised. Near the principal figure which is seated stands a small one whose head is missing. It holds in the right hand, which hangs down, a small cloth. The grave in this case consisted of a central space with two side chambers right and left and niches. In the stair-case entrance there were certainly over 20 clay statues packed together, all of them having been broken in pieces in antiquity.

2. Terra-cotta statue, H. 0,39 m. Grave 72, Nekr, II. Type the so-called "mourning" Penelope like CLXXXV, 3 only here of better style and better proportioned. Pupils rendered plastically.

In the same grave were found no less than eleven small black attic kylikes with graffiti of 1—2 Cyprian syllabic characters, The water jug too (figured above in Pl. LXIII, 2 (= CLXXX, 3 and 4) came from the same grave. The terra-cotta statue lay, as usual, in the entrance to the grave and broken to bits.***)

3. Clay statue H. 0,435. Grave 69, Nekr. II. Pupils rendered by slight depressions.

The missing portions are recognisable, being supplied by plaster of Paris. This figure too must have been put together long ago out of many pieces. In the same grave were found black Attic vases not only those of the 4th century B. C. but also a few specimens of the 5th. This statue is also somewhat more severe in style than the other three figures in this plate.†)

4 = Winckelmannsprogramm. Pl. I.

The terra-cotta statue, H. 0,755 m. I excavated myself, at my own expense in 1885 between Nekr, I and III in Negers' territory, near the last house to the south of the village of Poli; the spot must be counted as belonging to the same large cemetery to which our sections I and III belong i. e. Munro's western nekropolis. Now in Berlin. (Cf. Pl. CCXVIII, M. O.-R. first tomb).

The grave, in the approach to which the statue lay broken to bits and with it the remains of two other seated statues, is figured in Pl. CLXXV, 13 It is similar throughout to grave CLXXV, 12 (cf. also CLXXXVI. 2).

This fine seated monumental figure, discussed in detail by Herrmann (W. Progr. p. 41—42) and considered by him to be the work of an Attic artist of the end of the 5th century B. C. belongs, like the others in this and the preceding plate and like No. 3 on the last plate but one, to a school of Graeco-Cyprian local art which certainly was much influenced by Attic work and which extended its activity over a period of 100 years or more. The counterpart of these Cyprian and pure Greek terra-cotta statues of Marion-Arsinoë is presented by the life size terra-cotta statues of the Bumo sanctuary. (Cf. p. 350) This very statue here figured, which I excavated first of all in 1885, and which led definitely to the discovery of the towns of Marion-Arsinoë where art is so full of Greek elements, shows traces of having once being painted. These and other terra-cotta statues were first overlaid with a coat of white slip, on which the colour could be better fixed and which prevented its being so easily absorbed by the porous clay. Traces of red painting are preserved in this case. The polychrome technique of the vases in Pl. LXIV, 2, 4 and 7, where the little figures are painted white, flesh tint, red-purple and sky-blue oblige us to assume similar polychrome technique for the larger number of these terra-cotta statues. (Cf. also Plates LXVIII and CCII, 2 and 3, CCVIII, 1 and 2).

Plate CLXXXVIII.

The figure of a horseman which came from Amathus and is now in the possession of Herr Albert Brockhaus at Leipzig is 19¹/₄ cm high; its length from the tail-piece of the horse to the nostrils is about 13 cm; the length of the basis 15 cm.

The motive conceived in this and similar fashion is a very frequent one for Cyprian genre-figures which are for the most part of votive origin. The youthful figure mounted on the horse is beardless and is exceptionally broad and fat. In fact one person who examined it, i. e. the Indian savant Dr. Hermann Brunn-höfer of St. Petersburg took it, Herr Albert Brockhaus tells us, to be a woman. But against that there is the flatness of the breast and the pointed conical cap, the ordinary male head-gear, which indeed so far as I

*) R. Meister—Griechische Dialekte II, p. 175, No. 25, 1 ἀρὰ Διί.
**) Parts must be restored in plaster of Paris, in order to make it possible to put and keep together this terribly shattered group.
***) First published by me in Harper's Weekly, vol. XXXI. 1887, p. 408.
†) Published on the same page of the same publication.

know is still worn in Cyprus. Below this cap the hair, divided into long parallel locks, falls down over the back of the neck between the shoulders. The features have suffered somewhat from corrosion but seem to have been treated with a freedom that shows comparative emancipation from archaic severity. The absolute nudity of the figure presents no difficulty if it represents a god, a hero or a dead man heroized. Such an explanation would however so far as I know stand alone, whereas in the case of all the other numerous mounted figures (Cesnola-Stern Cyprus Pl. XXXVII, 2—4, 6. Cesnola Salaminia Fig. 249, 250, Döll, Coll. Cesnola Pl. XIV, 18—22, 24, cf alsn Pl. CXCII, 15 and others) and in the case of similar representations (man or man and wife in chariot Döll 14, 18—16, horses or mules laden with baskets and wares, Figs. 12, 17—23, quadriga with two male figures; Perrot-Chipiez Histoire de l'art dans l'antiquité III, Fig. 114 &c) we are led to the conclusion that these figures are genre representations of daily life in antiquity. It is in accordance with ancient conceptions of which we find the expression as well in the earliest days of Greek civilisation (cf. Furtwängler),[*] e. g. in the lowest strata at Olympia, or in the later periods (Köhler, Ueber die Ehre der Bildsäule, in his Gesammelte Schriften Bd. VI, p. 308) that sacrificial offering to the gods should be made not merely in natura but also vicariously by means of copies of the object sacrificed on a larger or smaller scale, and that to the most complete form of offering belonged the dedication of the actual person of the worshipper, either effectively and actually accomplished or symbolically by the offering of some portion of the person (pars pro toto), e. g. of the hair, or by the setting and consecration of a portrait, be it in the form of a life-sized statue or only a figure in a group as in the present case.

It is quite possible that some piece of drapery e. g. an apron such as so often occurs in the case of male figures was originally indicated in the horse-man figure in colour. We must anyhow assume such colouring to have been employed to depict the straps which we have to conceive of as existing on the chest of the horse carrying the rosette which is modelled plastically.

Plate CLXXXIX.

Already described p. 467 with plates CLXXIV and CLXXV (CLXXV, 6 = grave II in this plate., CLXXV, 7 = grave I of this plate) and compared with analogous graves in other countries. These two grave-structures were excavated in Dec. 1888 for Sir Charles Newton in a hill near Xylotimbo in the Famagusta district (territory of the former principality of Salamis) and the plans &c, which I made with great care, are here published for the first time.

Ground plan and sections show that the interior of both graves were of almost the same size and height. But grave II had an imposing façade and further was adorned above-ground by an external structure that was superimposed all round the whole site. The greater part of this enclosure, which consists of stone slabs, is preserved and each stone that is still in situ is represented in the ground plan II, 6. In the perspective view II, 5 further, the condition of the grave is preserved. I cleaned it out and enclosed it by a broad outside gravel walk. To the architecture, only the blocks marked black in the ground plan II, 6, belong. The great stone blocks are laid one on the other without mortar. In the parts where the masonry consists merely of filling in with quarry and field stones, lime-mortar is freely used. The stone cave-entrances are hewn out of the conglomerate. In both graves remarkable corner stones were found built into the corners and of these I figure two specimens to the right of the view II, 5.

I am able, by the light of my Cyprian studies, and the graves excavated at Tamassos, to assert as proved that these graves were built at the beginning of the 6th or end of the 7th century.

The only remaining contents of the graves were the wretched clay vases figured in the same plate. These make it certain that they were re-used more than once, probably in Hellenistic days, but also make the original date certain as of about 600 B. C.

Plate CXC.

1. a and b. Bearded wreathed head of a statue (limestone) from Cyprus. From coll. Cesnola. Berl. Mus. Antiquarium.

The head is damaged at the back. Eyeball and lips are painted red. The forehead is surrounded by a double line of small curls which get thicker on the temples. The curls of the whiskers are of similar form and should be compared with those of the small head in Pl. XLVIII, 1. The moustache is only given in slight relief and the surface is marked by a number of finely modelled lines. On the hair is a double wreath; the one wreath of wine or ivy-leaves lies flat on the hair; above it is a crown of lance-shaped leaves from which hang down thick knobs. The treatments of the features shows that the artist had emerged from the archaic period. A cross fold gives vitality to the forehead; the arch of the eyebrows is rendered by a deep sunk line as in the head Pl. XLVIII, 1. The profile approximates very closely to that of Classical Greek art. The lines of the mouth are strong; there is no archaic smile. This head represents a date at the beginning of the 5th century B. C. — the period shortly before that is represented by the head already mentioned Pl. XLVIII, 1 published Halm-Album Pl. 53.

2. Female head wearing Kalathos (limestone) from Cyprus, from the Coll. Schönborn. Berl. Mus. Antiquarium.

The back is damaged. Many parts of the face are too damaged. The head represents the severe fine style of the 5th century B. C., it is more advanced than the former. The head is adorned by a Kalathos the woven circle of which is clearly rendered — it is decorated with alternate rosettes and lotus-

---

*) Furtwängler "Ueber die Bronzen Olympias" in the Abhandlungen der Akad. d. Wiss., zu Berlin, 1879. Holwerda, "Die alten Kyprier in Kunst und Cultus", p. 37 ff. Dümmler, Mittheilungen d. Deutsch. Arch. Inst., zu Athen, XI, 1886, p. 240.

flowers. The hair is parted in the middle and combed to the side in beautiful waving lines. The ear ornament is pure Greek, it consists of a rosette to which is attached a prism-like pendant.

3. Female head—from a statue (limestone). From Coll. Schönborn. Provenance uncertain. Berl. Mus. Antiquarium.

The back is cut off quite smooth, the front badly damaged. But there is no doubt that the head is substantially earlier than the one already discussed (No. 2), possibly older than the male head in No. 1. The mouth shows archaic severity, so does the treatment of the eyes. The crown is interesting. On it are alternate crouching sphinxes full face and flower sprays; the topmost border too is formed of erect lotus-blossoms; as in the head in LV, 8. A similar crown of terra-cotta from Cyprus is published in Fröhner. Coll. Gréau, p. 124, No. 533.

These stone heads No. 2 and 3 belong to the cycle of the images of the Cyprian Tanit-Artemis-Kybele Cf. Pl. CCXI, 1—4 etc.

Plate CXCI.

1 and 2. Clay statue of an ox from Cappadocia. Berl. Mus. V. A. H. 0,35 m, L. 0,57 m.

The body of greyish-brown clay is covered with a fine coat of red slip and then polished. The details are partly modelled, partly represented by depressions, partly by incised or engraved lines. Cf. p. 233.

3 = XCIV. 2. An almost life-size ox-head of clay. From the Nekropolis of Hagia Paraskevi in Cyprus.

Technique as in 1 and 2, and exactly the same as in many Cyprian clay vessels of the bronze period. The arm, too, on Pl. XL, 8, is of the same clay. Cf. the silver cow's head from Mykenae, Schliemann, p. 250 and 251, which stands near to this Cyprian clay head both in point of time and style.

4. Stone figure from the grove of Rešef-Apollo at Frangissa. Between two rams, Baal-Zeus-Hammon is seated on a throned, holding a horn of plenty in his right hand. Cf. pag. 194.

‡ 5. The upper part of a Graeco-Phoenician-Cyprian vase of very light, thin, faintly coloured clay. The vase is painted black, and on the neck is a cow's head. Cf. p. 237.

6 = CXXXIV, 6. Limestone group from Idalion. Berl. Mus. Antiquarium. Earlier acquisition by L. Ross.

Here we have a ram richly coloured. The back worked flat, the space between the legs left unworked: the surface thus afforded is painted with wicker-work pattern in red. The eyes, muzzle, nostrils and ears are also painted red. On the ram rests some object which is painted red but unrecognizable. Below that we have to imagine a support. It is painted green with red tufts — on the unrecognizable object, a human mask or face can be made out — its mouth is painted red, the nostrils also are given in red. The nose is damaged. The eyes are recognizable as rude depressions. The whole stands on a basis which extends back to a breadth of 0,050 m and of which the back edge is broken off. The edge in front and at the sides is painted red. Above the mask is a tray-shaped object hollowed out and its back half broken off just at the back of the ram. H. 0.085 m. (H. S.)

°7. A very beautiful Attic Rhyton, in the form of a ram's head. Marion-Arsinoë 1886. Grave 51. Nekr. III. The picture on the neck of the vase represents two maidens, with their skirts raised about their waists dancing round a fluteplayer. In the same grave were found the beautiful, pure Greek stele of Cyprian limestone, Pl. CLXXVI, 1 and the silver ring, Pl. CLXXXII, 38.

Plate CXCII.

1—13. Selection of Cyprian coins from J. P. Six. Du classement des séries Cypriotes. Extrait de la Revue Numismatique, Paris 1883, cf. p. 243.

1 = Six Pl. VI, 3. Silver coin of Nikodamos or Lacharidas. Obv. recumbent sheep — Rev. hooked cross.

2 = Six Pl. VI, 5. Gold coin, Euagoras I (410—374 B. C.) obv. Head of Herakles with lion's skin Rev. forepart of chevreuil.

3 = Six Pl. VI, 11. Gold coin of Nikokles (374—368 B. C.) obv. Head of Aphrodite or Artemis. Rev. Head of Athene.

4 = Six Pl. VI, 16. Bronze coin Euagoras II. Obv. head of Athene. Rev. forepart of bull.

5 = Six VII, 15. Silver coin, possibly of Paphos (circ. 480—460 B. C.). Obv. the river Bokaros in the form of a recumbent bull. Rev. small knuckle bone.

6 = Six VI, 7. Silver coin, Euagoras I. Obv. Herakles seated with club and cornucopia. Rev. recumbent chevreuil or human. headed horned quadruped.

7 = Six VI, 12. Bronze coin of Nikokles. Obv. Aphrodite. Rev. Dolphin. Cf. p. 202.

8 = Six VI, 20. Silver coin, date and place uncertain. Obv. lion. Rev. bull.

9 = Six VII, 14. Obv. River-god Bokaros as human-headed bull. Rev. Small knuckle bone.

10 = Six VII, 20. Silver coin of Gorgos or Onesilos. Obv. hooked cross. In the hook the syllabic character Ku. In the corners lotus-buds.

11 = Six VII, 21. Silver coins with head of sheep Date and place still undetermined.
12 = Six VI, 21. Silver coins, date and place undetermined. Obv. recumbent lion, above bird flying. Rev. forepart of lion.
13 = Six VII, 12. Silver coin of Stasinoikos. Obv. Head of Zeus. Rev. Head of Aphrodite.

°14. Terra-cotta H. 0,155 m. Aphrodite riding on swan. Excavated in 1881 for Sir Charles Newton from a Hellenistic grave at Salamis (near Enkomi).
In the British Museum. Similar replica but in better preservation published in Salaminia, Plate fac. p. 204. I saw several replicas of this type at the house of Alex. P. di Cesnola in Cyprus.*)

‡ 15. Richly painted rude Cyprian terra-cottas from Athiaenou, now in Vienna. Cf. Jahrb. d. k. deutsch. Arch. Instituts 1892, p. 115, No. 109.
Graeco-Phoenician island style. "Snow-man" technique.

Plate CXCIII.

The objects reproduced in this plate are discussed in detail on p. 191.
1 and 2. Tumulus of Sesönk. Humann-Puchstein, "Reisen in Kleinasien und Nordsyrien" Fig. 34 and 37.
2—5. Tumulus of Kara-Kusch. Humann-Puchstein op. cit. Fig. 40, 41, 53.
6. Votive column from Athens, Ross, Archäologische Aufsätze. Pl. XIV, 1.
7. Panathenaic prize-amphora. Ross, op. cit. Pl. XIV, 5.
8. Ross, op. cit. Pl. XIV, 6.
9. Column from a clay relief. Campana op. di plast. 5; Ross, op. cit. Pl. XIV, 4.

Plate CXCIV.

1a and b. Relief from Nineveh. Perrot II, p. 76, Fig. 13 and p. 77, Fig. 14.
A trinity of divinities seem to be represented here in procession; in front, on the throne, are seated two goddesses, behind is the horned principal god Baal-Moloch with axe and bundle of rods. The child who is carried behind the goddesses and in front of the god seems destined to be a human sacrifice.
2 = CXII, 4. The Griffins are represented as superior in power to mortals, are in fact, monsters who are tearing them to pieces.
3 = CXIV, 4. The griffin holds a human head between his front paws.
4 = CLI, 34. Representation of a human sacrifice.
5 = XXXII, 37 = CXIV, 3. Griffin tearing a stag in pieces. Below a Medusa or human head.
6. Cyprian cylinder. Cesnola Salaminia, Pl. XII, 12. Two men stand near two seated divinities, one of which has a child in its lap.
7 = CXIV, 5. Two quadrupeds tear a human being in pieces. Above hovers an eagle.
8 and 6 also. Salaminia, Pl. XII, 13. Similar representation, the child hovers between the two seated figures.
The representations in these plates are intended to illustrate human sacrifice and the dominion of divinities, daemons and mythical beings**) over mortals. (Cf. also the silver kylix from Idalion, p. 441, Fig. 257).

Plate CXCV.

Vase from Idrias in Karia. Perrot V, p. 329, Fig. 233 = Winter, Mittheilungen von Athen, XII, Pl. VI.
What has been found so far in the way of vases in Karia points to a connection with Cyprus. Further excavations in Asia Minor are much to be desired.

Plate CXCVI.

Four chariot scenes of stone, all from the same nekropolis and from the Graeco-Phoenician stratum of the 6th and 5th century B. C. From Amathus in Cyprus. All show traces of painting Cf. p. 284.
‡ 1. Biga, limestone. H. 0,15 m. Breadth of the slab 0,21 m. Cf. Jahrbuch des k. deutschen archäol. Instituts. Anzeiger 1891, 4, p. 171, Fig. 5. In Vienna. Obtained by me. Shews remains of red and black painting. Cf. p. 284.

---

*) The same or a similar motive, Aphrodite riding on a swan, appears on an Attic reed-shaped lekythos of Marion-Arsinoë. Journal of Hellenic Studies 1891, Pl. XIII, p. 317, Fig. 3. The motive must have been a very popular one on the island. It almost seems as if Attic vase-painters had painted this design on their vases actually with a view to the Cyprian market.
**) In our discussion on the representations of sphinxes and griffins, either singly or in pairs, in Cyprian Graeco-Phoenician art (pp. 430—433, Pl. CXII CXVII) we overlooked an instructive analogy, which A. S. Murray (A history of Greek sculpture, London 1880, p. 35) was the first to establish between Cyprian finds and Phoenician discoveries, found in Phoenicia itself. These important researches of Murray speak for the priority of the Cyprian works and their Graeco-Phoenicia character.

Genre-scene — The charioteer stands at rest between the two horses that are prancing to be off. A woman looks out of the tent-like chariot which is otherwise completely covered with draperies. A third person, probably a eunuch, follows the chariot and seems to be holding together the draperies which are stretched over the chariot, so that no profane eye may look into the chariot. It is a scene taken from actual harem life, just such a one as may be seen now-a-days in Cyprus. The very shape of the two-wheeled car hung over with drapery and semi-circular at the top is the same. In the same nekropolis has been found another such a two-wheeled close shut harem carriage, only without figures. It was sold in an auction held on the 15th and 16th of June 1891 at Paris, together with the quadriga and the procession car No. 4. (Cat. Fröhner-Hoffmann, Pl. III, No. 129.)

2. Limestone quadriga. H. 0,20. Of the horse only, 0,13 m. Breadth of the slab 0,24. Total length 0,275 m. Seems to be a war or procession chariot. The body of the chariot has two compartments. To the right in the larger compartment stands the charioteer, to the left either a warrior or the image of some divinity. Both are of frequent occurrence. The man is perceptibly bald, and the bald place on his head is painted with the same flesh colour as his face and the forepart of his head.

† 3. Limestone. H. 0,168 m. Breadth of slab 0,150 m. A biga. In Dresden. Obtained by me. A man in a pleated shirt (cf. the statuette in Pl. XLI, 1–3) crouches in the small backless, armless seat of the vehicle. The picture reproduces the painting which is of red colour.

4. Limestone. Four horse procession chariot. H. 0,29 m. L. 0,20 m. Cat. Fröhner-Hoffmann, No. 131, Pl. IV. (Cf. No. 1.) The same pleated garments are used both for the charioteer and in the colossal image of the goddess or her priestess or representative, as in the case of the car in No. 3 (and in the figures of Pl. XLI, 1–3). Painting in green*) white body colour and red. In this case the wheels are preserved; there are three, so that this chariot can drive along over a level surface — like a toy — without scratching. In spite of this we must regard it as a votive offering. With this group should be compared the procession chariot on the gold breast-plate. (Plate CXCIX, 3.)

Plate CXCVII.

1. Ionic limestone capital from the Acropolis of Kition, H. 0,45. Diameter at the base 0,44 m. From a new photographic view placed at my disposal by W. Dörpfeld. There is a bad reproduction of it in Perrot III, p. 264, Fig. 798. A comparison with the representation in Plates CLIX—CLXIII and CXXIV, 5 makes it all the more probable that as a matter of fact the Ionic capital took its rise from the lotus blossom and the Egyptian lotus capital, though Assyrian, Hittite and Asia Minor forms contributed to its development. They all finally culminate in Egypt Cypriots, Cyprian-Greeks and Phoenicians all took a prominent part in this formation of the Graeco-Ionic capital. The pure Greek form developed from Cyprio-Graeco-Phoenician which in their turn were preceded by Egyptian forms. The American writer W. H. Goodyear has rendered to archaeology a cardinal service by his investigations in the Egyptian origin and primitive form of the lotus, although some links in his chain of argument are missing. (Grammar of the Lotus.)**) Cf. p. 190—194

2 = CII, 1 = CXXXIV, 2 = p. 193, Fig. 167. Cf. 180, 192, 281, 426, and 443.

This limestone holy-water stoup or censer 0,95 m high was bought by me in the village of Voni on which account R. von Schneider (Jahrbuch-Anzeiger, 1891, p. 171) gives Voni as the place of provenance. On the contrary, the vessel was found in the ruins of Chytroi itself, to the north of Voni. The prototype given in this plate and taken from the original supplements other publications. The winged woman holds a winged sun-disc in front of her and leans on a pillar which forms together with her the support of the basin.

°3. Limestone ornamental lion with Cyprian inscription. Marion-Arsinoë, 1886. H. 0,38. L. 0,44 m. D. 0,16 m. Grave 117, Nekr. I. Head hewn off. The inscription runs according to W. Deecke and R. Meister:

Τιμόκυπρος, ὁ Τιμοκρέτεος ἐπίστασε Γιλ(λ)ίκαϝι τῶι κασιγνήτωι.

The lion plays, as we have seen, a conspicuous part in Cyprian art, but not till the 7th century B. C. (Cf. too the coins on Pl. CXCII, 8 and 12.)

° 4. Limestone water-stoup or censer from Cyprus. Only the foot in the form of a winged sphinx is partly preserved. From the sanctuary of Resef-Apollo at Frangissa (No. 4 in the list).

† 5. Limestone water-stoup or censer from Athienou in Cyprus. The nose of the sphinx which forms the foot is broken off. Cf. p. 199 and 443. Painted red and black. In front of the breast there is also a maeander pattern.

Plate CXCVIII.

° 1. Bronze mirror-handle reproduced almost on the original scale. Marion-Arsinoë, 1886, Gr. 94, Nekr. II. At present in Berlin. Cf. p. 220 and Furtwängler's report of acquisitions. Arch. Jahrb. III, p. 239 and 240.

---

*) Green paint occurs also elsewhere in Cyprus in the case of clay and stone figures at Tamassos, Frangissa and Idalion. e. g. Pl. LXVIII, 2. Great quantities of chariot scenes, for the most part quadrigas and images of war-chariots with warriors, were deposited as votive offerings on the altar in the grove of Resef-Apollo at Frangissa No. 4. These are chariots and horses of the sun.
**) Cf. supra, p. 104, Note 4. Goodyear is here clearly on the right road. Cf. also O. Puchstein, "Das Jonische Capitell". Winckelmannsprogramm 1887 and Koldewey, Niandria. Winckelmannsprogramm, 1891. Indepedently of Goodyear, I had included a large number of these Monuments in my investigations and had published them. A more complete collection including them, appear in "The Grammar of the Lotus". On the other hand I believe that I too have, by my own investigations, and by means of the monuments I myself excavated, added something to the history of the development of the Ionic capital and have shown the important share taken in it by the island of Cyprus and Cyprian art. C. Belger drew my attention to the bronze candelabra from Cyprus, figured in Pl. XLII, 8—10, each of whose branches ends in two lotus buds folded over the other, and reminds me of the lotus capitals and analogous designs. Particularly interesting is the comparison of these Cyprian bronze candelabra with those of the carved gems (Pl. LXXXII, 3) and with the capitals from Neandria (Koldewey, Winckelmannsprogramm, p. 34 and 36, Fig. 60 and 61).

Good Greek work. Eros seated with outspread wings on a small capital of Ionic style which grows up out of the spiral. Attention has often been called to the analogies between Etruscan and Cyprian discoveries. The nearest analogy to this Cyprian mirror-handle is Etruscan work of a similar sort.

†2. Marble figure for a fountain from the ruins of Neapaphos. L. 0,567 m. H. 0,262 m. Now in the Cyprus Museum. Presented by Mr. Tompson.

Eros asleep on a garment spread over a wine skin. Cf. supra p. 226 and 267. Good Graeco-Roman work, worthy of detailed publication. Of the replicas of this motive that exist in the Museums this Cyprian specimen seems to me to be by far the most important.

Figs. 3 and 4 are included in this plate only to utilize the space and to avoid having another special plate.

⁰3. Fragment of a heavy gold cylix. Marion-Arsinoë, 1886. Grave 92, Nekr. II.

The grave from which came the marble torso Pl. XXVII, 3. Ground plan and section Pl. CLXXIV, 2. The fragment of the golden cylix weighs 13½ lbs. Clearly only a fragment cut off from the cylix had been given to the dead man in his grave. On the bowl were two rows of acorns alternating with two of lotus blossoms in relief.

⁰4. Terra-cotta mask, reproduced almost in its original size, with two holes behind the ears and a hole above for suspending it. Dali 1885, No. 36 of the list. Worship of a sacred tree in which were hung numerous masks. Cf. p. 19 und 146.

Plate CXCIX.

⁰1, 2. Small shrine (terra-cotta) from Amathus. In the possession of Ohnefalsch-Richter.

In the interior of the shrine, whose outer edge is somewhat damaged, is a figure of exceedingly primitive shape; it has a mantle drawn over the head, the right arm is uplifted and carried to the face. The mantle has small buttons at the head level. At the inside edge of the shrine primitive volutes have been stuck on separately. On figure 1 there is one clearly visible. The two outside edges of the larger sides have each of them 6 knobs; the lowest on the left side is broken off. On the upper edge in the middle, there is the combined symbol of the sun and half moon which so frequently appears in Cyprus. Near to it are traces of larger knobs. At the back of the shrine beneath there are separate pieces added on which served as supports for setting it up. The grave in which this object was found is figured in Pl. CLXXV. 2.

Cf. p. 190, 235, 251, f and 300, note 5, as well as what was said above in the explanation of Pl. CXXXVIII and CXXXIX with respect to the breastplates and Aaron's in particular.

Again the Cyprian stone-capitals Pl. CLXII, 5, CLXIII,11 &c, should be compared with the diminutive primitive columns that bear capitals of obviously Ionic tendency.

⁰3. Embossed Gold plate from Kurion in Cyprus. Berlin Museum. Antiquarium M. J. 7932.

For the whole contents of the grave now in the Berlin Museum cf. Furtwängler, Jahrbuch des arch. Instituts, 1886, I. Anzeiger, p. 132. The gold plate was found in the terracotta sarcophagus there mentioned. The representation is both as to subject and treatment of the highest interest. The image of a goddess who clasps her breast with her two hands is led out on a two-wheeled chariot. While the image stands en face the charioteer is represented in profile. The treatment of the face reminds one of the Dipylon vases and certain Cyprian cylinders (Cf. Plate CXXVIII, 5). On account of the beak-shaped profile of the animals, Furtwängler thought they were griffins, but he did not explain them as such for certain as they had no wings. We find, the beak tendency, however, appears also in the profile of the charioteer. (Cf. further Pl. CLXXXII, 3.) The gold ring and gold pin figured in the same place came from the same grave. The style is the most primitive Cyprian. Similar gold plates may be seen in Pl. XXV, 10, 12—14. The plate has been already published in Reinach "Chroniques d'orient", p. 268, (6², 98—99). Cf. also the description and explanation of this breast-plate given above to Pl. CXXXVIII, and CXXXIX.

4 = Pl. CXXIV, 4.

5, 6, 7. Open limestone box from Tamassos. Berlin Museum. Antiquarium M. J. 8105, 6. Breadth 0,065 Height 0,090 m.

The principal side (No. 7) is distinguished by the design of a hunt in low relief. Two quadrupeds are represented of which one is horned, possibly they are a male and female chevreuil.

The hunter is depicted as though floating in the air with his bow drawn. Near him at the upper edge is a third and smaller wild animal, possibly the young one of the larger creature. To the right a tree on which are perched four birds. Round the tree are four swastikas. The back of the casket (No. 5) is decorated only with line ornaments, triangles placed opposite each other. The narrow sides (No. 6) are equal and on them are depicted two nude female figures in relief of the so called "worshipper type" which occupy quadrangular spaces surrounded by a double border. This type is very frequent in Cyprus as I have already noted (cf. Pl. LI, 6).

Cf p. 268, 285 and the text to Pl. CXXXIII, where reference is also made to the analogy with the Boeotian casket (1—4) with others from Cyprus (5—8) and with the Tamassos vase (p. 37 Fig. 38).

Plate CC.

†1 and 2. Stone capital from a house in Larnaka. Now in the Louvre. (Cf. supra p. 187). Cast in the Syrian department of the Berlin Museum.

This is a Cyprian imitation of Egyptian original. On a calix-shaped capital stands a head of Hathor, above this again a shrine. In the door of this stands a figure the significance of which cannot be precisely determined. At either side of the door is a Hathor head on a high pillar-like pedestal. They seem to represent in miniature the votive-pillars to which the capitals which alone are preserved belong. The double abacus is decorated below with a winged sun-disc above with star-shaped rosettes. The foliage and palmette pattern which runs at either side of the shrine is finely and carefully modelled. The capital is intended to be looked at all round. The narrower sides are carefully worked from a profile point of view. The back (Fig. No. 2) is somewhat differently decorated in the uppermost part. In place of the temple are groups of palmettes the decorative elements of which remind one of representations of the sacred tree. In the calix of the palmette two sphinxes are grouped in heraldic fashion. The whole scheme of ornamentation is closely allied to that of the well-known Cyprian stelae (cf. Pl. XXVI). These Hathor capitals too, seem to belong to unattached stelae. Ohnefalsch-Richter conjectures that their provenance is Kition (p. 187). No. 2 is published in Reinach Chroniques d'orient p. 178, (5², 347).

‡3. Exactly similar capital from another house in Larnaka. Now in the Syrian department of the Berlin Museum. 2715.

The abacus over the temple door has a border of dog-tooth and is decorated with a winged sun-disc. The back of this stele is exactly similar to the side figured. The narrow left side is damaged.

4. Fragment of a similar capital from the akropolis of Amathus. Now in Berl. Museum. Antiquarium M. J. 8171.

Of the Hathor head there is preserved the left roll of hair and the left ear. In place of the temple façade we have the figure of a man walking left who is taming two wild animals in the heraldic scheme. The back has suffered considerably. As to all front capitals of text v. p. 187.

I was the first to discover these remarkable Cyprio-Egyptian capitals and to recognise their importance for the history of art. Through my intervention they passed into the museums of Berlin and Paris. The capital that I found in conjunction with W. Dörpfeld on the slope of the akropolis hill at Amathus belongs to the same series but it unites in a curious way the influences of Egypt, Assyria and Greece, while the two capitals from Kition betray a more Cyprio-Egyptian tendency. The specimen from Amathus is indeed an imitation of an Egyptian Hathor-capital, but a very free one. About the Hathor head are no accessories borrowed from Egypt. On the other hand we do find an Assyrian motive, in fact that of the "animal tamer" standing between two winged horses, and in the renewing of its outlines and in style generally it has passed here into the domain of archaic Greek art. (Cf. supra Pl. CXI with text).

Plate CCI.

Plan of a part of the Akropolis of Kition called Bambula for shortness.

(Cf. supra. p 280).

The description begins below.
T.   The portion of ground yet untouched.
H.   A canal, for draining off the water, about 0,31 m deep and cemented throughout; it debouched into the ancient harbour which abutted on to our masonry at the east side.
C—G.   Masonry of buildings of at least two stories.
C.   Pavement slabs jutting out.
D.   Carefully hewn blocks of stone end up. ⎫
E.   A complete wall line of carefully hewn blocks. ⎬ Lime-mortar employed.
F.   Wall lines of roughly hewn blocks. ⎪
G.   Lime-mortar in stone partition walls. ⎭
A.   Long line of wall built of large free-stone blocks and rising to an impressive height. At A are depressions in the stone blocks which from their shape and size were intended to receive strong wooden stanchions.
B.   A reservoir of long curved shape, sunk vertically and rendered water-proof with lime-mortar.
I. J.   Two similar receptacles cut of circular shape.
K.   Here there was a round space in the stone wall which had belonged to a similar receptacle but it had been hewn away by the workmen before I reached the spot.
L.   Puteal in situ, disused well.
M.   Basis of pillar in situ.
N   Compact quadrangular masonry with small outshoots. N'.
Is there not an analogy between this and the quadrangular structure in the Dali-sanctuary Pl. VII, on which I thought the cone of Astarte rested? (Cf. Pl. LVI).
O.   Walls deep sunk, and round them a pavement with stone slate and still deeper sunk.
P.   Remains of a wall of gravel behind rough walls of quarried stone.
Q.   Remains of the lining of a vertical partition wall.
R.   Column standing high above the rest. Broken column in situ.
S.   Long quandrangular space which certainly formed the chamber for votive offerings in the sanctuary of the pair of deities Astarte-Mikal. On the north-east entrance wall, which unhappily was much broken away before I could get it drawn into the plan, stood still in situ the holy-water stoup decorated with palmettes in Assyrian style mentioned above. The votive-offerings lay here in a mound.
I figure the principal specimens here. Fig. 263. The terra-cotta vases, with one exception, belong to Hellenistic or Roman times. On the other hand the clay censer that lies to the front in the middle is early work and belongs to the sixth and seventh century B. C. It is not unlike a modern candle-stick

and its shape is characteristic of early times. Next came some male and female Cyprian heads, idols of Egyptian style, the goddess with the child (as in Pl. XXXVII, 9), a similar statue but of more Assyrian style, several cow-headed idols (one large one Pl. XCIV, 4) and the fragment of an incense-vessel mentioned by Ceme in the Jahrbuch des Instituts 1890. (Cf. supra p. 444 and Pl. CXXXV), &c.

In Figs. 264—266 the reader will see three views of the removal of the mound which was undertaken under the direction of Lieutenant (now Captain) Sinclair. It was the removal of this hill that led me to the discovery of the Akropolis of Kition and of the sanctuary of Asaure. Fig. 264 shows us from the east the line of high massive walls A made conspicuous by deep shading. On it about the left the spaces shown in outline and marked B, C, D, G, F.

Fig. 264.

Fig. 265.

Fig. 266.

Fig. 266.

Fig. 265 gives us a view of the same and from the east side, i. e. from the harbour of Kition, only at a greater distance. To the right at the top the broken column B is seen standing conspicuously on the raised ground while in the middle behind the seated figures and the horse is this ground space B.

Last Fig. 266 shows the hill Bamboula at still greater distance and from the east. The views are taken from the Graphic (London 1880 pp. 76 and 261, and are faithful reproductions of my original photographs.[*])

What was saved is due to the attention of Captain Sinclair, as are also the finds of Phoenician inscriptions that were made here (C. I. Sem. 56 and 67, cf. p. 171 and 185). The site was visited in 1887 by both Sir Henry Layard and Sir Charles Newton. Neither had any knowledge of early Phoenician structure. I myself at that date had had no experience. Thus it happened that these exceedingly interesting Phoenician structures did not receive the attention they deserved, and that many wall-structures were broken down long ago that ought to have been left standing or at least much more carefully measured than was done by me. Above all a number of exact sections ought to have been made, none of which unhappily were made. Also owing to the misfortune that befell me at Niccosia, I lost a number of my views of the hill, e. g. a view from the wall, and hence I cannot give so complete a ground

*) A detailed description of the site and the finds appeared in "Ausland 1876 pp. 970 994 in my paper " Neue Funde auf Cypern. Die Akropolis von Kition und ein Nekropolitum der syrischen Astarte ".

62

plan as was contemplated. To the S. W. the fortifications end in a tower. To the N. E a small staircase leading down to a lower level abuts on the space S. and N. On this staircase lay the figurine in
Pl. CCII, 5. This little staircase, which certainly led down to the little temple cellar, again corresponds
to the little staircase of Cyprian precincts and the chapels that lie near them.

It is only after the lapse of years and by means of experience gathered in countless other
excavations on the island that I have obtained a more exact knowledge of the measuring of Cyprian
Graeco-Phoenician structures. I am only able, however, to present to the reader of the present book a
portion of the material for the history of architecture that I have collected, and I hope on another
occasion to make further compilations to fill the lacuna. Had I know in 1879 what I now know,
something would have been done to in order to preserve for posterity at least adequate views and sections
of the Akropolis of Kition that was cleared away. Such views and sections alas, now are lost for ever
and belong to the limbo of lost hopes.

Plate CCII.

Cyprian Terra-cottas.

? 1. Statuette of peaceful Athene resting from battle, 0,21 m. high.

Greek grave of the Salaminian plain, excavated for Sir Charles Newton (1889), between the village
of Enkomi and the monastery of H. Varnavas. The treatment somewhat sketchy but of fine Greek style.
Badly published by me in the Athenian Mittheilungen VI p. 250, by Percy Gardner in the Journal of Hellenic
Studies (1881 pl. XVI), by A. S. Murray (History of Greek Sculpture H. Pl. 17) and by S. Reinach (Chroniques
d'Orient p. 188. (5² 851.) Adequately published here for the first time. Cf. p. 299.

‡ 2—4. Terra-cottas from Hellenistic graves at Kurion, which were found by peasants and by a
Limissiot Alexandros (since dead) in 1883 at Kurion.*)

2, High-girt Artemis richly painted. She caresses the dog painted sulphur-yellow.**)

3. Very charming lyre-player — female. Remains of red paint on the instrument.

More probably a musician or a temple attendant. In A. P. de Cesnola's Salaminia (Plate facing
p. 212) there is a very similar but even more beautiful figure from Salamis.

4. Woman in motion with torch. Possibly an Artemis or priestess of Artemis.

These Kurion statuettes remind one of the Kyrenaika finds.

‡ 5, 6 and 8. Terra-cottas from Kition, ? 7 from Salamis.

5. Veiled genre figurine of fine biscuit-like clay quite in the style of Greek terra-cotta
fabriques of Kition. Now in the possession of the engineer Mr. W. Williams (Nicosia), found by the
quarry-men of Mr. Sturgis in the Akropolis of Kition and indeed close to the little staircase and to the
north entrance to the sanctuary, west of M (Ground plan CCI).

6. Upper part of a draped figurine from the same akropolis. Was purloined by the workmen
and came into the hands of a barber. Clay with white slip. Quality same as e. g., p. 316, and
Fig. 233.

? 7, Excavated by me at Salamis in the same Necropolis as 1 in 1881. It is my opinion that
this mother in the long garment holding a child is no Aphrodite κουροτρόφος but a mere genre figure.
Cf. Pl. CCV, 4, 5, 7—9 and Pl. XXXVII.

‡ 8. Female draped figure from the salt lake near Kition. H. 0,20 m. She carries a jug on her
head. From the earlier collection of D. Pierides. Style and treatment of head, specially in the face,
resemble the former figure.

Plate CCIII.

5 a & b = p. 310—313, Fig. 221—223.
Artemis group from Kition, described p. 309—315.
Figs 1—4 are placed above it for comparison.
1 = p. 314, Fig 231. Gerhard. Akad. Abhandlung., XXIX, 6. 0,356 m. high. Figure in marble.
Formerly in coll. Rollin.
2 = p. 314, Fig. 229. Etruscan bronze figure — Gerhard. Akad. Abhandlung. XXVIII, 6.
Shoes with turned up toes. This particular shape of foot covering plays a conspicuous part
among the Hittites, Cyprian and Etruscans only.

---

*) Messrs. J. W. Williamson and C. Christian had managed to get rom island authorities a comprehensive permit for excavations
and that without any control exercised on the spot either by the Government or by the Cyprus Museum. They had the work carried on
without any of that archaeological supervision by a competent person which elsewhere has constantly been exercised on the spot. The
director and inspector of the excavations was the Cypriot Alexandros already mentioned, and who did not know how to write. The nekropolis, which contained great quantities of glass vessels (e. g. the glass vessels in Pl. LXV supra, the purple-red and white cylikes and the
blue-white alabastron) were discovered by Mr. Gordon Hake when he was excavating there in 1882 for the South Kensington Museum. The
English managers of the excavation expended something over £ 100, and realized, as they told me themselves, by the sale of the principals
collection after deduction of the third portion belonging to the museum the sum of £ 600.

**) The dimensions of these and some other figures and of those immediately following I cannot give at the moment as my note
are not to hand. They are, except where the contrary is stated, terracottas of small size.

⚲ 8 = p. 314, Fig. 230. Female draped figure of the so-called "Spes" type (limestone) from Marion. Berl. Mus. Antiquarium. M. I. 8138.

This figure is in fact the most interesting specimen of the Cyprian collection in the Berlin Museum, and is especially noteworthy because the rich colouring is perfectly preserved. The back is worked smooth up to the head and back portion of the neck. The height amounts to 0,179 m. It belongs to the mature archaic Greek style. The figure is draped in a long chiton with many folds and a himation. This is arranged over both shoulders so that in front it falls in a bow-shaped fold and one end rests upon the right arm which is bent. On the right side the mantle falls in the familiar schematic fashion. The folds of the garments are rendered plastically, the edges are painted with broad red stripes. On the chiton also the folds are painted red and the collar still remains. Specially interesting are the evident traces of painted swastikas. The coiffure is the same as in Pl. LIV, 2, 3. The tuft of hair is twisted round with a narrow handkerchief whose waving edges are sharply rendered in relief. On the handkerchief are stripes of colour, and indeed there are dark red stripes to be seen alternating with stripes consisting of rows of red spots in the rough stone. At the topmost paint of the globe-shaped coiffure appears a small portion of the black hair as in Pl. LIV, 5. The finely modelled hair on the brow is painted black. The features are rounded and delicate, the profile is still somewhat oblique. The eyebrows are very delicately painted in black, so are the eyelids and pupils of the eyes which are modelled in almond-shaped relief. Here therefore we find what we sought in vain among the other stone figures i. e. the rendering of the eyelids.

The finely cut lips are painted with thin red streaks, the eyelids are rendered in the same fashion. From the ear-lap hangs the red-bordered disk shaped ornament. The shell of the ear here again is modelled into three different parts as in Pl. LIV, 3. Here it has the look as if it were intended to represent not the ear itself especially but rather an ornament of the ear which is either very similar to or identical with the specifically Cyprian kind. We have seen with what tenacity this fashion was adhered to. The neck is adorned by a broad band outlined in red; to the middle of this is attached an ornament. A chain of tassels hangs down upon the breast. The figure in our plate is published in the Report of acquisitions of the royal Museum of Berlin Jahrb. d. arch. Inst. 1891, VI, Anzeiger p. 127. As regards the cap, Furtwängler cites the Κεκρύφαλος with the πλεκτὴ ἀναδέσμη of the Ionian women (cf. Helbig Hom. Ep. 2, p. 222 and Berl. Phil. Wochenschrift 1888, Sp. 458). In the same grave I found a second figure of the same size and otherwise identical but of finer modelling and better preserved as to outline and colour. It fell to the share of the Cyprus Museum; moreover I found a terra-cotta of the advanced archaic Greek style representing a seated goddess with both hands upon her knees, 0,112 m high, a type exceedingly common in Cyprus and especially in Marion-Arsinoë and which is identical with those found in Rhodes, both as to motive, style and material. (Heuzey, Figurines de terre cuite. Pl. XIV, 2.) We came also in the same grave on some Attic stamped terra-cotta ware of the 4th century B. C. and on the fragments of a Cyprian water-jug, brown, with painting in black (as in Pl. LXIV, 1—3) and on the fragments of another polychrome jug with red and sulphur coloured painting on white slip (as in Pl. LIV, 4—7). The fragments of this last lead me to conclude that it was an unusually large specimen, as the extant spout, that of an ox's head, is by itself 0,048 m high. The grave-structure is hewn out of conglomerate has a sloping dromos and is like the one figured in Pl CLXXV, 14. It has been used several times during the second half of the fifth and on to the end of the 4th century B. C. (Cf. infra Pl. CCXVIII, and explanatory text). The style and dress, especially of the cap, worn by our two stone figures remind us strongly of the corresponding Etruscan statues which are also contemporaneous, i. e. they fall about the time of the sixth and fifth centuries B. C.

Plate CCIV.

1. Seated goddess (terra-cotta) from Larnaka. From coll. Cesnola. Berl. Mus. Antiquarium. T. C. 6682, 37.

The figure is admirably well preserved. The goddess wears a long chiton and is covered by a cloak with fine folds which is drawn over the back of the head and leaves the right hand free. It rests on the upper thigh. The left hand rests on the breast and is completely covered by the cloak. The right seems to hold something. Besides the head-band which appears below the cloak the goddess wears a crown ornamented with rosettes. The back of it is missing. The hair falls down in long locks over the ears. The legs are not close together; the left foot is somewhat drawn back and brings into play an effective scheme of folds. The great side wings of the back support of the throne fall open. The style is of the 4th century B. C.

2. Group of a seated goddess and 2 priestesses (terra-cotta) from Larnaka. Berl. Mus. Antiquarium. T. C. 6223.

The heads of the figures have been fastened on but belong to them. The seated goddess represents the same type as the previous one. The position is somewhat more formal and legs are closely glued together. In the right hand the goddess seems to hold an attribute, possibly a kylix or fruit. The dress is the same as in the previous figure. Here then we have a well-established type. At both sides of the throne stand the hand-maidens on a smaller scale; their dress is thrown on the left leg, the right is unemployed. Their dress consists of a long chiton and cloak which is drawn over the head. They too, like the goddess, wear crowns. On the left arm they carry a sort of casket. Their attitude shows that these figures are hand-maidens of the goddess.

3. Seated goddess with fruit (terra-cotta) from Larnaka. From coll. Cesnola. Berl. Mus. Antiquarium. T. C. 6682, 42.

The type is the same in essentials. The position of the legs is somewhat freer than in No. 1. The cloak is arranged over the lower part of the body and is drawn backwards and laid over the head from which it hangs down on the left side, so that the upper portion of the body and the arm are left free. The right hand is in the same attitude as in the preceding examples but holds no attribute, the left holds an apple in front of the breast. On the breast there hangs a splendid piece of jewelry. The close clinging chiton which leaves the navel visible through it, has an overfold. Besides armlets the upper part of the arms wear triple clasps.

In conclusion a peculiarity must be noted which is common to all three figures. The feet have round the ankles ring-shaped rolls which can have no connection either with the drapery or the shoes, but must have been laid on separately like anklets. These rings are to be regarded as ornaments and occur also in the fragmentary feet LII, 8 and 9.*) The so-called "fetters" for the feet of the Aphrodite Morpho at Sparta must be explained in the same way. These gave rise to curious myths. (Cf. Paus. III, 15, 10. Curtius, Nuov. Mem. D. Inst. II, 874. Preller-Robert, Griech. Myth. I, 868.) Cf. p. 800 and 816.   (1–3. H. S.)

For comparison with the fetters for the feet of Aphrodite Morpho at Sparta I have indeed as yet not excavated any chains for the feet such as are mentioned in the Bible and as occur in Egyptian monuments (Pl. CCXIII, 3). We may, however, come upon such.   (M. O.-R.)

4. Small female head (terra-cotta) from Cyprus. From Coll. Gréau. Berl. Mus. Antiquarium T. C. 8275.

The head represents a common type; the cloak is drawn over the head and forms a back-ground from which the delicate little head stands out. The style is that of the 4th century B. C.

5. Head of a Persian (terra-cotta) from Cyprus. From Coll. Gréau (No. 684). Berl. Mus. Antiquarium T. C. 8273.

The head is covered by a handkerchief which conceals the ears, temples and chin, and is arranged above in the form of a Phrygian cap. The hair of the brow ripples out beneath. The upper lip has a small moustache. The style is certainly the free style of the 4th century B. C. Cf. the Persians in the famous mosaic of the battle of Alexander from Pompei in Niccolini "Case di Pompei", Tav. VII = Baumeister, Denkmäler II, Taf. XXI and S. 929, Abb. 1000.

6. Fragment of youth in oriental dress (terra-cotta) from Larnaka. Coll. Cesnola. Berl. Mus Antiquarium T. C. 6682, 48.

The head is preserved and the right arm resting on the head. The youth wears a Phrygian cap the side flaps of which hang down like lappets. The way the arms are crossed also shows that the dress is Phrygian. The position of the arm is explained by the action of the whole figure. The youth has been taken while dancing. A corresponding fragment of the dancer will be found in Heuzey. Terres cuites du Louvre, Pl. 16 bis No. 7; it also is from Cyprus. Both hands are uplifted and brought together. The whole dance motive is illustrated by a vase with figures from Melos also given in Heuzey, Pl. 87, No. 1. (Fig. 2 in the text.) The youth in Phrygian dress here has wings which leads Heuzey to call him the god Atys.

°7. Small female head (terra-cotta) from Dali, found in the Astarte-Aphrodite precinct so often mentioned (No. 8 in the list). Berl. Mus. Antiquarium M. I. 8015, 78.

·The head is noticeable for its great sweetness and charm. The hair is parted in the middle and frames in the brow and temples with graceful waving lines. The back knot of hair is, gathered up into a pointed cap. Style of the 4th century B. C.   (4–7. H. S.)

I have figured this beautiful little head here, because it stands quite alone among the thousands of other images and hence very possibly was dedicated by a worshipper from Kition at the sanctuary of Idalion.   (M. O.-R.)

8. Fragment of a seated goddess with a flower (terra-cotta) from Larnaka. From Coll. Pierides. Berl. Mus. Antiquarium T. C. 6282.

The front part of the figure is broken off at the neck; somewhat more of the back which is left unmodelled is preserved. The type is somewhat different from that above. The cloak is drawn over the crown; moreover the figure is in lively action. The right arm is raised side-ways and the pose of the head which holds a flower or attribute is specially full of delicate charm. By the movement of the arm the cloak is drawn upwards and makes a becoming background for the arm. Also the free style of the 4th century.

9. Fragment of a group of two lovers (terra-cotta) from Larnaka. From Coll. Pierides. Berl. Mus. Antiquarium T. C. 6245.

Both heads and the right arm of the maiden are preserved. The motive of the lovers kissing is very graceful and especially the arm resting on the youth's head. This group too is of the same period.   (8–9. H. S.)

Plate CCV.

1 = XXXIII, 7. Group of two seated goddesses — one with cylix, the other with flower (terracotta). From Coll. Pierides. Berl. Mus. Antiquarium, T. C. 6286.

The type of the figures correspond to the goddess in Pl. CCIV, 3. Upper part of body and arms are left free of the cloak; as in No. 8 of the previous plate, the cloak is drawn over the crowns. The left goddess holds a cylix in the right hand which hangs down; the left hand she rests on the other's shoulder. The right hand goddess holds a flower in her left in front•of her breast. On the left side of the group a piece is broken off so that the elbow of the left arm is missing; the hand with the flower is also damaged. The juxtaposition of two female goddesses dates from earlier days, as it seen by the group No. 8 of the same plate.

A corresponding group in Heuzey "Terres Cuites", Pl. 16, 1 (Demeter and Kore). Cf. text p. 817.

2. Group of three goddesses on a basis (alabaster) from Kition. Acquired by L. Ross. Berl. Mus. Antiquarium.

The type of the three figures is quite similar. They stand side by side with the weight on the right leg, the left unemployed, and are clothed in a long girded chiton and cloak. The cloak rests on the left shoulder, is drawn backwards from the front and draped over the head from which it hangs down on to the

---

*) I have frequently found large anklets in Cyprian graves and that in very early ones. They are usually of bronze and silver That they were meant for the ankle is evident by their position on the corpse.

left fore-arm. The extreme end is held in the left hand which hangs down. In all three figures the action of the right arm is the same. They hold the border of the cloak lightly in their hand on the right side. Everywhere are traces of red colouring. The execution is indeed very simple but shows that the style is of the fine period.

3 = XXXIII, 6. Group of two naked goddesses (terra-cotta) from Larnaka. From Coll. Pierides. Berl. Mus. Antiquarium. T. C. 6222.

The goddesses stand as if under a roof which is broken away at the left side. Body and face alike very roughly portrayed. At the upper edge are holes for suspension; the type is one that has already often been mentioned; the goddess grasps her breast with both hands. Cf. Pl. XLVII, 4 (from Limniti); L, 4 (from Dali).

4. Upper portion of a female figure holding a boy on her shoulder (terra-cotta) from Larnaka. From Coll. Pierides. Berl. Mus. Antiquarium. T. C. 6230.

The boy, who is completely nude, sits on the left shoulder as if riding. The right leg hangs down at the back and is not visible; the woman holds him fast by the left leg with her left hand. The right arm is raised but broken off about half-way across the upper arm. The motive seems to be that she is holding the boy behind with her right hand probably by his right arm. The left hand of the boy rests on the woman's head. On his face is a roguish smile. The woman wears chiton and cloak; this last is lifted up by the movement of the right arm; on the left arm also the folds of the cloak are visible, on her head is a high diadem. The hair is arranged as it is in the seated figures of the previous plate. From the ear hangs a disc-shaped pendant. Such types with boys are to be distinguished from the groups in which a draped female figure is carried on the shoulder as e. g. in Heuzey, Pl. 18 bis No. 3 (from Greece). Cf. p. 204.

5 = XXXVII, 5. Seated goddess with boy (terra-cotta) from Larnaka. From Coll. Cesnola. Berl. Mus. Antiquarium T. C. 6682, 44.

The torso only of the figure is preserved from the neck to about the navel. The goddess wears chiton and cloak, this last hangs down from the left shoulder; with the right arm, the hand of which is broken off, she is lifting it upwards. With the left she holds the boy by the left shoulder — for the rest the action of the boy seems to be that he is wriggling round with his little leg in her lap. The motive is full of charm.

6. Torso of nude youth (terra-cotta) from Larnaka. From Coll. Pierides. Berl. Mus. Antiquarium. T. C. 6248.

The figure is to be restored as standing with the weight on the right leg, the left free. The right hip stands out prominently. On the right upper thigh about the level of the scrotum there is a space, where something has been fastened on; the outline of this space can be seen even in the plate. Probably this is the remains of where a pillar or some other high object, which served as a support to the figure was attached. We have then here a Praxitelean motive.

7. Fragment of a seated goddess with a boy (terra-cotta) from Larnaka. From Coll. Pierides. Berl. Mus. Antiquarium. T. C. 6228.

Only the left side of the torso with the boy is preserved and the topmost portion of the back of the chair. The figure belongs to the same group as No. 5 in the same plate. The boy has reared himself up on the lap of the goddess. He had laid his right hand on her breast, while she supports his head with her left. With his left he supports himself. He has drawn up his left leg, his right, which is broken off, must be restored as stretched out. The goddess wears chiton and cloak — this last hangs down on the left side. A pendant hangs on the breast.

8. Goddess tending child (terra-cotta) from Larnaka. From Coll. Cesnola. Berl. Mus. Antiquarium. T. C. 6682, 45.

The upper part of the body only is preserved; the head has been put on but belongs to it. It is not clear from the motive of the figure whether she was sitting or standing. She is dressed in a long sleeved chiton and a cloak, which is drawn over the head and rests on the left arm. The child is carried on the left arm and is partly covered by the cloak, specially the lower part of the body; it rests its right arm on the breast of the goddess and in the left hand holds an apple; the goddess holds a second apple in her right in front of her breast. The motive is made the more charming as the goddess bends her head forward. A similar specimen from Cyprus in Heuzey, Pl. 15, No. 4. (Larnaka).

9. Seated goddess with child (terra-cotta) from Cyprus (?) Berl. Mus. Antiquarium. T. C. 6279.

The goddess sits with legs glued together in a chair without arms, and is completely enveloped in cloak. On her left shoulder is seated a child who is also enveloped by the cloak. The execution is very careless. Cf. No. 4 of the same plate.

All the terra-cottas of this plate (and also of the alabaster group 2) come from Kition and have been made there. The larger number (1, 3, 4, 5, 7—9) are very probably from the sanctuary of Artemis-Paralia (No. 7 of the list) the remainder (6) from graves in the neighourhood

Plate CCVI.

1—4. Figures of Athene, from Gerhard, Akad. Abhandlungen, Pl. XXII, 2, 4, 1 and 5, figured for comparison. The Gorgoneion seems to have originated in the disc of the moon or the breastplate. (Cf. the Cyprian figure No. 5 and p. 300). The group also of the seated Athene with two standing attendants near her reminds me of the Cyprian Artemis groups e. g. Pl. CCIV, 2.

? 5. Painted terra-cotta figure from Kurion in Cyprus. Hight 0,143 m. I excavated at Amathus, two just such terra-cotta figures with the disc in front of the body (but without eyes in the breast) from the grave depicted in Pl. CLXXV, 2, together with the little terracotta shrine figured in Pl. CXCIX, 1 and 2. Cf. p. 210, 251, 300.

† 6. P. 287, fig. 198. Seated Artemis-Rhea-Kybele with lions on either side. From the Artemis sanctuary at Achna, No. 1 of the list. Remains of red colouring. Cf. p 218, 237.

‡ 7—10. From grave of the same Graeco-Phoenician stratum at Amathus.

7. Small headless painted terra-cotta figure of a seated goddess.

8. Limestone statuette, painted red, of a recumbent male figure.

9. Painted limestone statuette. A white dog on red ground tears to pieces a green hare with red and white eyes. Cf. p. 286.

10. (Erroneously numbered 9 on the plate.) Dove painted red, limestone.

Plate CCVII.

1. Small female head (terra-cotta) from Larnaka. From Collection Pierides. Berlin Museum, Antiquarium T. C. 6231.

The whole of the right side is damaged: of the crown there is only a small stump remaining on the left side, the nose too is damaged. The back side is only partially modelled. The clay is light brown. The type is somewhat like that of the large head in Pl. XV. Style somewhat freer. Ear-ornament is the same. The crown rests on the handkerchief which is drawn over the head. In front fall the blobs of an ornament which is fastened on to the crown.

2. Small female head with crown (terra-cotta) from Larnaka. From Collection Pierides. Berlin Museum, Antiquarium T C. 6256.

The right side of the crown is broken off,the back is entirely gone; the nose too is damaged. The clay is light brown. The head is totally enveloped with a cloth, which lets only the eyes, nose and one part of the cheeks free.

3. Small female head with crown (terra-cotta) from Larnaka. From Collection Pierides. Berlin Museum, Antiquarium T. C. 6225.

The back is not modelled; the front of the crown is only represented. Clay light brown. Type same as in no. 1. Fine style of the 4th century B. C. On the head below the cloak rests a head band. The crown is of Kalathos shape. The ear-ornament is the same as in no. 1.

4. Upper part of maiden with a vessel on her head (terra-cotta) from Larnaka. From Collection Pierides. Berlin Musenm, Antiquarium T. C. 6238.

The back is worked smooth. The maiden wears a sleeved chiton. The vessel standing on her head and held with both her hands is preserved in a particular specimen in the Collection Gréau, v. Fröhner, Collection Gréau, p. 126, fig. 536. Another replica, in which the head and hands of the girl are preserved, is in the Louvre, v Heuzey "Figurines antiques de terre cuite" Pl. 16 bis, No. 3. The vessel is polygonal and with polygonal sides. In the central space which is arched is depicted a female figure with long drapery, moving towards the right. The spaces next, both right and left, are filled with diagonal lines. Style 4th century.

5. Small female head (terra-cotta) from Larnaka. From Collection Cesnola. Berlin Museum, Antiquarium T. C. 6682, 47.

The head is of the same type as no. 2; but there is no crown.

6. Small female head (terra-cotta) from Larnaka. From Collection Cesnola. Berlin Museum, Antiquarium T. C. 6682, 46.

The hair is parted in the middle and combed to the sides in beautiful wavy lines. In the middle of the forehead a knot is to be seen into which several strands of hair are gathered together from behind. On the head is a handkerchief, which, however, is not fully rendered at the back of the head, the whole back is shaped out with a knife to the form of the head. Fine work of the 4th century B. C.

7. Fragment of female figure with basket of fruit (terra-cotta) from Larnaka. From Collection Pierides. Berlin Museum, Antiquarium T. C 6240.

Of the figure, only the head, left shoulder, and left arm are preserved. On the forehead of the woman is a crown which is ornamented with alternate flowers and round discs. She wears a long sleeved chiton. The contents of the elongated basket are all sorts of different fruits, among which apples and grapes can be made out. Cf. p. 136.

8. Youth in Phrygian dress (terra-cotta) from Larnaka. From Collection Pierides. Berlin Museum, Antiquarium T. C. 6243.

The figure stands with the weight on the left leg, the right unemployed and leans with the left arm on a basin, raised on a high foot, the right hand rests on the hip. The youth wears a short girdled long-sleeved chiton and Phrygian cap, the ends of which rest on the shoulders. Whether he wears trousers and shoes cannot be determined. Both figure and basin stand on a quadrangular basis.

All these examples certainly come from the ateliers of Kition and from the salt lake. 1—7 might have come from the sanctuary of Artemis-Paralia. The type enveloped in a cloak e. g. 2 and 5 (similar replicas in Heuzey and Piot Hoffmann—Fröhner's catalogue) is also very characteristic of the types of Artemis-Paralia, who seem to have got confused with Kybele-Demeter and Persephone.

Plate CCVIII.

Kyprian Terra-cottas.

‡ 1—2. Kurion. ° 3. Marion-Arsinoë. † 4—8. Kition.

1 and 2 come from the same nekropolis and excavation as CCII, 2—4 and were richly painted.

Group of comedians. The little man, who plays the part of a satyr, is embracing a tall slim veiled woman who repels him. On the male figure are remains of a sulphur coloured garment and flesh coloured mask.

2. Eros and Psyche. Eros has yellow wings, the wingless Psyche a rose coloured garment.

3. Small terracotta from Marion-Arsinoë. Amor and Psyche are winged. Of Hellenistic date.

4. Group of two comic actors. The one to the right has a pointed beard, the other represents a woman.

5—8. Four comic actors. For 1—8 cf. p. 221 and 256.

Plates CCIX—CCXII.

Cf. Pl. XI—XII. Find from the sanctuary of Artemis-Kybele. No. 1 of the list. The hand only with the seal (figured in Pl. CCX, 22), comes from a stone statuette from the sanctuary of Artemis-Apollo (no. 12 of the list) between Achna and Xylotimbo, and the terracotta figure in Pl. CCXII, 6 = 7 comes from the Artemis precinct (no. 10 of the list) mentioned p. 11 infra.

Plate CCIX.

1, 3, 4, 9, 10. Stone heads. 2, 5 = 8 of terracotta, 8 = LXVIII, 6. All broken off statuettes.

1 is one of the less pure heads from the Achna precinct which are of Egyptian tendency. 2 an interesting head of Graeco-Phoenician style. 3 and 4 more archaic-Greek in style. 5, 6, 7 become more purely Greek. 8 and 9 (9=10) are instances of pure Greek art of the 4th century B. C. The last small head (enlarged in the plate) is directly related to the type of Artemis in Pl CCIII, 5.

Plate CCX.

1—2. Women figures carrying a hen. 3—4 carrying a dove, all wear the archaic priestly dress (cf. Pl. L, 1.)

5—7. Greek figures in Greek dress. While the previous examples stand rigidly, in these the supporting and unemployed leg are differentiated; e. g. 5 and 6.

Figure 5 holds only a broken object (cylix? bird?)

Figure 6 holds a bird and carries besides fruit or flowers in a piece of drapery that is caught up like an apron. Cf. p. 136.

7. The woman supports the left hand with the bird on a pillar and holds in the right a seal or a flower.

8. A small stiff figurine in archaic dress with a small typmpanon.

9—11. Portions of glass chain links set in silver. They were discovered in small jugs of the shape shown in p. 359, Fig. 253, 5. Clearly girls or women had dedicated their ornaments · to the goddess.

12—14. The ornament describe above, p. 306, belongs to the cult of Artemis and forms part of the dress of a priestess.

15—17. Lamps from the Artemis Temenos. The bulk of them are in shape like Fig. 16.

18—20 and 23. Idols of Artemis with stumps of arms 18 and 20 (as 1—8, 12—14) of terra-cotta, 19 and 23 of stone. Described p. 305 ff.

21. Stone censer with inscription. Cf. p. 328, note 2.

22. Hand with seal on which signs are engraved. Cf. p. 308 with note 3.

Many of these figures have abundant remains of colouring from former painting, e. g. Fig. 97 But the stone figures too e. g. 19 and 23 were painted and had saffron under garments and white over garments bordered with red.

Plate CCXI.

Contains only figures from the Artemis Temenos at Achana No. of the list. 1—6 of terra-cotta, 7 (= 8) and 9 (= 10) of stone. While the terra-cotta figures are all worked in the front only and cast in moulds the stone statuettes 7 (= 8) and 9 (= 10) are worked in the round. All are of Greek style and of the fifth and fourth centuries B. C.

Fig. 1. Upper part of a female figure with the bird in the right hand. Fig. 2 and 3 with the lamb (in the case of 3 partly broken away) in Figs. 4 and 5 the object held is injured and unrecognizable.

Fig. 5 represents a mere fragment of a specially large and very beautiful terra-cotta.

6. The drapery is specially fine.

The two stone figures 7 (= 8) and 9 (= 10) are specially life-like and the unemployed leg is much bent.

Fig. 1 and 5 are good examples of dress in which the armholes are caught together by buttons. Cf. Pl. CLXXXVII, 4, and Pl. LXVII, 11, p. 409 specially note 1.

Fig. 2 is of special interest as regards the colouring — bright green under- and red upper-garment.

Plate CCXII.

Fig. 6 (= 7) very ancient terra-cotta figure from the precinct 10 of the list. It may however belong to the 7th or 8th century B. C. All the remaining figures (from precinct Fig. 1 of the list) are to be retraced to the 4th century B. C. 1, 10 and 11 of stone, 2—5, 8 and 9 of clay.

With these figures should be compared the figures (published in Cesnola's Atlas, pl. CXVIII, 848,–854) from the grove of Pyla-Artemis Apollo (No. 27) of H. Lang.

No. 1 of our plate corresponds with 852 of Cesnola. The head is just the same and the hair frizzed in the same way, but without the veil and with quiver, quiver strap and stag (or dog?).

Here No. 10 resembles Cesnola's No. 850 only the torch that occurs is missing there and its place is supplied by a stag or roe.

Fig. 11 corresponds to Cesnola 849 with the dog and exactly the same dress with in Cesnola's instance the addition of quiver strap and quiver and the head preserved.

The headless statuette No. 5 with the stag at the side has a specially majestic effect. The fragment Fig. 4 belongs to a similar replica. Of special charm but also dignified in conception are the figurines with the high frizzed hair (2 and 3) but without any chain ornament (2 has not even earrings).

Fragment 8 belongs to an Artemis type described above, p. 309, in which the goddess turns back to grasp her quiver.

Fragment 9 a specially fine little terra-cotta figure, which like stone figurine 11 leans for support on a pillar (cf. p. 315).

At Salamis in the precinct near the cistern (No. 66 of list, Journal of Hellenic Studies XII, April 1891 p. 137) Apollo and Artemis were evidently worshipped. The editors in their description refer to these antiquities from Achna, now for the most part in the British Museum and figured in plates XI, XII, CCIX—CCXII. They mention heads in the severe Greek style with high crowns decorated by rows of cups, discs, rosettes, palmettes, Sphinxes (in fact vultures e. g. Pl. CCXI, 1, 3 &c., cf. p. 309) and figures with lyre in the left and with fruits flowers and animals — just such in fact as ours. Even a young stag occurs there. Then I found several specimens in better preservation and belonging to the Artemis - Kybele cult only, whereas there i. e. in Salamis (Cistern No. 66) the frequent warriors with shields and high caps and the scenes with chariots evidence the contemporaneous worship of Apollo.

Plate CCXIII.

1—4. Egyptian monuments figured here for comparison with those of Cyprus.

5—25. Cyprus.

1. From an Egyptian wall painting of the tomb of Ramses III. Wilkinson-Birch, "Manners and Customs" II, p. 32, Fig. 300 = Riehm Bibellexicon I, p. 840.

The man to the left pokes the fire with a rake, whose prongs turn downwards. The man to the right uses the same rake, but with the prongs turned upwards and takes some meat out of a pot with it

5 = Pl. VII, 2 (cf. p. 353). One of the six iron fire-rakes, which I found in a heap on the altar for sacrifice of the sanctuary at Dali. This Cyprian utensil thus entirely corresponds with that of Egypt.

2 Egyptian wall-painting from Thebes. From Wilkinson Birch, I. p. 227, Fig. 60 = Helbig Homerische Epos p. 113, Fig. 17. Carpenter and waggon-builder at work.

To the right a beam is being hewn or planed with a tool that very closely resembles that figured in 6, and this is used in the same way.

6 = Helbig Homerisches Epos, p. 114, Fig. 18. Modern Cyprian skeparnon. Helbig has made use of the drawing I sent him. I was the first to discover this implement, which plays so great a part in Homer, in use among the modern Cypriots and I informed Helbig of it. My attention was directed to it by the name. For it is called to-day by the Cypriots, as in Homer's days, σκεπάρνι and is used in many of the same circumstances now as then.

3. Egyptian wall-painting from Beni-Hassan. Women weaving and spinning.

7a. Part of an ancient spindle from H. Par. Cyprus Bronze-pin and terra-cotta whorl.

8a = CXLVI, 2B. Bronze spindle H. Par. Antique Bronze-period,

7b and 7c modern Cyprian spindles. 7b. from Pera, 7c from H. Andronikos. The latter decorated with geometric patterns and inlaid beads.

8b. Modern spindle of wood.

It is easy to see that in very primitive days there must have been spindles like this one, of cane and wood, which were afterwards copied in bronze.

4. Egyptian bronze and gilt ladles. From Wilkinson Birch II, p. 47, No. 314, 4 Exactly similar ladles are frequently found in Cyprian graves of the 6th century B. C.

9a and 9d. Modern spindles of wood painted with bright coloured red and green stripes, consisting of whorl, spigot and iron hook.

9a for cotton, wool 9d large and heavy for the wool of sheep or for goats' hair.

10—25. Antique whorls of terra-cotta and stone, all from graves of the bronze period. H. Par. 10, 12—22 of terra-cotta, 11, 23—25 of stone. The modern spindle 9d, that is heavy and very large, shows that many large heavy stone objects of the shape in Fig. 10 were used in spinning to weight the spindle. This heavy weighting was actually necessary to stretch the wool or goats' hair.

In general the further study of modern Cyprian customs, usages, implements, vessels &c. promises to throw light on many obscure questions of antiquity. When this study is pursued, it is surprising how the relations between east and west mount up. A thoroughly typical example which I could not include in the plates may be noted here.

On the inner side of the doors of the three stone royal graves that I excavated in 1888 at Tamassos (cf. Pl. CLXII, 5—7) wooden locks are set in the stone. The only way of opening these locks was to pass the arm throug ha round hole made in the wall or door and large enough to admit the arm and so insert the key in the lock and raise up the latch and so open the door.

The arrangement that A. von Cohausen notes (in vol. XIII of the Annalen des Vereins für Nassauische Alterthumskunde and Geschichtsforschung Taf. X, Fig. 2) in the courtyard door of the Szekler-House 1873 in the Vienna Exhibition, is in Cyprus the customary plan in all those shepherd's dwellings that are remote from towns and in inns used for the summer only. Key hand, and arm are inserted through a round hole and the door thus opened from the inside. Usually however the wooden locks of houses in towns are opened from outside, as public safety is much greater in the towns which are constantly inhabited than it is in distant and only casually inhabited huts and farmsteads. In Fig. 267 I figure the Cyprian wooden lock. There are still whole villages in which there is not a single iron lock in use. When I left Cypria in 1890, in the monastery of Metoschi outside the gates of Nicosia which belongs to the richest monastery of the island, Kikku, they had only just then bought a new wooden lock from one of the shops. In the Cyprian lock everything is made of wood, whereas in Syria and in Beirut and Tripolis a similar wooden lock is in use in shops but the key for it is of iron. Similar wooden locks to those in Cyprus are in use in other Eastern countries and also in the North of Africa. Von Cohausen figures in the same Plate X, Fig. 5 a wooden lock as used in the Hundsrück and the Westerwald. This shows in fact a marked analogy to the Cyprian specimens. In the German lock there are only three falling bolts that go up and down and raise themselves in and out of the main lock bolt. In the Cyprian kind there is a fourth falling bolt added and this again is made up of three narrow bolts. These last three small bolts are of irregular outline and must be notched to correspond with the wooden key so that its teeth may catch hold of the corresponding teeth of the last three bolts. In the picture we see the key in the lock. The bolts have fallen down by their own weight into the notches of the principal bolt and of the key. If the key be drawn out the lock remains locked. If the key be vertically raised the principal bolt can be pushed to one side and the door then opened. I have I hope in this plate collected sufficient examples to show the importance of approaching Cyprian studies in the way that I have inaugurated. Results of equal importance for anthropology, ethnography, archaeology and the history of civilization in general will thereby accrue cf. my essay and paper on "Parallelen in den Gebräuchen der alten und der jetzigen Bevölkerung von Cypern" (Parallels between the customs of the ancient and modern inhabitants of Cyprus) Verhandlungen der Berliner anthropolog. Gesellschaft, 1891, p. 84.

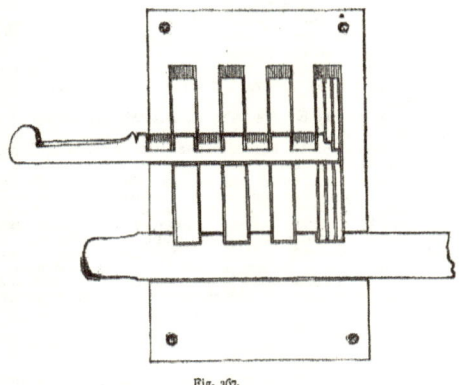

Fig. 267.

Plate CCXIV.

Cyprus and Naukratis.

Cf. supra p. 111 the story of the merchant Herostratos who brought a miracle working statuette of Aphrodite from Paphos to Naukratis.

No. 1. **Naukratis.** Upper part of a limestone statuette. Temenos of Apollo. Flinders - Petrie Naukratis I, Pl. II, 1. Presumably male. There is no characteristic female neck-chain.

No. 2. **Cyprus.** Upper part of female limestone statuette with neck chain. Temenos of Aphrodite at Idalion, No. 3 of the list.

No. 3. **Naukratis.** Fragment of a stone statuette from the town. A female figure holds a kid with both hands in front of her body. E. A. Gardner, Naukratis II, Pl. XV, 1.

No. 4. **Cyprus**. Upper part of the female limestone statuette published in full in Pl. L, 2.

No. 5. **Naukratis**. Female stone statuette from the Aphrodite temenos. A woman holding a lyre in her left, the plectron in her right. Naukratis II, Pl. XIV, 14.

Nos. 6 and 7. **Cyprus** = Pl. XII, 6 and 7. Terra-cottas from the Artemis temenos at Achna (No. 1 of the list). Women with lyre and plectron.

No. 8. **Naukratis**. Stone statuette of Aphrodite κουϱοτϱόφος from the temenos of Aphrodite.

No. 9. **Cyprus**. Limestone statuette of Aphrodite κουϱοτϱόφος certainly from a precinct of Aphrodite like our precinct at Dali No. 33, of the list. Cf. also our Pl. XXXVII, 1 and 8. From Cesnola Atlas Taf. XXXVIII, No. 251 from Athiaenou. I suspect in this case that the provenance is incorrectly stated. Very probably from Dali and from the site No. 33 of our list, which was thoroughly rummaged out in Cesnola's time.

10. **Naukratis**. Figurine of faience from the town. Player on the double flute.

11. **Cyprus**. Upper part of a limestone figure (probably feminine?) blowing the double flute. From Cesnola Atlas, Pl. XXVI, 46. Cf. Pl. XVII, 5, XLII, 3 and 6.

12. **Naukratis**. Upper part of a female stone-figure, which holds a lotus blossom in the right hand before the breast. From the Aphrodite temenos. Naukratis II, Pl. XV, 5.

13. **Cyprus** = Plate L, 3. Upper part of a female limestone statuette, which holds in her left hand a lotus-flower before the breast. From the Aphrodite-Temenos at Dali. No. 3 of the list.

14 and 16. **Naukratis**. Limestone and alabaster torso of male statuettes. Naukratis I, Pl. I, 4 and 8. (Cf. Naukratis II, Pl. XIV, 13) probably from the Apollo temenos.

15. **Cyprus**. Upper part of a limestone figure from one of the Apollo precincts at Athiaenou No. 25 or 26 of the list. (Cf. also archaic Greek marble torso, excavated in 1886 at Marion-Arsinoë Pl. XXVII, 3).

The Cyprian sculptors were influenced on the one side by Assyrian on the other by Egyptian art. It almost looks as if in Cyprian sculpture in stone Egyptian influence preceded Assyrian and vice versa in the case of terra-cotta. The Graeco-Phoenician and imitated Egyptian style, developed as regards stone sculpture in Cyprus. was brought in the seventh and sixth centuries B. C. to Naukratis but not the reverse road. The Greeks who were settled in Naukratis were plainly not Cyprian Greeks. Also there were, it would seem, no Cyprians at all in this colony of Naukratis, whereas they played an important part in e. g. the cemeteries and the settlement generally of Tell Nebescheh. In Naukratis there were Greek settlers who created a peculiar sort of terra-cotta work that does not occur either in Cyprus or in Nebescheh. The sculptors of Naukratis imitated the peculiar Graeco-Phoenician Egyptizing sculpture which had arisen in Cyprus and which developed later into archaic Greek style. For we see that the sculpture of Naukratis was of inferior artistic merit to the contemporaneous Cyprian sculpture of which it was an imitation. The statues too of Naukratis are smaller and less numerous than those of Cyprus, where at just the same time numbers of life-size and colossal works were executed both in stone and terra-cotta. The finds conform most precisely to the contents of the story told above p. 111. The worship of Aphrodite, her images, the style and technique in which they were wrought passed from Cyprus to Naukratis. The same is true of Reśef-Apollo. As in Cyprus, so in Naukratis Aphrodite and Apollo are the pair of deities who take the first rank in religious worship. E. A. Gardner's (Naukratis II, p. 56) statement that from our primitive male figures (14—16 of the plate) to the archaic statues of Apollo and even to the noble Greek statues of athletes there may be traced an unbroken series of development is true not of Naukratis but of Cyprus. It is also a mistake to say with Gardner (Naukr. II, p. 56) that the Cyprian images of the Aphrodite precinct (e. g. 2, 4, 9, 13 of our plate) must be explained as works of Phoenician art. Centuries before Homer the Greeks were settled in Cyprus (cf pp. 226 and 245). Pure Phoenician sculpture whether in stone or terra-cotta has never existed either in Cyprus or anywhere else. The whole sculptural art is from the beginning a Graeco-Phoenician mixture. It is preceded only by idols of board and pillar shape as in Pl. XXXVI, and XXXVII, 6 and 7 of terra-cotta and small agalmolite and steatite images as in Pl. CLXXII, 15a and b.

In the main however, but for this point, E. Gardner has assigned to Cyprian influence in sculpture in Naukratis its right place. On the other hand what Munro says, (J. H. S. 1891, 162) on Greek art in Cyprus must be noted as wholly erroneous. Munro thinks that Greek art did not come direct to Cyprus but by two indirect routes. The one route led from Greece along the borders of the Hellespont and Asia Minor. The other came from Egypt, i. e. from Naukratis, and is most perceptible in Salamis. But on the other hand Munro recognises that even the earliest Salaminian finds of statues, which are of terra-cotta from the site Toumpa, (No 67 of the list) show the greatest possible analogies to my finds at Frangissa (No 4 of the list). The influence of Attic Greek art came rather by sea direct to Cyprus and the best proof of this are the finds at Marion-Arsinoë (cf. infra, excursus). It begins in the early part of the 6th century B. C. But on the other hand it is at Cyprus that the Greek who came from and returned to Attica, absorbed and modified Graeco-Phoenician and oriental elements, which were in part earlier and in part contemporaneous with his own work. In general Cyprus and her artists have had, as has been frequently shown, a very important influence on the development of archaic Greek art and especially of sculpture. From Cyprus Graeco-Phoenician and archaic Greek styles of sculpture passed to Naukratis. The Doric and Asia Minor Ionic and Arcado-Achaean-Peloponnesian styles which preceded the Attic must have, at all events, in part, first found their way to the island by way of Asia Minor. As the Greek Attic influence in the main passed direct by sea to Cyprus, so also the Egyptian, Babylonian-Assyrian and North Syrian Hittite influences might pass to Cyprus either directly or indirectly. Their influence must have inevitably have been felt in connection with the exchange and barter that went on in the export and import of Cyprian copper. How far specific Syrio-Phoenician and Asia Minor influence from Cappadocia, Lycia, Lydia, Caria, Phrygia, Thrace were conjoined with these can only be decided by excavations undertaken on a large scale in these countries, which have been, so far as their relation to Cyprus goes, so little the subject of investigation.

Plate CCXV.

Limestone heads broken off statues. All from Apollo precinct (attested by incriptions at Voni near Chytroi No. 2 of the list). Cf. Pl. XL—XLII.
1. Head of the statue XLI, 9. Graeco-Phenician imitation; Assyrian style.
2 and 2a. Archaic Greek style. The head only was found.
3. Life-size head of a missing statue of the severe style of the 5th century B. C.
5 and 5a. Head of statue XL, 3. Fine Greek style 4th century B. C.
4 and 4a, 6 and 6a. Hellenistic heads.
7 and 7a and 8. Roman portrait heads. The greater part of the body belonging to head 7 was found present as far as the region of the lower thigh. Length 2,235 m. This colossal figure in a many folded toga belonged to the so-called "Cicero" type.

The heads of this plate, which were all set up in the Apollo precinct, take us over the space of full 600 years. The statues figured Pl. XL—XLII from the same site give us further links in this chain of Cyprian sculpture. We find among them types represented that imitate Egypt and also some that unite Assyrian, Egyptian and Greek elements.

I must also refer the reader to the descriptions of the finds in the sanctuary of Astarte-Aphrodite at Dali (No. 3 of the list. Pl. XIII, XLVIII, 3 and XLIX—LV, 1—4 and 8), of the Artemis sanctuary at Achna (No. 1 of the list Pl. XI, XII, CCIX—CCXII), of the Apollo sanctuary at Limniti (XLIV—XLVII), of isolated finds (e. g. XLVIII, 1, 2, 4 and CXC and others). The antiquities now in the Berlin Museum were treated most fully by Herr Dr. H. Schmidt *) and me, and we went into the question of the various tendencies in style. (Cf. also supra p. 348 and 349).

Plate CCXVI.

A contribution to the History of the development of Cyprian ceramic art illustrated by 32 Cyprian monuments.

Cf. the description, text and Excursus to Plates XIX—XXI, p. 352—356, Pl. XXII—XXIV, p. 358, LXXXIX; 1, 2, and 8, CXI, 2, CXVIII, 8, CXLVII—CL, CLII, CLXVIII—CLXXIII.

‡ 1. Black brightly glazed whorl. H. Paraskevi. Concentric circles with central dot, incised.
‡ 2. Red brightly glazed whorl. Incised band of lines, arranged horizontally and obliquely. In the triangular spaces are arches, which are filled in with parallel lines all running in one direction. Hagia Paraskevi.
? 3. Fragments of a large vase with red glaze and incised ornaments filled in white slip. A ring made of 8 concentric circles from which radiate ornaments made up of straight lines.
? 4—7, 12—14. Terra-cotta vases from the same rock grave at H. Paraskevi. All (up to 18) are made bright of red glazed clay and decorated with incised ornaments which are in part artificially filled in with white slip. Hand made vases of the bronze period. No. 6 (without handle; shape like Pl. XXXIV, 2 and CLXVIII, 2 e) comes towards the top of a shining black. The grave had been used several times. At the top burial layer lay the Graeco-Phoenician wheel turned vase with painted concentric circles. (13).
‡ 8. Red glazed vase in the shape of an ox. (Badly figured in Pl. XXXVI, 5). With incised ornaments, bands of lines and concentric circle patterns which are filled in with white slip. From a bronze-period grave. Hagia Paraskevi.
‡ 9. Animal-shaped vase from Parasolia. where was found the double headed Aryballos (Pl. CXIII, 3) made of clay with green glaze. Painted with bands of lines, groups of concentric circles and loop ornaments (which occur more frequently in Rhodian than in Cyprian ornaments.)

It is evident that the concentric circles that are painted on this early bird-vase of the iron period have their prototype in the animal-shaped vases of the bronze period (Fig. 8) where the concentric circles are incised and filled with white slip. At the same time one sees how the loop ornament so prominent in Rhodes may possibly have arisen in Cyprus from the concentric circle motive are have been brought thence to Rhodes to be there further modified (cf. supra p. 358 note 1).

10. Fragments of a vase with incised ornaments.
No less than 17 concentric circles drawn ond within the other ot size constantly diminishing to the centre; there is no centre dot. The Cyprian vases of this kind are in part, if not altogether, much earlier than the Mycenae vases with the so-called "annuals" of which one specimen is figured in 24, and have on each side 22 concentric circles. Certain it is that Graeco-Phoenician Cyprian vases like those in Figs. 23 and 25 have been influenced by Mykenae ones (like 24) it is equally certain that the Mykenae potters in making their so-called "annual" vases drew their inspiration from earlier classes of vases with similar incised rings to those in the Cyprian vase Fig. 10.

*) In the descriptions by Herr Schmidt (marked H. S.) the results of my investigations are utilized and the whole has been revised by me. As soon as I received from Herr Dümmler (and it was not till the end of October) the very full and excellent report of the excavations which had been kept back from me for six years it was a double gratification to me to find in Herr Dr. Schmidt so reliable a coadjutor, who could relieve me of a portion of the descriptive text to the plates. The main interest of the antiquities now in the Berlin Museum I only recently utilized for in giving an account of Cyprian sculpture centred in the Dali collection excavated by me from the Aphrodite Temenos (No. 3 of the list).—For this purpose an illustrated catalogue by Herr Dr. P. Herrmann which was deposited in the Archives of the Antiquarium and most readily made available by Herr Prof. Furtwängler could be used. This catalogue of Herrmann was based on my detailed report of excavations and on my detailed illustrated catalogue. My photographic views also had been utilized, which I had made in Cyprus to a large extent at my own expence, and of which I had sent prints. For the work however, new original views had been taken for the most part in the Museum.

11. Belly of a vase of the bronze period from H. Par. Brown clay unglazed. Ornaments incised and as yet unfilled with white slip.*)

16. p. 301, Fig. 210. Hand made water-jug, 0.50 m. high of gray clay, intended to hold a large quantity of water. From Alambra. The only ornaments are two nipples placed on the shoulder of the vase opposite the handle. The jug figured above p. 487, Fig. 306, 0,54 m. high from the same nekropolis and worked in the same technique is decorated in relief with alternate rows of nipples placed vertically one below the other and sunken.

I place here in Fig. 205, a small water-jug in use at the present day. In good Greek village houses the families of even the highest English officials ordinarily use the sort of jug made in the village of Kornu. The clay walls are thick and porous, which keep the water comparatively cool. These rude jugs, made partly by the hand only, are decorated with ornaments scratched in with a piece of comb. They have three feet, a beak-shaped spout and beneath it are depicted two female nipples.

16. Early iron period Graeco-Phoenician vase, which I excavated at H. Paraskevi is one of the few graves that belong to the transition time between the bronze and iron periods. With it the tripod vase Pl. CLXX, 10c of the bronze period.

The bronze daggers found with them are of shapes that belong to the bronze period.
The wheel-turned vase 16 is decorated only with two concentric circle ornaments on the shoulder, opposite the handle.

It is evident at once that the potter of vase 16 painted on concentric circles those same nipples which the potter of vase 16 indicated plastically in relief. The vase of the iron period (22) on p. 89, Fig. 60 also has three nipples in relief. It is also clear how one of the rows of plastic nipples (Fig. 21a) were developed rows of painted concentric circles (Pl. CCXVII, 12, 15, 10 &c.)

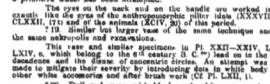

Fig. 205.

* 17 = CL. 8, CLXXII, 17 g. Vase from grave 17, Pl. CLXXII, Kalydata-Lion. Transition time from bronze to iron period. Turning on a primitive wheel has been attempted.

The eyes on the neck and on the handle are worked in relief exactly like the eyes of the anthropomorphic pillar idols (XXXVII, 6 and CLXXII, 17c) and of the animals (XCIV, 30) of this period.

* 19. Similar but larger vase of the same technique and from the same nekropolis and excavations.

This vase and similar specimens in Pl. XXII—XXIV, LXII, 1, LXIV, 8, which belong to the 8th century B. C. **) lead on to the time of decadence and the disuse of concentric circles. An attempt was at first made to mitigate their severity by introducing dots in white body colour, other white accessories and after brush work (Cf Pl. LXII, 1).

* 20. Dull red vase with black and white concentric circles. These placed vertically are intersected by horizontal ones (cf. also Title page Figs. 2 and 3). Excavated at Kition 1879.

Even this intersection of vertical by horizontal series of circles was borrowed by Cyprian vase-painting of the iron period from the incised style of Vase-decoration of the Cyprian copper-bronze period as a glance at our illustrations Figs. 4, 5 and 11 shows.

With Fig. 20 the vases found in the Cyprian graves at Tell Nebescheh in Egypt must be compared. They were buried there in the 7th century B. C. (Flinders-Petrie Tanis II., Pl. III.) But the Cyprian specimens (e. g. Fig. 20) are in part earlier and never later.***)

18. Excavated by me in 1883 at Kurion. Graeco-Phoenician vase of the iron period accurately worked on a good wheel. Ornaments in black and white body colour on a dull red ground.

The potter copied the plastic eyes of the vases from the close of the bronze period e. g. 17 and substituted painting for relief; (Cf. Pl. CLXXII, 10 L.) The vases on Pl. XIN, 1 and 4 show us in place of those eyes painted concentric circles and semicircles as here in Fig. 19.

From the illustrations Figs. 1—29 it is clearly evident that the Cyprians invented the concentric circle decoration and the manifold ones to which circular ornaments were put in the geometric system of decoration in Cyprus itself. It was not the Arcadians who brought this style from the

Peloponnese, where it never existed, nor did the Hittites bring it from North Syria,. where it cannot any more than in the case of Arcadia be proved to have been a native product*). Nor did this style reach Cyprus either from Asia Minor or from the Greek islands. It arose in Cyprus itself. Nor was the early civilisation of the Cyclades, as F. Dümmler states, brought to Cyprus at a previous date in the copper-bronze age or in the transition time to the iron age. These civilisations, like those which have been discovered below the lava at Thera, are only the outcome of the feeble local efforts of those islanders, which disappear when confronted with the wealth of Cyprian indigenous civilisation and monuments powerful alike in quantity and quality. Nor does what we have so far got from Asia Minor**) Phoenicia***), Palestine†), and Egypt††), justify the conclusion that Cyprian ceramic art, so far as it is characteristic of Cyprus was imported thither from other countries. It arose in Cyprus itself. How far Cyprian potters in the different periods of their art drew inspiration from the ceramic products of other countries should be clear \so far as we can judge at present) from the explanatory text to our Plates. Much still remains to be made out. As was said before we must first make further excavations in Asia Minor, Syria and Phoenicia as well as in Cyprus before we can advance our knowledge in the department of comparative archaeology and ceramics.

♯ 21. Upper part of a dull clay vase painted in faint black. On the neck is modelled roughly a human face with nose, eyes, ears and ear-rings.

♀ 22. Similar vase excavated by me at Tamassos in 1889.†††)

28 = XIX, 2, XX and p. 39, Fig. 40.

It is evident that even the iron age Graeco-Phoenician vases in the shape of masks and heads have their prototypes in the previous layers of the bronze age

♀ 24 = CLII, 8 right. A Mykenean vase with painted decoration in bright glaze excavated by me for Sir Charles Newton at Phönitschäs in 1883.

Whatever may have been the origin of this Mykenae class of ware, Cyprian potters of the iron age in making such vases as 28 and 25 have unquestionably been influenced by vessels like this present instance (Fig. 24).

25 and 25a. Graeco-Phoenician vase of the same date and stratum as 28 and 26. It is the stratum of the bronze fibula (p. 466, Fig. 260) and the gold ear-ring (Pl. CLXXIII, 19 i and in CLXXXII, 1) and of the painted swastikas (CLXXIII, 19, e, k, n, here Pl. CCXVI, 26). (From R. Virchow, "Ueber alte Schädel von Assos und Cypern p. 45).

♀ 26. Excavated by me in 1880 at Kition.

25 and 26 are executed in the same technique. The concentric circle ornaments bands swastikas and other figures are painted in dull black on a deep red ground which is slightly glazed.

The ground in this class of vases is always covered with a red slightly polished glaze on which the painted ornaments, which are always black, show a dull blueish shimmer. This class of ware which is so common in Cyprus was made contemporaneously with classes of vases like Fig. 23 and 20. The Tamassos grave which contained the vase on p. 87, Fig. 38 also yielded a vase of this technique like 25 and 26, on which the headless idol in Pl. LXXIII, 7 was painted. The vases too from Idalion in Pl. LXXIII, 3 and 6, 5 and 8 are of the same technique and made of the same clay as the vases in this plate Fig. 25 and 26.

27 = XXXVI, 6.

♀ 28. Upper part of a water-jug with a seated woman-figure holding a jug. Excavated at Kurion in 1883. Cf. Pl. XXII &c.

Hence this motive also of the woman-figure on the shoulder of the vase, which is Graeco-Phoenician and occurs in the iron age, has its proto-type in the pre-Graeco-Phoenician copper-bronze age. (Fig. 27).

♀ 29. Excavated by me in 1883 at Katydata-Linu from a grave of the transition time from the bronze to the iron age. In the Cyprus Museum.§)

♀ 30 = CLXXVII, 3. Cf. description supra.

It is evident that these classes also of Cyprian ware e. g. 28, 30 and analogous ones arose in Cyprus itself.

♯ 31 = CL, 19. This ring-shaped vase came from an early Graeco-Phoenician grave.

Found together with the vase in Pl. LXXIV, 5 and the vases in the shape of a duck and a boat (XCVIII, 6 and 9).

This shape too is developed from the ring-shaped vases of the copper-bronze age. (Cf. CLII, 9 and CLXX, 9 e).

---

*) Cf. supra p. 468 the explanatory text to Pl, CLXXVII, 1.

**) W. R. Paton. Journal of Hellenic Studies VIII, p. 66 ff. Excavations in Caria. Winter, Athen. Mittheilungen XII, p. 226 ff. Vasen aus Carien.

***) Observations made by me in the collections at Beirut and in the trade in antiquities in Syria, (especially Tripolis)

†) Researches of the Palestine Exploration Fund.

††) Work done by the Egypt-Exploration Fund.

†††) The terra-cotta vase excavated by me and described by Dümmler in Mittheilungen 1886, p. 228 and published Beilage 11, 5 belongs to the same class as 21 and 22 in this plate. It is the vase in shape of face with ears and large rings such as occur in the idols in the same stratum. Hence Dümmler is incorrect, when apropos of a defective publication of a face-shaped vase of this kind with large ear-rings he deduces these rings from metal technique. And this fact, which he misapprehends, leads Dümmler to the further deduction that the terra-cotta vases, with incised ornaments originally of earlier date (e. g. Pl CCXVI, 3—7, 10—12, 14 and 32 &c.) must be explained as imitations of beaten, embossed and engraved copper and bronze ware. This theory is untenable. I pointed out in reference to Plates XXXIV and XXXV that the real prototypes were vessels made of gourds of wood, palm-leaves and wheat straw. This kind of vase made of clay is in its original form much earlier than the production of the first copper cylix without ornaments. These terra-cotta vases appear even in the early strata where the small copper weapons are still very rare or not present at all. They seem indeed to be in part of earlier date than the first discovery of how to get copper from brass and the technique of its working.

§) Also published, but inadequately, by Dümmler in the Mittheilungen Athen, 1886, p. 209, Beilage 2, p. 14.

† 32.   Cask-shaped vase of red polished clay. Incised ornaments. From Hagia Paraskevi. Now in the Philadelphia Museum. Cf. supra Pl. XXXV, 1, 2, 3, 5, 6. CXLIX, 1, CLXXI, 11, i.

Wo noted how this class of terra-cotta vessel was imitated from a basket woven of palm leaves. We now see how in imitation of such tun-shaped neckless hand-made terra-cotta vessels of the bronze age corresponding shapes were made in the iron age and neatly turned on the wheel, a neck too being added. Moreover terra-cotta vessels like 25 which are pressed flatter and are like hunting-flasks have their proto-types in the bronze age and these also have a long neck (Pl. CL, 9).

When Dümmler examined on the spot the discoveries I had made in the cemeteries of Cyprus, which for the most part I made over to him for publication, it happened that I had investigated certain sites in which graves of the bronze and iron period lay near together but separate. That facilitated the examination, but led Dümmler to the erroneous conclusion that the distinction was a hard and fast one and sharply drawn, as if the fresh wave of population had suddenly swept away the old one. But that is not the case. As before, so later on I discovered transition graves from one age to the other. And finally I was able in 1889 at Tamassos to discover on the same site traces of a continuous civilisation beginning far back in the bronze age and continuing in an unbroken chain right down to Roman and Byzantine imperial times.

Plates CCXVII and CLXXVII.

Cf. p. 337—340. Cyprian gold- and silversmiths' art in Antiquity.

In the copper-bronze age silver is the first of the precious metals to make its appearance, then come isolated instances of gold and electron.

Gold spirals (Pl. CXLVI, 3 B, p) appear side by side with those of silver (3 B, m and o)*), glass (3 B, q) and bronze (CLXXXII, 10 and 11) all from Paraskevi.

These spirals of the Cyprian bronze-copper age (exactly similar specimens occur at Hissarlik, Pl. CXLVI, 3 A, c) were taken on in their simplest form in the iron age, e. g. of silver at Marion Arsinoë (LXVII, 5) or ornamented, first made of bronze and then coated with gold-leaf. Specimens with protome of griffins from Marion Arsinoë (Pl. XXXIII, 28) and from the same place with enamelled silver knobs (Pl. XLVII, 8), with lions' heads at Katydata (CLXXXII, 16) with human heads at Marion Arisinoë (CLXXII, 2, 24). These metal spirals then begin very early and are at first of copper or bronze. But silver ones also appear in isolated cases in very early earth graves**) of the copper bronze period.***) The decorative ornament at the ends was developed at a date not much before 600 B. C. into flowers and heads of animals and mythical beings. The spirals with the griffin protome (bust) XXXIII, 28 belongs to the first half of the 4th century. The latest of these metal spirals which as a rule are found in pairs near to the ears of the corpses, occur in graves of the 4th century B. C. Those with human heads belong to the latest kinds, of which a specimen is figured in Pl. CLXXXII, 24. In the Hellenistic period they are superseded by the regulation earring with heads of animals and human heads. (CLXXXII, 8 and 9. CCXVII, 13—17). These large spirals were somehow attached to the ears, the smaller ones possibly also in the ears.†) This is evident from the place where they are found, and from the fact that they occur in pairs.

On the other hand, it seems that the numerous small spirals which occur together with the large ones or without them near the same body, have in fact served as hair slides or ornaments. So far, Helbig may be right. (Homerische Epos). Possibly however, the question has still to be asked whether the large and small spirals alike served as our hooks do to keep together pieces of drapery. The small spirals would thus serve as buttons to hold together the armholes and the larger ones would keep the dress on the shoulders. (Cf. Helbig' Epos p. 201).

Jui. Naue has attempted on the strength of communications I have made to him and the Cyprian copper spirals he has been allowed to examine to explain these as currency rings, and has compared their weight with that of Cyprian coins. It is easily conceivable that these ornamental rings were used also for purposes of barter just as now-a-days glass rings are still used as payment in trade with savage peoples. Since then I have weighed various sorts of Cyprian antique metal objects of various periods and found that most of them were manufactured of a definite weight. Gold and silver—as well as copper and bronze—wares and even presumably those made of iron were sold as the raw material was, by weight. That is the method and fashion in which we know the ancient Hebrews of the Old Testament gave their commissions to metal workers and concluded their bargains. The same sensible practice is in force now in the East generally and also in Cyprus. On the value of the weight of the metal a certain percentage is added as payment for the work. If then, on occasion these spirals served as the means of barter in trade we need not therefore regard them as current coin, for they persist as we see down into the 4th century B. C. when the custom of striking coin was universal throughout the island. The Cypriotes were certainly in possession of an adequate supply of minted coin at the beginning of the 6th century B. C. I excavated one of the earliest Cyprian coins (obv. Sphinx, rev. incuse square) in grave 92 Nekr. II. Marion Arsinoë) cf. Pl. XXVII, 3. and CXCVIII, 3) and this grave belongs to the beginning of the 6th century B. C.

Besides the rare silver and the still rarer gold and electron spirals we meet so far in the Cyprian copper-bronze age for the most part only rude round perforated beads of gold (Plate CLXXIII, 22 m)††) and settings of gold and silver for clay beads, beads of stone and faience and stone cylinders. A clay bead of this period set in gold from a grave in Hagia Paraskevi now in the Museum at Düsseldorf in Pl. CCXVII, 7, a similar one in Pl. CLXXIII, 22, 1, (H Paraskevi) an agalmatolite bead set in silver (H. Par.°) also in Pl. CLXXIII, 22a (cf. p. 464). Cylinder settings of gold from Cyprus in Pl. CXLVI, 5, B, a and b (cf. p. 451).

---

*) In the note on p. 451 I discuss the differences of colour, oxydization and chemical composition of the silver ornaments. The expert has in most cases in these a ready indication whereby he may distinguish between the finds of the copper-bronze and the iron ages. The same applies though in a more limited degree to gold and to colour. Cf. above, note to the explanatory text to Pl. CXLVI, 5 B, a and b.

**) Pl. 455, Pl. CXLVI, 3 B, m, u and o.

***) Cf. p. 455 note and 463.

†) It is impossible in the case of many of these spirals that they could have been put in the ear itself as earrings. The hole required for that would have had to be too large; also the long spiral ring would have hindered the movement of the head. On the other hand it is clear from the ear, that it is possible to bore very large holes in the ear. The columnar idols too e. g. Pl XXXVII, 6 show further that the goddess and her attendants wore two very large rings in their ears. The male statuette from the precinct of Apollo at Tonmpa (No. 67 of the list), published by Munro-Tubbs in J. H. S. 1891 Pl. IX, has in its ears two rings painted yellow and suspended one from the other which in conjunction might quite well represent the coils of a spiral.

††) In Hissarlik we find not only the same gold cylinder and bead settings as in the early Cyprian bronze age graves (cf. Pl. CXLVI, 5, A) but also gold beads similar in technique and colour (cf. for Cyprus Pl. CLXXIII, 22 m and for Hissarlik Ilios p. 559, Fig. 900).

A pair of rude gold rings that are too small for earrings and too large for fingers were excavated in 1893 in a grave of the bronze age at Tamassos, exactly similar ones practically interchangeable as to technique and colour of gold were found at Hissarlik.

A very clumsy electron ring from a bronze age grave at Psammatismeno with an engraved design of early Babylonian style (reproduced full size in Pl. CCI. 15, cf. p. 456) is so far the only Cyprian example of a finger ring made of one of the precious metals in early times.

We turn to the earliest type of the gold earring, frequent in the Graeco-Phoenician iron age (Pl. CLXXXII. 1 and CLXXXIII. 19, 1). It only occurs in those early iron age strata in which occur such silverly the fibulas of gold (Furrov III. 3, 491, Fig. 596[***] and bronze (p. 460 Fig. 591), the term cotta vessels such as those in Pl. CCXVI. 23, 24 and 26, XIX. The painted swastikas and the plate which I discussed above on p. 393 note 1 and of which I give another example in Fig. 295. This plate was excavated at Tamassos in 1890 and also has the swastikas as ornaments. It is painted with dull black and blood-red geometric patterns on the dull brownish ground.

This kind of earring has been discussed on p. 481 under 5—7 Pl. CXLIII. The ear-ring illustrated here came in long was found at Tamassos in 1889, in the stratum of tombs from which the plate shown on Fig. 295 and the vase on p. 77 Fig. 35 came. I found ear-rings like these in which the exhibit another mulberries applies (Cf. p. 456[***]) at Tamassos and Kurion and also at Amathus. They were but inserted into the ear itself but fastened to it by ribbons or strings ending in bows. I evidently represents a similar ear-ring without the mulberries. True, a gold pendin is passed through the eyelet of the ring, but I suppose that it was placed there by the finder. Alexandros, a Greek of Limassol, who died some years ago. I could not myself go down into the grave as I had injured my foot and the shaft was too wide. The gold breast-plate illustrated in Pl. CXCII. 3 was found in the same grave.

The gold breast-plates CXCIX. 3 and XXV. 10, 19 and 12 come from the same stratum. The bronze kylix of Idalion Pl. CLXX. 1 belongs to the same period and the same stage of artistic development. The provenance of the kylix is marked on the map Pl. II No. 12 (cf. p. 943) and is close to that of the vases on Pl. CCXVI. 23. Both belong to the same stratum as the gold and bronze fibulas, the swastikas, plate and cask-shaped vessels (e. g. Pl. CCXVI. 25 and 26) and may therefore be dated before 550 B. C.

The next class of ear-rings[***] begins at the end of the 7th century and occurs very frequently in the 6th century (XXV. 5). These earrings which were always hung into a hole bored in the ear, are shaped like a bead. With their appearance the berry-shaped ear-rings cease. These boat-shaped earrings Pl. CLXXXII. 9, continued to be made in various varieties and were at late as the 4th century B. C. While the berry-shaped kind (like CLXXXII. 1) were only made of gold and that of a very red colour similar to gold of the bronze period, the boat-shaped kind occur in red and in pale gold and also in silver. The earliest variety is very roughly hammered and shows the dull red colour of the most ancient gold. But parallel with these in the 6th century B. C. occur others made of silver (sometimes granulated) silver gilt and electron. Indeed the pair of ear-rings which I found in 1894 in excellent preservation in a grave at Kurion illustrated about half actual size on Pl. CLXXXIII. 4), seem from the circumstances of the discovery to belong rather to the 7th(?) than to the beginning of the 6th century B. C. In this example the carving consists of two rings one within the other each forming a boat-shaped ornament. One of these rings is made of granulated silver which has suffered from oxydisation and the other of electron, the well known mixture of gold and silver. From the oxydisation and the fact that the two parts were found stuck together it is evident that they were worn in one.

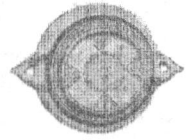

Fig. 99c

Along with these ear-rings I excavated several simple silver spirals, a series of silver rosettes (which had been sewn on a garment, ribbon or fillet one of these in Pl. CLXXXII. 2), 18 rectangular pieces of silver leaf with busts of two female divinities (Pl. XXV. 14, p. 295), fragments of a silver girdle (like XXV. 1—6 and a breast-ornament in the shape of a calf-head of coloured porcelain with gilt muzzle. The silver boat-shaped ear-ring (CLXXXIII. 6) may be dated as early as the 6th century. I was led to this conclusion by the fact that I found it at Marion-Arsinoe in Grave 19, Nekropolis II in 1886 together with a kylix of Chalcylion and another of Harmston, and by other circumstances of the discovery. The gold boat-shaped ear-ring with toothed edge and ornamented with granulated work (CLXXXIII. 7) which was found with the painted vase (LXIII. 5) must be as early as the 5th or quite the beginning of the 6th century. In the same period we must place the gold boat-shaped earring granulated but without the toothed edge (CCXVII. 18). The silver boat-shaped earrings (one in Pl. CXXXIII. 8) with cord shaped wires belong to the middle of the 6th century B. C. and come from the same grave (Marion-Arsinoe, Grave 49, Nekropolis III, 1886) as the spirals with human beads (one in Pl. CLXXXIII. 9d).

---

[*] Cf. also J. H. S. 1889, p. 195.

The ear-rings which show fine drawn out points ending in eyelets in or under the muzzle of an animal (c. g. CLXXXII, 8 and 9, CCXVII, 13—17)*) from the circumstances of discovery can hardly be earlier than the beginning of the 4th century B. C. The eyes of the heads and the toothed patterns are sometimes filled in with cellular enamel and sometimes not. In Hellenistic or pre-Roman graves which can be dated in the 5th or 2nd century B. C. I found ear-rings such as those in Pl. CCXVII, 14 (e. g. Grave 7, Nekropolis III, Marion-Arsinoë, 1886) with lions-heads not enamelled with glass. In these instances the gold is very pale in colour. The ear-ring in Pl. CLXXXII, 9 comes from a late Hellenistic grave (Grave 9, Nekropolis III, Marion-Arsinoë, 1886) while the accompanying ear-ring with dolphin head certainly belongs to the Roman imperial time and in its careless execution shews the decadence of art. Hollow discs and beads are hung on a wire behind the head. This pair of ear-rings with dolphin heads was found by me in Grave 110, Nekropolis II, Marion-Arsinoë in 1886. The same grave contained pale gold worked into myrtle and laurel leaves which are peculiar to the Roman graves throughout the island, late Roman unpainted vases, a late amphora of slender shape, Roman glasses 'and a short iron sword of Roman shape. The formation of the grave was decidedly Roman.

Other Hellenistic and Roman ear-rings are illustrated and compared in Pl. CLXXXII, 12—15, 19 and 21.

A comparatively early Hellenistic period is illustrated by a pair of ear-rings with pendants formed by hovering Erotes (CLXXXII, 21). In the same grave I found a silver coin of one of the older Ptolemies, two grave ornaments made of earth and gilded, one of them in the form of two snakes coiled together (CLXXXII, 20), the other a small capital with a head in the centre (27), a small glass head (28) one glass and one silver figurine, links of ornamental chains, a large glass ring, (like the milk-white one in Pl. LXV) silver ear-rings with animal head of the type just described, a small gold ring with a ruby (in shape like CLXXXII, 25 from grave 24, Necr. III Marion-Arsinoë) and the cornelian scarabaeus illustrated in Pl. XXXII, 29 (cf. p. 366). Ground plan and section of the grave staircase are given in Pl. CLXXIV, 3.

To late Hellenistic or perhaps even to Roman times belongs the class of ear-ring with Erotes bent round the ring, so frequently found in different parts of the island of Cyprus (CLXXXII, 15).

The ear-ring in Pl. CLXXXII, 18 with rows of glass beads (grave 36 Nekr. I Marion-Arsinoë 1886) is late Hellenistic or Roman.

The ear-rings from the same excavation in Pl. CLXXXII 12, 14 and 19 are certainly Roman. The ear-ring Fig. 12 (grave 39 Necr. II) ends in a flower in front of which is applied a black and white bead. The ear-ring Fig. 14 (grave Nekr. I) ends in a bird resembling a crane, which hides its beak behind its right wing. To the less important class of Roman grave ornaments made specially for funeral purposes belongs the ear-ring (Fig. 19) with green glass in the centre (Grave 26 Necr. II). The fact that Roman glasses, lamps and imperial coins were found together in graves of Roman construction makes the dating certain.

The ear-ring in Pl. CCXVII, 20 also is late Roman. The metal is beaten into thin plates and cut out in half-moon shape. It is ornamented with wire beaten flat, heart-shaped leaves, circular flowers and bunches of grapes. This kind of ear-ring is found in Roman graves all over the island and reaches down to the Byzantine period.

A Roman ear-ring variety much worn by the common people is illustrated in Fig. 18, Pl. CCXVII. Only the vase - shaped ornament hung in the ring seems not to belong to it but to be older (cf. Fig. 5).

The colossal ear-ring CCXVII, 10 is unique. I can say nothing definite about its date as I never found another like it, but it gives the impression of great antiquity.

On the other hand the small chain to hang over the ear (Pl. CCXVII, 7) the neck-chain (12) and the metal plates with impressed heads (Pl. CCXVII, 8 and 11 and Pl. CLXXXII, 29 Idalion) are Hellenistic. The last are made of leaf gold and were only intended for the decoration of corpses and grave-clothes. The round flat button-shaped ornaments in Pl. CCXVII, 2 and 3 are made of thicker gold leaf and were evidently intended for daily wear. While ornament 2 shows decided Hellenistic stamp, ornament 8 is archaic or archaistic.

We pass now to the pendants, which were either used alone or in rows as breast-ornaments.

Reference should be made to the descriptions of Pl. XXV, 7, XXXIII, 2—15, 16—22, LXVII, 7, 9, 12 - 14, CXLIV, 1—10, 14 - 17, and also to Pl. CLXXXII, 18, a gold vase shaped ornament certainly of the 4th century B. C. (grave 43 Necr. III Marion-Arsinoë). Attic red-figured vases, Kyprian Graffiti. Cf. Pl. XXXIII, 18, a very beautiful one in the form of a two handled amphora from about the same period or earlier. (Exact circumstances of the find unknown).

Two hanging ornaments found in grave 142 Nekr. II. Marion-Arsinoë (Pl. CLXXXII, 22 and 23) certainly belong to the 6th century B. C. The first (22) belongs to a chain like the one in Pl. XXXIII, 15, but is older. The second (23) represents a flower.

The amulet Fig. 26 in the same plate and from the same excavation certainly belongs to the 4th century (grave 82, Nekr. II) and so do the gold chain-links with double holes found in Grave 23, Nekr. III and illustrated in Fig. 37. In combination with beads of the same shape made of green and dull yellow Faience they make a very pretty ornament.

The pendant for a ring (Grave 249, Nekr. II) an unengraved cornelian scaraboid, Fig. 36, also belongs to the 4th century B. C. We have seen two exactly similar ones in Pl. XXXIII, 12 and 14). (From grave 24, Nekropolis I).

A gold figurine in Egyptian style used as pendant amulet and talisman hollow inside to allow for the insertion of a written charm is illustrated in Pl. CCXVII, 4 (cf. p. 337 and 448, on the Teraphim). This again illustrates a very pronounced type and belongs to the 6th century B. C. just as certainly as does the gold pendant in the form of an acorn (CCXVII, 6) with which the acorns on the gold kylix of the same period (Pl. CXCVIII, 3) ought to be compared.

The large pendant (CCXVII, 9) in the form of a round disc (cf. p. 307) has a very imposing effect.

The finger rings of gold and silver with or without stones occupy a very important place. I have already mentioned an ancient Babylonian ring from the Kyprian copper-bronze period (CLI, 35). In the

_____
*) Similar ones from Egypt. (Pl. CXLIII, 5—7).

stratum of the bow-shaped fibulae (1000—650 B. C.) I have as yet found no finger rings, but from the 6th century onwards they are very numerous. The swivel rings with scarabaei and scaraboids and the rings with engraved metal plates are about equally numerous. The flat gems or unengraved stones (e. g. Plate CLXXXII, 25) set in gold or silver do not as a rule occur before the 4th century B. C. A ring of the 4th century B. C. from which the stone has been broken away is given in Pl. CLXXXII, 32.

In the same plate I give six examples of rings with engraving in metal (all from Marion-Arsinoë).
38. (Grave 51, Nekr. III). Silver from the 4th century B. C. (Grave of the Attic Rhyton CXCI, 7, &c.)
39 (= XXXII, 31). Ring of pale gold, 6th century B. C. (Grave 98, Nekr. II).
44. Silver (Grave 239, Nekr. II) 6th century B. C. early Attic vases.
45. Silver (Grave 235, Nekr. II) 6th century B. C.
46. Gold (Grave 179, Nekr. II). 6th century B. C. many early Attic vases in the same grave).
47. Gold (Grave 181, Nekr. II). 5th or 4th century B. C. I give here four further examples of swivel rings which all come from the same excavation at Marion-Arsinoë (35, 41 to 43).

35. (Grave 258, Nekr. II) Silver swivel ring with a silver box in which was placed a small scarabaeus made of dirty green porcelain which crumbled to pieces as soon as it was dug out certainly belongs to the 6th century B. C. In the same grave is a silver ring with a long quadrangular seal-plate. The engraved work has disappeared through oxydization and use. Three heavy silver spirals of 1½ coils each. Black figured Attic vases.

43. Silver swivel ring with electron setting. (Grave 106, Nekr. II). Certainly belongs to the 6th century B. C. Quantities of Cyprian water-jugs, among them some with bird features (e. g. Pl. XXII, and XXIII.)

41. Silver swivel ring in which an unengraved scaraboid made of black stone is placed without metal covering. Certainly of the 4th century B. C. Red figured Attic vases in the grave.

42. Silver swivel ring like 41. 4th century B. C. (Grave 35, Nekr. III). Bloodstone of a milk-white colour with red spots. The engraving is very beautiful but unfortunately cannot be reproduced. A man, probably Perseus, running and turning his head round holds a sword and a head There are two more rings also illustrated here.

40". Finger ring of silver, presumably a wedding ring, with two small flat surfaces in which stones were formerly set. Marion-Arsinoë Grave 244. Nekr. II. Certainly of the 6th century B. C. In the same grave a number of vases by the lesser Attic masters.

84 Gold ring with Cyprian inscription on the inner side. 4th century B. C. (Grave 6, Nekr. II, Marion-Arsinoë)
The small weavers' wheels Pl. XXXIII, 10 and 11, Pl. CLXXXII, 48—51 form another special feature of the graves of Marion-Arsinoë. Cf. p 368
48. (Grave 48, Nekr. III). Made of silver, almost indentical in size and shape with the gold weavers wheels of the 4th century on Pl. XXXIII, 10 and 11.
49. (Grave 42, Nekr. III). Made of silver. In the same grave were discovered the silver earrings (Pl. CLXXXII, 6) and the spirals plated with gold leaf. Pl. CLXXXII, 24. 4th century.
50. (Grave 12, Nekr. III) Made of silver with gold inlaid. Certainly a grave of the 4th century B. C.
51. Two silver weavers' wheels. (Grave 174, Nekr. II). Grave of the kylikes of Chachrylion and Hermaios. 6th century B. C. The silver boat-shaped earrings (e. g. Fig. 5) were found in the same grave.*)

Gold or silver leaf pressed into the shape of a mouth form another feature peculiar to the Nekropolis of Marion-Arsinoë. There are no instances of these earlier than the 4th century.
The gold mouth illustrated in Pl CXLIV, 13 comes from grave No. 24, Nekr. I. (Cf. Pl. XXXIII, 9—15 and p. 455. 4th century B. C. These representations of mouths come as far down as the Roman period.**)

Pl. CLXXXII, 33 represents a gold mouth from grave 26, Nekr. III. The grave is certainly Roman. It contained Roman glasses, Roman clay lekythoi, as I proved in 1880 in Salamis, Roman cooking pots and Roman lamps. The gold and silver representations of mouths in metal were used to tie over the mouths of corpses.

In explaining my illustrations of gold and silver ornaments I have given the dates only in those instances where I could be fairly certain. In order to save time and room I have omitted many other examples of Kyprian gold and silver work. Any one who is interested in the subject can find more information in the works of the brothers Cesnola "Cyprus" and "Salaminia" and in Perrot III. No second excavation will be able to rival Louis Palma di Cesnola's collection of gold and silver ornaments and vases belonging to all periods of Cyprian art and consisting of old Graeco-Phoenician gold and silver ornaments, silver kylikes and purely Greek metal ornaments of different periods from the 6th century B. C. down to the Roman time.
We now pass to the larger metal rings and bands of bronze, silver, gold and gilt bronze.
The bronze ring wound round with gold wire (Pl. CLXXXII, 30) comes from grave 54 Nekr. I Marion-Arsinoë, the ground plan and section of which are given on Pl. CLXXXIV, 4 and in the entrance staircase of which the terra-cotta statue given in Pl. CLXXXVI, 3 was found, 4th century B. C. The ring is too small for a bracelet and too large for a ring.
The small ring, Fig 31, of similar workmanship was found in Grave 106, Nekr. II of the same excavation together with the swivel ring Fig 43 and belongs to the 6th century B. C. It might have been used as a finger ring. We see then that this technique extends over at least 200 years.

*) Later on Munro seems to have found several of these silver weaver's wheels at Poll. (J. H. S. 1890, p. 56.) He describes them as "objects like candlestick tops," and makes the extraordinary suggestion—"They are perhaps intended to fit round the lip of the alabaster ointment bottles." (sic!) This is impossible. Even the little wheel which differs from the others in shape (CLXXXII, 57) shows by the projecting fillet on the narrow side that it could never have been used as a stopper to a vase. It is quite possible that these little wheels may have been sometimes worn as ornaments or used to fasten drapery. Two of the terra-cottas Pl. CCXII, 2 and 3) excavated at Achna (Artemis Temenos, No. 1 on the list) shew, fastened on the shoulders, large round objects very like these wheels. The beautiful gold wheels (Pl. XXXIII, 10 and 11) were found lying on or beside the upper part of the skeleton.
**) On p. 450 I stated (in accordance with Herrmann, Winckelmannsprogramm p. 28) that I was the first to find these metal mouth-shaped objects. This statement is not strictly correct, for in Cesnola's Salaminia, Pl. II, a very rude example is illustrated. Munro (J. H. S. 1890, p. 56) makes Herrmann responsible for the mistake and cites besides the above-mentioned example from Salaminia (II, 10) a metal covering intended for the mouth (Salaminia p. 17, Fig. 6b) but not shaped like a mouth. I may at least claim to have been the first to find in Cyprus in any considerable quantity, in graves shewing Greek influence, thin plates or leaves of gold and silver, more skillfully modelled in imitation of the human mouth. Similar mouth-shaped metal plates have been found on Egyptian mummies.

One of the bracelets, a very beautiful one from the end of the fifth or beginning of the 4th century, is illustrated and described in Pl. XXXIII, 9 and p. 368.

In the same grave on the same female corpse near the knee lay large silver snake rings. They were used as anklets, cf. Pl. CCIV, Fig. 1–3.

These bracelets and anklets begin very early and occur made of bronze in the Bronze period.

The Silver girdles with and without gilt, the best preserved example of which hitherto found is given in Pl. XXV, 1—4 (cf. p. 51 ff.) and is of silver, the buckle gilt, belong partly to the first half of the 6th century and partly to the 7th century. I called attention to these girdles in the Nekropoleis of three towns (Marion-Arsinoë, Kurion and Tamassos).

In different passages of this work I discussed silver and bronze kylikes and shewed (p. 434 and 440 &c.) how silver kylikes of real Egyptian style, one of which was found in Cyprus, gave an impulse to the manufacture of Kylikes which became so important an industry on the island.

In general the goldsmiths' work of Cyprus from the 7th century onwards is strongly influenced by Egypt and in less degree by Assyria. It is true that in silversmiths' work Assyrian influence is early felt but even here it seems to be overpowered by that of Egypt. The few objects of gold, silver and electron belonging to the Cyprian Copper-Bronze period shew technique as primitive as or even more primitive than the objects discovered in Hissarlik.

Plate CCXVIII.

My discoveries of the cemeteries of Marion-Arsinoë and the excavations organised there by myself and the Cyprus Exploration Fund.

Fig. 270 = Pl. CLXXIV, Fig. 1. (cf. p. 466).

On this map of the site No. II, is placed a little too much to the West. The map was however prepared from the English survey so that it may claim, although drawn on a small scale to be more correct than the rough plan made by Mr. Ernest Gardner and Mr. Munro given in Pl. CCXVIII.

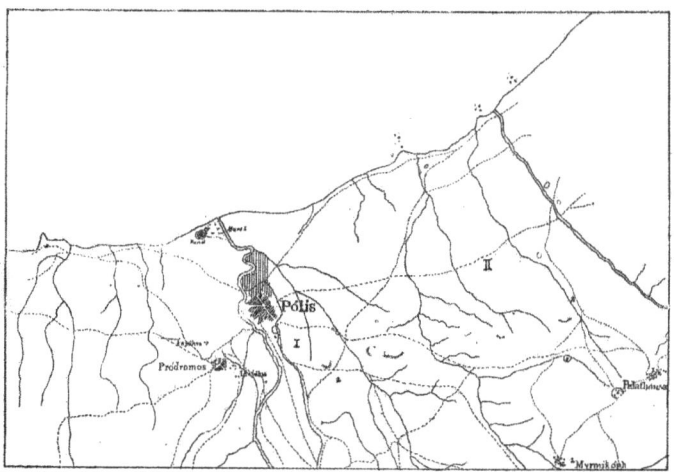

Fig. 270.

The **green colour filled** out with dots indicates the parts of the cemeteries which I excavated for C. Watkins in 1886 and which yielded such extensive finds. All the places where I found nothing are left blank, but as I finished the map not on the spot but in Berlin some places where I made discoveries are unmarked and in others the boundaries are drawn rather within than without the actual extent.

In 1885 I began my investigations at the point " **M.O.-R. first tomb** ", N.-E. from the star (*) at the green spot west of the road which leads to Poli and South of the last house, which belongs to a negro. Of the two terracotta statues found in the dromos of this first grave I give one in Pl. CLXXXVII, 4. (Cf. p. 472). The plans of the graves are in Pl. CLXXV, 13.

The second place where I began to dig (in 1885) is indicated by the green spot (Karpaga) N.-E. from the mark "Site K". The ground belonged to the then Demarchos of Poli. The beautiful bearded Greek head found there is given in Pl. CLXXXVI, 2 (cf. p. 471) and the grave itself in Pl. CLXXV, 12.

The third point where I dug in June 1885 lies further East on the ground belonging to the Turk Mullah Mehemed. It was here that I made the most important discoveries viz. the kylikes of Chachrylion and Hermaios, the alabastron of Pasiades, the marble torso &c. After the excavation of 1886 Mullah Mehemed's piece of land passed into the possession of Mr. Williamson and it is marked on the map as his vineyard. In 1885 I found there among other objects two interesting statuettes. The inferior one is illustrated in Pl. CCIII, fig. 3 and is enthusiastically described by Dr. H. Schmidt (p. 480). In the same piece of land I found in 1885 fragments of polychrome vases (like Pl. LXIV, 4 and 7) of oinochoës (e. g. LXIV, 1—3) and of glazed Attic ware. One of these graves excavated in 1885 is given in Pl. CLXXV, 14. In 1886 I began the excavations at Hagia Dimitrianos and marked the place I, I opened 127 graves which contained objects.

After seeking in vain on other sites I went to Mullah Mehemed's property (Mr. Williamson's vineyard) and numbered the second locality II. There and in the immediate neighbourhood 261 graves were opened. Then I came back to the neighbourhood of the village and opened 53 more graves, which I grouped together under Nekropolis III. As may be seen, I and III make up one and the same cemetery between them and correspond to Munro's Western Nekropolis, while my Nekropolis II corresponds to Munro's Eastern Nekropolis.

Plate CCXIX = Title Page.

Is to be found in the volume of text.

A new kind of Attic vase found and noted by me in 1886 in Marion-Arsinoë.

All the vases 1—8 come from the excavation begun at Marion-Arsinoë in 1886.

1. 0,14 m. high, the vases 2—6 are drawn to the same scale. Yellowish-grey clay, decoration in dull black. Formal pattern of concentric circles.

2. Reddish, dull clay, decoration in dull black. The Oinochoë is already somewhat more slender than 1. 1 and 2 from Grave 34, Nekropolis II (end of the 7th and beginning of the 6th century B. C.)

3. Still more elegant in shape, the neck longer and more delicate, the foot a more prominent feature. Decoration painted in white slip and black, direct on the clay ground. Horizontal circles intersect others that are vertical, as in 2. Nekropolis II, Grave 80. Grave of the 5th century B. C.

4. Similar shape to 2. Decoration in black and white on reddish ground. The intersecting circles are given up, the decoration is arranged horizontally. It consists of bands, rosettes of dots and little trees. Fourth century B. C. Grave 65, Nekropolis I contained many Attic red-figured vases.

5. Similar shape to 2 and 3. White slip and black ornaments on dark brown ground. Circles, lines and leaves arranged horizontally on the neck and foot, vertically on the body. Fourth century B. C. Nekropolis II, Grave 75.

6. Similar vase. Decoration in white slip and violet, and arranged only horizontally on dark green, dull ground. Between bands of lines is the egg ornament and wreath of leaves pattern. To the same class as 3—6 belongs the vase figured in CLXXVIII, 2 fig. 271 here. But, as in the case of 6, we have a second body colour added, i. e. violet red on the black ground. This vase most resembles No. 3, both in shape and decoration.

The clumsy shape of the Cyprian oinochoë, typical shape in 1 and 2, acted as an inspiration to the Attic potter (whether he worked in Athens or in Cyprus is all the same as regards results). He made for the Cyprian market imitations of this Cyprian shape of vase, which elsewhere has never been noted in Attic ware, but he made them of Attic clay, in Attic technique, and ornamented them with Attic designs. In the case of the oinochoë No. 7 (0,238 m. high) from Grave 113, Nekropolis II, the motive is Dionysos surrounded by a crew of Satyrs and Bacchantes.

In No. 8, an oinochoë 0, 27 m. high, we have the group of Herakles wrestling with the lion in presence of Athene and Iolaos (from Grave 113, Nekropolis II).

In both graves there were found a number of Attic black-figured vases from the first half of the 6th century B. C., and other things, which make it evident that these Attic vases made for Cyprus are of the same date.

The same grave 239 Necr. II, which yielded the silver ring, figured Pl. CLXXXII, Fig. 44, contained yet a third vase that belongs to this category, i. e. a somewhat larger and finer black-figured oinochoë of the same style. This fell to the share of the Cyprus Museum, and is still unpublished[*]. The vase-painter in this case selected the motive of the draught players, familiar on black figured Greek vases. Two heavily armed warriors are seated at play, while two others are standing, one on either side.

I am absolutely convinced that if further excavations were carried out, more instances of this class of Attic vases manufactured specially for Cyprus would be found[**]. As vases 1 and 2 are certainly earlier,

_____

[*] There was no time to reproduce the vase while the excavations were going on.
[**] I sent my report with the illustrations to Dümmler in his turn: he must have mislaid both for a very long time, for he has only just now sent them back to me. Hence Herrmann has never seen my report on this new class of oinochoë. But Herrmann in his Winckelmannsprogramm mentions (p. 37) Furtwängler's observation in these words: There were vases of the sort named with long neck and compressed about but decorated in the black-figured Attic technique among those sold by auction at Paris, as I know from word kindly sent me by Herr Prof. Furtwängler. Any further details he has forgotten. I have no knowledge of such vases either from originals or reproductions. I must content myself therefore with drawing attention to the fact and must forego any attempt at explaining this interesting phenomenon as this could only be done by an exact acquaintance with all the technical characteristics of the original.

and 3–6 (And all the numerous analogous instances are later than 7 and 8, it must be taken as proved that the Attic vase-painters developed their graceful oinochoës out of the clumsy Graeco-Phoenician oinochoë, e. g. 1 and 2, which dates as far back as and even farther than the 9–10th century B. C. This class of vase in its modified and rounded form, and so only, was manufactured down to the 4th century B. C. But the old stiff sort, e. g. Pl. CLXVI. 40, and Frontispiece, Fig. 1 and 2, is met with no more. Of this stiff, Graeco-Phoenician sort Fig. 2 is the latest instance that is typical in material, size, colour and decoration; it appeared in the stratum that belongs to the 9th century B. C. (found 1899 at Tamassos). Messrs. Munro (J. H. S. 1891, p. 329 sv.) and Tubbin (H. S. 1891, p. 91, note) have asserted that the primitive Cyprian ware with concentric circles goes down as late as Hellenistic or Roman days.— Tubbin even thinks those vases are abundant in Roman times, and that the finest examples came from graves of the 4th century B. C. and the Ptolemaic period. Munro (in 1891) regrets to have to contradict a great authority like Prof. Furtwängler who relies not only on information from me, and on the results of my excavations but also on his own personal inspection, made in Cyprus on the spot, both as regards my discoveries at Marion-Arsinoë (which I showed him in the Cyprus Museum) as well as those at Tamassos. He maintains, and rightly, that vases like that in the Frontispiece No 2 only go down as late as the 9th century B. C. and that those like 3—6 do indeed appear in the 4th century B. C. but then disappear utterly.

In discussing the water-jugs in Plate XXII—XXIV, LXII—LXIV, we have already seen how, in the 9th century B. C. a quite distinct form of jug was initiated, the concentric circles began partly to disappear, partly to be modified, and in the 4th century B. C. concentric circles disappeared entirely from the system of decorating employed for the Frontispiece. The groups of concentric circles are best preserved in a kind of amphora that is in shape related to that in Pl. CLXXVII. 2. The excavations I began in 1889 at Tamassos have only confirmed the results I arrived at in 1885 and 1885 at Marion-Arsinoë. I shall shortly return to this subject.

As to the class of Oinochoës that appears in the Frontispiece and its shape, I should like to draw attention again to the two vases in Pl. CLXXII, 17 d and e (Fig. 972 and 973). I excavated both of

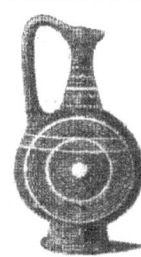

Fig. 474.

Fig. 474.　Fig. 475.

them in a grave of the transition period, between the Bronze and Iron ages, at Kaivdata-Leon i. e. 1300—1000 B. C. (cf. supra, p. 460). The collective contents of the grave are at Berlin. We note side by side in the same grave, the primitive hand-made jug (474) and the finely proportioned oinochoë, though even this is primitive compared to the vases 3—6 of the Frontispiece. The latter developed from the former simply because the Cyprian potter learnt the use of the wheel.

Excursus on Marion-Arsinoë.

1. The copper-mines of Marion-Arsinoë in relation to those of Tamassos and Soloi.

Munro and his friends have completely overlooked the general fact that the earliest Cyprian terra-cotta vases excavated by them and previously by me cannot with any certainty be dated earlier than the beginning of the 7th Century B. C. Also is the oldest settlement so far proved to have existed at Marion-Arsinoë, to which my Nekropolis II (Pl. CLXVIII, i. e. Munro's Eastern Nekropolis) belongs, there is no trace of the strata of the bronze Situlae (p. 460, Fig. 390), the clay-plates (p. 488, Fig. 359), the cask-shaped vessels (CLXVI, 34) the early sort of bird-vases (e. g. p. 97, Fig. 42, 43 and 84), the painted

*) Munro reproaches where e. g. I disagree with and giving references, out he does not give himself the trouble to make a thorough study of the literature of the subject. How I was invited by Messrs and the other gentlemen of the Cyprus Exploration Fund how they sometimes placed far more at detail always undertake made eager attacks upon me and my associates, will appear by what follows. But I find want my regrets that Munro made use of my ... H. S. a 329 note) and Colonel ... unable to support the inference about the manufacture of the blue-on-white glaze between two strata and considering them to Hellenic times. I had said once enough in the Mittheilungen (Athens 1881 p.199, that I had failed to enable in Kition together with Roman coins and Roman lamps a quantity of vases with concentric circles as ... and concluded therefrom that down to Roman times they found their way continued at Kition in quite cases to imitation of these old Cyprian models. But Munro overlooks the contradiction that I published in 1885 through M Richter in the Syrian Archäologischen Zeitung nr 346—6) l'ancienne d'abord a 179 and the detailed explanation of how I came to make the mistake. I had better quote the passage word for word.

"J'avais finalement à l'ouest de Larnaca découvert une longue ... des anciennes maisons d'époque 1885 ... Comme les anciens vases étaient mêlés aux anciennes lampes d'époque et aux pièces de monnaie d'époque plus romaine à Larnaca, j'en prenais à tort que ces poteries à cercles concentriques qu'ils avaient trouvés dans des couches inférieures ... M. Richter, chargé de fouiller dans ces couches inférieures et de ... supra ... dans le Mittheilungen de l'Institut allemand 1881 à 199 et à Berlin ... rapporte à une base ancienne que ... Hellénique de l'Art 1 III à 199 d'après le conséquence de M. Richter l'érreur le prenant cela tort à même temps que le tout périodes d'époque d'époque d'origine d'art ... Richter ne serait la correspondances et à quelques-uns les qualités précédentes qu'un archéologique un peut ... comme ... ...

"The reader naturally asks how I came to be myself deceived. I was beginning then in 1878—88 the vast excavations I ever undertook and I had had no previous archæological training. Besides then I had at the same time to superintend a photographic establishment for photographing, where I was managing and had also to earn my living by writing political correspondence and feuilletons. My salary was smaller then that drawn by the men placed in the excavations afterwards undertaken by the Exploration Fund.

Swastikas (ibidem) and the gold berry-earring (Pl. CLXXXII, 1). All the other strata, older than this, naturally do not appear i. e. the transition stages from the Copper-Bronze period and the Copper-Bronze period itself.

The journey I undertook in 1885 through a great part of Cyprus, at my own expense and at great personal sacrifice, had special relation to the ancient copper-mines and their entourage. By means of this journey and excavations undertaken later on I discovered that the copper-mine between Tamassos, Amathus and Idalion was the largest and earliest of all. It is only at Tamassos that we find all the strata represented, from the earliest down to the latest, i. e. down to the Christian era.

Next come the copper mines that can be made out in the kingdom of Solo, i. e. the valley which now goes by the name of Solias. These mines, situated near the modern villages of Katydata and Linu, and the Monastery of Panagia Skurgotissa (i. e. the Monastery of the Madonna of the copperslack) were, as is seen from the finds, discovered and worked out about 1500—1200 B. C., certainly not much before. The graves published in Pl. CLXXII, 16—18 and their contents point to the transition period 1200—1000 B. C. This period is not represented at Marion-Arsinoë.

The copper mines just on the edge of the mountainous district now called Tylliria, near Limni (cf. Pl. I) to the east of Marion-Arsinoë, were not opened before the beginning of the 7th Century B. C.

But as early as the beginning of the 6th Century there was no other place on the Island at which anything like so brisk an intercourse went on with the Athenians and Greeks of the mainland. The bay of Marion-Arsinoë (marked on the map Pl. I Chrysochu-Bay) opens to the west, and lies on the westernmost tip of the Island, near Cape Akamas. The copper mines were virgin soil, and yielded brass at a smaller outlay than in other parts of the Island where digging for brass had long gone on. The conditions were most favourable for transport, the distance between the mines and the shipping harbour was smaller than in the case of Soloi. I appeal to the reader, how could Messrs. Munro and Tubbs think of expressing even a general opinion of the developement of Cyprian ceramics, when in their excavations at Marion-Arsinoë they did not discover a singleg rave that dated certainly before 600 B. C. In Salamis too (where they only followed in my footsteps) they did not find a single grave of the 6th Century B. C., let alone earlier ones. If they did find earlier Graeco-Phoenician vases among the ruins, it was only a few fragments which came to light in the lower strata, and even these did not belong, as I satisfied myself, to the earliest classes of vases of the Iron age.

2. Results obtained by me and by Messrs. Munro and Tubbs at Marion-Arsinoë.

The plates that relate to Marion-Arsinoë (cf. Index) which accompany this book ought to make it clear that I succeeded in doing more in one campaign than Messrs. Munro and Tubbs did in two. And that depends not merely on the larger number of graves that I opened, but also on my having engaged in successful investigations in the West Nekropolis (Nekr. I and II, cf. Pl. CCXVIII) as well as in the eastern one (Nekr. II). The reason was that I possessed, first and foremost, local information, and had had years of practical experience in excavations, while Mr. Munro and Mr. Tubbs were seeing a grave opened for the first time. Add to this that my own notes, plans, drawings, water-colours, photographs and the work done under my direction by Messrs. Foot, Christian and J. W. Williamson, offer a wealth of material for evidence which Messrs. Munro and Tubbs fail to produce.

What F. Dümmler, A. Furtwängler, P. Herrmann and S. Reinach have spoken and written about my excavations all rests on information obtained from me.

The reason stated on p 498, Note, prevented my replying earlier and now prevents my replying in full. A part of the reports I sent in have been lost. Another, which I bring forward, is more than enough amply to meet the attacks which, directly or indirectly, Mr. Munro has levelled against me. It is almost comical to see how Mr. Munro, in the strength of his own ignorance first — in 1890 — wishes to instruct me and my learned friends, how he confuses the truth, only — in 1891 — to recant his errors and in somewhat confused fashion to arrive at conclusions which I had formulated five years before much more clearly and had entered them in my reports, and indeed had expressed openly, partly myself, partly by the verbal or written statements of my friends.*) And wherever Munro still tries to oppose Furtwängler and me he has fallen, as I showed in discussing Pl. CCXVIII, into very serious error.

It remains now for me to go more into detail on individual points so that it may not be thought any more that I have remained silent because I was in the wrong.

In the Journal of Hellenic Studies p. 3, at the end of the note, these words occur: — "Dr. Herrmann goes further and attempts to identify a separate site for the earlier and later foundations, but his ingenious argument is based on untrustworthy information and erroneous preconceptions v. J. H. S. X. pp. 281—282." Herr Herrmann writes in the Winckelmannsprogramm p. 6. "I borrow the facts for the following picture of the local conditions from the very exact Report of Excavations by Ohnefalsch-Richter, which now lies before me". Munro therefore can, by his "untrustworthy information and erroneous preconceptions," only mean my statements.

In J. H. S. 1890, p. 6, Mr. Munro directs an even more direct thrust at me. "Herr Richter (V. Das Gräberfeld von Marion, pp 7 and 12) is prepared to vouch for their bearing an essentially older character than the debris of Arsinoë," but from particular enquiries on the point I learnt that they were of the very poorest construction, exactly resembling the foundations of a modern Cypriote village, supposing the mud upper walls had crumbled away. We discovered precisely similar walls on the opposite direction on sites C and D. So far as they can be said to have any character at all, it appears to be of the very latest. Herr Richter seems here, as elsewhere, to have allowed himself to be misled in the interests of a preconceived theory."

_____

*) As I was not enabled to return to Europe before 1890 I was obliged to make over the publication of many of my discoveries to scholars who were my friends, discoveries which by rights I should have published myself.

On p. 12 he again speaks of, "Herr Richter's older settlement," and states that the graves abutting on to it, "had proved to be Roman." This row of graves will be found in Pl. CCXVIII, entered as Roman tombs.

Precisely what Munro says on the condition and character of the masonry discovered by me (Pl. CCXVIII) and called by me "older settlement, but going down to Roman times," (Foundations of ancient buildings discovered in 1886) speaks for my view. The masonry of the Cypriots of to-day is often undistinguishable from the masonry of their ancestors of the 2nd, 3rd, 4th and 5th centuries B. C. Munro need only have taken a look at the ancient, still extant foundations of the houses at Leontari Vouno, that date from 1500 –1200 B.C. (Pl. CLXV). Further I refer the reader to my ground-plan Plates IV—VII and the views in plates LVI and LVII, where I give instances of buildings which fall within a period extending from the 7th century B. C. down to Roman days. In 1889 too I excavated within the ring-wall of the town of Tamassos an ancient house with a little household sanctuary of the Mother of the Gods (No. 5 of the list) which was viewed by W. Dörp-feld and A. Furtwängler. The building, in the state it was found, dated, to judge from the objects found with it, from Hellenistic days In 1883 also I excavated a Roman house at Salamis, which Munro saw. The ordinary buildings and the poorer sanctuaries of Cyprus were made of sunburnt tiles in all times as they are now. But the stone under walls, except in the rare cases of buildings made of splendid hewn blocks, were decidedly more primitive in the 7th and 6th centuries B. C. than in the 5th and 4th, and more primitive in Helleni-tic than in Roman days. The ruins of poor buildings are so absolutely alike in ancient and modern times that it is impossible, unless other discoveries decide the question, to say which is modern, which ancient. Hence the attempt to throw doubt on my older settlement and make me a laughing-stock recoils on Munro himself. We shall shortly see moreover, that, as a matter of fact, there are other reasons for supposing that an "older" town lay near our Nekropolis I and III. Moreover, it will be evident directly that there were two towns of the name of Marion, an earlier one to the east, a later one to the west. On the ruins of the later Marion, destroyed by Ptolemy Soter, rose Arsinoë. It is possible however, that this earlier, easterly town did not bear the name of Marion.

Let us first however, follow up Munro's polemic, which is aimed at me, though covertly. In pp. 20 and 22, J. H S. 1890, these further words occur: "Dr. Herrmann has been led to suppose that early tombs are marked by a long δρόμος, but we found examples which cannot well have had one, and at least one comparatively late tomb which certainly had." In the same page he says: "I should doubt whether they, i. e. the tomb staircases, are to be confined to any particular period, as Dr. Herrmann supposes" (i. e. basing his statement on my report. M. O ·R).

In these two paragraphs are given my observations on the Dromos and staircase-graves which I placed at the disposal of Herr Herrmann. We shall shortly hear what this same Mr. Munro thinks on this point in 1891. But first let us see what, according to him, is the sum total of the results of the campaign of 1889 (J. H. S. p. 59, 1890).

"Scarcely less valuable are the recorded facts of the excavation. They have already proved service-able in furnishing a prompt refutation of certain erroneous theories about the site which seemed likely to gain credence and authority."

On the same page Munro mentions, for the first time, Dümler's proposal (based again on my researches) to assign the later graves of the western Nekropolis to the later town Arsinoë, and the graves of the eastern Nekropolis to the older town Marion. After having at first inclined to this view, one of the many expressed by Dümmler, he next comes to the following conclusion.

"Within this period occurred the gap beetween the destruction of Marium and the foundation of Arsinoë, but it is hopeless to attempt to distinguish among the tombs those to be assigned to the one or the other."

Neither Munro, nor presumably Tubbs, knew at the end of the first campaign which was Marion, which Arsinoë, they knew nothing of the difference between the grave structures of the East and West Nekropoleis. My distinctions between the grave structures, according as they have dromos or staircase entrances, they condemn. My "older settlement" is, according to their view, which they state as demon-strated fact, either Roman or modern Cyprian.

A year later, after the second campaign, Munro arrived at substantially different conclusions, which I print here from J. H. S. 1891, p. 327.

"Let us now try to gather and apply any larger conclusions which it appears possible to deduce from our evidence. It has already been pointed out that tombs 57 and 59 belong in character to the eastern nekropolis, from whi·h the rest of the western nekropolis, in spite of a considerable resemblance in the plain pottery, is sharply distinguished by the painted decoration of its Cypriote vases. In the one nekropolis only the usual geometric decoration, executed with mechanical precision in black and red on the natural or reddened ground, is to be found In the other only that system of decoration which we have termed the polychrome. The distinction is fully maintained in other classes of objects. In the eastern nekropolis the black-figure technique pre-dominates, vases in the red-figure technique are comparatively rare and of good style, in the western the black-figure technique disappears altogether, and the few red-figured vases exhibit the last degeneracy of the style. Porce-lain amulets occur in the eastern tombs, but are absent from the western. The terra-cotta figurines of the eastern nekropolis are very small and crude, the larger figures do not appear, in the western nekropolis on the other hand the larger figures are common and the crude little ones are scarcely found. Obviously the two nekropoleis are of quite distinct periods and the eastern is considerably the earlier. Can we more precisely define those periods? I think to some extent we can. There was found in tomb 40, as has been noticed, a silver coin of the Lion type, 480—400 B. C. The vases from tomb 57 may be probably assigned to the earlier part of the second half of the same century. Now tomb 40 belongs to one of the younger groups of tombs in the nekropolis. Both tomb 40 and tomb 57 are later in character than perhaps the majority of eastern tombs. If then these two date from the middle of the fifth century B. C. or thereabouts, the earlier tombs will extend from, say, towards the close of the sixth century over the first half of the fifth. None are probably so late as the fourth century. For the eastern nekropolis then we may assign the century 520–420 B. C. as a rough but probable date. Now are we to place the western nekropolis in the fourth century or the Hellenistic period? Is it to be connected with Marium or Arsinoë? I am inclined to think the latter, for the following reasons: (1) There is no transition from the one class of tombs to the other, no gradual substitution of the one kind of pottery for the other, but a new start which implies a decisive gap. (2) There is evidence of several tombs having been used a second time, and of two at least of the former burials having been of the fourth century. A repeated use involving the violation of a tomb is scarcely conceivable until two or three generations have passed away."

Munro now believes that "the general result of the work of Poli goes to confirms the suggestion of Dr. Dümmler that the eastern nekropolis is in the main to be connected with Marium, the western with Arsinoë."

But on p. 320 he himself concedes that in the previous year.

"One Roman tomb was discovered even this last season in the eastern nekropolis, and on the north side of the vineyard late tombs appear to be frequent, if not the rule."

He then enumerates the instances in which earlier graves appear in the Western nekropolis. Of these there are so many that the exceptions are in some sites more numerous than the rule and are of pre-Ptolemaic date.

After Munro has chopped and changed about in this fashion, his final statement culminates in these words.

"It would seem, therefore, that both nekropoleis were used by the inhabitants of both Marium and Arsinoë, but the later tomb-makers on the whole preferred the western, without, however, changing the character of large tracts even of that."

It will be seen that Munro, after asserting his dogmatic fashion his uncompromising conviction that the earlier Eastern nekropolis belongs to Marion and is sharply differentiated by all manner of fundamental differences from the later western nekropolis of the town of Arsinoë, throws the whole question into confusion again and concludes this time that the inhabitants of both towns, of Marion as well as of Arsinoë, buried their respective dead in both nekropoleis indiscriminately, the eastern as well as the western.

As to the question where the actual sites of Marion and Arsinoë are, Munro says not a word.

Whereas in the first year Munro was able to make no precise statement whatever as to the difference of character and date of the grave-structures in the eastern and western nekropoleis in the course of the next year he arrived at certain conclusions which are in part coincident with those that I had already demonstrated in 1886. He describes these relations in J. H. S. 1891, p. 299 – 301. The graves of the Eastern nekropolis are frequently of smaller dimensions, he says, than those of the western are and they consist of small irregular quadrangular cavities with blunt corners. I had already made that observation in 1886, Pl. CLXXV, 10 and 11 depict the two graves Nos. 113 and 119 in which the oniochoai in Pl. CCXIX, 7 and 8 were found. Hence they are graves belonging to the sixth century B. C. Munro himself now concedes that the graves of the Eastern Nekropolis (our Nekrop. II) almost always have a more or less lengthy dromos, that some have one of enormous length and that a staircase is rare. I have found as instances of graves with very long dromoi rich graves of the first half of the 6th century B. C, e g. grave 140 nekr. II, the grave of the Sphinx, of the Cyprian gems &c., Pl. XXVII and grave 92, East-Nekrop. II, the grave of the marble torso Pl. XXVII, 2, of the gold cylix Pl. CXCVIII, 3, of the early Cyprian silver coins &c. (Pl. CLXXV, 2). The observations made in the course of the excavations at Tamassos in 1889 confirm what was said of Marion Arsinoë. Munro found in his second campaign that the graves of the western nekropolis in contrast to those of the eastern were large and more regularly planned and more frequently provided with staircase entrances-like e. g. the grave that I excavated and cleared out in 1886 belonging to the western nekropolis I, No. 54 at Hagios Demetrios, Pl. CLXXV, 4, the grave of the terra-cotta statue (Pl. CLXXXVI, 3), of the polychrome jugs (e. g. LXIV, 4 and 7), of the Attic stamped ware with graffiti in Cyprian syllabic script. &c.

The following graves, i. e. the Hellenistic staircase grave, No. 41 East-Nekr. II (Pl. CLXXV, 3) with the large find of gold and silver ornaments (Pl. CLXXXII, 20, 21, 27, 28), the grave with niches (of the excavation of 1885) in the same place i. e. the East-Nekr. II (Pl. CLXXV, 16) again produce exceptions and varieties of type which go to show that graves in the East-Nekr. II may resemble types of the West-Nekropolis I. On the other hand the graves of the West-Nekropolis (— III, Pl. CXXV, 13) with the terra-cotta statue CLXXXVII, 4 and CLXXV, 12 with the terra-cotta head CLXXXVI, 2 resemble a current type of the graves of the East-Nekr. I.

The above remarks by Munro about the different contents of the graves in the East and West nekropoleis evidence very correct observations but to a large extent they can be adduced as evidence diametrically against Munro's own theories, they are however, I should be inclined to say, though correct in themselves, practically useless in part because they stand too much alone and can be easily refuted by my large generalizations.

I will first select some of Munro's own statements out of which we can forge weapons to fight their author himself.

In J. H. S. 1891, p. 327 Munro lays the greatest possible emphasis on the fact that the Cyprian vases found in the East Nekropolis together with black-figured Attic vases are quite different from those that are found in the West Nekropolis with red-figured Attic vases of the fine style. It is in the East Nekropolis only that we find vases decorated in exact geometric patterns with dull black and red on the dull natural clay ground, whereas in the same place there are no instances of polychrome decoration (e. g. as in Pl. LXIV, 4 and 7). The exact opposite is the case in the West Necropolis i. e. according to Munro the red-figured vases of mature fine style, attic stamped ware and Cyprian polychrome vases are all found side by side. Indirectly therefore, it is conceded that as early as the 4th century B. C. Cyprian vases with concentric circles have quite disappeared from the graves. Munro falls into the blunder of supposing that the oldest graves of the East Nekropolis only date back as far as 520 B. C. for he does not date the black-figured Attic vases early enough. In the same way he seems to date many red-figured vases some decades too late.

Next Munro maintains that porcelain amulets are found in the East Nekropolis, not in the West. To this we must take exception, for the very interesting bright coloured porcelain amulet in the shape of a crouching Bes (Pl. LXVII, 1) came from the West Nekropolis I, from the grave of Hagios Demetrios.

The terra-cotta figures of the East Nekropolis II are according to Munro very small and rude and there are no specimens of the large fine terra-cotta statues, while in the West Nekropolis the reverse is supposed to be the case. I regret to have to note that the beautiful Greek terra-cotta statues in Pl. CLXXXVII 2 and 3, were excavated from the East Nekropolis II (property of Mullah Mehemed, later Mr. Williamson's vineyard).

Next Munro asserts dogmatically once and for all that there is no transition from one class of graves to another, no gradual substitution of one kind of terracotta ware for another, but a new departure which necessitates a definite breach in time. That is utterly untrue. I need only point to Pl CCXVI, where vases from the 6th and 4th century B. C. from the two Nekropoleis East and West (II and I) are placed together and show us how the concentric circles persist and get modified. We have in both Nekropoleis a continuous development of craftsmanship. The difference is this, the town which buried its dead for the most part in the East Nekropolis II was at the height of its prosperity in the 6th century and beginning of the 5th century B. C., whereas the own which buried principally in the West Nekr. I—III flourished at the end of the 5th and into the 4th century B. C.

3. The site of the towns Arsinoë, Marion and their copper mines, iron founderies, copper works, bronze founderies and the cemeteries appertaining thereto.

A. Arsinoë.

As to the site of the town there can be no doubt*) (Pl. CCXVIII). The northern houses of the modern town of Poli stand on the southern extremities of the ruins of the town, and the southern houses stand on the site of the cemetery that abuts on the ancient town.**) The superincumbent layer of ruins and rubbish with its masonry fragments of marble and tiles is exactly like that of the late Hellenistic and Roman towns of the island only that the remains in the case of Arsinoë are less substantial and fruitful in antiquities than in the case of the sites of the larger towns like Neapaphos, Kurion or Salamis. That suits admirably what is told by literary tradition. After Ptolemy Soter in 312 B. C. had destroyed Marion and expelled its inhabitants the town was rebuilt under the name of Arsinoë but never again attained to any great importance.

B. Marion.

Either there were two Marions, one the earlier and more easterly (Pl. CCXVIII older settlement) near the East Nekropolis (II. Pl. CCXVIII) and a westerly one on the site of Arsinoë near the West Nekropolis I—III, Pl. CCXVIII or there existed towards the East an earlier town which bore another name and was more important in the 6th century B. C. than Western Marion.***)

Munro does not seem as yet to know how the ancient towns in Cyprus with their respective cemeteries were disposed. For the present I will only discuss the Graeco-Phoenician, Greek, Hellenistic and Roman graves ornaments and will explain them by means of two instances those of Idalion and Tamassos. In both cases the foundations of the towns goes far back into the first thousand year B. C. but does not extend back into the Bronze age. The débris of masonry that lies on the surface is or Roman date. Hence the towns had been inhabited for a period of a thousand years. The nekropoleis that surround the town in a circle enlighten us as to the date even without going below the soil. The people who laid the foundations of these Graeco-Phoenician towns and first inhabited them uniformly selected for their cemeteries the ground that abutted on the town all round in circular form. As at this date rock and earth graves were never made, the rocky places in the ground (and often too the firm conglomerate) remained unused, so did the beds of the rivers and the plots of ground prepared for over-flow or for artificial watering. The piece of ground lying in a ring immediately all round the town was first of all laid out by the oldest inhabitants for their graves, which according to prevailing custom or the wealth and position of the dead were used once or oftener. Each new generation had to move out further from the circular city wall to find graves for its families associations and individuals. Hence it follows that the age of the graves varies inversely with the distance from the town, assuming that the town is circular and the ground uniform. Hence the Hellenistic and Roman graves often are the most

---

*) Cf. Herrmann's Winckelmannsprogramm p 5.
**) Cesnola had already identified the ruins with ancient Arsinoë. Cesnola-Stern p. 196.
***) Munro had not then and has not now acquired the practical experience in the island that I did in the course of twelve years Otherwise he would presumably not only have been more careful in the polemic he opened up against me, but even possibly recognised the views that I took in 1885 and still defend What F. Dümmler and P Herrmann say about the cemeteries and settlements is again exclusively based on researches and communications made by me. I am in a position incontestably to complete these communications

distant from the town. As in the later Hellenistic and Roman times the custom of rock and conglomerate graves (which had previously been predominant in the bronze period*) came up again the rocky spaces in an earthy district and also those of hard conglomerate which had previously been left free were occupied by graves. The next step was to dig a row or several rows of graves in the neigbourhood of the city rampart, or in the rampart itself, that part having been formerly left free on purpose. It was only with reluctance that they came to re-use the old graves, but they made up their minds finally even to that and dug later Hellenistic and Roman graves above and between the earlier graves, e. g. I found round the circular wall of Tamassos, next to the wall and arranged in concentric circles, graves from the 11th—4th centuries B. C. and a large tract with graves not later than 600 B. C. while the graves of Hellenistic and Roman date were still further removed or else hewn in the standing rocks. But between the circle of graves of 600 B. C. (stratum of bronze fibulae) and the town wall close to and under the town rampart only one row of Roman graves had been dug.

Everywhere in Kition, Idalion, Kurion, Tamassos and Amathus I have observed that the earliest iron-period series of graves lay immediately near and round the city wall. It never happens that these older Graeco-Phoenician graves occur at a great distance from the town or are separated by wide spaces unoccupied by graves from the earth district.

I relied on this and other experiences for my plan of operations when I wanted to find graves worth opening where nothing was visible on the surface and no previous discoveries had been made. It was in this way that I discovered in 1885 the Tamassos vase (p. 37, Fig. 38) at Tamassos and the graves of the stratum of bent fibulae of a date before 600 B. C., and in 1886 the graves from the close of the 7th, 6th and 5th centuries in which the pieces of bronze armour &c., published in Pl. LXX were discovered.

We must now apply these experiences to my investigations and Munro's at the village of Poli tis Chrysoku (Polis tes Chrysochou).

a) Marion flourished in the 5th and 4th centuries B. C.

To this period belongs the West Nekropolis (I—III).

That Marion was situated near the modern Poli and Arsinoë I consider proved and that by me and my excavations.**) I have to show now that on the site of Arsinoë 100—200 years before it was founded another important town flourished. I discovered in the Nekropolis in 1886 alone 127 graves The main bulk of these graves belonged to the 4th century B. C. They were found for the most part on the plateau known as Hagios Demetrios. Munro calls this spot—though he only gleaned a scanty harvest after me—"the black-glazed site par excellence." The quantity of Attic red-figured vases, stamped Attic ware and Cyprian syllabic inscriptions on grave-stones and Attic vases was large, whereas of black-figured (and that late) vases only six came to light which I photographed together. It follows that a number of graves date back into the 5th and 6th centuries B. C. and this moreover is the time in which this town of Marion was first founded or, which is more probable, was moved bit by bit from the East—from the spot called "Outer Settlement" in the Eastern Nekropolis II—to the Western site on which Arsinoë was later erected.

Graves from the close of the 7th and beginning of the 6th century do not appear at all in Nekropolis I.

The group of graves discovered by Munro and Tubbs at Kaparga is on the whole somewhat earlier than Hagios Demetrios. I excavated tentatively here in 1885 (cf. p. 471, Pl. CLXXXVI, 2). Here a large percentage of graves from the 6th century B. C. was discovered. But Roman graves were also more frequent there and in 1886 I found a few near at hand which I have not marked in the map on Pl. CCXVIII. On the spot marked III, which naturally forms one continuous cemetery with Hagios Demetrios (I) and Kaparga, there were no graves found of a date earlier than the 4th century B. C. Here Roman graves were even more plentiful. But this plot of ground also was occupied by graves before the foundation of Arsinoë. It was here that I found in a grave the heap of coins of Alexander. The beautiful Attic rhyton also (Pl. CXCI, 7) comes from this district.

It is clear therefore that Arsinoë was built on the same site on which there was already an older town which could be no other than Marion and in 1886 I had already included in this double name the ruined site which lay north of the West Nekropolis on which Marion was situated before. It was destroyed at the close of the 4th century B. C. and Arsinoë built on its ruins.

b) The older town Marion of the 6th century B. C. or a town of another name.

With this the East Nekropolis (II).

The great bulk of the graves opened here (Pl. CCXVIII Mr. Williamson's vineyard) which yielded such rich results belonged to the 6th or 5th centuries B. C. The town was at the height of its prosperity as early as the 6th century, and to this period the nekropolis belongs. I found here the archaic Greek marble torso, the statue of the Sphinx, the Hermaios and Chachrylion kylixes, the Pasiades alasbastron (which nearly all belong certainly to the 6th century B. C.), earlier washing jugs with bird

---

*) Rock-tombs of Hagia Paraskevi. Pl. CLXXI, 14 &c.
**) Cf. Herrmann's Gräberfeld von Marion, p. 5.

faces (e. g. Pl. XXII and XXIII) and very early Graeco-Phoenician vases (e. g. Title page Fig. 1).—
Graves of the 4ᵗʰ century B. C. disappear here entirely. Only very few of Hellenistic date are
found. But all of a sudden north of the road to Limni a group of graves obtrudes itself which side by
side with very old graves includes a number of Roman ones. This series of graves I have marked
"Roman tombs" (Pl. CCXVIII).

Where is the town that belonged to the East Nekropolis? (II with the sites M. V. T.
Pl. CCXVIII)? We must exclude the supposition that the town that belonged to this extensive cemetery
which received most of the corpses in the 6ᵗʰ century B. C. could be Western Marion. They would never
have buried their dead so far from the town and that in a district which in winter would have been so
difficult of access owing to the damp nature of the ground. The town then that belongs to this
East Nekropolis must be sought in the immediate neighbourhood. More than ever I am convinced
that the earlier East town to which the East Nekropolis belonged lay on the plateau-like elevation (Older
Settlement but going down to Roman times, Foundations of ancient houses discovered in 1886 Pl. CCXVIII).
Otherwise how is it that this plateau is entirely free from graves while at its edge there is a whole
row of graves hewn in conglomerate and of Roman date? How is it that it is just here that there are
remains of foundation walls of houses which in this case I hold to be antique?

I have still to show why the older settlement in this case lay near the originally older
Nekropolis, and why even after the rise of Marion in the West and then of Arsinoë a small settlement
continued to live on down to Roman times, and so bodies were still buried there right down to
Roman times.

The key is given to us in Pl. CCXVIII by the arrow at the right edge of the map marked
"Heaps of slag". East Nekropolis II and the settlement belonged to the neighbouring works for
smelting copper where there was brisk business with the harbour whence the export of copper by sea
went on. Countless large heaps of slag show that the brass from the mines at Limni was for the most
part brought down and smelted here.*) As the mountainous district still called Tylliria abuts on the
district of the ancient copper mines i. e. Limni, I would conjecture that in Limni on the borders of
Tylliria we have the ancient copper mountain Tyrrias. F. Dümmler in the Jahrbuch 1887 p. 168 mentions
my conjecture as very probably correct. Our East Nekropolis II would belong then to this copper
mine on Tyrrias and to the copper foundry in the valley and the place for export trade in
connection with it. The bronzes found in precisely these graves of the East Nekropolis make it not
improbable that, side by side with the copper smelting, coppersmiths and bronze-casters plied their arts
and crafts on a large scale. They would then carry on trade not only in raw copper but in manufactured
utensils of copper and bronze, in vases and weapons.

----

*) This deserted copper mine of Marion Arsinoë near the modern place Limni, was intended have been to extended and restored
by a Copper-mine Co. in England. The works failed because the ancients had left nothing to be worked While they were looking for a
place suitable for embarking goods on the sea-coast, the people who were working for the Copper-mine Co. discovered in the sea the
remains of foundations made of copper slag. The ancients had themselves laded their copper just at the very spot the English had chosen

Conclusion.

How I carried on my excavations and specially what I dit at Marion-Arsinoë.

1. Mr. Munro on my researches.

It is at once my right and my duty to tell in accordance with facts what use I sought to make of my discovery of the cemeteries of Marion Arsinoë (already described under Pl. CCXVIII) and also how I and my discoveries which led the formation of the Cyprus Excavation Fund in 1887 were made use of by others.

But first about Salamis.

It was just the same as to Salamis and my excavations there although, Munro in that case did at least mention (J. H. S. 1891, p. 59) me and some of my publications. But neither he nor his colleagues are acquainted with the Revue Archéologique and S Reinach's Chroniques d'Orient or they do not choose to be acquainted with them, because S. Reinach speaks the truth based on what I told him.*) But further what Munro does tell of my discoveries at Salamis is so misrepresented as to give the impression that the discovery of the interesting temenos of Zeus**) was due to a mere chance and to peasants — a discovery which I am made to boast about — the words are (J. H. S. p. 59).

"Among the most important of Herr Richter's many services to Cypriote archaeology may be reckoned the accidental discovery of two marble capitals under the sand near the Forest Guard's house, which occurred while he was employed in the Forest Department and which subsequently gave us the clue to one of our sites."

On p. 66 Messrs Munro and Tubbs explain in still more unmistakeable language one of the principal services I have rendered to Cyprian Archaeology as follows.

"At two points, east and west of one another, the villagers had in digging for water brought to light a couple of bluish-white marble capitals in Roman-Corinthian style together with a base and two ἀγάλματα of limestone."

The principal service that I have rendered consists in the digging for water by the peasants who chanced when they were doing it to light on antiquities. I happened to be the Government official. For these gentlemen do not even say that the peasants were my workmen.

In company with Dr. Dörpfeld I visited the excavations when they were going on and at once forwarded to Messrs. Munro and Tubbs at Salamis my paper on "The Museum and excavations in Cyprus" that appeared in the "Repertorium für Kunstwissenschaft" 1886. In that I note as follows in 1886:

"Another great source of loss that eats like a cancer into the precious and irreplaceable treasures of antiquities, in part below the ground, in part above, in Cyprus, is the search for blocks belonging to ancient buildings which is scarcely now checked by Government.***) How often one or another of the island officials has shrugged his shoulders when I drew his attention to the fact that by this search for

---

*) Cf. S. Reinach. Chroniques d'Orient. Index sub. Ohnefalsch-Richter.

**) It is much to be regretted that Messrs. Munro and Tubbs did not at once excavate this site, which I had discovered, and in which, towards the north, important finds and presumably of remote antiquity could be expected It is in general to be regretted that these gentlemen did not complete any of the tentative excavations they began in seven places in the ruins of Salamis. This tentative work, this "Prospecting and not excavating", as the English officials call it, is only justifiable in cases when the actual excavations are carried out in the same or, at furthest, the following year and in cases where a trusty guardian is left in charge. Up to the present time nothing has been done, although three years have gone by, and there is no apparent intention of excavating these sites this year, which lie exposed to the will and pleasure of the peasants. The prohibitions in the Ottoman Code against employing ancient ruins as stone for building has indeed been revived under English auspices. But it will need a special body of police to make this prohibition a reality. The fact that I am able to lay before the reader in Plates II and III an exact plan of an almost complete ring wall at Idalion is due chiefly to the illegal search conducted by the peasants for building stones in the district of Idalion If anyone goes there now to check my statement they will find indeed some remains by help of which they will be able to appreciate the fact that my work is throughout reliable. But many remains that I myself saw and was unable to draw in had disappeared before I left the island. If therefore the Exploration Fund does not shortly make a thorough and systematic excavation of the island, these tentative works, this "prospecting" will have done more harm than good. It would have been better to have left the place untouched.

***) I possess the official correspondence on this point with the government seal, carried on under Sir Robert Biddulph and Sir Henry Bulwer.

blocks and this destruction of ancient lines of walls still buried in the earth the demonstration of the ground plan of an ancient building was made either more difficult or quite impossible. Worse still, in 1882, after refusing three times and being threatened with dismissal, I was obliged to consent, as Commissioner of Woods and Forests, to carry out the barbarian project of breaking building-stones in the ruins of Salamis, in order to wall round the wells which had been dug for the plantations and to build a Forester's lodge on the Akropolis of Salamis and on the citadel of the harbour.*) (sic!) I was sent in 1881 to the mouth of the river Pidias to look out government land suitable for plantations and to study the question of the drainage of its marshes and lakes. I chose out for plantations three pieces of land, one to the south and two to the north of Salamis. My propositions were accepted and the execution of the works was entrusted to me. But as somewhat later, Mr. Madon, my then chief (I acted as second Superintendent of work for replanting) was pleased to unite the land north and south of Salamis by a further plantation which was thus to extend over the ruins themselves and specially over that portion of the harbour of the largest ancient town in Cyprus that was covered by sand. I was obliged myself, half heart-broken, to carry out this barbarian undertaking. Naturally I did not begin the work till I had written to the government to say that there was still a great deal of unplanted land that might be planted out but that there was but one ancient town of Salamis to be excavated; further that an excavation of the city of Salamis conducted on rational lines must thanks to propitious circumstances be specially repaying, for, as history relates the town was destroyed more than once by earthquakes and then covered up for a long distance by sand blown and drifted up by the sea. At the present day a part of the city is covered in this fashion by sand as Pompeii is by ashes.

In 1880—1881 before Pergamon was begun, it was intended in Germany to excavate Salamis, and at my instance, and I was requested to draw up a report in which it should be stated clearly to what period the antiquities that might be looked for would belong, where and how they might be discovered, what were the topographical conditions and what the probable cost would amount to etc etc. Before I went further in this matter which so far was prosperous, I thought it my duty to communicate to Dr. Cobham, Agent to C. T. Newton, what were the desires and projects of the Germans at that date. The answer was that I had better break off the negotiations, for the British Museum had formed the definite project of undertaking very shortly excavations on a large scale and entrusting me with the direction.**) Instead of this, I myself, was doomed by fate in little more than the space of a year to further bring destruction on the ruins of Salamis, and instead of excavating the quarter of the harbour that was covered with sand, I had to sow it with acorns, pine needles and locust beans.

I now still hoped that a very obvious and substantial find of antiquities might check this barbarism. I had vertical shafts sunk in the ground at points **where I hoped to find not only water to water the plantations but also antiquities**. On the declivity of the harbour citadel and the N. E. end of the larger town (the ring wall of the larger and earlier town of Salamis and the second and smaller wall of the town of Konstantia built later over a portion of Salamis after frequent earthquakes can be clearly seen) I came deep down in the sand on the remains of Greek building of white marble and at the same time on fragments of limestone columns. I also lighted on large Graeco-Corinthian capitals of marble (of late date). When one remembers that in Cyprus marble when it appears must always have been imported, it was safe to indulge high hopes as regards this site, and all the more as nothing lay in sight above the surface. I next ran a pole down a second shaft and came on another part of the building and again on a huge Corinthian marble capital. My instructions were when antiquities came to light to stop the works, report the discoveries and work on in another place. I was now in search of water in another deep crater-shaped trough covered with sand which I took to be the outcome of another large ruined structure. At a depth of something over a metre at the bottom of this depression I came upon a pavement of greenish white marble, still in good preservation. I wrote, telegraphed, reported to the local government, to England, to Newton and to other English scholars. It was all of no use. I was to sow (sic) the Akropolis of Salamis and its marble buildings closely ranged together with trees. Only eight days later I received from C. T. Newton himself a letter which I still preserve. In it he wrote to me and told me as soon as I quitted the department of Woods and Forests to begin excavating on the site of the marble pavement and he would arrange with the government that the planting of trees should not be allowed to interfere. That was what Sir Chas. Newton wrote. Instead of this the whole plantation was enclosed by an iron fence and I received the strictest orders on quitting the Woods and Forests to dig only outside the plantations.

But as I had, as Superintendent, made use of the tendency to look for building stones as a means for a scientific investigation of Salamis, I had other sites ready and I excavated a portion of a bath belonging to a house of late Roman date. Although my work at the outset was most successful and I dug out a very interesting suadatorium with suspensurae in perfect condition and although I found an exhedra with a vestibule supported by two columns and a large mosaic design as pavement (together with many other important details) I was very soon obliged to leave off excavations for want of funds.

As the sandy soil, which though fruitful was heated by a burning sun, was not adequately watered at the right time the seedlings sown at and round Salamis to a considerable distance as good as perished. No trace remains except the pretty little house of the Superintendent, seen from a distance but with no Superintendent in it, and it too must too soon share the fate of the ancient ruins and fall to pieces. Hence, supposing money were forthcoming, nothing now stands in the way of an excavation of the Akropolis and the harbour quarter of Salamis.

---

*) On this point also I hold the letters necessary for evidence
**) In this case too I have epistolary evidence.

As we saw, this excavation ensued and cost me much labour while others made use of my discoveries.*) I can prove by eye-witnesses i. e. my former head intendant Trachana of Larnaka and my other intendant the peasant Panagotis of H. Sergis that I did in fact when digging for water and building stones with the workmen of the department of Woods and Forests look most earnestly for antiquities with a view to obtaining important finds and thereby distracting the government from their mania for planting. After sinking the first hole to the west in the temenos of Zeus I sank a second to the east in order to get an idea of the size of the building. I had upwards of 30 workmen for several days at work prospecting for water and antiquities (but not to excavate). After I had satisfied myself as to the extent of the discovery for which I can answer to the full, I had the shafts all filled up level even to the smallest holes. Other tentative borings, ostensibly in search of water, were really made much more to prospect for antiquities. But still, by the way, I sought for and found water.

Munro concedes at least in one place (J. H. S. p. 57) that I was commissioned by Mr. C. D. Cobham and Sir Chas. Newton, to excavate for the British Museum at Salamis.

2. Mr. Hogarth on my discoveries.

I now turn to Mr. Hogarth who also made my acquaintance in person and who wrote to me at Kuklia from Nikosia and in his letter acknowledged in the warmest terms the signal services I had rendered to Cyprian archaeology. Messrs Ernest Gardner, M. R. James and D. G. Hogarth were present when I showed my antiquities in the Cyprus Museum. If Hogarth did not know my work before, he learned in Cyprus how long, for whom and how I had excavated. The first Report of Excavations of the Cyprus Exploration Fund appeared in 1886. Three years before S. Reinach had published his paper "Fouilles et découvertes à Chypre depuis l'occupation Anglaise" in the Revue Archaeologique (5² 340—1) (cf Chroniques d'Orient p. 168 ff.) and this paper dealt almost exclusively with my researches as at that time there was scarcely anything else to deal with. In the Contemporary Review for 1889 A. S. Sayce wrote thus.

"It is in Cyprus, if anywhere, that the problems presented by early Greek archaeology will find their solution; and yet since our occupation of the island, not only has no attempt at systematic excavation been made, but foreign Governments, who might have undertaken the work, have been prevented from doing so. Such discoveries as have taken place have been made by private individuals often working illegally and in secret, and seldom, if ever, possessed of the means or the knowledge requisite for that systematic exploration which alone is of service to the historian. Had it not been for the fortunate presence of a German, Dr. Max Ohnefalsch-Richter, in the island, our knowledge of Cyprian archaeology would have been as scanty and misleading as it was ten years ago. Dr Ohnefalsch-Richter, however, has devoted himself enthusiastically to a work which ought to have been undertaken by Englishmen; besides excavating himself, he has kept a careful watch over the excavations which have been carried on by others during the last half dozen years. The result of his labours has been not only the discovery of several important archaic sites, but the introduction of order and arrangement into the archaeology of a country where all before was chaos. He has succeeded in assigning definite periods to the tombs and objects found in different parts of the island, and has thus furnished us at last with a criterion for deciding what is really to be considered belonging to the Phoenician epoch. Many of the Cyprian vases quoted as Phoenician by Professor Perrot in his magnificent volume on Phoenician art, now turn out to belong to an age earlier than that when the Phoenicians first settled in Cyprus."

Mr. C. D. Cobham himself, who acted as agent for the excavations I carried out for Sir Chas. Newton, had already spoken as follows in 1883 in the Journal of Hellenic Studies (A prehistoric building at Salamis by Max Ohnefalsch-Richter p. 111—116):

"The following paper owes nothing to my hand but its English dress. Its author, a young German gentleman, has been engaged for nearly three years past in conducting under my direction, with funds supplied by the kindness of Mr. C. T. Newton and his friends, excavations at different points in Cyprus. His enthusiastic and intelligent work has yielded many interesting and I hope some valuable results."

Now for Hogarth. In his "Devia Cypria" p. 60—62 he proposes as something apparently quite new those excavations at Cyprus which I had already so warmly supported. But from his own description it is apparent how casually he had investigated Salamis. He neither mentions my excavation, which could be seen from a distance and which looked in 1883 just as it did in the time of Munro and Tubbs in 1890, nor yet the site of the temenos of Zeus with the marble capitals which I had dug up from a great depth and which stood on the place where they were found.

In the Journal of Hellenic Studies 1888, p. 156 Hogarth writes—"Of the private explorations since the Occupation a few, such as those originated by the British Museum and carried out through Mr. Cobham of Larnaca, were conceived on a scientific basis, though a small scale; others again were of less value owing either to unscientific management, the dispersion of the objects as soon as found, or want of perseverance, and there was as much to be done in verifying and connecting their results as in breaking fresh ground."

On the next page, Hogarth mentions my excavations in 1886 as belonging to 1887 and their director as Mr. J. W. Williamson. Mr. Munro does the same. J. H. S. 1890. p. 2.

Rarely has it happened that a man who has in disinterested fashion sacrificed the best portion of his life to the systematic archaeological investigation of a country has been treated more unjustly.

As to the excavations directed by Mr. Cobham, the only ones that according to Hogarth were systematically and scientifically carried out, Mr. Cobham confined himself to consulting me as to what

---

*) I possess letters dating from as early as 1681 from English authorities who were exerting themselves in vain to raise large sums of money but who encouraged me to stay in Cyprus.

district I had better go to. It was always an important question what money I had to spend. It was only when I was excavating close to Larnaka that Mr. Cobham came upon my field of operations. I was left with an entirely free hand. I chose the plots of ground, I negotiated with the owners and excavated graves or sanctuaries without even telling Mr. Cobham beforehand anything about it. He left it entirely to me.

Anyhow, all the excavations I superintended, whether for the British Museum, the Museum at Berlin, for the Cyprus Museum, at private or public expense, were as a fact more scientifically carried on than the excavation directed by Mr. Hogarth by himself at Amargetti (No 58 of the list) of which he cannot give us so much as a ground plan. An excavation such as that I undertook for C. Watkins in 1885 at Dali (No. 3 of the list) may serve as an example, as also that which I directed for Sir Charles Newton in 1882 at Achna. (No. 1 of the list.) In fact, the private one undertaken for Mr. Watkins at Dali and the other at Poli tis Chrysokhou (Marion Arsinoë 1886) are really superior to the one undertaken for the British Museum at Achna because I had adequate funds to finish. In the Achna excavation funds ran short, although the whole business including my salary and the photographs taken did not amount to £ 25, Mr. Cobham recalled me to Larnaka. Hence I was obliged to break off the excavation and had not got as far to the S. W. as the end of the precinct and the wall masonry. Yet these excavations are according to Hogarth systematic and scientific, those at Dali (Pl. VII) for Mr. Watkins not. Again the model excavation at Voni (No. 2 of the list) which I undertook for the Cyprus Museum in 1883 (Pl. V, XL—XLII and CCXV) is placed by Hogarth under the rubric "unscientific". Hogarth knows the discoveries made there, he inspected them in company with Messrs. Gardner, James, A. H. Sayce and Percival, when I explained them to him in my capacity as Museum official. He cites them later in his "Devia Cypria", but in passing only. As to the duration and completion of the excavation not even the temple of Aphrodite at Old Paphos has been so thoroughly excavated. Towards the west, the earliest and possibly the most interesting portion of the precinct still awaits excavation. As far as regards Salamis the "Exploration Fund" has only made an occasional dip below the surface, as actually complete the excavation at the site of Toumpa possibly stands alone.

By its tentative digging in the sites of Salamis the "Cyprus Exploration Fund" is morally bound by the standard of the scientific and educated public to complete the excavation of that spot if it does not wish to incur the charge of fostering modern vandalism.

In any case, since the occupation of the island isolated excavations have taken place e. g. that by Messrs. Williamson and Co. (Mr. C. Christian was sleeping partner in this firm) at Kurion in 1883 more from a purely commercial stand point and without scientific intention. I have specially exerted myself from the beginning against such enterprises.*) I should like also to ask Mr. Hogarth how far they have succeeded in their first campaign in verifying and correcting the previous excavations that had taken place since the occupation, i. e. mine. For with four exceptions I had directed all these excavations. On the contrary I believe I may, without undue self-glorification, maintain that I am now the one who by the publication of a model book am correcting and supplementing the early and defective excavations of the Cyprus Exploration Fund at Leontari Vouno and the still more defective publication of its results. (Cf. Pl. CLXIV—CLXVII and p. 460 ff.). I hope thereby to have done a lasting service to science.**)

3. How I trained my workmen and directed my excavations.

When I began my first excavations I had to make practical use of the knowledge I had obtained in my scientific studies and the accumulated experience I had won as land-agent on a large estate. I looked all about for a long time till I got the most able and trustworthy workmen in Cyprus. The Larnakiote Gregori Antoniu especially approved himself as a skilled stone-mason, as foreman and as an active and indefatigable over-seer He accompanied me in 1885 through the island. As he was exceedingly quick in understanding I taught him my ways myself. He had to learn order and punctuality and to give attention to matters in excavating that he had never thought of before. The gentlemen of the Exploration Fund could not and would not employ me, but Gregori whom I had trained became at once indispensable to them while I from time to time went on digging with older Cypriots whenever Gregori became too exhorbitant in his demands. In the case of large undertakings I used to take at least from 6 to 12 skilled stone-masons with me through the island. Munro tells how the body of workmen had to be divided into two groups, stone-masons for the more delicate work and workers with shovel and pick. It was I who first made this division in Cyprus, and I too first employed women to carry up the soil in baskets and even to push the tramcars. Before then women had never been employed in excavating. It was a matter of great difficulty to overcome the popular prejudice on this point. Further I introduced the custom of pitching tents and that on the site of the work. When working at the graves I kept a

---

*) I have the official correspondence on this point. I made a representation on this point to the government in October 1883 and roused thereby no friendly feeling towards me in the minds of these gentlemen, which found expression in their letters to the government. They were so good later on to send me several letters from the government which they had received in answer to their communications. These documents are still in my hands.

**) Supra p. 230 note 2 I have shown most clearly how deplorable such maps as those of Mr Hogarth are, e. g. J. H. S. 1886 Pl. VII in which he writes below in the corner: "The whole of this plateau is a vast necropolis containing tombs of all dates". There is there no single instance of a tomb of the copper-bronze period with its various strata (cf. Pl. CLXIV—CLXXIII) Hogarth's Devia Cypria contains besides some new and good observations a mass of gross blunders as I explained in the Berliner Philologische Wochenschrift 1891 p. 997. Whoever conducted excavations in Cyprus in accordance with the advice given in Devia Cypria would leave untouched just those very places which have the best chance of yielding good results, as Hogarth gives advice about them based on superficial observation and defective information and experience.

number of posts in readiness. When the first object was found in a newly opened grave that grave had its post erected with a number on it. In the tent the contents of each grave were laid out separately and the finds of the several graves were separated off by a ring of stones round them. A number was attached at once to every object collected.

A workman specially trained for the purpose and having had ample practice had to look out for the fragments of broken objects as soon as they were brought to the tent. Many fragments were at once cleaned on the spot, where necessary carefully washed, heated with diluted vinegar, put together and cemented. For this work, which demands much intelligence as well as patience, I had trained a man from Dali, Loiso Anastasi, who knew how to write. He helped me too with my photography and finally developed all my paper negatives. He also became, by dint of pratice, a most accomplished packer. In the case of many breakages it was necessary to join with a coat of plaster of Paris or to fill up the missing places with this material to make the vase hold together. I taught workmen to do this when I myself experimented and learnt how. The whole system and method of conducting excavations has been thought out by me personally. Similarly, when I was excavating sanctuaries where soil had to be carried away in trucks, I had to adapt my method as far as was practicable to these circumstances. Whoever has paid a visit to my excavations has been satisfied with the arrangement and practical disposition and utilization of the labour at my disposal. From the beginning I insisted on the greatest punctuality, especially on the work being begun and ended at the time fixed. When first I excavated at Poli in 1886 there was serious insubordination before I could get the workmen into regular ways. Had I not had my own body of Daliote workmen with me to set a good example to the local peasants I might possibly never have established anything like order at Poli. For customs vary in various districts. On the whole however Greek workmen are much more go-a-head and industrious than the phlegmatic Turks. At times I could not remain continuously on the site of operations, or I might be excavating simultaneously at more than one site. The workmen never knew for certain from what direction I might come upon them, on foot or on horseback, to take stock of their work at a moment's notice. The diary of excavations I kept myself for the most part. I noted the contents of each grave one by one. Grave structures of interest were measured and had plans taken of them just like precincts &c. The photographs of antiquities, of excavations, sites &c., were always taken as soon as possible. Whensoever it was possible a fully illustrated diary of excavations was kept posted up and continued from the first to the last day. In the case of excavations on a large scale I always tried to get as many hands as possible so that by division of labour the work might be done as effectively as possible.

4. The practical arrangement of my excavations at Poli. Marion-Arsinoë.

I placed the contracts with landowners, which had been concluded in my name in 1885, at the disposal of Mr. C. Watkins, then Director of the Ottoman Bank at Larnaka, and that at cost price without commission. In my case, unfortunately, I acted all too disinterestedly, and tried to mediate between government, the local Museum and private enterprise. I proposed to Mr. Watkins to ask Herr Christian, Director of the Ottoman Bank, and Mr. J. W. Williamson, head of the English Club at Limassol, to share the undertaking at Poli tis Chrysoku. Mr. J. W. Williamson was at that time also acting for the English Cyprus Copper-mine Co. at Limni. I therefore proposed him to Mr. Watkins*) as paymaster and cashier. The society was formed. Mr. E. Foot, Government overseer, was sent with us, although I was at the time consulting Archaeologist and Superintendent of Excavations to the museum and had also represented the government. At the last moment, before the workmen began, my salary was substantially reduced by the very people for whom I had waived all my rights in the undertaking, but a small share of the profits was secured to me. I arranged the excavations at Poli exactly as I have described above, and trained Messrs. Williamson, Foot and young Christian (who unfortunately died of fever at Poli). At the beginning I was always on the spot at daybreak in order to get the workmen in working order. When I had done that I deputed this office to the others. At first too I kept the Diary of excavations accurately grave by grave and illustrated it fully with sketches. Later, when I found that Mr. E. Foot had great talent for drawing and was also a deft and conscientious worker, I taught him how to keep the diary-grave by grave. I have still in my possession Foots diary and list of antiquities. At first there is no statement of the arrangement of the graves, later this is added. When a large number of fine Greek vases were found I made preliminary tracing in water-colour myself, later E. Foot did them and did them better — the necessary reconstructions also — e. g. that of the silver belt Pl. XXV,—were drawn by him in admirable fashion. The increase of discoveries necessitated my presence more and more frequently in the town. We had by degrees filled 5 Magazines cram full with antiquities, for 441 graves had been open and all had yielded abundantly. I gave the practical direction as to the open-air work to Mr. J. W. Williamson, who had the assistance of young Christian as long as he was alive and of Mr. Foot. It was Mr. Foot's work to make the list of the finds of the graves and their contents, and Mr. Williamson measured the graves for me and sketched them roughly, so I had only to draw them out clean. At first I paid several visits to the excavations, then only one daily. Towards the end of the excavations the work accumulated to such an indescribable degree that I could not go every day to the site. Everything however was so well systematized and Mr. Williamson, with Gregorio's help, supervised the hands so efficiently, Mr. Foot kept the illustrated Journal in such

---

*) By forming this Company of three English capitalists, of whom one, and he a very able, practical man, was on the spot, I was at last able to carry through an excavation on a large scale. At the same time I had hoped to win Messrs. Christian and Williamson as my friends, a hope only partially realised.

masterly fashion and executed such admirable water-colour tracings one after the other, that I was able to do what was really wanted, i. e. concentrate my energies on my work in the town.

In the case of most of the finds, unless absolutely necessary, the fragments were not put together and cemented on the spot, but in my house and in the store-houses. That was a colossal piece of work. Moreover I had to take the great bulk of the photographs myself and to make the paper prints; that in itself was a gigantic task.*) Further, I myself did a number of the water-colour drawings of vases e. g. the water-colours reproduced in plates LXIII and LXIV &c., are by me. But, most important of all, I had to write the scientific report and put everything that was of importance on paper. This necessitated an extensive correspondence with the savants of the museums of Europe. Then those who had undertaken the scheme, with Mr. Watkins at their head, wanted to make money. Although the search for new strata of antiquities cost money, and although a great deal was paid out for water-colours, photographs &c., although no expense was spared to conduct the excavations in a systematic and scientific manner, the managers after expending ℒ 800 succeeded in clearing a net profit of ℒ 300. At the close of the excavations in 1886 we had not dug through all the plots of ground, and among those left untouched was one that I had first leased in my own name. Before I rode to Poli in the beginning of 1886 I had sent a sketch of the district to Mr. Williamson and had pointed out the pieces of land he would have to lease from the peasants. The site at Limni too, where later Mr. Tubbs excavated, first came to my knowledge and I had begged Mr. Watkins to lease the site. He commissioned Mr. Williamson to do it, and from him the Cyprus Exploration Fund got permission to excavate. But the principal finds made before this by the peasants came into my hands and have now gone to enrich the Berlin Museum. (Pl. XLIV—XLVII).

I hold therefore that I may justly claim to have discovered the cemetery of Marion-Arsinoë and to have been the actual leader and inspirer of the excavation of Poli in 1886. Dümmler's words in the Jahrbuch for 1887, p. 168 may appropriately be quoted here;

"The excavations in the extensive cemetery of ancient Marion tis Chrysokou, which Max Ohnefalsch-Richter was able to make, owing to the munificence of Mr. Watkins of Larnaka (in whose name only the permit was made out M. O. R.) surpass most of the previous enterprises in Cyprus, not only in the wealth and variety of the discoveries, but also, thanks to the systematic conduct of the excavations and the careful observation of all the circumstances of discovery, in the scientific value of the results arrived at."

For the first time in Cyprus we came upon a large importation of painted vases from Greece and as it would seem exclusively from Attica.

I conclude with A. Furtwängler's criticism on the first of the two Reports of Excavations of the Cyprus Exploration Fund (J. H. S. X, 1 f.) because it still holds good, and because Munro's puerile attempts (J. H. S. 1891, p. 329 and Essay in the Builder) could not shake the decision which Furtwängler arrived at on the spot. The Explanations of Plates, given above, (especially to the Title page) have thrown more light on the subject and shown that Furtwängler was right.

Berliner Philologische Wochenschrift 1890, p. 1671. Archaeologische Gesellschaft Berlin, November meeting:—Herr Furtwängler laid before the society the first part of vol. XI of the Journal of Hellenic Studies and discussed the paper contained in it by Munro and Tubbs on the recent excavations at Poli tis Chrysokou. (Marion-Arsinoë in Cyprus). The conclusions at which these archaeologists arrive as to the date of large classes of objects found in Cyprus are of a remarkable character. On the one hand they maintain that the finds are in general not dateable from their own peculiar characteristics, for, so runs the characteristic expression, "all the periods are much alike." (!) On the other they constantly assign a definite date and without giving reasons, but the date they do assign is always a late one. The well-known class of Cyprian vases with geometric decorations flourished, according to them), p. 91, Note) specially in Ptolemaic days and lasts far down into Roman times. Dr. Furtwängler next pointed out that the authors of the paper are qua archaeologists, inadequately furnished, viz they are unable to distinguish Attic vases from Cyprian, and still more unable to distinguish them from other Greek ware, and that hence the dates they assign are wholly worthless for scientific purposes. He also maintained that their attacks on the statements made by M. Ohnefalsch-Richter and P. Herrmann (Das Gräberfeld von Marion 1888) were quite unjustifiable. He then proceeded to speak of his own researches, of the great discoveries made previously in that nekropolis, with both portions which, i. e. that sold by auction in Paris and that which remained in the Cyprus Museum at Nicosia, he was acquainted. This latter half, which, by the great kindness of Mr. King Commissioner at Nicosia, was unpacked while Dr. Furwängler was in Cyprus, is specially important because the contents of each grave are kept separate. It can here be noted with absolute certainty how the early indigenous so-called Cyprian vase-painting, under the influence of Attic imported ware, modified itself step by step from the end of the 6th century B. C. onwards, and here and there lives on right down into the 5th and 4th centuries B. C. The time of the pure, unmodified Cyprian geometric style is entirely before the 5th century B. C. That the graves were used for a long period of time and were sometimes destroyed is true—so much the more important is it to hold fast to the certain chronology that a knowledge of vases gives us. Dr. Furtwängler ended with the hope that the English would be able to employ in the future better-furnished archaeologists to direct their deserving excavations in the island of Cyprus.

---

*) Imagine what it was to work with the wet collodion process in the East, in the hottest season of the year and in the open air.

5. The Cyprus Exploration Fund.

. When I was living in Poli in 1886 and making so many beautiful discoveries I came into relation with Mr. A. S. Murray, Sir Frederic Leighton, and Mr. A. H. Sayce.*) My discoveries at Tamassos and Frangissa, and still more at Marion-Arsinoë, had finally sent an electric thrill through the gentlemen in London. I received a letter saying that it was hoped £ 3 000 would be voted by government for the excavations. Nothing came of that. Instead, the Cyprus Exploration Fund was started, and I, who was the cause of it being started, was pushed on one side.

When the young archaeologists arrived in Cyprus and were to have begun digging. the Museum Council at Nicosia desired that I, their superintendent, should be sent as representative of the government and of the Island Museum, to the excavations of the Exploration Fund. This was a vote of confidence — the best possible by the best people in the island—English, Greeks, Turks, with Sir Elliott Bowill, the Lord Chief Justice, the Archbishop and the Kadi at their head. But the government rejected the proposition. Instead, it named Mr. Hogarth Inspector for the government, while Mr. Ernest Gardner acted as agent for the Fund. As Messrs. Gardner and James went off on a journey during the excavations, Mr. Hogarth resumed all offices in his single person, while I was pining at Nicosia without work and without pay though I still bore my long title, and was on paper, "Consulting Archaeologist and Superintendent of excavations". It was not till 1889 that, thanks to coming in contact with his Excellency Governor General Sir Henry Bulwer at Tamassos, I was able to revive an excavation for the Royal Museum at Berlin, which again had remarkably ample results. These will appear in a special monograph.

If I was put aside when I expected and had every right to expect, to be put in office, none the less have I followed with keen interest all the excavations that have been made subsequently to mine, and I shall follow still further with a constant and affectionate interest the fortunes of an island to which I am bound by ties of joy and sorrow that Time can never loose.

He who has traversed a long and toilsome road and looks back at last from the peak he has attained may well rejoice and offer his thanks to those who have accompanied him upon his way. — Such thanks I offer to my kindly readers.

From the topmost peak the wanderer sees, it may be, that he did not always take the shortest way, nor did he always withstand the temptation to wander from his upward road awhile.

If in this, my first great work, I have not availed to present my material, in itself all too abundant, in such clear and comprehensive fashion as I had hoped, I trust I may be pardoned.

---

*) I have in my possession a long correspondence on this point.

List of Illustrations in the Text.

63. p. 60 the same.
64. — Ornamentation of a whorl from Hagia Paraskevi.
65. — Incised ornamentation of a Trojan vase. From Schliemann, Ilios, p. 772, fig. 1532.
66. — the same. From Schliemann, Ilios, p. 773, fig. 1533.
67. — Incised ornamentation of a Trojan whet-stone. From Schliemann, Ilios, p. 773. fig. 1534.
68. p. 61 Picture from a Mykenae vase found in Cyprus. From Furtwängler-Löschcke, Myk. Vasen, p. 28, fig. 16.
69. — = LXXIX, 20 = XCIV, 3. Cylinder from Kephalovrisi near Kythraea.
70. — the same.
71. p. 62 Picture from the crater from Tamassos, p. 37, fig. 38.
72. p. 61 Engraving on a gold ring from Mykenae. From Schliemann, Mykenae p. 259, No. 334.
73. p. 62 Cylinder from the collection of the Duc de Luynes. From Ménant, Glyptique Orientale II, p. 82, fig. 87.
74. p. 63 Part of the warrior-vase from Mykenae. From Furtwängler-Löschcke, Mykenische Vasen, Pl. XLIII.
75. — Part of the crater from Tamassos, p. 37, fig. 38.
76. p. 65 Clay vessel from Haliki. From Furtwängler-Löschcke, Myk. Vasen, Pl. XVIII. 122.
77. — Amphora from Hagia Paraskevi. From Furtwängler-Löschcke, Myk. Vasen, p. 29, fig. 17.
78a and b, p. 65 = CXXI, 11. Cyprian steatite beads. From Cesnola, Salaminia, p. 145, fig. 138.
79a and b, p. 65 = CXXI, 10, the same Salaminia, Pl. XV, 61.
80. p. 65 = CXXVIII, 4. Cyprian cylinder. From Salaminia, Pl. XII, 9.
81. — the same; Salaminia, p. 124, fig. 117.
82. — Picture on a vase from Haliki. From Furtwängler-Löschcke, Myk. Vasen, Pl. XIX, 134a.
83. — Fragment of a vase from Charvati. From Furtwängler-Löschcke, Myken. Vasen, p. 67, fig. 36.
84. p. 67 Birds from a Cyprian vase. From Cesnola-Stern, XCII, 1.
85—88. p. 67 Vase painted with birds; from Mykenae. From Furtwängler - Löschcke, Mykenische Thongefässe, IX, 44.
89 (wrongly numbered 90) p. 69 Egyptian picture of a tamarisk. From Wilkinson-Birch, Manners and Customs of the ancient Egyptians II, p. 164.
90. p. 70 and 93 the same, Wilkinson-Birch III, p. 349. No. 588.
91. — (here wrongly numbered 95) the same, III, p. 350, No. 589.
92. — and 93 Reproduction on a reduced scale of XXI; the picture on the shoulder of the Cyprian vase XIX, 3.
93. p. 71 = CLXI, 3 Egyptian bouquet. From Prisse d'Avennes II, Bouquets peints.
94. p. 72 Egyptian wall-painting. From Rossellini.
95. p. 73 the same. From Perrot I, p. 453, fig. 256.

96. p. 74 Pomegranate tree from fig 95. From Wilkinson-Birch I, p. 376, No. 148.
97. p. 74 Pomegranate tree from a stele from Carthage From Perrot III, p. 460, fig. 335.
98. p. 74 (wrongly numbered 99) Egyptian picture of the God Min. From Wilkinson-Birch I, p. 405, fig. 174.
99. — Egyptian hieroglyphics. From Wilkinson-Birch.
100. p. 75 = CXXII, 1. Egyptian relief with Min, Anat-Astarte, Rešef. From Layard. "Cultè du cyprès." Pl. XI.
101. — = Part of a cuirass from Idalion. From Perrot III, p. 867, fig. 633.
102. — Portions of a silver girdle from Tamassos. The upper part repeated on CLX, 4.
103. — Reconstruction for the silver girdle from Marion-Arsinoë XXV, 1--4.
104. p. 77 Egyptian bracelet. From Prisse d'Avennes II, bijoux.
105. — Part of the silver girdle from Marion-Arsinoë XXV, 1--4.
106. p. 78 and 90 = LXXXIX, 7 = XCV, 3. Egyptian casket. From Wilkinson-Birch II, p. 200 fig. 399, 8.
107 and 108 p. 79 Egyptian basket. From Prisse d'Avennes. Vases du Tombeau Ramses III.
109. p. 80 Egyptian representation of a vintage. From Wilkinson-Birch I, p. 383 No. 159.
110. p. 83 = CLIII, 4. Babylonian cylinder. From Lajard, "Cultè du cyprès." Pl. IX, 2.
111. — Early Babylonian cylinder, found in Cyprus.
112. p. 84 = CLV, 1. Assyrian cylinder. From Lajard, Mithra XVIII, 2.
113. p. 85 Assyrian cylinder From Menant, Glyptique orientale II, p. 34, fig. 16.
114. — the same; Menant II, p 34, fig. 18.
115 — and 90 the same.
116. — the same; Lajard, Mithra XVI, 6.
117. — Inscribed cylinder. Lajard, Mithra.
118. p. 87 = LXXIX, 4. Cyprian cylinder. From Cesnola. Salaminia XIII, 20.
119. -- the same; Salaminia XIII, 17.
120. — the same; Cesnola-Stern LXXVI, 20.
121. — Assyrian cylinder in the Louvre. From Perrot II, p. 679, fig. 334.
122. — Cyprian cylinder; Cesnola, Salam. XII, 2.
123. — the same; Salaminia XII, 5. Cf. our Pl. LXXXVII, 7.
124. -- the same; Salaminia XII, 1.
125. — the same; Cesnola-Stern LXXVI, 13.
126. p. 88 Cylinder from Lajard, Mithra XXVI, 8.
127. — Chalcedony weight. From Lajard, Mithra, XVI, 7b.
128. p. 91 coloured; Pl LXI. Picture on the Cyprian Vase XIX, 1.
129. p. 90 Cylinder in the Berlin Museum V. A. 2116.
130. p. 92 Assyrian relief in the Berlin Museum.
131. p. 93 Jasper cylinder. From Lajard, Mithra XXVII, 7.
132. — Cyprian cylinder. Cesnola-Stern LXXVII, 24.
133. — Syrian cylinder. From Lajard, Mithra.

205. p. 293 = CIX, 9. Osiris soul from the Egyptian picture LXXII, 2.
206. — Siren from the Attic Kylix CX, 7, No. 4, from Marion-Arsinoë.
207. — = CIX, 6. Harpies on a Cyprian gem. From Cesnola-Stern, Pl. LXXIV, 1.
208. — = CIX, 1. Persian Cylinder. From Lajard, Mithra XLIX, 2.
209. — = CV, 8. Bearded divinity in the form of a bird. Cyprian terra-cotta figure. From Perrot III, p. 600, fig. 410.
210. — = CV, 7. Bronze winged figure from Wansee. From Perrot II, p. 584, fig. 281.
211. — Bronze winged figure from Olympia. From Furtwängler, Olympia IV, Bronzen, fig. 784.
212 and 212a, p. 293 = XXXIX, 3 and 3a. The same. From Furtwängler, fig. 783 and 783a.
213. p. 294 Siren from the Attic Kylix CIX, 11 and 12, from Marion-Arsinoë.
214. — Osiris soul from the Egyptian representation LXXIII, 1 = CIX, 4.
215. — Siren, inside picture on the Attic Kylix CLXXXIII, 2. From Marion-Arsinoë.
216. — Harpy from a picture on a vase. From Roscher, Mythol. Lexikon I, Sp. 1847.
217. — = CIX, 2. Harpy from the Harpy monument of Xanthos. From Roscher, Mythol. Lexikon I, Sp. 1846.
218. p. 295 = X, 3 = XXXVIII, 13 = CIX, 3 = CXXIV, 5. Terra-cotta chapel from Idalion. From Perrot III, p. 227, fig. 208.
219. p. 301 = CCXVI, 15. Red clay vessel from Alambra.
220. — = LXXXV, 7. Carthaginian stele. From C. I. S., Pl. XLIII, 269.
221—223, p. 310—313. = CCIII, 5a and b. Artemis statuette, from Kition.
224. p. 314 Coin from Eukarpia. From Wiener Jahrb., 1887.
225. p. 314 Coin from Tiberiopolis. From Wiener Jahrbuch, 1887, p. 6.
226. — Coin from Eukarpia. From Wiener Jahrbuch 1887.
227. — = CVII, 3. Etrurian Bronze figure from a candelabrum. From Gerhard, Akad. Abhandlungen, Pl. XIX, 3.
228. — = CVII, 1. Brass figure from the Troad. From Gerhard, op. cit. LX, 3.
229. — = CCIII, 4. Etrurian bronze figure. From Gerhard, op. cit. XXVIII, 6.
230. — = CCIII, 3. Draped female figure (limestone), from Marion-Arsinoë.
231. — = CCIII, 1. Greek marble statuette (female). From Gerhard, Akad. Abhandlungen, Pl. XXIX, 6.
232. — = CCIII, 2. Female marble figure of the fourth century. From Gerhard, op. cit. Pl. XXIX, 5.
233. p. 316 Enthroned female figure (terra-cotta) from the sanctuary of Artemis Paralia of Kition.

234. — Standing female figure (terra-cotta) from the same spot.
235. p. 321 Head of Herakles (Taken from the original, in the Berlin Museum).
236. p. 324 = LXXXII, 2. Graeco-Phoenician scarab. From Lajard, Mithra, Pl. LXVIII, 26.
237. — = LXXXII, 3, the same; Lajard LXVIII, 24.
238. — The same. Lajard LXVIII.
239. — The same. Lajard LXVIII.
240. p. 325 = XLIV, 2. Male head from Limniti
241. — The same.
242. — = XLVI, 10; the same.
243. — The same.
244. — = XLVI, 3; the same.
245. — = XVVI, 1; the same.
246 — The same.
247. p. 326 Bronze figure of Hathor, with a fish on his head. From Goodyear "Grammar of the Lotus", XLII, 7.
248. — = XIX, 4. Vase from Athiaenou.
249. — Qeb from an Egyptian picture. From Goodyear "Grammar of the Lotus", XLIII, 7.
250. and 257 p. 349. Portions of the decoration of the François vase.
252. p. 359 Outline and section of the tomb at Marion-Arsinoë in which the silver girdle and the ornaments represented on Pl. XXV, 1—7 were found.
253. — Vases from the same tomb.
254. p 431 Part of the silver kylix from Kurion, p. 53, fig. 52.
255. p. 434 Part of the bronze kylix from Olympia, CXXIX, 2.
256. p. 437 Hand-made vase from Alambra (0,54 m. h.).
257. p. 441 Silver Kylix from Idalion. From Perrot III, p. 771, fig. 546.
258. — Silver kylix from Athiaenou. From Cesnola-Stern Pl. XIX.
259. p. 468 Special plan of Nicosia and Lidir-Ledrai,
260. p. 466 Bronze fibula from a tomb near Kurion.
261. p. 467 Section of a subterranean passage at Pteria in Cappadocia. From Perrot IV, p. 620. fig. 304.
262. p. 470 Inside picture from an Attic kylix from Marion-Arsinoë.
263.–266 p. 479 Views of the excavation of the Akropolis of Kition. First published by me in the Graphic (1880).
267. p 487 Cyprian wooden lock
268. p. 490 Modern water-jug from Kornu in Cyprus.
269. p. 493 Terra-cotta plate. Taken from the original, which was found at Tamassos.
270. p. 496 = CLXXIV, 1. Special plan of Marion-Arsinoë.
271. p. 497 = CLXXVIII, 2. Vase from Marion-Arsinoë.
272 and 273 p. 497 = CLXXII, 17d and e. Two vases from Katydata-Linu.

I. Geographical Index.

Fig. 257.—2.) on the eastern Akropolis, Muti ton Arvili, Astarte-Aphrodite: 16 No. 29, III, 8, LX, 1; 17 note 3, 18 note 1, 203, 225 note 2, 229 f, XXXVII, 4, LVIII-LIX, 1, perhaps LIX, 2 and 188 Fig. 159—161, cf. 186 ff. 3.) Between the Akropoleis Rešef-Mikal = Apollo Amyklos (168 note 2 331): 16 No. 30, III, 6; Ground plan VIII = X, 8; 225 note 5, 230 f., 400; discoveries CLXIII, 9 (?), War-chariot 19 No. 41 image 206, Vessel for holy water 329, Conical idol 176—177; Herakles 319.—4.) Near 2, to the west Aphrodite: 17 No. 31, III, 7; Terracotta figures 136 note 2.—5.) on the northern slope of the western Akropolis, Aphrodite: 17 No. 32 III between 4 and 5; 343.—6.) West of Ambilleri, Aphrodite Kourotrophos 18 No. 33, II, 15, XCII, 2—7, CCXIV, 9 (?) 203—206, note 1 374 under XXXVII, 8.—7.) Cast of the old town male divinity 18 No. 34, II, 17, III, 17.—8.) S. E. of Idalion on the Aloupophournos, Apollo 18 No. 35, II, 16, 229 ff.—9.) In the village of Dali, Astarte-Aphrodite: 5 No. 3, II, 36, View of the Site XVI, LVII; Ground plan VII = X, 7; Space for votive gifts LVI; 5—6, 130 ff, 204, 225 note 3, 232, 235, 398—402; discoveries VII, 2—3, XIII, XVII, 4 (279 Fig. 189) XXXVII, 3, XXXVIII, 3—5, 11, 16—17, 20, XLVI, 11, XLVIII, 3, XLIX, 2—4, 6, L, 3—6, LI, 1—4, 6—12, LII—LV 1—4, 8, LXVIII, 1—3, LXXVI, 5—9, XCI, 1—3, CXXVI, 1, CXXXV, 3, CCIV, 7, CCXIII, 5, CCXIV, 2, 4, 13; Lamps 401 note, Masks 257, Horsemen and chariots 234, Dove cote 351 under XVII, 2—3, Animals 271 ff., Pomegranate 73—74, Sphinx 325 note 4, One male figure 255 note 1,°323.—10.) East of 9 Treecultus 18 No. 36, II, 37, CXCVIII, 4, 18 f., 25 No. 66, 142 f., 241, 257, 269.—11.) South of 9 cistern for religious use 18 No. 37, II, 41, 342. 12.) E. of Dali, goddess 18 No. 38, II, 21.—13.) North of Dali, Aminal divinity 18 No. 39, II, 31, 164 note 2.—14.) N. W. of Dali, Apollo II, 33, 342, Cultus of Melqart 320, of Sasam 183 note 1. Other discoveries I—III. Explanation (Nekropoleis included) X, 3, XIV, XIX—XXII, XXV, 11, XXXVII, 9, XLVI, 4, XLVIII, 2 (?), XLIX, 1,

6, L, 2, LI, 5, LXI, LXXIII, 3, 5, 6, 8, XCII, 3, CIV, 9 (249 Fig. 174), CIX, 3 (295 Fig. 218).= CXXIV, 5, CXXX, 1 (46 Fig. 49) (II, 12), CXXXIII, 5, CLIII, 3, CXCI, 6, CCXVI, 23 (39 Fig. 40).

Kalymna, Vase XCVIII, 7; 288.
Kamaraes, West of Akrotivi. Monolith Tria Litharia 26, 190 note 4.
Kameiros in Rhodes LXXV, 4, CII. 3, CVII, 5, 424 under XCVI, 12.
Kapthor 445 under CXXXVII, 5.
Kara-kusch in Commagene, grave mound CXCIII, 3 · 5, 191.
Karavostasi v. Soloi
Karmel Mountain and god 222 f.
Karpaso Promontory in the N. E. of Cyprus 26 f., 113, XLIII, 3, CXLIX, 19.
Karti-hadas(š)ti, Karthadašt, Assyrian name of Kition 89 note 5, 144, 163.
Katharina (Hagia) near Salamis CLXXV, 5 and 9, 214.
Katydata Linu, two villages in the Soliäs valley S. of the Bay of Morphu. Sanctuary of Astarte-Aphrodite 20 no. 53, 218 f., XVII, 5. — Graves CLXXII, 16—18 (CXLVIII, 11, CXLIX, 10, CL, 8, CCXVI, 17), 356. — LXV, 2—4, 7—10, 12, CLXXXII, 11, CCXVI, 29.
Kefa, Kefti 154 note 3, 164 note 2, 445 under CXXXVII, 5.
Kefti v. Kefa.
Kephalvorisi, Necropolis near Kythraea 61 Fig. 69 = LXXXIX, 20 = XCIV, 3; 61 Fig. 70.
Kerynia on the N. coast of Cyprus N. of Nicosia, 132.
Khorsabad-Niniveh LXXXVII, 14, XCVII, 3.
Kition between Larnaka and Skala 11, Phoenician Chittim-Kittim, Assyrian Karti-hada(š)ti 89, 144, 163; Acropolis, modern Bambula CCI, 229, 444 under CXXXV. — Cults: 1) on the Acropolis Mikal and Astarte 11 No. 9 168 f., 194, 229 f., Ground plan CCI, S., Discoveries XCIV, 4 (211 241), Inscriptions 168 f., 185 f. Cowheaded idols 211, πτωγοί 315, Vessel for incense 444 under CXXXV, Statuettes 373 under CXXXVII, 2, Terra-cottas 202, note 1. Dogs in cultus 154, 215. — 2) On the E. coast of the Salt Lake Artemis Paralia 11 No. 7,

314 f. Different elements in the principal goddess 256, 303 f., The Ashera beside her 99, 144 f., 168, Principal image CCIII, 5 = 310—313 Fig. 221—223, p. 309 f., Discoveries XVII, 2—3 (278 Fig. 187—188, XXXVIII, 12), XCIII, 4—6 (210, 297); presumably XXXVII, 5, XXXVIII, 6 and 7, CCIV, 1—2, 6, 8—9, CCV, CCVII, CCVIII, 4—8; 317 Fig. 233—234, cone 256, Dolphin monument 258. — 3) On the W. coast of the Salt Lake Ešmun-Melqart 11 No. 8, 28, 215 note 7, 214, 324. — 4) Opaon Melanthios 27 No. 72, cf. 22 No. 58, 255, 328. — 5) Ešmun-Adonis 28, 215 note 7, 320, LXXX, 5. — 6) On the Salt Lake Astarte-Aphrodite XXXVII, 2. — 7) Zeus Keraunios 319, 242. — 8) Baal Sanator 299 note 2, 319. — 9) Sasam 178, 183 note 1. — 10) Poseidon 183 note 1. Ancient buildings 214: 1) On the Salt Lake CXXV, 3-4, 466. — 2) Hagia Phaneromeni; 3) Monument of Mohammed's nurse. — Other discoveries at Kition and Larnaka XIX, 1, XXXII, 41 = LXXVIII, 7 = XCIV, 12 = CLVII, 4, XLVIII, 1 and 2, LXXIV, 5—8 = 58 Fig. 39 = CLII, 19, CIX, 5 = 291 and 290 Fig. 200, CLV 9, CXCVII, 1. CC, 1—3, CCII, 5-6, 8, CCXVI, 20, 26, 31, Vase 41, Sargon stele 95 Fig. 138 (89, 163). — Inhabitants 178, 183 note 1, 301.
Knidos in Cyprus; near the village of Gastria on the North shore of the Bay of Famagousta. Sacred precinct and monolith, 26 f. No. 68.
Kommagene, Grave mound of Sesönk and Kara-kusch CXCIII, 1—5, p. 191.
Kosci 13 note 1, v. Goschi.
Kotschini Trimithia, West of Nicosia 116.
Krete, gem XXXII, 3, Shields CII, 2, CXXIII, 1 and 7, CXXXI, 1, 2 and 4, Kylikes CXII, 5, CXXVIII, 1 and 2, CXXXI, 3, Writing on Bronze CXLV, 1, Place of manufacture Cyprus 98 note 1.
Krini Karava the ancient Lapithos 571.
Ktima on the West coast of Cyprus, the ancient Neapaphos (v. Paphos C.) 23, 116.
Kuklia on the S. W. coast of Cyprus, on the site of Palaipaphos, which v.
Kurion Assyrian Kuri 216, on the

X, 9, 233 ff., 438 under CXXVI, Discoveries XXXII, 35, 125 note 2, 323. — 2) Apollo 21 No. 55, 22 No. 58. — 3) Hera, Zeus, Polieus, Aphrodite 23, 286. — 4) Dionysos 253, 258 f. — 5) Bokaros 243, 253 f. Monoliths 22 f., No 57, XVIII, 2. — Finds in graves XXXVI, 1, 220, 259 note 1, 285 note 3. — C) Nea-paphos, Sanctuary of Apollo Hylates 21 No. 56, 22 No. 58, 229, 233 f. — Cemetery of Hagia Solo-moni XVIII, 1. — Figure of Eros CXCVIII, 2.

Paraskevi (Hagia) Necropolis of Lidir - Ledrai 460 f.; Graves CLXVIII- CLXXIII, 2—15, 22 a. 23; Discoveries XXVIII, 3. 4. 6. 9. 10, XXXI, 6. 8. 11. 13. 14, XXXIV, 2—4, XXXV, 2. 3. 5. 7. 9, XXXVI, 2. 5. 7—9, XXXVII, 6—7, XL, 8, XLIII, 2, LXXV, 7, LXXVI, XCIII, 1, XCIV, 2. 5. 6. 10. 14. 16. 20, CXVI, 9—10, CXXII, 2--5. 7, CXXVIII,5,CXXXIII,7,CXXXVII, 5, CXLVI, 1 B—9 B, CXLVII, 2. 6, CXLVIII,7—10. 12b and f.,CXLIX, 1—9. 11. 15—18. 20, CL, 3—7. 9 16—17, CLI, 2—34, CLII,1—7. 9—13. 15—16, CLXXXII, 10 and 11, CXCI, 3, CXCIV, 4, CCXIII, 7—25, CCXVI, 1—8. 10—14. 16. 21. 32; p. 29 Fig. 1—3. p. 30 Fig. 12 - 13, p. 31 Fig. 22—28; p. 33 Fig. 30, p. 34 Fig. 31. 33—34, p. 35 Fig. 35—36; p. 59 Fig. 58. 60. 61, p. 60 Fig. 62—64. 68, p. 65 Fig. 77; p. 83 Fig. 111; p. 275 Fig. 181—186, p. 31 note 2, 265, 269, 276 f.

Parasolia between Larnaka and Psematismeno XCIII, 3, CCXVI,9.
Pedaios modern Pidias, (which v.)
Pedalion modern Cape Greco, South-eastern promontory of Cyprus; Temenos of Aphrodite 12 No. 16, 16 No. 29, 225 note 2, 281.
Pera slightly to the north of the ancient Tamassos 7, 10.
Perga in Pamphylia, Coin with Idol of Artemis Pergaia LXXXIII,5.
Peristephani on Karpaso, Temenos 27 No. 69.
Persian works of art XXIX, 16. 17, XXXII, 17. 18, LXXVII, 5. 9. 10—12, LXXXVIII, 1, XCIX, 4. 6, CIV,4. 8. 13, CIX, 1, CXIX, 4.
Phaneromeni (Hagia) ancient building near Kition 214.
Pharangas N. E. of Achna, Sanctuary of Artemis 12 No. 14, 257 note3, 409 note4; cf. Achna 5.
Phasulla N. W. of Amathus, Cultus of Zeus Labranios (which

v.) 19 No. 46; Discoveries 226 note 5.
Phoenitschaes, Phoiniki-ais 452 note 2, N. of Idalion. Finds in Graves CLXXIII, 20 and 21, (CXLVI, 3 B, 30 Fig 29), XCIV, 9 and 25, CL, 12—15 and 18, CLII, 8 = CCXVI, 24, 239, 276, 271 under XXXVI.
Phoinikiais 452 note 2 v. Phoe-nitschaes.
Photios (Hagios) 1) near Athiae-nou 14 No. 25 and 26; 2) N. of Amargetti, sacred stones 167.
Phrourion, Promontory near Hyle; Human sacrifice to Apollo Hylates 233, 253, 327, 336.
Pidias river flowing into the sea near Salamis, the ancient Pedaios 10 f., 24, 25, 232, XLIII, 4.
Polemi S. of Drymu 117 v. Le-tymbu.
Politiko on the site of the ancient Tamassos 6, 10, 38 note 1. Woman of Pl. XXXIII, 6, modern straw plate XXXV, 4, p. 370.
Politis Chrysoku v. Marion-Arsinoë.
Pomos more correctly Bumo (which v.) 20 note 5.
Potamia N. E. of Idalion, v. Map II; Sanctuary of Resef-Apollo, beside it Melqart-Herakles 18 No. 40, II, 28.
Praeneste, Griffin's head CXVIII, 3, Silver kylix CXXIX, 1, p. 50, 200 note 1, 202.
Psematismeno in south eastern Cyprus, N. E. of Amathus; grave CLXVIII, 1, Discoveries XCIV, 9, CXLVII, 4 and 8.
Pteria in Cappadocia. Canal section 467, Fig. 261.
Pyla, N. of Larnaka Bay. Sanctuary of Apollo Magirios, beside it Artemis and Dionysos 15, No. 27, 257, 303 f., 329.

Rhodes. Works of art compared with those of Cyprus XXXII, 5, LXXV, 4, LXXXIX, 2, CII, 3, CIV, 1, CVII, 5, 424 under XCVI, 12; Influence of the art of Cyprus on that of Rhodes 358, note 1.
Rizokarpaso on the peninsula of Karpaso 27.

Salamis, Situation 96, Cultus sites 1) Zeus 23 f. No. 64, 243, ground plan X, 10.—2) Zeus Olympios 25 No. 65.—3) Apollo, Artemis and Dionysos 25 f. No. 66, 241, 257, 303 f. 485 under CCXII.—4) near

Toumpa, Apollo 25 No. 67, 232, 354, 426 under CI, 1, 495. — 5) Site of the granite pillars 23 No. 63. — 6) Aphrodite - Kybele 12 No. 17, 301, Cultus of Artemis 129 f., 302 f.; Athene, Agraulos, Diomedes 299f. Dionysiac inscription 256.—Grave chamber CLXXV, 5 and 9; coins CXCII, 244, 320; some discoveries XCVIII, 3, CXCII, 14, CCII, 1 and 7, 103, note 1, 259, note 1, 290, 31 note 2, 283 note 1.
Salt Lake, S. of Kition, which v.
Samal, v. Sendscherli.
Sardinia, LXXVII, 21, LXXXIII, 21, CXVII, 5. CXXIV, 3 and 6, CXLV, 2; 183.
Satrachos, modern Falias (Yialia) oder river Dali I and II, p. 5, 399 under LVI and LVII, 1.
Sendscherli in Samal, North Syria; Colossus 114 f., 246, Idols 33, terra-cotta vessels 98 note 1, Fibulae 356 note 1, gate masonry 346.
Sesönk in Commagene, grave mound CXCIII, 1 - 2; 191.
Sidon, XLIII, 8, LXXXIII, 17 CXV, 4.
Sinai, 222 f.
Skala, Suburb of Larnaka, 11.
Soliaes (Soliais), Valley S. of the Bay of Morphon. v. Katydata-Linu.
Soloi, modern Karavostasi, on the Bay of Morphon 20, 242.
Solomoni (Hagia), near Neapaphos XVIII, 1, 116, 166.

Tamassos in the centre of Cyprus between Pera and Politiko 6 ff., Name 216, identical with Temese 299, meaning 245 note 4, in ancient times 114 , 269, Sanctuaries. 1) Μήτηρ θεῶν 11 No. 5; 168, 218, 237, Discoveries 10, 19 No. 37, XCII, 6, Four-horse chariot 234; 2) Apollo, on the Pedaios, 10 No. 6, 232, XLIII, 4, Four-horse chariot 234. 3) v. Frangissa.—Discoveries in tombs: Vases XXXV, 10, LXXIII, 7, XCIV, 13 = CXXXVII, 6 = 36 Fig. 37, 37 Fig. 38 = 62 Fig. 71, 63 Fig. 75, CCXVI, 22, p. 105, Coat of mail LXX; Sword CXXXVII, 7; Girdle CLX, 4 = 75 Fig. 102 ,52 f., 76, 114); Ornaments XCIV, 11, CLXXXII, 2, 293 Fibula 355—356; Chests CXCIX, 5—7, 443; Sceptre 200; Candelabrum 378 under XLIII, 9—10, 417 under LXXXII;

II. General Index.

Errata and Additions.

(The work was originally otherwise arranged. In consequence of this and through the simultaneous printing of the German edition and the great amount of time and trouble, which the illustrations demanded, many errata, which require to be corrected, have crept into the text. Additions were also necessary.)

Page 4 line 3 for *ní ίωϱος* read . . . *αίδωϱος*.
„ 5 line 16 for in Egyptian read is Egyptian.
„ 9 note 2 for for. December read for December.
„ 23 line 18 for chapter will read chapter I will.
„ 25 line 7 for Salamil read Salamis.
„ 27 line 17 for flourishingn garde read flourishing garden.
„ 41 line 6 for tholy trees read holy trees.
„ 41 line 6 for cut read cuts.
„ 44 line 4 (from the bottom) for cut shows read cut, Fig. 48, shows.
„ 49 note 5 for dence read confidence.
„ 50 line 9 (from the bottom) for Plate XXIV read Plate XXV.
„ 56 line 23 for Plate XXVI, 3 read Plate XXVI, 1.
„ 56 line 23 for century or read century and the relief Plate XXVI, 3 in the middle of this century.
„ — line 31 for there but the group is read but the group is there.
„ 60 line 3 (from the bottom) for Mykenae and Kypros read 2. Mykenae and Kypros.
„ 61 line 5 for fig. 10 read fig. 33.
„ 62 line 1 for indicted read indicated.
„ 64 note 11 add Furtwängler-Löschcke, "Mykenische Vasen".
„ 82 line 5 for both must read in both must.
„ 84 line 18 for summit which read summit of which.
„ 91 line 6 for here. Two read here (Fig. 130) Two.
„ 94 line 23 for a eye (?) read an eye or vulva.
„ 96 line 22 for Xylolymbo read Xylotymbo.
„ — line 26 for neighbourhood made read neighbourhood of Salamis made.
„ 97 line 2 (from the bottom) for Kyprians, were read Kyprians were.
„ 99 line 18 for these Ashera read these Asheroth.
„ 102 line 13 for imitation read fulfilment.
„ — note 2 for stress in read stress on.
„ 109 line 13 for figures that read figures like that.
„ 115 line 23 for Pl. LXXVII read Pl. LXXVII, 2.
„ — line 24 after Adonis add (Pl. XCII, 5).

Page 124 line 20 for *Γυϱπιϭ(υ)* read *Γυϱπιαιου*.
„ — line 5 (from the bottom) after final add letter.
„ 138 line 20 for adopted the read adopted by the.
„ 153 note 3 for reil de lampe read cul de lampe.
„ 157 line 18 for with rays read with rays-
„ 214 note 3 for Phaneromein read Phaneromeni.
„ 216 line 3 for Melanthos read Melanthios.
„ — line 8 for Baal-Hamman read Baal-Hammon.
„ — line 19 for kinuar read kinnar.
„ 218 line 18 for wonderful read mournful.
„ 222 line 12 for approache read approached.
„ 223 note 7 for Chrysostom, a read Chrysostom. On a
„ 224 line 4 for Lithrodon read Lithrodonda.
„ — line 5 for spring I read spring, I.
„ 226 line 5 and 8 for Ba'alchamen read Ba'alschamen.
„ — line 27 for in whose return read in whose service.
„ 227 line 22 for lateral read natural.
„ 229 note 1 for it stown read its town.
„ 231 note 3 for its idolatrous surrounding read their idolatrous surrounding.
„ 234 line 4 for Dryum read Drymou.
„ — line 16 for that evidence read the evidence.
„ — line 23 for -join-stone read -stone.
„ 237 line 20 for and exercised read and who exercised.
„ 238 line 20 for can no read can not.
„ 239 line 10 for Psema tiomeno read Psemmatismeno.
„ 240 line 13 for XXXVI, 4—6 and 9–12 read XXXVI, 3, 4, 10.
„ — line 28 for Tanit image read Tanit.
„ 241 line 21 for Biblos read Byblos.
„ 245 note 7 for Trilogie read Trinity.
„ — note 4 for and become a read and had formed a.
„ 246 note 1 for fellows in read fellows see.
„ 248 line 4 for are afterwards read afterwards.
„ 250 line 28 for a Dipilon read Dipylon.
„ 259 line 9 (from the bottom). The coin figured on Pl. LXXXIII, 8 and described on pp. 102

note 3 and 168 comes from Myra and does not represent Europa but the Mother of the Gods.

Plate 272 line 5 (from the bottom) for in order that read in accordance with.

„ 291 line 11 (from the bottom) for Fig. 210 read Fig. 209

„ 307 line 2 for strap, a read strap or.

„ 309 line 7 for seized read seizes.

„ 329 note for attendarts, practire read attendants practise.

„ 335 line 26 for Argeiri read Argaei.

„ 338 line 24 for burnt work read wrought work.

„ 391 line 14 (from the bottom) for antiquarian read Antiquarium.

„ 395 No. 40 for reprodution read reproduction.

„ 402 line 24 for Dombined read combined.

„ 403 line 5 for the abrue read above.

Plate 411 line 8 for etitched read stitched.

„ 414 line 12 (from the bottom) for systematically. read schematically.

„ 425 Pl. XCVIII, 6. Height of the vessel is 0,13 m

„ 470 Plate CLXXXI add 4 and 5 Winckelmanns-programm p. 60, Fig. 43 and 44.
The provenance of the three vases, 3—5 is rightly given as Kurion, while 1 and 2 come from Marion-Arsinoë. On the Plate itself, through an oversight, there is no mention of Kurion, while Marion-Arsinoë is wrongly given as the provenance of all five vases.

„ 481 line 15 from the end of the description of Plate CCIII should stand the initials H. S. and at the end M. O.-R. The description of CCIII, 3 is partly by Herr H. Schmidt. See p. 489 note.

„ 526 sub. Lock for CCXI read CXXI.

Supplement to Plate VII.

Above on p. 345, in the explanation of the Plate, the German notes, printed on the Plate itself, have not been translated. They are, therefore, added here:

Ground Plan of the Sanctuary at Dali (Idalion) on the island of Cyprus.

Excavation and Plan by Max Ohnefalsch-Richter, Superintendent of Excavations in Cyprus (1885, February to April). Assisted by Mr. Sotherland, Royal Engineer and Surveyor.

Aphrodite Temenos. Dali I, 3; II, 36; VIII. XII—XV.
Explanation of signs &c. (More particulars in the text).
H. The Sanctuary proper.
S. Sacrificial space with hearth or altar for burnt offerings in the middle (A) and iron staves (e) for stirring the fire.
V¹. Unroofed space were votive offerings were set up.
V². Pillared walk leading, between O and V¹ to the Sanctuary proper (H). The rounded stones in the walls are river-pebbles, the angular ones mostly slabs or blocks of limestone.
ce. Lime mortar.
e. Iron hooked staves for stirring fire.
R and a. Cinders and ashes. The hearth.
F. Places where fires have been.
st, st¹, st² and f g. Stones which are important in respect of the architecture.
Col. Single Basis for a pillar, round top, the corners blunted.
y^3 y^4. Corners of a piece of masonry, perhaps the basis on which a cone stood.
hy. Fragments of a huge thick terracotta vessel, perhaps a pithos.
E. Entrance to the space for votive gifts.
P. Peribolos walls.
la. Spot where a number of lamps (all of the usual archaic open shell form) and some small and mostly unpainted vases (probably lekythoi) were found.
—.—.—. Approximate boundaries of the separate divisions.
The North wall of the space for votive gifts seems to have run East and West in a straight line (— β to ξ).
Later, when the gifts became too numerous for the allotted space. the court of the temple seems to have been enlarged by the addition of an irregular wall running in a zigzag. g and k. The large stones, mostly with quadrangular depressions, are pedestals for statues. On one of them a fragment of a stone statuette was found in situ.
The numerous stone feet to be seen in the court are fragments of statues and statuettes, mostly found in situ. Among them are some life-size and nearly life-size terracotta statues.
Traces of lime mortar (marked with a special mark on the plan) were found on some of the stone pedestals.
The most usual position for the votive statues is facing S E. or S.
The principal statue of the goddess herself has not been found.
All the votive gifts in human form are (with one solitary exception) figures of the goddess or women. The temenos was sacred to Aphrodite.
In the Apollo temenos at Voni I found (1883), with 2 or 3 exceptions, only male figures.
Spot ransacked by the peasants in 1883. In the same year I spent a few hours in digging at this spot and proved that walls must have stood there. These walls were probably removed by the peasants.